HOUSE
OF THE
PROUD

A Shattered Nation Novel

By Jeffrey Evan Brooks

Dedicated to my wonderful wife Jill, who fills my life with infinite love.

This is a work of fiction.

Published by CreateSpace Independent Publishing Platform

Cover art by Willow Clark

Message from the Author

House of the Proud is a sequel to my first book, *Shattered Nation: An Alternate History Novel of the American Civil War*. Between the two, a short novella, *Blessed are the Peacemakers*, was also published. All take place within the same fictional historical timeline and so can be seen as telling a single continuous story. At the same time, each can be read individually.

Allow me to provide a bit of background for those who have not read either of the two preceding books. In *Shattered Nation*, which takes place in 1864, Jefferson Davis decides against removing Joseph Johnston as commander of the Army of Tennessee in late July, 1864. Shortly afterwards, Johnston inflicts a crushing defeat on the Union forces commanded by William Tecumseh Sherman in the Battle of Atlanta (known to the North as the Battle of Peachtree Creek).

More bloody fighting follows as Union reinforcements are sent from Virginia to Georgia and Ulysses S. Grant arrives to take command in person. Although the Union forces outmaneuver the Confederates and inflict a defeat on them at the Battle of East Point, but a ferocious defense led by Patrick Cleburne manages to hold the city until Johnston wins the Battle of Fairburn.

Military failures in Georgia and elsewhere cause Abraham Lincoln's already shaky popular support to collapse. Consequently, he is defeated in the presidential election in November. A shaky and unofficial ceasefire takes hold until George McClellan, the Democratic candidate, assumes office in March of 1865.

In *Blessed are the Peacemakers*, delegations from both sides met in Toronto in the summer of 1865 to hammer out a peace agreement. John C. Breckinridge becomes the key player of the Confederate delegation as the two sides wrestle with questions of borders, whether freed slaves are to be returned, and other issues. Negotiation appear close to failing when Breckinridge cuts a secret deal with Hannibal Hamlin, giving in to demands that the Confederacy abandon claims for freed slaves in return for trade concessions. The peace treaty is signed.

House of the Proud picks up the story in early 1867.

A quick note on the "butterfly effect". Readers may note subtle changes in the historical timeline that appear, at first glance, to have little or nothing to do with the situation in North America. This is because any historical change, and certainly one as massive as the Confederacy winning the Civil War, will cause a ripple effect that will spread outwards, gradually creating more and more changes that will have ripple effects of their own. The "butterfly effect" was originally coined to refer to changes in weather patterns, credit generally going to the meteorologist Phillip Merilees, who rhetorically asked, "Does the flap of a butterfly's wings in Brazil set off a tornado in Texas?"

House of the Proud is envisioned as the second of five sequential novels in the *Shattered Nation* series. The three remaining novels will take place in the 1890s, 1920s, and 1960s, respectively. Other novellas that flesh out the timeline, like *Blessed are the Peacemakers*, will also appear, as will at least one collection of short stories. I also plan a few "sidequel" novels, which will take place in other theaters of war during 1864.

"I tremble for my country when I reflect that God is just, that his justice cannot sleep forever."

Thomas Jefferson on slavery

"Circumstances rule men. Men do not rule circumstances."

Herodotus

"The Lord will destroy the house of the proud."

Proverbs 15:25

PROLOGUE

1867
February 26, Night
Bergeron Plantation, St. Martin Parish, Southern Louisiana

Travis tried not to scream. If he could keep just prevent himself from screaming, a small sliver of his humanity might still belong to him and not to the overseer. He had managed to remain silent so far, even after more than a dozen lashes against his bare back. When the whip struck for the seventeenth time, the first slice in his skin opened. It felt to Travis as though hot coals were being pushed into his body. He clenched his teeth as hard as he could to avoid shrieking.

The overseer, a brutal old man known to the slaves as Big Jack, had bound him up against the whipping board and assembled the rest of the plantation slaves around him so that they would have to watch. Travis's hands instinctively strained against the shackles, but they were far too strong to break. With every new blow Big Jack landed onto his back, more of his skin was sliced open and the pain became more intense. It was as if his flesh was slowly being chopped into jelly. He could feel blood beginning to trickle down his buttocks and onto his legs.

Through the terrible pain, Travis berated himself for being so stupid. After a birthday party in the big house, there had been some leftover cake. One of the master's young daughters, Little Sally, had come running out into the field and offered a piece of the cake to Travis. Without thinking about it, he had momentarily put down his hoe and taken the cake. The moment he had bitten into it, however, the girl ran back to the house, screaming that Travis had stopped working and stolen her cake. It had all been one of Little Sally's mean-spirited tricks, for which she was well known.

He tried to ignore the pain and set his mind on the singular purpose of not screaming. Big Jack swung the whip against Travis's back for the twentieth time, although Travis had long since lost track of the number of lashes.

"Enjoy your cake, Travis?" the overseer asked in a shout. "Did you? Did you enjoy your cake?" His voice was full of hateful sarcasm and each new swing of the whip seemed more furious than the last. "What's the matter, boy? Cat got your tongue?"

1

Travis didn't know how many lashes Big Jack was going to give him. Fifty was the usual number for minor offenses. Each time there was a pause of more than a few seconds, he hoped against hope that the whipping was over. Nervously, he risked a glance backwards over his shoulder and saw Big Jack stepping closer.

The overseer was a vicious man and looked the part. Big and barrel-chested, a veteran of the recent war, he had a thick red beard and eyes that seemed to burn whatever they looked at. Even had he not been bound up on the whipping board, Travis could not have fought him for more than a few seconds. Through the fear and pain, he realized that Big Jack was holding something in his hand.

The overseer reached forward and roughly spread a large handful of salt into the open wounds on his back. Intense pain shot through Travis, from his head down to his feet. He screamed. It was an animalistic, primal scream that might have been heard a mile away. Big Jack laughed, pleased with himself for finally having ended Travis's stubborn silence. He picked his whip up again and cheerfully resumed the lashings.

The pain gradually forced all thought from Travis's mind except for a weak desire for his misery to come to an end. He would have been happy to die at that point. His lungs became so exhausted from screaming that they soon lost the power to do anything other than emit a pathetic moan. His feet gave way beneath him, but his shackled hands held him up. The dirt beneath him became slightly muddy as blood slowly dripped into it.

Finally, after what had seemed like hours but really had been only a few minutes, Big Jack stopped. Travis's memory of what happened next was hazy. He could vaguely hear the overseer giving one of his harangues against laziness and an exhortation to follow directions. Travis was too tired and in too much pain to make out the words, but he had often heard Big Jack give such speeches when he had whipped other slaves.

Travis numbly felt himself being taken down from the whipping board. He was helped by two other slaves as he stumbled uncertainly towards the slave quarters. He dimly sensed being laid down onto the dirt floor of his cabin. His mind was unable to form coherent thoughts. With his body broken and exhausted, Travis fell into an uneasy and fitful sleep.

He didn't know how long he slept. The sun set and night came over the plantation. Through the haze of his troubled slumber, it felt as though his back was on fire. At some point, someone came into the cabin and gently washed the wounds. His disordered mind thought for a moment that it might be his mother, but of course that was impossible. She had been sold years earlier, when he had been about twelve years old, after having had the gall to resist her master's attempt to rape her.

Another field slave, Bill, quietly tiptoed into the room. He carried a crumbly biscuit in his hand. He gently shook Travis's shoulder, careful not to touch any of the open wounds.

"Travis, eat this," he said urgently. "Eat it, but don't say nothing 'bout it. Big Jack says ain't nobody supposed to give you food for two days. If he finds out I gave it to you, I'll be whipped just as bad as you was."

2

Travis nodded. Bill had always been willing to take risks for him, which was more than could be said for most of the others. "Thanks," he said weakly as he clutched the biscuit and took a grateful bite. It had been many hours since he had eaten anything.

"Everybody talkin'. They say you got more lashes than anybody can remember anybody else ever gettin'. Big Jack must have been real mad. Damn that demon of a man! I hope Saul comes and kills him dead!"

"It hurts so much," Travis said faintly.

"Came in and washed you before. Just rest. Remember Betsy? Last time she got whipped almost as bad as you and it took weeks for her to heal up."

The thought of enduring the pain for weeks was almost too much for Travis, especially since he knew Big Jack would not permit him to remain in his cabin while his wounds healed. Most likely, he would be sent into the fields against the next morning, no matter how badly hurt he was.

"I gots to go," Bill said quickly. "Don't want Big Jack finding out I'm talkin' to you. Check on you later." In a moment, Travis was again alone in the cabin.

Awake but still in excruciating pain, his mind began to wander, sifting through various painful and disturbing memories. He remembered his last sight of his mother on her new owner's wagon, her tear-filled eyes looking at him longingly until she vanished down the road. He remembered his sister's slow death from consumption, two years later, robbing him of his last family connection. He remembered the dead body of Tom, one of his closest friends, who had tried to run away. Riddled with bullets and attracting swarms of flies, it had been left out for days in front of the slave cabins as a warning to the others, taken away only when the stench became unbearable.

More than any specific memory, though, his pain-wracked mind began to dwell on the toil and hopelessness of each passing day of his life. Since he had first been old enough to work in the fields, each day had been the same back-breaking and meaningless routine. He would be worked as a beast of burden harvesting sugarcane until the day he died. The Bergeron family owned him and controlled his destiny. His suffering mattered no more to them than the suffering of a donkey.

Only once had his life known any variance from this dread routine. Years before, rumors had swirled around the slave cabins that mysterious people known as the "bluecoats" were close by and would take them all out of slavery if they arrived. It did not happen, though, for they had all been marched to a different plantation several miles to the west, returning a few weeks later after the bluecoats had apparently left. The grief and disappointment of the Bergeron slaves had been intense, but Travis had wondered if the bluecoats had even been real.

He tried to sleep. If he could fall asleep, at least the pain would be dulled. Time passed. How much, he wasn't sure. He seemed perched on the thin line separating slumber from wakefulness. Exhaustion pulled him towards the former, but pain kept dragging him back to the latter. After some hours, he finally passed into the blessed realm of unconsciousness.

Travis did not stay asleep long, however. He was startled awake by a cacophony of gunshots, followed immediately by the sound of women screaming and confused shouts of men. More scattered gunshots followed and the screaming continued. Though still dulled by pain, Travis's mind came alive as it tried to make sense of what he was hearing. He could perceive that many people were running around outside and he began to make out the strange words that were being shouted by strong and unfamiliar voices.

"Saul! Saul and freedom!"

Travis inhaled sharply. Rumors of Saul had circulated throughout the local plantations for the last month or so. It was said that Saul was a warrior who led a band of black soldiers in the region, freeing slaves and killing whites. Travis had refused to believe the stories. Big Jack, for his part, had threatened to hang any slave who spoke Saul's name.

He forced himself up off the ground, ignoring the pain that flared through his back. Opening the door of his cabin, he saw black men wearing dark uniforms running down the row between the slave cabins, some of them wielding rifles. Off in the distance, the plantation house was on fire. The slaves were running to and fro, but Travis could hear the soldiers shout for them to stay in their cabins. One man, catching Travis's eye, motioned frantically at him and shouted.

"Stay inside! Shut the door and stay inside! We'll come get you!"

Travis could hear the thunder of hooves and he suddenly saw Major Bergeron and his two sons riding into the midst of the soldiers, like mounted ghosts coming out of the darkness. The owner of the plantation looked confused and enraged at the same time. The three men were firing their revolvers at the black soldiers, who raised their rifles and fired back.

The sight of black men fighting against white men, rather than submissively accepting violence, caused Travis's mouth to drop open in astonishment. Two of the black soldiers cried out and fell, dead or wounded, but a bullet then took down the horse of one of Major Bergeron's sons, throwing him roughly onto the ground. Several bullets then smacked into the cabin just a few feet from where Travis stood. Instinctively, he dove to the ground inside, leaving the door open.

Mary, a house slave that Travis did not know particularly well, dashed into the cabin, seeking shelter from the flying bullets.

"What happening?" Travis asked dazedly.

"Saul!" Mary exclaimed. "It's true! He's real!"

Travis desperately wanted Mary to be right. It was being whispered in the slave cabins that Saul and his men would free all the slaves in the South and take them to a place called Canada. Other, more fantastical stories were told. Some said Saul had magical powers that made him invulnerable to bullets, that he could make a man drop dead simply by saying his name, and that he was the man who had killed the devil Nathan Bedford Forrest during the war.

The sound of gunfire continued for some time, interspersed with occasional screams of pain and terror. Eventually, as though a blanket had been thrown over the plantation, all became quiet. Only the crackling of the burning house in the distance broke the silence.

"Come out!" an authoritative voice commanded. "It's over!"

Travis cautiously moved to the edge of the door and looked out again. Two of the black soldiers lay on the ground, unmoving. Puddles of blood were forming beneath their bodies. The three horses were dead and so was one of

Major Bergeron's sons. Major Bergeron himself was lying wounded on the ground, clutching a bloody leg, while his surviving son stood off to one side, his pistol on the ground and a look of fear and stupefaction on his face. Four black soldiers were leveling their muskets at the two white men.

Major Bergeron started to say something, but one of the soldiers rammed the butt of his rifle into the plantation-owner's wounded leg, causing him to cry out in agony. Travis was astounded. He had been terrified of Major Bergeron for as long as he could remember. Even when the man had been away in the army during the war, the thought of him was enough to cause Travis to shiver with fear. But now, he had been reduced to a pitiful, frightened shell of a man.

Another black soldier ran up. "All clear, boss," he said to a powerfully built soldier.

"Okay, up to the house with them," said the man, whom the others clearly looked upon as a leader. He then turned and called out to the slaves who, like Travis, were warily emerging from the cabins. "Don't fear, my brothers and sisters! Come with us! You're free now!"

The soldiers begin walking towards the plantation house, where the fire was continuing to burn out of control. The slaves followed, no one speaking. Travis went, too, wondering if the leader of the soldiers might be Saul.

The uniforms worn by the black fighters were ragged and torn, but undeniably blue. Travis wondered if the bluecoats he had heard about might be Saul's men, though the stories had always suggested that the bluecoats were white people. He was very confused. He could scarcely believe that what was happening was real and not a dream, yet he felt his soul filled with an exhilaration he had never experienced before.

As they came closer to the burning house, the flickering light cast by the flames allowed Travis to see the man more clearly. He was of medium height, but carried himself with a posture that made him seem taller than he actually was. He had a large, somewhat flat nose and dark eyes that seemed to pierce through the gloom of the night. Over his right shoulder to his left hip, he wore an old and raggedy sash that was red, white, and blue.

"Are you Saul?" Travis asked in wonderment.

The man turned and looked at him, smiling. "What do you think, my brother?"

It had to be Saul. Travis felt a sense of unrestrained joy, abandoning all skepticism. If Saul was real, then perhaps the rest of the stories were true, too. Perhaps he would take the slaves of the Bergeron plantation away to Canada, where they would be free. For just a moment, Travis imagined what it would be like to have no fear of whippings, to work only when he wanted to work, to never again experience insults without being able to respond, to own oneself rather than be owned by another. His heart leapt.

Saul looked at Travis carefully. "You're hurt. Did they whip you?"

"Yes."

"Today?"

"Yes."

Saul nodded and the walk continued. A safe distance from the burning house, there was a group of perhaps two dozen more black soldiers silently watching the blaze. With them, under guard, were the rest of the white people who lived on the plantation. The women and children of the house stood bewildered and terrified, clutching one another in fear. Among them was Little Sally, the girl who had gotten him whipped earlier. Four men, including Big Jack, were among the group. Between the group and the front patio of the house lay the bodies of three more white men.

Travis realized that there were now fires behind him as well. He turned and saw that all the slave quarters were in flames. So, too, were the rest of the plantation buildings. The black soldiers were clearly intent on destroying everything.

As Saul approached, the soldiers fanned out into a large semi-circle, their muskets still leveled at the white people who now stood in the center of their formation. The wounded Major Bergeron and his son were shoved into the group. Travis wondered if perhaps his lifelong tormentors might be tossed into one of the burning buildings.

"Please!" Major Bergeron said. "Please, don't hurt my children!"

His master's voice had a frantic, pleading quality that Travis had never heard before. The look in the man's eyes was one of utter panic and powerlessness.

Saul scoffed. "You don't want me to hurt your children, do you? Oh, how noble of you, white man. Tell me, how many children of slaves have you had whipped? How many children of slaves have you condemned to a life of servitude?"

Bergeron glanced anxiously at the slaves. "I'll give them all their freedom. Just don't hurt my children or my wife!"

"Freedom is not a gift you can give them, white man. In the eyes of God, they were free the moment they were born. You have stolen it from them, but now they're reclaiming it from you."

Travis was fascinated by the tone of Saul's voice. When he had asked him about the whipping a few minutes before, Saul's accent had been like that of any slave. When he spoke to Major Bergeron, however, it sounded refined and polished, like the wealthy New Orleans businessmen who occasionally visited the plantation. It was one more thing that Travis found confusing.

"Who are you?" Big Jack demanded, displaying an arrogance that seemed absurd under the circumstances. "What do you think you're doing?"

Saul turned to Travis. "Is this the man the overseer? The man who whipped you?"

Travis nodded.

"What's your name, my brother?"

"Travis."

Saul turned to one of the soldiers. "Isaac, give your rifle to Travis."

Without a word, the soldier stepped over to Travis and extended the gun to him. Hesitantly, Travis took it. He had never held a firearm in his life and did not know how to use it, but was conscious of the fact that it might accidentally go off.

Saul stood next to him. "Do you want to kill this man?" Two of the soldiers roughly hauled Big Jack in front of Travis and forced him down onto his knees.

Travis's mind was a storm of turmoil and confusion. He dimly grasped that his life had changed irrevocably in the last half hour. He yearned for freedom and frenziedly hoped Saul had come to bring it to him. Still, running away to Canada and killing another human being were two very different things.

"Don't do it, Travis!" Big Jack pleaded, a sharp fear suddenly entering his voice, banishing all pretense of superiority. "No! Please! Please don't kill me!"

"He whipped you like you was a worthless animal," Saul said, his accent shifting again to that of a field hand. "Lord knows what else he done to you and yours. You's got to do what you's wants to do now. All you's got to do is point it at him, put this part of the gun in your shoulder, and pull the trigger." He patted the butt of the rifle, as if with affection.

"I'm sorry, Travis! I'm so sorry! I'll never whip you again! I promise! Please! Please don't kill me!" His voice trailed off into a series of frantic, pathetic sobs, until he finally regained a momentary measure of control. "I don't want to die!"

Travis felt the burning pain in his back. He remembered a thousand insults from Big Jack, a thousand days when he had lorded it over Travis, a thousand days that he had laughed and drank whiskey while Travis had labored in the sugarcane field. He raised the rifle to his shoulder, as Saul had told him. He pulled the trigger, the gun discharged with a loud crack, and a hole as big as a man's fist was blasted through Big Jack's chest. The lifeless carcass tumbled over onto the ground.

The children shrieked in terror and the women held them closer. Some of them had begun to pray, certain that they would soon be killed themselves. The surviving men stood stoically, resigned to their fate.

Saul took Travis's hand by the wrist and led him forward to Big Jack's body. Pulling him down onto his knees, Saul shoved Travis's right hand into the bloody opening in the dead man's chest. The blood was warm and oozy. After he had done the same with his own right hand, Saul clasped Travis's hand firmly. Big Jack's still warm blood spurted out from between their clenched fingers. A rush of exhilaration filled Travis. Never in his life had he felt a sensation of power and now he had killed the man who had tormented him for almost his entire life.

"You is like me now," Saul said simply. "Follow me, and I promise you'll get to do this again."

Now a man stepped forward whom Travis had not noticed before. Although he stood among the black soldiers, he was white. He was not wearing a uniform, but rather a worn dark suit and broad hat. The man was holding a Bible in his left hand, patting it gently with his right.

He spoke. "The angels will come forth, separate the wicked from among the just, and cast them into the furnace of fire. There will be wailing and gnashing of teeth."

The crying among the women and children intensified. One of the men fell to his knees and began reciting the Lord's Prayer. Saul, his hand still covered in Big Jack's blood, strode over to them. They seemed to shrink from his approach, as though he was a horseman of the Apocalypse.

"The women and the children shall not be harmed," he said in his low, booming voice. "The men must die and we shall hang you from these trees. But you may go to your punishment knowing that your women and children are perfectly safe. We are not barbarians and do not wage war on the helpless. Unlike you, we are men."

7

"Go to hell!" Major Bergeron shouted.

Saul didn't respond for a moment, only looking at Bergeron with utter contempt and disdain. "You first," he finally said.

Twenty minutes later, the bodies of Major Bergeron, his son, and the other white men were hanging from the trees surrounding the burning plantation house. The roof of the building caved in with a resounding crash, eliciting cheers from the liberated slaves. Leaving the cluster of white women and children standing in the midst of the flaming plantation buildings and beneath the dangling bodies of their menfolk, the band of black soldiers and newly liberated slaves faded into the woods to the west.

CHAPTER ONE

March 1, Morning
Grace Street, Richmond, Virginia

The Richmond air was cold and crisp, as if to tell the citizens of the Confederate capital that winter had no intention of releasing its grip anytime soon. A thin scattering of snow had covered the ground during the night, though not enough to allow the children to make snowmen. The people on the sidewalks hurried along without conversing much with one another, all anxious to reach their destination and get out of the cold as quickly as possible.

Among the pedestrians walking west down Grace Street towards the center of town was John Cabell Breckinridge. He was a tall, well-built man who held himself with an erect and confident posture. His smile was warm and welcoming and his blue eyes sparkled with a clear and composed intelligence. People recognized him from a considerable distance, for the thick, brown whiskers that cascaded down from his face were legendary throughout the Confederacy, especially among the ladies.

Though he was only just past his forty-sixth birthday, he had already enjoyed a much more varied career than most. He currently held the position of Secretary of War in the Confederate Cabinet. During the War for Southern Independence, he had served as a major general in the Confederate army, fighting in innumerable battles in both the eastern and western theaters. Prior to secession, he had represented his home state of Kentucky in Congress and had served as Vice President of the United States during the Buchanan administration. In the tumultuous election of 1860, very much against his will, he had been the presidential candidate for the Southern wing of the Democratic Party. No man in the Confederacy could boast of a military and political portfolio that ranked with Breckinridge's.

This morning, as usual, he had emerged from the front door of his Richmond home at precisely eight o'clock. Holding a dark coat tightly around him to ward off the cold, he set off on his daily walk. His position in the Cabinet entitled him to a horse and buggy, which would have made the trip much faster, but Breckinridge found his early morning constitutional pleasant and refreshing. In any event, due to the time he had to devote to his work in the War Department, it was about the only exercise he was able to get.

As he walked down the street, most passers-by tipped their hats to him politely and received their own hat-tip and a cordial nod in return. On two occasions, though, especially well-dressed men passed by without the slightest acknowledgment, sternly averted their eyes. He was generally a popular man in the Confederacy, but Breckinridge knew that there were some in the country who emphatically did not wish him well. He knew why, too.

Breckinridge passed by the housing plot where workmen were hammering and sawing as they built the new residence for the incoming minister from the Russian Empire, whose arrival was expected in the next month or so. He turned left on Ambler Street and then right on Franklin Street, approaching Capitol Square. Ahead of him loomed the Capitol itself, an architectural masterpiece designed by Thomas Jefferson, who had modeled it on a Roman temple he had seen in Europe. Looking at it made Breckinridge think of his own family's connection to the American Revolution. His grandfather had been a friend and political ally of Jefferson and his great-grandfather had been one of the signers of the Declaration of Independence.

Until recently, the Capitol Building had housed both the Confederate Congress and the Virginia House of Delegates. The latter, however, had relocated to Charlottesville in January, as the state had decided it did not want to share a city with the national government of the Confederacy. Similarly, the handsome house that had previously been the residence of the governor had now been handed over to President Jefferson Davis. The city of Richmond was gradually reinventing itself, morphing from the capital of a single state into the capital of an entire nation.

Looking to the northwest of the Capitol Building, Breckinridge could see the imposing equestrian statue of George Washington, his arm outstretched as though he were pointing towards the limitless possibilities the people could grasp if they but had the will. Richmond wags had often observed that Washington's statue was pointing directly at the state penitentiary, which Breckinridge found amusing.

On most days, Breckinridge would have strolled on through Capitol Square toward Mechanic's Hall, the building just west of the Capitol that housed the offices of the War Department. But it was Friday morning, which meant Breckinridge would be attending the weekly meeting of the Cabinet. Rather than continuing to Mechanic's Hall, Breckinridge turned to the south, crossed Bank Street, and arrived at the Executive Office Building.

Before the war, the Italianate structure had been the United States Customs House. It had been taken over by the Confederate government upon the secession of Virginia and now housed the offices of the State and Treasury Departments, as well as the personal offices of the President of the Confederate States. There was talk of a grander structure eventually being built, but lack of funds meant that nothing had yet been done.

Breckinridge gave friendly greetings to the clerks on the ground floor, quickly ascended the steps to the second floor, and minutes later was being ushered into the Cabinet meeting room. It was a routine he had repeated a great many times since he had joined the Cabinet two years before. Inside the room, sitting around a large oak table, were President Jefferson Davis and Secretary of State Judah Benjamin.

"Good morning, John," Davis said, genuine affection in his voice. He rose from the chair and extended his hand.

"And good morning to you, Mr. President," Breckinridge replied as he shook. He nodded towards Benjamin. "Mr. Secretary," he said simply. Benjamin, his omnipresent smile never wavering, nodded politely in return.

Breckinridge took his seat. He knew both of the other men quite well and felt that they could not have been more different from one another. Davis had seemingly aged a century since he had become president six years earlier. His face looked as though it was chiseled out of granite and he appeared considerably thinner than he had been even a year before. Davis reminded Breckinridge of an old leather saddle that had been in use for too long. He knew how poor the man's health had become and was certain that, with the war won and independence secured, he was looking forward to the end of his term.

Benjamin, by contrast, projected gaiety and youthfulness even in his mid-fifties. Happily corpulent, well-dressed as always, his eyes seemed to penetrate into Breckinridge even as they concealed whatever thoughts were passing through his own mind.

As they waited for the other cabinet members to arrive, Breckinridge and Benjamin engaged in polite chitchat, discussing the latest social gossip of the Richmond upper crust, while Davis scribbled furiously on a piece of paper. Over the next six or seven minutes, the others arrived. John Reagan, the rough-hewn, tobacco-chewing Texan who served as Postmaster General; George Trenholm, the fabulously wealthy South Carolinian who headed up the Treasury Department; Stephen Mallory, the crusty Floridian who ran the Navy Department; and Isham Harris, formerly the Governor of Tennessee and now the Confederate Attorney General. Breckinridge genuinely liked and admired all these men, though he often thought they had more Cabinet meetings than was necessary and that they went on far too long.

"So," Davis said, finally setting down his pen. "What happened in Louisiana?"

"We're not quite sure, Mr. President," Breckinridge answered honestly. "It would seem that a bandit force of blacks, likely made up of men who served in the Union army, attacked a plantation owned by one Major David Bergeron. The men were all killed, either by shooting or hanging, though the women and children were left unharmed. The plantation buildings were all burned to the ground."

"The slaves?" Davis asked.

"Near as we can tell, they all ran off with the bandits."

"How many dead?"

"Eight, I think."

"What else?"

"According to Mrs. Bergeron, the leader of this bandit group was a man the slaves call Saul. They apparently told all sorts of stories about him. Also, there was one white man with the bandits, though nobody knows who he is."

"How mysterious," Benjamin said.

"When was the last time anything like this happened?" Davis asked.

"About a year ago," Breckinridge replied. "During the Great Disorder."

There was an uneasy muttering of agreement around the table. For just a moment, Breckinridge recalled those confusing months. The Treaty of Toronto had given the Union army three months to evacuate Confederate territory after the date of ratification. In most places, the withdrawal had been orderly enough, but in the more remote parts of Mississippi and Arkansas, as well as in some coastal communities of the Carolinas, many of the all-black regiments the Union had raised from freed slaves had mutinied and refused to depart. They, along with bands of white deserters from both the Union and Confederate armies, and simple ruffians, had taken to looting their localities in order to feed themselves and there had been much bloodshed.

Edward Pollard, the editor of the *Richmond Examiner*, had called the series of insurrections "The Great Disorder" and most other newspapers had soon begun using the phrase as well. The last few months of 1865 had seen much confused fighting as the Confederate army moved in to the lawless areas to regain control. There had been skirmishes and even some pitched battles between Confederate troops and some of the black units which had remained behind. Yet without officers to lead them and without access to supplies, most of the black regiments had fallen apart by early 1866. By the start of spring, the men who had made up the units had either been killed or had fled into Union territory.

"Surely this cannot be one of those groups of blacks," Attorney General Harris said firmly. "How could they have survived in the swamps and forests for more than a year, cut off from all support?"

"I don't know," Breckinridge replied. "But the description matches that of soldiers from the all-black Union infantry regiments. They were described as wearing old Union uniforms and carrying rifled muskets. Saul himself is described as having a United States flag wrapped around him like a sash."

"Well, Louisiana has lots of places to hide," said Postmaster Reagan.

"Anything else?" Davis asked.

"Yes, Mr. President," Breckinridge said. He shifted uncomfortably in his seat, not sure exactly how to phrase his next words. "This Saul fellow nailed a message for you to a tree."

Davis's eyebrows went up. "Message for me?"

"Yes, sir."

"What was the message?" Davis said, bemused.

"According to the telegram from Governor Allen, Saul's words were as follows." Breckinridge unfolded the paper to make sure he read the message correctly.

Tell Jeff Davis and his gang in Richmond that not all the sons of Africa have forgotten the ways of their warrior ancestors.

Silence descended on the men around the table. For a moment, Breckinridge thought he could hear the other Cabinet members breathing more deeply. An already chilly room became even more so.

"Fascinating," Benjamin said. "Not a bandit, then. This Saul is a political actor. He's trying to make a statement."

"Who cares what his motives are?" Trenholm said with a hint of irritation. "People were killed, a plantation was destroyed, and valuable slave property was stolen. Worse yet, stories of this so-called Saul will no doubt start to circulate among the slave population throughout the Lower Mississippi Valley. It will make the slaves there restless. The number of attempts to escape will surely increase."

"As interesting as these questions are, the matter before us today is what measures need to be taken in response," Davis said firmly. He took a deep breath. "I want to discuss two questions, gentlemen. First, does this raid require us to lodge a complaint with the United States? And second, what steps must be taken to hunt these bandits down?"

"What would be the point of complaining to the Yankees?" Attorney General Harris asked.

"It seems obvious that these men once belonged to the so-called United States Colored Troops regiments during the war. Wasn't it the responsibility of the Yankees to withdraw them from Confederate soil in accordance with the Treaty of Toronto?"

Breckinridge felt a tinge of alarm. "I would hesitate to make any statement that might seem accusatory," he said. "We went over this during the Great Disorder, after all. They told these men to come back to the United States and they simply refused. Why risk upsetting the Yankees? President McClellan acts every day like he wants to be our friend, not our enemy."

He spoke these words firmly, for he felt strongly on the issue. Since the ratification of the Treaty of Toronto in the summer of 1865, the United States had behaved like an aloof neighbor. President McClellan had been roundly denounced in the Republican newspapers for not maintaining a hostile attitude towards the Confederacy, but Breckinridge knew McClellan had more important things to worry about than the Confederacy. Tensions between the United States and the British Empire were on the rise due to illegal movements across the Canadian border by the Fenian Brotherhood, a group of radical Irish nationalists. Obviously, the last thing McClellan wanted at this time was to have trouble with the Confederacy.

Breckinridge refocused his attention, for Davis was speaking.

"So, perhaps something more like a statement of concern?"

"That's what I would recommend," Benjamin said. "A quiet statement. If we frame it as a protest or demand, we risk placing McClellan in a position in which he is forced to take a hard line with us to avoid losing face. That would play into the hands of Senator Sumner and the rest of the Radical Republicans. It would also damage our efforts to improve our image with the Northern public. It might be best to say nothing at all."

Trenholm chimed in. "We need a positive image in the North right now. Our first major bond auction in New York City started just a few months ago. So far it is doing reasonably well, but if there were a diplomatic tussle between us and the Yankees, further bond sales could be more difficult. This, in turn, would contribute to further inflation and make it harder for us to service the debt."

There was another uneasy stir around the table. Like nothing else since the end of the war, the specter of inflation and debt was haunting the Confederacy. To Breckinridge, it was as though termites were eating away at the foundations of the country, threatening to bring it crashing to the ground only a few years after it had been established.

In order to win the war, the Confederacy had been forced to feed and equip enormous armies for four years and build an entire war industry from scratch. To pay for it, the Confederacy had printed huge amounts of paper money not backed by gold or silver and had taken out loans from European bankers at stupendous interest rates. As a result, uncontrollable inflation had run rampant throughout the South. At times during the war, Breckinridge had expected the Confederacy to collapse for financial reasons long before its armies were defeated in battle. That it had survived at all was something of a miracle.

Now, even with the war over, both the national government in Richmond and each of the eleven state governments had to cope with an endless multitude of commitments. Richmond still had to pay for a sizable army, manage the post office, maintain consulates in Europe and the United States, and a host of other things. It had to do all this while trying to make interest payments on the massive debt it had already accrued.

The states, for their part, were trying to maintain and repair the transportation infrastructure that had been thoroughly wrecked by the Yankees during the war, for the revival of international trade depended upon the railroads linking the interior to the great port cities. This was a burden the states had to take on themselves, for the Confederate Constitution prohibited the national government from providing any funds for internal improvements. The states were also burdened with the huge cost of taking care of tens of thousands of disabled war veterans and servicing their own debts.

To cope with the fiscal crisis, a series of bizarre and disjointed tax measures had been enacted. Excise taxes on everything from cigars to whiskey had been put into place, sparking rage in hotel bars and billiard halls throughout the South. A type of stamp act had been put into place on official documents, drawing comparisons with the measure the British had imposed on the American colonies before the Revolutionary War. Import and export duties had been raised as far as the politicians dared, despite the anger this generated among the merchants and the fear that it inhibited the economic recovery.

Davis shook his head. "If the bond auction in New York does not go well, we may have to raise import duties yet again. That, needless to say, will infuriate the Wigfall faction in Congress like a stick stuck into an ant bed."

"Wigfall, Toombs and all the rest of those bastards can go to the devil, for all I care," Reagan spat.

"They may be fools," Trenholm said carefully. "But they carry great weight in Congress and the states. Moreover, they will oppose any policy of ours, no matter what its virtues. They fear the encroachment of centralized power here in Richmond."

"Hogwash!" Davis said harshly. "They are self-interested men of no principles whatsoever! Their only objective is to secure power and positions for themselves!"

"True enough," Benjamin said, waving his hand dismissively. "But let's not be distracted. With your permission, Mr. President, I shall draw up a communiqué to be wired to Ambassador Miles in Washington. We can review it at the next Cabinet meeting and make a decision then."

William Porcher Miles, a former South Carolina congressman, was the Confederate Minister to the United States. Breckinridge grimaced when he heard the name, as though he had smelled something rancid.

"Very well," Davis said, nodding. "And now, on to the question of hunting down these black bandits."

"Might it be best if we simply let Louisiana deal with this matter?" Harris suggested. "Surely the state militia is sufficient to run down a band of a few dozen fugitive blacks."

"Indeed," Benjamin added. "I don't want to be accused of overreacting and making more of this incident than is warranted. If this Saul fellow is trying to make some sort of political statement with these murders, the last thing we should do is inflate his importance. He's a mosquito, nothing more. We would be foolish if we turned him into a wolf."

Breckinridge nodded his agreement. He remembered the panic caused by John Brown's raid on the federal arsenal at Harper's Ferry in 1859. Brown had been a lunatic and his attempt to start a slave insurrection would have been comical had lives not been lost. Yet he had struck unimaginable terror in the hearts minds of Southerners. Breckinridge recalled the paranoia that had swept the South, the lynchings of blacks for no apparent reason, the rumors of abolitionist agitators infiltrating from the North. None of it had any basis in reality, but the very fact that so many people had believed it had made it dangerous.

Benjamin was still talking. "This Saul fellow and his renegades have burned down a plantation. Well, so what? There are thousands of such plantations across the Confederacy. On a national scale, this raid is insignificant. If the measures we take are too strong, we risk making him appear as a figure of actual importance."

"That may be," Davis said. "Yet if we do nothing, we shall be accused of standing idly by in the face of servile insurrection. Congress and the state legislatures will surely start their chattering." He paused for a moment and looked over at Breckinridge. "If I give the order, how long would it take for some regiments to be mustered into national service?"

"How many?"

"Five, perhaps?"

"That could be done within two to three weeks. Off the top of my head, were I to receive such orders, I would mobilize two Louisiana regiments and one each from Mississippi, Arkansas, and Texas."

Breckinridge said these words with confidence. Since the war had ended, he had bent himself to the task of reforming the Confederate Army and turning it into a peacetime force. A future war with the United States couldn't be ruled out, so there had never been any thought of going back to the prewar days of a tiny army that had little work to do other than patrolling the frontier. On the other hand, the state governments had refused to countenance the existence of a large army under the complete control of Richmond.

Throughout late 1865 and early 1866, even as the Great Disorder was being dealt with, Breckinridge had held a series of meetings with generals, congressmen, and governors to hammer out an appropriate plan. What had emerged was a hybrid army, control of which was shared between the national government and

15

the individual states. Each state retained general control over its own regiments, but individual units could be called up for service by Richmond. Several of these were on duty for the national government at any given time, manning critical fortifications along the border or along the coasts, as well as protecting the frontier of Texas from Indian attacks. The two major field armies, the Army of Northern Virginia and the Army of Tennessee, still existed, though they were much smaller than they had been during the war.

There was considerable debate over the constitutional implications of the new army system. Some, such as Senator Robert Toombs, believed that a state had the right to refuse to have its regiments called into national service. Since a Supreme Court had yet to be created, the question remained unanswered answered, which often made Breckinridge feel unsettled.

The regiments of the new Confederate Army were, for the most part, the same regiments that had fought during the War for Southern Independence. The men knew each other, had fought in the same battles, endured the same hardships and, for the most part, came from the same counties and towns. Such ties bound men together and created effective fighting units. As part of his reform plan, Breckinridge had intensively studied the regimental structure of the British Army, trying to fathom the secrets of its legendary *esprit de corps*. He had been helped in this by a long exchange of letters with his British friend Garnet Wolseley, Colonel of Her Majesty's Perthshire Volunteers, whom he had met in Toronto during the peace conference.

A few specialist units, such as the Corps of Engineers and some cavalry and heavy artillery units, were directly under the control of the national government, as was the small Marine Corps. A large proportion of these units were made up of soldiers from Missouri, Kentucky, and Maryland, which had never seceded from the Union. Tens of thousands of men from these border states had fought for the South during the war and had chosen exile in the Confederacy over returning to their homes when the fighting had ended.

Harris looked skeptical. "Five regiments? That would be more than two thousand men, yes? Surely we don't need that many to deal with what is likely just a small group of bandits."

"Quite so," Benjamin replied. "I agree that we must take action, but I don't believe mustering state forces into national service is warranted. Not yet, at least."

"What do you suggest, then?" Davis said, irritation creeping into his voice.

"Why not reinforce the Louisiana militia with a small number of regular troops and appoint a commander from the regular army?" Benjamin said. "That would avoid raising any undue alarm at mobilizing state forces, while allowing us to circumvent any charges from the opposition that we are not taking the matter seriously."

"The state of Louisiana would have to go along with that," Breckinridge said. "But I think Governor Allen would be amenable. I personally think Secretary Benjamin's suggestion is a good one."

"And who should be appointed to this command?" Davis asked.

"I would like an officer who would have the confidence of the people and is experienced in irregular warfare." He thought for a few quick moments. "I can think of no better man for a job like this than General John Hunt Morgan."

Breckinridge said this with some trepidation. It was well known that Breckinridge and Morgan were friends. Moreover, both men were Kentuckians and members of the somewhat controversial Orphan Society. Breckinridge feared accusations of favoritism. On the other hand, Breckinridge genuinely thought Morgan the best possible choice. His cavalry raids in Kentucky and Tennessee during the war had demonstrated his unrivaled capacity for partisan warfare.

"Morgan, eh?" Davis said, rubbing his chin. "What is his current posting?"

"General Morgan is currently commanding a cavalry brigade in the Army of Tennessee."

"Yes, well, I imagine that General Morgan is rather bored where he is," Davis said with a wry grin. "I am happy with Morgan, assuming the Cabinet agrees."

Breckinridge glanced around, seeing a succession of nods. Postmaster Reagan, however, cleared his throat.

"Mr. Reagan?" Davis asked.

"Might I suggest that Morgan's orders clarify that his role is to supervise and advise the militia, rather than command them directly? There has been a perception in some quarters that we here in Richmond have taken to dictating directly to the state governments. An advisory role for General Morgan would seem to me to be appropriate."

Davis looked at Breckinridge. "Any objections, Mr. Secretary?"

"None," Breckinridge said. This was not entirely true, for Breckinridge found Reagan's suggestion potentially troublesome. It would make Morgan's role hazy and uncertain and might lead to a disjointed response to Saul's depredations. However, he thought it inadvisable to say anything in front of the whole Cabinet. He knew from experience that the president did not like such disagreements aired at their weekly meetings. If he felt the need, he could discuss it privately with Davis later on.

Secretary Mallory cleared his throat. "Mr. President, I'd like to discuss the issue of proper funds for the proposed goodwill visit of the *CSS Shenandoah* to Brazil later this year."

Breckinridge felt a headache coming on. Cabinet meetings always ran on far too long and his mind was wracked with all the work he had to do when he finally reached Mechanic's Hall. Above all, he needed to send telegrams to General Morgan and Governor Allen and begin the process of organizing the cavalry force to be used against the bandits in Louisiana. Yet the meeting continued to drag on until well into the afternoon. Davis, Mallory and Trenholm spent a ridiculous amount of time talking over how to fund the visit of the navy cruiser to Brazil, a matter that Breckinridge considered to be of little importance, going over the same ground many times over.

Other issues were brought up and discussed, most of which had little or nothing to do with the War Department. Breckinridge spoke up when he felt like he had something worth adding, but otherwise remained silent and lamented over the lost time. Finally, when the hour hand on the clock was nearing three, the meeting thankfully came to an end. Handshakes were exchanged all around and, a few minutes later, Breckinridge was back out on the street, walking towards Mechanic's Hall. He felt tired, but knew he had to put in at least a few hours of work at the War Department before he could go home. Then, hopefully, he would be able to spend some time with his wife before exhaustion pulled him to bed.

March 6, Evening
Bridgewater Iron Works, Bridgewater, Massachusetts

Charles Russell Lowell stood a safe distance away from the workers as they labored to pour the molten iron from the crucible into the mold. The crucible, which reminded Lowell of an enormous teapot, was suspended from the roof with thick chains as the men used giant rods to tip it over. Elsewhere, men were banging away with hammers on what would eventually be railroad track. The roar of the furnaces, the shouting of the men, and the clanging of metal against metal created a cacophony of industrial sound, all being illuminated by the angry glow of the yellowish liquid iron.

The workers were mostly stripped to the waist, their hair tied back with bandanas and thick gloves on their hands. The intense heat caused all of them to glisten with a layer of sweat. His workers were good and strong men, like the men Lowell had commanded during the war. Indeed, many veterans who had served under his command were now employed at his ironworks.

Despite the intense heat and grimy air, Lowell wore a well-pressed gentleman's suit of fine New England cloth. This was not just because he liked the feel of a suit, even in such an unlikely place as an iron foundry, but because he wanted to send a message to his workers. He liked them and was happy to come among them, but he was not one of them. In the end, though they might share a form of camaraderie, they were common workers and he was a member of the Lowell family.

The foreman turned and looked at him, wordlessly asking for approval. Satisfied with the progress of the work he was seeing, Lowell nodded sharply and turned back toward his office. He enjoyed coming out onto the floor, to see the actual work being done at the ironworks, but his job largely kept him confined to his desk.

"Everything going well today, sir?" his secretary asked as he reentered his office.

"Quite well, William," Lowell replied, wiping a layer of sweat from his forehead. "I think those rails will be ready for shipment ahead of schedule."

"Very good, sir. Your tea is on your desk."

"Thank you, William."

He sat down at his desk, which was covered with a high stack of correspondence. Many of them, he knew, were from men desperately seeking employment. The massive influx of returning war veterans, as well as the hundreds of thousands of slaves freed by the Treaty of Toronto, had inundated the labor market in recent years. Combined with the drying up of wartime production contracts and a significant rise in inflation, a serious unemployment crisis was gripping the United States.

It pained him to read pleading letters from men who had served under his command during the war. Most of them were honest men and hard workers.

Many of them had families that needed to be supported. However, with almost seven hundred men already employed at the Bridgewater Iron Works, it simply wasn't possible to bring on any more workers.

Lowell set the most piteous letters aside for him to bring home later. He would see if perhaps his church or one of the philanthropic organizations he and his wife supported might be able to help them. He also made a mental note to inquire of other iron foundry owners whether they had any positions available, though he doubted that they would.

He picked up and quickly read through another letter, laughing out loud when he finished it.

"What's funny, sir?" William asked, looking up from the work he was doing at his own desk across the room.

"Did you see this letter from the Memphis and Charleston Railroad?"

"I did, sir," William replied. "They are offering to purchase rails from us at a very good price, I think. They've apparently gotten a loan from a bank in England to pay for it."

"I'm very flattered to be considered by a Confederate railroad company," Lowell said with scornful sarcasm. "But no iron produced by this foundry is ever going to be sold south of the border. By Plato, no!"

"Very well, sir," William said as he went back to his paperwork. Lowell thought he sensed something in the man's voice.

"You disagree, William?"

William thought for a moment before replying. "You are the boss, Mr. Lowell. We'll do whatever you tell us to do, of course. But since you ask, this deal would likely make our company a fair profit."

"Perhaps so. But would you want us to make rails that would be set in place by the labor of slaves? I would not be able to sleep at night."

"But with a new contract, we might be able to hire more people. So many people need jobs. And those who already have them are still afraid of losing them."

"I understand that, William. But there are still moral absolutes in the world."

Lowell knew that most of the other iron companies in New England shared his scruples against doing business with the Confederacy. Months earlier, when one foundry in Rhode Island had signed a contract with a Southern company to provide rails for the repair of the Virginia Central Railroad, a mob of abolitionists and free blacks had surrounded the company office and threatened to burn it down. Not surprisingly, the contract had quickly been cancelled. On the other hand, Lowell had heard that many iron companies in Ohio, Indiana, and Illinois were eagerly filling orders for Southern railroads. Across the ocean, according to the papers, English and French companies were even more interested, especially since their bankers were financing most of the work.

After a few minutes of silence, during which both men were focused on their respective paperwork, William spoke again.

"Sir?" he asked hesitantly.

"What is it?"

"I'm sorry, sir, but there was a matter I wanted to discuss with you. The Clayton brothers received a telegram yesterday. Apparently their mother has passed away."

19

"I'm very sorry to hear that," Lowell replied.

"I happen to know from talking with some of the boys that they wanted to go to Springfield to organize her funeral, but cannot afford to lose their pay."

Lowell didn't need to think. "Tell them they can go and they won't lose any pay." He paused a moment. "In fact, please find out the details of the ceremony. The company will pay for the flowers."

William nodded, saying nothing further.

Lowell pulled out his pocket watch. It was getting on towards six o'clock. His working day was coming to an end. He quickly neatened the papers on his desk and said goodbye to William. A few minutes later, wrapped tightly in his coat, Lowell mounted his horse and begin the short trip to the Bridgewater house where he lived.

It wasn't home. The elegant Lowell house in Boston, twenty-five miles to the north, was home. When he had first taken the job of running the Bridgewater Iron Works the year before, he and his wife Josephine had considered living in Boston, with Charles staying in Bridgewater only during the week. But having lived apart for so long during the war, in the early years of their marriage, Josephine had refused to be separated again. A comfortable if small house had been leased for their convenience and Josephine had decorated it elegantly. Still, it would never be home.

As he rode through the streets of Bridgewater, the feel of the saddle and the smell of the horse brought his mind back to the war, as it always did. When he has first enlisted in the army, he had been an aide-de-camp to General George McClellan, the man who was now President of the United States. It hadn't been until 1863, when he had been given a commission as a colonel, that Lowell had joined the cavalry. During the last half of the war, he had probably spent as much time in the saddle as he had on his own two feet.

He arrived at the house. After stabling his horse, he went through the front door and entered the foyer. As soon as he did so, he heard the delighted and excited voice of his daughter Anna.

"Father!"

Her face beaming, Anna scrambled down the stairs as fast as her awkward body, not yet three years old, could carry her. Lowell kneeled down just quick enough to scoop her up into his arms. She wrapped her little hands around his neck and he playfully spun her around in a circle. Anna squealed with delight.

"How are you, my dear?"

"Happy," she replied, burying her face in his shoulder.

"You are not causing any trouble for your mother or Mattie?"

"No, Father."

"And what of your brother, Robert? How is he?"

"Crying a lot."

"A lot?"

"All day."

Lowell laughed. Robert had been born just six months before and Anna was not yet entirely resigned to having a little brother. He wondered how Anna would react when Robert began crawling and getting into her things.

He spun her around one more time then tossed her up in the air, catching her as she fell back. She had been born in the confusing days following the 1864

20

election, when everything he had fought so long and so hard for had been falling apart. When he had returned from the war, finding the newborn girl waiting for him had made the defeat easier to endure. She was already displaying signs of an unusual intelligence.

He told her to go to her room and play, then went upstairs to his room and changed out of the clothes he had worn to the foundry. It simply would not do to have dinner wearing an inevitably grimy and sooty suit. His laundry bill was annoyingly high, but there was nothing to be done about it. A few minutes later, now suitably dressed, he went downstairs to the dining room.

"Good evening, darling," Josephine said as he entered. She strolled across the room to kiss him tenderly.

"And good evening to you, my dear. How has your day been?"

"Well enough. I attended a luncheon put on by the ladies of the Bridgewater Anti-Slavery Society. And you?"

"I continue my labors as a modern day Vulcan," he said teasingly. "We're almost finished with the rails for the B&O Railroad."

"Thank God the foundry won that contract. So many men would be unemployed without it."

"Indeed."

The two sat at opposite ends of the table. Their cook, Mattie, brought in the evening's dishes. An escaped slave from Georgia, Mattie had been with the Lowells for just over a year. She had prepared cod with beurre blanc sauce and a side of roast vegetables. Accompanying it was a bottle of Vouvray.

"I met Anna in the foyer. She seems to have had an enjoyable day."

"Mattie says so, yes."

"But Robert has been crying a great deal?"

"No more so than any other baby, I would think."

Lowell chuckled as he took his first bite of the cod. As with everything Mattie cooked, it tasted delicious.

"What's the news of the day?" Lowell asked his wife. He was usually so busy with his work at the foundry that he scarcely had time to glance at the newspaper.

"Sad news out of England, I'm afraid," Josephine replied. "The government has withdrawn the Reform Bill from consideration in Parliament."

"Well, that is unfortunate," Lowell replied. "I suppose we shall have to wait some time then before the voting franchise in Britain is expanded."

"Yes. The aristocracy in Britain appears more strongly entrenched than ever."

Lowell grumbled as he cut more of his cod. "The success of the Confederacy has discouraged progress the world over. Those who remain committed to reform have enough on their plate with the struggle against slavery."

"All too true, darling."

"What else?"

"The papers report that the British ambassador is going to lodge an official protest with Secretary of State Seymour on the matter of the Fenians."

Lowell's eyebrows went up. The Fenians were militant Irish nationalists based in the United States. Thousands of them had served in the Union army

21

during the war in order to gain military experience they could use against the British Empire. Rumor told of camps being established in upstate New York, from which a Fenian invasion of Canada was to be launched.

"Well, I can't say I blame the British for that," Lowell said.

"What does the president think he's doing, Charles?" Josephine asked. "His policy of allowing these Fenians safe haven in America will poison our relations with the British beyond repair."

"Irish immigrants voted for McClellan in large numbers in 1864," Lowell answered. "I suppose he feels he must pay his political dues. McClellan is a capable administrator, but he does not know how to think through to the logical conclusion of his policies. I served on his staff for many months and saw this happen time and again."

"Could this lead to a war, Charles?"

"I pray to God that the answer is no, Effie. I, for one, have had my fill of war and I am sure most of the country agrees. And this would be a war fought for a foolish purpose, not a war to set enslaved people free."

As he sipped his Vouvray, Lowell imagined what a war between the United States and the British Empire might be like. An invasion of Canada would be an extremely difficult campaign. Even though the Union forces would surely outnumber the British and Canadian troops, the logistical challenges and short campaigning season would work to the advantage of the defenders. Moreover, the Royal Navy was vastly superior to the fleet of the United States. They would surely sweep the seas of United States merchant vessels and blockade the ports of the North.

Lowell had to assume that McClellan understood this as well as he did, for the president was a man of great intelligence. This did not mean Lowell held him in any respect. McClellan's dishonest election campaign against President Lincoln in 1864 and his shameful acquiescence to so many Confederate demands during the Toronto peace talks the following year had completely tarnished him in Lowell's eye. As far as Lowell was concerned, McClellan was going to be damned as one of history's villains.

"I have left the most interesting news item for last," Josephine said. "There has been some sort of raid on a plantation in Louisiana. According to the papers, it was carried out by black men who are rumored to have once been Union soldiers."

"Is that so?" Lowell asked, his voice rising slightly with enthusiasm. "By Plato, how very interesting! What are the details?"

"They wore tattered Union uniforms and were armed with military muskets. The leader of this group of men – the Confederates refer to them as bandits – was said to be a man named Saul. Apparently he and his men took over a plantation, freed all of the slaves and burned all of the buildings, then killed the men and left the women and children unharmed."

"I don't much care for the executions of unarmed men, even if they are slaveholders. Still, we cannot expect otherwise from men who were slaves. They have every right to feel rage and hate. In their place, I should likely behave the same way. You say they left the women and children unharmed?"

"That's right."

"Even more interesting. If true, that would reflect a certain discipline among these so-called bandits. Not what one would expect from an unruly rabble."

Lowell considered what the news might mean. There had always been rumors of rebel slaves retreating into the forests and swamps of the Confederacy in the aftermath of the Great Disorder. Lowell himself had heard several such stories at dinner parties, at meetings of the Anti-Slavery Society, and in the lobby of the Unitarian Church after Sunday services. He had always dismissed the rumors as wishful thinking. The news Josephine had just related made him reconsider. Could a band of rebel slaves have survived in the wilderness for an entire year? If so, could this raid on a Louisiana plantation mark the beginning of a renewed armed resistance to the Confederacy? And what of Saul himself? Who was he? Was Saul the man's real name or was it a *nom de guerre*?

Lowell made a note to himself to keep an eye on the newspapers. If more stories of this bandit raid and the mysterious Saul were to emerge, he would take a particular interest in them.

"Could it be, Charles?" Josephine asked. "Could it be that this Saul and his men are survivors from one of the all-black regiments we formed during the war?"

"It's possible, yes," Lowell responded. "The lower Mississippi Valley was where large numbers of our all-black units were located. Besides, the discipline of these men suggests to me that they might have received military training. I can't think of any other explanation."

"It makes me think of poor Robert," she said sadly.

He nodded, understanding perfectly. Josephine's brother, Robert Gould Shaw, had been one of the great Northern martyrs of the war. As the colonel commanding the legendary 54th Massachusetts Infantry, one of the first all-black Union regiments, he had fallen at the head of his men during the doomed assault on Fort Wagner outside Charleston Harbor in July of 1863. Although the attack had been a bloody disaster, almost shattering the 54th Massachusetts, the courage of Shaw and his men had won the admiration of the world.

"I miss Robert every day," Lowell said. "He was more than a brother-in-law to me. He was a dear friend. He had such a loyal and kindly heart. I honestly cannot recall him ever doing a single unkind or thoughtless act. I hope that our son will be honored to bear his name."

Josephine nodded. "In the years since his death, I have been comforted somewhat by the thought that he died fighting to preserve the Union and to end slavery. That doesn't make me miss him any less, though."

Lowell nodded sadly. Robert Gould Shaw was far from the only friend and relation he had lost during the war. He thought of his brother James Lowell, mortally wounded at the Battle of Glendale in June of 1862. He remembered his beloved cousin William Putnam, killed at the Battle of Ball's Bluff in October of 1861. Far too many of the friends of his childhood, many of them his classmates at Harvard, had proudly donned the blue uniform and gone off to war, only to return home inside wooden boxes. Moreover, many of those who returned alive were missing arms and legs, and almost all of them had been shattered in spirit.

Then there were the men he had commanded during the war. He thought of the unruly but courageous troopers of the 2nd Massachusetts Cavalry, whom he had led against the guerrilla troops of John Mosby. He recalled the tenacity and bravery of the elite Cavalry Reserve Brigade, which he had commanded throughout the battles of the 1864 Valley Campaign. Hundreds of those men now lay in shallow graves across Maryland and northern Virginia.

He frowned, allowing a trace of bitterness to enter his mind. These men had sacrificed their lives to preserve the Union and destroy slavery. Yet when he looked at a map, he saw the Confederate States of America. Millions of blacks remained in chains. All of the death and suffering had been for nothing.

Lowell looked up at Josephine. "Do you think I'm a good man, love?"

She drew her head back in surprise. "Of course I do, darling. What sort of a question is that?"

He pursed his lips slightly and took another sip of Vouvray.

Josephine continued. "I would not have married you if I had not thought you were a good man, Charles."

"I know."

"Then why would you ask such a question as that?"

"So many died in the war, yet I fought in dozens of battles and never received so much as a scratch."

She nodded in understanding. "You have spoken of this to me before. I'll say now what I said then. You are no less brave and principled than my brother, or your brother, or any of your men who were killed. The fact that they died and you survived doesn't reflect on you at all. You were just more fortunate."

"My mind tells me that you are right, but my heart sometimes refuses to believe it."

"Perhaps God spared you for a particular reason. We can't know the mind of God."

Lowell chuckled. "I wish my grandfather were still alive. I would have enjoyed talking with him about the theological implications of that particular question." His grandfather, after whom he had been named, had been one of the most prominent Unitarian preachers in Boston and among the first clergymen in the North to speak out against slavery.

"I'm sure he would agree with me," Josephine replied.

"But if God granted me life when he has taken away the lives of so many others, do I have a right to live for myself and my family?"

"The iron you make at the foundry is helping to build this country. You give good, honest work to hundreds of men, allowing them to put food on the tables of their families. You are actively involved in the Anti-Slavery Society and half a dozen other reform organizations. You are raising two children. The world is a far better place because you are in it, Charles. I hope you realize that."

"Thank you, Effie. I am so blessed to have you in my life."

"I am glad," she said. "Now, what has Mattie prepared for dessert?"

Lowell smiled, but only outwardly. A few minutes later, as he dipped his fork into a dish of sorbet, he still could not shake the faces of Robert Shaw and James Lowell from his mind.

Few things in the world gave Senator Robert Toombs as much pleasure as smoking a good cigar while drinking a glass of excellent brandy. He reveled in the sensation of the tobacco smoke swirling about in his mouth as it mixed with the fiery liquid of the fortified wine. He felt relaxed, confident, and reassured that the world made sense.

Dinner with his guests had been quite good. His slave cook, with whom he was pleased, had prepared two large Virginia hams glazed in maple syrup. The conversations had been lively and pleasant, although Toombs had found it all rather tiresome. After a few glasses of wine, he had become impatient for the dinner to end so that the women would leave and the men could get down to business.

When the dessert of pound cake and iced fruits had finally been finished, the women had gone off to the drawing room, to talk about whatever it was women talked about when their menfolk were not around. The table cloth had been removed, the decanters and cigars brought in, and Toombs was now at liberty to begin the conversation that had been the actual purpose of the dinner party.

Toombs glanced around at the four other men in the room, which was rapidly filling with cigar smoke. There was Senator Louis Wigfall of Texas, on his way back to Richmond for the coming congressional session. He was a big bear of a man, with cold, intimidating eyes and a dark beard speckled with gray. The man had a violent streak, having killed men in duels before the war. Like Toombs himself, he had served as a brigade commander during the war with the Yankees, though without the distinction Toombs himself had achieved.

Then there was Governor Joseph Brown, a fellow Georgian. A beard as white as snow spilled down from his face like a child's bib, making him look older than his forty-five years. He had more the appearance of a quiet Protestant minister than a politician, which belied his fierce commitment to states' rights, slavery, and white supremacy. Politically, he and Toombs had alternated between alliance and enmity before the war, depending on the circumstances. His presence at this meeting was proof that their interests were once again becoming aligned.

Just to Brown's left was Senator Robert Hunter of Virginia. Sitting straight in his chair with a dignified, aristocratic bearing, he appeared considerably taller than he actually was. His expression was firm but not unfriendly. He had been a giant of prewar politics in his state, but had strangely never developed much influence in the Confederacy. Toombs was well aware that this was something Hunter himself was determined to rectify.

Finally, there was Alexander Stephens, Vice President of the Confederate States. Alone among the guests, he was not smoking. Stephens was ridiculously small, as if an unknown disease had stopped his body from growing when he had been a teenager, yet allowed his skin and face to continue aging. Sensitive, shy and bookish, he was unlike Toombs in virtually every way. Nevertheless, he was the one man in the room that Toombs counted as a genuine friend. The two of them had been devoted to one another for decades, ever since they had met as young Georgia lawyers trying to make their way in the world.

The Texan, the Virginian, and the three Georgians were very different from one another, not only in personality but in politics. Before the war, Toombs and Stephens had been Whigs, while the other three had been Democrats. Wigfall, Brown and Toombs had been outspoken secessionists, while Stephens and Hunter had opposed secession until almost the last moment. The single thing which united them, which had brought these five men together this evening, was the fiery hatred they all shared toward Jefferson Davis.

Toombs took another sip of his brandy as he listened to Stephens talk about his most recent meeting with Davis. He had decided not to say anything at first, wanting to let the talk about Davis grow heated and indignant, as he knew it would in such company. Like a blacksmith, he would wait for the metal to grow red hot before striking with the hammer to shape it into its proper form. Then, he would move the conversation toward the topic he wanted, just as he had planned when he had first invited the men to his home many weeks before.

"He just stared at me across the desk, as if he was a law school professor and I was a first year student," Stephens was saying. "I spent half an hour trying to get him to discuss our concerns regarding Cuba, and he never said anything aside from general platitudes."

"At least you got to talk to him," Wigfall said in irritation. "He has not deigned to give me a personal interview for many years."

"The vice presidency may be an office of no influence, but it does convey a certain prestige. He can't just ignore me like he can ignore all of you." This comment brought bitter chuckles from the men around the table.

"What exactly did you tell him?" Hunter asked.

"I expressed to him the position you and I have discussed by letter and which, if I am not mistaken, is shared by all of us here at this table. Cuba must become a part of the Confederacy. If Spain is unwilling to sell it to us, it must be taken by force."

"And Davis did not give a proper response?" Wigfall asked.

"He simply said he would consider the matter. A few days later, I received a letter from the Secretary of State saying that more pressing issues require the government's attention at this time and that the Cuba question would be considered at some point in the future."

Brown scoffed. "Davis had Benjamin reply, did he? Typical of him to use that fat, little Jew as his errand boy. He could at least have had the courtesy to reply in person. Insults aside, though, how can Davis be so blind on the Cuba question? Even he can't be that stupid! The island is the first step in expanding the Confederacy to the south and it is already in rebellion against its Spanish overlords. If we do not act soon, the British or the French might beat us to the punch."

"Even the Yankees might intervene in Cuba," Hunter said. "What better way to impede our ambitions in Latin America than to invade and occupy the island, blocking our path to the south?"

Wigfall shook his head. "Davis does not keep the Senate properly informed about any of the diplomatic dealings of the administration. Not only are our concerns about Cuba dismissed with scorn, but we are told nothing about the proposed treaty with France."

"Rumors abound, though," Brown said. "From what I hear, the treaty would make the Confederacy little more than an appendage of France. I don't much fancy the idea of swearing a loyalty oath to Napoleon III."

"Some apparently do fancy it," Stephens said. "Benjamin and Slidell have clearly been working for a long time to place the Confederacy in France's pocket. One wonders how much money the emperor is paying them."

"A Jew like Benjamin will do anything at the slightest sniff of a dollar," Brown said sneeringly. "I wish we had passed Senator Foote's constitutional amendment banning all Jews from Richmond when he proposed it back in `62."

Toombs listened as the rest of the men talked. Stephens aside, they were not his friends. They were nothing more than political allies, and likely temporary ones at that. He did not consider them close to his equal in intellect or integrity. Had they not been necessary for his plans, he would never have invited them into his home. Still, given enough brandy and cigars, almost any company was tolerable. Toombs admitted to himself that he was enjoying the proceedings.

Stephens shook his head. "We fought the war to free ourselves from the control of the government in Washington, but I see little to suggest that our current government in Richmond is any better. We pay more taxes to Richmond now than we do to our own state governments. The very brandy and cigars being enjoyed at this table were subject to excise taxes levied by Richmond."

"Excise taxes are bad enough," Wigfall said. "But I see no sign the Davis administration is planning on reducing the so-called War Tax anytime soon. The war has been over for nearly two years, yet Southerners still have to pay direct income taxes to Richmond. It's intolerable. It must be stopped."

"I don't see how a direct tax on income can be constitutional," Brown said.

Stephens chuckled. "Why should Davis care? There is as yet no Supreme Court to tell him what is and is not constitutional. And even if there were, I am sure he would simply ignore its rulings."

Hunter now spoke. "Had there been a Supreme Court from the beginning, we never would have seen such travesties as the mass conscription, impressment of goods, and outrageous taxes we all saw during the war."

"Well, at least we shall soon be free of Davis," Stephens said, relief in his voice. "Even he cannot ignore the six year term limit set by the Constitution. A new chief executive shall be elected in November. By this time next year, we shall have a new man in the presidential mansion."

Stephens glanced at Toombs when he finished saying this. The comment had been prearranged. Toombs now began to put his plan in motion.

"This is all true enough," Toombs said. "No one shall be happier to say good riddance to Jefferson Davis than myself. But let me ask you gentlemen this. All of the newspapers say that Robert E. Lee is going to run for president. The public may laud him to the high heavens, but we all know he is little more than the president's puppy dog, ever willing to fetch the stick his master tosses for him. He will surely continue the policies of the Davis administration."

Toombs tried to restrain the heat he felt. He despised Robert E. Lee and everything the man represented. He detested the aristocratic pretensions of the Virginia patrician class from which Lee came. He hated West Point and the whole idea of a professional army officer corps. Furthermore, Toombs had always felt that Lee had failed to give him credit for the actions of his brigade at the Battle of Sharpsburg, when it saved the right flank of the army. Toombs had sufficient reasons for loathing Lee, but even if he hadn't, he would have hated him simply for his close relationship with Davis.

"General Lee turned President Lee?" Wigfall asked rhetorically. "I have to wonder if Lee would be any better than Davis."

"General Lee is a great man," Senator Hunter said, a slight sharpness to his voice. "I think Senator Toombs is being quite unfair."

"I do not mean to impugn the man or his character," Toombs said quickly. "I merely wish to voice my concern that, should Lee be our next president, he will continue the policies of the Davis administration."

There was silence around the table. Toombs wasn't surprised. He knew these men, he knew their moods, and he knew how to manipulate their emotions. He knew that the brandy would loosen them up in the right way. Toombs had let them get worked up with talk of the tyranny of Davis and then had had Stephens move the discussion towards the president's coming departure from the stage. At that moment, he knew he could play on their subconscious fears that their freedom from Davis might not be on the horizon after all.

"We would be in an even worse position," Brown said sourly. "Lee is much more popular with the people than Davis is. The only person who holds the same level of public esteem is Joseph Johnston."

Toombs nodded, for he fully agreed. The two Virginia generals, one having commanded the Army of Northern Virginia and the other the Army of Tennessee, were already being hailed as the two military titans who had secured Southern independence by their brilliant victories. However, while Lee was an associate of Davis, Johnston hated the president with almost the same fervor as did Toombs himself. For all his animus against Virginia aristocrats and West Pointers, that was something Toombs could appreciate.

"It is nearly spring," Brown said. "The election is only eight months away. If we are to have any hope of setting our new nation on its proper course, we must agree upon our own presidential candidate, yes?"

"Indeed," Toombs replied. "That is precisely why I invited all of you here tonight."

"I thought so," Brown said. "If Lee does run, who would make a better candidate against him than Johnston himself?"

"That was my first thought as well," Stephens said after a moment's thought. "His victories at Atlanta and Fairburn were decisive in winning the war. And he certainly shares our distaste for Jefferson Davis. The loathing between those two is legendary."

"If Lee runs, Johnston is the only man who could have a chance of victory against him," Wigfall replied.

Toombs looked carefully at the Texan. "Senator Wigfall, you and General Johnston are friends. Do you think he would do it?"

Wigfall took a long pull on his cigar and then took a sip of his brandy before replying. "I don't think so, frankly. He's never been all that political, aside from the fact that he hates Davis. He does not have any strong political positions."

"He doesn't need any political ideas of his own," Brown said with a chuckle. "We can provide him with all the political ideas he wants."

"Perhaps," Wigfall said. "But I cannot honestly say that he fully shares our views on slavery."

Toombs drew his head back, as if in surprise. "Surely Johnston is pro-slavery!"

"I don't think he has an opinion one way or the other on the question," Wigfall responded. "He owns no slaves. His wife harbors emancipationist views, I think. She once told my wife that there would never be slaves under the roof of the Johnston household."

There was a rustling of discomfort in the room. They had fought a vicious war and sacrificed hundreds of thousands of lives to free themselves from the threat of abolitionism. It was distressing to think that some Southerners, otherwise gallant and patriotic, were not as devoted to the cause as they were.

"Wasn't Johnston linked to Cleburne's devilish proposal to free slaves and enlist them as soldiers?" Hunter asked. "I seem to recall some mention of it in the papers during the summer of '64, between the Battle of Atlanta and the Battle of Fairburn."

"Johnston neither endorsed nor condemned Cleburne's proposal," Wigfall said. "He told me that he considered it a political matter and therefore not relevant to his role as commander of the Army of Tennessee."

"I don't like that at all," Brown replied. "We can't afford to have anyone who would waver on slavery. He should have condemned Cleburne's proposal outright and then cast that little Irish fool out of the army."

"We should at least explore the possibility of his being our candidate," Toombs said. He looked again at Wigfall. "Could you perhaps sound him out and ask whether he would commit to a firm defense of slavery? And the other issues of concern to us?"

Wigfall nodded. "I can certainly try. I'm headed to Richmond after I leave here anyway, and I know Johnston will be in the city sometime in the next few weeks. But I can make no promises. Johnston is a man with his own mind."

"Very well," Toombs said, satisfied.

Toombs knew that he was taking a calculated risk by proposing Johnston, but he figured it was an acceptable one. Stephens had told him the stories of Johnston's alleged emancipationist views and the tacit support he had given to Cleburne's memorandum. He was gambling that these would make Johnston unacceptable to his assembled allies. By pushing Johnston's name first, Toombs hoped to disguise his own ambitions from the others.

"You all seem convinced that General Lee intends to become a politician," Hunter said. "I know him better than any of you. Despite what the newspapers say, I am not at all sure he intends to enter the presidential race."

"Why wouldn't he?" Toombs asked.

Hunter chuckled. "Because I don't think he has any particular desire to hold political office. Certainly not the highest office in the land. I think he is content in retirement."

Toombs found Hunter's comment incomprehensible, almost laughable. How could any man decline the opportunity to become the leader of an entire nation? The ability to wield such power, to have men defer to you, to bend the actions of a whole country to your will. What man would not want such power?

He remembered an anecdote he had heard during his days as a member of the Demosthenian Literary Society, the debating society of the University of Georgia. Julius Caesar and his retinue passed through a small village of uncivilized savages. One of Caesar's officers had made a joke at the expense of the villagers, mocking them for their primitive ways. Caesar had reprimanded the man, saying that he would rather be the first man in the uncultured village than be the second man in Rome.

Toombs recalled the awful night in the spring of 1861 during the Montgomery Convention. The Southern states had formed a new government and were set to choose the provisional president the following morning. Robert Toombs had been the first name on the list of most state delegations, a testament to his political prominence and his long history of defending Southern rights. Jefferson Davis was spoken of with respect but was considered a serious contender only by the Mississippi delegation.

Confident of his coming success, Toombs had ventured down to the barroom of the hotel to gab with the other delegates and perhaps secure a few more supporters. He had proceeded to drink far too much whiskey. Within two hours, he had been slurring his words, mouthing incomprehensible statements, and generally making a fool of himself. By midnight, his drunken antics had been the talk of Montgomery. The next day, Jefferson Davis was selected by a wide margin to be the first President of the Confederate States.

Simply thinking about that humiliating memory made Toombs cringe, but it would soon be time to set all things right. His plans had been carefully laid. By the end of the evening, he intended for his associates around the table to agree that Toombs himself would be their candidate in the event that Johnston proved unacceptable.

"If Lee does not run, whom do you expect Davis to put forward?" Brown asked. "Surely he will seek some sort of chosen successor."

Hunter took a quick sip of brandy before replying. "Word in Richmond is that he will be pressing Breckinridge to seek the presidency."

"Breckinridge?" spat Brown. "Damned Kentuckian! If it hadn't been for him, the Yankees wouldn't have run off with all the thousands of slaves they stole from us during the war!"

"That's the truth, by God!" Toombs said. He looked at Stephens. "Is it not so, Aleck? You were at the Toronto Peace Conference with him. You know the facts."

Stephens shifted uncomfortably in his seat, frowning. "I have no wish to impugn the Secretary of War. He is a man I both admire and respect."

"But you have told me that Breckinridge counseled giving in to the Yankees on the question of the slaves freed under that damn so-called Emancipation Proclamation. The truth is the truth, isn't it?"

The vice president waited a moment before replying. "It was his position that we should let the Union have its way on that question, yes."

Wigfall now spoke. "Minister Miles, who was also a delegate to the convention, has told me that Breckinridge also refused to support his efforts to get back the slaves we recaptured from those devilish black regiments the Yankees raised."

Stephens nodded. "Yes, that's so."

Wigfall went on, his tone becoming more accusatory. "And did Breckinridge also refuse to support pushing the Yankees on a new fugitive slave law?"

"Again, true."

Toombs, from the experience of a friendship that had lasted decades, could tell from Stephens's expression and tone that he did not like the turn the discussion was taking. Toombs had anticipated this and did not enjoy putting his friend into a disagreeable position. Still, it had been necessary to achieve his objective, for Breckinridge had to be seen as being just as unacceptable to those around the table as Lee.

"What is it with Davis and these Kentuckians?" Brown asked. "Breckinridge is made Secretary of War. Morgan and Buckner are given important army commands. All those useless would-be senators and congressmen, when their positions were abolished, were given plum jobs as postmasters or customs collectors in places they had never even seen. Perhaps these rumors about the influence of the Orphan Society are more credible than I thought."

"Not only that," Wigfall said. "Breckinridge has been happy to sit back and allow Judah Benjamin to act as a shadow president behind the mask of Davis. Why should we think Breckinridge won't keep that damn string-pulling Jew in the Cabinet if he becomes president?"

Hunter repeatedly jabbed his finger into the air like an angry professor. "Breckinridge proved at the peace conference that he is willing to compromise on slavery. No man who does that is fit to serve as president of this confederation. If he turns out to be the candidate of the Davis faction, we must do everything in our power to make sure he is defeated."

"If Johnston is our candidate, he should have little trouble beating Breckinridge," Brown said, sounding as if he were trying to reassure himself.

"Perhaps so," Toombs replied. "But as Senator Wigfall has already said, we cannot be sure he is solid on the slavery issue."

"What of Wade Hampton?" Hunter asked. "If anyone is solid on slavery, it's Hampton. He's the biggest slave-owner in the Confederacy, by some accounts."

"Hampton would be ideal," Stephens said. "His military record as a cavalry commander under Lee is beyond reproach. And he is perfectly sound on the question of state's rights."

"Perhaps," Brown said. "But he has only just been elected Governor of South Carolina. I am not sure he is ready to move on from that office to the presidency quite so quickly."

The discussion went on for some time, as different names were proposed and debated. It was suggested that Kirby Smith might make a good candidate, considering his military record and his well-known distaste for Jefferson Davis. James Longstreet was also briefly considered, though no one knew the man's positions on political issues.

Toombs glanced around the room, trying to gauge everyone's thinking. Very soon, perhaps within the next few minutes, it would be time for Stephens to propose that Toombs himself might make a good candidate. Ever so humbly, he would decline at first, but Stephens would ask him to at least consider the possibility. One of the other three would hopefully suggest that it was a good idea and the pieces would fall into place, just as he and Stephens had planned.

They never got the chance. The next name suggested was Pierre Gustave Toutant Beauregard.

March 14, Evening
Spotswood Hotel, Richmond, Virginia

Major General John Hunt Morgan applauded heartily as Breckinridge came to the end of his speech. So did all the other men crowded into the ballroom of the Spotswood Hotel. It had been a good speech, Morgan thought wistfully, but then Breckinridge didn't make any other kind.

Morgan glanced around the room, which was with a few hundred members of the Virginia Chapter of the Orphan Society. He knew practically everyone and some of them were close friends. Several were men he had personally commanded during the war. All of them were drawn together by a common experience. As Kentucky Confederates, they were exiles from their own land trying to make their way in a new country that was not entirely their own.

Breckinridge descended from the raised speaker's platform and the master of ceremonies, a major who had served in the 6th Kentucky Infantry, took his place.

"General Morgan? Would you please join Secretary Breckinridge by the statue?"

Morgan took a quick sip of his wine and rose from his chair, glancing down for just a moment to make sure nothing had spilled on his uniform. It wouldn't do to look ridiculous in front of so many people. He was relieved that his duties at this meeting did not require him to do any public speaking, for he hated nothing as much as talking to large groups of people. It was far better to leave that sort of thing to Breckinridge.

The statue in question was about seven feet tall and covered with a white curtain. The purpose of the day's gathering was the public unveiling of the sculpture. It depicted General Benjamin Helm, the commander of the Orphan Brigade who had been mortally wounded at the Battle of Chickamauga in September of 1863. The men of the Orphan Society had raised the funds among themselves and commissioned a French sculptor to do the work.

Morgan and Breckinridge were performing their ceremonial roles because they had been elected Grand Commanders of the Orphan Society at its first meeting the previous year. The third Grand Commander, Simon Bolivar Buckner, had been unable to attend the meeting because of his military responsibilities in Tennessee.

Morgan and Breckinridge stood together beside the statue, careful not to obstruct the view of the assembled Orphans. At the word of the master of ceremonies, they tugged strongly and the curtain fell away. The great bronze statue of General Helm was revealed. There was a momentary hush and gasp among the crowd, followed moments later by rolling cheers and applause.

The figure held a sword in its left hand and was pointing forward as if towards the enemy with its right. Morgan was stunned. The statue was so lifelike that he half-expected it to begin moving and speaking. It looked exactly as he remembered Helm, the expression on its bronze face reflecting the fierce determination instantly recognized by all who had known him.

The two grand commanders stood for a moment beside the statue, applauding along with the crowd, before making their way back to their seats at the head of the room. As the applause died down, well-dressed slaves entered the ball room with platters of food and trays of wine glasses. Soon, the Orphan Society was deep into its dinner and a low hum of conversation filled the air.

"Amazing," Morgan said as his took his seat. "It looks just like him."

"I'm relieved," Breckinridge replied. "The statue cost a fair amount of money. I'm glad it turned out so well."

"Is it true that Abraham Lincoln sent a contribution?" Morgan asked.

"Yes, he did," Breckinridge said.

"Don't you think that's inappropriate?"

"Why should it be? Helm was his brother-in-law."

"I'm surprised the Society didn't return his contribution."

"Some wanted to, but I said no. Lincoln has as much a right as anybody else to contribute. The war's over."

Morgan's plate of fried chicken was good but nothing special. He wished he could have had beer or whiskey rather than wine, but wasn't about to complain. For the next half hour, he and Breckinridge exchanged stories about Helm and talked pleasantly with many of the Orphans who came up to the table to say hello.

During the war, nearly thirty thousand Kentuckians had served in the Confederate Army, fighting in battles all across the South. Kentucky itself had never seceded from the Union and the last Confederate troops had been driven out of Kentucky in late 1862. When the Treaty of Toronto had been signed in 1865, the state had been confirmed as Union territory. Having fought and suffered for the South, the Kentucky Confederates had found themselves faced with a terrible choice. They could return home and live under the government of the United States or they could remain in the South and make the Confederacy their new home. Most had chosen the latter course.

The Orphan Society had been created to give these men a foundation on which to build their new lives in the Confederacy. Morgan, Breckinridge, and Buckner had been happy to be a part of it and honored to be chosen as the Society's Grand Commanders. A large number of the Orphans had remained in the peacetime army. Others had settled in various parts of the South, particularly in Tennessee and Virginia, assisted in findings jobs and homes by the Society. Quite a few of those jobs were middle-level government positions. Breckinridge had worked hard to find employment for his fellow Orphans and some newspapers had cynically suggested he had abused his administrative power to help them.

Chapters of the Society now existed in every state and in most major cities. Monthly meetings were held and, it had been decided, a great annual gala would take place in a different city each year. The first had been held in Atlanta the previous October. The second was expected to be held in Richmond in September.

"Still nothing from Louisiana?" Morgan asked.

"No," Breckinridge replied. "The woods and swamps throughout the area surrounding the plantation have been thoroughly searched. Nothing has been found."

"I suppose it's up to me to run this darkie down, then."

"You're leaving tomorrow, yes?" Breckinridge asked.

Morgan nodded. "On the first train. I should arrive in Baton Rouge in four days, barring delays."

"Good. The force should be assembled by the time you arrive. Five hundred Louisiana militiamen, backed up by one hundred troopers from the 1st Kentucky Cavalry Regiment. Almost all of the Kentucky boys are men you led during the war. Some of them, I believe, were fellow inmates with you in the Ohio State Penitentiary."

Breckinridge said this with a warm grin. In the summer of 1863, while the Confederacy had been reeling from the defeats at Gettysburg and Vicksburg, Morgan had led a force of two thousand cavalrymen on an epic raid deep into the heart of the North. For two months, they had ridden through Indiana and Ohio, burning bridges, cutting telegraph wires, damaging railroads, and generally raising havoc. Never before or after had any Confederate force penetrated so far into Union territory. Forty thousand Union soldiers were sent after him, diverting Northern strength from the front lines. Although the raid had ended with the capture of Morgan and most of his men, it had been breathlessly followed by the newspapers of the Confederacy, which had been desperate for uplifting news.

Confined to the Ohio State Penitentiary, Morgan and a few others had intrepidly escaped by digging a tunnel from one of their cells into a courtyard and then climbing over the wall, using a rolled up sheet as a rope. He had then simply boarded a train to Kentucky, where sympathetic locals had helped him escape back into Confederate lines. The Southern public was enthralled by Morgan's exploits. When he had arrived in Richmond that summer, his place as one of the most glamorous heroes of the war had been secured.

"I still don't understand why six hundred men are necessary. Surely it should be little trouble to run down a few slave bandits."

Breckinridge shrugged. "Why take chances? Better to have too many men than not enough."

"I suppose that's true," Morgan replied.

"And you read the orders carefully?"

"John, how can you think I wouldn't read them carefully?" Morgan commented with a grin. Inwardly, he was slightly affronted, but he knew that Breckinridge was a careful man who always wanted to make sure he had taken care of every detail.

"I'm meaning that portion of your orders specifying that your role is to advise the militia, not command it. You can give orders to the Kentucky cavalry, but with the militiamen, you will simply have to persuade them to do what's best."

"Yes, I read that part. Most annoying. Can we not rectify that? Rewrite the orders to give me full authority?"

"Sorry, my friend. Politics, you see. We don't want anyone complaining that the president is using this incident as an excuse to increase Richmond's power over the states."

"I understand. I'm sure the militia officers will defer to my judgement anyway. I won't have to issue any actual orders. I'll ask the militia to patrol the back roads and protect the larger plantations, while my horsemen will sweep through the forests and swamps to find these slaves."

"It's not very good cavalry country, to say the least."

"I know, but we'll do our best. They're trained to fight dismounted, you know. Assuming that the bandits are surviving on food they're stealing from plantations, my plan will hopefully cut them off from their sources of subsistence and force them out of hiding. Then we'll simply gobble them up."

"The sooner the better," Breckinridge said. "These slave bandits are responsible for the deaths of nearly a dozen white men. While there has thankfully been no panic among the people, opponents of the President in Congress are beginning to criticize the government for lack of action."

"Toombs?" Morgan asked as he forked another piece of chicken into his mouth.

"Him and the rest of the usual crowd of malcontents."

"I'm no politician. I leave that stuff to you."

Breckinridge chuckled. "You'd never win an election in this country, John. Every husband of every woman who wrote you a love letter during the war would vote against you."

Morgan laughed. He was well aware of the awe in which he was held by the women of the South, who reveled in the stories of his daring raids and his gallantry towards women and children.

"Well, if all those men would vote again me, perhaps it's for the best that I have no political ambitions," Morgan said. He paused a moment. "Who is going to run for president, John? It's already March. The election is just eight months away."

"Your guess is as good as mine," Breckinridge answered. "There's still no political party structure in the Confederacy. Everything is in flux."

"I would assume it would be some military hero. The newspapers say it will be Lee."

Breckinridge shook his head. "No," he said emphatically. "Lee will not run for president or any other office. He had said so to me personally more than once and left no room for ambiguity."

"Is that so?" Morgan asked, interested.

"He talked to me once of how he felt his father's political activities had diminished his reputation and that he would have preferred that his father had rested on his military laurels. And frankly I think he just doesn't have the stomach for politics. He wants nothing more than to enjoy his retirement and write his big book about the history of the Army of Northern Virginia."

"Oh, he's writing his memoirs, is he?"

Breckinridge nodded. "Working on them feverishly, in fact. He has his old aide Walter Taylor rummaging through the War Department archives practically every day."

"Well, that should make for good reading when he finishes." Morgan took a sip of wine. "What of old Joe Johnston? Will he run?"

"I don't know," Breckinridge said. "He keeps his own counsel out at his headquarters in Nashville. He is coming to Richmond later this week, though."

"If not Lee or Johnston, then who?" Morgan pressed.

"Like I said, your guess is as good as mine."

Morgan momentarily weighed whether he should ask the next question. "Well, why not you?"

Breckinridge chuckled nervously. "I have no desire for the presidency, John."

"Why not? It seems to me that you're the perfect candidate. You had a great political career before secession. You made your mark as one of our best generals during the war. You're in the Cabinet now. I can't see any better person than you."

Morgan knew he wasn't a subtle man and lacked the ability to read people. Nevertheless, he thought he sensed a certain uneasiness in Breckinridge, as though he wished Morgan had not brought up this subject.

"My duties at Mechanic's Hall take up far too much of my time. I would have neither the time nor the energy to spare to conduct a national political campaign."

"Stuff like that has never stopped you before. What does the president think?"

"I don't know. I have not discussed it with him."

"Well, for what it's worth, I think you should run. If you do, you'll have my full support and the support of every other member of the Orphan Society."

"Thank you, John. But like I said, I have no desire for the presidency."

Morgan shrugged, sensing that the discussion was over. Around them, the dinner continued. Morgan and Breckinridge engaged in a conversation blessedly devoid of business or politics, speaking of their wives and children. Morgan's wife Mattie had recently given birth to a son, an event which had given him great joy. He and Breckinridge reminisced about the winter of 1862, when the Army of Tennessee had been encamped near Murfreesboro. Morgan had gotten married to Mattie that winter and Breckinridge had served as an usher at the wedding.

Around them, the sound of the party grew louder as more and more wine was consumed. Boisterous laughter started to make conversation difficult. The decorum which had characterized the gathering an hour earlier slowly gave way to revelry and merrymaking. For just a moment, Morgan was reminded of many happy evenings around the campfires of his bivouacs during the war.

One man, more in his cups than the others, clambered up onto his table and began clumsily singing. Within moments, he was joined by nearly every other man in the room.

Let others bow submissively
Beneath a tyrant's will!

36

We will give ourselves to freedom
And fight for freedom still!
We'll plant our glorious standard
On Kentucky's verdant shore!
And rescue from the tyrant
Our homes forevermore!

Morgan stood and joined in the singing enthusiastically, but he noticed that Breckinridge remained in his seat. The Secretary of War had a smile on his face, but declined to lend his voice to the chorus that filled the room.

Yes, we'll march, march, march!
To the music of the drum!
And soon we'll free our native state
And welcome you at home!

As the song came to an end, the room filled with cheers and applause. Morgan laughed heartily as he sat back down, happy to see that someone had refilled his wine glass in the meantime.

"I really wish they wouldn't sing that song," Breckinridge said.

"We sang it during the war," Morgan replied.

"I know, but the war is over. The Yankee newspapers always talk about this song whenever they print stories about the Orphan Society. They say it proves we still want to incorporate Kentucky into the Confederacy."

Morgan shrugged. "It's just a song. Doesn't mean anything."

"Yet more proof you'd never make it in politics, John."

"How's that?"

Breckinridge paused a moment before replying. "Everything means something."

March 17, Morning
Home of Judah Benjamin, Richmond, Virginia

It was Sunday and, as usual on that day of the week, Judah Benjamin was lonely. He sat silently in his study, a half empty cup of coffee that had long since become cold sitting on the small table beside his chair. Beneath it was a short stack of newspapers. He intended to read them before the end of the day, but there was no hurry. For the time being, he was diverting himself with a copy of *Tristram Shandy*.

Most of the rest of Richmond was at church, where he could not go. He was not an observant Jew. He ate ham on occasion and did not attend synagogue very often. There were a few synagogues to which he might have gone had he been so inclined, but he had always turned down repeated invitations. He lent his financial support to the various synagogues and assorted Jewish charities, of course. Yet he knew that he could never fully embrace his Jewishness without weakening his position with the rest of Richmond society.

On the other hand, he could never have embraced Christianity, even for appearances, as Prime Minister Benjamin Disraeli had done in Britain. To do so would be an admission that he cared about what the Richmond gossip-mongers thought about him, and that was an admission he was unwilling to make. He was who he was and he was not about to let the Christians dictate such things to him. Jewishness was part of Judah Benjamin, for better or for worse.

He sipped his coffee and, feeling that the novel was not going well, set it down and picked up one of the newspapers. As he started reading, there was a knock on the front door of the house and, moments later, he heard one of his slaves answer it. There was a muffled conversation which he could not hear through the doors and distance. Perhaps it was simply some delivery boy. If it were anything important, he would be told soon enough.

Benjamin was reading a story concerning tensions between Britain and Russia in Central Asia when a slave knocked softly and entered the room.

"Master? A message has arrived from your office."

The slave handed him the paper and, without a word, withdrew from the room. Benjamin unfolded the message and read it carefully. As he did so, he became increasingly excited. He checked the clock and then rose from his chair, calling for his valet to dress him and for another slave to prepare his hansom cab. A few minutes later, now properly attired with his hat and waistcoat, he stepped out onto the light of day and clambered into his carriage, quickly calling for the slave holding the reins to begin moving. Moments later, they were clattering down the Richmond streets.

"Where to, sir?" the slave asked.

"St. Paul's," he answered.

The sidewalks were filling with people, for the churches were starting to empty of worshippers. They would be on their way to their various luncheons or tea parties, in clear violation of the strictures of their religion. Because he made no pretense of being observant in his own faith, Benjamin felt no hypocrisy in disdaining the lack of faith in others.

The great Episcopal church soon hove into view. St. Paul's was where most of the elite of Richmond society choose to worship and Benjamin spotted several prominent men gathered in little conversational clusters on the sidewalk in front of the building. Chief among them, of course, was Jefferson Davis, who was speaking with Flora Stuart, the widow of the martyred Jeb Stuart. The beautiful woman still wore a black mourning dress and, if the gossip was to be believed, she intended to do so for the remainder of her life.

Benjamin ordered the coachman to pull to the side of the road and then stepped out onto the sidewalk. He leaned back against the coach, lighting a cigar and waiting for the president to notice him. It would have been rude to interrupt the conversation, especially as Davis had few opportunities for purely social pleasures. It made Benjamin happy to see a genuine smile on the president's face, which was a rare event.

Others noticed Benjamin and looked in his direction, but no one approached him. Some, he knew, did not want to speak to him because they simply disliked him. Others, he supposed, felt that it was improper to speak to a Jew having just left church. It was something to which he had long since grown accustomed.

The president finally did notice him and met his eye. Benjamin smiled, wordlessly telling him that there was no emergency and that he brought good news rather than bad. Davis turned and continued speaking to Mrs. Stuart for a few moments. Then, he politely excused himself and walked over to the Secretary of State.

"Good morning, Judah."

"And good morning to you, Mr. President." He glanced around. "Mrs. Davis?"

"At home with Willy, who is sick."

"Alas, I hope the little one feels better soon."

"Just a cold, I think. What brings you here?"

"I have news from Slidell. I thought you would want to know it as soon as possible."

"Good news, I hope?"

Benjamin smiled. "Quite, I am happy to say."

"Well, then. Shall we walk?" Davis gestured down the sidewalk and the two men began strolling. "What is it that Slidell says?"

"The telegram arrived late last night," Benjamin replied. Although the transatlantic telegraph had been operating now for more than a year, he still found it astounding that people in Washington and Richmond could communicate more or less instantaneously with people in London and Paris. It had once taken the fastest steamship more than a week to carry the latest news between Europe and North America. Now it took a matter of minutes to send the same information across a wire by means of electricity. To Benjamin, it was a testament to the fascinating modern age in which he lived.

"And?"

"Minister Slidell believes that we have a better chance of getting France to sign a treaty of friendship and alliance with the Confederacy now than at any time since the end of the war."

"Well, that is quite a strong statement," Davis said.

"Indeed."

Benjamin thought for a moment over the history of their new country's relations with the European powers. Since the ratification of the Treaty of Toronto, an alliance with either France or Britain had been one of the chief foreign policy goals of the Confederacy. If such an association could be forged, many were convinced, the United States would never dare engage in another war with the Confederacy. The South's security would be guaranteed.

By early 1866, it had become clear that Great Britain would never sign a military alliance with the Confederacy. Large segments of its population were steadfastly opposed to slavery, with abolitionist organizations flourishing in London and most of the industrial cities. Having already signed a trade agreement with the Confederacy as part of the deal that had given the South diplomatic recognition, the British saw little to gain from a closer connection and were unwilling to risk a domestic political backlash. Davis and Benjamin had soon abandoned any hope of an agreement with Her Majesty's Government.

France, however, had proven to be another matter. Unlike the men who governed Britain, Emperor Napoleon III did not have to pay much heed to public opinion and consequently had greater freedom of action. While there was abolitionist sentiment in France, it was not as strong as it was in Britain and the emperor himself reportedly had no qualms about the slavery question.

More importantly, France had a good deal to gain from an alliance with the Confederacy. Over the previous few years, Napoleon III had created what amounted to a French protectorate over Mexico, installing a Hapsburg princeling named Maximilian as a puppet emperor in Mexico City. The United States had strongly protested this violation of the Monroe Doctrine, but had been unable to do anything about it while distracted by the War for Southern Independence. The Confederates, for their part, were happy to have a friendly power just over the Rio Grande.

Although Maximilian had the support of the Catholic Church and much of the Mexican aristocracy, he was opposed by liberal republicans led by a politician named Benito Juarez. The republicans had been defeated in several battles in 1866 by a large French army. Yet the republican resistance persisted and Maximilian could not yet rest easy on his throne. Obviously, Confederate support could make the difference between success and failure in France's attempt to bring Mexico into its sphere of influence.

"Slidell has been working on this for years," Davis said. "What are the terms the emperor is proposing now?"

"Most are rather technical," Benjamin answered. "He wants to make sure that grain and beef from Texas are provided to the French army in Mexico and other such things. But the sticking point is that Napoleon wants a lower export duty on cotton and tobacco shipped to France than is placed on cotton and tobacco shipped to Britain."

"Trying to undercut the competition, is he?" Davis said. "I'll defer to Mr. Trenholm on questions of tariffs, but it seems to me that if France has to pay less for our cotton than the British do, it means that the French will be able to produce their textiles at a lower cost and therefore export them to other countries at a price that will be competitive with British products."

"It is clever," Benjamin said with an admiring grin. "The production techniques used by the French textile industry are not as advanced as those used by the British. All things being equal, British cloth is cheaper than French cloth and usually of higher quality. But if the French can get their cotton at a lower cost than the British, it changes the equation."

"The British will be very upset," Davis pointed out. "Not only would they dislike losing out to the French, but they will claim that this violates the trade treaty we have already signed with them."

"And they would be correct," Benjamin said.

"It may be worth it, though, if it gets us a treaty with France," Davis said.

"Trade with Britain, the workshop of the world, is of vastly more importance to us than trade with France. We risk losing a favorable position with them at our peril."

"What's more important? A military alliance or favorable trade?"

"An interesting question," Benjamin replied. He left it at that, for it was obvious that Davis believed the former to be more important than the latter. Benjamin himself was not so sure, but did not want to give voice to his opinion. He had learned how to work with Jefferson Davis through long experience and one of the most important lessons had been that the president could not stomach outright disagreement.

Davis glanced sideways towards him as they kept walking. Perhaps he sensed Benjamin's true feelings and, unwilling to violate their unspoken truce, had chosen not to inquire further. "In any event, if we cannot offer the French the tariff deal they are asking for, I suppose Napoleon will walk away from the deal, yes?"

"That's what Slidell thinks. But perhaps we can offer him something better."

"What is that?"

"Napoleon III has successfully placed Maximilian on the throne of Mexico. He can remain there only as long as he has French troops in the country. Despite the success he has achieved, there is growing resistance in France to the steady drain of French soldiers' lives. Given time, the Habsburg princeling can build up enough support to be able to raise an army of his own. Until then, however, the regime is propped up only by French bayonets."

Davis nodded thoughtfully. "Go on."

"Perhaps we can provide him with some Confederate bayonets."

Davis stopped walking and turned to face Benjamin. "Are you seriously suggesting that we dispatch troops of our own to aid the French scheme to colonize Mexico?"

"It's not as crazy an idea as it sounds, Mr. President. Thousands of our veterans returned home to destroyed farms or wrecked towns, having lost their livelihoods. For men currently lacking employment, service in Mexico would be an attractive prospect. Moreover, we can make this offer on the condition that these men be paid and supplied by France rather than us."

There was another consideration that Benjamin carefully left unsaid, for he did not wish to impugn the integrity of Confederate soldiers. History was filled with examples of underpaid, uncared-for veterans turning their wrath against the government for which they had fought. Classical history was full of such events and, indeed, it had nearly brought down America itself after the Revolutionary War. If the most disaffected soldiers could be encouraged to volunteer for service in Mexico, it would remove a potentially destabilizing element from the political equation. That, needless to say, would be very useful.

"The United States might react badly," Davis said.

"They'll be distracted by this Fenian business. The time is propitious."

"I am not sure the people would look kindly on sending their sons and husbands to fight in a foreign land for a foreign power."

"It would be strictly on a volunteer basis," Benjamin replied. "Nobody who doesn't want to go would be sent. Besides, there are lots of fighting men in this country who have no families. Wars produce soldiers who, for whatever reason, don't want to stop fighting when the shooting stops. Not sure why that is, but I suggest we turn it to our advantage."

"How many?"

"You'd have to ask Breckinridge how many could be sent. And we'd have to see how many the French want and how many they could properly supply. We'd have to allocate it among the states, of course. Perhaps the big states could each sent a regiment's worth, the smaller states a few companies. Nothing very big. Not like the vast armies we mobilized during the war."

Davis nodded, turned, and resumed walking. Benjamin followed. A few minutes of silence passed as the president mulled over what his Secretary of State had said.

"It's an interesting idea, Judah. We'll consider it at the next Cabinet meeting. There are several political factors to consider, naturally. We will be accused by some of kowtowing to France. Many are already upset with the fact that we are violating Jefferson's precept against entangling alliances."

"Jefferson never had to worry about a superior industrial power on his northern border," Benjamin observed. "We live in a different world. We need friends. Besides, what happens in Mexico impacts the Confederacy directly. What better way for us to gain influence in that quarter then to send men to fight there?"

"Perhaps," Davis said. "In any case, I expect that the next president will be the man who will have to deal with it, more than I."

Benjamin waited a moment before replying. "Lee still will not budge?"

"No. He's resisting me more strongly than he resisted Grant at Cold Harbor."

"Is it time to put our plan into effect, then?"

Davis's face took on a more thoughtful look. "Yes, I suppose it is."

CHAPTER TWO

Senator Charles Sumner, Republican of Massachusetts, was leaning back in his chair, his arms folded across his chest, an angry expression on his face. Below his mass of disheveled hair and broad forehead, his dark eyes glared across the aisle toward the Democrat who was currently holding the floor.

The year before, in a move that reflected the increasingly bitter partisan divide of the nation, the Senate had changed the chamber's seating arrangement so that the two parties sat on opposite sides of the center aisle. Sumner was happy with the new system, as he preferred to put as much physical distance as possible between himself and the Democrats. This was especially true of Senator James Bayard of Delaware.

"While I applaud the members of the peace delegation for securing the cession of the northern Virginia counties for the purposes of improving the security of Washington City, the brutal truth is that our capital will be very difficult to defend in the event of any future conflict with the Confederacy," Bayard was saying. "During the war, we turned our capital into the most heavily fortified city on Earth, yet the enemy came within a hairbreadth's of capturing it in the summer of 1864."

Sumner frowned and shifted uncomfortably in his seat. He exhaled in exasperation, having heard this sort of talk far too often over the past few months. Nothing Bayard was saying was unexpected, though it made the words no less disheartening.

Bayard went on. "No one in this august body wants to preserve peace between ourselves and the Confederacy more than I do. But facts are facts. The nearness of Confederate territory to this city creates an unacceptable situation. However unlikely the prospect might seem, and despite all the measures we might take in placing this city in a condition for proper defense, the possibility of a Confederate seizure of Washington City by a *coup de main* can never be entirely eliminated. Therefore, I state my intention to vote for the bill put forward by the distinguished senator from New Jersey, the Capital Relocation Bill. It is a bitter yet necessary step we must take to ensure the security of our nation."

Sumner pursed his lips and shook his head. The Capital Relocation Bill, which would transfer the government from Washington City to Philadelphia, had been the first item on the agenda when the Senate had convened two weeks earlier. Sumner had immediately become the floor leader of the opposition to it, but it had proven an unequal struggle. Most Democrats were supportive of it and, to Sumner's disgust, several Republicans were as well. Edgar Cowen, a Republican from Pennsylvania, was supporting the legislation to shore up his support in Philadelphia. Sumner knew that at least two other Republicans were solidly supporting the bill because they genuinely worried about the military threat of the Confederacy, with at least two more leaning towards voting in its favor.

For the past several days, Sumner had been cornering his Republican colleagues in the halls and cloakrooms, trying to secure a commitment from them to vote against the bill. In most cases, he had succeeded, but Cowen had refused. He had told Sumner that he was sure he would be defeated for reelection if he failed to support moving the capital to Philadelphia. Several other senators had been frustratingly reluctant to tell him what their final vote was going to be. He had glumly concluded that the bill probably had enough votes to pass, but he was determined to make one last effort to block it.

Bayard was still speaking. "The bill currently before the Senate only specifies that the capital shall be moved. Precisely where it shall be moved will be decided later. I, for one, believe we should move the seat of government of the United States of America from Washington City to Philadelphia. Our capital should be the city where the Declaration of Independence and the Constitution were created, whose streets echo with the memories of legendary patriots. It was the destiny of that great city from the moment it was founded."

Sumner chuckled bitterly. The idea that Bayard cared one whit for patriotism or the ideals of the founding generation amused him. As far as Sumner could see, neither Bayard nor any of his Democratic colleagues had any convictions at all, save the furtherance of their own power and influence.

Fifty men sat in the United States Senate. The 1866 mid-term elections had been indecisive, with neither party able to claim a clear victory. When the 40th Congress had been seated just a few days before, Sumner's party held a thin majority, with twenty-seven Republicans facing twenty-three Democrats in the Senate. By contrast, the Democrats had maintained a solid majority in the House of Representatives. A mile down Pennsylvania Avenue, President George McClellan sat in the White House, treating visiting senators and governors with a disdain worthy of an Oriental monarch. Aside from the Senate, the other bastion of Republican influence in Washington City was the Supreme Court. There, Chief Justice Edwin Stanton and four associate justices appointed by Abraham Lincoln held a majority.

Bayard continued to drone on. "The city of William Penn and Benjamin Franklin reflects the best of our great nation, our spirit of commercial enterprise, our devotion to the principles of liberty and good government. No man of good sense can give me a single reason why it should not again serve as our nation's capital."

Sumner had been waiting for the right moment to intervene. He had one last card to play in his effort to defeat the bill, and that was his own thunderous voice. The comment about a man of good sense was a perfect opening. If Sumner was going to scupper the insanity about moving the capital, he would have to do it now. There was still a chance, albeit a small one, that one of his trademark feats of rhetoric might sway the wavering Republican votes to against the bill.

With an intentional loudness, Sumner pushed his chair back from his desk, then rose to his feet. "Will the Senator yield for a question?" The deep sound of his voice filled the vast hall.

Bayard, momentarily taken aback, looked at Sumner curiously for a second and then smiled. "I yield to the distinguished senator from Massachusetts for a question."

"It is true that your son has recently been purchasing real estate in the city of Philadelphia?"

There was an uneasy rustling throughout the Senate Chamber. A low but loud mummer quickly became audible, amid a few snickers from the ladies watching from the visitor's gallery. A few of the young pages dashed out of the chamber, no doubt to alert men in the lobby that Sumner was on his feet and that there were sure to be fireworks.

Bayard was silent for several seconds, grimly staring at Sumner. "I am not privy to all of the business dealings of my son, nor do I see how they might be remotely relevant to a Senate debate over a serious question of national policy."

"I note that you decline to answer the question with a clear affirmative or negative," Sumner noted dryly, his booming voice echoing throughout the chamber. "Will the senator yield for another question?"

"By all means," Bayard responded with a smug grin.

"Have you and the other sponsors of this bill fully considered its financial cost? Relocating the Congress, the offices of the president and the executive branch departments, the Treasury?"

"We have," Bayard replied. "We would not have put the bill forward otherwise."

"The Smithsonian Institution?"

Bayard's eyebrows went up slightly. "I confess I had not thought of that, but I'm sure it would not be difficult to move to Philadelphia."

"And what of the enormous expense the United States has poured into building the capital city here for nearly three quarters of a century?" Sumner asked. "How much time, labor, and money was spent constructing the very building we stand in? Now that the Capitol Rotunda is finally completed after decades of work, you would have us vacate? What about the White House? This lovely city was carved out from a swamp and now is the home of thousands of people. You would have us simply cast all of this away?"

Bayard faltered momentarily, his expression befuddled. The silence went on for nearly half a minute, generating mutterings throughout the chamber and light chuckling from the Republican seats.

"Senator, when the United States lost the war, it marked an epochal moment in our history," Bayard finally replied. "I support this bill not only for reasons of security, in that I do not think our national capital should be located in such a vulnerable position close to a potentially hostile neighbor, but because I think it would mark a decisive break with our unpleasant recent past and encourage us to focus on the future."

"I believe that the recent past has given our nation some unfinished business," Sumner replied. This statement caused another wave of uneasy muttering throughout the chamber.

"Perhaps the distinguished senator from Massachusetts could enlighten us as to the nature of this unfinished business he speaks of?"

"I shall certainly attempt to do so, though I am skeptical as to whether the distinguished senator from Delaware shall understand me." There was laughter on the Republican side of the aisle. "Simply put, moving the capital away from Washington City shall be an abject admission that the result of the recent war was definitive. I do not believe that it was, nor do I believe that we should act as though it was."

"The senator from Massachusetts will forgive me, and will forgive almost every other member of this body, for believing that the result of the war was quite definitive. That the Confederacy is an independent nation is now an established fact. The ink is long since dry on the Treaty of Toronto, which, I may remind you, was approved by the very committee over which you have presided for some years."

Sumner's mouth warped into an angry frown. Being reminded of the lowest moment in his political career stung badly. But what choice had there been that horrible summer of 1865? Had he not agreed to allow the treaty out of the Foreign Relations Committee, President McClellan would have repudiated the Emancipation Proclamation, thus condemning hundreds of thousands of freed slaves to bondage once again. Moreover, the people had been demanding peace at any price, sickened by four years of a bloody war they saw no prospect of winning.

For all that, Sumner would never forget the moment the Committee on Foreign Relations had voted to send the treaty to the full Senate, knowing full well that it would be ratified. It had been the darkest moment of his life, save perhaps the day in 1856 when he had been beaten nearly to death by Congressman Preston Brooks on the floor of the Senate. With a great effort of will, he prevented the memory of that day from sweeping through his mind.

Sumner glared across the chamber at Bayard, who was a perfect example of the kind of doughface Democrat he so detested. "Fighting between Britain and France lasted for more than a century between the 1680s and the final defeat of Napoleon in 1815," Sumner said carefully. "This long conflict was often interrupted by brief periods of peace marked by treaties. Why should we expect our conflict with the South to be any different?" He paused for just a moment, allowing a rustle of anticipation to build in the chamber. "For we are still in conflict with the South! Let there be no mistake! The treaty notwithstanding, we are and forever will be in conflict with the South so long as the detestable institution of slavery remains!"

Bayard turned to the rostrum. "Mr. President, I still hold the floor, do I not?"

The President Pro Tempore, Senator Daniel Clark of New Hampshire, nodded. "The senator from Delaware still holds the floor."

"That being so, I move for cloture."

There was a sudden hush and a quick sense of rising anticipation, as there always was before a vote on an important bill. Bayard, sensing that he could not

46

compete with Sumner in debate, had been smart enough to use the Senate procedures to simply cut him off. Clark called for a voice vote, but the yeas and nays sounded roughly equal and a motion was quickly passed to hold a roll call vote. In alphabetical order, the name of each senator was read out by the clerk, followed by that person calling out his vote to be recorded.

Sumner kept a running tally of the votes in his head and it briefly appeared as thought the outcome might go either way. By the time his name was reached and he called out his vote against the bill, however, it was obvious that it was going to pass. In the end, with all but one Democrat voting for the bill and five Republicans also in favor, it was approved by a margin of twenty-seven to twenty-three.

He sank back into his chair, defeated and dispirited. The House would pass the bill easily and McClellan would sign it without a moment's hesitation. Under its provisions, the government would shift from Washington City to Philadelphia over the course of the next three years. It would be yet another humiliating acknowledgment that the Confederacy was a permanent entity, rather than the ungodly but temporary aberration Sumner felt it to be.

He exhaled sharply. It was more than a year and a half until the 1868 elections. Sumner wondered how much damage McClellan and the Democrats could do before then. His friends in England, of whom he had many, were writing him regular letters detailing how respect for the United States had dropped sharply in Parliament and among the elite of British society. There seemed to be no effort underway to hinder the warming relationship between the Confederacy and France. Sumner was the chair of the Senate Foreign Relations Committee, yet McClellan had not asked his advice or opinion on a single matter since he had taken office. The rising tensions with the British Empire on account of the Fenian madness were deeply distressing to Sumner, but he felt powerless to do anything about it. As far as Sumner could see, President McClellan was as comfortable with the existence of the Confederacy as any ordinary townsperson would be with a new neighbor.

Sumner had suffered his first defeat in the new congressional session, and it was a bitter one. The thin majority the Republicans enjoyed in the Senate would matter for little if the Democrats could remain united and peel off a few moderate Republicans each time there was an important vote. The disarray within the Republican Party weighed on Sumner's mind. It might, indeed, sound the death knell of the republic.

He did not want to be in Washington City when McClellan signed the legislation. Instead, he would go back to Boston to rest, gather his strength, and consult with his political allies. If any important business came before the Senate in the meantime, he could rush back to deal with in. For now, though, Sumner was going home.

March 23, Evening
McFadden Ranch, West of Waco, Texas

The stony ground was covered with scrub and prickly pears, crawling with spiders and the occasional scorpion. Scattered about were Spanish oaks of various sizes, some seemingly growing sideways in a haphazard fashion. Among the sparse vegetation, a number of cows and goats roamed freely, chomping on the available grass, seemingly without a care in the world. On top of a slowly rising elevation sat the ranch house, with a wispy pillar of smoke rising from the chimney.

Half a mile south of the ranch house, James McFadden stood on an outcropping of limestone, carefully raising his pistol. There was an uninvited guest at the ranch that evening, in the form of an unusually large rattlesnake. It was the fifth he had had to deal with that week and McFadden was becoming heartily sick of the reptilian intruders.

The pistol was a Navy Colt revolver that had been given to him when, much to his surprise and reluctance, he had been promoted from sergeant to lieutenant in the Confederate Army in the wake of the Battle of Atlanta. He had made himself famous that day by capturing General George Thomas, commander of the Army of the Cumberland. No other soldier on either side of the conflict could claim to have taken prisoner the commander of the opposing army. McFadden himself didn't think much of this accomplishment, as it had been nothing more than good fortune and not due to any skill or daring on his part. Still, it had set in motion a chain of events which had changed his life and brought him to the happy place he now inhabited.

Carefully, silently, he pulled back the hammer on the revolver. As if sensing danger, the snake began loudly shaking its rattle, ringing out its customarily disconcerting noise. McFadden paid no mind. He had encountered innumerable rattlesnakes in his life and this one was going to be no different. He calmly squeezed the trigger of his Navy Colt and, with a flash and a bang, the head of the snake was blown cleanly off.

For just an instant, the acrid smell of gunpowder brought him back to the war. From the confused fight at Valverde in New Mexico in the late winter of 1862 to the bloody battles around Atlanta in the summer and fall of 1864, James McFadden had fought in more engagements than he cared to remember. He had carried many scars home from the war, not all of them physical. Yet, against all odds, he had made it home, which was more than could be said for many of his comrades in the 7th Texas Infantry.

He didn't bother with the reptile's carcass, as some bird would feast on it soon enough. The rattlesnake dealt with, McFadden holstered his pistol and glanced around at what remained to be done. He had been spending the afternoon trying to push the line of cacti farther from the ranch house, which required laborious and mind-numbing chopping of the plants from the root. He had more than a few needles in his hands, which was annoying but unavoidable. After several hours of hard work, he had succeeded in clearing only a few dozen square yards. It was frustrating to have worked so hard for so long with so little to show for it. He began thinking that his wife was correct and that he was wasting his time trying to clear this section.

He decided to head back to the house. Glancing at the sun, he could tell it was already late afternoon. Annie and Thad would be expecting him back soon. Hoisting his shovel and axe over his shoulder, he began the walk back. He took his time, sometimes stumbling over the rocky ground, watching as the shadows cast by the oaks gradually lengthened over the ranch.

McFadden loved his ranch. It had been built by his father, a Presbyterian minister who had come across the Atlantic from Scotland and settled in the area before the war. McFadden's father was buried there, as were his mother and two sisters, all of whom had died under a hail of Comanche arrows while McFadden had been off fighting in New Mexico. When he had returned from the war, his new wife Annie by his side, he had resolved to make the ranch work. He would not walk away from ground that contained the blood of his family.

It was not easy, for sure. Indeed, it had begun life as a farm rather than a ranch. But the hard soil of Texas west of the Balcones Escarpment made it very difficult to grow much in the way of crops. After a disastrous grain harvest the first year, McFadden had changed tack and purchased large numbers of cows and goats, who now wandered about the ranch at will, chewing the cud in blissful ignorance of their eventual fate. He was still not completely resigned to failure at farming, but ranching thus far seemed far more profitable.

McFadden was lucky, for he could afford to fail from time to time. His wife's father, who had died during the Union bombardment of Atlanta during Grant's attempt to capture the city, had been one of the richest men in Georgia. Annie had been his only child. It was not widely known among their neighbors, but the McFadden family was wealthy. They remained on the edge of the Texas frontier by choice rather than need.

He did not show off their money, partly out of genuine modesty and partly out of fear that people would try to harass or blackmail him. He could have purchased dozens of slaves to work his ranch for him, but though he employed some hired hands, he preferred doing as much of the work as possible himself. During his service in the army, he had seen more than a few fat and lazy plantation owners relaxing on their porches while slaves had labored on their behalf. McFadden had no liking for such men, especially as so many of them had avoided military service.

As he approached the ranch house, McFadden saw a familiar brown and white horse tied up out front. A smile crossed his face and he increased his stride, for Major James Collett had come to visit. A few minutes later, he walked through the front door.

The scene that greeted him warmed his heart. Annie was bent over the wood stove, making a beef and vegetable stew. Collett, his good friend and former commanding officer, was happily bouncing Thad on his knee, to the clear delight of both. It was a picture of contentment.

"Papa!" Thad squealed as McFadden walked through the door. Collett put the sixteen-month-old boy down and the boy clumsily tried to walk towards McFadden, only to fall to the ground. Rather than cry in frustration, he pulled himself up again and, holding his hands over his head and smiling broadly, walked the few yards to the door.

"Hello, you little devil!" McFadden said as he hoisted him up and kissed him on both cheeks. "I missed you today!"

"Papa!" Thad said again. It was, thus far, the limit of his vocabulary.

McFadden smiled at Collett. "A nice surprise to see you, James."

"It's always a pleasure to stop by, Jimmy," Collett responded. As they shared the same first name, an unspoken agreement had arisen between them as to what they called each other. It had taken some time for McFadden to stop referring to Collett by his rank.

"There's more than enough stew," Annie said. "I was about to offer Major Collett some of your apple cider."

"As long as you pour some for me, my dear," McFadden said as he set Thad down on the floor. He walked over to the table and firmly clasped Collett's hand. "It's good to see you, old friend."

The next hour passed quite pleasantly. The two men drained their ciders and refilled them a few times while they recounted stories of the war and anecdotes about former comrades. As the former commanding officer of the 7th Texas Infantry, Collett was unofficially in charge of keeping tabs on all the veterans, who were scattered across Texas. A great many of them, like McFadden and Collett, had settled along the frontier west of Waco. To pay its soldiers, the state of Texas had offered land grants on the frontier in lieu of hard currency. This also had the added benefit of settling the frontier with veteran fighting men, who might be called upon to serve in the militia in the event of more trouble with the Comanches. In addition to men from their regiment, soldiers from quite a few other Texas units had also settled in the area.

When McFadden had joined the 7th Texas in the spring of 1863, having served in other regiments during the fighting in New Mexico and Arkansas, it had perhaps three hundred men. But after fighting in the bloody battles at Raymond, Chickamauga, Missionary Ridge, and in the long retreat through Georgia towards Atlanta, the unit had been reduced to only about one hundred troops. It had fought gallantly in the Battle of Atlanta, only to be all but destroyed in the disastrous Battle of East Point, where dozens of men had been captured by the Yankees. Among them had been Collett. The few survivors had been led by McFadden himself after that. Such shared dangers and adventures formed close and unbreakable bonds between men.

"Is the beef stew good, darling?" Annie asked, concern in her voice.

"Quite good, dear," McFadden answered. Annie's look of concern relaxed into a smile.

He wasn't lying. Having grown up in an affluent Atlanta home, she had not learned how to prepare food, which had always been done for her by slaves. When they had arrived on the Texas frontier almost two years earlier, McFadden had worried about how she would adjust to such a dramatic change in her circumstances. His admiration for her had risen with every passing day, as she steadily evolved from the pampered Southern belle into a tough frontier wife. Just a month earlier, for the first time, she had killed a coyote with a shotgun.

Dinner was finished and McFadden and Collett switched from cider to whiskey. He noticed Collett's smile fade and his expression became more serious.

"Something wrong, James?"

Collett pursed his lips and nodded. "Truth be told, there is a matter of concern I wanted to discuss with you. Do you remember Alton Williams?"

McFadden thought for a second. "Strange-looking private with long gray hair, right? Got himself killed at Chickamauga?"

"That's the one."

"What about him?" McFadden couldn't fathom why Collett would be concerned about a man who had been dead for years.

"Not about him. It's about his widow, Mary."

McFadden grunted. He probably hadn't thought about Williams since his death and hadn't even known he had been married. "What about her?"

"The state gave her a land grant and she tried to start a farm with her little boy. He's ten or so, I think. But now the county has seized the farm for unpaid taxes. It's going on the auction block in Waco in two weeks."

"Judge Roden's doing?"

"Probably."

McFadden sneered. "Yes, well, I knew Judge Roden was a bloated jackass who'd do anything for a dime. But I didn't think that even he would sink so slow as to throw a war widow and her child off their farm."

Judge Lucius Roden, head of the Commissioners Court of the recently renamed Granbury County, was not a man much loved by his constituents. While most men of the county had been off fighting during the war, Roden had remained behind in Waco. He always maintained that his command of the local Home Guard had constituted military service, though it had done little more than confiscate livestock from local ranchers and then sell it to the army at an inflated price. Rumor had it that Roden had extorted money from locals by threatening to denounce them as Unionist sympathizers.

"He is a brute of a man," Annie spat. "I feel myself grow nauseous whenever I have to look at him."

"You're not the only one, Annie," Collett replied.

"Can anything be done for the Widow Williams?" she asked.

"That's why I came, though I hesitate to ask."

"Please, go ahead," McFadden said.

"You know I would never ask for money for myself. Times are tough, but I am not in any danger of being thrown off my land. The Widow Williams, on the other hand, is staring that possibility in the face."

McFadden nodded and gestured for Collett to continue.

"I've gotten together with some of the other boys from the 7th Texas and some fellows from the other regiments, too. We've decided to pool our resources to buy the farm when it's auctioned. Then, we can just give it back to the Widow Williams."

"Yes, well, you can count me in as well. I can't say for how much, but I shall certainly contribute."

Collett was one of the few men who knew how much money the McFaddens had to spare. The fortune of Annie's father had been quite large, though much had already been spent. A good deal had been distributed to the men once employed at the Turnbow iron foundry in Atlanta, which had been destroyed by the Union bombardment, to help them reestablish themselves. McFadden had also used a good portion of it on the ranch, especially in the early days when so much had needed to be done simply to get the place going again. McFadden was one of the wealthiest men in this part of Texas, but scarcely a man was aware of this.

The only indulgence that McFadden had allowed himself with the Turnbow money was the purchase of a respectable library. Slightly over three hundred volumes, the collection of books largely consisted of history, biography, and translations of Greek and Roman classics. It also contained many volumes of poetry, which he and Annie enjoyed reading to one another by candlelight after Thad had finally fallen asleep. It was a library that McFadden thought would have made both Robert Turnbow and his own father proud.

Collett went on. "I don't want you to give any more than you're comfortable with, Jimmy. I know you don't like to throw your money around."

"That's the least of it," McFadden replied. "I don't want Judge Roden getting wind of it. If he does, he'll try to find a way to get his hands on it." When he finished speaking these words, Annie looked over at him with concern on her face.

"That's the truth, by God," Collett said. "But if you could stand up to the Yankees, Jimmy, then a stupid, fat rascal like Lucius Roden surely won't be any trouble."

March 25, Night
Tuilieries Palace, Paris, France

The grand hall of the Tuilieries Palace was illuminated and decorated on a scale beyond anything anyone could remember. Innumerable gas lights and polished oil lamps cast a warm yellow glow that cascaded off the crystal chandeliers hanging from the ceiling and the enormous gold-rimmed mirrors that lined the walls. A full string orchestra filled the air with lovely music, the latest from the increasingly popular Camille Saints-Saens. All over, women in elegant evening gowns and men wearing fine suits or elaborate military uniforms moved gracefully across the floor, talking, laughing and sipping champagne.

Into the hall stepped John Slidell, Minister of the Confederate States of America to the court of Napoleon III, Emperor of the French. Old and frail, Slidell walked unsteadily, his daughter and his son-in-law supporting him on either side. His head, to which a few wisps of white hair still clung, appeared attached directly to the shoulders, as if the neck had been omitted from his body. His smile conveyed a cunning confidence, as if he were master of the world and tremendously amused by it.

Eyes turned to Slidell and his two companions when they entered the hall. This did not surprise the Confederate diplomat at all. His daughter Marguerite was considered one of the most striking and exquisite women in all of Paris. Her arrival in the city in 1862 had sent shockwaves through the salons of the city. His son-in-law, Frederick Emile Baron d'Erlanger, was one of the leading bankers in Europe. Despite holding hereditary noble titles from both Portugal and Austria, his reputation rested almost entirely on his immense wealth. Slidell was entering the reception with the embodiment of Beauty on one side and the embodiment of Money on the other.

"The emperor is putting on quite a show this evening," d'Erlanger said. "I don't think I've ever seen the Tuilieries done up so."

"It's only to be expected, darling," Marguerite replied. "It is not every day that the Emperor of the French welcomes the Czar of Russia to Paris."

Slidell chucked. "If I am not mistaken, the last Russian czar to visit Paris was Alexander I in 1814. And he did it at the head of an army of a hundred thousand men."

"I do not think he received the same welcome that his nephew is receiving tonight," d'Erlanger said.

The three of them laughed lightly as they took proffered flutes of champagne from the tray of a servant. Slidell sipped his and decided it was quite good. He had become a fair connoisseur of French wines since he had arrived in the country. His tastes had certainly evolved from what they had been in America, when he had drunk strong bourbon and mint juleps with the men of the South. In their drinking, as in so many other ways, the French simply knew how to live better than Americans.

For a moment, Slidell reflected on his strange place in the world. He wasn't even a native Southerner, having been born in New York. But he had settled in New Orleans, married into the Creole aristocracy, and gradually become more Louisianan than the Louisianans. His adopted state had sent him to Congress, where he had become a fierce defender of slavery and state's rights. Appointed ambassador to Mexico by President Polk in the 1840s, Slidell had played a significant role in sparking the Mexican War. Throughout the 1850s, he had represented Louisiana in the Senate. When secession came in 1861, the newly established Confederacy had named Slidell as its envoy to France on account of his diplomatic experience and his knowledge of the French language and culture.

Slidell had now spent half a decade in Paris. As the New Yorker had become a Louisianan, the Louisianan had become a Parisian. He had been seduced by the city's food and wine, its art, its music, its architecture, and, above all, its people. He did not intend to return to the Confederacy. He was in his mid-seventies, ailing and not expecting to live many more years. When his time came, he hoped and expected to be buried among the people of Paris.

Still, Slidell never forgot that he was a servant of the Confederacy. He had played a vital role in building support for the Southern cause in France during the war. His relationship with Napoleon III had developed into a respectful friendship. In helping to secure the independence of the Confederacy, Slidell felt he had done his duty for the South. His reward, he felt, should be to live out his years amid the delights of the most wonderful city in the world.

There remained one task to be done. All Slidell needed to do in order to finish his work was to secure a full treaty of friendship and alliance between France and the Confederacy. The protracted and complicated negotiations had now been going on for more than a year and he was finally seeing some real progress. When the treaty was signed and ratified, the Confederacy would be protected from any future Northern aggression. Slidell could then retire in peace.

"Would you two excuse me for a moment?" d'Erlanger said. "I think I see Alphonse Rothschild over there. I'd like to speak to him about these rumors that the Brazilian bond issue will be delayed."

"Very well, my son," Slidell said with a smile. "If you don't mind, tell him I am still waiting to hear whether his bank intends to purchase shares in the Memphis and Charleston Railroad."

"I shall do so, Father." D'Erlanger hurried off, vanishing into the crowd.

"I do wish my husband would learn to separate work from play," Marguerite said. "Galas such as this are meant to be enjoyed."

"He does enjoy them, my dear," Slidell responded. "And for men such as he and I, work never truly ceases."

This last point was brought home when Slidell noticed two men in conversation just a few steps away. One was a Frenchman he didn't recognize. The other was Montgomery Blair, the United States Minister to France. From a powerful Maryland family that simultaneously owned slaves and supported abolitionism, Blair had served as Postmaster General during Lincoln's administration. President McClellan had appointed him to his post in Paris in an effort to woo conservative Republicans over to the Democratic administration.

Blair frowned as Slidell and Marguerite approached. The Confederate found this amusing but not unexpected and now relished the opportunity to mix business with pleasure.

"Good evening, Minister Blair," Slidell said with a warm smile.

Blair stiffly nodded. "And you, Mr. Slidell." The Union diplomat had never addressed his Confederate counterpart by his official title. A lesser man would have been offended by the snub and Slidell knew Jefferson Davis would have been outraged had he known about it. Far better, the Louisiana man thought, to simply treat the insult as a compliment.

"You've met my daughter, the Baroness d'Erlanger?"

Blair's eyes flitted rapidly from Marguerite's head to her feet, unable to keep from focusing on her breasts for a fraction of a second. He awkwardly kissed her extended hand. Inwardly, Slidell chuckled. Despite having been in Paris for more than a year, Blair had yet to master French court etiquette.

"I read your pamphlet on the proposed international postal union," Slidell said. "If such a conference can be organized, the Confederate States will certainly send delegates."

"Oh?" Blair said. "Well, I suppose they would be welcome."

"You suppose? Why wouldn't they be welcome?"

"Of course, of course," Blair stammered uncomfortably. "You would be as welcome to participate as any other country."

"I am glad to hear you refer to the Confederacy as a country, Minister. I sometimes wonder if you recall that we are now an independent state."

Blair's expression hardened. "I do not like having to do so," he said firmly. "My family fought as hard as possible to strangle the Confederacy in its cradle. But history was against us."

"Or perhaps the will of the Lord was done," Slidell said. He had no particular use for religion himself, but he enjoyed employing it to needle the Yankees. Before Blair had a chance to respond, Slidell spoke again. "Please let me know if there is anything I can do to help bring about the conference. I believe your intentions very worthy and the Confederacy would benefit from an international postal union as much as any other country."

Blair nodded. "I will do so, sir."

Slidell smiled and he and Marguerite moved on. As they glided across the hall floor, Slidell observed all that was taking place around him. He noticed that the Prussian and Austrian ambassadors were studiously avoiding one another. Their two nations had fought a bitter war the previous year, resulting in high casualties in only a few weeks. Napoleon III, his ego boosted by the success he was having in Mexico, had mobilized the French Army to support the Austrians, forcing the Prussians to back down before they had won a decisive victory. More through luck than anything else, France had come out of the crisis with its influence augmented, while Prussia had been humiliated and Austria was now looked upon as beholden to France.

Slidell spoke with both men, making polite chit-chat and allowing them to ogle his daughter. During the brief conversations, Slidell was able to drop hints to the diplomats that their respective nations should not delay in appointing consuls to Richmond and might consider signing trade agreements with the Confederacy. His purposes accomplished, Slidell moved on.

Slidell had a pleasant ten minute conversation with the envoy from the Empire of Brazil. The two nations enjoyed good relations, as they were the only two significant nations that still continued the institution of slavery. Despite being competitors in international trade, each vying for maximum market share in cotton, sugar and tobacco, Brazil and the Confederacy saw one another as kindred spirits and natural friends.

D'Erlanger rejoined Slidell and Marguerite.

"Were you successful?" Slidell asked.

"I was, father," the banker replied. "He wanted me to tell you he has not forgotten about the railroad shares."

Slidell smiled. "Very good. The more European money going into our railroads, the better."

"Some disagree," d'Erlanger pointed out. "I read in the newspapers you send me that some members of Congress are proposing legislation limiting the amount of foreign investment in railroads. They say that it will give the foreigners too much influence."

"Wigfall and his friends, no doubt," Slidell said. "Would they rather have no railroads at all? Because that would be the result of such a law."

"Father, there is the Marquis de La Valette," whispered Marguerite.

"Ah, yes," Slidell said, steeling himself for the evening's most important piece of business. La Valette was the French Foreign Minister. Slidell considered him little more than the emperor's ear and mouthpiece, who made no significant policy decisions on his own. Still, he was useful as an indirect means for Slidell to communicate with the emperor.

"Minister Slidell," La Valette said pleasantly as the trio approached. "And Baron and Baroness d'Erlanger! I am so pleased to see you!"

"Would we miss an opportunity to see two emperors at once?" Slidell asked.

"It would have been three had Emperor Franz Joseph arrived on time," La Valette said with a slight frown. "So many rulers are coming from across Europe to attend the international exposition that we may have to start putting them up in hotel rooms, as we have run out of palaces!"

"Heaven forbid," d'Erlanger said with a smile.

"Why is Queen Victoria not coming?" Marguerite asked.

"I am not sure," La Valette replied. "There are many British exhibitors, obviously. But she declined our invitation without comment."

D'Erlanger took his wife's arm. "If you gentlemen will excuse us, we want to pay our respects to the Russian ambassador." The two of them glided away, leaving Slidell and La Valette alone.

"Might I have a few minutes of your time, My Lord?"

"Of course, Minister."

"I was hoping we might discuss the treaty for a few minutes."

"Business never ceases, does it?"

"Not for men such as us. And if business can be conducted in the midst of finery and decoration, so much the better."

"Very well. What is it you wish to discuss about it?"

Slidell nodded his head towards the north wall and the two men quietly strode in that direction. Along the way, both men took the opportunity to obtain new champagne flutes. Once they were out of earshot, Slidell began.

"I have been in communication with President Davis and the Cabinet since I received your last letter. They are gratified that the emperor appears more willing to conclude the treaty now than he did when we last discussed it a few months ago."

"You should not have been surprised. With the concessions you have offered on export tariffs, we would have been foolish not to reconsider."

"The tariffs are in place only as a revenue source," Slidell said. "In an ideal world, there would be free and unrestrained trade between our two nations. Alas, having accumulated such a heavy debt load from our war with the Yankees, we are obliged to find income wherever we can."

"But why are you willing to risk losing revenue you need in order to obtain our agreement on this treaty? Lowering the tariff to the same level that the British pay will cost you some of that revenue, clearly."

"We are more interested in obtaining an official pledge that France will provide direct aid to the Confederacy in the event of aggression on the part of the United States."

"I know this. I must again emphasize that this particular clause will apply only to a conflict between you and the United States, not any other nation. You must not think you can put more pressure on Spain to cede Cuba to you because we are willing to enter into this treaty with you. We shall not aid you if the Cuban question leads to war between the Confederacy and Spain."

"That is acceptable. We have no intention of going to war with Spain."

What Slidell said was true in a technical sense. Deeply in debt, the Confederacy was in no condition to enter into a conflict with a European power even were it inclined to do so. Still only enjoying its third year of peace after a devastating war, the people were in no mood to fight against anyone. But Slidell knew that a new president would take office in a year's time and that there were powerful factions determined to annex Cuba to the Confederacy, even if doing so required the use of force.

Slidell went on, speaking very carefully now. "On the matter of lost revenue due to abolishing our export duties, it would be very helpful if the French government extended a loan to the Confederate government to help us meet our obligations."

"You want money?" La Valette asked, his voice tinged with irritation.

"Only a loan to allow our government to adjust to the lost revenue," Slidell said quickly. "It would be a small price for France to pay if it gave you access to our cotton, tobacco, sugar, and other products on the same terms as the British." He paused for a moment. "Such a sweetener might even persuade us to abrogate our free trade agreement with Britain and allow you access to our commodities at a more favorable rate than your rivals."

La Valette pursed his lips. Despite having been allies against the Russians during the Crimean War barely over a decade ago, the traditional rivalry between France and Britain showed little sign of going away. Any measure that could strengthen the French economy while weakening the British economy put France in a stronger position.

Slidell went on. "Marquis, at the price of granting us an alliance against the United States and a temporary financial loan, France will be gaining our support in its quest to gain control of Mexico and secure a decided economic advantage over the British. All things considered, it is a very good bargain for you."

"You are persuasive, Slidell. I'll grant you that."

"I have not said the best part yet, Monsieur. President Davis suggested in his most recent telegram that, as part of a final agreement, we might be willing to dispatch troops to serve in your Mexican campaign."

La Valette's eyes widened in some surprise. It was a proposal that Slidell had not previously made. While the Mexican adventure was generally popular in France, as the people liked overseas success, it was beginning to sour on some due to French casualties. Replacing some of the French troops with Confederate soldiers, about whose lives the French could not have cared less, would greatly improve matters.

Slidell only wanted to drop the hint and not discuss particulars. As it was, he had timed the statement perfectly, for there was a sudden blare of trumpets, bringing all conversation in the grand hall to an end. Through a large door marched two single-file rows of soldiers. One was French, the soldiers wearing the red-and-blue uniforms and tall bearskin caps of the Imperial Guard. The other was Russian, the men decked out in blue uniforms and tricorn hats of the famous Preobrazhensky Regiment. All of the men were immensely tall and marching with precision.

The soldiers lined up in front of an enormous elevated platform with four thrones. They came to a sudden halt and for a moment all was quiet. Then the trumpeters began again and, walking with great solemnity, Emperor Napoleon III of France and Czar Alexander III of Russia entered the room. By Napoleon's side was the Empress Eugenie and next to Alexander was the Czarina Maria. All the guests were completely silent and still as the four of them ascended the steps onto the platform. When they took their seats on the thrones, looking out over the assembled guests in the grand hall, everyone broke into applause.

Slidell clapped along with the rest, his gaze resting on the Emperor of the French. He knew Napoleon III rather well and recognized that he was a man like any other, sometimes clever and sometimes foolish, as governed by his passions as anyone else. He also knew of the rumors that there was not a drop of Bonaparte blood in the veins of Napoleon III, for his mother had been notorious for her countless sexual affairs. For better or worse, the man was on the throne of France. Slidell knew that his whims would have a profound impact on the fate of the Confederacy. Despite the arrogance of its people, the Confederacy was a very small fish in a pond full of much larger creatures. Slidell knew, better than anyone else, how important it was for the new nation to find powerful friends.

As the party guests slowly resumed their conversations, Slidell bid his farewells to La Valette and began searching about for the Russian ambassador. It would be some time before his night was over.

March 27, Night
Robbins Plantation, St. Martin Parish, Southern Louisiana

Saul sat silently in the underbrush, observing the slave cabins and the plantation house beyond with his small field telescope. Sentries were marching back and forth amidst the cabins and slowly walking in a circle around the house, all shouldering rifles. Torches had been placed all around, clearly to provide illumination in the event of an attack.

He sighed. The destruction of the Bergeron plantation the month before had obviously frightened the Southerners, for the plantation owners were hiring men to act as guards. Economic times being what they were, there would be no shortage of war veterans needing to earn some money. His earlier raid had been carried out against virtually no resistance. This time, however, he and his men would be up against men who were at least as experienced as themselves in fighting, if not more so. He would have to depend upon the element of surprise and the cockiness of his opponents.

Saul carefully snapped his telescope closed. He was amazed that the thing remained undamaged after so long. It had been given to him by one of the white officers of the 84th United States Colored Troops, the regiment in which he had been serving when the war ended. He struggled for a moment to remember the man's name, before pushing the thought out of his mind. He was about to lead his men into a fight and could not afford to distract himself.

He looked behind him. Hidden amidst the vegetation were two dozen of his men. Circling around to the other side of the plantation was the second column of roughly equal numbers. If all went as planned, they would get into position and then wait for his signal to strike. Saul felt confident that, with a sudden attack, they could overwhelm the plantation guards with a minimal number of casualties. He would surely suffer more men killed than in the earlier raid, but he was expecting to replenish his troops with the slaves he was about to set free.

Saul had considered trying to alert the slaves in the plantation to prepare for the raid. They might have attacked the guards with their agricultural implements the moment they heard the first gunshots. He had decided against it, for the risk of detection was too great. Dr. Ferguson, the closest thing Saul had to a father, had taught him that many planned insurrections before the war had been thwarted by individual slaves who revealed the schemes to the white authorities in the hopes of being granted their freedom. How any man could be so selfish was beyond Saul.

It probably wouldn't matter. Saul knew how news travelled among the slaves on the various plantations. Even before he had destroyed the Bergeron plantation, the slaves within it had heard rumors of a force of renegade blacks hiding out in the wilderness. According to some, they had even heard of Saul himself.

He did not know why his men had taken to calling him Saul. He figured it was as good a pseudonym as any. Of the band of insurrectionists that had assembled under his banner, only Doctor Ferguson, the sole white man among them, and his lieutenants Troy and Silas knew his real name. Saul was determined that it remain that way, for it was better to be an enigma.

There was the stirring of some birds in trees perhaps fifty yards away. He pursed his lips in frustration. It was that sort of thing which could set the sentries on their guard. Since the men were almost certainly veterans of the recent war, they undoubtedly had experience in picket duty. Even the smallest noise or movement might alarm them.

Saul despised the Southerners with all his heart and soul. He remembered growing up on the sugar plantation, the endless days of unremitting labor, the agony of whippings and beatings, and the daily humiliation of his everyday existence. He had escaped from that life, but most of his people remained in unnatural bondage. The Southerners considered him inferior simply due to his black skin. They would cast him back into slavery if they could.

Saul was a man of the knife. He had run away to the bluecoats at the first opportunity, even though he was not sure at first that they were even real. He had been quickly recruited into the Union Army and fought at the Battle of Milliken's Bend two weeks after first shouldering a rifle. The white officers recognized in him an outstanding noncommissioned officer and he was moved from regiment to regiment, serving throughout the Lower Mississippi Valley in countless battles and skirmishes. He had been one of the leaders of the black bands of fighters during the Great Disorder. Unlike other bands, his men had remained intact in the swamps long after the fighting had ended. Whoever he was, Saul was a man who knew what it meant to be a soldier.

An hour-and-a-half had passed since the second column had departed on its march to the far side of the plantation. There was no way to signal back and forth without alerting the guards, so he had to trust that his men had done what he had asked them to do. The commander of the other column, who called himself Troy, was competent and Saul felt able to count on him. Troy's second-in-command was Silas, whom Saul had known for years and who was perhaps his most experienced fighter, but a man who liked killing a little too much.

It was almost time. He glanced over his shoulder at his men. Some of them were fellow veterans from the war, men who had been trained by the Yankees and had fierce discipline instilled in them. At least half of them had working rifles, the rest having to place trust only in their bayonets. Their faces were expressionless. The rest of them were mostly men freed during the raid on the Bergeron plantation or who had escaped into the swamps on their own. They were armed with hoes and scythes that had been adapted into crude blade weapons. They had no experience and appeared frightened and uncertain of themselves. He had instructed his veterans to stay close to the new men, to steady their nerves.

Saul understood these men, for he had been formed by the same experiences that had formed them. They had been conditioned from birth to fear the whites, to be subservient to them, to see themselves as inferior. It was this indoctrination, more than anything else, which kept the blacks from murdering the whites in their beds. Yet there was another element at work in their minds, too. A lifetime of mistreatment and humiliation had fostered a ferocious desire for revenge that burned within the soul of every black slave, male or female. Saul's task, when he rescued slaves, was to stoke that spiritual fire until it destroyed the mental stupor the whites had forced upon them. When that happened, it did so with explosive force. For many of them, tonight would be the night they became empowered.

He tensed, suddenly remembering a matter of grave concern. Ammunition was in critically short supply. Even those lucky ones who held functioning rifles would have to conserve their fire for fear of running out of bullets. He knew he was unlikely to find much ammunition on a plantation and was increasingly worried about how to replenish the supply. He shook his head. There would be time enough to think about that later on. For now, he had a plantation to destroy.

Saul raised his hand. He instantly sensed a tightening of tension in the men behind him. With a single movement, he swiped his hand forward. Without a word, his men rose and began moving quickly but silently towards the slave cabins.

"Look out!" one of the guards shouted, frantically pointing towards them. "Bunch of darkies coming out of the woods!"

Saul's veterans halted, raised their rifles, and unleashed a quick volley just a few dozen yards from their targets. The sudden crack of explosive gunpowder shattered the stillness of the night. Several of the guards fell, dead or wounded, some screaming in agony. The black insurgents then dashed forward without reloading. The new men followed behind them, brandishing their weapons and shrieking a battle cry.

The next few minutes passed quickly. It was not as easy as the first raid had been. There were perhaps twenty guards scattered across the Robbins plantation. Most survived the initial volley. Overcoming their initial surprise, they fought back. At first, Saul could hear several gunshots coming from many different directions, but it did not last long. Only a few of the whites had time to reload and get off a second shot before being cut down by the blades of the black fighters.

He strode into the main row between the slave cabins while his men finished off the guards. Frightened and curious eyes peered out from slightly open windows and doors.

"Inside!" he yelled. "We get you! Inside!"

Saul could hear more firing and shouting from the other side of the plantation. The second column had gotten into position as planned and launched their assault on schedule. If they were following their orders, a group of chosen men from the second column would head directly for the main plantation house. It was important that the main house be captured as quickly as possible, in order to prevent the guards from retreating there and barricading themselves within it.

The volume of gunfire began to diminish. Many of the white guards were killed outright. The more seriously wounded were put out of their misery with bayonets or scythes. As the two attacking columns linked up amidst the slave cabins, twelve of the white guards were taken prisoner, either unwounded or wounded only slightly.

During the planning of the raid, every man had been given instructions for what they were to do when resistance ceased. Twenty men surrounded the prisoners, who were sternly ordered not to speak or attempt to escape. Some of the others began moving through the slave cabins, informing their inhabitants that it was now safe to come out and trying to keep them calm. Most of the men scattered across the plantation, searching for food and other needed supplies. A few have been specifically detailed to find much needed ammunition, though Saul was doubtful they would obtain much of that critical commodity.

After giving orders to bring the prisoners in front of the plantation house, Saul walked in that direction himself. In the distance, he could see some of his own men standing on the front porch, which indicated that the building was in their possession. He could only imagine how surprised and terrified the Robbins family had to be.

"Saul!" the voice of Troy called out. "You all right?"

"I's all right!" he called back, irritated. The idea that he himself might be hit was not something he thought about much. He didn't really want his men thinking about the possibility, either, for it would likely erode their morale.

"We lost two," Troy said, trotting up beside him. "Frederick and Bache. But we got all of the white bastards. Either killed them or took them prisoner."

"Good," Saul replied. The deaths of Frederick and Bache were of course to be grieved, but that was the price of war. "Are your men doing their jobs?"

"Yes, boss! They are doing it, just like you asked them to!" Troy's voice betrayed excitement. The act of striking back against the white slaveholders, after having hid out in the swamps for a year, was clearly elevating the man's spirits. Saul wished Troy would act more level-headed. Excited men made mistakes. Besides which, Troy was an officer, and an officer was expected to set a good example for his men.

Saul noticed Silas shoving a rotund white prisoner forward using the butt of his musket. "Move along, you fat white bastard!" Silas shouted.

"Don't talk to them, Silas," Saul said sternly. "You know the rules."

Silas turned and looked at him for just a moment. The expression on his face was one of defiance and disrespect, but the man said nothing. The group of prisoners and the men surrounding them began walking up to the main house.

The slaves were now emerging from their cabins. Most looked confused and alarmed. Others gazed at their liberators in wonderment, as if they were figures from their dreams somehow made real. Some of the slaves pointed to Saul himself and whispered his name in hushed tones. As before, his reputation had preceded him. He thought that was good, not because he was vain, but because it served the larger cause. The more rumors that circulated about him, the more frightened the whites would become.

Now that the firing had ceased, the few women of the partisan band had emerged from the tree line and were now assisting their menfolk as they scoured the plantation for anything useful. Most of the women they had liberated in the February raid had fled north, hoping to reach the United States, but some had refused to leave and offered to help in any way they could. Some had even asked to be allowed to fight, though that was a step Saul was not yet prepared to take.

They arrived in front of the plantation house. The family was assembled there already and the prisoners were herded beside them. A mother was holding two young daughters close to her, quietly weeping. An older daughter, about sixteen, looked more annoyed than frightened. Aside from the guards they had captured, there were two other men. One, older and gray-haired, had to be George Robbins, the master of the plantation. On Robbins's right was a strong-looking man in his early twenties, most likely his son. Robbins and his son did not appear frightened, either.

Holding Robbins's hand was a very young boy, perhaps seven or eight, who looked disoriented but not scared. Saul surmised that he had been woken from a sound sleep and did not truly grasp what was happening.

"What is the meaning of all this?" the older son asked arrogantly.

"Isn't it obvious?" Saul replied. "We're freeing the people you have held as slaves and destroying your plantation."

Saul enjoyed the look of astonishment evident in the faces of the whites, just as he had when he had seen it at the Bergeron plantation. They were entirely unused to hearing a black man speak in the accent of an educated man rather than a field hand. Saul had Dr. Ferguson to thank for it, among many other gifts.

"You damn darkie!" the older son shouted. He took a step forward, but was then stopped by the leveled bayonets of three of Saul's men. He spat on the ground. "You're going to be hunted down like a dog and your body will be left on the ground for the maggots!"

Saul knew that this would not be his fate. His mother was a powerful practitioner of voodoo arts. The night before he had fled to the Union, he had confided his plans to her. She had not tried to talk him out of it. Instead, she had stripped him of his clothes and rubbed him from head to foot with a magical powder which, she said, would confer an immunity to all enemy weapons. Thus far, it had worked, for Saul had fought in scores of engagements during the war and no Confederate bullet or blade had touched his skin. He knew he was perfectly safe.

There was no point in explaining it to the white man who now stood before him. He shrugged. "If you kill me, you're only killing one man," he said. He waved his hand at the now free men and women walking up from the slave cabins. "Can you kill all of them? I am Saul. I know you've heard my name. If you ever kill Saul, a thousand other Sauls will rise in my place."

The teenage daughter stepped forward. "You think you talk so smart? You're not fit to wash my horse's turnips!"

Silas stepped forward and, before Saul could stop him, forcefully backhanded the girl across the face. She cried out in pain and surprise, with such volume that Saul wondered if she had ever been physically struck in her life. She collapsed in a heap onto the ground.

"Silas!" Saul roared, furious. He roughly grabbed Silas by the shoulders and pulled him away from the girl. Silas threw his own arms out to free himself from Saul's grasp and then defiantly pushed his face forward towards Saul, their noses mere inches apart. For an instant, Saul looked deeply into Silas's eyes, seeing nothing but rage and hate. He angrily jerked his head away from the whites. Silas waited before complying, so long that Saul began to wonder if he would refuse to obey, but then stepped away.

"You are animals," the elder Robbins said harshly.

Saul felt his temper beginning to fray. "How many women have you held as slaves? How many women have you whipped? You call us animals, yet your actions show you to be the true beasts."

The older son spoke again. "How dare you speak to us with such insolence? You're nothing but a damn slave!"

"Why, then, are you at my mercy and not the other way around?"

"Put down your rifle and let us each take a knife, darkie. I'll show you who's superior."

These words caused a rustling among both Saul's men and the captured white guards. He knew instantly that he could not refuse the challenge of the younger Robbins without losing face in front of his men. If he shot him dead, there would surely be some who believed he did so out of fear. Yet if he accepted the challenge, he ran the genuine risk of being killed.

He considered the younger Robbins. He was tall and well-built, likely stronger than Saul himself, standing with a self-confident attitude evident even under his suddenly diminished circumstances. It was a safe assumption that he had served in the army during the war, in which case he probably had considerable fighting experience. Yet Saul knew that he had the protection of his mother's magic.

Saul turned to Troy. "Give him a knife."

The white man sneered and stepped forward, cracking his knuckles as he did so. Saul withdrew his own bowie knife from its belt scabbard. He waved it around, remembering its weight and balance. He then turned to face his opponent.

The black insurgents backed up to give them enough space, though they kept their weapons leveled at the other white prisoners as the knife fight began. Robbins's eyes flared with anger as he dashed forward towards Saul. He slashed at him instantly, hoping to finish the fight within the first few seconds. Saul felt a certain relief as he ducked beneath the arc of the blade. An experienced knife fighter would thrust rather than slash, as the latter mode of attack was more easily avoided. The man he was fighting against was an amateur.

Saul was patient, either avoiding or blocking the clumsy attacks of Robbins and taking his time before striking back. Finally, however, an opportunity presented itself that was too good to pass up. Robbins slashed downwards towards Saul and, in doing so, thrust too much of his own body weight forward to maintain an even balance. Easily sidestepping his opponent's knife, Saul firmly clasped the white man's throat, lifted him bodily into the air, and then threw him roughly onto the ground.

Robbins's knife flew from his hand and landed several yards away. The man himself was dazed, but, after a moment, gamely tried to pull himself onto his feet. It was an easy matter for Saul to place his foot on the man's back and forcefully shove him back down. He then moved his foot up to the back of the man's neck.

"That was a fair fight," Saul said. "You see how easy it was for me to beat you? It would be even easier for me to break your neck right now."

Saul looked at the elder Robbins. The white man looked imploringly into Saul's eyes, wordlessly asking him to release his son. Deciding that there was no point in holding him on the ground, Saul lifted his foot off the man's neck and stepped back. The younger Robbins scrambled to his feet and stumbled back to his father's side.

The sound of breaking glass brought all eyes around to the plantation house, where some of Saul's men were beginning to throw torches in through the shattered window panes. Down below, flames began to lick the sky from the slave cabins as well. The Robbins Plantation would soon be nothing but ashes.

The plantation owner cleared his throat to speak. "Saul, when you raided the Bergeron Plantation, you left the women and children unharmed, yes?"

"That's right."

"Are you doing to do so again tonight?"

"I am. You need not worry about that."

"May I ask you for a favor, Saul?"

Saul's eyes widened slightly in surprise. "What is it?"

"You intend to kill all the men here, yes?"

"I do."

"Shoot us, then. Don't hang us like you did Bergeron and his people."

Saul considered this. The man he saw before him was a slaveholder who had denied freedom to scores of his fellow human beings. That being the case, he deserved death. Hanging was the common penalty for common criminals, while firing squads were for soldiers. There was a reason that the black troops who had executed Nathan Bedford Forrest had used a noose rather than a bullet.

"Sorry," he said simply.

Robbins pursed his lips and, for the first time, Saul thought he sensed sadness coming over the man. "Will you at least allow me to speak to my wife for a few moments?"

Saul inclined his head slightly. "Very well."

Robbins nodded and stepped over to his wife, who cried out and threw her arms around him. He spoke calmly to her in a whisper that Saul could not hear. She continued sobbing, but periodically nodded in response to whatever it was he was saying. He then bent down and hugged his two young daughters. The teenage girl, who had begun to cry as the reality of the situation finally dawned on her, was the last to be embraced. Robbins tussled the hair of the younger boy, who maintained an expressionless face, clearly not understanding what was going on.

"Be strong, Samuel," he said. "You're the man of the family now."

Saul reflected for a moment that, had little Samuel been only a few years older, he would have been strung up with the older men. As it was, the memory of seeing his father and older brother executed would surely stay with him for the rest of his life. Might he, one day, seek his revenge? After all, how many of the renegade slaves Saul himself now led were motivated by memories of a thousand insults and injuries done to their families throughout their lives?

Robbins turned and faced Saul. "Very well. I am prepared. Lead on."

Saul nodded. He didn't deny that this white slave-owner was brave, but that didn't matter. His men had already prepared the ropes. Fifteen minutes later, Robbins, his older son, and the remaining guards were dangling from the nearby trees. Saul and his band of insurgents, now joined by the liberated slaves from the plantation, vanished into the forest.

Breckinridge pursed his lips and shook his head as he read through the report from the Louisiana militia commander. The raid on the Robbins plantation followed the pattern of the earlier raid on the Bergeron plantation almost exactly. The guards who had been hired to protect the place had been quickly killed after being surprised. Then, just as before, the slaves had been freed, the buildings had been burned, and the men executed by hanging, leaving the women and children unharmed.

One raid could be dismissed as a singular occurrence, but two raids began to form a pattern. Some newspapers were now speculating that another round of slave insurrections was about to break out. It didn't surprise Breckinridge that some of the editors were blaming the whole thing on Jefferson Davis. The most scathing piece had been run by the *Charleston Mercury*, the most vehement anti-administration newspaper in the country. The newspaper's owner, Robert Rhett, all but accused Jefferson Davis of stirring up Saul's insurrection on purpose. Breckinridge was troubled to find himself mentioned in the last paragraph of the piece, where Rhett seemed to suggest that Breckinridge's willingness to compromise with the United States in Toronto had contributed to Saul's rebellion.

Breckinridge sighed. The forcefulness of the editorial was only to be expected, for Rhett was perhaps the most bitter and outspoken Fire-Eater in the Confederacy. As with most of his ilk, the hatred he had directed towards Northerners and abolitionists before the war had long since found a new target in the form of President Davis and his supporters.

There was nothing he could do about the newspapers, so Breckinridge turned his thoughts back to the situation in Louisiana. General Morgan had finally arrived on the scene. Presumably, with so many freed slaves having joined Saul's band, it would now be less easy to conceal, even in the vast swamps and forests of the region. Assuming that the militia cooperated with him, Morgan should have little trouble finding the insurrectionists. With any luck, Saul's second raid would be his last and the spark of slave rebellion would be snuffed out as quickly as it had been lit. Breckinridge trusted Morgan and felt he could count on him.

"Wilson!" Breckinridge called.

On the other side of the door, there was the scrapping sound of a chair being pushed back from a desk. A moment later, the door opened and the face of James Wilson, Breckinridge's chief-of-staff, appeared.

"Yes, sir?"

"Please send a telegram to General Morgan, requesting an immediate update on the situation as he finds it. I am tired of depending upon partisan newspaper accounts. I want a report from the main officer on the scene."

"Right away, sir." With a smile, Wilson closed the door and went about following his instructions.

Breckinridge smiled. Wilson had served as one of his chief aides during the war. In matters of administration and organization, there was no one better than Wilson. In all other matters, there was no one possessing more ineptitude. Wilson's clumsiness was a source of much hilarity to Breckinridge, who adored the young man.

Having dealt with the telegram to Morgan, Breckinridge picked up the next report he had to read. It had been sent to him by General William Hardee and detailed the progress being made in the construction of fortifications on the upper Mississippi River just below the border with the United States. The system the Confederates had relied upon during the war had proven woefully inadequate, leading to the fall of Memphis early in 1862. Should war ever be renewed with the United States, Breckinridge was determined not to let that happen again.

It was one of a thousand issues, some large and some small, that Breckinridge was trying to deal with in his capacity as Secretary of War. Although the army had been largely demobilized after the ratification of the Treaty of Toronto, it was still far larger than the prewar United States Army had ever been, with roughly a hundred and fifty thousand active soldiers scattered about the Confederacy. A force this size required careful management. There were promotions to consider, supplies to be purchased, fortifications to be strengthened or constructed, and a myriad of other tasks. Illegal or incompetent actions by officers during the war had left a backlog of courts martial to be dealt with as well, an unpleasant and sometimes controversial task.

During the war, the men who had held the office of Secretary of War had been little more than clerks, doing exactly and only what Davis asked them to do. When he had been asked to take the office, Breckinridge had made it clear that he would be cut from a different cloth and his own political and military eminence gave him the necessary clout. Breckinridge had gradually earned Davis's trust and had emerged as the most effective member of the cabinet, save perhaps for Benjamin. Davis still reserved the final say on the most important matters, but he generally listened to Breckinridge's advice.

Breckinridge had taken advantage of his position to push military innovations which had occurred to him during the war. He felt he had an advantage over the professional officers, for he had not had a military education and had not inculcated the powerful traditions of West Point. In addition to his highly regarded reformed militia system, he had created a Bureau of Military Intelligence, established a new and better method of inspecting cavalry horses, and reformed the old system of military departments. Much of this had been done over the objections of high-ranking officers, but Breckinridge's natural political skills had allowed him to smooth ruffled feathers.

He was so fixated on the report about the Mississippi River defenses that he almost failed to hear a muffled conversation on the other side of the door. A few moments later, Wilson entered the office again, a slightly confused look on his face.

"Sir? General Johnston is here to see you."

"Is he?" Breckinridge asked in surprise. "I thought his appointment wasn't until tomorrow."

"That's correct, sir. But the general expressed an urgent desire to see you immediately."

Breckinridge's eyebrows went up. It was very unlike Joseph Johnston to break a carefully arranged schedule. Whatever the cause was, he suspected that it was something important.

"Well, by all means, send him in."

A few minutes later, General Joseph Johnston entered the office. As usual, he wore an immaculate uniform and bore himself with a stately countenance. Though surprised at the man's appearance ahead of schedule, Breckinridge was pleased to see Johnston, for he greatly admired the army commander. Like Robert E. Lee, Johnston was what a Virginia gentleman was supposed to be. He was dignified yet kind, somehow so comfortable in his superiority that most people didn't resent it. Breckinridge and Johnston were colleagues who knew each other well, though not close friends.

As he rose from his desk and extended his hand, Breckinridge noted that the expression on Johnston's face was grave. That did not bode well.

"It's good to see you, Joseph," he said as the general gave him a firm handshake. "I did not expect to see you until tomorrow, though."

"I apologize for the breaking of protocol," Johnston said as he took his seat. "But unfortunately a situation has arisen that I believed required an immediate discussion with you."

"Nothing is wrong in the Army of Tennessee, is it?" The once mighty force, which had defeated the armies of both Sherman and Grant outside of Atlanta, had evolved into a collection of garrisons along the border between Tennessee and Kentucky, all administered from Johnston's headquarters in Nashville.

"Oh, not at all. The army in is fine shape, actually. As well as troops in garrison for months on end can be, at any rate. You will have my full report tomorrow. No, the matter I need to discuss with you is of another nature entirely. A nature which, I confess, is rather unfamiliar to me, though I expect not to you."

"Well, please enlighten me, General."

Johnston frowned and shifted uncomfortably in his seat, remaining silent. Breckinridge waited. He knew that Johnston was a man who disliked awkwardness, and was therefore willing to wait for him to speak.

"I'm sorry to say that there's a personal element to it, John. Can I trust that this conversation will be kept in confidence?"

"Of course."

"Very well. When I arrived in Richmond yesterday, I called on Senator Wigfall and his family. As you may know, Wigfall and I have been friends for several years."

Breckinridge nodded, for the friendship between Johnston and Wigfall was well known. He recalled that, in 1862, Johnston had stayed in the Wigfall home while he recuperated from the horrible wounds he had received at the Battle of Seven Pines. In Breckinridge's opinion, Johnston had displayed poor judgment by aligning himself so openly with Wigfall, one of the bitterest critics of Davis, but there was no point in saying so.

Johnston went on. "During our conversation, Wigfall informed me that certain eminent gentlemen have been putting my name forward as a potential candidate in the upcoming presidential election."

"Is that so?" Breckinridge asked, his interest in the conversation suddenly magnified.

"Yes. They did so without my permission."

"And what did you tell him?"

"I told him that I had no desire to run for office and that the idea was preposterous."

"I see."

"But he then told me that he had been authorized by these gentlemen to directly ask whether I would consider seeking the presidency and promising me their support if I accepted."

Breckinridge nodded. The election was only eight months away, yet in the absence of organized political parties, it was still unclear exactly who the candidates were going to be. Did Johnston's news indicate that the campaign to succeed Davis was finally beginning?

"Did Wigfall tell you who these men were?"

"Yes, but he told me in confidence. You understand?"

"Of course." Breckinridge assumed that Robert Toombs was involved somehow. The coalition of political figures opposed to the Davis administration was large but had never been well organized. There were many tensions between rival members. With the election approaching, perhaps they were finally coalescing.

"And you still said no?" Breckinridge asked.

"Of course."

"Just like that?"

"Indeed. I declined the offer immediately and I made sure he understood that my decision was final. I have no political ambitions, John. You know that. I would have expected Wigfall to have known that. It is well known that I do not like President Davis and that he does not like me. But that sad fact is rooted in personal differences that go back many years, as well as disagreements over military matters during the war."

"You do not disagree with his politics?" Breckinridge asked. Ordinarily, he would have considered it inappropriate to ask a general this question, but this conversation was obviously different.

"I am a soldier of the Confederacy," Johnston replied. "I leave politics to the politicians."

Breckinridge nodded, believing him. Johnston had to know that, if he had decided to put his name forward for the presidency, he would have easily won the election against anyone but Robert E. Lee himself. Breckinridge knew that Lee was not going to run, but this fact was not widely known to the public at large. Perhaps Lee had also told Johnston. In any case, Johnston was being offered a prize for which many men in the Confederacy would have given anything, yet he was turning it down.

Johnston went on. "I fear that this proposal for me to become involved in politics may taint my continued service in the army. That is why I felt it necessary to tell you at once."

"You need have no fear on that account, Joseph," Breckinridge replied quickly. "I would be the last person in the world to question your integrity."

"What about President Davis?" Johnston asked, concern in his voice. "He despises me and he despises Senator Wigfall. If this reaches his ears, I would expect him to ask for my resignation."

Breckinridge sighed. "We both serve at the pleasure of the president, Joseph. But I shall not bring this news to him. If he hears it from other sources and does desire your resignation, I shall argue against it."

Johnston pulled a piece of paper from his coat pocket. "I would be very offended if my integrity were questioned even to a slight degree. If you wish, John, I have already written a letter of resignation. Perhaps it would be better for me to resign now rather than have the president ask me to do it."

"Put that letter away," Breckinridge said quickly. "You won't need it."

Johnston held the paper for a moment, before smiling and putting it back in his coat pocket. "Thank you, John."

"There's no need to thank me, Joseph. It is I who thank you for bringing this to my attention."

"In that case, Mr. Secretary, I shall return tomorrow at the scheduled time to discuss my report on the Army of Tennessee."

"Very well."

Johnston rose, stiffly saluted, and walked out the door.

Once the general was gone, Breckinridge immediately began thinking about the implications of what he had been told. He had long expected the faction of anti-Davis politicians to unite and put forward its own candidate for the presidency. If it would not be Johnston, who would it be?

Breckinridge knew better than anyone how chaotic and disjointed the political situation in the Confederacy was. Prewar affiliations of Democrats, Whigs, Know-Nothings, and Constitutional Unionists had lost all meaning. Elections since the country's formation had largely focused on whether candidates supported or opposed President Davis. With the war over, new political combinations were beginning to appear. People who had once been adversaries were now allies, and vice versa. Politicians who had opposed secession were now lining up with Fire-Eaters. Even some regional associations were beginning to form, with representatives from the Trans-Mississippi often voting as a bloc in Congress. Thinking about it all reminded Breckinridge of a small ship sailing on a turbulent sea, the crew becoming increasingly suspicious of one another.

Breckinridge had always considered the Fire-Eaters unrealistic and dangerous. Before secession, they had been willing to tear the Union apart and inaugurate a bloody war rather than compromise with the North. Breckinridge considered it the supreme irony of his life that he had, in effect, become their candidate for president during the 1860 election, but that had not been his doing. Had he been able to avoid it, he would have.

Breckinridge knew that many newspapers, especially those friendly to the Davis administration, were speaking of him as a potential candidate if Lee declined to run. He had been one of the most prominent defenders of Southern rights before the war. He had been a successful military commander and one of the commissioners that crafted the Treaty of Toronto. He had earned a reputation for hard work and outstanding administration of the War Department. In many ways, he was the ideal candidate. Once it became public knowledge that neither Lee nor Johnston was going to run, the clamor for him to announce his candidacy would surely grow louder.

Yet there was a story from Breckinridge's past that only a very few people knew.

During the torturous negotiations that had led to the signing of the Treaty of Toronto, Breckinridge had secretly met with Vice President Hannibal Hamlin, one of the Union commissioners. Behind the backs of their respective delegations, they had worked out a compromise by which Kentucky would remain in the Union while Tennessee would be given the option of voting in a referendum to either rejoin the Union or remain in the Confederacy. In addition, Breckinridge agreed to drop Confederate demands for both the return of freed slaves and the enactment of a Fugitive Slave Law in exchange for trade concessions favorable to the Confederacy. Breckinridge and Hamlin had rallied the two delegations to agree to the compromise, without which the talks surely would have collapsed.

When they had made their deal, Breckinridge had assumed that only he and Hamlin would know what had actually happened, for the two of them had agreed to keep their meeting secret. He hadn't reckoned with the deviousness of Congressman William Porcher Miles, one of the other Confederate delegates. Unbeknownst to Breckinridge, Miles had learned of his clandestine meeting with Hamlin and had hired a man to follow him and report on what happened. Miles, therefore, knew that Breckinridge had deceived the rest of the Confederate delegation, ending any chance that the South might gain control of Kentucky, recover its lost slaves, and obtain a new Fugitive Slave Act.

During the signing ceremony, Miles had revealed to Breckinridge what he knew. He had threatened to use the information to destroy Breckinridge if he ever sought elective office again. The passage of nearly two years had not made the words Miles had spoken any less ominous. He remembered them as clearly as if they had been said to him the day before.

Breckinridge was not an easily intimidated man, yet he could not see a way out of the situation. How could he run for president without having the damning information exposed? Breckinridge had no reason to think Miles had yet told the secret to anyone. Now Minister to the United States, Miles seemed content to sit on the information and to let Breckinridge be. Were he to seek the presidency, however, Breckinridge had no doubt that Miles would go public. The consequences of that were impossible to predict.

If Miles had never issued his threat, Breckinridge was certain he would run. He remained an ambitious man and he felt he knew what was needed for the Confederacy to take its proper place among the nations of the world. Moreover, he feared what would happen if one of the Fire-Eaters won the election in November. As was proved by countless historical examples, from Oliver Cromwell to Maximilian Robespierre, attempting to run a country by ideology rather than pragmatism was a recipe for disaster. What choice did that leave him?

He decided not to think about it for the rest of the day. Instead, he tried to focus again on the paperwork on his desk. Pulling out writing materials, he began a letter to General Jubal Early, who commanded the Army of Northern Virginia from his headquarters at Winchester, to ask about a disturbing report he had received concerning the quality of artillery gunpowder.

Sitting silently in a stationary hansom cab across the street from Mechanic's Hall, Secretary of State Judah Benjamin watched as General Joseph Johnston stepped out of the front door, entered a waiting carriage, and rode away. He had been too far away for Benjamin to see the expression on the general's face, but that didn't matter. When he talked to Breckinridge, it would be easy to find out what happened.

Johnston had gone directly to the Secretary of War after his meeting with Senator Wigfall. An easy explanation would have been that Johnston had agreed with Wigfall's suggestion that he run for President and had gone to tender his resignation. Benjamin doubted this was the case, however, for Johnston rarely did anything quickly. Had he accepted Wigfall's offer, Johnston would have spent several days deciding exactly how to resign.

The second possibility, that Johnston was undecided about Wigfall's offer, also did not accord with the evidence. Had that been the case, there would be no need for Johnston to go to the War Department that day at all. He was scheduled to meet with Breckinridge the next day anyway. Nor would the meeting have been so short.

The most likely explanation, from Benjamin's point of view, was that Johnston had been horrified by Wigfall's offer to support his candidacy and had rushed to Breckinridge to explain what had happened. Like most aristocratic Virginians, Johnston was extremely touchy on matters of honor and protocol. He would not want the Secretary of War thinking that his behavior was anything less than faultless.

Johnston's carriage disappeared down the street. Benjamin waited, knowing that a long time would pass before Breckinridge emerged from Mechanic's Hall. The slave sitting on the coachman's seat on the back of the cab wouldn't mind, nor would Benjamin have cared if he had. Settling down in his seat, Benjamin contemplated the events that were transpiring.

Wigfall's attempt to get Johnston to run for president was the opening salvo of the 1867 presidential election. The gruff senator from Texas had made common cause with Toombs, Stephens, and undoubtedly others. Having been rebuffed by Johnston, they would turn elsewhere for a candidate. Benjamin needed to know who that person would be as soon as his enemies knew it themselves. The sooner he knew who the opposing candidate would be, the sooner he could begin dismantling him.

Benjamin had been by the side of Jefferson Davis almost from the moment of secession. He thought about how many times their experiment of a slaveholding republic had nearly failed. The Confederate armies had come close to disaster more times than Benjamin cared to remember. He had spent much of 1865 in London and Paris, obtaining desperately needed loans from British and French bankers; had he failed, the Confederate government would have collapsed despite having won its independence. Protected by its brilliant generals, guided

71

by the steady hands of Davis and Benjamin, the South had weathered all these storms.

Now another storm beckoned. With the electioneering for the first contested presidential election about to begin, the Fire-Eaters and their misguided allies would do their best to gain control of the government. If they succeeded, their foolish policies would surely bring down the Confederacy. Their determination to gain control of Cuba might lead to a war with Spain, which the country was decidedly unprepared to wage. The effort to conclude an alliance with France would be abandoned. The European governments would respond with disgust, destroying the Confederacy's foreign credit and making inflation even worse.

In addition to their imperialistic ambitions, the Fire-Eaters held political ideas that would reduce the Confederacy to anarchy. Benjamin had no problem with a strong government for the South, so long as it was free from Northern domination. The Fire-Eaters, though, seemed to want no government at all. If the Fire-Eaters won the election, the Confederacy would be fall into a chaotic state similar to the thirteen original colonies before the Constitution had been adopted. Unable to agree on anything, the eleven states of the Confederacy would soon be at one another's throats, especially since any state had the right to secede whenever it wanted.

Then there was the troubling possibility of a slave uprising in Louisiana. Benjamin hoped that the band of blacks led by Saul would turn out to be nothing but an outsized gang of ruffians easily dealt with by Morgan's cavalrymen and the militia. Yet there was always the possibility that it might prove to be something more. If the Fire-Eaters gained control of the government in the upcoming elections, they would surely overreact to the situation and initiate policies likely to encourage further insurrections in the future.

The Confederacy was a newborn child in a volatile world. It was heavily in debt to British and French bankers, whose governments might use the financial obligations to exert control over the country. To the north, the United States remained a dangerous potential enemy, nursing resentment over the lost war. Internally, the threat of a renewed slave uprising and severe economic distress threatened to knock down the weak pillars propping up the country.

If the Confederacy was to survive, it would need wise and pragmatic leadership. The Fire-Eaters were the antithesis of that, so Benjamin was determined to defeat them. To achieve this goal, he needed John C. Breckinridge.

Benjamin had waited almost two hours when he finally saw Breckinridge emerge from the front door of Mechanic's Hall. He knew that the Secretary of War made it a habit to walk to and from work rather than take a horse or carriage. As Breckinridge began strolling down the sidewalk, Benjamin thumped his gold-headed cane on the roof of the hansom cab, signaling the coachman to start. Moving slowly, the cab soon caught up with Breckinridge.

"Is that you, John?" Benjamin called from the window.

Breckinridge turned and looked at the cab in some surprise. Benjamin thumped his cane again and the coachman pulled to a stop.

"Why, hello, Judah," Breckinridge said with a smile. "Quite a coincidence meeting you on the street."

"Isn't it? May I offer you a ride home?"

Breckinridge hesitated just a moment. Benjamin could read his facial expression as easily as if it was a book and he saw instantly that Breckinridge was skeptical that this was a chance encounter. That didn't bother Benjamin, though. In fact, a little ambiguity could only serve his purposes.

"I don't see why not," Breckinridge said.

Benjamin opened the door and scooted to the side to make room. Once Breckinridge was seated and the door closed, he thumped his cane on the roof again to signal the coachman.

"Please take us to Mr. Breckinridge's residence!" Benjamin called.

"Yes, sir," the deep voice of the coachman replied.

Benjamin reached into his pocket and withdrew two cigars. "El Principe de Gales?" he asked as he extended one to Breckinridge.

"Why, thank you," Breckinridge said as he took the proffered cigar. "I may be a Southern patriot, but I cannot deny the quality of good Cuban tobacco."

Benjamin lit a match and soon the two men were puffing away.

"So, are you concerned with this news of another raid by Saul's bandits?" Benjamin asked.

"I am not sure," Breckinridge replied. "Now that Morgan has arrived, hopefully he can deal with the problem. My advice is that we wait and see."

"Is that what you will tell the president?"

"Yes."

Benjamin sighed. "I can only hope that you're correct. If Saul's little spark of rebellion flares into something larger, it can only spell trouble. We were terribly fortunate to escape a full-blown race war in 1865. We might not be so lucky again."

"True."

"Pray tell," Benjamin asked Breckinridge, changing his tone. "Rumor has it that General Joseph Johnston paid you a visit earlier today. Is this true?"

Breckinridge chuckled. "Word travels fast in Richmond. Yes, he did pay me a visit."

"But at our last cabinet meeting, you said that you would not be meeting with him until tomorrow."

"That's correct."

"So what was it Johnston wanted?"

Breckinridge waited a moment before replying. "He asked that the conversation be kept in confidence."

"Did he? Well, I apologize. I certainly would never ask a gentleman such as yourself to betray another man's confidence. What would happen to society if private conversations could not be kept private, after all? I am sure, in any case, that it was nothing that touched on public matters."

Breckinridge frowned. Benjamin didn't need him to say anything more. If Johnston had resigned, it would have been public knowledge soon enough and there would have been no need to keep the news confidential. It was clear to Benjamin that Johnston had rejected Wigfall's offer. Pestering Breckinridge for a confirmation would only unsettle him, which was the last thing Benjamin wanted to do.

"Have you read this morning's papers?" Benjamin asked. "The editorials, I mean."

"Yes, I have. The President is being hauled over the hot coals over the Saul business."

"You and me as well. They are accusing us of doing nothing while rebel slaves run amuck."

"One gets a little tired of hearing about how Davis is a tyrant and all of us in his administration are either incompetents or villains."

"Quite so. With the approach of the presidential election, such talk is only going to increase, you know."

"I wish I could disagree."

"We are only eight months away from Election Day, you know. Things are beginning to happen. Rumor has it that Toombs held a conference with several of our political enemies at his home recently. I am not one to smell conspiracies under every stone, but it seems likely to me that they are laying the groundwork for an organized presidential campaign."

"They need a candidate in order to mount a campaign," Breckinridge observed.

"True, true," Benjamin said. "They'll have one soon enough. Which is why we need to find one of our own as quickly as possible."

"I'm not sure I know to whom you're referring when you say 'we'."

"You and me, John. The rest of the cabinet. All those who support us. Call us whatever you want. The administration party? The Tories? The label doesn't matter. You and I want the same things for this young country. There are many who think as we do. If our enemies are going to rally behind a presidential candidate, we must do the same."

Breckinridge took a long pull on his cigar and glanced sideways at Benjamin. "And whom do you have in mind, Judah?"

"Why, you, of course," Benjamin said simply.

The Secretary of War frowned. "I was afraid you would say that."

"It must be you, John."

"Why?"

"Lee is not going to run. You and I know that. The people will know it soon enough. Most of the other possible contenders are sympathetic to our foes. Who else is there?"

Breckinridge pursed his lips and didn't reply. Benjamin allowed him a few moments to contemplate what had just been said. He had known Breckinridge in Washington before the war, when Breckinridge had been Vice President of the United States and Benjamin had represented Louisiana in the Senate. He had grown to know him more during their service in the cabinet together. They were not intimate friends, but Benjamin felt he understood how Breckinridge's mind worked. If he was going to persuade him to run for president, he would need to make use of the Kentuckian's natural ambition and sense of duty, while somehow negating his underlying desire to retire from public life.

"You want the presidency, John," Benjamin said. "One does not rise in politics as fast and far as you have without ambition. But you're better than most, for you actually want to use your positions to do some good. Believe me, if I had my pick of any man to succeed Davis, it would be you."

74

"Why don't you run yourself?"

Benjamin laughed. "Are you serious, John? The Southern people would as soon vote for Satan as vote for a Jew. Besides, even if I were as Christian as Martin Luther, I would be lucky to scrap together half a dozen votes outside of Louisiana. The people of New Orleans might tolerate my unorthodox marriage, but would they in South Carolina or Virginia? Never."

Benjamin thought for a moment about Natalie, the woman he had married in 1833. She had lived in France for the past twenty years, seeing Benjamin only intermittently during summer visits. Though it separated him from his beloved daughter Ninette, the distance suited them both. Benjamin, for reasons he thought perfectly reasonable, had never enjoyed fulfilling certain marital duties and Natalie had found consolation in the arms of other men. Divorce was never contemplated, but neither was any pretense of an ordinary marriage. He sent Natalie the necessary money that allowed her to maintain a luxurious lifestyle, while he made regular use of the connections of her influential Creole family. All in all, it was a satisfactory arrangement.

"What makes me such an attractive candidate?" Breckinridge asked. "I'm a Kentuckian. Like the rest of the Orphans, I have no real home in the Confederacy."

"You're as Southern a man as lives in the Confederacy," Benjamin replied. "You risked your life on the battlefield. You defended the rights of the South in Washington for a decade before the war. I don't mind saying it, John. You have one of the most brilliant political minds I have ever known. You know about administration, trade, finance, military affairs, and, most importantly, how to work through the political process. If you're not qualified to be president, John, then no one is."

"I appreciate your kind words, Judah."

Benjamin waited a moment. "But?"

"There are… complications," Breckinridge said carefully.

"What sort of complications?" Benjamin asked. He found Breckinridge's statement intriguing. Was it just an expression of a subdued desire to leave politics to spend more time with his family? Benjamin would have believed Breckinridge if he had told him so, though he would have believed very few others. Yet somehow Benjamin didn't think that was what Breckinridge meant.

"I'd really rather not speak of it."

Benjamin decided it was time to play the first of his cards. "Is it the *North Star*?" he asked with a smile.

Breckinridge turned sharply to look at him. "What do you mean?"

"There's no need for alarm, John. I know that you were a subscriber to Frederick Douglass's newspaper. But don't worry. Your secret is perfectly safe with me."

"How did you find out?" Breckinridge asked. "I thought I had that buried so deeply no one would ever be able to find it."

"I'm a Jew who got kicked out of Yale, yet I became a senator and a cabinet secretary. You don't get from where I started to where I am without being able to sniff out such things as this. But that's neither here nor there. Like I said, your secret is safe with me. My question is whether you're reluctant to seek the presidency because you once subscribed to a newspaper published by the most notorious abolitionist in the North and a runaway slave to boot."

He shrugged. "I suppose that's part of it. Had it been public knowledge, I should never have been nominated to run for president in 1860. I would more likely have been tarred and feathered and run out of the South."

"Perhaps so," Benjamin agreed. "Southerners can be rather uncompromising when it comes to such things. But as far as I can tell, no one but me knows that you subscribed to Douglass's paper."

"They might learn of it. You did."

"Yes. And when I did, I had the evidence destroyed."

This was a lie. The detective Benjamin had hired had found the old subscription list during a night break-in of Douglass's office. He had not destroyed it, but had stolen it and mailed it to Benjamin. It was now kept it in a hidden desk drawer in Benjamin's home. Such things were useful insurance against future events.

"Well, I guess I should thank you for that," Breckinridge said.

"The *North Star* is not a problem. I have taken care of it for you. So what's stopping you?"

"I have based my career on conciliation and compromise. If I run for president, I shall doubtless stir up a hornet's nest of opposition. Many men despise me for pushing the delegation in Toronto to give up the claims for the return of freed slaves and a new Fugitive Slave Act. If I announce a candidacy, they will do their best to destroy me."

Benjamin thought he sensed something in Breckinridge's tone when he mentioned his role at the Toronto peace conference. Were the complications of which Breckinridge spoke somehow related to that? Benjamin made a mental note to consider the question later.

"You have fought tough campaigns before," Benjamin said. "Besides, you've gone through a war since you last ran for office. At least no one will be shooting at you."

Breckinridge chuckled slightly. "If the Fire-Eaters put forward a candidate and I then announce my own candidacy, I will be accused of being a puppet of President Davis."

"So what? You'll be accused of many other things before the campaign is over. It won't be any worse than what your Whig and Know-Nothing opponents called you in Kentucky before the war. Or what the Yankees called you during it, for that matter. It won't make a difference to us."

"You keep saying 'we' and 'us'. What's in this for you, Judah?"

"You and I are on the same side, John. We both are working to establish the Confederacy on firm foundations so that it may take its rightful place among the nations of the world. But if Wigfall, Toombs, and their ilk gain power, you and I both know that it will all come tumbling down."

Breckinridge nodded. "The policies they support would be disastrous, I agree."

"Then you are duty bound to stop them. And you can only do that by running for president."

"Like I said, Judah, there are complications."

"Fine," Benjamin said sharply, a hint of irritation entering his voice. "Everything in life is complicated, especially in politics. I can see that you don't want to tell me what these complications are. That's all right. Every man is entitled to his secrets, after all. We'll deal with these complications as they arise."

"Whether I run for the presidency is a decision I shall make myself, Judah," Breckinridge said firmly. "Don't try to push me into anything. I appreciate your support, but I will decide whether or not to do this in my own good time."

"Time, unfortunately, is something we do not have much of. Our enemies are already beginning their campaign. I imagine that they are organizing in each state even now, laying the groundwork. We must match them. You must decide soon."

Breckinridge pursed his lips. "I do not like being bullied."

"And I do not like doing it. But I, like you, have no choice."

The Kentuckian fell silent. Again, Benjamin let him think things through. For the next few minutes, as the cab continued its way through the streets of Richmond, neither man spoke. Eventually, the horses were pulled to a stop.

"Secretary Breckinridge's home, sir!" the slave cabby called.

Breckinridge opened the door and stepped out onto the sidewalk. "Thank you for the ride, Judah." He paused a moment. "I need some time to decide. I shall give you my answer in a few days."

Benjamin nodded. "Very well, my friend. I shall see you soon."

He watched as the Secretary of War disappeared into the front door of his house, then thumped the roof of the hansom cab again. It was time to head to the evening's poker game.

CHAPTER THREE

April 5, Night
Home of Samuel Howe, Boston, Massachusetts

"So, you don't think it's a good idea, Charley?"

Lowell frowned at his friend Henry Higginson as they each took their seats at the long and elegant dinner table. It was covered with ornate dishes and glasses, decanters full of wine, and beautiful flower arrangements. All around, other guests were also taking their seats.

"I didn't say that, Henry. I think it's a wonderful idea. Inspired, even. I just wonder if it is the proper time to be pursuing such a project."

"What are you two rowdy boys talking about over there?" Josephine asked playfully, taking her seat beside her husband.

Higginson laughed softly. "I'm trying to persuade your husband to support my proposal for organizing an orchestra of musicians to give regular concerts in Boston. With sufficient funds, the players could be paid regular wages and ticket prices could be low enough that even the common people of the city could enjoy the music of the world's greatest composers."

"A professional orchestra," Josephine said. "A marvelous idea."

"Indeed, it is," Lowell said. "But why now, Henry? There are so many other issues confronting us. Veterans who need employment. Education reform. The millions of blacks still held in slavery in the Confederacy. Why devote time and resources to a musical venture?"

"Music to sooth the spirits of disillusioned men may help inspire them to use their lives in the service of causes higher than themselves," Higginson replied.

"Perhaps. It is, in any event, a very interesting idea."

"Would you be willing to talk with me about it later?"

"Of course."

Lowell turned his attention to the galaxy of illustrious people in the room. At the head of the table sat the hosts, Samuel Howe and his wife Julia. The two were well-known philanthropists, especially renowned for their efforts on behalf of the blind. Howe had also supported overseas revolutionary causes in France and Greece. Rumor had it that he helped fund John Brown's raid on Harper's Ferry. Around the table, Lowell saw the great abolitionist Wendell Phillips, the Unitarian minister William Henry Channing, former Governor John Andrew, and other members of Boston society's elite.

Two men in particular caught Lowell's attention. Senator Charles Sumner sat quietly by himself, observing the goings-on around the table with a studied disinterest. Lowell knew Sumner well and respected him enormously. It had been Sumner's influence that allowed Lowell to obtain his commission as the colonel of the 2nd Massachusetts Cavalry, paving the way for him to ascend up the chain of command. Lowell hoped to get the chance to speak to the senator before the evening was over.

The other man who stood out to Lowell sat at the opposite end of the table from the Howes and was, in fact, the guest of honor. Frederick Douglass, the runaway slave who had become the greatest orator and abolitionist in America, sat regally in his chair. The occasion for the dinner was to bid Douglass farewell as he embarked on a speaking tour of Europe.

The food was delicious. The first course consisted of oyster and turtle soup, after which broiled salmon and striped bass were brought out. The main course consisted of braised beef and a roast saddle of mutton, which Lowell enjoyed very much. Side dishes included sweet potatoes, boiled onions, and sautéed asparagus with garlic and cinnamon. Wines fit for each course were provided, a Vouvray from the Loire valley for the soup, an Alsatian Riesling for the fish and a fine Bordeaux for the meat.

As he ate the splendid dinner, Lowell couldn't help but remember the food he and his comrades had eaten while campaigning in northern Virginia. During the war, he and his men had subsisted mostly on hardtack eaten through with worms and salt pork so old that it had turned blue. Economic times being what they were, most of the men he had commanded were likely still eating food closer in quality to their wartime fare than what Lowell was enjoying this evening.

Lowell conjured up a bit of knowledge from the classical education he had received at Harvard. Cato the Younger, the great Roman patriot and enemy of Julius Caesar, had been a wealthy man on account of his family inheritance. Yet he had lived in a Spartan home, drank only the cheapest wine, and ate the same kind of plain fare that the average Roman ate. For this, he was lauded as a man of the people. The fact that Lowell could never have brought himself to do the same troubled his conscience.

"Where shall your speaking tour take you, Mr. Douglass?" Howe asked.

Douglass responded in a deep tone, his voice effortlessly filling the room. "I shall sail first for Dublin and speak there and in a few other cities in Ireland. I have been well-received in Ireland in the past and I hope to be welcomed again. Of course, with the newspapers full of stories about Fenian agitation, the climate may be different. People might not be as interested in hearing about slavery in America when there are so many other problems closer to home."

Lowell nodded softly, though he was unsure whether it was out of agreement or politeness. He did not know how he felt about the issue of Irish independence. He had spent considerable time in England and thought well of the nation and its people. If the Irish wished to be free, though, then obviously their wishes should be respected.

To Lowell, home rule for Ireland was a side issue. Of far more importance was the continued struggle against slavery. All other progressive ventures, no matter how worthy in and of themselves, had to be set aside until that great problem was solved.

"And after Ireland?" Howe asked.

"Then to London, the industrial cities in the north of England, and on to Scotland. We have many friends in Britain. I aim to rally them around the standard yet again and remind them that the abolitionist cause is not lost."

"You must persuade them, Mr. Douglass," Senator Sumner said. "If the people of Europe begin to shift their attention away from slavery, the feeling shall set in that the success of the so-called Confederacy has settled the slavery question for all time. The feelings of the people are fickle and their interest shall drift to other things."

"I fear you may be right, Senator," Douglass said gravely. "The defeat of our cause in the late war has dismayed the supporters of abolitionism the world over. I receive letters from Brazil telling me that the incipient emancipation movement in that country has almost entirely collapsed in the wake of the Confederacy's victory."

"The forces of reaction are on the march," Howe said sadly. "We all know about the failure of the bill to expand the voting franchise in Britain. Opposition to the rule of Napoleon III in France also seems to have declined precipitously and efforts at reform in Russia seem to have evaporated."

Lowell contemplated the conversation as he took another sip of his Bordeaux. Before the war, he had intently read the works of Theodore Parker and other social reformers. It had been hammered home to him at Harvard that the state of the world was not what it was supposed to be. It was his duty to use his life in such a way as to make the world a better place than it would have been had he never lived. Frederick Douglass had achieved this many times over, and Lowell was certain that God had a special place waiting for him in Heaven when his time came. As for himself, Lowell was less certain.

Douglass continued to describe his itinerary, laying out his proposed route through France, the Low Countries, the western states of Germany, and down to Italy. Lowell had travelled through much of Europe during his youth and fondly remembered the joys he had experienced in the Old World. Yet he could not help but reflect on the difference between his voyage and Douglass's. He had gone to Europe for his own pleasure and edification. Douglass, by contrast, was going to Europe in the service of something higher than himself.

"Such a long trip, Mr. Douglass," Josephine said. "You shall surely exhaust yourself."

"I am happy to suffer exhaustion, Mrs. Lowell, if it advances the abolition of slavery. The alternative is to do nothing in the face of evil, which is to die slowly as one's soul is gradually consumed by the guilt of complicity."

"Well, thankfully no one at this table can be accused of doing nothing in the face of slavery," Higginson said. "Everyone here has either put their fortune or their life on the line. I only wish we had been more successful."

"It is the slave himself who is the bravest of the brave," Douglass said. "So many thousands who journeyed north through the Underground Railroad before the war. So many thousands who risked death to escape to Union lines during the war. So many thousands who joined the ranks of the United States Colored Troops. Even now, we see in the actions of the brave Saul and his band of gallant men the actions of heroes."

"Saul?" Higginson asked. "The bandit in Louisiana?"

"The Confederates might call him a bandit," Sumner said. "I choose to call him a warrior. Any man who fights for the freedom of others is elevated above the level of mere banditry. He has already freed dozens of slaves."

"It may not last long," Andrew interjected. "Our newspapers might be crowing about the whole thing, but two small raids on plantations do not make a rebellion. If I understand correctly, the local militia is currently searching for him. Perhaps this little spark of resistance will be snuffed out as quickly as it ignited."

"Perhaps," Douglass echoed. "But I choose to be optimistic. Perhaps his raids are the beginning of something that may grow, like tinder being tossed onto a slowly smoldering fire, reigniting it into such a fury that it consumes the whole of the Confederacy."

Lowell noticed Sumner glancing around the table for a moment until his eyes came to rest on him. "General Lowell, you appear to be the man with the most military experience present here tonight," the senator said. "What is your opinion on the prospects of Saul's little rebellion?"

Lowell had not expected to come to dinner and be asked to speak to a roomful of the most eminent persons in Boston on questions of a military nature. Yet he immediately responded with a tone of confidence.

"Let us assume that Saul is more than just a bandit," he began. "Partisan warfare has a long history. William Wallace and Robert the Bruce employed it against the English. The Spanish employed it against Napoleon. I myself spent a year trying to put down the rebel partisan John Mosby in Northern Virginia and I freely admit that I failed. Men employing partisan tactics are capable of achieving great things."

"So you think Saul might succeed in expanding his rebellion?" Howe asked hopefully.

Lowell sighed. "Sadly, no."

"Why not?" Douglass asked.

"I believe that Saul and his men might live off the land as far as food is concerned. But I do not see how they could replenish their supply of ammunition. Their weapons, too, must be falling in some state of disrepair. Unlike other necessities, they cannot make good these losses by raiding plantations or subsisting off the bounty of nature."

"Meaning?" Douglass pressed.

"Meaning that unless Saul's force can obtain ammunition and replace worn out weapons, they shall inevitably be reduced to fighting with knives and their bare hands. And they will be faced by well-disciplined and well-armed militia, made up of veteran soldiers. No men, no matter how brave and gallant, can succeed in such circumstances."

"But others have," Sumner said. "You said so yourself. The Scots against the English and the Spanish against the French."

"The Scots under Wallace and Bruce fought in an age before the invention of gunpowder, when cold steel was all that mattered. The Spanish had the advantage of being constantly resupplied by the British."

"So there would be no hope?" Sumner asked.

Lowell paused a moment before responding, wanting to choose his words carefully. "There is always hope, Senator. But if I am required to state my

81

honest opinion, I can only say that the capture or death of Saul and his little band is a mere matter of time."

"That is sad to hear," said a guest Lowell didn't recognize. "I would have thought Saul's example would inspire other slaves to fight for their freedom as well."

Douglass sighed and sat back in his chair. "Perhaps that would have worked last year, but now I am more skeptical. When the peace treaty was ratified and the United States began withdrawing its forces, there was a frantic effort on the part of those slaves freed by the Emancipation Proclamation to escape into Northern territory. They naturally feared being returned to slavery when the Confederates reoccupied the territory being evacuated. But many men of the U.S.C.T. regiments tried to continue the fight. In many cases, Union commanders left behind supplies and ammunition for them."

Lowell remembered what Douglass was talking about, though it was not a pleasant memory. When the unofficial cease-fire had come into effect in late 1864, Lowell and his brigade were in the northern Shenandoah Valley, having just taken part in Sheridan's campaign against Jubal Early. The men had reacted with disgust and disdain, furious that all their sacrifices and the loss of so many good men had been in vain. There had been no U.S.C.T. units in Sheridan's army, but he could understand why many of his fellow officers had been willing to leave them supplies. He knew that he would have done so, had he been given the chance.

Douglass continued his story, telling his guests how the black troops had been defeated by Confederate forces in the last two months of 1865. Most of the survivors had fled into Union territory, while many prisoners had been returned to slavery. Some in the North had protested that this violated the Treaty of Toronto, which specified that black prisoners could not be returned to slavery. The McClellan administration, however, had taken no action, maintaining that the blacks who had remained to fight had become renegades. The treaty, therefore, no longer applied to them.

"Of course, there were rumors that some of these men escaped into the swamps, but those rumors were never verified," Douglass concluded. "Not until Saul and his men emerged, anyway."

"Exactly," Lowell said. "Saul and his men are obviously survivors from U.S.C.T. regiments. What else could they be? The reports tell of them wearing tattered Union uniforms and being armed with Enfield or Springfield rifles. They could not have simply sprung up from the ground like warriors sown from dragons' teeth."

"But how could they have survived in the Louisiana swamps for nearly a year?" Governor Andrew asked.

"A year is nothing," Douglass responded. "We know that thousands of fugitive slaves have inhabited the Great Dismal Swamp on the border between Virginia and North Carolina for a very long time. Others fled into the swamps of Florida and lived there for many years. If one is determined to be free, one can endure all manner of hardships."

Lowell nodded, enraptured by the voice of the great abolitionist. He found it astounding that the man who held Boston's elite entranced had once been a common field slave in Maryland. Lowell himself had been born into one of

America's most prominent families and been the valedictorian at Harvard, yet he scarcely considered himself worthy to serve as the black man's valet.

Douglass continued. "Some of the women and children rescued from the raided plantations have turned up in Illinois, having made their way north to freedom in small boats along the Mississippi, moving only at night. They speak of Saul's men emerging from the woods like ghosts, silent and dark. A fitting image, I think, for it is right that the South be haunted for the sins it has committed. But as General Lowell said, without weapons and ammunition, Saul cannot continue his struggle for long."

Sumner scoffed. "McClellan will do nothing," he said sourly.

"Indeed, he will not," Douglass agreed. "He cares nothing for the slaves and has always despised the abolitionists. Besides, even if he did care, he is too dependent on the political support of immigrants in the big cities, too many of whom see freed slaves merely as competitors for jobs. And with the tensions between the United States and the British Empire, difficulties with the Confederacy would be the last thing he would want."

"Perhaps individual citizens could do something," Lowell said. "Before the war, we helped slaves escape to freedom via the Underground Railroad. Now, why not help Saul, and perhaps other bands of insurgents, by smuggling weapons down to them. Rifles, ammunition, and such."

Lowell made this comment without really thinking it through. As he still viewed the Confederacy as the enemy, along with almost everyone else at the table, the idea of smuggling weapons and ammunition to Saul seemed all too obvious. He had simply spoken his thought as it had passed through his mind.

It was only after he had said the words that he realized he was advocating something strictly illegal. The Treaty of Toronto, for better or worse, had established peace between the Confederacy and the Union and specifically prohibited the citizens of each nation from taking any hostile action against the other. Smuggling war materials to rebel slaves would be akin to waging war against a nation that was at peace with the United States.

Lowell sat uncomfortably as the other guests remained silent. He realized that he had made a social *faux pas* and felt as though all eyes were suddenly on him. Douglass stared at him with raised eyebrows but an otherwise calm expression, leaving Lowell uncertain as to the enigmatic man's genuine reaction. The other guests remained awkwardly silent, either uncomfortable with the words he had spoken or embarrassed on his behalf.

Across the table, though, Lowell saw a very different response in Sumner's face. He almost failed to notice it, so mortified was he at the unease his words had caused. Ever so faintly, a very rare smile had crossed the senator's lips. His eyes were observing Lowell with a certain calculation and, just possibly, admiration.

"Ah, dessert!" Howe said, as the door opened and servants brought in more trays. The relief in his voice was palpable. The timely arrival of dessert allowed the conversation to move away from the subject of Saul's insurrection. With any luck, Lowell's rash words would be quickly forgotten and not mentioned by anyone afterwards.

Two desserts were offered, cherries jubilee and Connaught pudding. Both looked equally delicious to Lowell and he was tempted to take a serving of each.

He feared appearing greedy and indecisive to his fellow dinner guests, however, and so only took a serving of the pudding. He did not regret his decision, for it was quite wonderful, made all the better by a glass of excellent champagne that came with it.

Conversation shifted to more light-hearted subjects, including a new theater company that was being organized and a new school for the poor that was being opened with funds raised by subscription among the city's wealthier families. Some of the guests got into a polite debate over the merits of Darwinian evolution, which had been a common topic in recent months.

Lowell noticed, however, that neither Douglass nor Sumner seemed to engage in much discussion. Out of the corner of his eye, Lowell saw Sumner quietly get out of his seat, walk over to Douglass, and whisper something in his ear. He couldn't be sure, but Lowell thought that the two of them looked at him carefully, with Douglass then nodding his assent to something.

After fifteen or twenty minutes of pleasant banter, Howe rose from his chair and tapped his fork against his glass several times to quiet the table.

"At this time, I should like to invite Mr. Douglass, as the guest of honor, to make a toast."

Lowell, along with everyone else, shifted their eyes to the great abolitionist. Douglass rose to his feet. The room quieted, anxious to hear whatever it was that Douglass would say. He remained quiet for a few moments, gathering his thoughts. He then raised his glass and turned his gaze directly towards Lowell, meeting his eyes.

"'Sometimes the spark of generous fire revives in vanquished hearts again.'"

"Here, here," Howe said, somewhat uncertainly. He and the other guests raised their glasses and sipped their champagne, but it was clear from their hesitation that they did not quite know what Douglass had meant by the words he had spoken.

Lowell, by contrast, recognized the quote immediately. It came from the second book of Virgil's *Aeneid*, in which Aeneas recounted the story of the fall of Troy to Queen Dido of Carthage. When Troy had fallen to the Greeks, the cause that Aeneas and his comrades had fought for so long and so hard had been lost, seemingly forever. Yet Aeneas himself would go on to greater glory than he could ever have imagined.

Douglass turned his head and looked at Lowell, holding his gaze for a few endless moments, then turned to the rest of the table and accepted their raised glasses with one of his own. The servants had entered again, for the time had come for the table cloth to be removed and for the women to retire to the drawing room, leaving the menfolk to enjoy brandy and cigars in the dining room.

"Shall we take our leave, darling?" Josephine asked.

"Yes, my love," Lowell answered. "Considering the amount of wine I have already indulged in, I should think twice before indulging in brandy as well."

Josephine laughed softly. They said their farewells to the hosts and their friends. As they moved toward the front door, Lowell was surprised to see Senator Sumner walk up to him, just a slight trace of urgency in his step.

"Leaving so soon, General Lowell?"

"I'm afraid we must make an early night of it, Senator. My wife and I have far to travel to return home."

"I am disappointed. I was hoping to speak to you regarding a private matter."

Lowell's eyes narrowed. He could not fathom what Sumner could possibly want to talk to him about. Their interactions since the war had been few and minor.

"Well, sir, you are free to call on me at any time before you leave for Washington."

"Better still, General Lowell, would you do me the honor of joining me at my home? I shall not return to Washington until a week from tomorrow. While I cannot provide as sumptuous a meal as our hosts this evening, I am sure I could put together something for you. In any case, as I said, I wish to speak with you on a private matter."

The tone of the words and the look in Sumner's eyes told Lowell that something odd was afoot. This needled his curiosity, but he also knew he was greatly in Sumner's debt and did not want to disappoint him.

"Very well," he said. "Thursday evening?"

"Thursday evening would be quite agreeable," Sumner said. "I look forward to it."

The two men shook hands, and Sumner strolled back into the dining room, leaving a confused Lowell to walk out the door.

"What was that all about?" Josephine asked.

"I would tell you, my dear, but I do not know myself."

April 10, Afternoon
Selma and Meridian Railroad, just east of the Mississippi-Alabama border

"Joseph Johnston is a strange man," Toombs said as he stared out the window of the train, watching the landscape of western Alabama rush past them.

"How's that?" Stephens asked, looking up from the book he was reading.

"He said that he didn't want to be president. He has to know that if he ran, his election would be all but guaranteed. How could anyone turn down such an opportunity?"

Stephens shrugged. "Wigfall said he was not very political. You know those Virginians. Always obsessed with honor and dignity and so forth. And Johnston's vain. He obviously thought playing the role of Cincinnatus would make him look better in the history books than running for president. Maybe he didn't want to run against Lee, who is his friend. Maybe he didn't want to risk losing. Who knows?"

Toombs's reply was an irritated grunt. His foul mood had scarcely abated since he and Stephens had left Georgia. He now realized that his plan to persuade the others to support him in his quest for the presidency had not been carefully thought out. Having gone through a titanic war, the people of the South would surely turn to one of the great military heroes of the conflict for their next chief executive. Toombs's brief service as a brigade commander in Lee's army scarcely counted for anything when there were so many men with much more distinguished records.

"So now we will see if Beauregard takes the bait," Stephens said. They were travelling to New Orleans to personally ask the general to run for president.

"I have no doubt that he will," Toombs replied. "Johnston may want to play Cincinnatus, but Beauregard fancies himself a Napoleon. He'll leap at the chance of the presidency the way a child leaps at a piece of candy."

It hadn't surprised Toombs that the suggestion of Beauregard had electrified his political allies. Few men had such hold over the Southern imagination as Pierre Gustave Toutant Beauregard. He had commanded the Confederate forces that reduced Fort Sumter in the war's opening engagement, earning instant fame on both sides of the Atlantic. He had defeated the Yankees at Manassas in the first major battle of the war. He had not done well during his brief tenure in command of the western army, but had gone on to redeem himself later in the war by twice repulsing Union attempts to capture Charleston and heroically saving Petersburg from an attack by a vastly stronger Union army.

Yet his military record, impressive though it was, was only part of what made Beauregard so appealing. He had a certain mystique that was difficult for Toombs to understand. He was a Louisiana Creole, spoke French better than he spoke English, and was regarded by the ladies as dashing and handsome. For some reason, many people in the Confederacy continued to look on Beauregard as a man of destiny, certain to achieve infinite heights of greatness. None of this made any sense to Toombs, but that made it no less real.

"Johnston would have been far better than Beauregard," Stephens said. "He would have given Lee a serious fight for Virginia and North Carolina, which I think Lee will win against Beauregard. Still, if it cannot be Johnston, perhaps Beauregard is the next best choice."

"Perhaps," Toombs said. "Lee may take Virginia and North Carolina, but I think Beauregard will easily carry Louisiana and South Carolina. I am not so sure of the other states. But then, you and I have been through enough elections together to know how unpredictable they can be."

Stephens nodded. "Beauregard may be an egotistical blowhard, but the people hold him in high esteem. He will stand a good chance against Lee. And if Lee follows Johnston's course and chooses not to run, I think Beauregard would have the advantage over any other pro-Davis man."

"Including Breckinridge?"

"Yes, I think so."

"But Breckinridge has political experience. He has been through a great many campaigns and knows how to win them. Beauregard, if I am not mistaken, has only sought public office once in his life, when he ran for mayor of New Orleans."

"That's right. And he lost. This time, though, he'll have us to help him."

Toombs grinned. Thoughts of electoral votes and political campaigning inevitably cheered him up, for he had been a political animal for nearly three decades. He had gradually worked his way up through the Georgia state legislature, the House of Representatives, and finally the Senate, becoming known for his bombastic speeches and acerbic wit. He had started his career as a pro-Union member of the Whig Party, but by the late 1850s had evolved into a states' rights Democrat. John Brown's raid on Harper Ferry had finally pushed him into the arms of the disunionists. When Lincoln won the 1860 election, Toombs had been one of the loudest voices calling for immediate secession.

It was no surprise that many had expected Toombs to be the first president of the new Southern confederation when it was formed in early 1861. Again, the memory of his fateful drinking bout in the barroom of the Montgomery hotel stabbed at him. How could he have been so foolish? Still, it was not too late to set things to rights.

Toombs waited a moment before continuing. "We have not yet discussed the vice presidency, my friend."

Stephens sighed. "I was wondering when you would bring that up."

"You offered me your support for the presidency, Aleck, you recall."

"I know. I would happily have given it had there been any way. However, once Beauregard's name came up, the others fell into line around him instantly."

"I remember," Toombs said with a slight trace of bitterness in his voice. His plan to secure support for a presidential run had failed, but perhaps something could be salvaged from it. If Beauregard did become their candidate, Toombs might yet secure the vice presidential position. Assuming Beauregard's ticket was elected, Toombs would be sixty-three years old when the next election took place in 1873. That was old, but not too old.

"You want to be vice president?" Stephens asked. "You'd have far more influence remaining a member of the Senate. John Adams was quite correct when he said that the vice presidency is the most insignificant office ever conceived of by human imagination."

"The people of the country will know the name of a vice president far more readily than they will know the name of a senator," Toombs replied. "Besides, there are other ways to exert influence. Beauregard strikes me as a man who will need a great deal of guidance. Who better to provide that guidance than his vice president?"

Stephens nodded. "Well, you can rest assured that if you want the vice presidential nomination, you shall have my full support. But you know that I can guarantee nothing. Once we have our candidate, our next task is to organize a convention that will officially nominate him and choose the running mate. That process may be difficult to control."

"Yes, well, we have the remainder of this long train ride to discuss it, don't we?" Toombs replied. "Perhaps you and I could put a proposal together and mail a letter to our compatriots detailing it once we have determined who our nominee will be."

"A good idea," Stephens agreed. "And a reasonable way to pass the time."

They spent the next two hours talking over the idea of a convention, as the train slowly rumbled westward. With so many people disillusioned with the leadership of President Davis, they assumed it would be easy to gather a large assembly of influential people together. Many congressmen, senators, governors, and members of state legislatures would be eager to attend. Aside from politicians, there would also be military officers, newspaper owners, and wealthy merchants and plantation owners who could be expected to come in large numbers.

"We shall need to invite Governor Vance of North Carolina," Stephens said. "And Senator Foote of Tennessee. Both of them are avowed enemies of Davis and share our views on the matter of states' rights."

"Them and many others. Davis has made so many enemies over the past few years that I suspect our problem will be that too many people will want to attend," Toombs said with a broad grin.

Various cities were discussed as possible locations for the convention. Richmond, the capital, was an obvious choice, and holding the event there might help win support in Virginia. Atlanta and Nashville were considered, as well as Memphis and New Orleans. They also discussed Montgomery, with its immense symbolism as the birthplace of the Confederacy.

"We'll have to meet again with Wigfall and the others before determining a proper place," Stephens said. "It's not a decision easily made with an exchange of letters and telegrams."

Toombs and Stephens continued talking about the proposed convention. Obviously, the key players in each state would have to organize themselves into a committee to select delegates, otherwise anyone would feel free to show up and there would be no way to control the outcome. A central committee would also be needed to coordinate all this activity.

"Well, such a committee has essentially already been formed," Stephens said. "Isn't that what the meeting at your home with Brown, Wigfall, and Hunter was all about?"

"I suppose it was," Toombs replied. "But we'll need some more people. The five of us only represented three of the Confederate states."

"I'll draw up a list of names that we can go over," Stephens suggested.

"Good idea."

Stephens waited a moment before going on. "If we play our cards right, Robert, we will be building more than a simple nominating convention."

Toombs smiled. "Indeed, my old friend. We will be building a political party."

Their conversation waned as the train slowed to enter the station in Meridian, Mississippi. Toombs and Stephens stopped talking amid the bustle of many passengers disembarking and others getting on. A black newspaper boy came onto the car to hawk copies of the local broadsheet. Not having anything else to read, Toombs paid the boy a dime and pulled open his copy. If nothing else, it would allow him to pass the time before the train got underway again. The long journey had prevented him from getting any of the day's news.

He was glad to be sitting down, for the newspaper's headline left him reeling.

GENERAL LEE NOT RUNNING FOR PRESIDENT

"Aleck!" Toombs said quickly, shoving the paper towards his friend and pointing at the headline.

Stephens steadied his glasses and read. "Good Lord!"

Toombs hurriedly scanned through the lead article and found the text of Lee's statement, which the story said had been mailed to the editor of a

Richmond newspaper with the suggestion that he publicize it throughout the country.

Dear fellow citizens,

It has been suggested by many people on numerous occasions that I shall be a candidate in the forthcoming presidential election. I wish it to be known that I shall not, under any circumstances whatsoever, be such a candidate. Since I presented my resignation from the Confederate States Army to President Davis on December 31, 1865, I have had no ambition but to lead the life of a private citizen. I wish to stress that my decision is absolutely final and that nothing shall change my mind. My sincere hope is for the people of the Confederacy to enjoy the liberty and happiness that was earned by the blood of the men I had the honor to command in the field, but the tumult of politics I shall leave to younger and abler men than myself.

Sincerely,

Robert E. Lee

Toombs scoffed. "Idiot Virginians," he said harshly under his breath.

Stephens, however, was smiling. "Well now. It appears that we have a proper election ahead of us. Because if it's not going to be Lee, then I expect it will be Breckinridge. And a contest between Beauregard and Breckinridge is sure to be entertaining, to say the least."

"You're assuming Breckinridge will run," Toombs said. "We shall see."

April 11, Night
Home of Charles Sumner, Boston, Massachusetts

Sumner poured himself a glass of inexpensive Spanish wine as he awaited Lowell's arrival. Seven o'clock, the agreed upon time, was fast approaching. He had already eaten a simple dinner of lamb stew, for Lowell had said in his note that he would have already eaten. This suited Sumner. His meeting with Lowell might last ten minutes or it might last hours, but however long it turned out to be, he wanted no distractions.

His Boston home was small and sparse. He paid little attention to it, as he spent most of his time in Washington City. A lifelong bachelor, Sumner felt no need to decorate the house or indulge in elaborate furniture. A minimum level of ornamentation was necessary for those rare occasions in which he entertained guests, but otherwise the house, like most other things in Sumner's life, had a distinctly Spartan tinge.

As he sat in the front parlor, he wondered if he should feel guilty for what he was about to ask Lowell to do. Smuggling weapons to rebel slaves in the Confederacy was a deadly serious business. Under the laws of the United States, one could expect a lengthy prison sentence if caught. In the Confederacy, it would mean a swift execution. It was no small matter to ask someone to run such risks, especially a man with a wife and family.

Yet Sumner knew Lowell. During the war, Sumner had assisted Lowell's advancement through the ranks, using his influence to obtain his commission as colonel of the 2nd Massachusetts Cavalry. The two had also worked together to build support for the enlistment of black troops in the Union Army. By the end of the war, they had grown sufficiently close for Lowell to write Sumner with requests for political favors for friends and relatives.

Sumner admitted to himself that he had not thought much of Lowell when he had first met him in 1861. He had initially helped him only because of the prominence of the Lowell family. He had not expected such a boyish and bookish fellow to make much of a soldier. Being the valedictorian of Harvard was an impressive feat, but not one likely to indicate a successful warrior. No one had been more surprised than Sumner when Lowell had emerged as one of the most effective and energetic cavalry officers of the war. Hearing stories of the young man's bravery in battle, of countless horses being shot from under him, Sumner had daily expected to learn of Lowell's death. Yet he had ridden through the war without even being wounded, as if destiny were saving him for some particular purpose. Perhaps that was even true.

Lowell's abolitionist credentials were impeccable. His family had been abolitionists since virtually the beginning of the movement. His grandfather had been one of the first Unitarian ministers to speak against slavery from the pulpit. His uncle, the celebrated poet James Russell Lowell, was one of the most prominent anti-slavery activists in the country. From his wartime conversations and correspondence with Lowell, Sumner knew that the abolitionist fire burned in the young man's breast as hot as it did in his own. That was a boast few men in the country could honestly make.

Yet there was one more element to Lowell's character, beyond his personal bravery and abolitionism, which gave Sumner hope that he would agree to the proposal. It was a quality that Lowell shared with many of his fellows, those young New England men who had gone through Harvard and Yale in the years just before the war, their minds equally formed by the classical authors of Greece and Rome and the modern Transcendentalists. Men like Lowell yearned to experience life in some higher form, to seize life as Beowulf might have seized his spear. They were infected with an unacknowledged and unspoken ambition that saw life as a mountain that had to be scaled. If they didn't bother to try, if they decided to live a normal life of ease and comfort, they might as well have never lived at all.

It was this enigmatic quality, impossible to fully define, that had driven so many idealistic New England youths to join the Union Army when the war had broken out. Though the trauma of defeat had torn this idealism away from most of the survivors, it had endured in Charles Russell Lowell. Alone of the younger war veterans Sumner knew, Lowell still glowed with it. That, by itself, would have made him the perfect man for what Sumner had in mind.

The senator had already gone through his first glass of wine and poured another when he heard a soft knocking on the door.

"Come on in, General Lowell," he said, as he opened the door, with as much warmth as he could muster. "Would you like a glass of wine?"

"If you're having one, Senator."

He poured Lowell's glass, handed it to the general, and returned to his chair. Lowell, looking about awkwardly for a moment, soon took the seat opposite him, a small table set up between them.

"I appreciate the invitation to join you this evening," Lowell said hesitantly.

"It was not for social reasons, mind you," Sumner replied. "And if you do not mind, I would like to dispense with small talk."

"Very well."

"I'm afraid I wasn't born with the social graces of your family."

Lowell chuckled. "That's quite all right, Senator." He paused for a moment and sipped his wine. "You said you had a private matter to discuss."

"So to speak," Sumner replied. "It has to do with what you said at Howe's dinner the other night. About sending weapons and ammunition to Saul's band of insurgents."

Lowell sat back in his chair, a somewhat anxious expression forming. Sumner wasn't surprised to see him so uneasy, for he had to have understood the full implications of what he had said.

"My words were intemperate," Lowell said, using the tone a student might use to explain an error to his teacher. "I spoke without thinking. It was a mistake. It certainly was not my intention to advocate anything against the law. I do hope Mr. Howe was not offended."

"Mr. Howe was himself nearly arrested in 1859 on suspicion of providing money to John Brown. Do you think he'd care a whit about talking of smuggling weapons to rebelling slaves in the Confederacy?"

There was a pause. "I suppose not, Senator."

"You say it was not your intention to advocate anything illegal," Sumner said. "Yet the fact that you spoke as you did clearly indicates that you have thought about this question at some length."

Lowell did not respond right away, silently eyeing Sumner. When he did reply, a tone of caution had crept into his voice. "I do not think that any man in the Union who follows public affairs and who cares about the slavery question has not thought about Saul and his men, Senator."

"That's true, by God. Did you read the papers this morning?"

"I did," Lowell replied. "Another plantation burned by Saul's men and another two dozen slaves freed."

"Quite wonderful news, don't you think?" Sumner asked.

"I do," Lowell replied. "Every raid will strike more fear into the hearts of the slaveholders. But I also noted in the newspaper story that John Hunt Morgan shall soon arrive to take command of the militia charged with hunting Saul down."

"And you think they will succeed?"

"Sadly, yes. Saul's men must soon lose their ability to fight, for they cannot replenish their ammunition. And Morgan, by all accounts, is an effective general."

"Unless?"

Lowell sipped his wine. "Unless what?"

"What if someone did as you proposed and supplied Saul with proper weapons and ammunition?"

"As I said, Senator, my words were spoken in haste. I was merely expressing a thought, not suggesting any plan of action."

Sumner nodded slowly in reply, carefully studying Lowell while taking another sip of wine. He could tell that he was making Lowell uncomfortable, but that didn't especially bother him. He had been making people uncomfortable

91

throughout his career. Most politicians were subtle and deceptive, constantly compromising themselves and misdirecting others to achieve their objectives. Abraham Lincoln, whom Sumner counted among his friends, was a perfect example of this. Although it was often effective, it was not Sumner's way.

"I think you should do it," Sumner said simply.

"Do what?"

"Exactly what you said at dinner, General. I think you should smuggle a shipload of weapons and ammunition to Saul's men in Louisiana. It's a small band of men, according to the reports. Even a few hundred weapons would be tremendously effective."

Lowell frowned. Clearly, he was not surprised to hear Sumner say these words. Very carefully, he took a sip of wine and set his glass on the table.

"I thought you might say that, Senator."

"You are not immediately declining, I see."

Lowell paused a moment before responding. "The Union and the Confederacy are at peace. Neither you nor I like it, but there it is. Smuggling weapons to Saul's men would be no different than some Confederate citizen smuggling weapons to the insurrectionist Mormons in the Utah territory."

"There is letter of the law and then there is moral law, isn't there? The first is the work of men, the latter the will of God. One is higher than the other."

"You will find no disagreement from me on that point, Senator. You will recall that I participated in efforts to prevent the enforcement of the Fugitive Slave Act before the war."

"So if we must choose between obeying the laws of men or of obeying the laws of God, which do we choose? Obeying the laws of men is easy, while obeying the law of God can be much more difficult."

"My grandfather was the theologian in the family, Senator. I'm afraid I don't quite follow."

Sumner leaned forward and spoke quickly. "The war is not over, Charles. Yes, we failed to defeat the rebels. Yes, we signed a peace treaty with them. But never think for a moment that the war is over. Our two civilizations, North and South, cannot coexist side-by-side, with one nation being free and the other holding slaves. The two ways of life are irreconcilable. Sooner or later, there will be another war. You know that and so do I."

"Why not wait until that war comes of its own volition?" Lowell asked. "Why should we try to force the issue?"

"Because millions of slaves yet remain in chains in the Confederacy. Every day, their agony continues. While you and I live comfortable lives here in Boston, drinking fine wine and eating good food at fancy dinner parties, they toil away in the cotton fields day after day, whipped and beaten at the whim of their masters, seeing their families torn apart, condemned to a life of bondage from which there is no escape. Doing nothing while slavery persists for even a single day is not something a moral man can accept."

Lowell slowly nodded while he listened to Sumner, but said nothing.

Sumner sat back in his chair. "What is the source of your morality, Charles?" he asked.

"My faith in God."

"And?"

Lowell thought for a moment. "I want to be worthy of the respect of my wife."

"You married her during the war, yes? The sister of Robert Gould Shaw, if I'm not mistaken."

"That's right."

Sumner allowed himself a moment to remember Shaw, one of the great martyrs of the war. He had been so much like Lowell, one of the bright idealistic young men who had gone off to war. Unlike Lowell, however, he had not returned, dying under the guns of the Confederates at Fort Wagner while leading his regiment of black troops. Perhaps the mention of his brother-in-law, to whom he had been close, would help nudge Lowell in the right direction.

"You've made a good life for yourself since the war, Charles. The iron foundry is doing good business in spite of the hard economic times. You're providing jobs to veterans who would otherwise be without the means to support their families. I know how easy it would be to simply sit back and take no further part in public affairs. But you and I are not the sort of men to allow the persistence of slavery, the smallpox scar on the face of the world."

"And what if we do this?" Lowell asked. "Suppose we do smuggle weapons and ammunition to Saul and his men? What does that achieve in the long run?"

"Mr. Douglass spoke the other night of Saul being the first flickering of a fire that might soon burst into a flame. If Saul's little rebellion can be kept alive, if he can keep liberating slaves from plantations, than perhaps the dream of John Brown might become a reality. The longer Saul and his men survive and continue fighting, the stronger he will become. Do you not see it?"

Lowell nodded slowly, then looked up and looked Sumner closely in the eye. "How would this work?"

"There are others who are ready and willing to help, Charles. Men with money. I want you to meet with them. If they are agreeable, they will provide the funds and purchase the weapons and ammunition. They're not military men, Charles. Neither am I. Neither is Mr. Douglass. You are. You would need to inspect the weapons and supplies to make sure they are worth sending."

"A sound precaution," Lowell said. "With so many surplus weapons left over from the war, it wouldn't be hard for an unscrupulous person to pawn off second-rate rifles on someone."

"Exactly. Much more importantly, you'd need to accompany the shipment to New Orleans and ensure that they are delivered directly to Saul."

Lowell's eyes narrowed. "Why does that role fall to me?"

"Your ownership of the Bridgewater Iron Works is the perfect cover, don't you see? There are any number of reasons a businessman like you might want to visit New Orleans. Who else could go? Me? Mr. Douglass? That would be absurd."

"I cannot argue with you there, Senator. My foundry has received business offers from Southern railroads."

"I had not heard that, but it is good to know. Moreover, you have just the right experience for this sort of thing. When you fought against Mosby in northern Virginia, you learned the arts of subterfuge and intelligence-gathering, didn't you? I have heard that even Mosby himself said that he never faced an opponent more formidable than you. Hopefully it will not be a complicated matter to get this shipment to Saul, but we can't be sure. And if it is, we need someone reliable to take care of any unexpected eventualities. That person is you."

Lowell rose from his chair, glared down at Sumner for a moment, then began pacing back and forth across the room. He did this for more than a minute, occasionally rubbing his chin, then stopped and took up his glass of wine from the table.

"You are suggesting that I take a large shipment of illegal weapons into the Confederacy, get it past the customs officials without their learning what it is, and then somehow locate Saul and his band of rebels in the Louisiana swamps, even though they are doing everything they can to make sure no one can find them?"

"That's right."

Lowell shook his head. "You know, Senator, during the war I sent men on missions from which I doubted they would return. Many of them didn't, in fact, return. Suicide missions, you might say. What you're asking me to do sounds a lot like one of those suicide missions."

"But those men went, didn't they?"

"Yes, they did."

"Well, if they went, so can you. And you risked your life many times during the war. How would this be any different?"

There was a slight pause. "I would consider it unlikely that we would even reach Saul," Lowell said. "A suicide mission is only worth doing if there is a chance of success."

"I understand from Mr. Douglass, though he has declined to provide me with the details, that there is a man in New Orleans who says he can communicate with Saul."

Lowell's eyebrows went up and he returned to his seat. "Tell me more."

"That's all I know myself. The trouble is that we have no way of ascertaining whether or not what this man in New Orleans is being truthful. You will have to determine that when you arrive in the city."

"Going into the Confederacy myself entails a certain amount of risk," Lowell said simply. "I would consider my safe return extremely doubtful."

"Perhaps."

Lowell nodded and was silent for a time, mulling the matter over in his mind. Sumner waited patiently, nursing his wine, not wanting to hurry Lowell. The young man was making what could be one of the most important decisions of his life. Sumner wondered how much was at stake at this moment. Perhaps it was nothing more than the fate of a few dozen brave men in a swamp. Perhaps it was much more.

"You were right before," Lowell said finally. "When you said that the war is not over. No man of conscience can stand by and do nothing while slavery continues to exist. I lost too many friends and loved ones on the battlefield to be able to forgive and forget."

"So you'll do it?"

"Yes, Senator. I will."

Lieutenant-Colonel Garnet Wolseley was made for war.

"Your men look most impressive," he said with admiration to the man walking beside him. "Especially considering the long sea voyage."

"Thank you," replied Colonel Edward Bell, commanding officer of the Second Battalion, Royal Welch Fusiliers. "They always turn out very well for inspection. Luckily for me, they fight even better."

The two British officers marched down the parade ground, carefully studying the line of Welsh troops, stern expressions on their faces. The soldiers stood absolutely still, their eyes staring solidly forward. A stiff breeze ruffled their red coats and dark trousers, but not a single man moved even a fraction of an inch. It was as though they were all made of stone.

The officers were dressed differently than was the case in most British regiments. Five dark silk ribbons, known as 'the flash' dangled from the back of each man's neck. Steel scabbards, rather than the customary leather ones, were clasped to each officer's belt and each of them also wore a blue patrol jacket. These subtle variances were unique to this very special regiment.

Wolseley and Bell pressed on with their inspection, finding nothing amiss. Each weapon they inspected was perfectly clean, each uniform immaculate. When Colonel Bell put them through drill, they performed flawlessly. Wolseley wasn't surprised, for the Royal Welch Fusiliers were legendary. One of the most storied regiments in the entire British Army, it had been formed so long ago that it retained the archaic spelling of 'Welch' instead of the more proper 'Welsh'. Official efforts to correct the spelling error had been fiercely resisted by the men of the regiment, who protected their history with the same ferocious energy with which they fought against the enemies of the Queen.

They passed by the color guard, which held the regimental flag. Emblazoned upon it were the names of some of the greatest battles in British history. Blenheim. Minden. Waterloo. At these and many other epic clashes, the Royal Welch Fusiliers had played their part.

Impressed though he was, Wolseley did not know if he entirely agreed with the regiment's devotion to tradition. In many ways, he found the British Army hopelessly antiquated. In a dangerous world, with a large empire to protect and expand, Her Majesty's military needed to be as effective and powerful as possible. Clinging to ancient traditions might be a hindrance to that end. On the other hand, he knew the power of *esprit de corps* and unit identity. Such things bound men together to create formidable fighting forces and that was obviously to be encouraged.

"I am very happy to see the men armed with the Snider rifle," Wolseley said approvingly. The new breech-loading weapon had been approved for use just the previous year.

"They received them just before we embarked for Canada," Bell replied. "They are much more accurate than the old muzzle-loaders."

"Yes, and they can be loaded much more quickly and easily. The superior rate of fire will vastly increase the firepower of any battalion armed with the Snider."

"I was very sad to give up the old Enfield, which had served us so long and so well. Rather like parting from an old friend. But I suppose we must change with the times, as much as we might not want to."

"You're not opposed to the change, I hope."

Bell considered this for a moment. "I am not opposed to change in and of itself. I simply think that it should be delayed as long as possible and only enacted when there is no other choice. It seems to me that anything that changes makes the world worse for us. Therefore, it is in our interest that as little changes as possible."

Wolseley turned and glanced at Bell for a moment. He had met the man twice before, first during the Crimean War and then again in India during the Sepoy Mutiny. He felt a burning envy when he looked upon the Victoria Cross, the Empire's highest award for gallantry, pinned onto Bell's uniform. The Fusilier colonel had won it when he had single-handedly captured a Russian artillery battery during the Battle of Alma. Bell was a brave man, but Wolseley also considered him an example of the inflexible tradition that held back the British Army. He reflected on the fact that Colonel Bell was the son of a Lieutenant General and had therefore been granted a commission as a matter of course.

Wolseley, by contrast, came from a family of no wealth and few connections. He had clawed his way up to the rank of Lieutenant-Colonel through merit alone, an almost unheard of achievement in the British Army. He had paid a heavy price for his advancement. Though still only in his mid-thirties, Wolseley had earned more than a few scars fighting to expand Her Majesty's empire. He walked with a limp, the result of a bullet wound during the 1853 campaign in Burma. The left side of his face was deeply scarred thanks to a severe wound inflicted by Russian artillery at the Siege of Sevastopol during the Crimean War, which had also stolen the vision from his left eye.

As they came to the end of the Royal Welch's line, the two officers came upon one soldier who was standing at attention next to a goat. The animal, strangely enough, appeared to be standing at attention as well, staring straight ahead as though it was also worried about passing inspection. Wolseley wasn't surprised. The Royal Welch Fusiliers always took their honored goat, invariably named Billy, with them wherever they went. The tradition had been religiously followed by the regiment for at least the last century, but how the practice had begun was one of those mysteries that was lost in the shadows of time. No one knew. More importantly, no one really wanted to know. It was just the way it was.

Colonel Bell barked out a series of orders. With precision, the Welsh soldiers turned and marched back towards their barracks. Wolseley admired the marching skill the men demonstrated. He wondered if his own regiment, the Perthshire Light Infantry, could do as well.

An inquisitive look crossed Bell's face and he turned to Wolseley. "I say, old boy, were you the fellow back in the Crimea who suggested that our soldiers be taught how to read and write?"

"I am the man, sir."

Bell shook his head. "A dangerous idea, if you don't mind my saying so. I mean no disrespect, you understand, Wolseley. But what good would it do for us to have literate soldiers?"

"I think the more intelligent a soldier is, the better a soldier he will be." Wolseley decided against mentioning the fact that he was hard at work on a field manual to be read by enlisted men. It was a task to which he had devoted most of his free moments for the past two years.

"They would only fill their heads with nonsense," Bell protested.

"I respectfully disagree, Colonel. When I visited the armies of the Union and Confederacy during the late war in America, I found to my surprise that almost all the men in both armies could read and write."

Bell scoffed. "Yes, well, our men are not Americans. Let the Americans prattle on about politics and ideologies, not our men. Better that the Queen's soldiers focus on drill."

Wolseley said nothing in response.

"Shall we move on to inspect your militia?" Bell asked.

"Certainly," Wolseley replied with feigned enthusiasm. He was not looking forward to having a superior officer, and a winner of the Victoria Cross to boot, scrutinize his militia soldiers. As Deputy Quartermaster-General of British forces in Canada, it had been Wolseley's task for the previous few years to train the Canadian militia. Only about ten thousand British troops were in Canada, pitifully few to protect the colony should war ever break out with the United States. Only by supplementing their forces with local militia would anything like a respectable resistance be possible. With the Fenian threat growing, this was becoming a more serious matter every day.

Wolseley felt like a woman going to an evening party knowing that her dress was not nearly as elegant as those likely to be worn by other guests. The Royal Welch Fusiliers was a proper British regiment. Compared to them, his Canadian militia were pathetic amateurs. He had trained them rigorously, of course, but he was certain that any positive words from Bell would be made out of politeness only.

As Wolseley led Bell down the line of militiamen, whose uniforms were somewhat shoddy and whose arms were frequently found to be unclean, his embarrassment was intensified. Moreover, the militiamen were nowhere near as trim and fit as the Welsh troops they had just inspected. Many were rather plump and had puffy cheeks. As hard as he had worked to bring them into fighting condition, Wolseley had serious doubts about how well they would fare in a fight with the Americans.

His embarrassment emphasized his resentment at his exile in the Canadian backwater. He greatly enjoyed the hunting, but in every other way Canada was boring and frustrating. Around the world, in places like China, southern Africa, and the northwest frontier of India, the regiments of Queen Victoria were fighting on almost a daily basis. Yet Wolseley had been stuck in Canada for the past several years. He was unable to compete in the game of money and social connections to earn promotion, and would have been unwilling to do so even if he had. The only way to move up through the ranks was to earn distinction by fighting. He was so eager for battle that it felt like a burning inside his soul.

"Your militia seem solid," Bell said.

"I appreciate that, Colonel, but there is no need to flatter me," Wolseley said. "I know how they look."

"No, I am being sincere. Considering the material with which you have to work, I am impressed. If the Fenians cross the border, I am confident that the militia will be up to the task of defeating them."

"I do hope so. In any case, I continue to rigorously train them with all the means at my disposal. I want them to be more than a match for the Fenians."

Wolseley's analytical mind rapidly reviewed the trouble with the Fenians. Beginning in the 1840s, huge numbers of Irishmen had immigrated to the United States to escape the potato famine. Among them were large numbers of nationalistic revolutionaries who wanted to separate Ireland from the British Empire. America, with its silly notions of democracy and egalitarianism, had provided these agitators with a perfect environment in which to radicalize the arriving immigrants. The result had been the formation of the so-called Fenian Brotherhood.

Determined to free Ireland from British rule by force, thousands of Fenian sympathizers had enlisted in the Union army during the War for Southern Independence. This was done less out of devotion to the Union cause than to gain military experience they could eventually use against the British. By all accounts, these men had fought bravely throughout the war, suffering heavy casualties at battles such as Fredericksburg and Gettysburg. When the guns had fallen silent, untold thousands of Irish veterans, now trained in warfare and experienced in battle, had been discharged from the Union army. What these men were going to do was a matter of great concern to the Canadian and British authorities.

The failure of the Union war effort had done nothing to deter the Fenian Brotherhood from acting against the British Empire. Clandestinely assembling in northern New York, they had mounted several small-scale raids across the border into Canada. These had not done serious damage and, in and of themselves, were little more than annoyances. Rumor had it, though, that these forays had been only initial probes and that attacks on a much larger scale were to be mounted within the next few months. More infuriatingly, the United States government had done little or nothing to stop the attacks.

Wolseley and Bell came to the end of the militia's line and Wolseley ordered them back to their barracks. The sloppiness and laxity with which the Canadian soldiers marched embarrassed him further. Wolseley was glad that the joint reviews were almost over. The point had been to let the Canadian militiamen get a chance to see what real soldiers looked like. Now that they had, Wolseley could only hope it would inspire them to do better.

Bell turned to look at him. "I should like to extend an invitation for you to dine with us at the officers' mess, Colonel."

"I would be delighted," Wolseley quickly replied. In truth, he had mixed feelings. While he would enjoy the good food and fine wine sure to be served in the mess of a regiment as distinguished as the Royal Welch Fusiliers, he did not wish to become an object of pity. Moreover, as 'shop talk' was generally forbidden in such a dignified setting at the officers' mess, Wolseley would have to restrain himself from expressing his opinions about the state of the army or the snobbery of its senior commanders, something he found difficult to do. Yet he could hardly decline Bell's kind offer.

"Very good," Bell said, smiling. "I shall send you the details as to time and place."

"Thank you, Colonel."

"I bid you a good afternoon."

"And you, sir."

The two men exchanged salutes and Colonel Bell departed to see to the billeting of his men. Wolseley watched him go, feeling the envy burn. Bell was less than ten years older than he was and was already a decorated commander of one of the elite battalions of the British Army. Would Wolseley be in such a place in ten years? The fear that he would not gnawed at him unmercifully.

He strode across the encampment until he reached the small wooden building where his office was located. As he took his seat, he noticed that the first report on his desk described the preparedness of the second battalion of the East Devonshire Regiment, which had arrived from England a few months before. Happily, all seemed well with the unit.

He took a deep breath and poured himself a cup of tea. Now that he had finished his inspection, the remainder of the day would be occupied in endless paperwork that was his lot as Assistant Quartermaster-General in Canada. Wolseley didn't mind, for he had always been a man who loved absorption with detail. Were the battalions now arriving from Britain receiving the correct amount of rations? How fast was the average loading speed of a Canadian militiaman? How long would it take to move units by rail from one section of the border to another? What were the last known positions of the Fenian bands on the other side of the Saint Lawrence River?

Wolseley reveled in this kind of information. As he read through the various reports on his desk, his mind danced contentedly in an abstract realm of facts and figures. It was knowledge and expertise that would win the wars of the future. Of that, Wolseley had no doubt. The first inklings of it had been obvious in Napoleon's day. If he could make himself a master of such administrative work, it would greatly help him advance his career.

He was no fool, though. Even with the best organized system and the most accurate information, an army was only as good as the men that filled its ranks. He thought for a moment about the Royal Welch Fusiliers. Their uniforms were immaculate, their training impeccable, their discipline faultless. Wolseley agreed with the late Duke of Wellington that the enlisted men of the British army were the scum of the earth. It was their training and discipline that made them formidable, along with the sheer courage of its officer corps.

He thought back to 1862, when he had taken a leave of absence to visit the Confederacy and see the War for Southern Independence up close. He had been fascinated by the Confederate Army, whose men had been rough, undisciplined, and willing to express their own opinions to their superiors. Some units had even elected their own officers, an idea Wolseley found absurd. Everything Wolseley believed told him that such democratic and egalitarian attitudes should ruin an army, yet the Southerners had made formidable soldiers, regularly defeating enemy armies that greatly outnumbered them.

Perhaps the reason lay with the South's brilliant leaders, many of whom Wolseley had met. Robert E. Lee, perhaps the greatest general since the Duke of Wellington, had greatly impressed him. In Stonewall Jackson, he thought he had glimpsed a military genius of the highest order. Along with James Longstreet, Jubal Early, and all the other commanders in the Army of Northern Virginia, Lee and Jackson had created a group of leaders that could somehow mold the raucous and undisciplined Southern soldiers into an invincible fighting force.

Another factor that had favored the Confederacy was the simple fact that its men had been fighting to protect their homes and families from hostile invaders. Wolseley had considered the Northern rhetoric about abolishing slavery and saving the Union to be self-serving bombast. The South had found its own way to regulate the relationship between the black and white races, and Wolseley didn't think it was the business of any other people to interfere with it. He disliked and distrusted the abolitionist societies that existed back home in England, considering them troublemakers. As for the abstract idea of the American union, if the people of the South wanted out, they should have been allowed out.

As fascinating as the Southern army had been, however, there was little Wolseley had learned from his sojourn into the Confederacy that he could apply to his duties with the British Army.

They were two completely different entities, representing two completely different societies. The South was learning from Britain, however. The Confederate Secretary of War, John C. Breckinridge, whom he had befriended when he had been in Toronto for the peace negotiations two years before, was constantly sending him letters inquiring about various details of the British Army's organization, especially its unique regimental system.

The correspondence between Wolseley and Breckinridge was based entirely on personal friendship, for official relations between the British Empire and the Confederacy were not close. The abolitionist societies in Britain, who had the support of many members of the House of Commons, had made sure that London not draw too closely to Richmond. The Confederacy's flirtation with France, Britain's traditional enemy, had also raised suspicions among the decision-makers in Britain.

This made Wolseley sad, for it seemed to him that Britain and the Confederacy were natural allies. For all its expressed egalitarianism, the South was still an aristocratic society in which an established elite governed the nation, just as in Britain. Moreover, they shared a common enemy in the United States. If Britain ever did go to war with the Union, over the Fenian raids or for any other cause, it seemed obvious that it should have the Confederacy as an ally. Wolseley was not surprised that the members of Parliament failed to see this, for he considered most of them to be fools.

Wolseley relished the idea of a war between the British Empire and the United States. In his time, he had fought against the enemies of Queen Victoria in many exotic places around the world, but never had he faced what he considered to be a worthy adversary. The Russians had had good artillery, as the scars on Wolseley's face proved, but their army was otherwise shaky. The sepoy mutineers in India had been trained by the British and had fought bravely, but their lack of officers of quality meant that they had been easily defeated when fought on anything like equal terms. The Burmese and Chinese, needless to say, had fought so ineptly that beating them had scarcely been worth the bother.

The Americans, though, might be just the worthy adversary he was looking for. They were battle-hardened from their war with the Confederates, led by experienced and competent officers, lavishly equipped with the latest weaponry. Going into battle against the Americans would be a genuine challenge. Wolseley's pulse quickened at the mere thought of it.

He poured himself another cup of tea and concentrated again on the paperwork before him.

April 14, Noon
Granbury County Courthouse, Waco, Texas

The square in front of the courthouse was crowded with hundreds of people. Most of them were white, but there were some Tejanos. The auctioneer's stand had been set up on the courthouse steps and the auctioneer himself was already there, chatting with some local officials. Off to the sides of the square, vendors were peddling cornbread, peanuts, and mugs of beer and cider. The atmosphere was expectant, as everyone was waiting for the auction to begin.

It had been a long time since McFadden had seen so many people in one place. During the war, he had been a soldier in a vast army, accustomed to seeing thousands of men crammed together in enormous camps. Since his return to Texas, seeing more than a dozen or so people at any one time was an unusual event. Days would sometimes pass in which he did not see anyone aside from Annie or little Thaddeus. Hired hands came out to the ranch on a regular basis, but rarely more than three or four at a time. For the most part it was just the three members of the McFadden family and that was the way he liked it.

He had arrived in Waco the previous evening, riding his mustang Yellowjacket, the favorite of the three horses he owned. He had boarded at Grayson's Inn, which had been established the previous year by a returning veteran who had served in Terry's Texas Rangers. Though he preferred the solitude of his ranch, he still found himself visiting Waco about once a month, sometimes with Annie and sometimes by himself. These trips mostly involved various business matters or to retrieve his mail, but he also took the time to visit the shops. He occasionally had dinner with old comrades from the 7th Texas who happened to live in the area. Waco wasn't a boomtown like Atlanta, but it had enough aspects of civilization to make life on the Texas frontier a bit less primitive. For that, McFadden was thankful.

Having already had breakfast, he stood with his arms folded, watching the auctioneer's stand and waiting for the proceedings to begin. Collett had told him to meet him in the square, so until his old friend appeared he had little to do but wait.

Off to one side, standing amidst a circle of sycophantic hangers-on, was Judge Lucius Roden, the man who effectively ruled Granbury County. He was an overweight man with a red face, leading McFadden to conclude that he was

101

probably a heavy drinker. His larger-than-average lips were curled into an unpleasant and ominous smile, reminding McFadden of a cardsharp.

Thankfully, McFadden had avoided any involvement with Judge Roden. He doubted than the man even knew who he was, which was fine with him. McFadden's father had owned the ranch before the war and his title to the land was unquestionable. The Turnbow fortune made sure that he could pay his land taxes even though the ranch was not yet profitable, so he did not have to worry about his land being seized. Roden might be powerful, but even he was limited by the letter of the law.

"Jimmy!" a voice called.

He turned and saw Major Collett approaching with a woman by his side who McFadden assumed was the Widow Williams. In contrast to Collett, who wore his habitual smile, Mrs. Williams appeared anxious and tense. McFadden could understand why, as the proceedings about to commence would determine whether or not she would be allowed to remain in her home.

"Mrs. Williams, this is Captain James McFadden," Collett said. "Jimmy, this is Mary Williams."

"How do you do, ma'am?"

"Well, I suppose," she said. Her meek tone and pursed lips showed that she was lying. "I cannot tell you how much I appreciate what you and Major Collett are doing."

"It is nothing," McFadden replied. "Your husband was one of our comrades and a good man. We could not stand by and do nothing while his wife was forced off her land."

She nodded quickly, her eyes fearful and worried. For just a moment, McFadden recalled the death of Alton Williams at the Battle of Chickamauga. The 7th Texas had been participating in the grand assault which had broken the right flank of the Union army on that memorable day. The Yankees had turned and fled and the Confederates had chased after them, capturing many prisoners. Yet occasionally some stubborn groups of Northern soldiers would stop and try to hold their positions.

It had been in one such moment that Alton Williams had been shot through the head. As battlefield deaths went, Williams had gotten off easy, as he had been killed instantly. Far worse was to be shot in the belly, which virtually guaranteed a man a lingering, painful death. Equally bad was to be hit in an arm or leg and have it sawed off by one of the surgeons in a dirty field hospital, only to succumb to gangrene after a few nightmarish days.

McFadden shook the unpleasant thoughts from his mind. The war was over and had been for more than two years. With any luck, he would never hear the sounds of battle again.

He considered the Widow Williams, a small and slightly portly woman, not especially attractive. He wondered how grieved she must have been when she had received the dreadful letter announcing the death of her husband. To be left so utterly alone had to be terrifying. Perhaps it was not so terrifying as what one experienced on a battlefield, but battles last a few hours and are then over. The Widow Williams had been left alone forever.

He looked at Collett. "How much were you able to raise?"

Two hundred dollars. Lots of the boys pitched in. Quite a feat when you consider how tough times are."

McFadden nodded. He figured that the Williams Ranch, a few dozen acres of sparse and cactus-ridden ground, would be valued at around three hundred dollars. With any luck, McFadden wouldn't have to put up for than forty or fifty dollars of his own money for them to regain the land. Though he was determined to help Mrs. Williams, he didn't want to set tongues wagging throughout Waco about how much money he had.

"Major Collett!" a voice called. "Captain McFadden!"

He turned to see Daniel Jones, a man who had been a private in the 7th Texas. Having been captured by the Yankees during the retreat from Missionary Ridge in the fall of 1863, Jones had spent the latter part of the war in a Northern prison camp, thus missing the Atlanta Campaign. McFadden had known Jones only slightly during the war, but had become more familiar with him since his return to Texas, as he had settled on his land grant only a few miles away from him.

"Hello, Daniel!" Collett said as Jones approached. "Good to see you!"

"And you, Major. Is this Mrs. Williams?"

"I am," she replied. They shook hands.

Jones looked contrite. "I am sorry that I was not able to contribute money to saving your ranch," Jones said. He frowned. "I'm afraid that my affairs haven't prospered the way I hoped they would."

"That's all right, Mr. Jones," she replied. "Times are very hard."

"That's true. In fact, that's why I'm here. I'm selling out."

McFadden frowned. "I'm very sorry to hear that, Daniel. I've enjoyed having you as a neighbor. I know your land hasn't produced as much as you thought it would, but surely you can give it one more year?"

Jones shook his head. "No, I'm tapped out. One more year would ruin me."

"What are you going to do, then?"

"California," Jones said. "Pretty much everything I own can fit in my saddle bag. Whatever I can make from today's auction I'll take with me and set up in San Francisco or some other place out there."

"You'd be willing to live in a place under Yankee rule?" Collett asked.

"There's jobs out there, I'm told," Daniel replied. "A man's got to work, Yankee rule or no."

McFadden nodded. Jones was far from the first man to tell him he was giving up on the Texas frontier and heading across the Rocky Mountains. With economic prospects in the South not appearing very bright, there was a steady stream of Confederate veterans heading westward. The days of the gold rush might be over, but California was still spoken of as a land of milk and honey, where anyone willing to work hard could make a life for himself and his family. McFadden himself was skeptical, not knowing why California should be expected to be any less forgiving a place than Texas.

The auctioneer took his place on the rostrum.

"Welcome, everyone!" The man's clear voice rang across the crowd and everyone became quiet. "We are ready to begin. I hope you fine fellows are ready for a morning of buying and selling land, because that's what I'm all about up here. Let's start with the tract on the north bank of the Brazos River called the Hewitt Ranch. Do I hear fifty dollars?"

The auction thus began and it went on for some time. Tracts of land throughout Granbury County were up for grabs. According to the schedule, after the land auction was over, livestock would go on sale. McFadden was hoping to purchase some Hereford cattle for his ranch, as it would improve his stock. If any goats were on offer, he might consider buying some of them, too.

Within a very short time, McFadden stopped thinking about livestock, for he noticed a dismaying pattern to the land sales. Almost all the bids were being made by the cluster of wealthy-looking men standing around Judge Roden. Within the crowd itself, some men bravely offered up to a hundred dollars or so before reaching the limit of their resources, upon which the rich men easily snatched up the tracts on offer with higher bids. The men standing by Roden looked jubilant, while most of those in the crowd looked disappointed, even ashen.

McFadden wondered how many of the saddened men in the crowd were facing the same predicament as the Widow Williams. How many of them had had their land confiscated by the county and were now desperately trying to buy it back? For them, it was not a simple land investment, but a matter of trying to save their homes. McFadden's stomach tightened when he considered that many of the men had wives and children to worry about.

The disheartening scene continued to unfold. A tract of land would go on the block and a bidding match would be launched between a rough-looking man in the crowd and one of the fat cats standing near Judge Roden. Inevitably, the poorer man would be outbid and the hammer would come down in favor of the richer man. All too often, the man in the crowd would sadly shake his head and began to walk away.

"I don't like this," McFadden whispered harshly to Collett. "Not one bit."

"What do you mean?"

"Look at those fat bastards over there. They're buying up every single land tract! Did all these poor fellows have their land taken by the county, too?"
Collett's eyes narrowed and he glanced around the crowd. "I don't know. I hope not. I thought it was just an ordinary land auction. Lots of the boys are talking about selling their land and headed out to California like Jones, aren't they?"

"Have you heard about any other people having the same problem as the Widow Williams?"

"Yeah, sometimes. But surely it happens a lot. I mean, times are tough. Not everyone is able to pay their taxes."

McFadden shook his head. "Not right. What we're seeing here is damn near criminal."

"The problem, Jimmy, is that the county judge is the fellow who decides what is and is not criminal around here. Seems to me he's the one doing it."

The auctioneer announced another tract of land for sale, describing its acreage, location, and the fact that it bordered the Brazos River and therefore could be easily irrigated. "Do I hear fifty dollars?" he declared.

A man in the crowd held up his hand. "Fifty!"

"Isn't that old Jack Weller?" Collett asked McFadden.

"Weller? Sergeant Weller, of the 10th Texas? I believe you're right." McFadden hadn't known Weller especially well, as he had served in a different regiment. But the 7th Texas and the 10th Texas had been brigaded together, so the two units had generally been in close proximity. McFadden remembered Weller as a good soldier and an unusually religious man.

"Fifty-five?" the auctioneer asked. One of Judge Roden's friends casually raised his hand and the auctioneer pointed to him. "Fifty-five! Do I hear sixty?"

It went on for some time, but the result was never in doubt. Weller was able to bid as high as a hundred-and-twenty-five dollars before he could go no further and the richer man outbid him. The hammer came down and the friends of Judge Roden had acquired yet another bit of land. Weller's lips tightened and his eyes moistened.

The auctioneer's voice rang out again. "Now we're taking bids on the next ranch up the Brazos, the Williams Ranch."

"That's mine," the Widow Williams whispered urgently. "Judge Roden's friends have gotten every tract so far!"

"Don't worry," Collett said. "We have enough money to keep your ranch."

"Are you sure?" she asked, frightened.

"Don't worry about a thing."

"Do I hear fifty dollars?" the auctioneer asked.

Collett raised his hand and the auctioneer acknowledged him. "There's fifty! Do I hear sixty?"

As McFadden had expected, one of Roden's cronies raised his hand. He was a portly man with a wart of his nose large enough for McFadden to see even from a distance. "Sixty here!" the man cried.

"There's sixty! Do I hear seventy?"

Collett kept bidding, matched each time by the wart-nosed man. As the amount approached one hundred dollars, the auctioneer seemed to slow down, shifting into increments of five rather than ten. He clearly expected the bidding to stop soon, as it had in all of the previous cases.

"One hundred and twenty!" the wart-nosed man said triumphantly, turning aside slightly to grin at Judge Roden.

"One hundred and thirty!" Collett shouted defiantly. This caused a rustling in the crowd, not only because the amount being bid had gone beyond that of any of the previous sales, but because the respective tones in the voices of Collett and the wart-nosed man seemed to promise something unusual and perhaps exciting. It was as if a duel was about to commence.

McFadden glanced over to Judge Roden and his people, noticing a furrowed brow on the face of the man who ruled Granbury County. The bidding man also looked confused and irritated, but continued to bid.

"One hundred and thirty five!"

"One hundred and forty!" Collett replied.

It kept going, to the undisguised delight of the crowd and the evident anger of Judge Roden's group. McFadden looked at the Widow Williams. Her face was tightly drawn and her lips firmly pursed. Her breathing was quick and sharp. It was evident that she was terrified.

"Two hundred dollars!" Wart-Nose finally thundered, glaring at Collett as if daring him to continue.

Collett hesitated. Two hundred dollars was the limit of the funds he and the fellow veterans of the regiment had been able to raise. He looked over at McFadden, for this was the moment where it would be up to him.

"Two ten!" McFadden said sharply.

The entry of a new player into the mix caused another round of muttering in the crowd. McFadden heard several people say his name and was surprised at being so widely recognized. He hadn't known that many people in Waco even knew who he was, but there was no time for considering the question.

"Two hundred and twenty five!" the wart-nosed man shouted, exasperation clear in his voice.

"Two hundred and thirty!" McFadden instantly shot back. He did his best to maintain a level tone, hoping that the appearance of nonchalance would deter the man from continuing further.

His opponent looked flummoxed and glanced to Judge Roden as if for encouragement. Roden himself glared down at McFadden, staring deeply into his eyes. McFadden recognized the menace, yet he was not intimidated. He had faced death a hundred times during the war. If he could charge the muskets of the Yankees at places like Chickamauga and Atlanta, he wasn't about to be frightened by a fat politician who had avoided military service.

"Two hundred and forty!" the wart-nosed man replied. Upping the ante by a full ten dollars was clearly a ploy, but the man's voice now betrayed uncertainty.

"Two hundred and fifty!" McFadden shot back.

"Two hundred and fifty-five!"

"Two hundred and sixty!"

McFadden kept his eye on Wart-Nose, but noticed Judge Roden leaning over to another one of his cronies and whispering something in his ear, eyeing McFadden all the time. He assumed that Roden was asking the other man if he knew who McFadden was.

The auctioneer glanced back and forth between McFadden and the wart-nosed man, before directing his question to the latter. "Are you finished, sir?"

Roden's friend paused a long moment before replying. "Two hundred and sixty-five!"

"Two seventy!" McFadden replied instantly, again striving to maintain the appearance of indifference. Annie would surely be surprised, since he had said he wouldn't spend more than thirty dollars or so. Yet she would not be angry, for she didn't want to see the Widow Williams tossed off her land any more than he did.

"Two seventy five?" the auctioneer asked, his eyes on the wart-nosed man. The man rubbed his chin for a moment, then slowly shook his head. The auctioneer slammed his hammer down. "Sold for two hundred and seventy dollars!"

The crowd erupted in cheers and applause. It was a triumph for them no less than for McFadden, Collett, and the Widow Williams, for they had seen the rich cronies of Judge Roden given at least one black eye.

The Widow Williams was crying. "Thank you, Major Collett! Thank you, Captain McFadden!"

Judge Roden began pushing forward into the crowd. McFadden sensed his approach before he actually saw him. Rudely shoving aside the people in his way, he soon loomed up in front of McFadden. Having seen him from a distance, McFadden was initially surprised at the man's size. Yet it seemed much more fat than muscle. The look in the man's eyes, more than his physique, was what made McFadden feel a sense of danger.

"Who the hell are you?" Roden demanded.

"Captain James McFadden," he replied. "Late of the 7th Texas Infantry Regiment." He spoke the name of his unit clearly and proudly. There was, after all, a big difference between one of the most fabled regiments of the Confederate Army and the local Home Guard units Roden had commanded, who had spent the war chasing deserters and harassing Unionists.

"You may have heard of him, Judge Roden," Collett said, trying to sound pleasant. "You're looking at the man who captured General Thomas at the Battle of Atlanta. He was mentioned in the dispatches by General Joseph Johnston himself."

Roden grunted in reply. It was obvious to McFadden that Roden didn't care one whit about his service during the war. "What business do you have depriving my friend over there of the land tract he wanted?" he snarled.

"Not sure what you're getting at, Judge," McFadden replied. "It's a land auction, isn't it? I have as much right as he does to bid on anything I want."

"See here, McFadden, or whatever the hell your name is," Roden said. "I run this county. As long as things go the way I say they are supposed to go, everything's smooth and easy and everybody stays happy. But when some nobody that I never heard of shows up and throws a bunch of mud in my friend's face, I'm not happy. Understand?"

McFadden didn't reply, for he couldn't believe the words he was hearing. He thought for a moment that Roden must be insane. The stories he had heard about the man were disturbing enough. Yet insanity wasn't what McFadden saw in front of him. It was simply the face of a cowardly and cruel man, clever without being intelligent, willing to step on others for both his own profit and simply because he enjoyed it.

"I asked if you understood," Roden said.

"I think that my understanding and your understanding are two different things," McFadden replied.

"I don't like the sound of that," Roden said. He took a step forward, thrusting his face towards McFadden. "Believe me, I am the wrong person to have as your enemy. If you ever cross me again, I will make you pay for it."

A fire welled up inside McFadden. His first instinct was to pull his bowie knife out of its scabbard and run it through the judge's belly, yet he knew that if he did that the law would see him dangling from a rope. He would do nothing that would endanger his ability to take care of Annie and Thaddeus. Yet he couldn't allow Roden to have the last word.

"If you think you can intimidate me with crude threats, Judge, you've got the wrong man. I fought in seventeen major battles during the war. I can't even remember how many skirmishes I fought in. How many did you fight in?"

Roden scowled, then turned and walked off. McFadden willed himself to calm down and his heartbeat slowly returned to normal. He had not felt so angry and flustered since he had left the army. It had been an unpleasant reminder of the man he had once been.

"I'd lay low for a while, Jimmy," Collett advised. "Maybe he'll forget about it."

"Maybe," McFadden replied. "Maybe not."

April 14, Noon
French Quarter, New Orleans

Toombs looked out the window as the carriage rumbled through the streets of New Orleans, a place which he had always found mystifying. With over a hundred thousand people, the city was by far the largest in the Confederacy and it was still growing. Yet it was more than the size of New Orleans that Toombs found puzzling. The city had a unique atmosphere that seemed fully Southern yet strangely alien at the same time.

The French Quarter was alive with noise and energy. The sidewalks were crowded with people passing by storefronts jammed with merchandise of every conceivable description. Lines were forming outside the more popular restaurants and the smell of cooked shrimp permeated the air. On many corners, newspaper boys were waving copies of *The Picayune* while shouting its headlines. A cacophony of voices, French as well as English, filled the air.

Of all of the sights Toombs could see out his carriage window, the strangest was that of black men dressed in fine suits and carrying themselves with confidence as they strolled through the streets. New Orleans was home to thousands of free blacks, some of whom had acquired considerable wealth. Like so many of his fellow Southerners, Toombs did not know quite what to make of this. Better, therefore, not to think on it too much.

Among the major cities of the Confederacy, New Orleans had been the least touched by the hardships of war. Captured by the Union early in the conflict, the Crescent City had endured three years of enemy occupation until the last Northern troops had departed on January 1, 1866. As much as he hated the Yankees, Toombs had to admit that they had administered the city well. The streets and gas lights were all in fine repair, an effective system of garbage collection had been instituted, and trade had continued. Because of this, even as cities like Atlanta and Richmond had not yet fully recovered, New Orleans had continued to flourish almost as though the war had never happened.

Whatever the political tumults that went on around the city, it remained one of the keys to the world economy. Its warehouses bulged with cotton and sugar that flowed in from surrounding states and vast amounts of corn and grain that came down the Mississippi River from the Union. From New Orleans, these commodities were shipped out to Europe, Latin America, and points beyond. The trade brought wealth and prosperity to New Orleans, as well as thousands of people looking for work.

Toombs glanced over at Stephens, who was quietly reading a newspaper as the carriage bumped along the street. Toombs had caught himself up on the news while they had been eating breakfast at their hotel that morning. Things seemed eerily calm. President McClellan had signed the bill relocating the capital from Washington to Philadelphia, a matter Toombs considered irrelevant. There was unrest with the Mormon population in the Utah Territory, but that was nothing new.

More seriously, in London, there had been a series of fiery speeches in the House of Commons denouncing the McClellan administration for not preventing Fenian bands from crossing into Canada from New York. It was amazing to Toombs that news from Europe could now reach North America in a single day rather than three or four weeks. The transatlantic telegraph had changed everything.

Stephens sighed and folded up the newspaper. "I am not looking forward to this meeting," he said.

"Why is that?" Toombs asked.

"Beauregard is a pompous blowhard. He has an amazing talent for talking endlessly without ever actually saying anything. I fear that this meeting will last far longer than it needs to."

"And you have great difficulty in tolerating fools," Toombs replied with a grin. "But don't worry. Beauregard is one of the most easily flattered men I have ever met. If you ever find yourself in difficulties during conversation with him, just make some comment about how wonderful or brilliant you think he is. Tell him his military skill rivals that of Napoleon or something like that. He'll stop talking in order to bask in the glow of his own magnificence."

"Well, you know him better than I do," Stephens said. He paused a moment before going on. "And, unlike me, you have a genuine reason for disliking him."

Toombs chuckled. "I assume you're referring to the misunderstanding he and I had back in `63?"

"Misunderstanding? He had you arrested, Robert."

Toombs laughed again, finding the memory amusing. While commanding a unit of Georgia militia near Savannah, which was in the military department then commanded by Beauregard, Toombs had an altercation with a railroad official who was supposed to be transporting his men. What should have been a minor problem had snapped his always fragile temper. To vent his frustrations, Toombs had harangued his men for half an hour, denouncing Jefferson Davis as a tyrant and hinting that a military coup might be necessary. The men had been thoroughly shocked and the unfortunate railroad official had concluded that the politician-turned-general had gone insane. Declaring the speech to be tantamount to treason, Beauregard had arrested Toombs. Though he had not been confined for long, the newspapers had a field day. In truth, Toombs had been delighted, for the whole episode had only given his speech against Davis greater exposure.

Toombs had disliked Beauregard to begin with and the incident had only increased his contempt. As far as Toombs was concerned, all West Pointers were elitist snobs who thumbed their noses at men like himself. He thought Lee and Johnston were overrated fools and most of the corps and division commanders were hapless idiots. The true strength of the Confederate Army lay in the quality of its ordinary soldiers and citizen-officers like himself.

Toombs's distaste for West Point was more than a personal whim, though. He felt very deeply that a professional standing army was a threat to the political liberty of the Southern people. A national army was absurdly expensive, requiring oppressive taxation and increasing debt. Even worse, it might be used by an unscrupulous president to overthrow the constitutional order and set himself up as a dictator. Better a system of militia run by the states than any kind of standing army with a professional officer corps.

These thoughts were still drifting through Toombs's mind as the carriage slowed to a stop in front of an attractive house built in the Greek Revival style and painted a warm yellow. Although lacking a dome and being set in the middle of a crowded street, it reminded Toombs somewhat of Monticello. The coachman called down, saying that they had arrived at General Beauregard's house.

Toombs and Stephens clamored out onto the sidewalk. The front porch was reached by a staircase off to the side, as if the builders had not wanted to harm the aesthetics of the house's façade by including stairs directly in front. A few moments later, they were knocking on the door.

A liveried slave answered within seconds.

"Vice President Stephens and Senator Toombs?"

"Yes," Toombs said impatiently.

"Very good. General Beauregard has been expecting you. If you will please follow me."

The slave led them to a drawing room. The walls were painted the same warm yellow as the exterior of the house. A large mirror hung over an elegant marble fireplace and a pianoforte occupied one corner of the room. Comfortable-looking blue upholstered chairs surrounded a small table set on a carpet in the center. Toombs glanced at the portrait on the wall, snickering to himself when he realized that it was Napoleon Bonaparte.

"General Beauregard will be with you shortly," the slave said. "Please help yourself to a drink in the meantime." He gestured to a whiskey decanter on a small table against the wall, then withdrew from the room.

Stephens sat down in one of the chairs, clearly tired by the long carriage ride. Toombs poured himself a whiskey before sitting in the chair across from the vice president.

"That preening little rooster intends for us to cool our heels, does he?" Toombs said.

"Don't jump to conclusions," Stephens replied. "Perhaps he has a legitimate excuse."

"The vice president and a senator have called on him, for God's sake!"

"Calm down and enjoy your whiskey."

Toombs sighed and took a sip of his drink. As always, the taste of whiskey flowing over his tongue and down his throat had a calming effect. Being a connoisseur, Toombs could tell instantly that it was expensive and high-quality liquor. Nevertheless, as the minutes passed and Beauregard did not appear, Toombs became increasingly agitated.

"Where is he?" he loudly asked after ten minutes had elapsed. "This is unacceptable!"

"Let him have his moment," Stephens replied. "Surely he knows why we've come. It will be by flattery that we will achieve what we came here for."

"If he is not here in the next two minutes, I am leaving."

110

"Remember that Beauregard is the vehicle through which you may achieve your own ambitions," Stephens said calmly. "Through him, we can make you my successor in the vice president's office. And in six years, you can vie for the ultimate prize yourself."

Toombs pursed his lips. Stephens knew him too well. Without a word, Toombs downed the entire contents of his glass in a single gulp, then rose from his chair to get another. Moments after he had finished pouring, the slave who had greeted them reappeared in the doorway.

"Gentlemen, may I present General Beauregard."

The slave stepped back into the hallway and Beauregard entered the room, a serious expression on his face. He looked exactly as Toombs remembered him from their last meeting, being of medium height and unremarkable build. Yet his eyes had a penetrating quality to them. His bushy mustache and thin goatee were quintessentially French. Although he was wearing an impeccable uniform, he struck Toombs as resembling a Caribbean pirate captain.

Beauregard bowed his head respectfully to Stephens. "Mr. Vice President. It is very kind of you to call on me here at my home." His Creole French accent made his words somewhat difficult to understand.

"Thank you, General Beauregard," Stephens answered, rising from his chair.

Beauregard looked at Toombs. "And Senator Toombs. It is good to see you again."

"And you didn't even have to arrest me this time," Toombs said as he strolled back to the table.

Beauregard smirked slightly but did not laugh. He gestured toward the chairs. "Please sit."

"Thank you for receiving us," Stephens said. "You are no doubt a very busy man."

"My work on the river fortifications keeps me very occupied," Beauregard said tiredly. "Fort Jackson and Fort St. Philip proved utterly inadequate to protect New Orleans from the enemy during the war. However, our defenses have been considerably improved. If the Yankees, or any other enemy, attempt to take New Orleans in the future, they shall find it a much more difficult task."

For the next several minutes, Beauregard droned on about the new fortifications he had designed and was now constructing. He spoke of interlocking fields of fire, different types of coastal artillery, underwater torpedoes, and other technical topics of little interest to Toombs. Beauregard seemed very proud of some sort of device he claimed to have invented which was designed to catch enemy warships in a massive chain. Toombs almost interrupted the general several times, but quick glances from Stephens persuaded him to remain silent. Toombs marveled at his friend's ability to feign curiosity about a subject of which he had little understanding and no interest. Beauregard might as well have been speaking to an empty room.

"I'm sorry," Beauregard said after an interminable amount of time. "I am sure I am boring you."

"Not at all," Stephens said. "The defense of the Confederacy is a topic of interest to everyone. However, there are some matters we would like to discuss with you."

"Oh?" Beauregard asked. "And pray tell, what is it you wish you discuss?"

Stephens paused a moment before continuing, glancing at Toombs for just a moment. Toombs nodded, almost imperceptibly.

"It is well known that you have little love for President Davis," Stephens began cautiously.

Beauregard grimaced, as if he had smelled something bad. "If I may ask, are we speaking today as private gentlemen? Or are we speaking in our official capacities, you as members of the government and myself as a general officer?"

"We are speaking as private individuals," Stephens said.

"In that case, I can say that I believe Jefferson Davis is a vile, despicable man who thinks of nothing but his own ambition. He's a fool. Almost all the problems our new nation faces today can be laid at his feet. I believe we would have won the war much sooner had we had a chief executive with any intelligence. The strategic mistakes Davis made cost the lives of many thousands of Southern soldiers. Had the right man been at the head of our affairs, we would be in a much stronger position today."

"Perhaps it will not surprise you to know that we heartily agree with you," Toombs said.

Beauregard laughed. "It surprises me not at all. I have read your speeches, Senator. The words you typically use to describe the president – tyrant, despot, dictator, and so forth – are quite appropriate, in my opinion. In my view, we have freed ourselves from the rule of an oppressive government in Washington only to find ourselves in thrall to a would-be monarch in Richmond."

"An apt description of the problem, General," Stephens said. "Davis continues to ignore the wishes of the states, abandoning the principle of state sovereignty for which we seceded in the first place. The state governments might as well not exist, as far as he is concerned. He continues to levy direct taxes upon the people. He continues to delay in establishing the Supreme Court. He continues to ignore calls for the acquisition of Cuba."

Beauregard nodded quickly. "The last is the most important point to me," he said with urgency. "The expansion of our Confederacy to the south is our national destiny. Cuba is the obvious first step. If it means war with Spain, as I expect it will, I am ready to lead our forces to victory."

Toombs frowned. The tone with which Beauregard had said the last sentence filled him with dread, for the Creole general seemed to relish the prospect of another war. Toombs was suddenly convinced that Beauregard would happily support a strong central government centered around a single dynamic individual, provided that Beauregard himself was that individual.

He felt a brief tug of indecision. Was it wise to put Beauregard, a man of such enormous personal ambition, forward as a presidential candidate? Would they be able to control him? Toombs thought for a moment that perhaps they should have approached James Longstreet, a popular figure who might have won the election but who didn't suffer from delusional beliefs that he was infallible. Or perhaps they should never have chosen to select a military figure at all. He wondered if it was too late for them to change course.

Toombs comforted himself with the thought that Beauregard did not appear to be a deep political thinker. It was glory and position that Beauregard was after. Such a man could easily be manipulated into adopting the positions that Toombs, Stephens, and their allies wanted.

"But why are we even speaking of Davis?" Beauregard asked. "His term will soon be up. And even he is not foolish enough to attempt to throw out the Constitution and remain in office beyond the six years allocated to him."

"I will tell you, General," Toombs said with conviction. "The rumors swirling around Richmond these days are that Davis wishes to hand-pick a successor who will continue his policies. It is even possible that his plan is to continue to rule the Confederacy through a puppet president."

Beauregard's face darkened. "If that is the case, it poses a serious threat to the future of our republic. The newspapers have said that Lee will not be running, so who is the man being groomed as Davis's successor?"

"We are not entirely certain," Stephens replied. "But we suspect that it may be John Breckinridge, the Secretary of War."

Beauregard nodded. "I do not know Breckinridge well. We served together at Shiloh and he acquitted himself well. A good general for a man with no military training. But then war should be left to the professionals."

The last sentence struck Toombs like a fist in the face. He had to restrain himself from launching into a tirade against the travesty of a standing army and a professional officer corps. In an instant, his mind recalled a dozen historical examples of ambitious generals who had overthrown legitimate governments. Caesar in ancient Rome. Cromwell in England. Napoleon in France. He glanced for a moment at the portrait of the French emperor on the wall. Any man who would glorify a tyrant like that surely had the inclination to become a tyrant as well, if the opportunity presented itself.

A few moments earlier, Toombs had reassured himself with the thought that Beauregard had no political convictions. Now the idea frightened him. An ambitious man with no principles was, in fact, a dangerous man, for there would be nothing to restrain him from trying to accumulate all power to himself.

"General Beauregard?" Toombs quickly interjected. "I am very sorry, but I must speak with Vice President Stephens out in the hallway for just a moment."

Beauregard looked at him quizzically. Stephens had a momentary look of trepidation but quickly recovered. "Of course," Beauregard said with seeming calmness.

Toombs gestured with his head towards the door. Stephens pursed his lips and hesitated just long enough to register his displeasure, then rose from his chair and followed Toombs out into the hallway. The door closed quietly behind them.

"What is this, Robert?" Stephens asked urgently. His expression was one of irritation.

"This is a mistake, Aleck. We're making a terrible blunder. Making Beauregard our candidate will be like letting the wolf into the henhouse. He will be worse than Davis a hundred times over!"

"Calm yourself," Stephens said quietly but urgently, glancing uncomfortably back toward the door. "Look, Robert, we have come too far. We are committed. As we speak, Wigfall and the others are working on the assumption that Beauregard will be our standard bearer. They're lining up support on that assumption. We've come too far to go back."

"It's not too late," Toombs said urgently. "We could leave here and send a telegram to Wigfall within the hour. Perhaps we could approach Longstreet or some other general. I am sorry, Aleck, but I suddenly cannot shake the fear that we are about to make a terrible, terrible mistake."

Stephens whispered harshly. "We went over this again and again at the meeting in Georgia, Robert. Beauregard is our man. We all agreed on that! If we break this thing off now, our political coalition will fall apart. Potential supporters will see us as disorganized and incompetent. It's too late, my friend. Either it's Beauregard or it's no one!" The last sentence came out almost as a hiss.

For an endless instant, Toombs stared hard at his old friend. As always, he couldn't disagree with what he was saying. There was no going back. Yet neither could he shake the feeling that putting Beauregard forward for the presidency might place the Confederacy in deadly peril.

Toombs sighed. "Very well. Let's go back in. Mistake or not, if we're going to do this we might as well do it properly."

They reentered the room. Beauregard looked at them with raised eyebrows.

"I am sorry, General Beauregard," Stephens said apologetically. "Senator Toombs suddenly remembered a personal matter he needed to discuss with me."

"I understand," Beauregard replied. His tone made it clear that he did not believe this but was not going to address the issue.

Stephens and Toombs returned to their seats. "Now, what were we discussing?" Stephens asked.

"You mentioned that Secretary of War Breckinridge may be a candidate for the presidency and that, if so, he is likely to be under the influence of President Davis."

"Ah, yes," Stephens said. "It is true, I am sorry to say."

Toombs sat glumly in his chair, picking his whiskey up from the table and taking a large swallow. He wondered if the scene playing out before his eyes would be discussed by future historians as the beginning of the end of the Confederacy.

The Creole general was still talking. "Of course, I am aware of the disdain felt by many people in our Confederacy towards Breckinridge on account of his actions during the Toronto peace conference. I believe he gave too much away when he agreed to allow the Yankees to keep the slaves they had stolen from us during the war. And he should have pushed harder for plebiscites in Kentucky and Missouri that might have allowed those states to be incorporated into the Confederacy."

"As a man who was also a delegate to the peace conference, I agree with you," Stephens replied. Toombs could sense in his old friend's tone and body language that he was not completely comfortable as he spoke these words, but he doubted Beauregard noticed anything.

"So, if we may get to the point, gentlemen," Beauregard said. "You are telling me that Jefferson Davis wants to maintain control of the Confederacy by personally selecting his successor and that this man is likely to be John Breckinridge?"

"That's about the size of it, General," Toombs said. He knew he had no choice but to go all in, just like a man who had no choice but to throw all his chips in at the end of a poker game. If he did manage to obtain the nomination for vice president and Beauregard did go on to win the election, perhaps he could be a moderating force on the ambitious general. In any event, dangerous as he thought Beauregard to be, it was still true that the man remained Toombs's own pathway to power.

"Well, then, what are we to do?" Beauregard asked. "More importantly, why do you feel the need to seek me out in regards to this matter?"

Stephens answered. "We are here, General Beauregard, to ask that you seek the presidency in the upcoming election. We are ready to offer our full support. We are already in the process of organizing our political friends and allies in all eleven states. If you are willing to be our standard-bearer, we will back you to the hilt and defeat the designs of Jefferson Davis."

Toombs felt a tightening in his stomach as his friend spoke these words. Beauregard's face betrayed no reaction. It was obvious to Toombs that the Creole was not surprised by what he had heard. He had probably discerned the purpose of the meeting from the moment he had received their initial telegram several days before.

"Tell me more about your plans," Beauregard said. "Being a candidate in an election is rather like being the commander of an army during a military campaign. If one is not properly prepared at the beginning, defeat is all but certain."

"We will be fully prepared," Stephens said.

Toombs and Stephens spent the next twenty minutes outlining their plan to summon like-minded politicians, military officers, and other influential citizens to a convention, while also organizing committees in each of the eleven Confederate states. The three of them discussed what city should host the convention and Beauregard recommended several names be added to the list of invitees, mostly officers with whom he had served during the war.

"So you agree to be our candidate?" Toombs finally asked.
Beauregard rose from his chair, a stern look on his face which struck Toombs as rather too theatrical. The general paused for a moment before responding.

"Gentlemen, when destiny calls you forth, you do not decline its offer. Yes, I shall be a candidate for President of the Confederate States of America."

CHAPTER FOUR

Sumner looked out the window as the train slowed to a stop inside the terminal. Many people were crowded along the platform, no doubt eager to board for journeys westward. Sumner, though, had reached the end of his trip. He held tightly to a carpetbag in which he had placed his most important items. He would have to trust the porters for the handling of his luggage.

When the train finally lurched to a halt, Sumner rose to depart, along with about half of the passengers on board. He had to push past the crush of people trying to board at the same time, restraining the urge to berate them for their rudeness. Sumner traveled on trains often enough to know that it would have done no good in any event. He could not understand why, but rail travel always made people less polite.

He finally pushed his way past everyone. He expected that it wouldn't take more than a few minutes to hail a hansom cab and his luggage should soon be on its way to his residence. With any luck, he would be home within the next half hour. Afternoon was only just settling into evening, so he looked forward to a night of rereading some Greek or Roman classics over a glass of wine. Perhaps he would settle on Livy, for it had been some time since he had read Livy.

"Senator Sumner!" a familiar and friendly voice called.

He turned and was greatly surprised to see William Seward approaching. The man who had served as Lincoln's Secretary of State was beaming a great smile out from beneath his large and distinguished nose. Seward's blue eyes sparkled with warmth and intelligence. As he came close, he eagerly extended his hand.

"Secretary Seward," Sumner said as he shook hands. "Well, this is a pleasant surprise. I am delighted to see you."

"No more so than I, my old friend."

"What brings you to Washington City?"

"I am here to see Frederick."

"Ah, yes," Sumner replied. "I am sorry I have not yet had the chance to call on your son since his election to the House last November. I assure you that I have intended to do so."

"I take no offense. I am sure you have been very busy."

116

Sumner allowed himself a rare smile. Seward's warm countenance brought forth recollections of happier times. He remembered how supportive Seward and his wife had been after he had suffered the brutal attack by Preston Brooks. He remembered how closely they had worked together during the war when Seward had served at the head of the State Department. It had been their joint efforts, in late 1861, which had prevented war between the United States and the British Empire during the Trent Affair.

They had not always agreed. Sumner had constantly pushed the Lincoln administration to adopt harsher war measures against the Confederacy and a more aggressive approach towards emancipating the slaves, with Seward often counseling Lincoln toward more moderate policies.

"Will you join me for dinner?" Seward asked. "We could talk about the old days."

Sumner hesitated. He was tired after his long train journey and had already set his mind on a quiet night of reading. Yet he could not turn down Seward's offer without appearing rude and he was genuinely pleased to see him. His mind was made up by the memory of many dinners at the Seward house in days past, which had always been characterized by delicious food and fine wine.

"I would be delighted."

"Good!" Seward said. "Come along, then. I telegraphed ahead for a hansom cab. I am sure there shall be room for two."

A few minutes later, the two men were rolling through the streets of Washington City, heading west on D Street. Sumner glanced out at the people walking to and fro along the sides of the streets. He did not care for Washingtonians by and large, for Washington City was a Southern town in many ways and more than a few of its residents had exhibited pro-Confederate sympathies during the war. Moreover, Sumner felt he had little time to consider the feelings or concerns of ordinary citizens. He was not, and didn't pretend to be, a man of the people.

"How is Mr. Lincoln?" Sumner asked Seward.

Seward sighed. "As well as could be expected, I suppose. His relaunched law practice in Springfield is keeping him busy." Seward paused for a moment. "You heard about poor Mary Todd, I am sure."

"Yes, I did," Sumner said sadly. The former first lady, to whom Sumner had been especially close, had been so distraught with her husband's defeat at the polls that she had collapsed into a depression so severe that she had been institutionalized. Even worse, Lincoln had also been forced to contend with the enormous debts Mary Todd had run up with high-end stores in New York City during the war, which had effectively ruined his finances.

"He keeps his spirits up, though. I'm sure that doesn't surprise you. You remember old Abe, don't you? He could face despair and nearly succumb to it, but would pull himself back out of the abyss every time."

"Yes, that's true," Sumner said. "I remember when I toured the battlefield at Antietam with him, not too long after the fighting had taken place. There were still bodies strewn about everywhere. Really a ghastly scene. And Lincoln made a joke! I couldn't believe it. How could a person make a joke at a time like that? I reprimanded him for it, but immediately regretted it. For he nearly broke down in tears, saying that humor was the only way he could keep the melancholy at bay."

Seward nodded. "Lincoln carried the whole cause on his shoulders. To lose in the end was the bitterest blow."

"Indeed."

Seward's face then brightened. "You'll be happy to know that I am sending him to Europe. He's always wanted to go. He says he can't afford it, so I am paying for him. I refused to take no for an answer. He leaves in June."

"That sounds like a lovely idea. I would be happy to write letters of introduction to my friends in England. Not that he'll need them, of course. His own fame will open all the doors he might want opened to him."

"Write them anyway," Seward said. "If nothing else, it will remind Abe how many true friends he still has."

They turned right and headed north on Fourteenth Street, passed by the Willard Hotel, then turned left on G Street before pulling to a stop in front of the Seward residence. He had not sold his elegant house in Washington City when he left to return to New York in the spring of 1865. People commented that this suggested that a run for the Senate might be in Seward's immediate future. As it was, the house was currently being used by his son.

Sumner found it touching to see Seward and his son reunited. The two men embraced warmly as they walked through the door and exchanged exuberant words of greeting. Sumner wasn't surprised at the open display of emotion, for he knew how much Seward cared for his family. He recalled the terror he had seen in Seward's face in July of 1864, when there had been a rumor that one of his sons, William Jr., had been killed at the Battle of Monocacy. He also remembered the tears of joy on Seward's face when word arrived that his son was alive, having only been slightly wounded.

Not for the first time, Sumner wished he had a wife and family. As quickly as the thought entered his mind, however, he thrust it out. Sumner's life was consecrated to the destruction of slavery. No desire for personal happiness could be allowed to get in the way of that.

Dinner with Seward and his son Frederick was pleasant. The food and wine were as good as he recalled from the wartime days when he had been invited to the house for dinner. After an appetizer of turtle soup, a dish of roast mutton and a variety of vegetables were brought out for dinner, all accompanied by an excellent Burgundy wine. Sumner marveled at the fact that he had arrived at the Seward home unexpectedly, yet its staff was still able to present him with a meal more delicious than anything he could have expected at any of the Washington eating establishments he frequented.

The conversation during dinner was agreeable but light. Frederick brought his father up to date on the latest gossip from the Washington social scene, news of what was currently showing at Ford's and Grover's theaters, and other such things. Sumner said little, only offering a brief opinion when either of the other men specifically asked for it. He had little time for such trivial things. As they moved through a dessert of almond cake with a bottle of Château d'Yquem, Sumner found himself wishing he had declined Seward's offer of dinner. Much as he was pleased to see his old friend, he now found himself wanting to be in his own study, sipping his own wine, rereading Livy.

"Shall we move into the study for some brandy and cigars, gentlemen?" Seward asked as the table cloth was removed by two black servants.

"Certainly, Father," Frederick said at once. "Senator Sumner?"

"By all means," Sumner said, hoping he sounded sincere. He told himself that he should join them, though he wanted to return home. After all, he had often been quietly reprimanded by his friends for not being social enough. Lincoln himself had told him many times to adopt a more amiable attitude.

Seward's study was a place where Sumner felt more at home than he did in the dining room. Hundreds of books lined the walls, arrayed in elegantly carved bookshelves. Interspersed were chairs and two sofas in the French style. A small fire was burning inside a large marble fireplace, casting a yellowish, dancing light throughout the room.

Sumner was not much of a brandy drinker and the name of the bottle that Seward grandly announced meant nothing to him. Frederick offered Sumner a cigar and the three men were soon filling the study with smoke. As Sumner took the first hesitant sip from his snifter, he finally heard a question in which he had a genuine interest.

"So what is the latest political news?" Seward asked.

Frederick let out a sardonic snort. "I wish I had happier tidings, Father. Little has changed here in Washington that would give you much cheer. McClellan continues to lord it over us. Our narrow majority in the Senate means little, as the Democrats control the House and will not consent to voting on even the most innocuous legislation sent over from the Senate. Since I took my seat in the House, I have not gotten to vote on anything I felt worth voting for. In short, nothing is being done while the country faces troubles on many fronts."

"It is worse than that, I am afraid," Sumner said. "The increasing split between the Moderate and Radical Republicans is deeply upsetting to me. The Capital Relocation Bill would have been defeated in the Senate had the Republicans remained united. As it was, enough Moderates voted for it that it passed." Sumner knew that both Seward and his son aligned with the Moderate faction, though to his credit the younger Seward had voted against the Capital Relocation Bill in the House.

"I read that in the papers," Seward said. "Very discouraging."

"It's worse even than the newspapers say," Sumner replied. "The Democrats seem happy to do nothing but enjoy the delights of holding power. The Radicals in the Senate have put forward all sorts of legislation to assist the refugee slaves along the border with the Confederacy. Much of this legislation, I am proud to say, I sponsored myself. But when they pass in our chamber, the House refuses to even bring the bills up for a vote. At times the Moderate Republicans and the Democrats in the Senate come together to vote them down in our chamber anyway."

Seward chuckled bitterly. "Well, the idea of any of the Democrats, much less McClellan, doing anything for the slaves is laughable. And while the Democrats remain in power, we can do nothing on their behalf, either." His tone suggested that he was trying to steer the conversation away from the Moderate-Radical split.

"I suppose not," Sumner said quietly. Seward was correct that the engines of the government were powerless to help the slaves, but Sumner reminded himself that the abolitionist cause was far from powerless. There were more ways to influence events than through the use of government power. His thoughts turned to Charles Russell Lowell, no doubt back in Boston planning his illegal mission into the South. He wondered for a moment if he should bring Seward into the confidence of the conspiracy and decided against it. The fewer people who knew about it, the better.

"The only thing the Democrats seem willing to do is encourage the Fenians in their struggle against the British," Sumner said. "So long as there is the possibility of a war against a foreign enemy, the Democrats can speak as though any opposition to their policies is disloyal to the nation."

Seward nodded sadly, sipping at his brandy. "And it gets them the Irish vote, even in regions that are normally our strongholds. Every day more Irish immigrants arrive in New York City and they are met by Tammany Hall men almost as soon as they get off the boats. They help them find a place to live and to get a job, so long as they vote for their candidate in the next election. It's no surprise that the Democrats gained control of the state legislature last year. Until the Republicans regain it, I shall not be able to return to the Senate."

It's not just in New York," Frederick said. "Out in places like Chicago and Cincinnati, local Democratic officials promise everything under the sun to the newly arriving immigrants. From Ireland, yes, but also from eastern and southern Europe, as well as the existing class of urban working poor. More than anything else, they promise to keep blacks from taking away their jobs."

"Demagoguery," Sumner said with disgust. "It's been the tool of ambitious and faithless men since the days of Greece and Rome. By focusing the attention of the working class on the idea that blacks may steal their jobs, the Democrats appeal to both their fear and their self-interest."

"Right out of Machiavelli," Seward commented.

"True, which makes it all the more sickening," Sumner said. "I do hope Salmon Chase is successful in the upcoming gubernatorial election in Ohio. Were he to win, it would send a clear message that the principles of virtue and liberty have not been entirely lost in that part of the country."

Seward shrugged. "I think Chase only sees winning the Ohio election as a first step towards a bigger thing," he said dismissively. "He wants to run for president next year."

Sumner wasn't surprised by the disdain in Seward's voice. He knew that Seward had a tense relationship with Chase, who had served in Lincoln's cabinet as Secretary of the Treasury while Seward had been Secretary of State. Yet Sumner thought he sensed something more behind the words Seward was speaking.

"Is he the only one who wants to be the Republican standard bearer next year?" Sumner asked.

Seward smiled and took a long sip of his brandy. "No," he said simply. "And let's leave it at that."

"Certainly," Sumner said. Between Chase and Seward, Sumner would not have known whom to choose. He considered both men to be strong opponents of slavery and gifted with enormous talent and intelligence. Either man might serve as the candidate to oust McClellan from office. Yet the Radicals would be supporting Chase and the Moderates would be supporting Seward. Sumner was a Radical through and through.

Sumner remembered the vicious political struggle between Seward and Chase in 1860, when the two men had grappled with one another for the Republican presidential nomination. The surprise victory of Abraham Lincoln, whom no one had considered important even a few months earlier, had taken everyone by surprise.

They talked on for another hour, mostly about the recklessness of the pro-Fenian policy of the McClellan administration, but Sumner felt the weight of sleeplessness combined with a heavier than normal consumption of alcohol begin to wear on him.

"Gentlemen, I am afraid I must take my leave."

Seward nodded. "My coachman will take you home."

"I am much obliged, both for the coach and for this very pleasant evening." Sumner rose from his chair and Seward followed him to the door while Frederick went to fetch the coachman. As they stepped outside, Seward's face suddenly became more serious.

"Charles, I would like to speak to you about the presidential election sometime."

"Of course, William."

"You are one of the first people to whom I am telling this. I do intend to be a candidate for the Republican nomination. I hope to have your support."

Sumner didn't respond right away, looking deeply into Seward's eyes. "Well, we shall have much to discuss, won't we?"

Seward's smile returned. "An understatement if ever there was one."

April 18, Night
Bridgewater Iron Works, Bridgewater, Massachusetts

Lowell had never expected his iron works to be the setting for a conspiracy. It was a special place to him, as sacred in its own way as the great cathedrals he had seen during his European travels. Not only did it give men the ability to earn livelihoods and care for their families, but it represented the hopes and dreams of an entire nation. The iron that came out of it, destined to be formed into bridges, railroads, and great buildings, was a manifestation of the idea of progress. More importantly, it was made by free men being paid wages, not slaves driven to work by the whip.

Lowell wondered if his iron foundry was being sullied by the meeting of plotters. Yet could a conspiracy in opposition to slavery sully anything? Should Brutus and Cassius have been ashamed to make their plans to slay the tyrant in the back rooms of their own homes? Lowell didn't think so. If anything, the meeting did the building honor.

It was approaching midnight. The building was silent and empty but for the three men in the office. A few oil lamps and candles provided the only illumination, creating a bubble of yellowish light inside the darkness of the building's vast interior. Lowell sat at his desk, almost as if this were an ordinary business meeting. Sitting in chairs opposite him were two fellow members of the conspiracy, Franklin Sanborn and George Stearns.

Lowell knew Sanborn quite well, as they had both been students at Harvard together and both had been active in various New England charitable enterprises. Unlike Lowell, however, Sanborn had not served in the army, choosing instead to focus his time and energy during the war on various relief efforts. Stearns was a much older man than either Lowell or Sanborn, a successful businessman who had bent his energies to the recruitment of black soldiers during the conflict with the Confederacy.

Both Sanborn and Stearns were fervent abolitionists who were willing to countenance violence in pursuit of the cause. Both had been clandestine supporters of John Brown's 1859 raid on Harper's Ferry, with Stearns going so far as to purchase the weapons Brown and his men used. Sumner had told Lowell that the two men were willing to provide financial assistance to the effort to smuggle weapons to Saul's rebels in Louisiana and assist in various other ways.

The meeting had been set up by Sumner. Both men had arrived, half an hour apart, long after the sun had gone down. Lowell doubted anyone had seen them enter the ironworks and, even if they had, he doubted anyone would have thought anything of it. It probably would have been perfectly safe for the two of them to arrive together at any time they wanted, but it didn't do to take chances. That was a lesson he had learned the hard way when matching wits against John Mosby in the forests of northern Virginia.

Lowell realized that his mind was already reverting back to that of a soldier. Asking Sumner to communicate to Sanborn and Stearns how they were to surreptitiously enter the ironworks had been the first active decision he had made as a member of the conspiracy. He had crossed his Rubicon the moment he had told Sumner that he would go to New Orleans. That had not been an easy decision. Yet now that he was committed, he found the whole thing somewhat easier, though he was troubled by the fact that he had not yet told Josephine.

"So, you're really willing to do this?" Sanborn asked as Lowell poured him another cup of tea. "You're willing to risk your life to get weapons to Saul?"

"He and his men need the means to fight," Lowell answered. "The Southerners have dismissed his efforts up to this point as simple outlawry. What do a few burned out plantations matter, or a few dozen freed slaves? Nothing, in the grand scheme of things. But if we can furnish weapons and ammunition to him, it could become a genuine slave revolt. A slave revolt that might spread like wildfire throughout the South."

"And what if it doesn't work?" Stearns asked. "What if you succeed in getting these weapons to the insurgents and they are still defeated?"

"I'm quite sure Saul's men would prefer to die fighting with rifles in their hands rather than be slaughtered like animals. I know I would."

Stearns nodded slowly and looked over at Sanborn. It was clear to Lowell that the two of them were sizing him up, trying to ascertain whether he truly had the stomach for what was being asked of him. He was determined to show that he did and he wasn't about to be intimidated by the fact that these were men who had shaken hands with John Brown.

"Senator Sumner told us that you could be relied upon," Stearns said. "I am beginning to believe that he was right."

Sanborn smiled. "I never doubted it. I knew you at Harvard. Even though you were a few years behind me, your determination and pluck stood out to me.

The way you overcame your consumption was, frankly, inspiring. When I heard all the stories of your exploits during the war, I wasn't surprised."

"Thank you," Lowell said, embarrassed. He never liked it when people spoke of him as though he were a hero. The real heroes were the ones who had not come home. Besides, when he had returned to New England at the end of the war, it had been as a veteran of an army that had failed to win.

"Well, I need no more convincing," Stearns said. "You're the man for it, Charles. Sumner says so. Douglass says so. Sanborn here says so. And I say so." He paused a moment and took a sip of tea. "Now, you need to know how we're going to do this."

"Indeed," Lowell said. "It's easy to decide to ship these weapons to Saul. But I confess I do not know how we shall do it. That, Sumner told me, was the purpose of tonight's meeting."

"There is a way," Stearns said, a curious smile crossing his face. "You see, Saul has communicated with Douglass and other prominent black abolitionists. All very secret, you understand. He sent them a letter, asking them for help."

"Did he?" Lowell asked, surprised. "When?"

"About two months ago."

Lowell was confused. "But that would have been before the raid on the Bergeron plantation."

"Quite right," Stearns said. "Saul's uprising has been in the works for some time. Perhaps since he and his men first retreated into the woods in 1866."

"And how did this message reach Douglass?" Lowell asked. "Surely he didn't just drop it in the post."

"No, he sent it through a third party. A fellow in New Orleans named Andre Gardet. A wine merchant in the city. A free black who is secretly in touch with Saul. I think it goes without saying that none of us should speak this man's name outside of this room. Nor should you write it down. Commit it to memory."

"How does he get messages to and from Saul?" Lowell asked.

"I have no idea," Stearns replied. "And I don't know if Douglass has any idea, either. If he does, he didn't tell me. Perhaps some sort of coded message. Perhaps invisible ink. But it doesn't matter. What matters is that he can get messages to and from Saul. If you get to New Orleans with the weapons and contact him, he can tell you how to get them to Saul."

"Do we know this for sure?" Lowell asked. From his days hunting Mosby in northern Virginia, he knew that people were often very fickle about sharing information when they might expect retaliation.

"No, we don't," Sanborn admitted. "But it's the best possibility we have of reaching Saul. And if this Gardet fellow weren't willing to help, why would he have sent along Saul's message asking for assistance?"

"It seems rather shaky and uncertain," Lowell said, concerned.

"We're fighting a war against the slave-owners," Stearns said. "What in war is certain? You will at least have a better chance than old John Brown had. He went into Harper's Ferry knowing that he almost certainly wouldn't come out alive. You, at least, have an even chance. All you need to do is get to Louisiana, deliver the weapons, and then get out again."

Lowell frowned. Before and after every battle he had fought, he had thought long and deeply on the possibility of his own death. During actual combat, however, the thought had never even crossed his mind, for he had been unalterably fixated on the twin goals of protecting the lives of his men and taking the lives of his enemies. The enterprise on which he was now embarking would not be a battle, but the same way of thinking would be at work. He did not want to die, yet he had always been willing to risk death in pursuit of what was right. Now, with two children, he felt somewhat less certain.

It didn't matter, though, for it was useless to have doubts now. He had told Sumner he was going. Douglass had presumably been told. He had now promised Sanborn and Stearns. It was too late to back out now, even if he wanted to. And while the faces of his wife and children might seek to pull him back from the brink, the memories of brothers, cousins, and friends slain during the war would drive him ever onward.

"And we know how to get in touch with Gardet?" Lowell asked.

"Yes," Stearns said. "As I said, he's a wine merchant. He has an office."

"Very well. Now, Sumner says that the two of you will arrange the financing of the weapons purchase itself?" Lowell asked.

"Oh, yes," Stearns answered, as if that were a simple matter. "But you will need to inspect them."

"Yes, Sumner said as much," Lowell replied. He thought a moment. "What else will be involved?"

"Well, we need to find someone who will be willing to ship the supplies to New Orleans, which won't be an easy task. There are plenty of smugglers, of course, but not many who would be willing to ship a cargo that potentially involves dangling from a noose."

Lowell chuckled. It was refreshing that such a morbid topic could be dispensed with by a joke.

Stearns went on. "False papers will be needed. We'll have to manufacture a story for you to explain why you are in New Orleans. We'll send word to Gardet that you're coming. And if..."

"No!" Lowell said sharply.

"I'm sorry?" Stearns asked, taken aback.

"No, we should say nothing to Gardet. That is absolutely out of the question. Not only would we have to worry about the communication being intercepted by the Confederates, but it would place in Gardet's hands a very valuable chip that he might be tempted to cash in."

Sanborn's eyebrows went up. "Douglass says we can trust Gardet."

"How do we know the Confederates don't have him under some sort of surveillance? Besides, in a matter of this sort, I shall prefer to strictly limit the number of people on whose trust I have to depend. It would be better if he doesn't even know we're coming. When I show up at his door and demand the information necessary to get the rifles to Saul, it would be best if it were as a bolt from the blue. Besides, even if he is completely trustworthy, which we can only assume he is, it would be best for him to be kept in the dark as much as possible. Men who know something worth knowing tend to slip up, even without intending to do so. Who knows? He might talk in his sleep to his wife."

"Well, you know better than I do, I suppose," Stearns said.

Lowell didn't want to sound presumptuous. He was an experienced hand in the game of clandestine operations, while Sanborn and Stearns were amateurs at best. Yet they would be the men financing the operation. He did not want to adopt a tone that they might find offensive. Moreover, the whole thing was the brainchild of Sumner and Douglass. If the conspiracy were a chessboard, he was certainly not the king or the queen. He might be charitably described as a bishop.

He suddenly wondered why this should be so. He had been brought into the conspiracy rather than formulating it. His money was not going to be financing it. Yet it was he, not the others, who was going to be risking his life to ensure its successful completion. It was he who would one day shake hands with Saul somewhere in the Louisiana swamps as he turned over the priceless weapons.

"Nothing must be done without my express approval," Lowell said firmly.

Stearns glanced to Sanborn as if for support. He had a bemused and irritated look on his face. For a moment, Lowell was reminded of a boy who had just had his toy snatched by a playmate.

"Of course," Stearns finally said.

They spent another half hour going over the various details. How the money would be forwarded and from where the weapons and ammunition would be purchased. Lowell persuaded them to include other materials as well, not only medical supplies like bandages and medicines, but such mundane things as pots and pans for cooking food, knapsacks, socks and shoes. Men who had not served in the army failed to appreciate the critical importance of such seemingly trivial things. They discussed what sort of man they would need to captain the ship to New Orleans and whether the person should be brought fully into their confidence.

"I am feeling reassured," Lowell finally said. "I believe our plan is a good one. I have no concerns."

"Don't you?" Sanborn said. "Have you told your wife yet?"

April 20, Afternoon
St. Martin's Parish, Southern Louisiana

General Morgan was riding at the head of his column. Behind him were one hundred of his best Kentucky cavalrymen, whom he had personally handpicked to accompany him to Louisiana. They were men who had followed him throughout the war, fighting in battle after battle against the Yankees in Kentucky and Tennessee. He knew all of them by name and would have trusted any one of them with his life.

The prospect of fighting against rebel blacks had cheered the men when he had told them about their new assignment. The routine business of patrolling the border with the United States provided little in the way of excitement and these were men to whom boredom was anathema. Unfortunately, since their arrival in Louisiana a few weeks before, not much had happened that could be called exciting. They had patrolled back and forth along the main roads throughout the parish, sent small groups through the thicker parts of the wilderness, following rumors and reports of Saul's activities. Yet they had yet to see a single insurgent. Morgan was beginning to wonder if he was on a fool's errand.

Worse, the climate was positively miserable. The thick and humid air and oppressive heat was quite the contrast to the fresh air and cool breezes that characterized the Cumberland River Valley where he and his men were normally stationed. Morgan knew his men well and was certain that the nature of the region was wearing on their morale.

He was distracted from these thoughts when a horsemen cantered up beside him. Morgan was happy to see that it was Colonel Basil Duke, his brother-in-law, whom he had persuaded to come along on the expedition as his second in command.

"News from the militia, John," Duke said as he slowed his horse to match the walking pace of the column. "Looks like this Saul bastard raided himself another plantation."

"Another one?" Morgan asked.

"Yes, sir," Duke replied. "Two nights ago. In St. Landry Parish this time."

"That's north of here, right?" Morgan asked, trying to remember the details of the map.

"That's right. Saul raided some place called the Malveaux Plantation. Why do these Frenchies have to have such strange-sounded names, John?"

Morgan ignored the last question. "How many slaves were stolen this time?"

"Not sure. Two dozen, at least. Heard tell that this place was bigger than the other two. Might be that Saul's getting more ambitious."

"The attack was the same as before? The white men were killed and the women and children allowed to live?"

"That's what the militia officers told me. But there were a couple of interesting things. They described what one of the female survivors said. At one point, one of the plantation owner's older sons was trapped in a room, but did not have a weapon. One of Saul's men was about to fire his rifle through the door and Saul shouted for him not to waste ammunition. They broke down the door with the butts of their rifles instead."

"That is interesting," Morgan said. "It might indicate that this band of outlaws is running out of bullets."

"Another thing. Apparently one of the slaves, the plantation valet who had been with the Malveaux family for decades, refused to go with Saul and said he wanted to stay with the white women. In response, Saul ordered the man's throat to be cut."

"Well, that's not very friendly, is it?"

"No, sir," Duke replied with a grin. "Very discourteous, if you ask me."

Morgan was glad that Duke had agreed to accompany him to Louisiana, for not only was he married to his sister Henrietta but was one of his closest friends. He had served as Morgan's deputy commander on many expeditions throughout the war. He valued Duke's intelligence and intrepidity. Having him with him was reassuring, as Morgan was beginning to have serious doubts about his assignment in Louisiana.

According to the orders he had received from Richmond, Morgan had direct command only of the hundred Kentucky cavalrymen. He had no real authority to give orders to the Louisiana militia, but only to give them advice. Many of the officers had turned to him for direction, as he was the highest ranking officer present and due to his reputation. But some officers, more vain or stupid than the others, had failed to cooperate at all. Some had not even replied to his requests for information.

He had asked for the various units of the Louisiana militia to cordon off the main roads and paths through the forests and swamps in the areas where the raids had taken place, hoping to pin Saul and his bandits in a limited area. That being done, the Kentucky cavalrymen and some of the more mobile militia units were now sweeping through the area, hoping to flush Saul out.

Rumors abounded and many eye-witnesses had told breathless tales of seeing large numbers of armed blacks in the wilderness. None of the information was reliable, though. The more cooperative militia officers reported that, upon arrival in the areas where Saul had allegedly been sighted, they invariably found nothing. On two occasions, the remains of a campsite abandoned a few days earlier had been found, but nothing else.

Other disturbing reports were also reaching Morgan's ears. Plantation owners were reporting an increase in the number of slaves trying to escape. Mysterious fires were breaking out at some plantations as well. Throughout central and southern Louisiana, plantation owners were hiring large numbers of men to guard their property. Disquiet was steadily turning into paranoia.

Men had flocked to join the units of the Louisiana militia that had been called up. Indeed, there were many more men than Morgan thought were needed. The militia officers had actually sent many of them back home because they lacked the money to pay for their food and ammunition. Some refused to leave, pledging to pay for their own supplies, which created its own share of administrative problems. Morgan found it all faintly ridiculous.

"John, look up ahead," Duke said quickly.

Morgan did so. A lone black man, looking to be in his fifties and wearing the tattered clothes of a plantation slave, was walking in their direction, seemingly oblivious to their presence. He was unarmed and appeared harmless.

"Boy!" Morgan barked. "Stop there!"

The man looked up at the mounted men in surprise. He froze and said nothing.

"Come forward, boy!" Morgan shouted. "Show us your pass!"

All slaves travelling between plantations were required to carry passes. This had been the case for decades. Saul's recent depredations had caused local authorities to tighten security and increase slave patrols, so the request to present his pass should have come as no surprise to the man.

Morgan found it unusual that a slave should be walking down the road anyway. Slave-owners throughout the region had been told to clamp down on allowing their slaves to travel between plantations. This particular fellow was the first black man that Morgan had seen all day.

"I told you to come here, boy!" Morgan shouted again. "Show us your pass!"

The man bolted into the woods as though struck with a shock of electricity. This took Morgan by surprise and he didn't react for four or five seconds. He spurred his horse up to the point where the man had been standing on the road, seeing instantly that the area into which he had fled was not suitable for horses.

"Dismount!" he shouted to the column. "After him! Get him!"

Against skilled soldiers like the Yankees, Morgan might have been cautious, but he reminded himself that he was up against runaway blacks, who surely lacked the ability to plan anything like an ambush. With skilled precision, the men of the company dropped from their saddles. Every fourth man took the reins of the horses of three of his comrades. The three-quarters of the troops who were not so encumbered gripped their Enfields and dashed into the woods after the fleeing black man.

Morgan and Duke ran along with the company. As his feet found their way across the marshy ground, Morgan wondered what had caused the man to flee. Clearly, the black man had been doing somewhat he wasn't supposed to be doing. The possibility flashed through Morgan's mind that he could be a courier for Saul's men.

"Don't shoot him, boys!" Morgan yelled. "Take him alive! Double whiskey for whoever catches him!"

The men laughed and whooped with delight as they ran forward, as if it were all a grand fox chase. Through the underbrush, Morgan glimpsed their quarry trying desperately to escape.

"Get him!" people were yelling. "Get that darkie bastard!"

Some of the cavalrymen on either side of him were running faster than Morgan was and so were catching up to the fleeing black more quickly. The general didn't like this. He was only in his early forties, after all, and should have been able to keep pace with his younger troops. Yet he could feel himself getting tired, while his soldiers continued running at full speed and shouting their war whoops. Duke was easily outpacing him, now several yards ahead. He gritted his teeth and kept going as fast as he could.

The next few seconds seemed to unfold very slowly. He thought he noticed their quarry jump slightly, as if he were running over a low obstacle like a log or large stone. He also thought he heard the man give off some incomprehensible shout. A moment later, Morgan saw four or five black men rise to their feet directly ahead. It took a fraction of a second for Morgan to grasp what was happening. Before he could do so, the black men raised rifles and fired.

The explosive cracking sound of gunfire instinctively caused Morgan and several of his men to dive to the ground. One man was too late, hit by a bullet that blew a hole through his chest, causing an eruption of blood to burst out his back. He fell dead instantly. There was a cacophony of shouted curses and expressions of confusion from Morgan's soldiers. As the sounds of more gunshots and screams rang out, Morgan realized to his horror that he and his men had been led into an ambush.

"Halt!" Morgan shouted. "Aim and fire!"

It took a few seconds, but scattered shots began to signal return fire against the ambushers. Morgan glanced about frantically, trying to determine exactly where his men were. Running after the fleeing man, who he now realized had been nothing but bait, had caused his troops to become hopelessly disordered. There was no semblance of any formation.

His trained ears were listening to the gunfire being directed toward his troops. In addition to the initial line of black men he had seen, there were now shots being fired from both the left and right. Morgan could not tell how many, but it was a large number. Clearly, the aim of the ambushers had been to catch them in a crossfire and they had succeeded.

"Fall back!" Morgan shouted. "Fall back to the road!"

It was the only thing to do. If they stayed where they were, out of formation and not knowing the strength or deployment of their attackers, they might be cut to pieces. By retreating back to the road, they could rally and assume a proper formation. Then it would be a fair fight, which they would surely win.

The men picked themselves up and dashed back the way they had come. Veterans to a man, they had instinctively sensed the need to fall back just as easily as he had. As they jogged back towards the road, several of them tried to reload their Enfields while moving, a difficult and dangerous task that none but the most experienced soldiers could successfully perform.

"After them!" a strong and fierce-sounding voice shouted.

Even as he ran, Morgan was stunned to hear this and it felt as though he had been punched in the gut. The full impact of what was happening suddenly hit him. His Kentucky veterans, whom he had led across a hundred battlefields, were being chased by a gaggle of black bandits. The leader of the band had given his men an order to pursue the Confederates. To Morgan the words represented the most sickening kind of insult imaginable.

He could hear scattered gunshots and screams behind him. Tossing his head over his shoulder for just one moment, he saw a horrifying sight. Two black men had grabbed one of his soldiers, a young man barely in his twenties, and were dragging him to the ground. One of the black assailants was raising a scythe over his head in preparation to strike, while his trooper screamed in terror. Morgan looked forward again and continued his flight. He heard a crunching sound and the man's scream stopped abruptly.

As he ran, his feverish mind couldn't help but imagine what headlines the newspapers would run when they learned that he had been bested by black men. During the war, the newspapers had lionized Morgan as the man who had ridden undefeated across Kentucky and carried the war into the Union itself. Yet he knew how fickle public opinion could be. If they thought they could sell more newspapers by doing so, the press would turn on him in an instant. Having once been a hero, Morgan would be subject to the most abject humiliation. He would also be blamed for the deaths of his men.

"No!" he shouted. He stopped in his tracks and turned around, drawing his sword as he did so. "Rally to me!" he shouted, waving his saber over his head. "Rally to me, my boys!"

Some of his men stopped beside him, turned, and raised their weapons. Over the next thirty seconds, two dozen of his men stopped fleeing and came into position on either side of him. At first, none of them fired for fear of hitting their own men. When the last of the Confederates came into line, however, they raised their Enfields. A thin line of blacks, some armed with rifles and others armed with improvised blade weapons, were coming at them.

"Fire!" Morgan yelled.

The Confederate line unleashed a ragged volley of rifle fire. Without additional orders, the men began reloading and firing at will. It had been their customary method of fighting during the war and Morgan was pleased that they remembered their skills. Morgan saw two or three of the black attackers let out sharp screams of pain and fall as bullets hit them. He pulled his pistol from its holster and began blazing away at their black enemies.

He glanced around. His men had arranged themselves into an irregular line and were firing back at their attackers. Perhaps eighty men had dashed into the forest ten minutes earlier. Morgan could now see perhaps forty or fifty of his men. How many of the missing were dead, and how many were simply separated and trying to return, he didn't know.

He couldn't see Duke, but thought he heard his voice shouting encouragement to the men. He didn't have time to worry about his brother-in-law. From where Morgan was standing, he could see black fighters in front of the line. But they continually rose to fire and then ducked down into the underbrush, making it impossible for Morgan to guess their numbers. There was also fire coming in at them on both flanks, which meant that not all of their enemies were directly in front of them.

Morgan was astounded. He had never encountered black soldiers during the war and had not given much credence to reports that they had fought well. He had assumed that Saul's men were simple robbers and bandits. Not in his wildest dreams could Morgan have suspected they would fight in anything like an organized manner. Not only that, but they were using effective tactics, skillfully employing cover and maintaining a disciplined skirmish line.

"Company! Kneel!" Morgan shouted. "Keep firing! Give the darkie bastards hell, boys!"

"Hell is where you're going, slaveholder!" a booming voice answered from the other side of the fighting.

It was the same voice that Morgan had heard earlier, which had ordered the blacks forward in pursuit. He suddenly locked eyes with the man who had spoken. He was not tall, but appeared strong and menacing. He carried no rifle, but wore a dirty colored sash that might have once been a battle flag. The man was staring back at him. For an endless instant, their eyes met. There was a fierce look of hatred on the man's face and a total absence of fear.

Morgan knew instantly that the man was Saul.

The two sides were separated by perhaps thirty yards, but the thick underbrush made it seem much farther. They sniped at one another, with men on both sides rising to fire and then ducking to reload. Morgan had expended all six bullets in his revolver and struggled to reload as quickly as possible. Men on both sides were falling, dead or wounded.

The sight of his men being shot down by blacks filled Morgan with ferocious rage. Yet what happened next made him even more furious, even as it confused him. From the line of black soldiers shooting at his men, astonishingly, he could hear the sound of singing.

John Brown's body lies a-mouldering in the grave,
John Brown's body lies a-mouldering in the grave,
John Brown's body lies a-mouldering in the grave,

Morgan felt his blood boil. The blacks were mocking them. Never in his life had he felt so helpless and humiliated. People he considered inferior, who should have been laboring in the cotton and sugar fields, were killing his men and openly taunting them while doing it. It was a situation that no Southern white man could endure.

"Fix bayonets!" It took only two or three seconds for his veterans to obey this command, turning their rifles into deadly spears. "Cold steel, boys!" Morgan yelled. "Charge!"

With a blood-curdling shriek of rage, the Confederates dashed forward with murderous intent evident on their faces. They wanted revenge as much as Morgan. They had faced death a hundred times before and they were not about to flinch in the face of men they considered less than human.

Morgan could hear Saul shout out something, though he could not make out the words amidst the battle cries of his own men. In an instant, the line of black soldiers split in two and dashed off in opposite directions, ducking down into the underbrush and seeming to vanish. Morgan's mouth opened in shock.

The Confederate charge sputtered out instantly, for suddenly there was no enemy to charge against. The men halted and looked at one another in confusion. Some glanced back at Morgan as if looking for guidance, but for once he had none to give. The maneuver the blacks had just carried out was unlike anything he had ever seen before. It could not have been carried out by untrained troops.

"Halt!" Morgan shouted. "Reload! Form up!"

His men responded quickly to these routine orders. In less than twenty seconds, every man had reloaded his rifle. They glanced back over their shoulders, expectantly waiting for orders to pursue the retreating blacks.

Morgan said nothing. His mind was racing. The ambush had been skillfully staged. He was furious with himself for having been so completely duped. During the war, the Yankees had rarely caught him flat-footed. Part of him desperately wanted to run down the bandits and kill every last one of them.

Yet Saul's fighters had split into two groups and he did not know which one to follow. Neither had seemed larger than the other and he did not know where either of them was going. If he elected to pursue one group, he risked being attacked from the rear by the other group. Indeed, that might have been what the rebels had intended. He also had to consider the possibility that there were more insurgents out in the woods. If he ordered his men after the bandits, he would be taking a significant risk. More of his men might be killed.

Duke dashed up to his side and he was relieved to see his brother-in-law unhurt. "Are you all right?" he asked.

"Yes," Morgan replied quickly, his breathing coming heavily.

"What do you want us to do, sir?"

Morgan thought quickly. With the last charge, Morgan's men had seemed to scatter the bandits and were now in possession of the ground. They could, therefore, claim a tactical victory. Now was the time to hold onto one's cards.

"Deploy skirmishers," he ordered. "See to the wounded."

There was a muttering of discontent in the ranks when they heard Morgan say this to Duke. Ordinarily, Morgan did not mind when his men expressed their disapproval. He certainly had made many decisions during the war with which the men had not agreed. As long as they followed orders, it didn't much matter. Yet as his own confidence had just taken a severe beating, the questioning on the faces of his men bothered him to no small degree.

A thin line of skirmishers advanced, forming a cordon to protect from any resumption of the enemy attack. Morgan considered this unlikely, but he was not about to take chances. He sent some men back to check on the horses and the troopers holding them. Meanwhile, the members of the company took stock of their losses and tried to help their wounded comrades.

"Sir!" Duke shouted after a few minutes. "Over here!"

He walked over. Duke was standing next to an enlisted man. On the ground was a slain insurgent. Morgan did not immediately see why Duke had called him over and felt a tinge of irritation.

"Tell him what you just told me, private."

"What's this?" Morgan asked.

"They shot him, sir," the private said.

"What do you mean?" Morgan asked in confusion. He looked down at the dead black again. The insurgent had a wound through his leg as well as through the head.

"The darkies, sir. When they dashed off just now. This one was on the ground, because I shot him in the leg. One of the other darkies stopped for a moment and shot him in the head."

"My God," Morgan said, his eyes widening in surprise.

"Why would they do that, sir?" the private asked. "Kill their own man?"

"They couldn't move him, so they killed him to make sure he wasn't taken prisoner."

Duke grunted. "Surprised that a darkie would think so carefully," he said.

Morgan didn't reply, for he found himself lost in thought. If Saul was willing to have his own men killed rather than see them fall into the hands of the enemy, then the Confederacy was dealing with a man of far more strength of will than any simple bandit. Morgan thought of the report that Saul had killed a slave on the last raided plantation because the man would not go with him. He thought back to the face of the man he had seen across the lines, who had shouted back defiance at him. He remembered the cold, formidable look in the man's eyes.

Reports came in. The skirmishers had advanced through the area over which the men had earlier retreated, trying to account for the dead and wounded. They told him that they had found the bodies of fifteen black men, though their weapons had apparently been taken by their comrades. For their part, eight Confederate soldiers had been killed and twenty wounded. Of the wounded, seven appeared likely to die, having been shot through the belly.

For Morgan, the most unsettling part of the report was that three men were missing.

"James!" Annie called from the porch. "There are some men coming!"

She said this with concern but not alarm in her voice. McFadden, on his knees in the kitchen as he struggled to light the wood in the stove, sensed something was amiss. He rose to his feet and walked out onto the porch. Holding his hand up to shield his eyes from the sun, he gazed out toward the group of men on horseback. There looked to be about half of dozen of them.

One of McFadden's most prized possessions was a pair of field glasses that had been given to him by General Patrick Cleburne in the aftermath of the successful defense of Atlanta in 1864. On the ranch, of course, the gift had a very practical value. He stepped back inside for a moment, snatched the field glasses from the shelf near the door where they were kept, and scanned the group.

Judge Lucius Roden was riding in front. Behind him were five men armed with carbines. They were perhaps a quarter of a mile away, meaning that they would be at the house in a matter of minutes.

"Annie," McFadden said sternly. "Take Thaddeus and go to the shelter. Now!"

She said nothing and did not change her expression. Her face might as well have been carved out of stone. She stepped inside and McFadden could hear her speaking softly to their son as she lifted him out of his crib and carried him out the back door to their hidden shelter. It had been built with the idea of Comanche raids in mind and was also useful in the event of tornadoes. McFadden had never expected to use it in such circumstances as this.

He had no idea what Judge Roden had in mind, but he decided to assume the worst. McFadden loaded his two Enfield rifles and placed them against the wall next to the door, dropping his old ammunition pouch on the floor next to them. He retrieved his Navy Colt revolver from its regular place near his bed and made sure that all six chambers were loaded, while placing several more cartridges in his pocket. Finally, he belted on his bowie knife. By the time these preparations were complete, Judge Roden and his posse were pulling their horses to a stop in front of the house.

"McFadden?" Roden's voice called. "Are you home?"

"What do you want?" McFadden replied. He picked up one of the Enfields and pulled back the hammer. He discounted Roden himself as a threat, but the five men he had brought with him were obviously dangerous. If it came to a fight, he would have to rely on the fact that he was within the house, which provided a certain amount of cover, while they were out in the open within a clear field of fire. But odds of five-to-one were never very good.

"Just dropped by to chat with you is all," Roden's voice said. "You're one of my constituents, ain't you? Why, we're practically neighbors, you and me."

McFadden hesitated just a moment, then stepped out onto the porch, cradling the Enfield in his arms. If he needed to, he could duck back inside the house at a moment's notice. He didn't want Judge Roden to think he was afraid.

"Ah, there you are, McFadden," Roden said with a sickening grin. "I was afraid you weren't going to be in the mood to be hospitable."

McFadden didn't reply, staring instead down at the figure of Judge Roden on his horse. Looking at the fat politician made McFadden wince, as though he had smelled something bad.

"Aren't you going to invite me in for a friendly drink?" Roden asked.

"Friends aren't normally escorted by an armed gang."

Roden looked taken aback and McFadden had to resist the temptation to believe his expression was genuine. The man was, after all, a politician. Such people were adept at making people believe whatever they wanted them to believe. McFadden didn't want to trust Roden.

"Tell you what," Roden replied. "How about I tell my boys to wait out here and I come inside by myself? I'm not armed. Even if I was, an old soldier like you could kill me before I had a chance to let out a single juicy fart, ain't that right?"

McFadden considered this. He had to admit that what the judge said made a certain amount of sense, for Roden himself presented no serious threat. Perhaps he had simply come to talk after all.

"Come on in."

Roden dismounted from his horse without much in the way of grace. One of his men also dismounted and took the horse's reins as well as those of his own mount. Roden walked up the steps and came through the front door. McFadden walked in behind him. The judge glanced down at the other rifle and the ammunition pouch situated, then back at him.

"You got me all wrong, McFadden," Roden said. "I didn't come here as anything but a friend."

"After what you said to me at the land auction, you'll forgive me if I think otherwise."

"Yes, well, that was unpleasant, I admit. I was upset. And I do apologize. Sincerely. May I sit?" He gestured to one of McFadden's chairs.

McFadden nodded hesitantly. While keeping a careful eye on Roden, he set the Enfield against the wall. He then poured two glasses of whiskey, handed one over to the judge, and took the seat opposite him. His Navy Colt was still in its holster and his bowie knife could be drawn at a moment's notice.

"Like I said, I was upset," Roden began. "You see, that piece of land you bid on, which I know you gave back to that poor widow after you bought it, was supposed to be for a friend of mine. It's adjacent to land he already owns. He was simply trying to expand the size of his ranch, you understand."

McFadden nodded slowly, trying to figure out what Judge Roden was getting at. "I was trying to make sure that a poor war widow was not thrown off her land. Had she been, she would have had no way to support herself."

Roden held up both hands. "I know, I know, I know. You were doing an honorable thing, McFadden. I respect you for it. More than that, I admire you for it. I don't want poor widows thrown off their land any more than anybody else. But it's business, you see."

"I don't follow," McFadden said.

"Well, I'm going to tell you something that I haven't told too many people yet. You see, I'm going to be running for the state legislature in this year's election. That friend of mine who wanted to buy that plot of land? He told me that he'd help bankroll my campaign if I helped him get it. I didn't think any help

134

would be necessary, to be honest. I certainly didn't expect you to show up and bid so high, using all that money collected from your old regiment."

McFadden's eyes narrowed. He wondered how Roden had learned of the manner in which the veterans had raised the funds to save the Widow Williams's ranch. After a moment, he chided himself for being so stupid. Roden was the head of the county commissioners' court. He was in a position to know pretty much anything he wanted to know about what went on in Granbury County.

"Truth be told," Roden went on. "If I had known that you and your friends felt so strongly about it, I might not have bothered. I need the votes of people like you and your friends. That's what it's all about, right? That's what we fought the war for. Democracy. Equal rights for all white men. You know what I'm talking about, right?"

McFadden could tell he was being sweet-talked and didn't appreciate it. "What exactly is it that you want, Judge Roden? Why are you here?"

"Well, I want your help," Roden said, gesturing across towards McFadden. "I've been checking up on you since our little disagreement at the land auction. You didn't just capture General Thomas at the Battle of Atlanta. From what I hear, you are the man who destroyed the reserve ammunition train of Grant's army while the Battle of Fairburn was going on. Isn't that right?"

McFadden shifted uncomfortably in his chair. The fact of which Roden had just reminded him, unlike his capture of General Thomas, was not widely known. Even most of the veterans of his regiment were unaware of it. He couldn't imagine how Roden had learned of it. Clearly, the man sitting across from him was more resourceful than McFadden had given him credit for.

"I'm not sure what possible help you think I might be for you," McFadden replied. "You want to run for the state legislature? Then run for the state legislature. The people will vote for or against you as they please."

"You could help me a great deal, McFadden," Roden said. "Lots of men who fought in your brigade have settled here in this county. Hell, I persuaded the folks down in Austin to change the name of this county to Granbury to honor your old commander. These men respect you. They look up to you as a leader. The veterans from Hood's brigade and the other units respect you, too. If they were to hear that you were backing me, they would be more likely to back me as well."

"I think you exaggerate whatever influence I might have. I have never expressed any opinion on political issues. I'd like to avoid becoming involved, honestly."

McFadden wasn't lying. Politics was not something he cared to think about. After all, it had been foolish and hot-headed politicians in both the North and South who had plunged America into the war in the first place. Better, he felt, to focus on his own family and do his best to stay out of harm's way.

Many of the men he had fought alongside had never been able to stop talking about politics. They had droned on and on about state's rights, the unfairness of Northern control over the House of Representatives, the constitutionality of secession, and the right of the Southern people to self-determination. McFadden hadn't really disagreed with these things, but he hadn't thought of his wartime service in such terms. He had joined the army because, at that particular time in his life, he simply liked to fight.

Judge Roden was still talking. "Just think of it, McFadden. You and me together on the stage. If you get up and talk to the crowd first, introducing me before I give my speech, then all the veterans in the audience will take notice. They'll be more likely to vote for me. And they'll talk to their friends and tell them that, you see. Like ripples in a pond after you toss a rock in it. It would be a tremendous help, McFadden, I don't mind telling you."

"Why should I help you?"

"Why shouldn't you?"

"Well, maybe whoever runs against you would make a better state representative."

McFadden expected Roden to laugh at this, for the man was making a strong effort to charm him. Instead, Roden's eyes became ominously dark. McFadden again felt the same air of menace he had sensed in front of the courthouse on the day of the land auction. As instantly as it appeared, though, the expression vanished from Roden's face and he resumed his amiable visage.

"I'll tell you what, McFadden," Roden said after a pause. "If you help me, I can arrange for the commissioner's court to look the other way if you forget to pay your land tax. How does that sound?"

"I don't think so," McFadden answered instantly. Roden's words made him furious. He was enraged by the politician's insinuation that he might be open to a bribe. It was also obvious to McFadden that, if he took Roden's offer, he would be beholden to the man. Were there ever to be trouble with Roden in the future, the fact that McFadden hadn't paid his taxes in the past could easily be dusted off the books and used against him.

He wondered why Roden was going to such great lengths to persuade him to help his campaign. Roden must know that he was not much loved in the county and held his seat at the head of the commissioner's court more through intimidation than anything else. Perhaps moving from one elected position to another was a greater risk than he had run in recent years.

"Surely there is something I can offer that you want," Roden said, exasperation entering his voice. "As County Judge, I am in a position to help you in many ways, McFadden."

He thought for a moment, then decided to test Roden. "Perhaps one thing, Judge."

Roden's eyebrows rose. "Yes? What is it?"

"At the auction, I noticed that lots of ordinary folk, including many veterans like myself, were losing their land after being outbid by richer people. Like the Widow Williams, they were people who had had their land confiscated after they had failed to pay their taxes."

Roden grunted in response and said nothing.

McFadden went on. "Perhaps the court could implement a policy of forgiveness on those who are late in paying their taxes? Maybe the court could allow them to pay a little bit at a time rather than the whole all at once? I would consider such a policy very helpful to the people of this county. It might persuade me that you were a man worth supporting for higher office."

The judge's friendly expression vanished and was again replaced by that of smoldering anger. Carefully, he raised his whiskey to his lips and took a long sip. For a long time, he said nothing.

McFadden did not expect Roden to agree with his proposal. He was calling the judge out on what he considered a crime. He had thought more and more about the disgraceful scene at the land auction in the days since it had happened. He remembered the stories his father had told him about the Highland Clearances, when politically connected men had used unscrupulous means to acquire land from the poor Scots who lived on it, then drove them out with exorbitant rents and other corrupt, yet legal, means. This had been what had forced his parents to leave their beloved Scotland and immigrate to Texas in the first place.

The same thing, McFadden was convinced, was beginning to happen on the Texas frontier. Texas, unlike the states farther to the east, was not yet dominated by the wealthy owners of enormous plantations. A much greater portion of the land in Texas was owned by smallholders, especially on the frontier. The first Anglo colonists who had come with Stephen F. Austin in the 1820s had set the pattern, which had been followed by waves of additional settlers over the years. Following the failed 1848 revolutions in Europe, new arrivals from Germany and other parts of Europe had added to the mix. Although some larger plantations were starting to develop in the eastern part of the state, much more land remained in the hands of smallholders than was the case in the rest of the Confederacy.

What McFadden had seen at the auction, however, was evidence that this was changing. The men who ran Texas clearly wanted their state to be more like the rest of the South. Returning veterans, or the smallholders who had managed to hold onto their land through the hard times of the war, were going to be squeezed out by men who had made their money through profiteering or other foul means. Judge Roden was a perfect manifestation of the travesty that was starting to happen.

"Folks got to pay their taxes, McFadden," Roden said simply. "Not my fault if they decide not to."

"They don't decide not to," McFadden said sternly. "They can't. Times are hard."

"It's not my job to help lazy people avoid their responsibilities."

"No, clearly not," McFadden said. "I think you see your job as doing favors for your rich friends, crushing any of the ordinary common folk who get in your way."

Roden sat back and folded his arms across his chest, a look of intense irritation on his face. "You're an arrogant little son of a bitch, ain't you?"

"You're not the first person to tell me that."

"I came here to ask you a favor. You've been nothing but disrespectful."

"You should be thankful that I am not saying everything that I'm thinking."

Roden paused a long moment before replying. "I offered you my friendship because I thought you were a man respected by many of our neighbors. Now I see that you're nothing but a damn fool."

"Sorry to disappoint you, Judge."

Roden assumed a thoughtful look. "I'm beginning to wonder if your land's value has been properly assessed."

"What do you mean?"

"Well, you say you're not interested in having your land taxes lowered. Would you like to have them increased? Doubled, perhaps?"

McFadden felt a tightening of his stomach. "If you think you can intimidate me with threats, Roden, you have no idea who I am."

"I know that any man with a wife and child has a lot to lose."

Despite the warm air blowing through the door, McFadden felt as though an icy chill had suddenly washed over him. The full import of Roden's words struck him with the force of a fist. He reached behind him and pulled out his bowie knife, waving it slowly in front of him.

"Listen to me carefully, Roden. If I counted correctly, I killed thirty-seven men over the course of the war. I would not think much of adding a thirty-eighth. Don't you ever threaten my family again. Do you understand?"

Roden surprised McFadden by showing absolutely no sign of fear. He exhaled a sound that was half a laugh and half a snort and rose from his chair. "Well, I shall take my leave, then. Think on what I have said to you, McFadden. I hope to have your support in the coming campaign. If not, that's just too bad."

The judge strolled out the door and down the steps towards his horse. McFadden rose and followed, picking up his rifle as he stepped onto the porch. The five men were still there, waiting on their horses. Clumsily, for he was far from a graceful man, Roden climbed into his saddle. After one final, sneering glance at McFadden, he tilted his head away from the house. His men spurred their horses and were off. Minutes later, they vanished over the horizon.

McFadden stayed on the porch a long time, cradling his Enfield, his mind lost in dark and troubling thoughts.

April 22, Morning
Mechanic's Hall, Richmond, Virginia

Breckinridge sat in his office, intently reading the latest report from General Patrick Cleburne, who was serving as a military observer with the forces of Emperor Maximilian I of Mexico. His job was to monitor the struggle between the Imperial Mexican Army and its French allies against the republican rebels, reporting back not only on political and military developments, but any new tactics or weapons he saw being used which might be of interest to the Confederate army.

Despite the fact that the man had no formal military education, appointing Cleburne to the post had been a good idea. His brilliant performance in the Atlanta Campaign had played a key role in securing Confederate independence, but he was distrusted and despised by many people in the country for his proposal that slaves be emancipated and enrolled in the army. When his promotion to Lieutenant General had been rejected by the Senate, Cleburne had been so disillusioned that he had considered resigning. Breckinridge, not wanting to lose such an immensely talented officer, had offered Cleburne the post in Mexico and Cleburne jumped at the chance. It had all worked out quite well, Breckinridge thought.

The report from Cleburne made for very interesting reading. The French Army had begun using a new breech-loading rifle they called the 'Chassepot'.

The weapon fired standardized cartridges through a bolt action mechanism, making it very easy to reload even when lying down. According to Cleburne, a soldier could fire up to fifteen shots a minute with the Chassepot and it had a range of fifteen hundred yards. Using this new weapon, the French troops and their Mexican allies had been able to easily defeat the rebels in a number of engagements.

The implications were enormous. The Chassepot's range and rate of fire rendered all other firearms obsolete. Doing the math in his head, Breckinridge figured that a single regiment armed with Chassepots could probably decimate an entire division armed with old Springfield or Enfield rifles, provided they had enough ammunition. The United States would surely begin importing large numbers of Chassepot rifles for its own use.

More disturbing was the thought that factories throughout the North would soon begin producing their own rifles modeled on the French design. The Confederacy, by contrast, lacked the industrial capacity to produce the weapon or the financial resources to import them in meaningful numbers.

Breckinridge made a note for the report to be forwarded to Josiah Gorgas, his Chief of Ordnance, and prepared to write a reply to Cleburne. He also reminded himself that the subject needed to be brought up at the next Cabinet meeting. Funds would need to be allocated to import at least some Chassepots. At the very least, some specialized units might be equipped with the new weapon.

There was a soft knocking on the door and Wilson entered.

"Telegram from General Morgan, Mr. Secretary."

"Thank you, James," he replied, taking the proffered envelope. He had been expecting to hear from Morgan for a few days.

Secretary Breckinridge,

I must report that I have fought an engagement with what I believe to be the main body of insurgents. My company of dismounted cavalry, under my personal command, was ambushed by the bandits. Several of the bandits were killed and they were eventually driven off. Eleven of my men were killed and seventeen wounded. I must also report that three of my men are unaccounted for and may have fallen into the hands of the bandits.

I must reluctantly acknowledge that the insurgents behaved in a disciplined and organized manner throughout the engagement. They are clearly men who have received military training and had carefully planned the ambush.

General Morgan

Breckinridge tensed and his heart quickened. Up until that moment, Breckinridge had considered the matter of Saul to be of little importance. He and his bandits had raided a few defenseless plantation and killed a few dozen people. The Comanche Indians made as much trouble on the Texas frontier in a bad week as Saul had in Louisiana in two months. Yet Morgan was now telling him that the black insurgents had taken on a unit of the Confederate Army and given it a bloody nose in a fair fight. Davis and the Cabinet, including Breckinridge, had been assured that a minor commitment of troops and the appointment of Morgan would solve the problem. The telegram had ended that delusion in a single moment. Breckinridge felt as though a cold bucket of water had just been dumped on him.

During the war, a fight with a few dozen casualties would have been ranked as an insignificant skirmish. Breckinridge knew that this did not matter. The war was supposed to be over, after all. Men were not supposed to be fighting and dying any longer. More crucially, the men who had killed these soldiers were not Yankees but renegade slaves. Saul's little rebellion had just taken a big step towards becoming a genuine insurrection.

Breckinridge rose from his desk and moved towards the door, walking quickly.

"Everything all right, sir?" Wilson asked as Breckinridge passed him.

"It's all right, James. I need to see the president immediately. Mind the store until I get back, won't you?"

"Of course, sir."

A few moments later, Breckinridge was walking across the lobby of Mechanic's Hall and stepping out onto the streets of Richmond. The sidewalks were crowded with people. Most of them had happy, pleasant expressions on their faces. Breckinridge wondered how long the gay atmosphere would last once word of Saul's ambush of Morgan reached the newspapers, which it inevitably would. Up until this point, the depredations of Saul and his men had created surprisingly little public comment. Perhaps people didn't want to be reminded of the fear that had accompanied the Great Disorder in late 1865.

The ambush Morgan had suffered would make it much more difficult for people to remain in denial. Breckinridge had no doubt that the Yankee newspapers, especially those aligned with the abolitionist cause, would have a field day with the news, trumpeting it into a much larger event than it actually was. This, in turn, would feed Southern paranoia all the more, creating a self-perpetuating cycle of fear and anger. The ghosts of Nat Turner, Denmark Vesey, and John Brown were returning to haunt the South.

Breckinridge soon arrived at the Executive Office Building. Seeing the serious expression on his face, the guards and clerks in the lobby waved him right through and he soon bounded up the stairs two steps at a time. He reached the desk of Burton Harrison, the president's personal secretary.

"I need to see President Davis immediately," Breckinridge said. "It's urgent."

"He asked not to be disturbed, Mr. Secretary," Harrison said automatically.

"Dammit, man, didn't you hear me? I said it's urgent!"

Harrison's eyes widened in alarm. It was very unlike Breckinridge to display such anger. "He's meeting with Secretary Benjamin right now."

"Good. Better that he's here, too."

Harrison rose from his chair, knocked on the door, opened it, and stuck his head in.

"I'm sorry to bother you, Mr. President. I know you asked not to be disturbed, but Secretary Breckinridge is here and says he must see you immediately."

"Is that so?" the voice of Davis responded from the other side of the door. "Very well. Send him in."

Breckinridge pushed past Harrison and entered the office. Davis and Benjamin were sitting on their respective sides of the president's enormous desk, the Secretary of State smoking a cigar. Without waiting to be asked, Breckinridge took the seat next to Benjamin.

"We may have a serious problem, Mr. President."

The slightly amused expression that had been on Davis's face faded immediately. "What has happened?"

"A unit of Morgan's men hunting the bandits in Louisiana was ambushed by Saul's force. Several are our men were killed and the insurgents escaped. Morgan reports that the ambush was carefully and skillfully executed."

He let that sink in for a moment. Benjamin looked completely unperturbed, but Davis's expression reflected alarm.

"How is that possible?" Davis asked.

"I am not sure, Mr. President. Morgan's report was very brief and lacked full details."

"Is there any way to keep word of this from spreading to the newspapers?"

"I doubt it, Mr. President," Breckinridge said. "We shall have to notify the families of the men who have been killed, obviously. Once they know what has happened, the rest of the country will know in short order."

Davis thought for a moment. "Perhaps the official notification could get lost in the mail, so to speak?"

"Attempting to conceal word of what has happened will make us look foolish when the news does get out," Benjamin observed. "And it will, Mr. President. A story this big will be found out by the newspapers sooner or later."

Davis began drumming the desk with his fingers and staring intently at the wall, focusing his thoughts. Having encountered this reaction several times, Breckinridge was wise enough to remain silent. Nearly a full minute passed.

"The people will be gripped by fear," Davis finally said.

"No doubt," Benjamin replied. "The people in Louisiana are already scared. Now they will be terrified. All the old fears of the slaves murdering their owners in their beds will resurface."

"What does Morgan say specifically?" Davis asked Breckinridge.

Breckinridge pulled the telegram out of his coat pocket and quickly read through its contents.

"Morgan was in direct command of this force, you say?" Davis asked.

"Apparently so," Breckinridge replied. "I can only assume that the consequences might have been worse had the ambush happened to anyone else. Morgan escaped from countless traps during the war, after all."

"He's also reckless," Benjamin said. "Maybe he got cocky. Maybe that's why this misfortune happened in the first place."

"My thoughts exactly," Davis said. "He is a talented officer, but forces under his command are not known for their discipline. During his last raid into Kentucky in 1864, his troopers became so disorganized that some of them abandoned their units to loot civilian property."

Breckinridge sensed where the discussion was going. "Seeking to cast blame at a time like this is unwise, Mr. President. General Morgan has my full confidence and shall continue to have it unless and until circumstances greatly change. As I said when I first proposed Morgan for this command, he is skilled in unconventional warfare and that is the kind of officer we need for an assignment like this."

Davis looked Breckinridge hard in the eye for a moment. "Very well, John. But what do we do now?"

"I will be drafting my reply to General Morgan as soon as I return to Mechanic's Hall, Mr. President. I intend to ask him for a more detailed account of what has happened and inquire as to his future course of action."

"So you are still content with Morgan deciding how to proceed?" Davis asked. "This incident has not shaken your faith in him?"

"Perhaps he was reckless and underestimated these insurgents, Mr. President. How many officers have not made mistakes? It is my expectation that, having experienced a setback, Morgan will be more cautious in his operations. Now that he knows what these blacks are capable of, Morgan will be better able to devise a proper strategy for eliminating them." He paused a moment before going on. "He will also want revenge. That's always a good motivator, in my experience."

Davis thought on this for a few moments, finally nodding. "Very well, John. But I want you to appreciate how this is going to look when word of it reaches the newspapers. Our fine troops, led by one of our most distinguished officers, trounced by a gang of blacks? Morgan is about to appear the fool in front of the entire Confederacy."

"All the more motivation for Morgan to redeem himself, Mr. President."

"True. But if another such thing happens, we must be prepared to remove Morgan from command. Consider who you might call upon to replace him, if you please."

"I will do so, sir," Breckinridge replied. Agreeing to think about something was always easy to do.

"Might reinforcements be in order?" Benjamin inquired. "I hesitate to ask, of course, as I know nothing of military matters."

"I am not sure," Breckinridge admitted. "I will have to wait until Morgan has submitted a more detailed report. In any event, I stand ready to muster five regiments into national service if it becomes necessary. Mr. President, do I have your permission to do so if I believe the situation warrants it?"

"You do," Davis said immediately. "Of course, as we have previously discussed, I don't want our actions to inflate the threat posed by these insurgents. But I give you authorization to deal with the problem as you see fit."

"Our political enemies are going to take advantage of this," Benjamin said. "Toombs, Wigfall, and all the rest of those vipers will blame this debacle on us and use it to persuade the people that we are incompetent."

Davis sat back in his chair, not speaking for several moments. When he did reply, his voice betrayed exhaustion. "Of all the alterations we made when we wrote up the Constitution in Montgomery, I think none was as beneficial as the limit of the president to a single term in office. If I were under the pressure of reelection, I am sure I should go mad."

Breckinridge felt an unexpected wave of sympathy for Davis in that moment. He could see how much the president had aged since he had first taken office in 1861. Never a particularly healthy man, Davis had been steadily worn down by the stresses of his position until he was a pale shadow of the man he had once been. Even the end of the war had done little to ease the pressure on

Davis, as the problems facing the Confederacy in peacetime were nearly as daunting as those they had faced during the war.

Were he to run for the Presidency, Breckinridge knew, the same thing would undoubtedly happen to him. He was still only in his mid-forties, but he knew that the war had left him mentally and physically exhausted and his subsequent service in the Cabinet had given him no rest. Were he to be elected president, he was not entirely sure he would survive the six year term.

Benjamin was talking. "I'll speak to the newspaper editors friendly to the administration, encouraging them to mention this engagement as a minor setback of little importance. However, I think it would be helpful if you made it clear to General Morgan that a success against these insurgents is now even more necessary."

"Morgan knows that he's expected to defeat these blacks," Breckinridge replied. "I don't think he needs to be reminded. He might even take it as an affront."

"I'm not especially concerned with how he will take it," Davis said. "Make it clear to him that we expect some progress in the immediate future and that he must ensure that nothing like this ambush happens again."

Breckinridge waited just a moment. "I will do so, Mr. President."

"And when he provides a more detailed report, you will let me know right away, yes?"

"Of course, Mr. President."

"Good. Was there anything else?"

"No. I should be getting back to Mechanic's Hall." Breckinridge rose to leave.

"Oh, John," Benjamin said, holding up an envelope. "This is a copy of a letter I received from Slidell in Paris, about the new curriculum at French military academies, or some such thing. I was going to send it over to you, but since you're here, I'll just give it to you."

"Thank you, Judah," Breckinridge said as he took the envelope, thinking little of it. Reports from Confederate diplomats overseas that touched on military matters were forwarded to Breckinridge as a matter of course. He shook hands with Davis and Benjamin and, a few moments later, was walking down the street back towards Mechanic's Hall.

He tried to push thoughts of Morgan or the upcoming presidential race from his mind as he walked back to his office. It would have been a great relief if he could have simply enjoyed a walk on what was a pleasant spring day. Yet his mind remained clouded by worrisome doubts. What if Morgan suffered another setback? Breckinridge had appointed Morgan, so another failure would reflect badly on him as well as on Morgan. Would that impact his chances of winning the presidency?

The last thought bothered him. Was running for president really the right decision? He had told no one but his wife of his intentions, so he could still reverse himself and no one would be the wiser. If he did change his mind, he would have to do so in the very near future, perhaps within the next few days. If he waited too long before announcing his candidacy, there would not be enough time to properly organize a campaign. As the Confederacy did not have organized political parties as yet, getting a presidential campaign put together would be vastly more difficult than it had been for him in 1860. Since the moment Lee had publicly announced he was not running, newspaper speculation about Breckinridge's intentions had sharply increased. He had received letters from old friends and political allies asking him whether he planned on running and promising their support if he did. More than anything else, though, his recent conversation with Benjamin had made the issue crystal clear.

If he did run, he knew his opponents would bitterly denounce him for his role at the Toronto Peace Conference and that William Porcher Miles would surely release the information about his secret dealings with Hannibal Hamlin. That might be enough by itself to destroy whatever chances Breckinridge had to win the election. If it were coupled with further cases of Confederate soldiers being bested by rebel slaves in the swamps of Louisiana, the situation would be even grimmer.

Common sense argued against a run for the presidency, Breckinridge told himself. Yet if he did not run, who would stand against whichever candidate the Fire-Eaters put forward? With Lee out of the running, no one else that Breckinridge could think of would have the reputation among the people to compete with the energy and organization that the Fire-Eaters would surely bring to bear once they settled on their candidate.

He remembered the day he had stood with his friend Garnet Wolseley on the battlefield in Quebec where the British had defeated the French in 1759. He had made the decision then to seek the presidency, only to be faced with Miles's blackmail threat shortly thereafter. Since then, he had avoided thinking about the question for as long as he could. His time, however, was clearly up. He would have to choose.

Breckinridge reached Mechanic's Hall and was soon sitting down at his desk once again. He lit a cigar and decided to clear his desk of extraneous material. Writing his response to Morgan would require time and concentration, so it would be best to get trivial matters out of the way first.

He opened the envelope that Benjamin had given him and withdrew its contents. To his surprise, it was not a letter from Slidell. It took him a moment to overcome his confusion and realize that he was holding a page from the subscription list to Frederick Douglass's newspaper, the *North Star*. There, right in the middle of the list, was his own name.

So Benjamin had not destroyed it, after all. He could easily have used it to blackmail Breckinridge. Politically, it would have been much more devastating to Breckinridge than anything Miles might say to the press. Miles could do a great deal of damage, but in the end it would simply be his word against that of Breckinridge.

There was a short note in the envelope as well.

Dear John,
I don't really think I need this anymore.
Judah

Breckinridge chuckled. He took a few puffs on his cigar, filling the office with smoke, then touched the corner of the subscription list to the red-glowing tip. In an instant, the piece of paper ignited. He held it as it was consumed by the flame, dropping it into his ashtray just before his fingers would have been singed.

Writing the response to Morgan would take about an hour. After that, it would be time to start planning his presidential campaign.

April 23, Night
Insurgent Camp, St. Martin Parish, Southern Louisiana

Saul's standing orders to his men were to keep noise to a minimum and not to make fires any bigger than necessary. The swamps and forests of southern Louisiana were vast and full of places in which to hide. Even a group as large as Saul's could vanish into the wilderness almost without a trace. Still, it didn't do to take chances and Saul's instructions minimized the possibility of discovery.

Over the past few nights, however, the men had not been as assiduous in following these orders. They had laughed more, talked more loudly, and generally carried themselves with a jaunty and almost giddy air. They were continually speaking of their recent fight with Morgan's cavalry, each man recounting his own deeds in increasingly improbable detail. A pleasant cloud of good cheer seemed to hover over the camp. It was, Saul thought, the feeling of victory.

The engagement with Morgan's men, by any rational account, had not been a victory. It had been Saul's men who had run away in the end. The fifteen men he had lost represented a significant portion of his fighting strength, while the Confederacy could throw as many men into the fight as it liked. Morgan had not pursued them as Saul had hoped, thereby avoiding the second ambush he had planned.

Still, it felt like a victory to Saul's men, and that was what mattered. The very fact that they had stood toe-to-toe against regular Confederate soldiers, led by one of their ablest commanders, and gave as good as they got, represented a triumph. The Confederate soldiers they had fought against now knew that they were up against men equal to themselves.

No one knew this better than the three men on the ground off to one side of the camp. Gagged to prevent their speaking, and tied with ropes behind their backs that bound their hands and feet together, the three Confederate prisoners looked pathetic and helpless. On the night after the battle, in their first hours of captivity, the looks of terror on their faces had been intense. It had been obvious that they expected to be killed at any moment.

Saul had issued strict orders that no physical harm was to come to the prisoners. They had been given food and water, although no more than they needed to avoid hunger and not any of the meat. Considering the limited amount of food his insurgents had for themselves, Saul considered this generous and he was not overly concerned with the comfort of his prisoners.

Not much had happened in the few days following their fight with Morgan. Saul had ordered his column to move deeper into the wilderness and farther away from the roads. He expected that the Confederates would take a few days to recover from the surprise of the ambush and that they would be careful in their pursuit from now on. At the same time, knowing the Southern character as well as he did, Saul knew that they would be burning with a desire for revenge and a determination to erase the humiliation that had been inflicted upon them. Morgan and his men would be back to settle the score soon enough.

When word had reached Saul that the commander of the enemy forces chasing him was named Morgan, he had asked Ferguson if he knew of the man. None of the regiments in which Saul had served during the war had ever fought against Morgan and he had not heard of him. The white doctor had told him what he knew about the Kentuckian, explaining that he was a cavalryman known for long raids behind enemy lines. Based on what Ferguson had told him, the man was a master of irregular warfare and unconventional tactics.

Yet Saul had led Morgan and his unit of Kentucky cavalry into an ambush with almost dismissive ease. The Confederates had recovered quickly and fought well, it was true. They had inflicted heavy losses upon Saul's men. Still, they had proven themselves to be anything but invincible. Saul's men would not be afraid of them.

He sat on a log, watching his men cheerfully eat some of the pork they had obtained from one of the recently looted plantations, laughing and talking. Off to one side, the three prisoners sat sullenly, not moving and trying to ignore everything going on around them. Saul sensed Dr. Ferguson coming along beside him.

"What are you going to do with them?" Ferguson asked, sitting down beside him on the log.

"The prisoners?"

"Yes."

"I don't know," Saul answered honestly. "I never gave any thought to what we would do if we were to capture any of the enemy. I assumed that our men would not take prisoners."

"You killed the men on the plantations," Ferguson said. "How would executing them be any different?"

"There are rules to warfare," Saul replied. "You taught me that yourself. One of them is that prisoners are not be to be harmed. The men on the plantations were criminals because they owned slaves. We don't know if these men own slaves. Most Confederate soldiers don't."

"Well, in any case, I'd keep Silas away from them. He will mistreat them, no matter what your orders are."

Saul nodded. Silas was always causing trouble. The man was a skilled fighter and the best man in the band when it came to scouting, but otherwise a thorn in Saul's side. Both Ferguson and Troy disliked Silas, and Saul was not fond of him either.

"So what do we do?" Ferguson asked again.

"Like I said, I'm not sure."

"Well, you need to decide soon. It won't be easy to constantly detail men to guard the prisoners. They'll slow us down and perhaps try to signal to the enemy where we are. And they're eating a portion of our food, too."

"If you have any ideas, let me know."

Ferguson nodded and moved off. Saul watched him go. He knew how much he depended on the white man. Being born and raised on a plantation, Saul was aware that he knew little of the larger world. It had been Ferguson, in the Union camp at Milliken's Bend in mid-1863, who had taken Saul under his wing and taught him how to read and write. It had been difficult and frustrating at first, struggling with the mystery of the little black squiggles on paper. He had almost given up many times, but Ferguson had been patient and encouraging, acting in a completely different manner than any white man Saul had ever known.

Slowly, the little black squiggles had begun to make sense. As if a fire had been ignited in his mind, Saul very quick advanced from basic sentences about cats and dogs into deeper works. He remembered the morning when he had picked up a newspaper account of a battle and read it without assistance. At that point, he had begun to press Ferguson to give him more and more books, a request the white doctor had been happy to oblige. When not on duty, Saul had sealed himself in his tent, reading book after book. With the aid of a single dictionary, he found that he could read any of them almost effortlessly.

Saul did not know who his father was. Many of the old women on the plantation had told him that his white master was his father and that was certainly possible. Yet in all ways that mattered, his father was Stephen Ferguson. He was the one man from whom Saul was willing to take advice.

He rose from the log and walked over to the three prisoners. Seeing him approach, they cowered backwards to the extent that their restraints permitted them. When they had first been taken into the camp, they had appeared stunned and mystified at their predicament. The next morning, they had breathed defiance and spoken harshly towards their captors, as if the black men would untie them if only they shouted loudly enough. Then Saul had ordered them gagged. Now, three days after having been taken prisoner, the captured Kentuckians seemed to have settled into a strange sort of ennui.

Six guards with leveled rifles stood around the three men. Saul gestured for the gag of the largest man to be removed.

"What's your name?" Saul asked. When they had first been captured, they had refused to say what their names were. He hoped that the intervening days of terror had softened their attitude.

The Confederate soldier took a deep breath, gratefully sucking in the air that had been hindered by his gag. Then he looked up at his captor.

"You darkie bastard! Why don't you stop toying with us! If you're going to kill us, just do it and get it over with."

"We're not talking about whether or not I am going to kill you. I asked you what your name is."

The man hesitated only a few moments more. "Nathaniel Johnson. But what the hell do you care what my name is?"

Saul knelt down, bringing his eyes level with Johnson's. "You're Kentuckian?"

"Yes."

"Where in Kentucky are you from?"

"Why the hell should you care where I'm from?"

"Do you have a favorite kind of whiskey?"

"Shut up!" Johnson spat. "What the hell sort of game are you playing, darkie?"

"Is it really so hard? To talk to me as you would talk to any other man?"

The prisoner drew his head back in confusion and didn't respond. Saul wasn't surprised, for he had seen the same reaction on the face of many another white Southern enemy. To an ordinary man like Johnson, Saul could only be some sort of vague black subhuman, fit only for manual labor.

He did not wait for Johnston to respond to his last question. He stood and walked away, leaving the prisoners behind. For the next few minutes, he strolled through the camp. As he passed them, his men quieted their conversations and muttered respectful greetings. He replied by nodding sternly down on them, disdaining to speak. He had learned from observing the white officers of the U.S.C.T. regiments during the war that it was important not to develop too easy a familiarity with the men. Doing so would undermine morale and discipline, for it fostered a permissive attitude, in which orders became merely suggestions and soldiers had to be persuaded to do their work.

He almost chuckled to himself at the irony. He was fighting against the slave system, in which men held tyrannical power over those who worked for them. Yet to fight against it effectively, he had to hold what amounted to tyrannical power over the men he commanded. Yet he had made it clear to his men that they were free to leave at any time. They were soldiers, not slaves. Moreover, he endured every privation that his men endured. There was a difference between leading men fighting for their freedom and exploiting men to do manual labor for one's own aggrandizement.

Saul understood the great gulf that necessarily had to exist between himself and his men. Dr. Ferguson was the only person he could really talk to on anything like an equal level. Saul knew the infinite loneliness of command. Yet he loved his men dearly. He had no children, but he was certain that he knew what it felt like to be a father, for each one of the men under his command was like a child to him.

For just a moment, he wondered if perhaps John Hunt Morgan, his enemy, cared as much about his men as Saul did. He then stopped in his track, stung by the power of an idea that entered his mind.

April 26, Evening
British Army Camp, South of Montreal, Canada

To his knowledge, Wolseley had never encountered a man as smart as himself. He had certainly met men he thought greater than himself. The Confederate commander Robert E. Lee, whom he had met during his sojourn in the South in 1862, was one such man. His friend Charles "Chinese" Gordon, whose mystical religious belief was so intense that Wolseley wondered if he actually talked to God, was another. Yet when it came to raw intelligence, Wolseley was convinced that he was in a class all his own.

This occasionally made social events difficult for Wolseley. His head spun with radical ideas for how to reform the British army and these concepts were not always welcome among the aristocratic men who ruled the institution. Moreover, what was termed 'shop talk' was generally forbidden by the traditional etiquette of the officers' mess. He would have to hold his tongue, which was never an easy task for him.

Still, as he marched across the camp towards the stone building in which the Royal Welch Fusiliers had set up their officers' mess, Wolseley admitted that he was looking forward to dinner. The arrival of more British regiments in Canada was a boon to his social calendar, for he could sit down with men from the home country rather than the provincial Canadians. If nothing else, the dinner he was about to enjoy was certain to be a civilized affair with food and wine of high quality.

Wolseley had never known quite what to make of the Welsh. As a product of the Protestant community of Dublin and its environs, Wolseley reserved the right to treat both the English and the Irish with a measure of contempt. To the former, he was too Irish; to the latter, he was too English. It was an obvious solution to generally disdain both. Englishmen, in Wolseley's experience, were too haughty and affluent for their own good, so secure in their superiority as to be insufferable. The Irish Catholics were little better than barbarians, so ill-educated and easily swayed by their ignorant priests. Farther north, the Scots were surely the best fighters of the British lot, though the Scottish officers were far too cliquish.

The Welsh, though, were different from the rest of the peoples who made up Britain. They kept to themselves and were too small in numbers or influence to be much bother to the English, Scots, or Irish. To Wolseley's mind, the Welsh were like the second cousin whose name no one could remember at the family reunion. That said, Welsh soldiers in Queen Victoria's army had earned a reputation for bravery and tenacity far greater than their small numbers would seem to justify. Of the Welsh regiments, the Royal Welch Fusiliers was possibly the best.

The two privates standing guard on either side of the door saluted and stomped their feet as he approached. One turned sharply and opened the door for him. He entered the mess and looked around with admiration. Although the Royal Welch had only arrived in Canada a few weeks before, the mess was so elegantly decorated that it was as if they had been here for years.

The center of the room was taken up with a long table, on which several candles were glowing and dozens of silver place settings were sparkling in the warm, reflected light. In a stone fireplace in the center of the wall, several logs were blazing and crackling. Mounted reverently on the wall opposite the fireplace were the regimental colors. Along the wall on either side of the fireplace were portraits of former commanders of the battalion and a few photographs of officers and men assembled together on the parade ground.

He saw Colonel Bell speaking to a cluster of other officers. All held glasses of sherry in their hands. Bell turned and looked at Wolseley as he entered.

Wolseley stopped short. "Permission to enter the mess, sir?" As Bell was both his superior and the commander of the battalion, it was customary to request such permission, though the idea of its being refused would have been absurd.

"Permission granted. Glad to see you, Wolseley. Fancy a sherry?"

Wolseley gracefully tilted his head in assent. Bell snapped at a servant, who approached with a silver tray full of glasses. Wolseley took one and sipped. It was far from the greatest sherry he had ever tasted, but it was better than any commonly encountered in Canada.

Bell introduced him to the other officers one at a time. The young subalterns appeared timid and reluctant to speak, which was only to be expected. Some regimental traditions even dictated that subalterns never express opinions on anything until they had put in at least three years of service. The older officers seemed to Wolseley like fine gentlemen. A few of them he had met before, having served in close proximity to them in either the Crimean War or the Indian Mutiny.

Wolseley was tired and wanted to sit down, yet he knew he had to remain standing until Colonel Bell directed the men to the table. More and more officers began arriving. Wolseley circulated among them and they greeted him cordially. Yet he felt distinctly out of place. He was a guest in the mess, surrounded by men who were as close as brothers. All were polite to him, but none went out of his way to make him feel welcome.

He listened to the conversations swirling around him. Some of the men were discussing the latest horse racing results from Wales. Others were stridently debating whether Wales should form a football association similar to that which had been recently formed in England. There was no talk of politics or religion, which was strictly forbidden. Nor did any of the men discuss women, as convention decreed that no female ever be specifically mentioned by name in the mess.

Wolseley sighed and sipped his sherry, not especially wishing to join in any of the conversations. He paced around the room, looking at the portraits of the battalion's former commanders. As he did so, he came upon an old-looking set of keys in a glass case set on a red pillow. He looked at them quizzically for a few moments.

"Those are the keys to the postern gate of Corunna," said Colonel Bell, who had seen Wolseley's confusion and walked over to him.

"Are they? How fascinating. How did your battalion come to have possession of them?"

"I was told the story by some of the older soldiers when I was a young officer. You know about the battle itself, I'm sure. It was in 1809. Napoleon had our small army in Spain surrounded. We were trying to hold the walls of Corunna long enough for the Royal Navy to take our men off and get them back to England."

"I don't think there's a single soldier in Britain who doesn't know the story," Wolseley said.

"Yes, but did you know that the Royal Welch were the last battalion remaining onshore at the end of the evacuation?"

"No, I was not aware of that."

"We held the French off long enough for the rest of the army to board the waiting ships. Then we fled from the walls and dashed for the ships ourselves. The last man through the postern gate near the docks, a captain, decided it would be a good idea to lock the gates. He had to use his bayonet as a lever to turn them, though, for they were so rusty. I don't know why he bothered keeping the keys. He could have simply tossed them in the water while boarding his ships. In any case, he did keep them and now the regiment keeps them as a memento of that glorious day."

"Very fitting, Colonel."

"Thank you, Wolseley." Bell turned to address the room as a whole. "Please take your seats, gentlemen."

The assembled officers, numbering slightly more than three dozen, strolled to the table and stood behind their chairs. No one actually sat down until Colonel Bell himself did. Wolseley, as a guest of honor, sat just to the right of Bell. Conversation largely ceased as the dinner was brought out. The main course consisted of large slabs of roast beef, accompanied by leek soup and meatballs made from pig's livers. It was all washed down by a serviceable Portuguese red wine.

"So, you told me that you enjoyed the hunting here in Canada?" Bell asked Wolseley.

"Beyond words," Wolseley said. "There is so much more open space here. So different from England. It's like India in its wide variety of animals to be hunted, without annoying natives getting in the way. It is more difficult to find quality servants, though."

"Alas, such is life. All postings have their advantages and disadvantages."

"I find the latter more common here in Canada than the former. Not much goes on here. Of course, with this Fenian business. . ." He stopped short and looked at Bell. "I'm sorry, Colonel. I am forgetting myself and beginning to talk about politics."

"It's all right," Bell said, lowering his voice so that others could not hear. "I shall wish to speak with you after the evening's pleasantries are over, for I have received orders to take my battalion down to the St. Lawrence River. We have received information that a large band of Fenians intend to cross the river sometime in the next month. We will be moving into a position to stop them."

Wolseley felt his heart beat a little faster at the thought of fighting. "Where is this information coming from?"

"Spies, most likely. I imagine it wouldn't be difficult to infiltrate an organization like the Fenians."

"Colonel, can I persuade you to take along a battalion of my militia? It would be good for them to see some action against the Fenians, for their own sake and for that of the public. The Canadian authorities are fearful that the militia cannot be counted upon. If we can point to a sizable action in which they performed well, it would do much to solidify public confidence."

"I'm sure that could be arranged," Bell replied. "Are you sure they are up to it?"

"I've trained them very hard. They will do well."

"Then I shall put in the request. I see no reason why it won't be granted."

"Thank you, Colonel."

Wolseley was not lying, for he sincerely believed it would increase public confidence for them to fight in a successful engagement. Yet that was not his primary motive. Wolseley above all other things yearned to be in a battle. It had been more than half a decade since he had last heard shots fired in anger when he had taken part in the storming of the Taku forts in China. For a man who lived and breathed for battle, it had been far too long. Even if it meant leading militiamen rather than proper British soldiers, Wolseley would leap at any chance for combat that came his way.

The dinner continued. As more and more wine was consumed, the officers began acting increasingly like children. A major bet a week's pay that he could stand on his head for more than five minutes. The poor fellow did not last more than a single minute before tumbling to the ground, to the uproarious laughter of his comrades. The president of the mess, a rotating office which this week was held by a captain, dutifully noted the amount the major would be required to pay into the mess account.

After a time, Colonel Bell nodded to the mess president. The man gave instructions for the servants to refill everyone's wine glasses. This accomplished, the president stood and began tapping his crystal wine glass with his fork. Instantly, the room became silent.

The captain serving as the mess president spoke loudly and clearly. "Mr. Vice. The Queen!"

At the other end of the table, the lieutenant who was serving as mess vice president rose. An instant later, all of the men rose to their feet as well, Wolseley included. Although some regiments preferred to conduct the toast to the sovereign while sitting, the Royal Welch evidently stood.

"Her Majesty, the Queen!" the vice president said, raising his wine glass.

"The Queen, God bless her!" answered the assembled officers.

Wolseley spoke as loudly and enthusiastically as any of the Welshmen. It was not just for show, either, for Wolseley was an ardent monarchist. The republican and egalitarian principles of the Americans made no sense to him. Given the rise of England from a poor island to a mighty empire that now spanned the globe, was it not obvious that a monarchy, with appropriate constitutional checks, was the proper form of government for a country?

"Mr. Vice. The Prince of Wales!" the mess president said.

"His Royal Highness, the Prince of Wales!" the vice president said, again raising his glass.

"The Prince of Wales, God bless him!" answered the officers.

The toast to the Prince of Wales caught Wolseley slightly off guard. He had momentarily forgotten that the Welsh regiments customarily toasted the heir apparent as well as the monarch. Yet he had realized what was happening quickly enough to join in the toast and take another sip from his glass.

Colonel Bell raised his glass and Wolseley realized that the battalion commander was going to make his own toast.

"Gentlemen, to absent friends."

"Absent friends!" all exclaimed as they raised their glasses to their lips yet again. Wolseley wondered if the men of the Royal Welch Fusiliers took the words of this particular toast literally or whether it was a reference to comrades who had died on previous campaigns. Perhaps it was for both.

Colonel Bell looked across the table at Wolseley. "Gentlemen, we have a distinguished guest with us tonight. A man who has fought in some of the same battles as the Royal Welch in the Crimea and India. Lieutenant Colonel Garnet Wolseley of the Perthshire Volunteers and Assistant Quartermaster General of Her Majesty's forces in Canada."

Some of the officers raised their eyebrows at the mention of the name of Wolseley's regiment. The lips of a few curled up into a slight sneer, for Welsh regiments generally disliked and distrusted Scottish regiments. It did not matter

152

that the regiment was recruiting mostly from London or that there was not a drop of Scottish blood in Wolseley's veins. The Welshmen knew that Perthshire was in Scotland and that made the Perthshire Volunteers a Scottish regiment in their eyes. He was content to ignore whatever disdain they felt. Healthy competition and rivalry between regiments was one of the secrets of British military superiority.

Bell continued. "I should like to invite our new friend to make a toast to the assembled officers of our battalion here tonight."

Wolseley had assumed he might be called upon to give a toast, since many regiments asked their guests at the officers' mess to do so. He had spent some time during the afternoon considering what he would say if such a situation arose and so did not hesitate.

He raised his wine glass. "To a long war or a sickly season," he said calmly.

"Long war or sickly season," the officers repeated before draining their wine glasses. It was a common toast given at the dinners of British officers. Casualties in battle or deaths from disease opened up positions that had been held by higher-ranking men, making promotion more likely for younger officers. Such advancement, of course, depended on whether the ambitious men survived themselves. Wolseley, for one, had long ago decided that the best way to advance up the ranks of the British Army was by seeking to get himself killed at every possible opportunity.

He so desired a war. What Colonel Bell had related to him about the Fenians meant that he might, at long last, see action again. Even better, if the Fenian matter continued to fester and grow until it led to an open conflict with the United States, the glory-seeking possibilities for Garnet Wolseley would be practically limitless.

April 29, Night
Théâtre Lyrique, Paris, France

Slidell leaned forward slightly in his seat, watching the action down on the stage of the Théâtre Lyrique. It was the third time he had seen Verdi's *Rigoletto* and he found that he enjoyed it more with each performance. At the moment, the Duke of Mantua was confessing his love for Gilda, the daughter of Rigoletto, who did not know who the Duke was and believed him to be only a poor student. As Slidell recalled the story, Rigoletto, the court jester who wished to protect his daughter from the romantic intentions of the Duke, would eventually hire assassins to try to kill the Duke. In the climax of the story, the assassins would accidentally kill Gilda instead, the culmination of a curse that had been put on Rigoletto in the opening scene.

None of the story made any sense, of course, but that didn't bother Slidell. Opera was about music and beauty, not storytelling. As the singers drifted across the stage, their divine voices filled the immensity of the Théâtre Lyrique with a kind of exquisiteness that was difficult to articulate or explain. Christina Nilsson, the Swedish soprano playing the role of Gilda, was one of the most captivating women Slidell had ever seen. He enjoyed simply gazing at her. Opera singers, Slidell had decided, were as close as human beings could come to being angels.

All around the theater, almost two thousand people sat in silence and stillness, watching the performance in rapt fascination. In sheer size, there was nothing in America that remotely compared to the Théâtre Lyrique. More impressive than its scale, however, was the grace and elegance of its architecture. It had not just been built, it had been lovingly crafted by men who were artists as well as laborers. The ceiling, the columns, and even the hand railings had been ornately carved. The illumination cast by countless gas lights reflected off crystal chandeliers and the gilding which covered much of the woodwork.

Slidell reflected for a moment just how lucky a man he was. He had lived in Paris now for more than half a decade, serving the Confederacy while simultaneously indulging in everything that made life delicious and pleasing. The wealth of his son-in-law meant that he never wanted for anything he desired. His wife had passed away the previous year from an unexpected illness, which of course was to be lamented, but such things happened to people once they reached advanced age. Though he sincerely missed his wife, her death did free him to enjoy the pleasures of high-end Parisian prostitutes on those occasions when he was able to overcome his physical limitations.

Best of all, his crucial diplomatic position allowed him to keeping playing the great game of politics which he so enjoyed and at which he excelled. The thought jostled him somewhat. As much as he was enjoying the opera, Slidell had not come to the Théâtre Lyrique exclusively for pleasure. There was work to be done. In particular, there was a man to be recruited.

He patiently waited for the intermission to come, enjoying the music, longingly looking at Christina Nilsson's beautiful face and figure. The opera went on, its unlikely story unfolding in the same ridiculous manner as it had the previous two times Slidell had gone to see it. Eventually, the singers left the stage, the orchestra reached a conclusion, and the lights increased. The previously silent crowd applauded gratefully and, with a loud murmur of chattering voices, rose as one to enjoy the intermission.

Slidell strolled into the immense lobby of the theater, purchasing a glass of Romanée-Conti and savoring the taste of the red Burgundy as the wine danced across his tongue. The large room was crowded with the cream of Parisian society. At a glance, Slidell could see wealthy businessmen, members of the French Senate, diplomats from across Europe, and a host of other worthies.

Looking through the crowd, Slidell spotted the first man with whom he wished to speak. Sipping his wine, he walked up to Jules Baroche, the French Minister of Justice. The position he held was a powerful one, for he controlled the courts and police forces of the nation. He was not the man that Slidell had come for, but the Confederate diplomat knew an opportunity when he saw one.

"Good evening, Minister," Slidell said as he approached, bowing his head respectfully.

"And to you, Minister," Baroche responded. "I trust you are enjoying the opera?"

"Beyond words. Miss Nilsson is as lovely as ever this evening."

"She is. Her voice is also quite charming." Baroche chucked at his own joke. "What may I do for you?"

Slidell smiled. With many French politicians, small talk and inane pleasantries could take up a great deal of time. In all nations, but especially in

France, men used such banter to waste time in order to avoid giving firm answers to any questions. Baroche was cut from a different cloth, however, and usually wanted to get down to business as quickly as possible.

"Do you know who Henri Rochefort is?" Slidell asked.

"Of course I do," Baroche answered in an irritated tone. "He's one of those annoying socialist newspaper editors."

"His paper has been running numerous editorials in recent months that are quite derogatory to the Confederate States."

Slidell had read Rochefort's editorials avidly, for he made a point to examine as many of the French newspapers as possible in order to remain abreast of public opinion. Rochefort had written piece after piece, each more blistering than the last, asserting that the victory of the Confederacy in the War for Southern Independence had been a setback to the freedom and progress of all mankind. According to Rochefort, the continued existence of slavery was a "transgression against human nature."

As far as Slidell was concerned, socialism made no sense and was not to be taken seriously as a political or economic concept. Rochefort and those like him were silly people who obviously resented being at the bottom of the social ladder. On the other hand, the editorials couldn't be ignored, for Rochefort's newspaper had a surprisingly wide and growing readership. With the increasing liberalization of the French Empire's political structure, the franchise for legislative elections was expanding and the kind of people who read Rochefort's editorials were gaining the right to vote. The Confederacy needed support among the members of the Parliament of France, for they would have a role to play in determining whether the treaty of alliance between France and the Confederacy would be ratified. This meant that Rochefort's editorials were a threat. Perhaps only a minor threat, but a threat nonetheless.

"Is that so?" Baroche said. "Well, I am sorry to hear that. But I am afraid I can do nothing for you, Minister. As you know, the emperor has recently decreed complete press freedom throughout France. Even idiots like Rochefort are free to write whatever they want, so long as they don't engage in sedition against the Empire."

"I'm not asking you to arrest him," Slidell said. "I was simply wondering if you might investigate him. After all, if he is willing to criticize the Confederacy so directly, perhaps he is planning sedition against the French government as well."

It was a very thin argument, Slidell knew. It didn't matter, though. He had communicated what he wanted to Baroche and that was what was important. His son-in-law had prepared the way with some expensive gifts for the Minister of Justice and members of his family.

"Well, I will see what I can do, Minister. Was there anything else?"

"No, Minister. I hope you enjoy the rest of the opera."

The two men bowed their heads to one another and walked off in separate directions. Slidell felt that he had accomplished his purpose. More likely than not, within the next few days two or three inspectors would visit Rochefort's office and question him about why he was writing editorials against the Confederacy. It would be, in effect, a warning shot. With any luck, it might cause the socialist editor to hesitate before printing another damning editorial.

155

The Rochefort matter was a minor issue. There were more important things to which he needed to attend. While trying to find the man with whom he most wanted to speak, Slidell ended up exchanging pleasantries with Romulo Díaz de la Vega, the diplomatic representative of the French-backed Mexican government of the Emperor Maximilian. Although nothing substantial was said during the brief conversation, Slidell was pleased to talk to the man. Good relations between the Confederacy and Mexico were important, after all.

Slidell felt a tug of apprehension. The intermission had only a few minutes to run and he had not yet achieved his primary goal for the evening. At that moment, however, he finally spotted his quarry. Extracting himself from a crowd of hangers-on was Napoleon-Alexandre Berthier, a member of the French Senate and one of the men who would eventually be asked to weigh in on the question of the treaty between France and the Confederacy. Slidell did not consider Berthier an especially intelligent or cunning man, but he had a following due to the fact that his father had been one of the great French marshals of the Napoleonic Wars.

"Senator Berthier!" Slidell said pleasantly as he approached. "I hope you are having a pleasant evening."

The hint of confusion on Berthier's face told Slidell that the Frenchman did not immediately recognize him. It took a moment for Berthier to recover. "Yes, indeed, Minister Slidell. I am enjoying myself very much."

"Might I have a moment of your time, sir? The intermission will be over soon, but there was something I wanted to discuss with you."

Berthier gestured towards one of the walls and the two strode over to it together. "Well?" the French senator asked.

"Negotiations between myself and your foreign ministry are proceeding well," Slidell said. "I expect a treaty between our two countries to be signed before the end of the year."

"That is well and good," Berthier said. "I hope you will not take it as an offense when I tell you that this issue is not one of great interest to me. Of course, I want France to have good relations with all well-meaning nations. But to the extent that I think about foreign affairs, I tend to think about Europe."

"Naturally, Senator," Slidell replied. "In your place, I should be of the same mind."

In saying these words, Slidell was being completely honest. As cosmopolitan a man as he was, Slidell was a Confederate and his mind was always focused on the interests of his own nation. Such matters as the squabbling of the various German states, the threat that Russia posed to the British Empire in Asia, the unification of Italy, or the expansion of French influence over North Africa were no concern of his except as they might indirectly impact the long-term interests of the Confederacy.

French policy-makers only cared about the Confederacy in terms of how it might assist the French imperial adventure in Mexico. Napoleon III knew that his efforts to install Maximilian as a puppet emperor of Mexico would be greatly enhanced if French warships had unrestricted use of Confederate harbors, if cattle and crops from Texas could flow unhindered to feed the French armies, and especially if Confederate troops were sent to help Maximilian directly.

Slidell knew, however, that there were many powerful elements within French society that opposed the Mexican venture as a vainglorious waste of resources. Why, they were asking, should the lives of French soldiers be put at risk in an attempt to take over a country on the other side of the world? Why should vast amounts of French money be invested in a backward country that was mostly desert?

Slidell had no doubts that the emperor himself was eager to conclude a treaty of friendship with the Confederacy. Yet he might hesitate in the face of outspoken opposition from the socialists and abolitionists who abhorred the Confederacy and those who simply thought the Mexican venture was misguided. To counter such opposition, Slidell needed to cultivate an influential group of supporters within the French political elite. Berthier, he had decided, was ideally suited to be the central figure of any such group.

"So what is it that you wish to talk to me about, then?" Berthier said.

Slidell took a careful sip of his wine. "You say that you have little interest in the proposed treaty between our two countries. Perhaps I could offer something to pique your interest?"

Berthier's eyes narrowed. "Such as?"

The Confederate diplomat glanced around to ensure no one else was within hearing. "You may have heard that the Yankees tore up the Southern railroads during the war in a very ungentlemanly fashion. We have put enormous effort into rebuilding them."

"I am aware of this, but I don't see how it relates to me."

"I'm talking about shares in our railroad companies, Senator Berthier. Construction is proceeding rapidly thanks to loans from various European banks. The Rothschilds. Barings. My own son-in-law. Now that the cotton is starting to flow again, it won't be long before the railroads start seeing substantial profits. I can easily arrange for a generous issue of bonds from several different railroads to be purchased in your name. Or whatever pseudonym you might prefer."

Berthier snorted with contempt. "I am quite wealthy enough, Monsieur Slidell. My father was one of Napoleon's most trusted marshals. When the present emperor took his rightful place on the throne, my name alone made me a distinguished personage in France. I have since done quite well for myself, I assure you."

"Yes, yes, of course, Senator," Slidell said reassuringly. "But I would caution you to remember that your present situation depends entirely on the continuance of Napoleon III on the imperial throne. If anything were to happen to him, your own position would be threatened. You mentioned your father. What ended up happening to him?"

Berthier gave Slidell an angry frown, which wasn't surprising. In 1815, during the confusing days after Napoleon's return from his exile on Elba but before his defeat at Waterloo, the elder Berthier had retreated to his estate and tried to remain neutral, despite Napoleon's entreaties to join him. The elder Berthier had then fallen to his death from an upstairs window of his chateau. Some said it had been suicide. Others said he had been murdered by agents of Napoleon's enemies. Either way, he had fallen victim to the chaos of the times in which he had lived.

Slidell went on. "I could arrange the purchase of a healthy amount of railroad shares and keep them in a secret account in the Confederacy. Think of it as an insurance policy. Have you considered what you'd do if, God forbid, Napoleon III ever were to fall? What if the radicals were to seize power and bring back the guillotine? Wouldn't it be sensible to have a place to which one could flee on the other side of the Atlantic?"

Berthier was silent for a few moments, then nodded slowly. "Why don't you come speak to me about this treaty of yours sometime, Slidell?"

Slidell smiled and finished off the last of his wine. "Happily, Monsieur."

The Frenchman smiled and walked slowly away. Bells rang softly, indicating that the opera was about to resume. Slidell got another glass of wine to take with him to his seat and followed the rest of the crowd back into the theater. He went back inside in a very good mood.

Berthier would be his man, Slidell was sure. Having a prominent French politician speaking on behalf of the treaty would be of tremendous benefit to Slidell's cause. With luck, Berthier would bring other leading Frenchmen over to his side as well, negating the opposition being raised against the treaty in some quarters.

For Slidell, the treaty was like the Holy Grail. If he achieved his goal, his name would be remembered in history. Yet it was far more than personal ambition that drove him in his diplomatic quest. For as much as he loved France, he was still a Confederate. Unless and until the Confederacy obtained a treaty of alliance with a major power, there was always the risk that the Union would one day embark on a war of vengeance. With so much financial trouble and political turmoil in the South, the country might prove unable to meet the demands of another war.

Those thoughts were for another time, though. For the moment, he was looking forward to gazing at Christina Nilsson again.

CHAPTER FIVE

May 1, Afternoon
Flynn's Alehouse, Waco, Texas

"He actually said that?" Collett asked. "He used those exact words?"

McFadden nodded. Now on his second glass of ale, he had spent the last half hour relating to Collett and a dozen other veterans of Granbury's Texas Brigade the story of how Judge Roden had come to his ranch and made his clumsy threat. Every man wore an angry expression on his face.

"Hope you don't mind, Jimmy, but I will be coming by your place every now and then. Just to check to make sure you and the wife are okay. I'll be bringing my old Enfield and my knife, too." This came from Charles Anderson, who had served in the 24th Texas during the war.

There were mutterings of agreement around the table. McFadden's heart warmed at the display of camaraderie. Over the course of the war, thousands of Texas men served in the various regiments of Granbury's Texas Brigade. Sadly, most of them now lay in shallow graves in Tennessee, Mississippi, or Georgia. But quite a few of those who did make it back had chosen to settle in the frontier region in and around Waco, where many of the land grants issued by the Texas state government were clustered. It gave McFadden a sense that the community of which he had been a part during the war continued to exist.

Daniel Flynn, the owner of the alehouse in which they had gathered and who had served in the 10th Texas during the war, stood up.

"Anyone want another?"

The table produced a chorus of voices, all in the affirmative. After determining who wanted ale, who wanted cider, and who wanted whiskey, Flynn walked over to the bar to fetch the drinks. The men knew that Flynn would not ask them to pay the price he charged for his regular customers, so they were eager to drink as much as they could.

"To hell with just protecting McFadden," said Robert Farmer, a veteran of the 6th Texas. "Why don't we just go down to Judge Roden's house and shoot the bastard? He's already run dozens of people off their land. He runs this county like it's his own private kingdom. Now he's threatening our own? I say we take the hide off the son of a bitch."

"I don't want any violence," McFadden said. "Son of a bitch or not, Roden is the elected judge of Granbury County. People can't just go around shooting elected officials."

"Why not?" Farmer asked. "A son of a bitch is a son of a bitch, if you ask me."

"Because we fought to create this country and I don't think we can just ignore the laws whenever we want. If we do, what did we fight the war for?"

"But Roden is the one ignoring the law, Jimmy," said Collett. "Worse, he abuses the law, using his position to enrich himself. Yes, he's an elected official, but we can't simply ignore what he's doing. If we do, we're just peasants."

"Right," Anderson put in. "And I didn't fight and bleed in the army for four years just to be a damn peasant to a fat jackass like Roden. They said it was a rich man's war but a poor man's fight. Well, we won the fight and now we're a free country. And I'll be damned if I'm going to let rich folks like Judge Roden lord it over poor folks like us."

Again, there were mutterings around the table. The serving girl had brought another round of drinks for everyone. McFadden knew that the more the men drank, the more upset they were going to get. It wasn't just Roden's threat to him that had angered his comrades. Many of them had already run afoul of Roden's exorbitant property taxes themselves. Those who had been lucky enough to avoid them thus far knew that their luck could run out at any time. It took quite a lot to frighten men who had seen the carnage at places like Chickamauga and Atlanta, but these veterans were frightened. Fear and anger made for a dangerous combination, McFadden thought.

Flynn sat back down at the table. "Why don't we just put the fear of God into him?" he asked. "Don't need to really do anything. Just show up in front of his house, holding our Enfields, and tell him that he needs to stop acting like such a damn rascal."

"He has his own armed men," McFadden said. "People he pays, I guess."

"Sometimes he pays them," Collett said. "Some of them serve as his guards or whatnot because they can't pay their taxes or because they owe him for something. Hell, even some of the men we fought with during the war are working for him now. Some of the boys from Hood's Brigade, too."

"Well, the last thing I would want is for there to be a gunfight between us and any of our former comrades."

"No men who marched with Granbury or Hood would open fire on their fellow soldiers!" Farmer protested.

McFadden pursed his lips and shook his head. "If they are working for Roden, it means they're either just as rotten as he is and they're doing it because they want to, or it means that they're desperate enough to ignore what they know is right. In either case, it's impossible to know what they'd do if we showed up at Roden's door, armed and ready for a fight."

"So what do you want to do, Jimmy?" Collett asked. "I know you. I don't think you're going to let this jackass get away with what he's doing. You're certainly not going to let him get away with the threats he's made toward you."

"Why does Judge Roden have it in for you, anyways?" asked Flynn. "Is he really that upset that you made him look the fool in front of his friends at the land auction and then wouldn't support his reelection?"

"No, I don't think so," McFadden said. "I've thought about it a bit. If he's trying to intimidate us, it means he's scared of us."

Collett's eyes narrowed. "Scared of us?"

"Why would he be scared of us?" Anderson said.

"Think about it," McFadden said. "Roden got himself elected county judge during the war, when all of us were away in the army. This year will be the first election he will have to contest with all the veterans back home. He wants to be elected to the state legislature and have his own people keep control of the county commissioners' court, but he's afraid that all the returned veterans might try to stop him and he's trying to bully us into staying out of the election."

"That makes sense," Flynn said. "One of the old ladies who comes in here once said that Roden won the last election by bribing one third of the voters, blackmailing another third, and getting the last third drunk."

"Sounds about right," Anderson said. "I don't think a single person in this county has voted for him because they thought he would be a good judge."

"And now he runs the county like it's his own medieval fiefdom," McFadden said. "I know you all came here to hear about what happened to me. But this isn't just about me. Roden has done a lot worse to a lot of other folks. And he could do it to any of us."

"I can say he's already been trouble to me," said Peter Morehead, a veteran of the 6th Texas who had not previously spoken. He paused a moment, clearly reluctant to speak further. Glancing about at his friends for reassurance, he went on. "Some clerk comes to the farm from the courthouse a couple of months ago when I was away. Wife told me about it later. She says that this fellow delivered a note from Judge Roden, saying that he'd increase our property tax unless she came and spent the night with him before I came back home."

There was silence around the table, but McFadden sensed an obvious increase in unease among the men. Muscles tensed, facial expressions hardened, and hands gripped their ale mugs more firmly. Men reached up to stroke their beards, gritting their teeth while they did so.

"We have to do something," Flynn said.

"Yes, but what?" Collett asked. "McFadden has already said that he doesn't want violence, and I agree with him."

McFadden took a long sip of his ale before replying. "Someone has to challenge Roden in this election. And other people are going to have to challenge his cronies on the commissioners' court. It's just like when we were in the army and fighting a battle where we had to attack the Yankees. If we can take their strongest points, we win."

"So you're going to run for the state legislature?" Anderson asked.

"No, not me," McFadden said. "I was thinking of Major Collett here."

Collett drew his head back in surprise. "Me? Why me?"

"You're the highest ranking officer of Granbury's Brigade that lives in Roden's district. You're smart and know how to speak. The people know and respect you."

"I could say much the same about you. Why don't you run yourself?"

These words took McFadden by surprise, as it had not occurred to him that he himself could be a candidate. To him, Lucius Roden was a problem to be solved, as he presented a threat to his family. The best way to solve it, McFadden

161

had concluded, was to ensure his defeat at the polls in the coming election. Collett would be a good candidate. Once the election was over and Roden had been dealt with, McFadden could simply go back home to his ranch and raise his family.

"Yeah, Jimmy," Farmer said. "Why don't you run yourself?" These words were followed by mutterings of agreement from around the table.

McFadden held his hands up and laughed nervously. "Believe me, I have no desire to be an elected official."

"Neither do I," Collett said. "But this was your idea."

"Maybe you both should run," Anderson said. "One of you for the state representative seat that Roden wants and the other for the county judge seat that he's trying to pass off to one of his cronies. After all, if all that happens is that Roden loses his race for the legislature, his people here in the county will still be running things. Nothing much will change. We poor fellows will still have our land taken away, or at least be taxed so much that we'll have to do whatever Roden and his cronies tell us to do."

"That's a good point," Farmer said. "You two are the officers, after all. It's only right that you should take the lead in this county." He paused a moment to take a sip of ale. "I think I can speak for all of us when I say that you'd have the full support of every man who served in Granbury's Brigade. And probably quite a few of the boys from the other outfits, too."

"Of course they'll have our full support," Flynn said quickly. "In fact, you're free to use my alehouse here as a gathering place. Sort of like a headquarters, I guess. You can stay here rather than try to ride back and forth between your ranch and Waco every other day."

McFadden tried to protest again, but his voice was drowned out by a chorus of near-shouts from around the table, each man exclaiming ideas he had for how to help elect Collett and McFadden. The notion of their former leaders running for political office, and the idea that they could help them, had instantly replaced the feelings of anger and resentment with a sudden sense of hope.

"Hold on!" McFadden broke in. "Major Collett and I haven't agreed to anything here. You fellows are acting like we have."

"Well, you sort of have to now," Flynn said.

"Why?" McFadden said. "I don't have to do anything I don't want to do."

"You said yourself that something needs to be done about Judge Roden," Flynn said. "You said that someone needs to challenge him in the election. You're one of our leaders, Jimmy. You commanded some of us during the war and all of us know and respect you. There's more than one office up for election in November, so it can't just be Collett. We need you. If it's not you, who is it going to be?"

This was followed by another collective response of excited voices. Some men clanged their ale mugs on the table as a show of how determined they now felt.

Collett leaned over and whispered in McFadden's ear. "What the hell have you gotten the two of us into, Jimmy?"

Benjamin strode eastwards down Franklin Street, leaving Capitol Square behind him and entering one of the less savory parts of Richmond. Night had fallen over the city, which suited Benjamin perfectly. He loved the first few hours after sunset, when the stresses of work faded from his mind and the delights of the night were about to begin.

The neighborhood east of Capitol Square, sandwiched between Franklin Street and the waterfront on the James River, was not nearly as lively as it had been during the war. Back then, the city had been filled with thousands of soldiers. It was a truth of history that wherever there were soldiers, there were prostitutes, swindlers, and other assorted riffraff. It had reminded Benjamin very much of the French Quarter in his beloved New Orleans, which he missed so much.

Yet if the area was not as exciting as it once had been, it still was the only place in Richmond where Benjamin felt truly at home. Men in various degrees of inebriation stumbled down the sidewalk, some accompanied by smiling prostitutes who were just as likely to rob them as to satisfy their lusts. Laughter and raucous piano music spilled out from innumerable drinking establishments and the smell of beer and cigar smoke filled the air. Benjamin inhaled deeply and gratefully. He was among his kind of people.

He turned right on Fourteenth Street. After walking a single block, he reached his destination at the intersection with Main Street. Johnny Worsham's gambling den was Benjamin's favorite place in Richmond. He strode up to its imposing door, which was flanked by two large, well-built black men, each wearing bowler hats and shabby gray suits. They had menacing looks in their eyes.

A hapless man whom Benjamin didn't recognize was arguing with the two blacks.

"Let me pass this instant!" the man said.

"If you don't know the word, you can't go in," one of the bouncers responded.

"You damn darkie!" the man shouted. "You have no right to treat me this way! I'll summon the police!"

The two bouncers made no reply and their faces remained expressionless. Benjamin wasn't surprised, for Johnny Worsham regularly paid off the police to leave his establishment alone. He had learned his lesson during the war, when the provost marshal had raided the place more than once. Benjamin had gotten caught up in some of these raids, escaping out the back windows to uproarious laughter and cheers.

The frustrated would-be gambler eventually gave up and wandered off down the street, muttering repeated curses under his breath. Benjamin strode up to the door.

"What's the word?" one of the bouncers asked in a deep voice.

"The beard has grown long."

Without another word, the taller of the two men tossed his head slightly towards the door. Benjamin walked forward as the other man opened it for him.

This led Benjamin into a short hallway. The front doors were closed behind him and he now faced another set of doors, beside which stood a clean-shaven white man with waxed black hair, wearing a spotless and well-ironed suit.

"Good evening, Mr. Secretary," the man said politely.

"Evening, Paul."

The man opened the second set of doors and Benjamin stepped inside the magical place that was Johnny Worsham's. The enormous room was big enough to hold several hundred people. On the far side was a stage, on which a dozen or so scantily clad girls were dancing to the music of a black minstrel band. Along the two side walls were long bars where well-dressed servers, both white and black, poured whiskey, ale and other drinks for cash-waving customers. In one corner, a staircase led up to a hallway with secluded rooms, whose purpose was obvious to everyone.

Most of the space of Johnny Worsham's was taken up by a depression three feet deep in the center of the establishment, reached by a few short steps. Within that lower level, tables were set up that catered to every conceivable kind of gambling vice. Backgammon players were throwing dice at some tables, while croupiers spun roulette wheels at others. Most of the space, however, was devoted to card games, principally faro and poker. The tables were crowded with men, some well-dressed and others quite scruffy looking, while crowds of onlookers jammed the spaces behind the chairs to watch the proceedings. Between the tables, voluptuous barmaids wearing low-cut bodices circulated with trays of drinks.

Many of Benjamin's close friends, including Jefferson Davis, had told him that he had to change his ways and avoid Johnny Worsham's. He paid them no mind. He needed to gamble in the same way he needed to eat and drink. He always felt a thrill when he picked up a hand of cards that had been dealt to him, knowing that the luck of the deal and his own wits might win or lose him a small fortune. It was like an antidote to some undiagnosed disease of his heart.

Benjamin knew that the public would be scandalized if the newspapers reported that the Confederate Secretary of State regularly visited such an establishment as Johnny Worsham's. That he did so was an open secret among Richmond's political class. In a certain sense, this made the experience all the more exciting for Benjamin, adding another layer of recklessness to what he was doing when he gambled. Yet he felt in no particular danger. Many of his political enemies also frequented Johnny Worsham's. They couldn't risk having Benjamin exposed without exposing themselves.

He walked down the steps and into the lower level. In most social settings, several of the people would have strolled up to greet him, but here he was looked on as a gambler like any other. Far from being offended, he much preferred it this way. He ignored the dice and roulette tables, for he saw no point to games of pure chance. Benjamin found a poker table with an empty seat and was preparing to take it when he noticed the man sitting on the other side. It was Senator Louis Wigfall of Texas, one of his most bitter and intractable political enemies. Benjamin smiled, for the evening was going to be more enjoyable than he had expected.

"May I join you, Senator?" Benjamin said in an affable voice.

Wigfall looked up at him. When he saw that it was Benjamin, utter loathing instantly became evident in Wigfall's eyes. He took a long pull on his cigar and then sipped from his whiskey glass before he deigned to reply.

"I don't play with Jews," he said simply, in a voice that was half a snarl.

"Is that so?" Benjamin said with a playful smile. "Will you at least light my cigar?"

Benjamin pulled a Cuban cigar from his coat pocket and leaned over the table. Onlookers waited quietly, hoping for Wigfall to explode in anger or do something else that would be equally entertaining. The burly Texan refused to give them the satisfaction, though, waiting just a moment before striking a match and lighting Benjamin's cigar with only a look of irritation.

"I can understand why you don't play with Jews, Senator," Benjamin said pleasantly, a smile on his face. "I know my people have a certain reputation for depriving people like you of their money. Perhaps you are wise to be cautious."

Wigfall sat up in his chair and sneered. "I'm not afraid to play against you, Benjamin. I just don't want to sully my hands."

Benjamin held up his hands in mock humility. "I take no offense, Louis. For what it's worth, I would prefer to play against someone else as well. After all, one garners little satisfaction in beating an inept opponent."

Darkness clouded Wigfall's face and the onlookers held their breath. Benjamin knew he was pushing the Texan to the edge and part of his mind told him that it was not a good idea. Wigfall was not the kind of man to shy away from a duel and his skill with a pistol was legendary throughout the South. To Benjamin, though, it was just another form of gambling.

Wigfall nodded to the chair. "Sit down, Benjamin." He then turned to the dealer. "Just me and him, okay?"

"Yes, sir," the dealer, a dapper young man wearing a dinner jacket, replied complacently. Three other players who had been sitting at the table stood and joined the crowd gathering around Wigfall and Benjamin.

Benjamin slipped into the chair as the dealer expertly shuffled the deck and slid each of them five cards. "What are we playing for, my Texan friend?"

Wigfall placed two dollars bills on the table. "Start with this?"

"Fine with me," Benjamin replied, putting the same amount down. He looked down at his cards. It wasn't a terrible hand, giving him a pair of queens and a jack. Benjamin elected to put only a single card down, to lure Wigfall into the belief that his hand was better than it was. He would have preferred another jack, but was happy enough when he drew another queen. "Check," he said.

Wigfall frowned nervously and put down two cards, a look of irritation crossing his face when he viewed the two new cards he drew. Benjamin did not think an unsubtle man like Wigfall would be very good at bluffing, but the Texan was a denizen of more than a few gambling dens, so he assumed it was not a good idea to underestimate the man.

"Show your cards, gentlemen," the dealer said.

Benjamin turned his hand over, revealing his three queens. Wigfall, who had only a pair of aces, threw his cards down onto the table and cursed. Benjamin maintained a placid expression as he took Wigfall's two dollars, easily containing his desire to laugh. Wigfall was a buffoon, like so many other such men he had met during his political career. He was a man who didn't think things through very well and who would cheerfully do something to gain himself a short term advantage no matter how detrimental it might prove in the long run. Moreover, he failed to understand that a person did not really achieve anything if all one did was irritate one's political enemy. Indeed, doing so was often harmful to one's own interest. Such men were easily manipulated.

Benjamin took a proffered whiskey from a tray held by a pretty girl as the croupier dealt out the next hand of cards. He looked across the table at Wigfall, his smile never wavering.

Wigfall sneered. "You got lucky once, you damn, dirty Jew," he said as he put two more dollars on the table. "You'll not be so lucky again."

"There's no luck involved, Senator," replied Benjamin, matching the bet. "We're not rolling dice here."

The dealer tossed out the hands of cards. Benjamin looked down to see a jack, a seven, a five, an eight, and a six. On its own, it was a useless hand, but he could put down the jack and possibly draw a nine or a four, which would give him a straight. The mathematical odds were not good, but the only other option was to fold. Deciding that fortune favored the bold, Benjamin put his jack down and was rewarded when he drew a four.

"Show your cards, gentlemen."

Wigfall grinned as he put down three kings, clearly expecting to win the round. Benjamin kept a placid expression as he put down his straight, relishing the dismay he saw in his opponent's face. The gentle applause of the crowd gathered around the table added to his delight as he took the money.

The eyes of the Texas senator flashed with red fire. This suited Benjamin fine, for angry men were apt to make mistakes. One of the lessons that had been the hardest for Benjamin to learn over the course of his life was simply never to get angry. It was far better to withdraw into his own mind and present the world with a countenance of amused mastery, so that they never quite knew what was actually going on in his head. Frustration never improved one's situation.

"You damn, dirty Jew."

"You already called me that, Louis. I think you need to expand your repertoire of insults."

"I can only describe what I see."

"And I would do the same, only there are ladies present."

This brought a chorus of chuckles from the crowd of onlookers around the table, which only made Wigfall more upset. He glared at the people until they quieted down, then stared across the table at Benjamin.

"Enjoy your joking while you can, Benjamin. The joke is going to be on you soon enough."

"How's that?"

"Your master's term is almost up. A year from now, Jeff Davis is going home and a new president will be sitting down in his chair. The protection you've had for the last five years will be gone."

"What makes you think I need protection?"

"The next president might not like you as much as Jeff Davis does."

Benjamin shrugged. "Why should I care? Perhaps I might run for Congress from Louisiana. Or maybe I'll just resume my law practice in New Orleans."

He wasn't lying when he said this. Even a person as dimwitted as Wigfall could tell, if only on a barely perceptible level, when a person was speaking the truth. Benjamin's earnest desire was to continue as Secretary of State under Breckinridge, but he was not averse to other possibilities. He hoped that Wigfall would pick up something from his tone and body language and incorrectly perceive some sort of advantage. If he did, it would be easier to draw him out and obtain useful information.

Across the table, Wigfall sneered and shook his head. "Run for Congress? Resume your law practice? Ha! You'll be lucky if you're not torn to pieces by a lynch mob. You've lorded it over us long enough. You know you can never be president yourself, since the people would never vote for a Shylock, so you've always tried to be the power behind the throne, the man who pulls the strings. You're nothing but a trickster, just like your Rothschild friends in Europe. You've done it long enough, I say. Your time in power ends with the next election."

Benjamin simply shrugged, his composed smile never wavering. He didn't allow anti-Semitic taunts to bother him in public, for to do so would be to display a sign of weakness. He had been attacked as a Jew all his life, of course, even on the floor of the United States Senate. He made no effort to emphasize his Jewishness, attending synagogue rarely and sometimes even eating pork when it was served at social events. On the other hand, he did not run away from his identity, either. He was who he was. The fact that Wigfall and others clawed at him for being a Jew was simply another obstacle that had to be overcome. If anything, it made Benjamin more determined to get the better of his enemies.

He grinned across the table at Wigfall, imagining for just a moment how comical it would be for the man to fall out of his chair and spill his whiskey all over himself. It made it easier to avoid anger.

"Are we ready, gentlemen," asked the dealer, who had tactfully remained silent during the exchange.

Benjamin and Wigfall both replied in the affirmative. The man shuffled the deck and expertly dealt the cards. The Secretary of State looked down at his hand to see a king, an ace, an eight, a deuce, and a nine. He kept his face expressionless, though he felt like frowning. He had nothing and the statistical chances of obtaining a winning hand were not good. He put down the eight, deuce, and nine in the hopes that he would pick up two useful cards, but came up with nothing.

Wigfall won the hand with three sevens and smiled a devilish smile, as though his momentary success was akin to conquering the United States. "Well, that's more like it."

"I wouldn't get so cocky," Benjamin replied. "It's still early. I have plenty of time to deprive you of your money."

The next hour went by quickly. Benjamin won slightly more hands than he lost, yet Wigfall seemed determined to play things out until the end. In any event, Benjamin knew he could absorb any financial losses he might sustain. Unlike Wigfall, he had the self-control to know when to quit. Moreover, Benjamin was carefully limiting the amount of alcohol he was consuming, sipping at his whiskey slowly, while Wigfall was ordering whiskey after whiskey almost as fast as he could drink them.

"You seem quite confident that the next president will be someone to your own liking," Benjamin observed after another round of cards had gone his way.

"Of course, you fool," Wigfall responded, his words slightly slurred. "We're picking him ourselves."

"Who's 'we'?" Benjamin asked.

"Me and some of my friends. I don't have to tell you anything. But we're the ones who are going to pick the next president. We're already arranging it. I'd be worried if I were you."

"Toombs?"

"Yes."

"Stephens?"

"That's right. Yes, your own vice president is against you. How does that make you feel?"

Benjamin took a pull on his cigar. He had already known that Toombs and Stephens, whose partnership was one of the few constants in Confederate politics, had formed an alliance with Wigfall. He wanted to obtain as much information as possible as long as he had Wigfall before him in a drunken state.

"Any others, Louis? I always knew that Toombs and Stephens were stupid enough to get involved with you, but I doubt anyone else would be so idiotic."

Wigfall laughed. "You think you're so smart, don't you, Benjamin? If you knew the names of all the people who are joining us, you'd be scared. I'm telling the truth here. You'd be scared out of your wits."

"I'm sure you can see me trembling on this side of the table," Benjamin said with heavy sarcasm. "I'm quite confident that any people who join your little movement will be irrelevant nonentities. And have you hired some random circus clown to be your presidential candidate?"

Wigfall slammed his fist down on the table. "Circus clown, you say? How about General Beauregard, Benjamin? Do you think he's a circus clown?"

Benjamin's eyebrows went up. "Beauregard? He's your candidate?"

"Damn straight he is! And he's going to beat anybody you and Davis decide to put forward, sure as hell. I know you're going to try some desperate trick to hold on to power. I know you'll try to get someone to run on your behalf, but whoever that turns out to be is going to be beaten by Beauregard. You can take that to the bank."

Benjamin's mind instantly recalculated the political arithmetic based on what Wigfall had just said. He could see why Beauregard would be an attractive candidate for the anti-Davis faction. His name resonated with the people thanks to his military exploits, while the mutual loathing between Beauregard and Davis would inspire the Fire-Eaters. He was quite popular throughout the Confederacy, especially in Louisiana and South Carolina.

In short, Beauregard would be a formidable opponent.

Breckinridge, too, was a popular man. He had been the most admired statesman in the South before the war and his military achievements had further enhanced his reputation. Yet he lacked the exotic charisma of Beauregard and, more importantly, his role in the Toronto Peace Conference had turned many of the wealthy plantation owners against him. While Benjamin had no doubt whatsoever that Breckinridge would be an excellent candidate and, if victorious, an outstanding president, he had to admit that he was doubtful about his ability to defeat Beauregard. The Creole general might have little political experience, but he would be backed up by Wigfall, Toombs, and the rest of their cabal.

"So, Beauregard, eh? I thought you said your candidate wasn't going to be a circus clown."

"Who do you have who can beat him?" Wigfall sneered. "Lee was your only hope and now he's not going to run. Who does that leave you with? Nobody. No other man popular with the people is going to support you. Except maybe Breckinridge, but Miles will take care of him for us."

Benjamin's mind focused on those last words. "Ambassador Miles?"

"Of course, you idiot," Wigfall said, the liquor now causing his voice to slur even more. "He's got Breckinridge in his pocket. He won't run. If he does, Miles will ruin him."

Along with the knowledge that Beauregard was to be the candidate for the Fire-Eaters, Benjamin knew instantly that the existence of some sort of connection between Breckinridge and Miles was the most important piece of information he had obtained this night. Almost certainly, it was the source of the unnamed complications Breckinridge had referred to the day they had ridden in the carriage together. Benjamin knew he needed to find out what it was and deal with it as soon as possible.

"One more hand?" Benjamin asked.

"Fine by me," Wigfall responded.

"Ten dollars?"

Wigfall hesitated just a moment, before nodding quickly. Both men put their money on the table as the dealer slid them their cards. Benjamin smiled when he saw a flush, for though he had no pairs, all of his cards were spades.

"Check," he said.

Wigfall looked at him with a frown, then chuckled slightly. "You must think I'm stupid."

Benjamin didn't reply, merely staring back at him across the table and leaving the implication floating in the air. Wigfall put two cards down and seemed happy with those he drew.

"Show your cards, gentlemen."

Wigfall's hand contained only a pair of aces. When Benjamin put down his flush, the people gathered around the table laughed and gently applauded.

Wigfall frowned, his frustration evident. "Well, that's that," he said sourly. "I can't say that I've enjoyed this evening, Benjamin. But like I said, it won't be long before I don't have to put up with your arrogance or see your ugly Jewish face ever again."

Benjamin smiled. "Well, if I have anything to say about it, Louis, you're going to have to put up with my ugly Jewish face for a long time to come."

May 7, Night
Commercial Wharf, Boston, Massachusetts

"How many crates?" Lowell asked.

"Ten," the man replied.

"And twenty rifles to a crate?"

169

"Yes, sir."

The enormous warehouse was one of dozens along the Boston waterfront, packed to the brim with the products and commodities of world trade. Lowell and two other men stood quietly in one corner of the warehouse, a single lantern making a small pocket of light amidst the otherwise enfolding darkness.

Beside Lowell stood Stearns, his face grave yet inquisitive. Not being a military man, he was deferring to Lowell on the technical matter of inspecting the weapons and supplies. As promised, Stearns had arranged the financing of the venture along with other abolitionists who had been brought into the conspiracy.

The third man was their clandestine contact, who had only identified himself as Macintyre. Sumner had apparently arranged the meeting with him and Lowell had not asked any questions about it. Far better, it seemed, to know as little as possible. So long as the weapons and ammunition were of a sufficiently high quality, where they had come from was irrelevant. Lowell trusted Sumner and, therefore, had to trust Macintyre.

"May I see the weapons?" Lowell asked.

Macintyre nodded and, without a word, wrenched open one of the crates with a crowbar. As claimed, there were twenty Springfield rifles neatly stacked inside, bunches of hay between them to provide cushioning during transport. Lowell picked one up and raised it to his shoulders in a firing position, inspecting it carefully. The weapon appeared clean and well-oiled, but various scratches and other markings told him that it was not newly manufactured. It was clearly leftover from the war, but that didn't matter as long as it was in good working order.

The feeling of the weapon in his hand brought him back to his soldiering days. For just a moment, a rush of memories flashed through his mind. Serving as an aide to General McClellan at the Battle of Antietam. Hunting John Mosby across northern Virginia while in command of the 2nd Massachusetts Cavalry. Leading his brigade during the campaign against Jubal Early in the Shenandoah Valley.

He sighed. His life was a very happy one. He had a loving wife, two beautiful children, and a successful career in which he was restoring his family's fortune and reputation. Yet he yearned to return to war. As a soldier, Lowell had been able to focus all of his mental and moral energy on clawing and tearing at the slave-holding villains of the South. He had been driven by motives of absolute purity, untarnished by compromise or ambiguity. The Confederacy was an aberrant evil, undeserving of mercy, which simply had to be destroyed. To be guided by such a single-minded purpose had been exhilarating and soul-filling. It was something he wanted to feel again.

"What do you think, General?" Stearns asked.

Lowell glanced into the crate to visually inspect the other weapons. "They seem to be in fine order," he replied. "We could inspect each one individually."

"They're all good," Macintyre said emphatically. "There's a glut of Enfield and Springfield rifles on the market, as you might imagine. It's very easy to get hold of high-quality weapons at low cost, even with the Fenians buying up so much."

"I believe you," Lowell said, carefully placing the Springfield back in the crate. "What about the ammunition?"

"Over there," Macintyre said, gesturing to another large pile of crates. "Forty boxes, each containing one thousand rounds."

"Is forty thousand rounds sufficient?" Stearns asked Lowell.

"It would sustain Saul and his men for a considerable amount of time, I should imagine. They do not engage in set piece battles as we did during the war, but rely on ambush and sniping from a distance, like the Spanish did when fighting against Napoleon. Such tactics use less ammunition. If we provided them with more, it might actually be a hindrance."

Stearns's eyes narrowed. "How could more ammunition possibly be a hindrance?"

"Because whatever advantage they might gain through more ammunition would be negating by the difficulties they would encounter in transporting it."

Lowell had spent countless hours during the war studying military history, hoping that it would improve his knowledge and abilities as an officer. Since learning about Saul and his partisan efforts, Lowell had frequently been reminded of the guerrillas who had fought without mercy against Napoleon in the early 1800s. Operating in small, roving bands, they had inflicted greater harm on the Emperor of the French than all the vaunted armies of Europe had done up to that point.

One fact that had stood out to Lowell was that the Spanish guerrillas could not have inflicted nearly as much damage had they not been supported by Britain in the form of weapons, ammunition, and other supplies. Had the guerrillas been poorly armed and unsupplied, the French could easily have hunted them down. Similarly, if Saul and his fighters received no outside support, the little rebellion they had initiated in the Confederacy would quickly be extinguished, like a candle flame with a glass placed over it. Two hundred rifles and a supply of ammunition might not be much in the grand scheme of things, but it was a start.

Lowell turned to Macintyre. "What else?"

"As requested, some crates of pots and pans, other cooking implements, shirts and trousers, shoes, and other such things."

Lowell nodded. Such things might not be as exciting as weapons and ammunition, but fighting forces which lacked such basic necessities would quickly cease to exist. He had learned that early in the war, when his time as an aide-de-camp to McClellan had taught him everything he needed to know about logistics.

"When will all this be ready to be loaded onto the ship?" Stearns asked.

"It's ready to be loaded at any time," Macintyre answered. "Once I get paid, it's all yours. I'll have nothing to do with it after that. You people will never see me again."

Lowell turned to Stearns. "We need to discuss the ship."

Macintyre spoke quickly. "It might be best for you not to discuss such matters in front of me. If I am ever asked questions, I would prefer to be able to honestly say that I know nothing."

"Very well," Lowell said.

"Now, if you are satisfied with the merchandise, why don't we settle up and I'll be on my way. Then you two can talk of whatever subjects you like."

Stearns gave Macintyre written instructions specifying the name of a British merchant house in Boston, which was owned by a wealthy abolitionist who lived in London. Macintyre was to visit that merchant house, which would issue him a check in the amount of the weapons, ammunition, and supplies. The paperwork, however, would show the purchase as being for tea and coffee. If done properly, it would be a difficult transaction for the authorities to unravel.

Macintyre smiled and nodded, satisfied with the arrangements. He tipped his hat and, without a word, walked out the door. Lowell and Stearns were left alone in the immense warehouse.

"Well, what do you think?" Stearns asked, leaning against one of the crates.

"I think we should proceed as planned," Lowell replied quickly. "We've purchased the weapons. We've already gone too far to go back."

"I agree," Stearns replied. "By handing the letter to that man and taking possession of these weapons, we have committed ourselves. Cortez burned his ships when he arrived in Mexico, so that he and his men would not be able to abandon their enterprise. We have just done the same."

"An apt metaphor," Lowell said.

"You are prepared to meet this Captain Naismith?"

Lowell took out his pocket watch and checked the time. "Indeed, I should be going. It is only a quarter hour until nine o'clock, which is when I told him I would meet him."

"Very well," Stearns said. "When we meet tomorrow, you can tell me what he had to say."

Lowell shook hands with Stearns and stepped through the warehouse door onto the cobbled waterfront of Commercial Wharf, one of the largest and most important of the wharves that encircled Boston. He knew it well, for he had started his working life as a clerk at the firm of Larkin and Stackpole, which maintained its office there. His Harvard education and family connections could easily have been leveraged into a much more prestigious post, but Lowell had wanted to learn the merchant's trade from the bottom up and had willingly taken a low ranking job.

In contrast to the silence and darkness inside the warehouse, the Commercial Wharf was alive with noise and activity, even at the late hour. Gangs of laborers, mostly black or Irish, were busy unloading cargo from innumerable ships and moving them about in wheelbarrows. Torches along the waterfront or being held aloft by foremen provided enough illumination for the men to do their jobs. In the sky above, a crescent moon was partially obscured by clouds.

The ships had come to Boston from every corner of the world, Lowell knew. Rum and sugar from the Lesser Antilles, wine and brandy from France, cigars and molasses from Cuba, all sorts of manufactured consumer goods from Britain, tea from distant China, and every other conceivable cargo from half the ports of Earth crammed the wharves of the city. Many ships were being loaded with grain, dried fish, and other commodities for exportation to Europe.

Lowell frowned when he saw bales of cotton being unloaded from one ship. Most likely, the ship had come from the Confederacy and the cotton he saw had been grown and harvested by slave labor. The Treaty of Toronto had ensured that the government could not impose strong tariffs on the importation of Southern cotton. That had been the price for Confederate recognition of the freedom of the slaves who had come into Union lines during the war.

He and his wife made sure that their own clothing was made from cotton imported from British India, where slavery was illegal. Many of their fellow abolitionists did the same, but Lowell knew that this enlightened policy was not followed by the vast majority of Northerners. Southern cotton was both cheaper and of generally higher quality, so Northern consumers preferred clothing made from it, slave-grown or not. Glancing about at the shirts and trousers worn by the dock workers and other people strolling past, Lowell imagined for just a moment how much blood and sweat of black slaves had been expended in creating them.

The idea filled him with anger. Yet he quickly comforted himself with the thought that, if his current enterprise was successful, he would be striking a blow against the vile institution. Indeed, he might be initiating a process that would destroy slavery completely and forever.

He came to a nondescript oyster bar, one of many that lined the waterfront on Commercial Wharf. It was where he had agreed to meet Captain Naismith. Lowell stepped inside and immediately felt a bit uncomfortable. The oyster bar was not a place that any member of the Lowell family would normally have visited. The ceiling was low and the walls were of dusty brick. A few sooty oil lanterns provided a soft illumination. A long table took up most of the inner space, with hard-looking working men crowded onto both sides with dishes of oysters and glasses of ale. All of them were chattering in loud and irritated tones.

Three men were sitting alone at small tables against the walls. Studying them, Lowell saw what he was looking for. One of the men had a book with a red cover on the table in front of him. That had been the agreed upon signal. He slid into the chair opposite the man.

"Naismith?"

The man extended his hand. "And you must be Charles Lowell. Honored to meet you, General."

"Thank you." Naismith's handshake was firm. He had a cautious smile, but the left side of his face was badly scarred in a way that gave him a sinister appearance.

"You're looking at this?" Naismith said, waving his hand lazily over his scars.

"I'm sorry," Lowell said in embarrassment.

"Don't be. It's the first thing people see when they look at me. I used to be handsome. My wife tells me that I still am, but I can look in the mirror as well as any man."

"It happened during the war?" Lowell asked.

Naismith nodded. "When I was a lieutenant on board the *USS Passaic* during the big attack on Charleston in September of 1864. A plunging shot broke through the deck armor, which had already been badly hit. It struck the ship's boiler and exploded, showering all of us in the engine room with super-heated steam. I was one of the lucky ones. At least I escaped with my life."

"I see," Lowell said. He thought of the many close-calls he himself had experienced during the war. He had fought through dozens of engagements and had never been wounded. Whatever scars Lowell brought back from the war were not physical ones.

"Oysters?" Naismith asked. "They're good here."

173

"I've already eaten, thank you."

"Then an ale. I must insist." Naismith looked over at the bar and snapped his fingers, a gesture that Lowell considered rude. He held up two fingers when the barkeeper noticed him and, a few moments later, a serving girl brought two glasses. Lowell sipped on the ale. Until his time in the army, he had had few opportunities to drink beer, as his social class tended to indulge in wine or high-quality spirits. As far as Lowell was concerned, a person drank beer in order to get drunk. Still, if drinking ale allowed this meeting to proceed more easily, he would drink it.

"So I understand you need to have some special cargo shipped to New Orleans?"

"That's right."

"Why not just write up a contract and ship it normally, then? Why this clandestine meeting?"

"I need the cargo shipped in such a way as to avoid having customs officials, or anyone else for that matter, find out what the cargo is."

"And what exactly is it?" Naismith asked.

The question caught Lowell off guard. He had expected Naismith to understand the need for secrecy and to avoid asking any unnecessary questions.

"Why do you want to know?" Lowell asked after a few moments of awkward silence.

"Look, if you want me to smuggle cargo past Union and Confederate customs officials, you and I must trust each other. The only way I know whether you trust me is if you tell me exactly what it is that I'm going to be smuggling for you."

Lowell considered very carefully what he should say. Most likely, Naismith suspected that the stipulation to avoid customs officials stemmed from a desire to avoid paying duties on the merchandise. In that case, the cargo could be completely innocuous. Were Lowell to tell Naismith the truth, however, the ship captain would realize instantly that smuggled weapons and ammunition could only be intended for the renegade slaves.

If Lowell told Naismith the true nature of the cargo, there was always the risk that Naismith would immediately alert the authorities. If that happened, Lowell and the other conspirators, including Senator Sumner, would be arrested. Even so politically inept a man as President McClellan would sense the opportunity to rid himself of political enemies and win goodwill from the Confederates. Even if Naismith didn't go to the police, the fact that their plan would no longer be a secret would force a cancellation of the entire operation.

An even worse possibility entered Lowell's mind. What if Naismith took him and the cargo all the way to New Orleans and then turned him in to the Confederates? He would stand to gain a hefty financial reward by doing so. In this scenario, Lowell would probably find himself at the end of a rope.

Naismith looked him carefully in the eye. "If you cannot tell me what the cargo is, General Lowell, I'm afraid you and I can't do business together."

"You have no love for the Confederacy, I would assume? You served against them during the war."

"You won't be able to draw me out like that, General Lowell. I've been in this business a long time. Either you tell me what this cargo is or there is no point in continuing this meeting."

There was something in Naismith's tone that told Lowell the captain already suspected that something more than avoiding customs duties was under discussion. Lowell decided that fortune favored the bold.

"Very well, Captain Naismith. I am asking you to transport to New Orleans a shipment of weapons and ammunition, along with some other miscellaneous supplies. From New Orleans, it shall be sent to the insurgent forces of the renegade slave commander known as Saul."

Naismith sat back, a satisfied smile on his face. "Now, was that really so hard?" He took a swig of his ale before speaking again. "I figured it was some such escapade. A man like you can afford to pay customs duties and wouldn't bother avoiding them. Now, you must be well aware that what you are proposing is a capital crime in the Confederacy. I believe it's called aiding and abetting servile insurrection."

"I am well aware of that fact."

"Punishable by death."

"I know."

"Yet you are willing to go through with it. Why?"

Lowell considered his response for a moment. "I believe with all my heart that slavery needs to be crushed. I have consecrated my life to this purpose and I will not rest until the chains of every slave have been broken. So many men gave their lives for this cause during the war. I don't want to believe that their deaths were in vain."

"But it is not just your life you are risking here. You are asking me to risk my life as well."

"And yet you did not get up and leave immediately," Lowell observed.

"No, I didn't," Naismith said. He took another drink. "When the shell burst open the boiler on the *Passaic*, it killed a lot of men. One of them was my brother."

Lowell understood perfectly. In a flash, he saw in his memory the faces of his brother James, his cousin William, and his brother-in-law Robert, all cut down in their prime by Southern bullets. Even had he cared nothing about slavery, Lowell would have felt duty-bound to avenge the deaths of his loved ones.

Naismith went on. "Every Confederate soldier killed by one of those guns will be a slice of revenge I earn for my brother's death, won't it? I'll carry your cargo to New Orleans, General. I'll do it and be very happy doing it, I don't mind saying."

"I'm glad to hear you say that, Naismith."

"How much cargo are we talking about here?"

Lowell and Naismith spent the next few minutes discussing the number of crates, their size and weight, and the manner in which they would have to be stored. Lowell quickly understood that he knew next to nothing about nautical matters compared to Naismith. He was pleased to see Naismith smiling and relaxed, quite happy at the prospect of smuggling weapons to rebel slaves so long as it hurt the Confederacy.

"There is one thing I must insist upon," Lowell said.

"And that is?"

"I must remain in direct control of the cargo at all times. Except when it's simply not possible, such as during meals and such, I do not want those crates out of my sight for the duration of the voyage."

Naismith chuckled and shook his head. "You really don't know anything about smuggling, do you, Lowell?"

Lowell drew his head back in some surprise. "What do you mean?"

"You're not going to want to draw any attention to yourself or your cargo, don't you see? The men who work the decks of merchant ships are mercenaries the world over. And there's no privacy on board ship. If any member of the crew notices anything strange about you or the cargo you're paying such close attention to, what do you think he's going to do? As soon as the ship docks in New Orleans, he's going to go straight to the customs office and the local police to report you as a smuggler. If his suspicions are confirmed, he'll get a nice little reward. And you and me? We'll get a hangman's noose."

"I admit I hadn't thought of that," Lowell said, feeling frustrated. It seemed so obvious once Naismith had explained it to him. Not for the first time since he had entered into the conspiracy, Lowell found himself wondering if he were the right person for this dangerous assignment. After all, there was a big difference between being a soldier and engaging in the clandestine smuggling of weapons.

"I was a merchant captain before the war and I became one again after it," Naismith said. "I'm not a smuggler, you understand. I'm a perfectly legitimate businessman. But I'm not going to say I haven't done a few such jobs on the side every now and then."

"It's good to hear that you have experience in these matters."

"I will smuggle these guns into the Confederacy for you, General. You just have to promise me that you will do what I say so that we won't get caught. Because if we do. . ."

"The hangman's noose. I understand."

"Good. Now, let's have another ale and get to work."

May 9, Night
Mechanic's Hall, Richmond, Virginia

"Anything else, sir?" Wilson asked.

"No, thank you, James," Breckinridge answered. "You can go."

"Staying late, are we?"

Breckinridge chuckled. "Yes, I am afraid I shall be burning the midnight oil yet again."

Wilson beamed a self-satisfied, almost cocky smile. "Well, while you sit here working too hard, I shall be romancing a lovely young lady."

"Ah, I see. Well done. What is the lucky girl's name?"

A look of chagrin suddenly crossed Wilson's face. "I. . . I don't remember."

Breckinridge laughed. "Well, that is one fact you might want to ascertain before attempting to romance her."

"Oh dear," Wilson said nervously. Without another word to Breckinridge, he bounded out the door in a great hurry. The Secretary of War chuckled at the typical example of his young aide's misadventures. Wilson was a master of administration, but inept in all other walks of life.

Breckinridge turned his attention back to his paperwork. Outside, the sun had already dipped below the horizon and the curtain of night was being pulled over Richmond. He lit a few oil lamps and candles when the illumination coming through the window was no longer sufficient. It was easy to lose himself in administrative details, such as an inspection report from the Augusta Powder Works or a letter from a Florida congressman expressing concern about the coastal defenses protecting Saint Augustine.

Not long after eight o'clock, there was a soft knocking on the door. There being no staff remaining to open it for him, Breckinridge rose from his desk and did it himself. Judah Benjamin stood on the other side.

"Come on in, Judah," Breckinridge said pleasantly. "I give you full marks for punctuality."

"The least I can do is arrive on time, John."

"Would you like a whiskey?" Breckinridge asked. "My friend Garnet Wolseley, a British officer in Canada, has just sent me a bottle of scotch."

"I would be delighted," Benjamin replied, taking his seat across from Breckinridge's. "I have not yet had the pleasure of sampling scotch, but I have been told it is good."

Breckinridge poured two glasses. He was happy that Wolseley sent him gifts of scotch, for Kentucky's decision to remain in the Union made it more difficult to acquire bourbon than it had been before the war. This seemingly trivial matter highlighted the fact that Breckinridge was an exile from the place of his birth.

He shook the thought aside. It had largely been Breckinridge's own doing at the Toronto Peace Conference that kept Kentucky in the Union, despite his own sincere wishes that it join the Confederacy. He had come to terms with the fact that the land of his birth was not part of the nation of which he was now a citizen. He chuckled for a moment, reflecting on the irony that he would soon strive to become the chief executive of that very nation.

Benjamin sipped his whiskey. "Oh, that's very good. I hope that Richmond stores begin to sell it soon."

"As do I," Breckinridge said. He sipped his scotch and sat down across from Benjamin. Between them, a small table held a map of the Confederacy. "Now, shall we begin?"

"How about a toast, first?" Benjamin asked. He held up his glass. "You're the candidate. You should do it."

Breckinridge held up his glass as well. "To the presidential campaign of 1867," he said simply. The two clinked glasses.

"Now then, let us get started," Benjamin said. "Let's begin with generalities. What do the people know about you, John? You were a Congressman and Senator before the war, but from Kentucky, which isn't part of the Confederacy. You were Vice President of the United States, which made your name well known throughout the South and led to your nomination for president on the Southern Democratic ticket in 1860. When secession came, you were the best known and most respected statesman of the South, aside from Jefferson Davis himself."

"I appreciate your kind words. It seems like a lifetime ago, doesn't it?"

"So it does. Ten years ago, you were presiding over the Senate as vice president and I was in that chamber as a member from Louisiana. Could you have imagined then where we would be today, members of the cabinet of an independent Southern Confederacy?"

"Never," Breckinridge admitted. "Had anyone suggested such a thing, I would have considered them mad."

Benjamin took another sip of whiskey. "As would I. But let us not get distracted. We must discuss your vulnerabilities. One of the first issues that our opponents will raise is that it took you so long to join the Confederate cause. You were still a Senator in Washington representing Kentucky for months after the First Battle of Manassas."

"My state had not seceded," Breckinridge said firmly. "There was no reason to leave Washington City. During all those months, I was upholding the right of the Southern states to secede and maintaining that Lincoln's war measures were unconstitutional, which I believe they were."

"You don't have to persuade me," Benjamin said. "I think you did the honorable thing. But you know that Toombs and Wigfall will try to make hay out of it, don't you?"

Breckinridge thought that Toombs and Wigfall were going to be the least of his problems. He remembered the threat of William Porcher Miles to expose his secret dealings with Hannibal Hamlin. Breckinridge had not yet taken Benjamin into his confidence on the matter, though he suspected that the time would soon come when he would have no other choice.

Benjamin looked at him squarely. "Is it true that you visited Lincoln in the White House after he had been inaugurated?"

"Of course I did. Why shouldn't I have? He was my friend. Still is my friend, in fact. His wife is my cousin."

"I see," Benjamin replied.

There was an awkward pause. The expression on Benjamin's face suggested to Breckinridge that a fuller answer was desired. "What else do you need me to say, Judah?" Breckinridge asked. "I see no reason why men cannot differ in politics, even in the most strident manner, and yet not remain on cordial terms personally. Besides, whatever we might have wanted, the fact of the matter was that Lincoln had won the election. It was basic decency for me to call on him to wish him my congratulations."

"If only the rest of the human race shared your opinion," Benjamin replied sourly. "Now, let's talk about your time in the army. We can be sure that the anti-administration faction will examine it carefully to find things to criticize."

They spent the next half hour going over Breckinridge's military record in excruciating detail. His organization of the Orphan Brigade and his participation in the battles at Shiloh and Baton Rouge, they both agreed, were great successes that no one could possibly disparage. At the Battle of Murfreesboro, however, Breckinridge's attack on the Union left flank had been repulsed with heavy losses.

"I wouldn't worry about that," Benjamin said. "It's well known that had more to do with Bragg's foolishness than any failing on your part."

"So it did," Breckinridge said, his tone becoming ominous at the sound of Bragg's name. "That damnable bastard had my division slaughtered for no good purpose. He ordered that attack just because he was angry and hundreds of my men were killed." For a brief moment, he remembered kneeling beside his mortally wounded friend, General Robert Hanson, knowing that there was nothing he could do to save him. He shook the traumatic memory from his mind.

"You served with distinction at Chickamauga, but, not to put too fine a point on it, it was your corps which broke first at the Battle of Missionary Ridge, leading to one of the greatest defeats suffered by Confederate arms during the war."

"It was complicated," Breckinridge grumbled. He did not like being reminded of Missionary Ridge, which was undoubtedly his worst moment as a general. He had thought the position impregnable, as the height had dominated all the ground before it. His overconfidence, and a careless flaw in the positioning of rifle pits at the base of the ridge, had allowed the Army of the Cumberland to smash through his line as though it had been made of paper. He had been disgraced and it had taken some time for him to recover his confidence.

Benjamin went on. He spoke of Breckinridge's famous victory at the Battle of New Market and his service with Lee's army at Cold Harbor. He then recalled what he knew about Breckinridge's role in Jubal Early's legendary raid on Washington City and the subsequent campaign against Phil Sheridan in the Shenandoah Valley.

"Nothing much for them to criticize there," Benjamin said after he concluded. "So we can predict that our opponents will cast aspersions on your military record when it comes to Missionary Ridge and perhaps Murfreesboro."

"Let them slander me as they will," Breckinridge said defiantly. "I have nothing to hide in my military record and I will proudly stand by everything I did during my time as a soldier."

"Let me ask you this," Benjamin said. "Did you support General Cleburne's proposal to free and arm the slaves?"

Breckinridge considered the question for a moment. "I had left the Army of Tennessee for Virginia by the time he openly advocated such a move. I will say that, had I been present at that meeting, I would have supported Cleburne entirely. It would have been the correct policy."

"From a military standpoint, perhaps. But certainly not from a political one. I will suggest that you keep your opinion of Cleburne and his ideas quiet between now and Election Day."

"That's common sense, Judah," Breckinridge replied with irritation. "I am glad that you are going to help me in this campaign, but you don't need to speak to me as though I am a political neophyte. I have been in this game just as long as you have."

Benjamin chuckled. "You're quite right, John. I apologize. Now, let's discuss your tenure as Secretary of War. Several enemies of the administration, and Robert Toombs in particular, have criticized us for maintaining a system in which regiments raised by the states are kept under the control of the national government in Richmond. As Secretary of War, you were the architect of this policy."

"It's an obvious policy," Breckinridge said tiredly. "We held exhaustive hearings in both the House and Senate on the question. I do not see how they don't understand the logic of it. If the central government remained dependent on forces provided only at will by the individual states, there would be no border defense at all. Or it would fall entirely on Virginia, Tennessee, Texas, and Arkansas, which would be unfair to those states."

"Which may help us in winning those states," Benjamin pointed out. "Let's keep that in mind for later. Now, the biggest problem we will face is your role at the Toronto Peace Conference. You pushed the delegation to agree to Union conditions that allowed them to bring out hundreds of thousands of slaves that had been freed under the terms of the Emancipation Proclamation. At the stroke of a pen, some of the Confederacy's wealthiest and most influential citizens lost property worth millions of dollars. Needless to say, they didn't take it well."

Breckinridge chuckled. "I don't need any reminding about that. You should have read the letters I received. And I will never forget the bitterness that characterized the Senate debate on treaty ratification. But what other choice did I have? The Union delegation would have refused to sign that treaty if it had not contained that provision."

"There is reality and there is the perception of reality," Benjamin replied. "In politics, the latter is more important." He paused for a moment and sipped his scotch. "So, while the Southern people as a whole have a generally favorable opinion of you, we will face intense opposition from many in the planter class, who blame you for allowing their slaves to escape into the North."

"Beauregard's campaign will be well-funded, to say the least."

"Yes," Benjamin replied. "It also means that we might as well not bother campaigning in South Carolina. You have no hope of winning there."

"You think so?"

"Yes, I do. Beauregard is wildly popular in South Carolina. They remember him as the man who reduced Fort Sumter and then repulsed the two great Yankee attempts to capture Charleston in 1863 and 1864. That, combined with the immense political power wielded by the planter class in the state, means that we can already count its eight electoral votes solidly for Beauregard."

Breckinridge frowned. "I wish I could argue with you, but I can't." He paused a moment to light a cigar. Without a word, Benjamin took one out of his own coat pocket and Breckinridge leaned over to light it for him. "What other states should we be worried about?"

"Louisiana, for one," Benjamin replied. "Beauregard is their favorite son. The Creoles would support him even if Jesus Christ himself were the other candidate. With their support, Beauregard will easily carry the state."

"The Creoles wield that much power?"

"And then some. Take it from a man who spent a lifetime in Louisiana politics."

"But you won election to the Senate from the state. So did your friend Slidell, didn't he? Surely you and he could work with your people to mount a credible effort there."

Benjamin pursed his lips. "I'm an optimist, John. I really am. But I'm also a realist. Beauregard is beloved in Louisiana. Even if we somehow won the vote in New Orleans itself, which is doubtful, Beauregard would sweep the rest of the state. Being a cautious man, I think we should place its numbers in the Beauregard column." He paused a moment to take another sip of whiskey.

"Now, South Carolina has eight electoral votes and Louisiana has six. If we assume he is going to win both, that would give Beauregard fourteen votes. And only forty-eight are needed to win the election."

"You're supposed to be encouraging me, Judah. Everything you've said thus far is, quite frankly, the opposite."

"Unfortunately, I'm not done being discouraging, John. I believe that your chances of winning Georgia are also rather slim."

"Why do you say that?" Breckinridge asked. His mind rapidly did the electoral math. With twelve electoral votes, Georgia was one of the big prizes. Adding its votes to those of Louisiana and South Carolina would give Beauregard twenty-six of the forty-eight votes needed to win the presidency. It would mean that the Creole general would be over halfway to victory.

"Our enemies largely hail from Georgia, you see. Vice President Stephens. Senator Toombs. Governor Brown. They will do everything they can to make sure Georgia falls into Beauregard's column in November, calling in every favor they can from every political ally they have."

"I can live without South Carolina and Louisiana, but Georgia is far too big a prize to give up without a fight. Surely there is some advantage we can find to counteract the influence of Toombs and the others."

"If you have any ideas, please express them."

"We will have our own influential supporters in Georgia," Breckinridge said. "Senator Benjamin Hill, for one. He has always been very supportive of the administration. And John B. Gordon, for another. He was one of Lee's finest generals and is now making his mark on Georgia politics. He and I served together in the raid on Washington City and the Valley Campaign against Sheridan. We could look to them for support."

Benjamin shrugged. "Can't hurt, I suppose. But I still would rate our chances in Georgia rather low."

"I can only hope you're being overly pessimistic," Breckinridge replied. "What is your opinion of the other states?"

"Virginia, Tennessee, and North Carolina will all be competitive. You're popular in all three and the political influence of the planter oligarchs is not as powerful there as it is elsewhere. Many Kentucky Confederates settled in those states as well and they will back you to a man. We'll have the Orphan Society as a ready-made campaign organization in some places. You're especially popular in the Shenandoah Valley, of course. It's good news, too, as those three together count for thirty-nine electoral votes. But make no mistake, Beauregard will run you a hard race in all three of them."

"I commanded many Tennessee troops during the war, as well."

"Always useful, that."

"What of Mississippi and Alabama?"

"In those states, which together count sixteen votes, we have the same issue that we have in South Carolina. Many in the planter class distrust you for your role in the Toronto Peace Conference. But those people are not as politically entrenched in those states as it is in South Carolina. Moreover, tens of thousands of men from those states served in the Army of Tennessee, some of them under your direct command, and they respect you. One could flip a coin on those two states."

"And what of Florida?" Breckinridge asked.

"Florida, I fear, is rather like South Carolina."

Breckinridge nodded, having concluded the same. "And your view of the Trans-Mississippi states, Texas and Arkansas?"

"Those are the most difficult to assess, in my opinion. They're still basically frontier states, you know, with little in the way of a settled political structure and there is not a firmly established planter class. My guess is that they could go either way. Of course, Wigfall is the most prominent Texas politician and he will do whatever he can to pull Texas into the Beauregard column."

Breckinridge took a long pull on his cigar and sat back in his chair, doing the electoral math in his head. If he counted South Carolina, Louisiana, Georgia and Florida in the Beauregard column, which seemed reasonable, his opponent would have twenty-nine electoral votes. To have even a chance of victory, he would have to win Virginia, North Carolina, and Tennessee and at least two of the remaining states. Disturbingly, he had an even chance at best in each of them. It was not inconceivable that he lose every one of them.

"This isn't going to be easy," Breckinridge said sourly.

Benjamin grinned. "That's putting it mildly, my friend."

Breckinridge took a moment to sip at his whiskey. Thinking about the electoral votes of the different states reminded him of many similar nights in 1860, when he had sought the Presidency of the United States. His candidacy then, as he himself had admitted, had been a forlorn hope. From the moment he had been selected as a candidate, he had known perfectly well that he had no chance of winning. As difficult as the upcoming election was clearly going to be, his odds looked better now than they had looked then. That was something, at least.

"What issues do you think Beauregard and his supporters will campaign on?" Breckinridge asked.

Benjamin chuckled. "If Beauregard had his way, the main question for the voters would be whether Beauregard is an actual god or merely a demigod. But we have to assume that Toombs and company will keep a tight leash on the poor fellow. They will play to those issues that have traditionally motivated voters."

"I agree," Breckinridge said quickly. "The Fire-Eaters are like an old brass band that can't think of new tunes to play. Even during the war, the criticism they leveled against Davis was nothing but a rehashing of their opposition to the federal government in Washington."

"Quite so. They will accuse you of wanting to centralize all power in Richmond at the expense of the states. They will say that you intend to maintain heavy taxation on a permanent basis. They will say that this proposed treaty with Napoleon III will reduce us to the status of a French province. And they will say that you have no intention of trying to acquire Cuba."

"None of which is true," Breckinridge spat. "Except perhaps for Cuba. We are in no condition to financially afford the cost of purchasing Cuba from Spain. We are in even less shape to try to acquire Cuba by force. It's a fool's errand, at least for many years to come."

"Talk like that in public and Beauregard and his friends will accuse you of cowardice."

"And I'll accuse them of stupidity." Breckinridge allowed himself a chuckle, but his face remained serious. "So, what shall be our plan for moving forward?"

"We must move quickly. Beauregard's supporters have already begun their work and we must catch up. You and I together must draw up a list of allies we expect will support you in every state and reach out to them. Committees must be formed everywhere if we are to have an effective campaign."

"I agree."

"With your permission, I shall approach friends here in Richmond and elicit their support, starting with our colleagues in the Cabinet."

For just a moment, Breckinridge pondered the significance of Benjamin's words. He was asking his permission to do something, as a subordinate might ask a commanding general for permission to move a brigade of infantry or reposition an artillery battery. In using those words, Benjamin was acknowledging Breckinridge as his leader. It was, in a sense, the true beginning of his campaign for the presidency.

"You have my permission."

"And might I suggest that you personally approach Senator Hill and write to General Gordon? With the Georgians, who will be wary of taking on Toombs and his friends, a request for support would be more effective coming directly from you than from me."

"A sound idea," Breckinridge said.

"Postmaster Reagan will be our man in Texas. He will back you, I have no doubt. Attorney General Harris can help us mobilize support in Tennessee, I think. But who shall we turn to for Virginia and North Carolina?"

"I'm not sure," Breckinridge said, frowning. "There were many prominent men in those states who supported my candidacy in 1860. Perhaps we could attempt to revitalize those groups of people?"

"Perhaps, but everything has changed in the last seven years. The war was the great dividing line of our lives, and we shall always think in terms of what happened before the war and what happened after it. The political affiliations of 1860 will likely have no particular bearing on how people will line up now."

"I can't argue with you there, Judah. Let's draw up lists of potential allies in each state, especially Virginia and North Carolina, and go over the names one-by-one."

"This is going to be a long night, John," Benjamin said with a twinkle in his eye. "How much scotch is in that bottle of yours?"

May 12, Morning
Home of John Slidell, Paris, France

Like most of his other luxuries, the elegant home in which Slidell lived on the Avenue de l'Impératrice was paid for by his son-in-law. It was three stories high and offered a pleasant view of the surrounding neighborhood. The westerly breezes helped cool the residence and also protected the neighborhood from the smoke created by the industrial centers in the eastern part of Paris. On days when the weather was fair, Slidell enjoyed morning and afternoon strolls through the neighborhood, often stopping to chat with his wealthy neighbors who gave him advice on where to buy the most fashionable clothes and furniture.

Slidell's son-in-law also paid the salaries for the household staff, which included a butler, a valet, a wine steward, two chefs, and a young Algerian boy who cleaned the dishes and did other menial work. A pair of old women kept the entire house completely spotless. Slidell believed with pride that his house was one of the best-run in the city.

He started the morning as he always had since moving into the house two years before. He woke only when his body told him to, which was often an hour or more after the sun had started beaming through his window. A pull of a rope rang a bell in the servants' quarters below and, minutes later, his valet would appear with a coffee tray. Not long after that, the valet would bring in his breakfast, which usually consisted of fresh bread from a bakery around the corner and cheese which had been purchased from a market near the center of town. As far as cheese was concerned, Slidell had a particular fondness for excellent camembert, but he was willing to eat brie as long as it was the variety made in the town of Meaux.

Slidell didn't bother rising from bed while he enjoyed his coffee and breakfast. As he ate, he feverishly read his newspapers. In addition to perusing half a dozen Parisian newspapers, Slidell read *The Times* of London and the most recent editions he could get of papers from the United States and the Confederacy. His favorite reading consisted of *The Advocate* and *The Picayune* of New Orleans, which reminded him of home.

He enjoyed his newspapers immensely, but Slidell would have had to read them even had he found the task boring. As one of the most important Confederate diplomats, he had to remain well-informed about the events taking place both at home and throughout the world. If he appeared ignorant of a topic of conversation at social and official gatherings, his credibility as a representative of the Confederate States might be undermined.

The news from around the world was interesting this morning. In Vienna, intense negotiations were going on between the Habsburg Emperor Franz Joseph and representatives of his Hungarian subjects, who wanted increased power in the imperial structure and were threatening rebellion if they didn't get it. Despite the recent success of Austria in thwarting Prussian ambitions, albeit with the help of the French, it seemed rather humiliating for Franz Joseph to be treated so disrespectfully by his own people. On the other hand, the recent resignation of the Prussian foreign minister, Otto von Bismarck, would likely bring some cheer to the Habsburg court.

Much of the newspaper print was devoted to what had been termed, unsurprisingly the 'Fenian Crisis'. According to *The Times*, the British government had lodged an official protest with the United States over the harboring of Fenian groups and allowing them to train and recruit members on American soil. Additional battalions of soldiers were being sent to reinforce British troops already in Canada.

The more Slidell read about the Fenian Crisis, the happier he became. President McClellan had responded to the British protest with a pretentious letter full of bombast, declaring that he would not be "bullied" by the "British bulldog". He had called for more funding for coastal defenses and preparations

184

to call up state regiments for active service. Considering the enormous amounts of artillery left over from the war and the immense pool of men with fighting experience, these measures were not just rhetoric.

Slidell thought that the tension between the United States and the British Empire was good news for the Confederacy. The more attention the Yankees focused on the threat of war with Britain, the less attention they would be paying to the Confederacy as it sought to secure its treaty with France. Slidell believed that every month that passed without any serious dispute between the Union and the Confederacy made it more likely that their peace would endure. As long as the Democratic Party held power in Washington City, decent relations seemed certain.

Once Slidell had finished eating his breakfast and reading his newspapers, he rose and dressed for the day. He made a point to keep the most fashionable wardrobe possible which, thanks to his son-in-law's money, was not difficult. In Paris, more than any city in the world, how a man dressed impacted how he was received by others. Slidell was therefore only satisfied with the finest frock coats, waistcoats, shirts, trousers, and hats. He carried a gold-headed walking stick with him at all times. His pocket watch had been custom-made at one of the finest watchmaking establishments on Bond Street in London.

Now dressed, Slidell set out for the Confederate Embassy, which was only a few blocks away. Compared to Slidell's opulent house, the embassy was a fairly mundane place, for Richmond insisted that it be paid for out of Confederate government funds and not with Erlanger money. Occupying a few rooms on the second story of a building that also housed two import-export companies, one British and one French, the embassy was comfortable enough but nothing to impress anyone. On those occasions when Slidell had held receptions for other diplomats or members of the French government, he had always done it at his home.

As he climbed the stairs to the second floor, Slidell considered how nice it would be to have an elegant embassy such as those used by the ambassadors from Russia, Austria, or the Ottoman Empire. Unfortunately, the Confederate government simply did not have the money. Saddled with an enormous debt load from the long war with the Yankees and still obliged to maintain a substantial army, Richmond simply could not afford to maintain high standards at its overseas missions. Part of his usefulness as a diplomat, Slidell was perfectly aware, lay in the fact that the money of his son-in-law allowed him to move in high circles of French society. Had he been reliant on funds from Richmond, the task would have been impossible.

He walked through the door and nodded briefly to the secretary of the legation, William Lowrey. The son of a general who had been mortally wounded during the Battle of Atlanta, Lowrey was an efficient administrator and quite good at his job. He handled much of the routine paperwork and sundry tasks that the embassy had to deal with on any given day. Slidell was happy to give him such responsibilities. He thought that the young man's fierce Baptist faith prevented him from enjoying the pleasures that Paris had to offer, but there was nothing to be done about that. Employing a talented war orphan, moreover, made Slidell feel he was performing a useful service to society.

Slidell slid into his chair and, without a word, Lowrey passed him the day's correspondence. As usual, the secretary had already sorted the letters by importance, placing those that required urgent attention in front. Lowrey took care of routine matters, such as helping Confederate citizens who had run afoul of the French legal system, without Slidell's intervention. This allowed Slidell to focus on more important things.

The first letter in the stack, Slidell immediately noticed, was from Judah Benjamin. Slidell tore open the letter and began to read. It was not an official communication, but a personal message intended to inform Slidell of political developments back home. With each new line, he became more fascinated. The letter confirmed the rumors which had already reached Slidell's ears that Beauregard had aligned himself with the Fire-Eaters and was preparing to run for president. Benjamin went on to tell him that Breckinridge was preparing his own campaign for office, which Benjamin's assistance. So it was to be Beauregard at the head of an anti-administration party against Breckinridge at the head of a more moderate one. Clearly, the 1867 presidential election was about to get underway.

Slidell immediately had mixed feelings. Beauregard was, strictly speaking, Slidell's brother-in-law, having married the sister of Slidell's wife Mathilde. For some years, Slidell had been happy to use his political influence on Beauregard's behalf, as when he had lobbied to have him appointed Superintendent of West Point just before secession. In truth, though, Slidell did not think much of the Creole general. The man was an arrogant dandy who talked much more strongly than he acted. Besides which, both Slidell's wife and sister-in-law were dead, rendering the family connection between Beauregard and himself so tenuous as to be practically nonexistent.

Benjamin, on the other hand, genuinely felt like a brother to Slidell. Slidell and Benjamin had a close friendship and political alliance that went back many years before the creation of the Confederacy. Together, they had largely dominated the politics of New Orleans during the 1850s, despite the fact that neither was a native Louisianan. They had stood by one another through much political turmoil and were bound by close ties of comradeship as well as mutual interest. If he had to choose between his loyalty to Beauregard and his loyalty to Benjamin, there was no doubt that he would choose Benjamin.

Personal issues aside, Slidell thought well of Breckinridge and immediately decided that he would make an infinitely better president than Beauregard. The Creole was too pompous and given to grand gestures to make a solid chief executive. He would likely spend more time designing stylish uniforms for the Confederate Army or thinking up grand names for Confederate warships than he would doing the hard administrative work necessary to run a government. That being so, it would be easy for the likes of Toombs and Wigfall to manipulate Beauregard for their own ends.

Breckinridge, though, struck Slidell as the kind of man born to be president. Regretfully, the diplomat didn't expect to be an active participant in the election. He could obviously not exert any meaningful influence while he was on the other side of the Atlantic Ocean. Still, he appreciated Benjamin's thoughtfulness in keeping him informed of political developments. Anticipating who the next

President of the Confederate States was going to be would surely assist him in his talks with the French.

Thinking about the treaty made him frown. While he believed that Breckinridge would make a better president than Beauregard, it might actually be easier for him to conclude his treaty with the French if the Creole general won the election. The French public would rejoice if Beauregard were to take office as president. They considered the Creoles simply as transplanted Frenchmen and would see Beauregard as one of their own kind. Many within the French governing elite, perhaps even Napoleon III himself, would also succumb to such an emotional response. With Beauregard in office, the conclusion of the treaty would become a much simpler matter.

He set the thought aside for the time being and opened the next letter. It was from E. Porter Alexander, an artillery expert who had served in the Army of Northern Virginia during the war, who had been sent by Secretary Breckinridge to study the latest European methods of designing and manufacturing cannon. The letter described what Alexander had learned from a recent visit to the Krupp Iron Works in Prussia. Slidell cared little for military matters, especially technical ones. He made a note to have the letter forwarded to the War Department and moved on to the third letter.

It came from Landon Haynes, the Confederate ambassador to the United Kingdom who had replaced James Mason the previous year. Slidell didn't much care for Haynes, considering him of mediocre intelligence, overly apt to quarrel and, what was worse, uncouth. He assumed that Haynes, who hailed from East Tennessee, had been given his diplomatic post mostly to mollify critics from that notoriously Unionist region who complained that they were underrepresented in the high ranks of the Confederate government.

A former senator, Haynes had had no diplomatic experience when he had been appointed to represent the Confederacy in England and had relied upon Slidell's guidance since arriving in London. One of the most annoying aspects of Slidell's job was the regular arrival of letters from Haynes asking for advice. This letter was different only in that the problem Haynes faced was genuinely serious.

Minister Slidell,

I urgently request your presence in London as soon as you can conveniently travel here. The abolitionist agitator, Frederick Douglass, has arrived in England and is embarking upon a speaking tour whose purpose is to defame our Confederacy and sway the British government against us. I require your council as to how best to meet this threat to our interests.

I am, sir, your most humble and obedient servant.

Minister Haynes

Slidell reflected on the contents of the letter. Abolitionist societies were far more numerous and active in England than they were in France. Men like Douglass, articulate and able to speak about slavery firsthand, were always able to whip up opposition to the Confederacy among the working classes in the English and Scottish industrial towns. For the most part, Slidell thought it best to ignore them. As long as the ruling class paid little attention to them, they could pose no real threat to the Confederacy.

On the other hand, Slidell considered Frederick Douglass a greater threat to the Confederacy than any man alive. Slidell was a firm believer in slavery and white supremacy, considering it a self-evident truth that the white man should rule over the black man. Yet he was not so ideologically blind as to deny that individual blacks might, on occasion, be capable of reaching above their level. Just as the white race sometimes produced geniuses like Isaac Newton or Leonardo da Vinci, the black race could sometimes produce men like Douglass, who far exceeded the intellectual ability of the average member of his kind.

The trouble was that naïve and idealistic people in the North and throughout Europe saw Douglass and took his obvious mental capacity as a sign that slavery was immoral. Some people went as far as to suggest that there was no inherent difference between the black and white races. Such misguided people, unfortunately, had as much right to vote as anybody else. Consequently, extremists like Charles Sumner and Thaddeus Stevens were able to get themselves elected to Congress. In Britain, Parliament was festooned with MPs who sympathized with abolitionism.

This wouldn't be the first time Douglass had conducted a speaking tour of Britain. Before the war, he had travelled throughout the country, whipping up antislavery feelings and fostering hostility to the South. This has made it difficult for the Confederacy to obtain foreign recognition from Britain and France during the war. Douglass had not come back to Europe since the end of the war and circumstances were very different now. Slidell could not begin to imagine the damage Douglass could do to the fledging slaveholding republic with his oratory.

The tour Douglass was making in England would certainly be reported in French newspapers. It was also possible that Douglass might cross the Channel and visit France after he was finished in England. Anti-Confederate newspapers, especially those associated with the socialists, would happily spread the abolitionist's propaganda. With negotiations on the proposed treaty between the Confederacy and France likely to enter a crucial phase in the near future, such a threat could not be tolerated.

Slidell quickly wrote back, telling Haynes that he would come to London as quickly as possible.

May 13, Morning
Morgan's headquarters, St. Martin Parish, Southern Louisiana

The Confederate battle flag waved lazily in the weak breeze just outside Morgan's command tent. Though it was only mid-spring, the humidity drifting through the swampy region made it unpleasantly hot and sticky. Morgan did not like it at all. He would have given anything to be back in the region of the Tennessee-Kentucky border, where the land was covered with grassy fields and forested hills. That was his realm. Louisiana, by contrast, was an unknown country to him. Duty had called him and so he had come, but he was far from happy about it.

Morgan and Duke stood on opposite sides of the small table set up in the middle of the tent, both hunched over the map of the local area. Eight small red and a couple of dozen blue pins had been inserted into the map in various spots, red to indicate plantations that had been raided and blue to indicate suspected sightings of the insurgents by local civilians or, more rarely, by militia units.

Morgan frowned as he looked down at the pins. The ruins of the Bergeron Plantation, the first to have been raided, lay almost exactly in the middle. Like a spreading forest fire, Saul's attacks were spreading out over a wider area. Thus far, no attacks had taken place outside of the cluster of parishes surrounding St. Martin Parish, but Morgan felt certain that they would soon do so unless Saul could be run to ground.

"Too far apart," Duke said, shaking his head.

"What do you mean?" Morgan asked.

"See here. This plantation was raided on April 29. And this one was raided on May 1. But they're sixty miles apart. No group of men could move that quickly through such rough terrain, no matter how light they were travelling."

Morgan pursed his lips. "So there's more than one group of bandits," he said. "At least two. There has to be."

"I don't see any other explanation."

Morgan sighed. It was yet another sign of the growth of the rebellion. "Mr. Davis in Richmond is not going to be happy to hear that."

"Like it or not, he's going to have to face reality. These blacks don't fight fair. And every slave they steal from the plantations becomes another soldier in their little army. They're getting stronger, not weaker."

Morgan did not like Duke's words, but he couldn't argue against them. Since the battle he had fought against Saul three weeks before, things in Louisiana had gone from bad to worse. Although there had been some scattered skirmishes, there had been no stand-up fights with the insurgents. It was clear that Saul was trying to avoid another direct encounter. At the same time, however, four more plantations had been raided.

There was only one gratifying development. Witnesses to the four most recent raids all reported that the insurgents had gone to enormous lengths to avoid using their ammunition. During the last raid, some of the white men had been able to escape because the men attacking them were armed almost entirely with improvised spears and modified agricultural tools, as the insurgents armed with rifles had been dealing with armed guards on the other side of the plantation. All of this told Morgan that Saul's force was poorly equipped and would soon run out of ammunition entirely. In the meantime, though, their elusiveness still made them a frustratingly difficult enemy.

"We're going to need more men, John. There's no way around it."

"Well, Breckinridge has said that he's ready to call up five thousand men. That would more than double the number of troops we currently have."

"I think we need them. If our estimates are correct, Saul's men have stolen more than two hundred male slaves. I think we can assume he has three or four hundred men at this point. Five thousand men might allow us to cordon off the region and hunt them down, but we can't do it with fewer than that."

"I'll send him a telegram this afternoon. Hopefully he will agree."

Morgan didn't say it to Duke, but he felt the biggest objection to mobilizing more troops would be political rather than military. The administration in Richmond was telling the newspapers two things. First, they were saying that Saul's uprising was not a very serious problem. Second, they were saying that adequate measures were being taken to deal with it. Neither of these things were true.

The presidential election was heating up. The newspapers were full of rumors that Beauregard was going to run for president, aided by a large number of Davis's enemies. Despite the denials Breckinridge had made at the Orphan Society dinner back in March, Morgan suspected that Breckinridge was considering running for president himself. If that were true, every decision the Secretary of War made was going to have to take political considerations into account. By mobilizing more troops, Breckinridge would essentially be acknowledging that the problem was serious and that adequate measures to deal with it had not, in fact, been taken.

Morgan wasn't concerned. He knew Breckinridge well and was confident that he would do the right thing, regardless of any political factors.

An aide-de-camp entered the tent with a confused look on his face. "General Morgan?"

"Yes?"

"I'm sorry to bother you, sir, but this was just received from one of the Louisiana militia scouts." He handed over a small piece of paper. "He says it was found nailed to a tree on the edge of his unit's camp."

Morgan's eyes narrowed and he quickly unfolded the paper.

Dear General Morgan,

I wish to inform you that I am holding three of your men – Nathaniel Johnson, Matthew Billets, and Jonathan McDonald – as prisoners. They were captured in the fight of April 20. I assure you that they are being treated well in accordance with the rules of civilized warfare. I offered them the opportunity to enclose communications to their families, which they declined to do.

I propose an exchange. I shall release my three prisoners if the Confederate government, in turn, sets at liberty one hundred slaves, fifty women and fifty men, from plantations in either Mississippi or Louisiana. The men would be taken under my own care, while the women would be transported to the United States.

If you agree to these terms, please inform me by firing four shots from a cannon at the Bergeron Plantation at midnight on May 20. I shall then contact you again to work out the details of the exchange. If you do not agree, the fate of these men shall rest on your shoulders rather than mine.

Respectfully,
Saul

Morgan had never been more stunned in his life. "I can't believe it," he said in a hush.

"What?" Duke asked.

Morgan passed the letter over to his brother-in-law. As Duke read through it, Morgan tried to comprehend the momentous import of the message. During the war, he had routinely communicated with Yankee commanders by sending messages under flags of truce. Wives or mothers who wanted to tend to their wounded husbands and sons often had to cross the lines to do. At other times, Morgan had arranged for the bodies of slain Union soldiers to be returned to their families in the North. Local prisoner exchanges were common, as was the

190

release of prisoners who had given their parole. These and many other circumstances had required some amount of communication back and forth between the Union and Confederate officers.

To receive such a message from Saul, however, was stunning and outrageous. Saul was addressing him as an equal, as though he and Morgan were both legitimate commanders of regular military forces. The idea of a black bandit speaking to him with such effrontery was almost unbearable, yet part of Morgan's mind could not help but admire the black man's impudence.

"Cheeky," Duke said as he finished reading. "Who does this Saul fellow think he is?"

"I don't care who he thinks he is!" Morgan spat. "I only care that we run the bastard down."

"What should we do?" Duke asked. "Should we agree to his terms?"

Morgan had been so surprised by the message itself that he actually had not considered what his response would be. "I have no idea."

"Can we be sure he's telling the truth about these three men?"

"He knows their names. I can't imagine how he would have found out the names of the three men who went missing in that skirmish. We never found their bodies. We can only assume that he does have them."

"I don't see how we could possibly negotiate with this darkie."

"Me, neither," Morgan said quickly.

"Should you just toss the paper into the campfire, then?"

"I don't want to condemn these three men to death if it can somehow be avoided. Besides, we should probably leave this decision to Richmond. I shall ask Breckinridge when I send him this afternoon's telegram. I'm sure he will be as surprised as we are."

"We might gain some sort of advantage from this," Duke said. "Saul cannot communicate with us without coming close. This business of firing cannons means he would have to be within earshot of that plantation."

"He's far too wily for that," Morgan said. "He will just send some expendable underling to listen for four cannon shots. Besides, a cannon shot could be heard more than a mile away in every direction. We could have a thousand men scouring the woods and find nothing. And they would run away at the first sign of trouble anyway."

"Perhaps play along, then. He wants to act like he's a real soldier, fine. Maybe offer to meet him somewhere under a flag of truce and then just shoot the bastard if he shows up."

Morgan found it extremely unlikely that Saul would agree to meet with him. Strangely, though, he found the idea of such a betrayal rather repugnant. He had used many a *ruse de guerre* during the war, but there was a limit to what was acceptable and what was not. An ambush being carried out under a flag of truce would be an obvious case of perfidy and hence illegal under the accepted rules of civilized warfare.

What Morgan found odd, though, was that he couldn't help but apply this thinking to Saul. Saul was a black man inciting slaves to rise against their masters. He was probably an escaped slave himself. Any black man in arms against the Confederacy should not be entitled to the respect a warrior accords to a fellow warrior. He should simply be hanged from the nearest tree. Why, then, was

191

Morgan disturbed at the thought of entrapping Saul by such a trick as Duke proposed? He didn't know, yet he thought it best to stop thinking about it.

"I will enclose the contents of this message in my telegram to Breckinridge," Morgan said. "We will base our response on his instructions. This is a policy matter for the administration to decide, not us."

"I suppose that makes sense," Duke replied, though is voice was uncertain.

Morgan laughed softly. "Quite a fellow, this Saul. Don't you think, Duke?"

May 14, Morning
Executive Office Building, Richmond, Virginia

"I am astounded!" Davis exclaimed as he finished reading Morgan's telegram.

"No less than me, Mr. President," Breckinridge said. "I had to read through it several times before I could believe it. But it's true. Saul is offering to exchange his three prisoners for a hundred slaves."

Davis's face looked like that of a confused and frustrated child. "But why? What does he gain? His force is probably already too large for him to keep it adequately supplied. If he wants more blacks, why doesn't he just raid another plantation? And what's this about freeing fifty female slaves and sending them to the United States? How does that help him in any way?"

Breckinridge appreciated the president's confusion, for he had experienced the very same reaction when he had read Morgan's telegram that morning. He wondered how Morgan himself had reacted when he had first been handed the message. Moreover, he wondered how others would react when the news inevitably got out.

"I think this Saul fellow is getting rather too puffed up with himself," Davis said sourly. "He thinks we're scared of him and that he can therefore dictate to us."

"I agree, Mr. President. It is an insult. I think that's the point."

Davis's eyes narrowed. "What do you mean?"

"What I mean is that we are dealing with a man who is far more than a simple bandit."

The president's eyebrows went up at Breckinridge's use of the word 'man' to describe Saul. Breckinridge wasn't surprised. White Southerners invariably described black males, no matter what their age, with the word 'boy'. It was so common, and had been for so long, that it was done without any conscious thought. It was a subtle means by which Southern society trivialized blacks and reduce their standing in the eyes of the whites.

Breckinridge went on. "Sir, do you remember the first message we received from Saul, when he raided the first plantation two months ago? The one he gave to the wife of the plantation owner?"

"Yes, I do. He told us that not all blacks had forgotten their warrior ancestors and that he wouldn't rest until all the slaves were free. Or some nonsense like that."

"Why do you think he sent that message?"

"I haven't the foggiest idea. Frankly, I don't much care."

"But you should care, Mr. President. We all should. Because if we are going to defeat Saul, we have to understand his motives. He's not just raiding plantations to steal food. We have to think of him in different terms. He's a revolutionary. He is, if you will, a black John Brown."

Davis scoffed. "John Brown was insane."

"If you'll forgive me, Mr. President, I must disagree. Sure, Brown might have been a bit unhinged in the head, but he knew exactly what he was doing when he raided Harper's Ferry. He didn't dream he could actually succeed in raising a slave revolt across the South. All he wanted to do was create the idea of a threat in our minds, you see. He knew how the South would react. And he knew that this reaction would help bring on a war between North and South over slavery."

Davis looked at Breckinridge across the table for a moment, leaning back in his chair. "And you're saying that Saul is doing the same thing?"

"I have thought long and hard about it, Mr. President, and can come to no other conclusion. He could disperse his men and have them all escape to freedom in the North if he wanted. He could easily escape himself, I imagine. So why doesn't he? Why does he choose to remain in the Confederacy and fight us? They must know that their little band by itself poses no real threat to the Confederacy. He is merely trying to create the idea of a threat in the minds of our people. Just like Brown did when he raided Harper's Ferry."

"And this message about exchanging the prisoners for slaves? How does that factor in it?"

"By presenting himself as a legitimate commander, communicating to Morgan as though he were Morgan's equal, Saul is attacking the very foundation of Southern society. The idea that the black man is inherently inferior to the white man is, as Vice President Stephens once memorably put it, the cornerstone on which our Confederacy is based. Nothing is more calculated to enrage a white Southern man and frighten a white woman as the suggestion of black and white equality."

Davis nodded. "Go on."

"This Saul fellow has been making fools of us for two months. One of our finest commanders has been chasing him about the Louisiana swamps but has been unable to catch him. Several of our men have been killed and three have even been captured. Dozens of white civilians have been murdered. Plantations have gone up in flames. Now he is affecting to communicate with us, speaking to us on level terms as though he were our equal. This is becoming more than the terror of an unknown threat just beyond the trees at night. This is becoming a challenge to the very foundation of Southern society, Mr. President."

Breckinridge hoped he was not coming across too strongly. He believed every word he said and felt that he had to push Davis in order to get him to understand. Yet he knew the temper of his chief executive quite well and did not want to push him too far. Davis was, after all, a man with an ability to shut his mind off from things he did not wish to acknowledge. These were words that Breckinridge felt Davis needed to hear, but he had to craft his speech in such a way that the president remained willing to listen.

Davis waved his hand dismissively. "This is all very fascinating, John, but when it comes to Saul, I'm not really interested in discussing abstractions. It's a military matter only. What I'm interested in is how we defeat the black bastard."

Breckinridge nodded. "Of course, Mr. President."

Davis looked up at him. "I do not mean to be rude."

"Of course not, sir," Breckinridge said. He was surprised for a moment. Davis normally did not go out of his way to be polite during such discussions.

"When Saul has executed the men he has taken during his plantation raids, the manner of death has always been by hanging, yes?"

"There have apparently been some cases of men simply being shot, but most of them have been hanged, yes."

"No reports of any kind of torture?"

"None whatsoever."

Davis nodded. "Well, we need to come to a decision. As concerned as I am about the fate of these three men, I'm afraid that I cannot acquiesce in their exchange for the slaves, as Saul demands. Think of the precedent it would set. We can't allow it."

"I understand, Mr. President. And I reluctantly agree."

"Please send Morgan a telegram to that effect."

"I shall do so as soon as I return to Mechanic's Hall."

"I know it's not easy to sign one's name to a paper that you know is going to lead to a man's death. I couldn't bear to sign the death warrants of men found guilty of desertion during the war. I pardoned nearly all of them. But in this case, I'm afraid we have no choice."

Breckinridge nodded again. He reflected again on whether he wanted the responsibility of being president.

Davis went on. "In any case, it won't be us that does the killing in this case. When you send the telegram to Morgan, I want you to reiterate that all means necessary must now be employed to defeat and destroy Saul. I'm tired of his excuses. Mobilize all the men you want. This black son of a bitch needs to be crushed."

"I agree, Mr. President. It's time for the gloves to come off."

"We haven't wanted to alarm the people by making the threat of Saul appear more serious than it really is. And we didn't want to give Toombs and his people political ammunition they could use against us. But with these new developments, I fear tipping in the opposite direction. People are going to be asking why he hasn't been dealt with already. And our political enemies will be throwing all the wood they can onto that fire, believe me."

"That's the truth, Mr. President. I'm rather surprised that Toombs and company haven't made more out of Saul up to this point."

Breckinridge had thought about this last point at some length, in fact. He had concluded that the Fire-Eaters were reluctant to talk about Saul simply because they didn't want to face the fact that black fighters might be equal to white men. Back in 1863, when the Union-organized regiments of black soldiers had begun appearing on the battlefield in large numbers, the response of white Southerners had been a strange combination of outrage and ignorance. At first, they had simply exploded in fury, with scathing editorials appearing in the newspapers and indignation being expressed by the men in the ranks. But when, in battle after battle, the black troops had proven to be brave and resourceful fighters, a bizarre sort of silence had replaced this, as if the South simply did not want to admit that black troops were fighting against them at all.

More disturbing to Breckinridge, however, had been the massacres carried out against wounded and captured black troops by Confederate soldiers. The slaughter of black prisoners at Fort Pillow in Tennessee by troops under the command of Nathan Bedford Forrest was the best known incident, but other such atrocities had taken place at the Battle of the Crater in Virginia, at the Battle of Olustee in Florida, and in other places.

For Breckinridge, the issue of Confederate atrocities against black soldiers was personal. In late 1864, after the unofficial cease-fire had taken hold across most of the country, a unit under his command in southwestern Virginia had fought and won a skirmish against a black cavalry unit that was raiding the area. The commander of the unit, General Felix Robertson, had given permission to his men to murder the wounded black troops after the fight was over and, according to some reports, participated in the killings himself. Breckinridge had tried to have Robertson arrested and put on trial for murder, but the man had disappeared. Despite Breckinridge's searches, he remained at large.

There was no denying the strange mental disconnect that the South had on matters of race. Being a Kentucky man rather than a native of the Deep South, Breckinridge felt he had a better understanding of this than a Mississippian like Davis or a Georgian like Toombs. Many members of Breckinridge's family were outspoken abolitionists. In conversations with his wife and with close friends, Breckinridge was quite frank in admitting that slavery was morally wrong and a stain on the honor of the South.

Yet Breckinridge was also a realist. If he wanted to play a role in helping the Confederacy take its rightful place among the nations of the world, he would have to keep his opinions to himself. If his personal views on slavery were widely known among the population, he would not have the slightest chance of being elected president. Judah Benjamin understood this perfectly, which was why he had dealt with the evidence that Breckinridge had once subscribed to Frederick Douglass's newspaper.

The more he thought about it, the more he realized that his feelings towards slavery was a major reason he wanted to be president. At best, Breckinridge thought slavery was a necessary evil for the time being, and even that was very debatable. At some point in the future, the institution would have to be cast into the ash heap of history, for the rest of the world would simply not continue to tolerate its existence. The Fire-Eaters, on the other hand, believed slavery to be a positive good and would defend it to the death. Were they to prevail, the Confederacy would be taken down the wrong road, which would surely lead to its eventual destruction.

"John?" Davis asked.

"I'm sorry," Breckinridge said, slightly startled. "I must have become distracted."

"That's all right," Davis replied. "This is a lot to think on." He paused a moment before continuing. "Besides, I imagine your mind if increasingly focused on your own upcoming presidential campaign."

Breckinridge smiled and slightly chuckled. "Benjamin told you, did he?"

"Yes, he did. And if I may say, I am delighted."

"That's very kind of you to say, Mr. President."

"I'm not trying to be kind, John. I'm being honest with you. Your service to the South, in Washington before the war, in the army, and with me in the Cabinet, has been without equal of any man. And I include myself in that category. You are a man of intelligence and integrity. In all honesty, I can think of no man better to succeed me in this office."

Breckinridge was genuinely touched. Although they had always been cordial with one another and had, in the two years since the war, developed a relationship bordering on friendship, it was still uncharacteristic of Davis to display such personal warmth. Breckinridge knew Davis to be a loving and devoted father to his children and husband to his wife, but had always been rather reserved with most of his male associates.

"I appreciate that very much, Mr. President."

"This time next year, I hope that I can address you by that title. Though I imagine that I'll be happier to leave this office than you will be to enter it."

"Well, we'll see. I don't expect it to be an easy campaign. Word is that General Beauregard will be running, supported by Toombs, Wigfall, and their friends."

"Beauregard is a pompous ass," Davis spat. "We would be much better off if someone had tied some heavy stones around his feet and tossed him into Charleston Harbor right after Fort Sumter surrendered. And as for those Fire-Eaters, they can go to the devil."

"Pompous ass or not, Beauregard will be a formidable opponent. I'd personally rate my chances as less than fifty-fifty."

"Don't be pessimistic. In any case, I shall help you in any way I can. I know I am far from the most popular man in the Confederacy these days, and I certainly don't wish to make it appear as though you are relying on my support, but if there is anything you can think of that I can provide, don't hesitate to ask."

"Thank you, Mr. President."

"And I want you to be your own man from the moment you officially announce your candidacy."

Breckinridge's eyes narrowed. "Do you want me to resign?"

"No. Dear God, no. I still need you in the War Department, what with Saul and everything. But I don't want you to feel constrained about what you can say to the newspapers, what letters you write to anyone, or anything else. Understand?"

"Completely, Mr. President."

"It's time for me to begin to pass the torch to someone else," Davis said, a rare smile crossing his face. "That someone else is you."

CHAPTER SIX

May 18, Afternoon
South of Canadian town of Augusta, just north of the Canadian-United States border

Wolseley stood impatiently, his arms folded across his chest. Colonel Bell stood next to him. While Bell had a cluster of subordinate officers standing around him, Wolseley had only a single aide-de-camp, Captain Redvers Buller. All of the men were expectantly looking southwards in the direction of the St. Lawrence River, where the Fenians were rumored to be.

Behind them, the 2nd Battalion of the Royal Welch Fusiliers were silently waiting. Just to their right was the Royal Regiment of Toronto Volunteers, whose grand name didn't change the fact that they were untried soldiers who had never been in a battle. All told, perhaps five hundred British soldiers and about the same number of Canadian militiamen were drawn up for battle. How many Fenians there might be, and how they were positioned, no one knew.

"These Indian scouts of yours are reliable?" Bell asked.

"Completely," Wolseley said, somewhat offended that this should even be a question. "They are born, live, and die in the wilderness. They can track better than the best English fox hunter." He was pleased to have certain knowledge that Bell himself lacked.

As if on cue, the four native scouts they had sent forward an hour earlier emerged from the trees ahead of them. They walked forward at a slow pace and had unconcerned expressions on their faces, which Wolseley found extremely annoying. He was in awe of the scouting abilities of the Canadian aborigines, but he often found them infuriatingly lazy and indifferent to proper discipline.

The leader of the four-man scouting band spoke when he stopped in front of the British officers.

"Fenians this side of the river. Built a stockade."

"How many?" Wolseley asked. The scouts were officially attached to his militia, so he felt justified in questioning them despite Bell's higher rank.

"Many. Twice as many as your men."

"Describe the stockade."

"Thousand yards from river. Made of heavy logs from trees they cut down when they crossed. Some men building a dock on the river. Many boats in the river."

"How far away is the stockade from where we are standing?"

"Not far. Twenty minutes march through the woods."

Wolseley turned to Bell and his staff officers. "Clearly, the Fenians are intending to establish a base camp and bring up more men and supplies."

"Quite so," Bell replied. "Rather cheeky of the Irish bastards, don't you think?"

"By establishing themselves on Canadian soil, they are presenting a direct challenge to British authority," Wolseley said. "They are seeking to move from rhetoric to action."

"Well then, we shall have to clear them out, won't we, Wolseley?"

"I agree completely, Colonel."

An extreme elation swirled through Wolseley. He had been enduring his tedious Canadian exile long enough. For the first time in years, he was going to see combat. The fact that he would be leading Canadian militiamen rather than proper British soldiers diminished his only slightly joy.

For the last year, he had been tormented by letters from his fellow officers of the Perthshire Light Infantry, his regiment. Even as he continued his efforts to train the Canadian militia, the Perthshire Light Infantry had been dispatched to the Northwest Frontier of India. They had been engaged in almost daily battles against the Pathan tribesmen that inhabited the region, with every officer being presented with ample opportunities for glory. Although he did not think it had been their intention, his brother officers had made him intensely jealous, almost resentful. In his next letter of reply, perhaps he would finally be able to repay the favor.

Colonel Bell knelt down and began sketching out his plan in the dirt. Wolseley, Buller, and the staff officers clustered around him.

"The Toronto Volunteers will approach the stockade directly, while the Royal Welch guide on their left flank. When the militia have the Fenians fully engaged and pinned in place, the Welsh will swing in and strike their enemy right. Two of the Indian guides can lead us to the most advantageous place from which to mount the flank attack."

"You want us to attack a fortified enemy that has double our numbers?" one of the Welsh officers asked.

"Of course," Bell replied. "There's nothing to it but to go straight at them with the bayonet. They'll break and run."

Wolseley felt he had to break in. "With respect, Colonel, I feel caution may be in order. The Fenians are veterans of the recent American war. They're seasoned fighters."

Bell shook his head dismissively. "The American armies were just two mobs of armed men brawling with each other across the continent. They never had to stand against disciplined troops like my Welshmen." Bell turned to one of the Indian guides. "You there! Did you see the weapons the Fenians were armed with?"

"Yes," the Indian replied.

"Well?"

The Indian's eyes narrowed slightly. "Well what?"

"Tell me what they armed with, dammit!"

"Springfield rifles," the Indian replied, not offended in the least by Bell's angry tone.

"There you have it," Bell said, turning back to the British officers with a satisfied look on his face. "Yes, they have numbers and will be behind a stockade. But they are armed with muzzle-loading weapons from their recent war. No match for the Snider rifles our Royal Welch have."

Wolseley nodded, acknowledging Bell's point. The rate of fire of the Welsh troops would be much greater than that of the Fenians. Unless Wolseley was mistaken, this engagement would be the baptism of fire for the Snider.

It bothered Wolseley somewhat that only the regulars were armed with the Snider. His own militiamen were armed with ordinary, muzzle-loading Enfields, which had the same rate of fire as the weapons carried by the Fenians. They would not have the advantage that the Welshmen had, but there was nothing to be done about that.

Bell went on. "I'll detach the light company and the grenadier company from the Royal Welch and attach them to the militia. They'll be under your command, Wolseley. The light company will deploy in a skirmish line and lead the way towards the Fenian stockade. I want you to place the grenadier company in the center of the militia's line to stiffen them. They'll be less likely to run if the grenadiers are there with them."

Wolseley nodded, for Bell's deployment made sense. Each British battalion contained ten companies, eight of normal line infantry, one of light infantry, and one of grenadiers. The light company was trained in loose order skirmishing, being made up of the steadiest and most imperturbable soldiers in the regiment, who also tended to be smaller and more agile. They were adept at using cover and employing irregular tactics. Their job was to scout the ground ahead of their comrades and, if contact was made, to feel out the position of the enemy.

The grenadiers had the opposite job. They were made up of the biggest, tallest, and toughest soldiers in the battalion. Their tall, black, bearskin caps made them look even larger than they actually were. Wolseley recalled how terrifying their appearance had been to the rebellious sepoys in India back in 1857. Whether the Fenians would find them as intimidating was yet to be known, but the presence of these formidable warriors was certain to strengthen the resolve of the untried militiamen.

"Everyone understand?" Bell said, glancing around. The officers nodded. "Very well. We'll advance in ten minutes. Place the troops."

"Come on," Wolseley said to Buller as they jogged back towards the militia battalion. His mind was racing, for so many things were happening at once. The militia he had worked so hard to train was about to receive its baptism of fire. He himself was about to go into battle for the first time in several years. There was the possibility of getting killed, but that didn't matter much to Wolseley. He was fairly certain that he would one day lose his life on a battlefield and felt there was no better way to die. He was a soldier, after all.

He stopped in front of the line of militia. The men of all ten companies looked at him expectantly.

"Men, the Fenians have crossed to this side of the river! This insult to the British Empire cannot be tolerated! We are going to attack them! Within the hour, if God be with us, every last one of them will either be dead or a prisoner!"

There was a round of cheers from the Canadian soldiers, though Wolseley felt it was not enthusiastic enough. He sensed that the men, while ready to prove their mettle, were also nervous and perhaps fearful. Fear was an emotion he did not associate with battle. In his very first skirmish, deep within the jungles of Burma, he had felt no fear whatsoever, nor had he in any of his fights since. Battle was simply his normal element. He felt more apprehensive whenever he crossed a railroad bridge. Still, he understood that few other men were made the way he was made and felt the need to encourage them.

"I have worked hard to train you, men! You are ready! The Fenians will be no match for you! Load and fire as I have taught you, then go at them with the bayonet! You're safer going straight at them than you will be if you run away! And don't forget that our Welsh comrades will be with us! God save the Queen!"

"God save the Queen!" the battalion roared as one.

He barked orders to Buller and to his ten company commanders. Eight of his companies deployed in a double line, four companies in front and four behind. Of the remaining two companies, one deployed out to the right as skirmishers to guard against any surprise Fenian flank attack, while the other stretched out to the left to maintain loose contact with the main body of the Royal Welch Fusiliers.

The Welsh light company arrived and took its position in front of the battalion, stretching out into a loose formation out to cover the entire length. At the same time, the grenadier company took its place at the center of the militia's line, bayonets already fixed on their Snider rifles. Wolseley felt they were ready.

Since Bell had specified that the Royal Welch were to guide on the Toronto Volunteers, it was up to Wolseley to order the advance. The designated ten minutes had elapsed and he had to assume that the Royal Welch Fusiliers were ready.

"Battalion!" Wolseley shouted. "Advance!"

The drums began beating and the battalion set off into the woods towards the south. Wolseley jogged ahead and took his place amidst the skirmishers of the Welsh light company, wanting proper British soldiers beside him and not caring if this exposed him to greater danger. He carried neither a pistol nor even a sword, contenting himself only with the walking stick he carried on account of his limp. He clamped an unlit cigar in his mouth. He had earlier decided to light it only in the aftermath of a successful engagement.

Glancing to his left and right, he looked with admiration upon the Welsh skirmishers. It did not surprise Wolseley that the faces of men on either side of him were hard and expressionless. These soldiers were among the best of the British Army. As with Wolseley himself, these were men who didn't simply experience the emotion of fear. Nor should they, in Wolseley's mind. These were men who had fought the Russians, the Indian sepoys, and other enemies of the Queen. They had won every time.

He looked behind him at the ranks of the Toronto Volunteers. What he saw pleased him. Their faces might not display the fearlessness of the Welsh soldiers, but neither did they seem disposed to run away. They were marching forward at a steady pace, just as he had trained them to do. The men gripped their Enfield rifles tightly, as though holding them more firmly would alleviate their fear. The grenadiers in the center, needless to say, looked less like men than emotionless moving statues.

The steady beating of the drums resounded throughout the woods. Behind the advancing line, the fifers had begun playing *The British Grenadiers*. Whatever else it was going to be, the assault on the Fenians was not going to be a surprise attack.

The light company began to outpace the main body of the battalion somewhat and the wooded terrain began to obscure Wolseley's view of the militia's line. This didn't bother him. It would be best if the skirmishers came upon the Fenian position well ahead of the main body, as it would give him more time to shift his units about should that prove necessary.

There was the sound of a gunshot ahead, then a second and a third in rapid succession. A few of the Welsh skirmishers dashed forward to investigate, quickly being lost to sight. More shots rang out and Wolseley distinctly heard the sharp zinging sound of bullets passing nearby. He was not foolish enough to duck, for he knew that by the time he heard them, the bullets were already past. Besides, it would not do for an officer to appear concerned about enemy fire.

He considered halting the battalion to give the skirmishers time to feel out the enemy, but the Royal Welsh Fusiliers were guiding on the militia's left flank. Any such halt could lead to confusion if the regulars failed to halt as well. He jogged forward at a quicker pace, catching glimpses of the light company troops firing at dark figures moving farther away. A new sound began to echo through the forest, for he was now hearing occasional screams of wounded men.

It had been a long time, but Wolseley easily remembered how confused a battle could be. As much as he might want to, he could not control what happened. He could only respond to events as best he could. It was clear to him that the light company was pushing forward against light resistance. There was no sign of the stockade the Indian scouts had reported, so Wolseley could only assume that the Fenians had sent out their own line of skirmishers.

He glanced behind him, making sure he could still see the advancing line of the Toronto Volunteers coming up. Somewhere off to left of their line, he knew, were the Royal Welch Fusiliers. Then he jogged forward towards the light infantry.

He came upon the body of a Welsh soldier whose head had been blown apart. It reminded him of a melon that had been dropped from a great height. A little farther on was the corpse of a Fenian, wearing a dark green uniform, who had been shot through the heart. For a moment, Wolseley wondered if the two men had shot one another at the same instant, an interesting if irrelevant thought.

Amidst the whirring of the bullets, which were increasing in number, he heard a rustling among the leaves beneath a tall tree. Investigating, he found that it was a wounded Fenian, shot through the leg and unable to move. He was writhing in pain and gritting his teeth in an attempt not to cry out. The man's Enfield rifle lay a few feet away and, despite his wound, he might have been able to reach it with a determined lunge. Wolseley picked up the rifle, tossed it as far away from the man as he could, and continued on.

It didn't take long before he reached the loose skirmish line that had been formed by the light company. Most of the men were using the trees for cover, emerging only for a second or two to aim and fire before ducking behind them again to reload. The captain commanding the company disdained to seek shelter, however, even as bullets splattered into the ground and trees around him. He walked back and forth among his men with his hands clasped behind his back, a blasé expression on his face, as nonchalantly as if he were out for an afternoon stroll. Wolseley took an instant liking to the man.

"Afternoon, Colonel," the captain offered pleasantly as Wolseley approached. "Unexpectedly hot, is it not?" The man's crisp and clean accent suggested that he had been well-educated, perhaps at one of the elite public schools like Eton or Harrow. Wolseley himself had been denied such an education, a fact of which he did not like to be reminded.

"It is, Captain," Wolseley replied. He looked over at the Fenians exchanging shots with the Welshmen. "What an amusing, inconsequential lot of beggars these Irishmen are. I had rather hoped for a more formidable challenge."

"They are good shots, I shall grant them," the captain replied, as a bullet smacked into a tree less than five feet from where they were standing. "They have already killed two of my men, I believe."

Wolseley reminded himself that the bulk of the Fenians were likely veterans of the War for Southern Independence. While he did not doubt that his prejudice against the Irish race was fully justified and that they could not stand against proper Anglo-Saxons, it would not do for him to be lulled into underestimating his opponents in this contest. The Irish were a duplicitous race whose strength lay in their cunning. They would certainly try to obtain any advantage they could.

For just a moment, Wolseley felt an anger arise from deep inside him. It was intolerable that this Irish rabble felt it had the right to challenge the authority of the British Empire. Were it not for the Empire, Ireland would not enjoy its peace, stability, good government, and sound economic practices. As far as Wolseley was concerned, the Fenians were motivated only by vanity and a desire for their own aggrandizement. They were nothing more than disobedient schoolboys. The sooner they were crushed, the better.

He turned to the captain. "Keep pushing that rabble, Captain. We should come upon their main position soon."

The captain nodded sharply. "Very good, sir."

Over the next few minutes, the advance of the skirmishers slowed, suggesting that the Fenian resistance was becoming stouter. Moving forward more quickly, Wolseley strained his eyes to look through the trees and thought he glimpsed the stockade. He jogged forward a bit more to get a better look. It appeared to be a fairly rudimentary structure of a few heavy logs piled on top of one another.

He walked back from the skirmish line and soon came upon the main body of the militia. He looked around for his aide-de-camp and soon picked out his face. "Buller!"

He was by his side fifteen seconds later. "Sir?"

"Bring up the battalion more quickly," Wolseley said sharply. "Prepare them to halt when they come within range of the Fenian stockade."

"Yes, sir," Buller said as he dashed back the way he had come.

Wolseley paused, feeling he had come far enough forward. To move closer to the stockade at this point would be useless. As the militiamen came up, their officers barked orders to halt. The light company of the Royal Welch broke formation and dashed around the flanks of the line to reform in the rear.

Wolseley fell back behind the ranks, where his orders could more easily be heard. They were about three hundred yards away from the stockade, well within firing range, but the heavily wooded terrain would make it difficult to hit anything.

Wolseley ordered the bugler to sound the officers' call and, within two minutes, all of the company commanders of the Toronto Volunteers were clustered around him, aside from those of the two companies out on either flank. The commander of the grenadier company of the Royal Welch also appeared.

His mind conjured up an elaborate plan in which the entire battalion would advance with each company starting one minute before the other, thus creating an *en echelon* assault. He immediately cast the thought aside. He would not have hesitated to conduct such an attack with a regular British battalion, but it was far too sophisticated for him to entrust to the militia with any degree of confidence. What was required was a plan simple enough for the officers and men to carry it out without having to think too much.

"Our orders are to pin the enemy in place," Wolseley said to them, over the sound of increasing gunfire. "Each company in the front line will advance within range, fire at will for two minutes, and then fall back. The companies in the rear line will then pass to the front and do the same thing. You will emphasize to your men the need to use the trees for cover. Understand?"

"Yes, sir," the officers replied in unison.

Wolseley looked at the grenadier commander, a giant of a man whose name he did not know. "The grenadiers will remain in place. I want you ready to spearhead a full-scale assault the moment the flank attacks goes in." Wolseley didn't say it, but he also wanted the grenadiers to remain in the rear to deter the militiamen from fleeing the battle.

He turned to Buller. "Go over to the left, find Colonel Bell, and tell him that we're in position."

"Right away, sir," Buller said. The man saluted and dashed off.

He turned back to the company commanders. "All right, gentlemen. Let's teach these damn Fenians a lesson they won't forget, shall we?"

The next few minutes passed quickly. More or less in unison, but without the precision that a truly capable regiment would have displayed, the four companies in the front rank stepped forward and passed beyond the tree line in front of the Fenian stockade. Almost instantly, a blast of musket fire hit them. Men began to fall, but the lines remained steady and the men fired back at the Irishmen. Although the stockade provided some protection, several Fenians were hit and tumbled to the ground.

The Canadian line fell back as ordered. Perhaps two or three minutes later, the companies from the second rank stepped forward and repeated the process. More men fell on both sides. Wolseley was not one to flinch from casualties, but he hoped that Bell's flank attack would come in quickly. If not, the men dying in front of the Fenian stockade would be doing so for no purpose.

He was beginning to wonder what was taking Bell so long when Buller approached at a run. The shaken expression on the face of his aide-de-camp, normally a level-headed fellow, instantly caused Wolseley to worry.

"Sir!" he yelled over the sound of gunfire. "Colonel Bell's down! Come quick, sir!"

A thousand thoughts flashed through Wolseley's mind in an instant, but he remained calm and acted quickly. "You stay here, Buller! Take command of the militia! Keep the pressure on the blasted Fenians!"

Without waiting for an acknowledgement, Wolseley dashed off to the left in the direction of the Royal Welch Fusiliers. Gunfire was coming from that area of the battlefield as well, though it was not nearly as heavy as that in front of the Toronto Volunteers. Presumably the Fenians had deployed skirmishers in this area, to protect their stockade from any approach from their right.

The Royal Welch Fusiliers had not yet commenced their swing to the right. In fact, the men of the battalion were standing at attention with concerned and angry looks on their faces. There was a cluster of men standing around a prone figure lying on the ground just behind the line and Wolseley ran directly towards it.

Colonel Bell was still alive, but only just. He had been shot in the belly, a terrible wound that was certainly fatal. The hole torn in his stomach was the size of a teacup and blood was pouring out of his mouth as well. He looked up at Wolseley, a look of disappointment evident in his eyes. One of his officers knelt down beside him and clasped his hand. Less than a minute after Wolseley had arrived, Bell stopped moving.

There was an endless twenty seconds of silence. Wolseley had scarcely known Bell but felt sadness at his death. The other men standing around him, however, had been close to their commander for many years and fought side-by-side with him in many bloody battles. What was mere sadness to Wolseley was, to them, deep anguish. Yet they were in the middle of a battle. There was no time for such emotions until later.

One of the battalion captains looked up at Wolseley. "Sir, you're the senior officer present."

"Yes, you're correct," Wolseley said sharply. "I assume command on the battlefield. Where is the battalion major?"

"Here, sir!"

He had met the man when he had dined at the officers' mess. He did not recall his first name but remembered that his last name was Mostyn. "Major Mostyn, you will go forward with the previous plan of swinging the battalion to the right and hitting the Fenian right flank. Do you have any questions?"

"No, sir!"

"Very good. I will speak to your men and then you will proceed."

Wolseley dashed to the front of the Royal Welch's line. Fenian bullets were still flying about and a few of the enlisted men had fallen. From off to the right, there was a much louder exchange of fire going on in front of the Toronto Volunteers. Wolseley had to hope that Captain Buller was doing his job of pinning the Fenians in place. A few bullets smacked into the ground near Wolseley's feet and he assumed that enemy sharpshooters were attempting to kill him. He paid no mind.

"Soldiers!" Wolseley shouted. "Your colonel is dead!"

There was a roar of fury and indignation from the ranks of the Royal Welch. Wolseley was momentarily reminded of the moment in the *Iliad* when Achilles learns of the death of his friend Patroclus. He pointed his walking stick towards the Fenian stockade, the right end of which was just visible through the trees.

"There are the men who killed him. Will you let him go unavenged?"

"No!" came the reply from the ranks.

"Steady, men! Today you fight not just for Queen and Empire, but to avenge your colonel!"

He walked over to the right of the Welsh line, from which it would pivot at an angle to the line of the Toronto Volunteers. This put Wolseley close to the center of the British force as a whole, which he judged to be the best location from which to direct the action. Major Mostyn barked out orders and the Royal Welch stepped off, wheeling to the right like a swinging door.

Wolseley ordered the militia company that had been on the left of the Toronto Volunteers line to redeploy behind the militia in order to reinforce it. After all, the Canadians were likely to have suffered significant casualties in their feint assault. There was no longer any need for the company to remain where it was, now that the flank attack was going in.

The Welsh reached a position where they were at right angles to the Fenian stockade. Wolseley noted that the enemy were not reacting with any particular speed, though many of them were shouting to the others to alert them to the presence of the Welsh. Wolseley thought on this for a second. Though the Fenians were experienced soldiers, they were no longer part of a well-organized army with an efficient command structure. With no official system of military justice and with no punishment meted out to soldiers who deserted the ranks, discipline was sure to be lax. That being the case, it was only to be expected that the movements of their units would be haphazard at best. Even the bravest soldiers needed thoughtful officers to direct them.

With a terrifying battle cry, the Welsh surged forward. Through the trees, he could see them go in, determined to punish the enemy for the death of their colonel. There was another explosion of gunfire as they approached the Fenian position and Wolseley knew it would not take long before they reached the stockade. Wolseley dashed back to the line of the Toronto Volunteers and, within a matter of minutes, had found Buller.

His aide-de-camp seemed pleased with himself. Having taken command of the battalion, he had carried out Wolseley's orders with efficiency. The different companies were continuing to advance, give fire, and fall back, just as he had asked them to do. They were using the cover of the trees as best they could, but the ground in front of the enemy stockade was sprinkled with dead and wounded Canadians. To Wolseley's delight, this did not seem to dishearten the militiamen, but rather to enrage them and spur them on to further efforts.

Wolseley and Buller held a hurried conference.

"Keep up the pressure on those paddy bastards. When you see the Welsh reach the stockade, drive forward, using the grenadier company as your spearhead. The Fenians will be too distracted by the incoming flank attack to resist. You should be able to roll right over them. Understood?"

"Completely, sir!"

Wolseley nodded and jogged back towards the Royal Welch. The flank attack was going to be the key element of the battle, so it only made sense for him to position himself there. Besides which, the scene of the hottest action was the place most likely for Wolseley to be hit. As he always told himself, the best way to earn recognition and advancement was to try to get himself killed at every conceivable opportunity.

In the two or three minutes it took him to reach the line of the Royal Welch, he allowed his mind a few precious seconds in which to ponder the consequences of what was taking place. What was supposed to have been a simple rounding up of criminals had quickly escalated into a full-scale battle involving more than two thousand men. A prominent British colonel had been killed and many more British soldiers and Canadian militiamen were sure to die before the day was over. It was absurd to Wolseley that such a large force of Fenians could have crossed the border without the American authorities having been aware of it. What had been diplomatic tensions between the two nations was soon to explode into a full-blown crisis, which might conceivably lead to an outright shooting war.

Wolseley found this prospect delightful for two different reasons. First, a war between Britain and the United States would provide a virtually limitless number of opportunities for combat. Second, this engagement was going to be front-page news on both sides of the Atlantic and he could be quite sure that the name Garnet Wolseley would be prominently featured. If the engagement were successfully concluded, he could expect to obtain a significant prize, indeed.

As he arrived behind the advancing Welsh soldiers, he sensed a certain hesitation in their advance. Pushing through to the front, he saw Major Mostyn pulling his sword from its scabbard. He jogged up to be beside him. Ahead of the battalion, however, Wolseley saw a forbidding sight.

The Fenians had erected a more extensive stockade than Wolseley had expected. In addition to stretching in a straight line across the front, it also tracked back towards the St. Lawrence River at right angles for a distance of a few hundred yards, as if to counter the very kind of flank attack that the British were currently launching against them. Rather than charging into an unprotected flank, the Royal Welch Fusiliers were about to run up against a wooden barrier shielding hundreds of armed men. The British troops might be armed with superior rifles, but that was a virtually useless advantage in a fight that was clearly going to be decided by the bayonet.

"There's nothing for it but to go straight in, Major!" Wolseley shouted over the sound of roaring gunfire.

The Welsh major nodded and raised his sword over his head. Back over his shoulder, he shouted to his men. Wolseley couldn't understand what he was saying, for he was speaking Welsh, but whatever it was had clearly been inspiring. From the ranks of the battalion rose a ferocious battle cry and the hundreds of Welsh soldiers charged after their battalion major towards the Fenian position. Wolseley felt like a shock of electricity was running through him. It would be the height of irresponsibility for him to join in the attack, for with the death of Colonel Bell he was the senior commander on the field. Yet he could not restrain himself. Despite being unarmed, he ran forward with the Welsh soldiers, swinging his walking stick around over his head as if it were a sword.

He could scarcely see the Fenians up ahead, but the volume of incoming fire increased markedly. Welshmen fell on either side of him and Wolseley expected to be shot himself at any moment. The attack was covering the short distance to the stockade with astonishing speed.

As the Welsh reached the wooden barrier, Wolseley saw a Fenian soldier climb on top of it and jump down towards one of his men, swinging his Springfield musket down as a club. The Welshmen, a giant of a man, simply held up his Snider at an angle and the Fenian impaled himself on the bayonet.

"Oh, well caught!" Wolseley exclaimed.

As they came up to the stockade, the fusiliers sought any way through or over it, responding with what Wolseley thought was customary British determination and ingenuity. Many simply tried to scramble over them as best they could, heedless as to how many enemy troops there might be on the other side. Others tried to pry the top logs loose with their bayonets or bare hands. On the far left of the line, some enterprising Welshmen dashed towards the open flank of the stockade in an effort to get around it.

Wolseley was astonished that the Fenians had not bothered to dig a trench in front of the stockade, which would have greatly impeded the attack. Nor had the position been laid out to take advantage of the natural features of the nearby terrain. It was yet more evidence that the Fenians were poorly led.

Bayonets were jabbed through the firing positions in the stockade and rifles discharged at point blank range. Screams of agony and yells of triumph soon echoed amidst the steady drumming of gunfire. Over the logs of the stockade and through the firing loopholes, men grappled with guns, bayonets, and their bare hands. Wolseley watched as a Welsh soldier whose Snider had been grabbed by a Fenian let go of the weapon and attacked the Irishmen by sinking his teeth into the man's forearm.

It was soon discovered that the logs were not well-secured to one another and soon several openings were created as the top logs came tumbling away. Despite the gunfire being leveled at them from the Fenians, the Royal Welch passed over and through the stockade as though it were an insignificant barrier. With a terrifying yell, they pitched into the Fenian ranks without hesitation.

"Such magnificent infantry!" Wolseley cried.

He crawled through one of the firing positions and entered the stockade. At almost the same moment, Wolseley heard a tremendous explosion of musket fire followed by a battle cry a few hundred yards away, towards the center. The diversion of the bulk of the Fenian force to face the attack of the Royal Welch had denuded the strength of that part of the enemy position. Now, led by the gigantic and fierce-looking grenadiers, the Canadian militiamen were swarming over the logs into the stockade as well. Buller had done his job even better than Wolseley had expected.

For five terrifying and blood-soaked minutes, a ferocious hand-to-hand struggle took place. In such fighting, it was virtually impossible for the Fenians to take the time to reload their muzzle-loading weapons, while it was a fairly simple matter for the men of the Royal Welch to place more cartridges in their breech-loading rifles. As a result, the Welsh advantage in rate-of-fire was greatly augmented.

Soon, fire was being redirected against the Fenian rear from the other end of the stockade, where Wolseley had not known any British troops to be. He soon learned that Buller, acting on his own initiative, had ordered the light company of the Royal Welch to swing around that side of the Fenian position. It was a very sound move. Wolseley was rather disappointed that he had not thought of it himself.

He could hear several voices in Irish accents screaming for retreat. As first individually or in pairs, then in ever increasing numbers, the Fenians began to flee from the stockade and run to the south, towards the St. Lawrence River. Those who remained, deprived of the support of their comrades, fought on until they were killed or captured.

The main body of the enemy was now in flight. Wolseley determined to go after them. For a few frantic minutes, he conversed rapidly with Major Mostyn and Captain Buller, struggling to get the men assembled into a workable formation and to detail some of the militiamen to guard the prisoners.

"Sound the charge!" Wolseley ordered.

As the bugle notes echoed across the battlefield, the British and Canadian troops ran forward. It was difficult for Wolseley to keep up with them. The limp caused by his old Burma wound slowed him down considerably. As he followed his men, he saw groups of Fenian prisoners being led to the rear, broken and discarded weapons, and killed and wounded men lying on the ground. Almost all of the latter were Fenians. Wolseley was delighted to see that relatively few of his own men had become casualties.

He breathed in deeply. The acrid smell of gunpowder permeated the air. To Wolseley, it might as well have been the smell of roses.

The Saint Lawrence River was not far off in the distance. With a little luck, the British and Canadian troops would drive the Fenians into the river and bag the whole lot of them. Wolseley imagined what the headlines of *The Times* back in London would be if he succeeded in capturing the entire Fenian force. Surely he could then escape from his Canadian exile.

He sensed the forward movement slow. He saw men who had previously been running forward now stopping to reload their weapons. His units were now rather intermingled, with Welsh and Canadian troops jumbled together. Officers dashed back and forth, forming the confused men into coherent lines and maintaining a fire in the direction of the Fenians.

Wolseley scrambled forward to see what was wrong. A small group of Fenians, not without courage, had stopped retreating and had formed themselves into a loose defensive position. There were so few of them that they surely could not stand firm for more than two or three minutes. It was quickly obvious to Wolseley that he was witnessing a delaying action. These Irishmen were sacrificing themselves so that their comrades could make their escape. That meant that the Fenians had to have boats with which to escape across the Saint Lawrence River.

He told himself that he had to act fast. Although his units were hopelessly intermingled, he found that both the British regulars and the Canadian militia were still responding to the orders of his officers without hesitation. He smiled, for it was a testament to the rigorous training he had given the militia as well as the natural discipline of the British regiments.

"Mostyn!" Wolseley shouted, seeing the major nearby.

"Yes, sir!" the man answered.

"Pull thirty or forty of your men out of the line, form them into an ad hoc company, and start to work your way around the enemy right flank. I'll maintain fire on the enemy position to pin them into place."

"Yes, sir!" Mostyn replied. He darted forward and began calling for soldiers to join him. Over the next few minutes, Mostyn led these men in a flanking movement that smashed into the Fenian right flank. The enemy position quickly collapsed and the chase was on again.

Wolseley struggled to maintain control of his men. His officers dashed back and forth, having given up completely on reforming their units and simply giving orders to whatever troops they happened to be near at the moment.

"Keep moving!" Wolseley shouted. "Keep pushing forward!"

At the limit of his vision through the trees, Wolseley caught a glimpse of the Saint Lawrence River. More and more Fenians were throwing down their weapons and raising their hands, but he could see far more crowding into boats that were pushing off the bank. In the river itself, there were several boats already being rowed frantically by men desperate to reach the American side.

His mind whirled for a moment. His orders were to defeat any incursion by Fenian rebels across the American border into Canada. His instincts told him to line his men along the bank of the river and fire into the Fenian boats, causing as many casualties as possible. Yet his orders had also provided strict instructions to avoid any provocation to the United States, no matter what the circumstances. Would firing on boats in the middle of the river constitute that? He wasn't sure and told himself to tread carefully.

There was not enough room in the boats for all the Fenians still fighting on the riverbank, nor was there enough time for them to get on board. As the bayonet-wielding Welsh and Canadian troops came within a few feet, most of them surrendered. A few boats just pushing off were forced to stop when British officers shouted that they would fire if they tried to escape.

Wolseley reached the riverbank and snatched up his field glasses. There were perhaps two dozen boats in the river, rapidly heading towards the American side. Some of his men were already lining up and taking potshots at them. In view of his great success in smashing the Fenian force, and the large numbers of prisoners he had taken, Wolseley decided that discretion was in order.

"Cease fire!" Wolseley shouted. "Cease fire!"

His officers took up the cry along the riverbank and, over the course of a minute or so, all firing had ceased. The Fenian boats that had successfully gotten into the river continued towards the American side without further hindrance.

A strange and uneasy quiet settled over the Saint Lawrence River, like a curtain coming down on a theatrical production. Where there had been the sound of gunfire and shouting men moments before, there was now only silence. The British officers struggled both to reorganize their men and arrange for the guarding of the Fenian prisoners. The gunpowder smoke slowly lifted from the scene.

As the extent of what he had achieved coalesced in his mind, Wolseley had to restrain the urge to scream like a Viking in the exaltation of victory. It would not do for the men to see such a display of emotion from their commanding officer. Besides, there were prisoners to process and wounded men to care for.

He took a deep breath, willing himself to calm down and maintain his professionalism.

Wolseley raised his field glasses to his eyes and scanned the American bank of the river. His eyes widened in surprise. To his astonishment, he saw a large body of United States infantry standing amidst the trees. At first he couldn't believe what he was seeing. He lowered his glasses for a moment and then raised them again, as if expecting that the soldiers would no longer be there. Yet there was no mistaking the blue uniforms.

Observing them carefully, Wolseley judged the force to consist of at least two regiments, totaling perhaps fifteen hundred men. According to what Wolseley had been told, any American soldiers on their side of the river were supposed to be trying to stop the Fenians from crossing into Canada. Clearly, that had not happened in this case. If so many American troops were nearby, there was no way the Fenians could have crossed the river without their concurrence.

There was no mistaking it. The United States government was intentionally turning a blind eye to the Fenian raids. Wolseley was no politician, but he was certain that this was an act of war against the British Empire.

As he continued to observe the American soldiers, Wolseley noticed a thickset and gray-bearded officer of medium height staring back at him with a field telescope. He was obviously a man of high rank, for several staff officers were standing beside or behind him, as though waiting for his instructions. He looked vaguely familiar. The expression on the man's face was one of profound irritation. He reminded Wolseley of nothing so much as an angry bulldog.

Concluding that the officer was likely the commander of the American force, Wolseley wondered what his name was. Seeing no reason not to be polite, he waved.

May 20, Evening
First Methodist Church, Waco, Texas

"I was expecting more people," McFadden said glumly.

"There are nearly a hundred people here, darling," Annie protested. "That's a pretty fair turnout, if you ask me."

McFadden pursed his lips and shook his head. In truth, he was less disappointed than he was nervous. He had never enjoyed speaking in front of lots of people and had always avoided it. Before the Battle his promotion from sergeant to lieutenant had been forced upon him, he had always turned down offers of advancement to officer rank largely because he did not really like talking to people.

Yet he knew how much his life had changed since July of 1864. Not only had the events of the war propelled him into a position of responsibility and a modest level of fame, but he had met Annie. She had transformed his soul in ways he couldn't have previously imagined. She had filled the hole in his existence that had been left by the violent death of his family and had brought him back from the brink of savagery.

He thought for a moment about how the McFadden who had existed before July of 1864 would have reacted to Judge Roden. Assuming the man's corrupt actions hadn't impacted him directly, McFadden admitted to himself that he probably wouldn't have cared all that much that Roden had been taking land from poor farmers. He was a very different man than he had been the day before he had rescued Annie from the waters of the Chattahoochee River.

People were milling about the church, holding their own conversations, sipping on the coffee that the church had thoughtfully provided. McFadden would have preferred to hold the event at the local Presbyterian Church, where he and his family attended services, but the minister there had politely told him that he did not want to host political meetings. McFadden took this at face value, but inwardly wondered if the man had simply been afraid of getting on the wrong side of Judge Roden.

Annie was trying to corral Thaddeus, who was laughing as he skillfully avoided her by running down a row of pews out of her reach. Normally, McFadden would have found this amusing but, nervous at the prospect of speaking to a crowd, he simply found it irritating. He wondered if perhaps it would have been better for Annie and the child to have remained on the ranch. On the other hand, he had been extremely reluctant to leave them alone there since Roden's visit with his armed posse the month before.

McFadden glanced at the clock. It was getting on towards six o'clock, which was when the meeting was supposed to start. He frowned. There were still only slightly more than a hundred people in attendance, and that was if he counted the wives who had been brought along by their menfolk. He considered delaying the start of the meeting until more people had time to arrive, but only about ten or so had arrived in the previous twenty minutes. If anything, people would start to drift away if the event was delayed.

Collett entered the sanctuary, an angry expression on his face. He marched right up to McFadden.

"Our posters have been torn down!" he said indignantly.

"What do you mean?" McFadden asked.

"The posters we put up about the meeting. All over town, they've vanished!"

"Vanished? How?"

"That damn Judge Roden is how! He had his people tear them down as soon as our people put them up! Damn bastards!"

"Mind you tongue, Major Collett!" Annie snapped. "You're in a house of God!"

Collett went silent, but his face still showed his furious anger. McFadden felt angry as well, for it was a cheap trick. Yet he was also upset with himself for being surprised at it. Considering what they already knew of Judge Roden's lack of ethics, why shouldn't they have expected him to tear down their posters?

McFadden wondered if the lower-than-expected attendance of the meeting could be blamed on Roden's little trick. That actually made him feel better, for he had come close to concluding that it had been due to lack of interest, or perhaps genuine fear of Roden. Aside from the posters, the only means by which information about the meeting had been communicated was word-of-mouth.

Belatedly, McFadden wished that they had placed a sort of notice in the newspaper.

"There's nothing to do about it now," McFadden said. "We just need to get started and hope for the best."

He walked to the front of the pews. He thought it would be disrespectful to talk to the crowd from the pulpit itself, so he stood in front of it. He instantly understood the advantage of having a pulpit, however, for he realized that he did not know what to do with his hands. People stopped their conversations and looked over him expectantly, waiting for him to begin speaking.

Looking out over the crowd, McFadden saw a man in the back, leaning against the wall, whom he had not previously noticed. He was around thirty, with a thin mustache and a head that seemed strangely too large for his body. He wore a felt hat and had olive skin of such a dark hue that McFadden wondered for a moment if he might be a Tejano or Mexican. Something about his eyes gave him a lazy yet also sinister expression.

McFadden realized that he had seen him before, though it took him a few moments to realize that the man had been one of the horsemen who had accompanied Roden to his house the month before. He looked over at Collett for a moment, caught his eye, and then slightly tossed his head towards the man. Years of service together allowed them to communicate wordlessly. Collett walked off to the side and whispered in the ear of Private Anderson, who then quietly made his way towards the back and stood next to Roden's man.

"Thank you, everyone, for coming out tonight," McFadden began. "I think everybody knows why we're all here. We're here because we all share the same problem, and that problem is Judge Lucius Roden."

There was a smattering of nervous laughter throughout the church. Glancing at Roden's man in the back, McFadden noticed him looking intently at each man one at a time. He seemed indifferent to the presence of Private Anderson, right next to him.

"We've all had to deal with him," McFadden went on. "Lots of you have been pressured to sell your land to him, whether you really want to or not and even when he's only offering you pennies for it. Some of you have seen your county land taxes raised for no reason. Some of you, like me, have had the displeasure of having him visit your home, accompanied by an armed gang, and having to listen to his insults and threats."

He looked over at Roden's man, who stared back at him impassively. McFadden sensed a tension in the crowd, perhaps even fear. The judge had held sway over the county for many years and people had learned to keep quiet about him. The people were not used to hearing anyone denounce him in public.

"The commissioners' court meets behind closed doors, with the people shut out. We all pay taxes, some of us a lot more than we can afford. We hear that money is being spent, but we're not told who's being paid. And where is the money going? Has anyone seen any roads being improved? Has anyone seen any bridges being built? Has anyone seen any schools being put up?"

There were nods and mutterings of agreement in the audience. McFadden was encouraged and went on.

"Roden was elected county judge when most of the men who live around here were off fighting for the Confederacy. Some of us fought in the Army of

Tennessee. Some of us fought in the Army of Northern Virginia. Some of us fought for Kirby Smith on this side of the Mississippi. While we were doing that, Judge Roden was busy lining his own pockets and doing everything he could to keep himself and his friends out of the army."

"He's too fat to serve in the army, anyway!" someone shouted, prompting laughter from the crowd. This seemed to break the tension.

"Fat or thin, the man's a coward!" shouted a veteran from Hood's brigade. "While he was out here getting rich, me and my friends were fighting for Marse Robert at Sharpsburg and Gettysburg! If Judge Roden had been there, he would have turned tail and run at the first shot and that's the Lord's truth!"

There were more laughs and cheers. McFadden did not want to lose control of the meeting, but neither did he want to waste the energy and enthusiasm he felt building in the people before him. He had what he hoped was an inspired idea.

"Who here wants to tell their story about how Judge Roden cheated them?"

A dozen hands went up. McFadden pointed to the one farthest back, a tall, gaunt old man with a haunted face. He stood up and, after a nervous pause, began to talk. He was a widower, whose two sons had gone off to war and both died, one at Pea Ridge and one at Mansfield. He had tried to care for his two bereaved daughters-in-law and his grandchildren, but Roden's ruffians had taken most of his cattle, saying that they were due to the county in lieu of unpaid taxes. Not only that, but they were constantly coming by his home and harassing his daughters-in-law despite their firm rejections of their advances. The story brought mutters of disgust and cries of protest.

The second man who asked to speak was a veteran of the 9th Texas who had lost his arm at Shiloh. After being sent home, he had held a job as a county clerk for a few years, doing good work and never making a serious error. Yet when a friend of Roden's had asked that a job be given to his wife's cousin, the veteran had been unceremoniously fired and his place given to the interloper, whom the veteran described as both an idiot and a drunkard.

One by one, people stood to speak, with each story of Roden's corrupt rule as infuriating and heart-breaking as the last. As each person said what they wanted to say, McFadden could sense a feeling of empowerment building up. Before this night, people throughout the county had spoken of the dishonest rule and fraudulent actions of Lucius Roden and his friends, but such conversations had been scattered and meaningless. Now, in the presence of fellow citizens telling similar stories, there was an emerging feeling of collective purpose.

McFadden kept the meeting going. He was reminded of how it felt to command soldiers in battle, as he had done during the latter stages of the Atlanta Campaign. He continually called on the eager people raising their hands, maintained order when overeager attendees tried to interrupt those already speaking, asked easy questions to make nervous speakers more willing to go on. Every now and then, he cast a glance back at Roden's man in the back, who continued to observe the goings-on without any obvious emotion.

Eventually, after more than an hour of people rising to speak, McFadden took control once again. He was proud of himself and more confident than he had been.

"It's high time that Granbury County kick Judge Roden out. All of his friends, too. He thinks that he's going to be the representative of our community in the state legislature down in Austin, where he can pull more strings and squeeze more money out of us. And by running all of his people for county judge and the other seats on the commissioners' court, he's determined to keep the county court in the control of his friends."

"But what are we going to do?" asked one woman in the crowd, who cradled a toddler about the same age as Thaddeus in her lap. "Roden owns the county. He owns the courts. He runs the militia. Half the people in this county will support him because they know they'll lose their jobs if they don't!"

"Roden doesn't run this county!" McFadden shouted. "We do! We're the people, and in a republic the people rule. That's what we fought the war for, isn't it? We fought the war so that we'd be allowed to govern ourselves. And I say that being ruled by a fellow like Judge Roden is no better than being ruled by the Yankees. You say Judge Roden owns this county? Well, I say that we need to take it back!"

McFadden had spoken these words loudly and without thinking them through. He was taken aback by the cheers and applause that exploded throughout the church. He looked down at Annie and Thaddeus, sitting in one of the front pews. His heart melted when he saw the toddler's beaming face and his clumsy clapping. He was proud of his father. Annie had a noble smile on her face.

As the applause went on, McFadden glanced up for a moment to Roden's man in the back. For an instant, his eyes met McFadden's, a look of contempt in them. He sneered slightly, then quietly stole out the door.

May 20, Night
St. Martin Parish, Southern Louisiana

Saul lay silent and still in the underbrush, perhaps a quarter of a mile south of the Bergeron Plantation. Four of his men were concealed within ten yards of him, but no one spoke. Indeed, no one made the slightest sound or movement. It was almost certain that Morgan's men were scouring the woods for them. It had been a risk to take this course of action, but Saul believed it was worth it.

He had no idea whether or not Morgan would accept his terms. From everything Ferguson had said about the Kentucky cavalryman and his own conversations about him with the prisoners, Saul was convinced that Morgan was a man of honor, as least as the white Southerners understood things. He surely cared about the lives of his three men and did not want them executed. Moreover, like most Kentuckians, Morgan was different from the men of the Deep South in that he did not seem to be a fanatic about slavery. It wouldn't matter much at all to Morgan if a few dozen slaves were released from their servitude.

Yet Morgan, unlike Saul, was bound by the instructions of higher masters. Saul doubted very much if Jefferson Davis would agree to the proposed exchange and Morgan surely had forwarded the question to him. Besides which, Morgan was not the kind of man who would willingly do something another man was trying to compel him to do. If someone pushed him, Morgan's natural instinct would be to push back. It was a quality to which Saul could relate.

Saul had carefully planned out exactly what he would do. If he did hear four shots, he would send a volunteer forward to speak with whatever men Morgan had arranged to fire the shots themselves. He assumed that Morgan would have anticipated this and would either be present himself or have men there empowered to treat with his own representative.

If he didn't hear four shots, it was a much simpler matter. The three prisoners would die.

He tensed, sensing movement nearby. Although he could scarcely make out their outlines in the dark, he could discern his four men also readying themselves to either fight or flee. Within easy reach, Saul had both a loaded Springfield and his bowie knife. His four comrades were similarly armed. If Morgan had been foolish enough to disperse his men into small bands which searching the area, he would very soon pay a heavy price.

The nearby movement soon revealed itself, as a deer quietly walked by, searching for something to eat. Saul relaxed. He was pleased with himself and his men, as even the wildlife was not able to discover them when they choose to conceal themselves. They had been in the wilderness for two years. They had learned its ways as well as the animals.

They waited. About an hour passed, though he did not know exactly what time it was. It was easy enough to tell time by the sun during the day. On a clear night, Dr. Ferguson could always tell them what time it was based on the positions of the stars, but he was not present. It was now perhaps two hours since the sun had set, meaning that it would be another few hours or so before midnight.

There was a sound that resembled a soft bird calling. It was the signal from one of his own men, a scout who had earlier volunteered to move closer towards the area around Bergeron Plantation and observe what was happening there. Another of Saul's men answered in the same manner. When Saul signaled with a few clicking sounds, the man fell down onto the ground beside him.

"Well?" Saul asked in a whisper.

"There's a cannon set up in front of the plantation building. And what looks like two or three companies of infantry."

He nodded, trying to conceal his mounting excitement. He snapped a quiet order and the scout took his place among his concealed comrades. If Morgan had gone to the trouble of setting up a cannon, it could only mean that he had agreed to the terms of the exchange. Moreover, it meant that Jefferson Davis had agreed as well. A sense of euphoria almost filled him. He, a previously powerless black slave, had made Morgan and Davis dance to his tune. Saul's mouth curled into a very uncharacteristic smile.

They waited another hour and longer. Saul remained still and silent, unmoving, happy in his triumph over his enemies, waiting only for the sound of the four cannon shots to confirm it. By making them do what he wanted them to do, when they would have avoided doing it if they could, he knew he had achieved a victory.

Saul began to consider what he would do with the released slaves. The women, of course, would be smuggled to the United States and thence to Canada, to guarantee their freedom. War was not the business of females, after all. The men would be given the choice of either escaping into freedom or

215

joining Saul's forces. Ideally, he would prefer them to do the latter, but his supplies of weapons and ammunition was critically short. If more than half of the men decided to join him, he would probably not be able to properly equip them. Too many of his men were already armed with scythes and improvised spears rather than firearms. It would also prove difficult to feed them.

Suddenly, the sound of a cannon shot reverberated across the land. Lying on the ground, Saul felt it in his body as surely as he heard it in his ears. He felt a sensation close to ecstasy. There was a rustling of excitement among the five men with him, who forgot the orders for absolute silence and muttered enthusiastic words to one another.

A second cannon shot was heard, and then a third. The sound echoed across the land and then faded away into the night. Saul strained his ears to hear, but there was no fourth shot.

He waited. Perhaps there was an issue with the artillery piece that needed to be resolved. Minutes passed and there still was no fourth shot. Had there been any problem with the cannon, surely it would have been fixed by now. The men began to look over at him, confusion and concern evident on their faces. The agreed-upon signal had been four cannon shots. Why would Morgan have fired only three? If he had declined the exchange, he could simply have not bothered to set up the artillery piece altogether.

Saul stood up, his exhalation vanished and replaced with rage. Morgan was not only rejecting his exchange offer, but was doing so in a direct and definitive manner. It was a calculated insult. Saul's mind thought through it. It was as if he and Morgan had been in a room together, Morgan had listened to Saul's offer, and then strode across the room and slapped him across the face for his insolence.

"Morgan says no," Saul said quietly.

There were a few minutes of silence. He sensed the same disappointment in his men that he felt himself. This wasn't a surprise, for in many ways they were an extension of Saul, as much a part of him as his own hands and feet. He then signaled with a few hand motions and, like shadows, he and his men rose from their hiding places. Saul assumed that Morgan would have his best scouts scouring the area around the plantation in the morning, hoping to pick up their trail and follow it back to their camp. He had already ordered his men to take the necessary precautions. The first few hundred yards were covered only very slowly, as they took advantage of any stone, puddle or exposed tree root that allowed them to place their feet on anything other than the soft soil.

The further they moved, the more comfortable Saul felt. After an hour, he ordered his men to march in a regular manner. He planned to move the camp the following day in any event. They made good time and with their way lit by the full moon. Saul led the way, with the men following behind in total silence.

Saul could not tell the time by the position of the stars, but Ferguson had taught him enough about astronomy for him to be able to know in which direction he was heading based on the position of Polaris, which he could pick out through occasional breaks in the canopy of trees. He thought deeply as he walked. Dejected, he felt angry at himself for ever believing that the Confederates would agree to his offer. In making the offer in the first place, he was hoping to place them in a condition were they would be forced to treat him as an equal. That they would never do. They were willing to let their own men die rather than deal with him on level terms. He dwelled on this for some time.

The six insurgents kept walking. After a few hours, they finally came up to the first outpost of the main encampment, which held two men about a thousand yards from the rest of their force. Moving quietly, they signaled using their bird calls and passed through without incident. Another few minutes saw them safely into the camp.

Troy, Silas, and Dr. Ferguson were on their feet as soon as Saul came within the light of the campfires. They hurried over to him.

"Well, boss?" Troy asked expectantly.

Saul shook his head. Troy and Dr. Ferguson looked disappointed, but Silas smiled.

"So we kill them?" Silas asked.

"Yes, but let me talk to them first," Saul said.

Silas looked confused. "Why? Just let me cut their throats."

"No. We'll shoot them."

"Shoot?" Ferguson asked. "I thought we were going to hang them."

"Waste of ammunition, boss," Troy asked. "Don't have much left, you know."

"Soldiers are executed by firing squads. That's the tradition. These men are captured soldiers. It's different than the men we take at the plantations. A soldier deserves to die a soldier's death."

"Won't the noise risk alerting enemy scouts?" Ferguson asked.

"Only if we fire more than once," Saul replied. "We will make the men fire at the same instant. Then we will move the camp."

This seemed to satisfy Troy and Ferguson, but Silas had a surly expression on his face.

"You disagree, Silas?" Saul asked. He immediately thought it had been a bad idea to ask.

"Since you ask, Saul, yes, I do. You think the white men would give us firing squads? They'd just hang us from the nearest tree, maybe after torturing us for fun. You ask me, we should do lots worse to them. Let me take my knife and cut them into little pieces. Make them die slowly and painfully."

"That's not how we do things, Silas," Saul said sternly. "It's not about revenge."

"Maybe not for you. It sure as hell is for me."

Saul imperceptibly glanced around the camp, seeing that the eyes of many of the men were focused on the conversation. This made him uncomfortable. Silas was an intelligent man and a good fighter, which Saul valued, but he also spoke his mind far too readily and had a very different perspective of their campaign than Saul had. Saul worried that the man's outspokenness was beginning to corrode the attitude of his men.

Saul now spoke more loudly, so that more of the men would hear him, switching to the tone of voice he used when talking to his ordinary soldiers. "Now you listen to me, Silas. You is wrong. You hear me? What we is doing, it's not about revenge. We is out to destroy the thing that's kept our people in chains all these years. Only way to do that is by changing people's minds, Silas. We got's to act honorable like. We got's to out-white the white men. Yes, we got's to kill these men, because we got's to send a message. The white men got's to know that they's sinning and need to be punished. But there's a reason we don't torture them. There's a reason we don't degrade them. It's the same reason we don't do nothing to the women and children."

He looked around, gauging the impact that his words were having. Then, he continued. "We got's to get the whites to see us as men, not animals. If we let the whites think we's animals, then they'll think they've been right about us all along. Don't you see, Silas?"

Without waiting for an answer, Saul turned his back on Silas and walked across the campground. The three Confederate prisoners were tied to a tree. They had clearly heard everything said, but Saul was impressed that none of them seemed to have fear in their eyes. He wasn't surprised, for they had surely faced death many times on the battlefield and had grown used to the possibility of dying. Now that they were about to experience its reality, at least they were to be freed of uncertainty.

"You heard?" he asked them.

"We heard," replied the prisoner named Johnson. "Just get it over with."

"Do you want to send messages to your families?"

Johnson considered this, glancing over at his two comrades. They nodded.

Saul brought Ferguson over to the prisoners. A growing number of the men in the camp were literate, as Ferguson gave regular lessons whenever paper and ink were available. Yet Saul felt that the Confederate prisoners would feel more comfortable with a fellow white man taking down their farewells. He shooed the other men away and moved off himself to give the prisoners their privacy.

Silas was standing by a campfire, looking surly. Saul felt a tinge of guilt. He valued Silas, for no one in the group was better at reconnaissance. He felt his earlier exposition had been good for the men to hear, but he regretted that it had been at Silas's expense. One of the most difficult tasks for Saul was maintaining morale, and this required focusing attention on individuals as well as the unit as a whole. He walked over to him.

"Didn't mean to make you look bad, Silas," Saul said.

Silas grunted. "You and I disagree on lots of stuff. You know that. We both know that."

"I need you on my side. If you're not, the whole group will start to fall apart."

Silas turned and looked him in the eye. "I don't get why you don't want revenge, same as me."

"Doesn't matter. Things are the way they are."

"Maybe."

Saul decided that it would be a good idea for Silas to leave the encampment for a while. He sensed that the presence of the prisoners had grated on the man's mind. Every man had his breaking point, as Saul had learned during the war. It was important to see when a man was moving in that direction and deal with it before it happened.

"Silas, I want you to go into New Orleans."

"What for?"

"Since the enemy turned down our offer, a letter must be delivered to the newspapers. Ferguson has already written it. I need you to visit our friend and have him send the letter."

"I haven't been in six months."

"I know, but I think it would do you good."

"I'd rather stay in camp, where I can fight."

"I know. And I appreciate that. But this is what I need you to do right now."

Silas frowned and exhaled sharply. "Well, if you say so."

Saul nodded and walked among the campfires for a moment. He spoke quietly to his men, stressing that there must be no mocking of the prisoners about to be executed. Under no circumstances were they to show any pleasure at their deaths. Their execution was to be a solemn event, a necessary evil.

He came back to the prisoners. Johnson and one of the others were kneeling in prayer before Ferguson, who sat on a tree stump quietly reading to them from the Bible.

"Wherefore laying aside all malice, and all guile, and hypocrisies, and envies, and all evil speakings, as newborn babes, desire the sincere milk of the word, that ye may grow thereby. If so be ye have tasted that the Lord is gracious. To whom coming, as unto a living stone, disallowed indeed of men, but chosen of God, and precious. Ye also, as lively stones, are built up a spiritual house, an holy priesthood, to offer up spiritual sacrifice, acceptable to God by Christ Jesus."

"Amen," said Johnson and the second prisoner.

The third prisoner sat on the ground, his hands tied around his feet. The look on his face was surly and angry.

"Not praying?" Saul asked.

The man hesitated before answering. "Not one for piety."

"Me, either," Saul admitted.

The prisoner let out a long, slow breath, then looked up at Saul with fire in his eyes.

"They're going to hunt you down, you know. They're going to kill you. One day your bullet-ridden corpse will be tossed to the dogs for food."

"I doubt it," he replied. He didn't bother explaining about how his mother's voodoo magic protected him from enemy weapons. The man wouldn't have believed him anyway.

"You know you can't win. There's less than two hundred of you. The Confederacy can send tens of thousands of soldiers."

Saul shrugged. "Numbers don't matter when a man is right."

"Whatever you say, you can't win. Why don't you get out of here? Escape to the North? Find yourself some Negro wench and settle down on a farm somewhere?"

Saul sighed. "For both of us now, how we are going to die is more important than how we have lived. You are about to die. Your choice now is whether to die with dignity as a brave man or die as a coward."

The man stood up, his eyes staring level into Saul's, filled with fire. "You'll see no cowardice in my face when the noose tightens."

"You'll not be hanged," Saul said reassuringly. "You're soldiers. You'll be shot like soldiers. Are you ready?"

Johnson and the other kneeling prisoner nodded quietly, clasping one another by the hands as they stood up. The third prisoner didn't nod, but simply frowned and sighed, as if tired of the whole thing. Saul motioned to his men. Some of them gently pulled the three prisoners together until they were standing side-by-side. Half a dozen others loaded their Springfield rifles.

The Confederates, to their credit, showed no sign of fear. They turned down offers of blindfolds. Without much in the way of ceremony, the six men raised their rifles, aimed, and fired. The white men were dead before their shattered bodies crumbled to the ground.

May 23, Night
Spotswood Hotel, Richmond, Virginia

The carriage came to a halt and Senator Toombs clambered out onto the street in front of the Spotswood Hotel. He hurried through the door, anxious to grab a stool at the bar, which was well-stocked with some of his favorite whiskies and whose bartender knew him well. He would limit himself to only one drink tonight, though, for he had much work to do before he went to sleep.

The day's session in Congress had been unusually boring. Most of their time had been taken up debating whether Francis Pickens, the former governor of South Carolina, would make a suitable Minister to Russia. Toombs had little problem with Pickens himself, who had spearheaded the secession movement back in 1860 and who seemed solid on states' rights. Yet Jefferson Davis had nominated him, which made Toombs instinctively suspicious. In the end, Pickens had been confirmed by a nearly unanimous vote.

He sat in his regular spot at the bar and ordered a bourbon. He was neither surprised nor disappointed to see Edward Pollard at the neighboring stool. The editor of the *Richmond Examiner*, Pollard regularly haunted the Spotswood bar in the hopes of speaking with the politicos who gathered there. He was one of the few journalists that Toombs actually liked, for he was nearly as hostile to Davis as was Toombs himself.

"Senator Toombs," Pollard said pleasantly.

"Pollard," Toombs replied, nodding.

"Please put the Senator's drink on my tab, friend," Pollard said to the bartender.

"Thank you," Toombs said, a genuine smile crossing his face. For a moment, he wished he had ordered a more expensive brand of liquor. "What can I do for you, Pollard?" It was common for Pollard to use Toombs as a source of information and Toombs was more than happy to comply.

"Any thoughts on the clash along the Union and Canadian border?"

Toombs shrugged. "Not really. Now that we're independent of the Yankees, they go to war with the whole rest of the world and I wouldn't care. Not our business."

"What about Saul?"

"What about him?" Toombs answered in an irritated tone. He was sick of hearing about the black bandit, who would surely be killed in the near future.

Pollard sensed his irritation and asked no additional questions about Saul, moving instead in a different direction. "Pickens's nomination is approved?"

"It is, as everyone knew it would be."

"Anything else interesting happen today?"

"Nothing of consequence. Some veterans of the Stonewall Brigade sent in a petition requesting government funds to build a pedestal for a statue at a proposed mausoleum to Jackson in Lexington. As you might expect, all the senators spent the rest of the day making long-winded speeches in honor of the man."

The bartender handed Toombs his drink and he took a grateful sip. In earlier years, he would have taken a few swigs from his flask during the Senate debates, but in recent months he had begun an effort to appear more sober. Stephens, one of the few people from whom he was willing to take advice, had been pushing him to cut down on his drinking.

"Want to tell me about these rumors about a convention in Montgomery?" Pollard asked, with a grin.

"What rumors are those?" Toombs was not at all displeased that Pollard knew about their plan, which would have been impossible to conceal in any event. He was curious to find out how quickly word was spreading.

"Word is that you, Wigfall, Stephens and some other fellows are calling for all office-holders who oppose the president to meet in Montgomery on July 1. Any truth to it?"

"Who told you?"

"Senator Caperton. He says he got a letter from you."

Toombs nodded. Senator Allen Caperton of Virginia was opposed to Davis and would likely join their movement. He had been one of the hundreds of congressmen, judges, and state legislators who had received a letter inviting him to the proposed convention. Now that the letters had gone out, the cabal had sacrificed some measure of control over the flow of information, but that was inevitable.

"So, it is true?" Pollard persisted.

"Oh, it's true, all right. You should come down to Montgomery to cover the thing. It's sure to be the biggest story of the year and you can take that to the bank."

"You're one of the ring-leaders of this?"

"Damn right I am."

"Have you decided on a candidate?"

Toombs shrugged. "Perhaps."

Pollard took a sip of his drink. "Tell you what, Senator. If you make sure to keep me informed of what's going on with this whole thing, I'll make sure you get favorable stories in the *Examiner*."

"It's a deal," Toombs said. He was a firm believer in the proverb that the enemy of his enemy was his friend.

"You'll tell me each piece of news before you tell anyone else?" Pollard asked.

"That I can't promise you. I like you fine, Pollard, but there are lots of newspapermen. But I'll consider it."

"Well, that's something," Pollard replied, frowning.

Toombs didn't want to leave the man disappointed. "I can tell you something, if you like. Something that no one else has yet."

Pollard's eyebrows went up. "Yes?"

"When we do announce our candidate, don't be surprised if he has a Creole accent."

Pollard considered that for just a moment, then his lips curled up into a smile. "Interesting. Very interesting, indeed. Thank you kindly, Senator Toombs."

Toombs finished his drink, said good night to Pollard, and went upstairs to his room. The Spotswood Hotel was his home whenever he was in Richmond. He liked it very much. It not only had a fine bar, but staying there gave him a certain amount of prestige due to its reputation as the finest hotel in the city. Only a few other congressmen could afford it. As the key member of the Senate when it came to fiscal legislation and the acknowledged head of the opposition faction, Toombs felt he deserved a certain sign of status.

A large pile of unopened mail lay on his desk. Since he represented one of the largest states in the Confederacy, he received many letters every day. Most were from constituents with legitimate problems, such as farmers trying to obtain restitution for livestock the army had confiscated during the war or widows of dead soldiers trying to obtain their husband's back pay. Toombs tried to help all those he could, for he was a conscientious senator and took his responsibilities seriously, but there was only so much he could do.

The fighting might have ended two and a half years before, but his letters showed that the scars of the war were only just beginning to heal. A quarter of a million Southern men had died. That was tragic in and of itself, of course, but it also meant that countless families were without providers and had been left destitute. Some communities had been so depopulated of white men that there were stories of plantations where scores of slaves loafed about unsupervised, doing no work at all.

Then there were the economic troubles. Thousands of patriotic people had supported the war effort by purchasing Confederate treasury bonds, but the languid economic recovery meant that they were still worth only a fraction of their nominal value. The Yankees had destroyed mills and iron works and laid waste to farms all over the South, but there was little available credit to finance reconstruction. In order to pay interest on its debt, both the Confederate government and the state governments had not reduced taxes from their wartime levels, with many people utterly unable to pay.

In view of all these problems, it was no surprise that his constituents called out to him for help. He referred most of the petitioners to the state government of Georgia, which hopefully might be able to do something for them. He sent along the requests of war widows seeking back pay to the War Department. When he could, Toombs wrote personal letters lamenting the fact that he wasn't able to help more. Times were hard for everyone, he would tell them. In many of his replies, he couldn't resist the temptation to say that most of the Confederacy's ills could be blamed on Jefferson Davis.

Looking through his mail as he poured himself a whiskey, Toombs smiled. He set aside the letters from his constituents back in Georgia. He would read them in due time. More interesting to him for the moment were the large numbers of replies to the letters he and his cabal had been sending out over the past few weeks, inviting them to the July convention in Montgomery.

Toombs spent the next hour and a half opening and reading each letter. With every new envelope he tore open, his mood became brighter. One after the other, the correspondents were replying in the affirmative.

He began keeping a tally of names on a piece of paper next to the growing piles of opened envelopes. Zebulon Vance, the Governor of North Carolina who had long opposed Davis. Howell Cobb, a congressman from Georgia. William Boyce, a congressman from South Carolina. It wasn't just politicians, either. Several prominent former generals with distinguished records of war service said that they would be attending the convention as well. John Wharton, a popular commander of Texas cavalry. D. H. Hill, a gifted if irascible commander who had served in both the Eastern and Western Theaters. Gustavus Smith, who had served in the defense of Richmond during the Peninsula Campaign.

The list kept getting longer, until Toombs had scrawled down nearly three dozen names of prominent office-holders or former generals. How many more names would be added to the list as the replies continued arriving in the coming days? It was becoming clear that the July gathering in Montgomery was going to be the largest and most distinguished such assembly in Southern history.

He belatedly realized that it should have kept track of the different states from which the attendees came. Working from memory, he jotted down the names of the states, going down the list. Most came from the Deep South states of South Carolina, Georgia, Alabama, and Mississippi, which was hardly a surprise. Yet there was also a respectable showing from Virginia, North Carolina, Tennessee, and the Trans-Mississippi states. No one was going to be able to dismiss the gathering as a purely regional one. It would represent the entire Confederacy.

Toombs reread the letter from Congressman Howell Cobb, who had been one of his political rivals for many years. He considered Cobb a man of little ability and hopelessly arrogant to boot. As was the case with so many of these men, only their mutual hostility to Jefferson Davis and opposition to the centralization of power in Richmond would hold them together. Toombs hoped it would be enough.

Cobb's letter contained a short paragraph that Toombs found especially interesting.

It seems to me that the purpose of a convention such as you propose is the creation of a genuine political party whose purpose shall be to defend the sovereignty of the individual states against the usurpation of power by Richmond. If that is the case, please forgive me for suggesting a name for such a party. It is a very simple name – the States' Rights Party.

For once, Toombs thought Cobb's brain had conceived a fairly good idea. The States' Rights Party was a short name that perfectly encapsulated what they were trying to do. It was dignified without being grandiloquent or pompous. Toombs thought it even had a certain pleasing cadence to the ear.

The concept of state's rights was the foundation of the Confederacy itself. Toombs felt that the very words – *states' rights* - should be carved into granite columns at the center of every town and city across the South. The need to protect state's rights, above all in regards to slavery, had been the cause of Southern secession in the first place. The victory of the Confederacy in the War for Southern Independence had, it seemed to Toombs, vindicated the idea of state's rights before the entire world. Surely it was sanctioned by God Himself.

Yet to Jefferson Davis and his cronies, including Breckinridge, the concept of states' rights meant nothing. Toombs remembered the conscription of men, the impressment of goods, the suspension of habeas corpus, the crushing taxation directly levied by Richmond, and a thousand other examples of dictatorial power that had taken place during the war. The war was over, but such usurpations continued unabated. The Richmond power-brokers were clearly determined to trample on the sovereignty of the states to fulfill their own personal ambition and lust for power. It had to be stopped.

There was another consideration, though. It was rather more difficult to articulate, but Toombs could sense it in the letters he read and he knew he felt it himself, too. The war had fundamentally altered Southern society, mostly in ways that made him uncomfortable. Before the war, the South had been comfortably governed by a relatively small number of wealthy men. While lip service had always been given to the notions of Jeffersonian democracy, the truth was that the South was an oligarchy, ruled by an elite for the benefit of the whole. Within the elite, some men came from distinguished families that had existed for decades, if not centuries. Other men, such as Toombs himself, earned their way into the elite on account of their own virtue, ability, and sheer hard work. This aristocracy, guided by a sense of *noblesse oblige*, governed the South with wisdom and integrity.

The war had thrown everything into chaos, casting the notion of oligarchic rule by the elite into serious question. Entire regions had fallen into anarchy as groups of bandits, deserters, and escaped slaves had wandered freely, extorting whatever they wanted and beating or killing anyone who tried to oppose them. Ordinary people in counties and towns had organized mass meetings and dared to question the decisions made by their elected representatives and governors. Even women, left behind on the farms and plantations while their menfolk were in the army, had found themselves taking on economic and political responsibilities that would have been inconceivable before the war.

It was as if Pandora's Box had been opened and the insanity of egalitarianism had poured out. Toombs and his allies needed to put it all back in the box and lock it up as tightly as possible. The South had seceded from the Union to preserve itself as a slave-based society properly ruled by an elite class. The more he thought about it, the more Toombs came to believe that the States' Rights Party could be the mechanism through which this ideal could be secured.

Toombs then frowned, as though he had forgotten something. His mind worked the question through until he realized what was amiss. He quickly looked over the list again, looking for a particular name. It wasn't there and Toombs instantly had a sense of foreboding.

Robert Rhett's name was not on the list. Toombs had assumed that the fiery South Carolinian, who had led the call for secession for many years before it had become fashionable, would have been among the first to respond to the call for the convention. Perhaps his response would arrive in a day or two, or perhaps the letter Toombs had sent to him had gone amiss. Postmaster Reagan ran an efficient postal service, but there were inevitably mistakes. Yet Toombs couldn't help but feel slightly ill at ease at the lack of a response from Rhett.

Rhett was so extreme in his defense of slavery and state's rights that even Toombs and Wigfall had difficulty taking him seriously. Worse, Rhett had a complete inability to conceal his disgust and disdain towards anyone who disagreed with him even in the most minor way. Unsurprisingly, he had few friends. Toombs would not have even bothered inviting Rhett to the convention were it not for the fact that the man owned the *Charleston Mercury*, one of the most widely read and influential newspapers in the Confederacy. Because of that, and only because of that, they had to have Rhett on their side.

Toombs told himself that he was worrying about nothing. Surely Rhett's reply would arrive sooner or later. He organized the letters and set them off to one side. Pouring himself another whiskey, he began to open the first of many letters of complaint from his constituents. It was from a farmer outside Atlanta who claimed that the army had taken two dozen pigs from him in 1864 and never paid him. Toombs had more than thirty such letters after he finished the first. Long before he had finished reading, with yet another whiskey only half-consumed on his desk, he had fallen asleep in his chair.

May 27, Evening
United States Capitol, Washington City

Sumner was furious. On his feet, his hands almost quivering as they gripped the edges of his desk, he glared across the chamber at Senator Daniel Voorhees, a Democratic Senator from Indiana. The words being spoken by Voorhees, a fervent Copperhead and McClellan supporter, made Sumner so angry that he was worried he would soon lose control of himself.

"Let us be honest with ourselves," Voorhees was saying. "The Thirteenth Amendment has no chance of being ratified now or at any time in the foreseeable future. On the other side of the Capitol, the House delegations of Delaware, Maryland, Kentucky, and Missouri remain staunchly opposed to the measure. The representatives from New Jersey have publicly stated that they will not vote for it. I doubt many members of the House from my own state would support it. Even if the amendment were to achieve the necessary two-thirds majority in the House, which I regard as impossible, I should be surprised were it to be ratified by any state legislature outside of New England. Believing that the country needs to move on from this issue, I therefore move that the Senate rescind its approval of the Thirteenth Amendment of April 8, 1864."

"Will the Senator yield?" Sumner roared.

Voorhees chuckled slightly. "I happily yield to the distinguished senator from Massachusetts. I must say that I am not at all surprised that he has risen to his feet."

There was a smattering of laughter throughout the chamber. Sumner took a deep breath. He knew that Voorhees was engaging in political theater, for there was no realistic chance that the Senate would vote to rescind its vote in favor of the Thirteenth Amendment. If nothing else, it wouldn't be worth the bother.

225

The Republicans were still in control of the Senate and the abolitionists remained a very powerful faction within the party structure.

Sumner understood that Voorhees was simply playing to an audience back in his own state of Indiana, which had been under the control of the Democrats since the 1864 election. Resentment towards free blacks was especially strong there, as they were seen by many poor Indiana whites as competitors for low-wage jobs. The idea of an office-holder exploiting the racial bigotry of his constituents in order to gain votes was positively sickening to Sumner.

"Does Senator Voorhees agree that slavery is an abomination?" Sumner asked.

"I am not sure how the question is relevant," Voorhees replied.

"I believe the question is more than relevant," Sumner said. "The United States of America claims to be a civilized nation, does it not? Allowing the continued existence of an evil abomination such as slavery in our midst detracts from our claims to be a civilized nation. The stunted pretender to nationhood to our south at least makes no bones about its barbarism. It proudly proclaims it to all the world. But we, in the United States of America, should at least not hide behind the mask of hypocrisy."

Voorhees cast a quick glance at Senator Clark at the rostrum. "I do hope that the distinguished senator from Massachusetts is not accusing a fellow senator of being a hypocrite."

"I cannot answer to whether you are or are not a hypocrite, Senator Voorhees, for you have declined to answer my original question, which was whether you agreed or disagreed as to whether slavery was an abomination. I know it to be so. When I think of women and children on the auction block, families ruthlessly torn apart, human flesh torn by the lash, labor extorted without wages, and freedom denied, how can I think it anything but an abomination? And how can I acquiesce in its continuation within the borders of the United States?"

"The senator from Massachusetts seems to forget that the state of Massachusetts has long since abolished slavery, as is its right as a sovereign state. As he represents the people of Massachusetts, and no one else, I do not understand why he speaks as he does. If he wishes for other states within our nation to also abolish slavery, I suggest he try to persuade them directly, rather than waste our time here in the Senate." He looked back up at Senator Clark. "I yield back the balance of my time."

"For what purpose does the gentlemen from Pennsylvania rise?" Clark asked, exhaustion evident in his voice.

Sumner turned to see Senator Charles Buckalew standing at his desk, signaling to the President Pro Tem for recognition. "Mr. President, I rise to present for the consideration of the Senate a bill to appropriate a sum of $1,500 for the pedestal and base of a proposed monument to General John Reynolds, tragically killed in battle at Gettysburg, to be located here in Washington City. The funds to pay for the sculpture itself are to be provided by the Society of the Army of the Potomac."

Sumner frowned and sat back down. Voorhees has made his point and then he had made his point. It was obvious that the Senate did not want to hear a prolonged debate over slavery this day. The fact that the President Pro Tem had been happy to move the proceedings on to such a mundane topic was proof of that.

Senator Buckalew went on for some time, describing the financial arrangements being offered by the Society of the Army of the Potomac, the proposed location of the monument, and others bits of minutiae. Sumner only half heard him, not finding the topic particularly interesting. He then felt a hand gently touching his shoulder. Looking up, he saw it was one of the young Senate pages, who leaned down and whispered in his ear.

"Senator Sumner? President McClellan urgently wishes to speak to you. He has sent Mr. Williams to bring you to the White House. He's waiting under the Rotunda."

Sumner knew that the 'Mr. Williams' referred to had to be Seth Williams, the president's private secretary. "Did he say what he wanted to talk to me about?"

"No, sir."

Sumner's lips curled into a frown. What could the president possibly want with him? He got up and walked out of the chamber, noticing that some of the other senators were watching him leave with looks of confusion on their faces. A few moments later, he stepped into the immense space beneath the Capitol dome. Several people were milling about and chattering among themselves, but Sumner's footsteps still echoed loudly. He spotted Williams, who was wearing a gray suit, and walked towards him.

"Senator Sumner," Williams said, trying to sound pleasant. "President McClellan urgently wishes to see you at the White House. If you will come with me, please." He gestured in the direction he expected the senator to go.

"What's the meaning of this, Mr. Williams?" Sumner asked abruptly.

"I'm sorry, Senator?"

"The president sending notes of summons into the Senate Chamber? It's unseemly and highly inappropriate. President McClellan does not have the right to order senators around like stage hands. He's not a Roman emperor, you know."

Williams stared back at Sumner incomprehensibly for a moment. "I'm sorry, sir. I did not mean to be rude. But my instructions are to bring you to the White House."

"And what if I say that I don't want to go?"

Again, the man's face was confused. It was clear that he had never considered the possibility that Sumner might not want to go with him. Sumner began to turn to go back to the Senate chamber when curiosity suddenly got the better of his irritation. He stopped and turned to him again.

"What is it that President McClellan wishes to speak to me about?" Sumner asked.

"He wishes to speak to you about the incident that took place on the border with Canada," William replied. "He wishes to have your views on the matter."

That was surprising. Although he was the Chairman of the Senator Foreign Relations Committee, Sumner had never been consulted by McClellan on anything before. If he was now feeling the need to break that precedent, the situation on the Canadian border had to be serious.

Sumner considered McClellan's embrace of the Fenian movement not only stupid but disgraceful. It could easily raise tensions with the British Empire until one or the other would be pushed into a position where open conflict became unavoidable. Any war with the British Empire would certainly prove disastrous for the United States. That McClellan was taking such a risk merely to maintain political support among Irish citizens was scandalous.

If he went to the White House now, he would have an opportunity to tell that to McClellan's face. That was too good an opportunity to pass up.

"Very well," Sumner said. "Lead on."

Williams led Sumner out of the Capitol and to a waiting carriage. Soon they were clattering through the streets of Washington City. Sumner stared out the window, not really noticing the people crowded on the sidewalks, his mind racing through a multitude of possibilities. The Fenians had stated their aims forthrightly enough, laying out their plans to invade Canada from bases within the United States. It was difficult to see how attacking Canada would help the Fenians achieve their aim of liberating Ireland from British rule. Yet the Fenians would be far from the first political movement to have a loose grasp on reality.

Sumner thought back to his many visits to Britain and the many friends he had there. He had first visited when he was a young lawyer, scarcely distinguishable from any of the other lawyers of Boston. Yet the British had inexplicably fallen in love with him. British nobles and aristocrats had hosted him at their country estates, he had been given special seating in the visitor galleries of the House of Commons and House of Lords, and he had been invited to dinner so often that he had never had to dine in his own lodgings. It had been an awakening for him, for up until that point he had been a shy and bookish man.

In later years, after he had made a name for himself as one of the champions of abolitionism, and especially after he had suffered the brutal attack of Preston Brooks on the floor of the Senate, the British people had lauded him to the high heavens as one of the greatest men of the age. He was far more popular in Britain than he could ever expect to be in the United States.

Sumner thought that a war between the United States and the British Empire would be a calamity scarcely less evil than the late war with the South had been. Whatever he could do to prevent such a tragedy, Sumner would do.

The carriage arrived in front of the White House and slowed to a stop. Blue-coated sentries armed with rifles slowly walked back and forth across the lawn. It was far more security than Sumner thought necessary, far more than Lincoln had ever had even at the height of the war. Sumner was certain that McClellan kept the men around the White House more as a statement of his importance than for any practical purpose.

Sumner was led in through the main entrance. Williams led him to the door outside McClellan's main office and gestured to a deacon's bench.

"Please wait here," he said. "The president will be with you shortly."

Sumner nodded, concealing his irritation that the man had failed to address him as a senator. He sat down and waited. Occasionally, men walked past without acknowledging him, some of them wearing military uniforms. McClellan had a presidential staff of nearly twenty men, almost all of them former staff officers from his days as commander of the Army of the Potomac. When

Lincoln had presided in the White House, he had had only three or four secretaries at any given time.

It was one of innumerable examples of McClellan's insufferable arrogance. He treated Congress almost as if it was a group of subordinates required to do his bidding rather than a separate and equal branch of government. When the Senate had rejected judicial, military or diplomatic appointments sent to them, McClellan had often simply sent the same name again the next day. During excursions out of the White House, McClellan rode about in a grand carriage drawn by four white horses, with an escort of cavalry in dress uniforms accompanying him wherever he went. Many of his fellow Republicans thought the situation laughable, but Sumner could only see an incipient tyranny in McClellan's behavior.

The door to McClellan's office opened and, to Sumner's surprise and disgust, William Porcher Miles emerged. The Confederate Ambassador to the United States was a dapper, handsome man with a very pleasant manner. At their first meeting the previous year, Sumner had instantly seen through his charm and found a man fervently dedicated to the preservation of slavery and white supremacy.

"Ah, Senator Sumner!" Miles said, extending his hand. "What a delightful surprise."

Sumner frowned, ignored the extended hand, and said nothing.

Miles withdrew his hand, but the smile didn't waver from his face. "Charming as always, Senator. What brings you to the White House?"

"The president asked me to come. I assume to discuss this Fenian business."

"Ah, yes. The Fenians. One must admire them, don't you think? Men who are willing to sacrifice everything in pursuit of freedom and independence. They have cheek, those Fenians."

The words irritated Sumner less than the polite tone with which Miles spoke them. "You are the last person in the world who has a right to speak about freedom, Miles," Sumner said firmly. "Your entire life has been devoted to holding millions of human beings in bondage."

"Oh, our peculiar institution? You really must expand the numbers of subjects on which you can converse, Senator. In any event, our black servants live much happier and more agreeable lives than the unwashed masses who toil in the factories of your industrial cities. How many thousands of poor women and children, crowded into those nightmarish tenement buildings, die every year from disease, hunger, and cold? Who are you to say that your way of life is better than mine?" Miles said all of this with a smile.

Sumner sighed and didn't respond, crossing his arms and focusing his attention on a blank spot on the opposite wall.
Miles continued. "I will be having a dinner party at my home next week. Would you like me to send you an invitation?"

"Send it if you wish. I shall decline."

"A pity. Now, if you'll excuse me." Miles bowed politely and strode off down the hallway. Sumner wished he could have washed his hands.

"Is that you, Sumner?" McClellan's voice called from inside the office.

229

"It is, Mr. President," Sumner answered. McClellan might neglect to address Sumner by his proper title, but he was not about to be so inconsiderate in return. He did not like it, but the fact remained that McClellan was the President of the United States. The office, if not the man, was deserving of a certain level of respect.

"Come in."

Sumner entered. It was his first time to be in the room since McClellan had taken office. Glancing around, he saw immediately that the office had completely changed since the days of Lincoln. Back then, it had appeared disheveled and disorganized, with newspapers and official documents strewn about everywhere. Lincoln had rarely sat at the desk itself, instead lounging languidly on a sofa against one of the walls. Ash trays filled with the remnants of William's Seward's cigars were on every flat surface. Sumner had often been at a loss to explain how Lincoln got anything done.

With McClellan, the contrast could not have been more striking. Everything was organized with military precision. The papers were piled meticulously, their sides at perfect right angles to the edges of the desk. There was not an ink pot or an oil lamp out of place. Everything had been dusted very recently and there was not a speck of trash on the floor. Somehow, though, the office seemed much less animated and alive than it had been when Lincoln was president.

With distaste, Sumner saw an outsized painting of McClellan himself filling up a large portion of one wall. It depicted the general on horseback, striking a Napoleonic pose, leading his men at the Battle of Antietam in 1862. Sumner knew perfectly well that McClellan had stayed far to the rear for the duration of the battle. Nor had the battle really been a victory, despite McClellan's earnest efforts to portray it as such.

Sumner recalled a line from Shakespeare.

Who knows himself a braggart,
Let him fear this, for it will come to pass,
That every braggart shall be found an ass.

"Take a seat, Sumner," McClellan said, gesturing to the chair opposite him. "Can I have anything brought for you?"

"No, thank you, Mr. President," Sumner replied as he sat down.

McClellan looked across the desk at him for a moment. He knew what he thought about McClellan, but he wondered what McClellan thought about him. It was well known that McClellan despised abolitionists, blaming them for the rupture of the Union, and Sumner was one of the most recognizable abolitionists in the country. He could assume, therefore, that McClellan had no love for him.

"You know the details of the incident on the Canadian border?" McClellan asked.

"I have read the newspaper accounts, Mr. President. What remains unclear to me is how the Fenian band was able to cross into Canada from our territory in the first place."

230

"Our army units along the border have orders not to permit the Fenians to cross the border," McClellan responded. "Apparently this band slipped through the cordon."

Sumner nodded. He wasn't sure if McClellan was being truthful or not about the orders given to the army. If the president was serious about stopping the Fenians, why had the army not been ordered to take control of their camps and disarm and disperse the men? It would have made no sense for them to allow the Fenians to arm and train their units on American territory if they seriously intended to prevent their crossing of the border.

"Why not have the army disarm the Fenian bands before they cross the border, Mr. President?"

McClellan shook his head. "Our policy is to permit them to train and arm themselves. Their quarrel with the British Empire is not our quarrel, but they have as much right to organize on our soil as anyone else."

"With respect, Mr. President, such an interpretation does not correspond with international law. Allowing a force intending to engage in military action against the British Empire to arm, train, recruit, and organize itself does, in fact, constitute a hostile act by the United States against the British Empire. It violates treaties between our two nations, going back to the Treaty of Ghent in 1814."

"I do not agree," McClellan said with irritation.

"It is not a subjective matter, Mr. President. The law is the law."

McClellan frowned and shook his head, as though Sumner had made a simple mathematical error. It was clear to Sumner that he was not used to being contradicted and did not quite know how to respond. In any case, Sumner was quite confident he knew more of the law than anyone else in America and infinitely more than the buffoon sitting across from him.

"I understand that you made many friends in England during your visits there," McClellan said. "Is that correct?"

"I have many friends and acquaintances in England, yes."

"In influential circles?"

"I suppose you could say that," Sumner replied. He did not like where the conversation was going.

"I do not like imposing on you, Sumner, but could you perhaps write these men, or send them telegrams, advising them that any retaliation by the British in response to this Fenian raid should not be directed against the United States. To do so would be an act of war."

"It seems to me that sending such a warning would itself appear provocative."

"That is why I am asking you to do it through your personal acquaintances, so as to avoid the necessity of a direct communication between our two governments. If the Secretary of State were to dispatch such a message, it would have the appearance of an ultimatum."

For the first time, Sumner thought, McClellan had made a decent point. Still, he would not allow himself to be exploited for the purposes of McClellan's foolhardy and self-serving diplomacy.

"Mr. President, if you sincerely wish to avoid war with Britain, you must resolve to take direct action against the Fenians."

"I have already explained to you why we cannot do that."

231

"With respect, Mr. President, you did not. You gave excuses. You could act against them this very hour if you so wished. Call in one of your secretaries and dictate an order to the commanding general of our forces along the Canadian border directing him to immediately disarm and disperse the Fenian bands."

"Your tone is not acceptable," McClellan said sternly. "I am the President of the United States."

Sumner was not intimidated, but restrained his urge to respond with the derision McClellan's petty comment deserved. "Mr. President, have you considered the dangers to our nation if war were to break out on account of this Fenian nonsense?"

"I know far more of war than you do, I must say. And of course I have considered it."

"I may not be a military man such as yourself, Mr. President. But I am well aware that the British forces in Canada have been strongly reinforced and that they are making great strides in training their militia. Moreover, our fleet is no match for the Royal Navy. If war were to break out, we might find ourselves stymied in Canada and subjected to a naval blockade. The people are in no mood for another failed war."

"The last war was a failure only on account of a president who refused to listen to my advice," McClellan said quickly, pointing his finger across the desk. "Had Lincoln done as I suggested, the war would have been won in 1862 and the Confederacy would not exist today."

Sumner doubted that very much, but decided not to say so. "That may be, Mr. President. But like it or not, here we are."

"Quite so. Now, will you help me or not?"

"I am uncomfortable using my personal friendships in such a capacity, Mr. President."

"You did so for Mr. Lincoln, did you not? During the Trent Affair?"

Sumner frowned, irritated that McClellan knew of that. When the Trent Affair had brought America and Britain to the brink of war in 1861, Sumner had indeed made contact with influential friends in England to help foster a peaceful resolution. Lincoln had later told him that his intervention had been critical to preventing war from breaking out.

"This situation is different from the Trent Affair, Mr. President. I would be willing to use my personal contacts to reduce the possibility of conflict. But what you are asking me to do, in delivering this stark warning, would seem more likely to increase tensions than anything else. It would make a conflict more likely, not less."

"I brought you here to ask for your help, Sumner. Are you going to help your president or not?"

Sumner stood from his chair and stared solemnly down at McClellan. "No, Mr. President. I am sorry, but I can be of no assistance to you in this matter. Our enemy is the Confederacy, not Britain. I can only advise you to disarm and disperse these Fenians bands and turn your attention to the Confederacy."

A look of confusion crossed McClellan's face. "We are at peace with the Confederacy."

Sumner shook his head. "Make no mistake, Mr. President. The Treaty of Toronto is nothing but a temporary truce. We can have no true peace with the

Confederacy. Between the North and South there is an irrepressible conflict, a struggle between two opposing civilizations. Another war with them is inevitable."

He thought of Charles Russell Lowell, still in Boston preparing for whatever fate destiny had in store for him. Part of Sumner wished he could have gone with him, to share in the danger. Yet he also knew that he would be more useful to the cause by remaining in Washington City.

Sumner asked himself whether he was being hypocritical. He condemned the Fenians for waging war on Britain from the safety of United States territory. Was he not doing precisely the same thing by buying weapons and shipping them to rebel slaves in the Confederacy?

The difference was that Britain was a civilized society which had long ago abolished slavery and enforced the ban on the transatlantic slave trade with its unmatched naval power. It was the birthplace of modern democracy and the world's greatest fountain of science and literature. The Confederacy, by contrast, had no redeeming qualities and did not deserve to survive. There could be no ethical dilemma in contributing to its destruction.

McClellan was talking. "I was elected to bring peace between North and South. It is my duty to maintain that peace. Your talk of an irrepressible conflict makes no sense to me. There is no reason we cannot live side-by-side as peaceful neighbors."

Sumner felt more disgusted by McClellan than he had in some time. The President was willing to remain at peace with the Confederacy, and risk war with the British Empire, because he calculated that it was to his best political advantage. Taking a soft line on the Confederacy satisfied the immigrant communities in the big cities and western farms, who did not want to compete with freed slaves for jobs. Supporting the Fenians secured the Democratic loyalty of the Irish community, giving the Democrats the ability to compete in New England as well. It made perfect political sense, but that made it no less immoral.

As important as the developing Fenian Crisis was, however, Sumner now realized that he had not given it nearly as much attention as it deserved. He had been so focused on slavery and the Confederacy that he had not fully seen the opportunity being presented to him until this moment. By asking such a favor of him, McClellan had revealed how important the Fenian business was to him. Properly used, it was a weapon with which he could strike at the McClellan administration, making its reelection less likely the following year.

Sumner made a decision at that moment. "It is my duty to inform you, Mr. President, that the Senate Foreign Relations Committee will be holding hearings on this Fenian business."

McClellan's face darkened. "That would not be a good idea, Sumner."

"Good idea or not, I feel the safety of the republic requires it."

The president rose to his feet, staring firmly into Sumner's eyes. "I will block any such action."

Sumner had to restrain the urge to laugh. "How? I think you need to reread the Constitution, Mr. President. You have no control over the Senate. The Republican Party maintains its majority there. I am the chairman of the

Foreign Relations Committee. If I choose for hearings to be held on the Fenians, hearings shall be held on the Fenians. There is nothing that you can do about it."

McClellan said nothing. It was not out of spite, Sumner could see, but because he was at a loss as to how to respond. He was a little man with a little mind. It saddened Sumner to think that the same office which had once been held by men such as George Washington, John Adams and his friend Abraham Lincoln was now in the hands of such an utter nonentity.

"I'll show myself out, Mr. President."

Sumner rose from the chair and calmly left the room.

May 28, Evening
London, England

Victoria Station was bustling with energy and excitement. Thousands of people were walking to and fro, trains were pulling in or out on different tracks, station employees were constantly changing signs announcing arrival and departure times, and the noise of the steam whistles mingled with talking and shouting so as to create an enormous echoing cacophony. It all reminded Slidell of a human beehive.

The British were so unlike the French, Slidell thought. They were much louder, for one thing. They also seemed in much more of a hurry. It was not his first visit to England, yet he never failed to be surprised at the sudden change that seemed to take place the moment he stepped off the ferry at Dover and his feet touched British soil. It was like stepping through a door and discovering that one had passed from a dining room into a factory.

Slidell's valet, a fine French fellow named Michel, went to fetch the hansom cab. The luggage had already been sent ahead to the Langham Hotel. For a few minutes, Slidell simply stood and watched the mass of humanity flow around him, fascinated and appalled at the same time.

His trip had begun when he departed Paris on May 26, taking the train to Calais. The crossing of the ferry the following day had been atrocious on account of the weather, with the boat being constantly tossed back and forth by the waves, yet it arrived in Dover in one piece. He spent the following morning in Canterbury, where he took the time to tour the town's famous cathedral, and finally boarded the afternoon train to London. Now, as the sun began to disappear behind the western horizon, he had finally arrived in the great city.

Michel returned and guided him to the hansom cab. A few minutes later, they were rolling through the streets of London, inarguably the greatest metropolis in the world. The streets were crowded with horses, trollies, carriages, and hansom cabs like that in which he travelled. As he looked out at the people crowding the sidewalks and the vast buildings they passed by, Slidell reflected that any city in the Confederacy would simply be swallowed up by London. His own New Orleans was the largest city in the Confederacy, with a bit more than one hundred thousand residents. London, by contrast, had more than three million people living within its boundaries. New Orleans would be smaller than one of London's outlying neighborhoods.

Paris and London were two very different cities. If Paris was exquisite and grand, London was immense and imposing. The architecture of Paris was feminine and graceful, while that of London was more masculine and designed to impress. Each was beautiful in its own way, but London was a much more utilitarian place, with far fewer of the fountains and statues that one found in Paris. Every person he saw seemed utterly preoccupied with his own business. Londoners appeared so insular that it was hard to imagine that the city was the capital of a great empire, whose power stretched from Canada to India and dwarfed that of any other nation in the world.

Slidell reflected on that thought for a moment. For all his pride in the Confederacy and love for France, there was no denying that, when it came to actual power, no one could compete with the British Empire. It truly bestrode the world like a colossus. The mighty warships of the Royal Navy steamed in every corner of the world's oceans. If they so choose, they could sink the fleet of any other nation in a single afternoon.

Even if the Empire had had no warships, it would still have dominated the world on account of its financial power. Having been the first nation to industrialize and embrace free trade, the British economy had enjoyed an extended boom for much of the post-Napoleonic era. All over Britain, smoke rose from countless factories. British manufactured goods had flowed out of Liverpool, Glasgow, and other ports. Even in nations outside of the British Empire, such as Argentina and Siam, railroads and ports were being built with British money and British equipment. Where British investment had gone, British influence had inevitably followed.

Slidell wondered if the same thing was already happening to the Confederacy, as British bankers were financing the rebuilding of many of the South's ravaged railroads. Her Majesty's Government had already sent gunboats to enforce the collection of unpaid debts from nations that had the temerity to default. Would Royal Navy cruisers steam over the horizon outside of Charleston or Norfolk someday? Having struggled so hard to achieve its independence from the Union, might the South find itself in thrall to the might of the British Empire?

The cab headed northeast for a short distance, coming upon the House of Parliament and Westminster Abbey. Though constructed centuries apart, the architecture of each magnificent building bore clear resemblances to each other, seemingly representing the long continuity of English history. In previous visits, he had attended services at Westminster Abbey and had observed sessions of Parliament. Perhaps he would have the chance to do so again on this trip.

They turned north, passing by Charing Cross. Slidell could see, off to the east, the great dome of St. Paul's Cathedral rising majestically above the rest of the city. It looked very much like the Capitol Building in Washington City, which wasn't a surprise as it had served as a model for the latter building. He thought the cathedral, designed and built by the great Sir Christopher Wren, was quite beautiful.

They soon arrived at the Langham Hotel. Slidell stepped off onto the sidewalk with Michel's assistance. He looked up at the grand building. It had only opened two years earlier, yet was already being described at the greatest and most luxurious hotel in the city. He had stayed in the hotel twice before and had enjoyed his visit on both occasions. Weary from travel, Slidell was anxious to get to his room and slip into the bed.

The ornate lobby was illuminated by dozens of gas lamps. Perhaps two dozen people were scattered about, but it was not loud. As Michel spoke quietly to the clerk at the front desk, a confused look crossed his face. He walked back to Slidell.

"I am to tell you, sir, that someone is waiting for you in the dining room."

"Did they say who?"

"They would only tell me that he is a man of importance, sir."

Slidell thought for a moment. "Very well. See to the luggage. I shall be up presently."

He left Michel and strolled to the dining room. Like the lobby, gas lamps along the wall filled the room with a soft light, which was complimented by candles on every table. Perhaps two dozen well-dressed people were there, speaking quietly at the tables or at the bar along the far wall. Most of the tables were empty, as the proper time for dinner had been some hours earlier. A piano player was filling the space with subdued music.

A waiter led him to a particular table. At it sat a man Slidell immediately recognized. It was Benjamin Disraeli, Prime Minister of the United Kingdom.

Slidell tried not to look surprised, which would have been unbecoming of a diplomat. In truth, though, he was astounded. He had not expected his visit to England to involve much in the way of intrigue, assuming that he would simply coddle Minister Haynes through his troubles, perhaps have a perfunctory meeting with Disraeli that wouldn't last more than twenty minutes, and then return to Paris.

Disraeli, though, obviously had other plans. The prime minister had gone to the trouble to learn Slidell's travel plans and arrange to be at the hotel when he arrived. Minister Haynes could not possibly be aware of this, for he would have taken great offense at not being present himself. Disraeli wanted to discuss something important with Slidell and he was eager to find out what it was.

Disraeli rose from his seat when he saw Slidell approach and extended his hand.

"Minister Slidell," he said warmly as they shook hands. "It is good to see you again."

"Thank you, Mr. Disraeli," Slidell replied. "And may I take this opportunity to congratulate you on your recent elevation to the prime minister's office."

Disraeli smiled and bowed his head as he resumed his seat. In January, the British government had experienced a shakeup in the wake of the failure of its Reform Act, which had been designed to expand the voting franchise to more of the working class. The previous prime minister, the Earl of Derby, had resigned. Disraeli, who as Chancellor of the Exchequer had been the true power in the government anyway, had succeeded him. Slidell believed the rumors which asserted that Disraeli had undermined passage of the Reform Act himself, since its passage would have been damaging to the Conservative Party. Very cleverly, however, he had adopted a public position in opposition to slavery in the Confederacy, Brazil, and East Africa, somewhat mollifying the liberal forces in the country.

Slidell knew he was about to deal with a master of the political game. Yet Disraeli didn't look the part of a national leader. He was a small man, rather sickly looking, with thinning hair and a head too large for his body. Slidell saw Semitic features in Disraeli's face, for the prime minister was Jewish by birth. Like Slidell's friend Judah Benjamin, Disraeli had overcome intense anti-Semitism to make his way in the world. Unlike Benjamin, though, Disraeli had taken the route of baptism and at least nominal conversion to Christianity.

"Have a drink, Slidell," Disraeli said as a waiter approached. "The bar here at the Langham is the best in the world, they say."

"Champagne, please," Slidell said to the waiter.

"For me as well," Disraeli said. The waiter hurried off.

"I must say that this is an unexpected pleasure. It is not often that I am surprised these days."

"I apologize for any appearance of impropriety," Disraeli said. "I wanted to discuss certain matters of importance to both our nations and I admit that I wanted to do so without Minister Haynes present. I know it is not proper, given that Haynes is the accredited representative of your nation to Her Majesty's government. But you are the more experienced diplomat and, given your personal friendship with Secretary Benjamin, have a more direct line to the administration in Richmond."

Slidell nodded. He understood exactly what Disraeli meant. The prime minister wanted to talk Slidell rather than Haynes because he felt he was worth talking to and that Haynes was not. It was as simple as that.

The waiter returned with two glasses and a bottle of champagne. "Taittinger, gentlemen?"

"That will be fine," Disraeli said, answering for them both. The waiter poured the two glasses, left the bottle on the table, and withdrew.

Slidell sipped his champagne and sat back in his chair. "I came to England in response to Frederick Douglass's speaking tour, but I gather that this is not the matter you wish to discuss."

The British prime minister waved his hand dismissively. "This won't be the first speaking tour he has done of the kingdom, nor do I expect it will be the last. There's nothing I can do about it, you understand. He's breaking no law by speaking out against slavery in your country. I cannot have him arrested, nor would I even if I could. It wouldn't be proper. Besides, the Queen is fond of him."

"I certainly don't expect the British government to take any official action on our behalf. My intention was to work with Minister Haynes on more mundane measures. Placing some articles critical of Douglass in the newspapers, organizing counter demonstrations, that sort of thing."

"He needs the help?" Disraeli asked with slightly raised eyebrows.

Slidell took a sip of his champagne. "Yes, I'm afraid he does."

Disraeli smiled. "Well, I wish you success. Douglass is the most persuasive of the speakers the American abolitionists send across the Atlantic every now and then. Having been a slave himself, he can speak to its unsavory aspects more compellingly that anyone else. Members of Parliament will ask for his blessing, for much of the voting public likes him very much. But Douglass's speaking tour is not what I wanted to discuss."

"So what exactly is it that you wish to discuss?"

"This unpleasant Fenian business."

"Is that so?" Slidell asked, sipping his champagne again. "Well, what of it? The position of the Confederate government is that the matter is no concern of ours, being a dispute between the United States and the British Empire."

Disraeli chuckled slightly and shook his head. "Your Confederacy is in its infancy. But then, even the United States is but a child compared to the ancient states of Europe. Do you really think that if your nearest neighbor becomes embroiled in a war, it will be no concern of yours? Was last year's war between Prussia and Austria no concern of Russia? Or France? Or Britain? You Confederates have won your independence. Congratulations. But I fear it will be a long time before you truly understand what independence means. If you think you can remain aloof from the rest of the world, you will be bitterly disappointed."

Slidell frowned, not wanting to be lectured by Disraeli. Inwardly, he wondered if the prime minister was correct. He knew that much of the Southern aristocracy wanted nothing more than to seal the Confederacy off from the rest of the world, treating it as nothing but a market for its exports of cotton, tobacco, and sugar. In this fantasy, the elite members of Southern society could enjoy their plantation lifestyle, profiting from the labor of their slaves and sipping their mint juleps amid their magnolia trees, without caring in the slightest what the rest of the world thought. As Disraeli suggested, if the people of the South thought that this vision would actually be their reality, they would eventually get a rude awakening. As an independent nation, the Confederacy was going to be part of the world, whether it wanted to be or not.

"Perhaps," Slidell said. "Perhaps not. But let us talk in specifics. What does the Fenian business have to do with the Confederacy? If I may be frank, Prime Minister, what is it that you want from us?"

"First, tell me if you agree with my assessment of the political situation in the United States. The McClellan administration depends largely upon the support of the Irish immigrant vote in the large cities. There is also a latent antipathy to England in much of the American population, going back to the days when you separated from us. This means McClellan must whip up antagonism towards Great Britain, up to and including giving tacit support to these Fenian terrorists who wish to cross the border into Canada in order to wrest that colony from the British Empire."

"I don't disagree," Slidell said.

Disraeli sighed. "Her Majesty's Government does not think much of President McClellan's judgement. We don't think he wants war, but we fear he may place himself in a position from which he cannot retreat. At least not without losing the political support of that bloc of voters most responsible for placing him in his office. If he does that, war might become unavoidable."

"Why does that worry you?" Slidell asked. "The Royal Navy could destroy the United States Navy in a matter of days, then blockade their ports until they are forced to seek terms. Even if they did manage to conquer Canada in the meantime, you could simply require them to give it back to you at the negotiating table."

Disraeli shook his head. "Going to war with the United States would not be the same as going to war with the King of Abyssinia or with some godforsaken Mohammedan tribe on the Northwest Frontier. I have no doubt we would win the war. How could it be otherwise? But it would be messy and expensive. Besides, history proves that once the dogs are war are unleashed, it's not easy to restrain them. No, we feel it is very important to avoid war with the United States if at all possible."

Slidell chuckled and nodded. The political leaders of the South had certainly found that out over the previous decade. No one who voted to break with the Union at the various secession conventions in 1860 and 1861 could have imagined the blood that was going to be spilled over the ensuing four years.

Disraeli leaned forward. "We want to make McClellan reconsider his position. There are various ways of accomplishing this, and we shall be employing all of them. But what I would like you to pass along to President Davis is the proposal that your government make a statement of support for the position of Her Majesty's government in this little Fenian dispute of ours. If the United States is made to think that the Confederacy will back the British in any open conflict, they might think twice before committing to war. After all, how many troops could the United States commit to the Canadian frontier if it knew it had to watch its back in Maryland and Kentucky, eh?"

"A simple statement of support for the British position is hardly the same as threatening intervention on your side," Slidell said.

"Perhaps not, but McClellan is the sort of man who might take it as such."

"Such a course of action would make it more likely that the Confederacy would be dragged into a war if one were to break out," Slidell replied. "My country, to be honest, is in no position to fight another war and won't be for a very long time."

Disraeli took a sip of his champagne. "Of course. I understand your reservations. In your place, I might also hesitate. We are, of course, prepared to sweeten the deal."

"In what way?" Slidell asked the question with skepticism in his voice. He did not like the way the conversation was going. A pragmatist, Slidell believed that the Confederacy must maintain its freedom of action as much as possible.

"I could talk to my friends at the Rothschild and Barings banks and perhaps persuade them to extend another loan to your government. If they were agreeable, I might even get them to agree to accept a postponement on the current payments or even reduce the interest rates they currently require you to pay."

Slidell nodded, having expected something along those lines. The bait Disraeli was dangling before him was tempting, indeed. Government debt was crushing the life out of the Confederacy and greatly damaging the credibility of the Davis administration. If Disraeli did what he proposed, it could be a tremendous weight off the shoulders of the South.

"How would you like this done?" Slidell asked.

"I think bringing the United States minister in Richmond in to see the president would suffice. And we would like for a few of our warships to pay a courtesy call in one of your ports. Charleston, for instance."

"That would not be popular among your own voters," Slidell pointed out.

Disraeli shrugged. "They will have forgotten by the time of the next election."

Slidell considered this. "I will forward your request to the president. I cannot tell you whether or not he will agree." His mind raced as he spoke. Disraeli's proposal might potentially upend all of Slidell's carefully arranged diplomatic efforts. Was it a threat to the treaty negotiations with France? Was it an astounding opportunity that should be seized? He wasn't immediately sure.

"Well, please let me know what President Davis has to say about it," Disraeli commented. "If you ask me, it's a small price to pay for such compensation. A few words to a diplomat, a visit from a couple of warships, and your fiscal problems are significantly eased."

"I don't deny the generosity of your offer. But I am only a messenger. I cannot act without the approval of President Davis."

"Of course, and I hope to hear of his agreement soon. In the meantime, I hope you enjoy your time in England. I would like to extend an invitation to you to be my guest at a session of the House of Commons."

Slidell's eyebrows perked up in genuine interest. "That would be delightful."

"In that case, I shall bid you good night." Disraeli rose from his seat, prompting Slidell to do the same. The two men shook hands and, with a smile and a nod, Disraeli took his leave.

Slidell sat back down. There was still considerable champagne in the bottle and he refilled his glass. There was no hurry to get to his bedroom and he was enjoying the ambiance of the dining room. He sat quietly in his chair for more than half an hour, reflecting carefully on his conversation with Disraeli. He saw his goal as clear as crystal. Yet he saw that the path towards that goal was strewn with dangers. If he failed, he might lose everything.

Michel eventually found him and gently prodded him to retire for the evening. With a certain reluctance, he rose from his table and walked back to the hotel lobby. He then had the fascinating experience of using a hydraulic lift to travel to the third floor. Slidell had heard about this new invention and did not attempt to disguise his amazement. At his old age, he greatly disliked climbing up and down staircases. He wished that the new contraption could be installed in every building he frequented, though he knew how expensive it was. Reflecting on how long it would be before a hydraulic lift would be seen in the Confederacy, he sighed deeply.

Ten minutes later, he was soundly and gratefully asleep in his bed.

May 30, Night
Bridgewater, Massachusetts

"You seem quiet, my dear," Josephine said. "Is something wrong?"

Across the table, Lowell looked up from his plate. Mattie had prepared a wonderful boiled chicken in oyster sauce, one of his favorite dishes, with a German white wine to go along with it. Yet he found it completely unappetizing. The last thing on his mind was food, no matter how good it might be. He had decided that tonight would be the night he would tell his wife his intentions.

"I'm sorry, Effie," Lowell replied.

"You've barely touched your food. I thought you liked this dish."

"I do. I'm afraid my appetite isn't very good this evening."

Her eyes probed him carefully. "It's not something at work is it?"

"No."

"But it is something."

He waited a moment before replying. "Yes, my dear."

Josephine didn't respond right away, instead going back to the chicken and wine for a few moments. She had always been patient with him. Not for the first time, Lowell felt that he was unworthy of her. How could she have married a man who was so full of doubts? Yet he knew she loved him. It was the greatest honor of his life.

She was so beautiful. He had thought so the moment he first saw her, many years ago. There might be more beautiful women in the world, but if so he had never seen them, and he had seen much of the world. He wondered if he was simply seeing her as so lovely because he knew that, upon his departure, he might never see her again.

"Does this have anything to do with your cryptic dinner with Senator Sumner last month? And the recent meetings that you have so reluctant to speak of?"

"Yes, it does."

"Well, let's have it, then."

Lowell laid it all out for her. He gave a broad outline, not revealing too many of the details. Aside from Senator Sumner, whose involvement she had already guessed, he used no names. Better for her not to know, he thought.

Through it all, her face betrayed nothing. Judging from her expression, he might as well have been describing a normal day at the ironworks. She even continued to eat and sip her wine as he talked. As he finished, though, she set down her silverware and sat back in her seat, her arms crossed in front of her. Gradually, her face took on the air of a very irritated woman.

"And you agreed to all this without once asking me my opinion?"

"I did," he admitted.

"Why?"

He thought on his words before he responded. "I suppose I was afraid that you would tell me not to do it. And then I would have to choose between betraying my wife and betraying my ideals."

"We share the same ideals, Charles."

"I know. But this is different."

"How? I watched my brother go off to fight the slave power and he died at Fort Wagner. You went off to fight, too. How is this different? In my eyes, you're just going off to fight again."

"The war is over. What I will be doing is against the law."

"If you are caught."

"Yes, if I am caught."

She paused for a moment, thinking hard. "I am sure you are planning for every eventuality. You wouldn't be you if you weren't."

"I am doing my best."

"And what if you are apprehended in the Confederacy?"

241

"I'd be put on trial for inciting servile insurrection."

"Death?"

"Yes."

She took a deep breath. "No possibility of acquittal?"

"The Southerners do not take kindly to men who try to raise their slaves up in revolt. Look how quickly they disposed of old John Brown."

She had pursed her lips and nodded, not surprised by the answer. "Are you asking for my permission?" she asked.

"If you do not want me to go, I will not go." He surprised himself by saying these words, which came out automatically. He had earlier pledged that he would go anyway, even if she opposed it. Yet seeing her face and looking in her eyes as they spoke of it, his courage lapsed.

"But you want to go."

He had paused before answering. "It's not a matter of wanting to or not."

"You have already told Senator Sumner that you will go?"

"Yes, I have."

"Why didn't you discuss it with me first? I am your wife, Charles." There was reproach in her voice.

"As I said, my love, if you do not want me to go, I will not go. I can send a message to the others this very hour telling him that I shall not be involved with the scheme."

Josephine said nothing in response, simply staring at him across the dinner table. At that point, Mattie brought in their dessert for the evening. It was a sponge cake filled with vanilla custard and topped with chocolate, a recipe that both Charles and Josephine enjoyed very much. On this night, however, they scarcely touched it. Their collective appetite had simply vanished. A bottle of champagne brought out to compliment the dessert had similarly been ignored.

"You have two children, Charles," Josephine said.

"I know."

"And you can just say that and expect it to be all right? What if you don't come back from this? The Confederates will kill you if they catch you. Am I to raise two children without the support of a husband?"

"How many men died in the war, Effie? How many of them left behind wives and children when they set off to fight against slavery?"

"Yet God spared you!" Josephine said urgently. "No bullet touched you during the war! It wasn't a mistake, Charles!"

"Perhaps God spared me for this very purpose."

Those words caused yet another long silence. Lowell finally begun to sip at his champagne a bit, waiting quietly as his wife mulled everything over in her mind. His heart was in his throat and he found himself wondering if he would have the courage to go against her wishes. For that matter, even if she said yes, the pleading look in her eyes might cause his resolve to falter.

"No, no," she finally said, smiling faintly. "You must go, Charles. It's not your destiny to grow old running an iron foundry in New England. No, you're right. We are both committed to the abolition of slavery. You must do this. You could no more decline to take this mission than you could disown me and the children."

"Thank you, love."

She waited a moment before replying. "If you didn't go, you wouldn't be Charles Russell Lowell."

CHAPTER SEVEN

June 1, Afternoon
Granbury County Courthouse, Waco, Texas

McFadden looked out over the square in front of the courthouse. It was the same place where, not many weeks earlier, the land auction had taken place. As before, the square was crowded with people. This time, to his amazement, they had come to see him.

Standing just to his left on the courthouse steps was Annie, holding little Thaddeus in her arms. McFadden knew little about political campaigning, but it seemed like a good idea to let the voters see that he was a dedicated family man. To his right stood Collett.

"Better turnout that at the church," Annie said to both of them. "I'd say there's a few hundred people out there."

"Yes, but how many of them are supporters and how many are just bored?" Collett answered.

"I guess we'll find out when we start talking," McFadden replied. He pulled out his pocket watch and saw that it was about ten minutes to noon, which was when they had told everyone they would speak. The Texas sun was already beating down on them through a sky utterly devoid of clouds. It was going to be a very hot day. From his experience, McFadden was already assuming it was going to be a scorching summer.

McFadden thought back to the events of the past month, since he, Collett, and their friends had made the decision to challenge Roden and his allies at the polls. As far as he could tell, things were going well. Flynn's Alehouse had become the de facto campaign headquarters. Lots of people had dropped by to ask about what was happening and many had offered to help in any way they could.

He had started coming into town every other day to talk with his friends about the campaign. Flynn had offered to let him stay at his place every now and then in order to spare him the trouble of riding back to the ranch each night. McFadden appreciated the offer, but felt it necessary to stay on the ranch. Roden, after all, had threatened his family and he refused to leave them alone at night.

Annie considered his concern touching but unnecessary. When they had arrived on the ranch in 1865, he had taught her how to use firearms. This had not only been for the obvious purpose of killing coyotes and hunting game, but for also for self-defense. The Comanches had been pushed to the west during a militia campaign in 1866, in which McFadden had participated, but there was always the chance that a raiding party might swoop in. Rather to his surprise, she had quickly taken to it and proven to be an excellent shot. If Roden's men showed up at the ranch to hassle his wife, McFadden expected them to find a very unpleasant surprise.

McFadden was also comforted by the fact that fellow veterans of the 7th Texas and other regiments were making a point to pass by his ranch every now and then to make sure everyone there was safe. The men who had stood together against Yankee rifles and artillery during the war were standing together still.

As far as the campaign itself, McFadden admitted that he and Collett were not entirely sure what they were doing. They had filed the necessary forms with the county clerk's office to declare themselves candidates in the upcoming election, McFadden for the state legislative seat and Collett for the county judge seat. Other friends and fellow veterans had become nominees for the other county offices. It had all gone very smoothly, to McFadden's thinking. They had begun raising money, mostly in small donations from fellow veterans, and had talked of taking out ads in the local Waco newspaper. McFadden felt that there was a lot more that they should be doing, but he was not sure exactly what it was. His utter lack of political experience, he feared, would prove a major problem.

Another thing that troubled him was the complete absence of any kind of response from Judge Roden. He had not come by the ranch again, nor had he sent any of the angry or threatening messages that McFadden had expected. Those people who had seen Roden reported that he seemed to be acting like his usual, arrogant self. McFadden had confirmed with the court that Roden was an official candidate for the state legislature, but the man did not seem to be actively campaigning at all.

"Getting on towards twelve o'clock," Collett said. "You want to go first or should I?"

"You can go first if you want to," McFadden replied.

"It's all the same to me," Collett said.

"I really don't mind."

Annie looked at them both sternly. "Well, one of you has to be the first to speak!" she said urgently. "I don't want my boys looking like idiots in front of the whole county!"

The conversation was cut short as a rather gruff-looking man began ascending the steps of the courthouse. McFadden recognized him as James Hegel, a deputy sheriff of Granbury County.

"Mr. McFadden! Mr. Collett!" he called. "I'm sorry, but you can't be here."

"Can't be here?" McFadden asked. "What do you mean?"

Hegel jabbed a finger at the growing crowd in front of the courthouse. "This is an illegal assembly!" He turned and faced the crowd. "You all go home now!" he shouted. His voice was filled with condescension.

"We filed for a permit," McFadden protested. "We have a right to be here!"

Hegel shrugged. "Your permit must have gotten lost in the mail."

"I didn't mail it! I handed it in to the court clerk myself!"

"Must have gotten lost, then. In any case, you have no right to be here, and neither do these people. Either they disperse or I will have to call in the other deputies to send them away."

"Is this the way it's going to be, Hegel?" Collett said sarcastically. "Roden says jump and you ask how high?"

"You know damn well that we have every right to be here," McFadden said. He turned and looked at the crowd, which was watching carefully. He gathered confidence from the looks on the faces of the people and turned back to Hegel. "We're not going anywhere."

"Let them speak!" someone in the crowd shouted. This was echoed by several hollers of agreement. There was unruly muttering beneath the yelling, which sounded ominous to McFadden even though it was in his own support. He had always found the underlying energy of a crowd of undisciplined people unsettling.

"All of you go home!" Hegel shouted. McFadden sensed a mounting panic in the man's voice. It suddenly became apparent to him that Hegel had not thought the situation through before he had approached them. McFadden glanced about at the nearby windows, wondering if Roden was watching.

He did not see the county judge anywhere, but his eyes landed upon a man towards the back of the crowd. He recognized him immediately as the same man who had come to watch the church meeting. He was smoking a long cigar, watching everything with a bored expression. McFadden couldn't shake the impression that the man was a hunter waiting for a deer to pass by.

Hegel followed his gaze and saw whom McFadden was looking at. His face became tensed by fear. At that moment, a grizzled older man with a peg-leg began clambering up the steps. He had a look of fury on his face. Reaching the cluster of men, he jabbed his fingers into Hegel's chest.

"See here, Mr. Deputy Sheriff," he said sarcastically. "You better let these men say their say or you'll have a couple dozen men of Hood's Brigade knock you flat on your ass and haul you out of here. You hear me, boy?"

Hegel's face became angry. He whipped his sheriff's badge from his pocket. "You're under arrest!" he shouted.

These words brought a momentary silence to the crowd. The peg-legged veteran laughed in his face. He cast a glance back into the crowd. "Under arrest, am I? What do you think of that, boys?"

"No!" roared several of the men in the crowd. McFadden could tell that they were former soldiers like himself. He could see anger in their faces and sensed the coming of violence. He did not like the disrespect for the law shown by the peg-legged veteran, but he could say nothing without appearing to side with Hegel. If the deputy sheriff tried to arrest the man, the other veterans would come to his defense. Most men on the Texas frontier carried knives or guns with them as a matter of course.

McFadden spoke urgently under his breath. "For the love of God, Hegel, get the hell out of here before somebody gets hurt!"

"But he'll-" Hegel stammered. The man looked back out into the crowd, where angry yelling had commenced again. McFadden noticed that his face had gone pale and he saw that the deputy sheriff was looking at the man in the back of the crowd. Without another word, Hegel turned and walked away from the courthouse steps, quickly disappearing around the corner of the building.

A shout of exaltation and victory rose from the crowd. McFadden simultaneously found this uplifting and unsettling. Hegel might have been one of Roden's underlings, but he still represented the rule of law in Granbury County. If his supporters were going to intimidate and threaten a lawman until he did what they wanted him to do, how did that make McFadden's side any better than Roden's?

He looked back at the mysterious man watching from the back of the crowd. He looked irritated but not angry, perhaps more weary than anything else. He kept smoking his cigar and, as McFadden watched, strolled over to a nearby building and leaned against the wall, clearly intending to watch the proceedings until they were over.

He was distracted from his observations when he realized that Collett had started speaking to the crowd. He decided to forget about the enigmatic onlooker and focus on what he was going to say. Unlike McFadden, his friend seemed to have no compunction about the manner in which Hegel had been chased away.

"Friends, you all know me. I'm Major Collett, and this here is Captain McFadden. We both marched with Cleburne and Granbury during the war, just like lots of you fellows out there." There was some cheering from some men in the crowd, but it passed quickly. "With your help, we're going to run Judge Roden out of this county just like we ran that deputy sheriff out of this square!"

There was a louder and more sustained burst of cheering. Collett went on.

"Now, I'm running for county judge. Captain McFadden here is running to be your state representative. Some other fellows we know and like are running for some other offices, too. We want you to look at us as a group, like we're a team playing bat-and-ball together, okay?"

"Why are you running?" shouted an old, hard-looking woman standing near the front of the crowd. She had an angry look on her face. "I been out here since the first white men settled these parts. I've seen lots of young men like you stand up and say that they're going to make things better, but none of you ever do. Glad you fought against the Yankees, boys, but why should I think you'd be any better than Roden or anybody else?"

Collett turned to McFadden, wordlessly suggesting that it might be better for him to answer this question. He stepped forward.

"Ma'am, we're running because people are suffering. Times are hard for everyone in the country and especially out here on the frontier. They don't seem likely to get better anytime soon. Fact is, they might be getting worse. The crops don't do well. The livestock don't do well. Every dollar that we earn seems to be worth less every month. Now, we're all neighbors and we help each other out. That's only natural. God tells us to love our neighbors as ourselves. But what's not natural is when we look to our local sheriffs and judges for help, ask them to do their jobs, only to find that they are not out friends but our enemies. Rather than meet their obligations to the people they are supposed to serve, they take advantage of us, instead! They tax us to the limit and, when we can't pay, they take our land away from us! They're in it for themselves, not us!"

The crowd cheered. Out of the corner of his eye, McFadden could see Collett looking at him with a smile on his face, not perturbed that he had answered the question. He went on.

"We fought against the Yankees because we knew we had to defend our rights. But what good is it to have defended our rights from the Yankees when they are taken away by our own kind? The Yankees aren't going to burn our farms and ranches here in Texas, but what good is that when they are taken away by Judge Roden and his friends, to be made into large estates for the rich folk?"

"Keep going, Jimmy," Collett said beside him. "You're talking like a general to his troops."

"My father came to this country from Scotland because rich folk there cheated him out of his land," McFadden heard himself say. It was as though his words were running ahead of his mind. "I don't want to see the same thing happen here in Texas. And I can promise you that I will do everything I can to stop it!"

The crowd cheered again. McFadden felt himself energized by the people standing before him. He didn't understand the sensation, having never before experienced it. It was like a fine warm whiskey that intoxicated him without leaving him inebriated. Something told him there was a limitless supply. His nervousness had vanished. The cheering of the crowd, the smiles he could see on the faces of the people, seemed to feed something within him and make him stronger.

"In the Old World, there's an aristocracy in every country. Earls, barons, dukes, and kings. They lord it over their peasants, believing that God granted them the right to do it. If Judge Roden and his friends get their way, they'll be lording it over us forever, just as if they were dukes and barons."

McFadden suddenly felt apprehensive, fearing that his words were too highbrow for the simple folk that made up the crowd. He did not want to sound too smart, which he sensed they might find off-putting. To his surprise, though, the crowd greeted his words with sustained applause.

"Do you want some aristocracy lording it over you?" he shouted.

"No!" the crowd roared back.

"Roden treats us like we're his darkie slaves!" someone in the back of the crowd shouted. "No white man in the Confederacy should be treated like he treats us!"

The crowd cheered these words, but they made McFadden suddenly uneasy. For an instant, he remembered a hundred conversations between his parents at the dinner table, when he had been a boy. Having come to Texas from Scotland, in which there had been no slavery, they had had a very different perspective than most of their neighbors, who had immigrated to the land from the Deep South. McFadden's mother had never made a secret of her opposition to slavery, while his father had always counseled that they had to conform to the norms of the society into which they had immigrated.

McFadden didn't think his mother had been wrong, but he had never really troubled himself about the slavery question. As far as he was concerned, its victory in the war meant that the Confederacy was going to deal with slavery in its own time and its own way. The wealth he and Annie had inherited from the Turnbow family meant that they could have afforded to purchase slaves, but they

248

had chosen not to do so. He never would have been able to get his mother's voice out of his head if he had.

On a deeper level, though, McFadden didn't want to own slaves because he was sure he would never feel completely safe if he did. How could he be sure a slave wouldn't cut his throat while he slept? He had read the newspaper accounts of the slave insurrection going on in southern Louisiana. Could any rational person blame the slaves for rebelling? McFadden was quite sure that, had he been a slave, he would have done precisely the same thing.

Now that he was getting involved in politics, McFadden could sense the trap that slavery presented. As a young man, he had watched as unscrupulous politicians forced a war on the people in the name of slavery, even though the vast majority of the men who fought and died had never owned a slave in their lives. He wanted to avoid discussion of slavery in this campaign if he could, especially as there were as yet few slaves on the frontier. If he could have his way, that's exactly how it would remain.

Collett, perhaps sensing his uneasiness, stepped forward and spoke. "You're right, my friend! He does treat us like we're his slaves. But we're not his slaves, are we?"

"No!" the crowd roared again.

"Then we hope you come out in November to vote for us!" Collett shouted. "We're counting on you!"

McFadden applauded with the crowd, happy to let Collett take the stage for the last portion of the speech. He glanced back towards where the heavyset man had been standing, but there was no sign of him.

June 2, Afternoon
Cheval Farm, Southern Louisiana

"Corporal, could you get me a cup of coffee?" Morgan asked. "I have a feeling this is going to take a while."

"Right away, sir," the man said as he scurried off.

Morgan sighed and turned his attention back to the frightened slave sitting in a chair in the middle of the barn, his hands firmly tied with a rope stretched taunt beneath the seat. Philippe Cheval, a farmer who had served in the Louisiana Tigers during the war, had graciously offered the use of his farm for the interrogations, which had now been going on for several hours. It was a time-consuming process and Morgan was becoming bored. Still, if any useful information were extracted from the slaves, it might prove worth the time and effort that were being expended.

Throughout the region, owners of plantations and large farms were reporting occasional and unexplained cases of foodstuffs going missing. Some slave-owners who allowed their chattel to earn their own money by doing extra work were also describing larger-than-normal purchases of potatoes, chickens, and the like by their slaves. Morgan was fairly certain that this missing food was finding its way to Saul and his partisans.

Reinforcements had arrived, so that he now had a full regiment of Kentucky cavalry rather than a mere company. While they had continued their sweeps through the swamps, the Louisiana militia had rounded up dozens of slaves from the plantations and farms which had reported the largest disappearances of food. Now, one by one, they were being brought in from a holding pen just outside the farm to be questioned.

Morgan had set up the large space within the barn with meticulous attention to detail. The slave being questioned sat on a small chair in the middle of the large, empty space. Lining the walls were two dozen Confederate soldiers, each of them chosen specifically by Morgan for their size, strength, and burly expression in order to be as intimidating as possible. They all cradled rifles with bayonets fixed, many also having bowie knives visible in their belts.

To make matters clear, a noose was hanging from one of the ceiling beams not far from the chair in which the slave was sitting.

"Who is Saul?" Morgan demanded.

The slave's eyes were wide with fear. He kept glancing at the soldiers along the walls or the noose dangling above him. Morgan actually felt some sympathy for the poor fellow. Morgan was a supporter of slavery, owned a few slaves himself, and had bought and sold slaves regularly during his business career before the war. Yet he was not so blinded by prejudice that he couldn't empathize with the man sitting in front of him. In his place, Morgan had no doubt that he would have been terrified, too.

"Saul? Don't know, sir," the slave replied, barely suppressing the panic in his voice. "Honest to God, I don't. They say that he fights against the white men. A ghost, some say. Some say he's not even real."

"He's real," Morgan insisted. "I know he does, I've seen him with my own eyes, so don't you dare lie to me. I want to know where he is and I think you know."

"No, sir, I don't! Honest to God, I don't!"

He looked deeply into the man's eyes and saw only fear. His first instinct was to conclude that the man was telling the truth, yet Morgan knew slaves were full of clever tricks. After all, each of them had spent a lifetime concealing their true thoughts from white people. Was it possible that such habits of mind could resist even the terror Morgan was trying to strike into the slave's heart?

Morgan turned and nodded to one of his men, an unusually tall and fierce-looking soldier. He set his rifle down and stepped forward, pulling his bowie knife from its sheath in a slow and menacing manner. He began walking towards the slave, leisurely waving the blade about in the air. The closer he got to the slave, the faster the slave's breathing became.

"Please, sir!" the black man pleaded. "Please! I don't know nothing!"

"We know you stole food and gave it to Saul," Morgan replied. "Tell me where Saul is or I'll have my friend here cut off one of your fingers."

"I don't know nothing about Saul, sir! Please!"

Morgan turned to the soldier. "Forget the finger," he said calmly. "Just cut his throat. I'm tired of his lies."

"Please!" the slave shrieked. "I'm not lying! If I knew something, I'd tell you! But I don't know nothing!"

The soldier held the knife just below the slave's neck. Morgan looked at him carefully. This was the key moment of this particular interrogation. Only the bravest of men could withstand the sheer terror of imminent death. The man obviously was certain he was about the die, for tears were streaming down his face and his breathing had been reduced to sharp, pathetic gasps.

"One last chance," Morgan said.

"Don't know nothing," the slave whimpered.

The soldier looked back at Morgan, wordlessly asking permission. It was clear that he was as unperturbed by the thought of cutting a black man's throat than he would have been by the thought of ringing a chicken's neck. If anything, the soldier seemed eager to do it.

The slave, terrified beyond imagination, still said nothing. Morgan was certain that, had the black man had any real knowledge of Saul, he would have revealed it at that moment. He had been telling the truth after all. Morgan held up his hand. The knife-wielding soldier, hesitating just a moment as if in protest to Morgan's decision, returned the blade to its sheath and stomped back to his old position along the wall.

The slave, thinking he had come within a hairsbreadth of death, collapsed into a fit of pathetic sobs.

"Take him out with the others," Morgan tiredly ordered. Two men walked forward to the chair. One cut the ropes with his knife. Together, they hauled the slave, whose face bore an expression combining confusion with infinite relief, out one of the side doors.

The slaves who had already been interrogated were taken to a different holding pen than those who had not yet been questioned. That way, those waiting to be brought in would have no warning of what was about to happen to them. Even better, they might draw the worst conclusions about the fate of those who had gone before them. It helped soften them up before questioning.

The corporal who had earlier been sent for coffee finally returned. Morgan sipped gratefully at the hot drink, which he loved so much. He also hoped it would reduce his fatigue. After several hours of interrogating slave after slave, he was becoming increasingly tired.

Morgan spent the next hour-and-a-half questioning eight more slaves, but those sessions of interrogation went no better than those which had preceded them. No information of any use had thus far been uncovered from any of the slaves. Morgan was beginning to wonder if the entire exercise was a waste of time, but he saw little alternative. Since the embarrassing ambush of his men by Saul the previous month, neither his roving bands of cavalry nor any of the infantry or militia units had been able to pin down the insurgents.

Within the same time, two more plantations reported having been attacked by men suspected to belong to Saul's gang. These attacks had been repelled by armed guards, which were now protecting all plantations in the area, but several men had been wounded and three killed. Losses among the insurgents were unknown, as no bodies had been found after the brief fighting ended. Morgan suspected that the insurgents were carrying away the bodies of their comrades so as to conceal their own casualties.

Wealthy landowners were besieging both Richmond and the Louisiana state government with complaints. The expense of hiring guards for every plantation was high and many plantation owners objected to having large numbers of uncouth men in such close proximity to their wives and daughters. The cost of shipping cotton and sugar from the plantations to the markets in New Orleans had increased due to the need to provide armed escorts.

Even worse, reports were coming in from all over Louisiana and even southwestern Mississippi of an increase in the numbers if slaves attempting to run away. In one case, a slave had tried to kill his owners as they slept in their bed, declaring just before being hanged that he had done it for Saul. In another, slaves had stolen liquor and gotten drunk, then set fire to a warehouse filled with cotton and danced around it singing Saul's name, entirely unconcerned with the punishment they would incur. It seemed as though the ties that bound the slaves to the plantations were starting to weaken. If Saul were not dealt with soon, they might well break.

Secretary Breckinridge was being as tactful as possible in his telegrams, but it was clear to Morgan that officialdom in Richmond was dissatisfied with Morgan's efforts thus far. In their eyes, it should have been a simple matter to run a small band of insurrectionist slaves to the ground.

Inside, he fulminated at the unfairness of it all. Saul's depredations were nothing compared with what the South had experienced during the confused withdrawal of Union forces during late 1865 and early 1866. It was the fear the name of the man invoked, rather than any actual damage he did, that alarmed the decision-makers in Richmond. Morgan figured that Breckinridge understood this, but he was less sure about Jefferson Davis.

He was about to tell his men that they were done for the day when one of his soldiers entered the barn with an interested look on his face.

"Next one might be important, sir. This darkie just told me he's a deserter from Saul's band."

Morgan's eyes lit up instantly. Nothing like this had yet happened. Could this be the break he was looking for? "Does he seem sincere?" he asked the soldier.

The man's face looked puzzled for a moment. "I suppose so, sir. He seems like he knows what he talking about, at any rate."

"Send him in. But tie him up like any of the others. Don't let him think he's getting any special treatment just yet." Morgan tried to keep the excitement out of his voice.

The gruff soldier nodded and stepped outside. A minute later, he returned with a black man, quickly pushing him down into the chair. As with the others who had been interrogated, the prisoner's hands were tied with a rope that passed underneath his chair. Once secured, the man looked up at Morgan with an expectant look in his eyes.

"What's your name, boy?" Morgan asked.

"Silas," the slave responded. "At least, that's the name my master gave me."

"Your name is whatever your master says it is," Morgan replied. "So Silas is your name."

The slave didn't respond. He seemed odd to Morgan, very different from the others. He certainly was tense, but he also seemed to display a certain detachment to what was happening around him. He looked up at the noose hanging in the middle of the room and frowned, but no more so than a man would when he saw a thunderstorm approaching. He didn't seem afraid.

"You say that you are a deserter from Saul?"

"That's right."

"Why should I believe you?"

"Because I'm telling the truth."

Morgan considered Silas for a moment. From the black man's mannerisms and tone of voice, Morgan recognized the type of man he was at once, for he had had many such men under his command during the war. Men like Silas couldn't speak without being sarcastic and vaguely disrespectful. Under his command, such men had often wandered away from their units to loot local farms or let prisoners escape in exchange for a little money. Blacks with such personalities made poor slaves, for they were likely to run away at the first opportunity and display a generally surly disposition. Such men were much more likely to desert than others and there was no reason that a member of Saul's guerrilla band should be an exception.

Morgan understood such men, for in many ways he was much like them. He didn't like authority. During the war, he had insisted on operating as an independent raider rather than as unit of a large army. Braxton Bragg, his nominal superior, had given him orders and Morgan had obeyed or disobeyed as he pleased. In his current role, Morgan followed Breckinridge's orders more because of their personal friendship than anything else.

"Can you tell me where Saul is?"

"He moves around a lot. Can't rightly tell you where he is on any one day or night."

"I think you know. You will tell me what you know right away," he demanded.

Silas smirked. "Or what? You'll hang me from that noose? You'll have one of your men shoot me or cut my throat? What good is that going to do you?"

Morgan did not like being spoken to with such insolence by anyone, least of all a black man. "I can make sure your death is especially unpleasant."

"Wouldn't be any worse than what my master put me through before the war," Silas said defiantly. "Except there'd be an end to it."

Morgan nodded to one of the soldiers on the wall, who stepped forward. In quick succession, he punched Silas's face three times. Blood spewed forth from Silas's nose and the slave's eyes momentarily had a clouded, groggy look.

"Tell me about Saul," Morgan demanded. "Tell me everything you know, right now. If you don't you'll be punished far more severely."

Silas didn't say anything in response. Recovering from the pain and sitting up straight in his chair, he spat on the ground not far from the feet of the man who had punched him. Without waiting for Morgan's permission, the soldier promptly pummeled Silas's face again four or five times, before kicking him in the chest so hard that the chair toppled over backwards. Silas grunted in pain and his hands flexed strongly but futilely against the ropes that bound him.

Morgan stepped forward and stood over Silas's prostrate form.

"Tell me," he repeated.

Silas coughed roughly and then breathed deeply for nearly a minute. "After that, why should I tell you anything?"

"If you do, the beatings will stop and your life will be spared."

"If you really think I can tell you what you need to know, then killing me won't get you anything."

Morgan frowned. During the war, whenever he had been faced with a superior Union force, he had always sought to avoid it rather than engage it in battle. There was no point in fighting a battle one could not hope to win. What Morgan was faced with here, he now realized, was an implacable foe. He could have his men continue to beat Silas for hours and it would do no good. It was equally clear that Silas was not afraid of dying. Yet he might have information that Morgan desperately needed.

"Pick him up," Morgan said. Two of his men set the chair back up properly. Silas's face was red and puffy, one cheek noticeably larger than the other, with blood streaming down from his nose and a gash on his left cheekbone.

Morgan took a chair of his own that had been propped up against the wall, placed it directly in front of Silas, and sat down. He silently considered the brutalized face of the black slave for more than a minute, not saying a word. Eventually, Silas's eyes regained their focus and stared back at Morgan.

"What do you want?" Morgan asked simply.

"I can tell you stuff about Saul," Silas replied. "Stuff that will make you and every other white man scared as a baby. But if you want me to do it, you need to give me something, too."

"What?"

"You can start by cutting this rope and letting me stand up."

Morgan motioned to one of his men. "Cut his ropes."

"Sir?" the soldier replied in confusion.

"You heard me, private. Cut his ropes."

The man hesitated for a moment, then shrugged. Quickly pulling a knife out, he sliced apart Silas's ropes and stepped back. Silas rubbed his wrists for a few second, then stood up with a sigh. He looked down at Morgan.

"A glass of water would be nice."

Morgan nodded to the corporal who had earlier brought the coffee. "Get him a glass of water."

Silas made a show of stretching his legs and arms before sitting back down in his chair. When the water arrived, he drank it gratefully and loudly, as though it was the first water he had had in weeks. Then, he looked again at Morgan.

"Maybe something to eat?"

"Don't push your luck."

Silas shrugged. "Okay."

Morgan waited for a moment, weighing whether he was following the correct course of action. The stick had failed, but perhaps the carrot would work. He would find out one way or the other.

"What's your story, Silas?" Morgan asked.

The black man shrugged again. "Slave on a Mississippi plantation. Don't know how old I am. One day back in spring of `63, bluecoats in Grant's army come through and tell us we are free. I joined up with the Union army and served in the 51st United States Colored Infantry. I learned to read and write." Silas glanced up at some of the soldiers lining the wall. "Probably better than some of your boys."

Morgan sensed the anger that rose in his men at these words, but their discipline held and they did nothing. "And when the war ended?" he asked.

"Did it ever end? Not for me, it didn't. You know that the black regiments tried to keep fighting when the Yankees left. But you beat us. Most of the others left, but some of us stayed behind."

"And Saul leads the remnants of your old regiment? The 51st, I think you called it?"

"No, not really. The old regimental numbers don't mean anything anymore. Saul's group is made up of men from lots of the old units, as well as slaves that have been freed or escaped since then."

"Who is Saul?" Morgan asked this question with a quickening pulse, for he sensed that he was very near to getting the answers he so desperately needed.

To Morgan's fury, Silas laughed. "You really don't know anything about him, do you?"

"Answer the question."

"Something to eat. Then more answers."

Morgan considered having his men beat the insolent black once again, but thought better of it. Silas clearly knew that he had the advantage over Morgan in the contest of wills. Morgan was a practical man. He knew he could get what he wanted from Silas by persuasion rather than coercion.

The next fifteen minutes passed mostly in silence. Silently expressing their disapproval with irritated expressions, some of the soldiers brought in some warm cornbread and a few slices of chicken, which Silas happily devoured. It became clear to Morgan than the black man had not eaten well for some time. He wondered if that had something to do with why Silas had deserted from Saul's band.

After he finished eating, the soldiers took his plate away. Morgan didn't wait before resuming the questioning.

"Okay, your belly's full. Now tell me about Saul."

"Well, first of all, his name isn't Saul. His real name is Henry. He came from a plantation of Louisiana. Just a normal field hand. The Yankees freed him and he joined the army, just like I did. Just like thousands of us, I guess." Silas paused thoughtfully for a moment. "They tell lots of stories about him, though. They say his mother practices voodoo and uses magical powers to protect her son."

Morgan noted this information in his mind. He considered the strange religious beliefs of the blacks to be childish and silly, but knew that they were very real the minds of the slaves themselves.

"Go on."

"Saul joined the army in 1863. Milliken's Bend was his first battle. He served in lots of different regiments after that, and fought in lots of battles. He's a good soldier. Killed lots of men during the war. Some say that he's the one who killed Nathan Bedford Forrest, but I don't think that's true."

"What unit did he serve in?" Morgan asked. "What was his rank? Was he a noncommissioned officer?"

"Sorry, but I don't know. I don't think anybody knows. It's all just rumors, you see. Saul doesn't talk about himself."

"What else can you tell me about him? What sort of man is he?"

255

Silas scoffed. "He's an arrogant ass is what he is. All puffed up about himself, thinking that he's the master now. He scares you white people and he knows it. So now he thinks he's been sent by God to destroy the Confederacy and free all the slaves. Might be a bit crazy, I think."

Morgan tried hard not to let his excitement be too obvious. He didn't want Silas to realize just how valuable he was, for he would undoubtedly try to drive a harder bargain if he did. Still, this was the first solid information that had been obtained about Saul and it electrified Morgan. He could not wait to write his next report to Breckinridge.

"Hoe does Saul keep his men supplied with food?" Morgan asked.

"We live off the land. We also steal from plantations. Lots of food is smuggled out to us from slaves still on the plantations."

"How is that possible?"

Silas smiled and shook his head. "There's so much about slaves that you white people don't know anything about. Even before the war, slaves snuck back and forth between plantations all the time. Visiting family and such. Sneaking food. It's not that hard, you know. And Saul and his boys are better at it than anybody." Silas waited a moment before continuing. "It wouldn't surprise me if some of his men are watching this farm right now, in fact."

Morgan had not considered that possibility. Nearly an entire regiment of militia was positioned in and around the Cheval Farm. There could be no possibility of attack, but observation from a distance was not impossible. In Saul's place, Morgan would have done it.

"Where is Saul's encampment?" Morgan asked urgently.

"He doesn't have one," Silas replied lazily. "If he did, you would find it, wouldn't you? He's a lot smarter than you think. He never stays in the same place. He moves around in the swamps and forests all the time. And not just him, either."

"What do you mean?"

"There's another group. He calls them columns. Two columns, you see. He tells them what to do, sending men running back and forth between each group."

"Two columns," Morgan said. He and Duke had already deduced this. Reports of attacks and sightings had often made it seem as though Saul were moving at an impossibly quick rate through the swamps. If there were two different groups of insurrectionists operating in the region, they could strike at different targets simultaneously.

On the other hand, Morgan had not considered the possibility of continually mobile columns, because he could not think of a way in which they could have been kept supplied. During the war, on his extended raiding operations, Morgan's forces had foraged for their food as they passed through one region after another, but the area of Saul's operations had been too small. He had assumed that there had to be some sort of central base camp from which Saul's men grew their sustenance.

"How many men in these two columns?"

"We started off with only a few dozen, but we've freed lots of slaves in the past couple months. Other people have run away from their masters to join us, too. I guess there are a few hundred people in each group. Saul has people whose job it is to sneak the women and children down to New Orleans to be sent away to other countries. Some try to move north along the Mississippi to reach the United States. Don't rightly know whether this works or not, since we never hear from those people again."

"How are they armed?"

"That's the big problem. Only a few of the men have rifles. Left over from the war. Saul goes to great trouble to keep them clean and such, but time wears away at them. Most of the men are armed with spears and clubs, some made in the swamp, others made from the tools they take away from the plantation. There's not much ammunition left, either."

Morgan nodded. That was something he had already realized from the eyewitness accounts of the recent raids. "These gatherings of food?" Morgan asked.

"From all over," Silas replied. "You'd be amazed. Slaves in plantations all over the place are involved."

Morgan nodded. He had wondered why Saul had not attacked plantations more often. Now, he knew. Plantations which remained untouched clandestinely provided him with a steady flow of food and perhaps other supplies. So long as they remained intact, Saul's men would not starve. Morgan wondered, therefore, why Saul had bothered to attack any plantations at all. What was he trying to accomplish?

"Your friend Saul is clever, I'll give them that."

Silas's face clouded. "He's not my friend. Why else would I be telling you all this?"

It occurred to Morgan that he hadn't considered Silas's own motives. There were any number of reasons that someone might turn against their own people. During the war, virtually every community in Morgan's own state of Kentucky had seen vicious and usually violent turmoil, as often as not with personal rather than political causes. Had Silas been wronged in some way by Saul? Maybe there had been a clash over a woman? Morgan didn't know, but then again, he didn't care.

"You say that these two columns move back and forth a lot. Do they use the same paths? Maybe the same campsites every now and then?"

"Sometimes."

"Can you lead me to them?"

"I might be able to."

He looked across at Silas, nodding satisfactorily. "I must tell you that, under the law, I am required to return you to the plantation you ran away from four years ago."

Silas's eyes widened. "After how I just helped you?" he spat, anger flashing in his eyes.

"We'll discuss that later. For the time being, you'll stay with me. If you promise to continue helping me, and if you perform your duty well, perhaps we can come to some arrangement when all of this is over. And you'll keep eating well."

Morgan pondered what he could do about Silas's status. Perhaps his master, assuming he could even be located, would be amenable to having the slave purchased directly. Conceivably, Morgan could claim that military necessity required him to impress Silas for government service. In any case, it could wait. Now that he had useful information about Saul and how he was operating, Morgan was determined to run his foe to the ground, no matter what the cost.

"I'll go along with you, Morgan," Silas said. "You just have to promise me one thing."

"What's that?"

"When you find Saul, you'll let me watch you kill the son of a bitch."

June 5, Afternoon
Palace of Westminster, London, England

Slidell sat in the Stranger's Gallery, looking down onto the floor of the House of Commons. It struck him as rather ludicrous that such an august and famous legislative body met in such a cramped and comparatively unadorned chamber. The famous green benches lacked arm rests and looked decidedly uncomfortable. Illumination was provided by a small number of simple chandeliers hanging from an austere ceiling. Considering what he had seen in many English palaces and noble homes, the House of Commons seemed intentionally plain.

Compared to the Luxembourg Palace in Paris, where the French Senate met, the House of Commons might as well have been a small warehouse. The United States Senate Chamber, where he had served for nearly a decade, was also far grander and more elegant. Yet it didn't matter. If ever there was a lesson in the difference between the appearance of power and the reality of power, it was the British House of Commons. Sparse though its meeting place might be, it was by far the most powerful legislative assembly in the world.

In Paris, the French Senate was merely an advisory body to Emperor Napoleon III. In Washington City, the United States Senate had to share power with the House of Representatives and compete with both an ambitious executive branch and dozens of state governments. The same was true of the Confederate Congress. The House of Commons, by contrast, had no equal in the British government. On the other side of the Palace of Westminster, the House of Lords quietly acknowledged its inferiority and now rarely fought legislation passed by the Commons. Even Queen Victoria herself held little real power in the British Empire. A common joke in London was that if the Commons passed a resolution that the Queen commit suicide by drowning, she would have no choice but to sign it and then leap into the Thames.

Looking directly down from the Stranger's Gallery, Slidell could see Disraeli sitting in his place on the front bench of the government's side of the chamber. On either side were the various ministers of the Cabinet and, behind him, the back-benchers of the Conservative Party. In the middle and to Slidell's left was the Table of the House, where the Speaker and a few clerks sat. At the edge of the table was placed the ceremonial mace, which ostensibly represented royal authority.

On the other side of the chamber sat the members of the opposition Liberal Party, with the stony and grim-looking William Gladstone sitting in its front bench due to his position as party leader. Slidell did not much care for

Gladstone, who viewed the world through moral eyes rather than practical ones. The Confederate diplomat had no time for idealists, who always made things worse rather than better. Good intentions meant nothing if they produced disastrous results.

"Order!" the Speaker was shouting. "Order!"

Few of the MPs listened. Opposition members were shouting and waving papers, while Conservatives behind Disraeli were also on their feet, yelling back to the Liberals to sit down. Through it all, both Disraeli and Gladstone sat quietly. Slidell could not see Disraeli's face, but assumed that it bore his habitual expression of amused detachment. Gladstone simply looked angry and annoyed.

"Raucous," said Minister Haynes, who was sitting next to Slidell. "You'd never see that in Congress, would you?"

"No," Slidell replied.

"People back home always act as though Englishmen are dignified and decorous. Five minutes of watching debates in the House of Commons would cure them of that particular delusion."

Slidell grunted in response. He would have preferred to come alone rather than in Haynes's company, but protocol had to be observed. He had spent the last week closeted in the Confederate consulate with Haynes, developing an effort to counteract the impact of Frederick Douglass's speaking tour. Letters had been written to the editors of various newspapers, asking them to limit coverage of the abolitionist's speeches. Meetings had been held with the representatives of the London Trades Council, suggesting that they advise their members not to attend rallies at which Douglass was going to speak. All this was common sense to Slidell and it had been a little disheartening to him that Haynes had needed his help on such simple matters. Slidell was considering voicing this opinion in his next letter to Secretary Benjamin, but had not yet decided one way or the other.

One member of the Liberal Party, waving more energetically than the others, had finally succeeded in being recognized by the Speaker. The other MPs quieted.

"Will the prime minister explain to the Commons what manner of preparations are being made for the possibility of war with the United States?"

Slidell leaned over slightly to Haynes. "Who is that?" He was testing him, for any diplomat worth his salt would be able to identify the important political figures of the country in which he worked. This particular MP, being entrusted by Gladstone with questioning the prime minister on a crucial matter, was surely important.

"I believe that is George Goschen, a member for London."

Slidell nodded as he watched Disraeli rise from the bench and address the Commons.

"I appreciate the concern of the Right Honorable gentleman regarding our preparations for war. We do not wish for war with the United States. If we can avoid it, we shall. Yet we cannot ignore the unfriendly, dare I say outrageous, acts of the government in Washington City, who are allowing armed fanatics to organize, recruit, and train on their soil. They are doing nothing to prevent these criminal bands from crossing into the Dominion of Canada. Three weeks ago, one of these Fenian bands killed a British colonel and had to be driven out of the country by our gallant soldiers. Can we tolerate such insults?"

This was greeted with stomping of feet and thumping of fists on the wooden frames of the benches. Slidell felt the anger of the British legislators, the fury at being disrespected, and the sense of being provoked by the temerity of a weaker power acting as though they were as strong as the British Empire.

"Wonderful, is it not?" Haynes said. "We were trying to negotiate an alliance with the French, but now it looks like we can have one with the British for the asking."

Slidell didn't respond, for he did not share his colleague's enthusiasm. The British were considerably more powerful than the French, yet Slidell felt an alliance with them would be much more problematic. The British, being more democratically inclined than the French, were likely to alter their foreign policies with each change of government. There was greater opposition to slavery among the British as well.

Yet this was utterly lost on Haynes. He saw that there was a chance for a pact with Britain and was eager to jump at it. He could not see that the circumstances that had made this possible were temporary and unlikely to be repeated. A British administration might seek an association with the Confederacy to serve their immediate ends but, the moment the political calculus changed, they would terminate the arrangement. By any rational standard of judgment, the Confederacy would be much better off allying itself to France than to Britain.

Goschen was replying to Disraeli. "I know I can speak for all my fellow members of Her Majesty's Loyal Opposition when I say that I share the prime minister's angry feelings towards the Americans in this matter. But my question to the prime minister stands. What manner of preparations for war are being made?"

Slidell frowned, not liking Goschen's use of the word 'Americans' to refer specifically to the United States. After all, he and his fellow Confederates were Americans, too. He put that out of his mind as he listened carefully to Disraeli's response.

"The Channel Fleet is preparing a number of warships for deployment to American waters. I do not feel it prudent to give more specific information, but I can assure the House that the force being sent is more than sufficient to deal with any eventualities. In addition, several battalions are being readied to reinforce our forces in Canada and, according to the authorities in the Dominion, the recruiting of the militia has been stepped up."

"These ships being dispatched," Goschen said. "I assume that they are to go to the Royal Navy's base at Halifax?"

"It is not prudent to disclose information of a military nature," Disraeli said. "I am confident that the Royal Navy will do as it sees best and I have complete faith in the judgement of its commanders."

"Can the prime minister assure this House that none of our warships will be using ports in the Confederate States of America as their bases?"

There was a murmur of discontent throughout the chamber, mostly on the Liberal side but among some of the Conservatives as well. The other people watching the sessions in the Stranger's Gallery glanced over at him, wondering as to his reaction to the display.

Disraeli seemed to falter for just an instant before responding. "As I said, it would not be prudent for me to discuss military details. I will say, however, that when our Empire is threatened and a friendly nation offers us the use of its ports, it would be foolhardy not to accept."

This caused an uproar from the Liberal side of the chamber. Gladstone's eyes flashed fire and he was instantly on his feet, waving for the attention of the Speaker. Goschen, deferring to his leader, sat back down.

"Mr. Gladstone!" the Speaker shouted.

"Will the prime minister tell this House whether or not Her Majesty's Government is proposing an alliance with the Confederacy?"

"I will tell this House that Her Majesty's Government is not," Disraeli replied instantly. "It is our policy that the United Kingdom remain free from any entanglements with foreign powers. Temporary associations of convenience can be considered, as when we fought alongside the French and the Turks during our war with Russia in the Crimea. But if the Honorable Gentleman is concerned that Her Majesty's Government is contemplating a formal arrangement with the Confederate States, allow me to put his worries to rest. We are not, nor do I expect to do so in the future."

"And is Her Majesty's Government considering, to use the prime minister's own words, one of these temporary associations of convenience with the Confederate States?"

"The Right Honorable Gentleman seems to be forgetting the fact that a powerful nation, which has a large army and which shares a long border with Her Majesty's territory, is acting in a very bellicose manner. One of Her Majesty's most distinguished officers, a winner of the Victoria Cross, has been slain, to say nothing of dozens of British and Canadian troops. If the American government does nothing to restrain the outrages of these Fenian bands, war is a very real possibility. Now is not the time for quibbling. It is my responsibility to see to the security of Her Majesty's possessions, a question on which the Right Honorable Gentleman is clearly an ignoramus."

These last words caused an explosion of anger from the Liberal side of the chamber and loud shouts to the Speaker for intervention. Gladstone's face turned red with rage. The Speaker pounded his gavel several times before the room quieted again.

"The prime minister will retract his last statement," the Speaker said sternly.

Disraeli bowed his head. "I do humbly apologize. I should not have called Mr. Gladstone an ignoramus. I merely meant to suggest that he has a comprehensive lack of knowledge."

More shouts of outrage erupted from the Liberal side, but the Conservative benches and the Stranger's Gallery were convulsed with laughter. Slidell grinned, delighted with Disraeli. Whatever the merits of the respective arguments, the papers would carry the story the following day that the prime minister had made the Leader of the Opposition look foolish and that would be what the people would read.

During the War for Southern Independence, Disraeli had favored a strictly neutral attitude towards the Union and Confederacy, while Gladstone had been castigated for making a very uncharacteristic statement of support for the South. It had been the Liberal government of Lord John Russell that had recognized the

Confederacy, but that had simply been a concession to reality. British politics were developing in such a way that the Conservatives led by Disraeli were generally friendly to the Confederacy, despite public objections to slavery, while the Liberals of Gladstone were decidedly less supportive of the new nation, though not necessarily hostile.

Gladstone shook with anger, but sat back down. Slidell got the impression that he was concerned he would lose his temper if he tried to talk and might embarrass himself. Slidell watched as another Liberal MP, directly behind Gladstone, leaned forward and whispered in his ear. Gladstone nodded at whatever was being said. Slidell didn't recognize the man, who then stood and asked for the recognition of the Speaker.

"Mr. John Bright!" the Speaker said.

Slidell tensed. He knew Bright by reputation, as did everyone else. During the war, he had been one of the most stridently pro-Union, anti-slavery members of Parliament. Some credited him with single-handedly derailing efforts by pro-Confederate MPs to pass resolutions recognizing the Confederacy in the fall of 1862 and the summer of 1863. He was known as a radical on free trade and a strong advocate of the working class.

"Mr. Speaker, I rise to state emphatically my opposition to any military cooperation with the Confederacy, no matter how insignificant and informal it might be. If Her Majesty's Government do intend to send any of our warships, even one, to provision itself in a port of the Confederacy, as some sort of demonstration of a friendly connection between our country and theirs, I can only say that it would be to the everlasting shame and discredit of England to do so."

This brought a chorus of shouts and protests from the Conservatives. The Speaker banged his gavel several times until silence reigned again. Bright continued.

"England has much to be proud of. We are bringing the fruits of civilization and good government to the dark regions of the world. We are bringing prosperity undreamed of to the masses of our people. But I believe our greatest achievement, and that of which we can be the most proud, is the successful campaign by the Royal Navy to exterminate the African slave trade."

This was greeted by applause from the Liberal benches. Bright seemed to take energy from this and continued speaking when the tumult had died down.

"The Confederacy is a nation. We cannot deny this. It succeeded in outlasting the United States, it has a functioning government, and it has signed treaties with other nations. Yet it is not a nation like other nations. It is a nation whose entire existence is based on the unspeakable evil that is African slavery! Can anyone doubt that this new nation, this disfigured and disgusting nation, would have come into being had it not been for the base desire of a handful of white men to keep in bondage many millions of blacks? Why did the South wish to separate itself from the North? Because they feared that they would otherwise no longer be allowed to work Negroes, to breed Negroes, to lash Negroes, to chain Negroes, to buy and sell Negroes, and to deprive Negroes of their blessed families. Their own vice president has blasphemously declared slavery to be the very corner stone of their so-called Confederacy."

Slidell felt his stomach tighten in alarm. He glanced over to one side, where reporters were busy scribbling down notes as they intently listened to Bright's speech. The man's voice seemed to echo as it filled the House of Commons. A few minutes before, Slidell had hoped that the next day's headlines would speak of Gladstone's humiliation. Now, he knew they would speak only of Bright's eloquence. As much as he wanted to deny it, Slidell realized that it was listening to a spellbinding piece of oratory.

"It is to the honor of England that we have bent our energies to the destruction of the detestable institution of African slavery. We never allowed it on our own shores. We abolished it in our colonies decades ago. We have committed the resources of the Royal Navy to the destruction of the Trans-Atlantic slave trade, not in pursuit of our narrow interests but simply in recognition of the divine truth that slavery is wrong. We are a nation that abhors and detests slavery. The Confederacy, by contrast, is a nation with slavery interwoven into its very fabric."

Slidell pursed his lips and shook his head. The debate was going very badly.

"I am not a warlike man, as is well known," Bright was saying. "I, too, am outraged by the actions of the Fenians and the unfriendly attitude of the government of the United States. But ally with the Confederacy? Ally with these slave-driving hypocrites who daily commit the foulest outrageous against the human soul? Never! I say it! Never! Never! Never!"

The Liberal side of the chamber exploded in a thunder of applause, stomping of feet, and thumping of fists on the wooden frames of the benches. The Speaker pounded his gavel to no avail, for nothing could diminish the celebratory noise.

Slidell noticed some of the reporters casting side glances towards him and Haynes. He was suddenly seized with the thought that their very presence in the Stranger's Gallery was now dangerous to the interests of the Confederacy. If he and Haynes looked displeased at Bright's speech, the newspapers would be filled with stories of their arrogance and condescension. Yet if they maintained placid expressions, it might be taken as a sign that they lacked confidence in their own government's policies. The newspapers always printed whatever made the best story, regardless of what was true, and Bright's ferocious speech was sure to be the main story of the coming day.

"We must leave," Slidell said urgently to Haynes. He stood to go, grabbing his hat and coat as he did so.

"Why?" Haynes asked.

"Quickly!" Slidell snapped.

Like a soldier having received a harsh order from an officer, Haynes rose as well. The two men walked swiftly out the back of the Stranger's Gallery. They descended the stairs and were soon passing through the Central Lobby and then St. Stephens Hall. Another few minutes of walking brought them outside into the bright sunshine of an early England summer. It was still chilly to Slidell, who suddenly remembered with fondness the warm humidity of Louisiana. Yet he worried that the chill he felt was not due entirely to the climate of Britain.

"Why did you make us leave so abruptly?" Haynes asked. "I was hoping to see Disraeli's riposte to Bright's speech."

"It doesn't matter what Disraeli says," Slidell answered. "The newspapers have their stories for tomorrow. It was better that we not be part of them."

"You think the papers will cover Bright's speech?" Haynes asked.

"Of course they will," Slidell said, a trace of harshness entering his voice. It his mind was already thinking of a means to turn this to his advantage.

June 8, Morning
Executive Office Building, Richmond, Virginia

"And Morgan trusts that this Negro's report is accurate?" Davis asked.

Breckinridge nodded. "He says that this Silas fellow seems very sincere."

Davis scowled. "If he had been sincere, he never would have abandoned his master and joined the Yankee army in the first place. He certainly never would have joined up with a vile brigand like Saul."

Breckinridge did not respond to this. Though no Fire-Eater, Davis was far more closely connected with slavery than he was. The president, after all, owned a large plantation in Mississippi. Breckinridge thought that, like most Southerners, Davis held a strange and unrealistic attachment to the institution, leading to odd conclusions about the loyalty and mental state of the slaves themselves. Breckinridge had learned from long experience not to challenge such assumptions, as such conversations did no good.

Davis leaned back in his chair. "So, this Saul fellow has no supply base and just wanders around the wilderness, bilking supplies of food from local plantations?"

"It's smuggled out to him by slaves within the plantations, apparently. It cannot be a large amount, though."

"And there is another group of bandits as well?"

"Yes, sir. Saul commands two groups, it seems. Morgan had already concluded this. How they communicate with one another, we don't know."

"Judging from the fact that Morgan's men don't seem able to find them, we can assume that they are trying to avoid our forces. Why don't they just disperse and make their way to the United States? Surely even a black man is not so stupid as to think he can launch a genuine uprising that would overthrow Confederate authority."

"We can only guess, Mr. President."

"I assume that Morgan is going to put this fellow's information to use and become more active against Saul?"

"Of course, Mr. President."

"Good. The newspapers have been chattering about the lack of progress, you know. And I've been besieged by congressmen from Louisiana who are demanding Saul's head on a spike."

"Morgan is doing the best that can be expected, Mr. President. It's a large country, you know. Thick with swamps and forests. Finding Saul's men is like searching for a needle in a haystack. And these blacks are experiencing at concealing themselves. For all we know, our patrols have come within a few hundred yards of them without knowing it."

"I appreciate the difficulties. I used to live in the swamp country, you'll recall. But if progress isn't made soon, and if there are more attacks, I don't think I will be able to keep Morgan in his current position. He shall have to be superseded."

"I hope it does not come to that," Breckinridge said.

"Now, was there anything else?" Davis asked.

Breckinridge went through the list of more routine matters. He wanted an appropriation of funds to purchase a few hundred Chassepot rifles from France in order to experiment with them and perhaps equip a cavalry unit with them. General Hardee wanted more artillery to be allocated to the fortifications in the upper Mississippi. There were a few other issues, most of which Breckinridge felt to be of minor importance, but he knew Davis would want to hear about them. The president had always enjoyed delving into details.

After the last item on the list had been discussed, the president paused for a moment. He took a breath, removed his glasses, and tiredly rubbed his sinuses. "May I ask you a question that does not specifically relate to your department's business?"

"Of course, sir."

"This request of the British to send a warship to Charleston. What do you think of it?"

"Secretary Benjamin says that if we accept, it would be taken as a sign of Confederate support for Britain over this Fenian business."

"Yes. Do you think we should do it?"

Breckinridge thought for a moment. He was not used to being asked about foreign policy. "Speaking for myself, Mr. President, I believe we should do our utmost to maintain a strict neutrality in this matter. The Confederacy is in no condition for another war and will not be for a long time. Our debt levels are disastrous and the war hasn't even been over for three years. Best to avoid doing anything that might antagonize the United States."

Davis listened carefully and nodded as Breckinridge spoke. "And yet, if the world's most powerful empire extends the hand of friendship, should we not grasp it?"

"That's your decision, not mine, Mr. President."

"True, true. But you are running for president yourself. You soon may be the one who has to make the decision."

The Secretary of War waited a few moments before replying. He had not spoken to Davis about his developing presidential campaign, which had not yet been officially announced, but he didn't doubt that Benjamin was telling Davis everything. Davis and Benjamin were often closeted together for hours on end, talking politics as much as policy.

"I have learned in life that when something seems too good to be true, it probably is," Breckinridge said. "I believe we should trend very carefully with the British. The circumstances that have caused them to reach out to us are temporary and unlikely to be repeated."

"But if war does erupt, it could poison relations between the British and the Yankees for a long time. London might then consider us their natural friends."

"I doubt it, Mr. President. We must always remember that the British people as a whole strongly oppose slavery. Being a democracy, the British government can only move in keeping with the feelings of the voters. My own view is that we would find ourselves out of favor with London as soon as the Fenian Crisis fades away."

Davis rubbed his chin, then motioned for Breckinridge to continue.

"And we have been working for some time to establish a relationship with the French, a nation more likely to favor a long-term association. If we drop all those carefully crafted efforts and rush into the embrace of London, we will lose whatever chance we have for an alliance with France. When the British drop us like a hot potato, the French will not be likely to want to resume negotiations. They will feel like a spurned girl at a dance."

David nodded slowly, then sighed. "Perhaps you're right. Benjamin appears to be of the same mind as you. Still, I do not want to rush the decision. The last thing I want to do is initiate policies in the last few months of my presidency that you disagree with, since you will be the one to work through the consequences of them."

Breckinridge chuckled. "You're assuming that I am going to win in November, Mr. President. That is far from certain."

Davis smiled. "I told you before that I am willing to help your campaign in any way I can. I meant it, John. Public opinion being what it is, it may be that my open support would do you more harm than good, but that will be for you to decide. I hope you do not mind, but I have already written to friends and political associates in Mississippi, urging them to support your candidacy."

"No, I don't mind. Thank you, Mr. President."

"Let me suggest that you move quickly, though, John. Beauregard and his new friends have a head start, so to speak."

That they do."

"When are you going to make a public announcement?"

"Soon, Mr. President."

"Well, as I say, let me know what I can do to help."

"Of course. Good day, sir."

"Good day, John."

The walk back to the War Department offices in Mechanic's Hall was brief. The day was beautiful, with the late spring air being comfortable and fresh. It should have been a relaxing walk, yet Breckinridge could not ease his mind. The possibility of a larger slave uprising in Louisiana was extremely serious, though he took some comfort from Morgan's news of a deserter who might provide useful information. He wished that he could focus entirely on either Saul's uprising or his presidential election, rather than both at the same time.

The thought occurred that perhaps he should resign from office when his campaign really got off the ground. Not only would it allow him to concentrate on the political battle that was sure to come, but it would allow him to avoid charges in the press that he was neglecting his duties in the War Department in order to focus on the presidency. On the other hand, with Saul's insurrection still a thorn in the Confederacy's side, might he be accused of abandoning his place just when he was most needed? It was hard to determine which course of action would harm him the least.

He arrived at his office and placed his coat and hat on the coatrack. Sliding into his chair, he began to attack the pile of letters and telegrams that had accumulated there since he had left to visit Davis a few hours before. The first letter, he was interested to see, was from none other than Beauregard. When he opened it, he was not at all surprised at its contents.

Secretary Breckinridge

Progress on the forts and fortifications downriver from New Orleans is proceeding according to schedule. I am confident that the city shall soon be impregnable to attack by any conceivable naval force. That being the case, I request a leave of absence for a period of seven months in order to attend to personal business.

I have the honor to remain, sir, your most obedient servant.

P. G. T. Beauregard

Lieutenant General, Confederate States Army

The personal business to which Beauregard was referring, Breckinridge knew, was running for president. He didn't begrudge him for it. After all, one of the hallmarks of a Jeffersonian republic was that any qualified candidate should be allowed to seek any office he wanted. During his congressional campaigns of earlier years, Breckinridge had never held any animosity towards his opponents even though the debates had sometimes veered into personal territory. That was just the way the political game was played, especially in Kentucky.

He did not dislike Beauregard. They were not close enough for Breckinridge to consider Beauregard a friend, but they had served together at Shiloh and had met occasionally since Breckinridge had taken office as Secretary of War. Privately, Breckinridge thought Beauregard a bit of a dandy, rather too quick to take offense, and too often given to grand exaggerations. Yet he never doubted Beauregard's patriotism and he respected his intelligence. He also thought Beauregard possessed considerable military ability, albeit not nearly as much as the general public seemed to believe.

It was not Beauregard that worried Breckinridge, but rather the political company the man was now keeping. Robert Toombs, Louis Wigfall, Joseph Brown, and their allies were, Breckinridge strongly believed, extremely dangerous to the future of the Confederacy. Their constant carping for Confederate acquisition of Cuba unnecessarily raised tensions with Spain and needlessly alarmed the other European powers as well as the United States. While Breckinridge believed in state sovereignty no less than any Confederate, they took the concept to such ridiculous extremes that the country would fall apart were their policies ever actually implemented.

Breckinridge knew most of them well from his days in Washington City before the war, though he had rarely socialized with the extremists on either side of the slavery dispute. He respected the intelligence and ability of Robert Toombs, especially on matters of fiscal policy, but also thought him reckless and bombastic, especially after a few drinks were in the man. He considered Louis Wigfall uncouth, untrustworthy, unprincipled, and even more given to drink than Toombs.

In the upcoming electoral contest, Breckinridge did not see Beauregard as the real enemy. The men he had to fear were his Fire-Eater allies.

Breckinridge pulled out a sheet of departmental stationary and wrote out a polite response granting Beauregard his leave. There was no particular reason to deny it. As he placed it in the small box on his desk for outgoing mail, Breckinridge reflected that the Confederate presidential election of 1867 had now commenced.

He spent an hour going through the rest of the mail and doing routine paperwork. He held a meeting with General Josiah Gorgas, the head of the Ordnance Department, about labor difficulties at the Augusta Arsenal and the feasibility of building a major arsenal somewhere in the Trans-Mississippi. He answered a few letters from congressmen, including one from Senator Toombs, complaining about the War Department being late in reimbursing citizens for impressed animals during the war. Being anxious about Saul and the presidential election, Breckinridge was happy to have some routine work with which to distract himself.

June 10, Afternoon
United States Capitol, Washington City

"The committee will come to order," Sumner said, banging his gavel down a number of times until the conversation in the room ceased. This took some time, for the meeting room of the Senate Foreign Relations Committee, on the first floor of the north wing of the Capitol, was much more crowded than it usually was.

He sat in the center of the long table. On either side of him sat the six other members of the committee. His three fellow Republicans sat to his left, while the three Democratic members sat to his right. All of them were looking in his direction, waiting for him to begin. In the back of the committee room, just in front of the heavy doors, reporters and other interested persons who had come to watch the proceedings sat in several rows of chairs. Off to the side, on a small secretary's table, sat Moorfield Storey, the young and hardworking committee clerk.

In the center of the room, directly facing the members of the committee, sat Secretary of War Benjamin Butler, the chief witness of the day's committee hearings. The expression on his face was a mixture of fatigue and irritation.

As he shuffled a few papers on the table in front of him and arranged his writing utensils, Sumner glanced down at Butler. Despite the fact that Butler was a fellow Massachusetts man, he saw absolutely nothing redeeming in the face looking up at him. The man was fat and nearly bald, with skin that looked like wax melting off of his face. To Sumner, Butler was a monster deserving nothing but loathing and disdain.

A Democrat before the war, Butler had joined the Republicans when Lincoln became president in 1861. Given a general's commission, he had gone on to prove hopelessly incompetent as a military commander and had faced well-grounded accusations of corruption during his administration of occupied New Orleans. However, he had come out strongly in favor of enlisting freed slaves in the Union army, which had momentarily endeared him to Sumner and the other Radical Republicans.

All that had changed in the summer of 1864, however. The moment Butler sensed the political winds shifting following the dramatic Confederate victory at the Battle of Peachtree Creek, he effortlessly shifted back to the Democratic Party, shocking the country's political establishment. He went on to play a crucial role in defeating Lincoln at the polls in the subsequent presidential election. His reward for this service had been the post of Secretary of War when the new administration had taken office in March of 1865.

Sumner found the very existence of Benjamin Butler offensive. It was bad enough that the man had no political convictions and was corrupt in the extreme. Added to that was the stench of infamous betrayal. Sumner not only hated Benjamin Butler, he hated the very idea of Benjamin Butler. All the better that he was now sitting at the table across from the Senate committee Sumner controlled, subject to his questions.

Sumner nodded to Storey. "Go ahead."

The young clerk rose from his seat and stepped towards Butler, a Bible in his hands. "Mr. Secretary, would you place your right hand on the Bible, please?" When this was done, Storey repeated the familiar oath. "Do you solemnly swear to tell the truth, the whole truth, and nothing but the truth, so help you God?"

"I do," Butler said.

"You may be seated."

Sumner began scribbling a few notes on the papers in front of him, writing down the questions he intended to ask Butler over the course of the hearings. He might have done this earlier, but he wanted to force the Secretary of War to wait a few uncomfortable minutes before the actual questioning began. Sumner was not a subtle man and thought the demonstration would be a clear indication as to who was the master of the committee room in which the drama was to be played.

Butler folded his arms across his chest and waited, his face not displaying the slightest sign of discomfort. As the minutes passed in uncomfortable silence, mutterings began amid the chairs behind Butler. It was clear to all that Sumner was subjecting Butler to a deliberate insult. It was equally obvious that Butler did not care.

Sumner sighed, tiring of the game, and looked down at Butler. "Would you please state your name and title for the record?"

"Benjamin Franklin Butler. United States Secretary of War."

"It has taken a great deal of effort to get you into my committee room, Mr. Secretary," Sumner said sourly. "It would have been much easier on both of us, and cost us much less in wasted time, had you come when you first received your subpoena two weeks ago. I would not have had to threaten you with arrest by the Senate Sergeant-At-Arms."

"I do apologize, Mr. Chairman," Butler said with a grin. "I was much occupied by administrative matters at the War Department and did not then have the time to appear before your committee. A great deal of paperwork, you understand. One must establish priorities."

There was a light amount of laughter in the chairs behind Butler. Reporters scribbled away on their notepads and, off to the side, Storey was doing the same, carefully taking down every word being spoken in his customarily neat shorthand.

"I believe your failure to appear before this committee until the threat of arrest, despite your subpoena, is simply the latest example of the gross disrespect towards the United States Senate exhibited by you and the rest of the McClellan administration. I will note your trivial apology, though I have strong doubts as to its sincerity." He paused for a moment before continuing. "Mr. Storey, will you please pass the Secretary of War the first document?"

The clerk stood from the desk and placed a piece of paper on the table in front of Butler, who placed his reading glasses on as he took it in his hands.

"Mr. Secretary, this is a copy of the Treaty of Ghent, signed on December 24, 1814, between the United States of America and the United Kingdom of Great Britain and Ireland. It is the treaty that marked an end of the War of 1812."

"I know what it is, Mr. Chairman."

"Would you read the first two sentences of Article One, if you please?"

Butler cleared his throat. "'There shall be a firm and universal peace between His Britannic Majesty and the United States, and between their respective countries, territories, cities, towns, and people of every degree without exception of places or persons. All hostilities by both sea and land shall cease as soon as this treaty shall have been ratified by both parties as hereinafter mentioned.'"

"This provision has never been rescinded in any subsequent treaty between the United States and Britain or by any legislative or executive act of the United States. Under Article Six of the Constitution, it is part of the supreme law of the land."

"I am aware of that, Mr. Chairman."

"Mr. Secretary, who are the Fenians?"

"I am sure that the Chairman knows who the Fenians are as well as I do."

"Please answer the question."

Butler chuckled. "Very well. As I understand it, the Fenians are a group of Irish nationalists who wish to separate Ireland from the British Empire."

"And they are active here in the United States, yes?"

"Yes, if what I read in the newspapers is correct. They hold regular mass meetings in New York City, Chicago, and other places. But it is the right of any American citizen to advocate for any political cause they choose. If an Irishman has immigrated to the United States and become a citizen, it is his right to want to free Ireland from British control, is it not? The Bill of Rights guarantees freedom of speech, freedom of assembly, and freedom of the press, does it not?"

"Peacefully advocating for Irish independence is not my concern. I have called these hearings to discuss the administration's support for the Fenian campaign of armed military action against British territories in Canada, which clearly violates our previous peace treaty with the British."

"I am not sure what you are referring to, Mr. Chairman."

"Do you believe that the support given by the present administration to the group of Irish radicals known as the Fenians constitutes a violation of the Treaty of Ghent?"

"Your question presupposes that the administration is giving aid to these Fenians, Mr. Chairman. It is not. Therefore, I cannot see how this treaty provision applies."

"You state that the administration is not giving support to the Fenians?"

"Correct, Mr. Chairman."

"Is the administration allowing them to recruit, arm, and train their units on American soil?"

"Well, that depends on what your definition of the word 'support' is. The administration is not actively doing anything to arm or train these Fenians, nor are we actively recruiting on their behalf. We are ignoring them completely. How, then, can you say that we are 'supporting' them?"

"If I might, Mr. Chairman?" asked Senator James Doolittle, a Republican from Wisconsin.

"By all means," Sumner said, gesturing for him to speak.

"Thank you, Mr. Chairman," Doolittle said. "Mr. Secretary, if a police officer stands quietly by while a gang of armed thieves robs a bank, can it not be said that the police officer aided the thieves in their robbery?"

"I do not think that is an appropriate analogy, Senator. It is the clear duty of the police officer to protect the bank. It is not the clear duty of the United States to protect the British Empire. We have no obligation to them."

"I must emphatically disagree," Doolittle said. "As you read from the provisions of the Treaty of Ghent just a few minutes ago, we are at peace with the British Empire. Allowing a hostile force to assemble, arm itself, and train within our borders constitutes a clear hostile act on the part of the United States. How would we respond if, for example, the British were permitting Mormon separatists to arm and train themselves in Canada before launching raids into the Utah territory?"

Butler shrugged. "Hypotheticals are of no interest to me, Mr. Chairman."

Sumner rejoined the conversation. "It is a well-known fact, Mr. Secretary, that a heavily-armed band of several hundred Fenians crossed the border from New York into Canada last month and fought a battle against British forces, resulting in large casualties on both sides. It is equally well-known that several regiments of the United States Army are deployed along the border with Canada. You cannot seriously expect this committee to believe that the Fenians could have organized and armed themselves without the army being aware of it."

"You and the other members of your committee are free to believe whatever you like."

"It is my understanding that the commanders of our forces along the border with Canada have been given orders to prevent the passage of the Fenians across the border. Is that correct?"

"I cannot answer that, Mr. Chairman."

Sumner's eyebrows went up. "I'm sorry?"

"I cannot answer that question without making public information of a sensitive nature which may impact the safety of the country. Moreover, as the Constitution clearly states that the president is commander-in-chief of the military forces, he is free to give whatever orders to the army and navy that he sees fit."

Sumner snorted in contempt. He glanced down at Storey. "Please note that the Secretary declines to answer the question."

"Yes, sir," Storey replied. There was confused muttering in the crowd behind Butler. Reporters increased the tempo of their scribbling.

"Mr. Secretary, might I remind you that you are under oath? If you refuse to answer the committee's questions, you may be found in contempt of Congress. And if you provide false answers to the questions, you may be guilty of perjury."

Butler didn't respond, but simply stared impassively up at Sumner.

Sumner went on. "The Fenian bands are armed with large numbers of Enfield and Springfield rifles. From where did they obtain them?"

"I don't know, Mr. Chairman."

"Do you know the name Thomas Sweeny?"

Butler paused a moment. "I do."

"Who is he?"

"He is a brigadier general in the United States Army. He saw extensive service in the late war with the Confederacy, in which he fought with great gallantry. I do hope that the Chairman does not intend to disparage his character in any way."

Sumner ignored Butler's obvious attempt to divert attention from the matter at hand. "He has recently been granted a leave of absence, with full pay, for an indefinite period. Can you tell me why?"

"He requested leave for personal reasons, if I am not mistaken. The Chairman will appreciate that in my position of Secretary of War, I oversee an army of several hundred thousand men, commanded by several thousand officers. It would be impossible for me to remember all such minor details."

"It is true that General Sweeny has been involved with the Fenian movement?"

"I don't know."

"Is it customary to grant leaves of absence with full pay and indefinite time limits to general officers?"

Butler held up his hands. "Whether it's customary or not does not seem to me to be of much importance. As the Secretary of War, it is within my purview to grant leave how and when I see fit." Butler paused for a moment. When he spoke again, his tone had subtly changed. "I might remind the Chairman that you were absent from the Senate for two years following the attack upon you by Representative Brooks."

Sumner winced, as though struck by a violent electrical shock. He had to restrain the urge to clasp the table for support. For a moment, he could visualize Brooks standing over him, bringing his cane down upon his head again and again with tremendous force. It was as if the attack was happening all over again. It had taken years for the nightly nightmares to stop, but even after nearly a decade they sometimes returned, even while he was awake.

Butler sneered up at Sumner, seeing the effect of his words with a clear sense of satisfaction. From the look in the man's eyes, it was clear to Sumner that Butler had intended what he had said to have just such an impact, being designed to throw off Sumner's concentration and disorient him.

Sitting just to his right, Senator Charles Buckalew of Pennsylvania saw his distress. Buckalew was a Democrat, but as much a man of integrity as that party produced. "Mr. Chairman?" Buckalew asked. "May I ask the Secretary a question?"

Sumner nodded, finding it momentarily difficult to speak.

"Thank you, Mr. Chairman," Buckalew said. "Mr. Secretary, what is the current disposition of United States Army forces along the border with Canada? I am asking because I want to be satisfied that they are properly deployed to prevent Fenian incursions into Canada, in accordance with the stated policy of the administration."

Sumner didn't listen as Butler and Buckalew went back and forth for the next few minutes. He was unconcerned with the geographic details in any event and the Pennsylvania senator had obviously asked the question only to allow Sumner some time in which to compose himself. He took a deep breath, forcing the brutal memory of Brooks's attack out of my mind by sheer force of will. The South Carolina politician, Sumner reminded himself, was dead.

After perhaps five minutes had passed, Buckalew looked back at Sumner. "I'm finished, Mr. Chairman."

"Very good," Sumner said. He again tried to clear his mind and focused on the next question he wanted to ask. "Mr. Secretary, who commands the forces deployed along the Canadian border?"

"Major General George Thomas."

Eyebrows went up on half the faces of the committee members. There was a rustling of murmurs in the crowd behind Butler. Even Storey, normally so imperturbable, glanced over his shoulder to see the reaction from Sumner at the name.

Sumner found the very name of George Thomas distasteful. For one thing, the man was a Virginian and had been a slaveholder. More important than that, though, was the manner in which the name of Thomas reminded Sumner of things he did not wish to be reminded of. Thomas had been the commander of the Army of the Cumberland when it had been smashed to pieces at the Battle of Peachtree Creek in July of 1864. The shattering of one of the Union's principal field armies had set in motion a chain of events that had led inexorably to the Treaty of Toronto the following year.

Sumner had heard it said that George Thomas was a man without a country. His fellow Southerners considered him a traitor for siding with the Union; his own sisters refused to acknowledge that they had a brother. To the people of the North, in turn, Thomas was the man who had lost the war. Why McClellan and Butler had chosen Thomas to command the troops deployed along the border with Canada was anyone's guess.

"I wish to inform you, Mr. Secretary, that I intend to subpoena General Thomas to appear before this committee, as well as General Sweeny."

For the first time, Sumner thought he sensed a disquiet in Butler's expression, an unease behind his tiny, dark eyes. "I do not believe their testimony would be of any particular benefit. There is nothing they could tell you that I cannot tell you myself. Moreover, I would not want to pull them away from their important military duties."

"May I, Mr. Chairman?" The question came from Senator James Harlan, a Republican from Iowa.

"Of course," Sumner replied. He was comfortable allowing Harlan to speak, for the Iowan had always been a dependable ally.

"Thank you, Harlan said. "Mr. Secretary, you say that these generals should not be pulled away from important military duties. Yet you have also informed

273

us that General Sweeny is currently on leave of absence. Even if the committee accepted your argument in regards to General Thomas, how could subpoenaing General Sweeny interfere with military duties of any kind?"

Butler shifted uneasily in his chair. "I was merely offering advice to the Chairman. I was speaking hypothetically. You are, of course, free to subpoena anyone you like. That is the prerogative of every congressional committee, if I am not mistaken."

"Quite right," Sumner said sternly. "It's refreshing to hear someone from the McClellan administration acknowledge that there is such a thing as the separation of powers." He looked to the men sitting on either side of him. "Does any other member of the committee have any questions?"

"I ask to be recognized," said Senator John Downey, a Democrat from California.

"Proceed," Sumner said tiredly. He did not care for Downey. He had served as the new state's governor in the 1850s and been defeated for reelection for his lukewarm support of the war effort. The year before, however, the ambitious man had reentered politics by getting himself elected to the Senate. There were strange rumors that Downey's long-term goal was the secession of California and the creation of an independent republic on the Pacific coast.

"Thank you, Mr. Chairman," Downey said. "Mr. Secretary, do you believe that the proceedings of this committee today are legitimate?"

"I do not, Senator."

"Why not?"

"The purview of the Senate Foreign Relations Committee is to consider legislation affecting the interactions between the United States and foreign nations. It seems to me that Senator Sumner, in calling these hearings, is simply trying to bring the McClellan administration, officers of the United States Army, and citizens of Irish birth or ancestry into disrepute for political purposes of his own."

"Thank you, Mr. Secretary."

The reporters scribbled furiously, trying to get down Butler's every word. Sumner scoffed. The short exchange between Butler and Downey had obviously been planned out beforehand. This did not unduly bother Sumner. He had been in the political game long enough to know that there was little to be done about such tricks.

Besides which, Sumner had tasted blood. Butler was clearly afraid of the possibility that Thomas and Sweeny would be brought to testify before the committee. As the session ended and the people in the room rose to leave, Sumner knew exactly what his next move was going to be.

June 11, Evening
Ballard House Hotel, Richmond, Virginia

"Ten percent?" Secretary of the Treasury Trenholm asked, his eyebrows going up.

"Yes, ten percent," Benjamin replied with a smile. "They are free to contribute more if they like."

The dozen men in the hotel room fell into a sudden and uncomfortable silence, which didn't surprise Benjamin. He had arranged the meeting of high government officials and had known what to expect. These were men who were in a position to dispense patronage and who had used that power well. Over the years, they had obtained literally thousands of jobs for their political supporters, many of which paid hefty salaries while involving little actual work.

"The administration has been very kind to you and your friends," Benjamin said, breaking the silence. "Now it's time for you to repay that kindness."

"You know that I support Mr. Breckinridge's candidacy," said Postmaster Reagan. "I will do whatever I can to help him win the election. Still, telling all employees of the Post Office that they are expected to turn over ten percent of their salaries every month for the rest of the year? That's a very steep demand. It's hard enough for many of them to get by as it is."

"Exactly what I was going to say," declared Douglas Cooper, Commissioner of Indian Affairs. "I have a lot of boys in my department who are having a hard time putting food on the table. And you want me to ask them to take a pay cut?"

"Would your people rather lose their jobs altogether?" Benjamin asked. "Because if Beauregard wins the election in November, that is precisely what will happen. They will be kicked out and the Fire-Eaters will put their own people in. They may groan about contributing ten percent of their pay, but it's a better prospect than finding themselves on the street. Don't you think?"

Again, an uncomfortable silence descended on the men in the room. No one raised any objection to what Benjamin said. He was certain that the single thought passing through all of their minds was whether Benjamin expected this policy to apply to them as well as to their employees.

Trenholm spoke again. "So, we can tell our people that, if Breckinridge is elected, they will keep their positions?"

"Breckinridge is a man interested in good and efficient government. Continuity is a positive thing. So if they are doing their jobs well, I am confident that he will keep them on. If they are doing their jobs poorly, he will kick them out. That's a better proposition than they are likely to get from a Beauregard administration, who will kick them out regardless of how good they are at their jobs."

Benjamin recalled an incident that took place when Breckinridge had been asked by Davis to become the Secretary of State, in late 1864. Breckinridge had agreed to accept only if he would be allowed to fire Lucius Northrop, the incompetent Commissary-General of the Confederate Army. Davis had objected, as Northrop was an old friend. Yet Breckinridge had insisted upon it, rightly asserting that Northrop's ineptitude and mismanagement had been responsible for severe shortages of food and clothing among Confederate troops. In the end, Breckinridge had gotten his way.

In Benjamin's mind, the Northrop episode was just one of a thousand examples that proved how good a man Breckinridge was and how fit he was to serve as the head of the government. He would conscientiously devote himself to making the administration run smoothly and effectively, no matter how many sleepless nights it cost him. Beauregard would be a very different beast, indeed. Obsessed with his own vanity, he would find the detailed work of administration boring and unappealing, leaving Toombs and Wigfall free to run it as they pleased, with their own people.

"I agree with you that we need to work for a Breckinridge victory at the polls," Reagan said. "But ten percent is quite a large figure to ask. Can we not reduce it to seven? Or perhaps five?"

Benjamin shook his head. "One of Beauregard's advantages in the race is that his campaign is going to be well-funded. Many rich plantation owners from across the South are already licking their lips in anticipation of writing checks to him. Everyone knows that this is shaping up to be a contest between Beauregard and Breckinridge and are just waiting for official confirmation of that fact. Once it's all out in the open, the landowning class will seize their opportunity to get revenge on Breckinridge for what he did during the peace negotiations."

"So you're saying we need to do this in order to compete with Beauregard on level terms?" Trenholm asked.

"Exactly correct," Benjamin replied. "Even if we do it, I doubt we'll be able to match the financing of Beauregard's campaign."

"But how is this money to be used?" Reagan asked. "To my knowledge, no official national committee or state committees have even been set up yet. There's no organization in place. If I am to ask all my postal workers to do this, to whom do I tell them to write their checks?"

Benjamin nodded, appreciating Reagan's characteristic common sense. "All that is in the works, I promise you. By this time next month, there will be a national committee in place. And there should be state-level organizations within a month after that."

"You'd better move fast," said Thomas Moore, former Governor of Louisiana and now head of the New Orleans Mint, which produced the official currency of the Confederate government. "I've been reading in the papers that Toombs and Wigfall have already organized a national committee and are just waiting until their convention in Montgomery to make it official. Rumor has it that their work in establishing state committees is already underway."

"They are ahead of us, it is true," Benjamin said, trying not to sound defensive. "If you ask me, that just emphasizes the importance of the money that we're talking about. With it, we might have a chance. Without it, we are sunk."

Benjamin thought the situation was far worse than that, though he didn't say so. The Fire-Eaters who were coming out in support of Beauregard were intensely motivated and needed no persuasion to throw all of their energies into the campaign to elect the Creole general. As he was learning, it often took more effort to coax people into supporting Breckinridge. Plenty of people to whom he had spoken told him that they planned on voting for Breckinridge, but it had proven surprisingly difficult to get them to commit to contributing funds or to actively campaign on his behalf.

He reflected on why this should be so. The Fire-Eaters were the minority in the Southern political class, yet they were far louder than anybody else and consequently their influence was out of proportion to their numbers. After all, no one paid attention to a quiet man of good sense if there was a yelling, gesticulating extremist in the room.

More to the point, a moderate man generally kept his mouth shut around an extremist, because no one wanted to be shouted at. Men like Robert Toombs,

Louis Wigfall, or Robert Rhett were more likely to shriek curses and obscenities than to make level-headed arguments. Wise men avoided being drawn into disputes with such people, just as they avoided poking sticks into piles of fire ants. If, despite their efforts, the vitriol of the extremists happened to be directed at them, they either ignored it, as Breckinridge did, or responded to it with a measure of good humor, as Abraham Lincoln had so often done.

Of course, an extremist might forego talking altogether and resort to violence. He remembered the famous incident of Congressman Brooks, an arch Fire-Eater, smashing Senator Sumner's head on the floor of the Senate. Granted, Sumner had only gotten what he deserved in Benjamin's opinion, but such undignified violence was not the way of the gentleman.

Why didn't decent men want to do battle with the Fire-Eaters? To Benjamin, the answer was simple: they didn't want to get their hands dirty, nor did they want to get their hands burned. This was an understandable attitude, but it was also one that might hand the reins of government over to ideologues who would prove to be the ruin of the South.

"These state committees that are being organized," George Rains, head of the War Department's Niter and Mining Bureau, said. "I assume you want us to serve on them?"

"No," Benjamin said. "I'd rather not have this fundraising operation be put too much into the public view. We're not doing anything illegal, but it still may raise eyebrows in some quarters."

"I assume you have discussed all this with Breckinridge himself, yes?" Trenholm asked.

"No, certainly not. In fact, I would very much prefer he not know about it."

This caused mutterings of discontent throughout the room. Men glanced at one another uncertainly. Benjamin felt a tinge of apprehension. He knew that he had asked for a great deal from these men and that it might not take much for his financing plan to collapse.

"Why haven't you spoken to him about it?" Cooper asked.

"Because it would be best for him not to know," Benjamin replied. "Breckinridge is very much a stickler for matters of honor, as you know. It's not enough that something be within the letter of the law. It has to be decent and proper, too. That's an admirable attitude, but not one calculated to raise much money."

"So you acknowledge that some might deem what you're asking as not decent and proper?" This question came from John Wood, Assistant Secretary of the Navy.

"Some might so construe it, yes."

Wood persisted. "If any of our employees decline to contribute this suggested ten percent of their salaries, am I correct in thinking that they will be fired?"

"You are."

Wood sighed. "Well, in that case, I must count myself among those who do not consider this proposal to be decent and proper."

"Look," Benjamin said firmly. "We can sit here and debate ethics all day. Beauregard's supporters are getting ready to converge on Montgomery for their

277

convention. Unless you want to hand over the government to the likes of Toombs and Wigfall, you will fall in line. We need money if we are to have a chance at winning this election. What I am proposing is the only way we will be able to compete with Beauregard's supporters for cash. Ethical or not, if we don't do it, the Fire-Eaters will take power and we will all lose our jobs anyway. Worse than that, this country will be set on a disastrous course."

Silence descended upon the room as Benjamin finished speaking. The Secretary of State scanned the eyes of each of the men, trying to divine their thoughts and intentions. He knew that all of them had to give their acquiescence, for if any single one refused it could be used as an excuse for the whole operation to be abandoned.

He decided to put them on the spot. "Unless there are any objections, I shall consider our plan as being accepted. So, are there?"

Again, there was silence. Benjamin knew how easy it was to be the second person to raise his voice in opposition to something, yet how difficult it was to be the first person to do so. Nearly a full minute passed, but no one said another word.

"Very well, gentlemen," Benjamin said with a smile. "I consider the proposal to be accepted, then. I'll contact each of you to go over specific details about where to send the money. Until then, I bid you a good evening."

June 14, Noon
Portsmouth, England

Slidell felt his stomach turn somewhat as his ferry began to move away from the dock and into Portsmouth Harbor, the first step on its voyage across the English Channel to Le Havre. His valet Michel was in much worse shape, his face turning green and looking as though he were barely restraining himself from vomiting. It was rather pathetic, Slidell thought, for the weather was quite pleasant, with sunny skies and a cool breeze. There was not the slightest disturbance in the water.

Disraeli had sent him a message saying that the crossing would be smoother if he took the ferry from Portsmouth to Le Havre rather than the more direct route from Dover to Calais. Slidell was not fooled into thinking that the British prime minister was concerned about the weather. He simply wanted Slidell to pass through Portsmouth. The Confederate diplomat had reasoned that if the most powerful man in the world wanted him to do something, he should do it.

As the ferryboat moved into the center of the vast harbor, Disraeli's purpose became perfectly clear to Slidell. All around him, seemingly for miles, there was activity. Thousands of workers crowded the docks, sawing wood and hammering metal, moving equipment and crates and supplies, in an enormous cacophony of noise and energy. It was like looking at an immense army of worker ants. Portsmouth was one of the busiest ports in the world, for it was the primary base of the Royal Navy.

From his seat on the ferryboat, Slidell could see literally dozens of British warships. Some sat at the docks, being painted, cleaned, or stocked with supplies. Others were gracefully sliding across the water, entering or leaving the harbor.

Slidell saw the *HMS Minotaur*, a four-hundred-foot-long iron behemoth, said to be the most powerful warship in the world, making its way out towards the English Channel. The *HMS Warrior*, the first ironclad Britain had produced, was moving in the opposite direction, returning from patrol. All around, frigates and cruisers darted back and forth across the harbor like so many rabbits. Slidell reflected for a moment that the naval power within Portsmouth Harbor alone could easily destroy the entire United States Navy.

In one particular dock, Slidell could see the *HMS Black Prince*, sister ship to the *Warrior*. She was a graceful-looking ship, not all that different from the great three-masted sailing ships that would have been familiar to Nelson. Yet she was built of iron, not wood, and was armed with the most advanced cannon the iron foundries of Britain could produce. The sails were there only to supplement the two powerful steam engines with which the ship was equipped. Workers swarmed over her, cleaning her hull, scrubbing her deck, bringing supplies on board, and performing all manner of other tasks.

One of the crewmen of the ferryboat pointed. "That's her, sir. The *Black Prince*. Fine-looking ship, don't you think? They're fitting her out to sail to your country. Couple of frigates going to go with her. At least, that's the rumor going around Portsmouth."

Slidell grunted in response, not deigning to speak to a man of such low rank. He was somewhat surprised that Disraeli still intended to dispatch warships to the Confederacy, as the British newspapers were filled with reprints of the speech John Bright had given in the House of Commons. Even some papers normally supportive of the Confederacy had become noticeably cooler in their coverage of the South. Slidell could feel public opinion sliding away from the South and towards the abolitionist cause. What was worse, he didn't feel there was anything he could do about it.

Haynes had asked him to remain in London for another week to help him deal with the fallout from Bright's speech, but Slidell had refused. There was urgent business to take care of in Paris and he had allowed his affairs there to drift during his excursion to England. Besides, Haynes needed to learn to do his job without Slidell's assistance. If he didn't, the man had no business being a diplomat. Slidell had no time for ineptitude.

The *Black Prince* began to fade from view as the ferry continued on its way. For a moment, Slidell wondered if Disraeli had picked the ship for deployment to the Confederacy as a subtle message. The name, of course, derived from the gallant son of King Edward III, who had defeated the French at the epic battles of Crecy and Poitiers. Yet how many people in the North American nations knew that? Might Disraeli have chosen the *Black Prince* as some sort of subtle reference to the black bandit Saul, whose exploits were now regularly being discussed in the British newspapers?

Michel finally threw up over the side of the boat, much to the amusement of Slidell and the other passengers. The ferry passed out of Portsmouth Harbor and into the body of water known as Spithead, which opened into the English Channel. The ferry pilot increased speed and the boat began chugging away to the southeast towards France. With luck, they would be in Le Havre by nightfall and Slidell could be on the train for Paris the next morning. He ordered coffee and sat back in his seat, trying to relax.

He had enjoyed his English sojourn, but was greatly looking forward to being back in France. He preferred the French, for he felt himself to be very like them. Besides, he knew he was an old and increasingly frail man. He wanted to be back in his own home. There, it would be easier to relax and contemplate everything that had happened in England.

Disraeli's offer of an alliance still stood, despite the shifting of public opinion. Confirmation of this would come when the warships sailed for Charleston. Shunting Slidell through Portsmouth so that he could view British naval power up close had been intended to illustrate what Britain could offer to the Confederacy. Clearly, Her Majesty's Government saw the grumblings of a few abolitionists as a small price to pay if it meant bringing the Confederacy onto its side in its dispute with the United States.

Slidell pulled a copy of the telegram he had received from Benjamin just before departing London.

Minister Slidell,

I thank you for your report on your meeting with Mr. Disraeli. I look forward to a more detailed report after you return to Paris. President Davis views the possibility of closer relations between the Confederacy and the British Empire with great pleasure. If you could speedily complete your full report and send it as soon as possible, that would be most kind.

I am, sir, your most obedient servant,

Judah Benjamin, Secretary of State

Years before, Slidell and Benjamin had agreed that any official communication which ended with the words 'most kind' was to be treated with skepticism. Benjamin was telling him that while Davis might view closer ties with Britain in a positive light, he himself did not.

Slidell shared Benjamin's doubt. At first glance, the possibility of an alliance with Britain would seem to be a golden opportunity. After all, Britain was the world's premier military and economic power. What nation wouldn't want Britain as an ally? Yet the more Slidell thought about it, the more disturbed he became.

Though ostensibly ruled by a queen, Britain was a democracy. The moment that the Fenian crisis passed, the British government would abandon its temporary connection with the Confederates due to domestic political concerns. In the meantime, every step the Confederates took towards the British would be one step farther away from the French, the traditional and natural enemies of the island nation to the north. He did not like the idea of throwing away all the work he had done to achieve a treaty with the French in pursuit of what would probably be only a temporary alliance with Britain.

On the other hand, Slidell sensed an opportunity. If Napoleon III could be made to believe that an alliance between England and the Confederacy was a real possibility, he would certainly become alarmed. The French were participating in the negotiations with the Confederates not just because they wanted assistance in their Mexican adventure, but because they wanted access to Southern cotton and tobacco at prices that would allow them to better compete with the British economically. If they sensed that this opportunity was slipping from their grasp, the French might become more eager to sign their treaty.

An agreement with France was sure to be more lasting than an agreement with England. The Bonapartists seemed secure in Paris, so it could be assumed that the Napoleonic dynasty was not going to end anytime soon. In England, governments came and went with every election, so no commitment from London could be taken for granted. Better a firm alliance with the strong power, Slidell thought, than a precarious alliance with the strongest power.

Slidell knew he would have to play a very careful game, indeed. He needed to persuade Disraeli that he was inclined to agree to his proposal for Confederate support in the Fenian matter, but not allow matters to reach the point of any signed, formal agreement. He would have to persuade Davis to agree to it as well. This would have to be done in such a way that didn't embroil the Confederacy in any new conflict with the United States. At the same time, he would have to make the French believe that a formal agreement between the Confederate and the British Empire would happen unless they did something to stop it. It would require bamboozling his own administration, the McClellan administration, the British, and the French.

Yet if he played all of his cards right, the end result would be the treaty of alliance between the Confederacy and France that had become the last great dream of his life. He might even be able to drag Disraeli along long enough for the prime minister to do what he asked regarding the easing of the South's debt repayments.

He couldn't help but smile. The challenge before him was one that Talleyrand or Metternich would have relished. As the ferryboat passed through Spithead on its way to northern coast of France, Slidell felt a thrilling sense of anticipation fill him. If he succeeded, he would surely go down in history as one of the great diplomatic masterminds.

June 18, Afternoon
Aboard the SS Vincent *in the Atlantic Ocean*

Lowell stood on the bow of the ship, staring out at the empty expanse of water all around him. Overhead, a small flock of seagulls drifted lazily in the breeze, cackling back and forth to one another. Only thin wisps of clouds were visible in the sky. The whole scene was strangely beautiful. He understood why authors like Herman Melville found the subject of the ocean so alluring.

He himself was no stranger to sea travel. The Boston in which he had grown up was a busy port, so ships and sailors had always been present in his life. He had traveled to Europe twice and had sailed to points up and down the Atlantic coast of the United States many times. Many of his Lowell ancestors had been wealthy merchants, owning ships that crisscrossed the oceans of the world.

Compared to the beautiful clipper ships that plied the seas between Boston and China, the *SS Vincent* was not a handsome vessel. An iron-hulled sidewheel steamer, she had obviously been built with function rather than form in mind. According to what Captain Naismith had told him, she actually started life as a British-built blockade runner in the service of the Confederacy. Captured by the Union Navy off Wilmington in 1864, she had then been put to use as a gunboat until the end of the war. Naismith had purchased her in Philadelphia the previous year, named her after a Union colonel who had died at Gettysburg, and had been moving cargo up and down the Atlantic seaboard for the past several months.

Now, of course, the vessel was being put to use in a way its original owners could never have conceived and probably would have found horrifying.

Despite Naismith's instructions, Lowell had been unable to restrain himself from occasionally slipping below decks to make sure that his crates were still stowed securely. He had been careful to do this only when the crew was quite busy and unlikely to notice anything. The weapons and ammunition being carried on the ship had become an obsession and he could not keep himself away from them. He was resolved to deliver them to Saul or perish in the attempt.

Lowell sighed. Whether it had been the right decision or not, he had gone forward. It was far too late to change his mind now. He had not only crossed the Rubicon, but he had crossed several Rubicons. The moment he had loaded the crates onto the ship, he had violated the laws of the United States. The moment the ship docked in New Orleans, he would be violating the laws of the Confederacy, too. Lowell was now a criminal. He knew that he could expect no help other than symbolic gestures if his plan was discovered. Senator Sumner could give the most articulate speech on the floor of the Senate and it would not save Lowell from the gallows.

For a brief moment, the memory of his last sight of his wife flashed through his mind. Josephine and their two children had seen him off at the Boston dock and he had watched them fade into the distance as the ship moved out to sea. The sight had torn his heart in two. The children had not understood that he was going to be gone for a long time. Anna had assumed he was simply going on one of his normal business trips. He had not been able to bring himself to tell her that he might not be coming back.

He had a moral duty to fight slavery, but did he not also have a moral duty to support his family? By again taking up the fight for abolition, was he abandoning his wife and children? Josephine might have given her blessing, but the children were far too young to understand and were therefore not capable of giving theirs. If he did die, what would they think of their father in future years? Anna was just old enough that she might have a hazy recollection of his existence, but Robert would not remember him at all. He sighed with sadness and regret.

He heard footsteps and turned to see Captain Naismith approaching him, a reproachful expression on his scarred face. Lowell wasn't surprised.

"You checked your crates again this morning, I noticed," Naismith said.

"I apologize. I wouldn't think a few occasional checks would be out of the ordinary."

"Probably not, no. But we're smugglers now and shouldn't take even the slightest risk. Like I said, if a single crewman files a report with the Confederate authorities when we dock in New Orleans, a search of the ship could be made and they'd easily find the rifles. You and I both know what that would mean."

"I know."

"And might I remind you that it's not just your own life you're risking. It's mine as well."

Lowell nodded soberly. During the war, he had never asked a soldier to do anything he would not do himself. He had willingly shared in the danger of battle, as the number of horses shot from under him proved beyond any doubt. That had made it easier for him to issue orders he knew would get many of his men killed. Naismith had known the risks of this mission when he agreed to it and could have backed out if he had wanted. Still, reflecting on the dangers they faced was only natural, especially during the monotonous voyage when there was little else to discuss aside from the routine running of the ship.

"Have you been to the South before?" Naismith asked. "I mean aside from the war, of course."

Lowell nodded. "Yes, back in 56'. Doctor ordered me to tour Cuba and the South for my health. So I went with a good friend of mine."

Naismith looked at him in some surprise. "Consumption?"

"That's right."

"You seem very healthy now."

"Well, I beat it."

Naismith chuckled. "You are an interesting man, Lowell. But what were your impressions of the South?"

"A dark place," Lowell replied.

"Very pretty though, didn't you think? Lovely climate. And those plantation houses are quite fine."

Lowell grunted. "I was struck by the cleanliness of the elegant houses of the white slave-owners when contrasted with the dirtiness and misery of the slaves." He thought for a moment. "I have always been an abolitionist, you see. It comes with being a Lowell. But seeing the slave system up close, seeing what it really meant, stripped of all the rhetoric of the Southerners themselves, seeing it with my own eyes. That turned me into what I am."

"Where did you go?"

"From Charleston in South Carolina all the way to New Orleans. We stayed at many plantations along the way. It was strange how decent and polite the Southerners were to us. They had to assume, as we were New England men, that we were abolitionists. Yet we were greeted warmly everywhere. It made me very uneasy. How could such refined and courteous people live with themselves, knowing that their entire way of life was made possible only through the labor of slaves?"

"Did you talk to any of them about it?"

"No, it never came up," Lowell replied. "It was as if there was an unspoken agreement between us not to mention it."

"Politeness and grace does not make one a moral man."

Lowell grunted agreement, then turned to look at Naismith. "You still think our plan is a good one?"

"As good as any, I suppose," Naismith answered.

Before leaving Boston, they had agreed that the best course of action was to bribe whatever customs official was placed in charge of the *SS Vincent*, telling him that the crates contained expensive scotch intended for wealthy customers in the city, on which they did not want to pay import duties. Included as part of the bribe would be a few bottles of the said scotch, which would hopefully add a layer of credibility to the story. If they were lucky, of course, the customs officials would be doing their jobs sloppily and might not even notice the crates. In that case, their elaborate deception would not be necessary at all.

Lowell scanned the skies around the ship's masts. "I haven't seen any albatrosses. Is that a good omen?"

Naismith shrugged. "Albatrosses are signs of good luck, actually. Just don't kill them like that fool did in that poem. But you never see them in the North Atlantic."

For a long minute, the two men stood in silence, staring off at the horizon as the sun began its long descent. The seagulls continued their cackling and the waves kept passing underneath the bow of the ship.

"I will leave you now, Lowell," Naismith said simply. "I must see to the ship." He touched the brim of his hat and walked backs towards the stern.

Lowell watched him go. He realized that he felt a measure of comradeship with Naismith, not unlike that he had felt towards his brother officers during the war. They were both enduring danger in the service of a cause and were both depending on the strength of the other to get them through it. For just a moment, memories of the 1864 Shenandoah Valley Campaign came rushing back to him. He recalled images of hundreds of thundering war horses charging towards the enemy, of the psychological shock of Confederate surprise attacks, and of simple burial ceremonies on quiet hillsides as they said goodbye to far too many slain friends.

With nothing else to do, he resumed his pacing back and forth across the deck, his mind unsettled.

CHAPTER EIGHT

June 19, Afternoon
Flynn's Alehouse, Waco, Texas

"He fired you?" McFadden asked in astonishment.

The old man sitting across from him, whose name was Joseph Swenson, nodded, his lips tightly pursed, sadness in his eyes. In his early sixties, he had not served in the war on account of his age and an old leg wound from the Mexican War. A widower whose only son had died of typhoid during the war, he had made ends meet by working at a local tannery and doing occasional odd jobs around town.

"Yeah, he fired me all right," Swenson said, trying to control his voice. "He says that because I was supporting you in the election, he didn't want me in his tannery ever again. Not only that, but he's telling all the other folk in town not to hire me, either."

McFadden sat back in his chair, his eyes wide with surprise. Swenson was a well-known and well-liked figure around Waco. The idea that someone could flippantly take away his livelihood was almost unimaginable. The owner of the tannery was known to be a friend of Judge Roden and a beneficiary of county officials.

"You going to be all right, Joe?"

"Don't honestly think so, Jimmy. I'm an old man, you know. Too old to be a ranch hand, for sure. Don't have much in the way of skills. That tannery job was all I could get."

McFadden felt a wave of sympathy. "Why don't you just tell them that it was a mistake?" McFadden asked. "Tell him you're not backing me and that you've always planned on voting for Roden. Maybe they'll give you your job back."

"It's too late. Someone saw me at the rally you had a few weeks ago. They had a guy there writing down the names of people who went. I've told other people I plan on voting for you."

"Then tell them you changed your mind."

"Won't make a difference. They want to make an example of me. They want other people to see what happened to me, so that they'll think twice before voting for you." He waited a moment, not wanting his voice to crack. "You soldiers look out for each other, but who's going to look out for an old man like me? Got no family, Jimmy."

"We'll figure something out, Joe," McFadden said without thinking. The moment after he said the words, he wondered whether it had been wise to do so. He could give Swenson some money, for the Turnbow inheritance meant that he had cash to spare. But if he did that, others would surely hear about it and might come with requests for help themselves. If he helped Swenson, he'd have to help everyone.

On the other hand, now that McFadden was trying to enter politics, wasn't it his responsibility to do whatever he could to help Swenson? The man was a constituent, after all, and it was the job of community leaders to help their constituents. By entering politics, McFadden had made himself a community leader.

McFadden talked with Swenson for some time. He promised to ask the pastors of the various churches, at least those who were not overly friendly with Roden, if there was anything they could do to help Swenson until he got on his feet again. He said that he would inquire with his fellow veterans if any work might be available for him. He asked about work that Swenson had done in the past, thinking that such information might be useful for him when he made his inquiries.

Eventually, Swenson and McFadden stood from the table and shook hands. McFadden almost shuddered when he saw the fear and despondency in Swenson's eyes as he turned and left the alehouse. He understood, though. The fear of being utterly helpless, of having no place to sleep but a back alley and nothing to eat but what could be foraged from rubbish, was enough to make a man's blood cold. McFadden himself had land and money, yet even he was not immune from the fear. Watching as Swenson left, he felt another pang of sympathy, sensing how he would feel if Annie and Thaddeus were taken from him by death, leaving him alone in the world.

He sighed. Since announcing his nomination for the state legislature, many people had been coming to him at Flynn's Alehouse with various requests for help. Most of the requests were perfectly reasonable, though he had to remind most people that he had to be elected before he could be of any service to them. The case with Swenson, however, was the most unusual one yet and it raised disturbing implications for the upcoming election.

Flynn walked in the door, having been out running an errand.

"Was that old man Swenson I saw walking away?"

McFadden nodded.

"What did he want?"

"Owner of that tannery fired him because he went to our rally."

Flynn's eyes narrowed. "Did he, now? Well, that's mighty spiteful, if you ask me."

"It is that."

"Not any worse than other stories I've been hearing, though."

He looked up. "What stories?"

"Well, old man Swenson's not the only guy paying the price for supporting you. Not everybody's getting sacked from their jobs, you see, but plenty of people who went to hear you speak or who have said they support you have been told that they won't have a job unless they fall in line with Roden."

"But most people in the district have their own small farms and ranches," McFadden said. "Can't be intimidated like that if you own your own land and grow your own food."

"True," Flynn said. "Not as much, anyway. But people are getting nervous all around. They want to vote for you, believe me. But they are scared of Judge Roden. Scared of what he'll do."

"Well, if we kick him out of office, he won't be able to do a damn thing."

"You've got to persuade people that you'll win, then, Jimmy. As long as people think Roden will still be running the county come November, people will still be scared of him." He waited for a moment. "You want a pint?"

"That'd be nice. Thank you, Flynn."

"Sure."

Flynn went to the bar to pour the drink. McFadden went back to the letter he had been writing before Swenson had arrived. A missive to the commanders of the Texas regiments that had seen action during the war, it had been Collett's idea. Since Roden was not a veteran and McFadden and Collett were, they had thought it might be useful to seek the endorsement of the commanding officers of the Texas units. They could then publish the list in one of the local newspapers, increasing their credibility as candidates.

The thought of newspapers troubled McFadden. The city's leading newspaper, the *Waco Herald*, was backing Roden and was acting as though McFadden didn't exist. The somewhat smaller *Waco Tribune* was also backing Roden. The *Waco Southern Confederacy*, founded only the year before by a veteran from Hood's Brigade, was decidedly anti-Roden and supportive of McFadden and Collett, but had only a small circulation compared to the *Herald* or the *Tribune*.

Assuming that they received a list of endorsements from Texas regimental commanders, McFadden knew that the *Southern Confederacy* would publish it but assumed that the *Herald* and *Tribune* would ignore it. It wasn't right or fair, but he was learning that politics was neither of those things.

He had two pints of ale before finishing the letter. He would now let Collett look it over, since it would be signed by both men. He would also quietly let Annie take a look at it before he declared it finished.

McFadden rose and approached the bar to pay his tab.

"On the house, Captain," Flynn said casually.

McFadden chuckled. "I'm not hurting for the money, Flynn."

"I know it. But you're bringing in plenty of business for me just by having your campaign headquarters here in my alehouse. Besides, I really admire you for what you're doing for folks around here. Takes a lot of guts to take on a man as powerful as Judge Roden. Least I can do is pass you an occasional pint on the house."

"Well, I appreciate it, Flynn."

McFadden stepped out onto the dusty streets of Waco. The sun was about halfway through its descent towards the horizon and it was time to head back to the ranch. Yellowjacket remained tied up to the hitching rail, having faithfully waited for his master for the past several hours. McFadden untied the mustang and quickly mounted him. If he made decent time, he would be back at the ranch before sundown and would have time to spend a few hours with Annie before going to sleep.

He had only ridden a quarter mile down the road when his instincts told him that something was wrong. A quick glimpse backwards confirmed his suspicion. Someone was following him. Hundreds of days spent on the picket line or on patrol had taught him the skill of absorbing the maximum amount of information from the quickest glance. It did not really surprise him to see that the man following him was the same man who spied on the church meeting and observed the rally by the county courthouse. He was riding a medium-sized gray horse and wearing a brown shirt, with a wide-brimmed sombrero hat. He had two bandoliers strapped across his chest and McFadden thought he could see two pistols in holsters on his hips. The man did not seem to be making any effort to prevent McFadden from noticing him. He simply wore the same bored expression on his face as the last two times he had seen him.

McFadden rode on. He turned right, then left, then right again, moving randomly down the streets. The man continued to follow him, still making no effort at concealment. It was as if he wanted McFadden to know that he was following him. McFadden turned right twice more to head back to the street where he had started and the man still shadowed him.

McFadden had stared death in the face so many times during the war that the idea of fear no longer meant much to him. He could not help wondering, however, if Lucius Roden was so unscrupulous as to be capable of sending someone to murder him. He was reassured by the fact that his fully loaded Navy Colt pistol was in its holster on his hip. One bowie knife was in its sheath on the other hip, while a second bowie knife was concealed in his boot.

The man was almost certainly aware that McFadden knew he was being followed. After his long circle through the streets, only a fool could think otherwise. He considered continuing home, supposing that the man had been asked to watch what he was doing in Waco and would give it up when he left the town. On the other hand, if the man did intend violence, he might simply be waiting until there were no eyewitnesses.

McFadden considered his options. Continuing on made no sense, but he did not want to sulk back to Flynn's Alehouse and have the man report back to Roden that he was afraid. Confrontation was the only course open to him. He turned down a small alley between two buildings, where no one else was. A minute later, he glanced back to ensure that the man was still following him. Then McFadden tugged Yellowjacket's reins and turned the horse completely around, walking back towards the man. There was no surprise in his eyes. He reined in alongside him.

"Why are you following me?" McFadden challenged.

The man chuckled. "To see where you're going, obviously. Why the hell else would I be following you?"

The man's voice came out of his mouth as sort of a hiss. Though he looked vaguely Mexican, with a brownish face and a thin black mustache and goatee, his voice had the accent typical to white Texans. His tone was disdainful, yet something about the way the man talked told McFadden that he was educated.

"Who the hell are you?" McFadden demanded. "I saw you at our church meeting. I saw you at the rally. Now you're following me through the streets of Waco. I want to know your name."

The man chuckled, as though it were all a joke. "Name's Rufus Walker. I work for the judge."

"Oh, is that so?" McFadden asked sarcastically. "And what kind of work do you do?"

"Whatever kind of work needs to be done." The tone was politely sinister.

"You're not from around here," McFadden said.

"New arrival. Been down in Mexico this last year. Rather nasty down there these days, you know. Thought it'd be a good idea to look for new pastures for a while. Know what I mean?"

McFadden knew about the war between the French-backed imperial regime of Maximilian and the guerrilla struggle of the republican forces, though he considered it no concern of his. According to what he read in the newspapers, the fighting between the opposing sides had been particularly brutal and bloody. Walker certainly gave McFadden the impression of a man who had seen a lot of killing. He had the look in his eye that McFadden knew all too well, for he possessed it himself.

McFadden nodded towards the bullets strapped across Walker's chest. "Those intended for me?"

Walker looked offended. "Oh, no! Well, not necessarily. The judge don't like what you're doing. He don't like all this messing around. He wants it to stop. And it will stop, my friend. He'd just prefer it be handled the right way, you know?"

McFadden remained tense, ready to draw his Colt the moment he saw Walker reach for one of his guns. But the man made no effort to do so, simply sitting on his horse as though he didn't have a care in the world. "What's the right way?" McFadden

"The judge wanted me to tell you that, when I got a chance. But I thought it was more fun to just follow you for a while. See how you react. You've got good eyes, McFadden. Must have been a good soldier."

"Answer my question."

Walker chuckled, in a way that seemed threatening and amusing at the same time. He held up a finger. "I'm going to reach into my pocket now. I'm not getting a weapon. Trust me?"

"No, I don't," McFadden said abruptly. He slowly pulled his Colt from his holster and pulled back the hammer, leveling it right at Walker. "Make any move I don't like and I'll blow a hole clear through you, understand?"

"Yes, yes, I understand," Walker answered, with irritation rather than fear in his voice. He carefully pulled an envelope out of his pocket and handed it over to McFadden. "There you go. One thousand dollars cash. From the judge. He asks for nothing in return. Just a favor from him."

"I'm not taking any money from that bastard. You go back and tell him that."

"Why not? I know you don't need it, what with your wife's family money and all, but you could just give it to some of your friends. You know, those brave old veterans who are trying to hold on to their land. Always going on about the poor veterans, you are."

McFadden felt his stomach clinch. He could not fathom how Walker knew about the Turnbow money. He was obviously dealing with a devious and intelligent man, not just some simple mercenary. At the same time, he felt himself tempted by the last thing Walker had said to him. He thought of old man Swenson, terrified at having lost his job. He could simply take the envelope and give it to him, solving all the man's problems in an instant.

Yet he didn't do it. McFadden knew that the moment he touched the money, even if he had every intention of continuing to oppose Roden's designs, he would be tainted. His own mind would start to see itself as indebted to the judge and, once word of what had happened leaked out, everyone else would think so, too. It was a trap, pure and simple.

"Tell him to take his thirty pieces of silver and cram them up his ass."

Walker sighed and placed the envelope back in his pocket. "Very well. I suppose we'll have to do it the hard way, then." Walker clicked his horse into a walk, turned it back the way he had come, and began walking away from McFadden.

"Tell your master that if he wants to keep his job, he needs to win the election," McFadden called.

"Oh, he will, he will," Walker called over his shoulder. "Don't worry about that."

McFadden watched until Walker turned his horse and disappeared around a building, then resumed his ride home. He was much less happy than he had been that morning.

June 20, Afternoon
Tuileries Palace, Paris, France

Slidell was not easily intimidated and he had visited the Tuileries Palace enough times that he was no longer nervous upon entering it. Yet the immense, magnificent, and incredibly beautiful building still filled him with awe. Its construction had begun as far back as the sixteenth century and the constant additions and improvements meant that it had never been truly completed. It was like a living, breathing thing. Legendary monarchs like Henry IV, Louis XIV, and of course the great Emperor Napoleon I had ruled from within its walls.

As Michel helped him from the carriage down onto the courtyard grounds, Slidell looked up at the immense façade of the palace. He sighed with a quiet sadness, for he doubted that any such building would ever be built in the Confederacy. The Tuileries Palace seemed to grandly shout forth the magnificence of emperors and kings. Though ruled by an aristocracy, his own country had to keep up at least the pretense of Jeffersonian democracy and proclaim that all white men were equal. The stately plantation homes across the South and their finest examples of public architecture like the Capitol in Richmond would always be held back, like a horse whose rider kept tugging backwards on the bridle.

Michel stayed behind in the carriage, while Slidell stepped forward supported by his walking stick. Let in by the guards who quickly validated his pass, he moved through the main gate and was soon winding his way through the vast labyrinth of interior corridors. The walls were decorated with magnificent gilded mirrors, ornate carvings, and fine paintings depicting the great events of French history. The grandeur of the Second French Empire sometimes became simply overwhelming. A person who saw too much of it gradually no longer saw it at all.

Slidell came to rest in the waiting room outside the emperor's personal office. Breathing hard from the long walk, he gathered his thoughts. He was not sure how long it would be before he was summoned. In his past visits, it had been anywhere from fifteen minutes to two hours. Napoleon III was a conscientious person and knew that Slidell was a frail old man, so would not keep him waiting any longer than necessary.

He had returned from his sojourn in England four days earlier. Only two days after his return, a message came from the emperor requesting a meeting. He had sent a telegram to Richmond informing Davis and Benjamin of this, but had not yet received a reply. Most likely there had simply not been enough time. The trans-Atlantic telegraph had revolutionized communication between Europe and the Americas, but no message was truly instantaneous.

Slidell was in no doubt of the subject Napoleon III wished to discuss. He knew that the French had any number of spies crawling about London, who doubtless had reported on Slidell's every activity while he was there. The emperor almost certainly knew about his meeting with Prime Minister Disraeli.

He assumed that Napoleon was going to try to nip the possibility of an alliance between Britain and the Confederacy in the bud. Having secured France's place as the dominant power in Continental Europe, albeit more through luck than anything else, he was now turning his attention to expanding France's influence overseas. His project for doing so in the New World depended on establishing Maximilian's hold on Mexico and an alliance with the Confederacy was an essential part of that plan.

This put Slidell in the enviable position, rare for a diplomat of a weaker nation, of being asked for something rather than asking for something. He was determined to play his unexpectedly strong set of cards as well as he could.

After perhaps twenty minutes had passed, one of the finely dressed clerks emerged from the room and spoke quietly but firmly.

"His Majesty will see you now, Minister."

Slidell rose, pushing himself up on his walking stick, and stepped into the office. As with everything else concerning Napoleon III, the room was so grand as to be numbing to the senses. On one wall was a portrait of Julius Caesar, while across from it was a portrait of the emperor's illustrious uncle. Behind the immense ornately carved oak desk were large bookshelves stuffed with leather-bound volumes Slidell was certain the emperor had never read.

Sitting at the desk, scribbling furiously, was Emperor Napoleon III. He was not a large or physically imposing man. Despite all the grandness with which he surrounded himself, there was still something comical about the man. Slidell often thought that the emperor looked like a man one might encounter in a New Orleans gambling den rather than ruling one of the great nations of the world.

Slidell had grown to know the emperor reasonably well during his time in France. Unlike most of the crowned heads of Europe, Napoleon III had fought tooth and nail to gain his throne. Two unsuccessful coups had failed to bring him to power and he had lived the life of an exile in London for a time. When revolutionaries had overthrown the monarchy and established a republic in 1848, he had managed to get himself elected president with the support of Bonapartists, for whom his very name was a talisman.

In 1851, in a well-planned operation, he had dissolved the National Assembly and declared the Second French Empire. The Bonapartist dynasty, it seemed, had been reestablished.

All of this meant that Napoleon III had been cast from a very different mold than the other rulers of Europe. He had never quite lost the instincts of a political streetfighter, which was sometimes an advantage and sometimes quite the opposite. Moreover, he always had the sense that his throne was somewhat precarious and that, were he to make the wrong move, he might end up an exile on some godforsaken island, just like his uncle.

The emperor rose from his desk, walked around, and extended his hand.

"Minister Slidell, thank you for coming to see me on such short notice."

"Think nothing of it, Your Majesty. I am always at your service."

Napoleon smiled, nodded, and walked back around to the desk. "Please take a seat. Can I get you anything?"

"Coffee, if you please."

The emperor rang a bell to summon a liveried servant, gave him instructions, and a tray of steaming coffee was laid before them less than two minutes later. Cream, sugar, and a selection of fresh fruit were also on the tray. Slidell smiled. He always had adored French hospitality.

"So, what is it that Your Majesty wished to discuss with me?" Slidell asked.

"I was curious as to whether or not you enjoyed your recent visit to England."

"It was pleasant, though I greatly prefer being in France to being in England. The climate is more pleasant and the people are more polite."

Napoleon smiled. "I understand that your counterpart in London wished your assistance in undermining the visit of the abolitionist Frederick Douglass."

"That is correct."

"He is coming to France after he completes his tour in England, is he not? I assume you will be doing the same thing here that you did in England. Writing pieces against him in the papers and so forth?"

"I am not going to do anything that would violate the laws of your country, Your Majesty."

"I would not especially care if you did, so long as you are discreet about it," Napoleon replied. "I am not enamored of your country's continued practice of African slavery, you know. I would greatly prefer it if your government began moving towards a program of gradual emancipation. But I do not believe that the issue should complicate relations between our two countries."

"Certainly not, Your Majesty."

The emperor waited a moment before continuing, looking deeply into Slidell's eyes. "I understand you had a meeting with Mr. Disraeli while you were in London."

"That's correct, Your Majesty." It would have served no purpose to deny it and Slidell was anxious to get to the heart of the matter.

"May I ask what you discussed with him?"

"He wanted to inquire as to the Confederacy's position regarding the possibility of war between the United States and the British Empire."

"Ah, yes," Napoleon said. "I believe in the rights of the nations and if Ireland wishes to be free, it should be free. But war between the United States and England would be most unfortunate. My uncle gloried in war, but I myself deprecate it." He paused for a moment, with a faraway look in his eyes. "I shall never forget the field of Solferino, so strewn with dead and wounded. War is an insult to man."

"It is, indeed," Slidell said. He didn't doubt the emperor's sincerity.

"What did the prime minister ask of you? I know Mr. Disraeli well enough to know that he does not meet with senior diplomats for no purpose."

Slidell decided to get right to the point. "He asked the Confederacy to make a statement of support for the British position. He further asked that, if war does break out, that the Confederacy join the conflict against the United States on the side of England."

Napoleon frowned, nodded, and sat back in his chair. He said nothing further for a full minute. He pushed his fingers together and fixed Slidell with a deep stare.

"I assume you realize that any kind of alliance between England and the Confederacy would not be received well by France."

"I am very sorry to hear that, Your Majesty. Perhaps if I assured you that any agreement of this sort would be directed against the United States only and would not involve France in any way?"

"But it would, whether you intended it to or not. Personally, I love England. I am on very friendly terms with Queen Victoria, as I am sure you know. The English people were lovely hosts to me during my unfortunate exile. Yet I must never forget that I govern France for the sake of France, and not my own sake alone. France and England are natural enemies. We have been since the emergence of our two nations from the Dark Ages. If the Confederacy and England become allies, it means that we must regard your country as less than friendly to us."

"I fail to see why," Slidell replied. "Your country fought alongside England against Russia not long ago. You recently signed a treaty with one another guaranteeing free trade between your two countries. Why can the Confederacy not be a friend to both France and England?"

Slidell knew he was playing a dangerous game. He had to make the emperor believe that he supported the proposed alliance with England, so as to gain leverage that he could use in the negotiations with France. Yet he had to be careful not to push Napoleon so far that he terminated negotiations altogether. Moreover, Slidell had to drag things out as long as he possibly could, because he still hoped that Disraeli might come through on his promise to intervene with the British bankers to alleviate the Confederacy's fiscal obligations.

"A friend is not necessarily an ally. The Confederacy can be a friend to both France and England. But if it becomes an ally of England, it becomes a potential enemy to France. You must understand this."

Slidell nodded, taking the point. France was busy trying to transform Mexico into what amounted to a client state, ruled by a monarch allied tightly to France. There were rumors of French plans to extend its influence over other former Spanish colonies in Latin America. The British Empire did not look kindly on any of this. A Confederacy allied to England rather than France could be a serious hindrance to French expansionism in the Western Hemisphere.

"I understand quite well, Your Majesty," Slidell said. "In your place, I would have the same concerns. But I am obliged to seek what is in the best interests of my own country. England has made offers to the Confederacy that we would be foolish not to consider."

"What offers?"

"A commitment to protect us from any future aggression on the part of the United States and an alleviation of our debts to British bankers."

"I see," Napoleon replied. "And how do you know this offer is genuine? More importantly, how can you be sure their commitment will not be cast aside the next time the Liberal Party wins control of the House of Commons? Their abolitionists, you well know, are not very fond of your country."

"Yes, I was reminded of that very forcefully during my recent visit to Parliament. But I also believe that the English are an honorable people and that they will keep their word." Slidell, in fact, did not believe this, but it suited him to say that he did. "In any case, there are abolitionists here in France as well."

"Yes, but they are not as loud as those in England."

Slidell chuckled and nodded, but said nothing. His silence was an invitation for the emperor to move the conversation into a different sphere, presumably towards the terms France might offer to counter those of England.

"You and the Marquis de La Valette have been meeting regularly to negotiate the proposed treaty between our two countries, yes?"

"Indeed."

"He has kept me apprised, of course. Please tell me what you think of the progress of negotiations. And please speak frankly."

"Very well," Slidell replied. "I must tell you that negotiations have moved much too slowly. They should have been concluded months ago. Had they been, I might point out, the question of an alliance between the Confederacy and Britain would never have come up."

"True," the emperor replied. "And this question of dispatching troops to aid our efforts in Mexico?"

"I have been in frequent communication with Richmond on that subject. We are prepared to dispatch an expeditionary force of fifteen thousand men. Needless to say, they would be experienced veterans of the war and led by commanders of proven quality."

The emperor nodded. "With such a force allied to my own army in Mexico, the republican forces would not stand a chance."

"I agree, Your Majesty," Slidell said. "But without a treaty of alliance, why should we send any help? And if the British are making an offer to us, why should we not turn to them rather than you?"

"Because we are more trustworthy. I will be sitting here in this palace next year, and for many years after that. When my time comes to meet my maker, my son shall sit on the throne. Disraeli? He could be thrown out of office at the next election. And then you'd have Mr. Gladstone to deal with."

Slidell sat back in his seat, saying nothing, keeping a placid expression.

Napoleon went on. "I don't like you're talking with the English. It makes me wonder if our negotiations should be discontinued."

"That would be unfortunate, Your Majesty," Slidell said quickly, hoping his voice concealed his disappointment. Rather than responding with a carrot, the Emperor had decided to respond with a stick. He tried to gauge from Napoleon's eyes whether or not he was bluffing. France wanted the treaty with the Confederacy, but it did not strictly need it. Was the emperor willing to risk losing the advantage he would otherwise gain if he thought he might frighten the Confederacy out of the embrace of England? He might, if he judged that the Confederates realized the shakiness that would characterize any agreement with the British.

Slidell wondered if Napoleon thought he could still have his treaty with the Confederacy without having to sweeten the concession France would have to grant. Answering that question would be the most difficult task of all.

An uneasy silence of two or three minutes passed. Slidell sipped his coffee and waited for Napoleon to speak further.

"Well, this has been an interesting discussion," he suddenly said, switching to his friendly tone. "I do hope it has not been unpleasant for you."

"Not at all, Your Majesty."

The emperor rose from his desk, prompting Slidell to do the same. He had to lean on his walking stick. A handshake was exchanged.

"You are coming to our next ball, are you not?"

"Of course."

"And bringing that lovely daughter and son-in-law with you, yes?"

"I do hope so, Your Majesty," Slidell replied. The emperor had never made a secret of the fact that he strongly desired to bring Slidell's daughter to his bed. To Slidell's knowledge, he had not succeeded, which might explain the fact that he asked about her almost every time they spoke.

"In that case, I bid you a good afternoon and look forward to seeing you again soon."

Slidell bowed. "Until then, Your Majesty."

As he walked through the halls back to his carriage, where Michel was presumably still waiting, Slidell reflected carefully on the conversation. He choose to see it as the first step in what might turn out to be a long process. Yet his goal remained unchanged. He had to play both the British and Confederate governments long enough for the French to become convinced that a treaty of alliance between them was truly possible, perhaps also gaining preliminary financial concessions from the British in the bargain. Then, he could scupper those negotiations in exchange for a treaty with France on terms the Confederacy could not otherwise obtain.

If he succeeded, he would be giving his country a priceless gift and giving himself an achievement that would make his memory immortal. If he failed, of course, he would be leaving his country friendless in a dangerous world and become an object of derision to his people. It was a dangerous game, indeed, yet that was exactly the sort of game at which John Slidell excelled.

With that thought still passing through his mind, he entered his carriage and was soon rolling through the streets of Paris on his way to dinner.

June 22, Afternoon
Rideau Hall, Ottawa, Canada

Wearing his finest dress uniform, his chest festooned with medals he had won in previous campaigns, Garnet Wolseley stood ramrod straight as he walked up to the main door of Rideau Hall. To him, the building looked as though a vain architect had attempted to create something as imposing as Buckingham Palace and failed spectacularly. The upper third of the façade had a decent carving of a British lion and a unicorn, but the bulk of the wall looked sparse and utilitarian.

Wolseley scoffed. Rideau Hall was the official residence of the Governor-General, the representative of Queen Victoria in Canada. It was supposed to reflect the grandeur and authority of the British monarchy. If this was the best the Canadians could do, they had a lot to learn.

Wolseley had arrived in Ottawa the previous day. He had frequently come to the town over the previous few years to meet with government officials and had always been struck by how much it changed each time he visited. Buildings were being constructed everywhere, new streets were being laid out, and piles of freshly cut lumber sat around all over the town to be used for yet more projects.

The previous year, the Dominion of Canada had officially been created by the Parliament of the United Kingdom in London, essentially making Canada into an independent nation in all matters aside from defense, foreign policy and constitutional matters. Wolseley was not sure how he felt about this. His experience with Canadians had persuaded him that they were a well-meaning but second-rate sort of people. He was not confident that they would prove capable of governing themselves without the steadying hand of England to properly guide and care for them. Moreover, he worried the Canadians might eventually decide to sever their connections with the rest of the British Empire altogether, as their neighbors to the south had done.

Wolseley also did not understand why the Canadians had decided to call the upper chamber of their Parliament the 'Senate'. To Wolseley, it seemed a dangerous flirtation with American-style democracy. Why could they not have followed the British example and created a Canadian version of the House of Lords? Had he been able to craft policy, matters would have been handled very differently, indeed.

He strode up to the two guards standing on either side of the door, dressed in immaculate red uniforms and wearing tall bearskin caps. He saluted and the two guards responded with rigidly perfect salutes of their own. Their eyes did not move. Wolseley's experienced eye saw immediately that these two soldiers were well-trained and had been in the service for some time.

"Lieutenant-Colonel Garnet Wolseley to see the Governor-General."

One of the guards turned without speaking and entered the door, while the other remained rigidly at his post. A minute of silence passed before the guard returned and resumed standing in his original position. Following him out, however, was a small, well-dressed man with a Yorkshire-accented voice.

"Colonel Wolseley? I am Robert Burnaby, the Governor-General's private secretary. If you would please follow me inside."

Wolseley did as told and stepped into the building. The appearance of its interior was more pleasing than its exterior, with attractive paintings on the walls and crystal chandeliers hanging from above. The hallways were filled with men going to and fro. He saw no one else wearing a military uniform and several people looked at him quizzically as he passed. Several pointed to him and whispered quickly among themselves.

"I apologize for the curiosity of our residents," Burnaby said. "It was impossible to keep the news of your visit secret and your name has been in all the newspapers of late."

Wolseley said nothing in response, for he could not think of any response that would have been appropriate. All his life, he had hungered after advancement, recognition, and glory. His fighting in the Crimea, India, and China had won him medals and promotion, but he had never been in the public eye until his recent battle with the Fenians.

Burnaby came to stop in front of a door. He knocked softly and opened it. "Colonel Wolseley for you, sir."

"Yes, yes," a harried voice said from within. "Please send him in."

Burnaby opened the door fully and Wolseley walked past him. The office was ornate. Wolseley immediately concluded that the Governor-General was attempting to decorate his office in as grand a style as possible in order to impress visitors from England. The desk was made of finely carved oak, the chairs were of the latest French style, and the tea service resting on the table in the middle of the room was made from fine silver and well-polished. Several paintings hung from the walls, one of which depicted the death of General Wolfe at the Battle of Quebec in 1759.

Rising from behind the desk was Charles Stanley Monck, Fourth Viscount Monck and Governor-General of the Dominion of Canada. He was a friendly and intelligent-looking man with a long, sweeping beard. He strode forward with a smile on his face and extended his hand.

"Ah, Colonel Wolseley!" Viscount Monck said. "I am delighted to see you. Thank you for accepting my invitation."

Wolseley bowed his head as he shook Monck's hand. "Thank you for extending it to me, Your Excellency. I am honored."

"Please, sit, Colonel," Monck said. "A cup of tea?"

"Thank you, Your Excellency."

The two men sat across from one another at the table and Monck poured Wolseley a cup of tea. Wolseley thought it telling that he poured the tea himself, rather than have a servant on hand to do it.

"You're from Ireland, if I am not mistaken?" Monck said.

Wolseley found the question startling. "Yes, Your Excellency. I was born near Dublin." He paused a moment before going on. "Of good Anglo-Saxon stock, I assure you."

Monck grinned as he sipped his tea. "You need not worry. We belong to the same tribe, you might say. I, too, am an Anglo-Irishman."

Wolseley bowed his head slightly. "I was not aware of that, Your Excellency." He instantly felt more at ease. The Anglo-Irish race to which Wolseley belonged was a peculiar breed. To the bulk of Catholic Ireland, they were as English as any Englishman, while the English themselves viewed them with a certain suspicion, as though their long residence in the Emerald Isle might have tainted them in some way. As far as Wolseley himself was concerned, the only thing especially Irish about him was his belief that Friday was an unlucky day.

Many great British soldiers had come from Anglo-Irish backgrounds, including the Duke of Wellington himself. Unlike Wellington or Monck, however, Wolseley was an Anglo-Irishman who did not come from a wealthy or aristocratic family. He had had to fight his way into the world.

"You and I can appreciate the dangers posed by these Fenians, both of us being Anglo-Irishmen, better than our friends in London," Monck was saying. "Don't you agree?"

"Indeed," Wolseley said. "If I may speak frankly, Your Excellency, these Fenians are no better than vermin. They must be totally destroyed."

"Well, you took a first step in that direction, didn't you?" Monck said with a smile. "Every newspaper in Canada and Britain is talking of your fight against the Fenians. You are quite clearly the man of the hour."

Wolseley shrugged his shoulders. "The Fenians were experienced fighters but displayed poor discipline. Their officers, if one can use such a word to describe them, could not control them effectively. Their Springfield rifles were no match for our Sniders. It was not a difficult matter to drive them back into the river. Our men fought with great gallantry."

"That is only to be expected of the British regiments," Monck said. "We are also delighted by the performance of the Canadian militia. Their courage and discipline was no doubt instilled in them by the superior training you have given them."

Wolseley sipped his tea and nodded slightly. "Perhaps."

"I don't think there's any question about it," Monck pressed. "All of the militia officers are singing your praises. Before your training program was implemented, the militia was little more than a rabble, likely to run away at the first shot. Now, I should not hesitate to field them against any army the United States might send across the border. And I have you to thank for it."

Wolseley slowly became alarmed. It was obvious that Viscount Monck was trying to sweet-talk him, which could only mean that he was soon to ask him to do something he might not want to do. He distrusted politicians and titled aristocrats, and Viscount Monck was both.

Monck rose from his chair and turned towards the liquor cabinet. Without asking whether Wolseley wanted any, he poured two whiskies and handed one to him as he sat back down. The purpose became clear immediately.

"I wanted to share with you some news which I think you will be happy to hear," Viscount Monck said with a smile. "I received a telegram from Her Majesty yesterday. You have been nominated to be a Knight Commander of the Order of Bath."

"A knighthood?" Wolseley asked, genuinely surprised.

"A knighthood, indeed. What better honor for the man who defeated the Fenians?"

"I am undeserving of such an honor," Wolseley said automatically. He did not believe this, but it seemed the proper thing to say.

"To you, Sir Garnet Wolseley!" Monck said, holding up his whiskey glass.

Wolseley did not reply with words but leaned forward to clink his glass with Monck's. He didn't know how he was supposed to respond. All his life he had striven for glory and recognition. To receive the honor of a knighthood, when he still had decades left in his professional career, was something of which he had often dreamed. The goal had always seemed far beyond his reach, but now Viscount Monck was telling him that he had achieved it.

"I am speechless, Your Excellency," Wolseley stammered.

The Governor-General shrugged. "It won't be official for a few more weeks at least. And the investiture ceremony will have to wait until you return to England. But I believe it is all but confirmed. Her Majesty is most pleased with your victory over the Fenian rabble. And that's not all. It would not surprise me if a promotion was in order."

The suggestion that he might be promoted from Lieutenant-Colonel to full Colonel was music to Wolseley's ears. That he was already held his current rank despite being only in his mid-thirties was little short of extraordinary. He attributed it mostly to the terrible wounds he had sustained in Burma and the Crimea and to the fact that he had never made a serious mistake in his army service. Every report he had ever filed had been filled out perfectly, every brass button on each of his uniforms had been impeccably polished, and the sun had never caught him in bed.

Still, Wolseley knew how things worked in Queen Victoria's army. If you had money, you could purchase commissions. If you had noble titles or the right social connections, you would be guaranteed speedy advancement. For a man like Garnet Wolseley, who had neither wealth nor family connections, reaching the rank of Lieutenant-Colonel had been an almost unbelievable achievement. To be granted a knighthood and earn promotion to full Colonel would be a triumph the likes of which the British Army had never seen. It was, after all, only one more step from there to being a brigadier.

Another thought crossed his mind and he suddenly felt a sting of remorse. "If you'll permit me, Your Excellency, I would like for us to raise our glasses to the memory of Colonel Bell. I have seen much of war, sir, and I confess that I never met a braver man than he."

Viscount Monck nodded eagerly. "Yes, we should do that." He raised his glass again. "To Colonel Bell, who fell fighting for his queen."

They both sipped their whiskey gratefully. Wolseley remembered Bell's last moments. The Russians hadn't been able to kill him in the Crimea, nor had the rebellious sepoys in India. Yet he had fallen to a bullet fired by a Fenian who was not even a member of a proper, legal army. It seemed unfair.

Viscount Monck suddenly changed his tone. "Pray tell, Colonel Wolseley, is it true that you are acquainted with John Breckinridge, the Confederate Secretary of War?"

"Yes," Wolseley answered. "When he came to Toronto to participate in the peace talks two years ago, he and I became acquainted. I dare say we became friends."

"You still write him regularly, yes?"

"Often, yes," Wolseley responded. His eyes narrowed, for he did not see where the conversation was going. "He has often requested information about how things are done in the British Army to assist in his restructuring of the Confederate Army. He finds our regimental system particularly interesting, it seems to me."

"Well, the more people following the British way of doing things, the better," Viscount Monck said simply.

"I quite agree, Your Excellency."

"What sort of man is he?"

"Quite an extraordinary one, if I may say so," Wolseley replied. "It is impossible not to like the fellow. He combines political and military gifts in a very rare manner. He has a highly intelligent and discerning mind. Above all, he is a man of scrupulous integrity and honor."

"Would you say he is a friend to the British Empire?"

Wolseley considered this for a moment. "I cannot say, sir. He certainly admires many aspects of it. He often tells me how he wishes his own nation could have the industrial and financial power of ours. But he is entirely devoted to the Confederacy, as is only to be expected."

Monck nodded thoughtfully, studying Wolseley. There was an uneasy silence for a moment and Wolseley sensed that the purpose of the earlier flattery was about to be revealed. Clearly it involved his friend Breckinridge, but he could not fathom what it was.

"Colonel Wolseley, I wish to put forth a proposal to you. You are free to accept it or reject it as you wish. But I will tell you that it comes directly from Prime Minister Disraeli himself."

Wolseley's eyes narrowed. "I understand."

"Her Majesty's government in London have asked me to prevail upon you to journey to Richmond. Your personal friendship with Secretary Breckinridge makes you uniquely well-qualified for the purposes of this mission."

"Which would be?"

"Everyone in London and Ottawa is concerned that the Fenian Crisis might result in an open war between the United States and the British Empire. While the government believes that any such war would inevitably result in a British victory, we wish to avoid war if possible. If it does come, however, we want to ensure that any such conflict is as short and inexpensive as possible."

"That is only good sense, Your Excellency," Wolseley responded. "But what does this have to do with my going to Richmond?"

Viscount Monck leaned forward. "Her Majesty's government want to present an offer to the Confederate government, through your friend Breckinridge. You see, approaches have already been made to the Confederates for a military alliance in the event of a war. We hope that Richmond accepts these offers, but considering your personal relationship with Breckinridge, we want you to ask him directly to use his influence to secure it."

Wolseley considered this. An alliance with the Confederacy made a good deal of sense. If war did break out and the Confederacy joined in on Britain's side, the United States would have to deploy most of its forces on its southern border rather than its northern one, bringing a measure of safety to the Dominion of Canada. British naval supremacy could then be brought to bear, forcing the United States to seek terms.

"Would it not be more appropriate for this task to be given to Her Majesty's minister in Richmond?" Wolseley asked.

"That is already being done, as a matter of course. I am sure that Disraeli himself is speaking to the Confederate representative in London, whoever he may be. But your particular relationship with their Secretary of War gives you a certain advantage, you see. You have easy entrée into the inner circles of the Confederate government. We want to make sure that the Confederate government understands that we are serious in extending this offer."

"Are we?"

Monck sat back slightly, surprise in his eyes. Wolseley realized that he had spoken improperly, for it was not becoming of a British officer to question the integrity of Her Majesty's government. Wolseley did not especially care, though, for he had genuine doubts whether London would follow through on its promises to Richmond.

"I'm surprised at you, Wolseley," Monck said in a slightly reprimanding tone. "I would have assumed that the Disraeli government had your full confidence."

"I am a soldier, Your Excellency," Wolseley replied. "I will follow whatever orders I am given. I am sorry if I spoke out of turn."

"So, will you accept this assignment?"

Wolseley wondered if he should be offended that his political masters had no compunction about exploiting his personal friendship with Breckinridge in such a manner. After thinking about it for a few moments, he decided he should not be. Were he in the position of the Cabinet in London, he would have done precisely the same thing.

Wolseley was not blind, however. Neither the knighthood nor the promotion to full Colonel were official confirmed. Until they were, they were nothing but offers which the government might withdraw any moment it wished. Were he to turn down the request Monck had put forward, it seemed likely that either the knighthood or the promotion, if not both, would vanish like smoke in the wind.

Still, he had no particular qualms about the situation. It was the way the world worked and he understood that. He desperately wanted both the knighthood and the promotion.

"If Her Majesty's government thinks it would be advantageous to send me to Richmond, than to Richmond I shall go," Wolseley said. "It is my duty to serve Her Majesty in any way she sees fits."

Viscount Monck smiled and raised his whiskey glass. "That's what I hoped you'd say, Colonel Wolseley."

"So, we have an agreement?" Toombs said.

The man across the table pursed his lips. He was a wealthy sugar planter who had a plantation near Bixoli, Mississippi. He was willing to make a hefty financial contribution to the Beauregard campaign in exchange from a promise that the administration, should it be elected, would not move to lower the import duty on sugar. Doing so, the man feared, would allow foreign sugar from Cuba and other Caribbean producers to undercut domestic sugar like his own.

"I'd be more comfortable hearing all this from Beauregard himself."

"Yes, yes, I can understand that, sir," Toombs said. "But you see, my friend, General Beauregard is a very busy man. I can assure you that I speak with complete authority. You have my word."

This wasn't true. Indeed, Toombs had not communicated with Beauregard about any of the deals he was making on his behalf. This did not unduly trouble Toombs, for the Creole general was only going to be the face of the ticket. The mind that was going to be making policy was Toombs. Being certain of this, he saw no reason not to start acting like it.

A room at the hotel had been set aside for official campaign business. Since he had arrived in Montgomery the day before, Toombs had been holding meetings with all sorts of people. Some, like the sugar planter, were potential sources of campaign funds. Others were office-holders from across the country ready to put their connections to work on behalf of the new party. The convention might still be a week away, but enemies of Jefferson Davis were already converging on the city to plan and prepare for the coming campaign. Some were those to whom Toombs and his colleagues had written their letters, while many others who had not been officially invited were showing up as well. Reporters were also beginning to swarm into the city, like moths to a flame, eager to cover the big story. Toombs found it all marvelous.

"So, do you want me to write you a check for the thousand dollars?" the sugar planter asked.

"Yes, and you can make it out to the States' Rights Party," Toombs said proudly. They had officially opened an account with an Atlanta bank the previous week. The political party Toombs had long dreamed of was beginning to come into being.

The check was written and handed over. Toombs placed it in an envelope which already held a few dozen checks of roughly the same amount. He had been making deals and giving promises since the previous evening. Like most politicians, he did not enjoy fundraising, for it was a demeaning exercise. Yet it was something that had to be done. Without money, a political campaign simply could not be mounted. It was like water for a man about to attempt a desert crossing.

"Much obliged," Toombs said. "My man Jim will see you out." He gestured lazily to the slave standing by the door.

The sugar planter rose from the table and strode toward the door, taking nothing with him but the verbal promise of Toombs. Jim opened the door and walked out with him. He would be gone for a few minutes while he escorted the man to the hotel lobby. It wasn't really necessary, of course, but such little touches made a visitor feel important.

He took a moment to sip a bit from his glass of brandy. He was making a strident effort not to drink to the point of intoxication, but his mood was so heady and exuberant that it was hard to resist. With Beauregard waiting patiently at his home in New Orleans, Toombs was the man people were coming to see and speak with. He felt like the Sun, with all the planets revolving around him.

It was a familiar feeling, this sense of euphoria. He had felt it during the 'secession winter' in late 1860 and early 1861, when the Southern states seceded from the Union, one by one, and met in Montgomery to form their new government. Toombs had been one of the leaders who had pulled the state of Georgia from the Union and everyone had naturally expected him to be a major player in the newly formed Confederacy. Many thought that the Presidency would be his for the asking.

Toombs had thrown his chances away with that single disastrous night of heavy drinking. Yet now he felt the euphoria again. Power, not just popularity and fame but genuine power, the ability to craft the events of an entire nation, was now within his grasp again. The events of 1861 had been forgotten and he was again the old Robert Toombs, defender of Southern rights against the despot. This time, he told himself, he would do it right. This time, he was sure, he would get the reward he deserved.

There was a soft knock on the door and the slave Jim came back in. Jim was a good slave, Toombs thought, neither bright nor clever. He did what he was told, no more and no less. He wished all slaves could be like Jim.

"Sir?" Jim asked, in the peculiar accent of a slave that only men from the Deep South could easily understand. "Next man to see you goes by the name George Bagby. Says he's a newspaperman, sir. Shall I send him in, sir?"

Toombs nodded impatiently. "Yes, Jim, send him on in." He knew Bagby, whose stories were written for several different newspapers across the South, including some in most of the major cities. Getting men like Bagby on the side of the State's Rights Party was a key strategy for the success of the Beauregard ticket. Yet Toombs recalled that Bagby had been generally supportive of the policies of the Davis administration during the war. This would be a delicate meeting.

Realization suddenly struck Toombs. He stood quickly and put the brandy glass away. Newspapermen who thought back to the events of six years before might recall the drinking bout which had ended his presidential ambitions. It would not do to be drinking brandy while talking to a reporter.

Bagby walked in, a big man with a bushy beard. Like most reporters Toombs met, Bagby's fingertips were smeared dark with pencil lead and he carried a small notepad with him. Something about him reminded Toombs of a man who had forgotten something important and was absent-mindedly trying to remember what it was.

"Evening, Mr. Bagby," Toombs said grandly. "Please, take a seat. Would you care for some coffee? Or perhaps some freshly squeezed orange juice?"

"Some water, if you have any."

"Certainly. Jim, can you fetch Mr. Bagby a glass of water?"

"Yes, sir," Jim said, disappearing back out into the hall.

Toombs sat back in his chair and rubbed his hands together. He had always enjoyed talking to reporters, who in turn liked interviewing him. He could always be counted on to provide bombastic and inflammatory comments that made wonderful newspaper copy.

"So, what can I do for you this evening, Mr. Bagby?"

"I was just wanted to ask you some questions, Senator. The convention you're organizing here in Montgomery has everybody around the country talking."

"Happy to hear it. We're expecting quite a few people, you know. And not just politicians. Lots of good men who served in the army during the war. And of course hundreds of regular Confederate citizens. All coming here because they are united in a common cause."

"That was going to be my first question, Senator. What exactly is the 'common cause' you are uniting all these men around?"

"Why, we need to reclaim our country." Toombs founds Babgy's question odd, for he thought the answer was obvious.

"From whom, Senator?" Bagby said. "We won the war with the Yankees. The Confederacy is a free nation now. So, exactly from whom does the country need reclaiming?"

Toombs scoffed. "Jefferson Davis and his minions are far greater enemies of the South than Lincoln and all the Yankees ever could have been." He watched Bagby's eyebrows shoot up and felt a slight thrill. Those words would be printed all over the Confederacy the next morning. He continued. "The enemy within is far more dangerous than the enemy from without, if you ask me. At least the Yankees had the courtesy to form armies and attack us directly, wearing uniforms different from ours. Davis and his administration have tried to eat away at the Confederacy from within, sapping away the liberties of our people like insects eating a tree from the inside out."

Toombs thought he heard some sort of commotion outside the hotel, but was focused on Bagby's response and so didn't pay much notice. Jim came back into the room with a glass of water, which he placed before Bagby and then withdrew to the wall, where he stood still and silent.

"Respectfully, Senator, your critics will say that Jefferson Davis is as Southern a man as you are. He was one of the staunchest defenders of Southern rights in Congress in the years before secession. He led to country to victory against the Yankees during the war."

Toombs's eyes flashed fire. "He also instituted illegal conscription, forced direct taxes upon the states without their consent, impressed the labor of slaves without the permission of their owners, and stole crops and animals from farmers without paying proper compensation!" He told himself to calm down, for he sensed he was becoming angry. He wanted to be able to control his words.

"Suppose you're right, Senator," Bagby said. "What of it? President Davis's term is up in March."

"Jefferson Davis is just one man," Toombs replied. "They are plenty of others who think as he does and would act as he has done if they were given the chance. A whole nest of vipers. See here, Bagby, there are two kinds of people here in the Confederacy. There are those of us who actually believe in the values of our Confederacy, who believe that our rights are worth protecting, who believe

304

that God granted us victory in the war for a purpose. And then there are those other people who think and act no differently than the Yankees, who think that we should chain ourselves to a foreign power, who think that we need a big standing army, who think that we should look to Richmond rather than to our own state capitals."

"And who are these other people?"

"Oh, they're all over the country, sad to say. Mostly in Richmond, of course. John Breckinridge and Judah Benjamin are the ring-leaders, believe you me. In my own state of Georgia, we've got Senator Ben Hill, doing whatever Davis tells him to do. You've got Postmaster Reagan, giving jobs to anybody who will line up to kiss Davis's ass and not to any man of true Confederate principles. These are only the first few to come to my mind, you understand. Believe me, there are thousands of such men across the country. And like I said, they are more dangerous than the Yankees ever were."

Bagby's face revealed nothing of his actual feelings, if he had any. He simply nodded and scribbled down some notes on his pad. There was silence for perhaps thirty seconds.

"So, Beauregard's your man?" Bagby finally said, looking up.

"He is, indeed. I am quite confident that the convention will nominate him on a unanimous vote."

"Unanimous?" Bagby asked.

"Yes, or at least very nearly so. Some of the state delegations may vote for favorite son candidates on the first ballot, but I am certain Beauregard will receive all the votes on the second."

"And who do you expect will be the party's vice presidential nominee?" Bagby asked this question with slightly raised eyebrows.

"Oh, that is not easy to predict," Toombs said with a smile.

"It isn't?" Bagby asked. "Because most other people I have talked to have said that you are all but certain to have it yourself."

"I will believe that when I see it. Until then. . ."

The sound of the commotion outside the hotel was growing louder and it finally registered in Toombs's mind. He strained his ears and began to make out what sounded like a crowd of people. There wasn't anything as loud as shouting, but if a large enough group gathered together the collective noise created by their normal chatter would gradually swell into a wave of sound. He had heard it many times at large political rallies.

"Do you hear that?" Toombs asked Bagby.

"Outside? Yes, I think so."

There was a knocking at the door. Toombs looked up at Jim, who instantly walked over to the door and opened it. It was John Baylor, a congressman from Texas who had come all the way from San Antonio to attend the convention.

"Senator Toombs! You'd better come outside!"

"Why?" Toombs asked, suddenly alarmed. "What is it?"

"A huge crowd has formed!" The man could barely contain his excitement. "They're asking to see you! They want you to make a speech!"

Apprehension vanished and a broad smile came over Toombs's face. A thrill filled him. Hundreds of memories from his campaigns for the Georgia state legislature and Congress decades earlier came flooding back into his mind. No one who had not experienced it could understand the sheer delight, the feeling of godlike power, which filled a man's soul when he spoke to a crowd of wildly enthusiastic and supportive people.

Toombs leapt out of his chair. "Follow me, Bagby!" he said as he dashed out the door. "I'll show you something that will make good copy!" The reporter grabbed his hat and followed Toombs out into the hall. They ran down three flights of stairs, so quickly that Toombs was afraid for a moment that he'd lose his footing and unceremoniously tumble to the ground floor.

They entered the Oriental Billiard Parlor, one of the chief amenities of the Exchange Hotel. Dozens of elegantly dressed men were playing pool, smoking cigars, and drinking whiskey. A few of them stopped and spoke quickly to one another when they saw him, then began to applaud. Soon, it was taken up by the entire room. Pool sticks were put down, whiskey glasses were taken up, and a chorus of cheering filled the room from one end to the other.

"Three cheers for Robert Toombs!" a powerful voice boomed out. "Hip hip!"

"Hooray!"

"Hip hip!"

"Hooray!"

"Hip hip!"

"Hooray!"

Toombs smiled broadly and raised his hand to acknowledge them as he strode through the Oriental Billiard Parlor. Their cheers and applause filled him and gave him strength. He felt that the people were with him, that he truly manifested their hopes and desires. He knew his purpose and felt that it was genuinely good and patriotic.

He passed through the billiard hall and towards the main doors of the hotel, entering a lobby above which hung a great red lamp. Beyond the doors, he could hear the crowd out on Commerce Street. He paused. When he stepped out onto the hotel steps, he wanted to look like a self-assured statesman, not a wild-eyed crazy man. He wondered for a moment if he had had too much brandy and might not be able to speak clearly. There would be nothing to do about that, though. He could not turn away from the crowd now. Besides, fortune favored the bold.

Glancing over his shoulder to make sure Bagby was still with him, Toombs strode up to the big doors at the hotel entrance and, pushing them both open at once, stepped out onto the large patio of the hotel.

There was an explosion of wild cheering and applause, the voices of women mixed in with those of men. There were hundreds of them, their faces animated and smiling, filled with joy at the sight of him. He saw some waving signs in the air, bearing messages such as "Down With Jeff Davis!" and "Defend Southern Rights!" It felt like a beautifully hot wind blowing into Toombs's face.

His heart soared and he raised his hands for quiet as he began to address the crowd.

Sumner shifted uncomfortably in his chair and tiredly rubbed his eyes. It was mid-afternoon and the Committee on Foreign Relations had been in session all day. The members were just now returning from the hour's break he had given them for lunch. They had spent the morning discussing the proposed purchase of the Russian territory to the west of Canada, known as Alaska. The Russian minister had indicated to Secretary of State Seymour that Czar Alexander II was interested in ridding himself of the land and would be willing to accept a decent monetary offer. Sumner was not opposed to the idea, for he favored the territorial expansion of the country. The McClellan administration, however, was not making the subject a priority, while members of Congress did not want to waste the money on a region so cold and barren that scarcely anyone lived there. The other members of the committee had shown little interest in the subject. Russia, it seemed, was stuck with Alaska.

It had been a wasted morning, Sumner decided. He was cheered by the thought that it was now time to focus on more important matters. Sitting before the committee at the witness table was one of the men whom Sumner had subpoenaed to testify on the Fenian crisis. He looked stoic and dignified, not in the least intimidated by the senators who sat looking down on them from above.

"The committee will come to order," Sumner said, gaveling the room into silence. He looked down at the two men in front of him. "Please state your name and place of residence for the record."

"James Adelbert Mulligan of Chicago," said the man.

Sumner had read up on Mulligan the night before. He had been born in Chicago of Irish immigrant parents and had emerged as one of the cornerstones of that burgeoning city's Irish community and a promising attorney. He had raised his own units of Irish soldiers in 1861 and led them throughout the fighting in West Virginia and the Shenandoah Valley, serving most conspicuously in the campaign against Jubal Early. An influential Democrat, he was now being talked of as potential candidate for the Senate or for Governor of Illinois.

Mulligan was the first in a series of Irish leaders that Sumner had subpoenaed to testify before the committee. He wanted to find out as much as he could about the workings of the Fenian Brotherhood and, more importantly, expose all the information to the public. Until he could get General Thomas and General Sweeny before him under oath, the testimony of men like Mulligan would have the best effect.

Sumner had Storey administer the oath to Mulligan. His voice, tinged with a heavy Irish accent, sounded firm and trustworthy. This was a man who was sure of himself.

"Mr. Mulligan, thank you for appearing before our committee today."

"Thank you, Mr. Chairman," Mulligan replied.

"Can you describe your involvement in the Irish independence movement?"

Mulligan looked deeply into Sumner's eyes before he replied. The Massachusetts senator saw an intense soul in those eyes, a man of deep conviction and integrity. Sumner knew that Mulligan was a Democrat, who had been a friend and supporter of Stephen Douglas before the war and who had strongly opposed the Emancipation Proclamation. Yet he did not strike Sumner as the kind of man who would willingly be a tool of McClellan.

"Mr. Chairman, in addition to my law practice, I edit an Irish community newspaper in Chicago. I have established an Irish debating society and been very involved in several Irish community organizations. In all these capacities, I have strongly promoted the idea of the separation of Ireland from the United Kingdom."

"Are you a member of the Fenian Brotherhood?"

"No, I am not. However, I believe in its cause. I believe that the British government has lorded it over Ireland for centuries, exploiting its land and humiliating its people, depriving the Irish race of its rightful place in the world."

"Have you been asked to join?"

"Several times, yes."

"If you believe in their cause so firmly, why have you not joined them?"

"Because I believe in the United States Constitution and the laws made under its authority. I believe that the activities of the Fenian Brotherhood are illegal, for the United States is at peace with England. I cannot, therefore, officially adhere to it in good conscience."

Sumner could have demanded the names of those who had approached Mulligan, but decided against it for the time being. He did not want to place Mulligan in an adversarial position. Not only would it have made the hearings more difficult, but he wanted a good relationship with Mulligan in case the man was ever elected to the Senate. Besides which, as far as the McClellan administration was concerned, the Fenians were not an illegal organization. "As you are a well-connected man, Mr. Mulligan, I assume you know a great deal about the organization of the Fenian Brotherhood, even if you yourself are not a member of it?"

"I suppose I know more than most people, Mr. Chairman."

"Are any members of the McClellan administration members of the Fenian Brotherhood?"

"Not to my knowledge, Mr. Chairman."

"Is there any communication between the McClellan administration and the Fenian Brotherhood?"

"Again, not to my knowledge. There are rumors, however."

"What sort of rumors?"

"That leftover weapons from the war have been turned over to the Fenian Brotherhood and that high-ranking officers have been granted leave to participate in the Fenian incursions into Canada."

"Mr. Chairman, may I ask the witness a question?" This came from Senator Downey of California, the Democrat suspected by many of plotting the creation of an independent nation on the Pacific coast.

"By all means," Sumner replied.

"Mr. Mulligan, you speak of weapons being delivered by the government to the Fenians. Have you seen these weapons yourself?"

"No, Senator."

"Do you have any direct knowledge of these alleged transfers of weapons? Have you, for example, spoken directly with anyone who claims to have taken part in them?"

"No, Senator. As I said, these are only rumors."

"Mr. Chairman," Senator Downey said. "I submit that this committee should not concern itself with vague rumors and unsubstantiated statements of hearsay."

Sumner ignored him. Senator Downey was clearly working with McClellan and could be counted on to make trivial statements designed to discredit the work the committee was doing.

McClellan clearly feared the possibility that the committee would uncover the direct link between the administration and the Fenians that Sumner was convinced existed. That was why he had been so angered at the end of their meeting at the White House. That was why Senator Downey was now trying to cast doubt onto the proceedings. If Sumner's hearings brought forth information that proved that the administration was providing direct support to the Fenians, rather than simply tolerating their existence, it would be a tremendous scandal. McClellan would come under pressure from every side and would surely be forced to back down from his pro-Fenian policy. Without government support, the Fenian movement might collapse. This, in turn, would eliminate the possibility of a war between Britain and the United States, a conflict which Sumner was determined to avoid at all costs.

As far as Sumner was concerned, a war with Britain would be nothing but a bloody and expensive folly. The Confederacy was the true enemy. For a moment, Sumner thought of Charles Russell Lowell, out somewhere on the high seas as he journeyed to whatever fate had in store for him in Louisiana. Saul had kept the embers of resistance alive. Perhaps Lowell could blow on those embers and ignite a fire that would bring the slave power crashing down. If that happened, the United States could not afford to be mired down in a conflict with Britain. It had to be ready to finish the business which had been so shamefully abandoned in 1865.

In exposing McClellan's support of the Fenians, though, Sumner was doing more than forcing the president to back down. He would be inflicting a political wound upon the president that would make his defeat in the 1868 elections much more likely. Whether the Republicans put forward William Seward or Salmon Chase, McClellan would surely be defeated if he could be humiliated before the public on the matter of the Fenians. With McClellan out of the way, the United States could again turn its attention towards destroying the slave power that lay to the south, perhaps even reincorporating it into the republic, righteously punishing the villains who brought about secession in the first place, and freeing the millions of black men and women still held in chains.

"Mr. Mulligan," Sumner continued. "Are you familiar with Thomas Francis Meagher?"

The Irishman paused uncomfortably for a moment. "Yes, I am, Mr. Chairman." The tone suggested to Sumner that Mulligan did not particularly like Meagher.

The Republican members of the committee looked at Sumner, unspoken messages of concern in their eyes. Mulligan was a Democrat, so going after him was perfectly fine. Meagher, the former commander of the famed Irish Brigade, was a different matter altogether. He was a Republican and had been a staunch supporter of Lincoln. He was also an outspoken Irish nationalist like Mulligan.

Sumner had subpoenaed him to testify before the committee as well and the man was expected to arrive in the next few days.

"Is Mr. Meagher a member of the Fenian Brotherhood?"

"Not to my knowledge, Mr. Chairman."

"If he was, it seems to me that you would know it."

"With respect, sir, I make it a point not to ask people whether or not they are members. If they are, I would prefer not to know."

"But you said that you agree with the purpose of the Fenian Brotherhood."

"With its purpose, yes. But not with its methods. I do not believe its actions to be legal."

"The McClellan administration does not seem to agree with you."

"Well, the president has his opinion and I have mine."

Sumner nodded. Democrat though he might be, this Mulligan fellow was indeed a man of integrity. For an instant, Sumner thought on Mulligan's words and became disturbed. He, too, venerated the Constitution and believed in the rule of law. Yet he was a member of a conspiracy to commit an act of war against a foreign power with which the United States was at peace. That foreign power might represent a monstrous evil, but it was a legitimate power nonetheless, for the United States had signed a treaty with the Confederacy and recognized its independence.

Sumner told himself that it wasn't the same thing. McClellan was stoking the Fenian movement purely for selfish political advantage, while Sumner, Lowell, and their co-conspirators were supporting Saul because it was the right thing to do. They were striving to free millions of enslaved human beings, not risking war merely to gather more votes in the next election. The difference between them was close to infinite.

He continued to ask question of Mulligan for about another hour. After some time, he began to feel his time was being wasted. He was not telling him anything about the Fenian Brotherhood that wasn't public knowledge. Still, simply by holding more hearings, he could keep the issue in the newspapers and therefore keep the pressure on the McClellan administration. He felt he would have to wait until he had a chance to interview General Thomas and General Sweeny before he got a chance at some real answers to what McClellan was up to.

While Mulligan was describing a public meeting of the Fenians that had taken place in Chicago the month before, a messenger came into the committee room and quietly handed Storey a note. The clerk looked through it quickly and Sumner noticed that his eyebrows shot up sharply. Storey glanced up at Sumner, wordlessly asking a question. Sumner nodded and the clerk rose from his desk to hand the chairman the note.

Senator Sumner,

I am directed by the President of the United States to inform you that, under his constitutional authority as commander-in-chief, he has given orders to General George Thomas and General Thomas Sweeny to the effect that they are not to testify before the Senator Foreign Relations Committee.

I am, sir, your most humble and obedient servant,

Secretary of War Benjamin Butler

Sumner drew his head back in astonishment, but quickly recovered. Considering the man giving the orders, he told himself, he really shouldn't have been very surprised.

June 26, Noon
Southern Louisiana

Morgan focused on his breathing, trying to keep it slow so as to remain as still as possible. He was crouched down in the underbrush, off to the side of what appeared to be an old Indian trail. On either side of him were scores of Louisiana militiamen, all of them veterans of the war. On the other side of the trail, under the command of his brother-in-law Duke, were a few dozen of his dismounted Kentucky cavalrymen. All told, nearly three hundred men were in position. He would have naturally preferred a larger force, but he had needed to move quickly and not worry himself too much over supplies. Besides, a smaller force was more easily concealed. In this game, guile was more important than brute force.

Beside him, crouched down as well, was Silas, the self-professed traitor to Saul. Directly behind the traitor were two of the militiamen, who had been ordered to shoot Silas at the first sign of his providing any assistance to the insurgents.

He took another swig of water from his canteen. This only slightly relieved his thirst, for the heat was oppressive. Mosquitos buzzed at his face. Morgan swatted at them, perhaps killing two or three. It was futile, of course. Like Yankee soldiers, mosquitos always came back in greater numbers, no matter how many were killed.

They had already lain in concealment for more than three hours, ever since the sun rose. Militia scouts and local civilians had reported an unusually high number of sightings of possible insurgents in this particular area over the previous week, so he had concentrated his forces here after Silas had told him about the Indian trail. As the hours passed, however, he could not help but wonder if he was wasting his time.

"You sure this is the trail he uses?" Morgan asked again, his voice a harsh whisper.

"He's used it before," Silas replied. "If he's in the area, he'll pass through here. Like I told you, he has no base. He just moves back and forth between different camping sites."

"You'd better be right," Morgan said menacingly. "If we stay here all day for nothing, there will be hell to pay. And I'll damn well make sure that you're the one to pay it."

Silas simply shrugged with the nonchalance to which Morgan had grown accustomed. The informer seemed not to care what happened to him. He was pleased to be eating a decent meal three times a day and to be drinking whiskey whenever he asked for it, which was often. Some of the troops had begun to resent the repeated provision of whiskey to the black man, but Morgan was happy to keep Silas in a perpetual state of near-inebriation, for it made him more talkative and less able to run away.

311

For the hundredth time, Morgan wondered as to Silas's motives. Was it really as simple as Silas wanting to escape the harsh life of an insurgent in order to eat food and drink alcohol with a roof over his head? Or was it something deeper? Silas had occasionally displayed something close to hatred when Saul's name was mentioned, so it seemed clear that personal animosity was involved. Silas had expressed no particular interest in political or ideological questions presented to him. He had claimed not to even know what abolitionism was, though Morgan found this difficult to believe.

Still, Silas's motives didn't matter to Morgan so long as the information the black man provided turned out to be useful. So far, it had not. Perhaps that was about to change.

"Psst!" one of the militiamen down the left of the line urgently whispered.

Morgan's thoughts about Silas vanished in a flash and he strained his ears to listen. Yes, there was something. It was a sound he had heard before. Dozens of men were approaching, but making an effort to move quietly. He couldn't see them yet, but he knew they were there. He could hear twigs snapping, dirt crunching under marching feet, and the low sound of people speaking softly to one another. Four years of war had sharpened Morgan's fighting instincts beyond the reach of most men and he trusted what his ears were telling him.

Saul was coming.

He felt the tension increase among his Louisianans. These were men who had fought under Lee and Johnston, surviving some of the most brutal battles in history. Morgan knew he could count on them.

There was no way to signal to Duke across the trail without alerting the enemy to their presence. Morgan had to assume that the Kentucky troopers had also detected the approach of the insurgents and were ready for the ambush. Morgan trusted Duke as he trusted himself, and not just because he was his brother-in-law.

The first insurgent came into view. An individual black soldier, clad in a tattered blue uniform. He held a Springfield rifle over his right shoulder and his eyes were intently focused on the ground ahead of him. Obviously he was the point man, leading the way for the others.

Morgan was struck by the fact that Saul had not employed flankers to guard against exactly this sort of ambush. When marching through potentially hostile territory, any column of infantry under a competent commander would deploy skirmishers in the woods off to the right and left of the march route to scout for any hidden enemies. Saul apparently had not done so. Did this reflect the man's own lack of experience? According to Silas, Saul had never risen above the rank of a noncommissioned officer in the Union army. Or did it perhaps suggest that Saul's fighters lacked the discipline and organization for such a task of deploying skirmishers to guard the flanks of a marching column?

Behind the point marcher, Morgan began to see a long column of dozens of black men. Some of them were also wearing old Union uniforms, but the vast majority were wearing ragged and threadbare brown clothes similar to what plantation slaves wore. Morgan guessed that these men were not ex-soldiers but slaves liberated by Saul's recent raids. The clothes they wore were probably all the clothes they had. These men, he quickly noticed, were armed not with firearms but with spears and scythes. Many had no weapons at all.

Morgan sneered. Spears and scythes would not be much use to the blacks in the engagement he had planned for them. No matter how brave and determined a man might be, a blade was no match for a rifle.

An endless two minutes passed by in silence. The point man continued walking, unknowingly leading his comrades into a slaughter pen. Behind him, the column of black insurgents continued on, oblivious to their coming destruction. Morgan forced himself to be patient. He wanted nothing more than to strike out at his enemies, but he knew he needed to lure them a few yards closer in order to catch them in the perfect killing trap.

The point man suddenly stopped, his head jerking up. He quickly raised his hand to signal his comrades to halt. Then he raised his rifle into a firing position. Clearly, the man had sensed something was amiss. Perhaps one of Morgan's men had made a noise just loud enough to be heard. Perhaps he had smelled something. It didn't matter.

"Now!" Morgan yelled.

On both sides of the trail, the bushes erupted in concentrated musket fire. The sound was like that of a tremendous clap and hundreds of bullets zipped through the air in an instant like so many deadly daggers. The point man was struck more than half a dozen times in less than two seconds, his body nearly being torn apart and his remains falling onto the trail in a lifeless heap. Others in the front of the black column were also hit. Screams of pain and fear rose from the trail below him.

Morgan frowned. The alertness of the point man had forced him to trigger the ambush a minute or two before he wanted, meaning that the main body of Saul's column was not in the killing space in which he wanted to catch them. Because of this, only about half of the column was being caught in the cross-fire, while comparatively little fire was being directed at the trailing half.

He wished he had artillery. A single cannon charged with double canister could have blown Saul's entire column to bits with two or three discharges. But it had proven impossible to move cannon through the swampy terrain and it would have risked giving away their position.

What was happening, though, was quite bloody enough. As Morgan watched, Saul's men below him were being cut to pieces. There were perhaps a hundred and fifty men in the column, only about half as many as Morgan had under his command. They were in a disastrous position, being fired upon from two sides from a higher elevation. Within a minute of his order to fire, Morgan could see nearly two dozen black fighters on the ground, either unmoving in death or writhing in pain from terrible wounds.

Scattered puffs of smoke became visible within the insurgent column and those black fighters who were armed with muskets began to return fire. Morgan could hear scattered cries from his own line of Louisiana militiamen as some of his men were hit.

He had given strict orders that his men were not to charge the enemy. With their advantage of position, combined with the fact that so few of Saul's men were armed with firearms, the logical thing to do was simply to stay where they were and pour fire into the insurgent column until it disintegrated, like an ice cube tossed into a pot of boiling water. If his men obeyed orders, they could utterly destroy Saul's force while suffering only light casualties in return.

Yet Morgan saw that his orders were not being obeyed, for several of his men began charging down into the mass of black fighters. Perhaps it was rage felt as their comrades were killed or wounded. Perhaps the sight of black men in arms against white men simply drove them into a frenzy. Whatever the cause, Morgan saw his carefully orchestrated plan fall apart as his men rushed down at Saul's men, shrieking the Rebel Yell.

"Stand fast! Morgan yelled. "Stay where you are!"

It was no use. In a matter of seconds, what had been a carefully planned ambush was transformed into a hand-to-hand melee down on the Indian trail itself. The sounds of rifle fire were soon mixed with those of fists smashing into faces and of the thick wooden butts of muskets crashing against one another. Shouted curses and terrible oaths filled the air. Most worrisome for Morgan, he saw that those of Saul's men who were armed only with improvised blade weapons were now able to use them at close range against his men. While he watched in horror, a huge black man plunged his scythe into one of his men, striking the tender spot between the shoulder and the neck where the jugular vein was located. An eruption of blood spewed forth and the Confederate let out a shriek of despair as death took him.

Morgan pulled his Colt revolver from its holster and dashed after his men. He was furious at them for their lack of discipline, but they were his men and he was not going to let them fight alone. He was not a strong man and no better than average in a fight, so he knew he was risking his life. Yet instinct drove him down into the brawl. For a fraction of a second, he wondered what the newspapers would say of him if he were killed.

He reached the trail. Perhaps three minutes had elapsed since he had sprung his ambush. Dozens of bodies littered the ground. Most of them were black, but a number of them were white. The rear end of Saul's column, which had escaped the worst of the opening fire, was now hurrying forward to help their comrades. Morgan felt an elation fill him, for he was finally grappling with Saul rather than chasing him about the swamps. Saul's men would find it far harder to defeat hardened Confederate soldiers in an open battle than it had been to raid defenseless plantations.

Morgan opened fire at close range with his Colt, quickly expending four of his six shots. He was careful in aiming, for fear of hitting one of his own men. He thought he hit at least one of the black fighters, but could not be sure amidst the melee. A big, burly black man lunged towards him, bearing a Springfield with a rusty bayonet affixed to its end. Suppressing his fear, he aimed and fired his two remaining bullets, hitting the man both times in the chest and knocking him backwards.

It would take a few precious seconds for him to reload his weapon and during that time he would be helpless. Seeing no other choice, he tossed his revolver away and drew his bowie knife. There was no longer any way for him to control the battle, for his units were hopelessly intermingled and no one would be able to hear any orders he shouted.

The trail between the two slight ridges was full of cursing men struggling viciously with one another. Morgan saw the Kentuckians charging down from the other side to join in the fight. He saw Duke leading them with a drawn saber, though he was not sure whether his brother-in-law saw him.

"Morgan!" a formidable voice shouted.

He turned and saw the man who had stood out to him at the last fight, who he was certain was Saul. He stood amidst the combat with a strange stillness, as if he was set apart in a different reality than the men around him. Vicious fury was evident in the black man's eyes. Morgan tensed when he realized that the insurgent commander was aiming a Springfield directly at him. There was nothing Morgan could do, for Saul was too far away for him to strike with his knife, yet so close that he could not possibly miss. An endless instant seemed to pass as Morgan prepared for death. He didn't think about his wife or his children. The only thought which had time to pass through his mind was how ironic it was that he was about to be killed by a black man.

Saul's eyes narrowed and he tilted his head ever so slightly. To Morgan's astonishment, the insurgent leader then aimed the Springfield towards the ground and fired. The bullet smacked into the soft soil directly between Morgan's feet. The Confederate commander was so startled that he fell backwards onto the ground.

He glanced back up, certain that Saul was going to be moving in for the kill. Yet the black warrior remained where he was. He seemed entirely oblivious to danger. Morgan could see him looking up the ridge to his left, where Morgan had been concealed before the ambush had been sprung. Up there, Morgan saw Silas, still being guarded by one of his men. The turncoat had an obvious expression of glee on his face.

"Silas!" Saul roared. "You traitor!"

Morgan pulled himself to his feet as two of his men dashed past him towards Saul. In a seemingly effortless series of movements, Saul smashed the butt of his rifle against the head of the first assailant, then brought the Springfield around and up, skewering the second man with his bayonet. With a look of contempt, he withdrew his weapon and pushed the mortally wounded man off to one side.

"Follow me!" Saul shouted, his booming voice clearly audible over the sounds of the fighting. "All men! Follow me!"

One of Morgan's men pulled the general to his feet. When planning the ambush, Morgan had expected Saul and his men to try to retreat back the way they had come and had given orders for one company of Louisiana militia to swing around to their rear and block their route of escape. He had to assume that his orders had been carried out, but instantly saw that it would not matter. Saul dashed up the ridge to his right, where the dismounted Kentucky cavalrymen had been positioned minutes before. Scores of his men scrambled after him, some providing covering fire for the rest as they sought to disentangle themselves from the fighting.

"Fire!" Morgan shouted. "Don't let them get away!"

It was useless. His men were too disorganized to respond to his orders. He shouted for them to form up by companies and reload their weapons. His men glanced about, looking for their officers. There was nothing but chaos and confusion. A few men tried to keep up a fire against the black fighters scrambling up the ridge, but they only managed a few shots before Saul and his force disappeared over the other side. Some enterprising troops chased after them but, upon reaching the top of the ridge and seeing that no organized groups of their own force were following, stopped to wait for orders.

Morgan cursed as a strange and unsettled silence descended over the Indian trail. He began to hear officers yelling for their men to reorganize, to care for the wounded, to count casualties. One of the company commanders thoughtfully began to deploy a skirmish line on the ridge behind which Saul had vanished, in fear that they might return and attack. It would take precious minutes to pull his units back together and get them under control. By that time, Saul and his men would be long gone. If there was one thing Morgan had learned about his adversary, it was that he knew how to move quickly through the Louisiana wilderness.

Anger and frustration began to boil up within him as his mind recounted what had happened. If Saul's point man hadn't sensed danger, the entire insurgent force would have walked right into the killing zone. If his men had maintained discipline and not charged, they could have cut Saul's entire force to pieces at minimal loss to themselves. He cursed again, loudly enough for many men around him to hear

Duke came running up to him. To Morgan's surprise, he had a delighted smile on his face. "Congratulations, John!" he said excitedly.

"For what?" Morgan demanded. "We let them get away!"

"John, look!" Duke said, waving his hand. "We must have killed half of the bastards! Took some prisoners, too!"

Morgan looked down the trail where the fight had taken place. It was crammed with scores of bodies, roughly evenly divided between white and black. Some were still twitching as the throes of death overtook them. Morgan winced at the realization that a great many of his own men had been killed or wounded, far higher casualties than he had expected. Yet, very slowly, he comprehended that just as many of Saul's men had been cut down. If, as they suspected, Saul had only a few hundred men, it represented a grievous blow to the insurgency.

"Count the black bodies!" Morgan snapped at Duke. "Right away!" He wanted to know how badly Saul had been hurt.

Duke's expression changed to one more serious. "Yes, sir!" he said as he dashed off.

Morgan took a deep breath, feeling the battle fever within him subside and calm began to return. He was mystified as to why Saul hadn't killed him when he had had the chance. The manner in which he had aimed and fired at the ground between Morgan's feet seemed far too intentional to have been any kind of accident. He walked up to his original position, where Silas was still sitting under guard.

"Trust me now, General?" Silas asked. "I told you they'd come this way and they did."

"I thank you for your help," Morgan replied. He did not like the feeling of being indebted to a black man, yet he could not deny that the ambush would not have been possible without Silas.

"Your men shouldn't have charged," Silas said. "They should have just stayed where they were and kept firing."

Morgan shrugged. "Saul got away. Where do you think he will go?"

"I have no idea. He saw me, you know. He knows I'm helping you. So he'll think about everything I know before he decides what to do."

Morgan frowned, for Silas was right. Without another word, he stepped away and walked towards the Indian trail, watching as his men collected the wounded. He noticed some of his men corralling a few black soldiers, either unwounded or only lightly so, holding leveled bayonets at them in a small semi-circle. It occurred to him that he did not know what to do with such prisoners. That decision would have to be left to Breckinridge.

He wondered what to do with Silas now. Since Saul knew he had turned traitor, the man's usefulness was greatly diminished, if not completely gone. Now was not to time to think on that particular matter, though.

Duke came jogging back up to him. "Got the count, John. Fifty-three dead blacks along the trail. We also have thirty-eight prisoners, most of whom are wounded."

Morgan nodded quickly. The ratio of killed to wounded was absurd and suggested to him that many of his men had killed foes who had been wounded or who had tried to surrender. It wouldn't have been the first time. He himself had never encountered black troops during the war, but he knew what had happened at places like Fort Pillow. He did not like the idea of murdering defenseless people, even if they were black, but he also didn't think he could do much to restrain his men.

There would be time to think on that later on. His earlier feelings of frustration faded in view of what he had accomplished. Perhaps as much as half of Saul's force had been killed or captured. That, by itself, was something to cheer about. More importantly, though, by tracking Saul down and defeating him in battle, he had shattered Saul's reputation for invisibility and invulnerability. The thought that he had probably shaken the insurgent commander's confidence to the core made him very happy.

He walked up the ridge on the opposite side of the trail and looked out into the woods, staring in the direction Saul and his survivors had fled. He stood there thoughtfully in silence for a few minutes. He again wondered why Saul had refused to kill him during the battle and still could not come up with an answer. Far from feeling grateful, however, Morgan only become angrier the more he thought about it.

"I'm going to run you down, you bastard," he said to the empty wilderness. "I'm going to run you down if it's the last thing I ever do."

June 27, Night
Exchange Hotel, Montgomery, Alabama

"Congressman Baylor has agreed to join the Texas state committee," Wigfall said proudly, waving a lit cigar in the air as though it were a banner of victory.

"That's good," Stephens replied. "I think each committee needs to have a member with military service that can be highlighted to the people. And Baylor, if I recall correctly, had a good service record as a cavalry officer during the war."

"And Baylor makes seven members, right?" Toombs asked. "Including yourself as chairman?"

"That's right." Wigfall reached for his glass of whiskey and took a slightly larger than average sip, clearly pleased with himself.

Toombs nodded. Texas, he thought, was likely to be a closely contested state in the upcoming election. Wigfall, Baylor, and other Texans sympathetic to their cause would be set against Postmaster General Reagan and many powerful politicians who seemed more likely to support Breckinridge. With only six electoral votes, Texas was not one of the bigger prizes, but Toombs had been through enough elections to know that even a single vote might be critical when the cards came down in November.

Watching Wigfall take another sip of his whiskey, which was the third drink he had poured himself since the start of the meeting, Toombs felt a burning envy. At the urging of Stephens, he had refrained from refilling his own glass after he finished his first drink. In retrospect, he should have consumed it more slowly, for he now ached for a second dram. Thinking about it made it difficult for him to concentrate on the matter at hand.

They were sitting in one of the hotel's private dining rooms. Two hours earlier, Vice President Alexander Stephens had gaveled to order the first official meeting of the States' Rights Party Central Committee. It had been decided that Stephens would be the Chairman, since his position as vice president gave him more prestige with the public than anyone else. The other members were Senator Wigfall, Senator Hunter, Governor Zebulon Vance of North Carolina, Senator Robert Barnwell of South Carolina, former General William Walker, and former Minister to the United Kingdom James Mason.

Toombs himself was not a member of the central committee. The ostensible reason was that as Stephens was sitting as chairman and General Walker was also a Georgian, it would not have not been proper for Georgia to have such disproportionate representation. This wasn't exactly false. In truth, though, the real reason Toombs did not want a seat on the central committee is that he wanted to avoid any encumbrances to his eventual nomination for vice president.

Although he was not officially a member of the committee, the others had invited him to the meeting as a matter of course. He was one of the driving forces in the creation of the States' Rights Party and everyone knew that he was going to play a major role in the party's operations. Besides which, Toombs told himself, they required his expertise on policy questions.

Things were proceeding quite well, Toombs thought. Now that the membership of the Texas committee had been finalized, party committees had been established for all eleven states. He was reasonably satisfied with the men composing them. These committees, in turn, would establish party structures in each state, holding meetings in cities, towns, and in the markets of rural areas to nominate men for congressional and state legislative offices.

More important than the state committees, as far as Toombs was concerned, were the large numbers of supporters streaming into Montgomery for the convention, which was due to begin the next day. Ordinarily, the practice of a political convention was to allow each state committee to select its own delegation, but there had not been enough time for that. The state delegations were having to organize themselves as they arrived in Montgomery. Toombs knew that this convention was going to be raucous and confused, but that would simply make it more interesting.

It was being quietly but firmly communicated to the chairmen of each committee that Beauregard had agreed to stand as the party's candidate for president. Toombs assumed that the committee chairmen would make sure that the delegates going to Montgomery would be ready to cast their votes for Beauregard when the time came. Newspapers had already printed electrifying headlines about the great Creole general's candidacy, even though it had not been officially announced. Toombs thought that it would be a relatively easy matter to have it confirmed at the convention itself.

"Are we finished on the subject of the state committees?" Senator Hunter asked.

"I think so, yes," Stephens replied.

"In that case, I think we should begin discussing the specific wording of our party platform."

Toombs couldn't help but smile. With the bothersome details about state committees out of the way, the more interesting and enjoyable work could now begin. Of course, no platform would be official until it was voted upon by the delegates at the upcoming convention. There was sure to be a good deal of haggling before that took place, but it was imperative to start work early. At the very least, a general outline of the platform was necessary.

"The first plank of the platform should be a general statement of our party's principles," Toombs said. "The supremacy of the states over the central government. The primacy of the legislative branch. And, of course, a firm commitment to protecting slavery."

"I'd go farther," Wigfall said. "Not only protecting slavery, but expanding it into new territories."

"Let's not bite off more than we can chew in the first plank," Stephens offered. "Perhaps the first plank can be as Robert has just described, with the second plank calling for the acquisition of Cuba."

"And northern Mexico?" Wigfall asked. "My friends back in Texas are eager to grab some of that land, I don't mind saying."

"That would greatly anger the French," Mason pointed out.

"So what?" Wigfall said, lighting another cigar. "Why should we care what a bunch of effete frog-eaters think?"

"Well, we are trying to obtain a treaty of alliance with them," Mason replied.

"We shouldn't be," Wigfall countered. "Let them eat their frogs and snails in Europe. In fact, I think we should include a clause in the platform saying that this foolish attempt to get France to sign a treaty with us should be stopped. Only a fool would want to chain our Confederacy to the throne of Napoleon III."

They spent the next ten minutes debating how to write their foreign policy proposals into the party platform. Toombs fervently desired the annexation of Cuba and opposed any treaty with France. He asserted that the Confederacy should avoid entangling alliances with overseas powers, as they would inevitably result in their country being dragged into the murky world of European power struggles. No good and much evil would come from that.

They slowly made progress. It was agreed that the first plank would be a general statement of principles, the second a call for the acquisition of Cuba, and the third a rejection of alliances with any foreign power.

"It should go without saying that the crushing of any slave insurrection needs to be specified in our platform," Senator Barnwell said. "The administration's response to what has been happening in Louisiana has been pathetic. Unless such rebellions are crushed instantly and ruthlessly, we can only expect more of them in the future. You ask me, Morgan should have killed every one of the black bastards weeks ago. Either way, we need to say something in the platform."

"We shouldn't be too specific," Stephens cautioned. "If we criticize the response of the administration for a weak response and then, a week or so later, Morgan comes out with a great victory, we will look foolish."

"There is a rumor that Morgan beat the darkies in a big fight yesterday," Walker said. "Heard it from one of the newspapermen, who said it came through on the telegraph a couple of hours ago. They say it will be on the front page tomorrow morning."

"We can change it in the next few days if we have to," Toombs said. "Now, we need to address the issue of taxes being levied directly from Richmond," Toombs said.

"Indeed, we do," Stephens replied. "You are our acknowledged expert on fiscal matters. What do you suggest, Robert?"

Toombs took a deep breath before speaking again. He had devoted countless hours of contemplation to the Confederacy's financial woes. The debt load being carried by the Richmond government was enormous, and added to that were the mammoth debts being shouldered by the individual states. Some shortsighted people suggested simply defaulting on these debts, not understanding the disastrous consequences that would result from such a course of action. Millions of patriotic Confederate citizens who had bought Treasury bonds would be utterly ruined, rendered unable to even put food on the tables of their families. Moreover, the government would never again be able to borrow meaningful amounts of money from the major European banks, as its creditworthiness would be reduced to nothing. It would also destroy forever any chance of obtaining loans from banks in the United States.

If it were a question of fiscal matters alone, the obvious solution would be for the Richmond government to assume the debt load of the individual states, restructure its payment schedule, and apportion a sufficient amount of revenue to pay it off in a reasonable time. This was what Alexander Hamilton had done in the 1790s and he had succeeded spectacularly in restoring the credit of the early American republic. Yet this course of action was anathema to Toombs, for it would help centralize power in Richmond by making the states even more dependent upon the central government. Another solution had to be devised.

"I am preparing a bill to lay before the Senate in order to address the fiscal crisis," Toombs began. He spent the next ten minutes outlining his proposal. The others listened intently, with the exception of Wigfall, who continued to sip from his whiskey and appeared impatient and bored.

The solution, as Toombs saw it, was to allow the Richmond government to continue levying import and export duties on commerce but prohibit it from imposing direct taxes on the people, while specifying that a certain proportion of the revenue of each state be provided to the central government as long as its debt remained outstanding. It would also require that the central government maintain a balanced budget, slowly paying down the debt. Once the debt was paid off, the transfer of state funds would be discontinued and Richmond would have to depend on customs duties alone. Hamilton's proposal in the 1790s had strengthened the power of the central government at the expense of the states, but the plan Toombs envisioned would have precisely the opposite effect.

Since Toombs didn't think the central government needed to be doing anything other than running the postal service, the federal court system, a few diplomatic missions overseas, and a small navy, he saw no problem with leaving the central government such a small source of revenue. Indeed, it would likely allow the customs duties imposed on importers and exporters to be quite small. In the meantime, the individual states could be left to pay off their own debts in their own time with whatever means they thought best. As far as the army was concerned, Toombs felt that the individual states should be in charge of maintaining their own militia units and should therefore pay for them on their own.

Toombs finished his presentation in about ten minutes. The committee members were silent for a time as they considered what they had just heard. Stephens replied first.

"I believe these proposals have much merit," the vice president said. "I would support including a plank in our party platform calling for their adoption."

"I agree," replied Governor Vance. "It solves the debt crisis without infringing too much on the sovereignty of the individual states."

"I agree as well," Hunter said. "A general summary of your proposal should form the basis of the fourth plank of our party platform."

Toombs felt enormous satisfaction at the reception his plan had received. The meeting went on for another hour and the group discussed other clauses they wanted inserted into the party platform. They decided to include a statement calling for the much-delayed creation of a Supreme Court to be hurried up, though Wigfall insisted that there should be a constitutional amendment requiring a majority of state legislatures, as well as the Senate, to approve any nominees for it.

"Anything else?" Stephens asked, looking around the table.

General Walker, who had been quiet up to that point, cleared his throat. "If I might add something that deals with the military?"

"Of course."

"There's been a good deal of talk in the newspapers about where the permanent military academy is going to be located. Some say it should be at the Virginia Military Institute, while others are calling for it to be located at the Citadel in Charleston. I would humbly suggest that the SRP endorse the Citadel."

"Why?" Wigfall asked tiredly.

"There's always been a good deal of muttering among much of the officer corps that there are too many Virginians in positions of high command. Placing the military academy in Virginia would cause a good deal of resentment. Besides, the national capital is in Richmond. I think it would give the appearance of too much influence being concentrated in a single state. Better for the academy to be located closer to the central part of the country."

"Better that there be no military academy at all," Toombs said under his breath. Stephens shot him a quick and earnest look, wordlessly asking him to remain silent.

"What's that?" Mason asked.

"I said that it would be better for there to be no military academy at all," Toombs said loudly. He hesitated for just a moment, then plunged on. "In fact, I would like to propose another plank of our platform. I think we should assert that the Confederacy have no standing army and that the organization of military units be left entirely to the individual states."

"What?" Walker asked, aghast. "But how would we organize armies in the event of another war with the Union? Or a war with Spain or another European power?"

"The states would come together to face any such emergency," Toombs said firmly. As he spoke, he recalled a hundred insults and indignities he had suffered at the hands of West Pointers during the war. "The last thing we need is an elite officer corps. The continued existence of a permanent standing army risks giving the national government an instrument with which to intimidate the people into submission."

Senator Hunter replied. "I think you may be exaggerating slightly, Robert," he said in a humorous tone.

"Exaggerating?" Toombs replied. "Hardly. Give a president control of his own personal army and they'll become just like the Praetorian Guard of some old Roman emperor. No, my dear sir. No, we must rely on our state regiments and no others. Let each state maintain their own forces and let each state appoint and train the officers for those units in whatever way it sees fit."

There was a long minute of tactful silence. Toombs looked around the table. "Are we in agreement? A plank calling for a prohibition on a standing national army."

"No," Walker said. "No, we are not in agreement. And I must say, Senator Toombs, that I resent the implication that the professional corps of officers is dangerous to the liberty of the country." He paused a moment before continuing. "I am a member of it."

He glared across the table at Toombs, who felt a sudden shudder of fear. Toombs did not commonly find himself in the company of men who could intimidate him. Walker, however, was a leathery old warrior who was said to have been wounded so many times that half his body was now made of lead. He was most famous for his fervent opposition to Patrick Cleburne's emancipation proposal, which had nearly led to Confederate troops opening fire on one another during the Siege of Atlanta in 1864.

"Perhaps this is one of those matters that we should let go," Stephens tactfully offered. "Don't you think, Robert? After all, we do have one more important matter to discuss before we adjourn for the evening."

Toombs didn't respond, his eyes still level with Walker's across the table.

"What matter would that be?" Senator Hunter asked.

"Well, we are all agreed that General Beauregard will be our candidate for president. But we have not yet discussed who shall be our nominee for vice president."

These words shook Toombs out of his confrontation with Walker and he looked quickly back at Stephens. His old friend was looking right at him, as if catching him from falling. Toombs cursed himself, realizing how foolish it would have been to pick a fight with Walker over a plank in the party platform. He would need the support of Walker if he wanted the vice presidential nomination. In his eagerness to describe his fiscal plan and his heated exchange with Walker, Toombs had quite forgotten the most important item for discussion.

Stephens went on. "Beauregard will make a fine presidential candidate, I think we all agree. But I think we need to make sure that we have an experienced politician by his side over the course of the campaign and, of course, once he takes office. Moreover, since we can count on Beauregard's candidacy giving us the states of Louisiana and South Carolina on a platter, I believe the second man on our ticket should be from one of the larger states. In short, I can think of no better man than my friend, Senator Robert Toombs."

"I second that," Wigfall said quickly, as had been prearranged. "Every voter in the country knows that the debt is our most serious problem and that Toombs is the man in government who best knows how to deal with it. Besides, with Toombs on the ticket, we can trust that Georgia will fall to us on Election Day. Combined with Louisiana and South Carolina, that gives us twenty-six electoral votes, more than half of what we need to win."

"I feel very uncomfortable having this discussed while I am in the room," Toombs said, doing his best to sound modest. He rose from his chair. "If you gentlemen will excuse me."

Toombs turned and walked out of the dining room, his heart pounding. He had worried that Wigfall might back away at the last moment from his commitment. Having heard the Texan's words before leaving the room, Toombs could assume that he had indeed kept his word. That was a good sign. Yet his mind and heart were tormented as he strode down the hall towards the bar. Could Stephens and Wigfall persuade the other members of the committee to support Toombs's bid for the vice presidency? Could the committee in turn persuade the various state delegations?

He sat down at the bar and gestured to the barkeep. "Whiskey, if you please. A strong one."

"Is Tennessee all right?" the barman asked. "I have some Kentucky bourbon, but it's a bit more expensive."

"I don't give a damn," he said urgently. "Just pour me a whiskey."

Toombs drank gratefully the moment the whiskey was placed in front of him. His mind felt strained and tense. All day, he had been straining in thought about the Electoral College, the various state delegations and committees, his fiscal reform bill, and a half dozen other things. Behind it all, of course, lay his ambitions to become vice president and, six years down the road, to take hold of the presidency itself.

He took a deep breath and glanced around the bar. Many people were looking at him. Some were reporters or politicians that he recognized. Perhaps sensing his mood, no one approached him to talk. He continued sipping his whiskey and, after a few minutes, lit a cigar. He was angry at himself for having spoken harshly to General Walker, who might now be refusing to support his vice presidential bid. He comforted himself that, if he failed now, it would at least be due to his principled opposition to a standing army, rather than because he had allowed alcohol to take control of him. The ghosts of 1861 never stopped haunting him.

Half an hour passed. Stephens walked into the bar, an earnest look on his face. He came up besides Toombs's barstool.

"Robert, General Walker says he will not support your bid unless you agree to the insertion of a plank in the platform calling for a permanent military academy. We've decided not to bother with advocating that it be in South Carolina. He simply insists that you agree to a military academy in principle."

"But I can't do that!" Toombs whispered harshly. "Aleck, you know me! All my life I've held to my principles. Now you want me to sacrifice them for the sake of one old general's endorsement?"

"Walker is on the central committee, Robert. His words will carry weight. Most of the other army officers who have come to join the party will listen to him." He paused a moment. "I think we need to do this."

Toombs shook his head.

Stephens spoke again, more quickly now. "Look, Robert, we have to make deals if we are to get what we want. And that is for you to be vice president. You know what will come six years later."

Toombs turned and looked his old friend dead in the eye. "What other deals are you making in there?"

"Governor Vance wants to be Secretary of State. I told him we'd push his name with Beauregard. If we promise that, he says that he can get the North Carolina delegation to vote for you for vice president."

Toombs shrugged. "He'd be as good as anybody else, I suppose."

"So can I go back in and tell Walker that you agree?"

Toombs waited a long moment before replying. "Fine."

Stephens left without another word, again leaving Toombs to his whiskey and cigar. Another half hour passed before he came back out to tell Toombs that the committee had agreed to a man to back him for the vice presidency.

CHAPTER NINE

July 1, Morning
Executive Office Building, Richmond, Virginia

"It's really incredible when you think about it," President Davis was saying. "During the war, we begged England and France to recognize us as an independent state. They refused until we had won our independence on our own. Now, they both come to us, hats in their hands, vying with one another to make us their ally."

"Incredible is the word for it," Benjamin replied. "But you should not become too enthusiastic."

"How could I not be enthusiastic?" Davis asked. "An alliance with either England or France would ensure our nation's future safety. The United States would never seek a war of revenge against us if they knew it would involve them in a conflict with one of the European great powers."

"Neither England nor France are eager for the opportunity to protect us, Mr. President. Nations have no genuine friends or enemies. Nations only have interests."

"True, but is it not equally true that the enemy of one's enemy is one's friend? These Irish nationalists are doing us a great favor by stirring up trouble between the United States and England. If England and the Union become enemies, we shall then be in a position to become England's friend, no?"

"Perhaps, Mr. President. But we must not be too hasty. If we rush to embrace this offer from the British, it may be seen by the French as a rebuke."

"Certainly, but if we have an alliance with England, we will no longer need an alliance with France. Why dance with the second-most beautiful girl when the most beautiful one wants to take the floor with you?"

Benjamin was not the sort of man to become alarmed, but he did not like what he was hearing from Davis. The president was getting swept away with the prospect of a British alliance. For himself, Benjamin was wary. Slidell had sent him a private telegram, laying out his fear that any agreement with Britain would be abrogated the next time a new administration took office in London. Moreover, the Minister to France felt that the general British reluctance to enter into firm agreements with other countries meant that they were not entirely sincere in their expressed desire for an alliance. Disraeli, Slidell was apparently convinced, was trying to pull a fast one on the Confederacy.

The Secretary of State trusted Slidell as he trusted few other men. They had stood side by side in Louisiana politics for many years before the war. Still, he couldn't help but wonder what his old friend was up to. He assumed that they still shared the same goal of an eventual treaty with France, given his stated concerns. Yet he could never be absolutely sure. Benjamin had to trust that Slidell knew what he was doing.

As the talk continued, Davis seemed to grow irritated that Benjamin didn't share his keenness for an alliance with Britain. Skillfully, he turned the conversation with the president towards other foreign policy matters that needed to be discussed. They went over a list of potential nominees for the position of Minister to Prussia. Davis was leaning towards nominating a Fire-Eater, so as to reduce the number of such people in Congress. Benjamin was opposed, believing that the Confederacy's image in European courts was already bad enough. They discussed plans for the Confederacy to join the proposed international postal union.

He then provided Davis a summary of the latest foreign news. The Austrian Empire was hosting a conference of German states to discuss reforming the German Confederation. Benjamin thought that this was a ploy to reduce distract popular attention away from the Hungarian agitation within the Habsburg realm. In Egypt, the Suez Canal appeared ready to open for seagoing traffic. In South America, the so-called War of the Triple Alliance between Paraguay and the combined forces of Brazil, Argentina and Uruguay continued to rage with undiminished fury.

Another item from the foreign press concerned the naval skirmishes between Spanish warships and Peruvian coastal defenses, ostensibly over a couple of insignificant Pacific islands. Some were saying that it was the first step in a long-term Spanish plan to regain control of her lost South American colonies. Benjamin thought such an idea absurd, yet he couldn't help but note the lack of response by the United States. Ten years earlier, any such European campaign would have been condemned as a violation of the Monroe Doctrine. The Spanish effort, small though it was, indicated that the European powers no longer recognized the Monroe Doctrine as having much validity. The same applied to the French effort in Mexico. It might not mean much right away, Benjamin thought, but the long-term implications were ominous.

"Is there anything else?" Davis asked tiredly.

"Not regarding foreign affairs, no."

"Very well. How goes the presidential campaign, then?"

Benjamin grinned. "Beauregard's supporters seem to be having a grand old time down in Montgomery. They've christened themselves the States' Rights Party. I've been reading the newspaper accounts. I believe that they are going to nominate Beauregard sometime today."

Davis grunted softly, nodding. "Well, I suppose it was inevitable that something like this would happen. It's a good thing that my political opponents failed to organize themselves during the war, when their antics might have brought about the defeat of our cause. They caused quite enough trouble as it was. I had hoped to avoid the creation of party politics in the Confederacy, but it was not to be. Alas."

"It was the same in the early republic, Mr. President," Benjamin said consolingly. "The writers of the Constitution did not foresee the rise of political parties, either. Jefferson did not want to create his party, but he felt he had no choice when he observed what Hamilton was doing."

"Indeed. And now that these fanatics have started their own party, the forces of common sense will have to follow suit in order to counter them."

"Probably."

"And Breckinridge will be the standard bearer," Davis said. "I shall pray earnestly for his victory, believe me. But whether Beauregard or Breckinridge is the next man to hold this office, I shall be very relieved when my time here is done."

"I know," Benjamin replied.

"I fear, though, that Breckinridge is not doing enough. He has not even officially announced his candidacy yet."

Benjamin rose from his chair, a smile on his face. "If you think that, Mr. President, you must not have read this morning's paper." Davis's eyes looked at him quizzically, but Benjamin simply smiled, nodded, and turned to leave the room.

As Benjamin walked through the hall from the president's office to his own, he passed by two government employees whispering excitedly to one another. One held a newspaper in his hands. "He's doing it! He's really doing it!" one said to the other as he tapped the paper. Benjamin smiled. He could see the fruits of his labor unfolded within steps of his own workplace.

Benjamin stepped into his office and sat down at his desk, on which lay a copy of the *Richmond Enquirer*. While the other three major Richmond papers generally excoriated Jefferson Davis and those who worked for him, the *Enquirer* was supportive of the administration. He picked it up and unfolded it. The headline was unambiguous.

BRECKINRIDGE RUNNING FOR PRESIDENT!

He read through the open letter that proclaimed Breckinridge's candidacy. It was what one would have expected. Declaring that he sought office not out of personal ambition but purely out of a desire to serve the Confederacy, the Kentuckian had laid out for the consideration of the people his long defense of Southern rights in Washington before secession, his service as a general during the military struggle with the Union, and his efforts as Secretary of War since the conclusion of peace. He affirmed his readiness to serve the country as President of the Confederate States of America.

It was simple, straightforward, and well-written. Benjamin had offered to write it for him, but Breckinridge, ever the man of integrity, had rejected this as dishonest. The Kentuckian had brought the letter to Benjamin for his perusal and suggestions before declaring it finished, however. He had then left it to Benjamin to do with as he saw fit.

The Secretary of State had had his clerks make several dozen copies of the letter after being sworn to secrecy as to its contents. That done, Benjamin mailed the letters out to every major newspaper in the Confederacy, from Virginia to distant Texas. He asked the editors of those papers to publish the letter on July

1, as he had learned that this was to be the final day of the convention in Montgomery. Benjamin assumed that this would also be the day that the nomination of Beauregard as the candidate of the SRP would become official, so the simultaneous release of Breckinridge's letter would serve to distract the public from that event and therefore reduce its impact.

As he read through the letter a second time, Benjamin reflected on the fact that men all over the country were also reading it at that very moment. The newspapers, of course, were clustered in the big cities like Richmond, Atlanta, and New Orleans. From there, like water spilled onto a table, the news would rapidly spread across the country. Smaller papers in local areas would pick up the text and reprint it, word for word. Within a matter of days, thanks to the miracle of the electric telegraph, there would scarcely be a man or woman in the country who did not know that Breckinridge was running for president.

He chuckled to himself, delighted at the success of his little plan. The SRP might have begun to suspect that they would face no serious opponent in the upcoming presidential race. Instead, they would be opening their newspapers in Montgomery on the day they were to nominate their own man and discover that they were going to be up against a truly formidable opponent.

The campaign was about to begin in earnest.

Benjamin's eyes narrowed when he noticed another news piece in smaller print on another page of the *Enquirer*. Edmund Ruffin, one of the most ferocious of the pre-war secessionist Fire-Eaters, had passed away in his rural home west of Richmond at the age of seventy-three. Funeral arrangements were already underway and the service would be held in Hollywood Cemetery in Richmond. It was rumored that South Carolina, where Ruffin had been especially popular, would be sending a state delegation to attend the service.

Benjamin's mouth curled into a mischievous smile, his mind already taking this seemingly insignificant information and forming it into yet another plan.

July 1, Evening
Exchange Hotel, Montgomery, Alabama

Toombs had wanted Stephens to be the convention president, but his old friend had adamantly refused to take on the leadership role. It had not been nervousness but practicality, the vice president had stressed. Stephens's voice was thin and squeaky and would surely be inaudible in the crowded hotel ballroom. The central committee had instead given the job to Wigfall, whose voice could boom forth like the fire from a cannon.

Looking out over the ballroom, Toombs could now see that Stephens had been correct. The Exchange Hotel ballroom was packed to the brim with people, who were moving back and forth and chattering boisterously. It was extremely loud, yet the voices were all excited and cheerful, there was much laughter, and the general feeling was one of exhilaration and hope.

He sat at a table close to the speaker's platform. Stephens sat beside him, a blanket draped over him despite the warm and humid air that filled the room. Many of the other more prominent attendees were also at the table, including

Senator Hunter and Governor Brown. Behind the rostrum set up on the speaker's platform, Wigfall was speaking with a group of Mississippi delegates.

Toombs took a deep breath. The next few minutes were going to be crucial. After nearly four days of ceaseless activity, the convention he had worked so hard to put together was moving towards a climax. It was exhilarating to know that he was experiencing an event that would be mentioned in the history books of the future.

He had slept perhaps three or four hours each night for the last three nights, flitting from meeting to meeting. He had subsisted on sheer nervous energy and enormous quantities of coffee. Only rarely had he actually found himself in the ballroom, where the convention was officially taking place. More often, he had wandered from hotel room to hotel room, or to the various alehouses and coffee shops in the vicinity, offering deals, making promises, and generally playing politics.

A Mississippi delegate had been angered when he learned that the job of tariff collector for the port of Biloxi had been promised to someone else; Toombs had swooped down to mollify the man with an offer to make him postmaster in Meridian. A Virginia delegate wanted his son to be given an administrative job with the diplomatic delegation in Brazil; Toombs promised to consider it. A Florida delegate from a sugar producing family wanted reassurance that an SRP administration wouldn't push for an abolition of the sugar tariff; Toombs had given an ambiguous answer that the man could interpret any way he pleased. These and a thousand other political transactions had filled Toombs's hours as the convention proceeded. He had never had so much fun in his life.

Through all of this, he had kept close tabs on the progress being made by the Platform Committee. News had filtered into Montgomery that General Morgan had won a victory over Saul's insurgents, so the proposed plank denouncing the effort against the insurrection as a failure due to the administration's incompetence was removed. It was replaced with a general statement asserting the responsibility of both state and national governments to crush any slave insurrection by all means necessary. After some intense debate, it was decided that the platform would not specify a desire to gain territory in northern Mexico.

Toombs had addressed the Platform Committee directly when it began discussions of his proposed fiscal policy, which was enthusiastically embraced as part of the platform. He bit his lip and said nothing when the Platform Committee approved a plank calling for the establishment of a permanent military academy to train officers of the Confederate Army. He was certain that they were making a great mistake and hoped to put it to rights later on. A plank calling for a national naval academy in New Orleans had also been approved. Toombs had no issue with this, as a navy was not the threat to the liberties of the people that a standing army could be.

"Did you read the paper this morning?" Stephens asked, leaning over to speak to him over the din.

"I did," Toombs said. "So Breckinridge has officially announced, eh? How devious of him to do it on the final day of our convention."

"Devious, indeed," Stephens answered. "And not really his style, if you ask me. I think Benjamin was the one who did it. Gave the letter out to the editors and told them the day to run it."

"Wouldn't surprise me. He's a shifty little Jew, that Benjamin. We're running against him as much as against Breckinridge."

Wigfall finished the conversation with the Mississippi men, who descended from the speaker's platform and took their seats at their table. Wigfall took a sip of something at the rostrum and then began loudly pounding the gavel. The noise level slowly dropped to a level above which he could be heard.

"There are three votes now before the convention!" his thunderous voice boomed through the room. "I don't think I need to remind anyone that this is the most important moment of our convention! The first vote will be on whether to approve the States' Rights Party platform as presented by the Platform Committee." He looked around the room for a moment to make sure everyone was ready to proceed. "I think we're ready. Voting will proceed by alphabetical order by state. Alabama?"

The Alabama delegation approved the platform unanimously, as did Arkansas and Florida after it. Two Georgia delegates voted against the platform. Toombs remembered that they both hailed from the Atlanta area and had strongly pushed for a plank calling for the relocation of the national capital from Richmond to Atlanta. It had all been for show, of course, allowing them to go home to their constituents and tell them that they had done their best. Had the passage of the platform genuinely been in doubt, they surely would have voted in favor. Three of Louisiana's twelve delegates voted no, which was a troubling proportion. Toombs assumed that they were sugar planters angered by the committee's refusal to enshrine protection of the sugar tariff in the platform. Yet Toombs wasn't worried, as Louisiana would be a solidly SRP state in the November election no matter what.

Mississippi and North Carolina both voted unanimously to support the platform, which told Toombs that the final vote was going to be overwhelmingly in favor. One South Carolina delegate voted against it as a protest against a specific statement of support for the Citadel as the location of the national military academy. Two Tennessee delegates voted against it. Toombs did not know why, but by that point it didn't matter. The Texas delegation approved it unanimously. Virginia, the largest delegation by far, did so by a vote of twenty-eight to two.

"The vote is as follows!" Wigfall said after everything had been counted. "One hundred and sixty-four votes in favor of the platform! Ten against! The platform is accepted!"

There was thunderous cheering and applause throughout the ballroom, quickly becoming so loud that it hurt Toombs's ears. Yet he was elated. If he overlooked the beastly provision about a national military academy, the platform as it had been written was a close summation of his political beliefs. The opponents of Jefferson Davis and his policies of centralization had been fragmented and at odds with one another for too long. Now they finally had something around which they could rally. The platform would be to the new States' Rights Party as a battle flag was to a regiment in the midst of a battle.

Wigfall looked down at Toombs, who nodded up at him.

"And now, we move on to our next vote!" Wigfall boomed. "We shall now select the man who shall be our candidate for the office of President of the Confederate States of America!"

Once again, tumultuous cheering and applause exploded across the ballroom, to which many delegates added by pounding their fists on their tables. It was clear to Toombs that the convention was becoming increasingly rowdy. Glancing about, he could see that most of the attendees were drinking copious amounts of alcohol. Doubtless they were doing so to steady their nerves, for everyone knew that they were witnessing a historical event.

Toombs and his allies had worked very hard to make sure that the vote for Beauregard would be easy and definitive. It was important that the public realize that the party was united firmly behind its candidate and that there had been no controversy about the selection. Alabama, Arkansas, and Florida all unanimously voted in favor of Beauregard, precisely as had been planned. When it came to Georgia, another part of Toombs's plan came to fruition.

"Georgia?" Wigfall asked loudly.

Congressman Howell Cobb, the chairman of the Georgia delegation, rose from his seat. "Georgia casts its twenty votes for Senator Robert Toombs!"

There was a sudden murmuring of confusion and discontent throughout the room, following by two competing choruses of boos and cheers. This was precisely what Toombs had expected. It had long been customary at American party conventions for a state to cast its first-round vote for a favorite son, even when that person had no realistic chance of obtaining the nomination. In this case, it had been carefully orchestrated. By having some of the presidential votes cast in his favor, Toombs was now in a position to present himself as the most viable vice presidential candidate.

Toombs stood from his chair and looked back at the Georgia delegation. "No, no!" he shouted, loudly enough for several people to hear over the tumult. "Beauregard! Vote for Beauregard!"

"Georgia casts its votes for Senator Toombs!" Wigfall exclaimed. He moved on with the state count. "Louisiana!"

Louisiana, Mississippi, South Carolina, and Tennessee all voted unanimously for Beauregard. North Carolina had a single delegate who voted for Governor Vance as a favorite son, but all its other votes went for Beauregard. It was when the voting reached Texas that something happened which Toombs had not expected.

The chairman of the Texas delegation stood. "Texas casts its twelve votes for Senator Louis T. Wigfall!"

As had happened when the Georgia delegation had voted for Toombs, this announcement was greeted with cheers and boos throughout the ballroom. Unlike Toombs, however, Wigfall didn't say a word in protest. He simply smiled and moved on to Virginia, which unanimously cast its votes for Beauregard.

The vote stood at one hundred and forty-one for Beauregard, twenty for Toombs, twelve for Wigfall, and one for Governor Vance. Under the rules of the convention, established on its opening day by the Rules Committee, a resolution needed only a two-thirds majority to pass, meaning that Beauregard was officially nominated. A thunderous cheer, much louder than those which had preceded it, rose from the delegates. It seemed to Toombs that it was literally shaking the wooden pillars that held up the hotel.

Stephens leaned over to him. "What's Wigfall up to?" he asked.

"I don't know," Toombs answered. "We never discussed having the Texas delegates vote for him. Look at his face. He's not surprised."

"You don't think he's aiming for the vice presidency, too, do you?"

Toombs face became angry. "He might. He is deceitful, after all. His support of our positions up to this point has been strangely conciliatory for him, now that I think about it."

"Don't worry yourself. Perhaps it is just vanity. Besides, in a convention contest, you'd beat him."

"I hope so."

It took several loud poundings of the gavel before Wigfall could bring the delegates back down to a volume level low enough for proceedings to continue. "We shall move on to our final vote of the session!" he shouted. "It is time to cast our votes to select our party's nominee for Vice President of the Confederate States of America!"

Toombs felt a sudden apprehension. What was about to happen was likely to be one of the most important events of his life. He had climbed the ladder of Georgia politics before the war, becoming one of the greatest statesmen of the South. He had felt he deserved to be named president in 1861. This time, he had planned everything with exacting care. Could it now be that Wigfall, the man he had thought was his ally but who was undeniably devious, was about to wrest the prize from his hands?

"Alabama!" Wigfall called.

"Alabama casts its eighteen votes for Senator Robert Toombs!"

No words had ever been more reassuring to Toombs. He had personally spoken with every member of the Alabama delegation and had been sure of their support. To see that his efforts had not been futile was an enormous relief.

"Arkansas!"

"Arkansas casts its eight votes for Senator Louis T. Wigfall!"

Relief was replaced by terror. The fact that Alabama had far more weight in the convention than Arkansas scarcely mattered, for Toombs had been as sure of the votes from Arkansas as he had been of those from Alabama. He had canvassed the Arkansas delegates several times over the past few days and had repeatedly been assured that they were for him. Wigfall himself had promised that he could count on the votes of Arkansas. That the state had gone to Wigfall told him that something was terribly wrong.

"Wigfall's gone behind our back!" Stephens whispered urgently. "All the time he said he was building support for you, he was building support for himself!"

"It can't be!" Toombs protested. "Someone would have told us!"

"Florida!" Wigfall bellowed.

"Florida casts its six votes for Senator Robert Toombs!"

So it was twenty-four votes for Toombs and eight for Wigfall. On the face of it, that sounded more than adequate. Yet Toombs could not imagine how many state delegations Wigfall might have swayed over to his side. He tried to calm himself. There was nothing that he could do at this point to affect the outcome and panicking was not going to help.

He noticed something that gave him encouragement. When the Florida spokesman had announced his state's support for Toombs, Wigfall's face had revealed a certain disappointment. This could only mean that Wigfall had thought it possible that Florida would back him and it had not. Perhaps the Texan's politicking had not been as thorough and as careful as Toombs's own.

It was no surprise when Georgia, the next state, cast its support to Toombs. Louisiana, however, split its vote, with six delegates supporting Toombs and six supporting Wigfall. That put the vote at fifty for Toombs and fourteen for Wigfall. One hundred and seventeen votes would be required for the nomination. Toombs was much closer to the number than was Wigfall, yet Toombs could assume that the twelve votes of Texas would go to his opponent and the big states of Tennessee, North Carolina, and Virginia had yet to vote.

"Mississippi!"

"Mississippi casts its fourteen votes for Senator Louis Wigfall!"

Now it was fifty to twenty-eight. This was much too close for comfort for Toombs. His mind franticly tried to devise some way to intervene. If he dashed over to the Mississippi delegation, could be make some last minute deal to get them to switch their vote? He shook his head. There were only minutes remaining. As the convention president, Wigfall could simply refuse to recognize the state if it called for recognition before the final vote was taken.

"North Carolina!"

"North Carolina casts its twenty votes for Senator Robert Toombs!"

"Relax," Stephens said. "You're too far ahead for Wigfall to catch up, even with the Texas votes in his pocket. South Carolina and Virginia will certainly back you."

Toombs nodded hurriedly. He was no longer concerned with losing the vote to Wigfall. What terrified him know was the possibility that he would not win the necessary two-thirds of delegates to confirm his nomination. If Tennessee and Texas went to Wigfall and South Carolina and Virginia went to him, it would only give him one hundred and twelve votes to sixty-two for Wigfall, meaning that neither of them would be officially nominated. A second round of voting would have to be held, in which case a dark horse candidate might emerge. All of his carefully arranged deals, promises, threats, and bargains could come unraveled.

"South Carolina!"

"South Carolina casts its twelve votes for Senator Robert Toombs!" Congressman William Boyce, the spokesman of the South Carolina delegation, shouted his response in an especially forceful tone, demonstrating his anger at Wigfall's attempt to steal the vice presidential nomination for himself.

"Tennessee!" Wigfall called.

This would be the decisive moment. If Tennessee backed Wigfall, Toombs would not have enough votes to secure the nomination and a second round of voting would be held. If Tennessee backed him, his nomination would secured. Senator Henry Foote, the chairman of the Tennessee delegation, stood from his chair. He didn't respond right away, looking around at the suddenly quiet ballroom. He had done the math as surely as Toombs and knew that the words he was about to speak would be dramatic.

"Tennessee casts its twenty-two votes for Senator Robert Toombs!"

This was greeted with cheers from most of the delegates, but its fair share of boos and hisses. Toombs scarcely heard it, for he felt a wave of relief pass over him. He was all but certain that Virginia would support him, which would mean that he would have the votes to secure nomination.

"Texas!" Wigfall called out.

"Texas casts its twelve votes for Senator Louis Wigfall!"

"Virginia!"

"Virginia casts its thirty votes for Senator Robert Toombs!"

Toombs glared up at Wigfall, whose face bore a look of disappointment that was impossible to conceal. He had gambled and failed, leaving Toombs victorious. Yet the very fact that he had gambled at all, attempting to steal the vice presidential nomination out from under him, was enough to make Toombs regard him as a deadly enemy.

"The final vote is one hundred and thirty-four for Senator Toombs and forty for Senator Wigfall," the Texan said. He gave an exaggeratedly formal bow of his head in Toombs's direction. "Senator Toombs is hereby declared the States' Rights Party's nominee for Vice President of the Confederate States of America."

There was a warm round of applause throughout the ballroom. Toombs stood and waved to the crowded room, a forced smile on his face. He was proud to have secured the nomination, but he had expected the vote to be smooth and easy. It had turned out to be nerve-racking and nearly disastrous. He was not sure what the delegates thought of him now.

"Speech!" someone shouted.

Others quickly took up the call. "Toombs! We want to hear Toombs!"

He walked up the steps onto the speaker's platform. Wigfall was there, warmly clapping and with a smile on his face. As Toombs approached, the rough Texan held out his hand.

"Congratulations, Robert!" he said. Only Toombs and Wigfall could hear one another over the tumult of cheering. "It worked out just like we planned."

"You're a rat bastard and you will pay dearly for this," Toombs said even as he shook Wigfall's hand.

They turned together towards the applauding crowd and smiled broadly, holding up their shaking hands for all to see. Toombs knew that the appearance of conciliation would be to his benefit. Wigfall no doubt felt the same way. It was important to make it look as though there were no hard feelings, yet Toombs knew his mind would begin plotting his revenge as soon as it had the time. Wigfall backed away from the rostrum, still clapping, then turned and walked down the steps to the floor, leaving Toombs alone on the speaker's platform.

He took a deep breath and looked out over the crowd. The cheering and applause reassured him and washed away the doubts and fears that had filled him a few moments earlier. These were his people, fellow laborers in the cause of securing the rights of the states against the national government and ensuring the survival of the Confederacy as a slave-based society ruled by an aristocracy of the rich and well-born.

"My friends, the time has come!" Toombs said, gripping the rostrum with both hands. Cheering erupted at the sound of his words, yet he continued on, forcing his voice up into a thunderous volume that could be heard above the din. "We have had our convention, approved our platform, and nominated our candidates! The campaign of 1867 has begun! Let us now join hands to begin the long struggle to regain the liberties for which our brave and gallant soldiers sacrificed their lives!"

He had written notes for the speech he intended to give once he had secured the vice presidential nomination. Yet he had decided against writing a formal, careful oration. He felt that his reputation as a great orator was well-deserved and generally eschewed the elaborate preparations and intellectual approach favored by his friend Stephens. Better, he felt, to speak with the power of deeply felt emotion.

"When the Southern states seceded from the Union and formed our Confederacy, we knew we were taking a step from which there was no turning back. We would not have gone through with secession had there been any other choice. Had the North been willing to accept our right to live our lives as we see fit, to protect our own unique institutions, and not to succumb to the tyranny of a foreign majority, there might have been no separation. There might have been no war."

There was a murmuring in the crowd. Toombs wondered if he should have mentioned the hypothetical conciliation with the North before the war. After all, he was speaking to a crowd largely composed of Fire-Eaters. It didn't matter, for the next part of the speech would give them plenty of bloody meat on which to chew.

"Yet the North refused to accept this and we exercised our constitutional right to leave the Union. Even then, the North sought to maintain their dominance by force of arms. Yet how poorly did they understand the gallant strength of Confederate manhood, who stood against vastly superior numbers and resources and hurled the foe back on countless legendary battlefields. We won our independence through our own blood and toil and now we stand forth, an independent confederacy, on the same level with the other great states of the world!"

This was met with sustained applause, which reassured Toombs that the crowd was with him. He continued.

"All of the armies and navies of Yankeedom could not subjugate our Southern Confederacy. Yet we have grown to realize that the true threat to our liberties and institutions are not the bayonets of foreign foes, but the enemy within. Like the serpent in the Garden of Eden, this enemy has slithered into our midst by appearing at first to be a friend. It has only been through bitter experience that we have learned that it is not a friend, but in fact a far more dangerous enemy than any conceivable combination of Yankees. I speak, of course, of Jefferson Davis."

This was greeted with an explosion of forceful jeering by the crowd, exactly as Toombs had expected. Denunciations of Jefferson Davis were exciting the crowd as much as if Toombs was tossing them handfuls of gold coins.

"The man we must reluctantly acknowledge as our president came to us in the guise of a great man. He promised to defend our liberties. Yet he ignored the wishes of the states. He implemented conscription without our consent, imposed direct taxes after swearing he would not do so, treated governors and congressmen as though they were but his serfs, and acting towards all the people of the Confederacy the way as master might act towards his own slaves."

He paused, feeling a sense of fire and rage rise among the crowd. Nothing could stock the anger of a white Southern man more than to insinuate that someone considered them to be on the same level with blacks.

"We've seen this before, my friends. Read through history. Julius Caesar. Oliver Cromwell. Napoleon Bonaparte. They came to their countrymen with protestations of friendship and were raised to high office, whereupon they made themselves dictators. It is only through the foresight of the men who drafted our Constitution, here in this very city six years ago, that the ambitions of Jefferson Davis will be thwarted, for in their wisdom they included the provision that no man may serve more than six years in the office of the Presidency."

Toombs took a quick sip of water before continuing.

"But let us not be tricked into complacency, for it is more than one man we are struggling against! There is, indeed, an entire faction in our Confederacy who share the aims of Davis, who want to centralize all power in a national government, who want to trample upon the rights of the states. We know the names of these people. We should not be afraid of throwing down the gauntlet in front of them."

He listed off names of congressmen who continued to support Davis, including Senator Benjamin Hill, his own colleague from Georgia. He spoke of Postmaster Reagan and the manner in which he appointed political allies of the President to run the post offices around the Confederacy. He spoke of Treasury Secretary Trenholm and his ability to make himself rich even as inflation continued to eat away at the country's economy. He excoriated Secretary of State Benjamin as a liar and a master manipulator, never bothering to mention the man's Jewishness. Toombs knew that the largely anti-Semitic crowd in front of him knew of Benjamin's heritage perfectly well and would draw their own conclusions.

"But what man carries the tyrannical banner of Jefferson Davis higher than any other? What man has supported and encouraged every centralizing action of Jefferson Davis? What man sold out his own state and handed it over to Yankee dominion? What man signed off on the Yankee theft of hundreds of thousands of our servants? What man was it whose incompetence got the Army of Tennessee routed at the Battle of Missionary Ridge?"

The crowd followed what Toombs was saying. "Breckinridge!" contemptuous voices cried out.

"That's right! John C. Breckinridge! The finest son of Kentucky!" These words were spoken with sarcastic derision. "And he is the man who, this very morning, has announced that he is running for president!"

The chorus of boos and hisses again echoed through the ballroom. Many of these people, Toombs knew, had been firm supporters of Breckinridge during the 1860 election. Their disillusionment might have begun, as it had for Toombs, as early as 1861, when Breckinridge waited several months after the firing on Fort Sumter to join the Confederate cause. Through his actions at the Toronto Peace Conference and his joining forces with Jefferson Davis by becoming a member of his Cabinet, Breckinridge had betrayed them all. It was not just Breckinridge's policies they hated, but the man himself.

"Our enemies have pushed forward Breckinridge, a Judas to the Confederacy, as great a traitor as Benedict Arnold, as their standard bearer. Contrast that with what the States' Rights Party has done. We are calling upon the man who fired the first shot in defense of Southern freedom at Fort Sumter. The man who defeated the Yankees in the first great battle of the war on the plains of Manassas. The man who defended Charleston and Petersburg in the face of incredible odds. The man who did not hesitate for a single moment to throw his life, his fortune, and his very honor into the struggle for Southern independence and the rights of the states. My friends, we have called upon Pierre Gustave Toutant Beauregard!"

The roar of cheering was enough to make the earth shake. Toombs thought that his eardrums were going to rupture. Restraining the urge to cover his ears with his hands and struggling to maintain a smiling face, he saw a messenger boy come running into the ballroom from the hotel lobby, frantically waving a piece of paper.

"He's responded, Senator!" the young man cried, barely being heard over the tumult. "General Beauregard's responded! Here's his telegram!"

Everything had run smoothly, Toombs was pleased to see. At his New Orleans home, Beauregard had patiently been waiting for word that his nomination for president was official. His response, carefully prepared in advance, had been sent immediately. In the age of the telegraph, communication between New Orleans and Montgomery was virtually instantaneous.

The appearance of the messenger in the ballroom had been carefully orchestrated. The telegram had actually arrived several hours beforehand. Toombs had asked the messenger boy to wait until the end of his speech, telling him the exact words that would serve as a signal for him to enter the room. The messenger dashed up onto the speaker's platform, while the crowd in the ballroom suddenly went silent. Toombs snatched the paper from the young man's hand and made a theatrical display of reading it. Then, a smile beamed across his face and he turned to face the crowd once again.

"Allow me to read the response of General Beauregard. 'It is with a sense of humility and a consciousness of my duty that I accept the nomination of the States' Rights Party to be the President of the Confederate States. Trusting in the blessing of Almighty God and counting on your support, I believe we shall restore the South to the right path of state sovereignty and equal rights for all white men.'"

For the final time that day, the ballroom of the Exchange Hotel exploded in cheers and applause. Toombs drank it all in. He had achieved his goals, having arranged the nomination of Beauregard as president and his own nomination as vice president. The unexpected interference of Wigfall had momentarily threatened to upset the cart, but he successfully overcame it. As he watched the convention break up into celebratory songs and heavy drinking, with people already making their way to the bar, he knew that he had taken an important step towards the fulfillment of his great ambition.

Now, of course, there was an election to win.

"So they made Toombs their vice presidential candidate?" Breckinridge asked.

"That's what the papers say," said Senator Benjamin Hill. "They also ran the text of the speech he gave. He takes you to task quite explicitly, I daresay."

"Well, it will make things interesting, that's for sure," Breckinridge said. "Can't say I mind, though. The last thing I would want is a boring election."

There were chuckles through the room. Breckinridge grinned as he took another sip of the piping hot coffee that had been put out for everyone. The laughter was rather more than the joke deserved, but men had a habit of flattering political candidates. This would be his first campaign since the 1860 presidential election, but memories of what it was like to run for office were flooding back into his mind, some pleasant and some not.

Now that he had officially announced his candidacy, there could be no turning back. He had no choice but to go all in and mount a full-scale political campaign. Breckinridge still felt somewhat affronted at Judah Benjamin for bullying him into running, yet he knew his fellow Cabinet member had the best interests of the country at heart. He also genuinely believed that he would make a good president and that the policies likely to be pursued by a Beauregard administration made up of men such as Toombs would be disastrous. Duty, as well as ambition, pushed Breckinridge forward.

He glanced around at the men in the room, which had been reserved by Benjamin as a campaign headquarters. Senator Hill, a pro-Davis Georgian, was only one of a dozen men who had come to the meeting. Some were men Breckinridge knew very well, such as Postmaster Reagan and Secretary of the Treasury Trenholm. Others were congressmen from various states with whom Breckinridge was only passingly acquainted. There was Congressman Duncan Kenner of Louisiana, who had promised to do all he could to support Breckinridge but glumly reported that victory in his state was impossible. There was Congressman Israel Welch of Mississippi and Congressman Charles Collier of Virginia, among a few others. Breckinridge thought the gathering a good sampling of the Confederacy, but noted that there was a smaller proportion of men from the Deep South than there was among Beauregard's supporters.

One of the more interesting fellows was Congressman James Kemper of Virginia, who had commanded a brigade in George Pickett's division in the disastrous charge on the last day of the Battle of Gettysburg. Both before and since the war, Kemper had served as an influential member of the Virginia House of Delegates and some were speaking of him as a potential candidate for the governor's office. If Breckinridge had his way, Kemper was going to play a critical role in his campaign.

The man in the room whom Breckinridge knew best, however, was sitting directly across the table from him. Congressman John B. Gordon was a man rapidly rising up the ladder of Georgia politics, where he was emerging as a leader of the faction opposed to Senator Toombs and Governor Brown. His popularity stemmed from his service as one of Lee's most brilliant brigade and division commanders during the war. Wounded several times, Gordon had been credited with saving the Army of Northern Virginia from destruction during the terrifying Battle of Spotsylvania Court House in May of 1864.

Breckinridge and Gordon had served together under General Jubal Early in Maryland and the Shenandoah Valley in the summer of 1864. Fighting side-by-side, they had developed a deep respect for one another and become close friends. With Gordon and Senator Hill on his side, Breckinridge felt he had at least a chance of winning Georgia.

Judah Benjamin himself was not present. He had told Breckinridge that pressing diplomatic business with President Davis prevented his attendance at the meeting. This might well have been true, considering the strange occurrences in relations with France and England. Yet Breckinridge suspected Benjamin was staying away as a calculated ploy. He was relying on Benjamin's political advice a great deal and assumed Benjamin did not want to make this obvious to their supporters, as it might undermine Breckinridge's credibility and leadership.

"So, the die is cast," Breckinridge said simply. "Beauregard is running for president, backed by the so-called States' Rights Party. I'm running against them and have asked for your help. If we don't win, the country will be under the control of ideological radicals who will surely run it into the ground."

"That's the truth, by God," Gordon said firmly. "Senator Hill and I are better acquainted with Senator Toombs and Governor Brown than the rest of you fellows. If they are the controlling hand behind Beauregard after that old Creole wins the presidency, I don't think it's too much to say that the very survival of the Confederacy will be open to question."

"As you know Toombs, I know Wigfall," Postmaster Reagan said. "A more disgusting man can scarcely be imagined. The thought of him having influence over the government quite frankly sickens me."

"I don't think anyone in this room doubts the gravity of the situation," Kemper said. "If Breckinridge loses, our country faces a disaster. But how do we win? This so-called States' Rights Party has a huge head start. They just finished a convention in Montgomery that was attended by hundreds of people. Committees have formed in every state and local organizations are springing up like weeds all over the country. Us? It's just the people in this room."

"You're right," Breckinridge replied. "No point denying it."

"We'll have to catch up, then," Senator Hill said.

"As I said, how?" Kemper pressed.

"Let's go over it state-by-state," Breckinridge said.

The group spent the next half hour discussing and debating their chances for victory in each of the eleven states of the Confederacy, much as Breckinridge and Benjamin had done two months before. All agreed that Louisiana and South Carolina were not worth fighting for. Beauregard was so popular in both states that he was sure to win no matter what the Breckinridge campaign did. Alabama and Mississippi, whose influential planters despised Breckinridge for what he had done in the peace negotiations, were discussed at length, the consensus being that they would be difficult but not impossible to win.

"What of the Trans-Mississippi?" Hill asked. "Arkansas and Texas?"

Breckinridge looked at Reagan. "John, you're our Texan. What do you think of our prospects?"

Reagan exhaled an immense cloud of cigar smoke before answering. "Wigfall's an influential man in Texas. Probably the biggest player in the state, in fact. He'll be ruthless and play every dirty trick he can think of to beat you, my friend."

"So are you saying Texas is a lost cause, too?" Gordon asked. "It may be one of the smaller states, but if things are tight its six electoral votes might be the deciding factor."

"No, far from hopeless." Reagan paused a moment, thinking. "In fact, I shall be leaving soon to return to Texas to campaign on your behalf. I'll organize all the friends we have in the state and put forth the strongest campaign possible to win there."

"Will you?" Breckinridge asked in surprise. "I can't ask you to do that. You have too many responsibilities as Postmaster."

"You didn't ask me. I volunteered. And I am going, whether you tell me to or not. My deputy can handle matters in my department until I return. You're a good man, John. I want to make sure that you're the next president and the best thing I can do is use my influence in my home state to win it for you. Besides, I am looking forward to going up against Wigfall and nailing that bastard to the wall."

Breckinridge smiled. "Well, thank you, my friend."

"One other thing," Reagan said. "My department gives me the ability to dispense patronage. Every sizable town has a postmaster, after all. You let me know who I need to appoint to what job and I'll do everything I can to help."

"Again, I thank you."

Breckinridge felt a familiar uneasiness. Whenever he had run for office in the past, whether it was for the Kentucky state legislature or President of the United States, he had found it difficult to ask people to make the necessary efforts on his behalf. He did not like to be beholden to anyone, nor did he want anyone to mistake his desire to serve the people as ambition. The fact that so many people had always been willing to stand up for him and work on his behalf without his even having to ask astonished him.

"I'll do everything I can, but I can't guarantee Texas will come down in our column come November," Reagan said. "Wigfall is powerful. And as for Arkansas, I can't say one way or the other."

"Arkansas is nothing," said Trenholm. "It has only four electoral votes."

"Which just might be the margin of victory," Breckinridge said quickly. "Now, what about the big eastern states? Virginia and North Carolina?"

"Absolutely critical," Gordon said. "Together they have twenty-seven electoral votes, more than half of the forty-eight we need to win. You absolutely can't afford to lose either of them. If you do, I see no chance of winning the election."

They spent the next twenty minutes talking about these two crucial states. It was hard to say whether Breckinridge or Beauregard would have the advantage. Both men had served in Virginia and were well-liked by the people living there. Breckinridge was wildly popular in the Shenandoah Valley and would certainly win those counties, but he might not do as well in the richer counties in the central and southern portions of the state, where most of the plantations were.

On the other hand, Virginia and North Carolina were not as economically dependent upon slave-grown cotton and tobacco as were the states of the Deep South. Slavery was deeply engrained in the two states, but not to the extent it was in places like South Carolina, Mississippi and Alabama. The rancor over Breckinridge's role in the Toronto peace negotiations was not as intense.

The discussion moved on to Tennessee. The eastern third of the state, mountainous and with limited agricultural potential, had never seen widespread use of slave labor and had generally supported the Union during the war. If its voters came out in large numbers, they would probably do so more to oppose Beauregard than to support Breckinridge. The western and central parts of the state, on the other hand, had much more in common with Mississippi and Alabama than with the Eastern Tennesseans. Winning Tennessee would require a very delicate political dance.

"Georgia will be one of the key races," Breckinridge said. "Senator Hill? Congressman Gordon?"

"The result will be balanced on a knife's edge," Hill said. "I think I speak for Gordon as well when I say that we will do everything we can to win the state for you. But the faction of Governor Brown, Senator Toombs, and Vice President Stephens is very strong. We've made some inroads against them, but they still effectively control the state. They'll work hard to win Georgia for Beauregard."

"No doubt," Breckinridge replied.

"Here's how I see it, gentlemen," Trenholm said. "We must win Virginia, North Carolina and either Tennessee or Georgia. That secures us thirty-nine electoral votes. The other nine votes have to come from some combination of other states, while acknowledging that Louisiana and South Carolina are unwinnable."

"That sounds about right," Breckinridge said. "I will be frank with all of you. Considering the head start that the States' Rights Party has on our campaign, and the political realities of the Electoral College and Beauregard's popularity, I would rate our chances for success as considerably less than fifty-fifty." He paused for a moment. "And perhaps I'm being generous to myself."

"If I may make a suggestion?" Kemper asked.

"Of course."

"I read your open letter to the papers very carefully. It was very good. You state your readiness to serve as president and you describe, in language no one could call haughty, your record of political and military service to the South. You spoke in general terms of ensuring that the Confederacy is respected abroad, maintaining peace with the United States, and keeping faith with the people. But no specific policies are mentioned."

"This is true," Breckinridge acknowledged.

"Yes, but it's not true for the opposition," Kemper pointed out. "Beauregard and his supporters have formed a political party, complete with a policy platform that is even now being reprinted in every newspaper across the country. We will need something similar. Otherwise, we will appear vacillating and disjointed in comparison."

"The people know what I believe," Breckinridge said. "I've been in politics now for twenty years."

"That's true, but you've been either Vice President of the United States, a general in the army, or the Secretary of War for Jefferson Davis during most of that time. In none of those positions were you able to speak freely as your own man. Only when you were representing Kentucky in the House or the Senate in Washington were you able to articulate your own specific ideas. That was a long time ago."

Breckinridge nodded, mulling this over. "You think I should write up a summary of specific policy proposals?"

"Yes, I do," Kemper said.

"I agree with Congressman Kemper," said Gordon. "The people see you as an honest man of integrity. They respect you for what you have done. But they will want to know your vision for the country."

"True, true," Breckinridge said. "I will have to do so." Breckinridge noticed Reagan frowning and shaking his head. "John, what troubles you?"

"Organization," the gruff Texan said simply. "Beauregard's people are organized. We are not. Promises of support mean nothing if they are not backed up by organization." He paused a moment before continuing. "We need a party of our own."

"He's right," Trenholm said quickly. "Toombs, Wigfall and the rest of the Fire-Eaters have organized themselves into a proper political party. If we do not follow suit, our already dim chances of winning the election will become effectively nonexistent."

Breckinridge pursed his lips. "I had hoped to avoid this."

"I am afraid you have no choice," Trenholm pressed. "They have already taken the fateful step of introducing partisan politics into the Confederacy."

"Very well," Breckinridge said. He looked at his watch. "I know most of you have commitments for the rest of the day and some of you are soon to return to your homes. That being the case, let me ask the group as a whole. Do we agree with the proposal that we form a political party?"

There was a muttering of agreements and several nodded heads.

"Do we agree that this meeting has been the first meeting of our party's national committee?"

Once again, the men in the room quietly expressed agreement.

"Very well. It is too late today to discuss this matter in any particular detail, but I shall write up a proposal and send it to everyone via messenger. We can discuss it next week. Those of you who will no longer be in Richmond shall receive the information by telegram. Thank you all, gentlemen."

The sound of scuffing chairs being pushed back filled the room and everyone rose to depart. Handshakes and expressions of goodwill were exchanged all around. People began filing out the door.

"James!" Breckinridge called to Kemper as he turned towards the door. "Might I have a moment of your time?"

"Certainly." His tone expressed surprise, but more curiosity than apprehension.

Breckinridge waited until everyone else had left, then shut the door. He gestured for Kemper to sit back down. Once they had both done so, he produced a flask.

"I'm done with coffee for the day. Join me in a swig of whiskey?"

"Happily," Kemper replied, taking the proffered flask and indulging in a healthy sip. "Oh, that's good. From your state?"

"It is."

"Still seems odd to me that Kentucky isn't part of the Confederacy. The South is the South, isn't it? They should be with us, along with Missouri and Maryland."

"Alas, the fortune of war dictated otherwise. The Fire-Eaters tell people that I gave those states away at the Toronto Peace Conference, but they don't know what they're talking about. I tried to pry them away from the Yankees, but they would have none of it. The deal we got was the best we could get."

"I believe you," Kemper replied. "You'll have to persuade the people, but not me."

"And I will be needing your help," Breckinridge replied.

"I know. I've already pledged my full support."

"I need more than that. I want you to be my running mate, James." He paused for a moment to let the words sink in. "I want you to be vice president."

Kemper's face froze, looking directly down at the floor. Very slowly, he raised his head until he was looking directly into Breckinridge's eyes. He motioned for the flask to be returned. Once it was in his hand, he took another healthy sip.

"I am sure there are other men who would be much better suited to the role, John."

"I don't think so. In any case, I want you."

"I've only just been elected to Congress, John. All my political experience is in the Virginia House of Delegates."

"Exactly. That's why I want you. You know Virginia better than anyone. Virginia is critical. If we don't win here, we lose the election. You can do the math as well as I can. If it's just between me and Beauregard, I'd expect Virginia to be a coin toss. With you on the ballot, the chances will tilt significantly in our favor."

Kemper thought for a moment. "Possibly."

"But that's not the only reason, Jimmy. I'll be honest with you. If anything happens to me while I'm in office, you'd be the president. I have to choose someone I genuinely think would make a good one. And I think you would."

"I'm flattered," Kemper replied.

Something about his tone troubled Breckinridge. "But?"

"Please don't rush me, John. If I'm going to do this, you have to give me your word of honor on a few things. I require guarantees."

"Guarantees of what?"

"I want a seat at the table, for one thing. People think the Vice Presidency is a powerless office. I don't want to be treated the way President Buchanan treated you. I want to be allowed to give you my thoughts and opinions on matters of policy."

"I would have it no other way."

"I need you to mean it. I want to be seen as a member of the Cabinet. I want to be at every meeting, free to express myself."

Breckinridge nodded thoughtfully. "That's the way it will be. You have my word."

"I also want to ask you a question very directly. And I need you to be perfectly honest with me."

"Am I anything less?" Breckinridge asked with mock irritation.

Kemper stared deeply into Breckinridge's eyes. "What are your personal feelings about slavery, John? Not your position in public. Not whatever your policy is. I mean what you yourself feel about it." He paused for effect. "I want you to answer this question as if God Himself had just asked it. And I won't agree to be your running mate unless I get what I am sure is an honest answer."

"Slavery is our peculiar institution," Breckinridge answered carefully. "It has been part of Southern culture since the days when we were tiny British colonies clustered on the Atlantic seaboard. It shows no signs of going away anytime soon. Our victory in the war seems to have solidified it. Our economy depends upon it. Without it, the fields of cotton, sugar, and tobacco would go fallow."

"That's all well and good," Kemper answered. "But how do you feel about it?"

"I don't like it," Breckinridge admitted. "Calhoun was wrong to call it a positive good. It's a necessary evil at best. You can't find a dozen men in the Confederacy who are willing to say that blacks are the equals of whites and I wouldn't count myself among them. But blacks are humans. They didn't deserve to be born into slavery. We can chatter on about how we bring the word of God to them, take care of them as if we are their parents. But it's all about the labor when you get right down to it. It's all about money."

"One could say that," Kemper said, in a tone which told Breckinridge that he was not surprised at his words. "So, if you were God, slavery wouldn't exist in this country?"

"No, it wouldn't."

"And what then of the relationship between the white man and the black man?"

"I don't know. But let me say this. I don't think slavery is something that the government can deal with. Some problems are simply too intractable for mere mortals to solve. I argued before the war that the United States Constitution did not give the federal government any authority to legislate against slavery. The Confederate Constitution specifically and forcefully enshrined this idea in its text, making it absolute. So even if I were so inclined, I am not considering using the powers of the presidency to challenge slavery in any way, shape, or form, regardless of my personal feelings. Barring some extraordinary and unforeseen change in the views of the people, which seems to be unlikely, it will take decades, perhaps a century, for slavery to come to an end. History has to be allowed to take its course."

Kemper grunted a response, rubbing his chin as he thought. "I am a Southern man, John. I can't say I agree with you on this. I'm not surprised to hear you say it, though. You've never struck me as being a full-throated defender of our peculiar institution. I'm not the only one who holds that opinion, you know. I fear that it will hurt our election chances."

"Toombs and his friends are attacking me on that score already, regardless of what the people think or say."

"Perhaps you can assure me that you will keep your personal feelings about slavery to yourself? If you and I are to be running mates, we must not appear to have any disagreements. I do not oppose slavery. This is something that I need from you. Unless I get that assurance, I cannot be your running mate."

"You have it," Breckinridge said without hesitation in his voice. He did not like being restrained in this manner, but he needed Kemper and was willing to give him what he wanted.

"Very well, then," Kemper said, extending his hand for Breckinridge. "We have an election to win."

July 3, Morning
Mississippi River below New Orleans, Louisiana

The sun was rising, casting long tendrils of flickering golden and yellow light westward across the wide expanse of the lower Mississippi River. The *SS Vincent* was steaming steadily north towards New Orleans. After nearly three weeks at sea, Lowell was about to arrive at his destination.

During the night, they had passed Fort Jackson and Fort St. Philip, which guarded the lower approaches to the city. Lowell had gazed up at the enormous structures with reluctant admiration, appreciating their immense ramparts and massive guns. During the war, the fleet of Admiral David Farragut had run past the forts after failing to reduce them by bombardment, forcing the surrender of the city. It had been one of the Union's greatest victories of the war. Lowell pursed his lips and shook his head when he reflected on the fact that it had all been for naught. Indeed, every Union victory in the war had been for naught.

As if to underscore the point, as the *SS Vincent* steamed slowly upriver, it passed by a formidable-looking casemate ironclad steaming in the opposite direction and flying the Confederate flag. To Lowell, it was a dark and frightening thing, rather like Frankenstein's monster. As it passed slowly past the port side of the ship, he could see four 32-pounder cannon protruding through the gun ports. A broadside or two from those guns could instantly reduce the *Vincent* to matchsticks.

"That must be the *Louisiana*," Naismith said, coming up alongside Lowell. "I read about her in the papers. Just launched a few months ago, I think. Their newest ironclad."

"Looks like a tough ship," Lowell admitted.

"This is one of two ironclads they have on the Mississippi River, or so I've heard. The other, the *Mississippi*, is up by Memphis."

"Interesting," Lowell replied tiredly. The Confederacy had had years to recover its strength after having been brought to the edge of defeat. Were war to break out between the Confederacy and Union again, the Southerners would be in a much stronger position than before, despite their economic troubles. He reflected morbidly on how they might become even more formidable if they were to become allied to one of the European powers.

Naismith went back to the poop deck to see to the navigation of the ship as they continued up the river. Lowell remained at the railing, looking out over the swampy ground a few hundred yards away. He was now entering the South, the land of the immense cotton and sugar plantations, where black men and women were enslaved by the thousands. He was entering a realm in which human suffering of untold magnitude was a fact of daily life.

Abandon all hope, ye who enter here. The line from Dante passed through his mind without any conscious thinking on his part. He took a deep breath, feeling cold despite the hot and humid air that surrounded him.

The Confederacy. The very name was abhorrent to Lowell. To him, it represented a summation of all that was evil and vile, a manifestation of all the darker impulses of the human character. He had struggled against it with all his might, only to see it triumph. Now, he was struggling against it again.

He had never been able to understand why the soldiers of the Confederacy fought so hard and so gallantly in defense of such an odious cause. He remembered the long ranks of men clad in gray and butternut, the Confederate battle flag fluttering in the breeze above them, on so many bloody battlefields. He saw again in his mind those men charging into the teeth of concentrated artillery and musket fire, coming on even as so many fell, bravely surging into the mouth of death itself. Why did they do it? How could people display such bravery on behalf of slavery? Were they, perhaps, nothing but simpletons deluded by their leaders? Might he consider ordinary Confederates to be victims as well?

Yet he hated them. He despised them for what they had done, for what had their courage and gallantry achieved but the shattering of the nation so carefully crafted by the revolutionary generation and the continued enslavement of millions of innocent blacks? They said that they had been fighting for self-government, but the average Southern white man was lorded over by rich aristocrats, so what had they really gained for themselves?

Within the cargo hold of the *Vincent* were the instruments by which the Confederacy might be destroyed and its slaves set free. Perhaps not immediately, for Saul's rebellion was only a small thing, like a mosquito biting an elephant. Yet if it could grow and gather strength, it could prove to be the first spark of an explosion that would change the world and help to make things right.

Hours passed. The *Vincent* continued its slow and steady ascent up the river towards New Orleans. With every passing minute, Lowell was being drawn deeper and deeper into the Confederacy. Numerous ships of different sizes and types were passing by the port side of the vessel, loaded with cotton for export to the United States and Europe. Every bale of cotton that went out brought more wealth to the elite planter aristocracy that ruled the Confederacy and perpetuated the slave system. Simply watching the ships pass filled him with anger.

The Mississippi River turned sharply as they passed by the site of old Ft. St. Leon and ran eastwards for about five miles before again turning north and then making a loop around to the west. The volume of river traffic increased as they approached the city. The *Vincent* had to slow down as the vessels ahead of them seemed to bunch up, clogging the waterway. In the distance, Lowell could see wisps of smoke rising, the telltale sign that they were getting close.

Another hour passed and the city gradually came into view on the north side of the river. It was a large city, perhaps as large as his own native Boston. The docks were crammed with shipping, flying not only the flag of the Confederacy, but the flags of Britain, France, Brazil, and the United States. Lowell could see immense amounts of cotton and sugar being loaded onto some ships, while large crates of imported merchandise were being offloaded from others.

A harbor pilot came out on a small boat and clambered abroad the *Vincent*.

"Who are you?" he asked in a tired and businesslike tone.

"We're the *Vincent*," Naismith answered. "Out of Boston. I'm the captain, Stephen Naismith."

"What's your cargo, Naismith?"

"Railroad machinery, mostly. Some shipments of wine and liquor for retail shops. Couple other odds and ends."

The harbor pilot nodded wearily, unconcerned. He instructed Naismith as to where to dock his ship and started to provide advice about the best approaches. The crew of the *Vincent* sprang into action as Naismith barked out orders. Another half hour passed, and the ship was slowly pulled into place alongside one of the immense docks lining the waterfront of the city, secured within thirty seconds by several large and strong ropes. The harbor pilot went on his way.

Naismith came up alongside Lowell.

"Well, here we are," he said cheerfully.

"What now?"

"We'll stay here for a while. We can't unload anything until the customs officers come on board to inspect the cargo. That will be the tricky part, but I think we'll be okay. If anything appeals to Southerners, it's fine wine and liquor."

"It's as good a plan as any, I suppose," Lowell said. "If it works, it works. If it fails, I suppose we hang."

"You seem rather blithe about it, if you don't mind my saying."

Lowell shrugged. "I have no more desire to die than anybody else. But everything is in God's hands, is it not?"

Naismith looked at him a moment. "I suppose so. I don't talk to that fellow much, to be honest."

Lowell nodded. He had never known sailors to be especially religious people, despite their lives being dependent on God's will so much of the time. Their devotion to drinking and whoring helped explain this. He half-wondered if the sailors made up for their lack of religion with their strange superstitions, such as their belief in good luck charms.

"Since I shall remain here to deal with the customs officers, perhaps you should venture to meet this fellow we're supposed to talk to?" Naismith offered.

"Now?" Lowell asked. "We've only just arrived."

"Why wait? Frankly, the longer those crates remain on board, the more likely they are to be discovered. My own inclination is to get them off the ship as quickly as possible."

"Makes sense, I suppose."

"Nervous about venturing into New Orleans?" Naismith asked with a slight smile.

"I feel like Daniel entering the lion's den."

"Well, God protected Daniel, as I recall. No reason to think He won't protect you as well. Just keep an eye out. Check every now and then to see if you're being followed. I'll keep the ship in preparation for a quick getaway, if that becomes necessary."

Lowell's eyebrows went up. He had not considered the possibility of flight. "Would we make it?"

Naismith laughed. "Almost certainly not. They'd telegraph down to the two forts to be ready for us. They'd block the river with that big chain they've got. If that somehow failed, those big guns would blow us out of the water. And there's that ironclad to consider. Still, an infinitesimal chance is better than no chance, don't you think?"

Lowell shrugged. "Perhaps."

"Off with you, then. When you return, we'll have dinner on board and you can tell me what he said."

Minutes later, Lowell had dressed and cleaned himself as best he could and was walking down the gangplank onto the dock. Soon, he was walking up Canal Street. He expected to be horrified by everything he saw, yet the faces of the people he saw were warm and friendly. He was more surprised than he should have been to hear many people conversing in French.

"It's Beauregard versus Breckinridge!" a newspaper boy was shouting, holding up a copy of the *New Orleans Picayune* for sale. "Beauregard versus Breckinridge! Get your copy here!"

Lowell thought about buying a newspaper to read about the developing Confederate presidential election, then decided against it. It mattered little to him whether Beauregard or Breckinridge was going to be the next Confederate president, for neither promised any alleviation of the condition of the slaves, much less their emancipation.

He considered hailing a hansom cab and simply giving the driver the address, then realized that this would be foolish. It was best to keep himself as nondescript as possible, so the fewer people he spoke to, the better. In any case, he was confident he could find his way to the shop on his own. He had studied a map of New Orleans on board the *Vincent* during the voyage, in much the same way as he had studied topographical maps of battlefields during the war, and had committed it to memory.

He turned right on Royal Street, walking northeast. The air was hot and heavy, almost oppressive, very different from the cool, crisp Massachusetts air he loved so much. All around him, the people of New Orleans were going about their business. He wondered how they would have reacted had they known what he was doing there.

A black couple passed by, dressed in fine clothes and with smiles on their faces, speaking to one another in polished French accents. Lowell was taken aback and he had to restrain his mouth from dropping open in surprise. He had known that there were a fair number of free blacks in New Orleans, but it was strange to actually see them. His mind revolted against the image of contented black people in the Confederacy.

Lowell arrived at the address he had been given and looked up at the sign hanging over the door.

Gardet's Fine Wines and Spirits.

He entered. The store was dark and dusty. Lining the shelves on every wall were bottles of wine, rum, gin, whiskey, and every other kind of drink. Three white customers were examining the merchandize quietly. A tabby cat lazily slept on the desk that jutted out from the back wall. Sitting behind the desk was a trim black man wearing a faded suit. He held a newspaper in his hands and peered at Lowell through a pair of octagonal spectacles.

"Can I help you, sir?" he asked, rising to his feet. "Don't recognize you, but I've got any kind of wine or spirit your heart desires."

"Mr. Gardet, is it?"

"Yes, I am. That's a Boston accent, by God. Am I right?"

Lowell smiled. "Boston born and bred."

"I can always tell. You Yankees all have different accents. I can tell the Boston men from the New York men from the fellows from the Old Northwest. The Southerners are the same. Texans sound different from Virginians. You know what I mean?"

Lowell nodded.

"Well, what can I do for you?" Gardet asked. "Come to find a bottle of wine to enjoy with your lady? Got a nice shipment in from Bordeaux."

"I think I'll just look around, if that's all right."

Gardet bowed his head. "Let me know if you need any help."

Lowell nodded and proceeded to examine the shelves. He was surprised to discover that the quality of the wine and liquor was actually quite high. Brandy and fine Burgundy and Bordeaux from France, Tuscan wine from Italy, sherry from Spain, rum from Cuba and Barbados, gin from England, and tequila from Mexico were all available. They were not cheap, but then New Orleans was a city of considerable wealth.

One customer left without buying anything, to Gardet's undisguised irritation. Lowell pretended to carefully study a bottle of French brandy while the remaining two shoppers paid for what they wanted and departed as well. Gardet then turned his attention to Lowell.

"Interested in that French brandy, are we?" he said pleasantly. "I've got a very nice bottle of Armagnac in the back if you want to look at it. Bit more expensive, of course, but you look like a gentleman who appreciates a fine product."

Lowell turned to Gardet, remembering the password he had been told by Sanborn and Stearns. "Do you have any wine from the Chateau Marron?"

Gardet tensed. "Chateau Marron, you say?"

"That's right."

There was a pause. "Not quite sure what you mean, sir."

"That's all right. In truth, I'd like to talk about a mutual friend of ours."

Gardet's eyes narrowed. "Mutual friend?"

"I'm talking about Saul."

A look of quiet terror came over Gardet's face. He bolted to his feet, then his body froze. "I'm sure I don't know anyone by that name, sir," he said, his voice quaking.

"Don't be afraid. I'm a friend." Memories came back to Lowell of farmers and their wives in Union-occupied northern Virginia, protesting that they didn't know anything about John Mosby. Lowell had gradually become adept and determining who had been lying and who had been telling the truth. Gardet, he could easily see, was lying.

"You should leave, sir," Gardet said urgently. "Closing up the shop early today."

"I'm a friend," Lowell repeated. "There's nothing to worry about. Besides, if I was the police, the way you're acting has already given you away."

Gardet looked sternly at him, fear rapidly being replaced with anger. He glanced down at something behind the desk, which Lowell soldierly instincts told him was a weapon of some kind. He himself was unarmed. For just a moment, he thought about how absurd it would be to have come so far only to be accidentally killed by the person who was supposed to be helping him.

"I'm here to help Saul," Lowell said. "I know you're his contact. I know you're how he communicates. I was told by Frederick Douglass himself."

Gardet's eyes narrowed. "Douglass sent you?"

"Yes."

There was a pause. "Who are you? Tell me your name."

"I'm Charles Lowell."

"Lowell?" Gardet said, turning the name over in his mind. "And you're from Boston. Not likely a Boston man would be in league with the Confederates."

Lowell chuckled. "That's true, by Plato. I was a cavalry officer in the Union Army, if that makes you feel any better."

A long and quiet minute passed. Gardet breathed deeply, making a physical effort to calm down. His eyes never strayed from Lowell's. "Please, sit," Gardet said hesitantly, gesturing to a chair across from him. "Get you a glass of wine?"

"You mentioned Bordeaux."

"Yes, that's right. Perhaps a Chateau Giscours?"

"Of course," Lowell replied. He was not familiar with the wine.

Gardet produced a bottle of wine, still eyeing Lowell warily. He popped the cork and poured two glasses with the proficiency of a skilled sommelier. He placed a glass in front of Lowell and sat back in his chair.

"I've worked hard to build this business," Gardet said firmly. "I won't allow anything to happen that might hurt it."

"I know. I promise that won't happen."

"I'm no good to anyone if I can't save my own skin."

"That's true for us all."

"I help Saul because I believe in him. I'm a free Negro and I think that all the Negroes should be free."

"I believe that, too. That's why I've come."

"So you're here to help?"

"That's right. But you need to help me if I am to help Saul."

"How?"

"Simple. I need to you to take me to him."

Gardet looked uncertain. "That might not be easy."

"But you communicate with him."

"It's all done very secretly. I've only set eyes on him once. He leaves letters to be sent north and I leave letters for him in agreed-upon secret locations. Very rarely, he'll send one of his men to see me, but no one has come in the last few months."

"How do you explain going out to these special places?"

350

"I have to make deliveries of wine and liquor to the plantations upriver. While doing that, I slip off to the secret places to retrieve and drop off the messages in the middle of the night."

"So you could leave a message telling him you want to see him, couldn't you?"

Gardet waited. "Possibly. But I swore to him that I would never take someone to meet him. It's much too risky. Besides, the papers said that Morgan beat him in a battle. He may have moved out of his old stomping grounds." "We have to try."

"Why? He's never mentioned you in any of his messages." He took a sip from his glass and his eyes became more steeled. "How do I know you're not a Confederate agent, using me to get to him?"

"I knew the password that your friends in the North gave you, didn't I?"

"Any number of ways the slave-holders could have sniffed that out."

"It's very unlikely. In any case, you'll just have to trust me. But I think you will, when I tell you why I need to see Saul."

"And why is that?"

"Because I have brought hundreds of rifles and vast amounts of ammunition for him. And if you can help me get it to him, his little insurrection can be turned into a revolution."

July 4, Afternoon
New York City

Aside from paying for his train ticket to New York and his passage from there on to Richmond, the British government had not offered to cover the expenses of Wolseley's trip to the Confederate capital. He might have chosen to lodge an official protest over this, but he knew that this would have been about as useful as ramming his head into a brick wall. The penny-pinchers at Horse Guards in London would have simply filed away his letter in a box from which it would never again see the light of day. Consequently, Wolseley had eaten his dinner in a distinctly mediocre restaurant and was now walking back towards a hotel that was far from the most elegant in the city.

He leaned on his walking stick as he moved along, occasionally feeling a twinge of tight pain from his old Burma wound. A light rain was falling, cooling the air slightly. It was still quite a hot and humid day, however. Though the surroundings of New York City reminded him somewhat of London, the air felt more like that he had experienced in India.

One reason that the government declined to pay for his travel expenses was because it assumed that any British officer with the rank of Lieutenant Colonel had to be a wealthy man who could easily pay his own way. Wolseley hated to be reminded that his family had no money. His heritage was not entirely undistinguished. One of his ancestors had served as a general alongside King William III at the Battle of the Boyne in 1690. Yet the Wolseley family had produced no extraordinary men in the last hundred and fifty years. His own father had never risen above the rank of major. It had taken a series of pleading letters from his mother to the Duke of Wellington himself to earn Wolseley a commission in the army at all.

He pulled his hat more tightly down over his eyes as the rain began to pick up. He did not like these times, when unpleasant memories of past slights intruded upon his mind. He had reached the rank of Lieutenant Colonel only because he had purposefully placed himself in those positions where it was most likely for him to get killed. God's grace had brought him through the maelstrom of battle alive, though far from unharmed. His useless eye and his lame leg were constant reminders of that. Meanwhile, idiotic and incompetent officers who had never heard a shot fired in anger were promoted ahead of him thanks to their wealth and family connections.

So long as Wolseley had campaigns in which to fight, as he had in the late 1850s in Burma, the Crimea, India, and China, he could count on advancing in rank as his courage couldn't fail to earn notice from the high command. Yet his long Canadian exile had robbed him of such opportunities until the Fenians appeared on the scene. Now, a single battle and the death of a single man had given him new opportunities to win glory for himself and restore the once-proud name of Wolseley.

His mind returned to the diplomatic assignment that had been given to him. He was to offer the Confederacy an alliance with the British Empire, but it would take effect only in the event of an open war between Britain and the United States. He liked the Southerners, having gotten to know many of them during his sojourn in the Confederacy in late 1862. Yet he wondered if it was wise for England to suggest an alliance with them. The Confederacy had won its independence, but it was still a weak state, like a child just learning how to walk. He also wondered if the South would consider it prudent to align itself with England. If history proved anything, it was that a weak state that allied itself to a strong state inevitably ended up under its control. He thought for a moment that there was a quote from Machiavelli that proved this point, but he could not immediately recall it.

These thoughts were moving back and forth in his mind as he pressed his way down the sidewalk towards his hotel. The rain began to let up. As he came upon one intersection, however, he found his way forward blocked by large numbers of people simply standing there, without moving. At the same time, he heard the music of a brass band and numerous drums blaring into the air. Several people were singing along to the tune, which Wolseley recognized even though he detested it.

Yankee Doodle went to town,
A'riding on a pony!
Stuck a feather in his cap,
And called it macaroni!

He tried to push his way past the crowd, but the people stood firm. It was then that Wolseley saw the parade going past in the street. Hundreds of men, dressed in fancy blue uniforms more suited to the War of American Independence than to the present day, were marching past. It took him a few moments to realize that this was intentional and that the parade was some sort of celebration rather than a procession of an active military unit.

"What is this?" Wolseley demanded of a nearby man. "What is the purpose of this parade?"

The man seemed surprised that Wolseley was addressing him. "What?" he said in a voice heavily accented with German. He shrugged his shoulders and it was clear to Wolseley that he had not understood what he said.

A feeling a profound contempt and disdain rose in Wolseley with the force of a tidal wave. He asked again, pointing to the men marching in the street and practically shouting into the man's face. "The parade, man! What is this parade for?"

"Oh!" the man replied. "July 4. Independence Day. Independence Day parade, yes."

It was difficult for Wolseley to understand the broken English of the man, who was clearly a German immigrant. He had not remembered that July 4, the date on which the American Declaration of Independence was signed back in 1776, was a holiday in the United States.

He nearly laughed at the absurdity of it. Why should the Americans celebrate the day on which they broke from Britain? Before 1776, with the guiding hand of England to aid them, the Americans had enjoyed protection from their enemies and, more importantly, peaceful relations among themselves. After 1776, however, the Americans had quickly fallen to squabbling amongst themselves, lurching from one political crisis to another, until finally the whole country had torn itself apart amidst a bloody war.

Wolseley smiled even while he shook his head. None of that would have ever happened had the Americans had the wisdom to remain within the British Empire. It was clear to him, and he assumed it was clear to the rest of the world, that the American experiment with democracy and egalitarianism had not only failed, but had led to utter disaster. Yet the Americans, such stubborn people, still celebrated Independence Day.

He decided to stop and watch the parade, for he was in no hurry. The blue uniforms worn by the marching men were, he now realized, reproductions of the uniforms worn by the Continental Army during the War of American Independence. American uniforms had changed drastically since then, while British troops still wore the red coats that their forefathers had worn at Bunker Hill. Wolseley thought this was quite foolish, for a man wearing a red coat stood out distinctly in combat, while a man wearing a darker color more easily blended in with the surrounding terrain. On a battlefield, this was a real advantage, yet the fools who ran the British Army were so mired in tradition that they failed to see even something that obvious.

Wolseley then noticed something that took him aback. Interspersed within the American flags being carried by the marchers or waved by the onlookers were a few green flags that had yellow Irish harps on them, which he recognized as Fenian symbols.

The men dressed as Continental soldiers passed by and were followed by what appeared to be a regular United States Army regiment. At its head were color bearers, one man carrying the United States flag and the other the flag of the regiment, which revealed it to be the 69th New York Infantry Regiment. The names of the battles in which the unit had participated were emblazoned on the flag, among them Malvern Hill, Antietam, and Gettysburg.

Riding at the head of the regiment was a man Wolseley thought he recognized. With a start, he realized that it was the gruff-looking Union officer whom he had observed across the St. Lawrence River. This was surprising enough, but Wolseley was even more astounded when he heard many of the people watching the parade booing and hissing as the man passed.

"Who is that man?" he asked the nearest person.

"Him? Why, that's George Thomas. He's the damn fool that lost the Battle of Peachtree Creek and got himself captured by the rebels."

"George Thomas," Wolseley repeated, nodding. He had read about Thomas in the newspapers during the war. "Why is he in the parade?"

"Don't rightly know. I think he commands the army here in New York State. Damn disgrace for Thomas to be riding with the 'Fighting 69th'. Damn disgrace, I say!"

"How interesting," he said, walking away from the man and continuing to look at Thomas. He was a powerfully built fellow, though not tall. The expression on his face was stoic and solid, entirely unconcerned with the abuse he could undoubtedly hear being shouted up at him. Now knowing his identity, Wolseley could understand why people were jeering, for Thomas's defeat at Peachtree Creek had played a critical role in the defeat of the Union cause.

"Here they come!" a woman with an Irish accent shouted.

"Three cheers for the Fenian Brotherhood!" a man shouted on the other side of the street. The crowd responded with enthusiasm, cheering themselves hoarse.

Wolseley looked in the direction people were pointing. A column of troops in green uniforms and with Springfield muskets on their shoulders was approaching. Wolseley frowned at the realization that the Fenian Brotherhood, whose men had invaded British territory and killed dozens of British and Canadian soldiers, was being allowed to parade freely through the streets of the largest city in the United States, without the slightest fear of arrest or interference.

The green-uniformed soldiers were followed by a swarm of freckled and red-haired children, dressed in traditional Irish outfits and dancing along the street. Two wore large placards over their bodies. One read 'FREE IRELAND' and the other read 'SUPPORT THE FENIAN BROTHERHOOD'.

Infuriated, Wolseley decided that he had seen enough and wanted to be on his way back to the hotel. Loudly cursing, he began to push his way through the people, intending to cross the street, parade or no parade, and move along.

"Out of my way!" he said brashly. "Get out of my way!"

"English!" someone shouted, pointing to Wolseley. "He's an Englishman!"

This was followed by a loud chorus of jeering and hissing. Several people shouted profane insults at him. He pushed his way onto the street and walked directly across, disordering the men of the 42nd New York regiment, which was now passing by. This generated several protests and curses from the disgruntled soldiers, but Wolseley ignored them and stepped up onto the sidewalk, pushing his way through the crowd on that side of the street.

"Get that Englishman!" someone with an Irish accent was shouting. "Get him!"

Wolseley suddenly felt a twinge of fear, not an emotion he often experienced. No number of enemy soldiers in an opposing army might frighten him, yet somehow an unruly mob of hysterical men, women, and children filled him with dread. Now through the crowd, he hurried along as quickly as he could on his hobbled leg, but he could hear the footsteps of several people following behind him.

"Hey, Englishman!" a mocking voice said behind him. "Stop there! We want to talk to you!" There was a tug on the back of Wolseley's coat.

He did not think that there was anything worth talking about with whomever was addressing him, but he was not about to allow the insult of his coat being tugged to go unpunished. He turned and quite calmly slammed the weighted end of his walking stick into the man's lower belly with all the force his arm could muster. Stunned, the man yowled in pain and staggered backwards.

A dozen or so men, some broad and powerfully built, stood before him. If he turned to flee, his wobbly leg would ensure that he could not outrun them. Neither could he hope to win a fight, being armed only with his walking stick. Nothing was left, therefore, but intimidation.

"Away with you, damned rascals!" Wolseley shouted, waving his walking stick.

"English bastard!" one of the men said in an Irish accent, stepping forward with clenched fists. "I'm going to show you how to fight."

As he had with the first scoundrel, Wolseley shoved his walking stick forward into the man's belly just below the ribcage, knocking the wind out of him. He staggered back, stunned but still on his feet. Wolseley considered smashing him across the head, then reconsidered. It was best not to escalate the situation.

A few moments of quiet followed, but the look of anger in the eyes of the men confronting him grew. Others were approaching from the direction of the parade. Wolseley was reminded of advice that had been given to him by Canadian hunters of what to do in the event he encountered a bear. Under no circumstances was he to turn and run, as the bear would then give chase and rapidly catch up to him.

"Let's teach this English bastard a lesson," someone in the group said.

"I think this fellow is about to have an unfortunate accident."

Wolseley sneered. Such brutes were not deserving of a vocal response. He clutched his walking stick tightly, ready to lash out at the first man who dared approach him. None of them did, however. Wolseley knew that his glare had a strange impact on men, though he did not know exactly how to explain it. He knew that as long as he showed no sign of fear, no one would dare attack him. Still, the situation could not remain stalemated for more than a few seconds.

"That's enough," said an authoritative voice.

Wolseley and the men surrounding him looked in the direction of the voice. General Thomas pushed his way to the front of the growing crowd, much to the surprise of everyone.

"What's going on here?" he demanded. "They told me that some ruffians were chasing an Englishman. I sincerely hope that is not what I see before me."

"What if it is, old man?" someone said. "What are you going to do about it?"

"There are three regiments marching down the street just a few hundred yards away. They'll come if I call them."

"You sure about that?" asked another. "Way I hear it, the soldiers don't much like being commanded by a traitor."

"What's it they call you, Thomas?" one man asked with a sneer. "'The Dunce of Peachtree Creek'? Isn't that right?"

Wolseley felt even more anger rise within him. He did not know Thomas, but the man was an army officer and deserving of respect. The idea that simple, unwashed city folk could abuse him in such an insolent manner infuriated him. It was not the way society was supposed to function.

He stepped forward slowly towards the man who had called Thomas a dunce. With a speed that took all the spectators by surprise, he grabbed the man roughly by the shoulders and spun him around, smacking him on his backside with his walking stick with such force that the victim yelped in pain.

"Away with you, stupid whelp!" Wolseley shouted. "Away with you!" The man was so surprised by the unexpected assault that he took off running. Wolseley, sensing the psychological momentum, waved his stick at the rest of the group. "All of you! Go back to your business or I'll give you the same treatment!"

Men began to back off, having weighed the risks. After the first few turned to walk away, an increasing number began to follow suit. The threatening glare of Wolseley's eyes did not let up, shining like a calcium light, as though he could physically push the threatening men away just by staring at them hard enough. A long minute passed, and the crowd of unruly men gradually dissipated.

Wolseley sighed and turned to Thomas. "Thank you for coming to my assistance."

"It does not appear that you needed any," Thomas replied. He looked carefully at Wolseley. "Do I know you, sir? You appear familiar to me."

"We have met, in a manner of speaking. We viewed one another through field glasses from opposite banks of the St. Lawrence River."

Thomas's eyes widened in surprise. "My Lord!" he exclaimed. "Yet I see it! You are the man I saw on the other side of the river."

Wolseley extended his hand. "Lieutenant Colonel Garnet Wolseley, at your service, sir."

"General George Thomas. But then, I suspect you already knew that."

"I did, indeed."

"Why are you in New York?"

"For personal business," Wolseley said simply.

"I see," Thomas said, nodding. It was clear from his tone that he did not find Wolseley's words convincing. In the midst of saber-rattling between the United States and the British Empire, the idea that a high-ranking British officer would be in New York City for personal business was highly unlikely.

"Would you care to have a drink with me, General Thomas?" Wolseley asked. "We might exchange war stories."

"Alas, I must get back to the parade that those hooligans dragged me away from. Then I am to speak to the troops as part of the Independence Day celebration. Not that anyone wants to hear the Dunce of Peachtree Creek talk about anything." He sighed. "I sometimes think President McClellan requires me to do such things simply to humiliate me."

Wolseley nodded sympathetically, but did not say anything in reply for fear of hurting Thomas's pride. He knew that the man was a Virginian who had stayed loyal to the Union and had proven himself a formidable soldier. He had never lost a battle until the ill-fated day at Peachtree Creek, when his army had been shattered and he himself had been taken prisoner. He could not imagine the depths of personal agony that had to haunt Thomas each and every day. Rejected by his own family, despised by the South, disdained by the North, Thomas struck Wolseley as a man for whom dishonor had to be a daily companion.

Yet Wolseley didn't see that in Thomas's face or hear it in his voice. He saw a stoic, proud old soldier, like a rock against which the waves of the ocean beat in vain. He recalled that the man's nickname had once been 'The Rock of Chickamauga', in memory of the day when his desperate stand against vastly superior numbers had saved a defeated Union army from total destruction.

"I do thank you for the offer," Thomas said. "Perhaps another time."

"Of course."

"Good day, sir."

"Good day." Wolseley turned to continue on towards his hotel, but was stopped short.

"Colonel!" Thomas said.

He turned back a moment. "Yes?"

Thomas waited a moment before speaking again, weighing his words. "Colonel Wolseley, I feel the need to tell you this. Had it been up to me, the Fenian band would never have gotten anywhere close to the southern bank of the St. Lawrence, much less across it. I am aghast at the loss of life that took place. Had I been able to prevent it, I would have."

Wolseley absorbed what Thomas said, then slowly nodded. "I believe you, General."

"Good afternoon."

"And you, General Thomas."

With that, Thomas turned and walked away. Wolseley resumed the walk back to his hotel, turning over in his mind the import of the final words Thomas had spoken.

July 6, Noon
Supreme Court Chamber, United States Capitol, Washington City

A tall portrait of John Marshall looked down upon the gathering from one wall of the ornate chamber housing the Supreme Court. It was only a few minutes' walk from where the Senate Foreign Relations Committee held its meetings, yet to go that distance was to enter an entirely different field of power. The differences between being a legislator who made the law and a judge who ruled on those laws was so vast that it was difficult for people outside of government to fully grasp it.

Now that the passage of the Capital Relocation Bill was final, the Supreme Court was already making preparations to move to Philadelphia. There was talk of constructing a new, grand building for it that city. The court had slowly expanded its influence over the years, so there was a feeling that it was not appropriate for it to be housed in the Capitol Building. Much as he regretted the movement of the government out of Washington, Sumner found this interesting. He was a man devoted to the concept of the rule of law and the Supreme Court was the highest manifestation of that ideal. It would be only fitting for the institution to have its own great edifice. It would have been infinitely better for it to be built in Washington rather than Philadelphia, but there was nothing to be done about that now.

Sumner leaned forward over the table, his eyes ablaze. Several other prominent Republican senators and congressmen were in attendance at the meeting. On the other side of the table sat Chief Justice Edwin Stanton, whose face bore its customary expression of exasperation mixed with glumness.

"The president is tearing up the Constitution," Sumner said urgently. "The right of Congress to subpoena witnesses is essential to its ability to perform its legislative tasks. No one can seriously believe that the president's powers as commander-in-chief extend to prohibiting citizens from testifying before a congressional committee."

"If we were talking about ordinary citizens, you would be correct," Stanton replied. "But both General Thomas and General Sweeny are serving army officers. McClellan is asserting that his authority to give them orders, and their constitutional requirement to obey the president's orders, allows him to prevent their testimony."

"Well, that's blatant nonsense," Sumner spat.

"Oh, I agree," Stanton said. "Do not mistake me, my old friend."

"Well, what is being done?" Sumner asked, irritation in his voice.

"A case has already been filed in the Court of the District of Columbia," Stanton replied. "It cites the president in contempt of Congress for issuing the order barring the testimony of the officers."

"And the officers themselves?" asked Congressman Thaddeus Stevens, the hard and austere Pennsylvania abolitionist. "Why not cite them for contempt of Congress as well? If you ask me they should be dragged into the Capitol in chains, if that's what it takes to get them to testify."

"I'd hesitate before filing any charges against the officers themselves," Stanton said. "We do not want to appear to be putting ourselves in opposition to the army."

Sumner almost smiled. Stanton had been elevated to the position of Chief Justice of the Supreme Court in the last official act of President Lincoln, the day before McClellan had been inaugurated. He was perfectly qualified for the post, having been one of the country's leading attorneys in the years before the war. Yet he never stopped thinking like a politician. His exalted position might theoretically be above politics, but no one doubted that he remained a solid Republican. Stanton had agreed to this meeting, which most people would consider highly inappropriate and perhaps illegal, because he was still determined to pursue the abolitionist cause.

"No, the people will not like it if we appear to be the enemies of the army," Sumner agreed. "And they are not constitutional scholars, are they? These two generals? They may genuinely not know what they should be doing. Better for us to remain focused on the president."

There was a muttering of agreement among the men sitting at the table. Congressman Fred Seward spoke up. "So this complaint has been filed in the district court. What happens now?"

"It will be upheld and McClellan will be declared in contempt of Congress. He can then appeal to the Supreme Court, if he wants to, but we all know how that would go."

There were chuckles throughout the room. Of the nine justices on the Supreme Court, five had been appointed by Lincoln, including Stanton himself. Of the remaining four, only Justice Nathan Clifford was considered overtly friendly towards the McClellan administration. Sumner reflected that, with the Republican majority in the Senate so thin and its actions so easily blocked by the Democratic House of Representatives, the Supreme Court was the true institutional opposition to McClellan within the federal government.

Stanton went on. "Of course, this presents a serious quandary. It's one thing for the court to declare McClellan in contempt of Congress and quite another thing to enforce such a ruling. We obviously cannot dispatch federal marshals to the White House and arrest the President of the United States."

"Why not?" Stevens said, moments before Sumner was about to ask the same thing.

"Gentlemen, please," Stanton said. "We must be cautious. We are in the opening stages of a constitutional crisis. Suppose McClellan orders a regiment of infantry to the White House to protect him? The marshals would not be willing to risk an exchange of gunfire, so they would have to simply let McClellan be. And that would make both the judicial and legislative branches of government look powerless. It would be a significant step in the direction of a military dictatorship in our country."

Sumner pursed his lips and nodded, for he had to agree with Stanton. A man of principle, Sumner did not much like having to take practical concerns into account when dealing with a moral or constitutional issue. Yet in this case he had little choice.

"I assume the President is claiming executive privilege in ordering these officers not to testify?" Stevens asked.

"No," Stanton said. "I was surprised by this at first. But it makes sense if you think about it. McClellan does not want the public to know of any direct collaboration between his administration and the Fenians. If he claims executive privilege, he would have to explain why keeping these men from testifying is in the interest of the country. In other words, it would be an admission that such collaboration exists, at least in some form."

"A fool," Sumner said bitterly. "McClellan is no better a president than he was a general."

"No doubt," Stanton said in a low, growling voice.

Sumner sighed deeply. He did not want a constitutional crisis any more than Stanton did, yet he was not a man to whom caution came naturally. Had it been otherwise, he never would have sought to persuade Lowell to undertake his illegal mission into the Confederacy. He thought for a moment about the Massachusetts cavalryman, who perhaps had arrived in New Orleans by now.

He closed his eyes and thought a thousand thoughts in an instant. The slave-holding Confederacy was the enemy, as evil and vile to him as Satan had to be to God. His every action ultimately had to be aimed at the destruction of that evil. The Fenian Crisis was a distraction, yet also an opportunity. War between the United States and the British Empire had to be avoided, for it made no sense for his nation to fight against the world's greatest power when its true enemy lay just to the south. Yet he could also use the Fenian Crisis to destroy George McClellan, who was an obstacle that had to be removed if the struggle against the Confederacy were ever to be resumed.

"Well, whatever is to be done must be done soon," Congressman Rutherford Hayes of Ohio insisted. "We need to pull the country back from the brink. The situation is getting out of hand. I assume everyone has read this morning's papers?"

There were mutterings of affirmation around the table. Sumner nodded, acknowledging Hayes's point. The Royal Navy had already dispatched a naval force that was expected to stop for resupply at a Confederate port. Meanwhile, several thousand British soldiers were on their way to Canada from other parts of the British Empire. At the same time, President McClellan had ordered several regiments moved from the border with the Confederacy northwards toward the border with Canada.

As far as Sumner was concerned, the convergence of British and American troops along the St. Lawrence River was akin to piling ever-increasing amounts of wood onto a pile. A simple spark could erupt into a conflagration. The battle between the British and the Fenians had already raised tensions to a dangerous level. If a skirmish were to take place between British and American troops, the result could be an all-out war.

At the same time, local Democratic committees across the country were sponsoring anti-British demonstrations. Several had taken place two days earlier as part of what were supposed to have been Independence Day celebrations. The British embassy in Washington City and the British consulate in New York City were reported to be under a virtual state of siege by pro-Fenian demonstrators. Rumor had it that the British minister had already packed his bags and was ready to depart at a moment's notice.

Sumner pursed his lips. "I don't care what we have to do, but we must get those two generals in front of my committee, under oath. If we can expose the connection between McClellan and the Fenians we can cripple his political credibility and ensure a Republican victory in next year's election."

"More importantly, we can squash this mad drive towards war," Senator Benjamin Wade replied. "Our country has already seen more three hundred thousand of its sons die. I don't think it has the stomach for another war."

"At least those men died for something," Sumner said. "Union and emancipation. Dying in service to a worthy cause is not a tragedy. Dying for one man's vanity and stupidity would be."

"Quite so," Stanton said. "And if we don't stop this war from breaking out, a lot of men are going to end up dying for nothing."

The curtain of night was being drawn over southern Louisiana, but the campfires of Morgan's Kentucky cavalrymen and Louisiana militia pushed back against the advancing darkness. Amidst their yellowish glow, men were talking, laughing, and singing. A few were playing banjos. The smell of burning wood mixed with that of tobacco, whiskey and pork sizzling in hot frying pans.

Morgan walked through the happy camp with a smile on his face, stopping to chat with the men every now and then, making bawdy jokes, clapping old Kentucky friends on the back. Unlike some commanders, he had never bothered to put much distance between his men and himself. Generals like Robert E. Lee and Joseph Johnston were men of such dignity and presence that it was as if they couldn't be brought down to the level of ordinary mortals. Morgan took the opposite tack. He wanted his men to feel that he was one of them. They followed him not because they revered and loved him, but because they simply liked and trusted him.

It had been more than a week since their successful ambush of Saul's insurgent band. Since then, their patrols had captured another dozen prisoners, men who had become separated from Saul during the confused fighting and had been trying to find their way back. There had been no new insurgent raids on plantations or any other target. All the prisoners had been taken to Baton Rouge, where they were being held under a heavy guard, until Davis and Breckinridge decided what to do with them.

Though his scouts had not yet picked up a firm trail, they had reported tantalizing evidence of disorganization, such as discarded equipment. In a few cases, they had come across still-warm embers of extinguished campfires. Morgan was confident that they were moving in the right direction and would soon come to grips with Saul again. The insurgent band, to Morgan's mind, was like a wounded fox, desperately struggling to escape. He and his men, by contrast, were the hounds that were soon to catch and devour them.

The scouts reported no sign at all of the second insurgent band. Morgan and Duke had discussed the possibility that the two had linked up sometime before the ambush, which would mean that the force they had defeated had constituted all of Saul's strength. If this were true, it was an even bigger victory than they had originally thought.

Morgan finished making his rounds through the camp and found his way back to his own tent. Basil Duke and some old Kentucky comrades were there, happily eating some chicken that had been roasted over the campfire and amusing themselves by tossing whiskey onto the burning logs to see it flame up.

"Enjoying the evening, boys?"

"Good food and good whiskey!" Duke replied. "What could be better?"

Morgan nodded. He took a proffered glass from one of the men and tossed back a generous amount of the bourbon before handing it back. He did not drink as much as many of his men did, yet he certainly enjoyed his bourbon. As a man of Kentucky, it would have been strange for it to have been otherwise. He was the commander, however, and had to take care not to become intoxicated.

There was a small tent set up near his and Morgan strolled up to it. Inside, eating and drinking by himself, was Silas.

"And how are you, my black friend?" Morgan asked, peeking past the tent flaps.

"Just fine." Silas took another enormous bite of his chicken and took his time chewing and swallowing before speaking again. "What's the word?"

"It seems that your former master died of typhus a year after the war ended. He didn't have a wife or children."

"Never married a woman, my old master didn't," Silas said with a sneer. "Used his slave girls as his wives, if you know what I mean."

Morgan ignored the unpleasant statement. "Anyway, the War Department is trying to track down his next of kin."

"I'm still going to be returned to slavery after all the help I gave you?"

"The law's the law, Silas. It has to be followed. Once his next of kin is identified, the idea is that the War Department will purchase you from them and then manumit you."

Silas grunted and took a sip of his whiskey, of which he was very fond. "Don't much like the sound of that. When white men make vague promises, they usually don't end up keeping them."

Morgan didn't blame Silas for being skeptical. There was, in fact, a good deal of debate going on between Morgan, Breckinridge, and Davis on the question of what to do about Silas. It was recognized that common decency required them to reward Silas in some way and they hoped that they might set an example that would encourage other blacks with information about potential uprisings to come forward. On the other hand, Davis seemed dubious about freeing a slave as a matter of government policy. Morgan had not told Silas any of this, of course.

Silas set his glass down on the little table he had in his tent. "When will I know?"

"Not sure."

"Would it make any difference if I gave you more information?"

Morgan drew his head back a bit. "I thought you said you told me everything you knew."

Silas grinned. "I lied." He chuckled for a moment. "I'm not stupid, you know."

"Get out here," Morgan said angrily. His first instinct was to beat Silas to a bloody pulp for withholding information. He did not like being deceived, yet he was less upset with Silas than he was with himself for being so easily fooled. Why had it not occurred to him that Silas might still be concealing information, like a chess player who keeps his queen at the back for as long as possible?

Silas, with his attitude of unconcern not sliding for a moment, stepped out of the tent and faced Morgan.

"What have you not told me?" Morgan demanded.

"Something important. Very important. I can tell you that Saul communicates with people in the North. Yankee people."

"You're sure?"

"Oh, of course. I was his courier myself two times, to the man in New Orleans who sends our letters along."

362

Morgan felt his heart increase its tempo. If what Silas was saying was true, it could be the most explosive news about Saul yet to emerge. Many throughout the South had been blaming the uprising on abolitionist agitators in the United States, though there was no direct evidence. If Silas could provide such evidence, the consequences would be immense.

"How?" Morgan asked urgently. "How does he do it?"

"You keep your promise to me and I'll tell you."

"I'm doing everything I can!" Morgan said in frustration. "I don't control the War Department, Silas!"

"That's your problem," Silas said. "I'm a black slave and you're a white man. Would you trust me if you were standing here in my place?"

Morgan frowned. He admitted to himself that Silas was right, yet obviously could not say so. He folded his arms and stared at the renegade, thinking carefully of what he could say to get him to talk.

"Tell you what, Silas. Let's say that the War Department doesn't do what it says it will do after your master's next of kin is found. In that case, I promise you that I will put up the money myself and purchase you from your master in my own name, then set you free."

Silas nodded slowly as he listened. He thought the words over in silence for a few moments before replying. "And why should I believe you?"

"You have my word of honor."

Silas chuckled bitterly. "And what's that worth? You Confederates always go on and on about your honor. If you were honorable men, you wouldn't have ever owned any of us black folk in the first place." He sighed deeply. "But I suppose that's the best I'm going to get, isn't it?"

"Yes."

"Guess I might as well tell you then," Silas said with a hint of sadness. "Saul didn't know I had deserted until the moment he saw me during the ambush. Didn't ever occur to you to ask why he was surprised?"

Morgan shook his head. "He had sent you off somewhere," he surmised.

"To New Orleans," Silas said. "I was to meet with the man who is our contact with our supporters outside Louisiana."

"What is his name?" Morgan said urgently. "Who is he?"

"His name is Andre Gardet. He's a free black that sells liquor and wine out of his shop on Royal Street. Very stupid white people pay lots of money for their drinking. Don't rightly know why. Whiskey is whiskey, if you ask me."

"Andre Gardet," Morgan repeated. "That's the name of the fellow in New Orleans?"

"Right. He sends shipments of wine and liquor to plantations up the river every couple of weeks on a flatboat and wagon, you see? When he does, he takes letters to Saul from people up North and takes delivery of messages Saul wants to send out. The messages are left in secret places. The hollows of trees, mostly. Every now and then somebody will be sent into New Orleans to see Gardet. Not so much in the last few months, though. Saul thought it was getting too risky."

Morgan thought fast. It was too late to send a courier this night, but it would be the first thing he would do when the sun rose the next morning. With any luck, word would be received in New Orleans before the end of the following day. This Gardet fellow could be in jail within thirty-six hours. Careful interrogation might reveal facts about Saul that even Silas had been unable to provide. More importantly, the extent of any Yankee involvement in Saul's activities might be uncovered.

"Thank you, Silas," Morgan said.

He strolled away from Silas's tent and back towards his own men. As he again began wandering among the campfires, laughing and joking with his men, he became conscious of an immense weariness sweeping over him. The months he had spent in the swamps and forests of Louisiana, the constant marching and riding, was enough to wear out a younger man than himself.

Though he enjoyed campaigning, Morgan wanted very much to return home. Hunting down renegade slaves in the bayou country was not nearly as enjoyable as matching wits with the Yankees on the green hills of Tennessee or Kentucky. There was little glory or honor in it. He had expected it to be easy and found it to be more difficult than anything he had ever attempted. Morgan considered war a great game, but hunting the rebel slaves was a laborious chore. Still, he was on the verge of final success. A few more days and Saul's band would be snagged as easily as fish in a barrel. Perhaps information from this Gardet fellow could help.

He realized that it was becoming difficult to keep his eyes fully open. Morgan began to make his way back to his tent. He needed his sleep, he told himself, for tomorrow the scouts might have located the remains of Saul's force and he could close in for the kill. He was tempted to have one more glass of whiskey, but decided that he did not want to keep himself awake any longer, nor did he want a headache when he awoke in the morning. It was time to sleep.

He passed by his brother-in-law and their old Kentucky comrades, wearily saying goodnight, and stepped into his own tent. Barely taking the time to remove his hat and uniform coat, Morgan fell heavily on his cot and felt sleep start to overtake him almost immediately.

He slumbered and dreamed. He saw the face of his deceased first wife, Rebecca, then imagined himself trapped in a dark room from which there was no obvious way out. It was an edgy, disturbing dream and he wanted to shake himself out of it. He nearly woke again, then settled down. He imagined coming into an enormous Masonic Lodge filled with his friends, yet somehow he could not understand the language they were speaking. A disembodied voice began shouting, as if in alarm. Yet his fellow Masons were smiling complacently, acting as though nothing were unusual. It seemed wrong. Morgan felt angry at the Masons for not responding to the cries of alarm and he berated them, but they simply shrugged their shoulders, not understanding his words.

He stirred awake on his cot, yet his ears could still hear the cries of alarm.

"To arms!" he could hear voices shouting. "Get your muskets!"

He came fully awake in an instant, shooting up off his cot and grabbing his uniform coat with a single movement. He stepped out of the tent and saw Duke standing there, as alert as he was.

"What's happening?" Morgan demanded.

"There's picket firing at the south edge of the camp. And some sort of fire."

"Fire?"

"That's what the men are shouting." Duke's voice betrayed the same confusion Morgan felt.

He glanced over at Silas's tent. Through the flaps, he could barely make out the face of the renegade, gazing out with concern. Morgan pointed to two soldiers standing nearby. "You men! Watch him!" He pointed back to Silas's tent and the men nodded. "Let's go!" he said to Duke.

They jogged through the camp towards the south end. Scattered firing was still going on, but it did not appear heavy. Everywhere, men had emerged from their tents and were gripping their weapons. There was no sign of fear, only alarm and puzzlement. Morgan ordered Duke to organize the men into their companies and prepare them for action. A night attack was the kind of tactic men like Saul preferred, but Morgan felt in little danger. The pickets had provided adequate warning. If Saul really were attacking, it would merely provide Morgan with a chance to destroy him.

As he approached the southern edge of the camp, he was joined by numerous armed soldiers running in the same direction on their own initiative. The musket fire he had heard earlier had faded into occasional single shots. It seemed that whatever had happened was already over. Yet he could see a flickering of flames at various points in the trees out in the distance, a few hundred yards away.

"What is that?" he asked a nearby soldier as he reached the line, pointing towards the flames.

"Don't know, sir," the man replied. "The pickets said the flames just erupted and then they were fired upon, so they returned fire. But whoever did it is already gone."

"Anybody hurt?"

"Bullet hit one fellow in the finger, sir. Nothing serious. But he's mighty annoyed."

Morgan nodded, then gestured for some of the men to follow him and he began slowly walking forward, pulling his revolver out of his holster as he did so. He approached the flames carefully, wary of any trap. He wondered if it was the correct thing to do, for conceivably the flames were designed to lure his men out into some sort of ambush. His men were fully armed and alert, though, so an ambush made no sense.

As he approached the flames, he saw that there were three distinct fires, each about five feet tall. The closer he got, the more detail he could make out. They appeared to be crude wooden structures, shaped vaguely like people, wrapped in flames. He smelled the odor of turpentine. Nothing else was in sight.

He ordered men to comb the area by squads to search for whomever had ignited the flames and fired the shots. Morgan also ordered water to be brought to put out the fires, for he suspected that they might have been intended to illuminate the southern edge of the camp for some reason.

Reports began to come back that there was no sign of anyone in the woods. Nothing made sense. He began to suspect that perhaps some sort of raid had been intended but had been called off just as it was beginning.

Duke came running up. "Everything all right?" he asked Morgan breathlessly.

"Far as I can tell," Morgan responded quickly. "What's the situation?"

"Everybody is stood to arms around the camp. No sign of anything."

Morgan frowned and shook his head. "They must just be trying to scare us. Don't know what they hoped to accomplish."

Duke shrugged. "They're just darkies. What do you expect?"

Morgan wanted to laugh, but thought better of it. He he had learned not to underestimate the insurgent leader. For all Morgan knew, had it not been for the assistance of Silas, Saul might still be running rings around him.

The thought of Silas made Morgan wonder what the renegade would think of the flaming wooden shapes. Perhaps, Morgan reasoned, they had some sort of symbolic meaning to slaves. He began walking back towards his headquarters to ask him.

The fires had been put out and the alarm was subsiding. As a precaution, patrols were sent out to scour the surrounding area and Morgan decided to keep the men at arms for a while longer. If nothing else, the burning wooden men would be an interesting item to note in his next report to Breckinridge.

As he approached the headquarters tent, with Silas's tent just off to the left, Morgan sensed that something was amiss. He could not see anyone. He jogged forward quickly, calling out for the two men he had left to guard Silas. There was no response. Coming closer, he saw two bodies lying on the ground by the dim light of the fading campfire.

"Alarm!" Morgan shouted. He called out to the nearest soldiers. "Where is your company commander?"

"Don't know, sir," one of them replied. "Think he went off to the south when those fires broke out."

Morgan reached the bodies of his two men, while nearby soldiers also converged on their commander. Both were face down in the dirt. He rolled over the nearest one and almost recoiled from the sight. The man's throat had been slit nearly from one ear to the other and a puddle of blood had formed underneath the corpse, soaking his shirt. One of his men, rolling over the other body, stepped back and cursed in fear and disgust as he discovered the same thing.

"God!" Morgan exclaimed. He realized that his hands were covered with the dead man's blood. "Private!" he shouted to a nearby soldier. "Get me some cloth to wipe this damn blood off with!"

Duke ran up, having been drawn by the shouting. "What the hell?" he asked in shock. "What the hell happened?"

"The bastards tricked us!" Morgan exclaimed angrily. "The shooting and fires at the south end were a diversion."

"But how they did get into the camp? How did they kill these men without making any noise?"

Morgan shook his head, frustrated, confused, and angry. He stormed toward Silas's tent, wanting to demand what had happened. However, when he pulled back the tent flaps, he saw no sign of Silas inside. The small cot on which the man had slept was overturned on the ground and the plate and cup he had been using were scattered on the dirt floor.

"Sir!" a soldier called. "Your tent, sir!"

Morgan turned and looked where the man was pointing. A bloodstained knife had been jabbed into the upright tent pole, pinning a piece of paper onto it. Morgan tore it off and quickly read it.

Morgan,
I could have killed you, too.
Saul

Morgan crumbled the paper in his hands and let out a howl of rage.

July 9, Morning
Flynn's Alehouse, Waco, Texas

"Well, who should I go talk to?" Robert Farmer asked.

"Anybody, I guess," McFadden answered. "Everybody. How the hell should I know?"

Farmer frowned, the frustration evident on his face. He had come to the alehouse eager to participate in the campaign and had clearly expected to be given more specific directions. McFadden, unfortunately, did not really know what to tell him. Having never before participated in a political campaign, he had no more idea what to do than he would have if he'd been asked to sail a ship across the Pacific Ocean.

He wished it could have been like a situation on a battlefield during the war, when he would have known precisely what needed to be done and therefore what he needed to tell his men. If the Yankees were occupying a position on elevated ground, McFadden would have known exactly how to deploy his men in order to outflank them. Had his men been ordered to hold a hill, McFadden would have known precisely how to position them to take maximum advantage of the ground. Yet it wasn't like that. He was in unknown territory, with no one to guide him. All of the people in Granbury County who knew anything about running a political campaign were aligned with Roden.

"Should I just stand on the street corner out here and hand these out to people as they pass?" Farmer asked, holding up a short stack of pamphlets.

"I guess that couldn't hurt," McFadden answered. "How many did I give you?"

"Fifty."

McFadden nodded, mentally calculating how much money they had spent printing the pamphlets Farmer now held in his hand. Annie had actually designed and written the piece, which consisted of two columns separated by a vertical line down the middle. On the left side was a description of the responsibilities of a county judge, such as enforcing the law, maintaining order, and administering justice through the commissioners' court. On the right side was a description of what Roden was actually doing, such as engaging in graft, using his deputy sheriffs to harass people, and other instances of corruption. McFadden wasn't sure whether the effort was good or bad, since he had nothing with which to compare it.

"Well, I guess I will go do that, then," Farmer said. "Might come back in after a bit, though. Hot out there."

McFadden chuckled. "That's fine, Bobby."

Farmer smiled, got to his feet, and strolled out the door. A few minutes later, McFadden could hear the man's distant voice trying to persuade passers-by to take pamphlets and occasionally engaging in earnest discussions with them.

He appreciated Farmer's support. Like other veterans of Granbury's Brigade, he had not only volunteered to come by Flynn's Alehouse and help out with the campaign, but had also kept his promise to ride past the McFadden Ranch every now and then to make sure he and Annie were all right. Though he still felt that he did not know what he was doing and felt somewhat apprehensive about taking on a man as powerful as Judge Roden, McFadden was warmed by the encouragement and assistance he was receiving from his friends.

On the other hand, support was beginning to trickle in from people he had never met. Ordinary ranchers and farmers from throughout the county and cottage industry workers in Waco had come to Flynn's Alehouse, asking to speak with him. A good many, perhaps the majority, came in with a certain timidity, clearly fearful of crossing the powerful judge. All of them brought stories of Roden's corruption. One fellow reported that he had put in a bid for a county contract to build a bridge over the Bosque River, having built similar bridges over the Brazos, only to be told he had to pay ten percent of the expected cost up front to Judge Roden himself. When he refused, the contract went to someone else, who had no experience in building bridges. Work on the project, near as McFadden could tell, had not yet even begun.

Flynn walked up to the table. "Get you another ale, Jimmy?"

"No, thanks, Flynn." He noticed something in Flynn's voice. "What's wrong?"

"Got a notice in the post. You know that the county judge has to approve a license from any place to serve beer or liquor."

"Of course."

"Well, our friend Roden has decided not to renew mine. Round abouts midnight on New Year's Eve, I'm going to have to either start serving nothing but coffee or close up shop."

McFadden sighed. "I'm sorry, Flynn. I should have expected that he would do something like this to you. Tomorrow I'll start running this campaign out of my own house."

"Damned if you will!" Flynn said, almost angrily. "No, from now on, you're getting your ale free of charge. Not going to let this bastard push me around, no matter who he is. Way I see it, if you win in November, so does Collett. That makes him county judge and he'll renew my license without a problem."

"If we win," McFadden said.

"You will, won't you?" Flynn asked. "You two never let us down during the war. You're not going to now, are you?"

McFadden pursed his lips. "I don't know how to do this. Not Collett, neither. It's like being asked to go into battle without anybody ever having shown us how to load and fire our rifles."

"Well, find somebody to teach you, then," Flynn said.

"Who? Everybody who knows how around here works for the judge."

Flynn smiled. "Nice to know something you don't for a change. Read the paper this morning. Looks like Postmaster Reagan is coming down from Richmond back to Texas to organize Breckinridge's presidential campaign in our state. Setting himself up in Austin, he is. Why don't you go down and ask him?"

"The Postmaster?"

"Yeah, our very own John Reagan."

"I know who he is," McFadden said quickly. "I don't see why he'd care to give us any help."

"Well, on Election Day, folks around here aren't going to just cast votes in your state legislative race or the county judge race. They're going to be casting votes for president, too. Roden and his crowd are Beauregard men, aren't they?"

"I don't know," McFadden admitted. He realized that this was something he should know and chided himself for yet exhibiting yet more evidence of his lack of political experience.

"Well, I hear tell that they're always going on about how smart Louis Wigfall and all his friends are. The States' Rights Party, isn't that what they call themselves? I hear tell that Judge Roden and his friends have formed themselves a little SRP committee for Granbury County."

"Have they now?"

"Sure as shooting. Ask around to get the details. Only heard it myself this morning, so it might have only happened last night."

McFadden nodded quickly. "This is good to know. I will ask around. Let me know what you hear from anybody coming into the alehouse."

"Sure thing, Jimmy. I would have pegged you for a Breckinridge man. You back him, don't you?"

"Been so focused on my own business I haven't given much thought to who should be president, honestly. But I always liked Breckinridge. Voted for him back in 1860. Seemed to know his business at Chickamauga. Heard he did well in other fights, excepting the one at Missionary Ridge. But then nobody did well there, did they?"

Flynn chuckled. "No, they didn't. We ran like rabbits."

"And I guess Breckinridge would make a good president. Doesn't seem to scream and shout much, does he? More of a common sense, down to earth kind of fellow, I think. Can't say I know much about what he wants to do if he wins."

"Me, neither," Flynn replied. "Wish I did. But if Roden wants Beauregard to win, it stands to reason that we should want Breckinridge to win, don't it? And if we can help him win the vote here in Granbury County, it would make sense for them to help us, wouldn't it?"

"Can't argue with you there, Flynn."

"Well, why not go down to Austin and ask him?"

McFadden thought this over. He knew he needed help. The campaigning effort he and Collett were putting together was confused and disjointed, no matter how he looked at it. If he could somehow tap into the effort being made by John Breckinridge's people to win the presidential vote in Texas, he might be able to get the help he needed. There didn't seem to be any other way to do it.

He sighed and nodded. "Yeah, you're right, Flynn. I guess I'll be headed down then soon as I can."

Flynn smiled. "Good. Now, you sure you don't want that ale?"

"You know, I think I will go ahead and have another."

Flynn smacked him lightly on the back and walked over to the bar to get him his drink. McFadden went back to looking over the pamphlet his wife had made. He took out a notepad and began writing down what he thought their next leaflet should say. When he was finished, he would run it by Collett and Annie during the evening.

He could still hear Farmer speaking earnestly to people passing by the alehouse out front, though he could not make out the words. As he wrote, McFadden began to hear the tone of Farmer's voice change from pleasant to hesitant, and then into angry and acrimonious. The volume rose accordingly, until Farmer was nearly shouting.

McFadden rose and strode outside to see what was going on. He saw Farmer engaged in an angry exchange with a Hispanic man. Both men were arguing loudly with one another in Spanish, which McFadden did not understand very well but which he knew Farmer spoke fluently.

"What's going on here?" McFadden asked.

"This son of a bitch is telling me that I have no right to hand out our pamphlets!" Farmer said, indignant.

"Who the hell is he?"

"Says he's a deputy sheriff of the country."

"Never seen him before in my life. He doesn't even speak English. Ask him his name."

There was a hurried exchange between Farmer and the man, who had a smug look on his face. Farmer turned to McFadden. "Says he doesn't have to tell us his name, only that he works for Rufus Walker, who works for the judge, who says I can't hand these pamphlets out."

The man grinned at Farmer spoke these words, then pulled out a badge and began ostentatiously waving it around. McFadden scowled. He noticed that the man was well-armed, with a bowie knife and two pistols in his belt. He himself was carrying his Navy Colt and he expected that Farmer was armed as well.

"Tell him we don't recognize his authority," McFadden said. "And then tell him to go to hell."

Farmer spoke a few words in Spanish to the man, whose eyes then flashed with a rage. He let out a series of angry curses which McFadden, even with his limited Spanish, understood perfectly well. With a quick motion that told McFadden that the man was no stranger to fighting, he pulled one of his pistols from its holster and raised it towards Farmer's face. McFadden was just as quick, bring out the Navy Colt and aiming it at the man's head. He did this without thinking. It was as though his mind had instantly gone back to the war, with one of his comrades being threatened by an enemy soldier. His instinct was to fire immediately, but he was able to restrain himself.

A long moment's silence followed. Farmer had not had time to draw his own weapon and stood motionless. Flynn emerged onto the porch, a sawed-off double-barreled shotgun in his hands, which he instantly aimed at the threatening man.

"Gun down!" McFadden said. He assumed that the man would understand perfectly, whether or not he spoke English.

370

The man smiled and, waiting just a moment, lowered his pistol and placed it back in its holster. He then began whistling and walking away across the street. For a few seconds, McFadden and Flynn kept their guns trained on him, before carefully lowering them as well.

"Thanks, fellas," Farmer said. "Didn't know handing out little pieces of paper was going to be so dangerous."

McFadden grunted, then looked across the street to where the man was walking. There was Walker, sitting on a rocking chair in front of one of the banks, a rifle cradled across his lap, smoking a cigar. Around him were half a dozen other men, some white and some Hispanic, armed to the teeth and wearing bandoliers across their chests. All were staring impassively at them.

"That your friend Walker?" Flynn asked.

McFadden nodded.

"Looks like he's brought some friends into town," Farmer said.

"A posse," Flynn observed. "Probably just for the election."

"I don't doubt it," McFadden replied. "Looks like I will have more to talk to Reagan about than I thought."

July 10, Noon
Hollywood Cemetery, Richmond, Virginia

Benjamin took a deep breath and looked around at the solemn scene. Hollywood Cemetery was hallowed ground, being the resting place of thousands of Confederate soldiers. This included several generals, among them Jeb Stuart and Richard Garnet. It was also the burial place of two Presidents of the United States, James Monroe and John Tyler. It was kept meticulously clean by a team of slaves who labored for hours each day.

A large crowd had gathered to witness the burial of Edmund Ruffin. In his will, the man already being described as one of the founding fathers of the Confederacy had requested burial in Richmond, so there had been no question that Hollywood Cemetery would be his final resting place.

Benjamin recollected meeting Ruffin on only a few occasions and could not say that he had really known the man. Yet Ruffin had been such a strong champion of secession and slavery in the years leading up to the war that it would not be considered odd for him to be at the funeral. As a Jew, he had not attended the church service that had been held earlier, but he felt it acceptable to take his place in the crowd at the graveside service in the church cemetery.

The rector of St. Paul's Episcopal Church, the Reverend Dr. Charles Minnigerode, was conducting the service, speaking with the German accent that betrayed his national origins. According to what Benjamin had been told, Edmund Ruffin had not been a member of St. Paul's. Still, the man had at least nominally been Episcopalian, though he had entertained all manner of strange ideas about religion, just as he had entertained strange ideas about agriculture and racial matters.

"Jesus said unto her, 'I am the resurrection and the life. He that believeth in me, though he were dead, yet shall he live. And whosoever liveth and believeth in me shall never die. Believest thou this?'"

371

Benjamin did not believe it. He was again reminded how, despite his lofty position, he often found himself very much alone in Richmond. He was Jewish, but did not feel especially close to his coreligionists. His public life was lived among the Christians. If he had a place of worship, it was Johnny Worsham's.

He shook the thought from his mind, for despite appearances he was here on a business matter. A very important business matter, in fact.

Many of the city's distinguished personages were attending the funeral, including members of both the Senate and the House of Representatives, prominent newspaper editors, and ministers from other churches. There were also quite of a few of the formidable women who composed the elite of Richmond high society, including Hetty Pegram and Mary Chesnut. Benjamin supposed that these women either not been able to find excuses or had simply been incredibly bored.

The funeral of Ruffin had attracted so much attention that some people had come from outside the state to attend. Georgia and both of the Carolinas had sent official delegations, though there had not been time for the other, more distant states to do so. Benjamin's particular interest, the true reason he was attending the ceremony at all, was a particular member of the South Carolina delegation. Standing in the crowd on the other side of the casket from him was Robert Rhett.

Like Ruffin, Rhett was one of the leaders of the prewar secession movement, who had begun calling for the South to break away from the Union years before most Southerners had ever dreamed of such a thing. His support of slavery was so intense and fervent that even many Fire-Eaters kept him at arm's length. Were it not for his ownership of the *Charleston Mercury*, the most widely read newspaper in the Confederacy, he would not have mattered at all. Benjamin considered him the most bitter of all the political opponents of Jefferson Davis, though there was an element of buffoonery in the man that made him less dangerous than he might have been.

He looked across the casket, past the mourning members of the Ruffin family, and stared at Rhett. The South Carolina firebrand noticed this and kept glancing at Benjamin, clearly wondering why the Secretary of State seemed fixated on him. It made Rhett uncomfortable, Benjamin noticed, which was exactly what was intended. Eventually, Rhett made eye contact with Benjamin and glared at him, wordlessly asking him to stop staring. Benjamin responded by giving him an almost imperceptibly salacious smile, separating his lips ever so slightly. Rhett, his fury contained only by the fact that he was at a funeral, fixed his eyes on the casket and did not allow them to waver.

Minnigerode was still preaching. "Jesus said, 'Let not your heart be troubled. Ye believe in God, believe also in me. In my Father's house are many mansions. If it were not so, I would have told you. I go to prepare a place for you.' Jesus, we can be assured, prepared a place for our friend Edmund, and we can trust he has gone there and is even now with Jesus. So shall we all be, one day." He glanced at Benjamin. "Those of us that are saved."

He sensed the snub and didn't mind. Minnigerode was a decent man and was only doing his job. Besides, it was far from the first time Benjamin had been slighted in public for being a Jew.

The ceremony ended a few minutes later and the assemblage of people began to break up with the appropriate level of solemnity. Some spoke quietly to the members of the Ruffin family before leaving. Benjamin stepped forward and offered condolences on behalf of the president, whom he explained had been unable to attend due to the pressures of his work. This polite comment had the virtue of being true.

Rhett was following the other members of the South Carolina delegation towards the gate that led out of the cemetery and back out onto the street. People were crowding together to pass through the gate, allowing Benjamin to easily catch up to him.

"Good afternoon, Mr. Rhett," he said pleasantly, extending his hand.

People turned and looked at what was happening. Rhett glanced about, judging whether he could simply ignore Benjamin without committing a social faux pas. Sighing, he shook Benjamin's hand.

"Mr. Benjamin," he said simply, then turned back towards the gate, which was still momentarily crowded with people.

"A lovely ceremony, I thought," Benjamin said wistfully. "The verses from Scripture were well chosen."

Rhett stopped and turned to him. "How would you know?"

"I may be a Jew, Mr. Rhett, but I am an educated man."

"Are you? From what I understand, you were kicked out of Yale without graduating."

"Yes, but not on account of my grades."

A few of the people passing through the gate into the street laughed at these words. Rhett, feeling that he was being made fun of, stopped and glared at Benjamin.

"What are you doing here, Benjamin?"

"What do you mean?"

"Exactly what I say."

"Why, I am attending a funeral, just as you are doing. I thought Edmund Ruffin was a great man and feel that his death is to be lamented."

"This was a Christian service."

"There is no law saying that I cannot attend, Jew though I might be. Besides, President Davis thought that sending a representative from the administration would only be proper."

Rhett's face transformed into an angry and contemptuous scowl of the sound of Davis's name. "I am quite sure that Davis doesn't care one whit for the death of a man who truly loved the South," he growled. "At least Ruffin saw the South as something more than a vehicle for his own ambitions!"

Benjamin gestured his hand away from the gate. "You seem upset, Mr. Rhett. Perhaps we might speak in private?"

"What could I possibly want to talk to you about, Benjamin?" Rhett spat.

"I thought you might want to hear my thoughts about the election."

Rhett's eyes narrowed and it was obvious to Benjamin that he had piqued the man's curiosity. His plan depended on Rhett agreeing to talk further. If he simply continued out the gate, he would have failed in his mission. He was tense, though the unwavering smile on his face did not show it. He felt an immense sense of relief when Rhett stepped away from the gate and out of hearing of the crowd, which was beginning to disperse into the street and move off in several directions.

"What about the election?" Rhett asked.

"It's looking like it will be Breckinridge against Beauregard."

"I know that!" Rhett said harshly. "I own a newspaper, for the love of God! Do you honestly think I'm not aware of who's running for president?"

"On the contrary, I am sure you are well aware of what is happening, which is why I wanted to talk to you. Breckinridge has asked me to speak to you, in fact."

"He did?"

"Of course. You control one of the most influential newspapers in the country. Which candidate you choose to support is obviously a matter of great importance."

Rhett's eyebrows went up. "He doesn't seriously think that I'll endorse him, does he?"

"Why wouldn't you?" Benjamin asked in mock surprise.

Rhett kicked his head backward and laughed uproariously. Benjamin had always thought that you could tell a lot about a person by how they laughed. Some people laughed fully and heartily, in tune with life. Listening to such laughter was like warming one's hands by a fireplace on a cold night. Rhett's laughter, however, was sharp and discordant, sounding the way medicine tasted. Benjamin couldn't imagine Rhett laughing except in mockery or disdain.

"Endorse Breckinridge? Davis's puppy dog? Never! He gave away hundreds of thousands of slaves at the Toronto peace talks! He told the Yankees that they didn't have to return runaways! You know that he doesn't own any slaves himself, don't you? You know that, right? And he supported that beastly abolitionist proposal of Patrick Cleburne and let that Irish jackass stay in the army! Why, we might as well have Abraham Lincoln for a president as John Breckinridge! I'm ashamed I ever supported the man, frankly."

Benjamin took a step backwards, affecting to be surprised by Rhett's vehemence. "I had no idea you felt so strongly on the subject," he lied.

"If you didn't then you're a damn fool. Don't you read my newspaper?"

"No, actually, I don't." He let that light insult float in the air while he quickly went on. "So, you would seem to have nowhere to turn, then. You won't support Breckinridge and Beauregard's people don't want anything to do with you. So where does that leave you?"

"Don't want anything to do with me?" Rhett stammered in disbelief. "That's what you think? You think I didn't go because they didn't invite me?"

"I don't know why you didn't go. Word in Richmond is that you refused to go when you learned they weren't going to let you serve on any of their committees."

"What?" Rhett asked in anger. "Lying drivel! They sent me one of their stupid letters. I didn't go because I didn't want to go!"

"Whatever you say. But I have it directly from Governor Vance that Toombs and Wigfall decided that they didn't want you involved in the States' Rights Party. Had you gone to Montgomery, you would have been just another pair of clapping hands in the crowd."

Rhett's face twisted into a look of rage, turning a strange color that was somehow a combination of red and white. For a moment, Benjamin was reminded of an angry schoolboy who had not been asked by the other children to join in their game of marbles.

"That's not all," Benjamin said, deciding to pour salt into the wound. "I understand that one of the conditions that Beauregard insisted upon when he agreed to be a candidate was that you not be involved in the campaign."

Rhett cursed loudly, which didn't surprise Benjamin. He knew that Rhett and Beauregard had once been friends but had had a vicious falling out during the final Yankee effort to capture Charleston in late 1864. Benjamin didn't recall the details, except that it had had something to do with Rhett's son, Alfred, who had been an artillery officer under Beauregard's command. Rhett, like most Southerners of his background, took matters of family honor rather too seriously.

Benjamin knew how vain Rhett was. He had held numerous political offices before the war, but had been humiliatingly trounced in the governor's race of 1860. In 1861, he had expected to be a contender for the presidency, only to be ignored by nearly everyone. He had managed to get himself elected to the Confederate Congress, but the voters had unceremoniously turned him out of office in 1863. All of these events had crushed Rhett's spirits and made an already touchy man apt to become furious at even the smallest hint of a slight. Moreover, it had made him mistrustful and apt to believe that insults and abuse existed where they did not. These were personal flaws that Benjamin was intent on exploiting.

Rhett, a look of fury on his face, folded his arms across his chest and leaned back against the fence, staring down at the ground with a miserable frown on his face. Benjamin let him stew in silence for a few silent minutes. Benjamin knew how to play on people's emotions the way a violinist played on his instrument. In Rhett's case, Benjamin knew he could use the fact that he was Jewish and that he had obtained high position within the Confederate government while Rhett himself had not, for his only real goal was to make Rhett angry.

After a while, Benjamin chuckled slightly. "You were once a great man, Rhett. Look at you now. You're just a pathetic, shriveled mass."

Rhett's eyes flashed fire. "Did you come here to insult me?"

"No. Like I said, I came on Breckinridge's instructions to ask whether you might endorse him. After all, since Beauregard and Wigfall have seen fit to keep you out of their little coalition, it's not like you have much of a choice."

Rhett looked at him carefully, then slowly smiled. "You think you're such a smart Jew, don't you Benjamin? No other choice, you say?" He raised himself from the fence and stood as tall as he could manage. "What if I told you that I am thinking about running for president myself?"

Benjamin laughed. "You? Run for president? I've never heard anything more ridiculous in my life."

"Ridiculous? Hardly! I have received dozens of letters from around the country, from Virginia to Texas, telling me that I should run. There are many people in the Confederacy who have not abandoned our founding ideals, you know. There are still many who remember that we are a nation founded on the principal of African slavery, and not the Jeffersonian nonsense your man

375

Breckinridge holds so highly. There are those who, like me, believe we must reopen the African slave trade, to hell with what the rest of the world says."

Benjamin suddenly looked alarmed. "Mr. Rhett, for once I'll speak to you directly. Believe me when I tell you that it would be utter madness idea for you to run for president. You would obtain no support and come out looking like a fool."

"I would have support! Believe me, I have received dozens of letters, all promising to help me if I choose to run. And I have my newspaper, you know. I could put together a campaign in a matter of weeks."

"I implore you not to go down this road," Benjamin said urgently.

Rhett smiled. "You're frightened, aren't you? You and Davis and Breckinridge. You don't want me to run because you know I'll beat you. That's it, isn't it! That's it!" Rhett threw back his head and laughed his sharp, arrogant laugh.

"You've taken leave of your senses, Rhett, and now I choose to take my leave of you." Benjamin turned his back on Rhett and began walking towards the cemetery gate.

"I'll run and win, Benjamin!" Rhett shouted mockingly as the distance between them grew. He continued laughing. "The people want me to run! You should read my letters!"

As Benjamin walked through the gate and out onto the street, his back to Rhett, he couldn't help but smile. There was no need for him to read Rhett's letters, for Benjamin had written them himself.

July 12, Noon
Outside of Point Coupee, Southern Louisiana

Lowell sat stiffly as Gardet snapped the whip at the horses to prevent them from stopping. The road was miserable and, indeed, scarcely deserved to be called a road at all. Due to recent rains, it was little more than a track of mud in which the wheels of the wagon were constantly getting stuck. Whenever the effort became too much, the horses pulling the wagon hesitated and clearly wanted to rest. The animals were weak and underfed, so Gardet had to snap the whip almost continually. The going was extremely slow.

Behind them, the second wagon was having similar problems. Lowell could hear Naismith curse under his breath every time they went through a muddy depression in the road, which seemed to try to suck the flimsy wheels into the ground. The black boy sitting next to him, whom Gardet had vouched for and brought along, found Naismith's discomfiture amusing and giggled whenever the white man cursed. For the first time, Lowell felt a certain advantage over Naismith, for the sailing captain was now out of his element. Lowell, from his time in the army, knew exactly how difficult it was to move horses and wagons through difficult ground.

They had left New Orleans five days earlier, travelling in a hired barge upriver to the town of Plaquemine, then setting off overland. Gardet had not had any trouble procuring the two wagons from a shipping firm with which he often did business. Lowell's wagon contained twenty crates of ammunition, while Naismith's contained another ten ammunition crates and the ten crates containing the rifles. The boxes containing the cooking implements, boots, and other sundry supplies were crammed on top of them. Both wagons were dangerously overloaded, but bringing a third wagon would have required them to use men from the *Vincent* crew as teamsters, which both Lowell and Naismith had decided was too risky.

While Lowell and Naismith worse decent clothes, Gardet and the young boy were wearing worn and somewhat ragged clothes not unlike those of field hands. It had been decided to make the two Negroes appear as slaves, with Lowell and Naismith impersonating slave-owners. It had been Naismith's idea and, somewhat to Lowell's surprise, Gardet had immediately agreed. If he had any issue with pretending to be a slave, it wasn't apparent.

Lowell knew that they were in terrible danger, for the countryside was being heavily patrolled by Morgan's men and Louisiana militia. The cover story they intended to use if they were stopped and questioned was ridiculously thin. Using receipts and order forms from Gardet's store, they would try to persuade anyone who asked that they were making deliveries of wine and spirits to wealthy plantation owners in the area. They had brought along some French wine and brandy, as well as some rum from Barbados, to try to make the illusion seem real. The bottles had been packed in the tops of the most easily accessible crates, with a thin layer of hay beneath them, but even the slightest effort of anyone searching them would reveal the weapons and ammunition. Lowell did not expect it to work, but it was better than nothing.

As they proceeded on, Lowell felt the same sensation he had experienced when the ship had been ascending the Mississippi River towards New Orleans, that of being drawn deeper and deeper into the Confederacy. As he passed by the small towns along the river and on the road towards the rendezvous point, the institution of slavery was on display for him like merchandize in a store window. Roughly half the people in the state of Louisiana were enslaved blacks and he had seen hundreds of them during his short journey. On three separate occasions during the barge trip, he had seen boatloads of chained blacks being carried down towards the slave markets of New Orleans. They had passed by sugar plantations and seen scores of slaves working mindlessly in the fields.

He was comforted by the thought that, in the two wagons, he was carrying the instrument of their liberation.

"Does it bother you, Gardet?" Lowell asked.

"What's that?"

"Seeing all these slaves working in the fields."

"Of course it bothers me," Gardet replied. "Why do you think I do what I do?"

"You just seem rather blasé about it."

Gardet shrugged. "I was born in New Orleans. I've been seeing it all my life. Doesn't shock me like it must shock a Massachusetts man like you. But that doesn't make it any less evil, does it?"

"No," Lowell replied. "If anything, it makes it more so."

Gardet grunted and they both fell into silence once again. Over the course of the journey from New Orleans, Lowell had found that his black companion was not much of a talker. He gave directions towards the rendezvous point in a matter-of-fact manner and made few comments about anything they had seen along the way. Aside from the fact that he had been born free rather than a slave, had received a basic education, and had been in the wine and liquor business a long time, Lowell had learned next to nothing about Gardet. The man had not volunteered any information about how or why he had come to be involved with Saul and the few leading questions Lowell had asked had been politely rebuffed. Lowell wasn't offended. After all, every man was entitled to his own secrets.

They proceeded on. Hours passed and the swampy surroundings seldom seemed to change. Again and again, Lowell raised his sleeve and drew it across his forehead, removing a thin layer of sweat which only came back again a few minutes later. The mosquitos were almost unbearable. He longed for the cool air and crisp oceanic breezes of Boston. With little conversation and not much change of scenery, he felt his mind drifting. It seemed absurd to be bored during such an important mission, yet the long journey was making it difficult for him to remain focused on his task.

The tedium was abruptly shattered when Lowell's ears heard the unmistakable sound of large numbers of horses. Glancing ahead, he saw what appeared to be a squad of Confederate cavalry emerge from around a bend in the road. He quickly counted eight men, which probably meant that a corporal would be in command. The sight hit him like a fist, for he had seen such horsemen many times on battlefields in Maryland and Virginia. Every instinct in his mind screamed for him to prepare to fight and he had to restrain himself from reaching for his LeMat revolver.

"Stay calm," Gardet said quietly.

Naismith whispered something in a harsh tone, but Lowell couldn't make it out before the cavalrymen came close. During the long voyage from Boston and the barge trip upriver, Lowell had practiced feigning a Southern accent, for his voice would otherwise reveal him as a New Englander and pique the curiosity of any patrol leader. Naismith told him that it sounded convincing enough, but Lowell remained uncertain. Still, it was a better option than attempting to explain the presence of a Boston-bred man in the swamps of Louisiana.

Without being told, Gardet pulled the horses to a stop as the troopers reined in beside them. Behind them, Naismith did the same. Lowell comforted himself with the thought that these men were looking for black insurgents and probably could not have imagined the possibility of white men smuggling weapons to them.

"Afternoon to you, gentlemen," Lowell said in his best Southern accent, tipping his hat.

"And to you, friend," said a trooper with corporal's stripes on his uniform, whom Lowell assumed to be the squad leader.

"Mister?"

"Gardet," Lowell answered. "Andre Gardet, of New Orleans." They had to assume none of the troopers were so familiar with New Orleans that they would know anything about the shop. Gardet's name was what was on the invoices and receipts, though, so Lowell had to use it.

"Pleased to make your acquaintance, Mr. Gardet," the trooper said pleasantly. "Corporal Thomas Morris, at your service. Mind if you tell me what you're doing out here?"

"Making deliveries. Own a wine and spirits shop in New Orleans. Got lots of clients on the plantations out here. Lots of wine. Some cases of rum. That sort of thing."

"Fella says he got liquor in that wagon?" one of the troopers asked.

Morris ignored him. "You might want to be careful round these parts, Gardet. Sure you heard tell that that bastard Saul and his bandits have been seen around here."

"Saul? I thought you fellas took care of him."

"Not us," Morris said. "Morgan's men. North of here. But we ain't sure if he got all of the darkies. Might still be some wandering around here, trying to cause trouble. Don't know their place, you know?" He tossed his head in Gardet's direction. "He's yours, yes?"

Unexpectedly, a revulsion swept through Lowell. Though he was only playing a part, and doing so for the greater good, everything within him seemed to rebel against asserting that the black man sitting next to him belonged to him as a species of property. He struggled to retain his composure, reminding himself that everything depended on being able to pull off the subterfuge.

"Yes, my boy Casca here."

Morris looked behind them at Naismith's wagon. "And you there! Your name?"

"James Sears, friend. Partner of Gardet up there."

"And that boy's yours?"

"This fella? Yeah, Vincent belongs to me."

Morris nodded, satisfied. "You know we're working hard out here, riding around in the swamps, keeping folks like you safe from Saul."

Lowell nodded. "And we appreciate it, Corporal."

Morris leaned forward in his saddle, a mocking grin appearing on his face. "Appreciate it enough to donate some of that liquor you have? I think you said you had some rum."

Behind him, the seven other horsemen glanced at one another and grinned. Lowell felt an intense alarm. He had no idea as to the character of these men. It occurred to him that they might simply decide to take the liquor for themselves, selling whatever they couldn't drink. If they did that, they would discover the rifles and ammunition and all would be lost. After all, he knew from his time in the army that soldiers loved nothing so much as alcohol.

"I'd be happy to, Corporal. But you see, I'd have a disappointed customer out here somewhere. And I'd be the one to swallow the money."

Morris's face clouded. "You'd leave us disappointed if you don't cough up, you know. And lots of bad things can happen to people out here in the swamps, don't you think?"

Lowell mentally calculated whether he and Naismith might be able to resist. He knew he could pull his LeMat revolver out and, using the element of surprise, get off a few shots before the troopers reacted. At best, though, he might be able to kill or wound three of the eight men before him. Behind him, Naismith might try to do the same, but was farther away and would not be able to aim properly, especially since Lowell and Gardet would be in his way. Even under the best circumstances, there was no way to take out the cavalrymen before being killed. If they died on the road, the weapons would never to Saul.

"I'm just a businessman trying to make a living, friends," Lowell said, trying to sound relaxed.

"And we're just poor country boys trying to keep you safe out here," Morris replied. "Seems like a jug of rum would be the least you could offer in compensation."

Lowell nodded. "That's a good point. I suppose I can let you have one jug if you promise to let us get on down the road. In fact, why not two? That'd be about four pints. Enough for the eight of you, I would think."

Morris and his men chuckled. "Sounds like a good deal to us," the corporal said.

"Okay. I'll get it." Lowell rose from the bench and dropped down onto the ground.

The laughter instantly ceased among the mounted Confederates, who exchanged looks of confusion. "What are you doing?" Morris asked.

"What do you mean?" Lowell replied. "I'm getting your rum."

"Aren't you going to have your boy do it for you?" Morris asked, pointing to Gardet.

Lowell stopped, realizing his terrible mistake. No Southerner would have done manual labor when he could have asked his slave to do it for him. Gardet sat on the bench, absolutely motionless, as if he had been changed into a statue. The soldiers suddenly tensed, sensing that something was amiss. The silence, for a long and edgy instant, was deafening.

"You!" Morris said to Gardet. "Boy! Get off your ass and get me some rum."

"Yes, sir," Gardet said, using a soft and deferential tone very different than what Lowell thought he had sounded like in his store. He hopped quickly from the bench and walked back towards the covered part of the wagon, pulling part of the top away and revealed the crates beneath it. Pulling a hammer and crowbar from the front of the wagon, he banged and pried until the lid of the crate came open.

Lowell's heart was in his throat. As he pulled the lid away, a few jugs of rum and bottles of wine were visible on top of a layer of packing hay. Beneath the hay, Lowell knew, were the rifles. If one of the soldiers got curious or if a sudden gust of wind came through, all would be lost. He, Naismith, Gardet, and perhaps even the boy whose name he didn't know would all be hanged and Saul's little band, if it still even existed, would be finished for good.

Gardet withdrew two jugs of rum from the crate and held them up from Lowell's approval. Upon seeing him nod, Gardet walked directly to Morris and held the rum up for him to take.

"Thank you," Morris said as he put the two jugs in his saddle bag. "My men and I will enjoy our dinner more tonight. Ain't that right, boys?" The seven troopers behind Morris hooted loudly enough for their horses to be disturbed.

"Well, it was my pleasure," Lowell said.

"You get on about your business. But keep a sharp lookout. If you see anything you think ain't right, report it straight away."

"I will."

"Well, then, let's move out, boys." Morris clicked his horse into a walk, followed by his men. Once they were past Naismith's wagon, they quickened to

380

a trot. Within two minutes, they were lost to view as they turned a bend down the road.

Lowell let out a deep breath, but said nothing for a while. He imagined that Gardet and Naismith felt exactly as he did. All of them had come within a hairsbreadth of disaster and had only avoided it because the Confederate troopers had been lazy. He knew how lucky they had been. By all rights, their quest should have ended.

"We'd better get moving," Gardet said. "Still a few days to the campsite. Saul might have got my message by now, if he sent anyone to check the drop site. We need to be there when he arrives. I doubt he'll wait around if we're not there to greet him."

"Yes," Lowell said. "Yes, you're right. Put the lid back on the crate and let's get going."

CHAPTER TEN

July 14, Night
Saul's Camp, St. Martin Parish, Southern Louisiana

Saul stood still and silent, looking grimly down at a large patch of freshly dug earth. The raid on Morgan's camp had gone like clockwork, precisely as he had planned it. Silas had been snatched from his tent and knocked senseless with a single blow from Peter, an especially strong insurgent soldier whom Saul had freed from the Bergeron Plantation and who had been specially chosen for the task. Frankly, Saul had been surprised that Morgan had so easily fallen for such a simple diversion.

Silas had regained consciousness about half the distance back to the insurgent camp. He panicked when he realized what had happened and made a strenuous effort to free himself. The ropes with which he was tied had proven far too strong for him, however, and Peter dealt him a solid punch to the face every time he struggled too energetically. A tight gag had prevented him for crying out for help.

There had been no ceremony about the execution when Silas had been brought back to camp. The gag was left on, for Saul did not care what the renegade might have to say to him. They had tossed him into the already dug grave and simply begun piling the dirt back down on top of him. The traitor hadn't been able to scream, but the look of abject terror in Silas's eyes was plain enough to Saul, who had stood at the top of the grave while his men calmly buried Silas alive.

While the traitor's torso and face were still visible, the men parades one by one around the rim of the grave. Most spat down on Silas. Two men urinated on him. All glared down on him with expressions of undisguised hatred. Silas's betrayal had cost the lives of many of their comrades. Not a single man had showed the slightest sign of sympathy.

In his frantic struggles, Silas managed to free his left arm from its bounds, but by that point his legs were already buried and he could not attempt to untie them. It wouldn't have mattered in any case, for Saul and the others would have simply pushed him back down into his grave again had he tried to crawl out. Very slowly, the level of dirt rose toward his face. The gag kept Silas from uttering anything other than muffled cries that reminded Saul of a sad dog. As the end neared, with tears streaming down his face, Silas reached up with his left hand, in a silent plea for mercy.

"Do you think your white friends will save you now?" Saul asked.

Two minutes passed before the last, squirming bit of Silas was covered over with earth. The men kept shoveling, though, and the strange, slow, wavy movements of the dirt for a few minutes longer indicated that Silas had not yet suffocated. Saul imagined the horror and utter anguish that must have roiled through the renegade before the last bit of life was snuffed out of him. The men had kept walking across the patch of dug ground until it was level. Somewhere beneath the soil, Silas had died a traitor's death.

Saul had never liked Silas, but had always counted on his hatred of the slaveholders to guarantee of his loyalty. The shock of a traitor within the partisan band had deeply unsettled him, even more than the fact that Morgan had inflicted such a sharp defeat on him and killed so many of his men. The raid to capture Silas had been a dangerous risk, yet Saul felt it had been necessary. The men had to be made to see the consequences of treason, and they had. He did not expect anyone else to go over to the enemy.

Now Saul sighed deeply as he looked at Silas's grave. They would move on tomorrow and no marker of any sort would be left behind. It would be as though the Earth itself had chosen to swallow Silas up and drag him down to hell. It was no less than he deserved.

The men were subdued and quiet. Once their meager supply of meat had been cooked, the fires were allowed to die out. There was no need for warmth at night in the midst of summer and illumination for conversation wasn't required because no one seemed to want to talk. More than at any time since the end of the war, Saul's men seemed content to sit silently, musing on thoughts of their own.

The morning's report had not been encouraging. They had linked up with the second column three days after the battle, but even so they only had a hundred and seventy-two men remaining. Three weeks before, he had had more than three hundred. Aside from those who had been killed or captured by Morgan's men, several had left the group to make their escape to the North. Saul had given them permission to go, on the assumption that men who remained to fight by choice would be more loyal. Now he was beginning to question the wisdom of that policy.

Making the situation even worse was the fact that only thirty-six men had functioning rifles. For them, Saul had less than fifteen rounds of ammunition per weapon and many of them would likely be too damp and old to fire anyway.

He walked through the camp, frowning as he saw the disillusioned expressions on the faces of the men. Following their thrashing by Morgan, they had been motivated by the desire to gain revenge on Silas for his treason. Now that this had been accomplished, he could sense a sagging of their spirits, a questioning of what they were doing, perhaps even feeling that their campaign against slavery was certain to fail.

For the first time since Saul had formed his band two years earlier, he felt that a collapse of morale was imminent. Worse, he did not know what he could do about it. Morgan's aggressive patrols had forced Saul to keep moving to stay out of their reach and the Confederate militia seemed to be growing in number with each passing day. He lacked the numbers and weapons to mount another attack on a plantation, all of which were now well-protected, both by the militia and by private guards hired by the plantation owners. If he made a wrong decision, or simply ran out of luck, they would be hemmed in and trapped. If that happened, they would all surely die. The best that could be hoped was to go down fighting, but with so few effective weapons, it was more likely that they would simply be shot down like animals or hanged in disgrace.

Saul saw Ferguson walking towards him, clearly intent on speaking to him. Saul would have preferred not to, for he was in a foul mood. He wanted to appear stoic and strong, so as to hearten his men. What worried him more than anything was the possibility that they would sense his own despair. He knew he carried their own burdens on his shoulders. If they saw him falter, they would lose all faith.

"Where's Troy?" Ferguson asked as he approached.

"I sent him to check the drop site."

The drop site was the place where their New Orleans contact, Andre Gardet, would leave them messages. Sometimes newspapers would be left as well, to allow them to remain informed on events in the outside world. Generally, though, the messages specified locations where crucial supplies had been left for them to gather. Gardet's notes had also provided a very thin sliver of contact with the abolitionists in the United States.

Ferguson frowned. "Why should we bother? There won't be anything there. We haven't heard from Gardet for months now."

"Doesn't hurt to look, does it?"

"No, I suppose not." Ferguson paused uncertainly and Saul sensed he was about to say something he did not want to say. "Look, Saul, I would like to talk to you. Away from the men."

Saul gestured to a spot out of hearing distance from any of the sleeping or sitting men and they walked over to it. "Well?" he asked.

"I've been thinking," Ferguson began. "Perhaps we're played out. Perhaps we should order the men to scatter and make for free territory."

Saul wasn't surprised to hear these words. He wanted to be angry, to reproach Ferguson for being a defeatist. Yet he couldn't do that, because the same thought had occurred to him. Saul was many things, but he was not a hypocrite. Besides, he lacked the energy to be angry.

"It's too early to make a decision like that," Saul muttered.

"Too early? Look around! The men are on the verge of falling apart. Silas changed everything by what he did. The men feel it's only a matter of time before we're all caught or killed."

"Well, if we all want to sleep in feather beds, slavery will survive forever."

Ferguson's face melted into a combination of anger and sadness. Saul immediately regretted what he had said. None of the men, least of all Ferguson, could be accused of laziness or lack of fortitude. They could all have gone north when the Treaty of Toronto had been signed, but instead they all chose to follow him into the swamps to carry on the struggle.

Saul spoke more gently. "If we abandon our campaign now, we will give up all that we have gained."

"And what have we gained, Saul? Hmm? A hundred or so freed slaves? What does that matter when there are two million enslaved people across the Confederacy?"

"It means a great deal to the people we've freed!" Saul snapped. "Dozens of women and children have been smuggled out through New Orleans or up to St. Louis."

"But that's not what you talked about when you started this," Ferguson said. "I remember exactly what you told me. You used the word 'crusade'. Well, it's not a crusade anymore. We're just a bunch of scared men hiding in the swamp from evil people who are hunting us. It's time to get out of here."

Saul shook his head and walked away, gesturing with his hands to indicate that he did not want Ferguson to follow. He didn't want to listen to any more of Ferguson's words, though he could not disagree with them. Indeed, while he would never admit to the white doctor, he had already concluded much the same thing himself. Yet could he bring himself to abandon the campaign? The very thought seemed to burn his soul the moment it started to arise in his mind.

One of his men walked up, pointing. "Troy's back, boss."

Saul looked and saw Troy coming into the camp. What he saw took him by surprise. He had expected his right-hand man to be wearing the same kind of gloomy expression as Ferguson, but Troy had a smile on his face. Saul had not seen any of his men smile since Morgan's ambush. His surprise turned to astonishment when he saw the reason for Troy's happiness, for the man was holding up a piece of paper.

"Can it be?" Saul asked himself aloud. He walked quickly over to Troy and, without a word, snatched the paper from his hand.

My Dear Joseph,
I write this letter on January 9. A man has arrived with a very large order of vegetables. I shall drop them off on January 20 at three o'clock.
Your Friend,
Andre

"What is it, boss?" Troy asked.

"A moment," Saul replied, deciphering the message in his head, using the crude code that existed only in his own mind and Gardet's. 'January 9' actually indicated 'July 9', meaning that the message had been written less than a week before. The word 'vegetables' indicated 'supplies', while 'three o'clock' was a reference to the third campsite in a set of locations that only Saul and Gardet had memorized.

What Saul did not understand was the reference to a man arriving. Were these words simply tossed in by Gardet for effect? Saul shook his head, for Gardet could have simply said that he had an order of vegetables without referring to any man arriving. Since their crude code lacked the words for anything so specific, Saul assumed that Gardet meant the words to be taken literally and that a man actually had arrived in New Orleans with a shipment of supplies for him. Who could this man be?

"What is it, boss?" Troy repeated.

"Gardet may have something that can help us."

"Guns?"

"Maybe. I hope so." Saul sighed and looked around. "Only thirty-six of our men have rifles. If we can reequip even of a few of the rest, it would make a huge difference."

"Where are we going?"

"Remember the campsite where we met Gardet back in January? How long would it take us to get there?"

"It would take us just two or three days if we didn't have to dodge Morgan's patrols. As it is, it may take us a week. Of course, if Morgan catches us in the meantime. . ."

"Then it won't matter, will it?"

Troy waited a moment before replying. "No, I guess it won't." He paused before going on. "Maybe going is too great a risk."

Saul considered this for a few seconds, before nodding sharply to himself. "We're going. After all, we have nothing left to lose."

July 18, Afternoon
Governor's Mansion, Milledgeville, Georgia

Toombs took a deep pull on his cigar as Stephens read from the telegram they had just received from Wigfall, who was headed back to Texas to coordinate the SRP campaign in that state. He told them that Postmaster General Reagan had left Richmond to return to Texas as well, most likely to manage the Breckinridge campaign out of Austin. Texas, though not a large state in terms of its electoral votes, was likely to be fiercely contested.

"Does Wigfall say what he thinks our chances are?" Toombs asked.

"No," Stephens replied. "Well, that's not true. He says that he will win Texas for us easily. But you know how he blows so much hot air. His estimates are worthless. I think we have a better than even chance of winning Texas, but shouldn't take it for granted."

Toombs grunted. He was happy to see Wigfall vanish far across the Mississippi River. The few meetings he had had with the man since his dastardly attempt to steal the vice presidential nomination from him had not been pleasant. Indeed, it had taken a great effort of will for him to simply shake Wigfall's hand. For his part, Wigfall had acted as though nothing had happened, protesting that the votes for him represented a misguided effort on the part of his friends and that he had not even known what was afoot. It was so obviously a lie that Toombs had not bothered to respond to it.

His inclination had been to boot Wigfall out of the SRP altogether, but everyone knew that he might be the difference between victory and defeat in the polls in Texas. Toombs had therefore swallowed his pride and done nothing to retaliate. Revenge against Wigfall would have to wait until after the election.

Toombs glanced around in irritation. "Where is the Governor?" he asked. They had come from their respective homes to meet with Governor Brown to discuss the specifics of the presidential campaign in Georgia.

"We've only been here ten minutes. I'm sure he's busy."

"I'm reminded of how that pompous ass Beauregard made us wait in his house in New Orleans."

"And how is our Creole friend? Have you been in touch since the convention?" he asked.

"Yes, I have sent him a few telegrams to keep him informed about campaign news. And he has forwarded letters and telegrams he has received from others."

"He's content to wait in New Orleans?"

"Yes, he says campaigning would be beneath his dignity. To paraphrase his words, he is waiting for the voice of the nation to call him to his destiny."

Stephens let out a hearty laugh, a rare occurrence for him. Toombs smiled, pleased at having amused his old friend. He took another pull on his cigar as he heard the door to the office open. Governor Brown entered, an angry look on his face. He held up a newspaper.

"Rhett's running for president," he said sourly.

"He's what?" Toombs said in surprise.

"He's running for president," Brown repeated. "He officially announced his candidacy in yesterday's copy of the *Charleston Mercury*. Every other paper in the country is running with the story today."

Toombs cursed and Stephens let out a deep groan. They all knew Robert Rhett in some capacity and none of them liked him. Indeed, Toombs couldn't think of a single prominent member of the SRP who liked Rhett. Some had tried to befriend him, or at least forge political alliances with him due to the influence of his newspaper, but all had ended up disillusioned and resentful at the sheer malice of the man. Rhett hated everyone and, consequently, everyone hated him.

Yet he had his newspaper. It seemed absurd to Toombs that such an unpleasant person would also happen to own and edit the most influential and widely read newspaper in the Confederacy. Rhett had played a crucial role in pushing South Carolina into secession in 1860. He had expected to receive great honors and high office in the newly established Confederacy and had been given nothing at all.

"It must be a personal vendetta," Brown suggested. "It wasn't until after Beauregard officially became our candidate that Rhett announced. Didn't they have some sort of feud in Charleston in 1864, when the Yankees were attacking the city?"

"Yes," Stephens said. "Something about Rhett's son. I don't remember the details."

Brown growled. "It doesn't matter why he's running. I don't care. But we can't ignore it."

"Why not?" asked Toombs. "Does anyone take Rhett seriously? The man's insane, if you ask me. Absolutely insane. Who's going to vote for a crazy man? I would be surprised if one out of fifty voters would even consider casting their ballot for that lunatic."

"Indeed," Stephens replied calmly. "And two percent of the vote could make all the difference in very close states. We can assume that those people who will vote for Rhett would vote for our ticket were Rhett not in the race. I do not believe that we can dismiss this. It will present a problem for us."

There was a momentary pause. "Well, what do we do, then?" Toombs asked.

Brown sighed and shook his head. "I'm going to Savannah to give a campaign speech the day after tomorrow. When I am finished, perhaps I could dash over the border and meet with Rhett, try to persuade him to drop out."

"He won't do it," Stephens said firmly. "You know him. Any effort to dissuade him will simply make him more determined."

"I agree," Toombs said.

"Then maybe I could offer him a carrot?" Brown suggested. "Do you think Beauregard might be willing to offer Rhett a position in the Cabinet?"

"No," Toombs said firmly. "First of all, Beauregard would never allow it. I don't know what it was that happened in Charleston, but they despise one another. Second, now that he's running for president, Rhett would see any office other than the presidency as unworthy of him. And finally, I personally would rather be damned to hell a thousand times than to serve as vice president in any administration that included Robert Rhett."

"I agree," Stephens said. "Besides, Cabinet posts can't be given away like seats at a dinner party. Every one of them is a position of enormous responsibility. Can you imagine Rhett running the War Department or the Treasury Department? It would be an utter disaster."

The three men sat silently after Stephens said these words. After a few moments, Brown rose and walked over to the liquor table, pouring whiskies for himself and Toombs. Stephens, he knew from experience, did not drink whiskey. After passing the drink over to Toombs, Brown resumed his seat and spoke again.

"So, if we can't convince Rhett to drop out, what should we do? I would be happy to attack the son of a bitch in my speeches. It would be nothing less than he deserves."

Stephens shook his head. "If we attack him, people will think that we fear him. It would just give him more credibility. Best to simply ignore him. He may have an impact on the campaign and he may not. Either way, we'll just have to live with him."

"I suppose," Brown said. "Well, no more talk of Rhett for the moment, then. Let's move on to how we're going to bring our own great state of Georgia into the Beauregard column come November."

They spent the next hour going over the internal politics of Georgia. With its twelve crucial electoral votes, Georgia would certainly be one of the great prizes. Together, Toombs, Stephens, and Brown made a formidable triumvirate that they hoped would ensure the outcome of the state's election. They discussed where they thought support for the SRP would be the strongest and where it would be the weakest, who owned which newspaper in which community, which members of the legislature were going to back the SRP and which were going to back the Breckinridge ticket. A thousand different variables went into these kinds of strategy meetings and Toombs had always found them almost as intoxicating as his favorite whiskey.

Strangely, though, Toombs did not find this particular conversation all that interesting. He felt himself beginning to drift away in his thoughts. Georgia was his state, where he had been born, grown to manhood, received his education, and started his political career. He loved Georgia, yet he knew he had long since outgrown it. His time as a congressman, both in Washington City before the war and Richmond after it, had given him a broader perspective. He had outgrown his home state. Georgia, he had realized, was not big enough for Robert Toombs.

"Does that sound agreeable, Robert?" Governor Brown asked.

"I'm sorry?" Toombs replied, snapping out of his distraction. He realized he had not been following the conversation for a few minutes.

"Aleck and I were saying that you might host a barbecue for the members of the state legislature who represent the northeastern districts. That's your territory, after all."

"Yes, yes, of course," Toombs replied, waving dismissively. "I'll make the arrangements."

Stephens looked carefully at him. "What is it?"

"What?"

"You seem distracted."

Toombs thought for a moment before replying. "I was distracted, I suppose. I apologize."

"What is it that distracts you?" Stephens asked.

"I was considering what needs to be done outside of Georgia."

"A great deal, of course," Brown replied. "Campaigning must be undertaken in every state. But Georgia is our state. We know it better than we know any other state. And it is one of the states that Beauregard absolutely has to win if he is to become president. And, if I may say so, if you are to become vice president."

"Winning Georgia will mean nothing if we don't win some of the other states. I am the vice presidential candidate, aren't I? I should be looking beyond my own state."

"I'm not sure I know what you mean," Brown said.

He made his decision quickly, without really thinking about it. "I have decided to undertake a speaking tour throughout the Confederacy. I think that this will be the best way for me to help our ticket win."

"What?" Brown asked, stunned. "A speaking tour through the whole country? What on earth gave you such a harebrained idea?"

"Joseph's right," Stephens quickly inserted. "You're the vice presidential candidate for the party. It would look indecorous for you to actively campaign. That's why Beauregard is staying in New Orleans. That's the way it's always been."

"No, not always," Toombs countered. "Stephen Douglas campaigned throughout the United States during the 1860 campaign, even in the South."

"Yes, and look where it got him," Stephens said. "He won only twelve electoral votes against Lincoln." During the 1860 campaign, Stephens and Toombs had found themselves at odds, for Stephens had supported Douglas while Toombs had backed Breckinridge. It had been the first time the two old friends had found themselves on opposing sides in a political conflict and both hoped that it would also be the last.

"Look," Toombs said. "I know it's not been the tradition for presidential and vice presidential candidates to actively campaign. But the Confederacy is a new nation. We're not bound by what the rules were when we were part of the United States. And the States' Rights Party is a new political organization. It needs to be set on its feet properly. If I can speak around the country, it won't just help Beauregard get elected president. It will help our supporters who are running for Congress, for the governorships, for the state legislatures. It will help build the States' Rights Party up into a permanent institution of Confederate life."

Toombs didn't say the rest of what he was thinking. If he could help get supporters elected to political office in 1867, they would owe him favors that he could call in in 1873, when it would be time for the next presidential election. If he could line up enough support early on, he could forestall any attempt by someone else to gain the SRP's presidential nomination six years hence.

Six years as vice president under Beauregard would be difficult to endure, Toombs knew. Yet he could do it if he kept his eye on the prize and he could use his influence with the other members of the SRP to make sure Beauregard didn't do anything foolish. Then, when his time came, he could enter the office of the presidency himself, with Congress and the state legislatures filled with politicians who thought as he did and who perhaps owed him for their positions. If a Supreme Court had been created in the meantime, it would be filled with men whom he had a large role in selecting.

Then Toombs would be in a position to craft the South into the kind of country he knew it should be.

"You're determined," Stephens said. "I've known you long enough to know I can't dissuade you. In that case, I wish you good luck."

July 19, Afternoon
Eberly House, Austin, Texas

"How long do you plan on staying, sir?" the young woman asked.

"Tonight and tomorrow night," McFadden answered.

"Your pleasure, sir," she replied. She pushed the registry book towards him. "If you could just sign here, sir."

He scribbled his name onto the book. "If I can finish my business early tomorrow, I may leave in the afternoon if there's enough sunlight to get me through to Round Rock."

She looked down at the book. "Well, James, there'll be a bed for you one way or the other." She gave him a warm and welcoming smile, leaning forward slightly in a manner that allowed him a glance down her blouse. It was an obvious offer. For a moment, he looked deeply at her. She was a comely woman, just over twenty, with dark red hair and sparkling eyes. He glanced back down at the registry book, forcing improper thoughts from his mind. Annie was his life and soul. Not only would he not give in to temptation, but he would not even allow temptation to enter his mind.

"How much?"

"Dollar a night," she said. "That gives you dinner and breakfast as well, but not lunch."

He pulled two dollar bills out and laid them on the counter. She waved her hand through the air.

"Oh, you can settle up when you leave, especially if you're not sure you're staying tomorrow. Here's your key."

"Thank you," McFadden said. It was not common for such trust to be displayed by the matron of a hotel. He walked up the dusty stairs to his room, leaving Molly behind in the lobby. Weariness drew him to his room, for it had been a long and hard ride from Waco to Austin. He had left the morning of July 18 and had gotten as far as Belton, where he had camped for the night. Up early the next day and on the road as quickly as possible, he had arrived in Austin in the late afternoon. Yellowjacket had neighed protests continually, not used to such long and hot rides, but he had remained as faithful as ever and McFadden had made sure to stop every time there had been a chance for the horse to get some water.

He collapsed on what passed for a bed, thinking for a moment that he had heard mice or rats scurrying about underneath it. He did not want to fall asleep, for he had not yet eaten dinner, yet he knew that if he remained on the bed that sleep would come whether he wanted it or not. McFadden pulled himself up and set out the few contents of his carpetbag. He pulled out a copy of *The Life of Joseph E. Johnston*, by Edward Pollard, which had just been published the year before and was the bestselling book in the Confederacy. With every word he read, he grew more proud that he had served under Johnston during the war, even if he considered Pollard's writing rather too complimentary for a serious work of biography.

He later went down to the dining room for dinner, finding it filled with two dozen other guests of the Eberly House. Molly Haskins was there and smiled continually at him, but he ignored her, focusing instead on the cheese grits and braised beef in front of him. Two of the other diners were fellow veterans and they chatted about what units they had served in and where they had fought, though he turned down an offer to join them at a nearby tavern when the meal was over. He retired back to his room and finally fell asleep.

Yet his slumber was fitful. He found himself stirring up every few hours, constantly drifting in and out of that hazy and mysterious realm that separates the conscious from the unconscious. It was hard for him to tell the difference between his thoughts and his dreams. Little Thaddeus was there, saying more words each day than he could say the day before. Annie was there, still so young and beautiful despite the harsh realities of being a wife on the Texas frontier. Yet Lucius Roden was there, too. McFadden had not laid eyes on the man for several weeks, yet his stink seemed to hover over the town of Waco and its surrounding small communities and farms, sticking to the good people and somehow not allowing them to clean him off. At some point in his incoherent dream, the figure of Rufus Walker emerged as if from a deep gray mist, staring at him like a hungry predator.

The sunlight woke him up. At this time of year, it came early. He came awake, splashed some water on his face, and then dressed in his second set of clothes. He went down to the dining room and had a breakfast of biscuits and gravy, washed down with a few cups of coffee. Not long after, he stepped out onto the dusty streets of Austin and began walking the few blocks southwards down Congress Avenue towards the building where his meeting was to be held.

The small front room of the office was crowded with other people. McFadden pushed his way to the thin, bored-looking young man at the desk when he walked in. "I'm here to see Postmaster Reagan," he said, loudly enough to be heard over the din of conversation.

"Well, who the hell isn't?" the man snapped back. He shoved a piece of paper towards him. "Sign here and wait your turn."

McFadden complied, ruminating to himself that a man apparently had to sign his name several times a day whenever away from home. He glanced about. There were benches all along the walls of the room, but every space had been taken up already. He frowned when he noticed an older, frail-looking man awkwardly standing in the middle and thought that some of the younger men sitting down ought to have given up their seats for him.

He began a long period of waiting. He knew no one in the room and had never been the sort of man who could simply walk up to someone and start a conversation. Annie had told him that this characteristic did not bode well for a budding politician, which he supposed was true. He wished he had brought the Johnston biography with him, but it made no sense for him to return to the boarding house for it now. Leaning against one of the thick wooden pillars jutting out from the wall, McFadden unobtrusively listened to the various conversations going on around him. After all, he had nothing better to do. Unsurprisingly, they all dealt with the election. He focused his attention, for he suddenly realized that this would be an excellent opportunity to gather information.

People were saying that Beauregard was likely to win the presidency, for the Deep South states were all but certain to cast their electoral votes for him and he would probably win at least some of the big states farther to the north, too. He also heard people say that the States' Rights Party was rapidly organizing across the Confederacy, while Breckinridge had only the beginnings of an organized campaign and nothing resembling a genuine political party. The men speaking said all this with concern and alarm, for they were all Breckinridge men.

Other conversations revolved around issues about which McFadden knew nothing. Two men were locked in a deep discussion about a proposal for the state government to buy shares in a proposed railroad that would link Houston with Vicksburg, thereby finally established a rail link between Texas and the rest of the Confederacy. McFadden considered himself an intelligent man, but he could scarcely grasp the meaning of terms like 'sinking fund' or 'preferred stock'. A group of other men were discussing what proportion of the state budget would be required to purchase artificial limbs for disabled war veterans.

An hour passed, and then another. McFadden did not fidget and only occasionally shifted his position against the pillar. At long last, the thin man said the words he had long waited to hear.

"McFadden! You're next!"

He walked across the crowded room and through the door to the back, closing it quickly behind him. Sitting at a desk, scribbling furiously on a piece of paper and chewing on a lit cigar, was John Reagan, Postmaster General of the Confederate States.

"Take a seat," he said with a hint of disdain. He took another thirty seconds to finish writing before he spoke. "So, James McFadden, yes? I've heard your name before. Weren't you the fellow who captured General Thomas at the Battle of Atlanta?"

"I was, sir."

"Well, glad to meet you, then," Reagan said, shaking hands across the desk. "I don't have any time for small talk, as you saw. What can I do for you?"

"I'm running for the state legislature in Granbury County. My opponent is Lucius Roden, who is currently the county judge. About a week ago, I learned that Roden and his cronies have formed an official county committee of the States' Rights Party in Waco and have tied their campaigns to its organization."

Reagan growled. "SRP bastards," he said. He tapped the cigar into his ashtray. "Waco is a sizable town with lots of votes. I wouldn't like to see Beauregard and Toombs have an uncontested grab at them."

"That's why I'm here," McFadden said.

"You're willing to throw in your lot with the Breckinridge campaign?"

"I am," he said. "And not just because Roden has aligned himself with the SRP. I like Breckinridge. First vote I ever cast was for him in the 1860 election. Seems like a man of common sense, if you ask me. Done a good job as a general and as Secretary of War. I like that. Never screams or shouts or foams at the mouth like so many other politicians. Seems like exactly the kind of man one would want as president."

"Well, I agree with you. That's why I'm supporting Breckinridge myself. I've worked with him a long time. He's a good man. And I can tell you, that Creole bastard Beauregard and all the other bastards who are supporting him are as big a bunch of devils as you'll ever meet. That's why I've come home, to do everything I can to make sure Texas goes for Breckinridge in November."

"Well, perhaps you and I can help each other, then. Like I said, I'm running for the state legislature. My friend James Collett, who served as a major of the 7th Texas, is running for county judge and we're basically a single campaign. Now, since Roden has joined the SRP, every vote cast for him is likely to be a vote cast for Beauregard, too."

"Yes, and every vote cast for you is just as likely to be a vote cast for Breckinridge. I understand. But what did you come here to ask me for?"

"Well, we need help. We've never run a political campaign before. We're having to learn as we go." He paused a moment before getting to the rub. "And to be perfectly frank, we need money."

Reagan grunted. "You're probably the hundredth person to come into this office today to ask for money." He sighed, then took a long pull on his cigar. He sat back in his chair and said nothing for nearly a full minute. McFadden felt uneasy and was relieved when he finally spoke again. "Tell you what, McFadden. First of all, I want you to write me at least once a week. More often if you think it a good idea. I've run lots of campaigns in Texas and I can tell you what you're doing right and what you're doing wrong. And I want to know everything, and I mean everything, that this Roden fellow is doing. It's just like war, you see. A general needs to know what the enemy is doing, and I'm the general here in Texas as far as the Breckinridge campaign is concerned."

"I understand, sir."

"As far as the money is concerned, I'll do what I can but I can't promise anything. There's only so much to go around and we need to put it where it can make the most difference."

"That's pretty much what I expected, sir. But we are in desperate need. Roden and his friends have a lot of money and they're lining the streets of Waco with posters, sending out letters, and even paying people to go around canvassing votes. We have some people who care enough to be doing this for free, but they have to work and don't have much time. Money would be a great help."

"Like I said, I'll do what I can. Now, in exchange for all this, are you and your friends ready to officially endorse Breckinridge? Form a local committee on his behalf up in Granbury County."

McFadden nodded. "We talked about it before I left to come down here. The deal was that if you promised to help us, we'd help you."

"Well, then, let's shake on it and consider the committee created." He extended his hand across the desk and McFadden firmly grasped it. "Anything else?"

McFadden frowned. "I'm worried about the possibility of violence, to be honest. Roden and his people aren't going to take opposition lightly. And he has brought in a fellow named Rufus Walker who has followed me and made threats. And Walker seems to have a posse of Mexican gunmen working for him."

"Mexican gunmen?" Reagan asked.

"Walker told me that he had been down in Mexico, though he didn't say what he was doing down there. I assume it had something to do with the war."

"If that's the case, these men of his might be mercenaries. Roden's bringing in some enforcers to help him keep control of the county. Mexico is in chaos these days, what with the war between the French-backed government and the republican partisans. Lots of fighting men streaming out of Mexico, looking for employment." He mused for a moment. "The War Department has a man down there. Patrick Cleburne. Well, you must have served under him, if you fought in Granbury's Brigade. Yes?"

"I did," McFadden replied instantly. At the sound of Cleburne's name, memories stirred in him. He remembered seeing the fierce Irishman riding his horse back and forth behind the lines in battle after battle, leading charges against the enemy position, disdaining to seek shelter. He remembered when Cleburne had personally brought word to him of his battlefield promotion from sergeant to lieutenant immediately after the Battle of Atlanta. Weeks later, McFadden had brought warning to Cleburne of the enemy advance on Atlanta. He recalled standing side-by-side with Cleburne in the middle of the night, saying a prayer over the body of his beloved aide-de-camp who had been slain before their eyes. More than anything else, he remembered the fateful meeting at which Cleburne had given him the assignment of infiltrating behind the enemy lines with an explosive device, which led to McFadden's successful destruction of the ammunition train of the Union army.

"Well, if this fellow Walker was down in Mexico, we might ask Cleburne if he has heard of him. If you write out a message, I can forward it to the War Department and they can send it on to Cleburne. I can include a message of introduction, so that he'll know who you are."

McFadden chuckled. "He'll remember me. Don't worry about that."

Breckinridge could sense the tiredness and restlessness in his colleagues, the urgency they all felt to be on their way. The Cabinet meeting, as usual, had taken up most of the morning and a large part of the afternoon. They had discussed an enormous number of issues, some of which Breckinridge considered important and some which he thought trivial. Considering the urgent need for action on so many different fronts, it irritated Breckinridge that Davis was willing to waste hours of precious time talking about immaterial matters.

Trenholm had started the meeting by providing a general summary of the central government's fiscal outlook. It was actually somewhat better than it had been at the beginning of the year, which surprised Breckinridge. The Secretary of the Treasury attributed this to investors buying more Confederate bonds on the European markets in the expectation that British and French bankers would renegotiate the interest rates on already existing Confederate debt. The bond markets craved stability over all else, Trenholm explained.

Benjamin brought the rest of the Cabinet up to date on the latest developments in the Fenian Crisis. Since the battle on the Canadian frontier two months before, in which Breckinridge's friend Garnet Wolseley had so distinguished himself, tensions had continued to rise between England and the United States. The McClellan administration was refusing to crack down on the Fenian Brotherhood and still claiming that there was no official connection between the organization and the federal government. The United States was sending additional troops to reinforce those already deployed along its northern border, while more British troops were arriving in Canada every day. As far as Breckinridge could see, everything was pointing to a grand battle somewhere along the border between Canada and the United States the moment war was declared.

"Are we done?" asked Stephen Mallory, the Secretary of the Navy, in a voice that revealed just how tired he was.

"One more item on the agenda," Davis said without joy. "I understand from Secretary Breckinridge that General Morgan is requesting instructions regarding what to do with the prisoners he has captured."

"That's right," Breckinridge said. "He has sent me three telegrams asking for guidance on the question, each more pressing than the last."

"I don't understand why this is a question," remarked Attorney General Harris. "These are armed blacks in rebellion against us. Morgan should simply hang them from the nearest tree. Set a good example for the rest of the darkies."

"It's not so simple," Breckinridge replied. "For one thing, if Saul and those insurgents he still has under arms hear about the executions, it will embitter them to further resistance. It would eliminate any hope of making a deal for them to surrender in exchange for their lives."

Harris scoffed. "I don't think any such deal would be proper, anyway. We're talking about rebellious slaves. They should simply be disposed of." He frowned broadly before continuing. "I'm frankly rather surprised that Morgan has not dealt with this little insurrection long before now."

"He's fighting against a capable opponent in terrain almost tailor-made for partisan warfare. He has done as well as anybody else and I think it's fair to say than he's done better than most others could have done in his place."

"Capable opponent?" Harris asked. From his tone, it was clear to Breckinridge that Harris was taking issue with what he perceived as words that expressed admiration towards a black.

Davis broke in. "Let's stay on task, gentlemen."

"There are other concerns," Benjamin said quickly. "For one thing, at least a large number of these captured blacks are escaped slaves, meaning that they are the private property of someone. I believe we have already begun efforts to track down the individuals who own these slaves. Also, Saul's little rebellion has largely vanished from the headlines on account of the Fenian troubles. That's a good thing, because I don't want the good people in London and Paris thinking about our peculiar institution while we are trying to make important deals with them. A mass execution would put the story back into the minds of the public, hurting us in the eyes of British and French public opinion just when diplomatic events have been moving in our direction."

"Yes, that's the clincher for me," Davis said urgently. "Nothing must be done to jeopardize our current diplomatic efforts with the Europeans." He thought for a moment, coming to a decision. "Tell Morgan to keep those slaves cooped up. We'll deal with them later."

"I will, Mr. President," Breckinridge said. He stole a quick glance at Harris, who simply shrugged his shoulders.

Davis sighed deeply. "Was there anything else?" The president looked around the table and saw everyone shaking their heads. "Very well. This meeting is adjourned. Good day, gentlemen."

With evident relief, the Cabinet members rose from their chairs and walked towards the door. Davis tiredly motioned with his hand for Breckinridge to remain sitting, which didn't surprise the Secretary of War. Once the others had filed out of the room, Davis looked across the desk.

"Who is this man again?" the president asked.

"His name is Garnet Wolseley. He's a Lieutenant Colonel in the British Army. The letter he sent me states that he has come to Richmond to deliver a confidential message from Her Majesty's Government."

"And this Wolseley is a friend of yours, yes?"

"Yes. He and I met in Toronto during the peace negotiations two years ago."

"You trust him?"

"I do. He is a man of honor."

"He's not one of those Darwinian freethinkers, is he?" Davis asked.

"Oh, not in the slightest."

"A man of God, then?"

Breckinridge thought for a moment. "I think that Wolseley's faith in God is only tempered by his suspicion that he is God."

"Very well," Davis said tiredly, not having the energy or inclination to laugh at Breckinridge's joke. The president sighed again. "Mr. Harrison!" he called.

The door opened an instant later and Burton Harrison, the president's private secretary, stepped in. "Yes, Mr. President?"

"Could you send in Colonel Wolseley?"

"Right away, sir." Harrison vanished out the door.

Breckinridge felt a certain tug of uneasiness. He knew Wolseley well. During the heady days of the Toronto Peace Conference, the two of them had spent many hours talking over whiskey at the bar of the Rossin House Hotel. They had visited the battlefield at Quebec during a break in the conference. A year afterwards, he had taken Wolseley on a tour of the battlefields in the northern Shenandoah Valley. Moreover, they had exchanged dozens of letters. Breckinridge was a man who made and kept friends easily and he liked Garnet Wolseley.

However, Breckinridge was unsure how Davis and Wolseley would react to one another. Both were men who were convinced that they had never met their superior and probably questioned whether they had ever met their equal. This flaw in their temperaments was made worse by the fact that they were both genuinely gifted and intelligent men. When two men of such personalities encountered one another, there were bound to be fireworks.

Less than a minute later, the door opened again and Colonel Wolseley stepped into the office. He was wearing the pristine red uniform of an officer in Her Majesty's Perthshire Light Infantry and standing so ramrod straight that Breckinridge was reminded of a wooden board. Breckinridge stood and extended his hand. The presence of the president precluded Wolseley from smiling, but his eyes sparkled with familiar friendship.

"Welcome to Richmond, Colonel Wolseley," said Breckinridge.

"Thank you."

Breckinridge gestured to Davis, who was rising from his chair. "Allow me to introduce President Jefferson Davis. Mr. President, may I present my friend, Lieutenant Colonel Garnet Wolseley of the British Army."

"A pleasure, Colonel," Davis said as he shook Wolseley's hand. "Please take a seat."

All three men sat down, though Wolseley remained bolt upright in such a way that his back never seemed to touch the chair. There was a long and awkward silence. Breckinridge watched as Davis and Wolseley sized up one another.

"So," Davis finally began. "Mr. Breckinridge tells me that you have come to deliver a message from the British government."

"That is correct, Mr. President. I was given the assignment by the Governor-General, the Viscount Monck, who in turn received it directly from Prime Minister Disraeli. They asked that I deliver the message in person, without anything written down."

"Yes, but why?" Davis asked. "I have already met with your Minister Elliot more than once about this Fenian business. He has communicated your government's request that we enter into an alliance in the event of war between the United States and England."

"Her Majesty's Government desire to communicate something to you through confidential and unofficial channels. Specifically, they wish for me to present to you an offer the nature of which must be hidden from public view."

"Is that so?" Davis said, his eyes coming alive for the first time in the conversation. "Minister Elliot has told me that if war should break out, and the Confederacy forms an alliance with the United Kingdom, that Her Majesty's Government would pledge not to agree to any peace without the consent of the Confederacy, shall employ the Royal Navy to protect the Confederate coast, and shall provide financial assistance to our government. What additional communications do you have to make?"

"Only this, Mr. President." Wolseley paused a moment for dramatic effect. "That if war should come, Her Majesty's Government will look with favor on any Confederate attempt to detach Kentucky from the Union and bring it into the Confederate States."

Breckinridge's eyes went up and he felt his heartbeat increase its tempo. Before the war, Breckinridge's loyalty to his home state had been the paramount allegiance of his political life. It had been a grievous disappointment to him that so many of his fellow Kentuckians had not followed his example and joined the Confederate cause, though he remained convinced that the majority would have done so but for the Union military occupation. At the Toronto Peace Conference, giving up the idea of a popular referendum that might have allowed Kentucky to join the Confederacy had been one of the greatest disappointments of his life.

If what Wolseley was saying was true, however, perhaps Kentucky might still have a future within the Confederacy. Assuming war did break out, much of the military strength of the United States would be focused along the Canadian frontier. If the Confederacy allied with Britain, having had two years to recover its strength since the end of the last war, it might be able to put an army into the field strong enough to advance north from Tennessee and seize control of Kentucky. Breckinridge had no doubt that many, perhaps most, Kentuckians would welcome the Confederate army as liberators.

For just a moment, Breckinridge imagined being able to again make his home in Lexington, to encounter old friends from his childhood on the streets walking to and from work, to drink good Kentucky bourbon a few miles from where it had been created. He relished the thought of breathing in fresh Kentucky air and feeling good Kentucky grass beneath his feet.

The rational part of his mind reasserted itself and Breckinridge rebuked himself for having such selfish and foolish thoughts. Having seen war for himself, he had no desire to see it again. In a flash, visions of the fields of dead and mangled men at Shiloh, Murfreesboro, Chickamauga, and Cold Harbor shot through his mind's eye. No matter how much he wanted Kentucky to be brought into the Confederacy, he could never countenance any policy that might risk another conflict with the United States. His role in the government was to ready the South to defend itself, so as to deter the North from launching another war. He always prayed earnestly that such a war never come.

All these thoughts passed through Breckinridge's mind in a moment. He refocused his attention onto President Davis, whose face revealed a surprise as strong as Breckinridge's own. Wolseley simply sat motionless, like a man carved out of wood, waiting for the two Confederates to respond.

Davis spoke first. "How can we be confident that this pledge will be honored by your superiors in London?"

Wolseley nodded towards Breckinridge. "My superiors sent me because they are aware of a personal friendship that exists between Mr. Breckinridge and myself. He can vouch for my reliability."

Davis turned to Breckinridge. "Mr. Secretary?"

"If Colonel Wolseley says that he speaks with the authority of the British government, I think we can take him at his word."

Breckinridge said these words automatically, but he had already sensed something strange in Wolseley's tone. He couldn't quite place it, but he felt that his friend was not being entirely forthcoming. There was something behind Wolseley's words that remained murky and mysterious.

Davis remained silent for some time, rubbing his chin and obviously deep in thought, all the while staring intently at Wolseley. The British officer looked back at the president impassively. For a moment, Breckinridge was reminded of the classic logical paradox of the irresistible force and the immobile object.

"Are you going to be long in Richmond, Colonel?" Davis asked.

"No, Mr. President," Wolseley quickly replied. "I have come to deliver my message. Having done so, I intend to return to Canada as quickly as possible, as I expect to be given an important command among the forces being assembled to resist the coming enemy invasion."

"I see," Davis said. "Well, I do appreciate your willingness to wait for so long before seeing me and I do apologize that our interview has been so brief."

"I am not offended, Mr. President. I have done what I came here to do and I am sure you will think carefully on what I have said."

"I will. Mr. Secretary, you might as well walk your friend out, as we are finished here."

"Thank you, Mr. President," Breckinridge said.

"I thank you and wish you a good day, Colonel Wolseley."

Wolseley nodded. "Thank you for your time, Mr. President."

Breckinridge and Wolseley rose from their chairs and exchanged handshakes with Davis, then turned towards the door. Moments later, they were in the hallway headed towards the stairs that led to the building's lobby.

"It is good to see you again, John," Wolseley said, now freed from the formality that the meeting with Davis had imposed.

"And you, Garnet," Breckinridge replied. "I am sorry that you have come so far for the sake of a five minute interview."

Wolseley grinned. "It was an interesting trip. I was nearly torn to pieces by a Fenian mob in New York City."

"Were you?"

"Indeed. Interestingly enough, it was none other than George Thomas who saved me from the rabble."

"Thomas?" Breckinridge asked, incredulous. "The Union general?"

"The very one."

"How astonishing!" Breckinridge said. "I am not sure if I ever told you, but it was Thomas who broke my line on Missionary Ridge back in '63."

Wolseley smiled. "I'm sure it was simply bad luck."

"Perhaps I can share the details with you over a drink?"

By this time they had descended the stairs into the lobby. As they talked, they stepped through the front door and out onto Main Street, directly across from Capitol Square. Not many people were out on the streets, for the pleasant spring weather of the past few months had been decisively replaced by the oppressive heat of the Virginia summer. Most people Breckinridge saw on the sidewalks were moving quickly, anxious to be indoors again as quickly as possible.

"I am staying at the Spottswood Hotel," Wolseley replied. "I am told that they have one of the finest restaurants and bars in the city."

"It is true."

"Then perhaps you could join me there tomorrow evening, after you have finished your work? I shall be departing the following morning."

Breckinridge smiled. "Count on it, my friend."

July 23, Morning
St. Martin Parish, Southern Louisiana

Rain had awoken Lowell long before he would have liked. The storm had started at three o'clock in the morning and had not stopped. Their tent was not of the same quality as those in which Lowell had camped during his army days and there was a good deal of seepage. Already thoroughly soaked, he had emerged from the tent, not refreshed by much sleep but still ready to face whatever the day brought.

It was the fifth morning he had awoken in the same camp site. Thus far, there had been no sign of Saul. The previous day, during the later afternoon, Lowell had thought he had seen a dark figure in the distance observe them for a few moments before scurrying away, but in retrospect it had probably been an animal. Lowell was not yet becoming discouraged, though he had begun to ask himself whether his hope was genuine or a forced effort of will.

The storm had eventually abated, though the drizzle continued. As the sun rose, the cloudy skies above took on a bland grayness, made more so by being filtered through the thick blanket of trees. Gardet had assured Lowell that they were camping in the correct place, though it did not seem like much of a campsite. The Massachusetts man wondered if Gardet truly knew where they were. Still, there was no choice but to trust him.

Lowell began a fire in order to make coffee. Before the war, he would not have had the slightest clue how to get a good fire going on a rainy day, but years spent as a cavalry officer had taught him a great many things. He also knew that there was nothing a man desired more on an early morning than a strong cup of coffee and no mere force of nature was going to deny him what he wanted.

The campsite was in a completely nondescript area of the woods several hundred yards off the nearest road. The distance was such that a person on the road would not be able to see the tiny clearing due to the foliage. Lowell and Gardet might as well have been two mice in the midst of a vast wilderness.

Six days earlier, they had arrived at the campsite. Lowell, Naismith, Gardet, and the young boy had endured several hours of back-breaking labor to move the ammunition boxes into the concealed area. They were not too heavy, but there were many of them. They would have preferred to rest for some time after completing this task, but they still had the even more arduous task of moving the rifle crates. Each box contained twenty rifles and were much heavier than the ammunition boxes, requiring two men to move each crate using rope handles on their ends. The crates containing the other supplies were fewer and were much lighter and easier to move. A few crates contained shoes and one was full of cooking utensils.

Gardet had complained of being tired throughout the work. This had not surprised Lowell, for the wine merchant was not a physically imposing man and clearly not used to this sort of labor. Lowell had prodded him to keep working by constantly reminding him what would happen if a random militia patrol or some of Morgan's cavalry happened to trot by while they were doing the work. They had worked as though their lives depended on it, which they did.

All that had been several days before. Naismith and the boy had hurriedly taken the wagons and headed back towards New Orleans. Fatigued beyond anything he had experienced since the war, Lowell had slept soundly that night in the tent Gardet had brought. The next day, they had covered the crates with rubber blankets to protect them from moisture and the near-certain rain. They had also piled shrubs and dirt on top of them to better conceal them from prying eyes.

Then had begun the long days of waiting. Lowell half-expected to be discovered at any moment. After all, theirs was a fool's errand if there ever was one. They were carrying an arsenal of weapons through a region infested with Confederate cavalry and militia patrols who were searching for any sign of Saul's partisans. By all rights, they should expect to be dangling from the end of a noose within a very short time.

There was no rational reason to expect their plan to work, yet somehow Lowell was certain that it would. He couldn't understand how he knew this, but he did. God would not have permitted him to come so far only to come to grief when he was so close to accomplishing his mission. God had to be watching over him, for he knew his cause was just. More importantly, he knew his wife and children were praying for his safety. That gave him a pronounced sense of safety, as if he were wearing a suit of magical armor.

The fire ignited and began to heat the water. He kept an eye on the flames for nearly twenty minutes until the water finally began to boil. He had already prepared the coffee and gratefully poured the boiling water through grounds into his pewter cup. He only wished he had some cream or sugar to go along with it.

Gardet emerged from the tent, drawn by the smell of the coffee. "How did you get that fire going in the rain?"

"Learned in the army," Lowell replied simply. "Want a cup of coffee?"

Gardet nodded. Lowell felt some sympathy for the colored man. His life had been utterly upended from the moment Lowell had walked into his wine store. Yet he had brought it on himself for having agreed to become Saul's clandestine agent in the first place. More importantly, he was only one of thousands of men who had risked their lives in the cause of abolition.

"Any sign of anyone?" Gardet asked.

"No," Lowell replied, thinking it a stupid question. Had there been any sign, Lowell obviously would have woken Gardet up instantly.

"Well, I guess we keep waiting, then."

"I guess so," Lowell replied. He was beginning to ask himself, however, how long they would wait if Saul failed to appear. Another day? Another week?

Each hour increased the chance of their being discovered by the Confederates. Yet having come so far, he could not simply abandon the enterprise. Lowell was already thinking ahead and had determined to bury the crates as well as they could if Saul did not arrive. He had had the foresight to bring along two shovels, though he knew that the work would be extremely difficult.

Hours passed. Lowell was left alone with his thoughts, for there was nothing else to do. He had brought along a copy of Milton's poems, but the rain meant that he would have had to go back into the tent to read them and he wanted to keep a lookout for any sign of Saul or roving Confederate patrols. He had little choice, therefore, but to sit on a tree stump as the rain drizzled down upon him. His hat at least kept his face reasonably dry, but he was still uncomfortable.

Lowell chided himself. Spending a few days out in the rain was nothing compared to what he had gone through during the war. Besides, he had survived the war without a scratch. Who was he to complain when so many good men had been killed, or horrifically wounded, or hauled off to a nightmarish prison camp like Andersonville? Who was he to complain when millions of black people remained enslaved on plantations across the Confederacy?

There was a faint rustling in the foliage at the edge of the tiny clearing. Lowell's eyes instantly focused on the spot. He thought at first that it was another wild animal or perhaps even simply a shifting of vegetation due to a sudden breeze, but for a fraction of a second he had a glimpse of a black face looking at him, before it withdrew like a ghost.

"Gardet!" Lowell whispered strongly.

The wine merchant had been sitting on a tree stump as well, lost in his own thoughts as the long hours of waiting passed. When he heard Lowell's exclamation, he turned to look in the direction Lowell indicated and rose to his feet.

There was movement there, Lowell could see. More than one person was approaching, but they were doing so stealthily. He began to sense more movement around the area. A memory from the war came back to him, that of a party of flankers moving around his position. He and Gardet were being surrounded.

Lowell held up his hands to show that he was unarmed and rose slowly from his tree stump. As he was a white man, Saul's men would probably regard him as an enemy. After all, Saul could not possibly know who he was or why he was there. He could only hope that the presence of Gardet beside him would give them pause before they opened fire.

Very slowly, almost like a snake, the first armed black man emerged into view. He had scarcely made a sound while he moved, earning Lowell's soldiery admiration. He glared at Lowell with fierce dark eyes and an angry expression.

"I'm a friend," Lowell said.

The man glanced halfway behind him and twitched his head forward as a signal to his comrades. On either side of him, two more men emerged from the underbrush and walked slowly forward. All of them were armed with Springfield rifles, though the metal parts of many of them appeared to be rusty. Lowell would have hesitated to fire a weapon in such a condition for fear of it bursting in his hands.

"Keep your hands up," said the first man, whom Lowell assumed to be the leader.

"I'm not armed," Lowell replied. He wondered if he was talking to Saul. Then he thought about how absurd it would be to have come so far and then be killed by the very people he had come to help.

Over the next minute, a dozen more men emerged from the tree line and proceeded to surround him. No one seemed concerned about Gardet, who stood off to one side as if he didn't exist. All the guns were trained on Lowell. He did not move a muscle, fearful that even the slightest twitch would bring a hail of gunfire.

His eyes moved from one face to another. The black men surrounding him looked dirty, lean, and worn, like old bits of leather that had been stretched and pounded to the point of falling apart. To Lowell, they almost appeared to be beasts rather than men, yet they carried themselves with a steely determination and pride.

One of the men, a bit shorter than the others, handed his rifle to the man next to him and stepped forward towards Lowell. His eyes sparkled with a ferocious intelligence and an almost unnatural confidence.

"Who are you?" the man demanded.

"I am Charles Russell Lowell," he answered, still holding up his hands.

"Your voice," the man said simply. "Yankee?"

"Yes. Late of the Union Army."

The man looked deeply into his eyes for an endless minute. Lowell could only guess at what he was thinking. However, every second that passed made Lowell more convinced that the man before him was Saul.

"Gardet?" the man said, then nodded towards Lowell.

"He's come to help," Gardet replied.

"Help? Help how?"

"He brought weapons and ammunition."

"Over there," Lowell said, pointing without moving his arm too quickly. "Have your men open the top crate there and bring you what they find."

The leader turned his head and looked and one of his men. "Do it," he said simply.

It took a few minutes. The man opening the crate motioned for two others to help him and they pried the lid up with their corroded bayonets. Lowell did not look at them while they worked, simply keeping his hands up and staring straight ahead at the leader of the band.

"Are you Saul?" Lowell asked.

"Be quiet," the man replied.

The three men finished wrenching open the crate and started shuffling around through the packing hay. Moments later, one of the men stepped forward and handed the leader a clean, well-oiled Springfield rifle. The leader took it in his hands and looked down at it. The grim expression left his face and his eyes widened as though he had just been handed a treasure of gold and silver.

"I brought two hundred of them," Lowell said. "All in prime condition. And I brought sixteen thousand rounds of ammunition for them, too."

"Sixteen thousand?" the leader asked in astonishment.

"He's telling the truth," Gardet said. "You can trust him, Saul."

"There are more rifles in this crate," one of the men said excitedly. "And there are a bunch more crates over here, boss!"

Lowell could sense a sudden shift in the mood of the men around him. The carefulness and severity that had characterized the black men when they first emerged from the trees was quickly being replaced by excitement and cheer. Smiles were breaking out on their faces and some of them were beginning to whisper animatedly to one another.

"Two hundred?" the leader asked. "Two hundred rifles, you say?"

"Yes."

He motioned for Lowell to put his hands down, which he did. The man then stepped forward and extended his hand.

"Lowell, you say?"

"Yes."

"I am Saul. And I thank you."

July 23, Evening
Spottswood Hotel, Richmond, Virginia

Wolseley was happy to be staying at the Spottswood Hotel, for he was told it was the finest establishment in the city and had a wonderful restaurant and bar. He and Breckinridge were already on their second bottle of Burgundy wine as they enjoyed a delightful dinner. The main course was Smithfield ham, which Breckinridge had told him was made from specially raised, peanut-fed hogs that came from near Hampton Roads. An array of roasted vegetables and sliced apples completed the meal.

Every table in the dining room was filled with well-dressed people, both guests of the hotel and affluent citizens of the city. Wolseley had noted several of the restaurant patrons looking at the two of them, which wasn't surprising given Breckinridge's candidacy for the presidency. Some of the men glared angrily in his direction, which likely meant that they were political opponents of his friend.

The conversation had been quite pleasant, as Wolseley had expected. As they ate, they recalled the many hours they had spent on the barstools of Toronto during the peace talks in 1865. They reminisced about when Breckinridge had taken him on a trip of the battlefields in the northern Shenandoah Valley the previous year. Wolseley regaled Breckinridge with the story of the epic fight against the Fenians on the banks of the St. Lawrence River, going to great lengths to describe the heroism of the Royal Welch Fusiliers and his own Canadian militiamen.

"And Mrs. Breckinridge is doing well?" he asked.

"Well enough, I suppose," Breckinridge responded. "I do have some concerns about her health, but I do not believe them to be serious. It is lovely to have had these two last years together in Richmond as a family. We saw little of one another during the war."

"Indeed," Wolseley replied. He thought for a moment of Louisa Erskine, the girl back in Dublin whom he called 'Loo' and hoped to marry one day. Matrimonial happiness was a desirable thing. After all, it made social occasions less awkward and it reduced the chance of being ensnared by some disreputable female on a distant foreign posting. In India, he had taken a Hindu girl as substitute wife for a time. It had proven more trouble than he had expected to discard her when the time had come to return to England. Had he had an actual wife, that complication might never have arisen.

Thoughts of marriage were distinctly secondary to him, of course. Garnet Wolseley was made for war and little else. He reminded himself of the ulterior motive he had for dining this evening with his friend Breckinridge. He had asked himself again if he had any moral compunctions about deceiving a man he liked and admired. Having weighed the pros and cons, he had concluded that he did not.

"How does Mrs. Breckinridge feel about the prospect of being the First Lady of the Confederacy?"

Breckinridge laughed. "She is quite apprehensive about it, in fact. She has told me that if women were allowed to vote, she would be sorely tempted to cast her ballot for Beauregard simply to keep me out of the presidency."

"And are things going well with your campaign?" Wolseley asked. He felt a slight trepidation, as he and Breckinridge generally avoided political subjects. Yet as his friend was a presidential candidate, the topic could hardly be ignored.

"Yes, I suppose so," Breckinridge replied.

"I hope you won't think it amiss of me when I tell you how excited I was to see in the Canadian papers that you had finally announced your candidacy. I've been following the story closely in the papers, as you might imagine. This Toombs fellow is quite a firebrand, don't you think?"

Breckinridge chuckled. "He is that."

"A nation-wide speaking tour? Is that common in America?"

"Not for a presidential or vice presidential candidate."

"I really don't understand these American elections," Wolseley said, letting his enthusiasm get the better of him. "Your Electoral College is an absurdity that could only have been dreamed up by a madman. The upper house of your legislature is chosen by men who were elected by the people, for God's sake! Who would have thought of such a thing? Can you imagine the members of the House of Lords being chosen in such a manner?"

Breckinridge laughed. "No. No, I can't."

"And a president as both head of state and chief executive? Quite insane, I say. Really, you must agree with me. But then, democracy is insane no matter where we find it. Ordinary people cannot be trusted to make proper decisions for themselves."

Breckinridge grunted a response. It was clear to Wolseley that he disagreed but was too polite to say so. The Kentuckian finally replied. "I own that I find the whole business distracting. It is very difficult to strike a proper balance between my duties as Secretary of War and my new role as a presidential candidate."

"Are you considering resigning?" Wolseley asked.

"Yes, in fact," Breckinridge said quickly. "It seems that we are finally dealing with Saul's rebellion. I need to focus entirely on the presidential campaign. If I win the upcoming election, I will obviously be president. If I lose, Beauregard will place his own men in the Cabinet. My days as Secretary of War are soon to be over, no matter what happens."

Wolseley grunted. "But what if war breaks out with the United States at some point in the next few months? Won't Davis need you to remain in your current post?"

"I pray God that this will not be the case," Breckinridge replied. "Too many good men died in the last war. I fervently hoped that I never have to see another."

Wolseley frowned. He had never understood such talk and was alarmed to hear it coming from Breckinridge. If he was to achieve his goal of persuading the Confederate government to ally itself with Britain, he had to push his friend in the right direction.

"What about Kentucky?" Wolseley asked.

Breckinridge pursed his lips and nodded slowly. "I will admit that what you said about my home state caused my heart to leap. I dream of returning to my home in Lexington, where are all my friends and the dearest recollections of my youth. The course I have taken by choosing the side of the Confederacy has made that impossible. I shall die an exile from my own land."

Wolseley nodded, hoping his face didn't betray his thoughts. He had been given no authority whatsoever to say to President Davis what he had said about Kentucky. There was no commitment on the part of the British government to help the Confederacy gain control of the state. Yet by pretending that such a commitment existed, Wolseley felt it more likely that the South would agree to Britain's offer, which in turn would make a way more likely. And war was what Wolseley desired above all other things. That he had told an outright lie and greatly exceeded his authority didn't unduly trouble him.

"But if this war does indeed take place and our two nations triumph together, you can return to Lexington at the head of a liberating army," Wolseley said. "Kentucky shall be freed from the Yankees and brought to its proper place as a member of your Confederacy. All will be as you wish it."

"You're a soldier, Garnet. I'm a politician. If I'm to serve the people, I have to subordinate my own wishes to the general good. I would love nothing more than to return to Lexington and spend my remaining years at home. But not if the price was thousands of young men losing their lives."

Dessert was brought out in the form of a Chester pudding, which Wolseley liked. A Bordeaux blend of Semillon and sauvignon blanc was brought out to go with it. Wolseley was pleasantly intoxicated, yet not so much that he had lost his wits. He was not pleased to hear Breckinridge's words. It sounded as though Breckinridge would work hard to avoid war with the United States.

"The people of Kentucky chaff under the Yankee yoke," Wolseley said. "You've told me this yourself. Isn't it true that martial law is still in effect in some parts of the state, even though the war has been over for years?"

"It's true."

"You may have it in your power to set your state free, John."

"If war comes, it comes. My own wishes are irrelevant. I don't want war to come, but the army is ready. I have seen to that over the last few years. But whether we go to war will be a decision of the president and Congress, not me. I don't decide matters of policy. I am merely a servant of others."

Wolseley shook his head. "President Davis listens to you, doesn't he?"

Breckinridge shrugged. "More than most, I suppose. Not as much as Benjamin."

"But you're running for president. He has to take your views into greater account now."

"I suppose that's true, for what it's worth. But why are you pressing me so hard, Garnet? You communicated the message from your government to the president already. You and I are supposed to be sharing this meal together as friends."

Wolseley thought for a moment, then nodded. "I am sorry, my friend. I hope you are not offended." He took a bite of the Chester pudding.

"Not at all," Breckinridge replied, a relieved smile crossing his face. "I value your friendship, Garnet, but we do not always see eye to eye. We've both been through war, but I cannot help but see it as anything but a bloody blunder. I will do whatever I can to keep it from happening again. It's my duty."

"Of course," Wolseley said as he sipped on the Vouvray. "We each must do our duty, after all."

July 24, Night
McFadden Ranch, West of Waco, Texas

Yellowjacket responded to McFadden's commands only with an obvious snort of protest. Like his master, he was exhausted by long ride home from Austin. As the sun gradually slipped below the western horizon, familiar trees and rock formations became apparent and it was clear that they were almost home. It had taken him two days to make the trip and most of it had been through the searing heat of the Texas summer. He might have had made better time had he not had to stop frequently to obtain water for himself and his horse. That didn't matter now, though. He was home, and that was the important thing.

He reflected back on the fruits of his trip to Austin. He had made a commitment to join forces with the Breckinridge campaign. By so doing, he had hopefully gained a measure of financial support. He knew that he could turn to Reagan, an experienced political campaigner, for advice as he went forward with his effort to win the state legislative seat. All things considered, it had been a very successful trip.

On the other hand, he felt distinctly uneasy. He remembered how awkward he had felt listening to the conversations going on around him while he had waited for his turn to meet with Reagan. The lack of a university education stung now more than it ever had in the past. Compared to most men of his acquaintance, he was extremely well-read, but that would not make him an expert on railroads, or tariffs, or taxation, or any of the other complicated issues he would be expected to deal with if he was fortunate enough to win election to the state legislature.

Ironically, he had thought often about Abraham Lincoln during his long ride home. During the war, of course, he had heard nothing good about the man from his fellow Confederate soldiers. One thing he did learn, though, was that the President of the United States had achieved his position despite lacking a university education. The lanky man from Illinois had, by all accounts, educated himself through his own extensive reading. As paradoxical as it seemed, McFadden was beginning to take inspiration from the man who had been the enemy commander-in-chief.

Yellowjacket's clip-clopping continued as the ranch house came into sight. Wisps of smoke drifted out of the chimney, suggesting that Annie was cooking dinner. He tried to click Yellowjacket into a faster walk, but the animal snorted in refusal and continued plodding along slowly. He did not like being away from Annie and Thaddeus. Having now been separated from them for just over a week, he was anxious to see them.

He reined in by the stable, dismounted, and tied Yellowjacket to the pole near the water trough. Hurriedly, he removed the saddle and threw a single layer of water on the animal's back, and walked quickly up to the front door. Walking inside, he was greeted by the welcome sight of his wife over the cooking pot and his son playing on the floor.

"Papa!" Thaddeus shouted, running towards him in joy.

"Hello, son!" he said, picked Thaddeus up and spinning him around.

"I am very glad to see you, James," Annie said with a smile, walking forward to embrace him. "When the sun started going down, I was afraid that you might not return this evening and we would have to wait until tomorrow for you to come home."

"It would take more than the Texas heat to keep me from my family," he replied, setting Thaddeus down and ruffling his hair. "What's for dinner?"

They had a beef stew washed down with cider. As they ate, he asked anxiously about news of what had transpired while he had been away. Thaddeus was making progress on saying "please" when asking for something and "thank you" when he received whatever it was he wanted. The cattle were doing well and the hired hands had all done their jobs as McFadden had specified. Fellow veterans had come by several times a day to check on Annie and Thaddeus, as they had promised.

"Oh, this came for you yesterday," Annie said, retrieving a paper from the desk and handing it to McFadden. "From the telegraph office in town."

To James McFadden,

Very interested to receive your telegram. I have made inquiries and it seems Rufus Walker is a mercenary of a very disreputable character, who has commanded small units for the republican forces in Mexico's civil war. Suspected of murdering prisoners and other crimes. I am told that he vanished from Mexico a few months ago. If this is the same man you have encountered in Texas, I warn you to regard him a very dangerous enemy.

Wish you well. Many fond memories of friendship.

General Patrick Cleburne

McFadden digested these words with growing concern. Obviously, Judge Roden had been so spooked by the thought of losing control of Granbury County that he had brought Walker in as an enforcer. In the days before he had left for Austin, it had become clear that Walker had a posse of men with him, who were probably also veterans of the war in Mexico. There had, as yet, been no violence associated with the election campaign, but McFadden wondered how long that would continue. If Roden was willing to bring someone like Walker in to do his dirty work for him, it suggested that he wasn't about to be squeamish.

"You look troubled," Annie said, bouncing Thaddeus on her knee on the other side of the table. "Is there some sort of bad news?"

"I'm not sure," McFadden said. "Telegram is from Cleburne in Mexico. He says our friend Walker is a dangerous fellow."

"Well, from what you've told me, that was already obvious."

"Probably a murderer."

"Ah," she said simply. "I see." She paused for a few moments, thinking the implications through. "Do you think that this means Roden would be willing to have you killed to keep you from beating him in the election?"

"Maybe," he admitted. "He doesn't seem the kind of man to have any scruples."

"Wouldn't that be too obvious?"

"I would think so. But he might use Walker to try to intimidate us. He tried to do it himself a few months ago, when he came here. He suggested that I had a lot to lose, what with having a wife and child."

"I'm not afraid," Annie said, matter-of-factly. "He can try to intimidate me all he wants. I don't care."

"Well, there's Thaddeus to consider."

Annie drew her head back in surprise. "Surely you don't think he'd be willing to harm a small child?"

"One never knows with a man like Roden."

"No man could be so depraved. I don't care what some people say, but somewhere, deep down within everyone, there is a soul and a conscience."

McFadden wished he could agree with her, but he had seen far too much during the war to allow himself the luxury. He did not fear for his life for his own sake, but he knew that his family depended upon him. The thought of any harm coming to Annie or Thaddeus, moreover, was almost too much for him to bear. He was unwilling to bring violence into the equation, but Roden and Walker seemed likely to have other ideas. His friends would be willing to protect him, he knew, but he was not willing to ask them to risk their lives to help him win an election.

The doubts about his capacity to serve as a state legislator reared up in his mind again. What, after all, did he know about public policy? He had not really wanted to enter the race in the first place, but had been pushed into it by his friends, more as an expression of their own discontent than out of any real expectation that he might win. With Walker and his gang entered the scene, with his beloved family potentially in danger, he did not think that any of them would think less of him if he withdrew from the race.

"Maybe this isn't such a good idea," McFadden said simply.

Annie's eyes narrowed. "What isn't?"

"Running for this state legislative seat. Hell, running for any kind of public office. The whole idea. It's ridiculous when you think about it. I was a soldier and now I'm a rancher. I don't know anything about the state legislature. And now I'm worried that people are going to get hurt. It's just not worth it."

"You're thinking of withdrawing?" she asked.

McFadden thought that over. "Possibly. I don't want anyone to get hurt."

She said nothing for a long moment, staring at him across the table. "I need to put Thaddeus to bed," she finally said, rising from the table.

She carried the boy to the little cradle they had set up in the bedroom. He could hear her muttering soft and comforting words to him and smiled. Family was what he wanted, not political influence of any kind. He wouldn't have known what to do with it even if he won the election, which he almost certainly would not. Even with Reagan offering his advice, McFadden had no idea how to run a political campaign. Roden would use Walker and his men to bully and intimidate the voters into casting their ballots for him. Others he would simply buy off. Maybe the sensible thing to do was to withdraw from the race and go back to the simple business of running the ranch and raising his son.

Ten minutes passed and the soft protests of Thaddeus gradually faded. Annie returned to the main room and quietly closed the door. McFadden felt reassured. His wife had always supported him in his decisions. She was the pillar on which he leaned more than anything else. It would be a difficult decision, but she would help him see that it was the right thing to do.

Annie strode over to the table and, rather than sit back down, walked around to his side and forcefully smacked him in the face with her right hand. He cried out as much in surprise and in pain. He looked at her face and was stunned to see it curled into an angry and contemptuous scowl.

"There!" she said harshly. "You're about to ask me what I think. Well, there's what I think!"

"What the hell are you doing?" McFadden asked. "That hurt!"

"And I'll do it again if that's what it takes to knock some sense into you. How could you even think of getting out of the race? It's too late for that, James! That ship sailed a long time ago!"

He was so astounded that he could say nothing and simply stared up at her. Annie gruffly walked back around the table and sat back down.

"I have never, not once since I married you, seen a trace of fear in you, James," she said. "You weren't afraid when you jumped in that river to save me, three years ago. You weren't scared of the Yankees in all those battles, were you? I'm ashamed to see it now. You think I'm not scared? Whenever you go off to Waco to shake hands with voters and do whatever else you do, I stay here with Thaddeus. I make sure I know where the guns are, and make sure they're loaded, because I don't know if Roden's people might choose that day to come. And what would all your friends think? They'd see you as abandoning them, like the scared man who ran away from the firing line."

"I'm not scared for me," McFadden protested. "I'm scared for you and Thaddeus."

"Well, don't be!" she snapped. "I will take of myself and I'll take care of Thaddeus. You just go win this election. Besides, James, it's too late. Roden already has it in for you. If you withdraw from the race, he'll still want to take his revenge, because you've made him look bad. All those meetings you've had and all those pamphlets you've handed out. You think Roden is just going to forget all that? And if he does agree to leave us alone, that would put us in his debt forever, don't you see?"

McFadden listened to what she was saying, finding it hard to argue. He had never seen his wife speak so forcefully and was so surprised that he didn't know how to respond.

Annie went on. "You must realize that you've burned your bridges, James. You did the moment you turned in that paper to the courthouse declaring yourself a candidate. You have to win this election. If you withdraw your candidacy, our reputation will be ruined and we'll be at Roden's mercy. If you lose the election, you can bet that Roden will find some way to take away our ranch and run us out of the county. There's really only one option, James. You have to stay in the race and you have to win it."

He slowly nodded. "Yes, I suppose you're right."

"I am right." She paused. "So, go win. And don't ever show fear in front of me again."

July 25, Morning
Saul's Camp, St. Martin Parish, Southern Louisiana

As he gratefully sipped a cup of steaming coffee, Saul watched Lowell instruct some of the men on how to load and fire their rifles. He had worked at it all the previous day and all that morning. Saul had to admit that the Yankee officer knew what he was doing. Moreover, he could tell that Lowell greatly enjoyed the work. Some of the insurgents had never held a rifle before and were responding quickly.

None of the exercises had involved the actual firing of the weapons. For one thing, even with the huge influx in the number of cartridges, only about eighty rounds per rifle were available. Besides which, Morgan's cavalry was still looking for them and it wasn't impossible that some units were close enough to hear the sound of gunfire. Sentries had been posted a good distance out to make sure there was no enemy within a distance where they could hear them, but the crack of rifle shots would carry much farther than that.

Saul had noticed a sharp change in the morale of his men. After the treason of Silas and their defeat by Morgan, emotions among the partisan band had fallen to near despair. Meeting Lowell and Gardet and opening the crates full of weapons and ammunition had changed everything. It had been like giving a full meal to man who was starving. Every man in the unit was now armed with a rifle, which had never been the case before. Even if his numbers had been reduced from a few months before, he could now count on vastly increased firepower.

He watched as Lowell continued his training. The night before, Gardet had told him what he knew about the man. He had apparently been a cavalry officer during the war, rising to the rank of brigadier general. He had used the correct password when he arrived at Gardet's store and had said that he had been sent by Frederick Douglass and his other supporters. He had also told Gardet that the Lowell family were one of the wealthy, prominent New England clans that had long supported the abolition of slavery.

Some of the men were using the new cooking utensils to prepare the best dinner Saul had had in a very long time, for the men had caught a feral pig and

411

boiled it in one of the new pots. The food was restoring the strength of the men both physically and spiritually. The previous morning, Saul had enjoyed his first cup of coffee in many months.

Having absorbed the sudden change in his situation, Saul's mind was already turning over plans for the near future. There were a few options. Morgan, having perhaps grown overconfident, had spread his patrols out in order to sweep a vast area, imagining that they were hunting a small band of frightened and ill-armed men. That might have been true a few days before, but no longer. He might be able to lure one of these small units into an ambush and wipe it out. That would be a victory sure to send chills down the spines of the slaveholders.

Alternatively, he now had the force to launch another attack on a plantation, no matter how well guarded it might be. Resuming such raids even after his defeat at the hands of Morgan would also send a strong message to his enemies. It might also allow him to replenish his manpower and, thanks to Lowell, he would be able to arm many newly freed slaves with firearms.

Lowell, having come to the end of the instruction session, dismissed the men, who were soon eating the stew that had been prepared for them. He took a swig of water from his canteen and walked over to where Saul was sitting.

"May I join you?" he asked.

"By all means," Saul replied.

Lowell sat down. "I hope you're enjoying the coffee."

"Very much."

"I debated whether to bring it. After all, one less packet of coffee would have meant one more packet of flour."

"No, I'm glad you brought it. It has been a long time since I enjoyed a cup of coffee." He waited a moment before going on. "Once again, Lowell, I cannot thank you enough for what you've done here. You've been the answer to my prayers, I don't mind saying."

"You are far too kind," came the reply. Lowell looked at Saul with a quizzical eye. Neither of them spoke for some time, simply sitting in silence. The Massachusetts man poured himself a cup of coffee and sipped at it carefully. He looked up at the insurgent leader again.

"Who are you, Saul?" Lowell finally asked.

Saul leaned back and sighed. "You really want to know?"

"Yes."

"Why is it so important to you?"

Lowell thought for a moment. "I don't know," he finally admitted.

"I'm nobody."

"That's not true," Lowell protested. "Newspapers all over the world have talked about you. They speak your name in hushed tones at dinner parties in Boston and New York. You're famous all over the world, Saul."

"I'm not important."

"Tell me your story."

"There isn't a story, Lowell. I'm serious. What is it that you want to know? I was a slave on a Louisiana plantation. I escaped when the Yankees came close and was made a soldier in the Union army. When the war ended, I kept fighting. That's it. Really, that's it. I'm not any different from thousands of others."

"You speak better than the rest. Not like an ordinary slave."

412

Saul nodded in the direction of Ferguson. "You can thank Doctor Ferguson for that. He taught me to read and write. He taught me the right way to talk. Nothing like you, though. You probably went to one of those fancy schools that rich white folk send their children to."

Lowell didn't answer, which Saul took as an admission that he was correct. He could see the vast gulf that separated him from a man like Lowell. It was not that he did not appreciate the Boston man. But though a man like Lowell could work for the destruction of slavery, he could never really know what it was like to be a slave. He might read books about slavery, but he had never experienced a single moment of actually being enslaved.

Saul looked into Lowell's eyes and saw respect there. He had known many white officers during his days in the Union army. Some had been dismissive racists, scarcely any better than the Confederates against whom he had fought. Others had treated him kindly but condescendingly, as if he were no more than a child. Only a few had truly seen him as a man fully equal to themselves. Looking at Lowell, Saul could see that he was like the latter group.

"Did you have a wife or children, Saul?" Lowell asked.

"No."

"If you ever do, let me know. I'll see what I can do to get them a good education."

Saul shrugged. "If I had any children, I'd rather see them killing slaveholders than going to some fancy school."

Lowell slowly nodded, though Saul was not sure if the man had fully grasped how serious his comments had been. "What about the rest of your family?"

"Don't know who my father is," Saul said without sadness. "I was told that my mother was freed when the Yankees marched past her plantation, but I don't know where she is or what happened to her."

"Would you like me to try to find out?" Lowell asked. "When I get back to the United States, I mean. I have many contacts with the people who are helping the black refugees."

Saul shrugged. "You can if you like. My mother can take care of herself."

He thought again of the voodoo spell of protection his mother has cast on him the night he had told her he was leaving to join the Yankees. Ferguson might speak of it disdainfully, but Saul still believed in it. The magic had never failed. He wondered if perhaps the arrival of Lowell and his priceless weapons had also been conjured up by his mother's magic. She was still looking out for him, wherever she was.

"What did you do during the war?"

"Milliken's Bend was my first battle. Just a few weeks after I escaped from my master's plantation. Killed my first slaveholder there. First of many, in fact."

"How many?"

"Don't rightly know. Twenty at least. Half with my rifle. Other half with my knife. I prefer the knife. More personal when it's up close."

"I suppose," Lowell answered. "I'm not sure I personally killed anyone during the war. I fired my pistol at the enemy all the time, but could never tell if the shots struck home."

413

"That's the difference when you do it with a knife. I could feel the warm blood of the eneny spill out of his guts onto my hands. And I'll tell you what, Lowell. That feeling was the feeling of freedom. Freedom for me and my people. It's a joyful feeling."

Saul could see that Lowell was uncomfortable, yet he wanted to talk to the Massachusetts man. He felt released, that he could unburden himself to this man in a way that he could not do with any of his soldiers or even with Doctor Ferguson.

"After Milliken's Bend?" Lowell asked.

"They moved me from regiment to regiment. I was promoted to corporal and then to sergeant. There were dozens of skirmishes and little battles. They moved me to the 84th United States Colored Troops. I fought in the Red River Campaign and lots of other places."

"Small fights can be the worst fights. I know it."

"You commanded men during the war, yes?" Saul asked.

Lowell nodded. "I led a regiment of cavalry. A brigade, later on."

"So you know what it's like ordering men to kill people? Ordering men to do things that might get them killed?"

"It's war. Men die."

"You say that like it's a bad thing. It's not a bad thing. Killing slaveholders is a good thing. One day, the enslaved blacks of the South are going to carve out their own country, but it's not going to happen until a lot of people get killed. It just has to happen. It's like when doctors dig into a wound with a knife in order to get the bullet out. There's a lot of blood and the patient screams and screams. But it has to be done if the bullet is going to be taken out, yes?"

"That's a good analogy." Lowell paused for a moment. "What did you do when the war ended?

Saul sighed. "I remember the night we were in camp and we told that Lincoln had lost the election. Not all the men understood why the white officers were so upset, but I did. Then there was the ceasefire, but it didn't seem to matter too much where we were. There was still plenty of fighting. Lots of slaves tried hard to get into the Union lines and we kept launching raids to help them, even when the generals ordered us not to. Discipline was starting to break down all over, you see."

"And then?"

"After the treaty was signed, they told us that we were being sent to the United States. Some of the men went, but some of us said no. Lots of men had wives and families still in slavery and weren't going to leave them behind. Others, like me, just didn't want to stop fighting. And so, I told some of the men that if they wanted to stay, I would lead them."

"And they followed you?"

"I was a sergeant by then, like I said. Lots of the men looked to me as a leader. We took our rifles and as much ammunition as we could carry. Some of our white officers looked the other way and let us raid the regimental depots for supplies before we left. I think it was in September of 1865 when we marched out of our camp. The Confederates started attacking us right away. Ever seen a wolf tearing at a deer? That's what it was like. At first we tried to fight as an organized unit, just like we had been trained. Some of the other regiments did the same thing, and there were lots of fierce battles during that winter. But we didn't have any experienced officers with us. There's a big difference between being a sergeant and being a captain. It was all very confused. But by the spring, we had broken up into smaller units."

"I remember reading about it in the papers," Lowell said. "It was heartbreaking. I was in Virginia when the orders to withdraw came. Sometimes I wish I had had the courage you had. I wish I had stayed behind to fight."

"You have shown that courage by coming here," Saul said.

Lowell nodded, but said nothing.

"After that, we were just trying to survive. I gave orders to my group, which was now made up of men from lots of different regiments, not just the 84th, not to engage the enemy except in self-defense. We hunted and fished for our food, and sometimes stole food from farms and plantations. A long time passed. But after a while, I knew that we had to choose between either fleeing to the North or doing something to keep up the fight. And last winter, I made the decision that we would fight again, even if it meant we would be killed."

"And that's when the plantation raids started."

"Right. And you know the story after that, don't you?"

"I know it very well. But what will you do now?"

"We were about to give up, I think. Try to get to the U.S. Many of the men, anyway. But you've restored their faith with these beautiful weapons. The food won't last long, of course, but we can find more. We've gotten by on very little these past few years. As for exactly what we shall do, I don't know yet."

"I think I should tell you, Saul, just how much what you have done has meant to people," Lowell said with great earnestness. "When your raids first started, people talked of little else in Boston. It proved that the fire of resistance and the desire to be free still burned in the hearts of the slaves, no matter that we had lost the war. It has ignited a fire in the minds of the Northern people, I don't mind telling you."

"All of them?" Saul asked skeptically.

Lowell paused before replying. "No, not all," he admitted. "But many."

"Not sure it will matter. But Gardet told me yesterday that a war between the United States and England might break out soon. If that's true, I doubt any help will come from the North. It will be too distracted."

Lowell nodded. "President McClellan is using the possibility of war to distract people from the slavery issue. He has not said one word about your rebellion, even when it has been on the front pages of the newspapers. He doesn't want people to remember that he and his Democrats were the ones who gave up on the war and left the slaves of the South in chains."

Saul thought for a long moment and an idea began to germinate in his mind. "Well, maybe I'll have to do something that he won't be able to ignore."

Lowell smiled. "I have something you might like to see. Something that might help with what you're talking about."

"What's that?"

Lowell opened his knapsack and pulled out a few pieces of paper. "This is a copy of the constitution John Brown wrote back in the 1850s. What he intended to be the government of the area of the South he set free from the slaveholders."

Saul was struck by an intense curiosity. He took the papers and read through the first few lines.

Whereas slavery, through its entire existence in the United States, is none other than a most barbarous, unprovoked, and unjustifiable war of one portion of its citizens upon another portion – the only condition of which are perpetual imprisonment and hopeless servitude or absolute extermination – in utter disregard and violation of those eternal and self-evident truths set forth in our Declaration of Independence:

Therefore, we, citizens of the United States, and the oppressed people who, by a recent decision of the Supreme Court, are declared to have no rights which the white man is bound to respect, together with all other people degraded by the laws therefore, for the time being, do ordain and establish for ourselves the following Provisional Constitution and Ordinances, the better to protect our persons, property, lives, and liberties, and to govern our actions.

Saul was fascinated. He knew all about John Brown. Rumors of the man had filtered through to his plantation even before the war had begun. In fact, Saul wondered if he might have had the courage to run away had he not heard of Brown. Ferguson had told him about Brown in great detail and Saul had also read as much as he could find on the man's life.

Captivated by intense curiosity, Saul quickly went through the rest of Brown's draft constitution, occasionally asking Lowell clarifying questions but otherwise remaining silent. The document asserted that all "proscribed persons" or members of the "enslaved races of the United States" could participate the provisional government and called for the choosing of people to serve as president, vice president, Secretary of War, and Secretary of State, as well as to serve in a legislative assembly and as judges. This seemed outlandish, but Saul was so enthralled that he overlooked this and went on.

The heart of the document were the provisions clearly designed for carrying on a war for the abolition of slavery. There was discussion of how to use captured property and how to deal with prisoners, a requirement that slaveholders who voluntarily gave up their slaves should not be molested, for putting to death deserters and anyone guilty of rape, and various other items. Clearly, Brown had written the document not as a genuine constitution for any kind of new state, but as the governing charter of a military organization that would continue to wage war until slavery is destroyed.

Saul looked at Lowell. "This is widely known?"

"Yes," Lowell answered. "It was published in 1859, at the time of Brown's raid on Harper's Ferry. It was also submitted as evidence at his treason trial."

Saul nodded. "This is what I needed. May I keep it?"

"Of course. I brought it for you."

"I thank you for this almost as much as for the guns."

"Whatever you're planning on doing, I want to help."

"You've already risked your life by bringing the guns to me."

"I will bring you more," Lowell said earnestly. "If I got these to you once, I can do it again. If you can free more men from slavery, perhaps I can bring you the rifles with which to arm them."

"It would take a long time for you to go all the way back to New England, get more guns, and bring them down here again."

"Yes, but now I know it can be done."

"The enemy will be much more watchful," Saul warned. "They will know what you have done. Even your chances of escaping back from Louisiana are not be all that good."

"Perhaps," Lowell said. "But I have to try. It's certainly a smaller risk than you are running."

"All I can say to you, Lowell, is that with the weapons and ammunition you have brought us, we can launch our revolt all over again." He thought for a moment before continuing. "In fact, I don't think it will be a revolt. It will be a revolution."

Lowell looked at him deeply, then stood up. He pulled the pistol from its holster and handed it over to Saul. "Take this. It's my LeMat revolver. It was given to me by my brother-in-law, Robert Gould Shaw."

Saul's eyes narrowed. "Name sounds familiar."

Lowell nodded. "He commanded the 54th Massachusetts Infantry. Killed at Fort Wagner."

The name of the unit was a talisman to Saul. "The 54th," he said quietly. "The first of us." He took the revolver from Lowell's hand, feeling as though he were being given a magical weapon. He considered it very carefully, turning it over to examine it. "I thank you for this gift. Rest assured, many slaveholders will be killed by it."

Lowell smiled. "That is why I am giving it to you."

July 27, Afternoon
Mobile, Alabama

It was far too hot and humid for Toombs's taste. He wiped his sleeve across his forehead to rid it of a layer of sweat and took a long swig from the glass of water one of the organizers had thoughtfully put on the podium for him. The uncomfortable temperature was made all the worse by the fact that he had been speaking at the top of his lungs for more than half an hour, haranguing a crowd that he thought numbered between three and four thousand. Yet heat and humidity were as much a part of the South as mint juleps, so there was little use complaining.

Toombs was in a good mood. He was delighted with the work that the local States' Rights Party committee had done in Mobile. The speaking platform had been erected with only a few days' notice and the park had been cleaned and roped off for the crowd with great efficiency. The city was a center of cotton export to the markets of Europe and did not look kindly upon the export duties imposed by the national government in Richmond. It would not take much to ensure that the city's voters came out in droves for Beauregard on November 5.

He had been introduced by Captain Raphael Semmes, the legendary commander of the *CSS Alabama*, who was both an SRP supporter and the most popular citizen of Mobile. The crowd was cheering, the faces beaming with smiles of approval. Toombs took heart from that, just as he had from the audience in the Exchange Hotel ballroom at Montgomery a few weeks before.

Some were holding up placard signs demonstrating support for Beauregard or opposition to Davis or Breckinridge.

Thus far, he had been giving his standard stump speech. He had reminded his listeners of how the Davis administration had imposed conscription and ruinous taxes upon the people during the war, how it had suspended habeas corpus and confiscated crops and livestock without paying for it. He had reminded the audience how the Davis administration had pursued a flawed military strategy that led to the disasters of 1863, and how it had only been the brilliance of General Joseph Johnston which had saved the Confederate cause.

"And we all know that Davis hated Johnston, don't we?" Toombs asked scornfully. The crowd jeered in apparent agreement. "Never listened to him. Denied him support. Denied him reinforcements. We can only thank God that Johnston had the brains and his men had the bravery to win the Battle of Atlanta. Just remember that they did it without any help from the Davis administration!"

The crowd cheered again. Toombs thought of digressing a bit and bringing up the rumors that Davis had been on the verge of replacing Johnston in the days before the general launched his famous surprise attack. If he spoke about it correctly, it could further cement the idea in the minds of his listeners that Davis was at best a fool and at worst a criminal. After a few seconds of contemplation, however, Toombs decided against it. In most of the speeches he had given in recent years, Davis had been the sole target of his vitriol. Now, however, he had to learn to direct his fire towards a new target.

"And who was by Davis's side when all this was going on?" Toombs asked rhetorically. "Who said nothing while Davis pushed conscription and confiscation? Who is sitting in Richmond right now, working to make the high taxes and high tariffs even higher? Who is sitting in Mechanic's Hall right now, saying that good Alabama boys like your own husbands, brothers, and sons should obey the orders of Richmond rather than the orders of your own state of Alabama? You know who I'm talking about, don't you? I'm talking about John Breckinridge."

There was a chorus of booing and jeering from the crowd and Toombs felt a jolt of energy. Now that the campaign was properly underway, and Breckinridge was the declared opponent of the SRP, he had fine-tuned the stump speech he routinely gave. It had to be less of an attack on Davis and more of an attack on Breckinridge. He had spent long hours going over with Stephens and others exactly how he would attack Breckinridge. This, the first big speech of his national speaking campaign, would be the opening salvo in the effort to tear the Secretary of War down, destroy his reputation, and ruin his chances for the presidency.

Toombs's first target would be Breckinridge's alleged reluctance to join the Confederate cause.

"Breckinridge may claim that he wants to be the President of the Confederate States, yet his record proves that he never wanted the Confederacy to exist in the first place! He opposed secession, when men of true principles knew that we had to leave the Union if our rights were to be protected. When our soldiers were fighting and dying at Manassas and Wilson's Creek, what was Breckinridge doing? Why, he was still sitting in the United States Senate, twiddling his thumbs, and even having dinner with Abe Lincoln in the White House!"

Toombs had always found it inexplicable that Breckinridge had remained on friendly terms with Lincoln. To Toombs, a man's politics was representative of the man's character. He could no more imagine socializing with a Yankee abolitionist than socializing with Satan himself. In Toombs's mind, if a man's politics were unacceptable, the man was unacceptable. There were no two ways about it.

He continued. "Breckinridge's supporters say he was a great general. A great general? How do you then explain the disaster at Missionary Ridge back in the fall of 1863? He had plenty of troops. It was a strong defensive position. He had had months to fortify it. Why, then, did he fail to hold it? One wonders if his well-known fondness for Kentucky bourbon got the better of him."

There was laughing in the crowd. In the aftermath of the disaster at Chattanooga, General Braxton Bragg had indeed accused Breckinridge of being drunk on duty. Word of this had gotten into the newspapers and surely many people in the audience would have some recollection of the controversy. By reminding the audience of the rumor, Toombs knew he was tossing a match onto kindling. The pro-SRP newspapers would have an easy time turning the unsubstantiated accusation into a fact. Toombs had been in politics long enough to know that if you repeated a lie often enough, it essentially became the truth by default.

Toombs went on to disparage Breckinridge's military record for the next few minutes, dropping more hints that he might have been drunk during battle. He subtly hinted that Beauregard would have won the Battle of Shiloh had Breckinridge done what was expected of him. He trivialized Breckinridge's role at Chickamauga and Early's raid on Washington. Of Breckinridge's famous victory at New Market, Toombs simply said nothing.

The crowd kept cheering, delighted by Toombs's delivery as much as by the words themselves. What they didn't know was that Toombs was only just getting started. Tying Breckinridge to the unpopular policies of Davis, questioning his commitment to the Confederacy, and belittling his military record were only preliminaries to the true heart of the speech. If Toombs was successful, he would leave his audience both astonished and terrified.

He held his hands on the podium and looked down for a few moments, waiting for the laughter and low chatter in the crowd to die down before he continued. His face became unusually solemn and the audience seemed to sense that what he was about to say would be more important that what had been said up to that point. When he spoke, his previously mocking and sarcastic tone had become much more serious.

"Our Confederacy is founded upon the great truth that the Negro is not equal to the white man. We acknowledge what to us is obvious, that the black man was created by God to serve the white man. We fought the war to free ourselves from Yankee rule because the Yankees were conspiring to destroy our sacred institution of African slavery. I believe this with all my heart. I know that General Beauregard believes it. But, my friends, I must tell you now that I question whether Mr. Breckinridge believes it."

A murmur of discontent rose from the crowd. To Southerners, accusing someone of holding abolitionist views was a very serious matter. It had led to more than one duel over the past several years. Toombs knew he was treading onto dangerous territory, yet the very thought excited and encouraged him. For Toombs was a gambling man when it came to politics. The more outrageous the words coming out of his mouth, the more at home he was.

"Mr. Breckinridge owns no slaves. Why not? He's a prosperous man. He could well afford a good house slave to fetch his coffee in the morning. I'm sure his wife could use some help with the household chores. Does he, perhaps, have some sort of moral objection when it comes to our peculiar institution?" He paused for effect. "Does he, perhaps, secretly adhere to abolitionism?"

There was a collective gasp from a large part of the audience. Toombs went on with renewed confidence.

"Breckinridge likes to talk about the role he played at the Toronto Peace Conference. Well, what was his role there? I'll tell you what it was. He was the man who cravenly surrendered to the Yankee demands that give up our claims to all the slaves they stole from us. In other words, he thought Abe Lincoln's so-called Emancipation Proclamation was perfectly valid. He said the Yankees could keep any slaves who run away to them now that the war is over. Why aren't there any provisions in the treaty to protect our peculiar institution? Ask Mr. Breckinridge for the answer."

Applause followed, but more polite and restrained than the previous cheering. Toombs sensed that they had heard the complaints about Breckinridge's betrayal of the country at Toronto so many times already, in newspaper story after newspaper story for two years, that it was not enough to ignite their passions. Still, it was good for him to remind the audience of it. Now it was time to move towards the really sharp edge of his speech.

"Then we have this slave uprising in Louisiana. Half a dozen plantations burned down. Scores of lives lost. Breckinridge is the Secretary of War. It's his responsibility to deal with such matters. So what does he do? He appoints his personal friend, John Hunt Morgan, to command the troops. And Morgan gets himself whipped by a pack of ill-armed darkies! How many good Confederate soldiers were killed by black bullets and black blades because of the ineptitude of these two?"

The crowd's reaction to these words was mixed. Toombs had expected them to cheer and applaud, but few did. He realized that he was getting off track by talking about Morgan. For one thing, he was still a popular figure due to his astounding exploits during the war. For another, he had recently achieved considerable success against Saul and it appeared that the rebel slave's rebellion was close to being snuffed out. Toombs made a mental note not to criticize Morgan in future speeches and to write letters to that effect to his allies suggesting that they also refrain from doing so.

"I read the newspapers, same as you. And I see that our boys have captured quite a few of these ungrateful renegade darkies. Breckinridge has ordered them all confined to a stockade while he figures out what to do with them. What is taking him so long? What is there to figure out? If you ask me, what to do with these rebels is simple." His voice rose in volume and intensity. "If any black man raises his hand against any white man, find a rope, wrap it around the darkie's neck, and dangle the darkie from the nearest tree until he stops twitching!"

This time, there was no restraint in the cheers and thunderous applause that exploded from the crowd. The audience transformed into a sea of red faces and raised fists when Toombs shouted his words. The mere suggestion that Breckinridge was treating black men as anything other than base and inferior beings was repugnant to the audience.

"Hang them!" a woman in the crowd started screaming. "Hang them all!"

In an instant, like a rush of wind across the prairie, the crowd had taken up the call and begun repeating it with a grim cadence.

"Hang them all! Hang them all! Now! Now!"

Toombs felt a tug of fear. He had given enough speeches to know when to worry about a crowd getting out of control and he had no wish for that to happen. There was always the possibility that rash young men in the audience, perhaps under the influence of drink, would charge off and attack the first black person they came across in the street. It wasn't that Toombs would have especially cared, but he wanted the newspaper accounts to focus on his speech and not on a riot. He also didn't want to cause any trouble for the local authorities, whose support would be important in the months ahead.

Yet Toombs could hardly bear to try to quiet down the audience. He delighted in the fact that his words had been the inspiration for such powerful feelings. Moreover, he knew the furious resentment that the idea of black equality brought forth in the hearts of Southern whites, even those far too poor to ever aspire to be slave-owners themselves. Even the lowest white man in Southern society could be proud of the fact that he was, at the very least, higher than the black slaves. This simple truth was the foundation on which the elite of Southern society, men such as Toombs himself, had built their rule. That was the way things had always been and, if he had anything to say about it, that's the way things would always be.

He finally held up his hands for silence. The crowd didn't quiet itself right away and many men had to loudly shush those who were still yelling until sufficient silence had fallen for Toombs to continue.

"Who will you vote for, my friends?" he shouted. "Who? Will you stand with Breckinridge, who thinks you're no better than blacks and wants to consolidate all power in Richmond? Or will you support General Beauregard, the friend of the people, and your old friend Robert Toombs? Tell me, by your cheers, that you'll stand with General Beauregard and Senator Toombs!"

They did as they were told, exploding into a thunderous ovation.

CHAPTER ELEVEN

Before 1861, the town of New Iberia had been a prosperous commercial town, where the sugar from the surrounding plantations and salt from the nearby salt works was loaded onto flatboats and steamers for shipment down the Bayou Teche to New Orleans. The war, unfortunately, had not been kind to New Iberia. In April of 1863, it had been captured by Union forces under General Nathaniel Banks after the small but vicious Battle of Irish Bend. For two days, New Iberia had been thoroughly ransacked and looted, with the women subjected to all forms of humiliation. The nearby plantations and salt works, the source of the town's wealth, had been destroyed. The end of the fighting had only deepened the community's misery, for a yellow fever epidemic in 1866 had carried off many of the town's people, particularly children and the elderly.

About a thousand people called New Iberia home, but as in so many other Southern communities, the women considerably outnumbered the men. The men of the town and its surrounding plantations had volunteered in large numbers during the war, serving in numerous regiments that fought in both the Eastern and Western Theaters, as well as closer to home. Some had joined the 10th Louisiana Battalion, known as the Yellow Jackets, and served throughout the war on the west side of the Mississippi River. Many had served in the 12th Louisiana, which had been virtually destroyed at the Battle of Atlanta. Others had served in the 8th Louisiana, which had fought under Lee and Jackson in the Eastern Theater. A local effort to bring the bodies of the men home and reinter them in the local cemetery had been ongoing since the end of the fighting.

The war and its aftermath had been very hard on New Iberia, indeed. The citizens could not have imagined that an even worse calamity was about to befall them.

It was midway between five and six in the morning. The sun had not yet risen, though the red glow was beginning to spread across the eastern horizon. Saul and his men had yet to see a single person as they walked up the main street towards the center of town. Their destination was the New Iberia Grand Hotel, which had only recently been completed. Saul could see it at the end of the street. He thought the name pretentious and ridiculous, for the building was a simple and rather unimpressive three-story wooden structure.

Saul's heart pounded, for he knew that the most important phase of his uprising against the Confederacy had just begun. Very likely he would not survive the next few days, yet he had never felt so alive. He was no longer a rat hiding in the swamps. He and his men had emerged from the wilderness to grapple with the enemy in the open. Their new weapons, Saul was sure, would give them the strength to match the best troops the slaveholders could send against them.

He glanced back at the men behind him. He could see that they had recovered their strength and morale. Saul gave thanks to Charles Russell Lowell for this. His arrival had brought hope to the men, and not just in the form of guns. Lowell had been living proof that there were people in the outside world who knew of their struggle and wished them well. He had shown them that they were not alone. When he had told them that he would return with even more weapons, they had believed him. Saul had believed him, too.

Yet there was more to it than that. Saul could see it in their eyes. They moved with a sort of cocky swagger, excited and delighted about this new chapter in their adventure. For the first time in more than two years, they were no longer hiding. Their presence in New Iberia was a statement of purpose. They intended to defy the Confederacy directly and openly. Like him, they were enthralled at the feeling of emerging from the darkness to match themselves against their enemy in a fair fight. Their partisan tactics had served them well, inflicting harm upon their foes, and kept them alive. Yet all of them had yearned for the chance to fight in the open, showing the slaveholders that they were men equal to themselves.

Saul thought back to the meeting he had had with his two lieutenants three nights before. When he told Troy and Ferguson what he intended to do, they had both been stunned. Ferguson had tried to talk him out of it, saying that attempting to capture a Southern town was akin to suicide. Troy, too, expressed skepticism, stating his opinion that they should return to their previous tactics of raiding plantations, as their new weapons would give them renewed strength.

His plan was simple. He would march the column as quickly as possible southwards and occupy New Iberia before anyone had a clue that they were anywhere near it. With nearly two hundred men, now well-armed and equipped, taking a town of barely over a thousand should not prove difficult. Once the town was occupied, hostages would be taken and a fortified position would be secured. There were many slaves in the town. They would be liberated at once and small parties would be sent out to the surrounding plantations to set free even more, who could then be brought back to New Iberia. As word quickly spread, the slaves in the surrounding counties would rise up on their own. New Iberia would become the center of a revolution that would consume the Confederacy like a fire.

Ferguson had protested that this was exactly what John Brown had hoped to do at Harper's Ferry in 1859 and he had failed miserably. Saul countered that there were big differences between what he planned to do and what Brown had done. First of all, Brown had gone to Harper's Ferry with less than two dozen men, some of them scarcely trained in how to use a rifle. They, by contrast, were going into New Iberia with nearly two hundred men, many of them hardened veterans. Moreover, the slave population around Harper's Ferry had been very small, whereas the plantations around New Iberia were large and had thousands of slaves.

"Brown threw a match onto a pile of bricks," Saul had said. "We're going to throw a torch onto a pile of dry wood."

Still, Ferguson and Troy had resisted. Saul understood their fear. Neither man was afraid of danger, but both were afraid of the unknown. The risk Saul was taking might utterly fail, leading to the destruction of their force and the end of their rebellion. It had taken all of Saul's stubbornness and persuasiveness to get them to agree to his plan. They had long since pledged to follow his orders even when they disagreed with them, but it was still important to Saul that they went along with him of their own free will. He was not sure he had succeeded in this.

The column was now approaching the New Iberia Grand Hotel, which his scouts had reconnoitered during the previous night. Standing near the center of town, it was one of the few buildings that had more than one story. As it was the recognized gathering place in town, Saul had decided to make it his headquarters. As they got closer, Saul made out the shape of a man sipping coffee on the porch in the pre-dawn twilight.

The man suddenly bolted to his feet. "What the hell?" he shouted disbelievingly as he caught sight of the column of black warriors.

"Hands up!" the man at the head of the column said harshly, raising his well-polished Springfield.

Without a word, the man dropped his coffee and raised both hands above his hand. Saul relished the sight of his terrified face, then began shouting orders. The men had been carefully briefed the night before and every soldier knew what his job was. Fifty men quickly took defensive positions around the hotel to guard against any surprise reaction by nearby militia or cavalry. While some stood to arms, others began gathering material to erect barricades and dig trenches. There was no indication that any organized enemy was nearby, for Morgan and his troopers were still fruitlessly searching for them farther north. Still, Saul was taking no chances.

Twenty selected men rushed into the hotel and darted up the stairs. Their job was to sweep through the rooms, rousing the still-sleeping guests and bringing them down to the lobby. Saul wished he could accompany them, for he would have enjoyed seeing the petrified looks of fear on the faces of the white men and women when black men with guns smashed down their doors and hauled them out of their beds. Whites had been inflicting terror enough on the blacks of the South for a quarter of a millennium. It was time for a measure of payback.

Ferguson would remain in the hotel lobby to speak to the hostages. He was to tell them that no harm would come to them so long as they remained quiet and did not try to escape. As he was the only white man in the insurgent group, Ferguson would be able to calm the hostages in a way that neither Saul nor anyone else in the band could.

That left about one hundred other men, who had been divided into five different groups. Each group had a specific mission. One was to remain in reserve near the hotel, ready to attack any groups of New Iberia citizens who armed themselves once word of the attack had spread. Saul had read carefully about what had happened to John Brown when he had taken Harper's Ferry. The half-crazed white man had been totally unprepared for the spontaneous resistance of the local townspeople. Saul was determined not to make the same mistake.

The second group was to move through the fancier houses of town and round up more hostages, especially prominent citizens like the mayor, the bank president, and other such people. The third was to raid the local militia armory and see if there was anything there worth capturing. Saul was not sure if there would be, since many of the militiamen from the town had actually been out looking for them. The fourth group was to cut the telegraph wires out of the town to isolate New Iberia from the outside world.

The fifth group had perhaps the most important assignment of all. They were to gather together the slaves of New Iberia and assemble them in front of the hotel. Saul's plan was to address them, inform them that they were free, and then put them to work in helping secure New Iberia for the revolution. With any luck, enough weapons could be gathered from the town to arm at least some of the male slaves. The women and children could be put to other tasks, such as securing food.

It was now light enough to see without difficulty. Saul stood regally on the front patio of the New Iberia Grand Hotel, supervising the work that his men were doing. A crowd of two dozen white people had already been gathered in the hotel's lobby, guarded by five of his men and being calmed by Ferguson. The rest of his men were swarming around the town, which had now awoken in great confusion and alarm. Bewildered people were running about in every direction. Women were screaming in terror and clutching children close to their skirts. There was scattered gunfire as some of the town's citizens grabbed their weapons and tried to fight back, but Saul's men quickly killed anyone they found holding a rifle or pistol.

As pandemonium swept through the city, the only place where order still seemed to rule was around the hotel itself. There, all was quiet and organized. Some of Saul's men had already begun digging trenches around the building. Nearby structures, which might have provided cover for sharpshooters or other attackers, were being torn down, the wooden being incorporated into the barricades being erected. Slowly, the New Iberia Grant Hotel was being turned into a fortress.

One of Saul's men came up to the steps of the porch, holding his leveled rifle at a well-dressed man walking with him. "Boss, this is Claude Delacroix. He's the mayor."

"Good morning, Mr. Delacroix," Saul said pleasantly. "A lovely day, is it not?"

"You're Saul?" the man asked in a heavy Creole accent. He seemed more mystified than afraid.

"Yes, and I am delighted to make your acquaintance. I have appropriated the Grand Hotel for my headquarters. Won't you please come in?"

The soldier pushed Delacroix up the steps and he continued walking into the hotel lobby to join the other hostages. Over the next hour, more people were brought in, including the editor of the only newspaper in New Iberia and the president of the New Iberia Bank. Eventually, more than two dozen prominent citizens of the town were crowded into the hotel lobby, to join another dozen people who had had the bad timing to be staying at the establishment when Saul's men marched in.

He motioned for Troy, who was overseeing the digging of the trenches around the hotel. He quickly joined Saul on the porch.

"Yes, boss?" Troy asked. His voice was flush and excited.

"Everything is going well. I think we're ready to move to the second part of our plan. You ready?"

Troy took a deep breath. "I'm ready, boss."

"Then you know what to do. We scouted out the nearby plantations last night. Take forty men and go."

"Will do, boss. And good luck. Never thought I'd see the day when we'd do something like this."

Saul allowed himself a smile. "Me, either. Give thanks to General Lowell."

Troy vanished to carry out his orders. For a moment, Saul was troubled by the possibility that he might never see his old friend again. For all he knew, Troy's group would be caught and killed by the militia before they got to the first plantation. Then again, he might succeed beyond their most sanguine hopes. Like everything else they were doing, it was a roll of the dice.

Satisfied that things were going well, Saul went inside to speak to the hostages. They were crowding together, whispering urgently to one another, fearfully eyeing the rifles and bayonets held by the men guarding them. He walked halfway up the stairs, then turned to address them all.

"Ladies and gentlemen, as I'm sure you are aware, I am Saul. And I hereby declare New Iberia to be a liberated town. My men and I now constitute the legitimate civil authority here. You will be detained here until such time as the Confederate authorities recognize the new order of things in this town."

He looked around at the faces beneath him. None of them spoke, but many continued to cast frightened eyes towards their guards.

"Does anyone have any questions?" Saul said.

"What about the women?" one man asked. There were about ten females among the hostages, all of them having been guests at the hotel. "Why don't you let them go?"

"I do not intend for any harm to come to any of you. For now, the women will remain among you, under my protection."

Saul had planned for this. The attitudes of the Southern whites towards their women were irrational and illogical, yet he felt he understood them. He had always left women unharmed during his previous raids partially because he knew it played on the absurd Southern notions of chivalry. In this case, though, he would keep them as prisoners. Nothing enraged a Southern man so much as the thought of a black man possessing a white woman, so the idea of white females being held hostage by armed black men was sure to madden his enemies across the Confederacy.

"What is it you are planning, Saul?" asked Mayor Delacroix. "You know you cannot remain here. This talk of a liberated town is insanity. The army is going to come and kill every last one of you."

Saul smiled. "Well, we'll just see about that, won't we?"

Without another word, he stepped back out onto the hotel porch. He then saw a sight that thrilled his heart more than anything else he had ever seen. Led by a dozen of his soldiers, a huge column of black people was approaching the intersection just in front of the hotel. Men, women, and children, they must have numbered over two hundred. Almost all of them had looks of confusion and alarm on their faces, which was only to be expected. He had seen the same look on the faces of people who had been rescued from the plantations they had raided. Yet the sight of so many freed slaves in a single place was something he had not seen since the war.

They came to a halt just in front of the hotel. Almost all of them looked up at him in a sort of dazed wonder. Surely they knew who he was, for he knew stories of his exploits had been circulating among blacks, both free and slave, all across Louisiana and perhaps beyond. He held up his hands for attention.

"My brothers and sisters, I have come to New Iberia to set you free!" he shouted.

"Hurrah!" shouted his soldiers, who held their rifles up and shook them in the air.

The newly freed slaves glanced at him, at the soldiers, and at one another. None cheered, but Saul had not expected them to cheer. Most simply looked confused. Many of the children were crying, clearly frightened by the unusual events happening around them.

"I am Saul!" he shouted, trying to make his voice sound as authoritative and strong as possible. "As God is my witness, none of you shall ever wear chains again! You were free the moment you were born, no matter what the whites say! They took your freedom from you and now we are taking it back!"

This was greeted not with cheers but with a collective look of uncertainty and confusion. Saul felt a sudden tug of apprehension. He had expected town slaves, being more in touch with the outside world, to more easily adjust to the idea of being free than plantation slaves. He had never had much contact with town slaves, however, so he sensed that perhaps he had miscalculated.

"The chains that once bound you are gone forever!" Saul shouted, hoping to keep the momentum of his speech going. "But this is only the beginning! New Iberia is now a liberated town! We are in control here! The whites will be banished, never to return! There will be no more white masters! We are all the masters of ourselves!"

Saul could see several people cast confused glances at one another. Clearly, the idea of not having a white master, of being the master of oneself, was difficult for these people to understand. He remembered the first time Doctor Ferguson had tried to teach him about Copernicus and the idea that the Earth actually went around the Sun. It had seemed absurd to him at the time and he had only begun to understand with the passage of time.

These people, though, didn't have the luxury of time to get used to the idea of freedom. The Confederates would react to the occupation of New Iberia within a matter of hours. Even assuming his men had been successful in cutting the telegraph wires, Saul knew he did not have much time. In choosing to capture a town, Saul knew that he was losing the advantage of movement and allowing the enemy to fix him in a particular location. The Confederates would be able to bring all their forces to bear against him, rather than spreading them out to search the swamps for him. It was the price that had to be paid for Saul's plan to have a chance to work.

"Will the white men come back?" one woman asked, her voice fearful.

"They will try," Saul admitted. "But look around you. Look at my men. We're soldiers. We fought against the slaveholders during the war and we've been fighting them ever since. We have guns and we know how to use them. We have more guns and we will give them to many of the men we have just freed. The slaveholders will try to come back, sure enough. But when they do, they will meet armed men ready to fight back."

"Yes!" shouted one man in the crowd, his face suddenly flushed with excitement. "Give me a gun, Saul! Give me one of your guns!"

"I want one, too!" another man exclaimed. "I want a gun! I want to fight!"

"Soon enough, my brothers. I promise I will give guns to all men who want them, long as we have enough."

An older man, most likely too old to shoulder a musket, stepped forward. "Is it true what they say about you, Saul? Is it true that you can't be killed?" The question caused a hush to settle over the crowd.

He thought for a moment, remembering his mother's magic. "The slaveholders have tried to kill me many times. Don't you see me standing here, alive?"

This was followed by a chorus of cheers, both from the freed slaves and his own men. He sensed the excitement, the unrestrained joy, which was coursing through the people in front of him. He remembered how he felt during the early morning hours of the day he had fled from his plantation and escaped into the Union lines. For just a moment, his thoughts turned to his mother. He wondered how she was, whether she were alive or dead, whether she had escaped slavery before the end of the war or still remained in servitude, whether she knew what her son was doing. Whatever her fate, he knew the debt he owed his mother. Her magic had protected him up to this point. Surely it would continue to do so.

Saul held up his hands for quiet and the cheering quickly subsided. "You are all free now. But you must listen to me. Unless we work together, the whites will come back. They will try to take your freedom away from you again. If we stand together, we can beat them. If we do not, they will beat us." He paused for a moment, letting these words sink in before making his plea. "My brothers and sisters, will you stand with me? Will you stand with Saul?"

The loud, sustained cheer of the newly freed blacks could have been heard for a mile around.

August 3, Evening
Home of John C. Breckinridge, Richmond, Virginia

"Your appetite seems to have improved," Mary said happily.

Breckinridge smiled as he swallowed another forkful of roast chicken. "Well, this freed woman you have hired is a very good cook. What is her name again?"

"Joan. She came with good references from Mrs. Lee, actually."

"Oh, that's interesting."

"I very much like the Lees. We should try to see them more often."

"That would be lovely," Breckinridge said as he took another bite.

"You know why Joan's cooking is better than any slave's would be?" Mary asked.

"Why is that, my dear?"

"She takes pride in her work, you see. She gets paid for what she does, so some of the fruits of her labor belong to her. Not the same way with slaves. Why should they feel pride in their work, even if it's good, since nothing about it belongs to them?"

"You're quite correct. I remember one incident during the war, when a large gang of slaves was being used to construct fortifications near Chattanooga. The foreman tried to organize them into teams and hold a competition to see who could finish their work fast enough. None of the slaves seemed interested. None of them would gain anything if they won the competition. There was no motivation for them to work any harder. They would do the minimum needed to avoid the lash, but no more." He paused thoughtfully for a moment. "In their place, neither would I."

She smiled across the table at him. "I am very glad you came home at a decent hour tonight," she said. "You said yesterday than you do not intend to work over the weekend."

"Yes, and that is still my plan. It has been far too long since you and I were able to spend any time together. As the presidential campaign heats up, I am afraid that we shall have even less."

"I know," she said resignedly. "I had some hope that you might want to return to practicing law when the president left office. But I never really thought you would. I knew you would stay in politics." She chuckled. "I must say, though, that I expected something more like a run for Congress rather than the presidency."

"Well, perhaps luck will turn your way and I will lose the election. Then I probably will go back to the law."

She laughed, which made him smile. He had always adored her light, pleasant, and soothing laugh. The fact that she was generally a happy woman was one of the aspects of his life of which he was the most proud. She was almost tailor-made to be a politician's wife, for she endured his heavy workload with good grace and even shared some of his ambition. Whether she admitted it or not, she was excited about the possibility of becoming First Lady. He asked himself again whether he would have been able to run for the presidency if he thought she opposed it.

Breckinridge greatly enjoyed the dinners he got to share with his wife. He only wished their children were present. His oldest and youngest sons, Joseph and John, were away studying at Washington College in the town of Lexington. His middle son Clifton was now a midshipman in the Confederate Navy, serving onboard the ironclad *Charleston*, in the harbor of its namesake city. The commander of the Charleston Squadron, Captain Isaac Brown, regularly wrote Breckinridge glowing accounts of his son's service and predicted a splendid naval career for the young man.

His daughters, Frances and Mary, were visiting relatives in Nashville, which was now home to many of the pro-Confederate members of their extended Kentucky family. There was more to this trip than a desire for his daughters to become better acquainted with their relatives. A prominent cavalry general, a South Carolinian named Pierce Young, had begun asking whether he might be allowed to escort Frances to church. Breckinridge had nothing against Young, but was uncomfortable with the idea of his daughter being courted by a man so deeply enmeshed in the South Carolina planter aristocracy. He had therefore thought it best for Frances to leave Richmond for a few weeks. If Young was still interested when she returned, Breckinridge could deal with it then.

For just a moment, he found himself thinking of his namesake son John, who had died in 1850 at the tender age of seven months. He had been a beautiful baby boy. It was impossible for Breckinridge not to wonder what little John might have become had he not been taken by the illness. He tried to suppress the thought, which only brought forth grief, but it was never an easy thing to do.

"I need to tell you something, my dear," he said softly.

"Yes?"

"I intend to hand in my resignation to President Davis this week."

She pulled her head back in some surprise. "Is that so? Why would you do that?"

"Morgan seems to have the troubles with the renegade slaves in Louisiana dealt with. There are no other especially pressing matters at the War Department. It is time for me to turn my full attention to the campaign. And I was hoping perhaps you and I might go away together for a few days. Perhaps to Wilmington or some other place along the coast."

She smiled. "That would be lovely. A little rest would do you good before the full commitment of the campaign takes hold."

He nodded. "Rest would be pleasant. It is certain to be a long and hard campaign.."

"I know," she replied. "But I'm ready. You can't allow Beauregard and his supporters to win. The country would fall apart and everything you've fought for would be lost."

"I'm very glad that you understand and agree with me. I couldn't do it otherwise."

There was a soft knocking at the door and Breckinridge quieted. He could hear the door open and his household servant, a free black man named Tom, speak quickly with someone. He recognized the voice right away.

"It's Wilson," he said.

"What do you suppose he wants?" Mary asked.

"Something pressing from Mechanic's Hall, I'm sure." Breckinridge pushed his chair back from the table and stood up, wiping his whiskers with the napkin. He was preparing to walk to the front door when Wilson entered the dining room. From the look on the man's face, Breckinridge knew instantly that something was very wrong.

"I'm very sorry to disturb you at home, Mr. Secretary," Wilson said quickly.

"That's quite all right, James."

"Good evening to you, Mrs. Breckinridge," Wilson said quickly, bowing his head towards Mary. He seemed highly agitated, yet still observed the rules of etiquette where females were concerned, which Breckinridge thought to the man's credit.

"And to you, James," Mary replied.

"I assume that you would not have come here unless there was a matter that required my instant attention." Breckinridge was worried that what he was about to hear would simply be another tale of his aide's poor luck and clumsiness, yet something told him that it was not.

"Well, sir, it's like this. When you left, I was working on that report about the supplies supposed to be delivered to the frontier posts in Texas."

"Yes," Breckinridge said, waving his hand to hurry Wilson along in the telling of the story.

"Just after you left, a telegram came in from a steamship company in Louisiana. Something about a rumor that Saul had captured the town of New Iberia."

Breckinridge laughed. Morgan had smashed Saul's force more than a month before. As far as Breckinridge knew, only a few scattered bands or individuals remained, hiding in the swamps and no more dangerous than common criminals. His mind had already moved on from Saul. Even though the bandit leader himself had not been captured, Breckinridge had begun to suspect that he was dead. The idea that Saul could suddenly reemerge and capture a significant town struck him as ridiculous, but his laugh faded when he saw that Wilson's expression remained deadly serious.

"Go on," Breckinridge said, suddenly grimmer.

"Well, I didn't think it was anything but a rumor and didn't want to trouble you about it. But a couple of other telegrams came in over the next hour or so, all talking about something happening in New Iberia. The telegraph lines into the town were down, which struck me as suspicious. I sent a telegram to Morgan, asking if he knew anything about it. I hadn't gotten a response from him before I left, but then we got this message from Governor Allen. I came here directly after it was received."

Wilson handed over a paper and Breckinridge hurriedly read it.

Secretary Breckinridge

Report from St. Martin Parish militia officers confirms that New Iberia has been in the hands of armed black men since yesterday morning. The group numbers perhaps three hundred. All reported to be armed with rifles. Several hostages are being held in the hotel at center of town, which is being fortified by the insurgents. The man telegraphing me personally spoke to New Iberia citizens who escaped and can be relied upon.

Please notify President Davis immediately. I urge you to take whatever action is necessary to deal with this emergency. On my own authority, I am mobilizing additional militia units, whose orders will be to recapture New Iberia and destroy the insurgent forces at once.

Governor Allen

Breckinridge was stunned. He felt as though he had been punched in the stomach. It had to be Saul, yet that seemed impossible. Moreover, how could so many blacks be armed with rifles? All reports since Saul's first raid on a plantation, including all those sent by Morgan, had been unanimous in saying that only a few of Saul's men had working firearms.

He found himself wondering if Morgan had been lying to him. Morgan had said that he had killed or captured more than half of Saul's men. If that were true, what was now occurring in New Iberia could not be happening. Morgan would not have been the first Southern general to exaggerate the extent of a victory. Breckinridge knew how vain his friend was and knew how badly he had been stung by the criticism of the newspapers over the past few months.

Breckinridge turned to his wife. "I am sorry, my dear, but I must go immediately."

"What is it, John?" she asked, deep concern in her voice. "Saul is still on the loose?"

"I cannot say until I have more information." He turned to Wilson. "Did you come in a carriage?"

"Yes, sir."

"I must speak to the president at once. Let's go."

He walked hurriedly to the front door, Wilson following close behind. Moments later, they were in the carriage rattling through the streets of Richmond. The twilight was fading fast and darkness was closing in. Few people were on the streets, as most people were at dinner. The summer air was unpleasantly warm and stuffy.

Breckinridge stuck his head out the window. "Faster, man!" he shouted to the coachman. "We must get there as quickly as possible!" The coachman responded by snapping his whip and urging the horses to greater speed.

It did not take long before Breckinridge and Wilson arrived in front of the President's House. A slave answered the door after Breckinridge loudly pounded on it.

"Tell the president that Secretary Breckinridge is here."

"Very good, sir. And what may I tell him this is about?"

"Just get him, dammit!" Breckinridge snarled angrily. The slave turned and disappeared into the house.

"The insolence of that darkie!" Wilson exclaimed. "Who does he think he is, asking about our business rather than simply following orders?"

Breckinridge grunted agreement but said nothing. He waited impatiently outside the front door for what seemed like hours. All the while, his mind raced. Governor Allen had said in his message that he was going ahead and mobilizing his militia. Constitutionally, he was perfectly entitled to do so. Yet Breckinridge thought the situation serious enough to justify having the War Department assume command of the militia. The last thing he wanted was a disorderly command structure.

Davis came to the door. He had the habitual look that combined irritation with concern.

"I assume that this is important, John," he said. "You're not in the habit of dropping by during dinner."

"I apologize, Mr. President, but yes, it is important. We have received a telegram from Governor Allen of Louisiana. It appears that Saul is not dealt with yet. In fact, his men have occupied the town of New Iberia."

"What do you mean by 'occupied'?" Davis asked.

432

"Just like it sounds. According to eye-witnesses, they have taken control of the town and are fortifying a position at a hotel. Been there since yesterday morning."

"What?" Davis asked in disbelief. "How can that be? Morgan said that he had Saul on the run."

"I share your astonishment, Mr. President. But it appears that Morgan's view of the situation was rather too optimistic."

Davis did not reply right away and he stared off into the sky for a few moments. Breckinridge was not offended. It take a few moments for the shock to wear off, just as it had for him.

"We need to assemble the Cabinet," Davis finally said.

Breckinridge turned to Wilson. "James, go back to Mechanic's Hall. Get all the clerks and whoever else may still be there and send them around the city to the homes of each Cabinet member. Tell them they are to assemble at the Executive Office Building."

"Right away, sir," Wilson said. He dashed back to the carriage and within moments was whipping the horse into a trot. Breckinridge would worry about how to get home later.

"Mr. President, I'd like your permission to bring the Louisiana militia fully into national service."

"We'd have to ask Governor Allen for his permission," Davis said sourly. "In the present climate, I doubt he'll give it. He knows he'd catch hell from the SRP bastards if he did."

"Are you sure?" Breckinridge asked. "Right now Toombs is making a series of fire-and-brimstone speeches attacking us for taking so long to crush Saul."

Davis scowled. "Of course. If we move to bring the militia under national control, they will say that you're out to crush states' rights. If we don't, they say you're soft on slave insurrection. You can't win, John."

"Me?" Breckinridge asked.

"Of course," Davis said matter-of-factly. "Now that you're the candidate, they see you as the problem, not me. You've been reading their speeches in the papers. Every day, they talk less about me and more about you."

Breckinridge fumed. "If only they would put politics aside until we can finish Saul off." His face brightened as a new thought entered his mind. "Now that Saul has come out of the bayou into the open, we have an opportunity to finally crush him. He may have pulled off this little coup of his and taken one of our towns, but he cannot possibly hold it. No partisan force can defend an entrenched position indefinitely in the face of a regular army. We will simply cordon off the town and move in for the kill."

Davis nodded. "Order Morgan to surround New Iberia will all the forces currently under his command. I'll wire Governor Allen about placing his militia under the control of the War Department to mobilize additional militia. I'm also going to wire Governor Pettus in Mississippi to mobilize some of his troops as well. But there's one thing, John."

"What's that?"

The president sighed deeply. "I know he's your friend and that you Kentuckians stand by each other. Orphan Society and all that. But Morgan has failed. If he had succeeded against Saul, none of this stuff in New Iberia would be happening. He failed and it's as simple as that. He has to go."

Breckinridge looked impassively across the desk for a few moments, then frowned. He couldn't argue with Davis, for he knew he would reach the same conclusion if he looked at the question objectively. "Who should replace him?"

"I've given it some thought, since we knew this was a possibility. Especially now that Saul has chosen a position to defend and abandoned his previous strategy of movement, I think we need an infantry officer, not a cavalryman."

Breckinridge tensed, fearing that Davis was about to suggest Braxton Bragg. If Breckinridge had to name the single man in the world he detested above all others, it would be Bragg. He would never forget the last day of the Battle of Murfreesboro, where Bragg's stubbornness and stupidity had cut Breckinridge's beloved Orphan Brigade to pieces. The man had been in disgrace since 1864, holding a quiet command along the Lower Atlantic seaboard, but Davis occasionally mentioned giving him a more prominent position. Breckinridge could never understand why, but Davis had something of a soft spot for Bragg.

"James Longstreet," Davis finally said. "He's in Little Rock, yes?"

"Correct. He commands the Department of the Ozarks."

"Good. It shouldn't take him more than a few days to reach New Iberia, then."

"I should think not." Breckinridge choose not to clarify with Davis whether he wanted Morgan removed at once and have the command taken by his deputy until Longstreet arrived. Without such a direct order, Morgan would remain in command for a few more days. He choose not to raise the question.

"Why don't you go back to Mechanic's Hall and issue the necessary orders?" Davis said. "I'll send a messenger to inform you when the other members of the Cabinet are expected." He leaned forward on the desk, gently massaging his temples with his forefingers. "Good God, John! I think you must be a madman to want to succeed me in this office!"

August 4, Morning
New Orleans, Louisiana

"Hurry up!" Naismith was shouting to the men working in the rigging of the *Vincent*. His voice sounded angry and insistent, as if he could make his men work faster if he simply yelled more loudly.

To Lowell's eyes, Naismith was acting in a perfectly businesslike manner. The captain and his executive officer were engaged in a long-running conversation using various nautical terms that meant little to Lowell. He himself was barely suppressing a mounting panic. They were supposed to have cast off more than an hour ago, but a host of problems had intervened.

The delay was maddening. Lowell was no sailor and knew he could do nothing to help. He had to stay out of Naismith's way, for the captain was well aware of the need to be off as quickly as possible and seemed focused on his task. Whatever the problem was, it was not Naismith's fault. It took all of Lowell's willpower to keep from pestering Naismith to hurry, to ask what the problem was, to yet again stress the need for an immediate departure.

They had arrived back in New Orleans the previous night. Most of the crew had been off the ship, carousing in the bars and brothels that filled the dockside of the city. It had taken virtually all night to round them up and get them back on board. Even then, many of them had been drunk and not as attentive to their duties as they should have been.

"Look alive, there!" Naismith shouted towards one particular sailor. Lowell looked. The man stood slightly wobbly, as though he had just been punched in the face, as he tried to loop a length of rope through a lashing. Lowell thought that the entire crew seemed sluggish and uncertain, but he also admitted that it was possible his increasingly frantic desire to push off was causing him to be more infuriated than he otherwise would have been.

"Get your paper here!" a newspaper boy cried on the waterfront, waving a copy of the *New Orleans Picayune*. "Saul's rebels take New Iberia! Get your paper here! Saul's rebels take New Iberia! Unbelievable, right? You read it here first, folks!"

Naismith was distracted from his labors long enough to steal a quick glance at Lowell. Their eyes met in understanding for just a moment before the captain went back to yelling at his sailors. Lowell fought the urge to cheer wildly. The day before Lowell had left the encampment, Saul had confided in him the plan to attack and capture a town. New Iberia was one of the targets he had mentioned as a possibility. It was small enough to take and hold, but large enough that its capture would garner national attention.

Lowell had left the boat that morning and had breakfast at one of the many coffeehouses near the docks. His real purpose had not been food, of which there was a sufficiency aboard the *Vincent*, but the obtaining of information. Coffeehouses frequented by sailors were the same the world over, whether in Boston or New Orleans, in that they were outstanding sources of gossip and rumor. As he had sipped his coffee and eaten his cornmeal biscuits, Lowell had listened in rapt fascination as men at the nearby tables spoke excitedly of Saul's seizure of New Iberia. It had just been a rumor, of course, but now the newspaper boy had confirmed it. Something of great magnitude was clearly going on in the town, it obviously involved Saul, and Lowell could assume that the weapons and ammunition he had provided had been the decisive factor in causing the insurgent leader to adopt this course of action.

Lowell had urged Gardet to escape with them, but he had refused. During the trip back to the city, the black merchant had become possessed of a strange sort of fatalistic euphoria. Over and over again, he had said to himself, "It will be what it will be." He had gone back to his wine shop with scarcely a word.

He didn't have any time to think about Gardet now. Instinctively, Lowell scanned the waterfront, expecting at any moment to see New Orleans police galloping up and demanding to be allowed on board the *Vincent*. Now that Saul had made dramatic use of the weapons Lowell had smuggled to him, it would only be a matter of time before the Confederate authorities figured out how he had obtained them. Evil they might be, but they were not stupid.

Lowell found himself unable to resist. He walked beside Naismith, who was busily trying to give directions to crewmen who were struggling with some portion of the rigging.

"Naismith!" he said urgently. "Let's get the hell out here!"

"I'm going as fast as I can!" Naismith replied angrily.

"Why can't we just cast off now?" Lowell asked. "The current will carry us south, won't it?"

"If the sails aren't set we won't be able to tack to avoid obstacles or other ships!" Naismith snapped. He calmed himself. "Besides, we don't want to look like we're in a hurry. Our friends on the shore may be watching."

"Why don't we get steam up and just use the propeller?" Lowell demanded.

"The damn stokers were busy at a whorehouse until an hour ago," Naismith replied. "They've only just started shoveling the coal. We're going as fast as we can. Now perhaps you should go below and let me do my job!"

Lowell walked away, but he didn't go below. He paced the deck, keeping his distance from the sailors as best he could while they ran to and fro. Every few minutes, he looked out over the dock for the police, yet they still did not come. He began to relax. Watching Naismith, he could see that the captain was feeling more reassured. He looked over at Lowell and nodded encouragingly.

Finally, after what had seemed an eternity, Naismith began shouting the orders Lowell had waited so long to hear. The mooring ropes were cast off and, after a last few New Orleans civilians who had been in board selling fruit had departed, the gangway was removed. Two rowboats moved into position to help pull the *Vincent* out from the dock while the sailors prepared to set the sails. Lowell felt immeasurable relief when he began to feel the ship moving beneath his feet.

At that moment, there was a sudden thundering of hooves on the dock and a dozen riders could be seen charging down the street toward the *Vincent*. They wore the uniforms of New Orleans police officers. As the ship was sliding backwards towards the main channel downriver, with a dozen yards between its moving deck and the dock, the riders drew up at the end of the wooden structure.

"Stop! Stop that ship!"

"What's that?" Naismith shouted, feigning confusion.

"I order you to stop!" The police officer looked towards the two rowboats. "You in the rowboats! Stop at once!"

Lowell's heart sank as the black boys in the tugboats followed the shouted orders, pulling their oars into the boats.

"Tie your ship back up, Captain!" the police commander shouted. "Prepare to be boarded!"

"You have no right, sir!" Naismith shouted back. "Article Sixteen of the Treaty of Toronto clearly states that-"

"Surrender or we will fire on your ship!" the police commander yelled.

Lowell came alongside Naismith. "Can we make a run for it?" he spoke urgently in his ear.

Naismith glanced at the unmoving rowboats in the water behind the Vincent, then looked around at the crew. "They won't tow us into the channel. Even if they would, it would take some time. The police will start shooting and they surely have more men on the way."

"We've got to try!"

Naismith shook his head. "The crew didn't sign up for anything like this. As far as they knew, we were on a normal trading voyage. As soon as the first

436

bullet is fired, they'll stop work and throw up their hands. Besides, even if we could get into the channel and get underway, we'd never make it past the Forts Jackson and St. Philip or that damn ironclad they have down there. We'd be blown to splinters."

"Dammit!" Lowell spat.

Dockhands had started throwing rope back onto the deck of the *Vincent* and the ship's crew had started to tie the ship back onto its moorings. Hired hands were not about to disobey the orders of armed police just because the ship's captain had refused to acknowledge them. Naismith and Lowell could only stand helplessly while the *Vincent* was pulled back onto the dock. In the meantime, the dock was quickly filling with armed men and Lowell realized that a local militia company must have assembled.

It took only a few minutes for the gangplank to be in place and for the police to stomp on board. The commander of the police force approached and stared sternly at the two of them.

"Your names?" he demanded.

"I am Stephen Naismith, captain of the *Vincent*. We'll be bound for Boston as soon as we clear up this misunderstanding."

"You're not going anywhere, Naismith," the man gruffly replied. "We caught that Gardet fellow the moment he came back to his store. He told us everything." He turned to Lowell. "And you are?"

A thousand emotions tore through Lowell's heart at that moment. He saw the face of Josephine, imagining her at their home in Boston at that very moment, anxiously awaiting his return. He saw the faces of his two children, so young and vibrant, with the entirety of their lives ahead of them. His action would throw his family onto the charity of the Boston community. They would be well taken care of, Lowell knew, but now his wife would go through life as a widow and his children would be deprived of having a father.

Then he thought of Saul and the two hundred men he had met in the bayou. He thought of the millions of black men and women in chains across the Confederacy. He knew he had been right to come into the Confederacy and to place in the hands of those who would be free the instruments of dealing death to those who denied them their freedom.

He drew himself up and stared fiercely into the eyes of the police officer. "I am Charles Russell Lowell," he said. "Do with me what you will."

August 4, Afternoon
New Iberia, Louisiana

Mounted on his horse in the northern outskirts of New Iberia, Morgan stared angrily at the pillar of smoke that rose from one end of the town. According to his scouts, a warehouse on the Bayou Teche had been set on fire by the insurgents. A vast quantity of sugar was being destroyed and with it, the wealth of many Louisiana sugar planters.

That was not the only thing being reported from the scouts. It was difficult for them to get very close to the enemy position, for sharpshooters were doing their best to keep them away. Some of his more intrepid men had finally managed to get close enough to study the area around the hotel with field glasses, though. Other reports were being gathered by the white citizens who had been driven out of the town.

The picture that was emerging was both terrifying and fascinating. New Iberia had now been under the control of Saul for four days. He had made his headquarters at the hotel near the center of town. According to the eye-witnesses, he had entered the town with between two and three hundred men, though some people had estimated his force to be closer to five hundred. Morgan was experienced enough to know that people tended to overestimate numbers, especially when they were frightened, as these people surely had been. Yet there was no denying that Saul had arrived with a force much larger than Morgan would have thought possible a few days before.

The insurgents had torn down and burnt several structures near the hotel, obviously to prevent them from providing cover to any attacker. This made good military sense and Morgan was not so bigoted that he couldn't give credit to Saul for doing it. Saul's men were also digging trenches and building barricades in the cleared areas around the hotel. According to some of the scouts, white prisoners were being forced to do much of the work, even to the point of being whipped. This last bit of information had been reported with horror and disgust.

Something else reported unanimously by the men and women who had fled New Iberia was the fact that numerous white hostages were being held by Saul at the hotel. Some of these people had just happened to be there when the city was captured. Others were prominent citizens who had been rounded up by the insurgents the day the town fell. No one knew exactly who was among the hostages or how many there were.

One final report from the scouts concerned something that was militarily insignificant but, in a certain sense, the most infuriating thing of all. From the top floor of the hotel room, the insurgents had draped a black flag. Exactly what it meant was a mystery, but Morgan assumed it was a statement of Saul's claim to New Iberia.

He could hear the sound of scattered gunfire off to one side of town, where his skirmishers were trying to establish a position closer to the hotel. Three of his men had already been killed. At least eight others had been wounded, some seriously, and had been carried back to the makeshift hospital that was being set up just outside of town. The presence of the hostages had held him back from launching an all-out assault as soon as he had arrived. Besides, not knowing the strength of Saul's position, he did not want to charge into what might turn out to be a bloody repulse. His reputation had already suffered enough.

Rage filled Morgan. For weeks he had been sending back to Richmond telegram after telegram, saying to Breckinridge and through him to President Davis that Saul had been thrashed and would not be a problem any longer. Just days earlier, he had wired Breckinridge to tell him that could expect Saul's capture within a matter of days. In a recent letter to his wife, Morgan had even begun making plans for his return home.

Instead, Saul had made a fool of him. Somehow the man had recovered and returned stronger than ever. The eye-witnesses who had fled the town had unanimously asserted that every single insurgent that had come into New Iberia had been armed with a Springfield rifle. The veterans among these observers had said that the weapons all appeared to be in good working order.

Somehow, Saul had managed to resupply his unit with weapons. Morgan could not begin to imagine how he had done this. The bastard seemed to have no end of tricks up his sleeve.

Duke rode up behind Morgan and saluted. "Sir! Beg to report!"

"Go ahead."

"The artillery is on its way, sir. But it won't be here anytime soon. They're having to come up all the way from New Orleans."

"New Orleans?" Morgan said in disbelief. "Good God, it could take them at least a day-and-a-half to get here!"

"I know," Duke said sympathetically. "But there's nobody closer."

"Who is it?"

"Both companies of the Washington Artillery, sir."

Morgan nodded quickly. He knew that the Washington Artillery had fielded a number of companies during the war, most of which had served in the East and only one of which had served in the West. Breckinridge's military reforms had seen it reorganized as a militia unit of two part-time companies. They would be experienced artillerymen, perhaps the best in the Confederate army. He only wished they would get to New Iberia more quickly.

"You intend to fire on the hotel, sir?" Duke asked. "We could burn the thing to the ground and not worry about casualties."

Morgan shook his head. "There are hostages there. We don't know who or how many."

"I understand, sir, but we can't let these damn darkies stay in control of the town! Lots of white men are going to die before we root them out. What's the difference between a soldier killed on the street and a man killed in that hotel?" There was anger in Duke's voice. He was as infuriated with the situation as was Morgan.

"There might be women or children in there," Morgan replied. "I'm not going to risk any harm coming to such innocents."

Duke pursed his lips tightly, but said nothing. No officer of the Confederate Army could willingly place the lives of women and children in jeopardy.

There was more firing from the eastern edge of town. Morgan sent one of his staff officers over to find out what was going on. His orders had been to secure a perimeter around the part of town firmly controlled by the insurgents, so that there would be no risk of their breaking out or of anyone coming in to join them.

The last part of the message was crucial. Apparently, after seizing New Iberia, Saul had dispatched teams of men to the nearby sugar plantations, where they had rounded up slaves and brought them back. Aside from burning a few warehouses, they hadn't bothered much with destruction and had allowed the white people to escape without pursuit.

It was unclear exactly how many people Saul had under his command. He had entered the town with a few hundred men. The number of slaves in the town and which had been brought in from surrounding plantations was uncertain, but numbered at least several hundred. Most of these were not men fit for fighting, but many no doubt were. They would not be trained in the use of firearms like Saul's core of soldiers, but anyone could throw a rock or swing a heavy piece of wood. More ominously, some scouts with telescopes had observed what appeared to be a line of black men being drilled in the procedures of loading and firing rifles.

The presence of the hostages in the hotel made Morgan hesitate about attacking, but it was not the only factor. In order to concentrate a sufficient number of troops to storm the insurgent position, Morgan would have to pack his men tightly together and have them charge down the streets, thereby presenting an unmissable target to Saul's men. Now that every single insurgent seemed to be armed with a rifle, such an assault would simply create a large pile of Confederate corpses and still leave the hotel in Saul's hands.

Street fighting had been extremely rare during the war. Breckinridge had fought a battle within the confines of Baton Rouge and there had been some fighting amid the houses and buildings in Gettysburg. Those had been the exceptions, however, for commanders had avoided fighting inside towns whenever they could. Not only was there the danger of civilian casualties to be considered, but houses and buildings limited troop movements and made maneuvers extremely difficult.

Suddenly, three sharp zinging sounds filled Morgan's ears, accompanied by tiny bursts in the dust a few feet behind the horses.

"They've advanced their damn sharpshooters again!" Duke shouted. He turned towards Morgan. "General, I strongly recommend that you withdraw out of range!"

"The hell I will!"

"Don't be a damn fool, John!" Duke yelled insolently. "You're the perfect target on that horse!"

Morgan knew his brother-in-law was right, but he was not about to be chased away by black men, no matter how much he had grown to admire their fighting qualities. Acting as lackadaisical as possible, Morgan calmly pulled out his field glasses and raised them to his eyes, calmly observing the windows from which the sharpshooters were firing, searching for the telltale puffs of smoke. More bullets whizzed past him, one so close that he distinctly felt the air move near his left ear. There was no need to duck, he knew, for by the time he heard the sound the bullets were already past him.

"You've made your point, John!" Duke called. "Let's walk back a bit, shall we?"

"I suppose," Morgan replied. He kicked his horse gently and began moving slowly away, careful not to let the animal move into a trot. Under no circumstances would he allow Saul to think that he had scared him away.

"Thank you," Duke said calmly. Morgan knew his brother-in-law was anything but a coward, yet the tone of relief in the man's voice was obvious. He suspected that Duke's concern was magnified by the fear of being killed by blacks. Dying in battle was honorable, after all, but not if the bullet in question had been fired by a man fit only for slavery. And yet, if the insurgents were fit only for slavery, how was it that they were now in a position to shoot at him?

As he and Duke slowly walked their horses out of range of the enemy sharpshooters, an officer whom Morgan didn't recognize. He was wearing a bright and colorful Zouave uniform.

"Major Thomas Powell, sir! At your service! 10th Louisiana Infantry! Just wanted to inform you of our presence on the field, sir!"

"How many men have you brought, Powell?" Morgan asked.

"Oh, I've got two hundred and fifty mighty eager fellows at your command, sir! Ready to have a go at these damn darkies just as soon as you give the word!"

"Where'd you serve?"

"Under Lee and Early from the Seven Days to the end, sir!"

"Good! Take up position on the west side of town. We're a little thin there. Your orders are to make sure no blacks get in or out of the town. If you see any white people who appear in distress or attempting to make their escape, you are to assist them. But no attack as yet, Powell. No going off half-cocked. Is that understood?"

"Completely, sir! Honored to serve under your orders, sir!" He saluted and dashed away.

Morgan smiled, delighted with the man's enthusiasm. He could understand it. For all its horrors, there was something about war that pulled men back to it. The beating of the drum, the thrill of constant danger, and especially the feeling of camaraderie among men fighting for the same cause. Major Powell and his men had not taken the field for two years. The prospect of shouldering arms together, as in their glory days, must have been electrifying.

If he was dismayed at the manner in which a Southern town had fallen to Saul's rebels, Morgan was quite gratified at how efficiently the militia system was operating. Breckinridge's reforms were proving their worth. As the telegraph and messengers on horseback had spread the word that there was trouble in New Iberia, the various militia units, each formed out of the core of the regiments that had brought honor and glory to their names during the War for Southern Independence, had turned out on their own initiative. Now they were making their way towards the town. With each passing hour, more Confederate troops were arriving, gathering around Saul's band likes hyenas swarming around a lion.

Morgan chided himself for thinking this way. Saul was no lion. He was but a black man. He might be more intelligent than the average black man and was undoubtedly clever, but he was a black man just the same. As he thought, though, unpleasant reflections entered his mind. He recalled how Saul had been in a position to kill him during the ambush in late June, but had intentionally fired into the ground by Morgan's feet. Then there was the insulting note Saul had left on his tent the night the surprise raid had carried away Silas, in which Saul had insinuated that he could have killed Morgan if only he had wanted to.

The insurgent leader had now made a critical error, however. In seizing control of a town, Saul had abandoned his previous partisan strategy of movement. He had chosen a specific piece of ground on which to make a stand. That meant that if Morgan could surround the insurgents and prevent them from slipping away, he could destroy them.

A thought entered Morgan's mind and he immediately turned to Duke.

"Basil, I want an order issued to all units in the area. They are to make every effort to capture Saul alive."

"Why?" Duke asked, confused. "Seems to me it would be a lot better just to shoot the bastard."

"That would be too good for him."

"You want a trial? Something like that?"

"That will be up to Davis and Breckinridge," Morgan replied. "Just make sure everybody knows."

"Will do."

"Good."

Morgan envisioned what he would do with Saul if the decision was up to him. His men might want to hang him from the nearest tree, but Morgan would not allow that. Instead, he would lock Saul in a small cage, fit for a wild beast, and drag him through the streets of New Iberia so that the people could jeer at him and bombard him with rotten vegetables. Then, he would systematically break the man's will. He would not kill him, but he would starve him, keep him isolated, and dose him with freezing water. He would do whatever he had to do to destroy the black warrior's spirit of resistance. When Saul's mind had been reduced to that of a pathetic child, he would put him to work picking cotton on some godforsaken plot of land, broken in both body and mind.

His lips curled into a sinister smile. It would be a small price for Saul to pay for the crime of making Morgan look like a fool.

A rider approached and reined in alongside him. He quickly withdrew a paper from his coat pocket.

"General Morgan! Message from the War Department!"

General Morgan,

It is my duty to inform you that Lieutenant General James Longstreet is on his way to New Iberia from Arkansas and should arrive within the next few days. He will take command of all forces operating against the insurgent forces of Saul. Until his arrival, you will retain command, but prepare to turn command over to him as soon as he arrives.

Secretary of War Breckinridge

August 6, Morning
State Department Offices, Richmond, Virginia

"He's here, sir."

Benjamin nodded sharply at the secretary and rose from his desk. He stood as tall as his rotund frame would allow, fixed a stern expression on his face, and clasped his hands behind his back. "Show him in."

Joel Parker, the United States Minister to the Confederate States, entered the office. He had a worried look on his face, which did not surprise Benjamin. He was a handsome man who, had fate placed him in a different role, might have done something larger than what he had thus far achieved. Parker had been a successful New Jersey politician before and during the war, running for and winning the governorship as a War Democrat. Had Benjamin been in McClellan's shoes, he might have appointed Parker to the diplomatic post as well. Even a man with McClellan's limited political instincts knew that he could not have appointed an out-and-out Copperhead to serve as the Union's representative to the Confederacy.

Parker took a deep breath and stepped forward to the desk. He extended his hand. "A pleasure to see you as always, Mr. Secretary."

Benjamin's hands remained firmly clasped behind his back. "I am afraid that I cannot shake your hand today, Minister."

Parker frowned, though there was no look of surprise. He sat down in his chair and, after remaining on his feet just long enough to emphasize the superiority of his position, Benjamin did the same.

"I gather from your demeanor that this meeting wasn't called to discuss anything pleasant."

"You gather correctly, sir," Benjamin said with great formality. "The issue before us is highly important and highly unpleasant. A former officer of the United States Army has been arrested in New Orleans for smuggling weapons and ammunition to blacks who are in arms against the authority of the Confederate government. Moreover, the blacks in question have used those very arms to capture a town in Louisiana, where they have killed several people and continue holding many others hostage."

"I am aware only of what I have read in the newspapers," Parker said. "I have sent a wire to Secretary of War Butler in Washington, inquiring about this Charles Russell Lowell fellow. I still await his response."

Parker was struggling to maintain an amiable voice. Benjamin almost always presented a friendly and humorous air, which he knew made his stern and uncompromising attitude all the more effective. Parker was not used to being put on the spot by Benjamin so directly and it clearly disoriented him.

"He claims to have been a brigadier general in your army," Benjamin said.

"As I have told you, Mr. Secretary, I await word from Secretary Butler as to the identity of this man. I can tell you firmly that I am entirely unaware of any plot and I have been as shocked and surprised by these extraordinary events as you have been."

"That means nothing," Benjamin replied. "If this is a conspiracy by the government of the United States against the Confederacy, there is no reason why the McClellan administration would choose to inform you about it."

"I find it ridiculous to suppose the existence of any such plot," Parker said. "My government is in the midst of a crisis that may lead to war with the British Empire. Why would we choose this moment to try to incite a slave rebellion within the Confederacy? President McClellan has always been anxious for peaceful relations to prevail between us. Your theory makes no sense, Mr. Secretary."

Benjamin didn't nod, but he knew Parker was telling the truth. It was highly unlikely that the McClellan administration knew anything about Lowell or the plot of the smuggled weapons. Almost certainly, the man had acted on his own initiative. Whether he was the agent of a larger conspiracy remained to be seen. When word had arrived of the man's arrest in New Orleans, Benjamin had scrambled to learn all he could about him. He had spoken directly with Breckinridge and exchanged a series of telegrams with Jubal Early, who was at his headquarters in Winchester. Both had recollected that Charles Russell Lowell had been a Union cavalry officer during the Shenandoah Campaign in the summer and fall of 1864, though neither could offer much in the way of detail.

A few hours before Benjamin's meeting with Parker, a messenger from Breckinridge had arrived, holding a telegram that the Secretary of War had received from John Singleton Mosby. The former partisan ranger had left the army when the war ended and was now practicing law in Charlottesville.

Secretary Breckinridge,

I read in the newspaper this morning that one Charles Russell Lowell has been arrested in New Orleans in connection with a plot to smuggle weapons to the Negro rebels in the Lower Mississippi Valley. It seems likely to me that this is the man of the same name who commanded the 2nd Massachusetts Cavalry in the area of my operations in northern Virginia during 1863 and 1864. I wish to acquaint you of the fact, if you find the information worth knowing, that Lowell is a highly intelligent man and always acted the part of an honorable foe. He was the most effective Union commander I ever went up against. I share the shock of the nation at the man's activities in Louisiana.

John Mosby

A few other snippets of information had arrived. The Lowells were apparently quite a prominent family in Boston, somewhat wealthy but not to the extent they had been a generation or so before, and famous for their abolitionist sentiments. The tidbit that had really piqued Benjamin's interest was the fact that Lowell was the brother-in-law of Robert Gould Shaw, the infamous commander who had led the all-black 54th Massachusetts Regiment in its attack against Fort Wagner outside of Charleston in 1863.

"So you are telling me that this Lowell fellow is some sort of renegade?" Benjamin asked.

"I am telling you that I know nothing for certain and cannot speak with any reliability until I receive further word from Washington. But speaking for myself, I would assume that to be the case." There was a momentary pause. "I assume that Lowell will be given the opportunity to speak with the United States consul in New Orleans?"

"Yes, yes, of course," Benjamin said hurriedly. "You must be aware, though, that he will be charged under Confederate law with aiding and abetting servile insurrection."

"I assumed as much," Parker said. "Again, I cannot respond officially until I receive instructions from Washington."

"Naturally."

Benjamin's mind worked at its usual speed. The interview with Parker was a necessary formality, but nothing important was going to come from it. He could imagine, at that very moment, a confused and panicky George McClellan fumbling about in the White House, not having a clue as to how to deal with the situation. The question in Benjamin's mind, as always, was how he could use this strange event to his advantage.

"Please inform President McClellan that Minister Miles is being recalled from Washington to Richmond for consultations," Benjamin said.

Parker's expression grew more concerned. "I hope you are not taking such a step rashly, Mr. Secretary." Recalling the chief diplomatic representative was generally seen as the first step in breaking off diplomatic relations altogether.

"It is not a rash decision," Benjamin replied. "President Davis and I spent quite a long time discussing it this morning."

"I think you and I need to focus on reducing tensions between our two nations. Recalling Miles from Washington will only exacerbate the situation."

"We have no wish to raise tensions, Minister," Benjamin said. "But let me suggest a hypothetical to you. Suppose a man who had been a high-ranking officer of the Confederate Army was arrested for smuggling large amounts of weapons and ammunition to Mormon separatists in the Utah Territory. Suppose also that these weapons were then used to murder a number of your citizens working on the Trans-Continental Railroad. Surely you cannot deny that this would be a matter of serious concern for the United States government?"

Parker considered this for a moment. "When you put it like that, Mr. Secretary, I suppose I can't. But I do not think that such an analogy is correct."

"So you are of the opinion that Lowell is nothing but a common criminal?" Benjamin asked quickly.

Parker hesitated. "Again, I believe I shall have to wait for specific instructions from Washington before making such a statement."

"So what can you say at this point?"

"The United States is gravely concerned by what is happening in Louisiana."

Benjamin grinned for the first time since Parker had entered his office. "Well, then, I believe we have nothing more to discuss at this time. I do hope that you'll keep yourself available to discuss matters as they arise?"

"Of course, Mr. Secretary."

"Very well. Good day to you, sir."

Benjamin sat back down without shaking Parker's hand. He pretended to begin writing on a piece of paper. The Northern diplomat waited just a moment, before turning and walking out the door without another word.

Benjamin thought the situation was extraordinary. Certainly, it represented one of the most astonishing set of circumstances that had arisen since the end of the war. There were many different factors to weigh. The most subtle was the withdrawal of Miles from his post in Washington. Lowell's illegal act had given Benjamin the excuse to bring the South Carolinian Fire-Eater back to Richmond without anyone thinking it unusual. It would indeed put pressure on the McClellan administration, which might have its uses, but Benjamin's true purpose had more to do with the presidential campaign than it did with diplomacy. Miles presented a threat to Breckinridge's chances of winning the presidency and it was now time to nip that threat in the bud, but he would think about that later.

President Davis was still excited about the prospect of an alliance between the Confederacy and Britain. Combined with the continuing Fenian Crisis between Britain and the Union, the Lowell matter would make it more difficult for Benjamin to dissuade Davis from that course of action. He resolved to talk to Breckinridge about it as soon as possible. Perhaps if the two joined forces, they could together discourage the president from sealing the alliance with Britain and move him back in the direction of France.

Benjamin began to speculate as to how news of Saul's seizure of New Iberia and the arrest of Lowell would be received in Europe. Judging from the wires he had been receiving from Slidell in Paris, Benjamin assumed that the increase in tensions with the United States could be turned to the Confederacy's advantage. Sensing a greater possibility of an alliance, the British might sweeten the deal by liberalizing the terms of their existing loans in order to entice the Confederacy in their direction. The French, not wanting this to happen, would in turn advance their own proposals. These new combinations would surely give the Confederacy more options than had previously been the case.

Of course, the abolitionists and utopian elements in Britain and France, with their silly newspapers, would probably proclaim both Saul and Lowell as heroes, but Benjamin did not consider such opinions as likely to have much weight. Best, he thought, to simply ignore them.

August 7, Afternoon
United States Capitol, Washington City

"Senator Sumner of Massachusetts is recognized."

There was a palpable groan from the Democratic side of the chamber as Sumner rose to his feet. Even some of his Republican colleagues appeared alarmed, doubtless wondering what he would have to say in response to the astonishing news that had come out of the Confederacy over the past few days. The President Pro Tempore, Senator Clark, had to spend nearly a full minute gaveling down the noise before Sumner was able to begin. In the meantime, pages had dashed out of the chamber to alert absent members that the Massachusetts senator was on his feet. Few men would want to miss the fireworks that were certain to follow.

The impassive expression on Sumner's face hid an inner torment. The Fenian Crisis, which had dominated his thoughts for weeks, had been forgotten, at least for now. He had read in the previous day's edition of *The Washington Star* of the arrest of Lowell as he had been attempting to flee New Orleans. This, Sumner knew, amounted to a death sentence for Lowell, who would not have a chance of escaping a guilty verdict in the trial that was sure to come soon. He was undeniably guilty of the crimes for which he would be accused. Sumner remembered how quickly the state authorities in Virginia had tried, convicted, and executed John Brown after his fateful raid on Harper's Ferry in 1859. Something quite similar was about to play out in New Orleans.

Yet Sumner and Lowell both believed in a higher law than that of mere men. An immoral law was no law at all in the eyes of God. Lowell, if anything, would have been guilty of a worse crime had he remained safe in Boston while Saul and his band of faithful warriors were hunted down and killed.

As true as this was, Sumner also found it difficult to shake Josephine Lowell from his mind. She had already lost her brother in the fight against slavery and now she would lose her husband, too. Sumner had played a role in both cases, for he had pushed the creation of the 54th Massachusetts Colored Infantry, the leadership of which had led to the death of Colonel Shaw, and he had persuaded

Lowell to undertake his mission to support Saul's rebels, which was now going to lead to his death as well.

Guilt was not an emotion Sumner often experienced. Lowell had known perfectly well what he was risking when he had decided to go to Louisiana, just as his brother-in-law had known what he was risking when he had taken command of his regiment. Josephine Lowell would certainly feel grief, yet Sumner hoped she would also feel pride. If her children were going to grow up fatherless, at least they would have an example of sacrifice by which they might be inspired. They might not get a chance to know their father, but they would be able to honor his glorious memory for the rest of their lives.

There would be time for these thoughts later. Now, he had a speech to make. He took a deep breath and the Senate became silent.

"Events of the most extraordinary nature are unfolding within the grotesque entity that calls itself the Confederate States of America," Sumner began. "Extraordinary and, dare I say it, exhilarating. Exhilarating, at least, to those unblemished Northern men who still uphold the virtues of freedom and liberty."

A muttering of discontent rose from the Democratic side of the aisle, requiring Senator Clark to bang his gavel three times quickly to stop the noise from becoming too loud.

Sumner went on. "The South has dismissed Saul as a common criminal. I suppose if being a black man who yearns to be free is a crime, then a criminal he is. The South says that Saul and his men are nothing but a ragtag band of thieves. I suppose that to free one's own friends and family from the chains of slavery is to be a thief in the Confederacy. But tell me, when was the last time that a ragtag band of thieves was able to capture an entire town? When was the last time a ragtag band of thieves was able to hold at bay the most feared soldiers of the Confederacy? This is not a band of thieves, but a band of warriors! A band of warriors who are guilty of one thing: fighting to free themselves and their people from the chains of slavery and despotism!"

He glanced around to gauge how the opening of the speech had gone. What he saw on the floor of the chamber did not surprise him. The Democrats were either gazing at him the way one looks at an inmate in a lunatic asylum or simply pretending not to pay attention at all. His Republican colleagues also had a mix of reactions on their faces. Some, Radicals like himself, smiled and nodded with each passing sentence, urging him on with their eyes. The more moderate members of his party appeared apprehensive, obviously worried that he would begin speaking in excessively extreme language. He was about to prove them correct.

"As these momentous events unfold, we hear nothing from President McClellan. The silence coming from the White House is more deafening that the loudest crash of the cannon. Millions of good Northern men are cheered by the success of Saul and his brave band of black warriors as they struggle against the Confederates. The enemy against which Saul fights is the same enemy that good Northern men fought on battlefields from Shiloh to Gettysburg, from Vicksburg to Missionary Ridge. President McClellan himself – perhaps he needs to be reminded – led soldiers against the Confederates when he commanded the Army of the Potomac. Less than three years ago, our men were fighting and dying in the struggle against slavery. Saul and his men are struggling still. What does the president have to say about it? The world wonders."

Sumner took a moment to glance at the visitor galleries. As usual, they were crowded with well-dressed ladies, the elite of Washington society come out to see him speak. Sumner cared little for their reaction to his words. He was more interested in the newspaper reporters scribbling down his words on their small notepads. In truth, he knew he was not really speaking to his fellow Senators, but to the citizens of the nation as a whole.

Sitting in the gallery, Sumner saw, was Sir Frederick Wright-Bruce, the British Minister Plenipotentiary to the United States. His presence reminded Sumner that he was also speaking to the powers-that-be in London and Paris, for his words would surely be reprinted in the newspapers of Europe. Sumner was still determined to do whatever he could to prevent the Fenian Crisis from sparking a war between the United States and the British Empire. It was unclear to him how the events in Louisiana would play into that particular state of affairs, but anything that focused the attention of the people of the North against the slaveholders of the South and away from war with England was a good thing.

He was already using every means at his disposal to expose McClellan's direct involvement with the Fenian movement and so humiliate the president until he had to back down. With Saul's capture of the town of New Iberia, Sumner could put yet more pressure on the president by calling upon him to speak out on what was happening. McClellan could not condemn what Saul had done, for even many Democratic constituencies in the North would not tolerate an open statement of support for the Confederacy. Neither could the president speak out in support of Saul without appearing to be actively opposing the Confederacy, thus contradicting the policy his administration had maintained since it had taken office. The wisest course of action for McClellan, politically speaking, was to say nothing at all. Sumner was determined to make that impossible.

"Will the Senator yield for a question?"

He looked over at the man speaking. It was an old nemesis, Senator Bayard of Maryland, one of McClellan's puppies and a man Sumner thoroughly loathed.

"I yield to the senator from Maryland for a question."

"Is it not true that Senator Sumner is personally acquainted with one Charles Russell Lowell, late of the United States Army, who we learn today has been arrested by Confederate authorities in New Orleans for smuggling weapons to the group of insurgents led by the man known as Saul?"

"It is true," Sumner said simply. Inwardly, he smiled. Bayard thought that he had caught Sumner in a trap and was about to embarrass him. The Marylander had been unaware that Sumner was not only unashamed of his connection to Lowell, but had been about to loudly proclaim it for all to hear. The unlooked-for question from the Democratic side of the aisle would only make the coming comments more dramatic.

"Perhaps the distinguished senator from Massachusetts could enlighten the members of the Senate on your personal relations with this criminal?"

"Gladly," Sumner said. "I have known Charles Russell Lowell since he was a boy. I watched him grow to manhood. The Lowell family is one of the most distinguished in the United States. It is a family that has given us poets, theologians, and captains of industry. And in the man of Charles Russell Lowell, it has given us a patriot of the highest order. In his service as a cavalry commander in northern Virginia, Charles Russell Lowell proved himself to be every inch a courageous soldier." He paused a moment for effect. "I am surprised and disappointed to hear the distinguished senator from Maryland speak of as gallant a man as Charles Russell Lowell in such a disparaging manner."

Bayard winced slightly and he abruptly sat back down. Sumner's comments were sure to be in the papers the next day and the Maryland senator now knew he would not come out looking well. Satisfied that he had put the Copperhead in his place, Sumner went back to his speech.

"So we have two men, Saul and Lowell, and that faithful band that fights on in the swamps of Louisiana. Gallant men. Honorable men. Men braver by far than any of us in this chamber here today. Saul could had fled to freedom whenever he wanted and Lowell need never have gone to Louisiana at all. They face death because they knew a truth of which our president apparently needs to be reminded: that what is merely expedient is rarely right."

Glancing about quickly, Sumner sensed that he had the audience firmly in his grasp. Encouraged, he went on.

"I call upon President McClellan to summon Minister Miles to the White House and demand that the Confederacy meet the following conditions. General Lowell must be granted full legal rights and due process. Any attempt by the men of the South to exact extrajudicial vengeance upon this gallant man must be treated as a serious breach of the diplomatic relations between our two countries. Lowell is, after all, a citizen of the United States. If the Confederacy refuses to abide by the laws which govern all civilized nations, then I would urge a citizen of the Confederacy residing in our own country to be similarly seized and subjected to the same treatment as that which Lowell receives."

There was an uneasy rustling and muttering among both his fellow senators and the people crowded into the visitor galleries. Sumner knew that McClellan, being a man of such obscene vanity and pride, would almost certainly reject Sumner's ultimatum simply to avoid the appearance of being unwillingly forced into anything. That was not the point. The Confederates were going to kill Lowell anyway, Sumner was certain. If McClellan refused to intervene, Sumner and his allies could blame him for Lowell not receiving a fair trial, which would serve their political ends quite effectively.

"Second, the president must demand that the Confederate authorities treat Saul and his men as legitimate military combatants and insist that they not be subjected to arbitrary execution. We have every reason to believe that a great many of these brave men are former soldiers of the United States. Though they may have disobeyed orders in refusing to be disbanded at the conclusion of the late war, they are still entitled to the same rights and privileges that all civilized nations recognize as the established laws of war. If they refuse, the president should consider such behavior to be an unfriendly act by the Confederate States against the United States."

These words were greeted with a stunning silence throughout the chamber. What Sumner was basically demanding was the first step in a long-established diplomatic process that could lead to an outright breaking off of relations and, conceivably, war.

"Third, the president must make the crisis in the Confederacy his primary focus. What is happening this day in the town of New Iberia may soon spread over the whole of the pretended nation to our south. A full-scale revolt of the slaves is possible. This means he must abandon his administration's foolhardy policy of support for the Fenians and make every effort to reestablish good relations between our country and England. I call upon President McClellan to disarm the Fenian war bands and arrest the ringleaders of the Fenian Brotherhood without delay."

Sumner knew that the Fenian business would vanish from the newspaper headlines for the foreseeable future. Reporters were always wary of boring their readers with the same story for too long and the Fenian Crisis had been on the front pages for almost three months. The newspaper scribblers were desperate for something new and the dramatic capture of New Iberia by Saul, combined with the arrest of Lowell in New Orleans, was like manna falling from heaven for them.

Yet Sumner did not want the Fenian Crisis to be forgotten altogether. His strategy depended upon emphasizing McClellan's callousness towards Saul and Lowell, but also his incompetence with respect to the British. He aimed to humiliate the president in the eyes of the public, ensuring that his time in office would be limited to a single term. In doing so, Sumner could ensure that war with Britain would be avoided and a future conflict with the Confederacy would be more likely. Once the Republicans regained control of the White House and the House of Representatives, all the pieces would be in place for the war for abolition to resume.

For, as far as Sumner was concerned, the war had never really ended.

August 8, Morning
New Iberia, Louisiana

"Good work, Troy," Saul said with admiration. "The slaveholders will think twice before they try to storm this position, hostages or no hostages."

"Thanks, boss," Troy replied.

From the hotel porch, Saul looked around again. All the structures near the hotel had been burned or torn down. Many of them had been stripped of their wooden frames before being set on fire, the pieces of which had been incorporated into the wooden barricade which, set in front of a low trench, now surrounded the hotel on every side. Two hundred men were in position, ready to repel any attacker.

The rest of his men were scattered throughout the now deserted town in small groups. The enemy soldiers were still hovering on the outskirts of New Iberia, having occupied a few buildings but being careful to remain out of rifle range. There had been occasional exchanges of fire, and Saul had sent forward his best marksmen a few times to shoot at the Confederate officers when their units were getting too close, but otherwise there had been no real fighting. Yet

Saul assumed that Morgan was not going to attack so long as there was a risk of danger to the hostages inside the hotel.

All told, Saul had about four hundred men under his command. The core of his fighting force were his one hundred and seventy seasoned fighters, many of whom had been battling the Confederates for more than four years. All of these men were armed with the new rifles smuggled in by Lowell. He knew he could count on them for anything and, newly armed and flushed with the capture of New Iberia, he knew their morale was high.

The remainder of his force consisted of the new recruits who had been freed with the capture of New Iberia or in the raids on surrounding plantations over the subsequent two days. These men had no training, but most had thrown themselves enthusiastically into the rebellion. All of these men were now armed with firearms as well, the steadiest having been given the few dozen leftover rifles from Lowell's delivery. The rest were armed with guns looted from a nearby militia depot, although they were poorly maintained Austrian-made Lorenz rifles, considerably inferior to the Springfields. He assumed that the best weapons of the militia had been taken by the men who had been sent north to serve with Morgan. On the other hand, there had been a good deal of ammunition, which was being stockpiled around the hotel.

Never since the beginning of his uprising had Saul commanded so many men, and never had they been so well-armed and equipped.

Saul knew that the Confederates could overwhelm him with massively superior numbers any time they choose to do so. Some of his units on the outskirts of town reported that enemy artillery had begun arriving. Saul knew that he would have no protection against cannon fire. This was the price he paid for choosing to capture and defend a specific position. Only the presence of the hostages protected them, but that had been his plan all along.

Saul turned and walked into the lobby of the hotel. Ferguson stood at what had been the check-in desk, reading carefully over the pieces of paper he and Saul had been working on since the night before. Upstairs, Saul knew, the hostages remained holed up in their rooms, guarded by a dozen of his men in the hallway who had been given strict orders to treat the captive whites properly and do nothing to unduly trouble them.

"Done?" Saul asked Ferguson.

"I believe so," the white physician answered. He handed the hotel stationary over to Saul, who read through it quickly.

To the Citizens of the Confederate States of America,

I have taken control of New Iberia, Louisiana, and freed its black residents whom you have held in slavery. I have also freed many more enslaved blacks from the surrounding plantations and brought them to the town. By right of military conquest, I declare that all authority of the Confederacy in the town of New Iberia is at an end and proclaim New Iberia to be a Liberated Town. It shall be the first of many.

New Iberia is hereby declared the capital of what we call the Liberated Territory. We further declare the implementation of the Provisional Constitution and Ordinances as promulgated by John Brown in 1858. As the territory under our control expands, it will continue to serve as the governing document.

I also wish to inform you that forty-nine white men, women and children are my prisoners at the hotel. Many others we have let go, to demonstrate our mercy. If any attack is made on my position, I am fully confident that my brave men can and will prevail and pile up the bodies of our enemies in front of our trenches. We are well-armed and well supplied with ammunition. But if, God forbid, it appears as if we might be defeated, all the prisoners shall be immediately executed.

Some will assert that my threat to execute my prisoners is proof that I am a barbarian. Perhaps it is. But how am I any more barbaric than a man who holds his fellow human beings in slavery, whipping them if they refuse to work and hanging them without compunction? For two hundred and fifty years, the white people of the South have held their black brethren in chains, in all violation of natural law and against the principles of the American Revolution that they claim to uphold. During the recent war with the United States, the slaves freed themselves in massive numbers and joined the Union Army to fight for the freedom of their people. We do not acknowledge the Treaty of Toronto. The war continues still and it shall not cease until every black man and woman in the South is free and slavery is utterly destroyed.

I have three demands. First, I demand that Confederate military forces currently deployed around New Iberia be immediately withdrawn to a distance of fifty miles. Second, I demand that all slave-owners within a radius of fifty miles immediately bring their slaves to New Iberia so that they might be set them at liberty. Third and last, I demand that the Confederate government recognize the status of New Iberia as a Liberated Town and the legality of the declaration of Brown's Constitution in the territory under our control.

If these demands are met, I shall set at liberty all the hostages under my control within forty-eight hours.

Sincerely,

Saul

"What do you think?" Ferguson asked.

"It's good," Saul replied instantly. "You've made copies?"

"Three."

"Okay, we'll send it over to the whites. They'll not allow it to be printed, though. We'll have to depend on rumors."

"Don't be so sure," Ferguson replied. "We'll send it across the lines to Morgan, who will forward it to his masters in Richmond. Somebody will make a copy of it, probably quite a few. It'll be a big story, after all. Any reporter who gets his hands on a copy will make sure it runs in his paper. The mere hint that a letter from you is appearing in that day's issue will cause sales of the paper to skyrocket. The whites of the South might be united in their defense of slavery, but any individual person can smell the chance to make money. Greed motivates men more than anything else."

Saul shook his head. "No. Fear is more powerful than greed."

Ferguson didn't reply, merely looking into Saul's eyes with a searching expression that Saul had seen many times before. He knew how much he owed to Ferguson. He was able to read and write because of him. He knew about things no slave knew anything about, such as astronomy and ancient history, because Ferguson had taught him about them in long discussions around the night's campfire. The white physician was as close to a father as Saul had.

Yet he could not help but feel that he was outgrowing the man. Ferguson was an educated man, who had graduated from college and even travelled to

Europe, a land which existed only in Saul's dreams. For all that, though, Saul felt that he was Ferguson's superior. Had he been blessed with all the advantages with which Ferguson had been blessed, and were a black man not inevitably seen as inferior to a white man, Saul was certain that he would have risen far beyond Ferguson.

The anger that always simmered below the surface of his spirit threatened to boil over for a moment. Everyone had but a single life to live and everyone had a natural right to use that life in an attempt to be happy. The slaveholders had robbed him of that chance, just as they had millions of other people. It had to be stopped.

"So you want to send one of the hostages out with this message?" Ferguson asked.

"Yes," Saul said. "We'll send Mayor Delacroix. Best that the letter he carried by a person with authority and credibility."

"I'll bring him down." Ferguson turned and walked up the stairs.

Saul took a deep breath. Whether the letter got into the newspapers or not, rumors of it would certainly began to circulate. He was positive that it would have its desired effect. It would strike fear into the hearts of the Confederates from General Morgan all the way up to President Davis himself. All the criminals who profited from the unpaid labor of their slaves, who daily inflicted violence upon the black men and women they claimed as their property, would be put on notice. The grotesque society that had built on the broken backs of the children of Africa was going to be destroyed.

He knew it wouldn't happen quickly. Almost certainly, New Iberia would be recaptured by the Confederates sooner or later, though he planned on making them pay a heavy price for it. Yet even if it was, word of what had happened in the town would inevitably spread among the enslaved black populations, just as the news of the advance of Union armies into Southern territory had spread in the form of stories of near-mythical bluecoats who had come to set the slaves free. The story would be different this time, for it would be a tale about something that blacks had done for themselves, rather than have somebody else do for them.

Saul allowed a dangerous thought to enter his mind. What if he could hold New Iberia? What if the words in his letter could be more than just rhetoric? Perhaps the slaves on nearby plantations had heard of his capture of the town and would finally rise up against their masters, diverting Confederate troops away and allowing him to maintain his position. There had often been talk that the slaves were just waiting for the right moment to murder their masters and take control of the plantations. This fear was why so many plantation owners slept with loaded pistols under their pillows.

Ferguson came back down, with Mayor Delacroix following behind him.

"Good morning, Mr. Mayor," Saul with pleasantly. "I trust you slept well."

Delacroix said nothing, glancing about the room uncertainly.

"I am releasing you," Saul said. "I ask only that you take a letter I have written and present it to General Morgan."

"Letter?" Delacroix asked. "What sort of letter?"

"I'm letting the Confederate government know what they need to do in order for the hostages to be released unharmed."

Delacroix nodded. "I see. That makes sense, I suppose." He paused a moment. "May I ask for something in return?"

"I'm letting you go. Isn't that enough?"

"My fellow hostages are complaining about not having any tea or coffee. You've provided food for them, but no coffee or tea."

"Coffee and tea?"

"They feel the want of coffee and tea very much."

Saul almost laughed. The white slaveholders were so tied to their luxuries that their minds had begun to consider them necessities. "I will see to it that the hostages be given coffee and tea, if any can be found." It would be amusing, if nothing else.

"Thank you."

Ten minutes later, after having allowed Delacroix to change his clothes and wash up, the man calmly stepped down off the porch of the hotel and walked down the street towards the Confederate lines on the outskirts of town, waving a white towel to ensure that nobody shot at him. He reached the enemy position and was then lost to Saul's sight.

August 9, Noon
Meridian, Mississippi

"Three hundred miles from here!" Toombs thundered, banging his fists against the podium. "Three hundred miles only! That is the distance that separates you and your families from murder at the hands of these darkie bandits! And why? Because our pathetic and incompetent Secretary of War, John Breckinridge, the man who now wants to be your president, was too weak to crush this rebellion when he had the chance!"

The people listening to him glanced nervously at one another. The crowd was not as large as those he had spoken to in Mobile or Selma, but still numbered a few hundred people. They were not very well-dressed, for Meridian was in a less prosperous of the Confederacy, removed from the opulence of the cities or great plantations. Moreover, the Yankee hordes under Sherman had burned much of Meridian to the ground in February of 1864 and recovery had been slow.

Toombs had made himself into a wealthy man, but he was not so far removed from the people that he could not relate to the poor. From long experience, he knew that the best way to inflame the emotions of the common white man was to talk about blacks. So long as blacks were held in slavery, poor whites could at least tell themselves that they were not on the lowest rung of the Southern ladder. As long as black slavery existed, the wealthy white aristocracy that ruled the Confederacy would have the support of the poor whites. This, almost as much as the need for unpaid labor for plantation agriculture, justified the protection of the South's peculiar institution.

"Do you doubt that the slaves in and around Meridian have heard of what's happening in New Iberia?" Toombs asked rhetorically. "Don't think they haven't. You know how clever they are. Since Saul started his rising in Louisiana, how many of the slaves you see every day have wondered whether they, too, might take up a knife and kill you in your sleep? How many, do you think?"

There were scattered black faces in the crowd, some holding umbrellas to shield white people from the hot sun, others holding the hands of children, and some simply standing around with unreadable expressions on their faces. Toombs wondered if his words might cause the whites to give in to paranoia. When John Brown had raided Harper's Ferry in 1859, the fear had been so intense that many innocent blacks had been hanged simply for being out on the road without proper papers. If similar incidents happened now, Toombs felt that the blame could be laid squarely at Breckinridge's feet for having failed to stop Saul in the first place.

"If you or any of your kin is struck down by a black wielding a knife, or any other sort of weapon, you can blame Breckinridge for it. He should have called up a whole brigade to crush these bandits when they raided the first plantation, months ago! Instead, he sent in only a token force and gave the command to one of his friends. These blacks have run rings around old Jack Morgan, just like Morgan used to run rings around the Yankees. Oh, how the mighty have fallen!"

Toombs reflected that the joke would have gotten a fair laugh at his earlier rallies, yet now it only generated a few nervous chuckles. He knew why. Simply put, the people were scared. Two weeks before, Saul had been the leader of a ragged group of bandits hiding in the swamp. A man might have been able to convince himself that the rebel leader didn't even really exist but was just a figment of the South's imagination. Now, though, this group of rebels was in control of a town and holding white hostages. How could people be confident that it wouldn't happen elsewhere, perhaps in their own communities?

Toombs was as shocked by the events in New Iberia as anyone else. He worried about the spread of the news through the slave quarters across the country just as much as did everyone else. Yet he had the mind of a politician. Within an hour of reading the first newspaper accounts of the town's fall, he was already altering his campaign strategy to take advantage of the new situation. He knew that a fearful population was more likely to vote for the ticket that promised strong measures than one which counseled moderation.

This being the case, he had sharpened his stump speech to cast blame directly on Breckinridge for the fall of New Iberia, disdaining now to even mention Jefferson Davis. He had sent out letters to other major figures of the SRP leadership, with the exception of Wigfall, laying out his new strategy. All over the Confederacy, he knew, his political allies were going to increase their attacks on Breckinridge to a fever pitch.

"And how did this Charles Russell Lowell fellow smuggle in cartload after cartload of weapons to these black bandits? Why wasn't Morgan patrolling the area to prevent such an occurrence? Yet more stupidity! Yet more incompetence! But I don't just blame Morgan. I also blame the man who gave him the command! Breckinridge has much to answer for! He's the reason you and your children are in danger!"

Men in the crowd nodded and he could hear people mutter agreements to one another. Women, Toombs noticed, clutched their children a little more closely and cast nervous glances at the blacks watching the proceedings.

He continued speaking in this vein for another half hour. He made no mention about the treaty with France, the acquisition of Cuba, taxes, or any of the other subjects he usually talked about. It wouldn't be right for this particular crowd of simple people. Fear was what moved folk like this and they were right to be afraid. What happened in New Iberia, it went without saying, could easily happen in Meridian.

"Who, then, will you vote for? Beauregard, the man you can trust to keep you and your families safe? Or Breckinridge, the man who placed them in danger in the first place? It's a decision that you will be called upon to make November 5. Join with the rest of the country and vote SRP!"

Timidity was thrust aside and the crowd roared its approval.

August 9, Afternoon
Flynn's Alehouse, Waco, Texas

It was starting to feel like a genuine political campaign, McFadden thought happily. The alehouse was full of men intently studying marked maps of the Waco streets and the nearby farms, memorizing the routes they were to take as they went door-to-door on behalf of his state legislative campaign, Collett's county judge campaign, and the Breckinridge presidential campaign. Children were being given broadsheets to paste up in specified locations around town.

The atmosphere was electric and positive. Excited chatter and laughter filled the alehouse. Flynn was passing out mugs of beer to the crowd, happy that the campaign was making him so much money. A supporter from a nearby farm had sent two pigs to be slaughtered, providing snacks of hot pork to the volunteers. A grizzled old black man, in exchange for some of the food and drink, was sitting in the corner and playing the banjo, an enormous grin on his face.

Many of those present were women, unable to vote but more than happy to work for the campaign. McFadden was quite certain that some of them had come in order to meet eligible men. In Waco, as in so many other Southern towns, war casualties meant that young women substantially outnumbered young men, so the females had to take what they could get. He was amused at the sight of gawky veterans with missing teeth being fawned upon by beautiful girls who would have paid them no attention before the war. The flirtatiousness evident as the men and women talked with one another added to the pleasant mood.

McFadden looked up and smiled as Collett entered the alehouse. His campaign for county judge and McFadden's campaign for state representative had always been essentially the same operation, and now they were jointly supporting Breckinridge's presidential run. Other friends were running for the lower seats on the county commissioners' court. If they won, they would have complete control of the county government and Roden's corrupt rule would be at an end.

"How are things?" Collett asked as he took off his hat, grabbed a proffered mug of beer from Flynn, and sat down at the table across from McFadden.

"Good, I think. We've got a lot of people out today, knocking on doors."

"Well, that's good. I'm thinking old Judge Roden is regretting talking to you the way he did the day of that auction, eh?"

McFadden grinned as he took another sip of beer. Things did indeed seem to be going well, with increasing signs of support from the people of Waco and the surrounding area. At first, many had been reluctant to openly favor those who wanted to kick Roden out of office, but slowly things had begun to turn around. Information had started to flow out, at first by word-of-mouth. Then the *Waco Southern Confederacy*, the smallest newspaper in the area, had regularly started putting out information about the meetings of the campaign, amid its denunciations of Roden and his cronies. When enough volunteers had begun showing up for people to start knocking on doors, the campaign had really started to get momentum.

Postmaster Reagan had suggested to McFadden that he, as one of the two leading candidates of the effort, get out on the streets to knock on doors himself. He had not enjoyed it at first. He wasn't a particularly outgoing person and felt embarrassed asking people for favors. Collett seemed to enjoy it, for he was a gregarious and amiable man. By contrast, when McFadden had made his first attempt at block walking, it had so thoroughly demoralized him that he had resolved not to do it again.

Annie had suggested that she go with him and that they bring Thaddeus along. McFadden had thought this idea silly at first, but it had soon proved to work very well. The adorable face and playful talking of their two-year-old had quickly warmed the hearts of strangers and Annie's natural charm had opened the conversation. After a minute or two, McFadden had been able to start making his pitch, speaking of the corruption of Roden, how his friends would change the way the county was run and how he himself would represent the district in the state legislature.

It hadn't always worked, of course. Quite a few doors had been slammed in their faces, either from genuine anger from Roden supporters, fear from those who feared Roden's wrath, or simply irritation from those who wanted to be left alone. Yet most people had wanted to talk. Many had expressed joy that people were working to get Roden out of office and quite a few had shared stories, sadly now quite familiar to McFadden, of how the county judge had intimidated them and bullied them in the past. He found that the more people with whom he spoke, the better he got at it.

Having Annie and Thaddeus go with him helped buck up his courage. What was more important to him, though, was simply having them with him so that he knew where they were and that they were safe. They would probably have been safe on the farm, but there was no substitute for having his wife and child actually in his presence.

"How many people are telling you that they will vote for us?" Collett asked.

"More than half," McFadden answered. "I think that as people have realized that we're serious about what we're doing, they've lost their fear of Roden and been more willing to openly support us."

"Some of the people who were threatened with losing their jobs stayed on our side anyway, even went out knocking on doors for us, and they haven't been fired."

McFadden took a swig of his ale. "Roden is turning out to be the big bully on the schoolyard. The other kids live in fear of him until someone has guts enough to stand up to him."

"That's the truth, by God," Collett answered. "And the kids who had the guts, turns out, was us."

McFadden shook his head. "No, it's all these people," he said, tossing his head towards the crowd of supporters in the alehouse. "It's all the people of Waco who are now willing to say they're voting against Roden, and out on the farms, too. They've been pushed around by Roden for years now and they're sick of it. They're the brave ones. You and me? What we're doing here is nothing compared to what we went through during the war."

"Any word from our friend Walker?" McFadden asked.

"None," Collett replied. "He and his boys are still hanging around at the bank across the street, smoking and drinking but not much else. Tough looking, but quiet as a little girl's doll."

McFadden wasn't so sure. He had looked in Walker's eyes and seen a dark and angry soul, like many men he had met during the war. They were the eyes of a man who thought no more of killing than a man would think of throwing away the parts of a steak that had proven too tough to chew. He had expected to see some sort of effort to keep his campaign from operating, but Walker and his men were doing nothing but watching. The only reason that this could be so, McFadden assumed, was because it was what Roden had ordered.

Not all the talk he overheard was about the campaign in Waco. News that the black bandit known as Saul had seized the town of New Iberia in Louisiana was on everyone's lips. The place was hundreds of miles away and, for all McFadden cared about, might as well have been on the far side of the Moon. Compared to the land of sugar plantations in southern Louisiana, there were few slaves on the Texas frontier. Nevertheless, the upswing in the fortunes of the famous black insurgent was certainly causing the whites of Waco to look upon their black servants with more than the usual scrutiny.

There was a sudden rustle of conversation among the crowd, causing McFadden and Collett to look up at the man coming through the door. He was well-dressed in a business suit and appeared simultaneously nervous and irate.

"Who is that man?" McFadden asked.

"By God, that's Robert Beckley, the owner of the *Waco Tribune*."

"Is it? What on earth is he doing here?"

Among the three newspapers now being published in Waco, the *Tribune* was the middle child between the *Waco Herald*, which was the largest, and the *Waco Southern Confederacy*, which was the newest and smallest. Both the *Herald* and the *Tribune* had been pro-Roden, refusing to run ads for the McFadden-Collett campaign and scarcely bothering to mention their existence in their pages.

Beckley saw McFadden and Collett at their table and, removing his hat, walked up to them. They rose from their chairs as he approached. "Afternoon, gentlemen," he said simply.

"Afternoon to you, Mr. Beckley," Collett answered. "Anything we can do for you? An ale, perhaps?"

Beckley hesitated, then nodded. "Yes, that would be nice."

Collett gestured to Flynn at the bar, who nodded and began pouring.

"Won't you sit down, Mr. Beckley?" McFadden asked, motioning to the chairs. The three men took their seats and, moments later, one of Flynn's tavern girls arrived with a tray of three frothing ale mugs. Beckley appeared uneasy, awkwardly trying to find a way to begin talking.

"I am sorry that I have not been to see you gentlemen before now," Beckley started.

"We are sorry, too," McFadden replied quickly. "You are, of course, free to support whomever you prefer between our campaign and that of Judge Roden. But I must say that I rather wish you at least mentioned our campaign. If one read your newspaper, they could be forgiven for not even knowing who I was or that I was running for the state legislature. And why not at least run the ads we asked you to publish? Our money is as good as Judge Roden's, isn't it?"

Beckley pursed his lips and nodded. "When you both announced your campaigns, I did not think you had the slightest chance. Judge Roden has been in political power for a long time. Granbury County operates as a machine that he controls like the conductor of a train. He told me not to cover your campaign. If I did, he told me, I would be sorry. I didn't see any benefit to refusing, but plenty of downside."

"No benefit?" McFadden asked, incredulous. "You're a newspaperman. You're supposed to report the news."

"There, there, Jimmy," Collett said. "Mr. Beckley has come to speak to us out of good intentions, I think. Perhaps we should let bygones be bygones."

"That depends," McFadden said, glaring at Beckley. "Are you going to cover our campaign now? Are you going to run our ads?"

Beckley took a swallow of his beer. "Yes, I am. Roden will be furious and I will probably suffer for it. But the alternate was not any more attractive to me."

"Why is that?"

"Because I received a message from the Postmaster General, John Reagan, who you know is in Texas to coordinate the Breckinridge campaign. He told me that if I didn't cover your campaign and let you runs ads, his postal workers were going to stop delivering copies of my paper to my subscribers."

These words took McFadden completely by surprise, yet they filled him with delight. Since he had met with Reagan down in Austin, the support that they received had been small but crucial. There had been a limited flow of campaign money and letters of advice from seasoned political campaigners telling McFadden and Collett the basics of how to organize their efforts. Small as this level of support had been, they probably would not have known how to get started at all had they not received it.

But if what Beckley was saying was true, and there was no reason to believe it wasn't, Reagan's actions had just had a major impact on the campaign. As hard as they were working to get more volunteers to knock on doors throughout the district, the best way to reach people was still through the newspapers. Being able to run ads in the *Waco Tribune* would greatly extend their reach to the people. Even better, people who had not taken their effort seriously had pointed to the absence of coverage in the newspapers as evidence. Now that idea would be thrown back in their face.

"Well, I'm sorry it took the intervention of the Postmaster General to make you see the light, but I'm glad you have," McFadden said.

"You might be a little more gracious about it," Beckley replied sourly.

"Oh, you think so, do you? You act like you're granted us some sort of favor, and against your will. It was a disservice to the people of this district to ignore our campaign up until now. You did it because Roden bullied you into doing it."

"Let's be generous to the man, old friend," Collett said. "Like I said before, let's let bygones be bygones. We should all be pleased with this. We'll get what we've asked him for and he'll get our money. It works out well for everyone."

"Well, Beckley could start by printing the letter we received from the Texas officers."

Collett nodded vigorously in agreement. They had contacted former Confederate officers, regimental and company commanders from Granbury's Brigade, Hood's Brigade, Terry's Texas Rangers, Walker's Greyhounds, and other units, asking for their support. Almost to a man, they had agreed to endorse McFadden and Collett and had signed their names onto a letter stating such. They had celebrated the night their one hundredth name had been added to the list. As far as they were aware, only about a dozen former officers had openly endorsed Roden. It was a distinction that they wanted the people to know about. Thanks to Beckley's turnabout, they would now get a chance.

"What do you think Roden will think of that?" Collett asked, after they had explained what the letter was.

Beckley pursed his lips. "Gentlemen, I hope you understand that I am doing what I am doing rather against my will. I personally will be voting for Roden on Election Day. I will open the pages of my paper to you, but that is all. You should not consider me an ally."

McFadden grunted out a response. He did not care for Beckley. Frankly, he did not care for men who only did the right thing when they had no other choice. Annie would never had respected him had he been that kind of man. The thought passed through his mind as to whether Beckley was married and whether his wife was proud of him.

Collett raised his mug of ale. "Everything else aside, I'll raise a cup to this day." With some reluctance, McFadden and Beckley raised their cups as well and the three clinked them together.

August 10, Morning
Executive Office Building, Richmond, Virginia

"Saul's men are dug in around the hotel here," Breckinridge said, pointing to the spot on the map. "They burned down or demolished all the buildings around the area to provide a clear field of fire, but left them standing at a distance of a couple hundred yards. This means that any attacking force will have to pack tightly together to approach down the streets, but then charge across open ground to reach the barricades. It's well done, to be honest. Any attack will suffer heavy casualties."

President Davis and the rest of the Cabinet looked down at the table, which was now covered with a map of New Iberia that a clerk had found in the War Department records. All had glum expressions on their faces. In the past few days, all of them had received the same severe shock that had been experienced by the entire country. Having thought Saul dealt with, they had been mentally moving on to other things. The capture of New Iberia had stunned all of them beyond measure.

"Heavy casualties need to be avoided," Davis said. "I don't want the newspapers of the world lauding this Negro as some sort of great warrior."

"They are already doing that," Benjamin pointed out. "People love an underdog, especially the British. The more he looks like a hero, the more our country looks like a tyranny. And the more fixated the world is on slavery, the lower our chances of concluding treaties or of obtaining loans."

"Benjamin is correct," Trenholm said sourly. "I received a telegram from our man in New York this morning telling me that bond sales have dropped sharply in the past two or three days. All the paperboys on every street corner are crying out the names of Saul and Lowell."

"All this is most interesting, gentlemen," Davis said impatiently. "What do we do about it?"

"Attack the bastard right away," Attorney General Harris said firmly. "Why are we holding back? We have thousands of men surrounding Saul by now. He's been in control of the town for a week and a half now. I say storm the building right now and overwhelm him with sheer force of numbers. Fighter or not, this Saul fellow cannot withstand the odds against him."

"That risks turning him into a martyr, just like the defenders of the Alamo," Breckinridge replied. "As the president just said, we need to avoid giving the newspapers material with which to build Saul up into something he's not."

"Every day he sits there in control of New Iberia does that much more effectively than if he killed a thousand of our men!" Harris protested. "No, I say we must crush him and crush him at once!"

"There are the hostages to consider," Benjamin replied calmly. "We would appear callous if we allowed dozens of white citizens to be murdered, especially as there are women and children among them."

Breckinridge was impressed by the sense of calm that Benjamin seemed to exude in the midst of the near-panic that had gripped the rest of the Cabinet since Saul's seizure of New Iberia. Of all of them, the Secretary of State had seemed the least surprised by what had happened. He never knew what was happening behind the man's enigmatic smile and, not for the first time, Breckinridge wondered if it had been a good idea to entrust so much of the presidential campaign to Benjamin. The man was undoubtedly brilliant, but despite having known him for many years, Breckinridge remained uncertain as to his motives.

Harris was talking. "I will regret the loss of life among these white hostages as much as anyone, but what is our alternative? Shall we simply sit back and let Saul do as he pleases? I hate to sound coldhearted, but thousands of women and children died during the war thanks to the Yankees. If we are to preserve our society, we have to be prepared to accept such sacrifices."

Breckinridge said nothing, but shook his head. During the war, he had been required to issue orders that sent men to their deaths. On a dark day in May of 1864, he had even had to order the young cadets of the Virginia Military Institute into combat at the small yet bitter Battle of New Market. Yet there was a difference between that and taking actions that caused the deaths of innocent civilians.

"I must agree with the Attorney General," said Secretary of the Treasury Trenholm. "I think Saul's actions in New Iberia have the potential to stir up trouble among the slaves throughout the region, if not the entire Confederacy. Remember the disturbances on plantations that we heard about back when Saul first started his depredations? Well, they're starting up again, worse than ever."

"What sort of disturbances?" Breckinridge asked.

"Slaves are running away in increasing numbers. Lots of those being recaptured say that they were trying to join Saul's men in New Iberia. So word of what is happening is certainly spreading throughout the slave populations on the plantations. Even more easily among the town slaves, where they overhear the paperboys and the conversations of the whites. Hell, there are stories that slaves as far away as South Carolina are starting to talk about Saul, like he is some sort of Moses destined to lead his people out of slavery."

"Maybe he is," Benjamin said with a wry grin.

This statement stunned the men gathered around the table, who looked hard at Benjamin, their eyes demanding that he admit his comment was a joke. Instead, he simply pulled a cigar out of his coat pocket, calmly lit it, and began puffing. Once again, Breckinridge remained mystified by the inscrutable nature of the man.

President Davis let out a deep breath. He glanced over the table at Breckinridge.

"John, has General Longstreet arrived at New Iberia yet?"

"Yes," Breckinridge replied. "He arrived and took command yesterday morning." The delay had irritated Breckinridge, but there had been nothing he could do to get Longstreet to New Iberia more quickly. The transportation infrastructure of the Confederacy remained dilapidated.

Davis nodded. "The question before us, gentlemen, is whether we go forward with an immediate attack on Saul's position or whether we hold back and hope that some opportunity presents itself to obtain the release of the hostages. I'll allow for one hour of discussion, then we must come to a decision."

They hashed out the question, going back and forth. Benjamin was for caution, while Trenholm and Harris were both for an immediate attack. Breckinridge himself could see both sides of the question and hesitated to commit himself. He dearly wished for more time to consider the matter, for he hated being rushed into decisions. He also regretted the absence of Postmaster General Reagan, who could have been trusted to be a voice of reason and common sense in the deliberations.

In the midst of their talking, a messenger arrived in the Cabinet meeting room and handed Davis a dispatch. The president unfolded it and quickly started to read through it.

"Is it about Saul?" Trenholm asked.

"Yes," Davis said, then returned to silence as he finished it. "It seems our Negro friend in New Iberia has become rather puffed up with himself. He released Mayor Delacroix and sent him into our lines with a letter addressed to the whole Confederate people." Davis then read the body of the letter aloud.

As Breckinridge listened, his blood turned to ice. Saul claimed that New Iberia would be only the first of many liberated towns. He demanded that the Confederate government withdraw its forces from New Iberia, free the slaves in the surrounding region, and recognize him as the leader of the town. It was utterly insane, of course, but if word of the letter leaked out, the effect on public opinion would be enormous. Throughout the South, Saul's status as a villain, the sort of being that mothers use to frighten disobedient children, would be cemented. In the North, and perhaps even more in Europe, however, Saul would start to become a mythic figure. He had been defeated, yet somehow came back stronger than ever to continue the struggle for the freedom of the slaves.

"Cheeky," Benjamin said with a grin after Davis finished reading.

"Who knows about this letter?" Harris asked.

"It came directly from General Longstreet," Davis replied. "So I assume no one."

"I would recommend that you send a telegram to Longstreet immediately, telling him to burn the letter," Harris said urgently. "And that we here in this room should act as though this letter never existed. We've talked many times of the need to avoid making this Negro into a martyr or a hero. If this letter gets into the papers, I think we can definitively say that we failed."

"Very difficult," Benjamin said. "Things like this will always get into the papers sooner or later. Telegraph operators between here and Louisiana have seen this letter. Probably many of Longstreet's staff officers. Saul may be a Negro, but he's a highly intelligent Negro. In his place, I would have tried to send the letter out in more than one way. By all means burn it, but don't be all that surprised when it is printed in the papers sooner or later anyway."

Davis grunted, not especially liking what he was hearing from Benjamin. He cleared his throat and spoke again.

"I will instruct Longstreet to burn the letter and speak no more of it. We should treat it as we did General Cleburne's emancipation memorandum back in 1864. Perhaps if we pretend it does not exist, we will have to worry about it no more."

Breckinridge thought that this was an extraordinary statement. He had supported Cleburne's proposal to free slaves and enlist them in the army and had openly said so to a number of people. The Confederate government had always prided itself, and Breckinridge thought rightfully, on the freedom of its press. Suppressing information of interest to the public was an exceptional and risky step to take. It did not surprise Breckinridge that, then as now, the issue that prompted the suppression had to do with slavery.

More than ever, he realized that the very institution which had prompted secession in the first place was, and always had been, the albatross around the South's neck. They would defeat Saul's rebellion sooner or later, but who could say that there would not be another Saul to take his place in a few years, if not a few months?

The Europeans loathed slavery and were becoming increasingly vocal about it. There was absolutely no reason to think that public opinion in foreign countries was going to change in favor of slavery. It was only going to become more intense against it. Breckinridge had read reports that membership in anti-slavery societies in Britain had increased every year since the end of the war, quietly promoted by Disraeli's government which wanted to distract progressive reformists away from issues more important to the Conservative Party. There were a great many people in the Confederacy who would cling to slavery with the urgency of a man trying to hold onto a lifeboat as his ship sinks. They would end up making their nation a pariah among the great states of the world.

Davis went on. "So, let's have it. Do we order Longstreet to attack or do we order him to hold off until a way can be found to free the hostages."

Breckinridge and Benjamin voted to wait, while Harris and Trenholm voted for an immediate attack. All eyes turned towards the president.

"We attack," Davis said simply. "I don't make this decision lightly, for I feel the burden imposed by the lives of those hostages. But we cannot allow Saul to remain in control of New Iberia for a moment longer. He must be destroyed once and for all." He looked at Breckinridge. "John, can you send Longstreet a message ordering an immediate attack with all his forces?"

"I can," Breckinridge said quickly.

"Then do so."

CHAPTER TWELVE

August 12, Afternoon
British Army Headquarters, Montreal, Canada

Wolseley sat bolt upright in an uncomfortable wooden chair, a steaming cup of tea on his desk, looking intently down at a map. It showed the positions of British and Canadian forces along the border with the United States. The known deployments of Union forces were also indicated.

Upon his return from his diplomatic sojourn to Richmond, Wolseley had found that his promotion to full Colonel had been approved and he had been made deputy quartermaster-general of all British forces in Canada. At thirty-four, he was the youngest officer ever to be placed in that position. It made him one of the chief advisors to General George Napier, commander-in-chief of all British forces in Canada. Wolseley considered Napier a first-class idiot, constantly babbling on about things of which he knew nothing and not fit to lead a company of schoolboys. The fact that such a buffoon could be raised to such a prestigious command merely through seniority and by being a member of the illustrious Napier family was yet another strike against the British Army, as far as Wolseley was concerned.

There was one advantage to having such an incompetent senior officer, though. Napier generally left Wolseley alone and allowed him to do his job without interference. This gave Wolseley enormous freedom of action in terms of the deployment of troops and the planning for the coming war with the Yankees. Though only a colonel, Wolseley fancied that he was the true commander-in-chief of British forces in Canada.

A steady stream of transport ships was entering the St. Lawrence River, bringing in reinforcing battalions from Britain and other parts of the Empire. There were already about twenty thousand British troops in the Dominion, backed up by several times that number of Canadian militia. All told, perhaps seventy thousand men were being deployed in strategic positions along the border.

It wouldn't be enough, Wolseley knew. According to his intelligence officers, the United States forces deployed on their side of the border already numbered perhaps one hundred thousand men. Wolseley also knew that, if the Fenian Crisis escalated into all-out war, there was essentially no limit to the number of men the Americans could hurl across the border. Nearly two million

Northern soldiers had served in the War for Southern Independence, giving the United States an enormous pool of trained military manpower.

He comforted himself with the knowledge that some of the battalions now arriving in Canada were among the finest in Her Majesty's army. Among those already marching for the border were the Royal Sussex Regiment, the Cornwall Light Infantry, and the Staffordshire Volunteers. Wolseley nodded approvingly when he read through a report indicating that the Black Watch, perhaps the army's most formidable Scottish battalion, was expected to arrive within the next week. They weren't the only Scottish unit, though, for the Gordon Highlanders and the Royal Scots Greys were already deployed along the border. Wolseley was especially thankful for the presence of the latter regiment, as it gave the British army in Canada some much needed cavalry.

Scanning yet another report, Wolseley's eyebrows went up when he saw that the next battalion slated to arrive was the Royal Irish Regiment. Wolseley knew that the bulk of the unit was recruited from the Catholic population in and around Dublin, rather than in the Protestant northeast of Ireland. He couldn't help but wonder if perhaps some Fenians had infiltrated the unit, then chided himself for thinking such a thing. Each man in the battalion had taken a personal oath of loyalty to Her Majesty and the Royal Irish had fought gallantly in the Crimea against the Russians and in New Zealand against the Maori. Surely they could be relied upon.

Wolseley had proposed, and Napier had accepted without comment, a plan by which each British battalion would be grouped with two Canadian militia battalions to form a number of brigade groups. It was a force like this that had defeated the Fenian incursion in what was now becoming known simply as the Battle of the Stockade. With a core of trained and experienced troops to stiffen the backs of the militia, each brigade would represent a strong fighting force.

At Napier's request, Wolseley had briefed Governor-General Monck on the plans for defending Canada from the expected American invasion. The brigades would operate either independently or as part of divisions to hold key points and contest the American advance towards the key cities of Montreal, Quebec, and the new capital at Ottawa. Little effort would be made to protect the border itself.

Monck had asked why each unit was not deployed directly along the border, stretched out so as to cover its entire length. That way, so the Governor-General had thought, no American troops would be able to enter Canadian territory. Wolseley considered Monck an intelligent man but never forgot that he had no military experience. Deploying the entire army along the whole length of the border would have prevented them from massing any strength at key points, thereby inviting an easy defeat. Wolseley was reminded of a French officer who had proposed such a defensive plan to Napoleon Bonaparte to protect France's eastern border. Napoleon had wryly commented that it was a brilliant plan, if the intention was to prevent smuggling.

Wolseley was immersed in the details of endless reports when Redvers Buller, whom he had chosen as his aide-de-camp upon being appointed Deputy Quartermaster-General, entered the office. He stopped and grandly stomped his boots on the ground, snapping his right hand up in a rigid salute.

"Good morning, Colonel."

Wolseley saluted in return, rather more lazily. "Morning to you, Buller."

"I have very good news to share with you, Colonel."

"And what would that be, Buller?"

A grin crossed the captain's face as he passed a telegram across the desk to Wolseley.

Colonel Wolseley,

It has pleased Her Majesty to appoint you, Garnet Wolseley, a Knight Commander of the Order of Bath. Congratulations.

Viscount Monck, Governor-General of Her Majesty's Dominion of Canada

Wolseley grunted. "So, the feckless bastards in London kept their promise, did they?"

"It would appear so," Buller replied. "Congratulations, Sir Garnet."

"Won't be official until I go through the ceremony."

"Yes, well, nothing says I can't start calling you that now."

Wolseley allowed himself a rare smile. "Thank you, Captain."

"Perhaps they'll make a Lord out of you one day, sir."

"God forbid."

He hoped his expression appeared blasé, for it wouldn't do to appear giddy in front of his subordinate. In fact, though, Wolseley felt such elation that he half-expected to be lifted out of his chair. That this telegram came as no surprise to Wolseley did nothing to diminish the sheer delight that filled his soul. From now on, he would be Sir Garnet Wolseley. The man who had once worked in a land surveyor's office in Dublin while having to beg the Duke of Wellington for an army commission was now a knight of the realm. Even the haughty dukes and wealthy aristocrats he so despised would be forced to accord him the respect he deserved.

Before the Battle of the Stockade, Wolseley had been a highly officer, yet his name had been entirely unknown outside of the army. Now, his name had been in the newspapers, he was holding meetings with the likes of the Governor-General of Canada and the President of the Confederate States, and the Queen herself had taken notice of him. It was a feeling of which he wanted more.

He looked down at the map again, imagining the epic battle that he was certain would soon take place along the border between Canada and the United States. Such an opportunity for glory did not come along more than once or twice in a century. When it came, he would be ready.

August 13, Morning
Confederate Headquarters outside New Iberia, Louisiana

Dawn had just arrived, but it was already hot and humid. The cluster of tents was full of activity as staff officers came and went, receiving or dispatching messages. Men leaned over small tables, studying maps of New Iberia and its environs. The sound of chatter was constant, as was the smell of coffee and cigar smoke. It was like a scene right out of the war.

All of this activity swirled around one particular officer, a tall, broad, and formidable-looking man. General James Longstreet had arrived and was now in command of all Confederate forces in and around New Iberia.

Morgan sat in a chair some distance away from Longstreet, who stood tall in the center of the command tent like a monarch surrounded by courtiers. Morgan burned with envy as he watched Longstreet issue orders, dictate messages, and dispatch staff officers on their various tasks. Still, he could not help but admit that Longstreet knew what he was doing. He had not known the man during the war, for they had served in different theaters of the war. Yet the stories he had heard of the man's effectiveness were certainly being born out.

He had asked Morgan to remain in New Iberia under his command, since he had experience with Saul and with the surrounding Louisiana terrain. Morgan had agreed, for he was a good officer and followed orders. Yet he would have strongly preferred to have simply been sent home. The humiliation of being superseded was intense, especially for a man as sensitive to public opinion as Morgan. During the war, he had thrived on newspaper stories about his daring exploits. This time around, the newspapers would only report that he had failed in his mission and been unceremoniously replaced.

"General Morgan?" Longstreet called, shaking Morgan from his thoughts. "Mind coming over here? I'd like your opinion on this."

Morgan stood from his chair and walked over to the table on which was spread a large map of the town and the surrounding area. Someone had circled the hotel in the center of town with green ink and scratched over the buildings closest to it, which had been torn down or burned by Saul. Farther out, the positions of the Confederate units were marked in red, with scribblings indicating their regimental identities.

"Go ahead, General," Morgan said.

"We have about five thousand men in position. If what your boys have told me is correct, Saul can't have more than five hundred or so fighters deployed around the hotel. Now, we've surrounded the town with trenches, to make sure no more blacks get in and that Saul can't get out. It's time to start planning the attack."

"So you're going at him?" Morgan asked.

"That's right."

"What about the hostages?"

Longstreet shrugged. "We'll just have to hope for the best, I suppose. Orders came through this morning from the War Department. We're to attack and overwhelm Saul at the earliest opportunity. But we're also under orders to keep casualties to a minimum."

"Not going to be easy," Morgan said. He pointed to the map. "The three streets that approach the hotel are not very wide. They will force us to bunch our attacking troops together, presenting an easy target for Saul and his men." He thought for a moment. "I would guess we will lose at least a hundred men in any attack. Perhaps more."

Longstreet grunted. "I agree. And since I'm ordered to keep casualties to a minimum, I have decided that we're going to go at this using siege tactics. The trenches we've already dug will constitute the first parallel, as old Vauban would say. We'll dig saps down three streets towards the hotel, zig-zagging the trenches so that Saul's men can't sweep them with rifle fire. Five hundred yards out, we'll dig another wide trench in which we can pack troops and keep them protected from enemy fire. That will constitute the second parallel. Then, we'll dig another line of saps until we get to the point of the burned-out buildings and dig a final parallel. That way, our men can be protected all the way up to the point from which they'll charge the hotel."

"Going to take a while," Morgan observed.

"A couple of days, at least. But I'll accept the delay if it means fewer of my men get killed."

"And if Saul's men sortie while we're digging these trenches?"

"I'd be delighted. I'm posting artillery to protect the sappers. If he tries to stop our digging, we can have the pleasant experience of blowing his men apart with canister fire. It would be suicide for him."

Morgan nodded. From a military point of view, Longstreet's methodical plan made perfect sense. There was nothing that Saul could do to stop them and it would allow the Confederates to eventually attack the hotel from a short distance, minimizing the length of time the attackers would be exposed.

"And what will you need from me?"

"When the attack goes in, I want you to command cavalry that will sweep around the outskirts of the city. Many of Saul's men will no doubt try to escape. I want you to make sure that they don't succeed."

"Very well." He paused a moment. "May I point something out, General?"

"By all means, Morgan," Longstreet said. "I was quite serious when I asked you to offer me your advice whenever you felt it valid."

"What if Saul demands a halt to the digging of the trenches, threatening to kill hostages if we don't comply?"

Longstreet frowned. It was obvious to Morgan that the idea had not occurred to him. "Well, I suppose we'll have to deal with that if and when it happens. In the meantime, the sappers will get started within the hour."

Morgan nodded. "Let me know if you need anything," he said, trying to keep the glumness out of his voice.

He strode away and sat back down. There was nothing for him to do for the time being. His Kentucky cavalrymen needed no attention. His face was expressionless, but inwardly he was fuming. Longstreet was being quite gracious, consulting him and making full use of his knowledge. That almost made the situation harder for Morgan. It would have been easier had Longstreet behaved poorly, as Braxton Bragg would have done, for that would at least have given Morgan an object on which to focus his resentment.

The activities of the headquarters swirled around him. He was in the midst of it, yet not part of it. He felt useless, not an emotion he normally experienced. Even the most frustrating moments of his hunt for Saul had been better than this, for at least then he had been doing something. Inactivity, combined with his humiliation, was almost too much to bear.

He considered asking for permission to return home. Surely Breckinridge would grant it. Morgan could return to the loving embraces of his wife Mattie, who alone could be trusted to remain true to him. Yet his mind recoiled the moment the thought had passed through it. Morgan was many things, but he was not a man who ran away. Longstreet had asked him to stay, and stay he would.

He thought for a moment of his glory days during the war. Sometimes he could close his eyes and imagine that he was once again behind the enemy lines, running circles around the Yankees, burning bridges and railroads, capturing hapless formations of Union soldiers and graciously releasing them on parole. Most of his activities had been in Tennessee and Kentucky, but he recalled the exhilaration of his raid into Indiana and Ohio in the summer of 1863. Never had Confederate soldiers penetrated so far into Union territory.

Morgan blinked. It had been a mistake to think of such things, for the memory made his current situation even more painful. The newspapers which had once trumpeted his name were now mocking him. The ladies who had once sent him longing letters of affection, some including requests for clandestine meetings, were now making fun of him in their parlor rooms.

Then there was Saul himself. Morgan couldn't help but think that perhaps his own arrogance had brought forth the rebel slave as some sort of nemesis, like a figure in one of those Greek tragedies that Breckinridge liked to talk about. He had humiliated Morgan at every turn. Even the successful ambush Morgan had carried out with Silas's help had been utterly forgotten.

He had read the newspaper accounts of the arrest of Charles Russell Lowell in New Orleans, who had apparently smuggled hundreds of rifles and other supplies to Saul. Clearly, it had been he who had allowed Saul to recover his strength after his defeat and come back stronger than ever. He had never heard of Lowell before. The mysterious Yankee was yet another block in the wall of humiliation that was building up around Morgan.

Morgan needed to do something, but what was needed was not escape. Indeed, he needed the very opposite of escape. On many occasions during his raids, the Yankees had thought they had cut off his lines of retreat and had him trapped. Whenever that had happened, Morgan had simply sidestepped them and attacked in a different direction, achieving victory with a dramatic flourish. What he needed to do now was find a way to recapture his glory with some sort of sensational exploit. The very thought that this might be possible suddenly enlivened him and, in a flash, he knew exactly what he needed to do.

He rose from his chair and walked towards Longstreet, who looked up as he approached.

"Let me go talk to him," he said firmly.

"Who?" Longstreet asked, confusion in his eyes.

"Saul," Morgan replied. "Let me go over to that hotel under a flag of truce and ask him to release the hostages."

Longstreet drew his head back in surprise. "Have you lost your damn mind, Morgan?"

"Not at all."

"You think those rebel darkies are going to respect a flag of truce? Do they even know what a white flag means? They'll shoot you down as soon as you walk within range of their Springfields."

"I don't think they will," Morgan replied. "When they see me coming down the street, they'll ask Saul what to do. He'll see that it's me and he will order them not to shoot."

Longstreet's eyes narrowed. "What makes you think that?"

Morgan's lips curled into a slight grin. "I've gotten to know the bastard pretty well these last few months. He won't want to kill me. He'll want to hear what I have to say."

"And what makes you think he'll release any of his hostages?"

"He wants us to think of him as an equal, don't you see? That's part of the reason he's been doing all this for the past several months. By putting us in a place where we have to ask him for a favor, he's placing himself on the same level with us."

"Don't much like that," Longstreet replied. "Don't think Davis up in Richmond will like it much, either."

"Probably not. But if it gets some of those hostages out of harm's way, it would be worth it. Don't you think?"

Longstreet shrugged. "If you want to do it, I won't stand in your way."

"Thanks," Morgan replied. He turned and addressed the nearest staff officer. "Lieutenant, I require a white flag, if you please."

Ten minutes later, Morgan had changed into a fine dress uniform, complete with a red sash and yellow color facings that marked him as a member of the cavalry. He would have put on his ceremonial sword, but the rules of parlay required him to be unarmed. In the meantime, the staff officer had brought out a flag of truce.

"Didn't think I'd need this in a fight against darkies," the man said sourly. It was clear that he did not approve of what Morgan was doing.

Morgan replied with a shrug. He couldn't care less what the man thought.

Longstreet walked up to him. "Still think you've lost your mind," he said. "But if you can persuade that bastard to give up any of the hostages, it will make my job easier. So, good luck."

"Thank you, General," Morgan said.

He took the white flag from the staff officer and turned to walk down the boulevard. Like most streets in New Iberia, it was wide, but it grew narrower as Morgan got closer to the hotel. He crossed over the Confederate trench, where men were already gathering to begin digging the saps towards Saul's position. Then, he entered the no-man's-land between the two opposing forces.

He held up the short flagstaff at an angle, so that the flag hung down towards the ground and was visible despite the lack of a breeze. Longstreet had asked if the renegades would even understand what the flag meant, but Morgan knew that the black men he was dealing with were soldiers. Saul had spent years in the Union army and so had many of his men. Morgan had developed a certain measure of respect for them. Longstreet, being newly arrived on the scene, had not had time to gain the measure of their opponents.

Morgan could feel the eyes that were surely watching him from the insurgent position. Even now, as every footstep was taking him closer to the hotel, someone was telling Saul of his approach. He could imagine the surprise the insurgent leader had to be experiencing. Morgan liked the thought, for he always enjoyed doing the unexpected and confounding his enemies.

As he drew close to the barricade Saul's men had constructed around the hotel, he could see half a dozen sets of eyes peering at him over the rough wooden ramparts. One man rose up and aimed a Springfield rifle at him. Almost instantly, the barrel of the gun was pushed down by the man next to him.

"White flag!" the second man said harshly. "No shooting!"

"I want to speak with Saul!" Morgan called out. He kept walking, until he was within twenty paces of the barricade. His military eye examined it closely. Based on how high the heads of Saul's fighters were, he could see that the trench was about three feet deep and the wooden wall was made up mostly of doors and heavy wooden boards piled on top of one another. In front of this were small but well put-together abatis, tangles of large tree limbs with sharpened branches. Any assault over such a defense would be difficult and costly, even if launched from that short distance that Longstreet envisioned.

"Who is you?" one of the black soldiers shouted.

"General Morgan!"

"What you want?"

Irritation welled up within him. "I just told you, dammit! I want to speak with Saul!"

"Go get the boss," one man said to another.

"Sharpshooters will get me if I leave the trench in daylight," the second man protested.

"I'm under a white flag," Morgan said. "They won't shoot at you."

"Yeah? Well, what's the promise of a white man worth?"

Morgan found this comment surprising and it took him a moment to reply. "If they shoot at you, I give you permission to shoot me dead. As you can see, I'm unarmed and defenseless."

"Go," the first man said. The second man rose up and walked swiftly back towards the hotel, disappearing inside.

Tense minutes passed. Morgan remained out in the open, wondering how many rifles were aimed at him from places where he could not see. He thought about his comrades hundreds of yards to the rear, watching him, perhaps expecting him to be killed at any moment. If some rash insurgent did decide to shoot him, he hoped death would come so quickly that his mind would not have time to realize what was happening. Yet the sound of gunfire did not come.

Saul appeared in the doorway of the hotel. Without fear, he stepped out onto the porch and strode down the steps. Morgan watched him as he came. When he had seen him before, it had been in the maelstrom of battle, glimpsed only for a few seconds amid confusion and noise. For the first time, Morgan was getting a good look at his nemesis. He was surprisingly small, but extremely well-built and strong. He might not have stood out among a gathering of field slaves, but for the fire in his eyes and the look of utter contempt that covered his face.

"What do you want, Morgan?" he called out.

"I want to talk to you." He noticed that Saul had a belt with a pistol holster.

"We're not going to surrender, if that's what you're going to ask."

"I'm not asking you to surrender. I know you won't."

Saul considered him for a moment. Then, to Morgan's surprise, he unfastened his pistol belt and set it down on the porch. He strode forward, clambering into the trench and then over the wooden barricade. Within moments, he was standing directly in front of Morgan.

The two stood there for some time, staring into one another's eyes. What was happening had to be shocking to the vast majority of observers on both sides. During the war, truces between the opposing picket lines had been common, but not with U.S.C.T. units. Blacks in arms against the whites of the South were considered too vile to treat with any respect or trust. Yet here was Morgan, talking with Saul as though he were an equal.

"You're not a coward, Morgan," Saul said. "That I'll grant you. You're the commander, yet you come forward knowing that any of my men could have shot you dead."

A twinge of disappointment tugged at Morgan. "I'm not the commander anymore," he said. "General Longstreet has arrived to take command."

"Longstreet?" Saul asked. It was clear from his tone that the name meant nothing to him. "Well, sorry about that."

"I don't care," Morgan lied.

"Hmm," Saul replied. "Well, say whatever it is you have to say."

Morgan took a deep breath. "I've come to ask you to release the hostages."

"Why should I do that? They're the only reason you haven't employed artillery."

"They're innocent people. Just happened to be in the town when you took it over. They have nothing to do with all this. Why not let them go?"

Saul laughed harshly. "Innocent? Hardly. Most of them own slaves. I know. I've talked with them. Anyone who owns even a single slave is guilty of a grave crime."

"I'm not going to argue that point with you," Morgan replied. Morgan had sometimes debated the merits of the Southern slave system with Northern men or visitors from Europe. He hadn't been able to convince them. He certainly knew he was not going to convince a man who had once been a slave himself.

"Anyone who holds another person in slavery deserves death," said Saul. "The men I'm holding are lucky that I haven't strung them up already, like I did with all the bastards on those plantations."

The intensity that was evident in Saul's eyes took Morgan by surprise. He had heard such talk from Northern men many times, but he had always considered them hypocrites. After all, was the lot of an illiterate German immigrant in some smoky New York factory any better than that of a slave on a Southern plantation? Morgan doubted it.

Hearing these words from Saul, though, was a different matter. He couldn't help but admit that, were he in Saul's place, he would feel exactly the same. It was a disquieting thought that had occurred to him many times, just as it surely had to every other white Southern man. Usually it was easy to push such thoughts aside. With Saul standing before him, a fiery look of fierce independence blazing forth from his eyes, it was more difficult.

Morgan decided to try a different tack. "You know, Saul, the whole world is watching what is happening here. There are reporters from half the newspapers in the country at our camp to cover the story. Folks up in the North and over in Europe think you're a big hero. But if innocent people die in this escapade of yours, that will change very quickly."

"You think I care what white people think of me?"

"Yes, I do," Morgan said quickly. "That's why you're doing all this, isn't it? You want to show all of us white people just how big and tough you are, don't you?"

"I'm doing all this because I want to free slaves."

473

"You're not going to free any slaves. All the people you've let loose here in New Iberia are probably going to be dead within the next few days. You know that and so do I. If they're lucky, they'll be recaptured and their masters will decide to put them back to work instead of hanging them."

"If any attack is made on my position, the hostages will be killed instantly. I think I've made that plain enough. So I don't see why I'm going to die. You can't attack me. And I'm not going to let go of the one thing which is protecting me."

"Orders have come from President Davis in Richmond. Our troops are going to attack and overrun your position, hostages or no hostages."

"Is that so?" Saul said. "Well, a lot of your boys are going to be killed before that happens."

"We'll do what we have to do," Morgan said firmly. "We're not soft people, you know. You think we'll flinch from a hundred dead? We'd lost that many during a medium-sized skirmish during the war." He paused a moment, gathering his thoughts. "You're a threat, Saul. The government has decided that it will pay any price to crush you. If hostages and soldiers have to die, so be it."

He couldn't be certain, but Morgan thought he sensed a moment of disquiet in Saul. Could the man have really expected that holding hostages and fortifying his position would protect him from attack? Perhaps Saul simply could not conceive of how determined the white South was to preserve its way of life. The brutal truth was that black slavery was the foundation upon which Confederate society was built. If it fell, so would the Confederacy.

Morgan had never been unduly troubled by this. He was not an intellectual man, but he knew enough history to know that slavery had always existed. Voices were now being raised against it in some places, which is why secession had been necessary in the first place. Had the Yankee abolitionists left well enough alone, there never would have been a war and thousands of dead men would still be alive.

Saul spoke again. "No, you're not soft people. I've known that since I first fought you at Milliken's Bend. But I don't understand you. I don't understand how you can call yourselves Christians while you keep blacks enslaved. I don't understand how you can have your fancy parties when you know that the food is being served by people whose lives have been stolen, whom you treat no better than farm animals. You say you're civilized people, but as far as I can see, you're nothing but barbarians."

"I see no point in arguing with you about it."

Saul thought for a moment. "The men you captured in that ambush you caught me in? Are they still alive or have they been executed?"

"They're alive. We sent them to Baton Rouge. Government in Richmond hasn't decided what to do with them."

"I'll release the hostages if you release those prisoners and let them join me here."

"That wouldn't be my decision. It would be Richmond's decision. I know that they would say no."

"Hmm," Saul replied thoughtfully. Then he looked up. "My letter?"

"What's that?"

"The letter I sent with the mayor. Has it been published in the newspapers like I asked?"

"No," Morgan replied quickly. "Longstreet burned the letter. Orders from Richmond came through. We're not to discuss that letter with anyone."

Saul pursed his lips and thought for a moment. "Am I a man, Morgan?"

The question caught Morgan by surprise. It wouldn't have occurred to Morgan to ask it. Morgan was a white man and Saul was a black man. They were both men in a certain sense, but Morgan saw the gulf between white and black as insurmountable.

"We're both men, Saul," Morgan finally replied. "But you call me a barbarian, while you threaten to murder innocent people."

"I learned it from your people. Whites don't give any more thought to killing a black slave than you would to wringing a chicken's neck."

"Aren't some of the hostages children?" Morgan asked. "Surely they're innocent. Why don't you at least let them go?"

Saul took a deep breath, but didn't reply.

Morgan went on. "You hanged the men at the plantations, but always let the women and children go free. The newspapers in the North and in Europe talked about that all the time. Made you out to be some sort of hero. Nice reputation to have, if you ask me. Why ruin it? If any children die during the fighting that's coming, they'll turn on you like jackals. All the people who have been calling you a hero will start calling you a coward and a villain."

Saul scowled. "I've already told you that I don't care what white people think."

"You and I both know that's not true. If it were, why did you bother writing that letter? Why would you bother trying to wave John Brown's stupid constitution around? You only came here to New Iberia because you care what white people think. You want to scare us so much that we'll give up slavery. Well, you do scare us. I won't deny it. But you won't scare the Confederacy so much that they'll let your fellow blacks go free. My people will fight forever to keep you and yours enslaved and they won't care whether the rest of the world thinks they're right or wrong."

Saul sighed deeply and was silent for several long seconds. "Why?" he asked finally.

"I don't know. It's just the way it is."

"For now." This was said with a grim determination.

"If women or children die because of your actions, the people who have been calling you a hero will start calling you a murderer of the innocent. You think that's going to make anyone want to abolish slavery? It will just make people angry and hateful towards you. You'll end up hurting your cause, not helping it."

Saul considered this. "I'll let the children go, Morgan. There's six of them. You take them back with you. But I won't let the women go. They're my protection. You Southerners may be willing to see your fellow Southern men die. You proved that during the war often enough. But the women are a different matter. I don't think you'll attack me as long as I am holding the women."

"I've already told you that we will."

"No, you told me that you've received orders. You and this Longstreet fellow might decide not to obey them."

"Then Davis will replace us with others who will."

Saul shrugged. "It makes no difference to me. But it's still an advantage for me to keep them. Now, take the children and go."

Saul turned and shouted orders to his men. A few minutes later, six confused and frightened-looking children, four boys and two girls, came outside. Two of Saul's soldiers lifted them over the trench, where they instinctively huddled around Morgan. The sight of a uniformed white soldier seemed to reassure them.

"It's all right, little ones," Morgan said. "You're safe."

"Go," Saul said sternly.

Morgan herded the six children back towards the Confederate lines and started to walk. After a few steps, he paused and turned back to Saul.

"Why didn't you shoot me during the ambush?"

"Since I didn't, you're in my debt."

Morgan's eyes narrowed. "What do you mean?"

"It makes no difference to me who commands the troops I'm fighting against. I owe you nothing, Morgan. But you owe me your life. I'm a better man than you. Whatever happens, that's going to bother you for the rest of your days."

Morgan was through talking. He turned and started walking back towards his own lines, gently pushing the children in front of him. He could see a crowd of Confederate soldiers staring down the street as he approached. As he came closer, a few men came forward without weapons and hoisted the children up into their arms, quickly dashing back to the protection of the Confederate trenches.

Just before reaching the trench himself, Morgan turned and looked back down the street. Saul had vanished. He turned and crossed over the trench.

Longstreet was there waiting for him. "Good job, Morgan," he said in his gruff voice. "You went out and risked your life to rescue the children. The newspapers are going to love it."

"I have a request, General Longstreet," Morgan said firmly.

"Yes?"

"I know you wanted me to patrol the town's outskirts with my cavalry."

"That's right."

"When the attack goes in, I want to go in with it."

"Hmm," Longstreet replied. "I suppose that's all right."

"Good." Morgan took a deep breath. "I want to be there for the kill."

August 14, Afternoon
Parish Jail, New Orleans, Louisiana

The shackles were far too tight. Lowell assumed this was intentional. He desperately wanted to slip his fingers between his skin and the metal rings so he could massage his wrists and ankles, but they were bound just closely enough to make this impossible. The feeling was somewhere between mere irritation and outright pain, but the fact that he could do nothing to stop it caused him more distress than the physical discomfort itself.

His wrists were connected to one another by a chain, as were his ankles. Each of those chains were, in turn, coupled to a larger and heavier manacle that was secured to an enormous ring on the wall. In the first few hours of his incarceration, he had tried to squirm in such a way as to allow him to stand up, only to find he couldn't. Quite purposefully, the police had set his chains so that he had no choice but to sit on the floor against the wall.

It was difficult for him to calculate how long he had been in the cell, to which the police had taken him immediately after his arrest. Underneath the door, he could make out a thin line of light. Lowell had tried to keep track of the number of times it had changed from a steady light, which would have indicated sunlight, to a flickering light, which would have indicated illumination provided by oil lamps or perhaps torches. He had tried to keep track of how many times the characteristic of the light had changed. He had long since lost track. He could have been in the cell for just a day or two, or he might have already been in the cell for more than a month. He simply could not tell.

The Confederate authorities had not been gentle with him when they first tossed him in the cell. For several hours, New Orleans police officers and two Confederate army officers had questioned him about the shipment of weapons. Lowell had told them nothing. They had threatened him with all manner of brutal treatment, but had not actually harmed him. His only response to their questions had been to ask to see the United States consul in New Orleans. It would not have mattered much if he had told them everything, but resisting the Confederates still gave him a sense of satisfaction.

That satisfaction, however, was rapidly fading. Since the interrogation ended, Lowell's only human contact had been with a black man who had brought him a plate of biscuits and a tin cup of water twice of a day. Each interaction had been but a matter of seconds. The man would simply open the door, step inside just long enough to place the plate and cup within reach of Lowell, then step back out and close the door again. Lowell had tried speaking to him the first few times he had come in, but the man had not responded. He assumed that the Confederate authorities had given him strict orders not to respond to anything Lowell said. It had been too dark to see the man's eyes, so he had had no clue as to his thoughts and feelings.

He wondered if Naismith was being confined in the same jail. Lowell spent long hours wondering what his sailor friend must be thinking or feeling at that moment. He had known the risks of taking Lowell into Louisiana. He had chosen to do so, at least in part, to avenge the brother who had died in the attack on Charleston. Lowell wouldn't blame Naismith if he was now bitterly regretting his decision.

Lowell could not know how long he would be confined by himself. He began mentally preparing himself to endure the ordeal of a long imprisonment. He remembered *The Count of Monte Cristo*, which he had read aboard ship during one of his trans-Atlantic crossings. He thought his plight might eventually become similar to that of Edmund Dantès, though there were obvious differences. First, Dantès had at least enjoyed the company of the mad priest.

Second, Dantès had no idea why he had been imprisoned, while Lowell knew only too well.

He would have given anything to read a newspaper. When he had boarded the *Vincent* on the morning of their attempted escape, the New Orleans docks had been filled with rumors that Saul had taken the town of New Iberia. Lowell thought he remembered hearing a newspaper boy proclaiming the truth of this, though his isolation was already beginning to affect his mind and he could not be entirely sure. Was Saul still in control of New Iberia? Might his capture of the town have set off the wider slave revolt for which he had hoped? Had Saul and his brave men been slaughtered by the Confederates? Of all things, being completely cut off from news of the outside world was the hardest.

He wondered what impact, if any, the events of New Iberia was having on the wider world. It might have been wise, at least from their perspective, for the Confederate authorities to keep word of what had happened from reaching the public. Yet despite how much he loathed them, Lowell had to admit that the Confederate government had always respected the freedom of the press. The fact that the newspapers in New Orleans had picked up the story meant that it had to have flashed across the telegraph wires throughout both the Union and the Confederacy, and shortly thereafter to Europe as well.

Lowell did not think that his own imprisonment would garner much in the way of public attention. Unlike the capture of a town, the arrest of two individuals would be easy for the authorities to conceal from the public view. He only hoped that someone had taken the time to inform Josephine of his plight.

The thought of his wife caused a wave of anguish to sweep over him. Would she consider his action a betrayal of her and their children? She had told him that she supported his going, but now that he had failed to escape, her feelings would surely change. Irrational thoughts began to march through his mind. He wondered if Josephine would even care that he had been arrested and imprisoned. Perhaps she would simply use it as an excuse to start a new life with another man, with Lowell's children tucked away in some boarding school, inevitably to be forgotten.

He tried to calm himself, understanding that the isolation would make it difficult for him to think coherently. Indeed, those friends of his in Boston who were advocates of prison reform had often spoken of the effect of long-term solitary confinement, considering it a form of torture. He had to avoid becoming paranoid and irrational. If he failed, his entire mind could become unhinged.

Lowell knew he had to find a way to keep his mind active. He tried to recall the names of all the officers and sergeants with whom he had served in the 2nd Massachusetts Cavalry, saying their names out loud. He started reciting his favorite passages from Virgil and Horace in Latin. When he could no longer continue that, he switched to French and started regurgitating Racine and Moliere. He started a conversation in his own mind between Hannibal and Napoleon as to which of them was the superior general. He did not know how long these mental exercises lasted, for he desperately tried to avoid contemplation of the passage of time.

He thought again of how close he had come to escaping. The *Vincent* had literally begun to move towards the river channel when the police arrived. Had a mere five more minutes elapsed, they might have gotten away. Perhaps they would have been caught at the forts downriver, but perhaps not. A line from Thucydides came to his mind: *So narrow had been the escape of Mytilene.*

A sound came from behind the door. Lowell was alarmed and a jolt of fear coursed through his body. He tried to struggle to his feet, but his chains held him down. There was a sound of metal scratching against metal as the door was unlocked and swung open. At first, Lowell thought it would be the black man with his food and water. To his surprise, however, three white men stood in the doorway. One stepped inside, carrying a small wooden chair that he placed on the other side of the cell. As he stepped back out into the hallway, another man entered with an oil lamp, flooding the cell with light for the first time since Lowell had entered it. Though the light was dim, Lowell had been sitting in darkness for so long that he had to shield his eyes as if from the sun. As the man sat in the chair, the door was closed and locked again.

"General Lowell?" the man asked hesitantly.

"Yes," Lowell answered weakly.

"I'm Edward Phelps, United States Consul in New Orleans."

Lowell nodded, trying his best to clear his mind. When he had first been arrested, Lowell had insisted on his right to speak to the United States consular officer, but the Confederates had ignored him. Lowell didn't know why he had appeared now.

"What day is it?" Lowell asked.

"It's Wednesday."

"Wednesday the what?"

Phelps looked confused. "Wednesday, August 14."

"I've been in here less than two weeks?"

"That's right."

Lowell was stunned. "It feels like I have been in here for an eternity."

"Yes, well, that is something you might have to get used to," Phelps said sardonically. "You may be in here for a while. You've created quite a stir, I must say."

A wave of dizziness caught Lowell, so intense that he would have fallen down had he been standing. He thought for a moment that he was going to vomit. He raised his hands to his head.

"I'm sorry," he managed to say. "Give me a moment."

Phelps said nothing and sat in his chair, waiting. Lowell tried to focus, but found it difficult. He could scarcely believe that Phelps was a real person and not some sort of illusion. He also considered the possibility that he was actually a Confederate, sent in to trick him into doing or saying something. The isolation had battered his mind.

"Phelps, you say?" Lowell asked.

"That's right."

"U.S. Consul in New Orleans?"

"Yes."

"Why have you come?"

"You're a United States citizen under arrest. And not for pick-pocketing a random person on the street, either. Your actions have set off a serious diplomatic incident between our two countries. I was ordered by President McClellan to interview you."

Lowell took a deep breath. Phelps was real and was probably not a Confederate agent. Besides, there was nothing Lowell would have been willing to say to Phelps that he would have cared to conceal from the Confederates. This was his first, perhaps his only, chance to communicate with the outside world, to make sure that Josephine knew what was happening, and learn what was happening in New Iberia.

"Naismith?"

"Dead," Phelps said without much emotion. "Some people apparently heard that the paddy wagon he was in contained someone accused of helping Saul. A mob blocked it from reaching the jail and pushed it over onto its side. Police say that Naismith split his head open and his brains spilled right out."

"By Plato!" Lowell exclaimed. He tried to keep his mind from recognizing the fact that he was responsible for Naismith's death. The ship captain had been a good man with a family that relied on him. He had begun to look upon the man as a friend. He willed himself to move on. Grief and guilt could come later. "And Gardet?"

"They hanged him."

Lowell nodded, not surprised by this. When he had first been told on the deck of the *Vincent* that Gardet had been arrested, he had assumed that the Confederates would simply kill him. After all, as a black man, Gardet had no legal rights.

"I'd like to protest my treatment," Lowell said carefully. "The conditions in this cell are intolerable."

"Oh, I will lodge an official protest. Don't worry. That's part of my job, after all. And I've already spoken about improving the conditions in which you're being held. But speaking frankly, you're very lucky the Confederates didn't simply hang you from the nearest lamppost the moment you were arrested."

Lowell didn't know what to say in response to this, so he remained silent.

Phelps went on. "Do you know that Saul has used the weapons you smuggled to him to attack a town? Lots of people are dead and it's your fault. The United States and the Confederacy are plunging into a crisis. The worst crisis since the war. That's your fault, too."

"I did what I had to do," Lowell answered. "President McClellan can stand by and do nothing while Saul and his men are slaughtered like animals, but I will not."

"Well, I'm glad you feel that you have done the right thing, Lowell, because you're going to suffer for it. That's why I've come. I have to tell you that you will be arraigned in court tomorrow afternoon."

"Court?"

"That's right."

"But I have no defense counsel."

"The court will provide an attorney."

"I would prefer an attorney of my own choosing," Lowell said. He knew that dozens of lawyers in Boston would be more than happy to represent him pro bono.

Phelps shrugged. "To be blunt, Lowell, it won't really matter a damn who represents you. Your conviction is certain. Even if there was any doubt about what you did, they'd still convict you. And there is no doubt."

"Of course not. I will proudly proclaim it on the floor of the courtroom."

The conversation with Phelps was sweeping away the mental cobwebs created by the isolation and refocusing Lowell's mind. He knew his conviction was certain and had known that such an outcome was a possibility from the moment he had told Senator Sumner that he would undertake the mission. Yet he had the example of John Brown before him. If he could present himself bravely, if he could speak eloquently in the courtroom, he could strike a blow against slavery every bit as damaging as Saul's capture of New Iberia. For when he opened his mouth in the courtroom, he would be speaking to the entire world.

"Has my wife been informed?"

"I don't know," Phelps admitted. "I'm sure she's read the papers."

"May I send her a letter?"

"I'll ask the Confederates, but I doubt they'll agree." Phelps paused a moment. "Have you considered the impact of what you have done on your wife and family?" The question was asked in a condescending tone.

"Of course I have, Phelps, else I wouldn't have gone."

"So why did you do it? I would not consider abandoning my family, no matter what the cause. You're going to die for nothing and your children will grow up without a father."

Lowell scoffed. "It's because of men like you that we lost the war."

Anger clouded Phelps's face. Lowell could see that, although only in his forties, Phelps had not fought in the war. He didn't have the hard look in his eyes of a man who had seen battle. The fact that he had been appointed to a lucrative diplomatic post suggested that he was politically well-connected. Lowell concluded that he was one of those Copperheads who had sat out the war while thousands of good Northern men were fighting to the death for Union and abolition.

"I'm here to help you, Lowell. You might at least have the courtesy of being polite."

"That's easy for you to say. When this interview is over, you're going home to a comfortable house. Me? I'll stay here in this cell, secured by these chains."

"And for that, you have only yourself to blame." Phelps rose from the chair. "I'll speak to the authorities about moving you to a more comfortable cell and allowing you to write a letter to your wife. Like I said, I doubt they'll agree, but I'll do what I can. I shall return soon. In the meantime, you shall have plenty of time to reflect on what has happened."

Lowell laughed. "I thought I did right the moment I did it and I will still think that the moment they put the rope around my neck. It's something that a man like you would never understand."

August 16, Night
McFadden Ranch, Texas

McFadden reined in Yellowjacket and dismounted, happy to be home after what had been a long day in Waco. He could feel the tiredness in his body and ached for sleep. He was surprised by how exhausting political campaigning turned out to be. When he first began, he had not seen how talking to people, shaking hands, writing letters, and so forth could be all that draining. It turned out to be one of the most tiring things he had ever done. When a day of campaigning was over, he was reminded of how he had felt during the war at the end of a long march.

What made it worse was the fact that he still had his ranch to tend. Without steady and back-breaking labor, cacti steadily encroached on the grazing ground of his sheep and cattle. Fences needed mending. Annie, yet again proving herself the perfect wife, was doing much more than her share of the work, getting up before dawn to milk and feed the animals, even as she tended to Thaddeus. Even so, the ranch was slowly deteriorating with McFadden gone every other day.

He worried about what would happen if he actually won the election. His duties as a state legislator would require him to spend several months in Austin every other year and even in Waco his job might be just as demanding as the campaign itself. What were the prospects of his ranch in the long term? Would he need to hire ranch hands? He did not want to add the burden of being an employer to what he already had.

The thought occurred to him that the obvious answer to his problem was to purchase a few field slaves. Even a single slave tearing out the cacti would make his life much easier. Yet McFadden did not want to do this. His mother's voice, gently saying that slavery was an evil that needed to eventually die, sounded in his mind whenever the thought of purchasing a slave occurred to him.

He cleaned and brushed down Yellowjacket and led the faithful horse into the stable. Making sure the trough was full of water, he patted the animal with gratitude, locked him in, and began to walk back to the house. He planned to eat quickly and retire to bed as quickly as possible. He could feel the clouds of sleep already beginning to form around his mind.

McFadden was feeling better about the campaign. Since his meeting with Postmaster Reagan a few weeks before, he felt a growing sense of confidence in his ability to win. His friends throughout the district were telling him that more and more people were saying that they intended to vote for him. His efforts to gain the endorsements of fellow former officers had yielded good results. Letters of support had arrived from throughout the state.

Judge Roden was still acting as though he did not exist, but rumors were swirling around Waco that the man was enraged at the success McFadden was starting to have. Walker continued to snoop around, but otherwise seemed to be doing little. McFadden was not as concerned about reprisals as he had been when the campaign began. Now that he was part of the Breckinridge political machine and had the backing of Postmaster Reagan, he felt a measure of protection.

Walking through the door, his tiredness vanished instantly when he saw Annie sitting in one of the chairs, staring earnestly up at him. He knew the look on her face, which was pensive and uneasy. She had obviously been sitting there for some time, waiting for his return.

"Annie, what is it?" he asked anxiously.

She didn't respond right away, simply staring up at him.

"Annie?"

"I . . . I killed a man."

"What?" McFadden almost shouted. "What do you mean?"

"A man came to the ranch this afternoon. He shot two of our sheep. I didn't know he was here until I heard the gunshots. I grabbed the shotgun and ran out the back to see what was going on."

"Are you all right?" he interrupted. He moved quickly beside the chair and took his wife's hand. Her grip was tight and he realized that she was more frightened than she was willing to admit.

"Yes, I'm fine. Thaddeus is fine. He's asleep. Neither of us is hurt."

"Who was the man?"

"I pointed the gun at him and yelled for him to stop. He looked at me and laughed. Said Judge Roden had sent him to teach us a lesson."

McFadden felt rage fill him. He had thought Roden's earlier threats had been bluff and bluster. Some of the men from the 7th Texas had taken to patrolling around the ranch every now and then, but that protection had tapered off when no threat had materialized.

"What happened then?"

"He told me that he didn't think the gun was loaded and that a girl like me wouldn't know how to shoot it anyway. Then he shot another one of our sheep. I told him that if he shot one more, then I would shoot him. And I told him to get off our ranch."

"And then?"

"He said that he had Judge Roden's permission to be here and that he didn't have to leave." She paused a moment, gathering the strength to go on. "Then he said that he thought I was pretty and started walking towards me. He said that he was going to have his way with me and that the sheriff wouldn't do a thing about it because he was Roden's man." She again paused. "He came up towards me, smiling at me, just leering at me. I told him he had one more chance to get off our land, but he ignored me. Then I pulled the trigger."

"You killed him?"

"Yes. I think he was dead before he hit the ground."

He exhaled deeply. "Good," he said firmly. "Damn son of a bitch. I hope he's roasting in hell even as we speak."

To McFadden's surprise, Annie suddenly burst into tears. Instinctively, he rushed to embrace her, wondering what was wrong. During the war, he had killed literally dozens of men. They were the enemy and he had no choice in the matter. Annie had merely been protecting herself from a man who intended to rape her. It was a clear case of a necessary killing. He couldn't understand why she was upset.

As she cried in his arms, clutching at him for reassurance, he began to understand. She was not a soldier and didn't think the way he thought. She was a woman who had never struck another person before, much less killed one with a firearm. She had crossed over a threshold that no one should ever have to cross. He tightened his embrace and let her cry.

As McFadden held his wife, his mind raced. Roden had obviously sent the man to intimidate him. He assumed that it had been Walker, though he wouldn't know until he saw the body. From what Annie had said, the man probably intended to kill a few of the animals and then leave. Maybe the man had threatened to rape Annie simply to frighten her, or perhaps he had been drunk. Yet it was just possible that Roden had ordered him to do it.

"When was this?" McFadden asked.

"About four hours ago," Annie replied through a sniffle.

"Where is his body?"

"Out in the back."

He gripped her more tightly. "Are you okay?"

She comported herself. "Yes, love. I'm all right."

He stood and walked out to the back porch of the ranch house, carrying a lantern with him. Lying face down in the dirt just at the bottom of the step, amid a swarm of flies, was the dead man. He kicked the body over and looked at the man's face. It wasn't Walker. It was a man he had never seen before. Unknown or not, he obviously was one of the many rough men Roden used for his dirty work. The fact that he had not returned from the McFadden ranch would soon come to Roden's attention, if it had not already.

The law was on their side. The man had trespassed on their property, killed their livestock, and threatened to assault Annie. She had been well within her rights to defend herself. Yet McFadden knew that none of this would matter. The law in Granbury County was Roden's law. Somehow he would turn the killing to his own advantage, perhaps by arresting McFadden on a charge of murder. That would neatly remove him from the campaign.

He went back inside. "Go to sleep, dear. Say nothing of what has happened. This man never came to the house. Nothing happened. It was a quiet night. Do you understand, my dear?"

"Yes."

"You did nothing wrong. You were defending yourself and your son."

"I know."

Minutes later, McFadden dragged the body into a grove of trees and started to dig a grave. He felt he had to move quickly, for it was possible that a posse of Roden's men might arrive at any moment, peddling some false story that would be the excuse for his arrest. As he shoveled, he wondered if Roden had sent the man with the intention that he be killed, not caring if the simpleton died if it meant he could gain some sort of advantage in the campaign.

He had to make the hole deep enough, otherwise the coyotes would dig the body up and devour it, scattering bits of human flesh all over the area behind the ranch house. It took almost an hour of back-breaking work, but eventually he kicked the body into the grave and started piling the dirt back on top of it. An hour and a half after he began, he patted down the replaced soil and covered it with bits of wood to better conceal it.

He could not allow this to happen again. Since Roden first came to the ranch with his bluster and threats, several veterans of the 7th Texas had offered to come to the ranch and provide security. Some had ridden by every now and then, simply to make sure everything was okay. He did not like asking for favors, nor did he want his friends to be unduly troubled, but neither could be accept leaving Annie and Thaddeus unprotected at home while he was in Waco for campaign work. He would ask some of the men to camp at the ranch, armed with their old Enfields, to ensure that no harm came to his family.

It was not supposed to be this way. A political campaign was supposed to be a free and fair exchange of ideas, in which the people made the decision as to which candidate would best represent their interests and cast their votes accordingly. Under those circumstances, McFadden could even accept defeat at the polls with good grace, because the people deserved the representative of their choice. Roden played by a different set of rules altogether, doing whatever was necessary to ensure his own reelection. Now a man had died.

This was not the kind of country for which he and his comrades had fought during the war. They had been told that they were sacrificing so that the South could be free from Northern domination, but all McFadden could see was an emerging aristocracy of wealthy men lording it over the common people. What difference did it make if the people who were trampling on liberty were foreigners from the North or fellow Southerners?

He came back into the house and found Annie snoring softly in their bed. He knew her life would never be the same, just as his had never been the same since he had killed his first Yankee out in New Mexico in 1862. He checked in on Thaddeus, finding the little boy sleeping peacefully, an utterly innocent and placid expression on his little face. He sensed the deep responsibility he had to protect his wife and child. Yet he also knew that he had to follow his ideals. When the morning came, he knew he would feel a renewed determination to defeat Roden. It might be a small part of the larger struggle now unfolding across the country, but it mattered to the people of Granbury County and it certainly mattered to the McFadden family.

August 17, Night
New Iberia, Louisiana

Saul awoke with a start and instinctively reached for the LeMat revolver Lowell had given him, which he kept within reach. He waited for any sound that might indicate what had woken him, but there was only silence. It was dark outside and he could not tell what time it might be. Deciding that it would be impossible to go back to sleep, Saul rose to his feet. His men had pulled down a mattress from one of the upstairs hotel rooms and set it on the floor of the hotel kitchen, turning it into a place where he could rest, though he had not been able to sleep for more than two hours at a stretch thus far.

He walked into the lobby, where a dozen or so of his men were sleeping on the hard floor, their rifles stacked against the wall. The snoring was so loud that Saul was amazed any man could sleep through it, but they were all so tired that it was not a problem. They lay so motionless that, but for the fact that he could see them breathing, he might have assumed they were dead.

It was dark enough that he felt comfortable moving out the front door and into the main trench. Confederate sharpshooters, posted in the windows of the closest buildings with British-made Whitworth rifles, would have made this suicidal during the daylight hours, but with the lights out in the hotel and the moon obscured by thick clouds, he would be effectively invisible. The Confederates had tried to light bonfires close enough to provide some illumination, but Saul's men had picked off the troops doing this and the enemy had soon abandoned the idea.

A long line of tired men stood along the wall of the trench, gripping their guns. A few had their feet up on the fire step, peering carefully out over the parapet at the enemy beyond, straining their eyes to pick some detail out of the darkness. The silence was eerie.

Saul climbed onto the fire step himself and looked out towards the Confederate positions. Every day, they inched closer to the hotel, as the enemy sappers dug their approach trenches. When the work had begun four days before, the Confederates had been about four or five hundred yards away. Saul had assumed that it would take weeks to dig such a distance. Yet the saps had approached with astonishing swiftness. They were now only about two hundred yards away.

The Confederate diggers were well within the effective range of the Springfield rifles carried by Saul's men, causing them to take precautions. The saps were being dug in a zig-zag pattern, so they could not be swept with gunfire. Moreover, as the saps slowly advanced, large wicker baskets filled were rocks and soil, called gabions, were being piled up in front of the saps to shield the workers. Although his men had occasionally taken potshots at the enemy sappers, Saul was doubtful if any of them had been hit.

The saps were approaching the hotel down three different streets. Saul had discussed the matter with Troy and both had concluded that the Confederates were now close enough to mount an infantry assault. A charge down the streets from four hundred yards away would give Saul's men enough space to inflict terrible casualties upon the attackers, but an attack from half that distance was a very different proposition.

Saul strained his ears in the darkness. He could hear muffled voices speaking to one another and the scratching sound of shovels against soil. Even during the night, the work was continuing. Every minute brought the Confederates closer to his position. He could see nothing, but neither did he hear any sounds to suggest that large numbers of men were being gathered in the saps. It sounded to him like the regular work details.

Satisfied that there was little chance of a surprise night attack, Saul went back into the hotel and crawled back onto the mattress. With any luck, he could sleep for another few hours before daybreak, when fighting would surely break out again. Yet sleep did not come. His mind was racing, going over the events of the past few days again and again. He tried to calm himself through sheer force of will, lying as still as possible and hoping exhaustion would pull him into slumber, but it was a futile effort.

The day of the occupation had been a momentous day, indeed. The experience of being in control of a Southern town was exhilarating. It did not take long, however, for Confederate militiamen to start arriving. At first, they came only in small groups of a few dozen men, who had been chased to the outskirts of town. For a dazzling day or so, Saul and his men had complete freedom in and around New Iberia. The whites had fled. Troy had brought in scores of slaves from nearby plantations. There had been a real sense that a slice of the Confederacy had been carved out in which slavery had been destroyed and the black people were free.

It had been fleeting. By the afternoon of August 2, word had spread throughout the surrounding counties and larger militia units were rapidly mobilizing. By that evening, sufficient numbers of troops had assembled around New Iberia to hem Saul and his now outnumbered force into the central part of town, in and around the Grand Hotel. Now they were trapped.

Realizing that sleep was not coming, he rose into a sitting position. The thought of failure burned at his spirit, but he told himself to rise above it. His seizure of New Iberia had surely stunned and terrorized people across the South and that was something of which he could feel proud. Simply by remaining where he was for as long as possible and killing as many of the enemy as they could, Saul and his men would be achieving something. In one of the books Ferguson had given him, he had read about the last stand of the Spartans at Thermopylae.

He was shaken from these thoughts by the sudden feeling that something wasn't right. He immediately rose to his feet, grabbed his LeMat, and dashed through the lobby, passing the still-sleeping men as he walked to the door. Glancing at the large grandfather clock against one wall of the lobby, he could see that it was quarter to three in the morning. Reaching the porch, he stared out into the darkness, but could see nothing. It seemed quieter than it had been earlier.

He moved forward cautiously and entered the trench. Moments later, Troy came up beside him.

"You should try to sleep, boss," Troy said gently.

Saul shook his head, straining his ears to hear anything from the direction of the Confederate positions. There was absolutely nothing. He could hear no coughing, no muffled conversations. The scratchy sound of digging had ceased. This unnerved him, for it suggested that the Southern troops were being silent for a particular purpose.

The clouds overhead were thinning and a ghostly moonlight was beginning to break through. Far in the distance, near the original Confederate positions, Saul could see what looked like tiny, glowing red dots, which he knew were the cigars being smoked by people. There were quite a few of them, suggesting that a group of men had gathered together for some reason. The glows occasionally grew in intensity before fading again as the men took pulls on their cigars. He imagined it was a group of officers standing together, as if to watch something. They were out of range of their rifles, else he would have ordered his men to pick them off. They seemed to simply be standing around, as if waiting for something to happen, and Saul felt a sudden alarm.

"You hear that, boss?" Troy asked.

"Yes," Saul replied. It was a strange shuffling sound. It might have been a wagon wheel, but it lacked the scratchy sound wood made against a dirt road, being somehow softer. It sounded familiar, but he could not quite place it.

"They're moving their gabions out of the way, boss!" Troy said urgently.

"Fire a volley at them!" Saul said quickly. "And light the fire!" The only reason they would be moving the gabions out of the way would be so that assaulting infantry could more easily climb out of the saps. The officers smoking cigars in the distance had come to watch the attack.

Troy turned and shouted to the men in the trench. "First company! Fire down the street!"

Saul kept his eyes focused in the direction of the enemy while scattered rifle shots erupted from the trench. In the darkness, it was impossible to tell if they hit anything. One of his men used a match to light a pile of kindling soaked in turpentine a few feet in front of the trench, which quickly burst into flames. The street was suddenly flooded with light and Saul saw that Troy had been correct. The space in front of the saps was no longer sheltered by the gabions. He trusted Troy's opinion for, unlike Saul, he had served at Port Hudson in 1863 and had some experience with siege warfare.

There was a thunderous crash, soon followed by a second and a third. Saul instantly recognized them as the blasts of artillery.

"Get down!" he shouted. "Reload!"

He heard a scream off to his left and turned just in time to see one of his men collapse, half his face ripped off by canister fire. The trench protected most of his men, but they ducked down as deeply as they could to avoid the terrible projectiles. He could hear them slamming into the front of the hotel behind him. They didn't explode, which meant that the Southerners were firing solid shot. No further artillery blasts were heard, and Saul realized that they had been intended only to force his men to take cover. That, in turn, meant that the cannon were probably the signal for the infantry attack.

A deep, enormous battle cry welled up from large numbers of men, shrieking the Rebel Yell like so many banshees. Saul looked over the rim of the trench and saw scores of men emerging from the Confederate sap and charging forward towards the hotel.

The men of Saul's line who had managed to reload pulled the triggers on their Springfields almost simultaneously and a ragged volley erupted from the trench. Several gray-clad soldiers fell, but it took only a few seconds for the rest to cover the distance from the sap to the trench. They halted a few yards short of the trench and fired a volley down into it, killing and wounding several men. Then, with another terrifying battle cry, they jumped down into the trench itself.

Saul fired his LeMat five times in quick succession, striking one man in the face and another in the abdomen. He wasn't sure if either wound was fatal but had no time to look. The fighting in the trench was wild and confused, with the men on both sides swinging their muskets like great clubs and jabbing away with their bayonets. The noise of rifle barrels smashing against one another mixed with the sickening squishy sound of bayonets skewering human flesh. Screams punctuated the clamor of battle. Illuminated by the yellow flickering of the bonfire, the scene struck Saul as truly hellish.

He had four rounds remaining in his LeMat, whose cylinder held nine bullets. He withdrew a few yards behind the trench, firing twice more at Confederate soldiers who had not yet entered the trench and were aiming their rifles at his men. He glanced about frantically, his mind working at a feverish pace. Down the street, he could see large masses of Confederate soldiers advancing. They were walking, saving their strength, but would be at the trench in a matter of minutes. The enemy was going to sweep over them by sheer force of numbers.

Saul had known that this would happen. Although Troy had freed dozens of slaves from the nearby plantations, there had been no uprising as Saul had hoped. Therefore, there could be no end to the drama except by his men being overrun and slaughtered. He had hoped to at least kill as many of the Southerners as possible, but it now looked like his men were dying much more quickly than the Confederates. It was turning out to be less a battle than a massacre.

He could think of nothing he could do to save his men, then had a sudden realization. Without taking an instant to think his plan over, Saul ran back into the lobby of the hotel and dashed up the steps in enormous strides. In the hallway on the second floor were five of his men, who had been guarding the hostages when the enemy attack had begun. As far as he knew, they were the only ones not in the trench.

"Bring out a hostage!" Saul shouted. "A woman! Quickly!"

"How about that Georgia plantation bitch who won't shut up?" one man asked.

"Anyone! Just hurry!"

The man opened one of the doors. "You there!" he yelled. "On your feet! Into the hall!"

The woman who came out into the hall looked to be in her mid-twenties and was wearing a scarlet nightgown. She was ravishingly beautiful, with dark hair and blue-green eyes. Saul expected the look on her face to be one of terror, but she only looked angry, resentful and arrogant. He conceded a respect for her lack of fear.

There was no time to ask for her name. He grabbed her arm and pulled her down the stairs with him. He knew what he was about to do was dishonorable, perhaps the most shameful thing he had ever done in his life, but he felt he had no choice. His men were being slaughtered and could not save themselves. What Saul had in mind was the only thing he could think of.

Moments later, Saul and the woman stood on the porch just in front of the doorway. In front of the hotel, the battle continued to rage in the trench. As he had feared and suspected, his men were being overwhelmed by a huge Confederate force. He could not see many bodies, since they were lying on the bottom of the trench. Three black soldiers lay dead behind the trench, apparently shot as they tried to escape into the hotel. Taking in as much as he could in a quick glance, Saul saw dozens of his men continuing to fight, but vastly more enemy soldiers were crowding into the trench and more were still approaching down the street.

"Stop!" Saul roared as loud as he could. "Cease fire!"

He held the women's arm with one hand and the LeMat revolver with the other, aiming it at her head. The arrogance vanished from her face and she was now frozen with fear. He wanted to whisper quietly that she was going to be all right, for he knew he was bluffing and would never harm her. The woman's terrified expression, however, served his purpose perfectly.

Firing slackened for a moment and several men, both white and black, looked up at the scene in the doorway in stunned disbelief. Then a few Confederate officers, seeing the implied threat, shouted for their men to stop firing. Scattered shots continued to ring out, however.

"Order your men to stop shooting!" Saul called towards a Southern officer who was looking right him. "Do it or I'll kill her!" He knew the Southerners wouldn't fire on him for fear of hitting the woman.

"Cease fire!" the man instantly shouted. "All men, cease fire!"

Saul knew what he was doing, for he understood the character of the Southern white man. Despite being capable of so much evil, Southerners liked to see themselves as honorable and chivalrous in the manner of medieval knights. This made them fiercely protective of their women. The image of a black man threatening a white woman with a gun was one of the most horrible a Southern white man could envision.

A stillness descended upon the scene. The flickering of the bonfire continued to illuminate the area in front of the hotel, but now the clouds were beginning to glow softly with the first hints of sunrise. The men in the trench, who had been struggling to the death just a few moments earlier, now stood silently in a stunned group, all eyes on Saul as he held the LeMat to the girl's head.

An officer materialized out of the gloom and walked confidently towards the trench. Squinting his eyes, Saul recognized Morgan. He paused when he reached the trench, looking at Saul carefully.

"Let the woman go, Saul. The game's up and you know it."

"The hell it is. Order your men to withdraw."

"I can't do that."

"I'll kill her."

"If you do, my men will kill you instantly."

"Is killing one black man so important that you'll let one of your own women die?"

Morgan frowned and looked down into the trench for a moment, considering his options. Saul watched him carefully, not allowing his hand holding the gun to waver. If he moved the pistol away from the woman's face, there was always the possibility that an over-eager soldier would fire at him.

The Confederate commander sighed deeply. "Saul, listen to me. These are all the men you have. We know it. The whole area is surrounded. We have more than three thousand men and more are coming in all the time. Why don't you release your hostages, starting with that girl there, and surrender?"

"We're not the sort," Saul said. "Besides, you'd just hang us all anyway. We already discussed this."

Morgan looked irritated and waited a moment to reply. "So what's it going to be, then, Saul? You think you can hold that gun to that woman's head from now until doomsday?"

"We have eleven more female hostages in the hotel. Withdraw your men or I will order them all shot."

"You know that can't happen."

"Then I'll give the order."

Morgan pursed his lips. "You've always avoided harming women before."

"You're not leaving me any choice."

"Please don't hurt me," the woman said pitifully.

Saul winced slightly, surprised that she had spoken. He jerked his head in Morgan's direction. "Tell him."

"Please do what he wants!" the woman cried. "I don't want to die!"

"Saul!" Morgan yelled. "You cannot do this!"

"Order your men away, Morgan!"

"I can't!" Morgan protested. His face then lit slightly. "Saul, if you release the hostages, then I'll pull back. All of them. The men, too."

Saul had not expected this. Truthfully, he hadn't known what was going to happen. Bringing the woman out onto the porch had been an act of desperation. He knew that Morgan couldn't simply abandon the attack when it was on the verge of succeeding. Had he done so, several of his men would have died to no purpose. By obtaining the release of the hostages, Morgan would have something to show for the attack.

Yet the hostages were Saul's ace-in-the-hole. If they were all released, there would be nothing to stop Morgan from wheeling up artillery and blowing the Grand Hotel to bits from a safe distance with explosive shells. Releasing them would be tantamount to a death sentence. Yet if he didn't, he and his men would die anyway.

"I will release the hostages if you pull back your troops."

"We are in agreement," Morgan said simply.

"And I require a ten-day ceasefire."

Morgan's eyes widened in shock. "Ten days? You can't be serious."

"You should know me well enough by now to know that I'm always serious. We need breathing room. You're a soldier. You understand that. What good would it be to me to release the hostages in exchange for you pulling back, if you just reform and attack again tomorrow night?"

Morgan's faced curled into a mask of anger and resentment. "I can't make a deal like that with you."

"Why not?" Saul replied. "You could make it with a white man, couldn't you?"

"You are a slave!" Morgan shouted furiously.

"No," Saul replied calmly. "No, I'm not. I'm not your slave or anyone else's."

"You should get down on your knees and thank God that I even deign to speak with you!" Morgan yelled. "Who the hell do you think you are, you insolent black bastard?"

Saul scoffed. The anger evident in Morgan's voice gave him a sense of satisfaction. "I'm the insolent black bastard that has already killed dozens of your men in battle and will kill every single one of the hostages unless you pull your men back to their original positions and grant me a ten-day ceasefire." He paused a moment. "I'll give you thirty seconds, Morgan. If you don't agree by then, I'll blow the head off of this beautiful white woman and order my men to kill the hostages."

"You'll be killed instantly if you do that," Morgan said quickly.

Saul thought momentarily of his mother's protective magic. "I don't think so," he replied.

Morgan turned and shouted to his men. "All companies! Pull back!"

Saul could see that some of the Southern soldiers were hesitating, wordlessly voicing their disagreement with Morgan's orders. Yet their discipline was too solid for them to disobey. They pulled themselves up out of the trench and walked unhurriedly back towards the sap from which they had emerged. Morgan stood in place as his men passed behind him, apparently unconcerned for his own safety.

"Why don't you start by letting that woman go?"

Saul released his grip on the young woman's arm. Instantly, the expression on her face transformed from fear back into rage. He could see the loathing in her eyes and for a moment was genuinely repelled.

"I am sorry, ma'am," Saul said.

She spat on the ground by his feet. "You're not fit to wipe my husband's boots!" she hissed as she stormed down the steps and away from the hotel. Ignoring the black soldiers, who parted like the Red Sea when she approached them, she reached the trench and was across it in a matter of seconds. She paused next to Morgan for just a moment, looking back at Saul, a deep incomprehension and antagonism clear in her gaze.

"Go," Morgan said softly. "My men will take care of you."

Saul looked through the door into the hotel lobby and was pleased to see that one of his men was standing there. "Go upstairs. All hostages are to be released. Send them down at once."

"Yes, boss." The man turned and headed up the stairs.

"They're on their way," Saul said to Morgan.

"Good."

Eleven women and fourteen men passed through the door and hurried past Saul. They moved urgently, as though they feared the decision for their release would be revoked if they tarried too long. Saul didn't blame them. In their minds, after all, they were living through a nightmare. It took only a few minutes for the released hostages to clear the trench and reach the waiting, friendly hands of the Confederate troops.

"I kept my end of the bargain," Saul said. "You keep yours."

Morgan turned to one of the officers. "Have the men fall back to their original positions. Order them to take up positions to ensure that none of these black bastards gets a chance to escape."

The Southern troops began to march away, the freed hostages going with them. Saul noticed the tenderness with which some of the soldiers threw their uniform coats over their sleeping gowns to protect their modesty. In minutes, the crowd of soldiers and freed hostages had faded away down the road.

Morgan now stood alone. Any one of Saul's men might have shot him, yet he remained there, utterly fearless.

"What did you do with Silas, by the way?" Morgan asked. "I forgot to ask you before."

"He received the punishment he deserved."

"You killed him?"

"That's right." He decided to spare Morgan the details. "What of my men? The prisoners you said were taken to Baton Rouge?"

"They were hanged."

Saul scoffed. "Some honorable warrior you are, Morgan."

"Orders from Richmond. Not my place to disagree."

"Feel free to tell yourself that. God might not agree. And you'll have to explain yourself to Him one of these days."

Morgan grunted once before continuing. "You might be interested to know that one Charles Russell Lowell was arrested as he tried to flee New Orleans. Just a couple of days after you took this town. He's going to be on trial for inciting a slave rebellion in a few days. My guess is that they'll hang him in short order."

Saul sighed deeply. The news wasn't unexpected, for he had given Lowell less than an even chance of escaping. He had spent only a few days in Lowell's company, yet the Boston abolitionist had become a comrade no less than Troy, Ferguson or any of his other men. He felt genuine sadness, for he knew that there would be no escaping the noose.

Morgan turned and began walking away.

"How many of your men did we kill this morning, Morgan?" Saul called after him.

"A few," the Confederate general replied over his shoulder. "But we killed a few of yours, too, didn't we? And we have more coming in every day. How many do you have left, Saul?"

"Oh, about enough for another killing."

August 18, Morning
State Depatment Offices, Richmond, Virginia

Benjamin looked down at the immense headline front page of the *New York Daily Tribune*, the Republican newspaper edited by the irrepressible Horace Greeley.

SAUL RELEASES LETTER TO PUBLIC!
DECLARES FREE BLACK STATE IN LOUISIANA!

Somehow, the letter Saul had written had gotten out to the public despite all their efforts to suppress it. Benjamin didn't know how. Perhaps a telegraph operator somewhere along the line had made a copy and handed it over to some Yankee reporter in exchange for money. Perhaps Saul had sent one of his men out with a copy who had then made it to St. Louis. It didn't matter. The letter would now be reprinted across the world over the next few days. Saul's reputation would now go from being a black Robin Hood to being a black King Arthur.

The capture of New Iberia was humiliating enough for the Confederacy, but Saul's letter would magnify the problem tenfold. Exactly at the moment when the presidential election and the diplomatic situation in Europe required public attention to be shifted away from slavery, events were conspiring to focus interest upon it. Worse, the press had two heroes in the form of Saul and Lowell around which they could center their coverage. As Benjamin knew very well, the newspapers would devote much more coverage to a story that had names and faces attached to it.

The arrest of Lowell only made the problem worse. In Saul, the newspapers around the world had a hero figure that they could raise to epic heights. In Lowell, they would have a martyr figure whose fate they could grieve over. To Benjamin's mind, it would have been far better if Lowell had escaped. It was the

493

worst of all possible worlds, as if the Almighty himself was conspiring to thwart the ambitions of the Confederacy.

Benjamin's mind wrestled with the implication, even as he carefully listened to the man sitting across the desk from him. William Porcher Miles, having returned to Richmond from Washington City, was giving his report. It was about what Benjamin had expected. There had always been considerable sympathy for Saul's insurrection amid the abolitionist strongholds in New England. News of his dramatic capture of New Iberia had apparently set off spontaneous celebrations in Boston, not unlike those which had greeted major Union victories during the war.

Similarly, there had been no denouncement of the illegal activities of Charles Russell Lowell. Far from it, in fact. Miles, a hint of amusement in his voice, told Benjamin about the rapid formation of something called the Committee to Secure the Release of General Lowell, which had started in Rhode Island and was now quickly spreading to other states. It was not clear what activities this organization intended to pursue, but its very existence was a clear indication of the state of Northern public opinion.

"So, you're telling me that there's no real voice in our favor?" Benjamin asked.

Miles shrugged. "If there is, I didn't see it. A few Democratic newspapers in New York City and Chicago, like the *New York World*, expressed the opinion that what Lowell did was illegal and harmful to good relations between us and the Union. But they did so quietly, without anything like the fervency of the abolitionists. Some papers are basically ignoring the Saul matter, mostly those whose readership is made up of poor immigrants who don't like the idea of blacks stealing their jobs. But most are celebrating him."

"That's disappointing," Benjamin said.

"Yes, but not surprising."

"No?"

"Not at all," Miles said. "You'll forgive me, Mr. Secretary, but having spent the last few years among the Yankees, I can tell you with full confidence what is going on in their minds. They elected McClellan and gave the Democrats control of the House back in 1864 because they were sick of the war and wanted it to end. They got what they wanted. Now, a couple of years on, the Northern people are starting to think they made a terrible mistake. Three hundred thousand of their menfolk died during the war and now they're starting to think it was all for nothing. They're deluded, of course, but I can't really blame them for thinking that way. Try to think how we would have reacted had we sacrificed so much and ended up losing the war."

Benjamin nodded, conceding Miles's point. "So they're still disposed to dislike us."

"Exactly. Now, McClellan and the Democrats are naturally terrified of this. They're only about a year away from their own presidential elections, you know. McClellan wants there to be good relations between our countries because he wants the people to think that he made the right decision when he made peace with us. The Republicans will try to stir up as much rancor towards us as they can because they know it will help them at the polls."

"I believe you're right," Benjamin said. "That's why McClellan is stoking the fire of this Fenian business. He wants the people focused in anger against the British, not against us."

"Precisely. But what with this black bandit taking control of a town and all the fuss that's going to be made over this Lowell fellow, the newspapers have all but forgotten about the Fenians and are again fixed against us instead. It's almost like the war isn't over."

"Is there any way we could influence public opinion in the North? Turn its attention back to the Fenians?"

"I doubt it," Miles replied. "There are some newspapermen who are sympathetic to us, outside of New England, anyway. But I think Lowell's trial is going to be followed closely by the public. Until it is over, we can't expect anyone to focus on anything else."

Benjamin nodded. The Ambassador to the United States had arrived back in Richmond two days earlier, in response to Benjamin's recall order. While the Secretary of State did not want an open breach with the United States, thinking such an event the worst of all possible outcomes, neither could they fail to respond in some way to the arrest of a former Union officer and the smuggling of weapons to Saul. In the diplomatic game, a recall of a representative for consultations was the appropriate response.

He considered Miles for a moment. The man had always been a useful tool. He had been a Fire-Eater before secession, but unlike most of that group, he had generally supported the policies of the Davis administration during the war. That, and the need to include a South Carolinian, had made him an ideal member of the delegation sent to the Toronto peace talks in 1865. Davis had not wanted to appoint him as Ambassador to the United States, but Benjamin had eventually persuaded him to do so. It quieted the Fire-Eaters at home, who might otherwise have accused them of kowtowing to the United States, and also sent a message to the Yankees that the South was not interested in compromising any of its ideals.

Miles had an agenda of his own, of course, and Benjamin was willing to let him believe that he was working for his own interests. Besides, Benjamin had to admit that he was genuinely fond of Miles. The man was like him in several respects, being a man who combined charm with a certain deviousness. When it came to being devious, however, Benjamin was quite sure he could run rings around Miles.

Benjamin had been somewhat surprised when Breckinridge had told him about Miles's blackmail threat. The Secretary of State did not like unexpected factors disrupting his carefully crafted political equations, but he always prided himself on his ability to adapt quickly. Within minutes of Breckinridge telling him of his backroom deal with Hamlin at the Toronto peace talks, and the threat of Miles to expose it, Benjamin had already devised a plan to neutralize the threat and make use of Miles at the same time.

They continued talking about public opinion and political events in the United States for some time. Miles described the developing split in the Republican Party, with the Radicals increasingly siding with former Secretary of the Treasury Salmon Chase and the Moderates lining up behind former Secretary of State William Seward. Miles made no effort to disguise his utter contempt for the abolitionists. Despite the growing unpopularity of the McClellan administration, the divisions within the Republican ranks gave at least some hope that the incumbent president would win reelection in the coming year. That, Benjamin had decided, would be very much in the Confederacy's interest.

Now it was time to move the conversation in a different direction.

"What think you of the election?"

Miles's eyes narrowed. "I just told you."

"No, I mean our election."

"Hmm," Miles replied. "I did not expect that my opinion on that subject would be of any interest to you."

"Consider it an unofficial conversation, then."

"Very well," said Miles, pausing a moment. "An unofficial discussion it is."

Benjamin noted instantly the change in the man's tone. Before, it had been a superior discussing matters with one of his subordinates, but now it would be a conversation between equals. Miles waited a moment before going on, looking warily into the eyes of the Secretary of State. It was as if Benjamin had put away one deck of cards and brought out another, while announcing that they were switching from poker to blackjack.

"Well, it shall certainly be an interesting contest between Breckinridge and Beauregard," Miles finally said. "My friends in Charleston are quite unanimous in their belief that Beauregard will carry South Carolina without difficulty. As for the other states, I cannot make any predictions."

"I see," Benjamin said carefully. "May I ask which candidate you intend to support?"

"I have honestly not made up my mind one way or the other."

Miles smiled and waited to see how Benjamin would respond. What he was really saying, it was immediately obvious to Benjamin, was that he was willing to support whichever candidate offered him the most. Under ordinary circumstances, Miles would not have had an important role in the election. His own political strength lay in South Carolina which, as he had just pointed out, was not going to be in play in November. Miles knew, however, that he had a trump card to play. He could leak to the press the information about Breckinridge's dealings with Hamlin in Toronto or he could keep quiet about it. Which course of action he choose, Benjamin was sure, would depend on what sort of incentive Benjamin could offer him.

Breckinridge had asked Benjamin not to make any deals with Miles, whom he understandably detested. Benjamin had given his word, but naturally had no intention of keeping it. He was determined that Breckinridge was going to be the next President of the Confederates States and, in his own way, he considered Breckinridge a friend. What he was about to do, he would do for Breckinridge's own good, as well as the good of the country. One of his great advantages in politics, he knew, was that he was not constrained by the code of honor that men like Breckinridge prized so highly. It gave him a flexibility that others lacked.

"I feel the need to be honest with you," Benjamin said.

"A rare thing, for men such as us."

"Breckinridge has told me about what happened in Toronto. I know that he made a deal with Hannibal Hamlin, that he concealed the fact from you and the other delegates, and that you discovered this fact and have threatened blackmail."

Miles shrugged. "It was obvious you knew from the moment we began this conversation."

"Which leads to a simple question, Miles. What is it that you intend to do?"

"As I said, I haven't made up my mind one way or the other."

Benjamin didn't reply, looking carefully at Miles, calculating, trying to pry through the man's facial expression. It was frustrating. Benjamin had always prided himself on his ability to read people. Whether they were dignified men of honor like Breckinridge or drunken fools like Wigfall, whether they were intelligent or stupid, people were normally open books to him. Miles, however, was a disquieting exception to this rule. His face might as well have been carved out of granite, an enigmatic smile not unlike Benjamin's own revealing absolutely nothing.

"Why did you threaten to blackmail Breckinridge?" Benjamin finally asked.

"I do not believe he fully embraces the values on which the Confederacy was founded. We are a slave-holding republic. I think Breckinridge feels that the latter is more important than the former."

"You don't?"

"No," Miles said calmly.

"You'd rather be a slave-holding autocracy than a republic without slavery?"

"Of course. What's so special about a republic, anyway? Your friend Breckinridge adheres to the discredited idea of Jefferson that all men are born with natural rights. They aren't. People are born neither free nor equal and it's nonsense to suggest otherwise. Liberty is an acquired privilege, you see. Only those whom God endowed with superior minds are deserving of it. I don't think it's a coincidence that all such people, certainly all such people that I've ever met, are white. If we have to one day give up either being slave-holders or being a republic, I shall unhesitatingly choose to give up the latter."

Benjamin shrugged. "I see no reason why we can't continue on as a slave-holding republic forever."

This wasn't true and Benjamin worried for a moment that Miles would sense his deception. Benjamin wasn't an idealist like Breckinridge and he did not especially care about the black people of the South, but it was clear to him that slavery was a doomed institution that could not possibly continue indefinitely. The question was whether it would end in a controlled manner, with the institutions of the South left intact, or whether it would end in a storm of fire and blood.

"I wish Breckinridge felt as you do."

"What makes you think he doesn't?"

"It's obvious. Just listen to what Toombs and Wigfall have been saying. Breckinridge doesn't own slaves himself. He endorsed Cleburne's abolitionist scheme during the war. In Toronto, he gave in to the Yankees on all the slavery questions. Before the war, when everyone was calling him the champion of Southern rights, he never defended slavery on its own terms. The most he would ever say was that it was a constitutional right."

"Isn't that enough?" Benjamin asked. "The Confederate Constitution has much stronger protections for slavery than did the United States Constitution. It's effectively impossible for anything to be legally done against slavery in our country, even if many people wanted that, which they don't."

"No, it's not enough. I don't want a man at the head of our nation against whom we need to pit our constitutional safeguards. I want our president to be someone who will defend slavery to the uttermost, no matter what the situation. I just don't think Breckinridge is that man."

"Then why haven't you already gone through with your blackmail?"

"I'm not sure I want Beauregard. I know him well. I served on his staff at the start of the war. He's a friend. But I am not sure he is the material out of which a good chief executive is made. Besides, I wanted to see what you had to say, first."

"What I was willing to offer, you mean."

Miles smiled. "Since you wish to put it in such language, let me simply ask you, then. What are you willing to offer me in exchange for my silence?"

"You already hold one of the most prestigious diplomatic positions. Only London or Paris could be considered higher, and even that's debatable."

"I know."

"You're not aiming as the Vice Presidency, are you? Breckinridge has already offered it to James Kemper."

"Yes, I know. A mistake. The people think Virginia already has too much influence. It will hurt Breckinridge in Georgia, especially. But no, I have no desire to be the vice president. It's a powerless office. Look what happened to poor old Aleck, after all. No, it would give me no means to stiffen up your man's softness on the slavery question."

Benjamin nodded, waiting a moment before speaking again. "I see. You want my job."

"I'm certainly qualified for it. I was mayor of Charleston and did very well, which proves I have all the administrative experience necessary for the State Department. I was a Congressman in Washington before the war and in Richmond during it. I think my service at the peace talks and as our ambassador to Washington has proven my diplomatic abilities. Honestly, I can't think of anyone better than myself."

"What makes you think I won't remain in my current post in the new administration?" Benjamin asked.

"Because you're not going to, obviously."

Miles was laying his cards out on the table. He wanted to be Secretary of State. Both men knew that if Breckinridge won the election and Benjamin asked to keep his position, the incoming president would probably agree. He could see what Miles was thinking. The South Carolinian thought he had the Louisiana Jew over a fire. Releasing to the press the information he had would seriously damage, if not ruin, Breckinridge's chances to win the election.

Miles clearly thought that Benjamin was willing to pay any price to ensure his silence, even the sacrifice of his own office. Yet Benjamin had an advantage Miles could never have guessed at, for he no longer had any intention of remaining in office.

"Very well. Secretary of State it is."

Benjamin relished the surprised look on Miles's face. It was not a common experience for him to engage in a duel of wits with an opponent of equal measure to himself. Having unexpectedly gained the upper hand was quite satisfying.

"Do you have the authority from Breckinridge to make this offer?" Miles said.

"Of course. I wouldn't have made it otherwise."

"I find that hard to believe."

"He doesn't want any trouble from you. So long as you give your word as a gentleman to fulfill your responsibilities as Secretary of State and to respect Breckinridge's position as president, he is comfortable with this arrangement."

Miles's eyes narrowed. Benjamin made a conscious effort to maintain a placid expression as the South Carolinian's eyes examined him carefully. He was telling a blatant lie about Breckinridge and he knew that Miles suspected it was a lie. He had to convince him that it was the truth.

"When will I hear this from Breckinridge?"

"Soon enough."

Miles nodded. "Very well. Until that happens, I shall keep what I know to myself. If I am promised the Secretary of State position by Breckinridge, I shall keep my mouth shut. But if it turns out that you have deceived me, I'll know soon enough and you can face the consequences."

Benjamin chuckled. Threats had never meant much to him. "So, do we have an agreement?"

Miles slowly nodded. "Yes, we do."

August 20, Evening
La Maison Restaurant, Paris, France

La Maison Dorée was Slidell's favorite restaurant. He thought a dinner there was about as near as a human being could get to heaven. The mirrors and gilding along the walls, the aromas of the delicious food and fine wines on every table, the soft chatter of wealthy and aristocratic clientele all combined to make a dinner there an intoxicating experience. Located at the intersection of the Boulevard de Gand and rue Cerutti, it had been the place for the elite of Paris to see and be seen since the early 1840s. The composer Rossini was a regular patron and it was said that the Prince of Wales ate there at least once each time he visited Paris.

The chef who presided over La Maison Dorée like an emperor was the great Casimir Moisson, said to be the greatest culinary master Paris had seen since the days of Marie Antoine Carême. The man made cookery into an art form, being no less a genius than Michelangelo had been in sculpture or Beethoven had been in music.

One of the most enjoyable aspects of La Maison Dorée was its selection of private rooms, where friends and colleagues could enjoy their dinners away from the prying eyes of ordinary people. Slidell had just sat down across from Senator Berthier. Several of Berthier's wealthy friends were also gathered around the table, brought together so that Slidell could persuade them to invest in the Confederacy's railroad reconstruction program.

It was no idle matter. Two years after the end of the war, the railroads of the South still functioned in a ramshackle manner, when they functioned at all. Almost every other telegram he received from Judah Benjamin or Jefferson Davis included an appeal to find money with which to finance the reconstruction program. The Confederate Constitution forbade the central government from providing funds itself and it would have been too cash-strapped to do so even if it had been permitted. European banks and private investors were the only possible source of help.

"There is money to be made, gentlemen," Slidell said with a warm smile. "As our nation recovers from the war, the production of cotton, tobacco, and sugar will slowly rise to its pre-war levels and eventually surpass them. All that produce needs to be moved from the interior of the country to the seaports. These railroads will not lack for freight."

"Yes," replied one of Berthier's friends. "But when will we see profits?"

"Soon enough, I am sure."

"That's rather vague," the man replied. "Five years? Ten years? I don't want my money being poured into some sort of bottomless pit. I would imagine it will take a long time before your railroads are in any shape to be making money."

"If French money doesn't rebuild our railroads, British money will," Slidell countered. "Wouldn't you rather see France, rather than your traditional enemy, reaping the economic benefits of investment in the Confederacy?"

The men at the table glanced at one another and many of them nodded. Slidell had learned early in his Paris days that using England as a bogeyman was always an effective tool when it came to influencing the French.

For a moment, he turned his attention to his plate, on which rested a dish of beef tenderloin with foie gras, covered in a Madeira demi-glaze sauce. Along with a glass of Château Lafite, it made for a wonderfully delicious dinner. His mind was already casting its thoughts towards dessert.

The men around the table talked. Some were bankers and others were simply wealthy individuals, but all were looking for places to invest their money in order to generate reliable and hopefully substantial returns in the years to come. Slidell understood finance and investment, for he had spent many years in the mercantile trade before getting involved in politics and had always kept his fingers in various business opportunities both in New Orleans and since he had relocated to Paris.

Amid the chatter, Slidell noticed that one man sitting at the far side of the table was strangely quiet. He recognized him as Jean-Baptiste Malraux, a wealthy banker and philanthropist. He had not spoken much thus far at the dinner and the look on his face was glum and unhappy.

"Is something troubling you, Monsieur Malraux?" Slidell asked.

"Many things," Malraux replied.

"Please tell me, so that I might alleviate any concerns."

"I will you tell, Monsieur Slidell, but I doubt you will be able to alleviate them." He cleared his throat, as the chatter from the other dinner guests quieted down. "I do not wish to have my hands sullied by investing in railroads that will be built by African slaves."

Slidell frowned. He was used to encountering anti-slavery feeling throughout France and it did not offend him. After all, he had served in the Senate in Washington before the war and locked horns with Northern senators on the issue almost every day. In France, abolitionist sentiments were usually voiced by working-class radicals or socialists, yet occasionally one found it among members of the upper class as well.

"It is a well-known fact that the Confederacy has developed a unique solution to the problem of having its whites and blacks live side-by-side in peace. But I see no reason why this should trouble any foreigner wishing to invest in Confederate railroads."

"I think it should trouble anyone who has a conscience. And even if it didn't, it should trouble anyone who is concerned with their own reputations." He looked away from Slidell to Berthier and the other dinner guess. "Tell me, my friends, what will your response be when the newspapers start running stories about your investments in the Confederacy? How will you explain that your money is going into business ventures which make use of slave labor, driven by overseers armed with whips?"

There were somber nods around the table, which alarmed Slidell. "Come now, my friends," he said quickly. "Some of you have already invested in various businesses in our country. I'm sure every one of you is aware that Gustave de Rothschild is considering financing the construction of a major iron foundry in Atlanta." Slidell knew that this project was of particular importance, as the new facility would have the capability to produce steam engines for ships, something the Confederacy currently lacked. Consequently, he had spent much time searching for money to finance it.

"That's not what I have heard," Malraux replied.

"What do you mean?" Slidell made a strong effort of will to keep the irritation out of his voice and the smile on his face.

"I heard tell at the stock exchange just before I came here that Rothschild is backing out of that plan."

"I have heard nothing of the sort. Why would he do that?"

Malraux looked at Slidell incredulously. "Why, all this business with Saul and Charles Russell Lowell, of course."

"Saul and Lowell?" Slidell asked, genuinely confused. Naturally, he was following the news of the fighting around New Iberia and the arrest and upcoming trial of Charles Russell Lowell. He knew that French newspapers were covering the two stories. Saul's dramatic letter declaring a free state around New Iberia had been reprinted in literally dozens of papers, much to his irritation. "I am, of course, aware of what is happening in Louisiana. I don't see what it has to do with this discussion over investing in our railroads."

"You are smart enough to understand, Slidell, if you would but open your eyes. You have worked very hard since you arrived here in 1862 to persuade all of us that the Confederacy is not based on slavery, even when all the manifestos issued by the Southern states upon secession said precisely the opposite. I've read articles you've written for the newspapers in which you've hinted that slavery will eventually die out, but I see no evidence of that and I have a very difficult time believing that this is what you really think." Malraux took a sip of wine before continuing. "The truth, Slidell, is that you're a trickster. Your Confederacy is based on slavery. We all know that and no evasion on your part is going to change that. The news coming out of Louisiana has fixed the attention of the world on your 'peculiar institution', as you callously call it, and the world doesn't like what it sees."

"I'm sorry you feel that way," Slidell replied. "But let me ask you a question. Why does French money flow to investments in Russia, a backward state governed by brutal oppressors? Why do your ships sail in and out of the ports of the Ottoman Empire, an Islamic absolute dictatorship? Why do you continue to import sugar, coffee, and other products from Brazil, whose economy is also based on African slavery? I sense no little amount of hypocrisy from you, Monsieur Malraux"

The Frenchman was unperturbed. "The Russians, Turks, and Brazilians are admitted barbarians. You Southerners, though, claim to be part of the civilized world. You cannot be civilized and adhere to African slavery, just as a husband cannot say that he is faithful to his wife if he sleeps with other women."

Slidell forced himself to smile. One of the key skills of a diplomat was to appear calm and pleasant when one felt very much otherwise. "I know that our peculiar institution gives pause to some Europeans. But why should it? Slavery still existed in your Caribbean islands as recently as thirty years ago. I can assure you, if you spent time among our people in the Confederacy, you would learn that it is entirely benign. Our slaves are happy and content, carefully fed and cared for by their loving masters. The blacks in the Confederacy are far better off than those who live in Africa."

"Happy and content?" Malraux asked sneeringly. "If that were true, why did they flee from the plantations during the war whenever a Union army approached? Why did they don blue uniforms and fight against you? Why has Saul raised the flag of rebellion in this town of New Iberia?"

"Allow me to explain, Monsieur Malraux. I-"

"There's nothing to explain, Monsieur Slidell. If what you claim about slavery in the Confederacy were true, then there would be no need for whip-wielding overseers to keep the blacks in line, would there be? Nor would this black warrior and his band of men be fighting with a gallantry worthy of Napoleon's Old Guard. Nor would this New England man have risked his life to give them the means to fight."

Slidell cast a glance at Berthier, looking for support. The nobleman said nothing, staring impassively down at his plate and refusing to meet Slidell's eyes. Slidell frowned, suddenly feeling himself alone among enemies. Rather than continue to engage Malraux, however, the Louisianan turned his attention to his plate, savoring a few forkfuls of his beef tenderloin and foie gras, followed by a long sip of his Château Lafite

Malraux addressed the other men at the table. "What we need to ask ourselves, gentlemen, is not just whether investment in these Confederate railroads would be profitable, but whether it would be wise. Even if we ignored our own moral scruples, the fact remains that the people of France are increasingly of the opinion that slavery is a hideous evil and that it should not be tolerated. Look at what is happening in England. Mass public meetings are being held in London and other major cities, calling for boycotts against any company doing business with the Confederacy. Do you want to end up like them?"

There were mutterings of agreement around the table. Slidell maintained a placid expression, but inside he was filled with rage.

Malraux turned to him. "I am afraid, Monsieur Slidell, that I cannot agree to your proposal that I invest my money in your country's railroad reconstruction program. I find the financial risk to be great, so I would hesitate even if there were no other objections. And there are other objections. I am a devout Catholic and I cannot in good conscience contribute to any project that would be done by the labor of slaves. And even if I had no moral scruples myself, I would not want the bad publicity that will inevitably follow anyone who does what you suggest."

"The coffee you drink every morning probably came from beans grown by the labor of Brazilian slaves," Slidell protested.

"If so, than we shall have to deal with that at some point, too. You do not seem to grasp, Monsieur Slidell, that the institution of slavery has no place in the modern world. And unless your Confederacy quickly rethinks its foundational institution, neither will it." Malraux glanced about. "And now, if you gentlemen will excuse me, I seem to have lost my appetite." He touched the corners of his mouth with his napkin, pushed his chair back from the table, and rose to leave.

There was silence at the table as Malraux walked out of the room. Slidell pretended to focus on his food and wine, smiling broadly. "Moisson has outdone himself tonight, don't you think, gentlemen?"

No one bothered to reply.

August 24, Morning
British Army Headquarters, Montreal, Canada

"You are quite sure of this?" Wolseley asked.

"Yes," the man replied in the strange accent unique to the American Indians. "Me and my boys, we've been there ourselves. Seen the whole thing. Rifles. Ammunition. Even two cannon. Enough weapons for two thousand men. Maybe more."

"Where exactly is it?" He could not have cared less that the Indian had crossed the American border without permission. As far as the Indians were concerned, nothing could be more irrelevant than a line on a map.

"Couple miles north of Chazy. Fenians tried to hide it, but my boys sniffed it out easy. Those Fenians, they're no good at stuff like that. Don't know nothing about..." He struggled for the word. "Concealment. They don't know nothing about concealment."

Wolseley nodded and jotted the fact down in the notes he was taking. He had long since memorized the maps of the border region between the United States and Canada. Chazy was a small town on the western shore of Lake Champlain. It was only about eight miles south of the Canadian border. In fact, if Wolseley mounted a horse and rode due south from Montreal, he could be in Chazy in less than a day. More importantly, this was a part of the border along which the St. Lawrence River did not flow. There was no natural barrier preventing the movement of large numbers of troops. Since the area was deeply wooded, it might be possible to slip a force across the border without being detected.

He looked up at the Indian scout, who went by the name Orenda. He had said he was a Mohawk, which Wolseley recalled was a subtribe within the larger Iroquois tribe. He would certainly have no love for the United States, traditional enemies of the Mohawk. Of the Fenians and their cause, Orenda probably knew little and cared less. It was enough that the man had been commended to him as a competent and effective scout by officers whom Wolseley trusted.

"How far south of the border?"

The Indian shrugged. "A mile. Maybe two."

"If I asked you, Orenda, could you led a force to this place?"

"Yes." The Indian's tone betrayed a slight irritation that this was even a question.

"Tell no one of this."

"Of course."

"You may go."

Without so much as a nod, Orenda turned and left the office. Wolseley had become used to the lack of deference by the natives. He had learned through experience that it was useless to do anything about it, so he no longer bothered trying.

Opening a drawer, Wolseley took out a map of the border region just south of Montreal. He considered the ramifications of the Indian's report. If the Fenians had established a large supply depot in the location Orenda indicated, it might suggest that they were planning to descend on Montreal in a *coup de main*. Wolseley scoffed, for such a move would be suicidal. Montreal was now garrisoned by nearly six thousand men. Most of the force was Canadian militia, but two regular British battalions, the Gordon Highlanders and the Duke of Wellington's Regiment, was also part of the city's defenses. If the Fenians were foolish enough to attack Montreal, they would be destroyed.

Would the Fenians be so rash as to do such a thing? Perhaps, if their aim was to spark a war between the United States and the British Empire. Yet Wolseley doubted it. For one thing, the Fenians would certainly be overawed by the defenses of Montreal. More importantly, though, Wolseley did not think that the American government would allow it. It was one thing to look the other way while small Fenian raids were mounted into Canada, such as the one he had repulsed with the Royal Welch Fusiliers back in May. It would be quite another to allow a major attack against the most important city in all of Canada. There would be no plausible way that the Americans could claim ignorance of such a major operation. Of course, it wasn't clear how much control the government in Washington City actually had over the Fenians.

There was a knock on the door.

"Come in!" Wolseley ordered.

The door opened and Buller entered, carrying two cups of coffee. "Morning to you, Colonel." He set one of the coffees on the desk in front of Wolseley.

"And to you."

"Was that our Iroquois scout Orenda I saw leaving?"

"It was," Wolseley replied. He then told Buller of the Indian's report.

"Interesting," Buller said when he had finished. "If they're stockpiling that much so close to the border, and right near Montreal, in fact, it suggests that they have decidedly unfriendly intentions."

"Quite so. I shall advise the commander-in-chief to reinforce the city with an additional British battalion and more militia."

"Do you think General Napier will agree?"

"He has followed all my advice up to this point. In addition, I shall direct that work on the fortifications south of the city be accelerated."

Wolseley was, in fact, certain that Napier would do what he said. The commander-in-chief of all British forces in Canada had proven so pliable and so impressed by Wolseley's competence and intelligence that Wolseley felt he had the man wrapped around his fingers. Wolseley was, in fact if not in name, the man in command of the defense of the Dominion of Canada.

"Read the paper this morning?" Buller asked.

"Not yet."

"You have heard about the cease-fire the Confederates made with the black insurgents in that town in Louisiana, yes?"

"Of course," Wolseley said, with a slight sharpness. He was irritated that Buller would think he was unaware of a story that had dominated the headlines for the past several days. Considering the prospect of a gigantic battle between the British Empire and the United States, Wolseley had not considered vandalism done by a few rogue slaves to be all that interesting. He was surprised that Saul had not been dealt with before now, but it was no concern of his. "The Southerners have brought in General Longstreet, who will deal with the problem."

"You know this Longstreet, as I recall?"

"I met him when I travelled the Confederacy in '62," Wolseley replied. "A fine officer, in my opinion. Quite friendly. More so than Stonewall Jackson, at any rate. His men were extraordinary. Their uniforms were all shabby and most didn't have shoes. They just wrapped rags around their feet. Yet under Longstreet, they were a truly formidable force."

"Their record certainly suggests it."

Wolseley was not interested in talking more of Longstreet or the rebellion of the slaves. "What does the paper say about the Fenians?"

Buller's eyes narrowed and scanned through a few pages. "Not much that I can see." He continued looking for half a minute. "Nothing at all, in fact."

"Nothing?" Wolseley asked.

"Not that I can see."

He gestured for Buller to hand him the newspaper. He flipped through it for nearly a minute, finding no specific mention of the Fenian Crisis. Virtually every news item dealt with the capture of New Iberia by Saul or the arrest of Charles Russell Lowell. There was, however, one item that caught his attention.

"It says here that the Royal Navy squadron in Charleston is leaving."

"Does it?" Buller asked. "I didn't notice that."

Wolseley frowned. The dispatch of British warships to a Confederate port had been intended as a symbolic statement to prepare public opinion for the announcement of the alliance between Britain and the Confederacy. He continued reading through the brief story.

"Looks like the *Black Prince* and the other ships are relocating to our base in Bermuda."

"That is a surprise," Buller replied. "They've only just arrived in Charleston, right?"

"Yes."

"Perhaps the government wants to back away from the Confederacy, what with all this talk of a liberated territory for slaves in Louisiana."

"What would that have to do with anything?" Wolseley asked.

"Well, you know. The government in London is very sensitive to what the people think. And all those abolitionists are pushing Disraeli not to have anything to do with the Confederacy, on account of their still being a slaveholding country and all. If everything's kind of quiet, he can get away with it. But now that this Saul fellow has gone and declared a free state for the blacks, and this unfortunate Lowell person has been arrested and will probably hang, things have changed. The papers back in London are now all talking about slavery in the South again."

Wolseley scoffed. "Every society has a right to organize itself as it wishes. If the Southerners want to maintain slavery, that's their choice. Who are we to tell them what they can and can't do with their own property?"

"Would you own slaves, sir? If it were legal in the Empire?"

"Probably not. But it's their choice, like I said."

"I suppose," Buller replied.

Wolseley scanned through the newspaper further. "I am mystified as to why the newspaper mentions nothing about the Fenians. All it seems to be talking about is the Lowell trial down in New Orleans."

"Oh, it's the big story," Buller said. "The trial of the century, some people are already saying. All the papers here in Canada and back home in England are hailing this Lowell fellow as some sort of hero."

Wolseley growled, finding this very frustrating. He had always been contemptuous of reporters, who flitted from story to story depending on the silly whims of the public. It could be that, having read continuously about the Fenian threat for many months, the public now wanted something new to fixate on. The New Iberia battle and Lowell trial seemed to fit the bill perfectly.

The more he thought about it, the more alarmed Wolseley became. If the attention of the public had shifted, the politicians in Washington City, Ottawa, and London would find the pressure on them greatly reduced. In this new age of public opinion, he knew that most great wars between major powers broke out because the respective national leaders were afraid of looking weak in front of their people. If the people were no longer thinking about the Fenians, however, there would be little for the politicians to fear and support for war would evaporate.

He pursed his lips and shook his head. It would be far better for Britain to cut the United States down to size now, when its industrial power was still comparatively small and when it was still reeling from its defeat in the War for Southern Independence. Twenty or thirty years from now, the United States would be much more powerful. Its industrial capacity would grow larger, it would be able to put ever more powerful armies into the field, and its navy might even become strong enough to challenge the might of the Royal Navy.

Moreover, with an ever-increasing Irish population, its hostility to Britain would only get stronger. The Dominion of Canada was far too tempting a conquest for the Americans to ignore forever.

It would be preferable to fight and win a short, sharp war with the United States now then a more difficult war later. With the forces in place, Canada could be successfully defended. At the very least, the British and Canadians could make its conquest so costly that the American people, having enjoyed the benefits of peace for only a few years, would refuse to shoulder the burden. In the meantime, the Royal Navy could shattered the American fleet, destroy the Union merchant marine, and blockade the enemy ports until its economy fell apart. Against the might of the British Empire, the United States could be crushed like the spoiled child it was. A hefty indemnity could be extracted and perhaps some territorial concessions as well.

This was all perfectly clear to Wolseley, yet it seemed entirely absent from the minds of the politicians in Ottawa and London. The exploits of Saul and Lowell in Louisiana had done more than distract the people from the Fenian Crisis and thereby given the powers-that-be the chance to allow tensions to cool off. They had also made the Confederacy appear even more distasteful in the eyes of the English public than it did before. It was all very unfortunate.

As Buller went on about the Lowell trial, Wolseley looked down at the notes he had made of Orenda's report. One jotted comment stated that the Fenian supply depot was perhaps a mile south of the border. Quietly, he scratched out the word 'south' and replaced it with 'north'.

August 27, Morning
New Iberia, Louisiana

"Just about time," Longstreet said simply.

"Yes," Morgan said. He looked to the east, where the first glow of sunrise was apparent. "Sun should be rising in about forty-five minutes or thereabouts. Still want us to go in right at dawn?"

Longstreet nodded. "That's right."

They were standing behind the Confederate barricade down the street from the insurgent position around the hotel. Longstreet was puffing on a cigar, standing still, seemingly without a care in the world. Morgan paced impatiently, wishing he could argue the sun into hurrying. It was deathly quiet. Confederate infantrymen manned the barricade itself, gripping their Enfield rifles, waiting like the two generals.

"The troops are in position," Morgan said. "They're ready to go in as soon as you give the word."

"Artillery ready?"

"Yes, sir."

Longstreet nodded again but said nothing more. Morgan had grown used to the Georgian's laconic way of talking. As he was a rather verbose man himself, it had taken Morgan a few days to get used to it and to accept that Longstreet was not trying to be rude. He certainly had grown to admire than man's organizational ability. There were now roughly ten thousand soldiers in

507

and around New Iberia, vastly more than were actually needed to deal with Saul and his small band of men. Militia units from as far away as Texas and Mississippi had assembled on their own initiative and made their way to the camps around the town.

Longstreet had been told by the authorities in Richmond not to turn any of them away, so he had assigned most of them to patrol the swamps and forests throughout the area, to make sure that none of Saul's men were trying to slip out of New Iberia to stir up trouble on the nearby plantations. Worryingly, several plantation owners had reported strange activities among their slaves, such as unexplained stockpiling of food, so the large numbers of troops had come as a welcome relief.

"Some copies of yesterday's New Orleans papers came into camp last night," Longstreet said, matter-of-factly. "Saw your name in them."

Morgan frowned and made a sound close to a growl. "I saw it." He had, indeed, read Toombs's editorial several times, becoming angrier each time.

"Not fair what old Toombs is saying about you. I wouldn't pay any attention to it. Man's a damn blowhard. I know it. I knew him during the war."

"Thanks," Morgan replied, not really wanting to talk about it.

"You know he's only attacking you to get to Breckinridge."

"I know. Doesn't make it any easier to take, though. I don't much like being made a fool of in front of the entire country."

Longstreet grunted. "Stupid old Toombs. Not right to question a man's patriotism. Not proper, you know? I know Breckinridge. He's a good man, through and through. Would make a good president."

"You intend to vote for him?" Morgan asked.

"Think so, yes. I don't mind Beauregard, honestly. Bit of a dandy, sure, but not a bad man. I just want a man of common sense at the top. Breckinridge is that man. You don't have to worry about him doing anything foolish."

"I hope the rest of the country is as wise as you are."

Longstreet grunted, then checked his pocket watch. "Light enough to read my watch. Getting on towards six o'clock. You ready?"

Morgan nodded.

"Very well. Let's go to it, then."

Longstreet withdrew his Navy Colt revolver, pointed it into the sky, and rapidly fired three shots in quick succession. Even though Morgan had known it was coming, the sudden cracking sound breaking the silence was startling. Longstreet waited five or six seconds, then fired the three remaining shots, completing the agreed upon signal to the artillery batteries.

For a few endless seconds, the echo of Longstreet's fire seemed to rise above the town of New Iberia. Moments later, the first boom of a cannon pounded the ears of all listeners within a mile, followed instantly by the blasts of several other artillery pieces. A storm of steel death flew through the air and impacted on and around the hotel where Saul's men were positioned. In an instant of fire, the controversial ten-day truce had ended.

Morgan stared intently down the street, trying to judge the effect the artillery fire was having. Whoever was in charge of the guns had elected to throw a variety of different projectiles at Saul's position. Solid shot was smashing into the building, while shells were exploding both inside and above, showering the whole area with shrapnel. So-called 'hot shot', cannonballs heated in furnaces until red hot, was also being hurled at the hotel in order to set fire to the wooden structure. With no hostages to worry about, there was no need to hold back. Almost instantly, he could see a small fire burning in one of the upstairs windows. As he watched, it slowly began to spread.

"Shells are a lot better than they used to be," Longstreet commented.

"What's that?" Morgan asked.

Longstreet looked at him curiously for a moment, before realization entered his eyes. "I guess you never had to use much artillery on those raids of yours, did you, Morgan? Thing was, when we fought the Yankees, the fuses in our shells would often explode early or just not go off at all. Sometimes half our damn shells wouldn't go off. Mighty frustrating, I tell you. All these shells are going off just fine, though. Just like Yankee shells, in fact."

"Ah," Morgan said. "Well, I know Breckinridge has been working hard to improve the quality of artillery ammunition."

"All the more reason to vote for him, then," Longstreet said. "I like fellows who can get things done." Longstreet tossed away the stub of his cigar, then calmly pulled out another one and lit it. He glanced at Morgan. "I'm sorry, General. Would you like one?"

"Thank you, no." Morgan's mind was too focused on the task at hand. The plan had called for the artillery to soften up Saul's position for half an hour, then the infantry assault columns would go in. With any luck, the artillery fire will have killed so many of the black fighters that the infantry would simply have to mop up a few survivors.

Longstreet had given command of one of the three assault columns to Morgan. He hadn't explained why. Perhaps he valued Morgan's experience, gained through months of fighting against Saul. Perhaps it was simply a sop to Morgan's pride after having been superseded in command and attacked in the newspapers. It didn't matter. Morgan felt indebted to Longstreet, for even a subordinate command allowed him a chance to recover his reputation.

Three streets led directly towards the hotel. Morgan's column had been assigned the middle street. Spearheading it would be his trusted dismounted Kentucky cavalrymen, men who had fought with him both against Saul and against the Yankees. Behind them would come the men of the 7th and 9th Louisiana regiments, men who had fought under Robert E. Lee and Jubal Early during the war. Morgan had no worries about the mettle of the men he would be leading.

He hadn't wasted much time thinking about the other two columns. The column to his right, he had been told, was made up entirely of Louisiana troops. The one to his left, by contrast, was a hodgepodge unit made up of Mississippi, Texas, and Arkansas troops. Having to deal with three assault columns instead of just one would hopefully disorient Saul's men.

Longstreet turned towards Saul. "I leave it to you to judge the time to begin the attack," he said simply. "You've fought these black bastards before, after all. The other two columns will go in when you go in."

"Thank you, sir," Morgan said quickly, over the din of exploding shells.

"We have plenty of ammunition," Longstreet said. "We might simply wait until they're all dead."

"No," Morgan replied. "No, that wouldn't do. In the end, this must be a hand-to-hand fight. We have to show that we can beat them fair and square."

Longstreet's eyes narrowed. "Why? They're all going to be dead inside of an hour no matter what happens. What do we care what they think?"

Morgan shrugged, deciding not to speak further on the matter. Inside, though, his mind went over the thoughts that had plagued him on this subject for the last several weeks. He wasn't really thinking about Saul and his men, but rather about the millions of other blacks held in slavery throughout the Confederacy. Try though they might to stop them, rumors inevitably spread from plantation to plantation. The name of Saul was on the lips of slaves all across the country.

That was dangerous. Indeed, it was much more dangerous than anything the Yankees had ever done. The whites might as well be sleeping on a powder keg. The disorder caused by the black regiments in the immediate aftermath should have been a wakeup call. Instead, the Southern people had assumed that life would return to normal after that problem had been dealt with.

Saul, needless to say, had disabused them of that notion in the most shocking manner. The bodies of white men dangling lifelessly from the trees around burning plantation houses had been a statement of purpose. The capture of New Iberia and the declaration of a liberated territory had been the next logical step. It was like an epidemic, Morgan concluded. If Saul's rebels weren't exterminated, their contagion would inevitably spread. The nightmare of Southern slaveholders, being murdered in their beds by their black servants, would become a reality.

Morgan knew he could not rest easy until he beheld Saul's dead body with his own eyes. If the rest of the white South had experienced what he had experienced in the swamps of Louisiana, he knew that they would feel the same way.

"If you are ready to begin, General Morgan, you may go to your command," Longstreet said.

"Thank you, sir."

Morgan shook Longstreet's extended hand, then left and walked briskly to the position where his assault column had been waiting. Crowded into the small alleys between some of the outlying houses and buildings, he had about one thousand men under his direct command. The other two columns were of a similar size, the idea being to simply overwhelm Saul through sheer force of numbers. Morgan took comfort in the fact that it would be impossible to fail. Casualties might be high, but the moment of Saul's demise was now at hand.

Duke was there, ever faithful. He didn't smile, but simply nodded sharply at Morgan's approach. Crouched down or seated on the ground, the troops of his assault column looked up expectantly at him. It was almost time. The faces of the men showed no fear, for they were all hardened veterans. All had faced death before.

"Ready?" Morgan asked Duke.

"Yes, sir."

Morgan sent a runner to Colonel Robert Beckham, the officer commanding the artillery batteries. As had been worked out carefully the night before, Beckham would halt the artillery fire as soon as he received word from Morgan to do so. The two other columns were under orders to charge at the same time as Morgan. It would take the runner a few minutes to reach the artillery command post. Then the assaults would go in.

"Get ready, men!" Morgan shouted. "We move out the moment the artillery fire stops!"

"We're with you, General!" someone shouted.

The plan was simple. When the artillery fire lifted, the men would dash from their hiding places and down into the saps that had been dug in the days before the truce, with the Kentuckians leading the way. The blacks had thrown broken furniture and other refuse into the parallel trench closet to the hotel, but they had not filled it in completely. Morgan's men were under orders to advance down the saps as far as they could, then climb out and charge towards the hotel. No one was to stop for any reason. With luck, the two other assault columns would converge on the hotel at the same moment as his own. If the artillery bombardment had the effect Morgan expected, the insurgents would be so dazed that they could simply be dispatched at will.

The last thought caused a momentary concern for Morgan. Longstreet had telegraphed Richmond several days before, requesting instructions on what to do with any prisoners they had taken. Breckinridge had replied that President Davis choose to leave that to the commander's discretion. Longstreet had decided to give the men no particular orders on the matter. This moved the responsibility from his own shoulders under those of his men, whom Morgan was sure would refuse to show any mercy.

A year earlier, this would not have troubled Morgan in the least. He was a white Southern man, fighting to preserve his people's way of life. If a black man were found in arms against the whites, he was killed, as had been required as far back as the days when Britain ruled America. Yet his experience in the swamps had changed him, he realized. He was not sympathetic to Saul in any way and knew that he needed to be destroyed. Yet killing the man in cold blood rather than combat was a different proposition. It bothered him, even if he was reluctant to admit it to himself.

He chided himself for worrying about such a thing at this moment. If his focus faltered even slightly, it could get men killed through simple carelessness. He might be a glory-hunter, but Morgan also cared about the men under his command and didn't want to lose any more of them than absolutely necessary.

The artillery fire ceased. It took a few moments for the ringing in Morgan's ears to lift, as when a brass band had come to the end of its song. He was gripped by the sudden anxiety that came just before going into battle. It was not fear, exactly, but certainly apprehension. He wanted to make sure everything went as planned and hoped that he would still be alive when it was all over. If he did die, he certainly wanted it to be in a manner that would look good in the newspapers.

"Let's go!" Morgan shouted. He dashed forward towards the first parallel, jumping down into it and moving quickly down the sap towards the hotel. He could hear his men following behind him. The sap extended a few hundred yards down the center of the street. It was deep enough that moving with a slight hunch would provide enough cover so that he wouldn't have to worry about enemy fire until they reached the parallel nearest to the hotel.

He could hear Duke's shouted voice behind him. "Come on, men! Come on!"

As he approached the end of the sap, he began hopping over the bits of refuse with which the insurgents had started to fill in the closest parallel trench. He then heard the familiar and comforting sound of the Rebel Yell, the ferocious and terrifying yipping noise made by the men during a charge, signaling the irresistible approach of a pack of wild predators.

Now, for the first time, he began to hear scattered gunshots. From the direction of the hotel, he thought he could hear the sound of Saul's men calling out warnings to one another. He glanced behind him and saw that the sap was full of gray-coated infantry, all gripping their bayonet-tipped rifles. The looks on their faces were furious and determined.

He reached the end of the sap, which formed a T-intersection with the final parallel trench. Before Morgan had time to think about anything, his instincts screamed at him to drop to the ground, which he promptly did. Immediately to his left, not more than five or six yards away, a flurry of musket fire exploded from within the parallel trench itself. The two men immediately behind Morgan screamed in agony as bullets punched through their bodies, splattering him with a shower of blood. Half a dozen insurgents, perhaps more, had concealed themselves in the parallel trench directly where it intersected the sap.

The insurgent ambush had thrown out a tremendous amount of gunpowder smoke. Morgan pulled out his revolver and fired blindly into the haze. He heard a man scream. As he scrambled to his feet, some of his men stepped around him and jabbed at the insurgents with their bayonets. Because the intersection was crowded with men trying to fight the insurgents in the parallel, the way forward for the rest of his men was momentarily blocked.

Morgan fired his pistol until it clicked for lack of bullets. He stepped back for a moment to reload. He was stunned when a black fighter suddenly emerged out of the smoke and raced the few meters towards him. Morgan tried to twist out of the way, but the man's bayonet lanced into the back of his right leg, near the top of the calf muscle. As the insurgent twisted the weapon, Morgan howled in pain and dropped his revolver, instinctively clutching his leg in a futile attempt to stop the pain.

The man withdrew the bayonet and was about to administer the killing stroke when his head exploded in a burst of red and pink slime, having been struck by a bullet at point blank range. Morgan looked to his left and saw that it was Duke who had saved his life. Duke did not pause for a moment, however, instead charging through the intersection and hurling himself into the hand-to-hand fight against the insurgents.

Within two minutes, all six of the ambushers had been shot or hacked to death, but not before they had killed five Confederates and wounded seven others, Morgan included. The vicious little fight in the trench had not only cost casualties, but had slowed down the impetus of the attack. A few crucial minutes had been lost, during which time Saul's men in the hotel might have been able to recover from the artillery bombardment and get into fighting positions.

His men began to scramble out of the trench and charge towards the insurgent defensive line ringing the hotel, where the attack ten days before had halted. Duke, brandishing his pistol, went with them. Morgan tried to rise to his feet, but this caused pain to scream through his right leg and he faltered.

"You all right?" one of his soldiers asked, grabbing his left arm to help hold him up.

He nodded, gritting his teeth against the pain, and waved the man on. He leaned against the side of the trench, while dozens of his soldiers filed rapidly past him, each clambering up to join in the charge. The sound of gunfire increased to an enormous level. He could hear the Rebel Yell from many different directions, which suggested that the other two assault columns had also converged on the enemy position. With great effort, he hobbled on his one good leg and pushed himself up into a position from which he could see what was going on.

The sight that greeted him was unexpectedly horrid. Dead and wounded Confederate soldiers lay strewn about in the space between the last parallel trench and the insurgent barricade, gunned down by Saul's men. The artillery had not seemed to weaken the enemy at all. The hotel was now a blazing wall of fire, casting a fierce yellowish glow over the whole scene. Astonishingly, he could see black fighters firing down on his men from the hotel windows, disdaining to escape the flames.

Morgan considered shouting for a withdrawal. Casualties were already running much higher than expected. Perhaps he could pull his men back to the start line and resume the artillery bombardment. After a few seconds, he abandoned the idea. It would be extremely difficult to conduct such a withdrawal with his own men and impossible to coordinate the movement with the other two assault columns. Besides, it would mean that the casualties already suffered would have been in vain. The men might refuse an order to retreat. There was nothing to do but push through the fighting to the end, no matter how many men died.

More and more Confederate soldiers were rising out of the parallel and charging forward. The insurgents poured as heavy a fire as they could from their own trench, taking a heavy toll of the attackers. He could just glimpse hand-to-hand fighting taking place in the defenses before the front porch of the hotel and could hear the familiar noise of metal striking metal and fists pounding flesh. The sound of the Rebel Yell echoed across the whole area, along with a strange sort of maniacal laughter, but Morgan thought he could also hear Saul's insurgents calling out encouragement to one another.

There was a trickling feeling down his leg. Morgan looked down and saw that the right leg of his pants was red with blood. He turned and shouted for a surgeon, realizing that if he didn't get a tourniquet on he might well bleed to death. A short man with eyeglasses scampered forward, instantly seeing the problem.

"Hold still, General!" the man shouted over the din of fighting.

Morgan nodded, and winced in pain as the surgeon slipped the coil around his leg above the wound. He tried to concentrate on reloading his revolver, in the hopes that distracting his mind would make the pain go away. The tourniquet was yanked tight, causing Morgan to cry out against the agony. Just as soon as the pain had become excruciating, however, it seemed to fade, being replaced only by a dense dullness.

"You need to move to the rear, sir!" the surgeon implored.

"Go about your business!" Morgan said harshly. "See to the more seriously wounded!"

Morgan finished reloading and again tried to prop himself up on his one good leg to see what was happening. There was still fighting going on in the insurgent trench, but many of his men had pushed past it and were struggling with the blacks in front of the burning hotel. He saw one of his men, a big soldier, trying to drive a bowie knife into a black fighter who was desperately gripping the man's wrists in a bid to stay alive. Everything was confused and difficult to understand. Gunpowder smoke combined with the smoldering of the hotel fire to produce an immense white cloud over the whole battle. The sounds of rapid gunfire came from almost every direction, combining with battle cries and the screams of wounded men to create a sinister cacophony.

Off to the left, he could see four or five insurgents on their knees, their hands raised in a plea for mercy. As Morgan watched, two were shot dead and the other two were run through with bayonets. His enraged men were obviously in no mood to take prisoners and they were not about to treat rebellious slaves with the same respect with which they had once treated the Yankees.

Morgan tried to pull himself up out of the parallel, only to give it up when his right leg again exploded in pain the moment he put weight on it. He let out a shout of rage, furious at being trapped away from the fighting while his men fought for their lives.

He noticed two men locked in combat on the porch of the hotel, dark figures against the backlight of the red and yellow flames, both armed with bayonet-tipped rifles. With a start, Morgan realized that the insurgent was Saul.

As he watched the unfolding duel, Saul smashed the butt of his rifle against his opponent's hand, causing the Confederate to drop his weapon. An instant later, the renegade slave rammed his bayonet into the man's belly. Morgan could see the point of blade punch out the other side of the soldier, who instantly began twitching like a stuck pig. Saul tossed the writhing body contemptuously aside, dropping his rifle while doing so. As Morgan watched in horrified fascination, Saul raised both fists into the air, like a boxer who had just won a match.

"Shoot him!" Morgan shouted desperately, pointing to Saul. "Kill him, dammit! Kill him!"

Most of the insurgents had apparently been killed, so dozens of white soldiers were standing around, uncertain what to do. Hearing Morgan's shouted orders and following the direction of his point, several soldiers raised their weapons and fired at Saul. At a range of less than a hundred yards, there was no way they could miss. To Morgan's amazement, however, Saul appeared entirely unharmed. A large portion of the overhand above the porch collapsed at that moment in a resounding crash, the flames licking upwards and illuminating Saul's face.

He felt the trickling down is leg again. Part of his mind told him that the tourniquet had come loose, yet he scarcely noticed. The black insurgent leader was staring directly at Morgan, as if he knew right where he was, disdainful of the fire raging around him and the bullets coming at him from every direction. He raised a clenched fist into the air and unleashed a primal, animalistic scream that Morgan could somehow hear over the din of the fighting. Morgan was not an easily frightened man, yet the shout of Saul was terrifying. Morgan was shaken by the thought, irrational though he knew it to be, that somehow Saul was turning into something beyond a human being, his yell manifesting the roaring rage of millions.

The hotel seemed to be falling apart. Morgan could hear the crashing of the second floor collapsing inside the building. Yet Saul just stood there shouting, the sound somehow filling the entire area and drowning out everything else.

Morgan felt faint and slipped down onto the ground. More and more Confederate troops were swarming past him, scrambling up out of the trench, and charging towards the hotel. He stood again, ignoring the pain in his leg. Behind him, the surgeon was saying that he needed to reapply the tourniquet. Even though the man was almost shouting, to Morgan the voice sounded strangely distant.

Morgan grimaced in pain as the tourniquet was tightened. He tried to ignore the pain by concentrating on the battle. Everywhere he looked, he could see his men and those of the other two assault columns. No living black soldiers were in sight, though many of their bodies were strewn about, their forms illuminated by the fire of the hotel and the red sun now coming over the horizon. The Confederate troops were now holding their rifles in the air and shouting in triumph. They had won. The rebellion had finally been crushed.

Yet Saul was nowhere to be seen.

CHAPTER THIRTEEN

September 2, Morning
Confederate States District Court of Louisiana, New Orleans

The courtroom had very high ceilings, whitewashed walls, and seemed to Lowell to be large enough to hold a grand dinner party. Aside from the large portraits of Jefferson Davis and John Calhoun that hung on the walls, it was set up like any courtroom in the United States. Lowell sat in the front left table, next to his court-appointed defense counsel, Donelson Caffery, a young man of little legal experience. At the table to his right sat the prosecuting attorney, James Eustis, the son of a Chief Justice of the Louisiana Supreme Court and a graduate of Harvard Law. A cluster of other lawyers were gathered around him at the table. Lowell recalled meeting Eustis a few times at Harvard, where their academic careers had overlapped. Thus far, Eustis had refused to even make eye contact with him.

Behind him, the two-thirds of the courtroom set aside for members of the public were crammed to the brim with onlookers. When he entered the courtroom twenty minutes before, his hands and legs still in irons and escorted by half a dozen armed guards, the crowd had jeered and hooted, obviously enjoying the spectacle. Most of the people were dressed to the nines, as though they were attending a party. Among the crowd were several newspaper reporters, including many from foreign papers. The world was obviously watching.

His own situation had improved, at least. The efforts of U.S. Consul Edward Phelps had gotten him moved to a more comfortable jail cell, with proper ventilation and natural light. He was still being held in solitary confinement, but was no longer shackled, had a bed on which to sit and lie, and had oil lamps and candles at night. He had not, however, been given permission to write letters to his family.

Lowell had not been given access to newspapers, but Caffery had told him about the fall of New Iberia to Confederate forces under the command of James Longstreet. He had been bitterly disappointed. Though he had not considered Saul's plan of sparking a wider slave uprising likely to succeed, Lowell had hoped against hope that it might. According to Caffery, Saul and all of his men had been killed in the fighting. Lowell earnestly hoped that this was not true.

Caffery sighed unhappily and folded his arms, frowning and shaking his head.

"What is it?" Lowell asked.

"Just want to get started," Caffery answered. "The sooner we start, the sooner we can get it over with."

"I am sorry to have caused you this inconvenience," Lowell said sincerely. Caffery had told him that some newspapers were denouncing him for agreeing to defend Lowell, insisting that he should have simply resigned rather than accept the assignment. Lowell supposed it was to Caffery's credit that he had taken the job. At least some Southerners had a semblance of respect for the rule of law.

"It's your own damn self you should be worried about, Lowell. You need to be making your peace with God, because nothing is going to save you. They're going to hang you as soon as the formalities of this trial are over. There's nothing I will be able to do about it."

"I am well aware of that."

Caffery looked at him. "I hope you know I mean no disrespect. I'm a lawyer, you're my client, and I'm going to do my job. I am required by my oath to represent you in this court to the best of my ability and I am going to do it. That said, I despise you and everything you stand for. A lot of my fellow Southerners died because of what you did. When you hang, I'm not going to feel the least bit sorry for you."

"I appreciate your honesty." He paused thoughtfully for a moment. "For what it's worth, I despise you, too."

Caffery scoffed but said nothing further. The crowd behind them continued jeering, shouting remarks about the length of rope that would he needed and how long Lowell's body was going to twitch before it stopped moving. When he set out from Boston on his journey, he knew that being arraigned in court was a possibility. Yet he had not really thought through what this might mean. As he listened to the crowd berate him, he was surprised to find himself feeling sympathy rather than anger. He found himself remembering Luke 23:34, in which Jesus asked God to forgive his tormentors, as they did not understand what they were doing.

He had been born and raised in the intellectually vibrant and cosmopolitan atmosphere of Boston, given an outstanding education, and raised in a social circle in which the abolition of slavery was held up to be the great issue of the day. It was only natural that he abhor slavery and bend his energies towards its destruction. Yet what if he had been born a Southerner, raised in a culture in which owning black slaves was seen as perfectly normal, and indoctrinated from birth with a belief that the institution of slavery had to be protected? If that had been the case, would he still have grown to hate slavery as an adult? Or would he have been no different from the members of the crowd who were now cheering for him to be executed?

He shook his head. It could not be like that. There were moral absolutes in the world and every human mind was capable of comprehending them. The idea that it could be moral for human beings to be held as property was simply unacceptable to anyone with a shred of decency. He could not understand how educated Southerners, men who otherwise seemed honorable and perhaps even noble, could fail to see this.

Lowell's thoughts vanished when the door near the judge's bench opened. The booming voice of the bailiff suddenly filled the room.

"All rise!"

Everyone stood from their chairs, including Lowell. During the ride in the paddy wagon from his jail to the courtroom that morning, he had toyed with the idea of remaining in his seat when the judge entered the room, as a visible expression of his contempt for the Confederacy and its pretended judicial institutions. After considering it, though, he had decided to stand like everyone else. He wanted to project civility, to better craft the public impression he was now determined to make. Saul and his rebels were beyond his help now. All he had left was his trial. If he used it the right way, he could send a powerful message to the Confederacy and the world beyond.

The bailiff continued. "The Confederate District Court for Louisiana is now in session! The Honorable Judge Edwin Warren Moise presiding!"

Judge Moise strode into the courtroom and quietly took his seat at the judge's bench. Lowell knew from the moment he saw the man's face that he could expect no mercy, for the eyes that looked out from the bench were cold and unfeeling. From what Caffery had told him, Lowell knew that Moise was a former speaker of the Louisiana House, a former district attorney for New Orleans when it was still a part of the United States, and one of the most prominent Jews in the state.

When Moise sat down, so did everyone else in the room. The crowd had gone silent the moment Judge Moise had entered the room. He put his spectacles on and, for several minutes, calmly read through the papers on his desk, acting as though the proceedings were nothing but a normal case.

"Call the docket," Moise said to the bailiff.

"Your Honor, today's case is the Confederate States of America vs. Charles Russell Lowell III of Massachusetts."

Moise looked at the attorneys. "Counselors, are you ready to proceed?"

"We are," Caffery and Eustis answered simultaneously.

Moise took a moment to read through the document in his hand, then looked sternly at Lowell. "General Lowell, would you please stand?"

Lowell rose to his feet, staring at Judge Moise with what he hoped was a defiant intensity. The judge, however, seemed entirely unimpressed.

"General Lowell, you stand accused of aiding and abetting servile insurrection. If found guilty, the penalty will be death by hanging. Are you aware of the crime of which you are accused and the accompanying penalty?"

"I am, Your Honor," Lowell replied. He was careful to make his voice sound as calm and dignified as possible. He did not want to give any of the onlookers or reporters any suggestion that he was either afraid or remorseful.

"You are aware of your right to a jury trial and your right to legal counsel?"

"I am, Your Honor."

"Very well. How plead you?"

Lowell drew himself up and spoke as forcefully as he could. "I plead not guilty to any wrongdoing, Your Honor."

This caused a hush of shock in the crowd and sent the reporters furiously scribbling. Judge's Moise's eyebrows went up in surprise. "You are telling me that you are not guilty of the crime of which you are accused?" Judge Moise asked.

"I do not say that, Your Honor. I say that I plead not guilty to doing anything wrong."

Moise frowned at him and shook his head. It was obvious to him what Lowell was doing. By technically entering a plea of not guilty, the trial would go forward in the full glare of the world's reporters. Yet by carefully choosing his words, Lowell was making a clear statement that, in his view, the crime of which he stood accused had been no crime at all.

"The clerk will note that the defendant enters a plea of not guilty," Moise noted dryly. "This court will reconvene on Wednesday, September 4. Adjourned." Moise banged the gavel and stood from his chair.

"All rise!" the bailiff said again, and everyone in the courtroom rose from their seats as Moise strode regally down from the bench and out the door. The crowd began to file out the main door to the courtroom as the guards walked forward to place the handcuffs on Lowell in preparation for taking him back to jail. He politely bade farewell to Caffery, who shook his hand without enthusiasm and took his leave. A reporter with a Deep Southern accent, perhaps an Alabama or Mississippi man, attempted to ask Lowell a question but was gruffly told by one of the guards not to speak to him.

He was led out a back door into the street, where a paddy wagon was waiting to take him back to jail. The guards pushed him inside, not forcefully but with enough strength to tell him not to resist. One of them, much to Lowell's surprise, spoke.

"Looking forward to swinging from the gallows, Yankee?"

Lowell shrugged. "As a wise man once said, 'When a man knows he is to be hanged in a fortnight, it concentrates his mind wonderfully.'"

September 3, Morning
Executive Office Building, Richmond, Virginia

"So we're sure that all the darkie bastards are dead?" Attorney General Harris asked.

"As near as we can tell, yes," Breckinridge answered. "Longstreet deployed militia in a *cordon sanitaire* all around New Iberia, covering every possible route of escape. Cavalry patrols scoured the entire area beyond that line, just as a precaution. There were no reports of any insurgents escaping." He paused a moment before continuing. "I am confident that none of Saul's men got away. All of them either died fighting or perished in the fire at the hotel."

"It's about damn time," Secretary of the Treasury Trenholm said tiredly. "This Saul fellow has been troubling us for more than half a year now. I feel like tonight will be the first night I will be able to sleep comfortably."

Breckinridge glanced over at Davis, who was slowly rubbing his temples and staring blankly at nothing in particular. He had seen the president do this on many occasions, but most often when he was deep in thought over a difficult problem or trying to evaluate the consequences of an important event. The Cabinet went silent, waiting for their chief executive to emerge from his thinking.

"How many men did we lose?" Davis finally asked.

Breckinridge pursed his lips. "I am sorry to report that our men did suffer heavily in the attack. The blacks put up a ferocious fight. One hundred and twenty-eight men were killed, and approximately four hundred were wounded."

Trenholm waved his hand dismissively. "Nothing compared to any number of minor battles during the war. Why are we acting as though these losses were at all heavy?"

"Because Gettysburg was a proper battle during a proper war," Benjamin replied quickly. "A war against a foreign power. A war against fellow whites. This was a fight against insurgent slaves, which is against the natural order of things. Every soldier of ours that falls to the bullet or the blade of a rebellious slave undermines the whole foundation of our Confederacy."

"I don't see how," Trenholm countered. "Our men went into that nest of vipers and killed every damn last one of them. Sets an example for the rest of the darkies, if you ask me. When they hear of what happened to the blacks in New Iberia, they'll think twice before thinking of rising up themselves. That's why we need to give the same treatment to any other insurgents that emerge from the ground."

"Exactly," said Harris. He looked at Breckinridge. "And I think we should also establish that if any such insurgency happens again, we will not condone our forces entering into any compacts with the rebel blacks like the ten-day truce Morgan agreed to in New Iberia."

"We've already discussed that," Davis snapped. "We are not going to discuss it again."

Breckinridge was happy to hear Davis say these words, for they spared Breckinridge the trouble of having to defend himself on that issue yet again. At every recent meeting of the Cabinet, Trenholm and Harris had denounced the truce that Longstreet and Morgan had arranged with Saul. It had become so heated over the past week that Breckinridge was no longer certain that he could count on the support of either Cabinet member in the upcoming presidential election. Harris had been especially vocal about the issue and had not spoken to Breckinridge in a friendly manner for some time.

Despite the opposition of his colleagues in the Cabinet, Breckinridge was not sure how he could have adopted any other course than the one he had taken. The truce had already been in place for a day when he learned of it via a telegram from Longstreet. He could not have countermanded the order without undermining the leadership of Longstreet and humiliating his friend Morgan, who had actually initiated the truce to secure the release of the hostages. Moreover, the honor of the Confederate Army was at stake. Having given its word, the army could not in good conscience go back on it, whether the other party was rebel slaves or white Yankees.

As Secretary of War, Breckinridge felt a deep responsibility to protect the honor of the Confederate Army. He had always been aware, and had been forcefully reminded during the peace negotiations in Toronto, of the many occasions during the war when Confederate soldiers had gone into a battle frenzy when fighting black troops and killed them even as they were trying to surrender. Breckinridge had been disgusted by these events, for whatever the color of their skin, the black soldiers in the U.S.C.T. regiments were soldiers of the United

States and therefore protected from unlawful killings under the accepted rules of warfare.

One officer under his own command, Colonel Felix Robertson, had engaged in precisely such a massacre during the confused fighting in southwestern Virginia in late 1864. Breckinridge's repeated efforts to find the murderer and bring him to justice had been frustratingly unsuccessful, but he had not yet given up hope of one day apprehending the man. If he became president, he had decided, he would spare no effort to find and arrest him.

Breckinridge had been unwilling to overrule Longstreet and Morgan for what he considered sound reasons. Yet he also hoped that the initiation of a truce between the black rebels and the Confederate troops would be looked upon positively by people in the United States and Europe. Assuming he was lucky enough to win the upcoming election, he would need that goodwill in order to have any possibility of progress on the diplomatic front.

"Enough about New Iberia," Davis said. "I frankly would prefer to never hear the name of that town again. What's the word on the Lowell trial?"

"He entered a plea of not guilty yesterday," Harris replied.

"Not guilty?" Davis asked. "Really?"

"Well, he insisted on using the words 'not guilty of any wrongdoing'."

"In other words, he's saying that smuggling weapons to Saul's men was not wrong," Benjamin said. "He's trying to do what John Brown did. He wants to use the trial as a platform to make a political statement."

"Never underestimate the power of martyrdom," Davis said. "John Brown might have been insane, but his actions at Harper's Ferry lit the fuse that set off the war. I don't want to see the Lowell trial do anything similar."

"We won't be able to avoid it," Benjamin said. "The law must run its course. If Lowell wants a trial, he gets one. Some people in the States' Rights Party are saying that we should just hang him without due process, but if we do that, we'd be trampling on our own constitution."

"The SRP doesn't care much about the Constitution," Davis dryly stated.

"I don't think that's a fair statement," Harris replied. The others looked at him in some surprise. It was not customary for any member of the Cabinet to dispute President Davis so openly. Whenever Breckinridge felt the need to do so, he did it privately. Harris himself looked rather surprised, leading Breckinridge to wonder if the Attorney General had accidentally voiced what was supposed to have been only an internal thought.

"I'm sorry?" Davis said.

Harris pursed his lips tightly and shook his head, like a man who had had so much that he could not stand it any longer. Suddenly, to Breckinridge's surprise, the Attorney General abruptly stood from his chair and looked angrily at him. Recovering himself, Harris turned to Davis.

"Mr. President? May I speak to you for a moment in private?"

Davis looked irritated, yet he could hardly deny the request. He looked at Breckinridge, Benjamin, and Trenholm. "Gentlemen, would you excuse us for a moment?"

With the sound of chair legs scuffing the floor, the three men rose from their seats and filed through the door into the hallway. Closing the door behind them, Breckinridge could immediately hear the muffled sound of Harris's agitated voice speaking in an urgent manner.

"What do you suppose this is about?" Benjamin asked.

"Not sure," Trenholm replied. "Harris did seem upset about something."

"I'm afraid, gentlemen, that Mr. Harris is taking issue with the New Iberia truce," Breckinridge replied. "That is what seemed to be bothering him the most."

"It bothers me, too," Trenholm said. "But I see no reason to be unpleasant about it."

The voices of Davis and Harris were barely audible through the heavy door. The three men standing outside could not make out the words, but soon it was clear that the talking had morphed into shouting. They stood in awkward silence for some time, not entirely sure how to respond to this unforeseen situation. After several minutes, Benjamin spoke, more to relieve the tension than anything else.

"Have either of you been to the theater lately?" the Jewish Louisianan said pleasantly.

"What?" Breckinridge asked, confused at the introduction of such a subject at such a time.

"The theater?"

"I have," Trenholm replied. "The Richmond Theater is putting on a production of *King Lear*, with Lawrence Barrett playing the title role. Quite good, I thought."

"Ah," Benjamin replied. "I shall have to attend."

The door swung upon and Harris, a look of fierce anger on his face, stormed past without saying a word. Breckinridge was stunned by the breach of etiquette. In his view, Harris was behaving in an entirely unacceptable and childlike manner.

"Come back in, you three," the commanding voice of Davis said.

Breckinridge, Benjamin and Trenholm strode back into the office, with the Secretary of the Treasury closing the door behind them. They retook their seats. The president sat still, looking down at his desk with a pensive expression.

"Attorney General Harris has resigned," Davis said simply.

"Yes, I gathered that," Benjamin said.

Davis looked at Breckinridge. "He also has told me that he intends to support Beauregard in the coming election. He is returning to Tennessee to campaign for the SRP."

Breckinridge sighed. Harris, being a former governor of Tennessee, would be a great help to Beauregard. When he thought he had the support of Harris, Breckinridge had rated his chances in Tennessee as slightly better than average. Without him, it was the opposite. Without Tennessee, he knew, he had no chance of winning the election.

"Well, that's unfortunate," replied Trenholm.

These words buoyed up Breckinridge somewhat. Trenholm might have disagreed with the New Iberia truce, but it seemed likely that he would continue to support Breckinridge for president.

Davis looked at Breckinridge. "I must say, John, that your friend Morgan has caused all of us a great deal of trouble. Yourself in particular. According to

Longstreet, it was Morgan's spur-of-the-moment decision to agree to this truce with Saul. It may have gotten those hostages out with their lives, but it has set off a political firestorm. Did you read Toombs's editorial?"

"Yes," Breckinridge replied quickly. The piece had been reprinted all over the South. People were talking about it everywhere. "I continue to stand by Morgan's decision. His actions saved the lives of all those hostages."

"At great cost to you. It may cost you the election."

Breckinridge shook his head. "You all know me well enough to know that I am not a man to embrace views I feel are wrong in order to curry favor with voters. What Morgan did was entirely correct. It got the hostages out and did not, in any way, undermine the military effort against Saul. After the ten days were over, we moved in and defeated them completely."

"I don't disagree," Davis said. "But it set a dangerous precedent, don't you think? Are we to parlay with rebel slaves in the same manner we did with the Yankees?"

"That is my concern," Trenholm said. "It raises these blacks to the level of ordinary soldiers."

"In Morgan's place, I should have done the very same thing," Breckinridge replied.

Davis grunted slightly, not wishing to speak any further. "If any of you have any recommendations for the Attorney General's replacement, please let me know by Friday."

The three remaining Cabinet members muttered their agreement. By the tone of the room, Breckinridge thought that the meeting was over. Davis was obviously upset by what Harris had done and he knew the man well enough to know that it was best to leave him alone at such times. He was ready to depart and head back to Mechanic's Hall.

Benjamin cleared his throat. "I have my own announcement to make," he said.

"And what is that?" Davis asked.

Benjamin chuckled slightly. "Well, since resigning from the Cabinet appears to be the fashion these days, I think it high time for me to announce my own departure."

"I'm sorry?" Davis asked quickly.

"I am resigning from the Cabinet as well. It is my intention to return to New Orleans to serve as the defense counsel to Charles Russell Lowell."

Breckinridge's mouth dropped open. He had been shocked many times in his life, but rarely with such force as this. It was stunning enough that Benjamin was announcing his departure from the Cabinet in such a sudden manner, but to do so in order to work as a lawyer for the infamous Lowell made it all the more surprising.

"Cabinet meetings are not a good place for jokes, Judah," Davis said, maintaining his composure.

"I assure you I'm quite serious," Benjamin replied dryly. "Lowell needs a good lawyer and, as you'll all recall, I was a fine attorney in my day."

"What is this?" Davis asked angrily. "Judah, have you lost your mind?"

Benjamin smiled, shook his head, and reached into his coat pocket for another cigar. He lit it and started smoking, as calmly as if he had said nothing unusual.

"My friend," Trenholm said. "You're not generally guilty of making decisions without fully thinking them through. But if you go to New Orleans to serve as defense counsel for Lowell, your reputation will be destroyed forever. He is an abolitionist terrorist and is directly responsible for the deaths of hundreds of Southern soldiers."

Benjamin shrugged. "Perhaps. Probably. But we're a constitutional republic, aren't we? Even the most despicable villains are entitled to fair representation in court." He paused for a moment. "John Adams defended the soldiers responsible for the Boston Massacre, did he not?"

"This is nonsense!" Davis said, his voice rising. "We need you here, running the State Department, not off in New Orleans on some quixotic legal quest! Lowell is going to be found guilty, and rightly so, no matter who his lawyer is!"

"I know," Benjamin said, puffing on his cigar.

"Then what on earth do you think you're doing?"

"My reasons are my own."

Breckinridge watched silently while Davis and Trenholm continued to argue with Benjamin. He was trying to recover from his shock. If Benjamin went to New Orleans, it would deprive Breckinridge of his advice and assistance just when the presidential election was entering the decisive stage. Breckinridge breathed deeply, trying to maintain a calm expression while thinking everything through. He almost agreed with Davis's suggestion that Benjamin had lost his mind.

Davis was yelling at Benjamin, accusing him of betrayal. It was clear that the president was outraged not only by Benjamin's actions, but by the manner in which he had announced them. Trenholm was berating Benjamin for wanting to help Lowell at all. Through it all, Benjamin replied in calm tones, smoking his cigar. Fifteen minutes after Benjamin made his stunning announcement, Breckinridge could still not believe it.

Benjamin rose from his chair. "Gentlemen, I can see that my decision has spoiled everyone's good mood."

"Good mood?" Davis asked. "I lose my Attorney General and then, mere minutes later, my Secretary of State deserts me, too. Not a good mood at all, sir. Not at all."

Breckinridge sensed the personal hurt in Davis's words. Almost from the beginning of the war, Benjamin had served successively in the Cabinet as Attorney General, then as Secretary of War, and finally as Secretary of State. While he knew the president valued his advice, Breckinridge also knew that Benjamin had been his closest confident in almost every matter since fate had made him the leader of the Confederacy. For Davis, it was not just a major political and administrative problem, but a personal matter as well.

"You shall have my formal letter of resignation tomorrow, Mr. President," Benjamin said. He cast a quick glance at Breckinridge. "In the meantime, I recommend that Ambassador Miles be appointed as a temporary replacement. Perhaps a permanent one."

This was a shock to Breckinridge even larger than Benjamin's original announcement. It felt like a punch in the stomach. He had confided to Benjamin about the threat of blackmail by Miles. What possible reason could Benjamin have for recommending Miles as his replacement?

"Miles?" Breckinridge asked, trying to keep unnecessary concern out of his voice. He could not voice his genuine feelings in front of Davis and Trenholm.

"Indeed," Benjamin replied. "His time in Washington has given him all the diplomatic experience one could hope for and he is well-acquainted with the international situation. Even better, he is already here in Richmond."

"Miles will do," Davis said quickly. "I'd prefer not to have to attend to such a matter at all." Davis paused and pursed his lips. "Benjamin, please reconsider what you are doing. I don't know your reasons. But I do know that this will hurt our nation in many ways and help it in no way at all. I urge you to put the needs of the Confederacy ahead of whatever personal motives you are pursuing."

"I assume you, Mr. President, that I am motivated entirely by the good of the Confederacy. I now bid you good day, gentlemen." Benjamin turned and soon vanished through the door.

"I'll talk to him," Breckinridge said urgently, rising from his chair and following. In a moment, Breckinridge was in the hall, walking quickly behind Benjamin, who was headed back to his own office. He could see that the Secretary of State was walking with a jaunty, even cocky, manner.

His own head was still spinning. From the moment he made the decision to seek the presidency, he had relied on Benjamin's advice and counsel. Breckinridge was himself a man with an enormous amount of political experience and high intelligence, yet he had to admit that Benjamin's political instincts were far superior to his own. If he was no longer to have Benjamin as an advisor, Breckinridge worried that he would start making mistakes that would reduce his already slim chances of winning the election. That, in turn, would put the Fire-Eaters in control of the Confederacy, which could well spell its doom.

"Judah?" he asked as he walked, approaching him from behind, yet Benjamin kept walking. "Judah!" he said more urgently.

Benjamin stopped and turned around. The smile that normally adorned his face was absent. "I know what you're going to say," he said.

"Do you?" Breckinridge asked. "I think the president is correct. I think you must have lost your mind."

"Believe me when I tell you that I have thought this matter through more thoroughly than any decision I have ever made in my life. I have to do it."

"I don't understand," Breckinridge said helplessly. "You can't help Lowell and I don't understand why you'd want to. In the meantime, you're abandoning me just when I need you the most. And what on earth possessed you to suggest a monster like Miles as your replacement? You know what he did to me. And if we're trying to stop the Fire-Eaters, why on Earth would you want one in such an important position as that of the Secretary of State?"

"I put Miles forward as my replacement in order to help you," Benjamin said, his voice uncharacteristically defensive. "It was the price we had to pay for his silence."

"What do you mean?"

"I offered him the Secretary of State position in exchange for his support in the election. He's agreed not to reveal what he knows about Toronto and to endorse you for president. It works very well, if you ask me. You have the danger of scandal removed and his backing will help shield you from some of the worst attacks that Toombs is now leveling at you."

"I'd rather go to bed with a syphilitic whore than accept the help of Miles!" Breckinridge exclaimed.

"I know," Benjamin replied. "That's why I had to do it all behind your back."

"Did you tell him that I had agreed to this?" Breckinridge asked accusingly.

"I did what I had to do to help you win."

"Did you tell him that I agreed?" Breckinridge said, more insistently.

Benjamin paused a moment before replying. "Yes, I did. And now you really have no choice but to go along with it. I know you're angry, but the same integrity that will make you such an excellent president also makes it hard for you to be elected to that position. That's why you need me to do your dirty work for you. I don't mind. I'm happy to do it. It's the kind of politician I am. But let's not fool ourselves here, John. You knew that all along. You wouldn't have accepted my help in the first place if you hadn't known you needed me."

Breckinridge took a deep breath and didn't reply. He did not like the insinuation that Benjamin was making, yet neither could he deny it.

"Miles isn't so bad," Benjamin said. "You think I've never threatened others with blackmail for political advantage? I basically threatened you, didn't I? The stuff about Frederick Douglass's newspaper. You wanted the presidency anyway, but you had to have thought I would be ready to use that information."

Breckinridge brushed this aside. "What about Lowell? Why are you doing this at all?"

Benjamin chuckled. "This is going to be the biggest trial in America since 1859. How can I resist?"

"You're talking about John Brown's trial. Well, Lowell is the most notorious abolitionist terrorist since Brown. If you defend him, your reputation will be ruined forever."

"No, just for now," Benjamin replied. The enigmatic smile returned to his face. "I'll die shunned and vilified, but a hundred years from now, my reputation will have soared to the high heavens."

Breckinridge's eyes narrowed. "What on earth are you talking about?"

"Please," Benjamin said with a hint of disdain. He was about to reply when he saw two secretaries from the treasury department approaching. He waited until they passed before he continued. "You know perfectly well what I am talking about. You, like me, know what our country must eventually do. Look at the reaction of the world to what has happened in New Iberia. Saul's declaration of a liberated territory above all. Do the newspapers in New York or London or Paris denounce Saul as a murderous terrorist? No. If anything, they trumpet him as some sort of hero. Why?"

"Because the rest of the world doesn't think about slavery the way we think about it," Breckinridge quickly replied. To him, this was so obvious that it didn't need to be mentioned.

"Yes, and that fact spells the eventual end of our Southern Confederacy. I'm no abolitionist. I owned slaves when I owned that plantation in Louisiana. But I'm not blind, John, and neither are you. Slavery will make us an international pariah. Already, Yankees and Europeans are turning to India and Egypt for their cotton, not because it's better or cheaper, but because it isn't grown by slaves. This will accelerate as times passes, believe you me. The more fanatically we hold onto slavery, the more it will eat away at us, dissolving us like a steady dripping of acid. That is, if it doesn't burn our new nation down in the fires of a bigger slave revolt."

Breckinridge was not sure if Benjamin had ever realized the extent to which he agreed with what he was saying. He thought back to the many conversations with his wife over the dinner table, with members of his family back in Kentucky, and with close friends. He was a Southerner, raised in a society in which the owning of black slaves was accepted as a matter of course. Yet he knew it was wrong. He had known it was wrong all his life. Moreover, he saw the truth of what Benjamin was saying. If not dealt with, slavery would eventually destroy the Confederacy. For self-interest, if for nothing else, it eventually had to be cast into the ash heap of history.

"If you think this, Judah, do you think that the war was useless?" It was a question Breckinridge had often asked himself.

"Oh, not at all. The South is now free to deal with its problems in its own way, rather than at the point of a gun. The Fire-Eaters think that the war meant that we won't have to deal with the problem at all, but they're wrong there, as they are in so many other places."

"But what does the Lowell trial have to do with any of this?"

Benjamin grinned again. "With my help, Lowell is going to say things that the South needs to hear. And the world needs to know that the South is listening. You see, the Confederacy has a cold. Lowell is a sneeze. I aim to make that sneeze so loud that no one can possibly ignore it." He paused a few moments to let the words sink in. "Now, if you'll excuse me, John, I have a few telegrams to send. Then I'm off to my home to pack."

Benjamin turned and strode on towards his office, leaving a confused and worried Breckinridge standing in the hall.

September 6, Afternoon
East Tennessee and Virginia Railroad, southwest of Knoxville

Toombs wished he could do something to make the train go faster. Events were moving rapidly, yet he now found himself moving through one of the most remote regions of the Confederacy, out of easy touch with his friends and allies. He had sent telegrams to Stephens and to Senator Hunter from the station at Knoxville, from which his train had departed a few hours before, but he would not be able to communicate with anyone until his train arrived at Lynchburg. Not for the first time, he cursed the slowness and inefficiency of the Confederate railroad system.

His speaking tour, he decided, had been a great success. He had barnstormed through western Georgia, Alabama, Mississippi, and Tennessee, making speeches almost every day. All told, he must have spoken to tens of thousands of people at dozens of different locations. Sometimes the crowds numbered only a few dozen. On other occasions, as at Mobile, Memphis, and Nashville, they were in the thousands.

Almost every crowd had been enthusiastic and supportive. Yet there had been a few occasions, all of them in Tennessee, where his speeches had been disrupted. One man had loudly shouted curses at him during a stop in Clarksville, claiming that he had served with Breckinridge and that Toombs had no right to criticize him. The soldier, in turn, had been shouted down by other people in the crowd.

One of the other disturbances had been rather more serious, though Toombs had not learned of it until after his speech was over. Apparently, during a stop in Shelbyville, a gang of Breckinridge supporters had been walking towards the church where he had been speaking, intent on interrupting the event. They were met in the street by members of the local SRP committee and a vicious fight broke out, during which one person had been seriously wounded with a knife.

According to the papers, violent confrontations between Breckinridge and Beauregard supporters were becoming more common all over the Confederacy. The general pattern had been an SRP-aligned speaker accusing Breckinridge of allowing Saul's rebellion to get out of hand, followed by ex-soldiers who had served with Breckinridge heckling the speaker, and a fight then breaking out in the crowd. There had been a sprinkling of more serious incidents, though, including an assault by a drunken crowd of SRP supporters on a pro-Breckinridge gathering in Greensboro, North Carolina.

None of this unduly troubled Toombs. Politics was a disorderly and vicious business, so occasional outbreaks of violence were only to be expected. It had been the same before the war. Toombs was an educated man and would have preferred that political questions be settled by rational discourse and debate. Yet he knew the character of his people well enough to know that hot-blooded Southern men were apt to take political controversies from the level of talking to the level of fighting, especially if they involved questions of race.

In every speech he made, Toombs did his best to push the question of African slavery to the forefront of the election. He wondered if he might be partly to blame for the rising tensions and violent altercations. If so, it was no matter. He was doing what he had to do to win. If brawls between hotheads resulted in a few injuries or deaths, it was a small price to pay. After all, the fate of the Confederacy was at stake.

The speaking tour was over. He sensed that he needed to be back in Richmond as quickly as possible. The drama in New Iberia had unfolded throughout his journey and the dramatic trial now underway in New Orleans would only add fuel to the fire of public outrage. The best place from which Toombs might take advantage of this, he now realized, was on the floor of the Senate.

While in Chattanooga two days previously, Toombs was surprised to receive a telegram from Isham Harris, telling him that he had resigned from the Cabinet in protest over the administration handling the New Iberia crisis. In particular, Harris said, he had been outraged that Breckinridge had acquiesced to the ten-day truce declared with Saul by Morgan and Longstreet. Cryptically, Harris had asked Toombs to meet with him as soon as possible upon his return to Richmond.

Toombs was intrigued. Was Harris willing to throw in his lot with the SRP? If so, he likely had damaging information about Breckinridge that could be used in the closing two months of the campaign. He had always given himself and Beauregard better than even odds of winning. Considering the way things seemed to be going, though, Toombs felt that their chances were getting better day after day. It events continued to follow their current course, likelihood would turn into certainty.

Then there had been the strange news that Judah Benjamin had also resigned from the Cabinet. Toombs had no idea what that could be about. Unlike Harris, the now ex-Secretary of State had issued no public statement regarding his reasons for resigning. Toombs knew that Benjamin was utterly loyal to Davis and had been effectively in charge of Breckinridge's presidential campaign, so there could be very little chance that his departure from the Cabinet was due to any policy disagreement, as had been the case with Harris. He could not imagine what Benjamin was thinking, but decided that it was a positive development. Much as he disliked and distrusted Benjamin, Toombs had to acknowledge that the man was a skilled political operator. The farther away from Breckinridge's campaign he was, the better it would be for Toombs.

He was distracted from these thoughts as the train began to perceptibly slow down. Toombs reasoned that they were about to arrive at the Knoxville station and his suspicions were confirmed when he noticed a few other passengers grip their carpetbags more tightly as they prepared to stand and disembark. To Toombs, it was just another delay on his journey back to Richmond.

The Congress had recessed back in June and was not scheduled to reconvene until after the November elections, but President Davis had issued a call for a special session in response to the crisis in Louisiana. Ordinarily, Toombs would have seen this as yet another tyrannical act by the president, but in truth he did not mind. Indeed, he was looking forward to getting back to the floor of the Senate. For one thing, he needed to put forward his bill for financial reorganization, which had been made a part of the SRP national platform. It would not only put the issue front and center before the people, requiring a response from the Breckinridge camp that they would probably be unable to provide, but would polish Toombs's own credentials for higher office and assist his effort to win the Vice-Presidency. Much depended on whether people thought he would be a good advisor to Beauregard on matters on policy. What better way to accomplish this than to present his bill?

More importantly, he needed to rally his allies in the Senate to excoriate the Davis administration on the handling of the New Iberia affair. The unconscionable delays in executing captured insurgents, the hesitation in launching a full-scale attack to retake the city from Saul, and then the absolutely unforgivable sin of agreeing to a ten-day truce with the rebel leader all demonstrated a policy of softness on the part of the administration. Action had to be taken to prevent this from ever happening in the future.

The train lurched to a halt and the conductor announced their arrival at the Knoxville station. Perhaps a third of the passengers rose to depart, the remainder, like Toombs, remaining on for the continuing trip into Virginia. A young black boy came on, peddling bags of peanuts. Toombs bought one, tipping the boy a copper penny. They would be in Bristol by nightfall, and he would have dinner in his hotel.

As the last departing passenger left the train, those who had been waiting to board now began to scamper on, fumbling with their carpetbags and scanning the seats to see which looked best. There were a few women travelling alone who, understandably, looked for seats in which they would not have to sit next to men. Some people glanced about, unsure about where to place their bags. Toombs smiled. As a politician, he was an experienced traveler and thought the antics of amateurs were amusing.

A man clambered aboard the train who required the assistance of the conductor, for his left arm was uselessly coiled up in a sling and a cork peg was in the place that his right leg should have been. Toombs was startled to recognize John Bell Hood.

"General Hood!" Toombs called out as he waved. "Over here!" He stood and walked forward. "I'll help with that," he said to the conductor as he took hold of Hood's bag.

Hood stared at him uncertainly for a moment. It was clear to Toombs that Hood was having some difficulty remembering him. "Senator Toombs," the Texan commander said finally.

"Yes, that's correct. It has been a long time, General. If you're travelling alone, would you care to sit with me? It's a long leg to Bristol, our next stop. A little conversation would be nice."

Hood shrugged and hobbled towards the seats Toombs indicated. It was plain to Toombs that the crippled general endured a measure of pain with every step, for the wounds he had sustained during the war had been truly horrific. Hood's arm had been mangled by an artillery shell at Gettysburg and the leg had been amputated due to a wound at Chickamauga. General Hood had suffered mightily in the service of his nation. For that, if for nothing else, he was worthy of admiration in Toombs's eyes, even if he was a West Pointer.

Though both men had commanded brigades in the Army of Northern Virginia, Toombs had to admit that he did not know Hood very well. The man's reputation was that of a fierce soldier, but the Richmond upper crust considered him rather dull-witted and had made him an object of ridicule for his persistent and disastrous courtship of the beautiful socialite Sally Preston. He was invited to dinner parties to serve as a military ornament, not for any social graces.

Hood had served as a corps commander in the Army of Tennessee, though he played only a secondary role in the decisive victory at the Battle of Atlanta. He had then been sent out to the Trans-Mississippi Department, where he served well in the fighting during the fall of 1864. Rumors still swirled in political circles that President Davis had been about to replace Joseph Johnston with Hood before the Battle of Atlanta, though Toombs was not sure how true such stories were.

"Care for some?" Toombs asked, opening his whiskey flask and offering it to Hood.

"Don't mind if I do," Hood said, taking it and indulging in a quick swig. "Not too much, though."

"It's a long trip. Good to have something to buck a man up, I think."

Hood chuckled in response, though he said nothing.

"Are you going to Richmond?" Toombs asked.

"Yes. I have some matters to attend to at the War Department."

"I am on my way to Richmond as well. I have been speaking throughout the country, but it is high time I return to the Senate."

"Yes," said Hood. "I have read about your speaking tour in the newspapers. I am sorry I did not get a chance to hear you."

"Well, you may visit the Senate anytime you wish. Feel free to consider yourself my guest if you choose to do so."

"Thank you."

As he moved into small talk, expressing his distrust of railroad timetables and his irritation at the frequent delays, Toombs considered where Hood's political opinions might lie. He knew that he had become close to President Davis while recuperating from his wounds in Richmond during the winter of 1863-64, but that this relationship seemed to fade sometime later. Perhaps it had something to do with the same rumors regarding Johnston.

He asked Hood to describe the campaign in Arkansas during the late summer and fall of 1864, which had been overshadowed in the newspapers by the dramatic events in Georgia and Virginia. Hood happily gave an account that was entertaining, though Toombs suspected that he played up his own role rather too much.

Toombs was never a man to miss an opportunity and his fortuitous meeting with Hood on the train was a chance to obtain a political advantage. After all, the man was considered one of the great heroes of the War for Southern Independence. If he could persuade Hood to publicly endorse the SRP ticket, it would be a boost to the chances of the Beauregard-Toombs ticket.

"If you don't mind my asking, General Hood, you mentioned that you were going to Richmond to deal with some matters at the War Department. What, exactly?"

Hood shrugged. "Hoping for a change of assignment, actually. Been out in the Ozarks since before the war came to an end. Second-in-command of the department under Longstreet. I took over for a while when he went off to deal with the slaves down in New Iberia. Guess it pushed me towards wanting an independent command. So I thought I might meet with some of the Congressmen from Texas and a few other friends, to see if they might put in a good word for me."

"Why not go directly to Breckinridge?"

"He's likely to be too busy to see me, what with his presidential campaign and all."

"Yes, well, there might be a shakeup in the command structure after the election. Beauregard has told me that he wants to reorganize the army high command."

"Has he, now?"

"Indeed," Toombs replied. "He has remained in New Orleans throughout the campaign, but he and I exchange telegrams regularly. Considering his military background, you can easily imagine that the army will be high on his list of priorities, especially if we ever come to blows with Spain over this Cuba business. And perhaps we'll end up fighting the Yankees again."

"Yes, perhaps we will." Hood paused and pursed his lips. "I suppose I might as well tell you that I myself am a Beauregard man."

"Ah, that is good to hear." Toombs was not sure if what Hood said had been true a few moments before. "May I ask why?"

"I like what you and all those others are doing with this States' Rights Party. Read your party platform and liked it. And Beauregard seems a good man. Never served with him during the war, but he did well enough. Seems likely to make a good president."

"And Breckinridge?"

"Don't really care for Breckinridge, honestly."

His politician's ear sensed a personal tinge behind Hood's words and Toombs immediately recalled that Breckinridge was a cousin of Sally Preston. Could he have played some role in her rejection of Hood? It was certainly possible. He sensed an opportunity.

"You might be interested to hear, General, that the SRP is circulating a letter for military officers and former military officers to sign if they wish to express public support for our ticket. We intend to publish it in the newspapers shortly before the election."

Hood glanced over at him for a moment, then gestured for the flask of whiskey. After taking a swig, Hood said, "Well, that is certainly interesting."

"I don't suppose you would care to sign it? You're a Lieutenant General, as I recall. I believe you would be the highest ranking officer to endorse our ticket. Your name would be prominent in the newspaper stories."

Hood grunted.

"Why do you hesitate? You just told me that you support him."

"I'm a serving officer. Not sure it would be appropriate."

"Why not?" Toombs asked. "You're a citizen, aren't you? You are free to support whomever you choose. Beauregard ran for mayor of New Orleans while he was still an officer in the United States Army, did you know that?"

"No, I was not aware."

Toombs paused for a moment before dangling his bait. "If you do sign, you can be assured of a favorable consideration from Beauregard when it comes to any changes in command."

"That's assuming Beauregard wins."

"Oh, he will, he will. I am confident we'll sweep all the states of the Deep South. We're doing well in Virginia, North Carolina, and Tennessee, too. All we need to do is win one of them, and we're over the line. In fact, I am not entirely convinced it won't be a clean sweep, with Beauregard winning every state."

"That would be impressive."

"Yes, and it may happen."

"What about Rhett's candidacy?" Hood asked.

Toombs laughed. "Rhett? That damn fool? He'll be lucky if gets one out of twenty votes in any state."

"Sure, but that might be enough to cost you one of the bigger states."

"I doubt it," Toombs said confidently. "Everything is moving in our direction. Breckinridge is being torn to pieces in the press, what with all the happenings in Louisiana. You've heard that Isham Harris resigned from the Cabinet in protest, didn't you?"

"Yes, but I read in the paper today that Ambassador Miles has endorsed Breckinridge."

"What?" Toombs asked. "That's not possible."

"Read it today in the *Knoxville Register*," Hood replied. He reached down to his carpetbag, fumbled around in it for a few moments, and produced a copy of the newspaper, handing it to Toombs.

The Georgia senator quickly devoured the story. At first, he assumed it had to be some sort of error, but he had learned to sniff out the truth or falseness of a newspaper while reading it. The story of Miles endorsing Breckinridge was written with a crisp exactness, including a public statement which sounded precisely like something that would come out of Miles's mouth. It had all the telltale signs of a real report.

Toombs was astonished. What could have persuaded Miles to do such a thing? Then he saw that the story also stated that Miles had been nominated by Davis to be the next Secretary of State now that Benjamin had resigned. Surely, Toombs reasoned, Miles had endorsed Breckinridge as part of a corrupt bargain with Davis to secure the seat in the Cabinet. What other possibility could there be? It was dishonest in the extreme, of course, and in an instant Toombs went from liking and admiring Miles to loathing the man. Never again would be speak to Miles unless forced to do so, he decided.

Yet troubling thousands were already entering Toombs's mind. Miles was far from a fool. He would only have done what he did if he thought Breckinridge had a good decent of winning the election. A few months as Secretary of State was not a prize worth seeking, after all, and Miles always played the long game. Did he know something Toombs didn't?

"Doesn't matter," Toombs said, as much to himself as Hood. "Miles must have lost his mind. This changes nothing."

"You'd have to persuade me that Beauregard's victory is certain. If I were to sign your letter and then Breckinridge were to win, it would be the end of my hopes for a long while."

"You have my word, General Hood. This election is in the bag. And if Beauregard wins, as I am sure he shall, it will make your dreams of an independent command much more likely to come true."

"I'm a soldier, not a politician," Hood said. "But I'm not stupid, Toombs. If Miles has done this, it makes me think that this election isn't as in the bag as you seem to think it is."

"We will win, Hood. Of that you can be sure. I am staking my future on it." He paused for a moment, then told an easy lie. "In fact, in the event that we lose, I intend to resign from the Senate."

Hood's eyes widened slightly. "You do?"

"What would be the point in remaining? My reputation and credibility will be ruined. If our ticket does not win, I see no future prospects for me, so why not retire from public life?" He made another rhetorical pause. "But as I said, I am entirely confident that we shall easily win on Election Day. Miles can say whatever he wants."

"Very well, then, Senator. I shall sign your letter."

Toombs grinned, satisfied with himself. Having a lieutenant general's name on the list of supporters would do much good. It wouldn't be necessary for winning the election, of course, because he was being truthful when he told Hood that he was certain victory was already guaranteed. Still, the greater the margin of SRP victory, the better. If nothing else, it would compound Breckinridge's humiliation, which would serve as a warning for all other public figures in the future who might consider going soft on slavery.

September 9, Afternoon
Confederate States District Court, New Orleans, Louisiana

"How did you acquire the weapons you distributed to Saul and his men?" Eustis asked.

"I bought them," Lowell replied calmly.

"From whom?"

"A black market arms dealer."

"His name?"

"I do not know his name. His identity was intentionally kept secret from me, so that he would not be compromised should I find myself in a situation where I would be questioned."

"A situation you are now in, General Lowell," Eustis said authoritatively. "For all the disgust I feel at your acts, I believe that you are a man of God and that you will not lightly dismiss the oath you took upon the commencement of these questions."

"I take no oaths lightly," Lowell said. "I shall answer all questions to which I can, in good conscience, provide an answer."

"Then you shall tell me the name of the man who sold you the weapons."

Aside from the verbal exchanges between Lowell and Eustis, the courtroom was unnaturally quiet. The heat was intense and Lowell could see several men and women in the audience fanning themselves in an effort to stay cool. He had expected the uncomfortable temperatures to keep people away from the trial today, but the seats were as crowded as they had been every day since the commencement of the trial. The looks on the spectators and reporters was somewhat bored, however, for the proceedings had been going on for several hours.

Judge Moise sat quietly in his raised chair, his arms folded across his chest as he looked down upon Lowell and Eustis. He made no move to restrain the questions of the prosecutor, though it was obvious to Lowell that they served no purpose in determining his guilt or innocence. Lowell occasionally turned to Caffery wordlessly asking him to object to some of the questions, but his defense attorney never made a move. Sometimes it seemed as if he had fallen asleep.

It had been this way all day, every day, for the past week. The previous Wednesday, after the jury had been seated, Eustis had made a fiery opening statement, continually glaring and pointing at Lowell, calling him an enemy of everything that the Confederacy stood for and everything its soldiers had died for. The speech lasted more than an hour and it was obvious that Eustis had gone to great lengths in preparing it. Caffery, by contrast, responded with a bland opening statement that lasted scarcely ten minutes, in which he addressed only the right of every man to a fair trial, no matter how heinous his crime. The subsequent two days had been more like a police interrogation than a legal proceeding, with Eustis continually grilling Lowell and Caffery making no real effort to stop him. The break for the weekend had been welcome, but now Lowell was back in the hot seat.

"General Lowell, I asked you again to name the man who sold you the weapons," Eustis said

"I cannot provide an answer that I do not know, Mr. Eustis. As I said, the man's true identity was never made known to me."

"He was being protected?"

"I suppose."

"By whom?"

Lowell saw immediately that he had stepped into another one of Eustis's traps. Lowell was not ashamed of what he had done and he wanted the world to know that there was still a strong element of the Northern population unwilling to accept the continuance of slavery. That said, he did not believe he had a moral right to expose the involvement of particular individuals without their permission. They might face serious legal consequences, perhaps even trial and imprisonment, and he was not going to have that on his conscience the hour of his hanging.

Irritation and anger caused Lowell to lose his composure and he decided to descend to ridicule. "Two men. Their names were Jefferson Davis and Alexander Stephens, the President and Vice-President of the Confederate States of America."

Laughter pealed throughout the courtroom and Judge Moise instantly began pounding his gavel for quiet. He looked down at Lowell in the witness stand, an expression of fierce anger on his face.

"I shall not have these serious proceedings marred with such absurd comments. This is neither the time nor the place for jokes. Do you understand, General Lowell? If you do not, I shall hold you in contempt and confine you in considerably less comfortable quarters than you currently enjoy."

"I understand, Your Honor," Lowell replied. He was surprised at himself and told himself to be more controlled. He had an important job to do, which would be his last service to God on this Earth and it had been childish and foolish of him to give in to the temptation to needle his enemies with a joke.

Eustis was resuming his questioning. "General Lowell, are you personally acquainted with Senator Charles Sumner?"

Lowell wondered what this could be about. "Yes, I am."

"Could you describe the nature of your relationship?"

"I come from a prominent Massachusetts family. Senator Sumner is a prominent Massachusetts politician. It is only natural that our paths should occasionally cross."

"A more detailed answer is expected," Eustis said.

"Very well. He and I worked together during the war to recruit men for the Second Massachusetts Cavalry Regiment. We also worked together to encourage the Lincoln administration to recruit liberated slaves into the Union army." Lowell paused for just a moment, sensing an opportunity. "After all, history proves that men who have been held in bondage their entire lives are eager and willing to cast off their chains and take up arms against those who would deny them their freedom."

Eustis looked up at Judge Moise. "Your Honor, I submit that the witness's answer is irrelevant to the matter at hand and that it be stripped from the record."

"Sustained," Moise declared. He glared down at Lowell in the witness stand. "I think that is quite enough from you today, young man. I am tired. I think all the members of the court are tired. We are adjourned until tomorrow morning. Bailiff?"

"All rise!"

Lowell rose along with every other person in the courtroom. The next few minutes no different than those which had taken place during the recessing of the court every day since the trial had begun. The guards reapplied his handcuffs and escorted him out the front door of the courthouse. As before, there was an angry crowd waiting for him. The moment he emerged from the door, the sunlight momentarily causing him to squint, a chorus of booing and enraged shouting rose up. The faces of the people in the crowd, which contained as many women as men and numbered at least a hundred, were contorted in irrational rage as they screamed.

"Hang him!"

"Kill the bastard!"

"You'll never take away our darkies!"

Soldiers drawn from one of the many New Orleans militia units held the crowd at a distance from him, their bayonet-tipped rifles held at the ready in case of trouble. The crowd made no effort to attack him, however. Lowell was not a man who feared much of anything, yet somehow the possibility of being torn to pieces by an angry mob filled him with dread. His guards soon pushed him into his paddy wagon and, with the snapping of a horsewhip, he was on his way back to his jail.

Two guards rode with him, never speaking. As they rode away from the courthouse, Lowell turned and looked through the bar-lined window at the crowd. He wondered if he saw, in the faces of the people, now fading into the distance, the common citizen of the Confederacy. It made his heart sink. He could understand that individuals could be evil, but it troubled him to think that a whole people could be evil. Was it possible for the Southern people to redeem themselves in the eyes of the world? Would they, one day, look back upon their unrestrained support for slavery with horror?

Lowell hoped so, and he hoped that the example he was setting in his trial would be a step in that direction. After all, the only way slavery could be ended without a massive and bloody race war was for the Southern people to accept the utter wrongness of the institution. He would use however much time he had left in service of that end.

They arrived at his jail and he was quickly escorted into his cell. It looked precisely as a jail cell was supposed to look. It was about ten feet by twenty, much of the space being taken up by a cot and most of the rest by a small desk and chair. Blessedly, there was a window through which the sunlight streamed. The view was out onto the alley behind the jail, but Lowell could also see a small stretch of a regular street down at the end. Seeing the denizens of New Orleans walk past reminded him that the real world still existed.

It didn't matter, though. His life was now playing itself out in only two locations, the courtroom and his jail. He would never see his wife and children again. All he had left was his trial. He would use it as a speaking platform for as long as he could, saying to the South what needed to be said, then go to the gallows with as much dignity and courage as he could muster.

Yet he was not pleased with how the trial was going. Though he was technically Lowell's attorney, Caffery was clearly trying to thwart his intentions. Lowell had said that he wanted the trial to last as long as possible, but Caffery had helped the court rush through jury selection the week before, when he might have easily used the process to delay things. The man seemed a competent enough lawyer, but clearly had no interest whatsoever in doing what Lowell wanted him to do.

His lunch arrived and he ate. The meals that the jail was now providing were better than those of his days of solitary confinement the previous month, but were nothing special. This one, like most of the others, consisted of a few small potatoes, a small piece of chicken, and a handful of rice. It reminded him of some of the meals he had eaten while on campaign during the war.

The jail had provided a copy of the King James Bible. He picked it up and began to read. He had reread the New Testament three times already. Lowell considered himself a devout Christian, though the influence of the New England Transcendentalists had shaped him into something of which many churchmen might not have approved. Additionally, Phelps had offered to bring him any books he wanted from the New Orleans library. He had requested volumes of Thoreau and Hawthorne, but they had yet to arrive. He frankly wondered if a Southern library would allow the works of abolitionist authors on its shelves.

He had also asked Phelps to obtain for him a copy of *The Consolation of Philosophy*, by the sixth century theologian Boethius, if one could be found. Lowell had read it many years ago and thought its message would comfort him in what were surely his final days. He wanted to be reminded that the only pain which could be inflicted upon him now was that which he would bring upon himself by succumbing to fear or regret. The Confederates would kill him, but if he willed himself not to be afraid and not to regret the choice he had made, there was nothing they could do to harm him on the level of the soul.

He thought he was holding himself up with admirable courage, though in a strange way his current situation was more difficult than solitary confinement had been. Then, he had simply been fighting to maintain his sanity. Now, much more comfortable and at ease, there was little he could do to avoid musing on his coming death.

Everyone died, of course. That was the one truly inevitable fact of life, the only thing shared by every human being. He told himself that he believed in a world to come, yet could he really be sure? Unless one counted Jesus himself, no one was able to come back and let people know the truth. It might just be that death was an endless, dreamless sleep, and there was nothing much to fear about that. It was not like he would be alive to be upset about it.

These musings were disrupted by the rough squeaking of the lock, then the heavy wooden scraping as the door was pushed open. One of his jailers, an uneducated but amiable maned named Matthew Styles, came inside.

"Packet from Mr. Phelps for you, sir."

"Thank you, Styles," Lowell replied. Styles was the only person in the jail or the court who had addressed him as 'sir'.

The packet contained the copies of Hawthorne and Thoreau that he had asked for, but a note apologizing that the only edition of Boethius he had been able to locate had been in Latin and he was trying to find one in English. Lowell sighed in irritation. He could read Latin as easily as English and would, in fact, have much preferred to read the book in its original language. He considered it odd that Phelps hadn't assumed this and wondered if the denial of the book was an intentional effort to aggravate him. The United States Consul was clearly unhappy to be dealing with the situation.

"What's the news, Styles?" Lowell asked. Since he had been denied newspapers, the kind jailer was his only real source of information.

"You're the news, sir," Styles replied. "Every newspaper, you're the headline. Walking down the street to get here this morning, all I heard people talking about was you. You're famous, sir."

"Famous, eh?" Lowell scoffed slightly. Fame wasn't anything he desired. He would happily trade being the most famous person in the world for the freedom of a single slave.

"Yes, indeed. The wife is awfully proud I'm you're jailer, I don't mind saying." He stopped smiling and recovered himself. "Not that what you did was right, sir. Indeed not. Very wrong, in fact. Very wrong."

"You're entitled to your opinion, Styles."

"Oh, a telegram for you, sir. From Richmond, sir."

Lowell's eyes narrowed. Who in Richmond would want to send a message to him? "Give it here, please."

Mr. Lowell,

You do not know me, but I certainly know you. I have resigned from my post as Secretary of State of the Confederate States and now wish to serve as your defense counsel. You will no doubt wonder as to my reasons for doing so. I shall explain as best I can when I arrive in New Orleans. If you wish to accept my offer, tell the judge that you wish to be represented by new counsel. Not wishing to waste time, I have decided not to wait on your response. I shall be on my way by the time you receive this telegram. I send you heartfelt greetings and look forward to meeting you.

Judah Benjamin

Lowell's eyes narrowed in mystified confusion. He knew who Judah Benjamin was, of course. The man had served as a pro-slavery Southern senator before the war and served in the Confederate Cabinet during and since the war. Lowell recalled Sumner was describing him in a conversation as highly intelligent but entirely unprincipled, like many other Southern politicians. The only unusual thing about Benjamin, as far as Lowell could see, was the fact that he was Jewish.

"I'll be going, sir."

"Thank you, Styles." The jailer closed the door, locked it, and Lowell was again alone in his private little world.

He read through Benjamin's telegram once more, which left him no less confused. It made no sense that one of the most prominent politicians in the Confederacy would want to serve as his lawyer. Was the man simply wanting to earn fame by being involved in a trial that was surely going to be remembered in history? That seemed too simple. Besides, Benjamin had to be aware that willingly serving as his lawyer, abandoning a critical post in the government while doing so, would surely earn him the wrath and hatred of his fellow white Southerners. Benjamin had cryptically said he would explain things to Lowell when he arrived. Until then, he would just have to wait.

Having nothing else to do until dinner, Lowell laid down on his cot. Yet his mind continued to swirl with questions about Benjamin. He wished more than anything that he could speak to someone knowledgeable about the man. He recalled that he was a Louisianan, which might have some importance since the trial was taking place in Louisiana. What sort of man was he, though? The confines of his jail cell prevented him from finding out, which was more frustrating than any physical restraint.

One thing was certain, however. Lowell was going to accept his offer. Far better to have a willing attorney than an appointed and unenthusiastic one like Caffery. Besides, Benjamin's involvement would add to the drama on the event, making them even more prominent in the newspapers. Since Lowell was determined to use his trial as a soap box to denounce slavery to a Confederacy largely unwilling to listen, any help in doing so would be most welcome.

He smiled, then gratefully reached for the Bible.

September 9, Afternoon
United States Capitol Building

Sumner pushed through the crowd in the hallway, not only congressmen and senators but clerks, reporters, lobbyists, and other assorted people there for various reasons. He disliked crowds in general, which he knew was a liability for a politician, yet he absolutely detested the gatherings of people that took place within the United States Capitol. Invariably every civilian visiting the place was there only to ask for an easy but well-paying government job, a favor for a friend or relative, or some other selfish indulgence. Sumner did not have a very high opinion of human nature and his time in the Senate had done nothing to improve it.

He sometimes wondered how it was that he himself maintained a sense of moral rigor in the midst of such a cesspool of depravity. He had seen many idealistic men come into Washington City as though on a white horse, eager to do good and improve society, only to fall into wickedness like Faust. What kept him from doing the same? Part of it, he knew, was the fact that he had no wife and children. Men who would refuse to sully their hands in corruption for their own sake were, he had learned, often willing to do so for the sake of their families. Others worried over the legacy they would leave behind after death, but Sumner was not a vain man and did not especially care how history would remember him, if it remembered him at all. He could focus all of his energies on the single cause of abolition.

His moral rectitude was, in his view, a suit of armor protecting him from the temptations the city threw in the path of men. He needed that armor now. Word had reached him that the Navy Department had cancelled two large shipbuilding contracts with firms in Massachusetts and turned them over to dockyards in Philadelphia. Additionally, the owner of the Springfield Armory had written him an urgent letter expressing alarm at a proposal by the army to reduce production there. An iron foundry making armor for the new ironclad, *USS Gettysburg*, had similarly reported rumors that its contract was to be cancelled. All these people were asking him to intervene with the McClellan administration. If he failed to do so, they warned, hundreds and perhaps thousands of men would lose their jobs. In the tough economic climate, many of these people would have no prospect of finding new work and a great many of them had families to support.

As much as it pained him, Sumner knew he had no choice but to ignore these entreaties. He sympathized with the men who would be made destitute, of course, but he was not about to be strong-armed by McClellan. Such pressure and retaliation might have had an impact on a lesser man, but it would not have the slightest impact on Charles Sumner.

Having struggled to force his way through the crowd in the Capitol hallway, he finally reached his destination, opening the door to the office of Congressman John Logan, a Democrat from Illinois, and stepping inside. He spoke to the clerk, a young man who was intent on reading a newspaper. Sumner was gratified to see that the headline was something to do with the Lowell trial.

"I'd like to speak with Congressman Logan, please."

"Did you make an appointment, sir?" the clerk asked without taking his eyes off the newspaper.

Sumner was irritated. "Young man, do you know who I am?"

The clerk looked up and his eyes widened in surprise. He struggled for a moment to find his words. "I'm terribly sorry, Senator Sumner. I will see if he is available right away."

The clerk rose from his desk and hobbled through a door leading to another room. Sumner then noticed that the man was missing his left leg and immediately regretted having been rude to him. Men who had suffered the loss of limbs during the war against slavery were always deserving of respect.

He had not chosen Logan at random. Sumner did not much care for Democrats in general, yet he had to admit that Logan was cut from a different stripe. The congressman had first come to Sumner's attention in the summer of 1861, when Logan had been one of the overconfident Congressmen who had journeyed out from Washington City to watch what was expected to be the Union victory at the First Battle of Bull Run. When the Northern army unexpectedly collapsed into a frightened rabble, Logan had grabbed a discarded musket and started blazing away at the advancing Confederates while trying unsuccessfully to rally the fleeing troops.

Logan had resigned from Congress shortly thereafter, raised a regiment of Illinois troops, and thrown himself into the war effort. Unlike the vast majority of politician-generals, Logan soon showed that he possessed considerable military ability, serving under Grant and Sherman in the Western Theater, eventually reaching the rank of major general and the command of a corps. By all accounts, he had demonstrated extraordinary bravery in battle, suffering wounds and having horses shot out from under him. During the fighting around Atlanta, the performance of Logan's corps had been one of the few bright marks in an otherwise disastrous campaign.

Returning from war, Logan had decided to remain within the ranks of the Democrats despite pressure from his wartime colleagues to throw in his lot with the Republicans. Sumner regretted Logan's decision, yet he had to admit that Logan certainly would not have made it into Congress as a Republican. Illinois, despite being the home of Abraham Lincoln, was locked tightly in the Democratic column and there was little sign that this dominance was going to end anytime soon.

Congressman Logan emerged from the back room. He was a formidable-looking man, with jet black hair and a large, flowing mustache of the same color. Combined with his dark eyes, it was no surprise that his troops had given him the nickname of 'Black Jack'.

"Senator Sumner," he said, bowing his head respectfully. "This is certainly a surprise. To what do I owe this unexpected pleasure?"

"I wish to speak with you."

"That much is clear. Well, come back here, if you please." Logan gestured towards his back office and Sumner followed him in. Both men sat down on either side of a small table and the clerk shut the door behind them. "So, what's this about?" Logan asked. "You're not in the habit of coming over to this side of the Capitol."

"I know," Sumner replied. He hesitated before beginning, not entirely how to start.

"Would you like a drink?" Logan offered.

"No, thank you." Sumner gathered his thoughts. "I feel the need to speak with a man of integrity on the other side of the aisle concerning the recent actions by President McClellan."

Logan smiled. "I am honored that you consider me a man of integrity. I am surprised, though, that you acknowledge the existence of men of integrity in my party. You've never concealed your contempt for Democrats in any of your speeches, and certainly not the ones you've been making lately."

"I cannot apologize for that."

"Nor would I expect you to," Logan replied. "I am a Democrat, Sumner. I was one before the war and I am one now. I do not agree with you when it comes to slavery and abolition. I think that you abolitionists have a lot to answer for. Your unwillingness to compromise with the Southerners is what led to the breakup of the Union." Logan paused a moment, looking at Sumner deeply. "The bill you laid before the Senate to grant diplomatic recognition to Saul's so-called 'liberated zone' in Louisiana caused a number of headaches, I don't mind saying. Many people on my side were furious. You forced them to either look ridiculous to their own voters or to appear to support slavery."

"I had to do it," Sumner said simply. "It was the right thing to do."

"It was not politically expedient."

541

"No moral act can ever be inexpedient. It is impossible for a man with a conscience to compromise with evil."

"The definition of evil varies from man to man."

Sumner nodded. "Possibly, but such a discussion is for another time."

"Very well. What are you here to discuss, then?"

He paused for a moment, considering how to approach the issue and choosing his words carefully. "It's widely known that you are not on good terms with the president."

Logan frowned. "Who says that?"

"It's an open secret in Washington City."

"Yes, well, I would be lying if I said I was pleased with the decision by McClellan to terminate the war in 1865. I understand that the people were no longer willing to go on fighting. The riots against the draft and the Copperheads winning so many congressional seats were proof enough of that. Perhaps there was nothing else to be done. Yet I can't help but feel he gave in rather too easily." He paused and shook his head. "So many of my men died assaulting the Atlanta defenses. More died at the Battle of Fairburn. I don't like to think that they died for nothing."

"Neither do I," Sumner said carefully. "But McClellan's crimes today go deeper, in my view. You have served in the army and you have served in Congress. You are an intelligent man. I am sure you understand the critical importance of maintaining civilian control over the military. These actions by the president, using the military to support an illegal organization like the Fenians and ordering military officers not to testify to my Senate committee, are deeply disturbing. Would you not agree?"

Logan sighed and waited a moment before replying. "I am not comfortable with the president's recent decisions, no."

"They are an unconstitutional abuse of executive power. The Supreme Court will certainly find this to be the case in due time. McClellan is so stubborn that he will ignore its ruling and we shall have a constitutional crisis on our hands."

"That would be very unfortunate," Logan replied, nodding his head. "It is an unsettled time. The threat of war with Britain is very real. The uprising in Louisiana and the Lowell Affair are pushing our relations with the Confederacy in a more hostile direction. Our country needs to be united and it is very far from being so."

"I agree."

"I am glad we see eye-to-eye. But why did you feel it necessary to come discuss this with me. What is it that you want?"

"I want you to introduce articles of impeachment against President McClellan," Sumner said simply.

Logan's eyes widened in surprise. "You want me to do what?" he said, incredulously. "Introduce articles of impeachment against President McClellan," Sumner repeated. "What he is doing is illegal and unconstitutional. It violates the separation of powers and sets the executive branch above Congress. It certainly meets the definition of 'high crimes and misdemeanors'."

"You're crazy, Sumner."

"I'm completely serious."

"No president has ever been impeached in the history of the United States."

"I know."

"Your man Lincoln did lots of questionable things when he was in the White House, didn't he?" Logan said. "Suspended habeus corpus, raised troops without congressional authorization, all sorts of things. You didn't want him impeached."

"Neither did you. What President Lincoln did was necessary for the war effort."

"Perhaps. But why do you want me to do this? First of all, it won't work. Even assuming you got every Republican in the House to support impeachment, I doubt you'd get enough Democratic support to obtain a majority. And even if you did, there'd be enough Democratic opposition in the Senate to keep you from getting the two-thirds vote you'd need to actually remove McClellan. And even if you succeeded, you'd end up with George Pendleton as president, which I very much doubt would make you happy."

"All true," Sumner replied. "But you misunderstand me. I don't really care about how far the process goes. I don't expect it to obtain a majority in the House. I merely want an impeachment motion put forward and for the vote to be reasonably close. The people need to be shown in the most dramatic fashion that what the president is doing is dangerous and unacceptable."

"Why me, though?"

"You're one of the few Democrats in the House that is known and respected around the whole country. What better way to demonstrate to the people the seriousness of the situation than to have you, rather than some Radical Republican, be the man to introduce the articles of impeachment?"

"What better way to frighten the president, you mean."

Sumner shrugged. "Take it any way you wish. He needs to be pressured to back away from his saber-rattling against the British. The Confederacy is our real enemy."

"You might just be prodding McClellan into assuming a more belligerent stance, rather than a less belligerent one. He does not like being pressured into doing things he does not want to do."

"He's a coward," Sumner replied simply. "He shied from combat during the war. If a major faction within his own party opposed him, he would back down."

Logan grunted and didn't reply for half a minute. "If I were to do this, the leadership of my party would not be happy. I might not be nominated again next year."

"McClellan is becoming ever more unpopular in the country. For every supporter you lose, you'll gain another. Besides, you could always come over to our side," Sumner suggested. "I know there have been some discussions."

"Your own party is having its troubles, you know," Logan said cautiously. "From what I've been hearing, the pro-Seward and pro-Chase factions on are on the brink of an open breach. It would not surprise me if your party goes into 1868 fielding two different candidates, rather like my party did in 1860."

Sumner pursed his lips and nodded. The two main factions of the Republican Party seemed more focused on battling one another for the presidential nomination than with thwarting the McClellan administration.

Whether Seward or Chase became the nominee, the Republicans stood a good chance of reclaiming the White House in the coming year. Yet if the party split, that opportunity might vanish like the morning fog on a sunny day, leaving the country with at least four more years of McClellan. He felt increasingly like a man without a party or, rather, a party of one.

Logan went on. "Before I give you a definitive answer, I need to ask you a question."

"Of course."

"Did you have anything to do with the arms smuggling operation of this Charles Russell Lowell fellow?"

Sumner shifted uncomfortably. "What do you mean?"

"Rumors are swirling that you know Lowell and that you met with him in Boston back in the spring, which would have been around the time his conspiracy was hatched. Some people are even saying that you helped arrange the financing of the arms purchase. I wouldn't be surprised if federal marshals come knocking on your door sometime soon." There was a pause. "So, what say you?"

"I do know Lowell. That much is true. I have long been friendly with the Lowell family. I helped gain him his officer commission during the war. I shall certainly not denounce him for what he has done."

"That's all well and good. But did you help him do it?"

Sumner considered denying the charge. Despite being a politician, lying did not come easily to him. Much of his appeal to the Northern public, he knew, came from his reputation for absolute integrity. He was able to maintain this reputation for the very simple reason that it was true. Yet was a lie in defense of righteousness a sin? On the other hand, if he claimed not to have helped Lowell and it later came out that he had, his reputation for truthfulness would be destroyed. He would be quite rightly accused of lying in order to protect his own skin.

"If I tell you, do you give me your word as a gentleman that you will maintain my confidence?" Sumner asked.

Logan gave a wry smile. "By the manner of your asking, I fear that giving you my word on such a question would place me in an awkward situation."

Sumner could not simply admit the truth, for Logan would be forced by his own sense of honor to go immediately to the authorities. Sumner had to remain free to continue his opposition to the president. If he were locked up in a jail, he would not be able to thwart the drift towards war with England or work to reunite the Republican Party in preparation for the struggles of 1868.

Weighing the alternatives, Sumner said nothing, simply staring impassively back at Logan. He knew that he was all but admitting the truth, yet he was giving Logan the ability to honestly say that Sumner had disclosed nothing.

"Well, I think we understand one another," Logan said.

Sumner nodded, feeling some of his control over the situation slip away. From the moment he had first approached Lowell after the dinner at the Howe's, he knew he had started down a very dangerous path. His own party was not in a position to help him and many fellow Republicans were probably not inclined to do so anyway. His actions had long since crossed the line into illegality. Logan had been quite correct when he said that federal marshals might come knocking on his door any day.

In that sense, Sumner had something in common with Charles Russell Lowell, now languishing in his cell in New Orleans and being subjected to a show trial that could only end with his execution. If Sumner was arrested and hauled off to prison, perhaps he could make use of it. Martyrdom, after all, had a long and glorious tradition. While he would not face the fate that Lowell was facing, going to prison for fighting against the enemy that more than three hundred thousand Northern men had given the lives to destroy would certainly catch the imagination of the people.

"So, will you do it?" Sumner asked.

"I will consider it. Beyond that, I can say nothing."

"I shall have to accept that." He rose from the desk and extended his hand. "Good day, Congressman."

Logan shook his hand firmly. "And you, Senator."

September 10, Noon
Milhaud Plantation, Assumption Parish, Southern Louisiana

"Ain't nothing here, General!" the sergeant shouted. "Regular bunch of darkies, near as we can tell. Seem harmless enough."

"Search everything!" Morgan replied. "Tear the slave cabins apart!"

The sergeant frowned, irritated that his words were being ignored and that there would be more work for him to do. Yet he duly shouted orders and the company of cavalry dismounted their horses, leaving one man out of each four to hold the mounts while the others moved forward. The men proceeded to kick down the flimsy doors to each slave cabin on the sugar plantation and move inside. Morgan could hear the sounds of light wooden furniture being tossed about. He doubted his men would show much respect for the property of the blacks.

The slaves themselves had been called out just before sunrise and were now arrayed in a single-file line in front of the row of cabins. They seemed resigned to the damage being done to their homes. Morgan could not help but feel a tinge of sympathy. After all, slaves owned nothing at all, not even their own bodies. Their few possessions were what their masters allowed them to have and they could be taken away at will. The pathetic cabins, scarcely stout enough to keep out the rain, were the only places they could ever feel at home.

"Tell me where Saul is or I will order all your cabins burned down!" Morgan said loudly. He remained on his horse, for dismounting caused intense pain in his right leg. His wound had been patched up by a regimental surgeon and there had been no infection, but it still hurt. Morgan preferred remaining mounted anyway, for it would give him a height and physical presence that would be intimidating to the blacks being questioned.

The slaves glanced at one another, uncertainty and confusion evident in their expressions. "Saul?" said one older male slave. "He's dead, ain't he? Thought you boys killed him dead in New Iberia."

545

Morgan glared down at the man as though in a rage, but it was entirely feigned. As far as he had been able to determine, Morgan himself was the last person to have seen Saul alive, immediately after he had killed one of his men on the flaming porch of the hotel. He knew that he would never be able to erase from his mind the sight and sound of Saul bellowing at the top of his lungs. However, the insurgent's body had not been found.

It was possible, of course, that one of the charred and unrecognizable corpses discovered within the scorched wreckage of the hotel had belonged to Saul. Yet Morgan's somehow felt certain that the insurgent leader had escaped.

"That what you heard?" Morgan asked the old man. "You heard he was dead?"

"That's right, sir."

"Who told you?"

The man looked hesitant. "Just what everybody's saying is all, sir."

"It's a lie!" said a much younger slave, scarcely more than a boy, in a quick and determined tone.

"You keep quiet, Willy!" the older slave said.

Morgan tapped his stirrups into the side of his horse and walked it forward a few feet, until he was directly beside the boy who had spoken. He looked down upon him, who suddenly appeared fearful. Morgan thought that, as far as the slave boy was concerned, he might as well have been the devil.

"What do you know, boy?"

"Saul got away is what they say!" the boy excitedly replied. "Old Man Henry up at the Dolmanet Plantation, just a few miles north of here, say that he passed through just two days ago. Says he gave him some food."

"Old Man Henry's a damn fool!" an elderly woman said contemptuously. "Would say anything to look important! He don't know what he's talking about! Made the whole thing up, he did!"

Other slaves joined in, loudly proclaiming their opinion about the reliability of Old Man Henry at the Dolmanet Plantation. Morgan watch the unfolding argument with dismay. He doubted that the young boy had any useful information. At best, he had heard a wild rumor, which had probably passed through half a dozen different mouths before it had reached his ears. It would be nothing worth acting on, yet the very fact that the rumor was floating about was a matter of concern.

The sergeant in charge of searching the cabins came up beside him.

"Just like I thought, sir. Nothing of any interest in these here cabins. No weapons. Nothing." There was a certain satisfaction in the man's voice.

"Take five men," Morgan said. "Ride to the Dolmanet plantation, north of here. Find the slave they call Old Man Henry and question him. Seems that some of these here darkies think he may know something. I expect you back at camp by nightfall."

"Very good, sir." The man moved off to follow his orders. Within the next few minutes, Morgan watched as selected men were told by the sergeant to mount their horses. The group then rode off for the north.

Morgan didn't expect anything to come from the venture. There had already been so many false leads. In the two weeks since the recapture of New Iberia, Morgan's cavalry had patrolled throughout the region, searching for any

546

sign of Saul or any of his men who might have escaped the town. He had ridden two horses nearly to death and had gotten very little sleep. No definite information about Saul had been obtained, certainly nothing that might disprove the idea that the man had died in New Iberia. Longstreet had told Morgan that he thought he was on a fool's errand.

He continued shouting questions at the slaves, warning them of dire consequences if they failed to answer. Yet every demand for information as to the whereabouts of Saul was greeted with the same frightened and confused answers as the first one. After a time, it became clear to Morgan that these blacks knew nothing of any use. The chatter about Old Man Henry was likely to have just been a bone they had thrown in hopes that it would satisfy him.

"Very well," Morgan said authoritatively. "I'm done here. I suggest you get yourselves ready for work."

"Sir?" a black girl in her early teens asked.

"What?"

She pointed to one of his men, who had just remounted his horse. "That there fella done stole my knife and fork. Seen them in his hand when he came out of my cabin."

"Shut your mouth, you damned black wench!"

She ignored him, apparently not in the least offended by his words, and continued speaking to Morgan. "Know it's just a knife and fork, sir. Nothing much to a rich white man like you. But it's all the tableware I got. And it's mine, you know?"

Morgan thought for a few moments, then slowly walked his horse towards the man who had taken the cutlery. "Give it back," he said.

"But she's a darkie, sir!"

"She needs to eat her food like everybody else. Besides, we'll get more cooperation from these people if we show them a little kindness."

The man frowned disrespectfully and tossed the knife and fork onto the ground in the general direction of the girl. He then spat on the ground and turned his horse away, walking it down the lane to move out of hearing distance. Morgan didn't respond to the display of insolence, which was directed at him more than it was the girl. So long as his men were willing to take orders and fight well, Morgan had never made discipline a high priority. There was a certain unspoken equality between Morgan and his troopers and he had no issue with any of his men expressing themselves so.

The overseer of the plantation arrived and shouted for the slaves to head to the sugar fields. Morgan assembled his troopers and moved on down the road to the next plantation.

They had only been moving about twenty minutes when Duke, leading a force of about fifty troopers, came up from behind. He had been investigating another nearby plantation.

"Anything?" Morgan asked.

"No, nothing," Duke replied tiredly. "Just like every other place we've looked into over the past couple of days."

"He's out here somewhere."

"Why do you think that?" Duke asked in a pleading voice. "How do you know he didn't die in New Iberia?"

"Saul got out, I'm sure of it."

"Well, I'm going to be honest with you, John. I'm tired. I want to go home. So do the boys. I think he's dead. You say that the last time you saw him, he was standing on the porch of a burning hotel, being shot at by hundreds of men. He's dead, John. Nobody could have gotten out of there alive."

Morgan grunted a response. He couldn't argue with the logic of what Duke was saying. Still, something told him that his nemesis was still alive. If he was, he still presented a danger.

"Oh, one thing I did hear at the last plantation," Duke said.

"Yes?"

"A teenage girl gave birth two nights ago. Folks said that she did it on her own, because the midwife was too drunk. But she insists that Saul appeared in her cabin and helped her deliver the baby."

"What?" Morgan asked, incredulous. "That's crazy talk."

"I know. Don't know why she said it. All the other slaves told her she was crazy, too, but she insisted that it had happened."

"I don't want to hear any ridiculous stories," Morgan said. "All I care about is finding solid information on Saul."

"He's dead, John," Duke said insistently.

"No," Morgan said, shaking his head rapidly. "No, he's not dead. He's out here somewhere and I'm going to find him."

September 12, Afternoon
French Foreign Ministry Building, Paris, France

Like every other senior government office in the France of Napoleon III, the office of the French Foreign Minister, known as the Salon de la Rotonde, was outsized and grand. The sunlight pouring in from the three enormous windows behind the Minister's desk flooded the room, bringing out the brightness of its yellow and gold-tinted walls. Framed tapestries, some more than a century old, lined the walls. On the desk was an elaborately carved inkstand that had belonged to Talleyrand himself. Sitting in a chair in front of the desk, Slidell might have felt intimidated had his mind not been clouded by feelings of anger and surprise.

"Monsieur La Valette, I do not understand," Slidell said.

"It's just as I said, Monsieur Slidell," the French Foreign Minister answered. "For the time being, our treaty negotiations have been put on hold by order of the emperor."

"But why?"

"He gave no specific reason. I would imagine that he is concerned with sparking a backlash of public opinion. I'm sure you read the same newspapers I do, Monsieur. Surely you can sense the mood of the people."

Slidell frowned. He had, indeed, been studying the newspapers as intently as ever and what he had been reading had been far from comforting. Before the insurgent force in New Iberia had finally been destroyed, the Paris papers had reported on the fighting with breathless wonder, as if it were an epic battle rather than a mopping up exercise. Worse, virtually every headline now was about the

Lowell trial taking place in New Orleans. Slidell couldn't understand it. Granted, the French took an unusual interest in events in Louisiana, with its large French population, but what was happening now was excessive. It was almost as if, for lack of any significant news, the Lowell trial was the only thing the editors had with which to attract readers.

Worse still, the stories were favorable to Lowell almost without exception. His arrest and trial had become a colossal *cause célèbre* that had captured the imagination of France. Editorials had been written in half a dozen Paris papers and others out in the provinces calling for Lowell to be spared from the death penalty or simply released altogether. One piece had even compared Lowell to Joan of Arc.

Slidell was used to hearing ill-informed statements against slavery made by foreigners. It was part of his job. Yet it was surprising and disheartening to see the outpouring of support for a man who was, as far as Slidell was concerned, a criminal and a terrorist. Lowell's actions had led to the deaths of hundreds of Southern soldiers. Yet the French papers were cheering him as though he were a hero.

"I know the mood of the people as well as you, Monsieur," Slidell replied. "But why should the emperor allow the fickleness of the public to sway him in this matter? The international situation remains the same today as it was when you and I first began negotiating the treaty. You want our help in Mexico. We want your protection from the United States. This is all still true. Why, then, should we suspend negotiations?"

"The emperor cannot ignore public opinion."

"Why not? His illustrious uncle certainly never paid attention to the prattling of a few discontented subjects."

"The first Napoleon had the luxury of ruling as an autocrat. It's a different world now, Slidell. The present emperor has to take into account a free press and a legislature that has real power. He can't just ignore the people."

Slidell grunted but said nothing in response.

La Valette went on. "I don't see why you're so surprised, Slidell. Half of your own time is spent wining and dining newspaper editors to print favorable stories about the Confederacy. You know the importance of public opinion as well as I do. You have no right to complain just because it seems to be turning against you."

"It's temporary. A month from now, no one will even remember the name Charles Russell Lowell."

"I wouldn't count on that. Have you heard the news from Marseilles?"

Slidell's eyes narrowed and he became even more worried. "What's that?"

"The local board of trade is organizing an effort to end the importation of cotton and tobacco from the Confederacy. They say that the Lowell Affair is shining so bright a light on slavery that they cannot, in good conscience, continue doing business with you Southerners."

Slidell snorted in contempt. "They're just cowards who are afraid that the agitation of the abolitionists is going to cost them money."

"What difference does the cause of their action make? It is the action itself that is important. This movement in Marseilles may just be the beginning. That particular board of trade is circulating a letter to other boards asking them to join them. Similar movements are taking root in Britain and other European nations, from what I understand from my people."

Slidell kept his face impassive, but he knew that La Valette was speaking the truth. Minister Haynes had written him from London to warn him that such measures were afoot in both Glasgow and Liverpool, two port cities that were critical to Confederate trade. According to his last letter, Haynes himself had seen a public meeting in London attended by over two thousand people, which had called for the end of slavery and the immediate release of Lowell. The attachés in other European capitals were saying more or less the same thing. The only place where anti-Confederate demonstrations were not being reported was in St. Petersburg.

"I would like to speak to the emperor himself, if that's possible," Slidell said.

La Valette shrugged. "I'll ask him. But as you know, he's exceedingly busy. Have your secretary file a request for an appointment. You know the procedure, yes?"

"Of course," Slidell replied. He had never been asked to go through some administrative routine before. "How long will this hold on the negotiations last?" Slidell asked.

"It will be maintained until the emperor says differently. This is his decision."

Slidell sensed something in La Valette's voice. "You disagree with him?"

"It's not my place to agree or disagree with the emperor. He commands me and I do his bidding."

"But you advise him. You can tell him that you think this is foolish."

"I have already given him my advice."

"Which was?" Slidell knew he was being rude and that La Valette might take offense. Yet he was grasping at straws.

La Valette sighed. "Under ordinary circumstances, I would probably tell you that the advice I give to His Imperial Majesty is confidential. However, I do not think he would mind if I told you that I approve of this decision. So long as the attention of the public is fixated on the question of slavery in your country, it simply isn't appropriate for us to continue discussing the possibility of a treaty of alliance with you." He paused before continuing. "It would be perceived by the people as, shall we say, dirtying our hands."

The last statement was a calculated insult, Slidell knew. He had not often been so clearly snubbed since his days in the United States Senate, when he had regularly clashed with Yankee abolitionists. It was not a feeling he enjoyed.

"If there is nothing else, Monsieur, I shall take my leave," Slidell said.

"Very well, Monsieur." La Valette rose from his chair and shook Slidell's proffered hand. Without waiting for him to leave the room, the French Foreign Minister sat back down in his chair and resumed reading some papers on his desk.

Slidell was offended as he turned his back and walked out of the room, leaning on his gold-headed walking stick. It felt as though he were being treated like the representative of an insignificant power, such as Portugal or Greece, rather than the Confederate States of America. He knew that President Davis would not be happy when he reported what had happened. Most likely, the man would be furious.

After winding his way through the maze of hallways leading out of the Minister's office, each door being opened for him and closed behind him by liveried servants, Slidell emerged onto the Quai d'Orsay. To the south, he could see the rising Dôme des Invalides, where the first Napoleon Bonaparte was buried, the one in whose shadow the current emperor labored. Compared to the man who had conquered Europe before he turned forty, the reigning ruler was a pigmy. Slidell had the humorous thought that he should walk over to the tomb and remonstrate with the body contained in the great coffin about the foolishness of the conqueror's nephew.

Michel, ever the faithful valet, was standing by his hansom cab, having waited there the entire time. Without a word, he opened the door and helped Slidell as the older man climbed inside. A few moments later, with a snap of the tiny whip, the horse began to walk and the journey home had begun.

Slidell would have to see Napoleon III in person. That much was clear. Only a personal interview with the emperor would allow him to argue the Confederacy's case directly and perhaps persuade the ruler of France to change his mind and resume negotiations. Yet he knew that the emperor would do his best to put him off. He would hide behind his own Foreign Minister and would make every excuse to avoid Slidell at social functions.

His stomach churned with a complex combination of unpleasant emotions. He was not accustomed to defeat. It was obvious that the suspension of talks on the treaty might be a prelude to their abandonment altogether, which would mean the end of Slidell's dreams for a Franco-Confederate alliance and the death of everything for which he had been working for the last few years. Rather than end his life on a high note, he might go to his reward as a disgraced figure.

He could only imagine how the other members of the diplomatic corps were going to be speaking of him when news leaked out that the Franco-Confederate talks had been broken off. Minister Blair was surely going to have a good laugh at his expense. Slidell might plead illness to avoid the next few social occasions, but he could not hide from them forever without suffering an even greater embarrassment. He could not neglect his duty, even if it meant suffering humiliation.

Then, he had a new thought altogether.

September 13, Afternoon
Ballard House, Richmond, Virginia

"Is there any good news?" Breckinridge asked the three men in the room. The entire committee had been unable to meet, so Breckinridge had sat down with Secretary Trenholm, Senator Hill, and his running mate Congressman Kemper.

"I'll be honest with you," replied Trenholm. "Not really."

"The endorsement of Ambassador Miles is a welcome development," Hill offered. "Very much a surprise, I must say, but welcome nonetheless."

Trenholm shook his head. "He's a South Carolinian and, though he carries some weight there, it won't be remotely enough to swing the state in our direction. In most other states it will go more or less unnoticed. Besides, people are already saying that he did it simply to secure the post as Secretary of State."

Breckinridge hoped his placid facial expression concealed his disgust. There was no undoing what Benjamin had done, but that did not mean he had to like it.

"If we're looking for positive news, we can at least give thanks that we're on the ballot in all eleven states," Kemper said. "The SRP filed a legal challenge against us in Mississippi, but the judge threw it out. Old friend of Jefferson Davis's, he is."

"Well, that's something, at least," Breckinridge said. "Every Confederate citizen will get to choose between me and Beauregard."

"Yes, but from the letters I'm receiving, it appears that the people are leaning increasingly towards Beauregard. The tide is settling strongly against us."

Trenholm, who had taken the mantle of committee chairman since Benjamin's departure, went on to describe an increasingly desperate political situation. Gordon had returned to Georgia and was making a series of pro-Breckinridge speeches throughout the state, but his audiences always appeared to be smaller than those appearing at rallies supporting the Beauregard candidacy. In distant Texas, Reagan was reporting strong SRP organizational efforts and comparatively mild ones for Breckinridge. The same was true of almost every state. Only in Virginia and North Carolina did the fight appear to be even.

The defection of Isham Harris had been devastating. He had given an interview to the press in which he had described Breckinridge's hesitation in ordering the final assault on the insurgent stronghold in New Iberia, his comments suggesting that this was due to some sort of desire to negotiate with Saul rather than fight him. The story had been reprinted in several other newspapers and many SRP speakers were denouncing him for being soft on the slave insurrection.

As he had listened to the members of his committee talk, it slowly dawned on Breckinridge that they had given up hope of winning in Alabama or Mississippi, placing those two states into the same unwinnable category as Louisiana and South Carolina. This had been made quite clear twenty minutes earlier, when Senator Hill had suggested that the committee stop sending money to local efforts in those two states in order to concentrate on Tennessee and Georgia.

As far as money was concerned, the playing field was a little more even. Breckinridge had finally been let in on the secret that government employees had been asked to contribute ten percent of their pay to the campaign, at the risk of getting fired. He was furious at first, but by the time he had learned of it, the operation had been going on for over a month. It was a *fait accompli*. Moreover, he had learned that not many employees seemed to mind the requested contribution, as they were genuinely Breckinridge supporters almost to a man.

The money that funded the SRP, by contrast, was largely being contributed by wealthy plantation owners in the Deep South. In 1860, when he was running for President of the United States, these people had been Breckinridge's strongest supporters. Since the Toronto Peace Conference, they had viewed him as the devil incarnate. He himself did not feel that he had changed his views or political positions all that much in the intervening time. The minds of men were strange things, indeed.

"It's New Iberia that is pushing people towards Beauregard and Toombs," said Hill. "Toombs is hammering home the idea that you appointed Morgan to the command to catch Saul simply because he's your friend and you're both Kentuckians. He's saying that if you had appointed a competent commander, Saul would have been caught many months ago and the New Iberia incident never would have happened."

Breckinridge frowned. "All lies," he said sourly.

"Of course, but the people are starting to believe it," Hill continued. "At every campaign rally, the SRP speakers are repeating the same thing. Morgan's incompetent and you appointed him out of favoritism. Given what Harris has told the newspapers, they are saying that you're soft on the insurrection and even favored letting Saul and his men go. They're also asking why it took so long for the black prisoners to be executed."

"And some of them are tying it back to the fact that you were said to have supported Cleburne's proposal for enlisting slaves in the army back during the war," Trenholm said.

"Well, I'm not going to respond to that," Breckinridge said.

"Perhaps you might make some sort of gesture suggesting a reprimand of Morgan?" Trenholm suggested. "And release a statement that, in retrospect, you think Cleburne's plan was a bad idea?"

"No," Breckinridge said firmly. "First of all, that would be dishonorable. Secondly, this is not the time to appear weak. If Beauregard's people want to hammer me, I need to project an image of strength."

"Benjamin's resignation from the Cabinet has made all of this much worse than it had to be," said Kemper. "I don't know what he thinks he's doing, but he has caused us an awful lot of trouble. It was well known that he was one of your key supporters, and suddenly he leaves the government and runs off to defend an abolitionist terrorist? Has the man lost his mind?"

"Perhaps," Breckinridge replied with a wry grin. "But there was no stopping him. Believe me, I tried. His mind was made up. For whatever reason, he thinks that he's doing what's right for the country."

"You think so?" Kemper asked. "Has it ever occurred to you that maybe Benjamin has been in Beauregard's pocket all along and this was just his way of ensuring your defeat at the polls in November?"

Breckinridge looked at Kemper in some surprise. The possibility had never entered his mind. He had been a politician for a long time and had gone up against some of the most unscrupulous opponents imaginable. Benjamin was certainly one of the craftiest political operators Breckinridge had ever met, yet he could not entertain the idea that Kemper had suggested. Benjamin had stood by Jefferson Davis since the earliest days of the Confederacy and his vision for the country had always been at odds with the Fire-Eaters. The anti-Semitism of the Fire-Eaters alone would have been enough to keep Benjamin out of their ranks.

"This is a bad time to start becoming paranoid, Jim," Breckinridge replied.

"I agree," Trenholm chimed in. "Benjamin is acting strangely, but he is not our enemy."

"I hope you're right," Kemper replied.

"Let us return to the matter at hand," Trenholm said. "Toombs is painting you as a secret abolitionist. He points out everywhere that you own no slaves yourself and picks at your role in the Toronto peace talks. Benjamin's actions and Harris's interview have only given more weight to this argument. You must do something to counter what he is saying."

"I'm not going to cave in to these bastards on anything," Breckinridge replied, irritation entering his voice. "What am I supposed to do? Go out and buy a random slave?"

"That might actually be a good idea," Kemper said. "Just a house servant."

"People aren't stupid," Breckinridge replied. "They'd say I only did it to shut Toombs up."

"In any case, you don't want to ignore Toombs. He's the SRP vice presidential candidate. He's not going to go away and people are listening to him."

Breckinridge nodded. "I agree. I have been giving this a good deal of thought." He paused for a moment, a calculated effect. "As you gentlemen know, the annual meeting of the Orphan Society will be on the last day of this month. I intend to use my speech to directly and forcefully challenge the accusations that have been leveled against me by Toombs and the rest of the SRP."

The three other men looked at one another in surprise. Breckinridge had expected this. After an awkward moment's silence, Hill replied.

"Are you not worried that this might draw attention to the Orphan Society itself? The SRP has not made it as much of an issue in this campaign as slavery, to be sure, but it has come up occasionally. Many people feel that Kentuckians have an unequal influence with the Confederate government. Some people speak of the Orphan Society in the same way that many people spoke out against the Freemasons back in the 1830s."

"People can see conspiracies whenever they wish," Breckinridge replied. "I think most Confederates value the sacrifices of their Kentucky brethren, who fought and suffered for the Confederacy even though their own state did not secede."

"Do you not think that making such a speech would appear inappropriate?" Kemper asked. "It's not proper for a presidential candidate to directly campaign for himself."

"I was asked to be the main speaker months ago, before I even announced my candidacy," Breckinridge replied.

"I think it is a good idea," Trenholm said. "Unorthodox, perhaps, but not overly so. But I think you need to carefully consider exactly what kind of speech you will be giving."

"What do you mean?" Breckinridge asked.

Trenholm looked thoughtful for a moment before answering. "It's not enough for you to respond to the SRP attacks. You need to do that, of course, but you need to do more. You need to counterattack, to use the military term. Toombs made statements damn near to treasonous during the war. He's an utter drunkard. Go after the bastard."

"I agree with that," Kemper said, nodding. "We've been so worried about being attacked that we haven't really done any attacking ourselves. The people need to be reminded why Toombs wasn't made president back in 1861. And

Beauregard? The man's a buffoon who think he's Napoleon. I don't think the people want two such men at the head of the country.

"Gordon, Reagan, and all our other surrogates are already saying that," Breckinridge replied. "It's one thing for the presidential candidate to defend himself. Quite another to attack the opposition."

"Unless it is articulated by you, the people won't hear it," Kemper replied. "It will just get lost amid all the ink the SRP is spilling in their attacks on you. For that matter, maybe I'd better get out there, too, just like Toombs has done."

Breckinridge frowned even as he nodded his agreement. He did not like politics to become a punching match. He would have infinitely preferred a calm and polite debate over the issues. Sadly, the world in which he lived was such that politics almost always became a no-holds-barred slugging match. Whatever else he was, Breckinridge was not a man who was going to take a punch without swinging back in return.

"One other thing," Kemper said.

"Yes?"

"Don't fixate on the opposition. Lay out your own vision. You have to make the case to the country for why you are the best choice. The SRP organized itself and had a big convention, so they have an official party platform that people can look to. The newspapers reprinted the whole damn thing in July. We have no such thing. What is your policy? What do you want to do if you are elected? The people need to hear it."

"I agree," Trenhom said. "Truth be told, John, you haven't really been all that forthcoming about what your governing policies would be. You say that you want peace and stability in order to focus on the economic recovery, and that's what your surrogates are repeating everywhere they speak. But having a detailed statement about your policies, rather like a party platform, would be a Godsend to the campaign. The newspapers would reprint it everywhere and people would clamber to read it. At this late stage, it would give your candidacy a boost that it desperately needs."

"Yes, I think you may be right," Breckinridge said.

Hill pursed his lips and slowly shook his head.

"Senator Hill?" Breckinridge asked. "What is your concern?"

"I don't disagree with the idea of making this big speech. But here is what I fear. You are a good speaker, John, but everybody has their bad days. Say you get up there and make the best damn speech anybody's heard since Cicero. That will certainly give us a boost and even the odds. But if your speech falls flat, that will be it. It will all be over. At this late stage, there won't be any time to recover from a fiasco."

Breckinridge thought for a moment. "Well, then I'll just have to make sure that my speech is a good one, won't I?"

September 15, Evening
McFadden Ranch, Texas

The area around the ranch house now resembled an army camp from the war. Tents were pitched everywhere and men wearing butternut jackets and gray trousers sat around campfires, drinking coffee and cooking meat. Enfield rifles were kept in four-weapon stacks, with bayonets interlocked, following exactly the camp regulations they all knew so well. Most of the men were armed with pistols and knives as well.

McFadden was vastly reassured by the presence of the veterans. He had been apprehensive from the beginning, but when the would-be assailant had come onto his ranch and threatened his wife, uneasiness had become genuine dread. He could not remain on the ranch himself if he was going to be campaigning in Waco. The only option had been to accept his comrades' offer to set up a permanent guard over his home.

At any given time, a dozen or more men were staying on his ranch, with a system in place to rotate guard duties each day and night. Some of the men participating were from his own 7th Texas, while most of the others were from the other units that had served under Granbury. A few veterans from other units had asked to join in as well.

Most veterans in the county had lined up behind the candidacies of McFadden and Collett, but not all of them. Some, disproportionately men who had served in the Trans-Mississippi, had aligned themselves with Roden. Many of these men, McFadden's allies complained, were siding with the judge merely because he was dispensing money and offering them reduced tax payments. Service in the Confederate Army during the war did not, in itself, make a man good and decent. It had more than its fair share of rogues, too.

The sun was about to vanish behind the western horizon when McFadden, riding Yellowjacket, came within view of his home. Thaddeus was marching back and forth across the lawn in front of the ranch house, using a stick in place of a rifle, to the delight of the soldiers. Near as McFadden could tell, his son was having the time of his life, with more playmates than he ever could have dreamed of. A soldier who was frolicking about with him saw McFadden approach and pointed him out to the little boy. Thaddeus, upon seeing him, ran out towards Yellowjacket, shouting his greetings as he always did.

Annie was on the porch, engaged in what looked like a friendly conversation with one of the men from the 5th Texas Infantry, who was standing a respectful distance from her. McFadden had no concerns about leaving his young, beautiful wife in the company of so many soldiers. He trusted her faithfulness without the slightest hesitation and she had never been a flirty girl in any event. Moreover, while his old comrades could be a rowdy bunch, none of them would have dared make approaches to Annie. They not only knew they would be would be rejected, but they knew they would then have to face McFadden's wrath.

As he reined in in front of the house, two soldiers walked up and offered to take care of Yellowjacket for him. McFadden awkwardly agreed. It felt strange to be in a position of authority again, even though he had commanded some of these men before. In his mind, they were all neighbors and on an equal footing. Yet as their candidate and the de facto head of the effort to reclaim Granbury County from Judge Roden, he was being looked upon as a leader. He never enjoyed the feeling, but he had grown used to it during the war. He would simply have to grow used to it again.

Annie greeted him happily and he sat down to a meal of pork cooked over the campfire. It reminded him of how he had eaten during the war. His mind went back to the heady days following the Battle of Atlanta, when Annie's father had donated livestock and produce to the men of the 7th Texas and given them the best meals they enjoyed at any time during the war. It was not long before Collett arrived to discuss the recent events in their two coordinated campaigns. McFadden insisted, however, that he have some pork and ale before they got down to business. The warm feeling of camaraderie was simply too pleasant to ignore.

After the sun had gone down, Annie put Thaddeus to sleep while Collett and McFadden sat down at the table, a mug of ale in the hands of each.

"Your day was long?" Collett asked.

"Long but fruitful," McFadden answered. "I finally met with that group of local shop owners. What do they call themselves?"

"The chamber of commerce?"

"Yes, that's the group. They wanted to ask me what I would do in Austin to help the local economy here in Granbury County."

"And what did you tell them?"

"Just as we discussed. I told them of our desire to keep taxes at a minimum for all Texans and to improve the roads that link Waco with other parts of the state. And I talked about our plan to seek state funds to clear the Brazos River of rocks and debris to make it navigable all the way from Waco to the Gulf of Mexico, which would make it much easier for local farmers and ranchers to get their goods to market."

This plan was one that McFadden and Collett had worked out together over several nights, using information from Austin provided by Postmaster Reagan. Judge Roden and his group of cronies had never discussed what seemed like an obvious project for the betterment of the community. Either they lacked the imagination for it, or they simply didn't care.

"And what was their reaction?" Collett asked.

"They loved the idea."

Collett smiled. "Well, that's good. Frankly, I think the very fact that they wanted to meet with you in the first place was a very good sign. Shows that they aren't afraid of Roden and that they think we stand a good chance of winning."

"That's what I think, too."

Collett went on to describe his activities for the day. He had joined the door-knockers in the morning, before the heat became too much to bear, walking around Waco neighborhoods and speaking to as many voters as possible. Overall, he felt very positive about the reactions he had received. During the afternoon, he had written letters to the pastors of the various churches around the community, inviting them to come and speak to him and McFadden about any issues they felt were important.

The two men were about to begin planning their activities for the next few days when one of the soldiers came in. Out of habit, he called them by their ranks.

"Captain McFadden! Major Collett! Come quick!"

"What is it?" McFadden asked.

"A big group of riders is approaching. All armed!"

They rose from the table and walked quickly out onto the porch. The soldiers in the yard had all risen and grabbed their rifles, ready for trouble. It seemed likely that they would get it, too, for McFadden saw by the light of torches and campfires that a large posse of men was approaching, some white and some Hispanic, half again as large as the group of soldiers in the yard. Riding at their head were Rufus Walker and Lucius Roden. It was the first time he had actually seen the judge in months. McFadden touched the Navy Colt in its holster to make sure it was still there.

"Evening to you, McFadden," Roden said scornfully.

"What do you want?"

Roden chuckled. "I see the months since our last talk haven't done anything to make you more polite."

"Not in the mood, Roden. What do you want?"

"Well, Deputy Sheriff Walker here needs to talk to you about something."

"About what?"

"About a murder."

McFadden's stomach tightened. He knew that the body he had buried behind the ranch house would come back to haunt him in some ways. His mind raced as he tried to think of what to do. To buy time, it seemed best to feign ignorance.

"Murder? What are you talking about? Whose murder?"

"Friend of mine, actually. As you can see, I'm all broken up about it. Fella went by the name Ed Adams." He gestured to one of the men of the posse, who dismounted from his horse and approached McFadden, holding out a slightly torn photograph. "Know him?"

McFadden took the photograph and looked. It was the same man he had buried the month before. "Never seen him before in my life."

"You sure about that?" Roden asked.

"Yeah, McFadden, you sure about that?" Walker echoed.

Both men leaned forward in their saddles, grinning like school bullies. The entire thing had been a set-up, McFadden could see. Adams, if that was even his real name, had been nothing but a dimwitted simpleton sent onto his property so that he would be killed and McFadden would be blamed for it. Simply getting rid of McFadden himself would have been too obvious, so Roden and Walker had decided on an altogether more subtle approach. They apparently had not cared in the slightest that it cost someone his life.

Annie stepped out onto the porch and it suddenly occurred to McFadden that she had been the only person at the ranch when Adams appeared. He himself had been in Waco at the time. According to what Annie had told him, Adams had suggested that he was going to rape her and that he said the judge wouldn't do anything to him if he did. It dawned on McFadden what the actual plan of Roden and Walker had been. He was willing to let Adams molest and assault Annie, knowing that McFadden would then hunt down and kill him in retaliation, or at least try to do so. Roden would then have had the excuse he needed to arrest McFadden and remove him from the scene before the election. They had not counted on Annie being willing to use deadly force in her own defense.

It was all so nasty and foul that McFadden almost couldn't stand it. He moved his hand towards his gun.

"Don't!" Collett said urgently. "It's what they want. Stay calm."

The men in the yard looked grim. None of them had raised their weapons into firing positions, but all gripped their Enfields tightly. It reminded McFadden of the tension he had always felt right before a battle. The men of Walker's posse, all mounted on horses, stayed a short distance away from the front porch, but had spread themselves out in order to hem McFadden, Collett, and their men in. If it came to a fight, Walker's men would have the advantage of elevation and of having their targets in a crossfire.

Roden turned to Walker. "Want to have a look around, Rufus?"

"He has no right," McFadden said sharply.

"Oh, don't I?" Walker asked. "That's right. I need the permission of the county judge." He looked at Roden. "How about it, Judge? Do I have permission?"

"You do, sir," Roden said with a chuckle. "You do, indeed."

Walker kicked his horse into a walk and began to circle around to the back of the ranch house, trailed by five other riders, two of whom carried torches. Without waiting for directions, two of McFadden's men moved quickly to block their path, their rifles held at the ready.

"Out of the way!" Walker roared, quickly pulling out his revolver and leveling it at the closest man. "I'm Deputy Sheriff. Judge says so. You're interfering with the enforcement of the law. If you don't stand aside, I will shoot you down where you stand."

Three of McFadden's men instantly aimed their rifles at Walker, unwilling to see their comrades threatened. For a brief moment, he feared that either they or Walker would be shot. If that happened, there would be an instant bloodbath in front of his house. He turned to Annie, who was still standing just outside the door.

"Go inside," he said urgently. "Take Thaddeus and get into the shelter."

"James," she whispered. "I need to tell you—"

"Quickly!" he said harshly. She looked deeply into his eyes for just a moment, a hint of reproach apparent, then disappeared inside.

"Stay here," McFadden said quickly to Collett. "Don't let the bastards in my house."

"Don't worry," Collett replied instantly.

McFadden walked after Walker, trying to ignore Roden's ugly and leering face looking down on him from his horse. Some of the veterans followed him, which in turn prompted more of Walker's posse to kick their horses into motion. A trail of armed men, mixed between the two groups, trailed after Walker as he rode around the ranch house.

"Over there," one of the other riders said to Walker, pointing. To his alarm and astonishment, he was pointing precisely to the spot where McFadden had buried the body the previous month. This could only mean that someone had been watching the ranch on the day the man had been shot. He damned himself for his foolishness. He had never imagined the depths of the depravity to his Roden and Walker could go and now he was about to pay the penalty.

Two of the horsemen dismounted and, at Walker's direction, began digging at the spot. Some veterans glanced over at McFadden, as though asking permission to stop them, but he said nothing and so they remained still, simply watching. He figured it would take them only a few minutes before they uncovered the body and he felt his life and world falling to pieces around him. They wouldn't bother with explaining how the man had come to be on the McFadden Ranch. Judge Roden was the law and he would simply make up whatever story he wished. With a dead body on display for all to see, McFadden was going to be found guilty of murder. Almost certainly, Roden would sentence him to be strung up in front of the Granbury County Courthouse in Waco.

There would certainly be violence, McFadden realized. His comrades would not be willing to see him arrested on what was obviously a trumped up charge. If Roden threw him in jail, they would simply break him out again. If Roden's deputy sheriffs and the men Walker had brought up from Mexico resisted, which they would have to do to maintain Roden's control, there would inevitably be shooting and people would get killed. The situation was about to reach the breaking point.

Whatever happened, his candidacy was over. Collett's would be over, too. If chaos and violence swept the county, Judge Roden, as the major authority figure, would be able to justify the use of extreme measures to restore order. If anything, the man might be hoping for McFadden's comrades to resort to violence so that he would have an excuse to clamp down on all of them.

As the men continued shoveling, McFadden's main concern became Annie and Thaddeus. He might ask some of his friends to escort them to Austin or Houston, or some other place where they might be safe. Whatever else happened, he had to make sure they were protected. He was tormented by the fact that if he had never challenged Roden, none of this would have happened. It no longer mattered whether it had been the right thing to do or not, because everything would be over the moment the men found the first sign of the body, which could only be seconds away.

It was at this moment that it first occurred to McFadden that it seemed to be taking a long time for the men to shovel away enough dirt to uncover anything. He remembered exactly how deeply he had buried the man and it seemed strange that nothing had yet been found. He also noticed that the expression on Walker's face had gone from gloating to concerned. McFadden's eyes narrowed and realization suddenly struck him.

The body was no longer there.

McFadden couldn't fathom how this could be. He wondered for a moment if coyotes might have dug it up, but if that had happened there would have been bits and pieces of human remains scattered all about the hole they would have made. Before Walker's man started digging, it did not appear as if the spot had been disturbed in any way.

More minutes passed and one of the men with a shovel grew increasingly frustrated and tired. He said something to Walker in Spanish, using an exasperated tone, but McFadden only recognized the word "here". Walker responded by loudly berating the man, the red glare of anger apparent in his face even in the dim light cast by the torches. After more yelling, the digger resumed his work with an increased intensity. McFadden watched in astonishment as he kept burrowing away, going deeper into the ground than he remembered going when he buried the body. There was no mistaking it now. The body was gone.

Walker kicked his horse into a walk and moved closer to McFadden.

"Where'd you put it?"

"Put what?"

"The body, dammit!"

"I told you! I don't know anything about a body!"

"Where is it?!" Walker shouted, as though the rancor in his voice could spook him into confessing.

"There is nothing here, Walker!" McFadden shouted back. "You're chasing a ghost, I think."

"I just might turn you into a ghost if you don't fess up," Walker replied, placing his hand on his gun. At this, some of McFadden's men raised their Enfields to a firing position and pulled back their hammers. For the first time since he had first met the man, McFadden thought he sensed fear in Walker. He clearly was flustered at not finding the body where he had thought it to be. Rattled men were more likely to make mistakes.

"There's nothing here and you know it, Walker!" McFadden said, keeping his own confusion from his voice. "I don't know what the hell kind of game you and the judge are playing at, but since there's nothing here, why don't you get the hell off my ranch?"

Walker kicked his horse, making it rear up and neigh loudly. McFadden took a step back, momentarily fearful that the horse might kick him. Walker turned the animal and kicked it into a quick canter, rushing back around to the front of the house. His men followed him and McFadden and his comrades scurried behind as quickly as they could. When he rounded the house, he could see Walker engaged in an urgent conversation with Judge Roden, whose expression was as flummoxed as Walker's had been a few moments before.

"Search everything, boys!" Roden yelled. "Tear every room apart!" The men of the posse began dismounting and storming up to the front door.

"Damned if you will!" Collett shouted. "Why don't you leave my friend alone, Roden? Ain't nothing here and you know it."

"Let your boy fight his own battles, Collett," Roden replied.

"We fight our battles together," Collett said. Then he turned and spoke loudly to the veterans. "Don't we, boys?" There was a roar of enthusiastic approval as the men held their guns high. The posse held back and looked to Roden for confirmation of the order.

McFadden walked up and placed his hand on Collett's shoulder. "We don't want any violence," he whispered.

"So what do we do? Just let him have his people rummage through your house? He has no right."

"He's still the county judge. Legally, he has the right."

"We're on the frontier out here, Jimmy," Collett said. "Let's just do it the old-fashioned way and fight it out. I think we'd win."

McFadden turned and looked at his men, clutching their rifles, just waiting for the word to open fire on the despised Roden and his posse. For an endless second, he weighed the odds. He could probably defend his house, but what then? Granbury County was filled with other veterans who supported their cause and would probably rally to them the instant they heard that a fight had broken out. Roden had his share of veterans he might call upon and Walker had obviously brought a reasonable number of armed men up from Mexico, but even together they probably would not match the number of supporters of McFadden and Collett. Moreover, while the men of the opposing camp were experienced fighters, his own followers were certainly better and had the priceless advantage of *esprit de corps*.

Assuming that fighting did break out and his men were victorious, McFadden and Collett could take control of the county and make sure that the elections were held on schedule. Even if they did nothing to influence the results, they would probably win, for Roden and Walker would not be able to intimidate voters any longer, if they survived the fight at all. Yet it was impossible to say what the politicians down in Austin would end up doing. If the SRP won control of the state government, they would probably annul the results and demand a new election. If Breckinridge's people emerged the winners, they might allow the results to stand. If nothing else, fighting seemed like a better option than letting Roden and Walker steal the election.

McFadden was about to shout to Roden that he refused to allow his home to be entered, when another voice was heard.

"You can come on in, Judge Roden!" Annie's voice called from the porch. McFadden turned and was stunned to see her standing there, holding Thaddeus in her arms, her expression one of utter disinterest. "Just you, though. None of these boys. I don't want mud on my floor, you understand?"

With that, she turned and walked back inside. McFadden was stunned. He turned to look at Judge Roden, who appeared just as surprised as he was. Nevertheless, after a few seconds of confusion, he awkwardly dismounted from his horse and started walking towards the door. McFadden followed.

Annie was sitting at the table, bouncing Thaddeus on her knee. "Here's how it's going to work, Judge," she said as they entered. "Your men can only come into my home if each one of them has one of my husband's friends beside him at all times and if you give your word that they will not damage our home or any of our possessions in any way. I worked hard to build this house and I won't have it wrecked. You won't find anything, but if you want to waste your time looking, that's your business."

Roden looked at McFadden. "Your wife gives the orders around here?" he asked sarcastically.

He didn't answer right away, as he mulled the idea over in his mind. It would allow the letter of the law to be followed, because Roden's orders for the house to be searched would be obeyed. Yet with his own men observing everything being done, he could be reassured that his property would be respected. Even if McFadden wasn't willing to use violence, he was willing to allow the simple possibility of violence work in his favor. If he accepted Annie's idea and Roden refused it, ordering his men into the house anyway, McFadden's veterans would surely resist with force. Roden knew that, too, which gave McFadden the advantage.

"Seems to me like my wife has a good idea, Roden," McFadden said. "How about we listen to her?"

A disappointed and frustrated expression came over Roden's face. "Fine," he said sullenly. He walked back out onto the porch and called his men in, asking some of the veterans to come in as well. For the next hour, every room of McFadden's house was searched. The posse went through every nook and cranny, but the presence of the veterans kept them from handling anything roughly. It also ensured that none of them attempted to plant false evidence.

"Ugly!" Thaddeus said, pointing to Roden. "Bad man!"

Time passed. McFadden stood with his arms folded across his chest, while Roden and Walker quietly whispered to one another on the other side of the room. One by one, the posse members came to tell the judge that they had found nothing out of the ordinary and certainly no signs of a dead body. Roden's expression grew more and more irritated.

"Let's go, boys!" Roden finally said, waving everyone to the door. His posse quickly lined up behind him and followed him out the door. A few men had been left outside to hold keep an eye on the horses and their torches continued to illuminate the area. Roden was helped onto his horse by some of his men, while Walker quickly climbed into his saddle without assistance.

McFadden, Collett, and Annie stood on the porch, surrounded by their friends, and watched as the posse prepared to depart. McFadden felt a profound sense of relief. Tomorrow morning, word of what had happened would begin to spread through Waco and the surrounding county and Roden would be made to look like a fool. It would discredit the judge in the eyes of the people and, since nothing incriminating had been found, reinforce his already strong image as a bully who abused his power.

"This ain't over, McFadden!" Roden said as he turned his horse. "Mark my words!"

With that, he kicked his horse into a canter and rode off, followed by Walker and the men of the posse. As their torches faded in the distance and the sounds of their horses' hooves died away, a profound silence descended upon the McFadden ranch. The veterans watched the posse depart, then looked up silently at the three people standing on the porch. Slowly, they walked back to their tents and camp stools, stoked the fires, and quietly resumed what they had been doing before Roden's arrival.

"When this is all over, I hope Judge Roden roasts in hell," Annie said firmly.

"I have no doubt that he will," Collett said. "He's viler than the worst Yankee we ever tangled with."

McFadden merely grunted, not wanting to speak. He was still confused as to what had happened to the body. Though Annie's careful ministrations over the years had brought him back from the brink of outright atheism, he was not generally a believer in divine intervention. Nevertheless, the disappearance of the body had all the signs of a miracle. He shuddered to think of how differently things would have gone had Roden's man dug up the dead man.

"I'm going home," Collett said. "Want to make sure that none of the posse head toward my place. Will you two be okay?"

"Yes," McFadden replied quickly. "We have our boys here. Thank you, old friend."

After a quick handshake, Collett left the porch, mounted his horse, and was off into the darkness. Annie turned and went back inside, still cradling Thaddeus in her arms. McFadden followed.

"Are you all right, love?" he asked.

"Yes," she replied. "Just a bit shaken. I thought they might burn the house."

563

"Our friends would have stopped them."

"Yes, I suppose they would have. But then there would have been a battle. I wouldn't have known what to do or where to take Thaddeus."

"You might have gone down into the shelter like I told you to."

"Well, someone had to stop the fight from breaking out."

"I just don't know what on earth happened to that man's body."

"I got rid of it."

These words, spoken so glibly by Annie, stunned McFadden. It took him a moment to respond. "What do you mean you got rid of it?"

"I thought something like tonight was going to happen. That Roden's men would come looking for it and use it against you. So I got rid of it."

"You dug it up yourself?" he asked, incredulous.

"Yes," she said simply. "Early one morning, before dawn. You'd already left for town."

"My God! Where is it now?"

"It's gone. I cut it up and fed it to the pigs. That ate every bit of it. Serves the man right, if you ask me."

McFadden's mouth dropped open in astonishment. There had been a time during the war, before he met Annie, when his soul had been so dark and angry that he had contemplated mutilating the corpses of the enemy soldiers he had killed, wanting to take their scalps in the manner of the Comanche warriors who had slaughtered his family. Yet he never went through with it. The thought had never occurred to him to dismember the body of the man who had threatened Annie. By disposing of the corpse in such a manner, it might as well never have existed.

She turned and looked him deeply in the eyes, challenging him. He suddenly saw his wife as never before. He had adored her almost from the moment he first saw her and had quickly fallen in her love with. She had been like a ray of light that had illuminated his own heart. Yet she had also seemed vulnerable and in need of protection, which he had been only too willing to offer.

Now, a different woman altogether stood in front of him. He never would have imagined that she had the toughness to touch a corpse, much less cut one to pieces. He knew that he could never have done it.

"Why, Annie?"

"I will do whatever it takes to protect you, James. And Thaddeus. Roden and Walker and their men? They're ruthless. I think it's time that you starting acting a bit ruthless in return."

"Ruthless," Thaddeus repeated in his toddler voice.

CHAPTER FOURTEEN

September 18, Noon
Confederate States Capitol, Richmond, Virginia

"Senator Toombs of Georgia is recognized."

Toombs rose to his feet, looking grave. It would be his first speech in the Senate for some time. Before the last regular session had recessed in June, there had been grumbling that Toombs was spending more time and energy on the election rather than on his duties as a senator. He was determined to put those tales to an end and was confident he would be able to do so.

As he glanced around quickly, assessing the mood of his fellow senators, Toombs took in the scene. It had taken some time to get used to the Senate Chamber in Richmond, but he had decided that he liked it better than the one in the United States Capitol. It was not as large, but it was grand and ornate enough for Toombs's taste. Besides, every Confederate senator represented a slave-owning state, which made the body infinitely preferable to the old one in Washington, which had become polluted with abolitionist agitators like Thaddeus Stevens and Charles Sumner.

This did not mean that there were not enemies to his vision of the Confederacy as a slave-owning, aristocratic republic, of course. As he inhaled deeply and prepared to speak, Toombs hoped that he was about to deal those enemies a heavy blow.

"Thank you, Mr. President," Toombs said to Senator Robert Jemison of Alabama, who, in his capacity as President Pro Tem of the Senate, was in the dais. "I shall endeavor to keep my remarks brief and to the point. I have often been accused in the past of enjoying the sound of my own voice rather too much. I should greatly dislike to add any credibility to such scurrilous rumors."

There was chuckling throughout the chamber, even among those members whom Toombs knew to be his enemies. He glanced up at the reporters and observers in the visitor's gallery and was gratified to see almost all of them staring down at him with intense anticipation. The special session of Congress was unusual enough to have garnered considerable attention in the newspapers. He was about to give them significantly more copy with which to work.

"In the last month and a half, we have been witnesses to scenes in Louisiana the likes of which have never been seen in the South. Like the Spartans of old, we have faced the terror of servile insurrection before. We use the names of villains like Gabriel Prosser, Denmark Vesey, and Nat Turner to frighten disobedient children. We have always weathered these storms in the past, thanks to the measures we have put into place to prevent and detect such conspiracies and also to the valor of our militia. But now we may add a new name, that of Saul. What the actual name of this particular villain is we may never know, nor does it matter. What does matter is that this outlaw, this adversary unleashed against us as if by the Devil himself, has laid bare many of the shortcomings of the current administration in dealing with this terrible danger."

"Will the Senator yield?" a voice boomed.

Toombs turned and saw that Senator Hill had risen to his feet. The man's face was flush with anger, which did not surprise Toombs. Hill had chosen to hitch his political wagon to the horse of Davis and Breckinridge, so it was only natural that he would try to find a way to soften the attack Toombs was about to make.

"For a question?" Toombs asked. He did not want to be tricked into surrendering control of the floor.

"Yes, for a question."

"I yield to my distinguished fellow Senator from Georgia for a question."

"Senator Toombs, are you implying that President Davis is responsible for the uprising of Saul and his temporary capture of the town of New Iberia?"

Toombs smiled. "I don't mean to imply that he intended for it to happen, no. But given the facts of the matter, I cannot draw any other conclusion than that the president's lack of foresight allowed this uprising to happen. His own, and that of others."

He could see that Hill was about to say something further, but stopped himself. Toombs felt a slight tinge of disappointment. Logically, Hill's next statement would have to been to ask Toombs to identify the other people. This would have allowed Toombs to shift his assault immediately to John Breckinridge, who, as Secretary of War, bore as much responsibility for the uprising as did Davis himself. That would have been more appropriate to Toombs's agenda. Yet Hill had spotted the trap a moment before it could be sprung and had held back. It was a disappointment, but not a serious one. He would have ample opportunity to excoriate Breckinridge in due time.

"I wish to convey my sincerest congratulations to the brave men under the command of General James Longstreet who successfully destroyed the insurgent force that had occupied New Iberia and to express my condolences to the families of those who gave their lives in defense of our Confederacy during the final assault. One day, the brave men who fell at New Iberia will be remembered no less than those who perished in such battles as Manassas, Chancellorsville, Chickamauga, and Atlanta. And rightly so."

Toombs went on for some time, reading the names of many of the men who had died in the fighting and providing a few tidbits about who they had been and where they had been from. He said the names of the wives and children of some of those who had had families. It was good political theater and would help him earn the goodwill of the public. Many people around the country, he knew, were comparing him to James Kemper, the opposing vice presidential candidate. Although Kemper's prewar political career had not been as stellar as that of Toombs, his military record during the war was longer and more distinguished. Linking his own name with those of the soldiers who had died in New Iberia posed no danger and would only improve his standing.

"Why did these gallant men have to die?" Toombs ask. "I shall answer. They had to die because of the incompetence of Jefferson Davis and John C. Breckinridge."

The tension was broken with these words and angry protests rained down on Toombs from the visitor galleries, prompting Jemison to bang his gavel for silence several times. Senator Hill was again on his feet, glaring at Toombs. On the other hand, Senator Hunter and a few others were loudly applauding from their seats.

There was no need for Toombs to go on with the words he might otherwise have spoken against Davis and Breckinridge. Thanks to his speaking tour, those words had already been spread throughout the Confederacy. He would let the accusation speak for itself and now move on to the more important matter at hand.

"Mr. President, I move to lay a bill before the Senate for its consideration, a copy of which has already been filed with the clerk." He held up his own copy. "I hold it here in my hands and invite any of my fellow senators to read it whenever they wish. It is titled 'A Bill for the Prevention and Speedy Suppression of Servile Insurrection.' The recent events in Louisiana make it clear to us that strong action on this overriding matter is necessary. I look to the executive branch and I see no action. I believe, therefore, that it is up to us in the Congress, and specifically we of the Senate, to act where the president will not."

"And what is in this bill of yours?" Senator Hill asked, disdain in his voice.

"Senator Hill of Georgia is not recognized," Jemison thundered from the dais.

"Be that as it may, I shall answer his question," Toombs said. "My bill consists of three principal articles. The first deals with the power of a state governor in regards to those suspected of inciting servile insurrection. As we sit here in Richmond, the trial of Charles Russell Lowell, the abolitionist terrorist, is underway in New Orleans. He has been caught red-handed in the act of bringing weapons and ammunition to Saul's insurgents. He is directly responsible for the deaths of all the gallant Southern men whom I named earlier. Yet he is being given an ordinary trial in our courts, as if he were but a common thief." He paused for a moment, looking about the chamber, measuring his words. "My bill would give the governor of any state the authority to execute anyone he suspects to be responsible for inciting servile insurrection."

There were loud mutterings of discontent throughout the chamber, which Toombs had expected. Senator Clement Clay of Alabama, generally a supporter of Davis and a man Toombs knew was backing Breckinridge for the presidency, rose to his feet. "Will the Senator yield for a question?"

"I yield for a question."

"Are you aware, Senator Toombs, that the bill you are proposing is unconstitutional? Specifically, it violates two clauses of Article 1, Section 9, of the Confederate Constitution, those parts which were taken from the Fifth and Sixth Amendments of the United States Constitution, written by James Madison. Your bill would violate the principle that all persons suspected of having committed a crime are entitled to due process of law and a fair and public trial.

567

You are trying to disregard principles of law that go back at least to Magna Carta in the thirteenth century."

"I do not think I need to point out to the Senator from Alabama that we are not talking about ordinary crimes. We are talking about servile insurrection."

"If the rule of law is to mean anything, then the law must apply in the same way, whether we are talking about a pickpocket or an inciter of servile insurrection."

Toombs could not help but grin, for Clay's riposte might have been tailor-made for his purposes. "Surely the distinguished Senator from Alabama is not going soft on servile insurrection, is he?" There were shocked gasps from around the room, but Toombs went on. "I, for one, believe that there must be no slackening of our resolve to prevent and defeat slave uprisings. I am rather surprised to hear contrary opinions from a member of this body."

Clay's face curled into a mask of rage. "You foul, stinking, worthless excuse for a man!" he roared. "You will retract that statement at once!"

Toombs restrained the urge to respond to anger with anger. Pleased with himself for having made Clay lose his composure, he decided to simply resume his talk about the bill. Since he still had control of the Senate floor, there was nothing that Clay or anyone else could do about it without violating the rules of the Senate.

"I shall move on to the second article of my proposed bill. Before the seizure of New Iberia by Saul, our forces had fought a single successful engagement against the rebels in which a number of them were taken prisoner. For reasons which are still not clear to me, nor do I think to anyone in our Confederacy, these rebel slaves were not immediately executed but were confined as if they were ordinary captives, such as when we captured Yankee soldiers during the late war. My bill would establish that any blacks found in arms against the Confederacy, or being strongly suspected of being such, are to be immediately executed. Such a question as this should not be up to the discretion of any governmental official. It should be firmly established by law."

The other senators listened to these words in attentive silence. Each individual state had its own special court system to deal with unusual criminal offenses committed by slaves, such as the murder of his or her owner or engaging in armed uprisings. Toombs was proposing to supersede state law with national law. In doing so, he knew he was perhaps going against his own principles of states' rights, but the issue of servile insurrection was so paramount to him that he thought it worth doing. This time, no one rose to oppose him.

"The third and final article of my bill involves regulation of the newspapers. We all know that the renegade Saul wrote, or had written for him, a sort of manifesto in which he declared New Iberia to be a liberated area. It's all nonsense, of course, and the vast majority of our own newspapers have appropriately refrained from publishing it. To my mortification, however, I have learned that a very few did, in fact, print the letter. No good and much evil can come from such irresponsibility, especially if it contributes to the spread of rumors among the slaves themselves. Therefore, the third article of my bill would empower the governors of states to suspend freedom of the press within the borders of their state should any form of servile insurrection break out."

Again, his words were greeted by silence. He looked around the chamber, disappointed that no one was rising the challenge him. Hill and Clay had both done so already and he had hoped that they would do so again, yet this time they refused to take the bait. Toombs was not overly disappointed. All things being equal, silence could be construed as acceptance.

"Does the Senator from Georgia wish to continue?" Jemison asked from the dais.

"No, Mr. President," Toombs said. "My remarks are concluded."

Toombs could feel the relief wash over the Senate chamber as he sat back down. He shuffled his notes a bit, while straining his ears to hear any whispered comments of response to his speech. Senator William Graham of North Carolina rose and began a lackluster speech about allocating revenue from the national government to the state governments in order to pay for increased slave patrols. Toombs disagreed with this, but had such a low opinion of Graham that he scarcely cared what the man said. Now that his own speech was over, he rapidly grew bored. No one else in the Senate, in his opinion, could match his rhetorical abilities.

He considered the impact his action was likely to have. Davis had gravely miscalculated when he called a special session of Congress, for the Bill for the Prevention and Speedy Suppression of Servile Insurrection was going to be news throughout the Confederacy over the next few days. Everyone running for any office, from the Presidency down to the lowest municipal position, was going to have to take a stand either for it or against it. What stand they chose would, in large measure, determine whether or not they would win their upcoming elections.

The bill was, Toombs was fully aware, unconstitutional. It violated the established rights to due process of law and jury trials, as well as the freedom of the press. The question that all office-seekers would now have to answer was whether they cared more about protecting the institution of slavery or whether they cared about abstract principles like the rule of law.

John C. Breckinridge, Toombs knew, held the rule of law above absolutely everything else, slavery included. He would oppose Toombs's bill, while Beauregard would support it. Yet again, the Kentuckian would place himself in a position where he could be attacked for tepidness on slavery. This was going to prove his undoing. More importantly, it would secure the Vice Presidency for Toombs and pave the way for his eventual ascendency to the Presidency itself.

September 21, Morning
Parish Jail, New Orleans, Louisiana

The clattering sound of the door being unlocked stirred Lowell from his quiet contemplation of the Bible. He stood from his cot and watched as the heavy metal door slowly swung open. One of the guards was outside, fumbling with the enormous ring of keys, but he stood aside as a portly, bearded man wearing a black suit and beaming a strange smile entered the cell.

"General Lowell, I presume?"

"Yes."

"I am Judah Benjamin."

"I assumed so," Lowell said, sitting back down on the cot.

For a moment, the two men simply considered one another from across the small space of the jail cell. Benjamin removed his hat and jacket and set both neatly on the desk before sitting down on the chair. He gestured for the guard to close the door, which he did. The rattling sound of the locking took a few seconds.

"You have followed my instructions?" Benjamin asked. "Informed the court that you wish to have new counsel?"

"I have."

"Well, as it happens, I am licensed to practice law in Louisiana. Would you like me to be your attorney?"

The humor was evident in Benjamin's voice, yet Lowell didn't smile. The man standing before him was, in every conceivable way, an enemy. He had been a pro-slavery senator before the war and one of the most important political figures in the Confederacy since the moment of its founding. By all accounts, Benjamin had been the right-hand man of Jefferson Davis.

"You may be my attorney," Lowell answered. "I already said as much in my telegram."

"I know, but I like to hear it directly. I am not much of a fan of the electric telegraph. I like old-fashioned things. Besides, most telegrams I receive are from my wife in France, asking for more money."

Lowell didn't respond, merely looking at Benjamin in some confusion. It did not seem to him an appropriate time or place for jokes. It was evident that Benjamin was putting on a show of being disarming. In his life, both in the army and in business, Lowell had often met people who took their time before getting down to serious business. Under normal circumstances, this was annoying. Under the present ones, where each hour was bringing Lowell closer to an inevitable death, it was exasperating.

"Harvard man, yes?" Benjamin asked.

Lowell nodded. "Class of '54."

"Valedictorian, I read."

"That's right."

Benjamin nodded. "Yale man myself. Or I would have been, had I not been expelled."

"What were you expelled for?" Lowell didn't especially care, but it was the obvious question.

"I was accused of gambling."

"Was it true?"

"Oh, absolutely."

"Gambling goes on all the time among college boys."

"Yes, but I was guilty of the additional crime of being a Jew."

Lowell nodded. His social class did not mix with Jews very often and Jewish students in the great universities were few and far between, but he had always deplored anti-Semitism. How a man like Benjamin could reach such a high position in a society so bigoted and stratified as the South was a wonder. Yet, listening to him talk, Lowell began to sense how he had done it. There was a calm charisma to the man. As much as Lowell didn't feel it appropriate, he realized that he might grow to like Benjamin, given enough time. Still, he wanted the chitchat to end and the serious talking to begin.

"Why are you doing this? Lowell asked Benjamin.

"Even the most despicable man deserves good legal representation. Your man Caffery won't provide that. I will."

Lowell shook his head. "You can't tell me that there isn't more to it than that."

"Why should there be? John Adams defended the British soldiers who killed those people in the Boston Massacre, did he not? You're a classically educated man. Don't you recall that Cicero said the job of an advocate is to provide the best argument for his client, regardless of whether the man is innocent or guilty?"

"But why you? You resigned from your Cabinet position and travelled all the way across the country to serve as my lawyer. Why?"

"Why do you think?"

Lowell shook his head, frustrated. "It doesn't matter. You might be one of the most famous men in the Confederacy, but it will change nothing. I'm still going to end up dangling from a noose."

"Of course you are," Benjamin replied with a smile. "No changing that, unfortunately. But that's what you want, isn't it?"

Lowell was taken aback by these words. "What do you mean?"

"It's why you came down here to Louisiana in the first place. You didn't really think Saul's rebellion would succeed, did you? No, Lowell, you came down here to die. Just like your brother and your brother-in-law died in the war. I read up on you. I know what sort of man you are. You came down here to be a martyr."

Lowell shook his head, slowly but sternly. "I am content to die for my beliefs. And I have hoped to use my trial to speak the truth to the people of the Confederacy. But a martyr? I have a wife and family. I have a life in Massachusetts. No, I don't want to be a martyr at all. I will be one, I suppose, but only because I failed to escape."

"Perhaps you genuinely believe that, Lowell. Maybe you're doubting it now, what with the reality of the trial. But if you didn't want to die, you never would have come."

"It was a risk I thought worth taking if it meant that I could help free slaves."

"I understand that. In fact, I respect it. And you are helping to free slaves, in a deeper way that just handing out a few dozen rifles. That's why I'm here to help you."

Lowell's eyes narrowed. "I don't understand."

Benjamin sighed and thought for a moment before continuing. "You thought you could free slaves by giving guns to the insurgents. That didn't work. It only got a lot of people killed, both black slaves and ordinary whites, who would otherwise still be alive. Saul's rebellion didn't really achieve anything."

Lowell pointed an accusatory finger at Benjamin. "It showed the South that the blacks will not meekly be held in bondage forever. They will fight. They proved that during the war and Saul proved it again this year."

Benjamin waved his hand dismissively. "That's never going to end slavery. You think Southerners are afraid to fight to defend their way of life? You fought in the war. You served in the Shenandoah Valley, yes? You know how ferocious a Southern fighting man can be. And that's when he's pitted against other white men. Against black slaves, whom they've been brought up from birth to despise and fear, they will be ruthless. Utterly and completely ruthless. You'll simply be unleashing something much more vicious and violent than the slaves themselves could ever be." He paused a moment. "You're aware of what happened in New Iberia, yes?"

Lowell nodded.

Benjamin went on. "Longstreet might have simply starved Saul and his men out, but that would have taken too long. The South was willing to let hundreds of its men be killed and to destroy a fair chunk of a major town, rather than let it remain in the hands of black rebels for just a few days. Irrational, isn't it? Doesn't make sense."

"I confess I don't understand it."

"You're a Northerner. Of course you don't understand. I've lived among these Southerners all my life. I know them better than they know themselves. They fear any sign of resistance among the slaves the way people in a plague-ridden city fear any sign of black bumps on their bodies. They will always descend upon any uprising with overwhelming force. To them, there is no other option."

Lowell nodded. "One can see that, given how they treated the black regiments during the war. They took no prisoners in those fights."

"Exactly. Look, if the entire United States was not able to bring down the Confederacy after four years of war, what do you think a bunch of disorganized bands of insurgent slaves are going to be able to accomplish? The white South knows all about keeping slave rebellions from happening."

Lowell shook his head vigorously. "No, Saul proved that's not true."

"Did he, really? Then explain to me why his was the first uprising of any kind since the end of the Great Disorder. Explain to me why Nat Turner's rebellion was the only major uprising before the war. The white South has had more than two centuries to perfect its system. All the laws preventing slaves from becoming literate, the whole complex system of travel passes and slave patrols, the militia system. They know exactly what they are doing."

"But the war changed everything!" Lowell insisted. "The slaves discovered that they could be free."

"Yes, but it changed things in another way, too. The Confederacy fielded enormous armies during the war. Now the South has hundreds of thousands of experienced killers waiting for the call to serve against any slave insurrection. Anytime a slave raises a weapon, he'll be faced by ten times his number of armed white men, military veterans, who will show no mercy against him. What's worse is that the United States is sitting there at the top of the map. Any slave who wants to be free is going to be focused on getting out of the Confederacy, not launching a rebellion. So there really won't be any incentive for the slaves to rise up, you see? A pot with a steam valve will never explode."

Lowell frowned and didn't reply. He admitted to himself that he had not been prepared for the possibility of total failure. There was a difference between what the mind said and what the heart believed. The cold, rational, military man in him said over and over again that Saul's rebellion was very likely to be snuffed out like a candle with a glass placed over it, even if he managed to get the weapons into their. Yet in his heart, Lowell had somehow believed that Saul would manage to defeat the Confederates, spark of wider uprising, and crush slavery throughout the South.

It had been a delusion, Lowell now saw. Saul and his band had been doomed from the very beginning. All Lowell had managed to do was get more people killed and condemn himself to a humiliating execution. His wife would live without a husband and his children without a father. He had taken his promising life and thrown it all away. Lowell took a deep breath and said nothing for a time, staring at the same spot on the floor. After a long minute, he looked up at Benjamin.

"What did you mean before? When you were accusing me of wanting to die. You said I was still helping to end slavery."

"Indeed, you are. That's why I've come."

"I don't understand." Lowell was finding Benjamin increasingly frustrating.

"Well, as it happens, you and I share the same goal. I want slavery to end as much as you do."

Lowell's face curled into a scowl. "I don't like being mocked."

"I'm quite serious," Benjamin said earnestly. "I would not admit it to many people, and certainly not the public at large. Come to think of it, I shall not admit it to anyone save yourself. They already have it in for me on account of my Jewishness, and for other reasons. But I am an abolitionist. An abolitionist of a very peculiar variety, I admit, but an abolitionist all the same."

"Lies," Lowell said. "I don't know much about you, Mr. Benjamin, but I know you were a pro-slavery, pro-secession senator before the war. I know you have served in the top levels of the Confederate government. They say it was largely through your efforts that Britain and France recognized the Confederacy after McClellan's election. Your entire life's work has been a defense of slavery."

"All true. And this vast wealth of experience has taught me that slavery must end. Not for the reasons which motivate you, to be sure. All that talk about equality and the rights of man? Sentimental nonsense. I'm done with sentimentality. But slavery will prove to be a curse to the Confederacy. It's as plain as day. In achieving our independence, we are like a man who has just begun to swim in the ocean." He paused for a moment. "What's that verse from the New Testament about the millstone?"

"Luke 17:2," Lowell answered. "'It were better for him that a millstone were hanged about his neck and he cast into the sea than that he should offend one of these little ones.'"

"Quite," Benjamin replied with a smile. "You see, slavery will be the millstone around the neck of the Confederacy. Look at what is happening in Europe right now. Britain and France both have reasons to seek an alliance with the Confederacy, yet slavery causes them to hold back. This will only get worse as time passes and, in the meantime, they're beginning to find sources of cotton in other parts of the world. The same thing is starting to happen in other parts of Europe. In the long run, slavery will make the Confederacy into an international pariah, perhaps tolerated, but liked by few and sought after by none. We shall be adrift in a dangerous world, without friends or allies. And the United States might one day seek its revenge."

"So that's it?" Lowell said contemptuously. "You only care that slavery makes you look bad to the rest of the world?"

"By God, no!" Benjamin said. "It's only the most obvious problem. Slavery undermines the Confederacy from within as well as from without. It's like a steady dripping of acid that is slowly corroding our soul. Some think, now that we have won our independence, that the rich folks can simply sit on the porches of their plantation houses and sip mint juleps while watching their slaves work and letting the centuries roll past them. History doesn't work that way. The world is changing. We must change with it."

As Benjamin spoke, Lowell mulled over his words. It was a point of view that the Massachusetts man had never really considered before. He had always seen the Southern slaveholders as unspeakably evil, which they undoubtedly were. They held the blacks in slavery for their own profit and aggrandizement. The idea that ending slavery might actually be beneficial to the South had never occurred to him before.

Benjamin was still talking. "You're an educated man. Think of the difference between Athens and Sparta. Athens was the wonder of the world, filled with philosophers, artists, historians, playwrights, and such. Sparta, by contrast, was so fixated on maintaining the helots as slaves that they stagnated into decay. They produced no great thinkers, did they? Whoever heard of a Spartan philosopher? They were great warriors, to be sure, but I'd much rather live in Athens than Sparta."

"And you think the Confederacy could become the Athens of the world?" Lowell asked sarcastically.

"Probably not, to be brutally honest. But if it tries to hold on to its slaves the way Sparta did, it won't ever have the chance."

Lowell nodded slowly, absorbing everything that Benjamin was saying. "What does any of this have to do with you wanting to be my attorney?"

"Ending slavery in the South isn't going to be easy. And it's going to take a long time. Decades at least. I won't live to see it. Maybe no one alive today will live to see it. The Confederate Constitution makes it almost impossible for the country to abolish slavery. And nobody wants slavery to end, not even the poor white people who don't benefit at all from the system. Look at what happened when General Cleburne's memorandum was made public. The man was a military hero, yet almost everyone wanted to run him out of the country on a rail."

"None of that answers my question."

Benjamin smiled and chuckled slightly. "Like it or not, you're going to be a martyr. I need you to act the part. If you go to your death with honor and dignity, showing no fear and holding true to your abolitionist convictions until the very end, think of the statement you'll make."

"That's all I have been thinking about since my capture."

"Yes, but not in the way you should be. You want to tell the South how evil you think it is, like an angry man throwing his water in another man's face. What is that going to accomplish? It's just going to make them more resistant to change. No, you need to change your perspective. The only way to win an argument, after all, is to get the other man to change his mind." Benjamin paused thoughtfully for a moment. "You don't get a woman to go to bed with you by telling her she is stupid if she refuses. You get a woman to go to bed with you by persuading her that she'd enjoy it."

Lowell frowned, not appreciating the crude analogy. He also didn't like the idea of becoming a tool of Benjamin. As far as Lowell was concerned, the South would never be persuaded to free its slaves. Abolition had to be forced upon the South from the outside, not done from within. Benjamin had the opposite perspective and Lowell found this disquieting. He had despised the Confederacy for so long that he did not like the feeling that his actions might benefit it, no matter how abstractly or how far in the future.

Benjamin went on. "Go to your death gallantly, and the Southerners will have no choice but to admire you. They're a warrior people, you know. They appreciate bravery. Your trial is the story of the moment. It's even overshadowing the presidential election in the newspapers sometimes. If the South remembers Charles Russell Lowell as a brave man who went to his death gallantly, it will it harder for them to hate abolitionists. And that's a step forward."

"So you want me to be Nathan Hale?"

Benjamin considered this. "Yes, I suppose. And just as he had one life to give for his country, you have one life to give in the struggle for abolition. You want to make it count or not?"

Slowly, Lowell began to nod.

September 22, Afternoon
British Army encampment, South of Montreal

"Your men look excellent, Major Mackay," Wolseley said as he walked down the row of dozens of well-armed, well-equipped men. The grenadiers of the Gordon Highlanders were among the most formidable soldiers he had ever seen, tall and powerfully built, with that gritty look of strength and confidence that so often characterized Scottish troops. Their kilts and bearskin caps gave them a frightening and intimidating appearance.

"Thank you, sir!" Captain Forbes Mackay, commander of the grenadier company, replied instantly, his voice projecting like a cannon shot.

"If we have to tangle with the Fenians, Major, do you think your men will be up to the challenge?"

"Without question, sir!" Mackay replied.

Wolseley nodded, pleased at the man's professionalism and enthusiasm. He had encountered the Gordon Highlanders both in the Crimea and in India during the Mutiny and considered them a fine regiment. Like most Scottish regiments, they were overly insular and tended to look down upon the English and the Welsh, but he could not question either their bravery or their loyalty.

He completed the quick inspection and dismissed the Highlanders, who shouldered their weapons and marched back to their tents. The camp was not large, containing only about four hundred men, divided more or less evenly between Scottish, English, and Welsh soldiers. Ordinarily, a camp was located in a clearing, but Wolseley had elected to have the men pitch their tents in a wooded area to better hide them from prying eyes.

The strike force being assembled was a curious blend of the British Army. He had detached the light companies and grenadier companies from the Duke of Wellington's Regiment and the Gordon Highlanders, the two battalions forming the bulk of the Montreal garrison. To stiffen them up, Wolseley had summoned the light and grenadier companies of the Royal Welch Fusiliers, men with whom he was familiar. Indeed, after his leadership at the Battle of the Stockade, the Fusiliers had made Wolseley an honorary member of their mess. Although his loyalty to the Perthshire Volunteers was unquestioned, he had to acknowledge that he had become rather fond of his Welsh troops.

Wolseley had rejected the idea of including any of his Canadian militia in the force, for the operation he envisioned would require a level of steadiness that only professional troops possessed. He had considered bringing in some companies of the Royal Irish Regiment, whose accents and knowledge of Gaelic might have allowed him to seize the Fenian supply depot through some sort of ruse. Having thought about it, though, he had rejected the idea. It would take only a single Fenian sympathizer to thwart his entire plan.

He had told no one of his intentions, not even Buller. If General Napier or any of the politicians in Ottawa got wind of what was going to happen, they would certainly try to stop him. Lacking his vision and intelligence, they would fail to see the simple logic of his plan. If all went as Wolseley hoped and expected, the spark of war would be lit between the British Empire and the Union. The time was propitious, for Britain was as strong as it had ever been. The Union was unsteady and weak, having lost the war with the Confederacy, but it would recover and become stronger as time passed. The time to nip its power in the bud was now.

Copies of the report of the Indian scout, altered by Wolseley to indicate that the Fenian depot was north of the border rather than south of it, was already on its way to the official files of the Canadian government and the British Army. When the time came, those pieces of paper would provide Wolseley with protection. The region was heavily wooded, after all, and it would be virtually impossible for anyone other than a team of surveyors to determine whether the depot was on the north or south side of the line. Besides which, his orders from London specified that he was empowered to do whatever was necessary to ensure the defense of Her Majesty's dominions and the Fenian arms depot was an obvious threat that had to be removed. To Wolseley, that overrode the portion of his orders which instructed him to avoid any conflict with the Americans. After all, he took "Americans" to mean soldiers of the United States government, which did not include the Fenians.

As he walked back to his command tent, Wolseley glanced at the small gathering of Mohawk Indians sitting in a circle near the center of the camp. Orenda, the chief scout, was talking to them in their native language, which sounded beastly to Wolseley's ears. Some British soldiers, many of them newly arrived in Canada, stared at the natives as if they were animals at a zoo, but Orenda and his people paid them no mind.

He returned to his command tent, which was not much bigger than any of the tents in which the men were sleeping. A small field desk and chair were set up for him. The six company commanders had each submitted a report on the fitness and health of their men, which Wolseley sat down and resumed studying intently. Officially, the excursion towards the border was a training exercise, designed by Wolseley to test whether the light and grenadier companies of different regiments would be able to function cohesively together in the Canadian wilderness. That was how he had sold it to General Napier, not that the fool needed much convincing.

Buller's head peeked through the tent flap. "Sir?"

"Yes, Buller, what is it?"

The aide-de-camp looked awkward for a moment. "The ammunition, sir."

"What about it?"

"I just went over the numbers. We have nearly two hundred rounds per man."

"Good," Wolseley answered. "That's exactly what I wanted."

"That's a lot for a training exercise, sir."

Wolseley's eyebrows went up. Buller's tone was skeptical and questioning, devoid of the deference with which he normally spoke. Clearly, he had finally begun to suspect something was amiss. Wolseley wondered how long it had taken Buller to work up the courage to speak to him about it.

Wolseley set the report he was reading down on the desk and looked up at Buller. "What of it?"

Buller took a deep breath. "What are we really doing out here, sir?"

Wolseley chuckled and pointed out the tent toward Orenda. "Remember his report? About the Fenian arms depot?"

"Of course."

"We're going to take care of that particular problem."

Buller's face showed astonishment. "I don't understand what you mean."

"We're going to march to that depot, burn it to the ground, and then march home."

"But the depot is on the other side of the Yankee border!"

"No, it's on our side of the border. By about a mile, or so Orenda tells me."

"I don't understand. Did he make another excursion after the report he gave us before?"

"No," Wolseley said calmly.

Buller didn't respond right away, as realization slowly dawned on his face. "You mean to cross the border?"

"Yes, I do."

"Do we have the authority to do that?"

"No, we don't."

Buller took a deep breath. Wolseley knew he would not object. He wasn't the sort of man to stand up to a figure of authority. He was very good at taking orders, but it took an enormous amount of effort for an independent thought to force its way to the forefront of his mind. Wolseley, sitting immediately before him, represented authority. Buller would follow whatever orders he was given. Still Wolseley decided to prod the man a bit.

"Do you wish to express an objection, Buller?"

"Sir?" Buller replied, confused.

"Do you wish to express an objection? I plan on taking these men across the border. We shall surely engage the Fenians on the Yankee side of the line. It's not impossible that we will encounter United States soldiers. If you have any objection to what I am planning to do, please say so now."

The confusion left Buller's face and he looked Wolseley in the eye. "I have no objection, sir."

"Good. Now, you told me about the ammunition. What about the food and our other supplies. It's possible that it will be a few days before we can resupply."

September 23, Morning
Mechanic's Hall, Richmond, Virginia

Breckinridge finished reading the report sent by Longstreet. Extensive patrolling by Morgan's cavalry around New Iberia had found no trace whatsoever of Saul or any of his men. The commanding general's opinion was that all of them had died during the fighting. Most of the bodies, likely including Saul's, had been burned beyond recognition as flames engulfed the hotel. All of them had been buried in a mass grave. In the unlikely every that any of the insurgents had escaped, they had only been as individuals or, at most, in twos or threes.

Saul's insurrection was over, as dead as if a stake had been driven through its heart. This had been clear for weeks now, but it gave Breckinridge relief to read it in an official report. The message did contain one caveat, however. General Morgan was still insisting on going on with his search, apparently not convinced that Saul had died in New Iberia. Knowing Morgan as well as he did, Breckinridge found this unsurprising. Saul had badly damaged Morgan's reputation, which the cavalryman prized above all other things. Having set his mind firmly on the destruction of Saul, he probably did not know what to do now that it had been accomplished.

Breckinridge set the report down, pulled out a piece of paper, and quickly wrote out an order for Morgan to return to the headquarters of the Army of Tennessee at Nashville and await further orders. It was the best thing to do for the time being. Technically, Morgan was still the commander of a cavalry brigade in the Confederacy's main army between the Appalachians and the Mississippi River, being only on detached duty in Louisiana. Yet it had been many months since he had last attended to his duties in Nashville. In the meantime, General John Wharton had been doing a solid job as his temporary replacement.

The Secretary of War hesitated to simply put Morgan back into his old place. For one thing, Wharton had become active with the States' Rights Party and Breckinridge feared accusation of using his official position to retaliate against a man for political purposes. More to the point, however, Morgan's time in Louisiana had raised many questions about his continued fitness for high command. Breckinridge had long defended him, both out of friendship and a sincere belief in his abilities. Yet the president, always suspicious of officers who had not been trained at West Point, now had serious doubts. Many members of Congress had also raised the issue. It was an open question as to whether it was politically expedient to return Morgan to his old command.

There was a soft knock on the door and Wilson entered.

"Sir? He's here."

Breckinridge set the matter of Morgan aside, now having a much more difficult and less enjoyable matter to face. He took a deep breath. "Very well. Send him in."

Wilson stepped back and William Porcher Miles entered the office, a smile on his face. Breckinridge felt a tightness grip his stomach. The door closed behind Miles, who then approached the desk and extended his hand.

"John!" Miles said boisterously, as if the two were old friends. "How are you, old boy?"

Breckinridge did not rise from his desk and did not even consider shaking Miles's hand. He simply sat in his chair, his arms folded across his chest, keeping his face as expressionless as possible and glaring up at the South Carolinian.

Miles gave a mimicked expression of disappointment and sat down in the chair. "Don't want to shake hands, do we? Well, that's okay. It's a free country. For us white men, anyway."

"You wanted to meet, Miles. Here we are. What did you want to say?"

"No need to be rude, John. We're Cabinet colleagues now. We'll be seeing lots of each other. We might as well be polite, don't you think?"

"The Senate has to confirm you before you're officially Secretary of State. It's not in session, as nearly everybody in Congress has gone home to campaign for reelection."

Miles waved his hand dismissively. "A formality, nothing more. A strong majority of senators have already said that they'll confirm me when they return to Richmond. In the meantime, I'm Acting Secretary, so I'm as much a member of the Cabinet as you are."

"When the Senate reconvenes, there'll be a new president. Maybe it'll be Beauregard. Maybe it'll be me. What makes you think either he or I won't nominate someone else?"

"Beauregard and I are old friends. I served as his aide-de-camp early in the war, did you know? He's probably a bit surprised that Davis has chosen me, but I expect he'll want to keep me on if he wins, though I haven't discussed it with him. As you for, well, that's what I wanted to come to talk to you about today."

"If you expect me to agree to you serving as my Secretary of State, you're even more foolish than I thought two years ago. If I am elected, there will be no place in the government for you."

"Why should it be so, Breckinridge?"

Breckinridge scoffed. "I'm sure you remember what happened at the signing ceremony of the Treaty of Toronto as well as I do, Miles. You threatened me. You said that if I ran for president you would destroy my reputation and ruin my career by revealing my secret meeting with Vice President Hamlin. I don't much like being threatened with blackmail, Miles. And as you can see, I am running for president, your threats be damned."

"Yes, I misjudged you. I freely admit it and I apologize."

The man's voice was smooth and a less cognizant man might have found it sincere, but Breckinridge was not fooled. Miles might have a reputation in Southern society as a charming, witty, handsome man, whose presence enlivened the drawing rooms of every elegant Confederate home. To Breckinridge, the man was simply a poseur, a man whose stylish dress and smooth voice concealed an unscrupulous and selfish brute. On a deep level, it bothered Breckinridge that such men existed. It was more than a simple personal loathing, however. Miles was a Fire-Eater as extreme as the worst of them. It had been such men, combined with the radical abolitionists of the North, who had torn the old Union apart by refusing to compromise. Yet Miles was even more dangerous, for he disguised his vulgarity behind a veneer of sophistication and refinement. He reminded Breckinridge of the line from *The Merchant of Venice* about the villain with the smiling cheek. Toombs might try to strike you in the face, but Miles would put his arm around you and speak pleasantly, ready at any moment to stick a knife between your ribs.

He remembered those weeks of complex negotiations in the summer of 1865, when he, Miles, Stephens and Reagan had laboriously hammered out an agreement with their Union counterparts to bring about an end to the war. It had been one of the most difficult things Breckinridge had ever done, and Miles had made it even more difficult by his insistence on an absolute defense of slavery in every form. He had continually pressed the delegation to demand a clause in the treaty for the return of fugitive slaves, making the negotiations far more problematic than they had to be. There had been no hint of compromise in Miles's attitude at any point in the discussions.

Breckinridge also recalled the comments Miles made when discussing the need for the Confederacy to secure control of Key West and Fort Pickens in Florida. Their status had been a bone of contention with the Union delegation, as those posts had never been under Confederate control. Breckinridge had wanted them on the basis of simple sovereignty and the desire to deny the Union coaling stations for another naval blockade in the event of any future war. Miles, however, had wanted them in order to use them as bases for an invasion of Spanish Cuba. Like all Fire-Eaters, Miles had imperialistic dreams, envisioning a slave-holding Confederacy that eventually stretched far to the south, perhaps even as far as Brazil. It was a vision, Breckinridge was convinced, that would bring the Confederacy into conflict with the rest of the world and eventually lead to utter ruin.

"Suppose I were willing to forget your past threats. Why should I want you to be my Secretary of State?"

"Why? Well, why not me? I've represented the Confederacy in Washington City these last two years. I'm a seasoned diplomat now. You're not going to keep Benjamin, whose antics with this Lowell trial are going to destroy his reputation beyond repair. Slidell in Paris is too old and wouldn't want the job anyway. Haynes in London has proven less than stellar, to say the least. I'm already Acting Secretary. You can even point out that you and I have worked together before. I am the obvious choice, my friend. Indeed, if you don't pick me, people will think it odd."

Breckinridge frowned, as much from Miles addressing him as a friend as from the fact that Miles was saying the truth. "Let us think ahead," he told Miles. "If I win the Presidency and you are my Secretary of State, it would present obvious problems. You and I do not see eye-to-eye on many issues. We found that out in Toronto."

"A Cabinet member serves at the pleasure of the president. I understand that. You'd be the band director and I would play on my trumpet whatever tune you asked me to play. You and I can have a gentlemen's agreement. When our administration takes office, I shall support you and your policies in every respect, unless and until my conscience presents an insurmountable objection. On slavery, for example. If that happens, I shall resign. In return, you agree not to remove me from office except in a similar case."

Breckinridge frowned yet again. A gentlemen's agreement was valid only if both of the contracting parties were actually gentlemen. Miles was emphatically not a person he included in that category. Moreover, he did not like the idea that Miles would bolt from the Cabinet if Breckinridge ever made a policy decision with which Miles disagreed. If he was going to be president, Breckinridge felt that he had to have complete freedom of action.

"How do you know I would keep my word if I made such an agreement with you?" Breckinridge asked.

"Because you're a man of honor. You'd keep your word, even if you gave it to a man you despised."

"And you?"

Miles grinned. "I'd keep my end of the bargain because it serves my own interests, as should be obvious. I was Mayor of Charleston, then I was a congressman, then I was a diplomat, now I'm Secretary of State. When your time in office is up, there's only one more rung of the ladder to climb."

"You'll forgive me for not wanting you to be president."

"Well, that will be for the Confederate people to decide, won't it? And I wouldn't expect your support. All I'd want is your assurance that you won't actively try to thwart my campaign."

"So, another agreement? First, I bring you into the Cabinet and keep you there? Second, I don't work against you if you run for president in 1873?"

"That's right, Breckinridge. A pretty good deal, if you ask me."

"Not in my eyes. All I get is your silence on my dealings with Hamlin in Toronto. I am not entirely convinced that such revelations would be the end of my presidential campaign."

"Allow me to sweeten the deal, then," Miles said.

"How? You've already told the newspapers that you've endorsed me. What else can you give?"

"I'm told that you're going to use your speech to the Orphan Society to attack Beauregard, Toombs, and the rest of the SRP leadership. Is that true?"

"I will be speaking on why I think their vision of the future of the Confederacy is wrong and mine is right, if that's what you mean."

"Trenholm told me that you intend to directly attack your opponents. Call Beauregard a vainglorious fool, call Toombs and Wigfall worthless drunkards, that sort of thing."

"I'd prefer not to," Breckinridge said forthrightly. "Making this speech a campaign event is unorthodox enough. I would hate to sully it further with direct personal attacks, which I have never been accustomed to making in any event."

"Then don't. Let me make them for you."

Breckinridge considered Miles more carefully. "How so?"

"Like them, I have been a Fire-Eater, as you call us. And I know Beauregard very well. You might say that I have been, up to this point, in the enemy's camp. The newspapers know it and so do the people. It makes little difference if Postmaster Reagan or Senator Hill or Secretary Trenholm attack the SRP leadership, because that's only to be expected. Let me be your attack dog. Everything is paralyzed in the government until after the election, anyway. Davis can handle things without me. I'll tour through Virginia, Tennessee, and North Carolina, which are the critical states, and tear your enemies to pieces in the face of the public."

Breckinridge thought this over. Miles was quite correct when he asserted that, because of his own background and reputation, his attacks on the SRP would be far more effective than anything he himself might have done. Having such a prominent Fire-Eater as Miles supporting his campaign would not only be useful in and of itself, but would give his candidacy the critical appearance of momentum. Some papers were reporting that his campaign was a lost cause. He needed something to jolt it back into life. His speech to the Orphan Society would be one part of it. The speaking tour Miles now proposed to undertake would perhaps be a second.

Yet everything Breckinridge believed in revolted from accepting Miles's help. He had long since felt his control over the course of events slip away. Benjamin had pushed him into running in the first place. He had been carried along as if by a river since that moment. Now he was finding himself, against his will, joining forces with a man he considered his most vicious enemy.

"Very well," Breckinridge said reluctantly. "You are a deceitful and conniving bastard, Miles."

Miles chuckled, not at all offended. "In that case, Breckinridge, you should get down on your knees and thank God that I am choosing to be on your side."

September 26, Night
Home of John Slidell, Paris, France

The burning logs in the fireplace cast a flickering orange and yellow light that illuminated Slidell's library. He sat silently in his reading chair, a glass of good but not outstanding Rhone wine in one hand and a copy of *A Clever Child*, the latest novel by Charles Dickens, in the other. He had been told the book was good by people whose literary tastes he trusted, but he was having a difficult time getting into the story and did not appreciate the leveling spirit that seemed to animate Dickens's writing.

The grandfather clock chimed, telling him that it was now quarter to midnight. He realized that he had been reading the Dickens book for more than half an hour and had not advanced more than five pages, so Slidell set the book aside and picked up the copy of *The Times*. He had read it earlier in the day, of course, but it was always useful to reread the news to ensure he had all the details committed to memory. The lead story on the front page was about some sort of disorder in the Balkans, instigated by Bulgarian nationalists who wanted to achieve independence from the Ottoman Turks. Below it was a story about a plan by some members of Parliament to introduce a bill that would end public hangings. Slidell shook his head in disapproval. Such leniency would only encourage greater outlawry.

The main item of interest on the American scene was the Lowell trial in New Orleans. *The Times* was reporting the shocking news that Judah Benjamin had resigned his position as Secretary of State to take on the role of Lowell's attorney. Slidell had, in fact, known about this before almost anyone else, for Benjamin had told him in a personal telegram, using the same secret code with which they had communicated during their days in Louisiana politics and still used occasionally. Slidell had been surprised, but not terribly so. After all, he knew Benjamin better than almost anyone.

The British papers were paying even more attention to the Lowell trial than were the French ones. Slidell was troubled by the clear belief among so many editorial writers that Lowell was some sort of hero. A few newspapers, mostly on the radical fringe, had published pieces calling for the Confederate government to unilaterally release Lowell, which struck Slidell as absurd. The man was a terrorist, his actions were responsible for the deaths of over a hundred Confederate soldiers, and it only made sense that he be subject to the ultimate penalty.

It was not just the glorifying of Lowell that bothered Slidell, however. His fundamental mission in France was to foster a positive opinion of the Confederacy among the people in general and the ruling elite in particular. Every news item that reminded the French that the Confederacy was a slave-holding nation made that more difficult. He was himself a believer in slavery as the natural state of relations between the black and white races, but he recognized that he was living out his last years in an increasingly liberal age, especially so far as Europeans were concerned. He was constantly being forced to defend something that he believed in but which most Europeans found abhorrent.

The uprising of Saul and the Lowell trial had focused the attention of France onto the institution of slavery in the Confederacy just as if a scientist were examining it under a microscope. It was this public focus that had brought a halt to the negotiations over the proposed treaty of alliance between France and the Confederacy. As the trial moved towards Lowell's inevitable conviction and execution, the European fixation on what was happening in New Orleans was only going to increase, especially now that Benjamin was involved. This, in turn, meant that it would become ever more difficult for Slidell to get the treaty negotiations going again.

Though he preferred to work behind the scenes, Slidell was not a passive person. From the moment the negotiations were suspended, he had been at work crafting a plan to restart them. As the clock struck midnight, he knew that a crucial part of that plan was about to unfold.

He set the newspaper aside and poured himself another glass of wine. He stood and walked over to the door that connected the library with the bedroom, listening carefully. He knew that such a plot as he had woven for tonight would not unfold precisely as planned. He might be waiting for some time. If so, he comforted himself with the knowledge that he had enough wine left in the bottle for at least three more glasses and he could always open another bottle if necessary.

Time passed. Slidell finished his glass and poured another. He was pacing himself, for he did not want to become intoxicated. His plan required him to play a particular role and play it to perfection, so he needed his mind to be as clear as possible.

The clock chimed that it was a quarter past midnight. There was still no sound from the bedroom. He waited. The clock struck half past midnight and there was still no sound. He continued waiting, walking quietly back to the small table beside the chair for another glass of wine.

Finally, he could hear a door softly open and close in the bedroom. He pressed his ear to the door and listened carefully. There was the sound of shuffling feet, a man's voice softly but urgently saying something, followed by the giggling of a female. He was unable to make out the words, as the couple was speaking quietly and his hearing was not what it had once been, yet the tone of the woman's voice suggested that she was playfully protesting whatever it was the man was doing. As the sound of a creaking bed was heard, what that was became obvious.

Slidell finished his glass of wine in a single, large gulp and set the glass down. He picked up his gold-headed walking stick and suppressed a smile. There was no reason not to have fun with the escapade, after all. He cleared his throat, steeled a stern expression onto his face, and shoved open the door.

As he strode into the bedroom, a ridiculous sight greeted his eyes. Had he not known precisely what to expect, he would have been shocked. As it was, the scene before him was hilarious. His daughter Marguerite was on the bed, clad only in her thin white undergarments which had been loosened so much that they appeared likely to fall off at any moment. Her elegant yellow dress lay crumbled on the floor at the foot of the bed. Hovering over his daughter was Napoleon III, Emperor of the French, naked from the waist down. It was clear that he had been so eager to make love to Slidell's daughter that he hadn't had any intention of undressing any more than strictly necessary, so his pretentious military uniform jacket was still tightly buttoned.

"What's the meaning of this?" Slidell roared with as stentorian a voice as he could muster.

"Father!" Marguerite cried as if in shock, disentangling herself from the emperor's grip and scurrying off to the side of the bed. "You told me that you were going to be at the spas in Vichy for the next week!"

"I cancelled my trip," Slidell said harshly. "I now wish I had not! I certainly didn't expect to discover something like this going on in my own home! Shame! Shame!"

"Minister Slidell," the emperor stammered. "Allow me to explain. . ."

"Be silent!" Slidell shouted, raising his walking stick as if to strike. "You may be the ruler of this country, but you have just crossed an angry father! To say nothing of an angry husband! I shall inform my son-in-law of these events at once!"

"Father, no!" Marguerite shrieked. "Please don't!"

Slidell glared at his daughter. "I am not surprised to find a Bonaparte engaged in such debauchery as this. But I always held you to a higher standard. Now I find that my beloved daughter is nothing but a dirty whore!"

Slidell turned and marched grimly back into the library. Behind him, he could hear his daughter collapsing into sobs, which he knew were feigned, while Napoleon fumbled to get his trousers back on. With his back turned to the hapless couple, Slidell smiled. So far, things were going as planned. He walked over to the table beside the chair and poured himself a large glass of wine.

"Minister Slidell!" Napoleon exclaimed. "Please, calm yourself!"

Slidell wiped the smile from his face, replacing it with a mask of fury. He turned and faced the emperor, taking a large sip of the wine. "At this moment, I would much prefer a totty of Caribbean rum to this glass of French wine. I thought we were friends, Monsieur! This is an insult not only to me, but to the Confederate States of America!"

Napoleon didn't respond, simply staring at Slidell in stunned silence. Marguerite slammed shut the door between the bedroom and the library, having played her role flawlessly. If Slidell had any qualms about using his daughter in such a manner, it was a moot point now. She had willingly embraced her part in the scheme, excited at being able to participate directly in her father's surreptitious work. Slidell also suspected that she relished the idea of allowing the Emperor of the French to come within a hairsbreadth of bedding her, as he had tried to do many times, only to see him thwarted at the last moment. Women were a strange lot and Marguerite was not an exception.

"Minister Slidell, may we talk?" Napoleon said piteously.

Slidell gave the emperor an angry glare. He ostentatiously drained his wine glass in a few rapid gulps. Slidell regretted this, for gulping good wine was a terrible waste, but it was necessary to maintain the illusion that he was furious.

Finished, he pointed sternly to one of the library chairs, on which the emperor immediately sat, the expression on his face like that of a contrite child. It was hilarious that one of the most powerful men in the world had been reduced to such a situation. Slidell took the chair on the opposite side of the carpet, taking deep breaths as if to calm himself.

He tried to imagine what was going through Napoleon's mind. Of course, the innumerable affairs of the emperor were an open secret throughout France. His personal secretaries often seemed to spend as much time sneaking women into the back rooms of the imperial palaces as they did on their official duties. As far as Slidell was aware, this was the first time he had been caught in the act by the father of one of his prospective mistresses.

"How am I to respond to this insult?" Slidell demanded.

Napoleon pulled a cigarette out of its case and lit it, puffing quickly. "I apologize for what has happened," he said, his voice calmer than it had been. "I am a man. Your daughter is one of the great beauties in France. I wanted her."

"And you just thought you could have her, didn't you? You Bonapartes are all the same, thinking you can just take what you want. Did it not occur to you that gratifying yourself with Marguerite would bring forth disastrous consequences to you? When my son-in-law learns of this, I would not be surprised if he immediately informs the Empress. She has an inkling of your infidelities, but how would she react to having one like this thrown in her face? I may forgive you, Your Majesty, but my son-in-law very likely will not."

Napoleon gazed mournfully into the fire. "I try to restrain myself, but I can't! Women adore the power of my throne and so many just throw themselves at me. The more I have, the more I want."

"You should take the example of your illustrious uncle. He had his affairs, but not nearly so many as you. More importantly, he never let them dominate his mind."

The emperor looked up at Slidell. "There is no need for you to tell your son-in-law about this."

"Why shouldn't I?" Slidell countered. "I love him as if he were my own son. He needs to know."

"Wouldn't it be kinder to spare him the humiliation?"

"I think you're more interesting in sparing yourself the humiliation."

Napoleon frowned. "Perhaps I might offer you a seat of honor next to me at the next great ball?"

Slidell laughed contemptuously. "You think you can buy me off with the offer of a better seat at a party? No, no, no. You'll have to do much better than that, Your Majesty."

"What is your price, Minister? You don't need money, clearly. What is it you want?"

Slidell poured another glass of wine. The moment had come for him to tread carefully. If he moved too quickly, the emperor might suspect that he had been caught in a ruse and his carefully arranged plan would collapse. He therefore was quiet for a few minutes, sipping at his wine, looking thoughtfully into the fire.

"Perhaps you might be a little more flexible on the matter of our treaty negotiations?" Slidell finally asked.

Napoleon drew his head back slowly, eyeing Slidell carefully. The Confederate ambassador was frightened for a moment that he might have tipped his hand. The emperor suddenly seemed less repentant and more wary.

"It would not be proper to allow a personal matter such as this to affect policy."

"You asked for my price. I gave it."

"So, it's to be blackmail, then? If I don't reopen the treaty negotiations, you'll tell your son-in-law what has happened?"

Slidell said nothing in reply, allowing silence to be his answer. He looked at the emperor without expression for a time, sipping his wine.

"I cannot," Napoleon finally said. "Do your worst, Monsieur Slidell, but the present political climate prohibits me from acting as you wish. Honestly, I am inclined to reopen the negotiations and conclude a treaty with your country, but even an emperor is limited in what he can do. The people are in a great state of agitation on the slavery matter. The trial of this Lowell fellow in New Orleans is being followed in rapt fascination. Saul has become something of a mythic hero. This proposed bill to execute without a trial people who help rebel slaves is being very poorly received in France. In such a climate, how could I announce to the country that we have resumed our negotiations? The people would be outraged."

"You're a Bonaparte," Slidell said firmly. "Since when did you care about the whims of the people?"

"We live in a different age, Monsieur. We live in the age of the nations, not the kings, and the nation is the people. I have granted the people the freedom of the press. I have given our assemblies genuine political power. If I were to do as you want, the people would use these instruments against me. Not to be rude, Monsieur, but I have weightier matters of state on my mind than the proposed treaty with your Confederacy. I have to keep Germany from unifying under the Prussian banner. I have to keep the British and the Russians in check. I have to protect Rome from those unseemly Italian nationalists. A treaty between France and your country is not a big enough prize for me to risk offending the people."

"You want to resurrect France's imperial ambitions in the Americas. An alliance with us is a necessary first step in that process. You won't be able to subdue the Mexican resistance without our help."

"Yes, yes, yes, I know. But not now. Perhaps in a few years, once matters settle down in both your country and mine."

Slidell didn't have many years left in his life, he knew. The idea of waiting was not acceptable. He wanted the treaty signed and ratified, ensuring that the Confederacy would be safe from any future aggression by the United States, before he breathed his last.

"You'll risk having this affair come into the open?" Slidell asked.

Napoleon chuckled slightly. "Oh, Monsieur. All of France knows of my fondness for the ladies. All of Europe, in fact. One more attempted seduction will not bother anyone."

"But the husband of this lady is not some court flunky. My son-in-law is one of the most powerful bankers in France. You owe him a great deal of money, as do many of your friends. Suppose that he calls all these loans in at once, by way of retaliation. He can make life rather uncomfortable for you and many of your friends."

Napoleon sighed. "Yes, I suppose. This will be rather more inconvenient." He thought for a few moments. "Monsieur Slidell, you and I are both reasonable men. I would like to keep this incident quiet, for the peace of mind of both my wife and your son-in-law. Surely you do not want him to feel aggrieved towards your daughter."

Slidell said nothing in response, worrying that any response he gave to this question might push Napoleon into sensing that he had been caught in a prearranged trap. Instead, he simply set his face in a determined fume and stared into the fire.

The emperor went on. "Do you recall, Monsieur, the treaty to enforce the ban on the African slave trade that your country signed with the British immediately after they extended recognition to you in early 1865?"

"Of course," Slidell replied.

"The British required it of you as a precondition of their recognition."

"I remember it well. I do not need you to remind me."

Slidell's mind briefly churned with memories of the heady days that had followed Lincoln's defeat in the 1864 presidential election. The Confederacy had been firmly established by the success of Lee's defense of Richmond and Petersburg and Johnston's tremendous victories at Atlanta and Fairburn in Georgia. It seemed only a matter of time before the incoming McClellan administration agreed to the peace talks that eventually were held in Toronto.

Judah Benjamin, meanwhile, had been feverishly working to obtain the long-sought diplomatic recognition from Britain and France. Despite all of Slidell's efforts, Napoleon III had been unwilling to act before the British. Her Majesty's government had agreed to extend recognition, but only if the Confederates first approved a treaty that gave the Royal Navy the right to search Confederate ships on the high seas suspected of being involved in the African slave trade. There had been some resistance among the Fire-Eaters, especially Robert Rhett, but as the Confederate Constitution already made the slave trade illegal and the prize to be won was so great, Davis had agreed. The Senate, after acrimonious debate, had ratified the agreement.

"Your country is an odd paradox, Monsieur," the Emperor said. "A slave-holding republic. The rest of the world doesn't like it. You're like the ugly lady that shows up at the party. I have heard from some of your people, and from you on occasion, that slavery is going to end at some distant point in the future. But I see no sign of this. The British extended you recognition only because you signed the treaty banning the slave trade as a gesture against slavery. They wanted your cotton and tobacco, of course, but they couldn't sell recognition to their own people without some sort of token action on your part, a subtle admission that slavery is a negative thing."

Slidell saw where the conversation was going. "So you're telling me that you require a similar gesture on our part now in order to reopen the treaty negotiations?"

"That, and a gentleman's word that the events of this evening will be kept quiet."

"What sort of gesture?"

"This proposed legislation about controlling newspapers and executing abolitionists must not become law, for one thing."

Slidell sighed. "I cannot control the legislative process in the Confederacy, as you well know."

"That is unfortunate."

"Something else, perhaps?"

Napoleon looked at Slidell thoughtfully. "You might let this man. . . what's his name? The fellow in New Orleans?"

"Charles Russell Lowell?"

"Yes, him. Perhaps you might let him live?"

"Surely you aren't serious. The man is a terrorist. If a man attempted to assassinate you, would you let him live?"

"Perhaps, if I thought it best for the nation."

"In any case, it's not up to me. It's up to the court in Louisiana. I don't expect him to escape execution."

Napoleon shrugged. "Well, you told me your price. I told you mine. I cannot sign this treaty under current circumstances, because the people would not stand for it. If the Confederacy were to make some grand gesture against slavery, however, those circumstances would change. Perhaps then we could move forward. Your country has done this before, with the British. I see no reason why it might not do something similar now, with us."

Slidell considered this very carefully. "I will look into it, Your Majesty."

"And keep this quiet, at least until you find out?"

"Yes."

"Very well," Napoleon said. "Perhaps we might formalize our decision over a glass of wine, then?"

September 28, Afternoon
Spotswood Hotel Ballroom, Richmond, Virginia

Breckinridge was surprised to feel nervous. Over the course of his political career in Kentucky, when he had fought in electoral contests for seats in the state legislature and then Congress, he had made hundreds of speeches. As vice president, he had made speeches to large audiences around the country on behalf of President Buchanan, albeit rarely on anything substantive or controversial. He had spoken to great assemblies of soldiers during his time as a general and in various different capacities since he had become Secretary of War.

He was not a shy man and had never understood those who had a fear of public speaking. Indeed, he usually found the experience enjoyable and invigorating, like taking a walk on a crisp autumn day. Yet Breckinridge couldn't deny that there were butterflies in his stomach. He knew that he was about to make the most important speech of his life, which was going to be covered by newspapers across the Confederacy and, indeed, the whole world. It would be a speech that would very possibly determine whether or not he was going to win the presidential election.

Breckinridge sat in a chair on the speaker's platform to the left of the podium, willing himself to remain still. The last thing he wanted the newspapers to print was that he appeared anxious before making his speech. It would be a few minutes before he stood to speak.

A man named William Simms was currently addressing the crowd. A friend of Breckinridge's, he had represented Kentucky in the Confederate Senate before the Treaty of Toronto had ended Confederate claims to the state and, with it, its congressional representation in Richmond. Since then, Simms had set up a successful law practice in Nashville and had become the head of the Tennessee Chapter of the Orphan Society. Breckinridge considered him a good example of Orphan success, a man exiled from his home state making a new life for himself in the Confederacy. He had been chosen to introduce Breckinridge.

It had been endlessly frustrating to Breckinridge that he had to run for president while simultaneously dealing with his pressing duties at Mechanic's Hall. Beauregard was under no such constraint, happy to wait quietly in his New Orleans mansion until the election had passed. On the other hand, Breckinridge wondered how much influence Beauregard actually had on the States' Rights Party and its campaign. It seemed far more likely that Toombs was the one calling the shots, as Breckinridge had predicted from the commencement of the campaign.

He sighed. Things were not going well. While efforts to organize local and state committees to support his campaign had been generally successful, he couldn't deny that they had not matched the organizational prowess that the SRP was demonstrating. From Reagan in Texas, Gordon in Georgia, and other state leaders throughout the Confederacy, Breckinridge was receiving discouraging reports. SRP rallies were larger than those organized by Breckinridge supporters and the people attending them appeared more enthusiastic. Miles had set off on his tour through Tennessee, Virginia, and North Carolina, but Breckinridge doubted that whatever good he would be able to do would be enough to counteract tide that was moving against him.

Newspapers were coming out with their endorsements. Before the war, most of the papers had been firmly Democratic in their loyalties, with only a few broadsheets adhering to a more independent stance or wistfully remembering the days of the old Whigs. With party politics only now beginning to grip the Confederacy, however, everything was in flux. Editors and owners were free to choose between Breckinridge and Beauregard and were being fervently courted by both sides. Unsurprisingly, most of the papers that voiced heavy criticism of Jefferson Davis had lined up behind Beauregard's candidacy, though not all. No one had been surprised that almost every newspaper in Louisiana, including the *Daily Delta* and the *New Orleans Daily Crescent*, had endorsed Beauregard. Worryingly, most of the papers in Georgia had as well, which surely showed the influence of Toombs and Stephens at work. On a happier note, Breckinridge had noted that most of the big newspapers in Tennessee, a crucial state, were endorsing him over Beauregard. Just before leaving for the speech that very morning, Breckinridge had learned that the *Daily Journal* in Wilmington, North Carolina, had endorsed him.

Most of the newspapers in South Carolina were supporting Beauregard, with one critical exception. The *Charleston Mercury*, naturally enough, had emerged as the mouthpiece of its owner Robert Rhett's quixotic quest for the presidency. Every day, the paper was publishing editorial pieces blasting both Breckinridge and Beauregard and advocating such extreme measures as the reopening of the African slave trade, the expulsion of all free blacks from the Confederacy, and making it illegal for slave-owners to free their slaves.

Breckinridge held Rhett in contempt and thought his views were an embarrassment to the Confederacy. He winced at the thought that men in the United States and Europe read Rhett's writings and might think them representative of mainstream Southern thought. Perhaps more worrisome for Breckinridge was the question of exactly how many of his fellow Confederate felt as Rhett did on the slavery question. If it were a majority, or even a significant minority, then the country could not succeed in the long run.

Rhett's presidential campaign had not gained much traction. His supporters had ensured that his name would appear on the ballot in every Confederate state except Texas and Arkansas, but he had secured few important supporters. The prominent pro-slavery academic James DeBow had published a piece supporting Rhett in his periodical *DeBow's Review* and there had a few scattered endorsements among businessmen and a few low-ranking military officers. No major office-holder had joined the Rhett bandwagon, however, nor did any seem likely to do so.

Breckinridge guessed that Rhett would gain a few percentage points of the vote in the Deep South and essentially nothing in the Upper South. Every vote that Rhett garnered was almost certainly a vote taken away from the Beauregard-Toombs ticket rather than his own. This would not be enough to make Breckinridge competitive in South Carolina, Florida, Louisiana, or Mississippi, but it might give him a slight chance in Alabama and could prove crucial in the all-important state of Georgia. It gave him at least a glimmer of hope amid mostly bad news.

The other factor which gave Breckinridge hope was the Orphan Society itself. Looking around the packed ballroom, he saw more than a thousand friendly faces, his brothers from his beloved Kentucky. Exiles like himself, he knew hundreds of them personally. All, he was certain, were going to support him to the hilt. Many had already donated money or volunteered their time to his campaign. That most of the Kentucky Confederates had settled in the Upper South might help give him an edge in the crucial states.

Breckinridge knew how much was riding on this speech. Having been scheduled before the announcement of his candidacy, he could give the speech without technically violating the taboo against presidential candidates actively campaigning for office. On the other hand, no one saw it as anything other than a campaign speech. It would be his only chance to personally respond to the vicious attacks being leveled against him by the SRP and to articulate his own vision of the Confederacy. It might be the moment that would make or break his chance to be the next President of the Confederate States of America.

Simms turned from the podium and looked at him, wordlessly asking him if he was ready. Breckinridge took a deep breath and nodded slightly. Simms turned back to the audience.

"It is now my distinct honor and privilege to introduce a man whom we all hold in the highest esteem. As a congressman and senator before the dark days in which our state fell under the Yankee sway, he fought for us in Washington with honor and integrity. During the war, he bled with us on countless battlefields. He commanded many of us and has always been our greatest advocate here in Richmond. Gentlemen, I introduce to you our Secretary of War and the next President of the Confederate States of America, Major General John C. Breckinridge!"

He stood from his chair and strode towards the podium as the ballroom exploded in a thunderous chorus of applause and cheers. He felt his nervousness vanish in an instant. The warmth and support of the Kentuckians filled him with energy and a strange calmness. The Orphans were his people and he felt at home with them in a way he never could with others.

Breckinridge set his notes down and gripped both sides of the podium, knowing from long experience at speechmaking that he had to find something to do with his hands to avoid looking foolish. He smiled broadly as the cheering and clapping continued. A single individual stood, then another, then another, until suddenly every man in the room rose to his feet and the applause reached such a loud crescendo that Breckinridge was convinced it could be heard halfway across Richmond.

He held up his hands for quiet. It took perhaps thirty seconds, but the applause began to die down. He waited until it had diminished to the point where he could be heard.

"My friends, I thank you!"

Breckinridge was surprised when this simple line was greeted by another explosion of cheers and applause, with everyone again standing from their seats to clap with irrational enthusiasm. It seemed to him that everyone in the audience was attempting to clap harder than everyone else, a strange phenomenon he had noticed at many political rallies over the years. He saw the intense looks in the eyes of the audience members and suddenly felt a heavy responsibility. These men were placing their trust in him, looking to him for the leadership necessary to bring their new country through the storms that were inevitably coming.

He was the one to do it, Breckinridge knew. His initial reluctance to seek the presidency had long since vanished. He was not a braggart, but he knew that he had the vision, the knowledge, the experience, and the integrity to do the job better than anybody else. The alternative was Beauregard, who would be dominated by Toombs and the rest of the Fire-Eaters. Down that road lay disaster for the Confederacy. Breckinridge alone was the man to save the country. He prayed a silent prayer that he was not succumbing to hubris and that he was seeking the presidency for the right reasons.

He held up his hands again and allowed the tumult to die down. "My friends, I thank you!" he said again. "I thank you from the bottom of my heart for such a welcome." He paused a moment for effect, taking a deep breath before going on. "We have been through a great deal together, all of us. We had to flee our native state and join the Southern Confederacy. We did so because the North was trying to deny the South its dearest rights and, while we are all Kentuckians, we are also all Southerners. We fought side-by-side during the war. I commanded many of you when I led the Orphan Brigade. At Shiloh, Murfreesboro, Chickamauga, and lots of other places, our blood mingled on the same hills and along the same creeks." He paused again. "It was always my dream to lead you back into Kentucky at the head of an army of liberation. Alas, fate decreed otherwise."

There was silence in the hall, just as Breckinridge had expected. The faces watching him were sad and somber. Many of these men, like himself, had not seen Kentucky since 1861. He went on, speaking of the terrible day in October of 1862 when he had been marching his division, including the Orphan Brigade, north from Knoxville towards the Kentucky border. Only about twenty miles south of the line, however, news arrived of the defeat at Perryville and the end of the Confederate campaign to occupy Kentucky. He spoke with genuine emotion, for it had been one of the saddest days of his life.

"I am sorry I could not do better. But the past is the past. We are all Confederates now. We could have returned to our state and lived under Yankee rule, but we have chosen to make new lives for ourselves in this independent Southern nation. I do not begrudge our fellow Kentuckians who chose to side with the United States. We all have choices to make in life. We, the Orphans, have chosen a particular path. It sets us apart, but we choose to embark on this journey together. Having done so, we must stand together."

There was warm applause around the hall. Breckinridge was pleased and took a sip of water. He wanted to finish this portion of the speech quickly, for the last thing he needed was too much attention to be drawn to the fact that he was a native of a state that had not joined the Confederacy. As it was the annual meeting of the Orphan Society, he could scarcely have ignored the fact and he did not wish to offend any of his fellow Orphans. Yet he needed to move on to the part of the speech that would matter. Moreover, he sensed that his audience was wanting and expecting him to do so as well.

"We have each striven to build new lives for ourselves in the Confederacy. Some of us have remained in the army and have continued to serve in defense of this new nation. Some of us have embarked upon new careers in business or the law. Others have resettled on new farms and begun to work the bountiful land of the South. And still others, like myself, have taken positions in government. I hope, in my tenure as Secretary of War, that I have proven to be useful to the Southern people."

He had carefully written that particular paragraph, seeking to pivot from speaking about Kentuckians to speaking about Southerners. He glanced over to the left side of the ballroom, where a cluster of perhaps two dozen reporters were scribbling down his words in shorthand.

"It is no secret to anyone in this room that I have been called upon to seek an office above that of my current post. I have been asked many times in recent months why I have accepted the challenge of seeking the Presidency of the Confederate States. Many of those who have asked me this question are here in this room. I feel obligated to explain myself to the people at large and I hope that my fellow Orphans will forgive me."

There was a muttering in the room. Breckinridge's words were not unexpected, but that made the occasion no less unorthodox. He felt a tinge of fear and regret, for he knew he was violating an American political principle that had existed since before the Revolution. It was unbecoming of a presidential candidate to actively campaign for the office; this fact was one of the pillars of the way politics worked in America. Breckinridge felt like a man telling God that he was choosing to disobey one of the Commandments. Yet he knew he had no choice.

"My great-grandfather signed the Declaration of Independence. My grandfather served in the administration of Thomas Jefferson and passed the famous Kentucky Resolutions, asserting the right of the states to control their own destinies in the face of the power of the federal government. Service comes naturally to the Breckinridge family. It is in my blood. Whether in the Kentucky state legislature, the United States Congress, the Confederate Army, or as the Secretary of War in our new government, I have always striven to serve the people of the South. I have always and will always do whatever is necessary to preserve the liberties of the South and to protect and preserve our unique institutions."

While writing his speech, he had sent copies of his drafts to some of his confidantes and advisors. James Kemper had told him that he needed to make a full and forceful defense of slavery at this point in the speech, but he had decided against it. He remembered the criticism that Alexander Stephens had received when he had described black slavery as the "cornerstone" upon which the Confederacy was built. That speech had been received very poorly in Europe and had made a mockery of the South's efforts to explain secession merely as a measure to protect its own freedom.

He could not ignore slavery, of course. Right or wrong, it was the reason the South had seceded and formed the Confederacy. The SRP was loud and boisterous in its open defense of the enslavement of the blacks. If he failed to make a statement in defense of the institution, they would tear him apart. Breckinridge recognized that slavery was an evil that eventually had to end, but he could not say so without destroying his chances of winning the election. If he lost the election, obviously, he could scarcely help lead the nation down the path he knew it must go.

"I will protect our institutions," Breckinridge repeated. "To the utmost of my ability, I will. There will never be any slackening of effort or lack of will on my part. If elected, I shall never allow any outsider to meddle in our affairs. Not the Northerners, nor the British, nor the French, nor anyone else. This was why we fought the war, is it not? The South governs the South. No one else does. If any man listening here today believes that I will falter or be found wanting in preserving our cherished rights, let him stand alone in his total error."

He paused, looking out at the crowd. There were neither smiles nor frowns evident on their faces. Every expression was one of attention and intense seriousness. It was exactly what he wanted.

"I have heard that certain persons, whose names I shall refrain from mentioning, assert that I am not a man who cherishes our Southern institutions. These misguided friends of mine claim that because I myself do not own slaves, that I shall not protect the right of any other man to do so. My friends, let me say that these people are completely and utterly wrong. I have held many offices over many years. I am used to being the subject of malicious slanders of all sorts. I take no offense. I merely point out that these people are as wrong as they would be if they claimed that the sun was blue or that two plus two equaled seven."

There was a slight chuckling in the audience. He didn't need to say the name of Robert Toombs for everyone to know precisely whom he was talking about. The jokes were not especially funny, but he knew that they would make it into the newspapers, and so would his stated commitment to preserve the institution of slavery. It left him sufficient ambiguity, however, to salve his own conscience and to allow foreign observers to draw their own conclusions.

"Yet I find this business of responding to my critics to be tiresome. I wish, rather to describe what I want to do if I am so fortunate as to be chosen by my fellow citizens to be the next president of the nation."

There was another uneasy murmur in the crowd, for he was going further in his break with protocol. Glancing over at the reporters, he could see raised eyebrows on many of their faces.

"The course I shall pursue, if elected president, can be summed up very easily. I want peace and political stability so that the country can recover from the war." He paused, letting these simple words sink it. He glanced over at the reporters, waiting for them to stop scribbling. "Let me repeat that. I want peace and political stability so that the country can recover from the war. That will be my policy, the North Star by which my administration will be guided."

He went on, describing the need to restore fiscal stability and bring the national and state debts under control, while not raising taxes any more than necessary. He stressed the need for the central government to cooperate with state governments in rebuilding the Southern railroad system, so that the cotton and tobacco would once again be able to flow to foreign markets. He wanted to get his position on these issues on the record, so that the newspapers would discuss his platform, but he did not want to get bogged down. While important, this part of the speech was not emotionally exciting and he did not want to lose his audience.

"Allow me to speak for a few moments on the matter of our foreign relations. We fought a long and vicious war with the United States to secure our independence. Having succeeded, we must strive to build a strong and lasting friendship with our neighbor to the north. An acrimonious relationship helps no one. Having separated ourselves from one another, I see no reason why our Confederacy cannot be on good terms with the United States, as we would hope to have with any other nation. We owe it to the next generation, on both sides of the border, to ensure that there will never again be conflict between the two great republics of the North American continent. In the event that the United States finds itself in a quarrel with any other nation, my administration will pursue a policy of strict neutrality."

Most of the audience listened quietly and some nodded their heads in agreement. However, for the first time, Breckinridge thought he heard disapproving grumbling. He wasn't surprised, for there had been chatter among the Orphans that the Confederacy should ally itself with the British Empire and launch a campaign to reclaim Kentucky in the event that the Fenian Crisis resulted in war. Breckinridge wondered what they would have thought had they been privy to what Garnet Wolseley had told him.

Breckinridge felt a profound sense of relief, however. In making clear his determination to pursue friendly relations with the United States, he had unshackled himself from Jefferson Davis. He knew that the chief executive would not be pleased with him, but it was not going to come as any surprise. As the day of the election drew nearer, Davis was gradually fading from the scene. Whether the sun would be rising on Breckinridge or Beauregard remained to be seen.

He went on. "I wish to make a few comments on the proposed treaty with France, of which I am an enthusiastic supporter. It has been said by some that signing the treaty would be akin to shackling ourselves to the ambitions of the Emperor of the French. Those who oppose the treaty have reminded us of the warnings of Washington and Jefferson against entangling alliances with other nations. Let me correct any misconceptions which might be held by any in this audience. First, we are not shackling ourselves to the French. The terms of the treaty call for us to provide assistance to the French in maintain a government in Mexico that is friendly to us. We should do this in any event, should we not? It calls for greater trade between the Confederacy and France. We should support this in any event, should we not? In exchange for this, France pledges to support us in the event of any future conflict with the United States. If, at any point in the future, we no longer feel that this treaty with France is worth continuing, we shall discontinue it and part on cordial terms. Were this a business deal, any one of us would see right away that it made for a good bargain. In my view, agreeing to such a treaty with France is a concession to common sense. Those who think otherwise are allowing themselves to be blinded by the prejudices of the past and refusing to acknowledge the realities of the present."

Breckinridge scanned the faces of the crowd and saw that he still held their attention. Glancing at the reporters, he could see them furiously scribbling away, taking his speech down word-for-word. He felt increasingly confident. Looking down at his notes, he saw to his surprise that he had not turned any pages since he began speaking. He habitually committed his speeches to memory before making them, but usually referred to his notes to know he was where he needed to be. Thus far, he hadn't had to do that.

"Allow me to say one more thing on the subject of foreign policy. Those running for office under the banner of the States' Rights Party have often asserted the need for the Confederacy to gain control of Cuba. Indeed, some have even suggested that we seize the island by force. I disagree. I am not opposed to one day welcoming Cuba into our Confederacy, but that should only be done through an honorable agreement with Spain and in accordance with the will of the island's inhabitants. My administration shall never indulge in imprudent imperialistic projects, nor shall I ever lead a government which would violate all accepted norms of the laws of nations by engaging in war except in self-defense." He paused for a moment. "I have seen too many young men slaughtered on too many battlefields. I have no desire to see more slaughtered in the swamps of Cuba."

These comments were greeted with warm applause. Those people who supported the acquisition of Cuba were almost entirely from the Deep South. Few Orphans that Breckinridge knew supported the idea with any enthusiasm and most were as strongly opposed to it as he was.

Breckinridge was on safe and solid ground at this point in the speech and felt comfortable. He could talk about policy all day if necessary, for he had a gift for getting to the heart of a matter and speaking of it in a way that made his hearers realize how relevant it was to their own lives. He knew, however, that his speech was about to move him into dangerous territory.

"I now wish to address the events that have taken place in southern Louisiana over the past several months. In my capacity as Secretary of War, I bore overall responsibility for the suppression of the slave insurrection in that quarter. If it was not suppressed as quickly as might have been desirable, I can only plead the difficulty of fighting in such a swampy wilderness and the ease with which the insurgents could conceal themselves. If the fault lies with any man, I take it entirely upon myself. The seriousness of the uprising was not apparent when it first began and I thought it best to avoid inflaming the situation if at all possible."

Eyebrows went up among the reporters, but Breckinridge paid no mind. The spokesmen of the SRP were denouncing him for the failure to easily suppress the Saul uprising anyway, so the appearance of taking responsibility would make him appear the bigger man. Besides, it was not the point he was trying to make and he hurried on to the next portion of the speech.

"The uprising would have been put down much more quickly and with less loss of life had it not been for the actions of the abolitionist terrorist Charles Russell Lowell. His smuggling of rifles and ammunition to the insurgents, under the nose of the authorities of the state of Louisiana, gave new life to an uprising that had been all but snuffed out. Fortunately, this man was captured and is now on trial in New Orleans. I fully expect him to be found guilty and to face execution."

He paused for a moment, taking time for a sip of water before continuing.

"It has been suggested by one of my distinguished political opponents, Senator Robert Toombs, that Lowell be summarily executed, that his crimes are so terrible that he does not deserve to be granted a trial. This suggestion has been taken up by other spokesmen of the so-called States' Rights Party, as well as by many of our country's newspapers. I must state that I emphatically oppose such an arbitrary and extralegal measure." He took a deep breath, for he was about to say the most important words of the speech. "Moreover, I charge all those who favor it are betraying the principles upon which our Confederacy was founded."

There was a sudden muttering in the crowd and a few audible gasps. It was bad enough to be a presidential candidate giving a campaign speech, but Breckinridge had taken it a step further by issuing a strong attack on the opposition. It was unprecedented, but having come this far, he had to push through to the conclusion. There was no going back.

"We are a new nation, forged in the fires of war. We are still emerging onto the world's stage, like a student who has just left university and now has to make his way in the world. In Montgomery, when we created our government, we pledged our Confederacy to be a nation of law, with its own unique institutions, to be sure, but a nation of law that can be respected among the other nations of the world. One of the pillars of the law is the right to a fair trial. Even John Brown was granted that right. If Lowell is denied a fair trial, if he is summarily executed as some of our fellow citizens have advocated, then we shall reveal ourselves to the world as a fraud, a pretender to nationhood, and not a country to be taken seriously."

He could see heads in the crowd nodding in agreement. Strengthened, Breckinridge went on.

"Another pillar of constitutional government is the freedom of the press. Seven decades ago, my grandfather passed the Kentucky Resolutions in response to the Alien and Sedition Acts, by which an aspiring tyranny sought to stifle dissent by shutting down those newspapers which questioned its methods and policies. Had I been there, I would have stood shoulder-to-shoulder with him, just as I now stand in defiance of any attempt to curtail the right of any man to exercise his freedom of opinion, whether or not I agree with him."

He had been careful not to mention the Bill for the Prevention and Speedy Suppression of Servile Insurrection by name. Yet he was now on record in opposition to its provisions. As a man devoted to constitutional government, he saw no other choice. He had to trust that enough Southern people felt as he did, and cared more about the rule of law than about slavery, to bring him safely through the election. If he was wrong, perhaps it was best not to win the election.

"We are not barbarians!" he said forcefully. These were the words he wanted the reporters to hear most of all, but to him they summed up the difference between his point of view and that of the SRP. He decided to repeat them. "We are not barbarians! We are the heirs of Washington and Jefferson, of Madison and Clay. The Confederacy must be a civilized nation, a nation of laws, and not descend into the realm of barbarism and mob violence. Down that road lies chaos. Down that road lies national disgrace and disintegration. Down that road lies the ruins of everything we fought the war to achieve."

Again, there was utter silence in the ballroom, yet all the eyes seemed attentive. He still had the crowd. The reporters went on with their scribbling. It was time to move to the end.

"I am not an ambitious man. Were it up to me, I should leave government service and grow old with my wife while watching my children grow into honorable men and proper women. But I cannot say no to the call of service. I am convinced that I can help move the Confederacy forward and I ask for your help and support in doing so."

Now the silence broke. In an instant, like the thunderclap of a storm one had not known was coming, a thunderous burst of applause filled the room. As one, the hundreds of Orphans stood up, clapping and cheering more loudly than almost anything Breckinridge had ever heard. Many began striding up to the speaker's platform, extending their hands up to him. He reached down and began shaking hand after hand. Within a matter of minutes, his hand was sore, yet he kept at it. It reminded him of the occasions when he spoke to soldiers just before leading them into battle. These men, he knew, would follow him.

It was a fitting analogy, he thought, for battle was exactly where he was about to lead them.

September 29, Afternoon
Granbury County Courthouse, Waco, Texas

"All right, Mr. McFadden," the man was saying. "But what about this whole business with France? You don't support that, do you?"

McFadden was taken somewhat by surprise at this question. "Well, my friend, I'm just running for the state legislature. Issues like our relations with other countries is the business of the government in Richmond, not the legislature in Austin."

"Course it is," the man replied. "But the state legislature chooses who Texas sends to Richmond to be in the Senate, don't it? And the Senate gets to say yes or no to treaties, don't it? So what you think about that would help tell me what kind of man you'd want to send to Richmond, see?"

"That's a good point," McFadden acknowledged. He had not previously considered it. "I'll be honest with you, friend, I'm not rightly sure whether I like the idea of the treaty with France or don't like it. Near as I understand it, it would help keep Mexico friendly to the Confederacy, which would be a good thing. On the other hand, I'm not sure I like the idea of our country being tied to anybody that closely. Best if we keep ourselves free from that sort of thing. But I promise you this. I won't vote to appoint anybody to the Senate unless he's a man I think is smart and honest and who will think everything through carefully before making a decision. How's that?"

The man's eyes narrowed and McFadden could see that he hadn't entirely convinced him. He was one of perhaps a hundred men to whom McFadden had already spoken that day in the square in front of the courthouse, which was filled with people on account of it being a market day. He had set up a table with apple cider and water and invited anyone who wanted to talk with them to stop by, while supporters fanned out across the town for another day of canvassing for supporters.

"But Breckinridge supports it and you support Breckinridge, don't you?"

"Yes, I do," McFadden replied. "But just because I support him doesn't mean I have to agree with him on everything, does it?"

"No, I suppose not," the man said. "Anyway, nice talking you." The man, whose name remained unknown to McFadden, began to walk away.

"Hope to have your vote on Election Day!" McFadden called after him.

"I'll think about it!" the man called back over his shoulder.

"He seemed pleasant," Annie, who was sitting next to him, observed after the man had passed beyond hearing distance. "Pleasant, but not easily persuaded."

"About what we should expect here in Texas," McFadden replied. "People are proud and have their own opinions. They don't like being told what to do." He thought about it for a moment. "If I win the election, I'm not going to be a leader. It will be the people I represent who will lead me. I will have to follow their orders, won't I?"

"Yes," Annie said. "But that's the way it's supposed to be, isn't it?"

He laughed and nodded, looking around as he did so. The square was filled with people buying and selling things. A lot of livestock trading was going on, along with people selling or trading peaches, watermelons, and other produce. Some of the local carpenters had set up displays of their sturdy rocking chairs and were hawking them as loudly as they could. It was a lively scene and McFadden enjoyed it.

On the other side of the square, occasionally visible through the crowd, was the table Collett had set up, following his example. They had discussed sitting together, then concluded that they would be able to speak to more people if they positioned themselves in different places. Every now and then Collett would wave at him, a smile on his face, so McFadden assumed that things were going well.

More people came up to speak to him. Some had specific local issues they wanted to discuss, such as whether state money could be used to build another public school. Others wanted to talk about broader concerns more suitable to the national race. To everyone who asked him about his views on slavery, he told the same thing. No, he didn't own slaves himself. No, he didn't oppose slavery. Several people wanted to know nothing aside from whether he was a Beauregard man or a Breckinridge man.

For the first time, he noted in his mind that it felt rather cooler than it had the week before. He prayed that the grip of summer was being released and the refreshing breezes of autumn were not far distant. He loved Texas and never intended to leave, but his adoration did not extend to the heat of the summer.

He was talking to yet another potential voter, who wanted to know if he was firmly committed to securing adequate pensions for veterans, when Charles Anderson, one of his fellow veterans and closest supporters, came running up to the table, an agitated expression on his face.

"Jimmy!" Anderson called. "You got to come right away!"

"What is it?" McFadden asked in alarm.

"Walker's boys! They've got Bobby Farmer!"

"Got him? What do you mean?"

"They've arrested him. But he didn't do nothing! Our boys aren't letting them leave!"

"Where?" McFadden asked urgently.

"This way! Follow me!"

He looked quickly at Annie. "Go back to the ranch at once!"

She nodded and rose to leave. McFadden bolted away from the table, following Anderson. They immediately left the square behind and began running down one of the main streets, passing not too far from Flynn's Alehouse. Minutes later, they came upon an ugly scene on one of the sidewalks. Farmer was surrounded by a dozen of Walker's men standing in a rough semicircle, though Walker himself was nowhere to be seen. Two held pistols at Farmer's head, while he stood still as a statue, a tense but angry look on his face. The rest of the posse had their guns out as well, aiming them at a group of McFadden's supporters just yards away in the middle of the street, some of whom had rifles held up in firing positions. It was obviously a standoff even edgier than that which had taken place at the ranch two weeks before.

"What's the meaning of this?" McFadden loudly demanded as he jogged up. He pointed to one of the men holding a gun to Farmer's head. "You there! Why are you holding that man?"

"Orders," he replied simply. "From Walker." The tone of the man's voice was one of utter contempt and disdain.

Something snapped in McFadden at that moment. All the disrespect for the law shown by Roden, the man ostensibly charged with enforcing it, had gnawed at him for months. The arrogance of Walker and the casual threats of violence towards his family had enraged him. It had been a miracle of restraint that he had not exploded long before now. Seeing a friend and former comrade being threatened with death, on top of everything else he had endured from these people, was too much to bear. He shoved aside two of the other men and, pulling out his Navy Colt, pointed it inches away from the face of the man who had spoken.

"Let him go or I'll kill you," he said coldly.

Seeing the look in McFadden's eyes, the man's face went from a mask of haughtiness to one of fear. The man instantly lowered his weapon and, after a moment, so did the other one. McFadden grabbed Farmer by the shirt and pulled him away from Walker's men, keeping his weapon pointed at them. The next few seconds seemed to last an eternity. His soldierly instincts were firing in his brain with an intensity he had not felt since the war. Walker's men were raising their weapons towards his friends as they backed away towards the center of the street. McFadden's friends, with Enfields or pistols raised, were backing slowly away across the street.

He heard the crack of a shot and saw white gunpowder smoke erupt from the muzzle of one of the guns being aimed in his direction. Beside him, Farmer's head exploded like a watermelon dropped from a great height. McFadden felt the hot blood of his friend splatter onto the right side of his face and into his hair. An instant later, though it seemed to happen slowly, weapons held by his own men and those of Walker were fired almost simultaneously. The street was filled with a cacophony of noise, gunshots mingled with screams of pain and terror.

McFadden pulled the trigger on his Navy Colt, hitting a man squarely in the center of his chest, even as he felt the lifeless body of Farmer collapse in his left arm. Though there was no doubt that he was dead, McFadden felt duty bound to remove the body to a place of safety, so he turned and dragged Farmer's body to the other side of the street, trusting to God that he would not be shot in the back.

Everywhere within his line of sight, people were crying out in alarm and running for safety. The acrid smell of gunpowder instantly brought his mind back to the war. He struggled through the door of a merchant shop directly across the street from where Walker's posse had been standing, lowering Farmer's body onto the floor. He was taken aback by the sight of the dead man's face, for it was entirely unrecognizable.

"What the hell is going on out there?" a man ducking behind the store counter demanded.

"Stay down!" McFadden shouted.

His comrades were scurrying into the store behind him, firing as they went. Two of the men were bleeding profusely from shoulder wounds and one was being carried in by two others, shot through the belly and crying out in agony. McFadden knew from experience that belly wounds were almost always fatal. He felt a jolt of anger and grief when he recognized the man as Jonathan Townsend, a man who had served with him in the 7th Texas and whom he knew well.

As they reached shelter, the men quickly began reloading their weapons. Some of the men peered out the door.

"What do you see?" McFadden asked.

"The bastards ran off," one of the others said. "I see two bodies on the ground, not moving. One other fellow on the ground out there, shot through the leg. Might lose the leg, but not killed, I don't think."

"Get out of my store!" the voice huddled behind the counter yelled.

Several of the men shouted apologies simultaneously, which struck McFadden as ridiculous under the circumstances. Still, he had no desire to remain in the merchant shop. At that moment, Walker's men were doubtless running to their master with word of what had happened. McFadden also wanted to be closer to where his own supporters might be expected to gather.

"We should get to the alehouse," he said sharply, speaking with the same tone of command that had been in his voice during the war. He quickly organized the men, tasking three men with carrying the wounded Townsend and another man to take Farmer's body over his shoulder, while the rest were to cover their movement if any trouble was encountered along the way.

They moved quietly and quickly. As they hurried down the side of the street as best they could, McFadden saw people beginning to gather, trying to piece together the events of the shootout. Seeing them, people began shouting questions and asking who had been killed or hurt. McFadden's men yelled back the names of Farmer and Townsend, adding that Walker's men had been the first to fire. Shouts of outrage followed and soon a crowd began to form, following McFadden and his men as they made their way to Flynn's Alehouse. People began calling for a doctor to treat Townsend, which might have been common sense, but which McFadden knew was going to be futile.

They reached the alehouse, where a crowd had already gathered. McFadden saw Collett among them, a look of intense concern on his face. His eyes focused on the dead body of Farmer and the wounded form of Townsend and McFadden saw his friend's face go red with fury. As McFadden and his group moved towards the door, Collett stepped forward.

"They shot first?" Collett asked.

"Yes," McFadden said quickly.

"Witnesses?"

"Half the town, I would think."

"How's Townsend?"

"Done for, I think," McFadden said as he passed through the door into the alehouse. "Poor bastards. He and Farmer get through the whole damn war and then are killed in a street fight with a posse from out of town."

They laid Townsend down on a table that had been rapidly cleared of plates and glasses. He screamed in pain, made worse by the despair evident in his face. He cried out repeatedly that he was dying. A doctor soon arrived and began tending to the wounded man as best he could. McFadden tried to push him out of his mind, for he knew he could do nothing to help him and could not afford to be distracted.

"What do we do now?" McFadden asked Collett. He was trying to prevent his friend from seeing how flustered he really was. He thought quickly about Annie and Thaddeus. Annie would, by now, be riding back to the ranch, where she would be protected by the men stationed there. Thaddeus had remained at the ranch and was likewise safe.

"I suggest that we put the alehouse in a state of defense. Roden will probably send Walker and his men to get us. Blood has been shed. I doubt it will end with what happened on the street."

They set to work. Men were gathering at the alehouse, armed and ready to fight. Tables were brought outside and turned onto their sides to form makeshift barricades. Holes were broken through parts of the walls to create small firing ports. Flynn piled ammunition behind the bar, which was seen as the safest possible place.

Townsend died about two hours after he was shot. McFadden and a few others stood silently about his body for perhaps a minute, in silent tribute to their friend. He had had no family that anyone knew of. Somebody recalled Townsend mentioning once that he was a Methodist and there was a brief discussion about whether to send for the local Methodist minister, but they quickly came to a decision that this matter could wait. In the meantime, the body was placed with that of Farmer's in the alehouse storeroom.

Allowing sadness to momentarily push out his concern, McFadden stepped out the door into the street in front of the alehouse. Glancing about, he was stunned to see that the crowd had grown to over a hundred men. Some were armed with shotguns and some with old Enfields and Springfields they had probably carried during the war. Most men also had pistols and bowie knives in their belts.

As he came out onto the street, the men began to applaud and cheer. It started slowly, but quickly built up into a loud roar. He was taken aback and had an instinctive moment of fear, even though he was the man being cheered. Amid the cheering, McFadden could make out scattered shouts.

"Let's go get the bastards!"

"They shot first!"

"Enough is enough!"

McFadden held up his hands for silence. Rather to his surprise, it became quiet very quickly. His mind raced as he tried to decide what to say. He sensed that he needed to calm the men down and prevent the situation from becoming worse than it already was. Through the confusion, though, he sensed an opportunity. If he led this eager assembly of men, a small army in the making, in an attack on Roden and Walker, the story would spread through Texas that he was a vigilante and he would probably be deemed an outlaw. On the other hand, if his faction remained quiet and did nothing, the story would be that Walker's man shot first and that he and his people had only acted to defend themselves.

"We will defend ourselves, my friends," McFadden said, loudly enough for all to hear. "We must watch each other's backs. But we're not going to go after them. We've done nothing wrong."

There were many shouts of protest and a large collective groan of disappointment. McFadden sensed he had to keep speaking to retain control of the crowd.

"Listen to me! We are not going to play Roden's game! They shot first! But if we go after them, we will look like the ones who started the whole thing. That's just what Roden wants, don't you see? Remember how Lincoln tricked us into firing on Fort Sumter, so he could say that we started the war? Same thing here, friends. No, we won't strike back. We will defend ourselves. We will defend one another. If Roden sends his hired hand Walker or any of his men to rough you up, or anybody that you know, protect yourselves. But don't do anything stupid. Don't do anything that puts us in the wrong. The election is barely a month away, boys. When it's over, Roden will be finished."

"There won't be an election, McFadden!" someone in the crowd shouted. "You think that Roden will let the vote go forward after this?" There were mutterings of agreement throughout the crowd.

"If there's no election, let that be on him, not us. The folks down in Austin will be on our side. But if we strike back, they might be on Roden's side. Let's not let that happen, okay?"

He turned and walked back into the alehouse. He wasn't sure of the impact his speaking would have on the crowd, but hoped that his refusal to lead them in violence against Roden would deter them from doing anything to further inflame the situation. In the meantime, he would wait to see if Roden and Walker decided to attack.

Afternoon faded into evening and evening into night. No attack came.

"I am placing a lot of trust in you, Benjamin," Lowell said as he took his seat at the defense table at the front of the courtroom. "I hope I'm not wrong to do so."

"You will find your trust vindicated, I assure you," Benjamin said warmly, leaning his walking stick against the table as he sat down. "I would not come all this way just to spend a few pleasant days in my hometown."

Lowell merely grunted in reply. He had spent several hours a day with Benjamin over the past week, both in the courtroom and in the confines of his cell, where they had talked over the details of the trial. He found that Benjamin drew forth from him a strange combination of respect and loathing. The man clearly had a brilliant mind and seemed genuinely friendly. Yet behind this façade, Lowell thought he sensed dark purposes and a complete lack of scruples. Moreover, he had begun to suspect that Benjamin was among that strange group who preferred intimate relations with other men rather than with women, a group whom Lowell had never understood.

The previous week of the trial had been anticlimactic. When Benjamin first took over as his defense counsel, Lowell had expected shift and sudden changes, yet events had unfolded with a mundane predictability. Eustis, the prosecuting attorney, had read the detailed reports sent in by Longstreet regarding the events in New Iberia, which made clear that the Springfields smuggled to Saul by Lowell had made the insurgent operation possible. A representative of the Confederate State Department, who had ironically been a subordinate of Benjamin himself until earlier in the month, presented what had been pieced together regarding Lowell's purchasing of the weapons. A man from the New Orleans Police Department gave evidence regarding the arrival of the *SS Vincent* and what had been gathered from the interrogation of Gardet.

According to what Benjamin had told Lowell, Franklin Sanborn and George Stearns, his co-conspirators, had fled the United States by taking ship to Europe, though their exact whereabouts were unknown. Charles Sumner was strongly suspected of involvement as well, though he had apparently chosen to remain in Washington City. Tellingly, Benjamin had not asked Lowell for any details regarding others involved in the plot. Any information Lowell might have given him would have been protected by the traditional confidentiality between lawyer and client, so the only conclusion Lowell could draw was that Benjamin simply didn't care.

The courtroom was slowly filling up. Lowell had grown familiar with many of the faces of the reporters, though he was not permitted to speak to them. Many of the socialites who had been attending the trial in the first days had stopped showing up, perhaps having become bored as the proceedings had grown technical and mundane. He frowned at the realization that, for many people, his trial was nothing but a meaningless spectacle, no more important than the latest theatrical production.

His guilt was obvious and he had made no attempt to disguise it. This fact was the key to the legal maneuver Benjamin had in mind. It had taken him quite a bit of persuasion before Lowell agreed to it.

"All rise!" the bailiff said loudly. Lowell rose along with everyone else as Judge Moise strode in the side door, his naturally regal bearing heightened by his formidable judicial robes. He took his seat with the same grave expression that had characterized his face since the first day of the trial. For just a moment, Lowell thought he saw a moment of eye contact between Moise and Benjamin.

Lowell took his seat, as did nearly everyone else in the room. Benjamin, however, remained standing.

"Your Honor?" Benjamin asked.

Moise looked over at him, a tired expression on his face. "Yes, counselor?"

"My client wishes to change his plea."

A murmur of interest and confusion filled the courtroom. Out of the corner of his right eye, Lowell could see Eustis sit up sharply in surprise. Benjamin turned his head slightly and grinned, pleased at the impact his simple words had had. Moise sighed and it was apparent to Lowell that he was not surprised. He glanced over at Benjamin, who responded with nothing but his habitual grin.

"Well, General Lowell?"

He stood up and looked at Judge Moise, then was seized by a moment of indecision. He and Benjamin had gone over the implications of what he was about to do very carefully the night before. There was no going back now.

"I wish to change my plea to guilty, Your Honor."

Gasps of astonishment filled the courtroom. The reporters, who had expected another day of dry testimony, frantically started scribbling on their pads. Eustis looked over at Lowell and Benjamin, eyebrows raised in an unspoken question. In the jury box, the men stared with narrow eyes down at Lowell. He imagined that they were trying to decide whether to judge him differently on account of his plea change. Moise remained the only person in the courtroom not perturbed by what was happening.

"The clerk will note that the defendant changes his plea from not guilty to guilty," Moise said simply.

The noise level in the courtroom rose, as people quietly asked one another what this development could mean or asked for clarification of what was being said. Moise eventually raised his gavel and knocked it heavily on his desk half a dozen times, until silence again descended. He sternly looked behind the tables of the two legal teams, glaring at the reporters and onlookers, as if daring them to make any noise again.

The next few minutes, Lowell knew, would be critical. Now that a guilty plea had been entered, Moise would be within his rights to ask the jury to deliver sentence. If that happened, they would surely return a sentence of death within an hour or so and Lowell would be dangling from the gallows the following morning. Benjamin had assured him that this would not happen, but had not told him how or why he believed this. He had to trust Benjamin, for he had no other choice. Still, it made him feel like a man dangling off a bridge from a rope, unsure of whether or not the rope was strong enough to bear his weight.

"Be seated, General Lowell," Moise said. "Counselors will approach the bench."

Benjamin and Eustis each stood from their chairs as Lowell sat back down in his. Moise leaned down over the side of the dais and spoke in an earnest manner, but so softly that neither Lowell nor anyone else in the courtroom could hear what was being said. At one point, Eustis formed an angry expression on his face, his whispers took on a harsher tone, and he jabbed a finger towards Lowell and then towards the jury box. Benjamin actually seemed to say little, but turned to look at Lowell and winked at him as the conversation drew to a close.

Mutterings had risen again in the courtroom as people speculated on the nature of the confidential conversation. As Benjamin and Eustis returned to their seats, Moise brought all to silence with a few powerful bangs of his gavel.

"In view of the change of plea by the defendant, we shall adjourn until Tuesday, October 2, when the court shall consider punishment. The defense wishes to have more witnesses testify and I see no reason not to grant their request." With that, Moise banged down the gavel one final time.

Eustis's face was a mask of anger, but Benjamin had a smug grin on his face. "Told you," he said quietly.

"All rise!" the bailiff said. Everyone stood as Judge Moise exited the room through the side door. The guards had started allowing Lowell and Benjamin a few moments to speak at the table before taking Lowell out to the paddy wagon. As the crowd of people began to file out of the courtroom, Lowell turned to his attorney.

"Well, you were right," he said. "Moise didn't send it to the jury, just like you said he wouldn't."

"Trust me now?" Benjamin replied.

"More than I did," Lowell replied honestly. "Now, how long can we drag out the sentencing phase of the trial?"

"Weeks, if we play our cards right."

"Weeks? Seems to me like it wouldn't take more than a day or two."

Benjamin chuckled. "Didn't you hear what Moise said about new witnesses?"

"Yes, come to think of it, I did. What's that about? You haven't called any witnesses yet."

"You're about to find out, General Lowell, that your trial has only just begun."

CHAPTER FIFTEEN

October 1, Noon
Confederate Headquarters, New Iberia, Louisiana

"No, General Morgan," Longstreet said firmly. "No, I cannot let you go back out. Your instructions from the War Department are to report to the headquarters of the Army of Tennessee at Nashville and await further orders."

Longstreet sat behind a desk in what had been a merchant shop before Saul took control of New Iberia and ran the people out of town. The place had been thoroughly looted during the insurgent occupation and all attempts to locate its owner had failed. Presumably the man had been one of those killed when Saul captured the town. It made a useful enough headquarters for the Confederate troops.

Morgan stood in front of the desk, his hat in his hand, a supplicant expression on his face. He felt more tired than he had ever felt in his life, even during his famous 1863 raid.

"But sir, I think he is still be out there," Morgan protested.

"He's not out there, Morgan. He's dead."

Morgan pursed his lips. "I'm sorry, sir, but I don't think so."

He did not like disagreeing with Longstreet, whom he had grown to respect since his arrival in New Iberia. Yet he did not think that Longstreet would take offense. They had developed a sufficient rapport with one another that they could speak freely. Longstreet had a reputation of disagreeing with his superiors, after all, and hypocrisy did not seem to be one of his character traits.

Longstreet sighed. "You've been riding around in the swamps and forests around this town for more than a month now. Have you seen any sign of Saul or any of his men? No, you haven't. Has anybody else? No, they haven't. Saul is dead, Morgan. He died here in New Iberia when we overran his position." He pointed out the window. "Want to know where he is? He's one of the burned bodies that we dumped in that mass grave over there. Covered in dirt and already being eaten by worms."

Morgan tried to choose his words, searching for those that would best express his mind. "I know everything points to that, sir. But I cannot accept it. I don't know why. I just can't shake the feeling that he's still alive."

"You've turned the campaign against Saul into a personal vendetta, Morgan," Longstreet observed. "Not healthy. Look, I know that this darkie embarrassed you. I know you didn't like what was written in the newspapers. I know you probably didn't like it when Breckinridge ordered me down here to replace you. I don't blame you for it. But you've got to give it up, you understand? Saul's dead. We're finished here. The militia have almost all gone home. I'm leaving to return to Little Rock the day after tomorrow."

"But sir, if I could just have a company or two of cavalry, I..."

"Morgan, the answer is no!" Longstreet said more forcefully. "You're a man who cares about his reputation. What do you think people are going to say when you've spent another month riding around the swamps, finding nothing? Or a month after that? People are going to start saying that you've lost your mind. And your Kentucky cavalrymen? They've been down here as long as you have and they want to go back to Tennessee. When are you going to be satisfied that Saul's dead?"

"It's these stories the slaves are telling," Morgan said carefully. "Yes, we've had no sure sightings of Saul or any of his men. But everywhere we go, we find slaves who say they've seen him. The stories they're telling are . . . well, they're strange, sir."

"Darkies love to tell stories," Longstreet replied. "Hell, half the ghost stories I heard over the campfire came from darkies. But they're nothing that should be acted on. They're just stories."

"I'm not so sure."

"During the war, if a darkie had told you that a ghost came up and told him the position of the enemy, would you have considered that reliable intelligence?"

"No, of course not, but these seem different. Why are they being told everywhere, all of a sudden? And why are they so strange?"

Longstreet's eyes narrowed. "Strange how?"

"I've been told by slaves that Saul walked through the walls of their cabins to tell them that they'll be free one day. I've been told that he has shown up at the sick bed of children and healed them with a touch. Hell, one slave told me that he saw Saul fly over his plantation during the night."

Longstreet laughed. "Flying, was he?"

Morgan didn't find it funny. "Yes, that's the sort of thing they're saying. And that's not all. They talk of him being invulnerable to bullets, being able to walk through fire without being burned, and all other sorts of things. There were never any such stories before. I don't think I've ever heard slaves talk of someone in such a way. Why now? And why Saul?"

"I don't really know and, frankly, I don't really care. All I care about is the fact that you've had hundreds of cavalrymen scouring every hut and hovel for scores of miles in every direction. What have you found? Nothing. No sightings of Saul or any of his men. That's solid military information, if you ask me. And from it, we can draw only one conclusion. Saul and all of his insurgents were killed in New Iberia." Longstreet paused a moment. "You're chasing a ghost, General Morgan. You need to give it up."

Morgan didn't respond. He wondered if Longstreet might be right. The thought struck him forcefully that he was acting like a fool. He wondered what his men were thinking of him, as they were the ones being ordered to ride around the area and kick in the doors of all the slave cabins. How many of them were writing disparaging letters to their wives back home, which might find their way into the newspapers? If what Longstreet was saying was any indication, many of Morgan's fellow general officers were already talking behind his back, questioning his judgement.

He took a deep breath. Longstreet was right. The longer he continued his fruitless search, the more ludicrous the whole thing appeared. Maybe the best thing to do to salvage what was left of his reputation was to return to his post in Tennessee. The diplomatic situation in North America was still tense and there was always the possibility of another war. If that happened, he could return to the kind of fighting at which he excelled. If he was successful, he could again become the darling of the Confederacy. The fruitless campaign against Saul in the Louisiana swamps would become just a footnote in an otherwise glorious career.

Longstreet eyed Morgan carefully. "Look, you did as well as anybody could have done. Probably better. You got trounced in that first ambush. No denying it. But then you gathered intelligence and were able to turn the tables on the bastard. Had it not been for that Yankee from Massachusetts sneaking in with all those weapons, you would have had him. It's not your fault that Lowell showed up. If the reporters come to ask me my opinion, that's what I'm going to tell them."

"Thank you, sir."

"But you have your orders. I expect you to follow them."

"Yes, sir," Morgan said, resignedly.

"Get yourself back to Tennessee. Then you can start putting all this behind you."

"I suppose," Morgan replied. He didn't believe it, though. He knew it would not be easy to forget his unfortunate time in the swamps, no matter how much he might want to.

October 3, Night
Home of Judah Benjamin, New Orleans, Louisiana

Benjamin liked eating alone. It allowed him to enjoy his food and wine with no company except his own thoughts, the best company he could imagine. He was taking particular pleasure in the taste of fine Creole cuisine, which had scarcely touched his lips in several years and which he dearly missed. He had asked his cook not to prepare anything fancy, just something indisputably Creole. The result was a dinner of gumbo, jambalaya, rice, and soufflé potatoes, washed down with a light pinot noir.

Aside from his cook and three house servants, all of whom were slaves, there was no one else in the house. It was entirely quiet, with only the crackling of the burning wood in the fireplace disturbing the silence. As he happily guided another spoonful of gumbo into his mouth, he looked around the dining room. Its walls were lined with gold gilding and hung with well-done art reproductions he had chosen himself. The furniture was in the latest French fashion, popular everywhere but especially so in New Orleans. Nevertheless, like every other room in the house, it had the telltale signs of underuse. Benjamin had scarcely set foot in New Orleans since 1861, having spent nearly all his time in Richmond.

The only interlude had been his 1865 excursion to Europe. It was nice to again sleep in his own bedroom.

The house was on Bourbon Street, in the heart of the city. It had passed through the war without any damage, which was more than many of his colleagues in the Confederate government could say. For this, ironically enough, he had to thank the Union army, which had generally protected private property in the city after it fell into their hands in 1862. Indeed, the only thing Benjamin discovered to be amiss was that someone had pilfered the expensive and elegant silverware set he had purchased for his wife, many years before.

He was pleased to have found his house in a state of habitation, for now that he was out of government service, he planned for New Orleans to be his home for the remainder of his days. Though it was a house intended for a family, he knew that he would live alone. Despite his occasional requests, he knew his wife Natalie would never return from France. She required the intimate embraces of a man to be satisfied and they both knew he would never be able to provide that. He bore her no malice. His only regret in that sphere of his life was that he only saw his daughter Ninette every few years. He hoped that he would be able to persuade Natalie that Ninette might return to New Orleans, perhaps after she had received a French education. It was a faint hope, but a hope nonetheless.

Judah Benjamin knew himself. He had long ago decided that he was not like other men. Ordinary rules of ambition or morality could not be applied to him. Other men craved adulation by the masses, or entry into the realm of the aristocracy, or the certainty that they would leave behind some solid memory in the history books. None of this interested Benjamin. What did he want, then? Even he didn't really know. The world was a chess set. God had set him in one of the seats and required him to play, but to what end he did not know. Sometimes he was not even sure if he was supposed to be trying to win. Maybe he might gain more by losing. Perhaps the game didn't even matter, though he made sure to play as though it did, just to be on the safe side.

He had convictions. His desire to help Breckinridge go forward to his destiny had been entirely sincere, as was his desire now to lead Lowell forward to his. Maybe he was but a pawn himself, waiting to sense the wishes of his real master and then try to bring them about in the real world. It was an old philosophical question, of course. To what extent was Benjamin really in control of his own actions? He would never know, but then no one did. In any case, it didn't matter.

He chuckled slightly as he sipped the pinot noir. Philosophical thoughts were all good and well, but now was the time to think about the future. In defending Lowell, Benjamin was not only doing his duty to an honorable man, albeit an enemy, and helping push the Confederacy on the path he knew it needed to take. He was also announcing his return to the legal profession. He was a well-known figure playing a crucial role in what was already the most famous trial of the decade. Granted, many newspapers were vilifying him for defending Lowell, but Benjamin knew that this would not matter for long. When the trial was over, he would lie low for a time, perhaps travel abroad for a few months, then return to resume his law practice in earnest.

Benjamin was one of the nation's leading experts when it came to wills and estates, the sale of personal property, and many other crucial elements of the law. Bigoted people might reject his services at first, but that would gradually decline as he began chalking up successive victories in various court cases. People inevitably followed their own financial interests and Benjamin knew that he would soon be able to count the wealthiest people of New Orleans in his client roster.

Benjamin's investments had done well during the war, as his unrivalled knowledge of the military and political situation had allowed him to time his purchases on the stock exchanges of New York, London, and Paris perfectly. Combined with the money he would make from his new practice, he would be able to spend the final decades of his life as a rich man. His dinners would always be excellent, his wine would always be exquisite, and on those nights when he choose to have company for dinner, he would be able to choose his guests from the cream of New Orleans society. As they ate, he would amuse himself with thoughts of their ignorance and absurdity, while they who had deigned to dine with a Jew would never know that the joke was on them.

It was a pleasant vision of the future, but he hoped he would be able to enjoy it in a stable and prosperous Confederacy. He had done everything he could to set the new Southern nation on the right path. He had helped birth it in Montgomery in 1861. He had been by the side of Jefferson Davis through four long years of war. He had secured recognition from the governments of Britain and France and financial backing from some of the greatest banks of Europe. Over the past year, he had ushered John C. Breckinridge into the presidential race. If he went down to defeat, of course that would be unfortunate, but it would at least have presented the Southern people and the world at large with a visible alternative to the Fire-Eaters.

His last act to perform in service to the Confederacy was to direct the final phase of the Lowell trial onto a path that would see his defendant die, but only after he was presented to the South as a gallant hero dying a martyr's death. Lowell was perfectly suited to play such a role. John Brown had been a half-deranged fanatic, an ugly and uncouth old man. Southerners could easily dismiss him. Lowell was a young, vibrant, attractive man from a distinguished and polished family. The aristocratic families who ruled the Confederacy could see themselves in him. He was a war hero, and Southern society respected heroic warriors even if they wore blue uniforms. Lowell would die, but in dying he would help change the way the South viewed those who opposed slavery.

That change would matter in the years and decades to come. The rest of the world would slowly become less tolerant of the South's 'peculiar institution.' It was already fashionable in some quarters to refuse to buy clothing made from Confederate cotton, choosing instead products made from Indian or Egyptian cotton. This attitude would only increase as the years passed. At the same time, technological changes would make the South's slave-based economy increasingly primitive. The wealth that was the foundation of the aristocracy's rule would slowly dry up, threatening their hold on power and increasing social unrest. The minds of the people would turn to the inevitable conclusion that slavery simply had to go.

When that alteration of the Southern mind took place, Charles Russell Lowell would be remembered. His memory would make the transition away from slavery easier for the South to bear. Ensuring that he died a heroic and dignified death would be the last service of Judah Benjamin to the Confederacy that he loved, even if it had often hated him.

He finished his dinner and rang the bell that sat next to his plate. Without speaking, one of the house slaves came in, refilled his wine glass, and removed the plate and silverware from the table. Benjamin rose and, taking his glass with him, strode through his house and out onto the narrow cast iron balcony that overlooked Bourbon Street. He looked down for a long time at the people going to and fro, talking and laughing with one another. Fashionable carriages passed by, intermixed with creaky wagons taking produce from the docks to the restaurants. He smiled. New Orleans was his home and he was happy to be back in it.

One of the slaves partially emerged from the darkness of the room behind him, like a shadowy wisp. "Master?" he asked, his voice timid and hesitant.

"Yes?"

"Telegram arrived for you, sir. Put through the mail slot just now."

"Give it here."

The slave complied, bowed, and vanished into the darkness of another room. Benjamin opened the envelope, which came from one of the most reliable telegraphic companies in the city and one known for its particular emphasis on confidentiality. He saw quickly that it was from Slidell, yet it contained only a single line of seemingly random letters.

Benjamin sighed and stepped back inside the house. He walked quickly to his study and opened a concealed drawer in his desk, where he kept the key to the substitution cipher he and Slidell used. He lit two candles and sat down, spending a few minutes scribbling on a piece of paper as he worked out the code. Then, he read through the simple statement Slidell had sent him.

The Emperor says that if Lowell dies, the treaty dies with him.

Benjamin realized instantly that his mission had changed.

October 4, Morning
Headquarters, Army of Northern Virginia, Winchester, Virginia

Breckinridge inhaled deeply, relishing the crisp autumn air of the northern Shenandoah Valley. It was an area he knew very well, having served there in 1864. Seeing the familiar heights of the Blue Ridge Mountains around him, the shape of which had been burned into his mind during the fighting, brought back powerful memories of the war.

Kemper had suggested that he leave Richmond for a few days following his speech to the Orphan Society, to help diminish the inevitable charges in the newspapers that he was inappropriately campaigning for the office of the Presidency. An inspection trip to the encampments of the Army of Northern Virginia seemed like the perfect excuse. He was close enough to Richmond that he could be back within a single day if any emergency took place, yet far enough so that the newspapers wouldn't be hounding him. Moreover, by attending to his duties as Secretary of War barely a month before the election, he would give the people the impression of diligence and dedication to his work.

The Army of Northern Virginia was organized in peacetime in much the same way it had been organized during the war, in that it was divided into three infantry corps and one cavalry corps. It was, however, considerably smaller. Each corps had only two divisions, and each division only mustered the strength that a single brigade might have fielded during the fighting. State regiments rotated their front line duty every few months and plans were in place for regiments to be called up to report to Virginia in the event of a mobilization, in accordance with the system Breckinridge had put into place.

The First Corps was based around the town of Warrenton, east of the mountains and not far from the heavily fortified Union base at Centerville. The Third Corps was located in Fredericksburg, around which nightmarish fighting had raged during the war. Winchester was the home of the Second Corps, arguably the most fabled of the three, which had been led to glory on many battlefields by Stonewall Jackson and Jubal Early. A small reserve division was based in the town of Staunton, where it could move quickly and easily to support any of the other three corps.

Inspection tours were a part of Breckinridge's role as Secretary of War. He enjoyed them enormously, for he loved getting out of Richmond and speaking to the ordinary soldiers who had fought to win independence and now stayed with the colors to protect it in peacetime. Simply due to proximity, he had made more tours of the encampments of the Army of Northern Virginia than any other force, this being his fourth. Only once had Breckinridge visited the camps of the Army of Tennessee, deployed along the northern border of its namesake state. His other major inspection tour, in the company of Secretary of the Navy Mallory, had been of the coastal defenses of the Atlantic seaboard from Fort Monroe down to the defenses of Savannah.

Breckinridge was due to inspect some of the regiments a few hours later, but always liked to engage in unscripted checks on how things were going. He had arrived the previous evening and, after a good dinner and a solid night's sleep, had awoken and mounted his horse, wanting to simply ride around and see for himself what things looked like. The encampment of the Second Corps bore little resemblance to the bivouacs Breckinridge remembered from the war. The men slept in sturdy wooden cabins rather than ragged white tents. Every man was outfitted with a clean uniform and wearing properly sized and well shined boots. Privies were well located away from water sources. All of this was in accordance with standard camp regulations Breckinridge had put into place, with the considerable help of Joseph Johnston.

"Glad to see that your men are following the official camp rules," Breckinridge said to the man riding beside him.

Lieutenant General Jubal Early, hunched slightly forward over his saddle due to his rheumatism, gave a huff of indignation. "You think I'd let them get away with being sloppy, John? You should know me better than that."

Breckinridge chuckled. He and Early had fought side-by-side through Maryland and the Shenandoah Valley. Most people did not like the irascible

Early, whose grating and biting jokes were almost always at someone else's expense and whose mastery of profanity was as legendary as his fighting ability. Yet despite their differences in temperament, Breckinridge quite liked Early. It was a counterintuitive quality that he shared with Robert E. Lee, who playfully referred to Early as his "bad old man".

"You've been doing well keeping them busy," Breckinridge said.

"Thanks. Lots to be done. The fortifications along the border are so strong that if the Yankees attacked with a million men, they'd just end up with a million corpses. But I have the boys always at work, because they can always be made better. Meantime, all the roads and railroads in this part of Virginia are back in tip-top shape. And when there's no work to be done, I have the men drill and march, drill and march, without letup. Better to keep them in shape, you know?"

"True."

"Your rotation system works wonders. If these fellows were professional infantry, expecting to be here for years on end, they'd get mighty frustrated after a while. As it is, these boys are here for six months or thereabouts and then they get to go home and a whole new batch of men shows up. All of them veterans. So they get to keep up their military habits and have their own lives back at home. Really a great system you put together, John."

"Thanks, Jube," Breckinridge replied, genuinely appreciative. He considered the regimental system the hallmark of his tenure as Secretary of War and always liked to hear complimentary things about it.

They rode on. They occasionally stopped to inspect a cabin, or a stable, or a field bakery, and once they stopped and inspected a hospital. It was strange to see only a few of the beds occupied, and those only by patients who were sick. Breckinridge did not like to remember the field hospitals of the war years, packed as they had been with fearfully wounded men, with piles of severed limbs outside filling the air with a repulsive smell and the desperate screams of terrified men drowning out all other sounds.

As morning moved towards noon, Breckinridge and Early rode to the main parade ground for a few scheduled events. Early had selected four regiments for Breckinridge to formally inspect: the 15th Alabama Infantry, the 10th Georgia Infantry, the 4th North Carolina Infantry, and the 1st South Carolina Cavalry. Breckinridge recognized a few of the officers of the North Carolina regiment, whom he had commanded during the 1864 campaign. Also present for the review was the Fauquier Artillery Battery, which fired off a few practice rounds from their cannon for the entertainment of the Secretary of War. The colonel commanding the guns caught Breckinridge's eye, for he seemed more of a master of artillery drill than any gunner he had ever seen before.

"Who's he?" Breckinridge asked, nodding towards the colonel.

"Him?" Early replied. "That's James Dearing. Good gunner, he is. Said to be from one of the first families of Virginia." The last sentence was drenched in sarcasm, for, as Breckinridge knew, Early held the average Virginia aristocrat in contempt.

"Why is it that nearly every Virginia officer I hear about is said to be from one of the first families of Virginia?"

"Don't know," Early said. "Probably because all the second families moved to Kentucky."

Breckinridge threw his head back and laughed heartily. Not many people would have considered making such a joke at Breckinridge's expense, nor would Breckinridge have found it particularly funny coming from anyone but Early.

The review went by quickly. The three infantry regiments conducted their drills perfectly. Breckinridge walked up and down their ranks, stopping occasionally by random soldiers to make sure their weapons were clean and their uniforms proper. The cavalry unit rode their mounts back and forth, executing commands given by their colonel with precision. All told, it took about an hour. The inspection over, the officers of the regiments shouted orders to their men, who formed up into marching columns and departed, headed back to their barracks.

"I think we're done here," Early said. "Lunch?"

"Certainly."

The two men remounted their horses and rode away from the parade ground, back towards Early's headquarters. They chatted about old army comrades and one another's families. Breckinridge learned that Early had become a father again, to a spritely boy named Robert Lee Early. Like Early's three other children, Robert had been born out of wedlock to Julia McNealey, a woman who sometimes was Early's companion but whom he vigorously asserted he would never marry. Breckinridge did not approve of Early's choices in this regard, yet it somehow did not diminish the affection which he held towards the unconventional Virginian.

Over a lunch of roast turkey, potatoes, and apple cider, the conversation between Breckinridge and Early took a more serious turn.

"I read your speech," Early said.

"And?"

"You always speak well, John. Saw little in it that I disapproved of. Maybe the Cuba thing. Wouldn't mind seeing our flag over Havana, I don't mind saying. All things considered, though, a very good speech. Certainly better than all the chatter that son of a bitch Toombs has been raising all over the damn country."

"I wish the newspapers were as enthusiastic as you are," Breckinridge replied.

"They aren't? Most of what I read was positive. Except for the horseshit from the newspapers that are already against you."

"Not as supportive as they need to be." Breckinridge frowned and shifted in his seat. "I'll tell you something, Jube. Wouldn't tell many people this, but you're a friend." He paused, suddenly uncertain whether to go on.

"What?" Early asked, still chewing his food.

Breckinridge sighed. "I'm going to lose this election. Beauregard and Toombs just had too much of a head start. My people haven't been able to organize. They'll sweep the Deep South, obviously. They'll win in two of the four big states, at least. Maybe all four of them. Hell, it's possible I won't win a single state at all. I may turn out to be a sacrificial lamb, just like when I ran against Lincoln in 1860."

"Not as bad as all that," Early replied. "Most of the people I talk to are for you all the way. Military people and civilians, both."

"They probably know we're friends. They're not going to want to tell you that they don't support me."

Early scoffed. "You know I don't tolerate any damn sycophants, John. If somebody disagrees with me, I expect them to damn well say it. No, I'm serious. I think there's a lot of support for you that you're not appreciating."

"We'll see, I suppose. But I'm not going to lie and pretend to be optimistic. I believe, a bit over a month from now, I'll be making plans to move to Nashville and set up a new law practice."

"Shit, John," Early said contemptuously. An angry and almost resentful expression formed on his face. "Not like you to talk like this. What the hell's the matter with you? Never heard you talk this way back during the war. Hell, if this had been your attitude when we went up against the Yankees at Kernstown, we never would have won the damn war."

"Just trying to be realistic, Jube."

"To hell with being realistic, John. I ought to slap you across the face, you damn son of a bitch. Secession wasn't realistic, given the odds against us when we decided to go up against the Yankees. That's why I argued against secession at the Virginia convention. But we won, didn't we? Buck up, dammit. If you think you're going to lose, you've already lost."

Breckinridge frowned and put a forkful of turkey into his mouth, but didn't reply.

Early eyed him warily. "This your wife's doing?" he asked. "Is she anxious for you to lose, so that you can get out of politics?"

"Not at all. Mary has been entirely supportive."

"Well, wherever it's coming from, this pessimism had better stop now. You've got one month, you bastard. One month in which to win this election. It's about more than just you, you know. If Beauregard wins, he'll put his own people in command of the main armies. The person he'll choose for Secretary of War will be whatever scoundrel kisses his ass the most. Either that or Toombs and Wigfall will make the choices for him. Either way, I'll be finished and so will most of our friends. And that's just me talking. The whole country will go to hell. You know that. They'll ruin everything, the people who back Beauregard. So busy shoving their heads up their own asses that they won't be able to tell which damn day of the week it is."

"I know," Breckinridge said.

"Then shut the hell up and win this damn election," Early replied forcefully. "I signed the letter your campaign sent me. The one calling on army officers to publicly state their support for you. I'm telling every son of a bitch I come across that I'm a Breckinridge man, through and through. Anything else I can do for you, all you need to do is ask."

"Well, I appreciate that, Jube."

Early leaned over the table. "In exchange for that, John, I want you to stop all this naysaying. You're going to win the election. You know why? Because you have to. I'm not willing to accept the idea that our country is going to be governed by the likes of Beauregard and Toombs, you understand." Early paused for a moment. "Hell, if they win the election, I just might order my men to get on the road to Richmond and-"

"You'd better stop that thought right there, Jube," Breckinridge said sternly.

"Why?" Early asked. "What did I say wrong?"

Breckinridge glared at him. "What you were about to say. Don't say it."

Early grinned mischievously. "I was going to suggest that my men go to Richmond and put on a parade. You know, for the ladies." He took a gulp of apple cider and then went on. "Whatever you think I was about to say, the situation will be very bad if Beauregard and Toombs win. There's not a stronger defender of slavery in the whole Confederacy than myself, but at least I believe in the rule of law. Those bastards don't give a rat's ass for it. If you let them win, they'll try to turn it into their own personal fiefdom."

"You talk as though it were just a question of me wanting it enough," Breckinridge replied. "It will be the people's decision. And right now, I think that they are turning towards Beauregard."

Early pursed his lips and shook his head. "That's too bad, John. If there's one thing I don't have much confidence in, it's the intelligence of the average voter."

A staff officer entered the room. "I'm sorry for interrupting, General Early, but I have a message for the Secretary of War from President."

"Well, he's sitting right here, lieutenant," Early replied. "Give it to him."

Breckinridge took the note from and read it.

Secretary Breckinridge,

With immediate effect, General John Hunt Morgan is to be removed from command of his cavalry unit in the Army of Tennessee, which he shall turn over to whatever officer General Johnston sees fit to appoint in his place. Inform General Morgan that he is to return to his home and await further orders.

President Davis

"Dammit," Breckinridge said. The fact that the message had not been unexpected made it no less welcome. He crumbled up the letter and flung it onto the floor. The staff officer quickly retreated out of the room and closed the door behind it.

"What is it?" Early asked.

"It's about Morgan."

"What about him?"

"Davis has ordered me to remove him from command."

Early grunted softly and nodded. "Has he? Well, why the hell did it take him so long? I'm sorry, I know he's your friend, but I don't much like those puffed up cavalrymen. Good for nothing in an open battle, frankly. Besides, he failed to catch that black bastard, didn't he? Removing him from command seems like the obvious thing to do."

Breckinridge shook his head. "It's not right. He did as well as anyone could. Saul scared everyone, so they need someone to serve as a scapegoat."

"Well, too bad it had to be your friend, but it will be for the best. By giving you a direct order, Davis took the decision out of your hands."

Breckinridge exhaled sharply. "Well, I suppose he is still the president. I had best issue the orders. I will write him directly, too. He deserves to know that I don't agree with the president in this matter."

"Of course." Early paused a moment. "It will be good for your chances of winning the election, you know. Morgan has been a ball and chain around your foot, since everyone knows he's your friend and you appointed him. And fairly or not, the whole country thinks that he failed in his efforts to root out Saul's bandits. By removing him from command, you will have dealt with this problem."

"I do not like having to compromise with my honor for political advantage," Breckinridge said firmly.

"If you're in politics, you're like a ship captain. Sooner or later, you'll run into a storm. True for everyone."

"Is it?" Breckinridge asked. "Or it is it just that others have been more willing to do it? God help us, Jube. I don't want to win the presidency only to lose my soul."

"You had best get used to it, my friend. If you win, you will be the final authority in all things. Then you will find out how hard it will be to keep your honor while leading a nation."

October 5, Evening
Spotswood Hotel, Richmond, Virginia

"Are you confident, Senator Toombs?"

"Am I confident?" Toombs replied. He smiled, amused by the naiveté of the reporter from the *Staunton Spectator*. "I am supremely confident. Our horse is several lengths ahead of Breckinridge and shows no sign of slowing down."

"What of Breckinridge's recent speech to the Orphan Society and the speaking tour of Secretary Miles? Aren't you at all worried that they might change public opinion?"

"Let me just add my voice to those who are condemning Secretary Breckinridge for turning his speech to the Orphan Society into a partisan event. It's one thing for a vice presidential candidate to actively campaign for office. I freely do that myself. But the head of a ticket? It's simply not done. Breckinridge would have been well advised to follow the example of Beauregard and maintain a dignified silence. But then, dignity is not a quality one usually associates with John C. Breckinridge, is it?"

"And Secretary Miles?"

Toombs sneered. "I think we all know a corrupt bargain when we see one. Davis promised Miles the portfolio of Secretary of State in exchange for his support for Breckinridge. It won't help him in the long run, though. Once I'm in office, there will be no place for William Porcher Miles in the government. No place at all."

The reporter's eyes narrowed. "You mean Beauregard, yes?"

"What's that?"

"You mean once Beauregard is in office, not you."

He backtracked in his thoughts for a moment and realized his mistake. "Yes, of course." He chuckled. "I apologize. I misspoke."

The assembled reporters laughed softly. Toombs decided to make a virtue of necessity and say no more about the mistake. It was a common belief that Toombs would be the power behind the throne once Beauregard was installed as president. It made little sense to do anything to dissuade people from thinking this. Furthering the speculation would help strengthen the idea that he would make a good president himself. Besides, it flattered his vanity.

There were roughly two dozen reporters around him, sitting in a loose circle at a cluster of dining room tables. Toombs had let Edward Pollard know a few days before that he would be available to reporters at the hotel during the evening hours and the ever-friendly Pollard spread the word rapidly. The result was a good turnout, especially for reporters favorable to the SRP cause.

He was drinking brandy rather than whiskey this evening. Stephens, who wrote him at least three letters a week, constantly reminded him to keep his drinking to a minimum. Yet as the election drew closer and an SRP victory appeared more and more likely, Toombs saw little reason to comply. He had made a sacrifice by curtailing his drinking for the past few months, so he felt entitled to loosen the rope a little bit.

"Senator Toombs, what do you make of the news from Paris that negotiations on the treaty of friendship between France and the Confederacy have been suspended?" This question came from a reporter for the *Mobile Register.*

"I'm delighted about it," Toombs said immediately. "I've always opposed the efforts of the Davis administration to shackle us to France. I hear tell that the French people don't like our peculiar institution and that's why the negotiations stopped. To hell with the French, I say."

"What do you want the focus to be on in terms of foreign policy, then?"

"The acquisition of Cuba, of course. As a first step towards the expansion of the Confederacy into the Caribbean and Latin America."

"It's been suggested by some that you favor taking Cuba by force if Spain refuses to sell it."

"I do," Toombs said with a smile. "I do, indeed. Not now, perhaps. But eventually."

The reporter glanced around at the other newspapermen in the room, gauging their reaction to what Toombs just said. "That simple? Cuba has been Spanish for centuries."

"So what? Its people are in revolt against Spain."

"True, but they might look no more favorably upon our rule than on Spanish rule."

Toombs frowned impatiently. "Cuba must become Confederate territory. And it will, sooner or later. Slavery has to either expand or die. I am unwilling to let it die. If we do that, why did we bother fighting the war?" He took a sip of the brandy, disappointed to find that it emptied his glass. "Taking control of Cuba, of course, will require a stronger navy."

"How would that be paid for?"

"Once my fiscal bill is passed, the finances of the Confederacy will be placed on a much stronger foundation. I am dismayed that it has not advanced through Congress already."

"Why hasn't it?" the reporter asked. "You introduced it several weeks ago, as soon as Congress reconvened."

"You're the reporter. You tell me. If I had to guess, though, I would suspect that Davis is pulling strings to keep it from becoming law before the election. He doesn't want me getting credit for any major accomplishment before the election, in case it makes the voters more likely to vote for the SRP ticket."

He gestured to get the attention of the barman, a free black named Bill, and held up his glass. Bill hesitated just a moment, as if to protest the fact that Toombs was ordering a third brandy. The barely measureable pause nearly threw Toombs into a paroxysm of rage, but the black man dutifully picked up a bottle of brandy, strode over to the table, and refilled the glass. There was a quiet pause among the reporters as Toombs sipped.

"Senator Toombs, do you care to comment on the letter of support that your ticket has produced from military officers?" asked a reporter for the *Raleigh Standard.*

"It's a fine letter, isn't it?" Toombs tried to focus his attention, remembering that North Carolina was going to be one of the critical states in the election. "Lots of well-known names on it. Just a few weeks ago I bumped into none other than John Bell Hood on a train and he practically begged me to add his name to the list."

"Yes, but the Breckinridge campaign has said that they are producing their own letter. Rumor has it that it will have many more names on it, and of more prominent officers."

Toombs's face clouded darkly. He did not like the tone of the North Carolina reporter. "More prominent? You know John Bell Hood defeated the Yankees in Arkansas, don't you? William Walker not only fought gallantly against the Yankees, but helped thwart Cleburne's dastardly plan to enlist blacks in the Confederate army. Evander Law was one of the greatest brigade commanders in the Army of Northern Virginia."

"Yes, but Breckinridge's list includes men like Jubal Early, William Hardee, Thomas Hindman, and Robert Rodes."

Toombs scowled. "Think about it for a moment. The man they are saying they support is currently the Secretary of War. For all we know, he simply ordered these men to add their names to the list. Maybe it's all corruption. Did you ever think of that? If you ask me, the men who signed our letter ought to be praised for their bravery, for they are taking a stand against the man who signs their paychecks."

"Breckinridge has already publicly said that he will take no action whatsoever against any military officer who endorses Beauregard," the North Carolina reporter replied.

"And you trust the bastard? Look, you've all read my speeches, haven't you? I think I've made it clear that Breckinridge isn't a man to be trusted. I frankly wouldn't trust him to pick up my mail, much less govern the country." He thought for a moment that he was becoming too heated, for the brandy was coursing through his system, but he was beyond caring. He knew his words were wise and it was the job of the newspapermen to report them.

More to the point, neither letter released by the respective campaigns included the names of the two men who might actually have swayed a large number of voters: Robert E. Lee and Joseph E. Johnston. The two Virginians, commanders of the principal Confederate armies during the decisive 1864 campaign, were beloved across the South. If they spoke, the people might listen. Thus far, though, both had chosen to remain silent. Toombs expected that they would not make their views public, for both men cherished their reputations and would not want to sink into the sordid business of politics.

For a time, Toombs had held some hope that Johnston would endorse the SRP ticket, for he had been a close friend of Louis Wigfall for a number of years. If Johnston had added his name to the letter, Toombs was confident that tens of thousands of veterans, and thousands of other men across the country who looked up to the general, would have been persuaded to vote for Beauregard on Election Day. It had not happened, which Toombs choose to add to Wigfall's growing list of failures. While it was a disappointment, he was more than confident of being able to win without Johnston's help.

Toombs went on. "Tell you what, boys. You want to know the character of John C. Breckinridge? Go and ask him why he refuses to support the Bill for the Prevention and Speedy Suppression of Servile Insurrection. He denounced it in his speech to the Orphan Society. Denounced it, by God! Said it was unconstitutional. Well, Breckinridge might choose to be soft on the question of slavery. Lord knows his record confirms that. I, for one, will never stand accused of that!"

The questions and answers dragged on. Toombs artfully declined to answer a question from a reporter who asked about rumors that he disagreed with the SRP platform on the issue of a permanent Confederate military academy. He clarified a few points about his fiscal reform bill. When a reporter asked his opinion on the possibility of a war between Britain and the United States, he said that he thought the chances of it had diminished, but then got laughs by saying that, if war were to break out, he hoped that both sides would lose.

He had a fourth brandy and he began to feel his senses becoming more and more dulled. He started to have some difficulty understanding the questions the reporters were asking him. He also could tell that he was becoming more irritable and that was likely to lead to no good.

He rose from his chair, steadying himself by placing his hand on the table. "Gentlemen, you must forgive me. It has grown late and I am very tired. I have enjoyed our conversations, but I am afraid I must retire."

The newspapermen muttered their thanks and rose to leave. Toombs watched them go, then he signaled to Bill for another drink.

October 7, Noon
Confederate States District Court, New Orleans, Louisiana

"The defense calls Colonel John Singleton Mosby to the stand," Benjamin said.

Even though he had known who was about to take the witness stand, Lowell's eyes widened as the short, unassuming man entered through the side door of the courtroom and proceeded to take the witness stand and swear the required oath. There was a rustling in the crowd, for Mosby was one of the great legends of the Confederacy's fight for independence, the South's most famous partisan ranger.

Lowell couldn't help but gaze at Mosby in wonder. He had never actually laid eyes on the man, yet for many months in late 1863 and early 1864, Mosby had haunted his dreams. Lowell had commanded the 2nd Massachusetts Cavalry then. His mission had been to eradicate Mosby's guerrillas from the region across the Potomac River from Washington City. He had failed. Mosby was not known as the "Gray Ghost" for nothing.

Time and again, Mosby's men had raided Union outposts, ambushed isolated detachments, and even abducted officers from their beds in the middle of the night. Lowell and his troopers would arrive shortly afterwards, only to discover that the partisans had faded into the woods like shadows. Trying to catch him, Lowell had frustratingly found, was like trying to grasp a handful of water. There had been many skirmishes, in which men on both sides were killed and wounded, but never had he been able to pin Mosby down.

As he sat down in the witness chair, Mosby shifted his head slightly and met his gaze. There was a strange warmth there, almost a look of camaraderie, which took Lowell by surprise. A faint smile crossed his lips and he gave a slight, friendly nod.

Benjamin was on his feet and strode over to the witness stand. "State your name and rank for the record, if you please."

"Colonel John Singleton Mosby, late commander of the 43rd Battalion, Virginia Cavalry."

"Do you recognize my client?"

"I do. He is Brigadier General Charles Russell Lowell, late of the United States Army."

"You've met him?"

"Not in person, no. But one might say that he and I have met one another on the battlefield."

"I assume, therefore, that you encountered General Lowell in combat during the war."

"Indeed, I did so on many occasions. When Lowell commanded the 2nd Massachusetts Cavalry, my men fought many skirmishes with his men. Later, during the fall of 1864, my men sometimes encountered his troopers when he commanded the Reserve Cavalry Brigade of the Union force known as the Army of the Shenandoah."

After a few more prodding questions from Benjamin, Mosby went on to describe many of the engagements his men had fought against Lowell's men. Judge Moise, the two respective legal teams, and the crowd in the back all sat enraptured as Mosby told his tales. Lowell nearly forgot that he was sitting in a courtroom on trial for his life and his mind went back to the war, to the endless forests of northern Virginia, to the open spaces and farmland of the Shenandoah Valley. As Mosby spoke, it was as though Lowell could hear the thundering hooves of his cavalry, the crashing sounds of heavy musketry and artillery fire, the triumphant shouting of victorious men and the screams of wounded men. The stories, interrupted only occasionally by clarifying questions by Benjamin, went on for half an hour.

"Would you consider General Lowell to be an honorable foe?" Benjamin asked after Mosby had finished.

"I would, indeed," Mosby replied.

Eustis was quickly on his feet. "Objection, your honor!"

All eyes turned to Moise, who raised his hands in a silent question to Eustis.

"I don't see how Mosby's opinion of Lowell is relevant to the matter of determining sentence on General Lowell for his crimes."

Moise looked at Benjamin. "Counselor?"

"General Lowell has pleaded guilty to his crimes. The jury will have to decide whether or not to execute or imprison him. With such a momentous decision before them, it seems to me it would be helpful for them to have an idea of General Lowell's character. Who better to provide it than our own gallant soldiers, who faced General Lowell on the field of battle?"

Moise nodded and looked back and Eustis. "Overruled."

"Your honor!" Eustis protested.

"I said overruled!" Moise said, much more sternly. He looked back to Benjamin. "Continue, counselor."

"You were saying, Colonel Mosby, that you considered General Lowell to be an honorable foe."

"Yes, I do."

"Why?"

"Many reasons. During the time he faced me around the outskirts of Washington City, he refused to adhere to the policy of burning the homes of civilians suspected of harboring my men, which his predecessors had done. He sent me a letter to notify me of this change in policy, which I very much appreciated."

"A letter?" Benjamin asked.

"Yes."

Benjamin picked up a piece of paper from the defense counsel table, walking back to the witness stand and handing it to Mosby. "Is this a copy of the letter in question?"

Mosby spent a few moments looking over the paper. "I believe it is, yes."

Benjamin looked up at Moise. "Your honor, I would like to submit for the record this copy of Lowell's letter to Mosby, outlining his refusal to burn civilian homes in northern Virginia."

Moise nodded. "Very well."

Lowell remembered the furious debate that raged within the high command of the Union forces around Washington City during that winter. Mosby's raids had become increasingly troublesome and had begun tying down large numbers of Union soldiers badly needed at the front lines. Some of the other Union commanders in the region had begun retaliating against civilians for Mosby's activities, but Lowell refused. He had learned that the Southern population could not be cowed into submission and understood that such harsh measures would only increase support for Mosby among the civilian population. More importantly, Lowell believed that war, acknowledged by all decent people to be the worst calamity that could befall a people, need not push good people into barbarism.

"Colonel Mosby, why do you think General Lowell made the decision to revoke the orders that required the burning of civilian homes?" Benjamin asked.

Mosby looked at Lowell for a moment. "If I had to answer simply, I would say because he is a man of decent and honorable character."

There was a rustling in the crowd and a series of low murmurs as people spoke softly to one another. The few words Lowell was able to make out were something to the effect of asking if Mosby had really just said what he had said.

"You're aware, Colonel Mosby, that General Lowell has pleaded guilty to inciting servile insurrection and smuggling weapons to rebel slaves, yes?" Benjamin asked.

"I am aware of that, yes."

"And yet you call him a man of a decent and honorable character."

"I do."

"You'll appreciate, Colonel Mosby, that many people in our Confederacy would not see that as even a possibility."

Eustis leapt to his feet. "Objection, your honor!" the prosecutor called, exasperation in his voice.

"What now?" Moise asked tiredly.

"Your honor, Mr. Benjamin is leading the witness onto a line of questioning which has absolutely no bearing on this case. It seems perfectly obvious to me that Mr. Benjamin has decided to use this trial as a soapbox to stand upon while he expresses his eccentric and heretical views about slavery to the country at large. I strongly urge that the questions to this witness be stopped and that the proceedings of this court move forward in a more orderly manner."

"Overruled," Moise said sternly. The look on his face told everyone that he could not have cared less about Eustis's objections.

Eustis glared across the courtroom at Benjamin, who simply looked back at him in an utterly blasé manner. Lowell was fascinated. His attorney walked towards the table just long enough to take a long sip from his glass of water, then strode back into the middle of the courtroom and resumed his questioning of Mosby.

"Colonel Mosby, you have spoken of General Lowell's refusal to burn civilian homes in northern Virginia. Is there anything else you know from your experiences with General Lowell that would lead you to believe him to be, as you say, a man of a decent and honorable character?"

"Indeed, there is."

"Would you please tell the court?"

Mosby took a deep breath. "It is not a story of a pleasant character. During the fighting in the northern Shenandoah Valley in late 1864, some of my men were taken prisoner by the enemy. Believing that they should be treated as bushwhackers rather than regular soldiers, General Sheridan had nearly a dozen of them hanged. In retaliation, I ordered the hanging of a like number of Union prisoners that had fallen into my hands." He paused a moment, gathering his thoughts. "They were chosen by lot. I must say I did not relish this experience. I am not a wrathful man, you understand. But I feared that if I did not take retaliatory measures, General Sheridan would have continued to execute my men, whose safety was always my chief concern."

"And where does General Lowell fit into this story?"

"Well, General Sheridan did not initially blink, you see. He ordered more Confederate prisoners hanged in retaliation for the executions I ordered. Measure for measure, I suppose one could say. General Lowell was ordered to send some prisoners that he had captured to Sheridan's headquarters for execution." Mosby looked at Lowell and smiled. "He refused to do so, even after Sheridan threatened to remove him from command for insubordination. In the meantime, a letter from me to General Sheridan arrived, which threatened further retaliation and gave information about the number of prisoners held by my men. There were no further hangings after that."

"So General Lowell's refusal to follow the orders of General Sheridan saved the lives of your men?"

"Absolutely. Of that I have no doubt whatsoever."

Benjamin looked up at Moise. "No further questions, your honor."

"Very well," the judge said. As Benjamin walked back to his seat, Moise surveyed the courtroom and checked the clock on the wall. He looked at Eustis. "Counselor, do you wish to cross examine?"

"No, your honor," Eustis replied, not even rising from his seat.

This surprised Lowell, though a quick glance to his attorney showed that Benjamin hadn't expected anything else.

"It is getting on towards five o'clock," Moise said. "Too late to call another witness. The court shall be in recess until tomorrow morning." He banged the gavel onto his desk and rose to leave.

Lowell then went through the now familiar routine of being escorted out of the courtroom to the paddy wagon. The jeering crowds had diminished, as people had grown tired of the spectacle. Today, however, the insults seemed rather fewer and more subdued than normal, even given the smaller number of people. Twenty minutes later, Lowell was escorted into his jail cell.

He spent half an hour reading the Latin text of Boethius, yet he found he could not concentrate. Mosby's words kept ringing in his head. Why, he asked himself, had he refused to burn the homes of civilians in northern Virginia? Why had he acted to prevent the execution of Confederate prisoners? After all, the people he protected had been slave-holders, or at least people who lived within the slave system and sacrificed to defend it. During the war, his conscience had revolted from barbarous actions, yet he had been willing to supply weapons to renegade slaves, who often burned civilian homes and executed men taken prisoner. Did the removal of direct involvement in an act truly eliminate a man's moral responsibility for the act? By aiding Saul, had he compromised his own honor?

His troubling thoughts were interrupted when the door opened and Benjamin entered. Instead of the habitual soft smile, however, Benjamin's expression was one of unusual seriousness. He had, however, brought along a meal of Creole gumbo, which Lowell found extremely unusual and highly spiced but not unpleasant.

"A very interesting day, I must say," Lowell said, after an uncharacteristically long silence from Benjamin. "It was very strange seeing John Mosby in the flesh. For so long, I half-believed him to be a phantom. And yet there he was, as real as anybody else."

"I am sure it was strange," Benjamin replied. "I thought it went well. His testimony will be reported in all the major newspapers. Things are going just as we discussed."

"I am glad to hear it, even if the story ends with me hanging at the end of a rope."

Benjamin only grunted, taking another bite of his gumbo.

"Who else will be testifying?" Lowell asked.

"I have lined up many of your former adversaries. Tom Rosser will testify tomorrow. Stephen Ramseur the day after that. I tried to get Jubal Early himself to come testify, but he did not answer my telegram. Knowing him as I do, he probably laughed and tossed it into the fire."

Lowell chuckled, yet he sensed something in Benjamin's voice that was out of the ordinary. "What else is there that you have to tell me?" he asked.

Benjamin looked at him carefully. "I feel that we have become friends of a sort over these past few weeks. Don't you?"

"I suppose," Lowell replied, after a slight pause.

"Then let me address you as a friend and not merely as a client. When we first met, we agreed that we were essentially going to use your trial as a public spectacle, to nudge Southern opinion in the direction we both feel it needs to go, albeit for different reasons."

"I remember."

"Well, my friend, I must tell you something. I am beginning to suspect that your life might yet be saved. I think it is not impossible that you might escape your death sentence in exchange for a lifetime, or at least a long time, in prison."

These words took Lowell completely by surprise. "By Plato!" he whispered harshly. "Surely you can't be serious."

"I am entirely serious. Listening to Mosby's testimony convinced me, as did the fact that Judge Moise seems to favor us. The more I think about it, the more possible it seems."

"But you said that no Southern jury would ever deliver any sentence except death. From everything I know about Southerners, I see no reason to believe otherwise."

"The jury is composed of New Orleans men, not South Carolinians or Georgians. We're talking about merchants, bank tellers, and wharf workers. Men from a cosmopolitan city. They rub shoulders with free blacks every day. New Orleans is a Southern city, to be sure, but it is very different from the rest of the south. No, if the other witnesses can keep pushing the jury in the same direction that Mosby started them along today, we might be able to generate enough sympathy that they will not be able to bring themselves to execute you."

Lowell's emotions swirled so much that he feared the gumbo he had eaten would come back up. He stood from his chair and walked in a circle around the table for a few moments, trying to gather his thoughts. Ever since the moment the *Vincent* boarded by the New Orleans police officers, he had been mentally preparing himself for death. He had been reading and rereading the Bible and his beloved works of philosophy, trying to absorb into his being everything they had to say about death and martyrdom.

He stopped, holding his fingers to his temples, breathing hard. He turned and glared at Benjamin.

"How can you tell me this now?" he demanded.

"What?" Benjamin said. "I'm telling you that you might yet live."

"I have been preparing to die. My death would mean something! If I'm tossed into a cell for the rest of my life, it will mean nothing. Just endless years of misery and loneliness. I'll be nothing but a pathetic wastrel, a figure for schoolchildren to make fun of."

Benjamin said nothing, looking back at Lowell with an expression that was simultaneously apologetic and determined.

Lowell went on. "What game are you playing, Benjamin? We agreed on what was going to happen. Are you trying to take from me my last chance to strike a blow against slavery? Why? Have you changed your mind about everything we discussed? Have you been lying to me this whole time?"

"No, I haven't," Benjamin responded harshly. "I've been more honest with you than I ever have been with anyone."

"Then why are you telling me that I might be able to live? I had resigned myself to my fate. I was ready to hear the jury read out the dreadful words. I was already dead, at least as far as it matters. I don't want any hope! I don't need any hope!"

Benjamin let out a deep sigh. "I'm your attorney. If I think there's a chance I might save your life, I am honor bound to try to do so." He pushed himself up from the table quickly, banging on the door to be let out.

"I'm supposed to be a martyr, Benjamin!" Lowell cried out as the loud metal door was swung upon. "It was what we agreed!"

Benjamin looked at him one more time, his enigmatic eyes seeming to pierce deeply within him, a look of strange sadness in them that Lowell could not comprehend. He stepped out and the door clanged shut behind him, leaving Lowell alone once again. Angrily, he sat back down in his chair, disdaining the remaining food, and held his face in his hands. More than at any moment since he had left Massachusetts, he felt totally and utterly alone.

October 9, Afternoon
French Foreign Ministry Building, Paris, France

As he waited to be summoned into the office of the Foreign Minister, Slidell clutched his walking stick with unusual rigidity, as if doing so would give him comfort. His bones ached painfully. He had been sitting in the waiting area for more than an hour and he longed to be reclining in his bed. Not for the first time in the past month, he reflected that his age was finally starting to catch up to him.

Concerned-looking bureaucrats walked back and forth, talking or whispering urgently to one another, shuffling official papers. There was trouble in Central Europe. In recent months, under pressure from Hungarian nobles, Emperor Franz Joseph of Austria had made some concessions, including the elevation of Hungarian to a co-equal place with German as an official language of the empire and an emphasis on Hungarian culture in the education system. A large faction of Hungarians, however, were dissatisfied with anything less than full political autonomy. Fears of a full-scale nationalist uprising, like those that tore Europe apart in 1848, were in the air. Even worse, no one knew if Prussia or Russia might be planning to take advantage of the situation.

Slidell knew that one of the pillars of French foreign policy was to prevent the unification of Germany under either Prussian or Austrian leadership. So long as Germany remained divided, its constituent states would be too weak to jeopardize France's claim to be the supreme power on the European continent. To this end, France had threatened intervention against Prussia when it had menaced Austria, forcing a mediation that humiliated Prussia. Slidell had been surprised by this, attributing the unexpectedly firm response of Napoleon III to an overconfidence brought on by his successes in Mexico.

If the Habsburg monarchy was torn asunder, Austria would be crippled and Prussia would become the strongest German power. France would no longer be able to play Prussia and Austria against one another. It was no surprise, therefore, that the men of the French Foreign Ministry were concerned.

The Hungarian crisis was yet another reminder to Slidell that affairs in North America, which meant absolutely everything to him and his countrymen, were considered a minor sideshow by the men of influence in the European capitals. It wouldn't have terribly surprised him if Foreign Minister La Valette had entirely forgotten about the proposed treaty between France and the Confederacy.

He sighed deeply. His long period of waiting did not appear likely to end anytime soon. Slidell also knew that news might arrive at any moment that outright rebellion had broken out in Hungary, in which case La Valette wouldn't be able to see him for several days and all his time waiting would have been for naught.

At least the enforced delay gave Slidell time to gather his thoughts. The distraction of the Hungarian crisis was only one of a number of frustrations bedeviling him, for the events of the previous month had been little short of disastrous. La Valette had made it clear that the question of whether or not to resume negotiations was entirely up to the emperor. Napoleon III, for his part, had made it abundantly clear that the negotiations were over unless the life of Charles Russell Lowell was spared. This struck Slidell as being unlikely in the extreme. Lowell was going to hang and it would be a miracle if his execution did not take place before the end of the year.

Benjamin not yet responded to the coded telegram Slidell sent him a few days before, but Slidell didn't doubt that he would immediately understand the implications of the message. Benjamin, Slidell knew, was a skilled attorney, but even his talents would not be able to overcome the fact of Lowell's guilt and the entrenched bigotry of a jury of Southern men. Yet Slidell had no choice but to hope Benjamin would somehow succeed, which was why he was at the Foreign Ministry in the first place.

Finally, after he had been waiting for more than two hours, one of the nameless secretaries approached him.

"Monsieur Slidell? The Foreign Minister will see you now."

He tried to rise and was surprised when the bones and muscles in his legs refused to obey and seemed to drag him back down to his chair. The secretary reached out and took hold of Slidell's upper arm, helping him to his feet. He composed himself and stepped forward, leaning on his walking stick as the secretary led him into the Salon de la Rotonde.

La Valette was seated at the desk, with three men standing around him, speaking urgently. When they saw Slidell approach, however, they became quiet and nodded their heads in a silent greeting. The office, normally meticulously clean, appeared disheveled, suggesting that the Foreign Minister had been working more hours than normally.

"We'll continue this discussion shortly, gentlemen," La Valette said to the men. "I must speak with our Confederate friend for a few moments. Please, Monsieur Slidell, take a seat." La Valette gestured to one of the chairs, which the secretary pulled out for him. A few moments after he sat down, the other men had left and shut the door, leaving Slidell and La Valette alone.

"I am sorry to keep you waiting, Monsieur, and I am sorry that I do not have much time for this interview. This Hungarian business may spiral out of control and I cannot even begin to predict what will happen."

Slidell shrugged. "I am sure that you will do your best to protect France's interests."

"It goes without saying that the Confederacy has no position on this matter, yes?"

"That's correct. Whether the Habsburg Empire is Austrian or divided between Austria and Hungary is a matter of indifference to us. I am here to discuss the treaty between our two countries."

"Yes, I heard about that little nocturnal encounter between you and the emperor at your home. You fooled him utterly, by the way. He remains convinced that your discovery of him in bed with your daughter was entirely a coincidence. But you don't fool me, Monsieur. I know a good trick when I see one."

Slidell said nothing in response.

La Valette went on. "The emperor told me what he told you. Even with all this Hungarian businesses, the people are still following the Lowell trial in the papers. It takes a lot more than some disorder on the other side of Europe to distract people away from the plight of a hero, after all. The people will not tolerate our government signing a treaty such as you propose if this man is executed."

"That is what I came here to tell you. Charles Russell Lowell shall not be executed."

The Frenchman drew his head back in surprise. "He shall not?"

"No, Monsieur," Slidell said. "You have my word on it. Lowell shall be allowed to live."

Slidell knew that he was promising something that was unlikely to happen and over which he had no control. Perhaps there was one chance in a hundred that this gamble would succeed. A man with more options might choose to sit and wait, for the fuss over Lowell's execution might be expected to blow over after a few months. Yet Slidell knew he couldn't wait. He could feel the strength of his body weakening and was not certain he would live more than a year or two longer. He would also likely be replaced as Minister to France after the election, for either Beauregard or Breckinridge would want their own man in Paris and Slidell's age was an obvious reason for putting a new person in place. If he did not obtain the treaty soon, he would never obtain it at all and his name would be utterly lost to history.

La Valette looked at him carefully. "I read the newspapers, you know. The trial seems to be a foregone conclusion. Lowell has already pled guilty, hasn't he?

It seems to me certain that the jury will sentence him to death. I'm rather surprised that the sentence hasn't already been issued."

"The reason that it hasn't is because Judah Benjamin is now serving as Lowell's attorney. There is not a finer legal mind anywhere on either side of the Atlantic or a more persuasive speaker."

"Yes, well, I know all about Benjamin. I met him several times when he was in France two years ago. Lowell needs more than a good attorney. He needs a miracle."

"Lowell will escape execution. I promise you."

"But how can you promise that?" He paused a moment and focused on Slidell's eyes. "What is it that you know which you aren't telling me?"

"That, Monsieur, I cannot reveal at this time."

Slidell knew of his well-deserved reputation for duplicity and was hoping that it would work to his advantage. He knew he was making his promise based on nothing but a forlorn hope, but La Valette couldn't be sure of that. He felt very much like a chess player who had lost almost all of his pieces, gambling that his opponent could somehow be tricked into thinking that one of his few remaining pawns was a rook. The fact that chance was involved, and a low chance at that, was infuriating. He hated not being in control of the situation, but such was fate.

La Valette sighed. "Well, it's interesting to hear you come in here and say that. But you'll forgive me if I require more than just your word. We will have to wait until the trial is over and sentence has been passed on poor Lowell. If he is sentenced to die, then this was a wasted visit on your part. If he is spared, then we shall talk some more."

"In the meantime, I would like an assurance from you."

"And that would be?"

"That when it is definitely declared that Lowell shall not die, the signing of the treaty between our two countries shall not be further postponed but shall take place without delay."

La Valette chuckled. "There are still some fine points in that treaty which we have not yet worked out. I might be willing to resume negotiations, but an immediate signing would not be possible."

Slidell pursed his lips. "Well, that is unfortunate. You see, at the risk of revealing a bit of information given to me in confidence, I can tell you that the prospect of an immediate signing of the treaty is part of why Lowell's life may yet be spared."

"Is it?" La Valette said. "How interesting. I do hope that one day you will be able to tell me this whole story." He sighed. "Well, I shall have to take your request to the emperor. Of course, after what happened at your house, I doubt he will be anything other than cooperative with you. Not because of his fears of scandal, but his fears of the security of those bank shares your son-in-law has provided to him and his friends."

"Yourself among them," Slidell pointed out.

"Yes, and thank you for reminding me."

"In the meantime, if we have an agreement, might we then resume talks, if only informally, on those fine points of the treaty you mentioned a moment ago?"

La Valette laughed again. "Ah, there is it! You are a clever man, Slidell, I grant you that. You have me. But it would be dependent on whether the emperor agrees, as usual."

"Of course."

"And you understand quite fully that if the jury returns a sentence of death on Lowell, the deal is off."

"I understand that, Monsieur. Indeed, if I understand anything in this world, it is that."

October 10, Noon
Flynn's Alehouse, Waco, Texas

"Granbury County Defense League?" Collett asked.

"You don't like the sound of it?" McFadden replied.

"Might be a bit long, don't you think?"

McFadden nodded and took another swig of beer. He glanced about, looking at the three dozen or so armed men pacing back and forth in the alehouse. More, he knew, were sitting out on the front porch, keeping an eye out for anyone who might have unfriendly intentions. Since the shootout in the street two weeks earlier, McFadden's friends were taking no chances. Waco was a frontier town and men generally armed themselves every day before leaving home, even if they intended only routine business. Yet blood had been spilled on the streets and the tension everywhere was now palpable.

Flynn himself remained behind the bar, pouring glass after glass of ale. Almost all of his regular customers were gone, fearful of the prospect of violence, yet the presence of all the veterans more than made up for his lost business. The bar owner himself was armed with two pistols and two bowie knives, his appearance alone a walking advertisement for his devotion to the cause of McFadden and Collett.

That cause had crystallized intensely over the previous two weeks. The loose organization that had characterized the twin political campaigns had coalesced into something more. The crowds of armed men who now gathered around Flynn's Alehouse and at McFadden's ranch were looking to McFadden and Collett for leadership. Admonitions to vote on Election Day, many had insisted, were simply not enough, especially as no one believed Judge Roden would allow a legitimate election anyway.

McFadden and Collett had decided upon two courses of action. First, urgent letters were sent to Austin addressed to both Governor Sexton and Postmaster Reagan, telling them what had happened and urgently requesting the intervention of the state government. McFadden expected little from Governor Sexton, who had not even deigned to respond to any of his previous messages, but Postmaster Reagan had not let them down yet. Perhaps he could push Sexton to restore some semblance of legal order in Granbury County.

Second, the followers of McFadden and Collett had begun to properly organize themselves. All the able-bodied men were members of the militia, of course, but Judge Roden had issued a decree that the militia should not muster before the election. McFadden and the rest had considered simply ignoring this announcement and mustering anyway, but it was felt better to create a new organization from scratch, formed directly by the citizens.

"You think the name is too long?" McFadden asked.

"Perhaps," Collett replied.

"Well, how would you make it shorter?"

"Not sure, but I'll tell you something else. I'm not really sure about the word 'defense' in it."

McFadden looked confused. "Why? We're talking about defending one another, aren't we?"

"Well, sure, but we're also talking about more than that. Some of the boys want to have a collective fund that everybody can contribute money to, which we could use to help our friends when something bad happens. Like if somebody is too hurt to work their ranch or they're robbed on the road or something like that. Not really defense, in the sense of arming ourselves and protecting each other, you know?"

McFadden shrugged. "Yes, I suppose so."

"And do we want to call it a 'league', too? Sounds like one of those radical European groups that those German refugees down in New Braunfels are always talking about. And you know, we don't want to sound provocative. We want the state government to help us, see? Maybe it would be best if the name was a little more mundane."

McFadden thought for a moment. "How about the Granbury County Assistance Organization, then?"

Collett frowned. "Well, that's just boring."

McFadden held his hands up. "Well, you think of a name, then."

Collett thought for a moment, then his eyes lit up. "How about just the 'Granbury County Association'. Men who join it can be called 'Associators'."

At first it sounded so simple that McFadden wanted to dismiss the idea out of hand. After considering it for a moment, however, the name quickly grew on him. It was simple, but sometimes simplicity had an elegance all its own. There was something else about the name, though.

"Sounds strangely familiar," McFadden said.

"It should. Didn't you ever read Ben Franklin's autobiography?"

"Ah, yes!" McFadden replied. "Of course. That time the Quakers refused to form a militia, Franklin just went ahead and did it on his own. Yes, the Philadelphia Association. That's what it was."

"How about that, then? It can cover mutual defense, like we talked about, but also all the other stuff. And it would be run by the members themselves, not the government, so Judge Roden can rant and rave all he wants, but won't be able to do anything about it."

"He'll try, anyway."

"Well, if he does, he'll come face-to-face with lots of angry men carrying guns."

They spent the next hour writing out their vision of the Association, based on all the conversations they had had with their friends, former comrades, and other concerned citizens in Waco and throughout Granbury County. Most importantly, its members would pledge to defend one another regardless of the source of danger. Be it Comanche Indians, outlaws escaping from the war in

Mexico, or corrupt officials of their own government, the members of the Association would stand by one another. They also talked about the proposed monetary fund for members who needed special assistance for certain reasons, with McFadden suggesting that some of it be used to help widows and orphans of members.

"And for the sort of stuff that got us into this mess in the first place," Collett said.

"What do you mean?" McFadden asked.

"When you helped that widow keep her land at the auction, all those months ago."

McFadden chuckled. "Seems like a long time, doesn't it?"

"Yes, it does."

Flynn approached the table. "Another round, you two?"

McFadden nodded. "Thanks, Flynn." He thought for a moment. "Say, did Roden ever tell you whether or not he was going to revoke your alcohol license?"

Flynn looked surprised. "Didn't I tell you? He revoked it last week. Sent me an official notice and everything. I told the lackey who delivered the letter to take it back to Roden and tell him to shove it up his ass. I'll keep serving beer and spirits as long as I want to and I couldn't care less what Roden thinks."

McFadden looked at the glass of ale in his hand and grinned. "So, this beer is being illegally served?"

Flynn's tone took on an uncharacteristic seriousness. "What's legal now? So what if Roden won an election awhile back? Everyone knows he bribed and intimidated people to get their votes. We weren't even all back from the war yet. What real right does he have to enforce the law or make rules for the rest of us? If you ask me, the fact that he abuses his power and tries to squash people like us to hold onto his office means that he has lost the right to be a judge, you know?"

McFadden nodded. He remembered reading his father's copy of John Locke's *Two Treatises of Government*. He had not enjoyed reading it, for he found it rather dully written, but his father insisted and took away his privileges until he had finished it. Locke said that people had a right to overthrow their government if the government stopped serving their interests. The American revolutionaries were following Locke's advice when they rebelled against the British in the 1770s. The secession of the Southern states, too, was in the tradition of Locke, though McFadden had never felt that it had had as much justification as the American Revolution.

What was happening in Granbury County was, McFadden had begun to think, a local manifestation of Locke's thinking. The rule of Judge Roden was corrupt and cruel, completely ignoring the good of the people he ostensibly governed. The people, therefore, were perfectly entitled to throw Roden out and put their own choices in his place. Ideally, this would be done at the time of the election and McFadden still hoped that this would be the case. Roden, however, had resorted to intimidation and violence, bringing in Walker and his Mexican mercenaries. Locke would have said that these actions delegitimized Roden and rendered his official status as county judge null and void. In large and small ways, from the formation of the Association to the refusal of Flynn to obey the order to shut down his alehouse, the people of Granbury County were expressing their belief that Roden no longer mattered.

He hoped that further violence could be avoided and the election allowed to go forward. If it was conducted fairly, the outcome would surely be an overwhelming victory for the McFadden-Collett faction and the crushing of Roden's power. McFadden did not doubt, though, that Roden would do whatever he could to prevent that from happening. Walker and his men had generally kept their distance from McFadden and his men since the shooting two weeks before. He hoped it would stay that way.

When the election took place, it would either bring about Roden's defeat and removal or force the state government to intervene when it became blatantly obvious that only corruption had kept Roden in office.

He heard a sudden commotion outside in the street. Instinctively, his hand went to his Navy Colt, expecting danger. Yet while there were unquestionably shouts of alarm, there was no gunfire. He exchanged a quick, confused glance with Collett and both men quickly rose and moved towards the door.

"What is it?" Collett asked as they stepped outside. "What's happened?"

"The courthouse is on fire!" a man shouted back.

"What?!" McFadden cried, incredulous.

"Just now!" the man cried back. "Whole thing went up like a damn tinder box!"

"Come on!" McFadden called. "They'll need help!"

McFadden dashed off, followed quickly by Collett and a few dozen of the men who had been waiting around the alehouse. A pillar of black smoke was rising into the sky in the direction of the central square and, as they got closer, McFadden began to hear the sinister crackling roar of a large fire. In minutes, the courthouse came into view. It was, indeed, wrapped in yellow and red flames.

Several men were already trying to pump up water from the nearest wells and form bucket lines in an effort to fight the fire. Without hesitation, McFadden and his men threw themselves into the work. It was the obvious thing to do, but he saw at once that it was a futile effort. The fire was raging to such an extent that the wooden structure was going to be a pile of ashes by the time it was put out.

McFadden took his place in the middle of one of the three bucket lines that had formed, quickly falling into the repetitive yet exhausting rhythm of taking a bucketful of water from the man behind him and passing it to the man in front of him.

"What started it?" he loudly asked the woman handing him the bucket.

"No idea," she replied. "But it was fast. One minute, nothing. Next minute, fire coming out of every window."

"Was anybody trapped in there?"

"Don't know!"

There was nothing to do but to keep grabbing and passing the buckets, which went on for over an hour. The square soon filled up with astonished onlookers, who kept a safe distance from the flames. Over the din of the fire, McFadden could hear a few people shouting that they had seen two men with cans of turpentine run into the building and run out again minutes later. He hoped this was just a wild rumor.

After a time, exhaustion ensured that he could not continue and he dropped out of the line, stumbling away from the heat of the fire and into the crowd. He looked at the courthouse. The roof was clearly about to collapse as its supports were gradually incinerated. The bucket lines were now useless, for it was clear that nothing was going to be saved. Yet the men and women continued tossing the water, stubbornly unwilling to accept defeat.

Some people, mostly women but also a few men, were in tears. For a moment, McFadden wondered why. The courthouse had been a wooden structure of no particular architectural distinction. Yet he quickly sensed the cause of the grief. Waco was a town on the edge of the frontier, menaced by Comanches, subject to droughts and epidemics, the livelihood of its people always at the mercy of market prices for crops and livestock. The courthouse had been a symbol of stability and reassurance, expressing the idea that there was a government to which people could turn for some measure of help and justice. That faith had already been shaken by Roden's reign of corruption. Now, it had literally gone up in smoke.

"Jimmy!"

McFadden turned to see Collett coming up to him. Like him, he appeared exhausted, having also put in his time in the bucket lines. "Are you okay?"

Collett ignored the question. "The voter rolls, Jimmy!"

"What?"

"The voter rolls! They were kept in the courthouse!"

Instantly, McFadden realized the terrifying implications of what Collett was saying. All voters in the county were required to have registered to vote by a certain deadline, which had passed the previous week. If a man's name wasn't on the list, he wouldn't be allowed to vote. McFadden and Collett, on the advice of Postmaster Reagan, had made sure that all of their supporters had registered to vote well before the deadline. However, the courthouse fire had destroyed everything within its walls, including the priceless voter rolls.

As he stood watching the yellow blaze consume what was left of the courthouse, the building's ceiling finally collapsed, bringing the whole thing down like a house of cards. McFadden couldn't help but wonder if the chances for a legitimate election had met the same fate.

October 12, Evening
French Quarter, New Orleans, Louisiana

Rain dribbled down onto the roof of the carriage, which sat motionless in a back alley. In the distance, thunder rumbled softly. Benjamin sat quietly, waiting. Thick, black clouds blocked the moonlight, so a single flickering candle and the red glow of his cigar provided the only illumination inside the carriage. Benjamin had brought a bottle of Armagnac with him and was slowly sipping his second glass, but was careful not to become intoxicated. The meeting he was about to have was so important that he could not afford to have his mind impaired.

Benjamin would have preferred to meet in one of the city's many gambling dens, or perhaps one of the better restaurants like Antoine's. This would have allowed him to mix business with pleasure. Unfortunately, it was necessary to keep the meeting strictly secret. New Orleans was renowned for the discretion of its eating and gambling establishments, but even the most careful person could not have guaranteed total confidentiality. A clandestine meeting in a back alley had turned out to be the only realistic option.

For a moment, he reflected on the fact that he was only a few hundred yards away from General Beauregard's house. The man himself was probably at home at that moment, enjoying his dinner and perhaps regaling some guests with embellished stories of his own military genius. The idea that Beauregard, a buffoon remarkable for nothing but his tireless self-promotion and Creole accent, might become the next president was almost absurd. It would have been laughable had the implications not been so serious. Worse yet, despite all the ground he had laid on Breckinridge's behalf, it seemed very likely to come to pass.

He sighed. The election was a separate issue. He needed to keep his mind focused on the Lowell trial, which, to his great surprise, had now become intertwined with the French treaty. He brooded for a moment on the telegram he had received from Slidell a week and a half earlier. It was not hard for Benjamin to make great mental shifts. It was rather as if, while playing a billiards game, he had intended to strike the cue ball into the red ball, only to have it whispered in his ear that he should knock it into the green ball.

So, Lowell had to live. Next to Breckinridge's victory in the upcoming election, the treaty with France was the most important goal the Confederacy had before it. Given responsible government and the promise of foreign protection from the United States, the new nation might endure long enough to become firmly established on solid foundations. Those were the facts and they could not be changed.

In late 1864, Britain had offered diplomatic recognition to the Confederacy only on the condition that there be some symbolic gesture against slavery. Without such a gesture, Her Majesty's Government would not have the political credibility to move forward. This was gained by having the Confederacy sign a treaty with Britain designed to tighten up the international ban on the African slave trade. Now the French were wanting the same thing, although they were willing to settle for a single man's life. The only problem was that Benjamin had no idea how to save it.

He took another sip of the Armagnac and then a long pull on his cigar, the combined taste and smell filling him with a momentary delight. He did not mind waiting, for he was perfectly happy alone with his thoughts. Moreover, being a very busy man, occasional periods of enforced quietude were rather welcome.

After a time, Benjamin heard the slave sitting on the bench thump his fist against the roof of the carriage, the agreed upon signal that the other carriage had arrived in the alley. Benjamin prepared himself. A few moments later, there was a soft knock on the door and it was opened by another slave. Judge Moise clambered into the carriage and took the seat opposite Benjamin.

"Good evening, old friend," Benjamin said warmly as the door was closed, leaving them alone.

"Good evening," Moise replied. He looked back out the window into the rainy darkness. "I wish I could say a pleasant evening."

"I don't know. I rather enjoy the rain. Would you like a glass of Armagnac?"

Moise shook his head. "No, thank you, Judah." He paused and pursed his lips. "I hope you don't mind my being forward, Judah, but I don't like this. I don't appreciate you asking to meet me like this. If anyone finds out, my reputation as a judge will suffer. It might even be grounds for impeachment."

"No one will find out."

"I certainly hope not. Still, I am nervous. So whatever you have to talk to me about had better be good. Had it been anyone but you, I should not have even thought to agree to this."

"Yes, well, we go back awhile, do we not? We both have had to make our way in the world of the Gentiles. We help each other out." He paused a moment. "You would not be a judge if it weren't for me, not to put too fine a point on it."

"Thank you for reminding me," Moise said sourly.

"And I know where the bodies are buried, so to speak."

"You speak of friendship and our shared Jewishness in one breath and threaten me with the next. Quite in character, I must say."

"It's not personal, it's business. In fact, it involves our old friend Slidell."

"Slidell? What possible interest could he have in the Lowell trial?"

Benjamin took a sip of brandy, then leaned forward to convey the importance of what he was about to say. "You know that we have been trying for a year now to get France to sign a treaty of friendship and alliance with the Confederacy. It would all but ensure that the United States would never attempt a war of revenge against us, as well as greatly improve our standing in the world. Slidell has been working hard to make this happen."

"I know all this," Moise replied. "The whole country knows. But I don't see what it has to do with the trial."

"I will be more frank with you than I would be with other men. After all, you know where some of my bodies are buried, too. Napoleon III wants to sign the treaty, but is fearful of doing so while French public opinion is so against it. Seems he doesn't have the stomach that his uncle had. But he needs some gesture against slavery from us that he can use to show the French press."

Moise nodded slowly in understanding. "You want Lowell to live, don't you?"

"That's right."

"You told me when the trial began that you wanted him to die. In as honorable and dignified a manner as possible, of course, but die nonetheless."

"I did. But the circumstances have changed. I have it from Slidell himself. The emperor says that if Lowell dies, the treaty dies. If Lowell lives, the treaty will be signed. You can understand, then, just how important the situation is."

Moise grunted and nodded. "Do we really need the treaty, though? We defeated the United States once already. As time passes and the peace is retained, we become stronger and more able to defend ourselves. This makes it less likely that the Northerners will ever launch a war of revenge, and more likely that we would win it even if they did. I must admit that I do not like this French treaty. Why should we support Napoleon III taking control of Mexico?"

"Better it be ruled by a friend than a foe. Or, worse yet, fall into chaos. Besides, the emperor has been good to our coreligionists."

Moise shrugged, as if this was of no matter. "Some say that we fought to free ourselves from Northern chains and that Davis is now just trying to shackle us to France."

"The treaty was my idea, not Davis's. Mine and Slidell's, I should say. And it would not put shackles on us. If we help them in Mexico, they will protect us from the United States. It's as simple as that."

"If Lowell lives?"

"If Lowell lives, yes."

Moise took a deep breath and said nothing for a long time. Benjamin allowed him to think, sipping on his Armagnac and puffing on his cigar. A low, distant rumble of thunder was all that disturbed the silence of the next few minutes.

"No," Moise finally said.

Benjamin was taken aback by the finality of the judge's voice. "No?"

"No, I shall not do it. I would not do it even if I could, and I cannot do it in any event. What do you expect me to do, Judah? Tell the jury that they are not allowed to sentence him to execution?"

"You have the right to give instructions to the jury before they deliberate," Benjamin pointed out.

Moise laughed bitterly. "If I told them anything other than to sentence Lowell to death, I would be lucky if I was only run out of town on a rail. More likely, I'd be hanged by the mob from the nearest lamppost. Good God, man! Have you considered how doing what you suggest would make us Jews look to the powers-that-be in the Confederacy? We have had enough difficulty fighting our way into any positions of influence in this bigoted country."

"We're no worse off here than our ancestors were in Venice or the Netherlands, and look what they achieved. No, the treaty is what I'm talking about. Using France to secure us against the United States. That's more important than our own concerns. I'm concerned about the entire Confederacy, not just us and our fellow Jews."

Moise looked at him with narrowed eyes. "More to it than that, methinks. What is it? You're not doing all of this just for the treaty. So what exactly is your game, Judah?"

Benjamin took another sip. "Lowell is not important as a man, only as a symbol. He is a piece of the puzzle."

"Perhaps, but I don't think I'm wrong in thinking that this is about more than the treaty to you. I've known you a long time, Judah. You can't lie to me. You said you would be frank, but you're keeping something from me now. What else is on your mind?"

"I'm not keeping anything from you."

"I know you better than that. Tell me, or this meeting is concluded."

Benjamin thought a few moments, taking a long pull on his cigar, considering just how honest he should be with Moise. He knew the meeting was not going well, so perhaps it was best to be bold. Besides, whether or not Moise agreed with him, Benjamin was certain that he would not betray his confidence. "Well, if you must know, I think that letting Lowell live would also have a salutary effect on our people."

"Our people? Southerners or Jews?"

"Southerners."

"How so?"

"Slavery will vanish. It is only a question of time. It will take decades, perhaps. Maybe a century. But it is destined to disappear. If it doesn't, we will eventually see an uprising that will make Saul look like a bit player. All other nations will despise us and we will be a pariah in the world. They will stop trading with us. Already cotton production is increasing in India and Egypt. No, slavery must disappear, sooner or later. And it would be best if we start preparing our people for the change now."

"And you think letting Lowell live will help this?"

"I wanted him to die in an honorable and dignified manner, so that he would win the respect of the Southern people. If the Crusaders could respect Saladin, then the Confederates can respect Lowell. And respecting the person with whom one disagrees is the first step in realizing that they may be right after all."

Moise frowned and shook his head. "I'm sorry, but I'm not having it. And I'm not going to help you. Slavery is ordained by God and it is the foundation on which the Confederacy is built. If the rest of the world hates it, so be it. I would rather live in a slave-holding republic isolated from the rest of the world than in a prosperous country in which a white man was no longer permitted to own slaves. After all, if slavery is to be abolished, what was the point of secession in the first place? What was the point of the war?"

Benjamin didn't respond, merely taking another sip of Armagnac. Getting into a debate on the question would not help matters. He was no abolitionist and did not want Moise to start thinking of him as one. Yet he was beginning to see that he had made a blunder in requesting the meeting. Benjamin did not think of himself as a man who made many mistakes, but he was willing to recognize it when he did. He wouldn't be able to persuade Moise to come around to his way of thinking.

"You will not help?" Benjamin finally asked.

"As I said, I could not help even if I wished to do so. And I do not wish to do so."

Benjamin pursed his lips and sighed. "Will you at least stick to our original agreement? Let my witnesses speak in spite of the prosecution's objections?"

Moise grunted. "I'll be frank with you, Judah. After tonight, I am less inclined to help you."

"Well, let me tell you who my final witness will be."

October 14, Night
Canadian-United States Border

Wolseley and his men had either already crossed the border or were about to cross it. It was impossible to know, of course, given the wooded conditions and the darkness of the night. Moving through the backcountry was necessary, of course, as Wolseley wanted to avoid encountering any United States troops before reaching the Fenian camp.

Behind him, the English, Scottish, and Welsh soldiers were moving quietly. He had deployed the three companies of light infantry in front, with the grenadiers bringing up the rear, so that the men best at skirmishing would encounter the enemy first and the troops more experienced in close quarters fighting could be brought forward at the best possible time. When the time came, they could quickly be deployed from column into line. All told, they numbered only about five hundred men, about half the size of a regular battalion, but they were the best troops from three of the finest regiments in the British Army.

Wolseley knew what he was doing. Only the most captious attorney in the world, splitting the tiniest hairs, could assert that Wolseley was acting within the bounds of his orders. He was empowered to protect Canada from Her Majesty's enemies, but no one in London or Ottawa would have ever dreamed that this authorized a foray over the border into American territory. His actions constituted an act of war by the British Empire against the United States. A handful of men crossing the border might be dismissed as an accident, but not five hundred men. Nor was it possible that the Americans would believe it was anything other than an action authorized by Her Majesty's Government. The wide latitude the men in London gave to the army in the colonies was playing to Wolseley's advantage.

Wolseley walked at the head of the column. Beside him was Orenda, the Iroquois scout, the airy and mildly irritated attitude as plain on the man's face as it had been from the moment he met him. Out ahead of the column, other Iroquois were screening the movement, moving about in a scattered manner and keeping an eye out for any possible enemies.

"How far?" Wolseley asked Orenda. His voice was soft, so as not to be heard by the men a few yards behind them.

"Half hour."

"We have crossed the border then?"

"Quarter hour ago."

Wolseley turned to him. "Why didn't you tell me?"

"No ask."

Wolseley chuckled. The natives of North America never failed to amuse him. He turned and looked behind him, seeing the cold and expressionless faces of the light troops that composed the front ranks of the column. He would need to deploy them in a battle line well before they came upon the Fenian depot. He turned back to Orenda.

"You will tell me when we are twenty minutes away from the depot."

"Yes."

"I don't want there to be any misunderstanding. I will need time to deploy my men."

"I will tell you," Orenda replied.

Wolseley decided that he had to be satisfied with that. The column continued on in silence. As they kept marching, he could sense a certain restlessness in his men. All knew that they were close to the border and moving south, so perhaps they were growing uneasy about crossing into American territory. No one said anything, however. British troops had implicit trust in their officers, instilled in them with endless hours of rigorous training. It was yet another difference between the British and the Americans, for British troops needed only to be told what to do, while the men Wolseley had observed in both the Union and Confederate armies had also to be told exactly why they were doing it.

Orenda turned to him. "Now." The words came out as casually as if nothing unusual were about to take place.

"How do you know?"

Orenda pointed to a small formation of rocks. "Recognize those."

Wolseley held up his hand and the company commanders behind him whispered harshly for the men to halt. As if on cue, the half dozen or so other Iroquois scouts Orenda had sent out slowly emerged from the darkness ahead, like ghosts manifesting themselves. They spoke softly in their native language to their leader, who then turned to Wolseley.

"Fenian camp ahead. Will go and see."

"Go ahead."

Orenda and his men vanished back into the dark woods. Moments later, Buller came up from the rear.

"The grenadiers are halted, sir. Shall I deploy them into line as we discussed?"

"Yes," Wolseley replied quickly. "When the Indian is back with his report, I shall advance the light troops. You will follow behind us. Maintain a distance of perhaps three hundred yards."

"Yes, sir," Buller said, before snapping a quick salute and dashing back towards the rear of the column.

Wolseley gave the company commanders of the light troops their orders for deployment. The Royal Welsh Fusiliers would take the center, with the Gordon Highlanders forming on the right and the men of the Duke of Wellington's Regiment on the left. Behind them, assuming that Buller was doing his job properly, the grenadiers would be aligning in the same pattern. The troops moved into battle lines with the precision of a machine, exactly as they had been trained.

There was now nothing to do but wait for the return of Orenda and his scouts. Wolseley considered lighting a cigar, but decided to wait until after the engagement was over. Standing still had the unpleasant side effect of making the cold less tolerable, for mid-autumn in this part of the world was not unlike winter in England. Wolseley could see his breath with every exhalation. Aside from scattered coughs and clearings of the throat, the men behind him made no sound. The full moon above cast a bright white light, interrupted only occasionally by puffy clouds.

Twenty minutes after the deployment, Orenda and his scouts came ambling back up to the line.

"Camp less than one thousand yards that way," Orenda said, pointing directly to the south. "If you march straight ahead, you'll come to it. Orenda led you very well."

"How many Fenians?"

"Not many. Maybe a hundred men. Very lazy. Ten or so marching around it in a circle. Very slowly. Not keeping an eye out. Others inside, cooking food.

Their uniforms not good. What's the word?" He thought for a moment. "Sloppy. Very sloppy."

Wolseley nodded. The picture Orenda was painting was typical of the Fenians, as near as Wolseley understood them. Though experienced soldiers and brave fighters, being part of a force in which any man was free to leave at any time, and therefore not disposed to follow the strict leadership of officers, inevitably caused discipline to suffer. Simple things like camp routines and guard duties, which armies depended upon, could never be conducted in a professional manner by groups like the Fenians.

"How big is the depot?"

Orenda shrugged. "If a regiment made a camp. About that big."

He turned to the three company commanders, who had come forward as soon as Orenda returned. Wolseley sketched out his simple plan. Of great concern was the danger posed by large amounts of musketry fire into the depot itself, which might set off the ammunition and cause an enormous explosion. This would kill all the Fenians, which was fine with Wolseley, but would also pose an unacceptable danger to his own men. Therefore, they would surround the depot and then call upon the men inside it to surrender. To achieve this, the Welsh company would advance directly towards the depot and close it off from the north, while the Gordon Highlander light troops would circle around and position themselves to the south, blocking any escape in that direction. The men of the Duke of Wellington's regiment, meanwhile, would establish a skirmish line screening the southern approaches to keep an eye out for any American troops.

"Any questions?" Wolseley asked.

The company commanders shook their heads and he dismissed them back to their formations. Wolseley looked at Orenda.

"Want to come along?"

The Iroquois scout shook his head. "No. White man's fight. Not our business."

"But you're our scout."

"For pay. We will leave you now." With that, Orenda and his men began walking back to the north.

Wolseley watched them go, reflected for a moment on how absurd the whole business probably appeared to an Indian, and then dismissed the man from his mind. He strode to the center of the line of the Welsh light troops. Ordinarily, he might have addressed the men to encourage them or describe briefly what they were doing, but the need for quiet precluded that. Instead, he simply raised his walking stick so that everyone could see, then turned and stepped off to the south.

The line lurched forward, the feet of the men crunching the grass as they followed him. A sense of thrilling excitement, similar to that he had felt just before the Battle of the Stockade, filled him. If his plan worked, there would be little if any firing. Still, the very possibility of combat was enough to cheer him, like a shot of warm scotch.

The trees were thick and boulders and rocky outcroppings were scattered throughout the area, which would have made it difficult for line infantry to maintain their formations. The light troops, however, were specialists at this sort of thing and shook their lines out loosely, so that the men parted and came back together to avoid obstacles, keeping their formation. The grenadiers, more used to tight formations, would have to move more slowly, but Wolseley trusted Buller to do his job. The heavy troops would only be needed if they ran into trouble, after all. As they advanced, the trees grew thicker and great clouds moved across the sky. A pale glow replaced the previously bright moonlight.

Wolseley thought he saw the yellow light of fires up ahead. He could also hear distant voices of men talking and laughing. Another thirty seconds of walking and the depot slowly came into his view through the trees. It looked like a typical army camp, although there were no trenches and the tents and campfires were laid out in a disorderly fashion. What was unusual were the large stacks of wooden crates that were piled up off to the sides, enough to contain enough rifles and ammunition to equip several regiments.

He stopped and raised his walking stick to signal for the Welsh troops behind him to halt as well. Looking in either direction, he saw that the English and Scottish companies were following his orders and moving on, the Scots moving by the right flank and the Englishmen by the left. It would not take long for them to circle around the Fenians and close the trap.

Orenda had mentioned sentries marching around the depot, but Wolseley could see no signs of any security measures. He quickly pulled out his pocket watch and saw that it was almost exactly ten o'clock. Perhaps one sentry detail had gone off duty, but the other had yet to take up its post. It was yet another example of the lack of discipline in the Fenian ranks.

He waited. Glancing behind him, he could see the gleaming bayonets of the grenadiers, showing that they were not far behind. The Fenians were being so careless, however, that Wolseley expected little need of his heavy infantry. He could see the Irish rebels clearly, lounging around their fires, cooking meat, talking and joking with one another. They were entirely unaware of the danger surrounding them, for the trees and the darkness concealed the British from view.

Finally, fifteen minutes after the Welsh light infantry had halted, Wolseley heard three successive gunshots at single second intervals, the agreed upon signal that the Scottish troops had arrived in position to the south. There was a series of confused shouts from the Fenians, as men demanded to know who had fired their weapons. Many of the men stood up, but some only with difficulty, leading Wolseley to conclude that they had been drinking. None of the Fenians made any effort to take up their weapons, however, and none seemed to consider the possibility that the gunshots had been anything other than an accidental firing by their own men.

"Fenian rebels!" Wolseley shouted. "You are surrounded by troops of the British Army! Surrender and your lives will be spared! If you open fire, you will be killed at once!" Wolseley raised his walking stick and stepped forward as he spoke, moving slowly. The Welsh troops behind him all raised their Snider rifles to their shoulders and stepped forward as well, matching his advance. Only yards now separated his men from the tents of the Fenians.

Confusion in the Fenian camp turned to consternation as Wolseley's words faded. Shouts of alarm and fear echoed as men rushed to grab their rifles and take up position, but there was little order. The men seemed to have had no prepared plan to deal with any threat to their camp. Only a few dashed out toward what should have been the opposing line, but froze upon seeing the formidable-looking Welsh soldiers. Wolseley assumed that similar scenes were being played out on the other side of the Fenian camp.

"Put your weapons on the ground!" Wolseley shouted.

Some of the officers and sergeants among the fusiliers repeated his orders for the Fenians to drop their weapons. A few obeyed, but others still gripped their Springfields, their eyes looking back and forth along the line of British troops. Most likely experienced soldiers, they had to know a hopeless situation when they saw one. Wolseley noted that many of them, in their hurry and confusion, had neglected to grab their cartridge boxes, which meant that they were harmless.

There were scattered gunshots from the other side of the Fenian camp, where Wolseley assumed the Gordon Highlanders to be. Some of the Fenians glanced nervously at one another, waiting to see if any man among them would pull the trigger. Wolseley's own men remained still as statues, their muskets leveled towards their enemies, waiting for orders.

There was no rapid escalation of gunfire that might have signaled a general engagement and the sound of the scattered shots faded into the forest. A tense silence followed. Wolseley stepped forward a few paces.

"Where is your commanding officer?" he demanded. He was not sure if the Fenians had even been sensible enough to appoint anyone to lead them. The men who had fought at the Battle of the Stockade had officers, though they had seemed able to exercise little control over their men. Perhaps the Fenians were so opposed to any form of authority that they had become like the French troops during the 1790s, trying to run battles by committee.

"Right here," said an imposing man with a strong voice, who stepped forward towards Wolseley. He had an angry look on his face. "General Thomas Meagher. And who are you?"

He recognized the name from the intelligence reports. Meagher had long been an Irish revolutionary and had led the famous Irish Brigade during the war with the Confederacy. By all accounts, fought with great gallantry. Wolseley reflected on the conundrum that misguided men fighting for foolish causes could sometimes be remarkably brave.

"Colonel Garnet Wolseley," he answered, relishing the title. "Of Her Majesty's Perthshire Volunteers."

Meagher scowled. "Mercenary sons of bitches, you and all of your men," he said, looking around at the rifles aimed at him. He stared back at Wolseley. "You know you are on the American side of the border, don't you, Colonel?"

Wolseley grinned. "You are mistaken, General. Crossing the border would be illegal. An act of war. No, we are on the north side of the border. In any case, the weapons you've stockpiled here are clearly intended for use in an invasion of one of Her Majesty's Dominions. That I cannot allow. You and your men will come along under guard with us and the weapons and ammunition you have stored here will be destroyed."

"The hell you say!" Meagher replied. He glanced about quickly. "Men, prepare to defend yourselves!"

Some of the Fenians raised their weapons, but not all of them. The discipline of the British troops held and none of them shot down the Fenians. Wolseley remained calm, feeling not the slightest trace of fear.

"There is no reason for you and your men to die, Meagher," Wolseley said. He pulled out his cigar and, as he spoke, lit it up and began puffing. "You're surrounded. We outnumber you five-to-one. We can see that some of your men neglected to grab their ammunition when they ran out. Besides, we have Snider rifles and you only have Springfields. You have no chance."

"Didn't have any chance at Fredericksburg, either," Meagher replied.

"Ah, yes! I've heard about what you did there. Well, your men died for nothing at Fredericksburg. Attacking that stone wall again and again. Why not save their lives this time? Order your men to put down their weapons."

Meagher looked around. "British soldiers!" he cried out. "Do not let yourselves be deceived by the rich aristocrats who use you as pawns to oppress the Irish! Why obey them as they swill their champagne while paying you nothing and leaving your families destitute!"

Wolseley scoffed. "If you think my men can be swayed by the revolutionary claptrap you feed your Irish guttersnipes, you're a much bigger fool than I thought you were, Meagher. I'll give you one more chance before I order my men to open fire. Tell your men to lay their weapons down and give up. If you don't, I'll give you the same treatment I gave the rebel sepoys in India."

These words caused a visible stir among the Fenians, for the brutal treatment the sepoys had received at the hands of vengeful British soldiers in the aftermath of the Indian Mutiny was well known to anyone who read the newspapers. Tales of Indian rebels being chained to the muzzles of artillery pieces and blown into fragments were all the more horrifying because they were true.

One of the Fenians dropped his Springfield, followed an instant later by two more. Meagher shouted for them to pick up their weapons and for the rest of the men to stand fast, but no one listened. The menacing stares of the Welsh troops and their leveled Sniders, combined with the obvious lack of Fenian discipline, were more than enough. Within a few seconds, as Meagher's face fell into deep sadness, all of his men had dropped their weapons.

Moments later, word came from the other side of the Fenian camp that the rebels there had given up as well. All was now quiet. According to the men of the Duke of Wellington's Regiment, there was no sign of anyone else nearby, and certainly no sign of any American army units. The Fenians, now prisoners, were marched a few hundred yards north and ordered to sit down, guarded by the grenadiers. In the meantime, the light troops of the fusiliers went to work, gathering the discarded Springfields and moving the crates within the camp together. When the time came, all of the war material the Fenians had gathered to invade Canada would be blown to kingdom come.

He summoned Buller, who appeared by his side a few minutes later.

"Your orders, sir?" the younger man asked.

"I'll get the depot ready for demolition. You will get word to the company commanders as to the order of march back to our side of the border. The Welsh and Scottish light troops will lead the way, while the light troops of the Duke of

Wellington's Regiment will cover the withdrawal. The grenadiers will march in the center and their job is to guard the prisoners. Any questions?"

"None, sir."

"Very well. To your business."

Buller dashed off to follow his orders. Under normal circumstances, Wolseley would have specified in his orders to the grenadiers that any Fenian trying to escape was to be shot, but that would not have served his purpose. He was happy that the Fenian supply of arms and ammunition was about to be destroyed, but it was only the largest of several dotted along the border. His goal was to create a diplomatic incident between the United States and the British Empire, which would exacerbate the tensions between them and draw attention away from the events in Louisiana, thereby reigniting the possibility of war. Escaping Fenian prisoners would spread word about what had happened, so it made little sense to shoot them.

While Buller and the company commanders were reorganizing the force to head back north, a picked group of men from the Royal Welch Fusiliers prepared to destroy the arms and ammunition the Fenians had gathered at their camp. An enormous pile of wooden crates had now been gathered. Kerosene brought along for the purpose was being splashed onto it, while a few men were dragging a spade through the ground to a point several score yards outside the camp, filling the tiny gulley with more of the flammable liquid.

Wolseley watched all this was a satisfied air. As he had in the Crimea, in India, in China, and at the Battle of the Stockade, he had pulled off a textbook military operation that succeeded through good planning and attention to detail. If his plan succeeded, the fire he was about to light on the Fenian weapons would spark a conflagration that would engulf the entire Atlantic world into a war, one in which the name of Sir Garnet Wolseley would become immortal.

The detachment of fusiliers, their work complete, backed away from the pile of wooden crates. A sergeant among them ran up to Wolseley.

"Done, sir," he said simply.

"Very well," Wolseley replied, taking a long pull on his cigar. "Return to your company and prepare to march."

The fusiliers ran past him back towards the north, clearly anxious to put as much distance between themselves and the coming explosion as they could. Wolseley himself felt no concern. The day he would die had been marked out by God long before he had ever been born. It was not going to be this day.

Alone now, Wolseley took another long pull on his cigar, bringing the lit end to a sparkling red incandescence. He calmly walked over to the end of the kerosene line and, with perfect nonchalance, dropped his cigar into the liquid. It immediately ignited, creating a fast-moving stream of fire that raced towards the pile of Fenian arms and ammunition. Wolseley turned and walked away, already reaching into his jacket pocket for another cigar. He sensed the instinct within him, telling him that he was in danger and needed to run, but Wolseley ignored it. Fear was as an enemy. It could be tamed and defeated, just as his other enemies had been.

As he walked north, using his cutter to prepare his new cigar, an enormous paroxysm of explosive force and heat detonated behind him. The sound punched at his eardrums, shattering the stillness and silence. He could see the red and yellow light reflected against the trunks of the trees, feel the heat that swept over him, and sensed the rush of air caused by the explosion behind him. It was like a hot and angry wind, reaching out without thinking to enemies it could not grasp. He didn't turn to look at it, for there was no need. He had seen bigger explosions in the Crimea, after all. He paused, waited for his hearing to recover somewhat, then started to walk north to catch up with his men.

He encountered them far more quickly that he had expected and under very different circumstances. He had expected the column to have gotten underway and already moved up perhaps a quarter of a mile from their starting point. Instead, they were only a few hundred yards ahead of him and, rather than being in a marching column, they had deployed into a battle line. Quickly, he searched for the company commander of the English light troops, the nearest formation.

"What's going on?" Wolseley asked urgently when he found the man.

"American soldiers are ahead of us," the man answered, his voice utterly businesslike.

Wolseley moved ahead, passing by the grenadier troops and the long line of Fenian prisoners who stood bemused. The heavy infantry of the Gordon Highlanders and the Duke of Wellington's Regiment had formed into line of battle, while those of the Royal Welch Fusiliers had sensibly arrayed themselves to prevent the prisoners from escaping. Just in front of the grenadiers, a line of light troops had also formed themselves into a line of battle, holding their rifles at the ready.

As he reached the front line, he found Buller standing out in front of the men and moved beside him. Looking out ahead, Wolseley saw a long double line of blue-coated American soldiers blocking their path northward.

"Well?" Wolseley asked Buller.

"They were here when we marched up. Never saw them coming. I ordered them to let us pass and they refused. That was a few minutes ago. Been standing here since then."

"Keep the men steady," Wolseley said. "If we have to fight our way out, so be it."

"Yes, sir."

Wolseley looked the Union line up and down. It stretched as far as he could see in either direction, vanishing into the trees to both the left and right. Though the Americans were gripping their rifles, they had not raised them into firing position. It was hard to make out any expressions in the darkness, but he sensed that he was facing disciplined and experienced men. No Fenians, these United States soldiers were no doubt being led by qualified officers. He walked forward, leaning on his walking stick with his right hand and holding his cigar with the other, so that he appeared unarmed.

"Your commanding officer?"

A familiar man, strong and stocky, stepped forward from the line. It was George Thomas. "Good to see you again, Colonel Wolseley," he said warmly. "And as was the case in New York City, I seem to have to bail you out of a mess of trouble."

Wolseley was stunned, but contained any outward expression of his emotions. There was no possibility of this being a chance encounter. Orenda and his Iroquois scouts had thoroughly reconnoitered the area and reported no

Americans close by. Confirming the suspicions that immediately rose, he saw Orenda and some of his fellow Indians standing in a group behind General Thomas.

"Deceiver!" Wolseley said harshly.

Orenda shrugged. "Yankees paid more."

Wolseley turned his gaze back to Thomas. "Perhaps you ought to order your men to let us be on our way, Thomas. It would be unfortunate if there were to be bloodshed here today."

"You are on the American side of the border, Colonel Wolseley. You have violated our territory. We would be within our rights to open fire and slaughter you all."

Wolseley sneered. "You think your Yankees can stand against the best troops of the British Empire?"

"Yes, I do. Were the odds even, I should still think so. As it is, my friend Orenda here tells me that you have only five hundred men. I have two brigades, one here before you and one approaching you from the south, each totaling more than a thousand men."

Wolseley fully expected that he would one day meet his death fighting a terrible battle against hopeless odds. He had always assumed that it would be against the French, or perhaps some nameless group of African or Afghan tribesmen. While he was happy to fight the Americans, it seemed somehow wrong for him to perish in combat against fellow speakers of the English language.

"What's the game here, Thomas?" Wolseley asked.

"Simple," Thomas replied. "You leave your prisoners with us and go home. Your men need not be harmed." He spoke again, more loudly, so that all of the British troops could hear. "That's right, Colonel. All you need to do is hand over the prisoners, who will be taken into custody by us and properly punished. And none of your men will die. You are, as I said, on the American side of the border. I would hate for this situation to get out of hand."

Wolseley frowned, furious. He knew he was checkmated. There was no reason to think that Thomas was bluffing about his numbers, for if Orenda had tipped them off to the whole operation, there would have been plenty of time for Thomas to assemble as many regiments as he wanted. Wolseley had made the fundamental mistake of placing too much trust in a native guide, an error which had led more than one colonial expedition to disaster.

The company commander from the Duke of Wellington's Regiment jogged up. "They're behind us, too, sir! At least three regiments of United States troops are marching up. Maybe more."

"Shall we form square, sir?" Buller asked urgently. Usually a deployment to receive a cavalry charge, forming a square was also useful if one expected to be attacked from more than one direction at the same time.

Wolseley thought quickly. In a fight, his men would be slaughtered. They might take quite a few of the Americans with them, but even such magnificent troops as his stood no chance against such large numbers of experienced, well-armed soldiers who held such an advantageous tactical position. The prisoners his men were holding would flee amid the confusion and a great many of them would probably die in the crossfire. He would surely be among the dead, leaving it easy for the British government to blame him for the border incident in the first place.

The death he saw coming was one in which there would be no glory.

He sighed deeply, then looked up at Thomas. "We release the prisoners and you allow us to march back to our side of the border?"

"That's the deal."

Wolseley turned to Buller. "Tell the grenadier officers that the prisoners are free to go."

"Even Meagher?"

"Yes, even that bastard."

Buller walked behind the lines, rather more slowly than he usually did. Perhaps he disagreed with what Wolseley was doing, but he was too good a staff officer to tell him that openly. It didn't matter. Wolseley turned back to Thomas.

"Well?"

"Shoulder arms!" Thomas called, his order being repeated up and down the line by the officers and sergeants. The Union men lowered their rifles from fighting positions and shouldered them. Thomas barked out further orders and several of the infantry companies slowly marched backwards in a wheeling pattern, opening a path through the line as though a gate was being opened through a fence.

Wolseley issued orders of his own, moving his men from line back into marching columns. That done, he gave the order to march. Uneasily but without incident, the British soldiers moved through the gap in the Union line and continued northwards, heading for Canada.

Wolseley stood still for a time as his column moved past him. After about half of his men had passed, he began walking as well. He passed close to Thomas.

"Where is the border, Colonel?" Thomas asked.

"North of here," Wolseley replied.

"Are you sure about that?"

"Yes."

Thomas smiled strangely. "I, for one, am not. Perhaps I have blundered and accidentally moved my men onto your side of the border. It seems to me that what we have here is a misunderstanding. Do you agree?"

"Not really sure what you mean," Wolseley replied sourly.

"That's fine. And thanks for helping with the Fenian prisoners. They won't trouble you any longer."

"What do you mean?"

Thomas chuckled. "A discussion for another time. For now, why don't you get your men back to their camp and you and I can both encourage all the boys under our command to forget everything that they might have seen or heard over the past few hours."

Wolseley did not know what to say in response, so he said nothing and resumed marching, moving alongside the column of men as it wormed its way north to Canada.

Lowell's cell was silent. Though his living conditions were vastly better than they had been immediately following his arrest, mere physical comforts did not reduce the stabbing pain of his personal isolation. Benjamin had assured him that he was trying to persuade the Confederate authorities to allow him to exchange letters with his wife and parents, but Lowell doubted that he was making this a high priority. There was the ever-present stack of books for him to read, but Lowell sat still on his bunk, staring at the wall. He had not moved for nearly an hour.

Even for a man as devoted to books as Lowell, there was a point at which he could simply read no more. Benjamin, in contrast to Edward Phelps, had made great efforts to procure Lowell whatever books he wanted. The enforced idleness of being in his jail cell whenever he was not in court or in the paddy wagon on his way to and from the court meant that he had little to do but read. For two-and-a-half months, he had read until his eyes hurt, but having completed the *System of Positive Polity* by Auguste Comte, Lowell had found himself unable to make himself read another book. He had tried several different authors and different genres, but for the past several days, he had found nothing interesting.

He knew the reason he no longer felt the desire to read. It was futility. A man read to improve himself, to make himself a stronger and more able agent of the Almighty to do good in the world. There was no longer any need for him to improve himself. Even if Benjamin was right in thinking that he might avoid the death penalty, he would be imprisoned for the remainder of his life. In either case, he would have no ability to meaningfully impact the world, so what point was there in improving himself?

The same applied, to a certain extent, to food. Benjamin was providing excellent fare from some of the finest restaurants of New Orleans, a city famed for its cuisine. Lowell found it all about as appetizing as the hardtack or desiccated vegetables on which he had subsisted during the war. Part of the enjoyment of good food was the promise that one would be able to enjoy the same dish again in the future. If Lowell was to die, each meal was one less that he would enjoy before his last supper. If Benjamin somehow persuaded the jury to imprison him for life, he could look forward to monotonous and unpleasant grub for the remainder of his natural life. Either way, the fine food he was currently eating seemed more like an absurd joke than anything else.

Benjamin had told him that he would make sure the Confederate authorities allowed him the use of paper and ink before his execution so that he would be able to write a letter of farewell to Josephine. Whatever else they were, the Southerners were gallant when it came to women and would never deny a condemned man the right to say goodbye to his wife. There would be no need to dwell on practical matters, for Lowell knew that his wife and children would be well provided for. His son would receive an excellent education at Harvard, just as he had, and his daughter would be brought up as a proper lady and eventually married off to an appropriate husband. There was no need for him to worry about any of that, so he would be free simply to express his love and his devotion for his family.

Lowell began wondering what it was going to be like to be hanged. He imagined having the hood placed over his head, then the noose wrapped around his neck. There would be a drum roll and the trapdoor below him would open. The whole point of being dropped from such a height was to allow gravity to snap the condemned man's neck so that death would be instantaneous. The real fear of every man about to be hanged was that his neck would be too strong or the drop not high enough, for if the neck was not broken, he would die slowly, his body twitching in agony until he suffocated and death finally took hold of him.

He reminded himself that he had faced death a thousand times on the battlefield, but this would be different. During the war, while riding into combat, he had always known that he might die, but he had never been certain that he would. There was always an even chance that he would come out of the engagement alive. That hope would not exist on the morning of his hanging. Lowell had no doubt that he would be brave as he mounted the steps to the gallows. He would have to be for his death to mean anything, for if he showed even the slightest trace of fear, the Southerners would be able to brand him a coward. Such humiliation would spell the ruin of his efforts to show the South that an abolitionist could be a man of honor and dignity.

There was a knock on the door, followed by the rattling sound of metal keys being clumsily inserted into the lock. The door slowly swung open, pushed by Styles, his good-natured jailer, and Benjamin strode in. Lowell stood to greet him.

"Good morning, Judah," Lowell said resignedly. "Off to court, are we?"

"Not today," Benjamin replied. "Judge Moise has declared that it will not reconvene until tomorrow morning."

"Why?"

"The official reason is that he is ill. He is not. He is, in fact, quite well and enjoying a hearty breakfast as we speak."

"What's the real reason, then?"

Benjamin didn't answer, but simply smiled and stepped aside. Then, to Lowell's astonishment, his wife Josephine stepped through the door and into his cell.

He had never been so surprised in his life and, for a long moment, he could not be sure whether or not he was dreaming. She was wearing a dark blue dress, her lovely hair pulled back tightly, her beautiful eyes looking eagerly at him. He had not seen her in four months, but now it seemed as though that time could have been an eternity or an instant.

"Josephine," he said. It was barely a whisper. He feared that if he spoke too loudly, she might vanish like the smoke from a blown-out candle.

"Charles," she replied, her voice equally soft.

"I shall leave you," Benjamin said, motioning for Styles to let him pass and to close the door. Lowell scarcely heard him and his eyes did not waver from his wife's face. A moment later, the door was closed and locked, leaving the Lowells alone.

They rushed to embrace. Lowell wrapped his arms around his wife's shoulders as tightly as he could, wanting to melt into her. They kissed one another's faces with an almost frantic intensity. Within a minute, both were

651

weeping, the moist tears of their sadness and love blending together on their cheeks.

"My love, my love," Lowell repeated several times.

"Yes, darling, I am here," Josephine said reassuringly.

"I have felt so alone," he said, fighting back tears.

"You're not alone. You have never been alone."

He pulled back from their embrace long enough to look questioningly into her eyes. "How did you get here?"

"Mr. Benjamin arranged it. I received the telegram just over a week ago, along with train tickets to St. Louis and then a river steamer down here. I arrived just last night. I wanted to come at once, but they would not allow me to come until now."

"Benjamin did this?"

"Yes."

Lowell felt dizzy and wanted to sit down, but he did not want to break physical contact with his wife. Still holding her hand, he sat down on his bunk and she sat down beside him, placing her other hand over his, looking at him with a nurturing eye as he stared at the floor.

"It's all right, darling," she said. "I have had time to recover from the surprise. You have not."

"Seeing your face brings me more happiness than I could have imagined," he replied, looking at her again. "My God, Josephine, you are so beautiful. I have looked at your picture so many times since I left Boston, but I have so longed to see your face again, one last time." He took a deep breath to recover himself. "The children?"

"They are both well. They are staying with your parents while I am away." She paused, a slight but bitter catch in her voice preventing her from speaking for a moment. "They both miss their father very much."

Lowell almost broke down at these words. The idea that he would never again see little Anna and the baby Robert gnawed at him terribly. The dangerous thought entered his mind that he would happily abandon his quest to destroy slavery if it meant that he could hold his children in his arms one last time.

"They're being well taken care of," Josephine said. "Higginson and your other friends have already launched an appeal for funds to pay for their education. It's amazing. People from all over the country are donating to it. Even people in England, supposedly."

"By Plato!" Lowell said. "If that's true, then people know what's going on down here? They know about the trial?"

"Why, of course, darling! It's been on the front page of every newspaper since the moment you were arrested. There have been demonstrations in cities all over the North in support of you. Boston. Providence. Buffalo. Even in New York and Chicago. You wouldn't believe the number of people who have been calling on me at our house."

Lowell smiled and nodded. "Since I saw the police coming down to stop the ship, this is all I have wanted. If the people are focused on my trial, then we can prove that abolitionism is not dead. Please, my dear, tell me everything."

He listened intently as Josephine related to him all the news he had been denied for the past two months. She told him about how the desperate fight waged by Saul and his men in New Iberia had captured the imagination of people on both sides of the Atlantic. She told him of the rumors that his exploits had caused Napoleon III to suspend negotiations on the treaty of friendship between France and the Confederacy, perhaps forever. Finally, she gave him the details of the attention being lavished on his trial by all the newspapers.

"It's amazing," Lowell said when she finished. "I never dreamed it would be so."

"I even received a telegram from Abraham Lincoln, offering me his prayers and telling me that there is no man in the world braver than you."

Lowell chuckled. "Well, at least I will be remembered after I am gone. That's something, at least."

The strange happiness that had been evident on Josephine's face faded instantly. "Don't speak so. Mr. Benjamin says that you may yet have a chance at life."

Lowell's cheer vanished, replaced by irritation. "He should not have told you that. I don't want you to have any false hope. Nor do I want any false hope myself. I have resigned myself to death, my love. You must do the same." It required all of Lowell's steely nerve to say these words.

"But that's why he brought me here."

"What?" Lowell said, stunned. "What do you mean?"

"I am going to plead with the jury for your life."

Lowell pulled his head back in surprise, then quickly stood and begin pacing around the small space of the cell, trying to comprehend what Josephine had just said. "You mean that Benjamin has brought you here to testify?"

"That's right. Mr. Benjamin says that the words of your wife, pleading for herself and for our children, may move the jury in the direction of mercy."

"But I don't want mercy!" Lowell protested. The feelings awoken by the sight of his wife vanished in a flash. "If the jury doesn't sentence me to death, none of what I have done will matter! No slaves were freed in New Iberia. All I have left is my execution. It's the only way that I can still strike a blow for the freedom of the slaves."

"But Charles, we're talking about your life! You may not have to die!" She choked up and wiped away some tears. "I don't want to lose you like I lost my brother."

"And what kind of life would it be, my love? I'd spend my life rotting in a prison cell. Year after year, I'd waste away. What would that be but a slow torture? No, I'd rather die quickly than spend my life inside the confines of a prison."

"But you would be alive, Charles! Alive! I would know that you are here, living and breathing, thinking of me and the children. We could even visit you here. Your children would get to know their father. You would be allowed to see them grow up."

He shook his head, fighting back tears. "No! I would rather them know me as a picture on the wall and know that I was a martyr for justice than to see me in the flesh as a prisoner. What kind of father could I be to them? I'd be like some perverse animal at an exhibit!"

She began to sob. "I cannot bear the thought of your hanging. I know what you're trying to do, Charles. I respect it. I hate slavery as much as you do.

653

But there are times when the duties of a wife must come before the duties of an abolitionist."

Lowell frowned. "Part of the duties of a wife is to obey the wishes of her husband. I do not want you to do this."

The next twenty minutes were filled with angry shouting. Lowell tried again and again to persuade his wife not to testify. She adamantly refused. No amount of argument on his part could change her mind.

"I don't care what you say," she finally declared. "I will do my best to persuade the jury to spare your life. I could not be at Fort Wagner to try to save my brother, but I can be here for you and fight for your life." She stood and walked towards the door, loudly banging on it. "I'm ready to go!" she shouted to whomever was on the other side.

"My love, I don't want our last parting to be done in anger."

"This will not be our last parting, Charles. You shall see me again. In the courtroom, where I shall do my very best to save your life."

CHAPTER SIXTEEN

October 16, Afternoon
First Methodist Church, Waco, Texas

"These things happen, McFadden," Judge Roden said, holding up his hands helplessly. "The fire was an unfortunate accident. I'm just glad that I had dismissed all the county employees early that day, so that no one got hurt. A happy coincidence, I must say." He was grinning like a child as he spoke these words.

"Your credibility with the people of this community was gone a long time ago, Roden," McFadden replied harshly. "Everyone knows that your men started the fire. They were seen running away from the building right after the flames were first seen. It spread so fast that there had to have been turpentine already spread throughout the building."

The meeting had been arranged through the efforts of the Reverend John Westerfield, the head of First Methodist Church, who had said he wanted to help avoid any further bloodshed. Since the courthouse fire, there had been two vicious street fights between supporters of the rival camps. The first resulted in only a lot of bruises and broken bones, but the second one had seen one of McFadden's supporters shot in the shoulder and one of Roden's backers stabbed in the waist. Only luck had kept anyone from being killed, as had happened the previous month.

McFadden and Collett had agreed to meet with Roden only reluctantly and after much prodding from Westerfield. In the end, they decided that they had little choice. If they refused to meet with Roden and the violence had gotten worse, they could suffer the blame for it. Moreover, McFadden and Collett respected Reverend Westerfield and were unwilling to go against his wishes. So they had agreed to the meeting, though they were not happy about it.

The two of them sat on one side of a table set up in the center of a large room that was usually used for community dinners. Roden sat on the other side, seemingly bored with the whole thing, while Reverend Westerfield had taken a chair at the table's end, reminding McFadden of the dealer at a card table. No one else had been allowed into the room and Westerfield had made the three men swear on the Bible that they were not carrying weapons of any kind.

Outside the church, McFadden knew, were dozens of armed men from both factions. An informal ceasefire had been agreed upon, with both sides pledging not to draw their weapons until the results of the meeting were known. McFadden was not sure if this agreement would hold, though. There was little reason to assume Roden would honor any agreement at all, and Walker and his men were surely nearby.

"It was an accidental fire, McFadden. They happen all the time." He chuckled softly.

Rage filled McFadden. "You're lying. Everybody in the county knows it. What's worse, you know that we all know it and you just don't give a damn. I really don't know how people like you can live with themselves. You're scum, Roden. Complete and utter scum."

Roden smiled, glanced over at Westerfield for a moment, and shrugged. "Well, I am naturally sorry to hear you say that, McFadden. I had hoped that we might become friends at some point. But rather than trade insults, why don't we look to the matter at hand, shall we?"

"Which is what?" Collett asked.

"Well, with the voter rolls destroyed, the election in Granbury County will obviously have to be postponed. After all, state law says that the deadline for registering to vote passed on October 1. Very unfortunate timing, that. Indeed, it may be that we will have to simply maintain our current offices as they are until the next election."

"That will not happen," McFadden said sternly. "You'll see blood in the streets if you ever try it, Roden. Mark my words."

"You hear that, Reverend Westerfield?" Roden said, looking at the minister. "McFadden here is threatening violence."

"I don't think he is threatening it," Westerfield said. "He is simply stating what he thinks is a fact. And I, frankly, agree with him."

"Well, if bloodshed does occur, it will be the fault of you and that damn Association of yours," Roden said, looking back at McFadden. "An illegal, armed gang, as far as I can see. I've already notified Governor Sexton of the threat it poses."

"Well, why don't you call up the militia, then?" There was an uneasy silence for a moment, before McFadden went on. "We all know why, of course. If the militia were summoned, it wouldn't follow your orders."

"They would follow my orders," Roden responded sternly. "Whether you like it or not, I am the county judge. And I plan on remaining the county judge."

"By any means necessary, it seems," McFadden said sourly. "Legal or illegal, is that it? Well, I have also written to Governor Sexton, as well as Postmaster Reagan, explaining what really caused the courthouse fire."

"The fire was an accident, like I said."

"We'll see what the folks in Austin have to say, won't we?"

"I suppose. In any case, the election can't go on with the voter rolls destroyed and the deadline for signing up already passed." He paused and looked over his shoulder at the armed men behind him. "There is no choice, McFadden. The election is off for the time being. Like you say, we have to wait and see what the authorities in Austin have to say about it."

It went on like this for another frustrating hour and McFadden found himself increasingly annoyed. Despite all the objections of McFadden and Collett, Roden simply refused to acknowledge that the courthouse fire had been anything other than an accident, nor did he accept any possibility aside from an indefinite postponement of the election. It was clear from the look on his face that Reverend Westerfield didn't believe this any more than McFadden did, but the minister was unwilling to violate his pledge of neutrality in the discussions. Many times, McFadden rose to leave, only for Westerfield to plead with him to stay and try to talk things out.

"Look," Collett said in exasperation. "There's no point in talking to you any longer if you won't admit that the fire was intentional, something which is obvious to all of us in this room and to everybody in Waco."

"Accident," Roden replied, the grin on his face an invitation for Collett to get him to change his mind.

McFadden's anger boiled over and he rose from his chair, leaning over the table and glaring into Roden's eyes. He was about to launch into a tirade of profane insults when there was a sudden pounding on the door, which silenced all discussion.

"Who is that?" Westerfield asked, clearly happy that something had caused a distraction before McFadden spoke.

The minister rose from his chair and walked over to open the door. Standing on the other side was a tall man whom McFadden didn't recognize, heavy but powerfully built.

"Reverend Westerfield?"

"That's right."

The man strode into the room and towards the table. McFadden thought he looked to be between fifty and sixty, with a leathery face well marked with scars. He walked with the jauntiness of supreme confidence and an utter lack of concern for what anyone thought about him. McFadden's military instincts told him at once that this was a man who knew all about fighting, yet he also sensed a certain warmth and felt no threat.

The man stopped at the end of the table and looked over the three men sitting there. "So, you are the Roden, McFadden, and Collett I've been hearing about, I assume."

"Who the hell are you?" Roden asked.

The man chuckled. "Name's Bigfoot Wallace, of the Texas Rangers. Governor Sexton sent me up here to Waco, after word of what happened at the courthouse. Seems like you boys have been a bit rowdy. We'd like for things to calm down, if you take my meaning."

"Bigfoot?" Roden asked, incredulous. "What the hell kind of a name is Bigfoot?"

"Well, name's William, truth be told. My pappy named me after some Scottish fellow. But people started calling me Bigfoot, on account of the fact that I've got big feet." To prove his point, he lifted his right leg and planted his foot squarely on the table, easily able to do so thanks to his height. McFadden thought putting his foot on the table to be rather rude, but somehow it felt perfectly natural for a man like Wallace to do it.

"I wasn't told any Texas Ranger was coming," Roden protested. "I'm the county judge. I should have been notified."

"Well, I'm notifying you, Judge. In fact, here's the letter from Governor Sexton." Wallace pulled a piece of paper from his jacket pocket and handed it over to Roden. As the judge read through it, a look of increasing gloom coming over his face, Wallace turned to the other side of the table.

"McFadden? Collett? Pleased to make your acquaintance." He extended his hand. As he shook it, McFadden could feel the calluses of a man who had done more than his share of hard work in his life. He decided that he liked Wallace quite a bit.

Roden finished reading the letter, grunted, and threw it down on the table like a petulant boy. "Unacceptable," he said.

"What do you mean, Judge?" Wallace asked, taking a seat. Reverend Westerfield had also rejoined the gathering, looking upon Wallace with restrained astonishment.

"You think you can just walk into my county and start saying how things are going to be?" demanded Roden. "You think that you can push me around like I am some bandit leader or Comanche chief?"

"Not about pushing anybody around, Judge. Governor Sexton just asked me to restore order. And that's exactly what I intend to do."

"How, exactly?" McFadden asked. "Don't get me wrong, Wallace, I am delighted that you're here. We've been waiting for some sign that the folks down in Austin will take our concerns up here in Waco seriously. But now that you're here, what's going to happen?"

"Well, first of all, we're going to solve the problem of the voter rolls that were destroyed when the courthouse burned down." He turned and looked at Roden. "Accidentally, I'm told?"

"Yes, accidentally," Roden responded.

"Right. And the water in the Gulf of Mexico is yellow, not blue. Well, I suppose it could be yellow if somebody pissed in it long enough. That what you're doing, Roden? Just pissing into this county long enough to turn it yellow?"

Roden glared at the Texas Ranger but said nothing. McFadden was delighted at the judge's discomfiture. He sensed that a major shift in their struggle against the power of the judge was taking place right before his eyes and he relished it.

"How are we going to solve the voter roll problem?" Collett asked.

"Well, the Governor had issued a special order extending the deadline for registration in Granbury County to November 1. I'm in charge of it. Judge Roden here and some of his deputy sheriffs will cooperate, I'm sure. And I plan on deputizing the two of you, and some fellows from this group of yours. What's it called?"

"The Granbury County Association."

"Right, them. I'll deputize you and some of your people. We'll set up shop in front of what remains of the courthouse, and maybe a few other places, and get everybody signed up. It will be a lot of work, but I think we can do it."

"The Association is an illegal body!" Roden protested.

"Not according to Governor Sexton, it's not," Wallace replied. "Constitution protects freedom of assembly, you know."

"I'm very glad to hear this," Reverend Westerfield said, relief evident in his voice. "If I might express my chief concern, Mr. Wallace, the men on both sides

658

of the political divide here in Waco are habitually going around armed and ready to fight. Men have already been killed. How will you and your men keep order?"

"My men?" Wallace said. "Why, my dear reverend, I came alone."

"Alone? How can you expect to keep order by yourself?"

Wallace chuckled. "You obviously don't know much about the Texas Rangers, do you? No, the people on both sides, these so-called Associators and Roden's people, are going to behave themselves from now on. I can assure of you of that, Reverend. If they don't, they're going to find themselves on my bad side, which means that they'll be on the bad side of the State of Texas." He paused a moment. "Never a good place to be."

"If there is to be violence, our people will not start it," McFadden said firmly.

"Well, thank you, Mr. McFadden." Wallace narrowed his eyes a bit. "Say, aren't you the fellow who captured General Thomas during the war?"

"I am, sir."

Without a word, Wallace stuck his hand out again for another handshake. "I am honored to meet you, sir."

Roden spat out a disdainful grunt at this. At that moment, McFadden noticed out of the corner of his eye that another person had appeared at the door. He looked and was disheartened to see Walker, who stared at Wallace with a questioning expression. He entered the room and walked to the table.

"Who is this?" he demanded, pointing to Wallace. "My boys say he pushed his way past the line outside the church and just barged in. Is he causing you any trouble, Judge? If he is, I can take care of him for you."

Wallace seemed not in the least intimidated or upset by Walker's word. Instead, Wallace looked at his face with an inquisitive gaze, like a man trying to solve a mathematical problem.

"What?" Walker asked, seemingly unsettled. "What are you looking at?"

"Nothing," Wallace said. Yet a strange smirk crossed the Ranger's face.

"This is Bigfoot Wallace," Roden said resignedly. "He's a Texas Ranger, sent here by Governor Sexton. Says he's going to work with us and with the Associators to register voters by November 1."

"The hell you say!" Walker roared, glaring at Wallace.

What happened over the next seconds stunned McFadden. It took place so quickly that he had no time to grasp what was happening. He saw Walker reach for the pistol on his right hip. Before he had had time to draw it, Wallace's gun was already out. He spun about and was pointing the barrel of his weapon directly at Walker's forehead before the man had been able to raise his gun.

Reverend Westerfield cried out in alarm. Roden simply looked astonished, unable to believe what was happening. McFadden and Collett, the only men in the room with military experience, tensed up and prepared to dive for cover. Walker froze and time seemed to come to a halt for an endless instant.

"I'd put that gun back in its holster if I were you," Wallace said.

Walker was as still as a statue. Very slowly, he returned his pistol to its place, then carefully extended his arms outwards to show Wallace that he was unarmed. Wallace took a few steps back, keeping his gun aimed at Walker's head the entire time. He gestured with one hand towards the chair next to Roden, which Walker immediately took.

"It's a very bad idea to try to get the drop on a Texas Ranger, even an old one like me. You're not going to pull it off, I assure you. Only reason I didn't blow your damn head off is that I don't like the idea of spilling blood in a church. Try something like that again, you're a corpse. If I see you out on the streets with a gun, or even a knife, I'm taking your scalp. Understand?"

Slowly and reluctantly, Walker nodded.

"Good," Wallace said, holstering his pistol. "Don't want any unpleasantness in the house of God, after all. Judge Roden, why don't you take your boy here and go tell your people the new situation. I'm going to have a few words with McFadden and Collett here." He sat down in one of the chairs and calmly put his feet up on the table.

Roden and Walker rose and walked towards the door. Wallace called out to them just before they passed through it.

"One more thing, boys. I'm to report to Governor Sexton himself once a day by telegraph. If anybody gets me with a knife in the back in some alley, or if I happen to eat some oatmeal with something bad in it, he'll be among the first to know. And he won't be happy about it. Understand?"

Neither Roden nor Walker replied, merely looking at the Ranger for a few silent seconds before turning and continuing out the door. Collett looked at McFadden, wordlessly expressing his astonishment and infinite relief.

"Well, gentlemen," Wallace said. "Now that they're gone, let me just say that Governor Sexton wants to see Judge Roden defeated next month. He hates the damn bastard. Don't think that we need to engage in any shenanigans to achieve that. All we need to do is get people registered and hold a normal election. Given a fair chance, the people will vote him out. I'm not wrong, am I?"

"No, you're not," said McFadden firmly. "Roden is a hated figure. If the people are allowed to vote, he'll be kicked out like a teacup kicked by a mule."

"Good. So, let's get to work, shall we?"

October 18, Afternoon
Confederate States District Court of Louisiana, New Orleans, Louisiana

"And your family supported the match?" Benjamin asked.

"Yes, they did," Josephine Lowell answered from the witness stand. "My brother Robert, especially."

Benjamin looked at her quizzically. "The Shaw family is wealthier than the Lowell family, if I am not mistaken."

"Yes, it is. Many times so, in fact."

"Such things are important to aristocratic families in New England, aren't they?"

"No more so than among aristocratic families in the South, I should think."

Her voice was both light and low, blending together a tender femininity and a deep seriousness. More than anything else, though, Josephine's voice resonated with intelligence. Benjamin wasn't surprised. Though he had met the woman only a few days before and had spent only a few hours speaking with her, he had realized the power of her mind almost at once. Josephine Lowell was no ordinary woman.

Benjamin knew that most Southern men, especially well-off and educated men such as those in the jury, had a strange relationship with their womenfolk. On the one hand, they treated them as children who needed to be protected and coddled, sometimes almost as porcelain dolls to be set upon a dresser and kept clean. On the other, they held them in high esteem and could easily be swayed by whatever it was they thought the women wanted. The average Southern man viewed women, just as he viewed blacks, in quite contradictory ways. Benjamin himself had a very different relationship with women, as he could never see them as desirable objects in the way that most other men did. This allowed him to respect the minds of intelligent women for their own sakes, and this was certainly true of Josephine Lowell.

They were in the third hour of her testimony. The early objections raised by Eustis as to the relevance of Mrs. Lowell appearing as a witness had been firmly squelched by Judge Moise, who appeared to be sticking to the terms of the informal agreement he had reached with Benjamin. The prosecuting attorney had finally stopped objecting altogether, seeing little worth in further complaints. Now he simply sat glumly in his chair, watching the proceedings with seemingly only a passing interest.

"So why did your family approve the match, if, as you suggest, a Shaw marrying a Lowell was marrying beneath her?"

"My parents adored Charles." She looked slightly surprised at her own words. "They still adore him. They admired his willingness to serve in the war, they respect his work and the work of his family on behalf of the unfortunate poor of Boston. My brother Robert was a close friend of his. And after we announced our engagement, it was not long before my parents began to look upon Charles as their own son."

Benjamin noticed that Josephine was bothered by the fact that she had referred to Charles in the past tense, as if he were already dead. Perhaps she might as well have been right. Benjamin was gambling that the men of the jury would be so overcome by the respect shown to Lowell by his former enemies and the undeniable love between him and his wife that they would forgo execution and sentence Lowell to life imprisonment without the possibility of parole. If he succeeded, the treaty with France might yet come to pass. Yet Benjamin had not deluded himself into thinking he had much of a chance Were he at the poker table back at Johnny Worsham's, he could flatter himself to think that he had a pair of eights in his hand.

He glanced over at Charles, who was staring impassively down at the center of the table. Benjamin could sense the tension in the man's muscles, like a rope being stretched out tightly. He how hard it was for Lowell to maintain his composure as he listened to his wife describe their life together, the life that he loved, the life he was likely to be soon departing. He had asked repeatedly that Benjamin not put his wife through the ordeal of taking the witness stand, asserting that it would be emotionally traumatic for her. He did not mention how hard it was going to be for him. Thus far, Lowell had held up remarkably well to the prospect of the hangman's noose, but Benjamin was worried that he was now approaching the breaking point. Were he to break down, it might hurt their chances, for Southerners did not respect a man who couldn't maintain his composure and steadiness.

Josephine went on to describe their wedding, which was held on Staten Island in the fall of 1863. Though the wealth of their families might have made the affair one of the great social events of the season, they had elected to have a very simple ceremony. It had not seemed proper to indulge in extravagance when so many men were dying. Nor had the newlywed couple enjoyed a honeymoon, for Lowell returned to the camp of his regiment immediately after the wedding concluded.

"He was denied leave?" Benjamin asked.

"No. He did not ask for it."

"Why not?"

"He felt it was his duty to return to his men as quickly as possible."

"Why? There was no fighting going on in Virginia at that time. The two armies were about to settle in to winter quarters, as I recall."

"Even so, he saw it as his duty."

"You were disappointed?"

Josephine shrugged. "I am his wife. Had I not understood what it would mean to be married to a man like Charles, I should have married someone else."

For a flicker of a moment, Benjamin thought of his own wife Natalie, who had chosen the life of an expatriate in Paris rather than remaining in New Orleans with him. Listening to Josephine's words gave him a moment of regret, for it was clear that the marriage of Charles and Josephine Lowell was built on a foundation of trust and understanding, which he himself had distinctly lacked with Natalie. He had not told her of his sexual proclivities until after they had exchanged their vows and were alone in their wedding bed, much to her chagrin. After he had tried and failed to overcome the issue, he couldn't blame her for first finding solace in the arms of other men and eventually fleeing to Europe. That they had remained married was itself something of a surprise, but then their marriage had been based on political and financial advantage. That of the Lowells, by contrast, was clearly based on a deep and abiding love.

He shook away the personal thought and focused on the work at hand. If it was clear to him how much Josephine and Charles loved one another, it would also be clear to the jury and to the audience watching so intently.

"You lived with him in camp, yes?" Benjamin asked.

"That's right. Throughout that winter, until the fighting resumed in the spring."

"I must say that it is quite uncommon for a women of high society, used to living in elegant mansions, to choose to live for months in a dirty army camp, surrounded by rough men."

"I wanted to spend as much time with Charles as I could." She paused a moment. "Besides, if the gallant men fighting for the Northern cause would endure the hardships, so could I."

There was a brief rustling in the crowd and some quiet murmurings. Benjamin looked at her with a subtle sternness. During their private conversations in the days leading up to her testimony, he had warned her against profuse praise of the Union cause, which would only antagonize the jury. Knowing that she had an excellent education, he had used the example of Homer and the Trojans, telling her that he wanted the men of the jury to see her husband in the same light as the Greeks had seen Hector, that of a gallant enemy who deserved great respect. He had told her that she should not mention slavery under any circumstances. By extolling the Northern cause rather than her husband as an individual, she had come close to crossing this line.

Josephine went on to describe her departure from the camp when the spring campaign of 1864 got underway, her daily terror at seeing the postman approach for fear that he would bring a letter announcing Lowell's death, and her great relief whenever she received a message from him telling her that he was all right.

"He was never wounded?" Benjamin asked.

"No."

"Not once? It is my understanding that he fought in several battles in the Shenandoah Valley."

"That's correct. But the bullets never touched him. He had many horses shot out from under him, to use the army expression, but he himself was never hit."

"Astonishing."

Josephine waited a moment before replying. "I like to think that my daily prayers kept him safe. But then, many a wife prayed for the safety of their husband only to see him die. Northern and Southern wives alike."

Out of the corner of his eye, Benjamin could see at least two of the jury members slowly nodding. He smiled. Josephine's innate charm was working, tugging on the heartstrings of the Southern men, who could not help but respect and admire her. He knew the odds were still against success and that they would likely still vote for execution, but the display of her love for Charles, combined with the respect already demonstrated by his former enemies, might indeed be enough to save Lowell's life. If he succeeded, the treaty with France would be signed and the security of the Confederacy would be secured, at least for the time being.

He looked over at Charles, who still sat silent and still, not meeting the gaze of his wife. Benjamin could not fathom what was going through the man's mind. He would ask him after the day's proceedings were over. He knew that Lowell was still angry with him for placing his wife in a position of such vulnerability, but the personal wishes of his client were not anything he was concerned about. Securing his life, with all that it now represented, was the only thing that mattered.

It was time to wrap up the testimony. Going too long might prove counterproductive and he could not risk Josephine going off into a tangent of abolitionist talk, which would undo all his carefully crafted plan. Though she had given him her word that she would not venture into that territory, she was an idealistic woman prone to speaking her mind. She might lose her composure, as he had seen happen with witnesses in many a previous trial.

"Mrs. Lowell, you are aware of the crimes your husband has committed, yes?"

"I am aware."

"Are you proud of what your husband has done?"

The woman looked at Lowell for a long moment. This was a question on which Benjamin had carefully coached Josephine and he knew the response she was going to give.

"My husband is a good and gallant man who has always done what he believes to be right," she said, not a hint of acting in her voice. "I regret the loss of life and, in retrospect, I am sure he does, too. But I am and always will be proud of him."

Out of the corner of his eye, Benjamin saw Lowell shift in his chair and noticed that he had turned his head toward him. Glancing over, Benjamin saw a look of fury in his eyes, though the face around them remained inexpressive. It was surely the coached words about regretting the loss of life that had bothered him so much, since Lowell emphatically did not regret it. Benjamin could understand how placing those words in the mouth of his wife was outrageous from Lowell's point of view, but it was something that had to be done.

"No further questions, Your Honor," Benjamin said quietly. He strode around the table and took his seat.

Lowell leaned over. "How dare you do this to her!" he whispered harshly in Benjamin's ear.

"What's done is done, Lowell," Benjamin whispered back. "I'm trying to save your life. You might show a little gratitude."

Judge Moise, looking bored and tired as usual, looked over at the other table, where Eustis was still waiting. "Counselor? Your witness."

The prosecutor rose from his chair and walked, very slowly, towards the witness stand. The room, already quiet, went strangely more silent, as if there had been a flash of lightning and people were now waiting for the thunderclap to follow. Josephine eyed the approaching Eustis carefully, sizing him up. Benjamin had told her not to worry much about him, as he did not think much of his abilities as a trial lawyer. More importantly, Benjamin was sure that his agreement with Judge Moise would allow him to object to any questions he deemed inappropriate, giving him the ability to protect the woman.

Eustis cleared his throat, while everyone in the room waited, silent and expectant.

"Mrs. Lowell, it is clear that you love your husband very much."

"Yes," she replied simply.

"I want to ask you about another man you have loved. Your brother, Robert."

Benjamin quickly rose to his feet. "Objection, your honor."

"What is it?" Moise asked.

"I fail to see how Mrs. Lowell's brother is remotely relevant to these proceedings."

Benjamin had no doubt that Moise would uphold the objection and Eustis would be prevented from grilling Josephine about her brother. Indeed, he was surprised that the prosecutor had even bothered to bring it up. Everyone knew that Robert Gould Shaw had led a regiment of black troops during the war. Perhaps Eustis had simply wanted the newspapers to note the fact.

"Overruled," Moise said in a monotone voice. "Proceed, counselor."

Benjamin was stunned. His mouth nearly fell open. "Your Honor!"

"Yes, counselor?" Moise asked.

"I…" Benjamin struggle to find the words he wanted to say, which was an unusual and unpleasant experience for him. "The purpose of these proceedings is to determine whether or not the crimes for which General Lowell has pleaded guilty merit the death penalty. How can the man's brother-in-law, who died before General Lowell married Mrs. Lowell, have any bearing on this question?"

Moise looked at Eustis. "Counselor?"

"I wish to inform the jury of what kind of family General Lowell chose to marry into. I believe it reveals a good deal of just what sort of man he is."

"Very well," Moise said. "You may proceed."

Benjamin sat back down in his chair, feeling as though he had just been punched in the gut. Moise had betrayed him. Maybe he had been too forceful or too arrogant in their secret meeting. It didn't matter. He had lost the advantage and now Eustis, of all people, was going to inflict significant damage on his chances of keeping Lowell alive.

For a fraction of a second, Benjamin wondered what the prosecutor would have thought had he known the true import of the court proceedings and known what was at stake in the courtroom. Might he have pulled back, or even fallen on his sword for the good of the nation? Benjamin shook his head. Men like Eustis always put themselves first and their country second. Besides which, there was no way that Benjamin could have communicated the message to Eustis, at least not in any way that would have been persuasive.

"Your brother was Robert Gould Shaw, wasn't he?" Eustis asked Josephine. "Yes."

"Commander of the 54th Massachusetts Infantry, yes?"

"That's correct."

Eustis turned and looked at the jury. "We all know of this regiment, don't we? It was made up of blacks. It was the first of many such units. Thousands of our slaves were stolen from us by the Yankees over the course of the war, after Lincoln issued his sickening, so-called Emancipation Proclamation. The Yankees took the farm implements out of the hands of our slaves and put muskets in their place. Then they taught them how to use those muskets to kill good, Southern white men. How monstrous! How against the laws of nature!" He looked back at Josephine. "Your brother led that band of malcontents, didn't he?"

"I already answered that question, sir," Josephine replied sternly. She was looking at him with an expression of utter disdain and contempt.

"You said you were proud of your husband. Are you proud of your brother?"

She took a deep breath. "The pride I feel for my brother is beyond what a man like you could comprehend."

Benjamin saw that Eustis was taken aback by Josephine's defiant response. He was clearly not used to being spoken to by a woman in such a way and it took him a moment to recover himself. "You're proud of him, you say? He commanded former slaves who took up arms to slaughter their former masters."

"That is incorrect, sir. The men of the 54th Massachusetts were free blacks from the North, not freed slaves from the South. I would have thought that a man such as you would have been aware of this. But it makes no difference, because I would have been proud of my brother either way. More so, in fact."

665

Eustis turned for a moment, his hands clasped behind his back, and looked at Lowell for a moment before turning again to Josephine. "Your husband? Was he involved in the formation of the 54th Massachusetts?"

"Yes, he was. He helped recruit men for it and helped many of his friends obtain commissions as officers to command it. He also used his connections with influential politicians to gain support for the regiment."

"So he supported this dastardly project?" Eustis asked in mock horror.

Benjamin watched as Josephine looked at Lowell for a long moment. The courtroom had become completely silent, waiting for the defendant's wife to say words that might sway the jury. Benjamin knew how intelligent Josephine was, that she could easily utter a vague and halfhearted response that would mean little to the men of the jury. That would be the correct course of action if she wanted to save his life. Yet he also knew her to be a woman of fierce abolitionist convictions who would not bear to allow her husband's efforts in that struggle to be trivialized.

"He strongly supported, with every fiber of his being, what he rightly saw as a great and worthy mission to help the oppressed blacks of the South break the unnatural chains that have bound them and to free the world from the sickening stain of human slavery."

There were loud gasps throughout the room. Even the eyes of Judge Moise, normally so imperturbable, widened in shock at the words. Benjamin quickly glanced around to gauge the reaction of the jury and the audience behind them. What he saw made his heart sink, for there was nothing but outrage and shock on the faces of everyone he could see. Words such as those Josephine Lowell had just spoken might have been common enough in Boston, but this was New Orleans, the greatest city of a slave-holding nation. It was entirely possible that many people in the room had never heard such talk before. It was as much of a shock to them as if someone had slapped them across the face.

Eustis was as taken aback as anyone else. "It's not normally customary for a lady..."

"It is evil!" Josephine said sharply, her voice filling the courtroom. She suddenly stood in the witness stand and shouted loudly enough for all to hear. "And it is an evil that will be extinguished! Maybe not now! Maybe not for years! But it will be gone!" Josephine ignored the banging of the gavel and kept shouting. "My husband and I want to see a hundred Sauls spring from the ground and a hundred New Iberias go up in flames! We don't want it to stop until the plague of slavery is purged from this sinful land by fire and the sword!"

People in the audience began standing up and yelling.

"Hang her, too!"

"Yes! Don't let her leave!"

"Abolitionist bitch!"

The guards around the room suddenly stood to attention, sparked out of their passive observation of the proceedings by the realization that they might have to keep order amidst an unruly crowd. Moise slammed his gavel down on the judge's bench several times in quick succession, continuing for nearly thirty seconds before a measure of quiet was restored.

"Silence!" Moise shouted. "I will clear the courtroom unless there is silence!"

Yet the crowd would not be quieted. Some were now standing, gesturing frantically towards Josephine as they shouted, their faces red with hatred and rage. A few men had pulled knives from their belt and waved them menacingly in the air. Some women approached the rails separating the legal teams from the crowd and spat in the direction of the witness stand. Reporters scribbled on their pads with urgent speed, trying to capture in words as much of the scene as they could.

Benjamin looked on with horror, his plan falling apart before his eyes. Even if the jury had been inclined to spare Lowell's life, which was questionable, Josephine's outburst had assured that they would now vote for execution.

In the midst of the tumult sweeping the room, Benjamin noticed that Charles and Josephine Lowell were strangely serene. They completely ignored the shouted threats of the crowd and the banging gavel of the judge, silently gazing into one another's eyes, shielded as if by a magic sphere from the furious upheaval around them. They both smiled. As Judge Moise shouted for the bailiffs to clear the room, Josephine mouthed the words "I love you" to her husband just before the guards pulled him from his seat and towards the door of the courtroom.

October 19, Afternoon
British Army Headquarters, Montreal, Canada

Wolseley was increasingly frustrated, not to say mystified. Five days had passed since his confrontation with the Union Army. As soon as he had seen his men back to the camp, he rushed back to Montreal to discover the impact of the incident on relations between the British and the Americans. He knew he would have to explain his actions to his superiors, but he was not concerned about that. His belief that General Napier was a complete dunderhead had only been strengthened the longer he had worked with him. Although the story that the depot had been on British rather than American territory was very thin, he was sure Napier would swallow it easily.

When he reached Montreal, however, Wolseley was surprised to find that no one seemed to have a clue that anything untoward had happened on the border. The troops he had led, of course, were still encamped and not able to easily communicate with the outside world. Yet Wolseley had expected word of what had happened to be instantly transmitted by the Americans and, via telegraph, rapidly to spread around the world. Within an hour of his arrival, it became clear to Wolseley that no one except himself was aware of what had happened. It was as if the whole incident had only taken place in his imagination.

He now paced back and forth outside General Napier's office, irritated and unamused, waiting to be summoned. The staff officer who had greeted him had said that the commander was dealing with some important matters and would be with him as soon as possible. This had made Wolseley more than a little upset, for what could be more important than the border incident? It was true that no one had been killed, but British forces had crossed the border and there had nearly been a full-scale battle between British and American troops.

The newspapers were saying nothing. All their attention remained focused on the trial of the Massachusetts abolitionist down in New Orleans. Wolseley could not have cared less about that matter, not being concerned in the slightest about either slavery or the fate of a single man. It infuriated him that his countrymen were paying such close attention to it, when war still seemed possible between Britain and America. Yet he couldn't deny that the newspapers, and with them the feelings of the people, had moved on from the pitch of war fever that had swept both countries a few months before. It was like a popular play at a West End theater, which had its run and was now closing down.

The door to Napier's office opened and a staff officer came out.

"General Napier will see you now, Colonel Wolseley."

"It's about time," Wolseley replied, unable to contain himself. "I have been waiting for nearly thirty minutes."

The man stepped aside and Wolseley strode into the office. Napier was sitting behind the desk, looking as though his mind was clouding over as he studied some piece of paperwork. His eyes slowly rose to greet Wolseley as he approached. Of average height and build, Napier had never struck Wolseley as being an impressive-looking man. He always gave off the impression that a strong puff of wind might knock him over.

"Ah, Wolseley. Good to see you. Take a seat please."

"Sir, I have been trying to see you since the moment I returned. I have very urgent information concerning an incident that took place on the border five days ago."

"Oh, I already know about it. I have a telegram from General Thomas right here."

Wolseley's eyes narrowed in confusion. He quickly took the paper from his commander's extended hands.

General Napier,

In the interests of avoiding any confusion that might have unfortunate results, I wish to inform you that a Fenian supply depot was destroyed by forces under my command on October 14. It was very close to the border between Canada and the United States, and because there was considerable noise and flames, a British unit I believe to have been under the command of Colonel Garnet Wolseley was apparently alarmed enough to investigate. As far as I am aware, no lives were lost and no forces of either side intentionally crossed the border.

Please do not hesitate to communicate with me if there are any unanswered questions. In tense times, unfortunate situations should be avoided.

General Thomas

"But that's not what happened!" Wolseley protested.

"What do you mean?" Napier asked tiredly. "Seems pretty straightforward to me."

"We destroyed the depot!"

"I don't know what you mean, Wolseley. Thomas here says that his men did it."

"He's lying!"

Napier's head drew back in surprise. "Lying? Why on earth would he lie about something like that?"

Wolseley thought quickly, trying to answer Napier's question in his own mind. Since the moment Thomas allowed his men to continue unmolested back to the Canadian side of the border, he had been trying to understand the strange American general. Were their positions reversed, Wolseley would have simply surrounded Thomas with his superior forces and attacked. Why had he let him go, and why was he now claiming that his men had destroyed the Fenian depot?

He knew little about Thomas. Their only meeting prior to the border incident had been their brief and strange encounter on the streets of New York City back on July 4. When he had learned the identity of the man who commanded American forces in northern New York, Wolseley had read up on him. Thomas seemed like a good-enough soldier, especially considering his performances at the battles at Stones River and Chickamauga, though the disaster at Peachtree Creek had ruined an otherwise stellar career.

As his mind raced, he recalled one particular aspect of Thomas's career. It had once been rumored that Thomas had been offered command of an army when the commander had been accused of not pursuing the Southerners out of Kentucky with sufficient speed. Thomas apparently thought the charges were unfair and had declined the appointment. A man like that was likely to place principle above his own ambition. Wolseley could respect a quality like that in a person, though he would never have done what Thomas did. What was good for Garnet Wolseley, obviously, was good for the British Empire. Thomas, clearly, was cut from a different stripe.

In an instant, it was clear to Wolseley what Thomas was doing. He was claiming that American forces had destroyed the depot because he was actively trying to prevent a war between Britain and the United States. He had known all along that Wolseley was going to cross the border, thanks to information provided by the traitor Orenda, and had made his plans accordingly. That was why he had not positioned his troops to resist the British the moment they crossed the border, and why he had not given them orders to open fire when they might have easily slaughtered all his men. There had been no bloodshed, which meant that the whole incident could be swept under the carpet by the politicians in both Washington and London, if that was what they wanted.

Thomas had said in New York that he did not approve of the Fenians himself and would have prevented them from crossing into Canada had he been able to prevent it. For whatever reason, Thomas was acting to maintain the peace between the two countries.

Even as his mind unwrapped the game Thomas was playing, he remained confused. A war between Britain and the United States would surely have given Thomas the opportunity to redeem his tattered reputation as a soldier. Why didn't he grasp the chance with both hands, as Wolseley himself would have done? It made little sense. Thomas was a soldier, after all. In Wolseley's mind, a soldier should be concerned with enhancing his own glory and reputation at every opportunity. Decisions of war and peace should be left to others, even to the politicians whom Wolseley so despised. Thomas, it seemed to Wolseley, had proven himself to be nothing but an abject coward.

"What do you mean when you say that you destroyed the depot?" Napier asked, his eyes narrowed in pathetic confusion. "Thomas says that the depot was on their side of the border, so how could our troops have been involved?"

"Because…" Wolseley stopped, trying to think through what to say. If Napier had a telegram from Thomas, then that version of events was doubtless already in the hands of the political leaders in the capitals of both nations. There was nothing Wolseley could do about it. He had not made allowance for the possibility that Thomas would want to cover up the incident, for such an idea seemed outlandish.

"Do you think having our troops so close to the border caused Thomas to act against the Fenians?" Napier asked.

Wolseley looked at his commander, contempt for his lack of intelligence burning within him, and quickly considered his options. If he tried to tell the real story, everyone in Ottawa and London would ask why. With the Americans claiming that they, and not Wolseley, had destroyed the depot, his action would make no sense. Rather than being viewed as a justified preemptive act in defense of Canada, it would be seen only as a reckless action that could have only harmful effects on the British Empire.

He could not keep himself from frowning. "I'll explain everything in my report, sir," Wolseley said glumly.

"Yes, please do," Napier said. "Oh, and there's more. Seems the Americans finally woke up. Their destruction of the Fenian supplies that you apparently saw yourself is only one part of what's happening. The American troops are shutting the Fenians down."

"What do you mean?" Wolseley asked.

"Their camps. All along the border. United States troops have closed them all down. Some of the Fenian leaders, from what I understand, are being taken into custody. The troops are apparently being let go, but ordered far away from the border under threat of arrest. I'd prefer if they arrested the whole bloody lot of them, personally, but we can't have everything, can we? In any case, over the last week, the Fenian threat has basically vanished."

"I don't believe it!" Wolseley said. He was not accustomed to being at a loss for words.

"Quite refreshing, isn't it? The Americans doing what we ask them to do? London is very pleased. Now they don't have to worry about paying for a war with the United States, which would have been terribly expensive."

Wolseley's heart sank. If the Americans were really doing what Napier said, all possibility of an open conflict between Britain and the United States was over. His dreams of leading a force into a glorious battle against a worthy enemy were gone. The idea of remaining in exile, training Canadian militiamen to fight a war that would never come while other British soldiers were fighting epic battles around the world, filled him with despair.

"Is there anything else, sir?" Wolseley asked, suddenly very tired.

"Oh, indeed! Word came through for you from London. Seems your time in the New World is at an end. You are to return to England and report to the depot of your regiment, there to receive new orders."

Wolseley's eyes widened. "I'm going back to England?"

"That's right. Her Majesty will be presiding over the investment ceremony for the Order of Bath next month. I am quite certain that you do not want to miss it. If you do, it may be some time before your knighthood becomes official."

670

"Well, yes, that is the case," Wolseley said uncertainly. He was so discombulated by what he had learned over the past few minutes that he almost felt dizzy.

"In that case, I bid you farewell, Colonel," Napier said. "You have done sterling service here in Canada and I am in your debt. Safe travels." He rose and extended his hand across the table.

Wolseley shook Napier's hand and the two men exchanged salutes. The colonel then turned and marched out the door, his mind trying to piece together exactly how his plan had gone so strangely wrong.

October 22, Morning
Waco, Texas

The square in front of the burned-out courthouse was full of people lining up in front of the table provided by Flynn's alehouse. Local storeowners, always keen on snapping up any opportunity for profit, had sent slave boys into the crowd to hawk newspapers, sell small bags of peanuts, or fill pewter cups with weak beer. Waiting in lines inevitably bored men, who were happy to fork over a few coins for any momentary distractions.

McFadden watched it all with wonder. As one of the candidates in the upcoming elections, it would not have been proper for him to have helped work the table at which citizens were being registered to vote, but that scarcely mattered. Wallace had deputized half a dozen men, most of them members of the Association, to do the work and they were doing it quite well.

The special order from John "Rip" Ford, the Texas Secretary of State and the man in charge of state elections, had been posted all over Waco, extending the date for voter registration to Friday, October 25. The reaction had been electric. All over town, men who had assumed that the destruction of the courthouse would rob them of their chance to cast a vote had put aside their work and headed towards the central square to register. Wallace had printed thousands of copies of the state form a man had to fill out. The table, moreover, had a public notary ready to witness each signature, including the marks made by men unable to write.

At the same time, the Association had sent riders out into the outlying farms and smaller communities throughout the county, informing everyone of what was happening and encouraging them to come into Waco to register before it was too late. McFadden and Collett had been asked by other Association members if it would be all right to send wagons and teams out to pick up men in the farms and take them into town, making it as easy as possible. They had immediately given their enthusiastic consent.

There was little for McFadden to do, so he simply sat on a bench on one side of the square and observed the proceedings while sipping on a mug of beer and reading a newspaper. The air was crisp and cool, with autumn having now banished summer and firmly established itself. It felt pleasant to be outside. Watching the men waiting in line to register, McFadden could not have been more pleased. The enthusiastic response to Wallace's last-minute registration effort was so strong that McFadden found himself wondering if more people would end up being able to vote than had been the case before the courthouse fire. If so, it would be poetic justice to Roden and his friends, who deserved nothing less after their disgraceful attempt to derail the election.

He turned his attention back to the newspaper for a few moments. As a political candidate, he was making a strong effort to keep up with the news from around the country. Most of the stories dealt with the presidential election and did not make McFadden very happy. Breckinridge appeared to be behind Beauregard in most of the major states, with some people saying that it wasn't impossible for the Creole from Louisiana to win all eleven states in the Confederacy. The State's Rights Party also appeared posed to do very well in the congressional and state legislative races, as there was no effectively organized opposition to them on that level.

Another story gave a summary of what seemed to be the closing events of the Lowell trial in New Orleans. McFadden, consumed with his campaign for the state legislature, had not followed the story very closely. When asked about it by voters and the occasional reporter, he said that Lowell had obviously committed a gross crime and deserved whatever punishment the jury sought fit to give. Privately, though he deplored Lowell's behavior, he couldn't help but admire the courage of a man who had ventured into hostile territory, knowing he was very likely to be caught and executed, in service to his ideals. McFadden might not share those ideals, being ambivalent about slavery himself, but one could admire courage in any man.

There was one item from the United States that was interesting. The Union army was apparently dismantling the training camps of the Fenian Brotherhood along the border with Canada, thus greatly reducing tensions between the United States and Britain. This seemed like such an obvious thing to do that McFadden couldn't understand why it had not been done long before. He was briefly startled to see the name of George Thomas mentioned in the story as the man who had issued the order to dismantle the camps. McFadden smiled as he recalled the memorable day back in 1864 when he had captured the Union general during the Battle of Atlanta. McFadden's eyes narrowed when the final paragraph said that Thomas had also announced his retirement from the army.

McFadden put the newspaper down and took another swig from his mug of beer. He noticed some friends in the line to register to vote and waved at them. Whatever the fate of the election around the nation, he was now convinced that he was going to win in Granbury County and become a member of the state legislature. Most of his colleagues in that body, if the newspaper story was to be believed, were going to be members of the States' Rights Party and probably a lot more like Roden than like him. It was worrisome, but there was nothing to be done about it just then.

"Jimmy!"

He turned to see Collett walking up to him.

"What are you doing here," Collett asked him. "Shouldn't you be out knocking on doors or something?"

McFadden shrugged and tossed his head towards the line. "I wanted to see this."

Collett looked into the square. "See what?"

"All these people who want to vote. Nice, isn't it? Ordinary folk wanting to have a say in how they're government works."

"I suppose so," Collett replied, sounding tired.

McFadden chuckled. His friend had always been more cheerful and less introspective than he.

His eyes were drawn to Wallace himself, standing tall and strong behind the men seated at the table who were registering voters. The man's arms folded across his chest, a look a self-assured confidence on his face. He had spoken with Wallace several times since his first meeting a week earlier and had come away liking him more every time. Wallace had told him that he personally favored the success of the Association in the upcoming election, but also made it clear that he would only ensure a fair and level playing field. He would not, he said, do anything to give McFadden and Collett's people an unfair advantage of any kind. The attitude of decency and fair play was, to McFadden, as refreshing as the cool autumn air now passing through Waco.

Wallace noticed his gaze and waved a greeting, which McFadden returned. The Texas Ranger then gestured for them to come down to the table to talk. McFadden rose from the bench and he and Collett strode through the square towards Wallace. Friends and old comrades waiting in line to register said hello as they passed by.

"Grand morning to you," Wallace said warmly as they reached the table. "These boys here, now my deputies, have registered over three hundred people already today. And, as you can see, they are still lining up in droves to get signed up."

"Glad to hear it," McFadden said quickly, thinking for a moment of the hard work that needed to be done on farms and ranches across the county. The needs of the community and one's civic duty meant that a man all too often had to set aside his own personal concerns. His own ranch had fallen into disrepair since he had embarked on his campaign and was only now being brought back into a proper state thanks to the efforts of the veterans who remained camped there as protection for him and his family.

"May need your help in just a bit, by the way."

"Of course," McFadden said. "What can we do for you?" The tone of the Texas Ranger suggested to McFadden that he was about to ask them for something akin to moving heavy boxes.

The smile not fading from his face, Wallace tossed his head towards the other side of the square. McFadden looked and saw Walker, perhaps ten of his men following behind, entering the area from a side street and walking purposefully towards the line of men waiting to register. McFadden instantly felt a sense of alarm and his heart began beating rapidly, instantly jerking his body into a state fit for combat.

"It's all right," Wallace noted quietly. "Notice that they are coming in unarmed."

Carefully examining the approaching group, McFadden saw that Wallace was correct. Even the knives and pistols men usually carried around in a frontier town like Waco were conspicuously absent.

"Why would they do that?" Collett wondered aloud.

"They want to make sure they don't give me a chance to arrest them," Wallace said. "I wouldn't have done so, but they're being very careful. They're up to something, sure as hell."

Walker and his men ignored McFadden, Wallace, and Collett and instead began speaking to the men in the line, fanning out to talk to as many of them as possible. As the conversations began, McFadden heard voices rapidly become loud and angry. One of McFadden's fellow veterans, a fellow named Bernard Jackson, left the line and came up to him.

"Jimmy! Walker and his jackasses are telling people in line that they'll pay them and give them free whiskey if they don't register to vote!"

Wallace laughed. "The old carrot and stick routine, is it? Well, I'll put a stop to this. You tell old Walker to get his ass over here, right now, or I'll have him arrested for disrupting these proceedings."

Jackson nodded and went to get Walker, who appeared before the table a few moments later.

"What the hell do you think you're doing, Walker?" McFadden demanded. He regretted the words immediately after saying them. Under the circumstances, it would have been better to let Wallace do the talking.

"What?" Walker replied. "We're just inviting some of these fine people to have drinks with us. And some cash we happen to have handy. Times are tough, you know. Neighbors should try to help each other out. Nothing illegal going on here."

"That depends," Wallace said authoritatively. "Are you offering alcohol and money in exchange for these men not registering to vote?"

"What's it to you, Ranger?"

"Because I'm sure I could find some statute or other telling me that such action would be illegal interference in an election. And if I didn't find it, I'm sure I could make something up and lock you up anyway. By the time anyone managed to get you and your boys released, November 5 would be way in the past and McFadden and Collett here would be running the county. Wouldn't like that, would you?"

"These idiots?" Walker said with a harsh laugh. "They couldn't run the outhouse of a cheap brothel!"

"Well, you're likely to find out anyway, seeing the way the people around here are likely to vote. And if you don't take your men out of this square this instant, I'll lock you all up and you will find out for sure. Understand me, Walker? Besides, it's plain as day that what you're doing isn't working. Take a look."

Walker glanced behind him and McFadden followed his eyes. None of the men were getting out of the voter registration line, despite the entreaties of Walker's men. Some were simply refusing to listen, while others were angrily protesting and pushing the interlopers away. McFadden found it odd that Walker had thought attempting to bribe or cajole them away from registering was going to work. Perhaps he and Roden were becoming desperate.

Walker thought for a moment, than spat on the ground by Wallace's feet. "We'll go drink by ourselves, then. Better company. Know this, Ranger man. When this election is over, you and I are likely to encounter each other again. And I wouldn't be surprised if something bad happened to you."

Wallace chuckled, quite unimpressed by Walker's words. He leaned over the table and gestured for Walker to step forward. Awkwardly confused for a moment, Walker did so and Wallace bent forward to whisper something in his ear. McFadden watched in wonder as, for the first time, he saw fear cross the face of Walker. It was quickly replaced by anger and he turned and stormed away, waving for his men to follow. They did so, and the men waiting in line to register laughed mockingly as the group vacated the square.

"What was that?" McFadden asked. "What did you whisper into his ear?"

"I just told him that I thought he was ugly," Wallace said with a grin. "Now, if you gentlemen will excuse me, I need to get back to work."

"Right," McFadden said. "Thank you, Mr. Wallace."

"Bigfoot, if you please."

McFadden chuckled. "Thank you, Bigfoot."

As they walked away, Collett suggested that they go to Flynn's Alehouse for a drink.

October 23, Morning
United States Capitol Building, Washington City

"The Senate Foreign Relations Committee is now in session!" Sumner said loudly.

The conversation in the audience rows behind the witness table dimmed but did not vanish. He banged the gavel several times, irritated at the arrogance of the people who presumed to continue talking after he had told them to stop. After about thirty seconds, the conversation finally died down. A few people who had been speaking to others quickly rushed back to their seats, as if a theater production were about to begin.

Sitting at the witness table was George Thomas, dressed in civilian clothes rather than in an army uniform. This was because of the momentous news that had come down from New York in the past several days, which had brought the Fenian issue back to the forefront of Sumner's thinking. First, there had been the unsubstantiated reports of some sort of border incident between British and American forces, near a Fenian supply base. The details were hazy, though all accounts were clear that no one had actually been killed. The report from Thomas stated that forces under his command had discovered the Fenian depot and blown it up. He had gone on to say that British troops had been nearby but had not been involved. Sumner could not quite put his finger on it, but the report seemed strange. Clearly, there were unanswered questions.

Almost as soon as this incident had taken place, Thomas had given orders for his troops to disarm and take into custody the men of all the organized Fenian units deployed within his department. The ease and speed with which this had been done proved that Thomas had been planning it for quite some time. There had only been resistance at one place, with three Fenians killed and one of Thomas's men slightly wounded. Hundreds of Fenians had been rounded up and were now being held in makeshift camps, though in quite comfortable conditions. The weapons and ammunition that the Fenians had stockpiled had been disposed of, though the reports were not clear on exactly how.

The third item of news was perhaps the most shocking. As he had been reading of all the other developments in the *New York Times*, Sumner received a telegram from Thomas himself. He had it out in front of him and, still amazed days after having received it, quickly read through it again.

Senator Sumner,

I understand from the newspapers that you wish for me to testify before the Senate Foreign Relations Committee regarding what I know of the Fenian issue, particularly the relationship between the McClellan administration and the Fenian Brotherhood. I will be on my way to Washington City shortly and earnestly wish to testify as soon as it can be arranged. Any objections to my testimony on the grounds that I have been ordered not to do so by the Secretary of War can now be dismissed, as I have this morning resigned my commission in the United States Army, effective immediately.

George Thomas

It was one of the most astonishing telegrams Sumner had ever received. In a moment, the entire situation seemed to have changed. He had been fixated on the Fenian issue for months, until the battle in New Iberia and the arrest of Lowell shifted public attention to events in the Confederacy. The possibility of war with Britain had faded quickly and although he had continued referencing the Fenian matter in his speeches denouncing President McClellan, Sumner had spent more time and energy speaking about Saul and Lowell than anything else.

Congressman Logan had not filed articles of impeachment against President McClellan, despite Sumner's initial hopes that he would. When he thought about it, Sumner wasn't really that surprised or even very disappointed. Logan had only promised to consider it and Sumner was sure that he had. Of course, depending on what Thomas was about to say, Logan might have reason to reconsider.

Sumner glanced around. Moorfield Storey was ready at the small secretary's table and Sumner had paper and ink ready in case he needed to send him any sort of message. Every committee member was present, for none wanted to miss out on what was sure to be a newsworthy event. The Democrats, unsurprisingly, looked apprehensive, no doubt worried about possible revelations that could damage their party. The Republicans, on the other hand, seemed almost giddy with expectation.

He looked down at Thomas. He had never met the man before and was not disposed to like him. He was, after all, a Southerner who had owned slaves before the war. It was admirable that he had remained loyal to the Union after his state of Virginia had seceded, but that only partially counterbalanced the sin of owning other human beings in the first place. Yet Sumner could not help but feel sympathy for the man seated at the witness table below him. Thomas seemed sad, but also solid and strong. He had lost many of his friends and all his family save his own wife and children when he had remained loyal to the Union. His defeat at Peachtree Creek, the greatest disaster to befall the Union during the war, had ruined his previously sterling military reputation. McClellan's manipulation of him with regards to the Fenians, which Sumner now hoped to expose to the world, had only rubbed salt into his already gaping wounds.

It was clear that Thomas was a man of ironclad integrity. Had he been otherwise, he would not have resigned his commission and volunteered to appear before the Committee. Sumner could respect that, for such honor and honesty was rare in the world.

"Please state your full name, sir, for the record," Sumner asked.

"George Thomas," he replied. "My current residence is New York City."

"I notice that you are not appearing in uniform, sir."

"I am no longer an officer of the United States Army, Senator. I resigned my commission four days ago."

"On October 19?"

"That's correct, sir."

The man's voice was respectful in tone, which Sumner appreciated. It also conveyed an underlying strength of character.

"Before your resignation, Mr. Thomas, what was your assignment?"

"I was commander of the Northern Department, which covers the area along the Canadian border from the Great Lakes to the Atlantic Ocean."

"There has been trouble there, yes?"

There was scattered laughter in the audience, light and easy. Sumner was confused, as he had not intended to make a joke. He had never understood humor and thought that it only clouded conversation. Sarcasm had its uses in humiliating opponents in debate, but being funny for its own sake seemed a waste of time. He banged the gavel a few times, probably more than necessary, to restore quiet.

"Yes, Senator," Thomas replied. "My tenure as commander of the Department of the North has been disturbed greatly by the actions of the Fenian Brotherhood."

"I think we are all well aware of who and what the Fenian Brotherhood is," Sumner said. "But perhaps you could sum them up in a sentence or two, for the benefit of anyone who might read the record of these hearings in the future?"

"Very well, Senator. The Fenian Brotherhood is an organization of Irish nationalists who wish to detach Ireland from the British Empire. They are active both in Ireland itself and here in the United States. Many Fenians here in the United States have attempted to attack British territories in Canada."

"May I ask Mr. Thomas a question, Mr. Chairman?" This came from Senator Charles Buckalew of Pennsylvania.

"Go ahead."

"Mr. Thomas, do you agree or disagree with the stated goals of the Fenian Brotherhood."

Sumner sighed. Questions of this type were all too common in politically sensitive committee hearings, intended to draw out the witnesses into making statements that could be used to discredit their testimony. Somewhat to Sumner's surprise, Thomas answered right away without hesitation.

"Who rules Ireland is a matter of little interest to me," Thomas replied. "It seems a matter for the people of Ireland and the British government to resolve. My only concern with this matter was following the orders I received from the War Department."

"And what were those orders, Mr. Thomas?" Sumner asked.

Thomas hesitated for a moment. The committee room was quiet, for this was the moment for which everyone had been waiting. Sumner knew that the

677

words spoken by Thomas in the next few minutes could help determine the political fate of the United States.

"Mr. Chairman, the president and the Secretary of War have publicly stated that the army was attempting to stop the Fenian incursions into Canada. In truth, I received orders that the men under my command were not only to do nothing to stop them, but actually to assist them in certain ways."

Sumner felt his stomach tighten. If what Thomas had just said was true, then the McClellan administration had been guilty of an act of war against the British Empire. Moreover, the president had done it unilaterally, without any approval from Congress. It was what Sumner had suspected all along, but to hear it proven still came a shock.

"In what ways were you ordered to help the Fenians?" Sumner asked.

"I was told the locations of the Fenian camps and supply depots and ordered to keep my men away from them. Surplus arms and ammunition were turned over to the Fenians. I was told the times and places where Fenian incursions were to take place and ordered to have my men assist them by clearing roads through the wilderness."

"You have copies of these orders?"

"I do not, Mr. Chairman. The orders were transmitted to me verbally by representatives of the Secretary of War. I wrote them down myself after the persons departed, but they are in my own handwriting."

Sumner frowned. Benjamin Butler was far too clever a man, and had been playing games like this for so long, that he could run rings around a man of integrity such as George Thomas. He would never leave fingerprints that could be easily followed.

"May I ask a question, Mr. Chairman?" inquired Senator Garrett Davis, the pro-McClellan Democrat from Kentucky.

Sumner had expected Davis to interject something at the earliest opportunity to discredit the proceedings, and Thomas's admission that he did not possess physical copies of the orders from Butler seemed like the ideal moment. However, if Sumner refused him permission to question Thomas, it would appear to the nation that he was not being fair and objective.

"Go ahead."

"Mr. Thomas, forgive me if my question seems direct, but if you have no copies of these orders you claim to have received from the War Department, why should we accept your claim that you received them at all? In other words, how can we be assured that you did not simply make the whole thing up?"

Thomas bristled at the Democrat's words, for he was clearly not a man used to having his honor called into question. "I have sworn an oath upon the Bible to speak truthfully to this committee, Senator. If you do not think that is enough, I cannot help it."

Davis scoffed. "I'm sorry to say, Mr. Thomas, that we live in an age where oaths don't seem to mean what they meant in the past. Some years ago, a man might be taken at his word. I wish I could say that it was still so."

Sumner decided to regain control of the proceedings and interrupted Davis. "Mr. Thomas, can you provide any evidence for your receipt of these verbal orders?"

"I can, Senator."

"What is it?"

"The man sent by the War Department to transmit these orders verbally was Seth Williams, a former staff officer with the Army of the Potomac and a man closely associated, I believe, with President McClellan. I did not consider the orders he gave me to be proper, especially in regards to the manner in which they were given to me. Verbal orders might make sense in the heat and confusion of a battle, but considering the situation I was in, it seemed designed entirely for concealing the activities of the forces under my command from public scrutiny. I therefore ordered my chief-of-staff, Colonel William Whipple, to have Mr. Williams followed. He compiled a list of the hotels where he stayed during his forays to my headquarters and collected receipts proving his presence at those places. I also asked Colonel Whipple to conceal himself in my office during some of Mr. Williams's visits and secretly listen to what he told me."

It all seemed so absurd, Sumner thought. A President of the United States giving orders to his army to allow an illegal group to carry out military actions against a foreign power, while members of that very army were resorting to clandestine means to investigate the veracity of the orders in question. It was too convoluted, but that was how real life unfolded.

"How did you know the orders transmitted by Williams were legitimate?" Sumner asked.

"I didn't, and I told him that I would not consider any such orders valid unless they were delivered to me through proper channels. The result was a meeting between myself and the Secretary of War, which took place in New York City in January."

Sumner realized at that moment that the hearings were going to be long and complicated, probably stretching over several days. As Thomas kept talking, describing a series of meetings with Butler over the course of many months, he could sense that his fellow committee members, shifting uncomfortably in their seats, were coming to the same conclusion. It was possible, though doubtful, that the former general's testimony would dig up any unambiguous proof that McClellan and Butler were guilty of a specific crime. McClellan was a bumbling fool, but Butler was one of the canniest political operators on the face of the earth and had clearly been in charge of the whole thing.

Still, Sumner knew he did not have to have either McClellan or Butler declared guilty in a court of law, but only in the court of public opinion. Looking behind the witness table, he could see newspaper reporters scribbling down the former general's words. They would be in headlines across the country the next day. All over the country, Republicans and disillusioned Democrats would have yet more reasons to distrust and despise the man serving as president. George Thomas, Sumner was beginning to understand, was going to provide more than enough rope for him to hang both McClellan and Butler.

Whatever happened, Sumner was going to make sure that McClellan was not going to be in the White House after the next year's election. Suspicions of illegally fostering the Fenian movement would morph with McClellan's dismissal of the plight of Charles Russell Lowell, creating an image in the public mind of a foolish and heartless man. Whomever the Republicans put forward as their candidate would surely be able to beat McClellan at the polls. Then the unfinished business with the Confederacy could be properly addressed.

A rare smile crept onto Sumner's face, and he interrupted Thomas to ask for the specific dates on which he had met Butler in New York City.

October 25, Evening
Home of John C. Breckinridge, Richmond, Virginia

"You're barely touching your food," Mary Breckinridge observed to her husband. "In fact, you haven't had much of an appetite in the last few days."

"I know," Breckinridge replied. "I apologize."

He was genuinely sorry for his lack of hunger, for the chicken pie and broiled sweet potatoes looked delicious. Moreover, he did not want to disappoint his wife, who was sometimes sensitive about her cooking skills. No matter how hard he tried, however, he could not force himself to eat. It had been this way for some time and he knew he had lost weight over the past month or so.

She looked at him carefully. "It will all be over soon, my dear," she said understandingly. "Two weeks from now, the votes will all have been cast, the results will be in, and we will know what the future has in store for us."

He nodded, even as his mind raced. The news coming in from all corners was universally negative. Miles in Tennessee was reporting that the SRP appeared in control, placing the final touches on a huge effort to get their supporters to vote on Election Day. Georgia was completely gone, according to his supporters there. Although Breckinridge still had many pockets of strong support, they appeared powerless against the organizational advantage of the SRP or the furious emotions whipped up by the New Iberia insurrection and the Lowell trial.

"I shall be happy when it is over," he said, taking a deep breath. "I do not expect to win, truth be told. I will consider my defeat to be a disaster for the Confederacy, but I cannot deny that a quiet return to my legal practice would be nice." He chuckled. "If it were anyone but Beauregard and Toombs, I might even prefer to lose."

"No, you wouldn't," she said sharply, but with amusement. "You can't play that game with me. With other people, perhaps, but not with your own wife. This is very different than the election in 1860, which we knew from the start was a lost cause. You want to win this election and you believe you should be able to win it. If you lose, you will see it as a great rejection."

He pursed his lips, sighed deeply, and tried unsuccessfully to focus on his food. A single bit of the chicken pie was all he could manage before his exasperation returned. "I am not a man given much to complaining," he said. "But you are my wife. I can complain to you, if no one else. I cannot help but think all of this is utterly unfair."

"How so, darling?"

"I have given my life to public service. For Kentucky. For the United States. For the Confederacy. I wouldn't be saying this to anyone but you, my love, but shouldn't I be given at least some measure of recognition for all I've done? If I am rejected at the polls, it will make me feel as though nothing I have ever done in all my years in public life has been noticed by anyone. That none of the sacrifices I have made are appreciated by anyone. It will be a terrible feeling?"

"I know," Mary said understandingly.

"And Beauregard? A good general, but a man who has never done anything for the people. Toombs? Please. Nothing but a drunken rabble-rouser. It's the fault of men like him that there was even a war in the first place. We might still be a united country with the North, on our way towards dealing with the slavery issue in due time, had it not been for Fire-Eaters like him."

"You've always said that the radical abolitionists in the North were equally to blame."

"Yes, yes, perhaps they were. But at least I can respect them for standing up for the blacks. I can't say so publicly, of course, but there it is. The Fire-Eaters? They stand for nothing but their own selfish interests, cloaked in the language of liberty and states' rights. And if you ask me, hundreds of thousands of people are dead because of what they did."

Mary shrugged ever so slightly. "The past is past, as you often remind me. We have to accept the world for what it is."

He nodded. "Yes, we do. I believe that God watches over us and wants us to be happy, but I also believe that it is the choices we make ourselves that determine our fate. I don't see this election turning out the way we had hoped. I will probably win Virginia and perhaps North Carolina. That may be it, my dear. Georgia is lost to us. Tennessee as well. I can do math as well as anyone. I just don't see any scenario in which we obtain enough electoral votes to win."

"Well, my dear, perhaps it is best for you to be coming to this conclusion before the votes are cast, rather than being held in suspense on the night of the election. I would hate for us to be awake all night until the sun rises, waiting on tenterhooks as the telegrams come in, desperately hoping."

He watched his wife as she took a sip of wine, her eyes carefully judging his reaction to what she was saying. He tried to keep his face composed, but was certain that his expression betrayed his disappointment in what she was saying. No one came close to knowing him as well as Mary did, so what would have been invisible to others was clear as day to her.

He began to reply, but she continued before he could speak. "I will say, though, John, that I do not quite share your pessimism. I think you may yet emerge the winner. We can't know what Tennessee will do. You served there for much of the war, which Beauregard did not, and you directly commanded many Tennessee soldiers. Plus, we have the natural affinity that Tennesseans and Kentuckians have for one another. That may give you an advantage you haven't considered."

"Perhaps," he said, acknowledging her point. His colleagues did not know it, but his wife was as astute a political observer as any of them, and better than most. His stomach relaxed somewhat and he indulged in a few bits of his food and a sip of his wine. "I thank you, my dear. Talking to you always leaves me happier than I was before."

"Well, John, that is the job of any wife. Especially a politician's wife."

"I have to be prepared for the likelihood of defeat, though. That being the case, I'd like you to look at this for me."

He pulled a piece of paper out of his pocket and handed it across the table. She took it, unfolded it, and began to examine it rather as a mother would examine her child's schoolwork sent home by a demanding teacher.

"Your concession letter?" she said after a moment.

"That's right."

She sighed deeply as she read through the paper, her eyes darting back and forth across the page with studied focus. "Too many adjectives, dear," she said disapprovingly. "And you make yourself out to be more humble than I know you really are."

He chuckled slightly. "Well, I cannot sound arrogant, can I?"

She finished and handed the paper back across the table. "No, but you certainly are far too reconciliatory. You talk of accepting the results of the election, which is fine and even admirable. Democracy and all that. But Beauregard is a buffoon and Toombs is a drunkard. Better simply to leave them unmentioned, than to praise them as decent men and call for the people to rally around them. If you win, they should certainly not do the same for you."

"To say anything else would not reflect well upon my honor."

"You men speak so grandly about your honor. If you ask me, you should remove the sections where you speak kindly of your opponents. Simply say you accept the results and remain ready to serve the Confederacy in whatever capacity the people see fit. What would be wrong with that?"

"Nothing, I suppose. But I want to be the bigger man, so to speak."

"You already are, John. In any case, I still believe you shall not need this letter. I retain faith in the wisdom of the people to see you as the rightful leader and the man who this country needs at the head of its affairs. Put this letter in the drawer of your desk. If you need it, you can revise it later. And if you don't you can hold it to a candle when we celebrate your victory."

"Your optimism never fails to inspire me, love."

"Pray tell, John, can I read the letter you intend to release to the newspapers in the event of your actually winning the election?"

He felt a sting of surprise. "I'm sorry, my dear, but I haven't written one yet. Truth be told, I highly doubt I will need one."

She chuckled. "Well, write one anyway."

October 29, Afternoon
Chatham Manor, near Fredericksburg, Virginia

"And your family is well?" Joseph Johnston asked.

"Yes," Robert E. Lee answered. He smiled, happy to feel genuinely proud of his children when so many other men had to feign happiness when it came to their own. "Rooney and Rob remain in the army. Rooney leads one of the cavalry divisions in the Army of Northern Virginia. Rob commands an artillery battery. General Early tells me that they are both doing a fine job. He would be honest with me, if anyone would."

"And Custis?"

"In his first term in the Virginia House of Delegates. He is lobbying strongly for Virginia Military Institute to become a national military school. A West Point for the Confederacy, if you will."

"An institution that will be sorely needed, in my view," Johnston said. "No one knows better than you and I how urgently the Confederacy requires trained officers. Thousands of men learned war through experience during the struggle with the Yankees, yet there is no substitute for a sound military education. And we will need trained engineers for more than just military purposes."

"I agree," Lee replied. He thought for a moment about the political battle raging across the country and the oft-repeated assertion by Robert Toombs that a professional army was a danger to the republic. To Lee, such notions made no sense. If the Confederacy were to be a proper nation, it needed a proper army, and a proper army required proper officers. How this was not immediately obvious to everyone was a mystery to him.

It pleased Lee greatly to be entertaining his old friend and comrade Johnston in his new home. Their old home, Arlington House, now lay outside the Confederacy, for the Treaty of Toronto, to his wife's everlasting grief, had ceded the Virginia counties directly across the Potomac River from Washington City to the United States. This had left the Lee family temporarily without a place to live. By happy chance, Chatham Manor, a fine mansion across from Fredericksburg, had been offered for sale at about the same time. A subscription undertaken by veterans of the Army of Northern Virginia had raised enough money to buy the house, which had immediately been offered as a gift to Lee. It had been one of the most heartwarming episodes in his long life.

They had settled into the house in late 1866. Without a slave workforce, the fields of the estate lay fallow, but Lee had plans to use hired labor to plant them the following spring. In the meantime, much work had to be done on the house. Along with the steady work on his memoirs, the refurbishment of the manor and the estate was a welcome way to keep busy. Since his retirement from the army, Lee had experienced excessive leisure for the first time in his life. He was not sure if he enjoyed it.

"So, I understand that you have joined me in retirement?" Lee asked.

Johnston smiled. "Indeed. Two days ago, I handed Secretary Breckinridge my letter of resignation. It seems the proper time, what with the change in administration soon to come. The Army of Tennessee is in fine shape. I want to spend my remaining years, however many the Good Lord chooses to bless me with, with Lydia."

"Congratulations, old friend," Lee said with genuine warmth. He did not say so, but Lee suspected that the main reason Johnston had waited so long before retiring was because he wanted to wait out the administration of Jefferson Davis and prevent anyone from suggesting that his great enemy had pushed him out of his position. He knew the depth of their loathing for one another better than most, yet he had been able to stay above their fray and remain on friendly terms with each of them.

"Did you recommend anyone to succeed you in command?" Lee asked.

"Yes," Johnston replied. "I suggested that Breckinridge appoint General Hardee to the command."

Lee nodded. "A fine soldier and a fine man. He would do very well."

"And I recommended that General Cleburne he appointed to replace Hardee in command of Northern Department of the Mississippi River. It is my understanding that Hardee will recommend the same thing."

"Breckinridge would do it, if Davis allows him. But I don't think he will. The public remains deeply suspicious of Cleburne, on account of his proposal to free slaves and enlist them in the army. I have never met the man, but he seems a fine soldier. His defense of Atlanta against Grant was little short of amazing."

"It was. A natural military genius, if I may say. One wonders how much further he might have gone had he received a proper military education. It was very unfortunate that his memorandum became known to the public. You and I might have agreed with him, at least as an intellectual exercise, but the people are not ready for such great changes."

"Clearly not," Lee observed. He remained dismayed by the attitude of the Southern people towards slavery. He himself did not approve of the institution and owned no slaves. He believed that it would end in God's good time. Over the course of his life, he had watched as Southern society went from viewing the institution as, at best, a necessary evil towards viewing it as a positive good, which never failed to sadden him. Its corrosive effect on the morals of the people was as plain as day and it had brought on the twin disasters of secession and the war.

Johnston set his teacup down on the small table between the two of them. Seeing that it was almost empty, Lee leaned forward, took the porcelain kettle in his hand, and refilled it.

"A fine tea service," Johnston observed.

"Thank you," Lee replied. "It was sent to me by a man in England as a gift." He thought for a moment. "I cannot immediately recall his name. He said it was simply an expression of his esteem."

Johnston chuckled slightly. "I have received similar gifts from European admirers, people I have never met nor am ever likely to meet. Tea services like this one, watches, a fine walking stick. At first, I thought to send them back, but my wife pointed out that it would be a needless expense and the gift-giver might feel offended. Besides, I think she rather likes most of them."

"It suits Mrs. Johnston to be the wife of a famous man, does it?"

"No more than it suits Mrs. Lee, I am sure."

Lee smiled and took a sip of tea. "Remember when we were young engineering officers working on the coastal defenses of Savannah? Laboring away in those swamps on the coast?"

Johnston smiled. "I could have saved every penny for months and not afforded a tea set like this one. And yet, they are very happy memories. Sometimes I feel like those days were only a few short months ago. And sometimes they seem like another lifetime."

"Indeed. Could you have imagined then the path that our lives have taken?"

"Never," Johnston replied firmly. "Seeing the Union to which we swore oaths broken by misguided men, both North and South. Leading armies of tens of thousands against those who had once been our comrades. So many Americans slain by other Americans. It has been a strange path for us, my old friend."

Lee sighed. "The war pained me greatly. I'm sure it was the same for you. We are old beyond our years for the burdens we have had to bear. The news of your retirement makes me happy beyond measure. You are healthier than I. You always have been. But you need the quiet and tranquility of retirement as much as I do."

"Perhaps. Speaking of retirement, how is your book progressing?" Johnston asked.

"Well enough," Lee answered. "Since my resignation, I have blessedly had few responsibilities of an official capacity. I can devote myself to settling my family in its new home and taking up the trade of a writer."

"Your army was one of the most magnificent that ever marched," Johnston said. "It is right and fitting that its commander be the one who chronicles its deeds."

Lee smiled and set down his teacup on the small table between them. A few years before, such a comment might have been tinged with jealousy, for the Army of Northern Virginia had been Johnston's before it was Lee's. The chance bullet that struck Johnston down at the Battle of Seven Pines had changed that. Lee had been told, by men he considered trustworthy, that Johnston had looked upon Lee's victories with something of an envious eye.

Yet if that had ever been true, it no longer was. The battlefield triumphs Johnston won with the Army of Tennessee at Atlanta and Fairburn were enough to ensure his own immortality as a great military leader. They could speak to one another as equals, which was how Lee preferred it.

"Writing the book is more difficult than I anticipated," Lee said. "The War Department has been happy to make its archives available to me, but sorting through them is a monumental task. Secretary Breckinridge has been kind enough to grant Colonel Taylor an extended leave of absence, allowing him to assist me while staying on the army payroll."

"Most kind of him," Johnston replied.

"Yes, well, he is a great and a good man. I met him in Washington before the war, but I did not appreciate just how good a man he was until he came to Virginia in 1864."

"A natural leader of men," Johnston said. "I saw better than you the care he took for his soldiers and the deep and abiding love that existed between him and the men under his command. A brilliant mind and a conscientious heart. It is my hope that he becomes our next president."

It was a clear hint that Johnston wanted to discuss the presidential election and Lee felt slightly uneasy. He had always studiously avoided most political discussions, having learned from long experience that they never produced much good and could produce much evil. He had never seen a man change a firmly held opinion after an argument, though he had seen many altercations and even broken friendships on account of political disputes.

Yet he could not deny that he was deeply troubled by the political disorder that seemed to be rising in the Confederacy. He was dismayed when he read that supporters of Beauregard and Toombs were organizing themselves into a political party, for he had hoped that the Confederacy might fulfill the wishes of George Washington and avoid the formation of parties altogether.

As he learned more about the policies being proposed by the States' Rights Party, Lee became even more uneasy. The idea of risking a war with Spain in order to acquire Cuba seemed both dangerous and immoral. The Confederacy would not recover from the struggle for its independence for some time and a war with a European power was the last thing it needed. The fact that the SRP attempted to blame Davis and Breckinridge for the uprising by Saul seemed both disingenuous and dishonorable, for no one could have predicted such an event. Opposition to the treaty with France seemed absurd, for if the Confederacy was going to survive in any future war with the United States, it would need a strong ally. The men who had led the American Revolution had made every effort to find French support against Britain, and when they did so they had ensured their country's independence. While the financial proposals of Toombs seemed reasonable enough, Lee thought that the bulk of the SRP platform was far from desirable.

"Speaking to you as a friend, I can say that I intend to vote for Breckinridge on Election Day," Lee said simply.

"I am glad to hear it," Johnston replied. "My friend Wigfall is very disappointed in me, I am sad to say. He wanted me to run for the office myself. When I refused to endorse Beauregard and Toombs on top of that, I believe that my friendship with him suffered an irrevocable breach."

"That is disappointing," Lee said, though this was false. He had never understood why a man like Johnston would associate with a man like Wigfall, who struck Lee as nothing but a drunken rogue. Toombs was little better. Lee did not like the idea of having such men at the head of the affairs of the new nation.

"Did you happen to receive their letter?" Johnston asked. "The one asking for endorsement for the SRP and its ticket?"

"I did not," Lee said. "I imagine that they did not bother sending me one as they knew I would refuse and did not want to risk the appearance of rejection. I have received many letters from old comrades who did get the letter, however. Some signed it. Most did not. My sons all received personal visits from SRP representatives, pushing them strongly to endorse Beauregard. I suppose that, if they could not have me, they thought they could settle for my children."

"And?"

"They all told the men to leave at once, naturally." He could not suppress a grin of amusement mixed with pride.

"Have you been approached by Breckinridge's men?"

"Not directly, although Jubal Early has been pushing me hard to issue an endorsement. He is not a man who concerns himself with proper manners, that one."

It sounded like chiding, but Lee could not help but like Early. In his disdain of proper form, his lack of concern for what people thought about him, his unorthodox relationship to the mother of his illegitimate children, he was everything Lee was not allowed to be. Early seemed to understand this, and could therefore take chances with Lee that no one else could. The constant stream of letters from Winchester, pleading with Lee to publicly endorse Breckinridge, was but the most recent example of this.

"I, too, have heard from his people." He paused a moment before continuing. "I will admit that I have considered publicly endorsing Breckinridge."

Lee nodded slowly. "You and I must be very careful about such things, Joseph. We carry a great weight on our shoulders. The people, rightly or wrongly, regard us as heroes for our victories in the war. Our every action is scrutinized and carefully considered. By God, when I journey into Fredericksburg to purchase something at a store, it is reported in the Richmond newspapers as though it were an event of national importance. Our opinions on such matters, if publicly stated, would carry a weight very disproportionate to their value. In a republic, our views should matter no more than those of any other citizen."

"If only that were true, Robert."

"And we are military men, not statesmen."

"So was George Washington, my friend. And endorsing a candidate is a far smaller step than doing what Washington did, for he took up the reins of government himself."

Lee felt himself stiffen up. He sensed that Johnston wanted to push him but was being careful about it. The two had known each other for more than four decades and knew how to read one another like books. Lee felt his formerly pleasant mood beginning to darken.

"You and I have both earned a distinguished place in the hearts of our people," Lee said. "Whether or not we deserve it is open to question. I do not feel I do, for I feel myself a miserable sinner like any other. The common ordinary soldier who served in my army during the war is a far better man than I. But the people think otherwise. An open endorsement of Breckinridge? It would sully our names like a cloth tossed into a muddy puddle."

Johnston nodded slowly, eyeing Lee carefully. It dawned on Lee that Johnston had not come to Chatham merely for a social visit, but had been waiting for an appropriate time to bring up the subject of endorsing Breckinridge. He felt a tinge of resentment at this realization, but did not allow any hint of it to appear on his face.

"It is more than the good opinion of the people we must consider, my friend," Johnston said. "It is the opinion of posterity as well."

"I don't follow."

"I do not mean to sound arrogant, but the events in which you and I have been involved have been historical in scope. Men will be writing history books about the battles we fought and the armies we commanded for centuries to come. Our names will live on long after our wretched bones are deposited in the ground."

There was an uncomfortable pause, for Lee did not know how to respond. He could not deny the truth of what Johnston was saying, but to acknowledge the truth of it would be an act of hubris and pride, twin sins that Lee always strove to avoid. To avoid speaking, Lee took a long sip of his tea.

Johnston, seeing his hesitation, went on. "If Beauregard and Toombs are elected, you and I both know the course that our country will take. It will not be good. It could well be disastrous. Breckinridge, by contrast, is a sensible man of good judgement. He is the man who must lead our new nation through the storms to come. You and I both know how much weight our opinions carry. One day, men will ask why we did nothing when we might have done something."

Lee nodded, very slowly. "You're saying that we have a responsibility to act."

"It would be a small thing, really. Nothing but a short letter with both of our names on it."

"That would not be a small thing and you know it. It would be the leading story of the newspapers for days after it was released. And would it matter? How many voters would be swayed by our opinion on the matter?"

"A great many, I should think. But even if it had no result, you and I would at least stand in the eyes of history as having done something to prevent our nation from going down a dark path. Having fought to make our nation free, is it not our responsibility to help make our country into the prosperous and flourishing place we know it should be?"

"It would result in heavy criticism of us from one side of the political balance." He paused anxiously. "I do not like public criticism." For just a moment, he remembered some of the newspaper articles that came out after his defeat at Gettysburg.

"We can endure criticism now from one of the political factions. What I am concerned about it is people will say decades from now, a century from now, when they look back at us and ask why we said nothing in the face of the coming disaster." Johnston paused for a moment to gather his thoughts. "You and I both revere General Washington. He risked his reputation to serve in the Constitutional Convention, though he did not want to. Imagine how different our historical memory of him would be today had he done nothing, had he remained at Mount Vernon, and the country had collapsed into chaos. Historians would be forever asking why he had not done something to stop it."

Lee considered this. Many of the friends who had suggested he himself seek the presidency had used the Washington comparison, knowing the enormous admiration Lee held for the great hero. His entire life, in more ways than one, had been modeled on Washington's example. He found himself wondering what Washington would do if placed in his situation.

"Do you intend to endorse him yourself if I decline?" Lee asked.

"No," Johnston said. "This is something you and I have to do together. Our strange position in the minds of the people means that if we failed to speak with a single voice, all the chatter would be about why we disagree rather than the contents of my letter."

Lee nodded. He sipped his tea carefully, mulling things over in his mind. He asked himself to consider the two possibilities. On the one hand, Breckinridge was a man he had full confidence in. As a politician, he had been a man of rare integrity and had always possessed a sense of duty absent from nearly every other politician Lee had ever encountered. He had been a successful soldier, despite having received no military education, which told Lee that his was a mind that could adapt easily. Finally, he was a warm and caring person. Placing the affairs of the nation in his hands would allow Lee to sleep easily at night.

There was also the matter of Breckinridge's running mate, James Kemper, a man Lee knew well and respected enormously. He had not yet been able to bring himself to write the portion of his memoirs that would deal with the third day of the Battle of Gettysburg, when Kemper commanded one of the brigades of Pickett's division that Lee sent forward in the most disastrous assault of his military career. Kemper was grievously wounded in the attack. Lee initially despaired for his life, prayed for his survival, and thanked God when the man pulled through. He knew Kemper was a good and intelligent man, an ideal vice president.

He could contrast that presidential ticket with the one put forward by the States' Rights Party. Beauregard was an intelligent man and a generally good soldier. Yet Lee thought him vainglorious, more interested in securing glory for himself than in performing his duties conscientiously. Humility was a necessary character trait for a successful leader and Beauregard did not know the meaning of the word. He was also given to flights of fancy and unrealistic projects. Having him as president would be like having a man uninterested in navigation as the captain of a ship heading towards rocky waters.

Then there was Robert Toombs, a man Lee deeply disliked and distrusted. His loud-mouthed bravado and well-known proclivity for drunkenness revealed a man who was simply not in control of himself. Had a man such as he asked for permission to court one of his daughters, Lee would have immediately refused. Given the fickle nature of fate, there was always a chance that the man serving as vice president would become president. Moreover, with Beauregard's lack of political experience, it stood to reason that Toombs would exercise disproportionate influence over the president and possibly use the office as a means to seek the higher office himself in six years.

Lee did not have to think long to decide between Breckinridge and Beauregard. He had known for some time for whom he would vote on Election Day. The question Johnston was proposing, however, was of a different sort. Would it be honorable for him to presume to intervene in the election by making his endorsement public?

"I am uncertain," Lee said simply.

"I understand," Johnston replied. "I do not mean to push you, old friend. But is it not true that we still have a duty to the South, even in retirement? It was our duty that compelled us to resign from the old army and follow our states, misguided though we thought them to be. It was our duty to lead the armies of the Confederacy, risking our lives and enduring enormous hardships while doing so. You speak of concern over public criticism. I understand that. But we still have our duty, do we not?"

"We do," Lee replied. In his mind, there was no more sublime concept in the world than that of duty.

"The States' Rights Party is going to win the election, unless some great change takes place. I do not mean to sound arrogant, but our word carries great weight with the people, especially the tens of thousands of men who fought under our command. If we were to issue a simple statement that we intend to vote for Breckinridge, it could be the great change that might swing the election to Breckinridge. You must agree."

Lee thought for a moment. "I agree."

"Then, I ask you, do we really have any choice in the matter?"

Lee found himself shaking his head. Just as he had no choice but to follow Virginia when it had seceded, just as he had no choice when he had been called upon to lead the main Confederate army, he had no choice now. He never really had any choice, he realized.

Lee set his tea cup down and called for a servant to bring pen and paper.

October 31, Afternoon
Parish Jail, New Orleans, Louisiana

It took the jury less than an hour to pass a sentence of death on Charles Russell Lowell. He had stood with the rest of the court to hear the jury foreman read out their decision in a bland and somewhat stilted voice. Lowell had expected the man to speak with glee or satisfaction, but he appeared grave and serious, rather like a New England man would.

The audience had responded in a very different manner. The moment the word 'death' was spoken, it erupted into a chorus of cheers. Women hugged and men shook hands as though congratulating one another for some great accomplishment. Others jeered at Lowell, yelling out that he was going to Hell. For nearly a minute, there was loud pandemonium in the courtroom until the banging gavel of Judge Moise brought it to an end.

Lowell himself had felt nothing. As the mayhem swept around him, he had remained still as a statue, like a man standing in the eye of a hurricane. He had expected nothing less of the jury, for it was simply an extension of the Confederacy itself. It could not forgive him for arming black men so that they might kill white men.

Moise had announced from the bench that the sentence would be carried out in December, which confused Lowell. He had assumed that he would be hanged within the next few days. Before he could ask Benjamin to inquire as to causes of the delay, however, Moise had dismissed the court and the guards had gone through the long since familiar routine of moving him from the court to the paddy wagon to take him back to jail.

That had been less than an hour ago. Lowell was now being escorted back into his cell by Styles, his emotions swirling within him. Knowing beyond the shadow of a doubt that one is going to die is a far different thing from merely suspecting it. The moment the foreman had read the sentence, Lowell had felt his soul start to separate from his body. He now existed in a strange sort of limbo, no longer fully alive but not yet dead.

"Is there anything I can do for you, sir?" Styles the jailer asked as Lowell passed through the door into the cell. The tone of the man's voice betrayed sympathy for him.

"Styles, perhaps you could take all these books out of the cell? I shall not be needing them any longer."

"All of them, sir? No one's said when your…" The jailer was at a loss for words for a moment. "Your appointment, sir. No one has said when that will be. Might be a few weeks yet."

Lowell grunted. "Leave the Bible and that volume by Boethius." He could, at least, reread the Word of God and the *Consolation of Philosophy* as many times as possible before they pulled him out of his cell to take him to his execution.

"Very well, sir. I'll send someone to pick up the others presently." He moved towards the door.

"And Styles?"

"Yes, sir?"

"I no longer want any fancy food. Bread and water will be fine from now on."

The jailer's eyes expressed confusion. "Customary to give the condemned man whatever he wants for his last meal," he said.

"Bread and water, if you please."

"Very well, sir."

Styles turned and left, rather more quickly than usual. With a metallic screech, the heavy door closed and locked. Lowell let out a deep breath and stood for a long time in the center of his cell, arms folded across his chest. The events that had brought him to this point flowed through his mind, as though he was watching a stage play. His meeting with Sumner, his decision to go, the clandestine preparations, his telling Josephine, the sea voyage of the *Vincent*, the journey to find Saul and their meeting in the wilderness, his capture, his trial, and now this. It had been a strange journey, indeed.

Had it been worth it? Lowell knew that this question would torment him from now until the moment the trapdoor on the gallows opened beneath him. Had he traded away his life for something worthy? Saul's uprising had failed, but it had struck terror into the heart of the Confederacy. In his trial, he had forced the South to look upon a brave man who was not afraid to die in the cause of abolitionism. He had focused the attention of the world back onto the evil of slavery, painting the vile Confederacy with wicked colors. No one could deny that his actions had struck fiercely at the slave-holding power. Yet still Lowell had to ask whether it had been worth it. The price he was now to pay, after all, was very steep, indeed.

He sat down on the cot and picked up Boethius. He had lost count of how many times he had read it since he had first stepped into the cell. A particular line occurred to him, and he quickly flipped to the page on which it was printed.

In every adversity of fortune, to have been happy is the most unhappy kind of misfortune.

These words forcefully brought back memories of the beautiful face of his wife as he embraced her, of the loving smiles of his son and daughter as he lifting them into his arms, of a thousand delightful evenings with friends and family around Boston dinner tables. People said that he was rebuilding his family's fortune and reputation, that he might be Governor of Massachusetts one day, perhaps even President of the United States. He thought of his travels in Europe, seeing the magical places that he had previously only seen in his dreams. He could have gone back to Europe whenever he had wished, taking his family with him. He thought of his heady school days at Harvard and the many friends he still had from that idyllic time in his life.

Lowell had known true happiness. He could have kept it, had he simply told Sumner that he would not go. His happiness had not been taken from him, for he had chosen to walk away from it. That, at least, was a sort of consolation.

He read through more of Boethius, though he knew it by heart and probably could have simply recited it in his own mind. At this point, reading Boethius was like talking to an old friend. Since he would never speak with nor see his actual friends again, at least not in this world, it would have to do. He would alternate between Boethius and the Bible for whatever time he had remaining.

There was a loud series of three knocks on the door, which was then unlocked and opened. Styles appeared, nodded quickly, then stepped aside as Judah Benjamin entered the room.

"Charles," he said simply, a hint of sadness in his voice.

"Hello, Mr. Benjamin."

Styles withdrew back into the hall, then closed and locked the door, leaving the two alone.

"I am sorry I could not do better," Benjamin said. "The odds were stacked against us from the start. Your wife's outburst infuriated the jury so much that death was the only choice they were going to make."

Lowell shrugged. "Don't apologize. I'm getting what I wanted. I told you, just as I told her, that I wanted to be found guilty and I wanted the verdict to be death. It was the best way to strike at slavery. My death will mean something. What would have been the point to be allowed to live a life of permanent and pathetic imprisonment? No, Judah, this way is much better. It's what I want."

Benjamin sighed, but said nothing. When Lowell first met Benjamin, the Jewish attorney happily agreed to put on a legal show to highlight the abolitionist cause before seeing him sentenced to death. He was not sure what had caused him to change his mind so abruptly in the middle of the proceedings, but events had made that irrelevant. The sentence had been passed and there was nothing that Benjamin could do about it now.

Lowell went on. "As for my wife, she did what was right and what I wanted her to do. You turned her from her course at first, but she righted herself in the end. I am proud of her."

"She is back in the United States," Benjamin said reassuringly. "There were fears for her safety if she took a ship from the docks, as a mob was forming at every rumor of her departure. So she was secretly sent by train to Memphis, then by river steamer to Louisville. She'll be back in Boston within the next few days."

"If any mob had come face to face with my wife, I should have feared for the safety of the mob," Lowell replied.

Benjamin smiled. "I came to tell you that Judge Moise will not schedule your execution until after November 5. He worries that the two events coming together will create public disorder."

"November 5?"

"The election."

"Ah," Lowell said. "I had forgotten." In truth, he had thought little about the election at all, since it didn't matter to him whether Beauregard or Breckinridge was the next President of the Confederate States. "How long after?"

"He hasn't decided. Perhaps a few weeks, to give enough time for the people to settle down."

"You will tell me when he has scheduled it?"

"You will obviously be notified, though perhaps not by me. I am returning to Richmond, where I have unfinished business."

"Are you? When will you be leaving?"

"Tomorrow morning."

"Then we shall not meet again, shall we?"

"No, I suppose not."

He waited for a moment. "Do you believe in the afterlife, Judah?"

"I honestly have never given it much thought," Benjamin replied. "Impossible to know either way."

"I didn't ask whether you knew. No one knows. I asked whether you believed."

Benjamin shrugged. "That's just semantics, Charles."

"Maybe for you. Not for me. You're a frustrating man, Judah. This will be our last meeting, yet I still have no idea who you are behind that placid expression of yours."

"A woman whose judgement I respect once told me that I was like a blank page between the Old Testament and the New Testament."

Lowell frowned. "That explains nothing."

"Exactly. But what I believe isn't important. What is it that you believe? After all, you are the one who is going to find out soon enough."

"I don't think this is all there is," Lowell said. "Man is born with innate senses beyond those of mere sensory experience. The moral sense. The aesthetic sense. The sense of the ridiculous. Something like that tells me that I will continue to exist after my body expires on the gallows. One day, I will be reunited with my wife and children. With all my old friends who died in the war. With my parents. Yes, I believe that."

"Well, I hope that you find comfort in that."

Lowell considered Benjamin carefully. He was not going to presume to inquire deeply into the man's religious beliefs. What difference would it make anyway? What difference did anything make, at this point?

"What are the newspapers going to say tomorrow?"

"I imagine that they will say that you took the news of your sentencing with stoic courage. It's only the truth, after all."

"That is good. Let them see a brave man die in opposition to slavery in such a way that they will never forget it."

"They won't," Benjamin said reassuringly. "You have made that impossible. You'll be like a bug bite that the South can't scratch. The English might burn Guy Fawkes every November 5 as an act of retribution, but every Englishman knows his name and, whether they admit it or not, they fear him. You have accomplished that."

"Saul is the one they should fear. I was merely an accomplice."

Benjamin grunted softly. "You know that Saul's body was never found."

Lowell felt a stirring of energy. "What's that?" he asked.

"Saul's body was never found. There is no doubt that he died in the fighting or was trapped in the burning hotel when its roof collapsed. But they never did find his body. Looked everywhere for it, but without any luck."

"I see," Lowell replied.

Benjamin hesitated a moment before continuing. "I'm told that slaves are telling strange stories about Saul, all over Louisiana. That he comes to them in the night and in their dreams, that kind of thing. Silly nonsense, of course. Slaves believe in ghost stories as easily as children. But it seems unusual that so many of them are talking about the same sort of thing."

"Yes, it does." He could not help but wonder if Saul had, indeed, somehow escaped from New Iberia. Even if he hadn't, Lowell hoped that the man's ghost would continue to haunt the South. His own example, of white men from the North willing to die to bring the slaves the means to fight, would throw kindling onto the fires of such fears.

"You have a will?" Benjamin asked.

"Yes, I prepared one before I left Boston."

"Very well. I will leave you know, Charles."

Benjamin stepped forward and extended his hand, which Lowell shook firmly. Whatever he thought of the strange Jewish man who had come into his life at its end, he was grateful for his help.

"God give you strength to be brave on the scaffold," Benjamin said.

"I know He will."

CHAPTER SEVENTEEN

November 1, Evening
Spottswood Hotel, Richmond

"And who will be the Secretary of War in the Beauregard administration?" a reporter from Alabama asked.

"Good question," Toombs replied. "Fact is, Beauregard knows so much about military affairs that he might as well serve as his own Secretary of War. Not sure exactly who will fill the post, but there will certainly be more than enough qualified applicants." He took a moment to sip on his nearly-empty glass of whiskey. "It will be important that every region of the Confederacy be properly represented in the Cabinet, obviously."

The reporter frowned slightly. "But you won't give us names?"

"Not right now, no."

"What about Secretary of the Treasury?" another reporter, this one from Georgia, asked.

"Same thing. We'll find qualified people and every region of the country will be represented. As far as the Treasury goes, I know as much about finance as Beauregard knows about war, so maybe we won't need anybody for that, either."

Toombs laughed exuberantly and the assembled reporters glanced uncertainly at one another. About a dozen men, representing many of the most widely-read newspapers in the Confederacy, were gathered at a few of the tables nearest the bar, where Toombs held court on a barstool. With the election less than a week away, it seemed to Toombs rather like a victory celebration already.

"Another whiskey, my good man," Toombs said to the barkeeper. Over the past few weeks, he had increasingly ignored Stephens's advice to restrain his drinking. The more his confidence in the election result had risen, the more whiskey he had consumed. He still recalled how the drunken scene in the Exchange Hotel in Montgomery had cost him the presidency six and a half years ago, but that now was but a distant memory. He was riding into the vice presidency on the coattails of General Beauregard. Six years hence, he would be running for the presidency from a position of strength.

He no longer had any doubt that the SRP was going to win the election. The question to Toombs now was merely what their margin of victory was going to be. SRP members were going to form the majorities in the House of

Representatives and the Senate, as well as in most state legislatures. As one of the major figures within the party, arguably the most influential of them all, Toombs would be more powerful in Southern politics than he had ever been. He had played his cards right and he soon would be able to start cashing in his chips.

The questions went on and Toombs happily answered them all. Yes, the proposed treaty with France was going to be scrapped. No, they were not going to back down on Cuba. When asked whether any former Breckinridge supporters would be allowed to become members of the States' Rights Party, Toombs merely laughed and took another sip of his whiskey.

As the questioning entered its second hour, a young boy entered the bar and quietly walked up to a reporter, handing him a note and a newspaper. The newspaperman handed the boy a coin and sent him on his way before unfolding the note. Toombs scarcely noticed until he saw the man's eyes widen in astonishment. The reporter quickly unfolded the newspaper and looked at the headline. He then gently elbowed the man next to him and passed the paper to him. The second man likewise received whatever news it contained with amazement.

"What's this?" Toombs asked, amusement in his voice. The liquor in his system made everything seem a game, so it did not occur to him immediately that the note might contain bad news.

The reporter who had initially received the note looked up at him. "Senator Toombs, I've just been informed that General Robert E. Lee and General Joseph E. Johnston have announced their endorsement of John C. Breckinridge. Do you have a response?"

Toombs laughed at first. Lee and Johnston had largely vanished from his mind, for it had long ago been clear that neither would seek office themselves. There had appeared no possibility at all of gaining the backing of either man, so Toombs had simply dismissed them as not worth thinking about. His initial assumption was that the man was making some sort of joke. When he saw the seriousness in the reporter's eyes, however, he quickly cooled and momentarily focused through the whiskey-induced miasma.

"Who says so?" he asked angrily.

"Today's copy of the *Fredericksburg Gazette*." He held up the newspaper so that Toombs could read the headline.

Lee, Johnston Support Breckinridge!

Toombs was taken aback, as if he had been slapped in the face. It had not been mentioned in the Richmond papers that morning, so it could only have happened the previous day. If a credible paper had the information, it would be flashing across the telegraph wires even as they sat in the hotel bar.

"Give that here!" Toombs snapped to the reporter holding the paper. The man stood from his chair and leaned forward to hand the newspaper over, his facial expression showing how much he was irked by Toombs's rudeness. The senator could not have cared less. He quickly read through the editor's note on the front page, which explained that the letter the Fredericksburg Gazette was reprinting had been delivered to their office on October 30. A day had been spent verifying its authenticity and it had been reprinted after confirming that it was genuine.

Toombs quickly read through the letter itself.

Reluctant though we are to make any public comment on political matters, we believe that extraordinary circumstances surrounding the current election make it our duty to the country to express our views. The Confederacy, still newly born, is facing grave challenges and requires competent political leadership.

We agree with one another that John C. Breckinridge is by far the best choice to serve as the next chief executive of the Confederate States. His long defense of Southern rights in Washington City before the war, his gallant and effective service as an officer during the war, his successful representation of the Confederacy at the Toronto Peace Talks, and his outstanding tenure as Secretary of War all bear witness to his capacity to serve as president. His personality honor, sense of dignity, and unquestioned Christian piety all reveal the qualities of a true gentleman. Moreover, James Kemper is also a man of high achievement and outstanding personal character who could be trusted to assume the office of presidency if it ever became necessary.

While we acknowledge the patriotism and intelligence of General Pierre Gustave Toutant Beauregard and Senator Robert Toombs, and hope and expect that they will continue to serve the Confederacy well in the future, we cannot but express our considered view that Breckinridge and Kemper are the men the Confederacy need at the head of their government at this crucial time.

Your obedient servants,
General Robert E. Lee and General Joseph E. Johnston

"Cowards!" Toombs spat. He disdainfully dropped the newspaper onto the floor and quickly downed a large portion of his whiskey in a single gulp. "Fools! Two idiots who were lucky enough to win some battles against the Yankees and now they think they're so smart. Who are they to tell anybody that Breckinridge would be better than me, eh?"

Rage filled him, fueled by liquor. He recalled that he was now almost done with his third whiskey and made the decision that he would certainly have a fourth now. He was so angry at this latest development that he felt entitled to another drink. The pressures of being effectively in charge of the Beauregard campaign and the States' Rights Party as a whole were bad enough, but to have the two greatest heroes in the Confederacy come down against him just as the very moment when success seemed in his grasp was infuriating. He swore to himself at that moment that he would make them pay.

"Senator Toombs, do you have any reaction?"

"Reaction? I'll tell you my reaction. Lee and Johnston are two worthless fools who have no more business talking about politics than do the pigs down on my plantation. Everyone thinks that they're these great heroes. They're not heroes. I served under both of them during the war and let me tell you this. Neither of them had a clue what they were doing. Fools, I tell you! Fools!"

He finished his whiskey, loudly smacked the glass down on the bar and ordered another. Some of the reporters glanced at one another with raised eyebrows and ambiguous, while others were frantically scribbling away, determined to get down every word Toombs was saying. Toombs, dulled by alcohol, could only hazily sense the feeling of urgency and expectation that had suddenly seized the journalists.

"You say that neither Lee nor Johnston knew what they were doing," one reporter said. "Could you elaborate on that?"

"I could elaborate on that all the rest of this damn day! All the rest of this damn week, for that matter. Look, you people write about Lee and Johnston as if they are great generals. They are not great generals. They got lucky once or twice, perhaps, but honestly the war would have been won a lot more quickly and easily if somebody like me had been in command, rather than stuffy West Pointers like them!"

"I'm sorry, Senator," one reporter said. "Are you saying that you think you would have been a better general than either Lee or Johnston?"

"Damn right I am!" He turned and looked at the barkeeper. "Where's that whiskey I ordered?"

The man leaned over the bar and whispered to Toombs. "Sir, you've already had three. Since you're talking to reporters, I thought you might want to..."

"Give me another whiskey and give it to me now!" Toombs said harshly, fire in his eyes. Reluctantly, the man poured another drink, pushed it across the bar towards Toombs, and then retreated out of sight.

"Senator Toombs, how do you think these comments by General Lee and General Johnston will impact the election?" a reporter from Mississippi asked.

"They won't," Toombs said firmly. He could sense that the whiskey was impacting his judgement and tried to tell himself to remain calm. Too late, the thought passed through his mind that Stephens had been right and he should have minimized his liquor consumption until the election was over. There was nothing to be done about that now, though. It was in his bloodstream and filling his mind, combining with the anger and jealousy he felt towards Lee and Johnston. He could no more control what he was saying than he could have controlled the movements of a wild horse.

Toombs felt himself to be a great man, but felt that the Southern people had never fully appreciated him. The adulation in which the people held Lee and Johnston grated on him enormously. Why should they achieve such reverence, but not him? After all, he had been pushing secession with all his might while the two Virginians had been debating whether or not to remain loyal to the Union.

"Why would anyone listen to these two old fools?" Toombs asked, unaware that his words were now becoming slurred. "Just two damn old fools, if you ask me. Would have been better if they had taken Lincoln's offer to lead the Yankee armies. Don't raise your eyebrows at me. I'm being completely serious here. You know what those people learn at West Point? Yankee ways, that's what! Lee and Johnston are just Yankees, really. I frankly wonder if they're disappointed that we won the war."

The reporters were frantically scribbling away, taking down every word Toombs was saying. One of them, a South Carolinian he knew to be sympathetic to the States' Rights Party, stopped writing and spoke with concern in his voice.

"Senator Toombs, you've obviously had a long day and must be very tired. Perhaps you'd like to retire to your room and we can resume our discussions in the morning?"

"The hell you say! Look, if Lee and Johnston get to have their say in the papers, I should get to have mine, right? No, I'll be here at the bar all night. You people can ask me anything you want and I'll tell you exactly what I think."

So it went on for another hour. The bartender refused to serve Toombs a fifth whiskey, which enraged him and caused him to yell at the man for nearly five minutes. Some of the reporters left, anxious to get their copy to the printers as quickly as possible. Eventually, his words now almost impossible to understand, Toombs drifted off to sleep on his barstool. The remaining reporters then departed and the hotel owner sent a slave to try to wake the vice presidential nominee and escort him up to his room.

November 5, Noon
Waco, Texas

McFadden stood in line, waiting his turn like everyone else. At Annie's insistence, he was wearing his best suit, the one which he wore whenever they were able to go to church. When he had arrived in the courthouse square where the voting was to take place, many people offered him their place so as to allow him to get to the front more quickly, but he had refused. Although he was reasonably confident that he was about to be elected to the state legislature, he did not want the holding of an important public office to go to his head. He wanted to continue to see himself as an ordinary citizen like everyone else and that meant taking his place at the end of the line.

Besides which, even as the citizens of Granbury County were lining up to cast their votes, the election campaign was not over. If McFadden were seen passing to the front of the line, Roden's people would immediately begin shouting that he was disrespecting the other men, hoping thereby to sway a few men at the last minute.

Four tables were set up on the western edge of the square. Wallace had arranged matters very carefully to ensure that the voting went off without a hitch and that neither side would have cause for complaints. At each table were clerks sent north from Travis County, as Wallace has determined that the Granbury County officials were loyal to Roden and could not be trusted. The clerks accepted the voting tickets of each voter after determining that their names were on the rolls. Overseeing the process at each table were four men, two chosen by Roden and the other two by the Association. Wallace himself strode back and forth behind the tables, his careful eye not missing a thing. The night before, the Texas Ranger had paid for posters to be put up around town informing people that he would not tolerate the carrying of firearms into the town square while voting was in process.

McFadden chatted a bit with the people in line nearest to him, but was too overcome by what was happening to be able to talk much. Many of the people crowding into the square, hopefully a majority of them, were voting for him. Their ballots were a democratic expression of their confidence in him, their expectation that he would be a good state representative, and their belief in him as a good and decent man.

This thought generated a sea of emotions within McFadden. Before Annie had come into his life, he had been a creature of violence and anger. He had always avoided responsibility of any kind, declining promotion to lieutenant several times until Patrick Cleburne essentially forced him to accept it. When he came home from the war, somewhat famous for his capture of General Thomas at the Battle of Atlanta, he was surprised that so many people in the community looked to him for leadership and guidance, for he had never thought of himself as a person of any trustworthiness. In becoming a man in whom people could have trust and confidence, he had Annie to thank.

Since the land auction so many months before, he had gradually felt his destiny being taken out of his hands, as if he were an actor in a play rather than a person in control of his own life. He was not upset about this and it would not would have mattered if he had been. The closer he came towards winning the election, the more deeply he felt the responsibility that would soon rest on his shoulders. Whatever duty his fellow citizens felt proper to bestow upon him, McFadden was determined to do it to the very best of his ability.

He glanced down at the ticket in his hand, a narrow piece of paper. Thousands had been printed for distribution to the voters of Granbury County by the Association and McFadden was sure that Roden and his people had done exactly the same. Along the top were the names of the Texans chosen as the slate for the Electoral College by the Breckinridge campaign, men who had sworn to cast their votes for John Breckinridge for president and James Kemper for vice president when they convened in Richmond in a few months. Below them was the name of a candidate for Congress aligned with Breckinridge and, below that, was McFadden's own name marked for the state representative slot. Seeing his name on the ballot still seemed strange.

Just over an hour after he got into the line, he finally arrived the voting table. A few people around him applauded, though not loudly. The look on the Roden men standing behind the table was sour, while his two supporters were positively beaming.

"Voting today, are we, McFadden?" Wallace asked with a grin.

"I am," he replied. "Seems a good day for it, no?"

He held the ticket in his hand. He wrote his name at the bottom, under the eyes of the clerk, who then crossed the name off of the voter roll. It was then a simple matter to drop it into the ballot box, yet he found it strangely difficult to do so. He stood there for a moment, uncertain, wondering if it was proper to vote for himself. He chided himself for being absurd and slipped the ticket into the slot. He immediately felt a profound sense of relief. He had voted, he had done his own civic duty, and now it was simply a matter of waiting until the votes were counted and the result made known.

Wallace had told him the night before how that would be done. At five o'clock, the boxes would be sealed and no more votes would be allowed. If anyone were still waiting in line to vote, they would be out of luck. The boxes would be taken to a secure location that Wallace had not revealed and the votes would be counted by the clerks from Travis County. Armed guards would be posted at the doors to prevent any possible interference. With any luck, the counting would be done by about seven or eight o'clock, be certified by the clerks, and then telegraphed to Austin.

Having cast his vote, McFadden left the table and began walking towards Flynn's Alehouse. Friends and supporters still waiting in line called out greetings to him, to which he raised his hat. He noticed a few, however, trying to get his attention and pointing into the middle of one of the other voting lines. Looking in the indicated direction, McFadden saw Judge Roden waiting to vote, his arms folded across his chest, a look of intense anger on his face. Their eyes met for a few moments, until Roden looked away.

He left the square and walked the short distance to Flynn's Alehouse. Annie and Thaddeus were supposed to meet him there for the victory celebration, as was Collett, who had voted earlier in the day. As he got closer, he could already hear banjo and fiddle music and hear loud laughter and happy conversation. Much of it, no doubt, was fueled by the whiskey and beer freely flowing from the bar. When he entered, he was not surprised to see dozens of his friends and supporters crowding every table, drinks in hand. Annie was talking with several women at one table, while Thaddeus was standing on another on the other side of the place, loudly singing one of the Scottish songs he had been taught.

He did not purchase an ale for himself at any point during the next few hours. Men argued fiercely with one another over who should have the honor of buying McFadden his next drink. Everyone who spoke to him told him that the election was certainly in the bag, for they had voted for him, everyone they knew had voted for him, and they didn't know anybody who had voted for Roden. Everyone seemed optimistic, almost as if the election results had already been announced.

Hours passed. After five o'clock, several people came running into the alehouse to say that Wallace had shut the voting down on schedule, leaving several disappointed people waiting in line. The boxes had been secured and loaded onto a cart, soon to be taken away to be counted. McFadden figured that it would only be two hours, three at the most, before he received news that he had won the election.

He allowed himself to think briefly about the rest of the country. All across the Confederacy, he knew, scenes more or less identical to what he had seen in the courthouse square were playing out. Despite having all his attention understandably fixated on his own race, McFadden was nervous about the outcome of the presidential race. He badly wanted Breckinridge to win and was worried that a Beauregard victory would lead the Confederacy in a difficult direction. Moreover, since he had run against the SRP in Granbury County as an avowed Breckinridge man, McFadden knew it would make his life much easier if Breckinridge were the next president.

The local newspapers, of course, had reported the dramatic disclosure that Robert E. Lee and Joseph E. Johnston had endorsed Breckinridge a few days before. That had persuaded many people in Waco, who had previously been inclined to cast their state legislative vote for McFadden but their presidential vote for Beauregard, to switch their support to Breckinridge. He couldn't know how widespread this feeling was, though. Based on what he had read in the papers, the outcome of the presidential race in Texas was balanced on a knife's edge.

When six o'clock came, Flynn lit the wood in the fireplace to replace the fading sunlight and ward off the coming chill. The conversation seemed to diminish a bit and people increasingly glanced at the clock, wondering how long it would be before word of the official results came in. McFadden felt a steadily increasing tightness in his stomach. Glancing about, he could see an apprehensive expression on the face of his wife. The waiting was unbearable.

It was at this point that shouting was heard from somewhere outside, distant but clearly coming closer.

"Quickly!" the voice cried. "To arms! To the square! Quickly!"

The men rose from the tables almost as one and scrambled out the front door, leaving their womenfolk behind. McFadden was one of the first ones onto the street. He saw Robert Brown, a man whose name he knew but nothing else, running down the street waving his arms.

"What is it?" McFadden yelled. "What's happened?"

"Roden's men shot Wallace and ran off with the ballot boxes!"

"What?" Collett cried, incredulous.

"They shot Wallace! Hit him in the chest, I think. Then they stole the cart the ballot boxes had been loaded on and drove off with them!"

"Arm yourselves!" The cry went up from many men at the same time and generated a confused rush to and fro across the street as men sought weapons.

"Come on!" McFadden called to Collett. The two men dashed down the street towards the square. Glancing back over his shoulder for a moment, he caught a glimpse of Annie standing in front of the alehouse door, Thaddeus in her arms, watching him go. There was no time to worry about her now, but he was confident she could take care of herself and their child without any help from him.

They reached the courthouse square minutes later. Dozens of armed men were milling about, angry and confused. Shouted questions brought back shouted responses, confirming the earlier claim that Wallace had been shot and Roden's men had absconded with the ballot boxes. There was a cluster of people off to one side. McFadden and Collett went over to them and found that they were standing around Wallace, who was lying on the ground in obvious pain. A doctor was tying a large white cloth around his left shoulder.

"Wallace!" McFadden said, kneeling down beside him. "What happened?"

"Bastards got the drop on me, just as we were about to take the wagon away. Dammit! First time since I was a kid that I let someone get the drop on me. Stupid, stupid, stupid."

McFadden looked at the doctor, wordlessly asking a question.

Wallace replied first. "Oh, I just need to be patched up a bit. Not the first time I got shot, you know. Lost count of the number, actually. Don't worry yourself, McFadden. No lowlife like Lucius Roden is going to kill the likes of Bigfoot Wallace."

"He shot you himself?" Collett asked.

"No," Wallace said, grimacing in pain. "No, it was that Walker bastard. But it might as well have been Roden, you know? His people are like his fingers. Just parts of him, really. But we have to find those ballot boxes!"

"Where would he have taken them?"

"We should talk about this later," the doctor said. "We need to get Mr. Wallace somewhere more comfortable."

"No!" Wallace said. "This is more important! We've got to find the boxes."

"Why wouldn't he just burn them?" Collett asked. "Or toss them in the river or something like that?"

"Destroying the ballots won't help. We'd just rerun the election and he knows that. No, he needs to alter the ballots, take out the votes against him and leave the votes for him. Then get them down to Austin to be certified before we get a chance to do anything about it."

"How could he get away with that?" McFadden asked. "Everyone in Waco either already knows what he's done or will know in the next few minutes. If he sends the results down to Austin, everyone will know they're fake."

"They might not care, if the SRP wins the election. People always want to line up with the winners, McFadden. If we're looking at an SRP president, an SRP Congress, and an SRP legislature, they might overlook what's happened here. Hell, they've been overlooking everything else Roden has been doing, until I came here, didn't they?"

McFadden heard something out of the ordinary and turned to see a group of armed men entering the square from the direction of Flynn's Alehouse, some carrying torches. To a man, they were veterans and supporters of his. It looked little different from a column of infantry marching in loose formation, something he had seen a thousand times during the war. The men walked directly towards him, stopping only a few yards away.

"What do you want us to do, sir?" one of the men at the head of the column asked.

"Form yourselves into groups of ten men each!" McFadden said loudly. "We have to comb through the entire town, and the surrounding countryside, to find where they have taken the ballot boxes. I know all of you. I went through the war with a lot of you. We've worked hard these last few months to take our town and our county back from Judge Roden. Let's not let him steal it away from us, all right?"

There was a roar of approval, with men raising their Enfield rifles over their heads and shaking them in a way that reminded McFadden of Crusader knights.

"All of you are deputized," Wallace said weakly, gesturing in the general direction of the crowd. "All of you. Texas Ranger deputies. You hear?"

"We hear you, Wallace," Collett said. "Now, let's get to it, men."

November 5, Night
Mechanic's Hall, Richmond, Virginia

It was almost midnight, yet Breckinridge was not even slightly sleepy. He was exhausted, it was true, but nervous energy continued to course through him and keep him fully awake, helped by cup after cup of coffee. The telegraph office in Mechanic's Hall had been turned into his de facto campaign headquarters, with the machines clicking away every few minutes to bring in election returns from across the length and breadth of the Confederacy.

Aside from the clicking of the telegraphs, it was almost silent in the room, despite the presence of more than a dozen people. President Davis sat sternly in a chair facing one of the telegraph machines, his back as erect as an ironing board, constantly snatching the scribbled paper out of the operator's hands and reading it to himself before announcing to the room what news it contained. Secretary Trenholm paced back and forth, his arms crossed across his chest, a grim expression on his face. Other supporters, mainly members of Congress and government officials, waited quietly. Secretary Miles was also there, having returned from his speaking tour of Tennessee. The room was filled with cigar smoke as nervous men went through one stogie after another.

Varina Davis and Mary Breckinridge, the outgoing First Lady and the woman whom everyone hoped would be the incoming one, sat quietly on a sofa that had been brought into the room for them. They quietly whispered to one another every few minutes, but otherwise remained silent and waited for news with the same fixation as the men. His ever-loyal aide Wilson was also present, quietly moving among the others to make sure coffee cups were filled and everyone had everything they needed.

Senator Hill and Congressman Gordon were not present, having returned to Georgia to cast their votes and speak at some last minute campaign rallies. Neither was Postmaster Reagan, who had remained in Austin. Yet they seemed almost present in the room, for some of the telegrams arriving were coming directly from them.

As much as he missed his most important Georgian and Texan supporters, who had been such an important part of his presidential campaign, Breckinridge wished most of all that he could speak to Benjamin. He had heard nothing from the former Secretary of State since he left for New Orleans more than a month before. Still, it had been the Louisiana Jew who pushed him into running for president in the first place and who had essentially organized the campaign from absolutely nothing. If Breckinridge won the contest, Benjamin would deserve much of the credit.

His chances of actually winning, seemingly nonexistent only a week before, now appeared much higher. The moment that the endorsement of Lee and Johnston had hit the newspapers, Breckinridge had begun to hope once again that he might have a chance. It was impossible to overestimate the weight of the opinion of those two extraordinary men. It had been their victories which had secured the independence of the Confederacy. Their virtuous and honorable personal characters, personifying everything that the aristocratic South liked to imagine itself to be, only added to their mystique with the people. When Lee and Johnston spoke, the people would listen.

Only slightly less important than the endorsement of the Virginia generals had been the story that hit newspapers all across the South the next day. Robert Toombs, in a rambling and apparently incoherent interview with reporters at the Spottswood Hotel bar, had denounced Lee and Johnston in vicious terms. Reading between the lines, Breckinridge was certain that the vice presidential nominee had been three sheets to the wind. Launching a personal attack against the Confederacy's two greatest heroes was akin to walking into a Baptist Church and denouncing Jesus Christ. Breckinridge could only hope that the news would disseminate across the country in time to affect voting. Given the miracle of telegraphy, there was a chance that it might.

The two related events had seemingly changed everything on the very eve of the election. The old electoral calculus that revolved around winning Virginia, North Carolina, Tennessee, and one or two other states had reasserted itself. Breckinridge tried not to become excited, for he did not want to indulge in false hope. A week earlier, he had all but accepted defeat. To now go through the emotional turmoil of again thinking he might win and then to be defeated after all would make an already terrible blow even worse.

He remembered the night in 1860 when it had quickly become clear that he had lost the 1860 election and was not going to become President of the United States. That had been easy to accept, for he had never wanted the nomination in the first place and had not expected to win. Moreover, he was consumed with worry that the election of Abraham Lincoln would lead to secession and war, as indeed turned out to be the case. His own political career had been the least of his worries.

It was very different tonight. He was close to achieving a goal that many men would give anything to obtain. If he were rejected by the voters, the very people he had fought for during the war, pain would be inflicted on his spirit that would not soon fade. He also felt that the election of the other party would spell doom for the future of the country he had striven to create. As he paced the floor of the telegraph office, he knew he was living through the most important night of his life.

"What news?" he asked loudly, addressing the whole room. "Any new returns?"

"Not in the last fifteen minutes," Kemper said. There was a calmness in his voice, yet also a hint of exasperation. Breckinridge understood, for it was foolish to think that they wouldn't have told him of any new information the moment it arrived.

Almost as soon as Kemper had spoken, however, the machine in front of Davis began clicking. The operator hurriedly jotted down what was being received and handed it over to the outgoing president. Breckinridge momentarily wondered what it was like to be one of the telegraph operators, always privileged to have the newest information before giving it over to those in power.

Davis shook his head. "A return from Alabama," he said glumly. "We have won Etowah County by three hundred votes."

"Isn't that a good thing?" Mary Breckinridge asked from the sofa. "You sound disappointed."

"It's bad news, I'm afraid, my dear," Breckinridge replied to his wife. "Etowah County is in the northern part of the state, where we expected to have the most support. If we were to have a chance at beating the SRP in Alabama, we would need to win such counties by a much heavier margin in order to counteract the success they are having in the southern and central parts of the state."

"I see," she replied.

"And it follows the pattern we have been seeing all night. We win the northern counties by smaller majorities than the SRP are winning the central and southern counties, which have larger populations anyway." He shook his head. "I'm afraid Alabama is slipping away from us."

Davis spoke next. "So, as South Carolina and Louisiana have already come down against us, if we add Alabama to the Beauregard count, that gives them twenty-three electoral votes. They're already almost halfway to victory."

"What's the latest count in Virginia?" Trenholm asked.

Kemper glanced down at his notes. "We are at about seventy-two thousand and the SRP is at seventy thousand. Very tight. Most of the counties that still haven't reported are either in the Shenandoah Valley or in the southern part of the state. The former will back us, but I am less sure about the latter."

"I have a suggestion," Varina Davis said pleasantly. "Wouldn't it be better if we all went home and went to sleep, then find out who won when we wake up in the morning?"

This comment generated laughter throughout the room, as the First Lady had no doubt intended. Breckinridge smiled, for he had always liked Varina and appreciated her ability to put people at ease. He looked forward to seeing how Mary would fare as First Lady of the Confederacy, but finding out first required that he win the election.

"What's the status of North Carolina?" Breckinridge asked.

"We're very narrowly behind at the moment," Kemper replied. "Thirty-five thousand to thirty-six thousand, or thereabouts. We were ahead just half an hour ago. That one will be very close, indeed."

"And Tennessee?" Miles asked.

"We're ahead, but by less than a thousand votes."

Breckinridge inhaled deeply and nodded. The three states he absolutely had to win were effectively even. He had as good a chance of losing each of them as he had of winning, which was not a good place to be. And even if he won Tennessee, North Carolina, and Virginia, he would still be nine electoral votes short of the forty-eight required for a victory. Those nine electoral votes would have to come from somewhere.

He turned to Wilson and spoke quietly. "Get me a drink, James. Wine, not whiskey."

"Sorry, sir," Wilson replied. "You told me earlier than you wouldn't want any alcohol."

"I know. Forget what I said earlier."

"Right away, sir." Wilson hurried out of the room.

"When is the last time we heard from Hill and Gordon?" Breckinridge asked.

"About an hour ago," Trenholm said. "According to their last message, we were behind by ten thousand votes."

"How many counties left to report?"

Trenholm pursed his lips. "Less than a third. And some of them are from the southern counties."

Breckinridge nodded. Georgia was much like Alabama, in that Breckinridge had stronger support in the more sparsely populated northern counties than he did in the southern counties, where the large plantations were to be found. As time went on, he began to feel that Georgia, too, was slipping out of his hands. This was not especially surprising, as it was the home state of Robert Toombs, but this made the fact only slightly less disappointing. It was hard to accept that the hard work of Hill, Gordon, and his other Georgian supporters had been for nothing, but that was the nature of politics.

One of the telegraph machines began clicking away again, causing all the quiet conversation to cease for a moment. The operator scribbled the words down and handed the paper to Trenholm.

"We have won Augusta County in the Shenandoah Valley by nearly eight hundred votes. That pushes us up in Virginia. We're now three thousand votes ahead. I'm going to go ahead and say that I think we will win the Old Dominion tonight."

"You've been saying that for weeks," Mary Breckinridge observed dryly.

"Yes, but what we've said up to the moment the votes are cast doesn't matter. Now, we're counting the ballots. And based on what we're seeing, I think we're going to win Virginia." He turned to Kemper. "We're talking about your state, James. Do you agree?"

"If a few more counties vote the same way as Augusta, then I'll be willing to agree with you. Until then, I'm withholding judgement."

"Suit yourself, my friend."

Wilson returned to the room with glasses and a few bottles of Spanish red wine, as well as an ice bucket. Within a few moments, he was pouring servings to almost everyone in the room. Rather to Breckinridge's surprise, Wilson managed to avoid spilling a single drop, leading to a quip that perhaps he should be a waiter rather than an aide to the Secretary of War. He held up one bottle for Breckinridge to see, thicker and heavier than the others.

"I thought I'd bring some champagne, sir. To be opened when you're declared the winner."

"Thank you, James," Breckinridge replied. "Alas, it might be sometime tomorrow before we have a chance to open it."

"I'll put it on ice until then, sir." He pushed the champagne bottle into the ice bucket.

"Telegram from Memphis," Davis said, reading quickly through the latest message. "Returns have come in from several western counties, which seem to be splitting their votes between us and Beauregard."

"That's good news," Trenholm said. "Since we're winning the eastern part of the state quite handily, splitting the vote in western Tennessee is as good as winning them."

"We're only running even with Beauregard in the western part of the state thanks to Rhett," Kemper pointed out. "In the counties we are winning, the margin of victory is smaller than the total number of votes Rhett is receiving, small though it might be. We can assume that those voters would be supporting Beauregard were Rhett himself not in the race."

Breckinridge chuckled. "If we win Tennessee, I will have to confront the supreme irony of giving my sincere thanks to Robert Rhett, a man I despise."

"Whatever the reason is, Virginia and Tennessee are looking promising," Miles said. "If we can win them and North Carolina, we have a chance."

Several minutes of silence followed, with people pacing and forth and seeming to concentrate on their wine. Varina Davis and Mary Breckinridge had a quiet and somewhat forced conversation about the progress a mutual friend of theirs was making on the remodeling of her house, which was ignored by the men. Breckinridge sensed that even the two ladies were simply talking to fill the silence.

Another telegram arrived. Davis read through it, frowned, and sighed deeply. "I am ashamed to say that my own state of Mississippi has moved irrevocably into the Beauregard camp. The latest returns show us down by five thousand votes. There's no way that can be overcome, even if the remaining counties favor us strongly."

"Which they won't," Miles said dejectedly. "Mississippi is lost to us."

Breckinridge did the math in his head yet again. South Carolina, Louisiana, Mississippi, and Alabama together had thirty electoral votes, only eighteen shy of the forty-eight needed for victory. Georgia now appeared almost certain to fall into the SRP column as well. If it did, its twelve electoral votes would bring Beauregard and Toombs to the brink of winning the prize. He took a larger than normal sip of the red wine in his hand, almost draining the cup.

Wilson was looking out the window. "There's a crowd forming outside," he said matter-of-factly.

Breckinridge and some of the others came to see. Several dozen people, perhaps as many as a hundred, were gathering together in the grass at the foot of the building. Some were holding pro-Breckinridge signs and the mood appeared friendly. Word must have spread through the city that Breckinridge and Kemper were following the returns at the Executive Office Building.

"Should I go out and speak to them?" Breckinridge asked the room.

"I'd wait," Davis advised. "There's nothing to say to them so long as the outcome is in doubt. But I'd start thinking about what you want to say."

Breckinridge chuckled slightly. "Hard to do when I have no idea whether I will win or lose."

"Unfortunately, the telegram I hold in my hand would seem to lend credence to the latter possibility," Trenholm said, his eyes reading through the latest report. "All Florida counties have now reported. Beauregard has just over seven thousand votes, while we came out with only about five thousand five hundred. Florida's in the bag for the SRP."

"Damn," Breckinridge said, gritting his teeth. With Florida's three electoral votes, the total for the other side now was at thirty-three. If he counted Georgia in the SRP column, it was really at forty-five, just three shy of victory. By contrast, although he was feeling better about Virginia and Tennessee, he could not conclusively count on any electoral votes for himself yet. As his mind did the math, he conceded that he was almost certainly about to be defeated. The endorsement of Lee and Johnston, he reflected sadly, had not had the impact for which he had been hoping.

Several minutes of total silence passed and the telegraph machines remained quiet. Breckinridge folded his arms across his chest and paced back and forth continually. He knew it was irrational, but he kept trying to think of some way in which he could still change the course of events. It was absurd, clearly. All the votes had been cast and only the counting remained to be done. His destiny was entirely out of his hands, assuming that it had ever been in his hands to begin with,

"Wilson, will you do something for me?" Breckinridge asked.

"Of course, sir. What is it?"

"Could you go outside and suggest that the crowd return to their homes? Tell them that it will likely be several hours before the result is firmly known and that I do not want them to risk their health by waiting in the cold."

"Very well, sir," Wilson replied. He quickly disappeared out the door.

"What word from the Trans-Mississippi?" Breckinridge asked the room. "We haven't had any returns yet from Texas or Arkansas?"

"About half the counties from Arkansas have reported," Trenholm replied. "We're ahead as it stands, but not by much."

"And Texas?"

"No returns yet. Reagan has sent us a few messages from Austin, but only to tell us that voting seems to have ended and he is awaiting results."

"Can we send him a message?"

Trenholm looked surprised. "Yes, we can, John. Anytime you want."

"Tell him that the moment he receives word of any county's returns, he is to inform us immediately, before he does anything else. Understood?"

"Of course, John."

It was a stupid thing to ask, Breckinridge knew, for Reagan would obviously do this anyway. Yet Breckinridge felt a burning need to do something, anything, other than simply wait. Sending an utterly useless message to a friend seemed as good a thing to do as any.

The machines began clicking again. Davis, who had scarcely gotten out of his chair at any point over the previous few hours, immediately snatched the paper out of the operator's hand.

"It's from Gordon in Atlanta," Davis began. He shook his head as he read through the message. "Returns from the southern counties are very unfavorable to us. We're losing by somewhat more than we expected."

"Here, let me see," Trenholm said, taking the paper from Davis's hand. He looked intently at it, then scribbled on scratch paper of his own. "That's close to three-quarters of the counties reporting. We're too far behind. Georgia goes to Beauregard."

There were groans of disappointment throughout the room. In response to the news, Varina Davis and Mary Breckinridge loudly and ostentatiously asked Wilson to pour them more wine, which generated some much-needed laughter. The wine was still being poured when the telegraph machine began clicking once again. Davis again read through the message the moment the operator had scribbled it down.

"More Virginia returns. We appear to be leading strongly in the southwestern counties. That's more than four fifths of the counties reporting and we are leading the state by eighty-five thousand to eighty thousand. I think we can definitely call Virginia for us."

All eyes turned to Breckinridge, who paused for just a moment before nodding his agreement. The room erupted into cheers and applause, shattering what had been a gloomy atmosphere. Breckinridge was unable to suppress a slight smile, but he was under no illusions that the situation had changed. Although he could now count Virginia's fifteen electoral in his column, those were the only electoral votes he could depend on in the face of the forty-five Beauregard had garnered.

"The first returns from Texas," Davis announced, as he read through yet another message from the telegraph machine. "Counties in the eastern part of the state. Looks like Beauregard is slightly ahead."

"That is not good," Mary said.

"It's too early to draw any conclusions," Davis replied.

Wilson came back into the room. "They won't leave, sir," he said to Breckinridge. "They say that they are in this with you until the end and that they'll go home only when they know that you've either won or lost."

"Rather like us, then," Miles said.

"Can we do anything for them?" Breckinridge asked. "Perhaps brew enough coffee to distribute to them?"

"I will see, sir," Wilson said, disappearing out of the room again.

At that moment, Breckinridge decided that he would keep Wilson on his staff in the event that he won the election and became president. The man was clumsy and often foolish, but his heart was always in the right place and Breckinridge knew he could always count on his loyalty. It probably wouldn't matter, though, since it still seemed quite unlikely that he would win.

The thought was still passing through his mind when the machines began clicking again. Davis could scarcely keep the excitement out of his voice.

"Looks like almost all the Arkansas counties have reported, but we're only just now getting the word out of Little Rock. We're ahead by twenty-six thousand to twenty-four thousand, with only a few counties left to report. I think we can claim the state!"

"That advances us to nineteen electoral votes, doesn't it?" Mary Breckinridge asked.

"It does, my love," Breckinridge replied. "In other words, we remain far behind. My own feeling is that this will be but a consolation prize."

"Cheer up, John," Miles said emphatically. "North Carolina and Tennessee are within our grasp. If we win them, that will push us to forty-three votes at a stroke. Forty-three to forty-five, with Texas still undecided."

Breckinridge winced slightly. He did not like the fact that Miles was in the room, let alone that he had committed to making the odious man Secretary of State if he won. Breckinridge was able to distance himself enough from the election returns for a few moments to reflect on the dangers and advantages that would result from the shady and squalid deal he had made with Miles. He had gained silence about his double-dealing in Toronto and support from at least some of the Fire-Eaters, but would the price be worth it? He was not comfortable with the idea that he had made a pact with the devil.

He could not deny that Miles spoke the truth, though. Now that he could count Virginia and Arkansas in his column, if he could win Tennessee and North Carolina, everything would come down to Texas.

Another hour passed and this scenario increasingly seemed likely to come to pass. Counties in western and central Tennessee generally split their votes between Breckinridge and Beauregard, while the eastern counties continued to strongly support Breckinridge. He knew he would face criticism for this after the election was over, for eastern Tennessee was generally Unionist and not friendly to slavery. That was a problem for another time. For now, he only wanted to win and was willing to take whatever votes he could get.

North Carolina, too, seemed to slowly turn in Breckinridge's direction. Results from several counties in the central part of the state came in, in which Breckinridge led by a hundred or so votes each. Taken together, this pushed him into a narrow lead. The western counties, more remote and mountainous, did not report as quickly, but Breckinridge had a consistent lead in all of them. As with eastern Tennessee, they were less dominated by the slave-owning planter class that formed the bulk of Beauregard's support.

"What news from Texas?" Breckinridge asked after several minutes of near silence.

"Still neck and neck," Davis replied.

Breckinridge looked at the clock. It was almost two o'clock in the morning. Two of his congressional supporters, who had indulged in rather more wine than the others, had fallen asleep on a sofa, one leaning against the other as if they were a married couple. The sound of their snoring infused the room with a palpable sense of exhaustion.

Breckinridge walked up to his wife. "Why don't you return home, love? I'm sure you're tired."

She snorted in amused contempt. "John, if you think I'm leaving a minute before you do, you have lost your mind. You and I are in this together and I'll be by your side until the final result is announced." She then leaned over and kissed him gently.

"Another return from Texas," Davis said. He shook his head. "Still basically a tie out there."

"This is excruciating!" Varina Davis said. "How much longer can this last?"

"Another hour or two at the least," Trenholm replied. "If any of the states are very close, however, we might not be able to verify the results for several days."

"Lord, help us," the First Lady said.

The telegraph machine clicked again and Davis took the message. "Tennessee. From Coffee County. You're up by five hundred votes there, John."

"That's outstanding," Trenholm replied. "That makes our margin in Tennessee now over two thousand votes. How many more counties are left to report there?"

"Less than a quarter, I think," Davis replied. "And lots of them are from the eastern part of the state. I think it's safe to say that Tennessee is in our column."

Amid the clapping, Breckinridge did the math in his head yet again. He now had thirty-one electoral votes to the SRP's forty-five. If nothing else, his fears of losing every single state had not come to pass and, if ultimately defeated, he could now bow out of the public limelight with some semblance of dignity. There still was a path for victory, however.

As the clock ticked past two forty-five in the morning, returns from Texas continued to slowly trickle in and paint a picture of a state split almost precisely down the middle, while Breckinridge continued to gain ground in North Carolina. A few of his supporters, saying that they were unable to remain awake any longer, made their apologies and departed. A small crowd of supporters remained outside.

"Maybe you could just wave at them from the window, sir," Wilson suggested. "No need to make a speech or anything."

"Not a bad idea, that," Davis seconded. "They've been waiting in the cold for many hours, after all."

Breckinridge went to the window and opened the blinds. He was surprised to find that the crowd was much larger than he had expected, as it numbered at least four hundred people. They cheered when they saw him, bringing a smile instantly to his face. Many called out his name. He waved down at them with a grand gesture, then stepped back from the window. He was not yet ready to speak to them and would not be until the results were known.

"Can we declare victory in North Carolina yet?" Mary asked. "We've been moving steadily up there for the last two hours and now have a thousand vote margin."

"There are still a quarter of the counties to report," Davis replied. "Those votes are more than enough to eliminate a thousand vote margin. We need to wait just a little longer."

Over the next fifteen minutes, returns arrived from four more North Carolina counties and two Texas counties. The former continued to pattern of a small but steady Breckinridge lead, while the latter had Breckinridge ahead in one country and Beauregard ahead in the other, each by a nearly identical amount.

"I think we can call North Carolina for us," Davis said. There was little joy in his voice, only exhaustion.

So now it was forty-three electoral votes for Breckinridge against forty-five for Beauregard, with only the six votes of Texas yet to be decided. Everything now hinged on the Lone Star State.

Varina Davis fell asleep on the sofa. Mary Breckinridge was obviously able to stay awake only through great effort. Davis remained seated, his back still ramrod straight in the chair, while Trenholm and Miles paced back and forth, waiting for the telltale clicking of the telegraph machine.

As they waited for the final verdict from Texas, Breckinridge realized two troubling things. First of all, if he won Texas and became president, the margins by which the SRP had triumphed in the Lower South meant that he would have lost the popular vote. He would be entering office even though more citizens had voted for Beauregard than had voted for him. Moreover, it was becoming clear that Congress was going to have an SRP majority, meaning that he could expect ferocious opposition to his policies from the legislative branch. He told himself that he could worry about this later, after his victory had been declared, but as time passed and fewer results came in from Texas, these two disquieting facts dominated his mind.

It was close to four o'clock in the morning when Davis, scratching away with a pencil, said, "Texas stands at thirty two thousand nine hundred and fourteen for Beauregard and thirty-two thousand eight hundred and twenty-seven for us, a margin of eight-seven votes."

"Eighty-seven votes!" Trenholm exclaimed. "To have an event of such massive importance separated by less than a hundred votes!"

"God is having a laugh at our expense, clearly," Breckinridge said. "How many counties remain to report?"

"I'm not sure," Davis said. "We have had no results for the last fifteen minutes. It might be over."

"Over?" Mary Breckinridge asked. "What do you mean by that?"

"I mean that the last Texas county might have already returned. I have quite lost track of how many we have."

"Is Reagan still at the office in Austin?" Breckinridge asked.

"I believe so," Davis replied.

"Wire him immediately. Ask him how many counties remain."

As Davis barked out a message to the telegraph operator, Breckinridge's mind swirled. Could he have failed to win by a margin of less than a hundred votes, in an election in which hundreds of thousands of people had cast ballots? Could the fate of the new-born Confederacy have been decided by such an insignificant margin? It seemed entirely unfair and he wanted to rail against fate for having mocked him so mercilessly, though he knew it would do no good.

"Reagan says that one county has yet to report. He says there's some sort of trouble there."

"Where?"

"Some godforsaken place called Granbury County."

November 6, Noon
United States Capitol Building, Washington City

As he waited in his office, Sumner read through the newspaper with deep interest. When the morning's edition of the *National Intelligencer* had gone to press, the outcome of the presidential election in the Confederacy had still been in doubt. Sumner had heard nothing since to suggest that this situation had changed. According to the story, Texas remained undeclared and neither side would have a majority without the six electoral votes of that state. The unresolved election was the talk of Washington, with almost everyone excitedly expounding on what they thought was going to happen.

Considering the Lowell trial and the Fenian Crisis, Sumner had not given much thought to the presidential election taking place in the Confederacy. It did not much matter to him who won. What he wanted to see were signs of political instability in the South, for he expected the rotten structure to eventually collapse upon itself. If a vigorous election could be successfully carried out, it would mean that such a downfall had been sadly delayed.

Strangely, though, he found himself hoping for a Beauregard victory. He had known Breckinridge slightly before the war, when the man had served as vice president, and knew him to be a man of integrity. That, in itself, made him dangerous. Throughout the years leading up to the war, Sumner had never understood why seemingly good and decent men, like Breckinridge or Robert E. Lee, could support so odious a cause. Their example gave the Confederacy the appearance of a moral foundation that it utterly didn't deserve. Better by far for the next administration of the Confederacy to be headed by a clown like Beauregard and a drunkard like Toombs.

The other major story in the paper dealt with the gubernatorial election in Ohio, which Salmon Chase appeared to have won decisively. This would disappoint those Republicans who wanted Seward to be their nominee in the 1868 presidential election, but Sumner considered it very good news. Chase had run on a principled abolitionist platform, supporting immediate passage of the constitutional amendment to finally abolish slavery in the United States. It was an open secret that he would seek the Republican nomination the following year and Sumner expected him to take a hard line against the Confederacy. He still was not sure whether he would back Chase or Seward.

Storey entered the room. "Sir, I'm told that he will begin soon. You might want to head over there."

Sumner nodded and rose from his desk. He folded the newspaper and placed it down carefully, for he wanted to finish the story later. He then strode out and through the Capitol. All around him, people were chattering urgently about the election in the South, entirely unaware that a political event of equal importance was about to unfold practically under their own feet. He crossed through the Rotunda, not bothering to look up and see the great dome and the fresco depicting George Washington in heaven, which he had seen thousands of times. Sumner crossed over into the side of the building where the House of Representatives held sway, noting only a few curious glances by people who wondered what he might be doing there. When they found out, Sumner thought with a slight grin, they would be astounded.

He climbed the stairs to the visitor galleries and took his seat as if he were an ordinary observer. Below him, the vast chamber of the House of Representatives was spread out. It had its own majesty, but was very different from the Senate Chamber. Everything seemed more crowded, noisy, and busy, with little of the stately elegance that characterized the other side of the Capitol.

Below, a representative named Andrew Rogers, a Democrat from New Jersey whom Sumner did not know, was speaking urgently. Sumner made himself concentrate on what the man was saying for a moment. It apparently involved the Mormon separatists in the Utah Territory and whether or not the federal government had the constitutional power to suppress writings that supported secession when there was not an actual rebellion going on. He hoped that Rogers would finish soon, so that the real action Sumner had come to see could then begin.

Rogers finished speaking. After a few moments in which the sounds of quiet chatter and shuffling of papers filled the chamber, Sumner glanced over to one particular seat and saw Congressman Logan rise up.

"For what purpose does the gentleman rise?" the Speaker of the House, Representative Samuel Marshall, asked tiredly.

Sumner watched as Logan took a deep breath and looked up at him in the visitor gallery for a long moment. The Illinois Democrat steadied himself, knowing that what he was about to say would define his political career, for better or for worse.

"Mr. Speaker, I rise to offer a resolution for the impeachment of President George Brinton McClellan."

There was a stunned gasp from every person in the vast chamber, followed by an instant and eerie silence. Even Sumner, who had known what Logan was going to say, couldn't help but feel astonished at what had just happened. Never before in the history of the republic had there been an attempt to impeach the

President of the United States. Logan seemed to fix his gaze at a point on his desk and did not glance around.

"The gentleman from Illinois is recognized," Speaker Marshall said carefully, his tone clearly betraying his strong disapproval of what Logan was doing.

"My resolution consists of two articles, which I shall proceed to read. Article One. That President McClellan did knowingly and willfully conspire to wage war against the United Kingdom of Britain and Ireland without the approval of Congress, in violation of Article One, Section Eight, of the United States Constitution, by illegally arming and equipping a military force and allowing it to use the territory of the United States for attacks upon British territory. Article Two. That President McClellan knowingly and willfully conspired to keep from Congress knowledge of military actions that brought the United States into danger of war with a sovereign power."

A congressman sitting in the center of the chamber, whom Sumner did not recognize, shot to his feet. "Logan, have you lost your mind?" he shouted. All around him, there was a chorus of concerned agreement. Marshall banged the gavel loudly several times, but for a moment it was no use. Several representatives close to Logan approached him and asked him urgent questions, clearly trying to get him to stop. He angrily shook his head and pointed back to their seats.

Sumner did not blame the other Democrats for being astonished and upset. Following his first meeting with Logan nearly two months before, Sumner had approached him several more times, slowly pushing him towards the idea of impeachment. When General Thomas moved against the Fenian bands and testified to Sumner's Senate Committee, putting the evidence out for all the world to see, Logan had finally agreed. There followed intense negotiations with reluctant Republican leaders, who promised Logan support in his reelection campaigns and the chairmanship of the Committee on Military Affairs whenever the Republicans regained control of the House of Representatives. For his part, Logan agreed to switch to the Republican Party the moment the outcome of the impeachment effort was determined.

It was a wild time, Sumner told himself. The war had inflicted such damage on the old political system that it was almost unrecognizable from what it had been before 1860. The Moderate and Radical factions of the Republican Party, led by Seward and Chase respectively, now looked so distant from one another that they might as well have been two different political parties. The Democrats, for their part, were aligning into pro-McClellan and anti-McClellan wings. What 1868 would bring, as McClellan prepared his effort to be reelected, was anyone's guess.

Sumner did not mind the chaos and disorder to which he was contributing. In fact, he welcomed it. The forces of reaction, which always held back progress towards the equality of man, thrived best in calm waters. Change only happened when the seas were turbulent and rough. If established norms and long-held precedents had to be shattered in the struggle against slavery, so be it.

He sat back in his chair and listened for the next hour as several Democrats rose to denounce Logan's measure and just as many Republicans rose to applaud it. It was refreshing to see a few Democrats offer measured support for the resolution, tempered by calls for its withdrawal if the president somehow

715

explained himself. Sumner smiled. It was going to be an interesting few days in the United States Congress.

November 8, Night
West of Waco, Texas

The sun had disappeared over the western horizon, but fingers of orange and yellow light still reached up and illuminated the clouds. McFadden and Collett moved quickly over the uneven ground, trailed by twenty armed men. A few hundred yards behind them, half a dozen young boys were watching the horses from which the group had just dismounted. Up ahead of them, two of their scouts were lying down on the crest of a small rise, peering intently at something on the other side. The group slowed down as it approached the scouts. McFadden and Collett waved their hands to tell the men to fan out on either side, just as if they had been deploying their men during the war.

It had taken two days for them to track down the path Roden's men had taken after they absconded with the ballot boxes. It had not been especially difficult, as Roden's men had little experience with this sort of thing and made no effort to cover their tracks. Some members of the Granbury County Association, by contrast, had served with Terry's Texas Rangers or had served as scouts in the previous year's campaign against the Comanches. They knew the business of reconnaissance. It had only taken as long as it had because Roden's men had kept on the move, never staying in one place for very long.

As his men fanned out, McFadden laid flat on the ground and crawled up to the point where the two scouts were situated. Below, spread out in the space of a dry riverbed, were seven men sitting around a campfire. Sitting among them, sipping almost continually from a flask, was Walker. Simply seeing the man caused a deep revulsion in McFadden. He liked to believe that every man had some core of goodness in him, but he could not bring himself to believe that about Walker.

Off to their right was the wagon, the ballot boxes still secure in its bed. It did not appear to McFadden that they had been tampered with, which was a good thing. Wallace had told him that Walker would not destroy the voting tickets but would fraudulently alter them to make it look like Roden had won the election. McFadden guessed that the need to keep moving had prevented them from doing so as yet. The horses were still hitched to the wagon and showed no signs of being cleaned or cared for.

He thought for a moment about Wallace, who had insisted on coming along despite his gunshot wound and was waiting in the back with the horse-holding team. McFadden admired and was jealous of the man's supreme self-confidence and was immensely grateful to him for what he had done since arriving in the county. He represented, in McFadden's mind, the ideal servant of the people, with Roden as his antithesis. He hoped that he would find a way to stay in touch with Wallace when all of this was over.

Wallace had said that Walker had to be taken alive and that he should not be shot under any circumstances. McFadden was curious as to why these instructions were so explicit and he sensed that Wallace had some particular interest in Walker, but he had decided not to press the point. There were, after all, more important things to worry about.

As for Roden, he had been arrested by some of the men Wallace had deputized immediately after the theft of the ballot boxes, charged with conspiracy to commit election fraud. He had protested that his arrest was illegal and threatened retaliation against anyone who cooperated with Wallace, but nobody paid him any attention. His legitimacy had been fading in the minds of the people throughout the election campaign and had almost entirely vanished when the courthouse fire happened. Once McFadden and Collett organized the Association, people began looking to it, and not the county government, as the true authority in the area. In a sense, the arrest of Roden had only made plain what had already been true.

McFadden surveyed the scene below him. It was clear that Walker, and probably some of the other men, were drunk. They were probably also exhausted, having had little sleep over the past two days as they tried to outrun their pursuers. Their failure to post any kind of guard or picket was an inexcusable case of negligence that would have gotten any officer cashiered during the war. McFadden was reasonably sure that Walker had some sort of military experience, yet his inability to grasp something as basic as posting a guard was telling.

"We can take them without shooting," Collett whispered. "Look, they're all tired. If we can just get around them so that they can't get away, then shout down for them to give up, they'll throw down their weapons. Just like that time we took that scouting party of Yankees a couple of days before Chickamauga, remember?"

"Right," McFadden answered. "I'd start by shooting the horses of the wagon, so they can't hitch up and run out of here fast."

"Even if they did, we'd catch them. It wouldn't take more than a few minutes for us to run back, mount our own horses, and get after them."

McFadden nodded. He and Collett gestured with their hands for their men to circle around Walker and his people. Slowly and silently, they moved, crawling on all fours or crouching low on the ground to take advantage of the cover provided by shrubs. There was still enough light to see, but that would not last very long. The waxing moon was in the sky, but was obscured by heavy clouds.

It did not seem like it would be difficult. Even as he watched, one of Walker's men fell fast asleep, hurried along by a hefty dose of whiskey. They were dealing with undisciplined men who might not be afraid to kill but were not used to going up against trained and experienced soldiers. During the war, men such as Walker had either deserted or been killed early on, leaving only the hardened souls behind.

Ten minutes passed, which McFadden thought was more than sufficient. He pulled out his Navy Colt pistol and looked over at Collett, who nodded. He took a deep breath.

"Walker!" he shouted. "Walker, you and your men are surrounded! Throw down your weapons and surrender! If you don't all of you will be killed!"

There was a scramble of terror in the tiny campsite as men tried to grab their weapons. One tripped and fell over the fire, shouting out in pain as the legs of his pants were scorched. Walker himself pulled two pistols out and pointed them up in the direction of McFadden's voice, but didn't fire as he could not see him clearly. The gathering darkness, an enemy to movement a few minutes earlier, was now working in McFadden's favor.

One of Walker's men fired a shot at the shadowy figures of one of McFadden's men on the other side of the campsite. The crack of gunfire removed any hesitation and within an instant a rain of bullets fell down upon the campsite. Before McFadden's eyes, almost every man in the campsite was struck and fell, dead or wounded. One man seemed to be hit by four or five bullets within a single second, his riddled body collapsing instantly. Another was hit in the head and fell dead like a sack of potatoes.

McFadden had told his men beforehand of Wallace's order that Walker be taken alive. Even as his men were being torn to pieces before his eyes, he remained unharmed, which told McFadden that his men were following their instructions. He blazed away with both pistols in both directions, screaming in rage, not aiming at anyone in particular. If he kept shooting, eventually he would hit something.

"Can you get him in the leg?" McFadden urgently asked Collett. He had always regarded his friend as a better shot than he himself was.

"Think so," he replied. He pulled back the hammer on his pistol, took careful aim, and fired.

Walker's kneecap exploded in oozy red. His shouts of defiance melted in a scream of pain and he collapsed on the road, his two pistols flung out of his reach. The echo of Collett's final shot faded like a ghost and soon the only sounds were the groans of the wounded men and the crackling of the campfire.

McFadden slowly rose and began to scamper down into the campsite, keeping his Colt ready in case any of the wounded men were foolish enough to continue resisting. He kicked some of the unmoving bodies to make sure they were dead. Of the six men that Walker had around the fire a minute before, four were dead and two others were wounded so badly that McFadden assumed they would die in the next few minutes. Their leader was immobilized and in excruciating pain, but would probably survive unless his wound became infected.

McFadden called to one of his men. "Go back to the horses and see if Wallace can come forward!"

"Right away, sir!" The man dashed off.

Two men walked in and leveled their rifles at Walker, who lay unmoving on the ground, clutching his leg. He looked up at McFadden. "You miserable bastard!" he said through clenched teeth. "Why'd you kill my boys and not me?"

"Shut your mouth," McFadden ordered. He didn't feel the need to explain that Wallace had ordered him taken alive, nor that he was sorely tempted to disregard that instructions and put a bullet in his head anyway. The man lying wounded in front of him had been the cause of much trouble and disorder in his community for the past several months. He had threatened his family, disrespected his property, and tried to undermine the rule of law. He had never showed the slightest remorse for what he had done, but positively reveled in his devilry. Such men, McFadden believed, were the cause of most of the ills of the world. Still, he kept his peace.

One of Walker's wounded men, who had been shot in the belly, stopped moving during the few minutes of waiting. McFadden had seen countless men

718

die during the war and didn't think much of it. Shots to the stomach area were almost always fatal. The other wounded man, shot in the shoulder, might survive long enough to be strung up on the gallows for his crimes. He hoped the same was true for Walker himself.

"What did you do with Roden?" Walker asked, his voice a pained gasp.

"He's been arrested," McFadden said.

"Arrested? I would have thought you would have shot him."

"Wanted to," McFadden said. "Certainly would have made me feel better. But the law's the law. That's the difference between order and chaos."

The fire was still crackling, unconcerned with the bloodshed that had happened around it, and some of the men were now warming their hands over the flames and sipping a bit on the whiskey the outlaws had been drinking. Helped by one of McFadden's men, Wallace slowly hobbled up to the crest above the dry riverbed and then down into the campsite.

"Well, well, well, look what we have here," he said with a grin on his face.

Walker looked disappointed when he saw Wallace. "Thought I killed you."

"No bullet fired by the likes of you is going to take down Bigfoot Wallace. Now, you're under arrest for trying to overthrow the law and order of Granbury County."

"Go to hell!" came the reply.

"Oh, probably one day I will. But you'll be going first, Walker." He paused thoughtfully for a moment and his grin grew larger. "Or should I say Robertson?"

McFadden's eyes narrowed in confusion and he glanced down at Walker, who now had a look of horror on his face.

"Yes, you hear right, you bastard. I know you that you are Colonel Felix Huston Robertson. You're also under arrest for murdering wounded and helpless Union soldiers in 1864. You've been a wanted man for some time, you have."

"What's this?" McFadden asked.

"This fellow that's been causing all this trouble is not named Walker. He's Felix Robertson, who shamefully wore a colonel's uniform during the war. Seems that he killed a lot of helpless men after a battle in Virginia late in 1864. Old Breckinridge has had the word out for years to bring this fellow in and put him on trial for it. We got ourselves a real fat turkey here."

"But they were blacks!" Robertson protested.

"Don't matter," Wallace said simply. "A man's a man in the eyes of the law, ain't he? Anyway, you're going to answer for everything you've done. Soon as we get back to Waco, you're going to be put in a paddy wagon to head down to Austin to go on trial for what you've done here in Granbury County and they'll be sending a telegram to Richmond to find out what to do about the other charges. I don't expect it will be long before you're dangling from a rope."

"Just shoot me now, then."

"Nah," Wallace said. "What would be the fun of that?"

A few men were ordered to put together a makeshift stretcher using material from the campsite. While this was going on, McFadden, Collett, and Wallace examined the ballot boxes in the wagon. They appeared undisturbed, sealed with the same red tape that had been tied around them before they left the courthouse square in Granbury County, which surprised McFadden. Wallace explained that it would have taken a good deal of time for Roden's people to fabricate false ballots using the real ones and that they probably had been heading to a secure location to do the work.

"When we bring these wagons back into Waco, I'm sure that the clerks will validate the ballots in them. With the tape still secured, I see no reason to suspect any tampering. And if they do, they'll just rerun the election."

"I rather wish they would," Collett said. "We'd win by an even bigger margin, after all these shenanigans and without Roden and Walker trying to intimidate everyone."

"You mean Robertson," McFadden replied, still amazed at the events he was witnessing. "When did you find out that Walker was really this Robertson fellow?"

"Why, I knew it from the moment I saw him."

McFadden drew his head back in surprise. "Then why didn't you just arrest him at once?"

Wallace looked pensive for a moment. "Well, you see, the wounded soldiers he murdered were blacks. You know, those slaves set free by the Yankees and then enlisted in their army. I can arrest him now, after all the other stuff he did, but to arrest him right then only for killing blacks during the war? I frankly thought that the people of Waco might not have thought he had done anything wrong. Nobody complained when Forrest's troops killed all those blacks at Fort Pillow, you know. Breckinridge has wanted this fellow brought in for a while, but I couldn't do it right away because I didn't know how the people of Waco would have responded."

McFadden frowned, but nodded. He was no abolitionist, but killing a helpless black man was more or less the same as killing a helpless white man as far as he was concerned. He doubted that the people of Granbury County might have thought the same way, though. If word had spread that a man had been arrested for killing blacks fighting against the Confederacy, the arrested man might have been sprung free from jail by a mob. Opinion might even have shifted towards Roden in the election. It would have added more disorder to what was already a volatile situation. All in all, things had worked out quite well.

"Well, now that the stretcher is ready, let's put that piece of filth on it, hitch up this wagon, and head back to Waco," Wallace said. "Shall we, boys?"

November 9, Noon
Parish Jail, New Orleans, Louisiana

Lowell looked resignedly down at the small stretch of street he could see from his window. A little girl in a yellow dress was walking past with her mother. Aside from the fact that the woman was quite a bit plumper than Josephine, he could imagine for just a moment that it was his wife and daughter, coming to pay him a visit. For the hundredth time that day, he fought back tears.

As far as the state of his mind and soul were concerned, he was in the worst shape since his arrest. Not knowing when he was going to go to the gallows, whether it would be the next day or the next month, was excruciating. If he only knew the date, then he could concentrate his mind. The ambiguity was the troubling thing. He could pick up the Bible or the copy of Boethius, but they were bringing him less comfort with each passing day.

It was strangely worse than the days he had spent in solitary confinement, when his conditions could only have been described as medieval. He tried to do now what he had done then and devise ways for his mind to be occupied. He now regretted sending away most of the books, for they would have been useful in this regard. Of course, Lowell at that time had expected his execution to come within a few days. Now, he had no idea how long it would be.

Lowell wondered if the Confederates were toying with him. Simply by leaving him in suspense and not saying anything to him, were they trying to drive him into madness and despair? When the rational part of his mind could assert itself, Lowell told himself that this was an absurd thought. They had nothing to gain by doing that. When it came to dealing with abolitionists, the Southerners were people of bloodlust and not the sort who would derive any pleasure from subtle mind games.

There was a loud knocking, followed by the long-since familiar metal screech as the door to the cell swung upon. There was Styles, with his tray of food. It was standard prison fare now, a few biscuits, some rice, and two cups of water. Occasionally there were potatoes and a few slices of poorly cooked pork, but not very often. Lowell did not mind. It was no worse than what he had eaten when he was in the army and he had grown tired of the Louisiana cuisine provided by Benjamin. What he would have really liked, he admitted to himself, was a bowl of New England clam chowder. He wondered if the prison authorities would be willing to make such a dish the night before his execution.

"Doing all right, sir?" Styles asked.

"Well enough."

"I have a letter for you, sir."

The guard's voice was slightly hesitant and apologetic. Lowell noticed that his hand quivered slightly as he handed the envelope over. He opened it and read through it at once. Printed on official letterhead from the Confederate District Court of Louisiana, it was a simple and short message informing him that his execution would proceed on December 2. He quickly did the math in his head.

"Twenty-three days," he said to himself. "Twenty-three days separating me from the day I meet my maker."

Styles said nothing, placing the tray of food carefully upon the tiny table in the center of the cell. Lowell found himself wondering for a moment why he was not to be executed on December 1, then realized that that date would fall on a Sunday and the Confederates never carried out executions on the Sabbath. He laughed at the thought that a nation which held millions in slavery and killed those who tried to set them free would care so much about offending the Lord.

"Can I do anything for you, sir? Maybe bring some of your books back?"

"Actually, Styles, could you ask the warden to procure a copy of *Phaedo* by Plato? I should like to read about the death of Socrates."

"Will do, sir," Styles replied. By the man's tone, it was clear to Lowell that Styles had no idea who Plato or Socrates were, but that didn't matter. He assumed that the prison warden had at least gone to university and therefore would be familiar enough with Plato to get the right volume.

He already had a copy of the King James Bible, so he could read about the trial and execution of Jesus. Perhaps it was the height of arrogance, but Lowell now realized that his own situation bore an uncanny resemblance to the plight in which both Socrates and Jesus found themselves during their last days. All had been tried and found guilty of something that had not been wrong in the sight of God. Jesus and Socrates had perished for it and now Lowell would do the same. Socrates had had a relatively painless death from drinking his hemlock, while Jesus had suffered the worst agony imaginable on the cross. Lowell wondered what it would be like for him. Would he be lucky enough to have his neck snapped easily, bringing death in an instant? Or would his neck remain stubbornly unbroken, in which case many excruciating and nightmarish minutes would pass before he finally died of suffocation? He would not find out until December 2.

"Oh, and I require writing materials, Styles. Pen, paper and ink, if you please."

"Very well, sir."

He took a deep breath, finding himself invigorated by knowledge of the date on which he would be executed. The uncertainty was gone and now he could resume his struggle against slavery. The Confederates would never refuse him the right to pen farewell letters to his loved ones, for their pretended gallantry would be exposed as a farce if they did so. So he would write a letter to his wife, a letter to his parents, and a letter to his children to be read by them when they were old enough to understand it.

He would, of course, pour out all the genuine love he felt for his family in these letters. He knew it would be a terrible emotional struggle to put pen to paper for the last time. Lowell decided quickly that he would write the letter to his parents first, then the one to his children, and leave the missive to his beloved Josephine for the last. It would be easiest that way, he thought. He knew that the paper would be stained with tears.

Yet it was not going to be about him, in the grand scheme of things. He would write a fourth letter, addressed to his wife, but written in such a way that she would know it was intended by him to be published in the Boston newspapers. It would thereafter be reprinted in other newspapers in the United States and Europe. His mission of becoming a martyr to the anti-slavery cause, an object of admiration and sympathy around which the minds of men could rally as soldiers might rally around a flag, would be accomplished.

His entire life had been devoted to the destruction of slavery. If his own destruction was necessary to advance the cause, then so be it. When his lifeless body dangled from the gallows and his testament was being reprinted across the world, the evil of slavery would be exposed again, more visible than it had ever been before. Minds would be changed. Attention would be focused. The Confederacy would have proved once again how vile an entity it was, a smallpox scar on the face of the world.

Lowell's death would be Lowell's victory and the Confederacy's death. For the first time in a while, he smiled, for it was a comforting thought.

Toombs paced back and forth incessantly, an enormous frown upon his face, his hands gripped firmly behind his back. On the table, the aroma of roast chicken and potatoes rose from his plate, which would normally have made him ravenous with hunger. Yet he had not touched a bite, even though he had not eaten a proper meal for nearly a week.

"You've been pacing back and forth for nearly an hour," Stephens said from the table, where he himself was eating. "Why don't you try some of this food?"

"I have no appetite," Toombs replied. "Nor am I likely to have one until we know the news from Texas."

"It could come today. It could come a week from today. We can't know. So you might as well try to relax and enjoy some of this food."

Toombs merely grunted. The situation had frayed his nerves to the breaking point. Granbury County remained the only place in Texas that had yet not reported its returns, due to some vaguely described attempt by a local candidate to steal the ballot boxes. Until that country reported in, the vote tally in Texas stood at thirty-one thousand four hundred and ninety five for Beauregard, thirty-one thousand three hundred and thirty-one for Breckinridge, and two thousands four hundred and forty-seven for Rhett. It was such a close margin that the result from Granbury County had to be tallied up for the outcome in Texas to be determined.

As Granbury County went, so it had become clear, so would the Confederacy. When the dust settled on November 5, the Beauregard-Toombs ticket had won South Carolina, Georgia, Florida, Alabama, Mississippi, and Louisiana, for a total of forty-five electoral votes. The Breckinridge-Kemper ticket had won Virginia, North Carolina, Tennessee, and Arkansas, for a total of forty-three electoral votes. Each side needed the six electoral votes from Texas to secure victory, which meant that each side needed to prevail in tiny little Granbury County.

"Some whiskey, perhaps?" Stephens suggested.

Toombs looked at him quizzically, for his friend had spent many years trying to gently persuade him to reduce his consumption of alcohol. "Am I annoying you that much?"

"You are starting to," Stephens admitted. "There is nothing we can do about anything at this point, Robert. The outcome is out of our hands. All we can do is wait."

Toombs pursed his lips, turned, and continued pacing back and forth. He and Stephens had departed Richmond on November 2, taking the early morning train together. This has been scheduled far in advance, for both men wanted to return to Georgia in order to cast their votes. The timing was fortuitous, however, for Toombs needed to escape Richmond to avoid the tumult raised by his comments about Lee and Johnston. He had been drunk when he made them, unable to control his actions, and should have known that they would be taken badly when they were reported in the Richmond papers.

From what he was being told, however, the outrage being directed against him was unprecedented. A mob had formed outside the Spottswood Hotel, believing he was still in the city, and nearly stormed the building to look for him. Almost every newspaper in the Confederacy, even those that had backed his candidacy, had condemned what he had said about the two revered generals. When his train had arrived in Atlanta, he had to depart the train virtually in disguise, wearing a thick-buttoned coat and broad hat so that no one would recognize him.

With the uncertainty of the presidential contest and the outrage caused by his comments, it felt good to be back on his own estate, in his own house and surrounded by his own slaves. Here, if nowhere else, Robert Toombs was in control of what happened. The thought calmed him.

"I think I will have that whiskey," he said. He clapped his hands loudly and a slave appeared in the doorway a few moments later. He ordered his drink and the black servant disappeared to fetch it, having never spoken a word.

"I think it will do you good," Stephens said. Then his tone turned reproachful. "I do not approve, mind you. Drink is what caused many of your current problems. If you had not been drinking when you were speaking to those reporters, you could have avoided a great deal of trouble."

"Yes, yes, thank you, mother," Toombs said with bitter sarcasm. "Whiskey is not my problem at the moment. The voters in a tiny Texas county that nobody has ever heard of are my problem right now. When will the godforsaken returns come in?"

Toombs had sent one of his slaves to wait at the town's telegraph office. The moment a telegram was received, he was to take it directly to the house, which should have taken only fifteen minutes. Only with effort had Stephens been able to persuade Toombs not to remain in the telegraph office himself.

"This is all Rhett's fault, you realize," Toombs said, still pacing. "If he had not stupidly tried to run for president himself, we would have beaten Breckinridge in North Carolina and perhaps Tennessee as well. The vote in Texas wouldn't matter."

"That's true."

"That son of a bitch will have a lot to answer for if Granbury County gives the victory to Breckinridge. Good Lord, the arrogance of that man! The stupidity! What in the world was he thinking?"

Stephens shrugged. "I would encourage you to remain positive. We know nothing about this county in Texas. Maybe it's strongly supportive of the SRP. And even if it does go to Breckinridge and he wins the election, you're still a member of the Senate. And we know that both houses of Congress will have SRP majorities in the next term."

Toombs waved his hands, as if to brush all that aside. Even with congressional majorities, the SRP would not be truly in power if Breckinridge held the chief executive's office. If he won the Vice Presidency, he could guide Beauregard on matters of policy with a supportive Congress behind him. His path to the Presidency in 1873 would be clear. As a Senator in opposition to the president, everything he wanted to do would be thwarted by the Kentuckian.

"Have I worked this hard and this long to have everything depend on a few frontier fools in Texas?" Toombs asked.

"There is nothing to be done about it, Robert," Stephen replied, more earnestly now. "The people must have their way. It is astounding that it has come down to this, but history is filled with unlikely situations."

There was the sound of one of the exterior doors opening and shutting loudly. Then they could hear rapidly approaching footsteps. A slave, nearly panting through the exertion of running, appeared in the doorway.

"Master!" he said, trying to catch his breath. "Davey's coming up the road, whipping his mule like there's no tomorrow."

"Come!" Toombs said to Stephens, who rose from his chair and followed quickly. Davey was the slave sent to the telegraph office. It suddenly occurred to Toombs that he might have been able to return to the house more quickly if he had simply been given a saddled horse rather than a wagon. He shook the foolish thought out of his mind instantly, however. Blacks could not be allowed to ride horses in the manner of white men. It would have been absurd.

They soon emerged on the front porch and could see the wagon approaching. Toombs dashed forward and Davey pulled his mule to a halt as he came close. The slave reached down and handed Toombs an envelope, which he snatched out of the man's hands. He considered tearing it open and reading it at that moment, but it was very cold and he wanted to return indoors. He strode back up the steps and through the front door, followed by Stephens, and went into the drawing room. He sat down in one of the chairs close to the fireplace, where several logs were burning, and hurriedly opened the telegram. Stephens stood in the center of the room, looking at him anxiously.

"It's from Wigfall," Toombs announced, his hatred of the man momentarily forgotten as he scanned through the message to find the numbers that would mean the difference between victory and defeat.

"What does it say?" Stephens asked anxiously. "Who won?"

"He says that Granbury County voters went for Breckinridge by five hundred and ninety-one votes to three hundred and sixty-nine votes, with only twenty-seven votes going to Rhett." He tried to do the math in his head and found that he could not concentrate sufficiently to do so. Angrily, he reached over and rang the bell sitting on the side table.

"So few votes for Rhett out there," Stephens mused. "But then there aren't many slaves out on the Texas frontier and Rhett talked about nothing else."

A slave appeared in the doorway. "Bring pen, ink and paper!" Toombs thundered. "And be quick about it!" The black man, clearly frightened by the certainty of punishment, vanished instantly.

A few endless minutes of agonizing waiting followed. Toombs's mind raced and his stomach seemed suspended in a sea of acid. He tried to do the math in his head and still could not do it. He told himself to remain calm and that the numbers would not change and it did not really matter if he found out in the next few minutes or the following day. It did not matter. When the slave finally returned with the pen, ink, and paper, Toombs placed them on the table and waved the servant away.

He dipped the pen in the ink and started frantically scribbling away, while Stephens looked over his shoulder. He calculated the change in the Beauregard vote first. Thirty-one thousand four hundred and ninety-five plus three hundred and sixty-nine added up to thirty-one thousand eight hundred and sixty-four. In the Breckinridge column, thirty-one thousand three hundred and thirty-one plus five hundred and ninety-one added up to thirty-one thousand nine hundred and twenty-two. Heartlessly, the numbers stared up at Toombs from the table.

"Breckinridge won Texas by fifty-eight votes," Stephens said resignedly.

Toombs let out a primal howl of rage and shoved everything off the table. The ink stand flew against a fine French sofa, splattering it with dark blue splotches. He then kicked the table over, smashing a fine china service. He gripped his hair with his hands and turned around, wanting to go somewhere but unsure of where that place would be.

"Calm down," Stephens said quietly. "You're allowing yourself to become unbalanced."

"That man!" Toombs said bitterly. "That damned Kentuckian! He has ruined me!"

"This isn't about you, Robert. It's about the country."

"Well, he will ruin the Confederacy, too! The man's a fool! He's an abolitionist! Everything we have worked for will be lost!"

"That's not true. You need to calm down. Take a seat and have a drink." Stephens turned and called down the hall. "Bring Senator Toombs a drink!"

Toombs collapsed in a chair, his head in his hands. He almost wished for death. Not only had his ambitions for the vice presidency and eventually the presidency been destroyed by a few voters in a small Texas frontier county, but he had been humiliated in the face of the entire Confederacy. It seemed a far, far worse blow than what had happened in Montgomery in 1861.

Stephens spoke comfortingly. "You are still a Senator," he said. "Our party has secured a majority in Congress. You are going to be one of the most important leaders in the coming political struggles. I know that this is a bitter blow, Robert, but you will rise from it and be stronger."

"That man," Toombs muttered. "That damned Kentuckian."

A slave arrived with a glass and a decanter of whiskey. Moments later, Toombs was sipping his alcohol, feeling the pain numb almost instantly. He resolved at that moment that he would drink as much as he wanted as often as he wanted for the next few days. There was, after all, no reason he could see to bother remaining sober.

November 14, Afternoon
Home of John C. Breckinridge, Richmond, Virginia

"Thank you for coming, my friend," Breckinridge said as he shook the hand of Congressman Williams Wickham. "You'll find food and refreshments in the living room. I do hope we get a chance to speak at greater length before the day is over."

"As do I, Mr. President-Elect," Wickham replied. "But I imagine that you'll have so many guests that you won't be able to do more than say hello to them all."

"You may be right there, sir," Breckinridge said with a smile.

Wickham nodded and moved along towards the living room. Breckinridge then greeted the next arrival, Father John Barry, head of the Catholic congregation at St. Patrick's Church. Breckinridge shook hands with him and exchanged a few pleasantries, even as his mind worked through the probable criticisms he would receive for allowing a Catholic priest into his home. Then he moved on and the next person, a Richmond judge, shuffled over an extended his hand. The line of people behind him seemed to stretch halfway across the city.

The house was filling up rapidly with well-wishers. His wife Mary, to Breckinridge's astonishment and relief, had organized the levee to perfection, even though final preparations had not been finished until just after the critical news from distant Granbury County in Texas came in two days before. A wagonload of roast turkey was procured, along with enormous quantities of side dishes, for a few hundred people were expected to flow through the house over the course of the day. Barrels of cider and several cases of celebratory champagne were being opened and consumed, though on a dignified level.

Since the doors opened at two in the afternoon, men and women had filed past him in the receiving line almost continually. He had long since lost track of how many people had shaken his hand, though the ever faithful Wilson was keeping careful track of everyone. Still, Breckinridge couldn't stay in the line forever. His hand ached from so many firm handshakes and he felt he needed to circulate among the guests in the living room for genuine conversation. More urgently, however, was the need to answer the call of nature.

Ten minutes later, Wilson had successfully extracted him from the front parlor, with appropriate apologies being made to the people still waiting in the receiving line. Soon Breckinridge was in the dining room, a glass of celebratory champagne in his hand. He discovered that it was little different from greeting the guests at the door, however, as a never-ending stream of people came up to him to shake his hand and offer their congratulations. The room was very crowded and many people had moved into the library or the guest room. Some had even ventured out into the small backyard, despite the cold temperatures.

Breckinridge smiled as he saw Jefferson Davis slide between two ladies to approach him and extend his hand.

"Do you know what Washington said to Adams at the latter's inauguration?" Davis said.

"If I ever did, I have forgotten," Breckinridge replied.

"He said, 'I am fairly out, and you are fairly in, and we will see who will be the happiest.'"

Breckinridge smiled. "He was a wise man, that Washington."

"Indeed. I have little doubt that you will say something similar to your own successor six years from now." He paused a moment. "Only a madman would want to be president for his own sake. I remember I was tending my flower garden at my plantation in Mississippi when the messenger came to tell me I had been chosen as president by the Montgomery Convention. I would rather the burden had been placed in any other hands than mine. The last six years have been the most troubled of my life. I can only be happy that the burden is now lifted from me, though I feel a sense of guilt to be placing it in your hands."

Breckinridge nodded slowly. "What will you do now?" he asked.

"Back to Mississippi. Restore my estate at Brierfield. Then, who knows? Perhaps write my memoirs, as General Lee is doing. I honestly don't know. And, strangely, the uncertainty makes me happy."

"You might run for the Senate," Breckinridge said. "Lord knows I will need allies in Congress."

"You will, indeed, my friend. You might have won the Presidency, but the SRP will be in firm control of both the Senate and the House of Representatives. They will do their best to thwart you at every turn. Alas, I shall not be the one to help you there. I shall certainly speak and write on your behalf, but whatever the future may hold for me, I believe I have had my fill of public office."

"I wish you nothing but the best, my friend."

"And I, you, Mr. President-Elect. Now, as I have taken up too much of your time already, I shall go and see what trouble Varina has managed to get herself into."

With a smile and a nod, Davis moved off to another part of the room. Breckinridge only had time for an occasional single sip of his champagne as guest after guest came up to speak with him. His stomach panged with hunger, but he could not break away from the well-wishers long enough to get any food. Across the room, Mary chatted pleasantly with several other ladies. Wilson, standing near the center of the nearest wall, watched over everything like a sentinel. Breckinridge waited for his clumsiness to show itself and, five minutes after the end of his conversation with Davis, Wilson spilled a glass of champagne all over one of Mary's chairs. The atmosphere was so pleasant and happy, however, that this caused nothing but good-natured laughter.

Breckinridge exchanged a few pleasant words with Senator Hunter, who had come to offer his congratulations despite having been one of his staunchest opponents during the campaign. Joseph Mayo, the Mayor of Richmond, talked with him for a few minutes about the proposal to construct a more appropriate building to house the government's executive offices. Mary Chesnut, an old friend, embraced him with a warmth and eagerness that embarrassed Breckinridge, loudly assuring him that she had known he was going to win the election all along. When a break of a few seconds between well-wishers miraculously took place, Breckinridge waved for Wilson to come over.

"James, I'm positively starving. Could you get me a plate of food and perhaps arrange for me to eat it in the library? I would just need a few minutes free from all these people."

"Right away, sir."

Wilson moved off to the kitchen. Breckinridge was soon besieged by another set of guests. Everyone in the city, it seemed, wanted to speak to Breckinridge and almost every conversation followed the same predictable pattern. The person would approach Breckinridge, offer his congratulations, and then ask for something specific. A Baptist minister wanted him to attend a coming Sunday service, as it would add prestige to his congregation to have the president-elect in the pews. The owners of the Tredegar Iron Works reiterated their desire for a contract to construct armor plating for a planned ironclad. A bank owner wanted information on when the next government bond issue was going to come out. Some merchant he had never met asked for an appointment to be postmaster of Greensboro, North Carolina. To all of them, Breckinridge tried to be as courteous and as noncommittal as possible.

Wilson came back. "Sir, I have a plate of food for you in the library. I cleared everyone out for a few minutes, but Mr. Kemper wanted to speak to you if that's possible."

"Yes, tell him to come. And bring some champagne, would you, James?"

"Of course, sir."

Breckinridge made polite apologies to Fitzhugh Lee, the nephew of General Lee and a cavalry commander in the Army of Northern Virginia. With no little relief, Breckinridge entered the library, saw Kemper waiting for him, and relished the silence as Wilson shut the door.

"Thank God," Breckinridge said. "Those people are attacking me like the Yankees at Missionary Ridge."

Kemper laughed. "Comes with the office, my friend. I am under assault as well, you know, though not with the same vigor. Of course, all the people who come to me do so only because they want me to say something to you."

"I hope we shall be free of this soon, when the administration takes office in March and all positions have been filled."

"Perhaps," Kemper said. "Or perhaps it will just get worse then."

The plate of warm roast turkey and vegetables beckoned and Breckinridge hurriedly devoured several bites. He knew he had only a few minutes to eat and speak with Kemper, so his ordinary proper table manners would have to be set aside. He washed down his food with a few hefty sips of his champagne.

"I am glad we have the chance to talk, James," Breckinridge said. "I wanted to reiterate something to you."

"What is that?"

"When I served as vice president in the Buchanan administration before the war, the president essentially ignored me. I was asked to perform the occasional ceremonial duty and preside over the Senate, a powerless and thankless activity, but otherwise I might as well have not even existed. With Mr. Davis, it was worse, for he and Mr. Stephens became outright political enemies."

"This is all sadly true," Kemper said.

"I don't want either of those things to happen with us. As I said when I first asked you to be my running mate, I intend to make you a full member of this administration. I want you to attend Cabinet meetings. I want your opinion on the issues that will surely come before our administration. There will be many tasks I will have for you, but you will never be ignored. Do you understand?"

Kemper nodded soberly. "I do, John."

"I shall have to confide in you about many things, and I ask your word as a gentleman that any such conversations will remain strictly between us."

"Of course."

"And I will need your loyalty and support in the difficult days we have ahead of us. Our administration will not have a supportive Congress. Most of the state governments are also under the control of the SRP. This will be a time to build bridges."

Kemper's eyes narrowed. "Build bridges?"

"Yes, we have to quiet the opposition and dissipate their fears. To do that, I am going to take several steps as soon as I take office in March."

"Such as?"

"As you know, General Johnston has resigned as commander of the Army of Tennessee. I intend to name General Beauregard as his replacement."

Kemper's eyes widened, but his surprised expression was quickly replaced by a smile. "A wise move, that," he said approvingly. "A lesser man than you would seek to punish your former opponent, not elevate him to one of the chief military commands of the country. You will appear magnanimous before the entire country."

"That's what I want," Breckinridge said. "Besides, in army command, Beauregard will have plenty of opportunities to satisfy his own vanity without having to meddle in politics. Let him design new uniforms and hold as many grand reviews as he likes, so long as he doesn't seek to rally political opposition to us."

Kemper nodded. "Very prudent. Very prudent, indeed."

"And I intend to move on creating the Supreme Court as soon as we can. I will need your assistance in this, for there is no way our choice of justices can fail to avoid becoming controversial in the extreme. We will need to ensure regional representation and we shall have to nominate some men who might have failed to support us in the recent campaign."

"Naturally."

Breckinridge already had in mind a choice for Chief Justice, though he decided against telling Kemper. There would be ample time to tell him before he made his nominations public. The creation of the Supreme Court, it had become clear, was a matter of overriding importance. The SRP had roundly criticized Jefferson Davis for failing to get on with the process, accusing him of not wanting a Supreme Court so as to rule as a dictator. By making the Court his earliest priority, Breckinridge hoped to avoid being subject to the same charge.

"And Cabinet appointments?" Kemper asked.

"We will get to work on them tomorrow."

"Good. For one, I think that Trenholm should remain at Treasury. The man has worked wonders."

"Perhaps," Breckinridge replied. He actually had a different choice for Treasury, but did not wish to tell Kemper just yet.

They talked further about many other issues, including finalizing the treaty with France and perhaps sending a special envoy to Madrid to discuss the Cuba question. The latter was seen as more a gesture to the SRP than a genuine attempt to gain the cession of the island. Breckinridge also asked Kemper's opinion on the advisability of arranging a meeting between himself and President McClellan, to discuss outstanding issues and foster better relations with their great northern neighbor. They had talked over all these things many times over the previous few months, but now that they had won the election and were certain to take office in March, their discussions had taken on a much more serious quality.

Kemper shook his head. "So many pressing matters. It is going to be a long six years."

"Yes," Breckinridge replied. "But think of the good we can do for our people. It falls to few men in history to have such an opportunity. We should make the most of it."

Wilson quietly opened the door. "Sir, the guests are becoming anxious for you to return."

"You cannot keep the people waiting, John," Kemper said with a smile.

Breckinridge sighed deeply. "Once more into the breach, dear friends."

They slipped through the open door and back into the crowded living room, where they were greeted with applause. Though he would have thought it impossible, the crowd had grown even larger during the few minutes he had spent with Kemper in the library. A swarm of people advanced to shake his already sore hand. Glancing about, Breckinridge noticed that President Davis and his wife had departed.

Amid the crowd, Breckinridge saw the familiar face of Judah Benjamin, who seemed to stand in a small bubble of quiet and calm amid the human tumult around him. Breckinridge smiled at the sight of his friend. He had not known that Benjamin had returned to Richmond from New Orleans. Patient as always, the former Secretary of State sipped his champagne and waited for the crush of well-wishers to subside before approaching the president-elect.

Breckinridge had naturally followed the newspaper accounts of the Lowell trial very carefully. He had not been surprised when the abolitionist New Englander was found guilty and was still confused as to why Benjamin had abandoned his governmental responsibilities to go off and serve as the man's defense counsel. It seemed quite out of character for him to indulge in quixotic quests. Yet Breckinridge had concluded that he would never really understand Benjamin and, in fact, doubted if anyone ever would.

Benjamin was finally able to gently elbow his way to Breckinridge and extend his hand.

"Congratulations, John," he said warmly. "I knew that you could do it."

"Thank you, Judah. I am very glad to see you, I must say. It does my heart good."

Breckinridge thought quickly over the contributions Benjamin had made to his candidacy, besides persuading him to be a candidate in the first place. He had been largely responsible for the early strategy, had taken the lead in raising campaign money, and probably done many things behind the scenes of which Breckinridge was unaware. He had no doubt that, had it not been for Benjamin, he would not be the president-elect. When history wrote the story of the 1867 Confederate presidential campaign, Judah Benjamin would deserve to be a prominent figure.

Yet Breckinridge doubted that he would be. Benjamin was a slippery, shadowy man, always wanting to remain in the background, as if he were a minor character in a story he himself had written. Most men wanted credit and recognition for what they did and were outraged when they didn't get it, but not Benjamin. He was always content to stand back and simply smile.

"I am glad you have come to Richmond, my friend," Breckinridge said. "It would not have felt right to celebrate our success without your presence."

"It's your victory, not mine," Benjamin replied. "But I am very glad to be here."

"What are you going to do now?" Breckinridge asked, straining to hear over the noise of the crowded living room.

"I am going to resume my law practice in New Orleans. My representation of Lowell has given notice to everyone in the Crescent City that I am available for council yet again. I have a few letters already from prospective clients. Aside from that, I believe I will simply enjoy myself."

Breckinridge leaned in more closely, to minimize the chance of being overhead. "Cannot I persuade you to remain in the government? Miles has to remain Secretary of State, as we discussed, but I will need someone I can trust to serve as our minister in Washington City. Or London or Paris, if you prefer."

Benjamin shrugged. "If you extend an offer, I shall naturally consider it. But my mind is already moving on to other things, John. My advice to you would be to find someone else to fill those posts."

"I hope that, even if you do return to private life, I might be allowed to seek your advice and counsel every now and then. I have always considered your opinion to be very valuable, and no one understands the problems facing our country better than you do."

Benjamin smiled and laughed softly. "I shall always be at your service, Mr. President-Elect."

With that, Benjamin shuffled out of the way so that the man behind him could walk up and speak to Breckinridge. A few minutes later, Breckinridge noticed Benjamin slipping out the front door.

November 14, Afternoon
Richmond, Virginia

Benjamin inhaled the cold Richmond air deeply, letting it fill his lungs as he walked down the street. He twirled his gold-topped walking stick, almost like a boy playing with a toy. Out of government service, with the Lowell trial over and done with, he felt liberated, freer than he had felt in many years. His wealth, secured in British and French government bonds and other stable assets overseas, was sufficient to provide for his needs even if he never made another penny. Detractors could say whatever they wanted about him and he would remain unconcerned. However many years remained for Judah Benjamin, they would be happy ones, free from care.

He had not lied when he told Breckinridge that he would consider a diplomatic appointment. Yet New Orleans beckoned, the city he loved so much, the only place in the world where he truly felt at home. He knew he would most likely turn down any offer the new president might make. Far better to remain home, wrapped in the sights, sounds, and smells of his own beloved city.

Benjamin had returned to Richmond to put his affairs on order, arrange for his furniture, books, and other possessions to be shipped to New Orleans or sold, and see to the leasing of his Richmond home to some credit-worthy politician. He also had to meet with Secretary Miles to discuss a few outstanding matters concerning the State Department.

All those were minor concerns, though. Judah Benjamin still had one great task to complete on behalf of the Confederacy before he vanished into quiet retirement.

He strode confidently up towards the door of the Presidential Mansion. Until the previous year, the house had been the home of Virginia's governor. It had been handed over to the national government upon the relocation of the state government to Charlottesville and making it the presidential residence had been the obvious thing to do. Benjamin did not quite care for the Federal-style architecture, considering it rather too forceful and personally preferring the Greek Revival style.

He knocked loudly on the front door and waited. The cold wind whistled past him for a few moments, as if trying to tell him secrets that he could not understand. Benjamin had always been a man of secrets. What he was about to tell Jefferson Davis might well be the biggest secret of them all.

A slave answered the door and his expression revealed his surprise at seeing Benjamin.

"Mr. Secretary," the black man stammered. Then he corrected himself. "I'm sorry. Mr. Benjamin. How do you do today?"

"I do well. I need to speak to the president."

"Come in, sir," the slave said, standing aside and then closing the door behind him before taking his coat and walking stick. "Please wait in the drawing room. I'll go see if my master's available."

Benjamin walked into the drawing room, stood for a minute in front of the fire to warm himself, then took a seat. He could hear the muffled sound of a conversation somewhere else in the house and recognized the voice of Davis. A few moments later, Davis entered the room.

"I didn't expect to see you here today, Judah," Davis said. "I thought we were going to dine together tomorrow night."

Benjamin rose and shook Davis's extended hand. "Yes, well, I would like our final dinner together to be a personal affair only."

"So you are here to discuss government business?"

"I am."

Davis smiled and took the chair opposite Benjamin. "Well, what could we possibly have to discuss now? You're a private citizen again. I will soon be out of office and on my way to a happy retirement. If you have government business to discuss, why not do it with Breckinridge?"

"You are still the President of the Confederate States until the official inauguration three months from now. And what I come to ask for is something that must be done immediately."

"I see," Davis said, rubbing his chin. "And, pray tell, what is it that you want me to do?"

Benjamin paused for a long moment before replying. "Mr. President, you need to issue a pardon for Charles Russell Lowell."

Davis sharply drew his head back in shock. "Issue a pardon? For Lowell?"

"That's right."

"Have you lost your mind, Judah?" Davis asked. "Or is this some sort of joke?"

"Neither, Mr. President."

Davis rose from his seat and glared at Benjamin, his eyes flashing fire. For a moment, Benjamin was expecting the president to unleash an angry tirade. He could see the telltale twitching of the veins in Davis's head and the habitual tightening of his lips. Yet no tirade came. Davis recovered himself, turned, and walked over to the fire, his arms across his chest. He stared into the flames for a few silent minutes.

Benjamin waited. He knew Davis better than anyone other than his wife and was unconcerned. The president often took time to fully absorb unexpected or unpleasant developments and usually did so in silence. Benjamin had often joked to himself that he should bring a good book to meetings with Davis, so as to pass the time while the president thought things through.

Finally, Davis turned and looked back at Benjamin. His look was still unpleasant. "Why on earth would I do that?"

"It is necessary."

"You'll have to do much better than that, Judah. You're not a crazy person, so I am sure you have some reason to ask me to do such a thing. Yet I must confess I can't think of what that might be. The man was found guilty of the worst possible crime a man can commit against the South. He smuggled in arms to slaves, and slaves used those arms to kill white people! There was a great deal of opposition to even giving him a trial, for God's sake! And you want me to pardon him? To just let him go?"

"That's right, Mr. President."

"Again I ask. Why?"

Benjamin opened his mouth to reply, then stopped and gestured for Davis to sit back down. Only when the president had done so did Benjamin speak. "Why do you think I left Richmond to serve as Lowell's defense counsel in New Orleans?"

"Frankly, I assumed it was a silly quixotic quest. I thought you wanted to offer a snub to the Richmond elite that so often slighted you."

"It was none of that," Benjamin replied. "Far from it. As I explained to Breckinridge, I did it in order to make a statement to the South. Not to the current generation, mind, but to those of the future. Slavery must end, my friend. You have admitted it to me yourself, after forcing me to swear that I would never reveal what you said to anyone. I went to New Orleans to make Lowell into a martyr. From the moment that he dangles from the gallows, the memory of his name will echo across the world. And people will ask how slavery can be right when it was hated by such a man as he."

"I don't understand," Davis said. "If that's what you wanted to achieve, why do you want me to pardon him?"

"Because other matters have intruded upon my plan," Benjamin replied. "Slidell informs me that Napoleon III will reject the treaty of friendship with us unless our government makes some sort of gesture against slavery, even if only a symbolic one. The emperor has said that he will sign the treaty if Lowell lives, but he will refuse to do so if he dies."

Davis's eyes widened. "Why didn't you tell me this before?" he asked, exasperated. "You could have sent me a telegram, using our old code."

"Because I wanted to spare you the political storm that you would have endured. It seemed to me that I could have persuaded the jury to imprison him for life rather than execute him. I might have succeeded, too, had not his wife exploded forth with her denouncement of slavery and the South on the witness stand. Or perhaps his sentence was unavoidable. I don't know. In any case, I did not want you to be involved, because it would have been a source of nothing but trouble for you."

Davis stood from his chair, locked his hands behind his back, and started pacing back and forth across the room. "If the French reject the treaty, we can no longer turn to the British. The Fenian Crisis is over. The British would now have nothing to gain and much to lose by aligning with us."

"Correct."

"So we will be without friends in the world."

"No friends worth having. What difference will it make if Brazil signs an alliance with the Confederacy? It can do nothing to help us against the power of the United States."

Davis turned and stared hard at Benjamin. "But the emperor says that he will certainly sign if Lowell lives?"

"Yes, according to Slidell."

Davis sighed. "It doesn't matter. I cannot even consider doing what you ask. The man is guilty and flaunted the fact in the face of the world. He expressed no remorse or regret. I am sure he would do it again if given half the chance. What message would I be sending to our people if I allowed him to live?"

"Not one the people will appreciate," Benjamin acknowledged. "There was a reason we hanged John Brown as quickly as we did. We wanted to set an example to others that we would respond mercilessly to efforts to instigate a slave uprising. But perhaps it will be a message that they need to hear. If you grant my request, my mission to make him into a martyr will have failed, but we can still have it put into the minds of our people that our country will have to one day move on from slavery."

"I am merely thinking the matter through, Judah. I have no intention of honoring your request. I would be insane to do so. I am set to leave office in a few months and I do not want my path home lit by my own burning effigies. I would be in genuine fear for my life. Besides which, it would hobble Breckinridge in his efforts to set up his own administration, since he is so closely tied to me."

"That's why you need to do it. Breckinridge isn't in office yet, so he will be free to denounce you as hotly as the Fire-Eaters. In fact, that is precisely what I will advise him to do."

Davis snorted. "You'd have me ruin my own reputation forever?"

Benjamin tried to think of words to say that might loosen the president's determination, which he had done successfully so many times over the years. Yet of all the times he had had to get Davis to change his mind, Benjamin realized that this would be the most difficult. Worse still, it might be the most consequential.

"Mr. President," Benjamin said respectfully. "Imagine a world in which neither France nor Britain aligns itself with us. None of the other powers of the world can lend the military support that they can. As you've already pointed out, an alliance with Britain is now out of the question. But an alliance with France can still be achieved. In the meantime, the election that will take place in the United States next year may very well bring the Republicans back into power, both in the White House and in Congress. Our country is independent, but we are still much weaker than the Yankees. Many of the Republicans will be looking for any excuse to launch a war of vengeance."

Davis grunted, but said nothing. He continued to pace back and forth.

Benjamin continued. "We have a worthy adversary, Mr. President. What we need is a worthy ally. You can give us one with a single scratch of your pen."

"At the cost of my own reputation," Davis said sourly.

"The Southerners living now will condemn you without reserve, it is true. What of it? Take Varina and go on an extended trip to Europe. You'll be celebrated there for pardoning Lowell, feted across the entire Continent. That's what old Abe Lincoln has done. He had tea with Queen Victoria and met with the Pope, according to the papers. By the time you come back, things will have died down. And as for your reputation, you might suffer now, but you will be praised by future generations of historians for your wisdom and foresight."

Davis pursed his lips and shook his head, leaving Benjamin to wonder if the president had really understood the words he had just spoken. The president continued to pace, while Benjamin remained sitting.

Benjamin went on. "You must also consider the impact on relations with the United States. McClellan is collapsing. Even now he is fighting off an attempt to impeach him, introduced by a member of his own party. He'll probably survive this, but he will be politically crippled. As I said, the Republicans will be back in power sooner or later. However, if the Confederacy has pardoned and released Lowell, their efforts to stigmatize us as a gang of devilish thugs will be made much more difficult. The abolitionists will be thwarted. It would be a cunning move."

Davis still continued to pace, saying nothing.

Benjamin continued. "You say that your reputation in the Confederacy will be destroyed. It will be, at least in the short term. There's no use sugar-coating it. But a hundred years from now, after slavery has been cast aside, you will come to be seen as a visionary."

"Even if you're right, why should I care?" Davis asked sourly. "I won't be there to see it. And I care nothing for what the people think."

Benjamin wanted to chuckle but restrained himself. He knew that Davis and almost every other politician obsessed over public acclaim, whether they admitted it not. They basked in the adulation of the people, drinking in their cheers and applause the way a man wandering in the desert would drink water from an oasis. Benjamin himself was immune to such addictions, which gave him a certain freedom of action denied to other political figures. Davis was at bottom an ordinary politician who wanted to believe the people loved him. Yet Davis was also an intelligent man of integrity, who genuinely wanted to do the right thing for his country. Benjamin wondered which element in the man's psyche would win the battle clearly raging in his mind.

Davis stopped pacing and stared into the fireplace for a long time. Benjamin waited. The president sighed deeply, shook his head, and turned back to Benjamin.

"No," he said simply.

"Mr. President, you have no choice."

"I don't like it when you say that to me," Davis replied, his voice becoming heated with anger. "The man's a terrorist. He's guilty. Many Southerners are dead because of him. No, I look forward to confirmation that he's been hanged and expect that God will not have mercy on his soul. I don't have a choice? Yes, I do. I choose not to pardon this evil man."

Benjamin frowned, disappointed. "You and I have long been friends," he said.

"I know, but friendship has nothing to do with this."

"I say that because I don't want to say what I am about to say," Benjamin said slowly. "Mr. President, throughout my tenure in your Cabinet, I have kept a very detailed diary."

He said nothing more, allowing those words to hang in the air like cigar smoke. Davis's stone cold face hardened even more, staring daggers down at Benjamin. His glare was too much even for Benjamin, who looked away from the president and into the fireplace.

As a member of the Confederate Cabinet from the earliest days of the Davis administration, when it had been birthed at the Montgomery Convention, Benjamin had been the president's chief confidante on every conceivable issue. Davis had told Benjamin, without hesitation, exactly what he thought about every well-known figure in the Confederacy, male and female. Always wishing to appear decisive in public, Davis had let his guard down with Benjamin in private, willing to reveal his own torn feelings on a great many matters. Over time, he had become more than a political advisor, morphing into a personal counselor as well. Davis had revealed secrets to Benjamin that he had revealed to no one else, his wife alone excepted. Benjamin knew about the financial assets Davis had moved out of the country, of the favors he had done for his congressional backers and the dirty tricks he had played on his opponents, of the string-pulling Davis had engaged in to get military and government appointments for his incompetent family members.

Moreover, Benjamin had become a close friend of Varina Davis during his Richmond years. The Richmond gossip-mongers would positively salivate over the stories he could tell of his late night conversations with the First Lady, with their revelations about the marital infidelities and other scandals of the Confederate upper class. Even if Davis could endure his own humiliation, Benjamin knew he could not stomach the humiliation of his wife.

Davis looked at him. "Publish and be damned."

Benjamin remained composed. "I also kept copies of correspondence that I considered especially important. You'll recall, for example, the exchange of messages we had with the actor from Maryland named John Wil-"

"Stop speaking!" Davis roared, silencing Benjamin instantly. The president's face became a mask of rage, kept from exploding only by the man's tight emotional control. Another endless minute passed until Davis spoke again. "So it's to be blackmail, then?" he asked. "It was an awful scheme. We should never even have considered it."

"But we did consider it. And I have the proof, which I can release to the public."

"You'd be implicating yourself as well."

"I will do what I feel is necessary for the good of the Confederacy," Benjamin replied.

"Why is this New Englander so important to you? Did he become your friend during the time you were his lawyer?" Davis paused for a moment, his voice becoming contemptuous. "A special friend, perhaps? Maybe people would want to hear about that, by God!"

Benjamin chuckled at the clumsiness and crudity of the implied threat. His homosexuality was widely known, even if it was not widely talked about. Benjamin scarcely cared if word of it was published in the newspapers. It might complicate the resumption of his legal practice, but he had enough money in any event.

"You are free to discuss anything you know about me with anyone you wish," Benjamin replied calmly. "However, I think it best if we come to an arrangement in which neither of us violates the confidence of the other. I have already explained how this is possible."

"Get out, Judah!" Davis snapped. "Leave this house at once! I cannot stand here and be spoken to in this manner. I am very sorry to say it, but our friendship is at an end. You alone are responsible for it. Now, get out before I find it impossible to control my anger!"

With perfect composure, Benjamin rose from his chair and politely bowed. "Good day, Mr. President," he said simply, then walked back to the foyer. The slave standing by the door opened it, handed him back his things, and the former Secretary of State strolled back out into the cool autumn day, twirling his walking stick as if he had not a care in the world.

CHAPTER EIGHTEEN

November 15, Afternoon
United States Capitol Building, Washington City

Sumner had decided not to watch the vote from the Visitor Gallery. He was afraid that his presence in the House chamber might inflame the anger of Democrats, possibly causing some representatives who might be inclined to vote for impeachment to change their minds at the last instant. Instead, he now paced back and forth across the length of the meeting room of the Senate Foreign Relations Committee, which was crowded with other Republican senators, their staff members, and other assorted hangers-on. The room was filled with cigar smoke, but few men spoke. Every now and then, Sumner glanced at the door, watching for the messenger boy who would bring word on the outcome of the vote. Everyone was tense and expectant, unsure of what was going to happen.

Everyone in the room could sense that they were experiencing an unprecedented moment in history. No one could tell what the result was going to be. The conversations were quiet, more whispering than talking, as if any loud noise would prevent them from finding out the result when it finally arrived.

Senator Benjamin Wade of Ohio, one of the few men in Congress whom Sumner considered as zealous in the abolitionist cause as himself, strode up to him.

"You caused this, Sumner," he said sternly. "You're the one who pushed Logan into doing it. Any regrets?"

"None," Sumner replied.

"This has never been done before. Not once in the history of the republic."

"We've impeached federal judges before."

"Yes, but never the President of the United States."

"Well, why would the men who wrote the Constitution have written the impeachment process into the Constitution if they didn't expect it to be used from time to time?"

"I suppose that's true. My fear is that, now that this particular cat is out of the bag, impeachment will become a regular occurrence whenever the White House and the Capitol Building are controlled by opposing political parties."

"The future will take care of itself, Senator Wade. Right now, I'm concerned about President McClellan."

Wade shook his head. "He won't be impeached, Sumner. We don't have the votes."

"If only a small chunk of the Democrats vote for impeachment, we will win. Since Logan was the one to introduce the resolution, we have credibility."

"And suppose McClellan is impeached. The Senate is so narrowly divided that we won't have the two-thirds vote necessary to convict. You are usually right, Sumner, but you're wrong on this one. President McClellan isn't going to be removed from office."

"We will see."

Wade nodded and, with a thin smile, moved off to speak with someone else. Sumner continued his pacing. Wade, he acknowledged, was probably right. Sumner considered it possible but not likely that the House of Representatives would vote to impeach. If it did, it would be well-nigh impossible to persuade a sufficient number of Democratic senators to come over to their side and vote to actually remove McClellan from office. All things considered, Sumner thought the odds of complete victory were perhaps one out of ten.

If they somehow succeeded, as many people had already pointed out to Sumner, Vice President George Pendleton would assume the office of president. The man had been an out-and-out Copperhead during the war, openly sympathetic to the Confederacy and still vocally pro-slavery. Yet this did not deter Sumner. If Pendleton did assume power, it was only a year until the next presidential election. There would be little time for him to settle into his administration and enact any damaging policies before the people could kick him out of office. The disarray in the White House should make it easy for the Republican Party to emerge victorious.

Sumner leaned back against the wall, crossing his arms and lazily watching his fellow Republicans mill about in the room. He was used to waiting and was not impatient. Listening to the chatter in the room, Sumner could hear people saying more or less the same thing that Wade had just said to him, asserting that there was very little chance of McClellan actually being removed from office.

He knew he had little in the way of a sense of humor, but he wanted to chuckle. People could be so daft. Could they not see that, even if McClellan were not removed from office, the proceedings now underway represented the *coup de grace* to his administration? No matter what happened, McClellan would be discredited and humiliated in the face of the public. He would be rendered largely powerless, just a year before he would be up for reelection. Either way, Sumner was convinced, the Republicans would emerge from the controversy as the victors.

One of the messenger boys dashed into the room, nearly gasping for breath after running across the immense building. "They've started voting!" he exclaimed. He didn't wait for a response, but sprinted back out as quickly as he had come. This news, not at all surprising, generated increased chatter among the Republican politicos.

Senator John Hale of New Hampshire, another old ally of Sumner's, approached.

"Well, now it comes down to the numbers."

Sumner shook his head. "We'll fall short. By at least two dozen votes, I think. But it doesn't matter. We've crippled McClellan as surely as if a surgeon hacked his leg off. We will regain the Presidency and the House next year."

"Our own people will have to settle on a candidate," Hale noted sourly. "If these divisions between the supporters of Chase and the supporters of Seward can't be healed, we may go into the elections as a split party, just like the Democrats did in 1860. That would spell trouble."

Sumner frowned. Sumner did not want to speak of such things at what was supposed to be a triumphant moment, but he couldn't deny that Hale was right. Salmon Chase had won the gubernatorial election in Ohio and was certain to seek the Republican nomination for president in the coming year. His ambitions would run headlong into those of Seward. Sumner knew that he would have to bend his energies towards bridging the gap between the two rivals and their supporters.

Lincoln had been able to bring Chase and Seward together during his presidency, but Sumner knew didn't have an ounce of Lincoln's political talents. He thought for a moment of the ex-president, recently returned from his extended European sojourn. Perhaps when the dust had settled from the impeachment vote, Sumner might visit him in Springfield. It would be good to see Lincoln again and it would be useful to gain his insight into the coming presidential election.

"What think you of Breckinridge?" Hale asked.

Sumner shrugged. "A tight election, to be sure. But it matters little to me who is president down in the Confederacy. Whoever it is, they will seek to maintain slavery and therefore we must oppose them."

"Breckinridge is, at least, a man of integrity. Perhaps we will be able to work with him in some capacity."

"I can't think of any way in which we would want to work with them," Sumner replied. "And I have a hard time describing any of those people as men of integrity. Refusing to free the oppressed Africans makes them evil, to a man, without a single exception. Once our party is again in control of the government, we can begin to deal with them again."

He thought for a moment of Lowell, now awaiting execution in New Orleans. The man had done what he had gone to do and placed the villainy of slavery on display for the whole world to see. He would be remembered as a martyr. It was already clear that the efforts of the South to improve its image with the European nations had been badly damaged by the trial, which had received extensive newspaper coverage on the other side of the Atlantic. Rumor had it that the French had abandoned all thought of signing a friendship treaty with the Confederacy. If Lowell's conviction had played even a minor role in that, it was worth it.

Hero though he was, Lowell was but a single man. What did a single life matter in the grand struggle against the slave power? He felt no guilt over sending Lowell to his death. Lincoln, after all, had sent more than three hundred thousand men to their deaths in his failed attempt to crush the Confederacy. Had there been three hundred thousand men like Lowell, Sumner would have told all of them to go and fight against slavery, even if it cost them their lives. He knew he would grieve when he read news of Lowell's hanging, but if Lincoln could endure it, so could Sumner. Guilt was not part of his temperament.

He looked again at Hale. "Chase or Seward, man? Let's hear it."

"Chase," Hale said unhesitatingly. "I admire Seward enormously, of course. But I fear he might be conciliatory with the Confederacy and I doubt Chase will be."

"Some say that Chase is too ambitious," Sumner replied. "That he's seeking the presidency for personal reasons only."

"Do you think that? If it were true, he'd have gone over to the Democrats when Lincoln removed him from the office of Treasury Secretary. No, he's as strong an abolitionist as they come. Yes, he's ambitious, but who among us isn't? Chase will be my man next year. I'm sure of it."

Sumner nodded, filing the information away in his mind for later use. He would need to get a solid idea of what level of support the two primary contenders had among the Republican leaders before he made up his own mind on which way to jump. He also had to consider the possibility that there might be a sudden, unexpected emergence of another challenger with enough heft to gain the nomination. After all, no one had expected Lincoln's victory at the Republican National Convention in 1860.

Another messenger boy, just as out of breath as the last one, arrived at the door, leaning against the frame to steady himself. All conversation immediately ceased. Since the last page had brought word that voting had commenced, this one likely brought news of the result.

"The vote failed!" the boy said breathlessly. "A hundred and seven votes to eight-six! The president is not impeached!"

The room was filled instantly with a chorus of voices expressing disgust and disappointment. A few men cast accusatory glances in his direction, as though it were his fault that the impeachment vote had failed. Sumner was not surprised, however, and refused to allow his countenance to be shaken. He would have been pleased had McClellan been impeached, but he had never really expected it to happen.

He did the math in his head. The House of Representatives was currently divided between seven-four Republicans, a hundred and fourteen Democrats, and two members of the so-called Bluegrass Party, a regional group of Kentuckians that generally supported the Democrats and were loyal to McClellan. This meant that twelve Democrats had joined with the Republicans to vote for impeachment. It was about what Sumner had expected.

"Well, that's that, I suppose," Hale said. "Now we can close the door on this whole sordid Fenian affair. McClellan will stay in office, but you have made sure he was thoroughly cashiered for what he did. No wonder that he has moved to put as much distance between himself and the Fenians as he can."

"Indeed," Sumner replied. Since the dismantling of the Fenian camps by Thomas, followed by the now-retired general's testimony in the Senate, the McClellan administration had moved against the Fenians with an urgency in complete contrast to their previous attitude. Many of its leaders had been arrested and arraigned in court on conspiracy charges. This had already created a firestorm against McClellan among the Irish immigrant community, which delighted Sumner as it would further ensure his defeat in the coming presidential election.

He politely excused himself from Hale and left the chamber, strolling back towards his office. It was time for him to move past what had happened with Lowell, to forget Saul, and to put the Fenian matter behind him. He would go home to Boston for Christmas and return when Congress came back into session in March.

Sumner felt liberated. It was less than a year until McClellan would face the challenge of reelection. There was much to do.

November 18, Morning
Mechanic's Hall, Richmond, Virginia

Morgan sat quietly, holding his hat on his lap, dressed in a pristinely clean uniform. The lobby of Mechanic's Hall was filled with young men, mostly secretaries and army officers, coming and going. He listened to their excited chatter as he waited. The question of who was to succeed Breckinridge as Secretary of War was clearly the question that occupied everyone's mind. Some were saying that Joe Johnston would be the ideal choice, now that he had officially resigned from the army. Others were saying that John B. Gordon would be the man.

He himself did not especially care who would lead the War Department. Indeed, he found it difficult to care who was going to be the next president. He had cast his ballot for Breckinridge, to be sure, for the man was a good friend. Yet Morgan increasingly felt that the Confederacy was no longer his country.

This fact was brought home by the fact that scarcely anyone in the War Department lobby had even noticed his presence. Three or four men had come up to greet him and shake his hand, but that was all. A few years earlier, during the war, a crowd of people would have formed around him, asking him to tell stories of his exploits and hanging on his every word. Now, he was just a disgraced general, like an old horse that had once come in third place in a few races.

Morgan knew who was responsible for this. His stomach churned as he thought again of the black warrior who had emerged from the swamps of Louisiana. He told himself for the hundredth time that Longstreet and all the others were right and that Saul had died in the burning hotel in New Iberia. His mind believed it, but his heart somehow could not. In quiet moments, he admitted that he still believed Saul was out there in the swamp, ready to rise again like a phoenix. It was a thought that gave him chills.

Most people had put Saul and his rebellion out of their thoughts completely, especially after the Lowell trial finally ended. All mention of it vanished from the newspapers. Partly this was because everyone's attention was focused on the presidential election and its incredibly narrow result, but there was more to it than that. His fellow white Southerners, Morgan realized, didn't want to think about Saul because they did not want to acknowledge what the man represented. The black slaves, despite all the Confederate propaganda to the contrary, were not content to remain in servitude. If they had found a leader to foment a rebellion once, they could do it again.

Morgan found himself especially disturbed by the strange stories the slaves had reported to him about Saul during his intensive search around New Iberia after the recapture of the town. Stories told of Saul moving through the region like a ghost, displaying magical powers and telling the slaves that he would eventually return and free them all. He couldn't understand why, but Morgan found these stories much more troubling than the thought that Saul might actually still be alive.

Astoundingly, these rumors of Saul's miraculous survival and supernatural powers were spreading across the entire South. From what Morgan had learned, even slaves as far away as Georgia and Tennessee had been told the stories and were now repeating them. It was well-known that plantation slaves communicated with one another across great distances, despite efforts to suppress this. The farther from the Louisiana swamps, the more colorful and disconcerting the stories became.

Morgan had been told by a friend of an incident on a sugar plantation in the Florida Panhandle. The owner woke up one morning to find the words *Saul Lives!* scrawled in black paint across the side of a warehouse in enormous letters. He had not believed before then that any of his slaves had even heard of Saul. When the culprit was identified and beaten to within an inch of his life by the overseer, he claimed that Saul had come to him in the night and told him to paint the message.

Many of his fellow whites greeted these stories with mocking laughter, but Morgan knew better. Having seen Saul face to face, having fought him in battle, he understood their import. The slaves, so quietly as to escape the notice of their masters, were being filled with a spirit of resistance and had found a talisman to inspire them. Slaves could only be kept in slavery if they were convinced that freedom was unattainable, but the war had revealed to the slaves that liberation from their bondage was possible. Saul, alive or dead, now offered to lead them to freedom.

Morgan blamed himself for it all. Had he been more efficient and less overconfident, he could have snuffed out Saul's rebellion in its very early days, before he received the weapons from Lowell that allowed him to attack New Iberia and become a legend. His failure to do so not only cost many Southern lives, but now presented to the Confederacy the prospect of a much greater and more dangerous slave revolt in the future. All of the mocking humiliation heaped upon him by the newspapers that once celebrated him as a hero was richly deserved, in Morgan's opinion.

James Wilson, the aide of Breckinridge's whom Morgan knew slightly, approached.

"Hello, General Morgan," he said pleasantly. "The president will see you now." He looked puzzled, then corrected himself. "I'm sorry, I mean the Secretary of War will see you now. If you'll follow me."

Morgan rose and followed Wilson up the stairs to Breckinridge's office. As they walked, there were a few glances in his direction. He could hear two people have a quick, hushed conversation about why Morgan had come to the War Department. The truth would surely have surprised them.

744

A minute later, he was shown through the door. Breckinridge was hunched over a desk, furiously going through papers, looking more annoyed than Morgan had ever seen him. It surprised him, for Breckinridge had always struck Morgan as the most level-headed and easy-going man he knew. Seeing him with pursed lips and a deeply worried expression was a new experience.

"Hello, John!" Breckinridge said warmly. "Come on in. I'm sorry. I'll be with you in a moment."

"Is something wrong?" Morgan asked as he came close to the desk. "I can come back."

"No. By God, no. For all I know, this will be our only chance to meet. Since the election results were finalized, everything has been chaotic here. I'm trying to get ready to take office as president while also getting ready to hand over the War Department to my successor. Lots of administrative nonsense to take care of. You understand."

"Of course, sir."

He looked over the pile of papers again for a few moments, then gave up. "I'll find it later. A blasted report about a ranch we've established in Texas to breed cavalry horses. A small matter, perhaps, but I want to make sure it's taken care of. But it can wait. Please, take a seat, John." He gestured to the chair across from him and both men sat down.

"I appreciate you seeing me, Mr. Secretary. I know you're extremely busy with the transition."

"Why so formal, John? We're old friends."

"I know. But I come here for a solemn purpose. Formality makes it easier."

Breckinridge frowned. "Don't like where this is going. What solemn purpose do you speak of?"

Morgan pulled a letter from his coat pocket and handed it over to Breckinridge. "This is my official letter of resignation from the Confederate States Army. I'd appreciate it if it were approved immediately."

Breckinridge sighed and quickly glanced through the letter, which was very short and without embellishment. The president-elect shook his head. "Why, John? You still hold my confidence and I am going to be president in three months. Hell, I was planning on making you the head of the cavalry in the Army of Tennessee."

"I appreciate that, Mr. Secretary. I really do. But the people would only say that it's favoritism on your part. I would not accept the appointment if it would generate such chatter, and it would also hurt you politically."

"Fine. You can have a post out of the public spotlight, then. That ranch in Texas I just talked about? Well, there will be a new officer in charge of our cavalry horse program. You know horseflesh better than any man alive. The post is yours if you want it."

Morgan simply shook his head, fearing that the emotions welling up within him would cause embarrassment if he tried to speak. He knew that Breckinridge, a man more loyal to his friends than anyone alive, would stretch the bonds of his precious integrity on his behalf. He would not allow him to do it. In a way, it would be even more dishonorable than the humiliations inflicted upon him by Saul.

"John, I'm not saying this because I'm trying to flatter you. We need you. Our new country is still in a very precarious position. The election showed how divided we are politically. The slavery question threatens to make us an international pariah. The Republicans in the United States are regaining their strength and will probably win back the presidency next year. I need people I can count on, both in the army and in the government. You're one of those men. Please reconsider this, John."

"No, Mr. Secretary. No, I cannot. The people have completely lost faith in me. I have become a figure of amusement. A clown. And my failures let loose a slave rebellion that was only restrained with difficulty and much loss of life. It will get worse, Mr. Secretary. These stories about Saul spreading across the land? They're like the dark clouds on the horizon before a thunderstorm. And when that storm breaks, people will blame me for it. They'll blame me for not stopping it when I had the chance. It will be better for everyone, for you and the country, if I am far, far away."

Breckinridge sat back in his chair and thought for a moment. "Where will you go?"

"I have received an offer from the Khedive of Egypt, offering me command of one of his cavalry divisions. I have decided to accept. I shall depart from Norfolk for Cairo two weeks from now. Mattie and the family will follow in the new year."

"Egypt, eh?" Breckinridge said. "Well, that's not too surprising. Lots of good officers heading out there, Yankees as well as our boys. As a matter of fact, I received a telegram from Cleburne just two days ago telling me that he will be resigning and going to Egypt. What's the name of the fellow who's recruiting all of you? The Khedive?"

"Ismail Pasha," Morgan replied. Morgan had met the official of the Egyptian government in Nashville shortly after he had returned to the headquarters of the Army of Tennessee. He had not taken the offer seriously at first and, in fact, had initially assumed it was some sort of subterfuge to trick him out of money. The more he had looked into the matter, however, the more credible the offer had appeared. Finally, a telegram received from the Confederate chargé d'affaires in Constantinople had confirmed that the man was who he said he was.

The offer promised a generous salary sufficient to ensure that Morgan would be a wealthy man within a few years. He could play the mercenary in some godforsaken desert for a while if it meant that he could put his humiliation behind him.

Breckinridge frowned. "Ismail Pasha? I'll just call him the fellow who's stealing some of my best officers." He looked sternly at Morgan. "You're abandoning me, you know. All these years of friendship, and you're abandoning me just when I need my friends the most."

"I can do nothing by remaining here," Morgan protested. "I'm just a liability for you now. People don't respect me any longer. They ridicule me! No, it's better for me to go, both for you and for me. I can start over someplace else, and you won't have me around to be an embarrassment to your administration."

"You're not an embarrassment," Breckinridge said.

"Yes, I am. And you know it. In the last days of that damn speaking tour of his, Toombs was attacking me as much as he was attacking you. And the newspapers said that his audiences cheered every word. Better for your presidency if I just vanish and have the people forget me. That's why Cleburne is leaving too, I bet. You can't have him around because of his emancipation proposal and you can't have me around because of my failure in Louisiana. Really, we're doing you a favor by leaving."

Breckinridge pursed his lips and shook his head, but said nothing in response right away. Morgan stood respectfully, giving the president-elect time to consider all that he had said. He knew Breckinridge couldn't deny that Morgan's quiet departure would be useful to his incoming administration. Yet he also knew that Breckinridge's loyalty to his friends and fundamental integrity meant that his disappointment was not feigned.

"From what port did you say you will be sailing? Norfolk?"

"That's right. I'm heading back to Nashville tomorrow to prepare the family and put my affairs in order. Then I will depart."

"Then you will pass through Richmond on your way to Norfolk. I shall insist that you and I dine together, in a place where the public will see. I want the people to know that you still hold my confidence and that you are not leaving because I asked you to. And I want a chance to say a proper farewell to my good friend."

Morgan was genuinely touched. "Very well, Mr. President-Elect."

Breckinridge rose from his chair and took the letter of resignation from Morgan. "I accept this. With great reluctance, I must say, but I accept it."

"Thank you, sir," Morgan said. He snapped his body to attention and gave a slow, formal salute, which Breckinridge returned. Not trusting his emotions to speak any further, he turned and left the room without another word. That he was no longer an officer of the Confederate army struck him with nearly physical force. From the highs of his glory days behind Union lines in countless raids to the lows of being outwitted by a black bandit in the Louisiana swamps, it had all ended with the simple handing over of a piece of paper. He assumed that his career was at an end and his coming service to the Khedive would simply provide the money for a comfortable retirement.

In fact, the adventures of John Hunt Morgan had only just begun.

November 19, Morning
French Foreign Ministry Building, Paris, France

Slidell had always detested the sense of urgency. For one thing, he was an old man and his body was increasingly frail. The stress that came with having to act quickly was not healthy. More than that, though, it simply seemed undignified. He liked life to move at the pace he choose and did not like to have to conform his actions to outside influences. The life of a diplomat, sadly, required him to do so more often than he would have preferred.

Whether he liked it or not, Slidell felt the nervous energy of urgency flowing through his veins as he walked as quickly as his delicate body would allow. The steady thumping of his walking stick against the floor seemed to echo through the grand hallways, overcoming the noise of the conversations swirling around him. His valet Michel followed behind him at a respectful distance.

Everything had been in flux since the telegraph had brought word of Breckinridge's triumph in the presidential election. Considering his age, it was expected that the new president would choose someone new to represent him in Paris and that Slidell's days were therefore numbered. Indeed, some of the dinner invitations he had received had been phrased in the tone of farewell messages. He had happily explained to his friends that, though his days of service to the Confederate government were soon to be at an end, he had no intention of returning to the other side of the Atlantic. He had resolved to end his days amid the people of Paris.

What troubled Slidell was the fact that the Foreign Ministry had stopped communicating with him almost entirely. Aside from a few routine discussions with low-level bureaucrats about wine exports and sugar imports, Slidell had not had any real contact with the French government at all. The day news of Lowell's sentencing was received, Slidell received a short, terse note from Foreign Minister La Valette, telling him that negotiations on the treaty of friendship, which had been placed on hold, were now definitively terminated. That this news had been expected made the message no less forbidding.

Slidell had been playing the political and diplomatic game long enough to know that nothing was ever permanent. La Valette might say that negotiations had been ended, but Slidell knew they could always be resumed if he could provide the right incentive.

A telegram from Benjamin had provided hope. It was an exceedingly dim hope, but hope nonetheless.

Tell the French that Lowell will not be executed. Trust me.

Slidell could not see how Benjamin could come through on his promise. Lowell had been sentenced to death by the District Court of Louisiana. It was done. He could only assume that Benjamin was pursuing the only legal remedy left, which would be a presidential pardon. Davis would technically be within his rights to issue such a pardon before Breckinridge was inaugurated, but Slidell found the idea absurd. While he admired many aspects of the man, Slidell had always believed Davis to be stubborn and overly concerned with his reputation for strength and solidity. Benjamin was a persuasive man, but he might as well appeal to a brick wall as to Davis.

The only other possibility was that Benjamin would resort to an illegal attempt to break Lowell out of his confinement and assist him in escaping New Orleans. Strangely, Slidell did not put this past Benjamin. He knew the man well enough to know that he was capable of almost anything. Yet Slidell also knew that such a scenario would not help him with the French. What Slidell needed was a sign that the Confederate government would make some gesture against slavery and Lowell surviving by escaping that government's justice would not provide this.

Still, Slidell had nothing to lose by trying to play this final card, even if it turned out to be chimerical. The Foreign Minister had declined his official request for an interview, apparently happy to do nothing until word arrived regarding Slidell's successor. Slidell had always been scrupulous about observing diplomatic protocol, but desperate times called for desperate measures. If Slidell was going to have one last roll of the dice, it would help to be as dramatic as possible.

As he approached the enormous door to the Salon de la Rotonde, the clerk sitting at the desk in front of it glanced up and was about to ask him his business. Slidell ignored him, marching past as though the man were not even there.

"Monsieur Slidell!" the clerked cried, shooting to his feet.

Slidell pushed on the door, but it was locked. He banged on it with his walking stick as loudly as he could.

"Open this door!" Slidell said to the clerk. "Open it at once!"

"Monsieur, what do you think you're doing?"

Two uniformed guards stepped forward and he raised his cane as if to defend himself. Not wanting to suffer the indignity of being walloped by a septuagenarian, they held back from trying to restrain him. The result was an awkward standoff. The officials and visitors in the hallway froze and stared at Slidell and the guards, stunned at what they were seeing.

The door to the Salon de la Rotonde opened and Foreign Minister La Valette emerged, a quizzical look on his face. "What the devil is going on out here?"

"I am very sorry, sir," the clerk said. "Monsieur Slidell appears to be unwell."

"I am perfectly well, thank you very much!" Slidell shot back. "I must speak with you, Monsieur La Valette. As you declined my request for an appointment, I decided to adopt a more direct approach. Now, may we go into your office?"

The Foreign Minister laughed heartily, as if the whole thing were being staged for his own amusement. "Well, my Confederate friend, I am currently speaking with the Turkish ambassador about a matter of grave importance. I do not like things being done out of their normal channels." He paused, looking carefully at Slidell. "Still, I can see that you are in earnest. I shall make some time available when I am finished with my current meeting. In exchange, will you promise not to batter down my door with that walking stick of yours?"

"Very well," Slidell said. He sat down in one of the waiting chairs without another word, as Michel took his customary place beside him. Still with an amused smile on his face, La Valette returned to his office and closed the door. Slowly, the clerk sat back down, the guards resumed their earlier station, and the people who had stopped to watch the proceedings went on their way.

Slidell waited. His feigned anger might have been indecorous, but it was a price worth paying if he could deliver his message to the French. Nearly an hour passed, but he never suspected that La Valette was having him cool his heels, for there were genuine reasons for the French Foreign Minister to be locked in discussions with the ambassador from the Ottoman Empire, given the instability generated in the Balkans by the Hungarian Crisis.

Eventually, the door opened and the ridiculously attired Turkish ambassador emerged with La Valette. A few more pleasantries were exchanged between the two of them and the Ottoman diplomat went on his way, pointedly declining to say anything to Slidell. For a moment, he wondered whether this was a calculated rudeness, then dismissed the question as irrelevant.

"All right, Monsieur, let's speak," La Valette said, sounding tired. "I do not have much time, however."

"I require little," Slidell said as he rose to his feet, assisted by Michel. He followed La Valette into the Salon de la Rotonde and the door was closed behind them. The Foreign Minister went to the desk and Slidell took the seat in front of him.

"Well, what is this all about?" La Valette asked. "I must say I am surprised. It is very unlike you to become agitated. And it was my understanding that you would be wrapping up your business with my ministry in preparation for handing things over to your successor, whomever he turns out to be."

Slidell did not reply right away, not wanting to be diverted by the minister's words into a direction he did not wish to go. He stared deeply into La Valette's eyes. "The agreement was that the treaty would be signed if the Confederacy made some symbolic gesture against slavery."

"That's what the emperor said to you himself, if I am not mistaken."

"A man named Felix Robertson has been apprehended in Texas. He was wanted for the crime of allowing his men to murder black Union troops who were lying wounded on a battlefield in late 1864. He shall be tried and put in prison."

"Well, that's very nice," La Valette said, a hint of sarcasm in his voice. "Based on the big speech your president-elect gave a few months ago, I know your Confederacy is trying hard to persuade the rest of the world that you are not barbarians. But the French government considers the matter of the treaty to be closed. We have already explained this to you. The arrest of some criminal out on the frontier is not going to change that. The issue was decided the moment Charles Russell Lowell was sentenced to death."

"The executive branch of the Confederate government does not control the courts."

"Yes, and that is too bad for you, isn't it?"

Slidell leaned forward, trusting Benjamin because he had no other choice. "Lowell will not be executed."

La Valette was taken aback and the amused smile vanished from his face. "I'm sorry?"

"He won't be executed. I have been assured of that."

"By whom?"

"That I cannot say."

"Then why should I believe you? The court found him guilty and sentenced him to hang. You just said yourself that the president doesn't control the courts. I don't see how his fate can be avoided."

"It seems likely that Jefferson Davis will issue a presidential pardon for Lowell before he leaves office."

La Valette laughed. "That will be the day! I have never met the man, but everything you have told me about him, and everything I have read in the papers, tells me that he's just another one of your stubborn Southern slavery apologists. He also seems very touchy regarding his reputation. He would no sooner pardon Lowell than he would leave all his wealth to Abraham Lincoln in his will."

"But you will soon see the truth of what I say. The news will soon arrive announcing either Lowell's execution or Lowell's pardon."

"I suppose that's indisputable."

"So I only ask you to be prepared to sign our proposed treaty as soon as word arrives that Lowell has been spared."

The Foreign Minister laughed again. "All right, Slidell. I'll humor you on this. I'll speak to the emperor about this. I'm sure he'll find it as amusing as I do."

"France still has much to gain from entering into this treaty. Your control of Mexico would be assured and your economic situation vis-à-vis England will be much improved."

"I know all this. I supported the treaty, you know. In and of itself, I like it. It is just public opinion we have to worry about. I will frankly say, Slidell, that I personally think you've gone mad. I think you're so personally invested in the success of this treaty that you have concocted a fantasy of your president being willing to pardon Lowell because it is now the only possibility that the treaty will be signed. But I will bring this to the emperor out of respect for your long tenure here in Paris."

"Thank you, Monsieur. And as for me having gone mad, you may well be right."

November 20, Afternoon
Westminster Abbey, London

Wolseley stood erect, clad in a uniform of an officer of the Perthshire Volunteers which he had ensured was meticulously cleaned and ironed for the occasion. He was icily calm, even though he knew that this was perhaps the greatest day of his life. Although he had already been notified of his knighthood, it would not become official until Queen Victoria herself had completed the investiture ceremony.

During the voyage back across the Atlantic to England, it had occurred to Wolseley that he might refuse to accept the honor of the knighthood. After all, there were honors more illustrious than being made a Knight Commander of the Order of the Bath. It was entirely possible that, by accepting it, he would risk being passed over for greater honors in the future. He had no doubt that his greatest glories on the battlefield were yet to come. He might have held out for the Order of the Thistle, or even the Order of the Garter. It was too late to change his mind now, however, so he might as well get on with it.

He stood in King Henry VII's Chapel of Westminster Abbey, an immense room with a high vaulted ceiling in the Gothic style. Sunlight flooded in through countless small stained-glass windows, illuminating the whole area magnificently with different colors. Banners representing members of the Order of Bath hung from the ceiling. Though a military man through and through, Wolseley had studied art and architecture and could appreciate beauty when he saw it. This part of the most famous abbey in the world was nothing if not beautiful.

Beside him were two other men who were being made Knight Commanders. One was Henry Hugh Clifford, a fellow officer he knew only slightly and whose career seemed focused more on staff work than actual fighting, though he had won the Victoria Cross in the Crimea. He seemed a decent enough fellow, and Wolseley never undervalued the importance of good staff officers, but it was obvious that the man's knighthood was due more to his being the son of a baron than anything else. The other man was not a soldier at all, but an engineer who had built a number of bridges and railways in India and whose name Wolseley had already forgotten. Wolseley was a man who liked progress, but the idea that construction of infrastructure should rank with great feats of warfare seemed silly to him.

A few dozen members of the Order flanked the room, all clad in their elaborate Mantle of the Order of the Bath, a long, silky robe-like garment similar to that worn by university graduates, except that it was colored red. Sitting near the altar on the far end of the chapel was a woman Wolseley had often thought of and for whom he had bled and nearly died on the battlefield, but had never seen before this day.

Clad in the same mantle as the other members of the Order, waiting to conduct the investiture service, was Her Majesty Victoria, by the Grace of God, of the United Kingdom of Great Britain and Ireland, Queen, Defender of the Faith.

This would be the first investiture service of the Order of the Bath in many years. For many years, the Queen had inducted new members in fairly simple ceremonies in Buckingham Palace. She had largely been in seclusion since the death of her beloved husband Prince Albert some years before, but was now emerging from the shadows and resuming her public role as monarch. Rumor maintained that her reappearance among the people was mostly due to the influence of Prime Minister Disraeli.

"We are ready to begin!" said the herald. He didn't need to speak very loudly, for his voice rang through the chapel like a bell. Wolseley was momentarily taken aback, then marveled at how the acoustics built into the design of the room allowed a voice to be heard so clearly.

Wolseley took a deep breath, wondering who would be chosen to go first. It mattered not at all, of course, yet somehow he could not help but obsess over the question for the next few seconds. He felt the eyes of all the other knights on him, feeling as if they were all trying to figure him out, open him up like a box to see what was inside. They would fail, naturally. Garnet Wolseley was who he was and no one else had any right to question him. With smug satisfaction, he reminded himself that he was undoubtedly smarter than anyone else in the room, the Queen included.

"Colonel Henry Hugh Clifford! Step forward!"

He felt an involuntary tug of disappointment at not being selected before the others, but quickly pushed the thought out of his mind. He watched as Clifford walked forward at the precise speed that they had all been briefed beforehand to use. What happened next was an extreme anticlimax, considering how so many men would have given almost anything to receive the honor being bestowed by the monarch. Clifford knelt before the plump little woman on the knighting stool and then remained still as she lightly touched with a sword first the man's right shoulder, then his left.

"I knight thee, Sir Henry Hugh Clifford, Companion of the Order of the Bath," said the queen.

Clifford stood up, a beaming smile on his face, while a page stepped forward with the burgundy mantle and helped Clifford put it on. He then retired back down the way he had come and resumed his previous place.

The engineer from India went next and the simple ceremony was repeated. Wolseley felt suddenly impatient, wanting to get everything over with so that he could go back to his rented lodgings and write a letter to Louisa to discuss their upcoming wedding. If nothing else, it would be fitting for him to sign his name with the much coveted "KCB" at the end of his signature.

Finally, the call came. "Colonel Garnet Wolseley! Step forward!"

He strode towards the Queen, purposefully walking ever so slightly faster than he had been told to walk, though he doubted anyone noticed. He reached the altar and, while Clifford and the Indian engineer had kept their eyes focused on the ground near Queen Victoria's feet, treating the woman's face as if it were a bright sun, Wolseley stared directly up into her blue eyes. Her face betrayed a hint of displeasure at his effrontery, but while he respected his monarch as much as any other British soldier, debasement did not become him.

"Kneel," she said sternly.

He did as told, and she performed the same simple ceremony as she had with the other two, touching the sword onto his right shoulder, then his left. "I knight thee, Sir Garnet Joseph Wolseley, Knight Commander of the Order of the Bath."

The page came forward and helped Wolseley put on the burgundy mantle. He willed himself to keep a straight face throughout these few minutes, though he could not deny how his heart leapt. He was about to retire back to the place from which he had started, when the Queen's voice unexpectedly echoed through the chamber again.

"Gentlemen," she said gravely. "I wish to speak to Sir Garnet alone. Please leave us for a few moments."

The assembled knights glanced uncertainly at one another and there was a chattering of confused whispers which the acoustics of the chapel strangely magnified. People asked one another if they had heard the Queen correctly, what this strange development might mean, and who this Garnet Wolseley fellow was in the first place. Yet there could be no disobeying the Queen's command and the assembled men quietly shuffled out the door.

Wolseley had no idea why the Queen wanted to speak to him without the others present, but he was determined not to show any bewilderment or uneasiness. He stood to attention, his face as straight as a plank of wood, looking up at the monarch's face. Slowly, the chamber emptied of other people. With a magnified echo, the great door was closed, sealing the two of them inside.

"Your Majesty," Wolseley said simply.

"Sir Garnet," she said with a sort of haughty pleasantness. For a long moment, she looked down on him from the throne that had been placed near the altar, considering him as a cat might consider a mouse, albeit an especially arrogant one. A strange smile spread over her face, yet she did not speak.

"I am at your service," he said, hoping to coax her into saying something.

"I am glad to hear it," she replied. "Sir Garnet, you very nearly caused a war between the British Empire and the United States, a war which would have entailed considerable loss of life and great expense of money. You did so without any authorization from my government. You took units of my army across the border of a powerful nation with whom we were not at war."

"Your Majesty, there must be some…"

"Do not say that there must be some mistake. There is no mistake, Sir Garnet. You might have pulled the wool over the eyes of that fool General Napier and quite a few others, but you cannot fool me. I know everything that happened. Events of a most astonishing kind, I may say."

The emotion of panic was not one that came easily to Wolseley. He could have probably counted on his fingers the number of times he had experienced it over the course of his life. Yet at this moment, he felt himself on the verge of shaking in fear. How could he have thought his actions wouldn't have been discovered? Now he stood before his monarch, the ruler of the world's most powerful empire, with everything laid bare.

She snorted, but more in amusement than contempt. "You should feel fortunate that the facts have not become more widely known, else serious repercussions might have fallen upon your head. In the future, I hope you shall leave questions of foreign policy to my ministers and follow the orders you are given."

"I shall, Your Majesty." Wolseley spoke these words in the tone of a disobedient child being disciplined, yet relief swept through him the moment the Queen spoke, for it meant that he was not going to be punished for what he had done.

She smiled. "I am pleased, Sir Garnet. I know what happened. Prime Minister Disraeli knows what happened. Only a few others. You covered your tracks well. I would like to let this matter end here. The Americans are agreeable to this suggestion. What say you?"

"I agree, Your Majesty." There was really nothing else he could say.

"Good. I want fighting soldiers, Sir Garnet. I have been told a great deal about you in the past month. I know how well you fought in India and the Crimea. They tell me that you have a keen and original mind, which is frankly rare in my army. You certainly have displayed initiative, if greatly in excess of what I desire."

"Thank you, Your Majesty." He was beginning to recover his nerve.

"You are headed to the Northwest Frontier with your regiment, yes?"

"That's correct, Your Majesty."

"A dangerous place, the Northwest Frontier. The tribes there are good fighters. I have often thought that they would make fine soldiers in our Indian army if they could only be reduced to obedience. Try not to get yourself killed. I want our Empire expanded, you understand. Glory is all well and good, but you must remain alive to be of proper service to me, Sir Garnet."

He allowed himself a slight chuckle. "Of course, Your Majesty."

"Off with you then. And make sure that head of yours remains attached to your shoulders. Something good might come out of it one day."

He bowed his head. "Your Majesty," he said simply. Then he slowly began walking backwards, careful to observe the form of not turning his back to the Queen and trying to keep his posture as straight as possible. She grinned, clearly amused at seeing him struggle to perform this feat. He heard the door open behind him and kept backing up until he was out of the chapel. He sensed the other men of the Order around him, still whispering excitedly as to what the Queen's actions might mean. Then the door closed, cutting off Wolseley's view of his queen.

No one approached him to ask what had happened. Wolseley snorted a slight laugh, then turned to leave Westminster Abbey and go home to write his letter. Then, his thoughts could turn towards his departure for India.

November 21, Morning
Mechanic's Hall, Richmond, Virginia

Toombs sat glumly in the chair outside of Breckinridge's office, having now waited for more than twenty minutes. He could feel the stares of the men passing by, who, being War Department employees, were almost certain to have voted for Breckinridge in the election. A few politely said hello to him, but he could imagine the internal sneering and mockery going on in their minds. It was only with great effort that he kept himself from denouncing them as the fools they doubtless were.

For the time being, Mechanic's Hall had become more than the Confederate War Department. It had become the hub of the incoming Breckinridge administration, with congressmen and other officials coming and going as regularly as military officers. When he arrived, he had encountered Congressman John Gordon leaving the building, whom rumor said was in line to succeed Breckinridge as Secretary of War. Their handshake had been exceedingly stiff and formal.

As he waited, Toombs fumed. In the week since the terrible news was received from Texas, he had felt like all of his dreams had been shattered like a crystal vase. He could not fathom a way that he could put them back together. He was not going to be the Vice president, which ruined his plans for seeking the presidency six years hence. He might run anyway, for he was still one of the most influential members of the Senate. Yet his credibility within the SRP, the very party he had been so instrumental in creating, had been terribly damaged. He had thrown all of his energies into the effort to defeat Breckinridge and it had all been futile. In the words of one SRP-aligned newspaper in Alabama, Toombs had been weighed in the balances and found wanting. Other elements within the SRP would surely seek to supplant him as the party's de facto leader.

Rubbing salt into the wound, it had become clear that he and Beauregard had won the popular vote and that the Breckinridge-Kemper ticket had only prevailed due to the mechanics of the Electoral College. The SRP had won their six states by considerable margins, while Breckinridge had taken his five states by very narrow ones. Toombs could recall some discussion at the Montgomery Convention, when the delegates were debating the new Confederate Constitution, of doing away with the Electoral College. Although most had supported the idea, nothing had been done in the end because it hadn't been considered a priority. As these thoughts passed through his mind, Toombs reflected that he had yet another thing to be bitter about.

Despondent over the election results, he had returned to Richmond for the lame duck session of Congress. Upon arrival, he was dumbfounded to receive a request from Breckinridge for a meeting. He could not imagine what the president-elect wanted to talk to him about. At first, he assumed that the man only wanted to gloat about his victory, but as much as he detested him, Toombs had to admit that Breckinridge was not a petty man. He had considered declining the invitation, but curiosity and a sense of patriotic obligation persuaded him to go. If word got out that he had been invited to meet with the president-elect and refused, the people would see him as a sore loser.

So he had come to Mechanic's Hall that morning and was now waiting impatiently. He felt more tired than he had in a very long time. During the heady days of the campaign, he had felt energized, as if he was a much younger man. Between Election Day and the final verdict from Texas, he had been kept aloft by sheer nervous energy. For the past week, however, he had been utterly deflated, almost unable to rise from bed in the morning. It had taken a great effort of will to come to the meeting with Breckinridge.

The door opened and, to Toombs's astonishment, Stephens emerged. He rose to his feet quickly as his friend closed the door behind him.

"Aleck! What are you doing here?"

"The same thing you are doing here, most likely," Stephens replied.

"I'm sorry. When they told me that Breckinridge was meeting with the vice president, I assumed that they meant Kemper."

"Not surprising," Stephens said. "One might have thought I was useless, now that I am on my way out."

"What did he want to talk to you about?"

"He asked me…" Stephens's voice trailed away and he glanced back at the door from which he had just emerged. "You know, I think I will let Breckinridge himself tell you."

Toombs scoffed slightly. "Not like you to be cryptic with me."

"With anyone else, I wouldn't be. But Breckinridge is the president-elect. For that reason alone, he is deserving of our respect."

"I'll respect the office," Toombs replied. "Not so much the man."

"I'd advise you, as your friend, to respect both." He paused a moment. "And when he asks you what he is about to ask you, I advise you to say yes, just as I did."

Stephens walked off down the hall, leaving Toombs to wonder what his words meant. Whatever the outcome of his own meeting, he imagined that he would have plenty of time to discuss it at length with Stephens later on. In a world of such dramatic and speedy changes in fortune, it comforted him to know that he always had a friend to count on in Stephens.

He took a deep breath, then loudly knocked on the door three times.

"Come in!" the voice of Breckinridge called from within.

Toombs straightened himself, molded a stoic expression onto his face, and opened the door. There was Breckinridge, the man who had defeated him, the man who had made him appear a fool before the entire South, the man whom Toombs was sure would lead the South down the wrong path. He was sitting behind his desk, bolt upright in his chair, appearing strong and vibrant to Toombs's eyes. As Toombs closed the door behind him and walked toward the desk, Breckinridge rose from his chair and extended his hand.

"Thank you for coming, Senator Toombs," the president-elect said. "I confess I was uncertain whether you would agree to meet with me."

Toombs unexpectedly found himself uncertain whether he should shake Breckinridge's hand. He had not thought about it before. He knew that decorum and decency required it of him, but the thought of any display of cordiality with the man who had destroyed his ambitions seemed an insult and an outrage. He felt the anger welling up inside of him again and forced it back down through sheer force of will. He made himself extend his hand and shake Breckinridge's.

"Please, sit," the president-elect said, gesturing to the chairs.

"Allow me to congratulate you on your election, sir," Toombs said stiffly, forcing the words out of his mouth.

"Thank you, Senator." He frowned. "I understand that this must be a difficult interview for you. Were I in your place, I should be most unhappy and uncomfortable. It speaks well of your patriotism that you agreed to come."

"Alas, you are not in my place."

Breckinridge nodded slowly. "I know what it's like to lose an election."

Toombs scoffed. "You hardly know how I feel. You knew you were going to lose to Lincoln in 1860. That can't compare to what I've just gone through."

"Senator Toombs, if I may say so, you would have hated the Vice Presidency. Of that I have no doubt. When I was vice president before the war, I felt every day that I was in a straightjacket. You would have been unable to express your opinions on any topic, unable to intervene in the debates of the Senate, unable to have any real impact on anything at all. You're not the sort of man to bite your tongue, Toombs. Trust me, being vice president would have driven you mad."

"Do you expect me to be grateful to you for winning?" Toombs said derisively. "You'll have to do much better than that, Breckinridge. Now, why did me to come visit you here? I don't like you. I don't mind saying it. But I have never known you to be a cruel man, so I hope that you have not dragged me into your office just so you can mock me."

"That would be the farthest from my intentions. What would I gain by doing that? No, Toombs. No, I asked you here today because the election is over. It is time for us to come together for the good of the Confederacy."

"You can wish that all you want," Toombs said. "I am already deep into discussions with my colleagues in the States' Rights Party. We will be in control of both chambers of Congress in the coming year, as well as most of the state legislatures. We will be able to block any policies you wish to enact and we plan on doing so."

"All of them?" Breckinridge asked.

"All of those with which we disagree, which will essentially be the same thing."

Breckinridge nodded slowly, saying nothing for a moment. "What of your fiscal bill?"

Toombs was confused. "What?"

"Your fiscal bill. The proposed reforms to the system of government revenue that you laid before the Senate. What if I told you that I planned on making that one of my highest priorities after I assume office?"

Toombs laughed. "You won't do that! You and Davis have always opposed shifting the means of revenue collection from the national government to the states."

"Davis did. I didn't."

"But you never spoke out about it."

"Davis was the president. As a member of the Cabinet, it was not really my place to voice disagreement to the public. Down that road lies chaos. But now I'm the president. I have read through your bill very carefully and frankly I think it is very good legislation. Perhaps not what I would have put forward, but probably better, to be honest. You understand fiscal policy much better than I do. That was obvious to me before the war. Now, I am willing to put the weight of the Presidency behind this bill to assure its passage. If I do, would the SRP oppose me?"

Toombs had difficulty believing what he was hearing. He knew that he would never have spoken to Breckinridge in a friendly or welcoming manner had the SRP won the election, nor would be have considered adopting any of Breckinridge's policy proposals. To the victor went the spoils, as far as Toombs was concerned. That indisputable fact of political life was as true for his time as it had been for the Romans in the time of Caesar.

It had to be a trick, Toombs thought to himself. Breckinridge was trying to derive some sort of advantage by pretending to accept an important part of the SRP platform. Perhaps the president-elect thought that he could divide the SRP and bring many of its members into whatever party eventually formed out of his own supporters. Perhaps he was simply trying to build some sort of bridge to his erstwhile enemies in a desperate ploy to get support for his unsteady administration.

"All right," Toombs said. "So you're saying you'll sign my fiscal bill. Thank you. Was there anything else?"

Breckinridge frowned slightly, piqued at the petty slight. "Yes, actually. There are many things I want to discuss with you."

"Well, what?"

"It's not enough to just pass the bill. The fiscal situation of the Confederacy is in terrible shape. It has been since the war ended. I need your help to fix it. That's why I want you to serve in the Cabinet as the Secretary of the Treasury."

"Secretary of the..." Toombs drew his head in amazement. A moment later, confusion turned to anger. "I did not come here to be insulted, Breckinridge!" Toombs spat.

"I'm not trying to insult you," Breckinridge said quickly. "I'm completely serious. I want you to be the Secretary of the Treasury."

"Hogwash! You're toying with me! What, do you think I'll jump through your hoops like a dog doing tricks because you dangle a Cabinet position before me? Davis tried that trick once. Made me Secretary of War. I didn't like it and I quit. I wouldn't have him for a master and I won't have you!"

"Senator Toombs, you're misjudging me completely. I am not making this offer out of any desire for political advantage. I truly think you're the right person for the job."

"What about Trenholm?"

"He's being made our minister to London. Listen to me, Senator, I'm being completely open and genuine here. I've already informed General Beauregard that he will be made commander of the Army of Tennessee, effective on the day of my inauguration. Your friend Stephens? I intend to nominate him as the first Chief Justice of the Supreme Court, the establishment of which I intend to make one of my top priorities. He accepted. I've already agreed to discuss the names of the other justices I shall nominate with Stephens before doing so."

Toombs didn't reply, sitting back in his seat and folding his arms across his chest. An ugly sneer formed on his face. He was not going to fall for any of Breckinridge's tricks.

Breckinridge was still talking. "I'm trying to reach out to the SRP, don't you see? Raphael Semmes supported Beauregard and denounced me. Well, I am promoting him to admiral and making him commander of the Gulf Fleet. Governor Vance of North Carolina? I'm asking him to be the Minister to the United States. Don't get me wrong. Most of the positions are going to people I know and trust. But I want to bring you and your people in, too. There's no reason we can't work together for the good of the Confederacy."

"Why?" Toombs demanded. "This is all some device to trick us. Well, the SRP is not going to be tricked. Why would you do any of this, bringing us into your government?"

"Because it's not about me, dammit!" Breckinridge thundered, anger finally entering his voice. "The country is divided. The election proved how deep our divisions run. The abolitionists no longer provide us with a common enemy. The Confederacy will only stand now if good men on both sides of the election now join together and govern with one voice."

Toombs stood from the chair and turned his back on the president-elect. He saw a whiskey decanter and glasses on a small table against the wall and, without asking permission, strode over to it and poured himself a glass.

"Get me one as well, won't you?" Breckinridge asked, a strange mix of conciliation and hostility in his voice.

Toombs poured another glass and walked over to smack it down on the desk so forcefully that it might have broken. He then paced back and forth before Breckinridge, taking a sip of whiskey every few seconds. He frowned and shook his head, trying as hard as he could to comprehend why Breckinridge would be so willing to make overtures to the SRP.

For what he would later remember as an infinitely long moment, Toombs actually considered accepting Breckinridge's offer. As Secretary of the Treasury, he would be able to implement the fiscal reforms he had long advocated. Breckinridge had already told him that he would support his legislation, which meant that they would easily become law at some point in 1868. He might go down in history as the man who saved the Confederacy from financial collapse.

More importantly, as a member of the Cabinet, he would be a full participant in discussions about crucial policy decisions for the next six years. The people would see Toombs as one of the key members of the government, and rightly so. If the administration succeeded, he would be seen as part of the reason for its success. It was entirely possible that the post of Secretary of the Treasury would be a better springboard for a run at the Presidency in 1873 than the Vice Presidency would have been.

As quickly as the thought passed through his mind, however, Toombs angrily rejected it. The thought of being one of Breckinridge's men, of taking orders from him, of having to defend him when people criticized him, was simply too terrible to contemplate. It was Breckinridge who had destroyed his plans and humiliated him. He would not kneel before a man like a suppliant. It was out of the question.

Toombs spun on his heels and faced Breckinridge again. "Did you not read in the papers what I said about you during the campaign?" he demanded.

Breckinridge laughed harshly. "Yes, I did. Every word of it."

"Well, I will not unsay a single word. Damn you, Breckinridge! You're a damn bastard! A damn Kentucky bastard! I'd sooner kiss Abraham Lincoln's ass than serve in your Cabinet! No, Breckinridge. I will stay in the Senate. And I will do my best to make sure that everything you want to do never gets done! If I have anything to say about it, you'll be remembered as an enormous failure!"

Toombs downed the remainder of the whiskey in a single gulp and threw the glass, which shattered against the desk where Breckinridge was sitting. With that, Toombs turned his back to the president-elect and walked determinedly towards the door, opening it so forcefully that it banged against the wall with a loud crash.

He heard Breckinridge shout some final words to him as he slammed the door closed, but he could not make out what they were. Feeling he had been victorious, Toombs held his head high as he strode through the hallways to the front entrance of Mechanic's Hall and back out onto the streets of Richmond. Breckinridge's offer had been a siren song, offering the prospect of power and influence, but only at the cost of his soul. Toombs felt deeply proud of himself for having rejected it. Now, it was time to meet with his fellow SRP members of Congress and begin to plot out a strategy of resistance.

November 23, Morning
Parish Jail, New Orleans, Louisiana

Lowell was dreaming. It was a strange dream. He was standing amid salt-incrusted rocks just a few yards from a seashore, with waves crashing against them every few seconds, tossing pillars of water into the air. Staring out towards the horizon, his eyes took in the image of the wine dark sea. He instinctively knew that the waters were the Aegean Sea and he was somewhere in Greece. All around him were some of the greatest minds of the classical world, engaged in an animated discussion. He could somehow recognize the philosophers Plato, Socrates, Aristotle, Seneca, Cicero, and others among the greatest thinkers of the ancient Greeks and Romans.

Yet Lowell could not hear any of the words the men were speaking. He could see their lips moving, he could observe their facial expressions, but the content of their conversations was entirely blocked to his understanding. He was in the presence of his heroes, but despite all his education, despite all his reading, despite all his attempts to make himself a better man, he could not hear what they were saying. He felt anger and despair and began loudly yelling at them, begging for them to speak in a way that he could comprehend. Yet they paid no attention to him at all.

Another man approached, whom Lowell somehow knew was Boethius. Unlike the others, Boethius was looking intently at Lowell and walking in his direction. He held a book in his hands, which he was holding out towards Lowell, offering it to him. It was a big, thick book, with a covering of red Moroccan leather. The cover title caused Lowell's heart to beat more rapidly, for the book was called *A History of Slavery in North America, from 1619 to the Present*.

Lowell took the book and opened it. The picture on the front page depicted the arrival of slaves at the Jamestown Colony in 1619. He started to flip through the book quickly, noticing through glances on successive pages discussion about the failure of the Constitutional Convention to address slavery, about the invention of the cotton gin reinvigorating slavery when it had appeared to be on the decline, about Denmark Vesey's attempted uprising in 1822 and Nat Turner's rebellion in 1831.

Boethius stared at him intently as he kept flipping through the pages. He saw that a chapter of the book was devoted to the attempted compromises in Congress to hold the nation together even as the slavery issue started to tear it apart. It described the rise of the Fire-Eaters in the South and the abolitionist movement in the North and the political turmoil that drove the country inevitably towards civil war.

Lowell's heart began to pound as he realized that he was only about halfway through the book. Boethius had given him a history from the future. He momentarily found this astounding, but as it was a vision coming to him in a dream, he choose not to question it. He continued perusing the volume, finding an illustration of Saul and then one of himself, standing before Judge Moise in the New Orleans courtroom. He had only to continue reading through it to learn what the ultimate fate of slavery in America was going to be. With trembling hands, he flipped to the next chapters, only to discover that they were blank pieces of paper.

"No!" he shouted. "No! Please, Boethius! You need to tell me!"

Suddenly, a loud, repetitive clanging sound began ringing, causing the assembled classical thinkers to look around in confusion. Storm clouds were rapidly gathering above them. Yet the dream was already fading and Lowell found himself shifting uncomfortably in his cot, the cobwebs vanishing from his mind.

He opened his eyes, dimly perceiving the faint light of an early morning coming through his window. The banging sound continued, persisting from his dream-state into his wakefulness. Lowell realized that someone was banging on the door and rose into a sitting position.

"Wake up, Lowell!" an unfamiliar voice shouted from the other side of the door. "We're coming in!"

With a rattling of keys and a metallic screech, the door slid open. Lowell just had time to swing his feet off the bed and stand before he was confronted by three armed guards wearing Confederate Army uniforms rather than the garb of prison guards, and one man wearing a stiff business suit. None looked happy.

"You are leaving at once," the man in the suit said sternly. "Come with us."

Lowell's courage, unsteady as he was still not fully awake, faltered momentarily. "My execution is not supposed to happen for another week!"

The man scoffed. "You're not being executed, Lowell. You're going home. You've been issued a full pardon by President Jefferson Davis. I don't have the first damn clue why he did it. God knows I disagree. But orders are orders."

"What?" Lowell asked, utterly dumbfounded. "I don't understand."

"I don't, either, Lowell," the man replied. "But Davis did it and he's still the president. Now, listen to me. I'm under very strict orders to get you the hell out of here before word spreads about what has happened. There's a French ship waiting for you at the docks to take you out of the city. If the people find out before we get to there, a mob is going to form and lynch you without hesitation. Now, let's go!"

"Wait!" Lowell said, struggling to comprehend what he was hearing. "This doesn't make any sense. Why am I not to be executed?"

"I don't have time to answer your questions, dammit! Besides that, I don't have the damn answers for you, anyway! You ask me, you should have been hanged from the nearest tree the moment you were arrested, but it's not up to me. Now, do you have anything to take with you? Because we're leaving this cell in less than a minute. If you value your life, don't do anything to slow us down."

Lowell felt dizzy and nearly fell down onto his cot. For a moment, he thought what he was being told could not be possible, for even if Jefferson Davis had pardoned him for some reason, the rest of the Confederate government would refuse to accept it. Then he remembered that the Confederate Constitution was almost identical to the United States Constitution and both gave the chief executive blanket authority to pardon whomever they wished. If Davis really had pardoned him, then, legally speaking, it was as if he had never violated Confederate law at all. He was not guilty of inciting servile insurrection or anything else.

His heart leapt at the thought that he would be reunited with his wife and family as a free man, no longer burdened by what he had done. He imagined embracing and kissing Josephine, sitting down to dinner with her again in their dining room, twirling around with her on the dancefloor at a fashionable Boston party, or simply gazing into her beautiful eyes after making love with her in the middle of the night. He imagined seeing the joyous smiles on the faces of his children as they ran toward him to be picked up, feeling pride as his little daughter started to learn how to read or his baby boy took his first steps, and watching them grow from children into an honored man and a dignified woman.

Lowell had forced such thoughts from his mind in the months since his arrest, for they only pushed him towards despair and spiritual collapse. If the man was telling the truth, the wall he had carefully constructed in his heart had just been broken and all the emotions could pour through it without anything to block them. He could go back to Boston and live the life that he had always wanted to live.

"Lowell?" the man said impatiently. "Didn't you hear what I said?"

He scarcely noticed that the man was speaking, so quickly was his mind working. He felt dizzy. Lowell was able to see past thoughts of his family and consider for a moment the larger implications of being pardoned. He couldn't fathom why Davis would have done it, but he saw in an instant that it wrecked

762

his plan for striking a moral blow against slavery. The Confederacy, by pardoning him, would appear to the world to be conciliatory and civilized, precisely the opposite of what it actually was. Rather than being branded as villainous and devilish, the Confederacy would come out of the entire episode appearing merciful.

"I don't wish to go," Lowell said suddenly, as he realized the game Davis was playing. "No, I want my execution to go forward."

The man in the suit looked confused. "Why the hell would you want to die? You're pardoned. There's not going to be any execution. And you're coming with us to get on the ship, whether you like it or not."

"No!"

The man laughed incredulously, then turned to the three guards. "Get this damn crazy Yankee. We don't have time for this."

The men stepped forward and grabbed Lowell by the shirt, tugging him quickly out of the cell. Aside from the courtroom and occasional excursions to the jail yard for exercise, the barred room had been Lowell's entire world since the moment he entered it. He had expected only death to free him of its confines. Now that he was truly liberated, even if the circumstances made no sense to him, he did not know whether to shout for joy or for rage.

The guards hustled him into a waiting paddy wagon, where a slave quickly clicked the horses into a trot the moment the door slammed. Looking through the window, Lowell could see that the sun had yet to rise, but the rose-colored glow of dawn was beginning to emerge on the eastern horizon. Street sweepers and a few others were at work, but few other people were out. Some looked questioningly at their wagon as they dashed by, wondering what they might be doing.

The man in the suit called repeatedly for the slave driving the wagon to hurry. As he began to think more clearly, Lowell realized that the man's fears of a mob were quite justified. It would not take long for word of Lowell's release to spread through the city. Indeed, it had probably started to do so the moment he stepped out the front door of the jail, for a few people had been standing nearby and his face was now well-known. When it became clear that he was being taken to a ship rather than to the execution ground, the people of the city would certainly become enraged. It would have all the makings of a ferocious riot, like the one that had killed Naismith. It was no wonder that the Confederates were anxious to get him out of the city as soon as possible.

They came to an abrupt stop as they reached the dock. Lowell glanced through the window and saw a three-masted ship flying the French Tricolour. The door was opened and Lowell stepped out quickly. A man was sitting on horseback close by.

"Get on the damn ship and get the hell out of here," the man in the suit said sternly.

"I have no clothes or money," Lowell replied.

"Not my problem. Get on the ship."

A man on board called down in broken English. "You Lowell? You come on. You now come on."

"I speak French," Lowell replied in that language.

"Oh, very good," the man replied quickly in French. "I'm Captain Daviau. There's the gangplank. Come on aboard. We have food and a change of clothes for you. I'm told that we need to cast off immediately." He glanced over at the horseman. "Go!" he said sharply, as if announcing the start of a race. With a kick and shout, the horseman galloped off.

Lowell said nothing to the Confederates who had taken him there. There was no need. He stepped off of the soil of Louisiana, walked up the gangplank, and boarded the ship. Even docked and secured, the slight shifting he could feel under his feet brought his mind back to the weeks he had spent on board the *SS Vincent*. He felt a tug of grief for the memory of Captain Naismith.

Daviau walked up to him and extended his hand. "Good morning, Lowell. I am honored to have such a famous man as a guest. We'll be underway in an hour or so. In the meantime, I have my cook preparing breakfast for you."

Lowell glanced around. "I've become rather familiar with ships, Monsieur. It appears all is ready for departure, so why not leave at once?"

Daviau smiled. "Because I am under orders to notify the French consulate that you have safely been delivered to us. It is very important, I am told. I have sent a messenger. As soon as he returns, we shall be on our way."

Lowell did not understand why the French government would care that he had been released and was now on board a ship. He thought of pressing Daviau for more details, but decided against it. Looking down at the dock, he saw that the four Confederates who had brought him to the dock had gotten back into the paddy wagon and were now driving away.

"Breakfast, you say?" Lowell asked.

"Poached eggs, ham, and champagne."

The idea of tasting champagne for the first time since leaving Boston filled Lowell with a delight that momentarily pushed everything else out of his mind. He went with the captain to his quarters and sat down to breakfast. He still could not understand what had happened, much less why, but it was now beginning to dawn on him that he would have plenty of time to figure it all out.

Forty minutes later, the messenger returned and announced that he had delivered the news to the French consulate, which in turn was sending a telegram to Paris. Shortly thereafter, the ship weighed anchor and embarked on its journey to take Charles Russell Lowell home.

November 26, Afternoon
Tuilleries Palace, Paris, France

Slidell had worn his finest suit for the occasion, which was only natural, as it was the culmination of a lifetime of service to the South and marked the climactic end to his political and diplomatic career. He stood tall, feeling so strong that he might have done away with his walking stick entirely. More so than at any other time in his life, John Slidell felt proud of himself.

The room was positively glittering, with the sunlight coming in through immense windows and being reflected in every direction by the mirrors and gold gilding on every wall. Around the walls, various flunkies of the French government and diplomatic observers from other countries stood to watch the treaty signing. Slidell took amused satisfaction from the fact that Minister Blair of the United States had been invited yet had declined, pleading illness.

On either side of Slidell stood Marguerite and the Baron d'Erlanger, their expressions of gratification mirroring his own. The treaty meant more to them than the simple success of their father or father-in-law. The elevation of the relationship between France and the Confederacy to an outright alliance would elevate Marguerite's social standing to new heights, for she would be seen as the female personification of that alliance. For the Baron d'Erlanger, it promised new financial opportunities to expand his already vast wealth. Many who had previously held back from doing business with him on account of his Confederate connection would now have second thoughts. The treaty, above and beyond what was stated in its provisions, gave the Confederacy a new level of credibility in the world.

Slidell noticed how Marguerite had cast disdainful smirks towards Napoleon III a few times, and how the emperor had responded simply by gazing at her with barely suppressed lust. He recalled the hilarious and eventful night when he had caught the emperor on the verge of bedding his daughter and the role that incident had played in what was now transpiring. History often worked in strange ways.

Slidell's suit had been made by the most respected clothing designer in Paris, yet it was nothing compared to the elaborate imperial costumes worn by Napoleon III or Foreign Minister La Valette, festooned with medals and ribbons. Slidell sighed at the thought that the Confederacy, though an aristocracy for all practical purposes, still had to maintain the façade of being a Jeffersonian republic, while the French could openly celebrate the virtues of nobility and monarchy. Not for the first time, Slidell wondered how he might have fared had he been born a Frenchman.

The treaty sat on a table in the center of the room. The emperor sat at a large white marble desk directly behind it. Two pens, made from ostrich feathers, sat in front of the parchment, ready for use.

The treaty text had not changed in any appreciable way for the past few months. The crucial clauses remained precisely the same. The French Empire pledged to provide direct military assistance to the Confederacy in the event of another war with the United States. In exchange, the Confederacy guaranteed support for the French presence in Mexico, beginning with the dispatch of an expeditionary force of several thousand men who were to serve under French command. Various other technical details relating to trade and other issues were included, but the real meat of the agreement was contained in the two main clauses.

The moment of the signing was at hand. Napoleon III made a speech, asserting his friendship for the people of the Confederacy and the commitment of both sides towards improving the lives of the people of Mexico. He then droned on for much longer than was necessary on the greatness of France and its destiny to bring enlightenment and progress to the dark places of the world. Under normal circumstances, it would have struck Slidell as grandiloquent, but if there was ever an occasion on which grandiloquence might be forgiven, it was this.

Slidell's speech, by contrast, was shorter and more restrained. His age was rapidly catching up to him and he no longer had the powerful voice that had once thundered in the chamber of the United States Senate. He thanked the French people for their friendship, expressed his respect and admiration for the person of the emperor personally, and said that he and the Confederate people looked forward to a future of strong friendship with France. He struggled to make his voice heard in the enormous room, but all of the observers remained courteously quiet as he had spoken.

The master-of-ceremonies, decked out in an even more elaborate costume than that of the emperor, stepped forward with a sycophantic smile on his face. "Minister Slidell? Minister La Valette? Would you come forward to the treaty-signing table, please?"

His walking stick thumped the ground as Slidell stepped towards the achievement for which he had striven so long and hard. He was surprised by his own nervousness, but his hands shook slightly and he felt his heartrate increase. He reached the table and supported himself by placing his hands on it. Two copies of the treaty, beautifully copied onto parchment by a French court official, lay before him. One would remain in France, while the other would be sent back to Richmond for ratification by the Confederate Senate.

Baron d'Erlanger had expressed some concern that the Confederate Senate might refuse to ratify. After all, the SRP had expressed contempt for the proposed alliance with France throughout the recent election campaign. Slidell was unconcerned. For one thing, the newly elected SRP senators would not take office until March and debate on the question could technically began right away, as the contents of the treaty would be in Richmond via telegraph before the end of the day. There were a sufficient number of Davis loyalists in the current Senate to ensure the treaty's ratification. A signed and ratified treaty would be greet the members of the incoming Congress as a fait accompli.

Even if legislative tricks were used to force a delay until the seating of the new members in March, Slidell was unconcerned. With the end of the election, many formerly opposed SRP politicians had quietly indicated that they were comfortable with the French agreement. Expanding Confederate influence into Mexico in partnership with the French was better than not doing so at all, many had pointed out. The rich opportunities for increased trade with France were also likely to benefit most SRP constituencies.

Minister La Valette would sign for France, as it would violate protocol for the emperor to sign it unless the other signing party were a fellow monarch. Slidell did not mind in the slightest. It was the way things were done, after all.

The Frenchman signed first, with a rather blasé expression on his face. To him, as Slidell realized, this was little more than a simple business deal, no different than if he had been signing an agreement with Brazil or Japan. He picked up his pen and, without the slightest delay or hesitation, quickly scribbled his name down onto the paper. He sighed, clearly anxious for the whole thing to be done so he could move on to something else.

Slidell took more time, for this was the finale to his life and he knew it. He held the pen in his hand, feeling its weight and judging how best to hold it as he signed, for he wanted his signature to be bold and strong. He worried that his old hands might shake and put down something entirely unreadable, so he knew he would have to hold the pen tightly. He looked at his daughter and son-in-law, who had been so faithful and supportive through the entire drama, and smiled. He glanced at Napoleon III, the complicated man whose own ambitions and foibles had made the event possible and who would now begin playing a role as a foreign protector of the Confederacy.

He took a deep breath, held the edge of the desk with one hand to steady himself, and signed the treaty with the other. "It is done," he said as he set the pen down.

The room filled with polite applause from the assembled worthies. Marguerite stepped forward to embrace her father and help him walk to a waiting chair. A few French officials came forward to shake his hand and offer their congratulations, though others were already leaving the room. Slidell sat down with an immense smile on his face, almost unbelieving that he had finally achieved his great ambition as a diplomat. The Confederate States of America was now allied to one of the European great powers, which meant that it was effectively protected from any attempt by the United States to undo the results of the War for Southern Independence.

The price being paid was high, of course. Many Southern soldiers would no doubt lose their lives fighting in Mexico. Many elements within the Confederate military establishment would denounce the transactions, declaring that they made the Confederacy a French puppet state. Yet it would be worth it. Now the Confederacy would recover from the war and settle its internal problems without fear of attack from their old enemies.

A reception at the Confederate Embassy was planned for later that day. It would not be a lavish affair, for the strange circumstances had allowed for little time to plan anything grand. It would be his last official event as the Confederate Minister to France, for he planned to send a telegram to Richmond the following day announcing his resignation.

He had only a few years left, Slidell knew. They would be years of good food and fine wine, enjoying the company of his daughter and son-in-law and perhaps grandchildren in the near future. Through however much time remained, he thought to himself, he would be able to say that he had done good service to the government which had sent him to Europe. That would be satisfaction enough.

November 28, Morning
Home of John C. Breckinridge, Richmond, Virginia

"Would you like another cup of coffee, darling?" Mary asked.

"No, thank you, dear," Breckinridge replied. "I fear I have had too much already."

"Suit yourself," she replied. "Let me know if you need anything. You've been chained to that desk all day."

"I want to make sure I have it right," he said, peering intently at the words he had already written.

"Would you like me to read it again?"

"Not yet. Maybe tonight, after I have worked on it a bit."

"Very well."

She left the study, leaving Breckinridge alone. Although he still had a few months before he would give his inaugural speech, he had decided to carve out time each day to work on it. Considering the crush of other business, he was afraid that he would end up having to hurry the writing for it during February if he did not force himself to work on it now.

Breckinridge had decided to take Thomas Jefferson's first inauguration as his model for both the ceremony and the speech. He wanted it to be simple yet dignified, fit for a government that was supposed to be based on individual liberty and the rights of the states. He had copies of both of Jefferson's inaugural addresses in front of him, as well as those of Madison and Monroe, some of the writings of George Mason, and several speeches of Henry Clay.

He took a deep breath and read through what he had already written. He wanted the speech to be about twenty minutes long. One of the benefits of using Jefferson's speech as a model was that Jefferson, like Breckinridge, had been elected after an especially bitter campaign that left the country angry and divided. Jefferson had tried to tie the nation back together rather than rub salt in the wounds of his defeated opponents.

Breckinridge was trying to do the same thing. The promotion of Beauregard to command of the Army of Tennessee and the declaration that Stephens would be Chief Justice as soon as Congress passed the necessary legislation to finally create the Supreme Court had been only the initial steps. Toombs might have turned down the opportunity to become Secretary of the Treasury, but Breckinridge planned on embracing the man's fiscal legislation anyway and would praise the bill in the speech. The fact that this would certainly enrage Toombs only made the idea more pleasing in Breckinridge's mind.

Throughout his political career, Breckinridge had always tried to be a man who pulled people together rather than drive them apart. Excoriating one's opponents was for the weak-minded and weak-willed. It was easy to do and might help win an election, but it was no policy for a governing administration. He wanted to set a different tone, to bring the people of the Confederacy together rather than drive wedges among them. It was time for the South to move forward and take its place as one of the nations of the world.

For decades before the war, Southern politicians in Washington had fixated on the issue of slavery and the gradually increasing efforts by Northerners to legislate against it. This had turned them into reactionary and paranoid men, always ready to see an abolitionist plot in every speech made by every Northern congressman. When Lincoln was elected, the Southern states had bolted from the Union without even giving the incoming president a chance to demonstrate any goodwill and willingness to compromise. If it was going to succeed as a viable nation, the Confederacy had to abandon such thinking. If they didn't they would surely tear themselves to pieces.

Breckinridge felt the weight of the responsibility on his shoulders. Davis had been made president during the confusing early days of the Confederacy. Breckinridge, by contrast, was the first choice of an actual election by the people and it had been a rancorous election, indeed. The world was watching to see whether the slave-holding republic would be able to transfer power from one administration to another and still maintain a level of political stability. Of course, Davis and Breckinridge were political allies, making the process as easy as possible. Breckinridge did not want to imagine how difficult the transfer of power would have been between Davis and Beauregard.

There was a knocking on the front door and Breckinridge heard Mary open it and have a hurried conversation with someone. The door then shut again, yet no one approached the study. Breckinridge smiled. His wife was protecting his speech-writing time with the vigilance of a sentinel. Since the election, dozens of people had come calling at his home every day, but between eleven o'clock and noon, as he and Mary had agreed, none would be admitted, giving him time to devote to what would be the most important speech of his life.

He looked at the clock. It was fifteen minutes to noon and he sighed with regret that his time alone would soon be at an end. Breckinridge liked people and reveled in a drawing room filled with friends and supporters, yet he also valued his solitude and he knew that such moments as this would become all too rare in the coming six years. He decided to set the speech aside for the remainder of his time, leaning back in his chair and pulling a Cuban cigar from his coat pocket. Moments later, he was puffing away, filling his study with the pleasing smell of burning tobacco.

Breckinridge took a deep breath and tried to clear his mind from thinking about the speech. For a moment, he tried to focus on things that had nothing to do with politics. He wondered what Mary would be serving for dinner. He thought of his children and what they might be doing at that moment. He might be the incoming president, but he was also determined to remain John Cabell Breckinridge. He felt the tug of thoughts about fiscal policy or post office appointments, but fixated his mind on other things. He had perhaps ten minutes before his wife starting letting callers into the house again and was determined to enjoy them.

Yet he could not. As much as he tried to think quiet and comforting thoughts for the precious few remaining minutes left to him, the facts of the task before him broke through his desire to relax as easily as a cannonball passing through a piece of paper.

His desire to bring the country together was probably doomed to failure, he knew. The SRP would not support his policies and he would have to oppose a great deal of the legislation that they would push in Congress. Already, Breckinridge knew, Secretary Trenholm and Senator Hill were holding discussions among the various men who had supported Breckinridge to organize their own political party, tentatively being called the Southern Democrats. Adding to the political muddle, Governor Vance of North Carolina, who had never sat comfortably with the rest of the SRP, was rumored to be launching his own group, which the newspapers were calling the Liberty Party.

Far from being united, the Confederacy looked likely to be just as politically divided as the United States had been on the eve of secession. It almost made Breckinridge wish that the French treaty had not been signed, for the possibility that the Union might one day launch a war of vengeance would have made it easier to hold the people together in the face of a common threat. He chuckled at the irony that the alliance with France could give the Confederates just enough security to allow them to destroy themselves.

He would have six years in office. Simply holding everything together would be an achievement. The magnitude of the task before him seemed unspeakably immense. The debt crisis required continued taxation and the smallest possible level of government spending. He would have to fend off unrealistic SRP demands for the acquisition of Cuba. He would have to deal with whatever fallout resulted from the dispatch of Confederate troops to Mexico to help the French. The foreign relations of the new nation would be encumbered by the institution of slavery.

Breckinridge frowned. Slavery. It was the lynchpin of why the Confederacy existed, yet he knew it was also a terrible moral sin and the albatross around the neck of the Southern people. It poisoned their relations with other countries, it stifled their own economic development, and it instilled a sense of moral depravity in Southerners from the youngest age. Slavery was not only the infliction of unspeakable suffering on the children of Africa, but it was what held his own people back from reaching their full potential and, he thought, their true destiny. Breckinridge would cut it out like a cancerous tumor if he could, freeing his people from its burden and setting the long-suffering blacks free.

Yet he knew it was beyond his power, just as it had been beyond the power of Jefferson sixty years before. The SRP would block even the tiniest movement towards a more liberal attitude on slavery and would politically crucify anyone suggesting anything other than their orthodox position. Breckinridge might revere Jefferson, but the SRP revered John Calhoun.

That was only the simplest aspect of the problem. As a thought experiment, Breckinridge imagined what would happen if he could simply wave a magic wand and end slavery the following day. The blacks would be set loose, without any education or experience in how to provide for themselves. What would become of them? Moreover, could he blame the millions of blacks if they took the path of Saul, grabbed anything that could be used as a weapon, and started killing the whites who had held them in servitude? In their place, would he do any different?

The words of Jefferson came to his mind without conscious thought.

We have the wolf by the ear. We can neither hold him nor safely let him go.

In this, as in so many other things, the Sage of Monticello had been correct. Yet it would be Breckinridge's task to begin the process of letting slavery go. He knew he could tell no one of this, except his own wife. The moves would have to be quiet and subtle, rather like a night march of soldiers to get into position for a surprise attack at dawn. Of one thing Breckinridge was certain, though. If the Confederacy was still insisting on maintaining slavery by the time the twentieth century began, it would have failed as a nation.

The ghost of Saul loomed over Breckinridge's thoughts. On the face of it, the man had not mattered. A dozen or so plantations burned, a town held for a few weeks, and a few hundred men killed. Troubling, to be sure, but less costly than a single medium-sized battle during the war. Yet the example set by Saul had been terrifying and there was always the possibility of others following in his wake. Reports were still being brought to Breckinridge of slaves across the Confederacy telling strange stories about the man who was quickly becoming an underground folk hero. Breckinridge had no clue whether there was anything to be done about that, for how could he stop the slaves from whispering to one another at night?

He sighed deeply. Glancing at the clock, he saw that it was nearly noon. At any moment, Mary would begin letting callers into the house again. With the greatest reluctance, he rose from the chair and stretched his back, sad that his momentary solace was coming to an end. He steeled himself for an afternoon of forced smiles and trite pleasantries exchanged with people he hardly knew.

Glancing quickly at the bookshelf, his eyes fell on a copy of the King James Bible. It occurred to him that he should probably put some biblical references into his speech, for Southerners were a devout people and the absence of any mention of God would surely be taken very badly. Breckinridge himself was a believer, in any event. He had already made the decision that he would attend church services every Sunday, unless a serious emergency required his immediate attention. Not only would it be good for the people to see him in the pews, but he also knew he was going to need God's help now more than ever.

He pulled the Bible off the shelf, ready to place it on the desk next to the copies of the speeches he was using as models. Absent mindedly, he opened it at random and let his eyes fall on the first passage he noticed.

Through wisdom is an house builded, And by understanding it is established.

Breckinridge smiled. He was not a credulous man, but he playfully allowed himself to wonder if the Good Lord had prompted him to open the Bible onto that particular verse. He closed the Bible and set it down on the desk.

The clock chimed twelve times. He sighed again, opened the door, and strode to the drawing room, where Mary was waiting. She had set up a tray of sliced meats and cheeses for the visitors that were about to arrive. Breckinridge would snack on them whenever he had a chance, which would have to serve as a substitute for a real lunch. A coffee service had also been set out. Mary, Breckinridge thought with a smile, was going to make an excellent First Lady.

"Ready?" she asked.

"Does it matter?"

"Not really."

"Well, in that case, I suppose I'm ready. Who is coming?"

"The minister from the Austrian Empire is scheduled to arrive at twelve thirty. Congressman James Leach of North Carolina is supposed to arrive at one o'clock. But, given what has happened over the last few days, we can expect lots of unannounced callers as well."

"Indeed. Well, let's get on with it, shall we?"

November 29, Morning
McFadden Ranch, outside of Waco, Texas

"I don't want to look like a banker," McFadden protested. "This is ridiculous!"

"What's ridiculous about it?" Annie protested. "You don't know what good clothes look like, James. This looks very nice, if you ask me. It reminds me of the clothes my father used to wear."

"Your father was a wealthy man. I'm a rancher."

"Well, you're going to be a state representative. It's an important job and you need to look dignified. Besides which, your friends put together the money to buy this suit. If you refuse to wear it, you'll be insulting them."

McFadden frowned, but he could sense the irritation and lack of patience that was entering his wife's voice. Experience had taught him to back down quickly when Annie began speaking with such a tone. One was foolish to provoke a storm when there was no need to do so.

He stood in front of their bedroom mirror, seeing himself clad in a suit of black clothes made by the finest tailor in Waco. It was a strange vision. For years, the image that looked back at him from the mirror had been wearing an army uniform. When the war ended, it had been the garments of a simple farmer. Now, as a new phase of his life was about to begin, it would be the suit of a politician.

"I really look okay?" he asked.

"You look grand, darling," she replied. "I am only worried that the beauties of Austin may try and tempt you away from your wedding vows."

He chuckled, momentarily recalling the girl from the Eberly House who had tried to do just that when went down to visit Postmaster Reagan months earlier. He was a virtuous man who would never think of being unfaithful to Annie. In other ways, though, he worried about what the future might hold for him. After all, there were countless stories of men being elevated to political office with the best of intentions and the greatest desire to do good for the people, only to succumb to the temptations of power and influence. A great many men rode into politics as if on a white horse, only to end up wallowing in the mud as just another corrupt politician.

McFadden had launched his bid for the office of state representative largely against his will, having been pushed by his friends and neighbors into doing it. He had agreed because he had felt it necessary that someone in the Granbury County community stand up to the bullying and de facto autocracy of Judge Roden. He had not had the slightest clue what running for office actually entailed and he had at first been certain he would be defeated. Yet the process had changed him greatly. He had become a leader of the community and a symbol of their determination to be self-governing men, to be free from the dictates of a corrupt county judge and his cronies.

He had felt himself grow as the campaign had proceeded. Now that he had won and would soon be off to Austin to be sworn into office, he felt himself a new man. It was about more than just himself and his family now. He was responsible for the well-being of an entire community. Moreover, he would be playing a role in the governing of an entire state. He would even be called upon to select men to represent Texas in the Confederate Senate, which meant that he would have a voice, albeit a very small one, in the direction of the entire Confederacy.

From a simple rancher, he was being elevated by the people of the county into a position of influence. With that, he knew, would come temptations. Men with money would approach him with bribes. Opportunities to advance himself at the expense of his constituents would surely appear. He prayed that he would have the moral strength to reject those enticements and remain true to his promises.

"I really look good, love?"

"Yes, dear," Annie replied. "I am getting rather tired of reassuring you about it."

He sniffed the air. "Roast pork for dinner?"

"Yes. And some vegetables from the garden. It's almost ready."

He nodded, looking forward to finishing the fitting of his clothes so that he could change back into something more comfortable and eat. Annie fumbled about with the measuring tape that the tailor had sent over with the clothes. She seemed to know exactly what she was doing as she assessed exactly what alterations needed to be made, periodically scribbling them down on paper. He doubted the wife of any of his friends would know where to begin on such matters. It was a reminder that, though she was now a frontier wife, she had been raised amid wealth and privilege in Atlanta. She knew all about fine clothes, though that phase of her life had ended years before.

The thought jolted something in McFadden's mind. Annie had never expressed any regret or reluctance about exchanging the patrician lifestyle of her past for that of the Texas frontier. When he had asked her, she had only replied that she wanted to be wherever he was and nowhere else. Did she, perhaps, see his elevation to the state legislature as the beginning of some sort of restoration of her former way of life? They were both still young and there was no telling what course his political career was going to take. He might be in the state legislature for some time. It might eventually lead to bigger and better things. Was Annie envisioning exchanging their ranch for a fine house in Austin? Was she imagining that they might one day leave the Texas frontier for the fine life of Richmond?

The future was open, to both them and the country. McFadden would follow it wherever it would lead.

Thaddeus strolled into the bedroom, playing with a toy Confederate soldier. He looked up at his father.

"Papa look different."

"Thank you, Thaddeus," McFadden replied. He turned to Annie. "That's a compliment, isn't it?"

"I would take it as one." Annie's look then became serious, as the little boy began marching the soldier in a circle around his parents, humming a martial-sounding tune. "It will be hard on the boy to be separated from his father for months at a time."

McFadden sighed. "Yes, well, we shall have to figure that out. Perhaps we could all go to Austin together when the legislature is in session."

"I am told that most men leave their wives behind."

McFadden chuckled. "That's because most of them like being out of the sight of their women so that they have indulge themselves in the taverns, gambling houses, and brothels. That's not an issue with me."

"I should hope not. Now I very much want to come so that I can keep an eye on you. But what about the ranch? It's one thing for us to be gone for a day or so. But the legislature is in session from January to the summer, every other year, yes?"

"That's right."

"And that's not considering the possibility of special sessions called by the governor."

"Right."

"Well, we can't leave the ranch by itself for months at a time. We'd come back and all the cattle would either be dead or someone will have taken them. The vegetables will have rotted in the ground or been devoured by weeds. The house will have fallen apart."

"Perhaps members of the Association could help," McFadden suggested. "Some of our boys are handymen who move from ranch to ranch doing odd jobs. I'm sure we could ask some of them to stay here while we are in Austin and keep the place up."

Annie's eyes narrowed. "So you've decided to keep the Association going?"

McFadden nodded. "We made the decision last night. I was going to tell you over dinner. The Association is not only going to keep going, but we're going to put a more permanent organizational structure in place for it. We're even going to rent an office in town to serve as a headquarters for it."

"But what for?" Annie asked. "Roden's in jail and is likely to be there for a long time, since I can't imagine any court finding him innocent of the corruption charges. Walker, or Robertson or whatever his name really is, has been handed over to the army and last I heard was being taken to Richmond to face charges. All their underlings are either in jail with them or are now lying very, very low and desperate to avoid causing trouble. Collett's going to be country judge."

"I know all this, love."

"What I'm saying is that the Association was formed to get rid of all the corruption in Granbury County. You've done that. It's served its purpose. Why keep it going?"

"Because it can serve a role in helping this community. Look, just because we kicked out the bad guys doesn't mean hard times aren't going to be over. People are still in debt. People are still having trouble putting food on their tables. The Association can help everybody. Through the churches. Through the Masonic Lodge. Through the veterans groups. It will pull them all together, you see?"

Annie picked Thaddeus up off the ground. "I suppose. Let's eat."

They walked out of the bedroom and into the kitchen, where the smell of roast pork was beginning to emerge from the stove, combining with the smell of burning wood to make McFadden instantly hungry. He sat down at the table and poured himself a glass of apple cider and Annie stirred a pot of some sort of soup. Thaddeus resumed the marching of his toy soldier on the floor.

"You know, people from other parts of the state have asked about the Association," McFadden said. "One fellow who was passing through from Jefferson on his way to Austin. One fellow from Fort Worth. I'm told by some of our friends that the Association is being talked about in lots of places. People want to create something similar in their own communities."

"Well, they can do whatever they please," Annie said. "What difference does it make to us here in Granbury County?"

"Because the problems we face are bigger than just those in any one county. Roden was far from the only corrupt official in Texas, after all. Everywhere we have poor farmers and veterans back from the war who are faced with efforts by rich men and crooked politicians who want to cheat them out of the little they have."

Annie frowned. "What did we fight the war for, then?"

"That's the question. Look back east, where you're from. In all the states east of the Mississippi, you have a planter aristocracy that runs the government. The common folk are totally shut out. During the war, men said that because we fought and bled for the Confederacy, the rich folks would have to listen to us after we have won. But I don't see that happening. The rich folks are still in power everywhere. Some of them are good people, like Bobby Lee and Joe Johnston. But most of them are just corrupt bastards like Roden. And whenever the common folks try to stand up, the rich folks just start screaming about the black slaves and everybody goes quiet again."

"The rich folks aren't in power here," Annie said. "Not in Granbury County, I mean. Roden tried to set himself up like one of those planter aristocrats. But you beat him."

"But some other corrupt fellow will show up sooner or later and try to do what Roden did. Which is why we need to keep the Association going. And need to encourage more groups to form in other places. To make sure that Texas doesn't become just like South Carolina or Mississippi. Common folk like us need to have a say in how the government works."

"Look out, Papa!" Thaddeus called as he marched his soldier across McFadden's foot.

Dinner was finished twenty minutes later. They had to remind Thaddeus to remain in his chair several times, as he constantly attempted to descend to the floor in order to resume playing with his toy. As he tussled the hair on his boy's head, McFadden knew that he couldn't bear to be separated from him for such a long time.

"So you're all right with leaving the ranch in the hands of the Association while we are in Austin?" he asked.

"Yes, I am," Annie said with a smile. "We'll have to make careful arrangements, of course. And I expect to be allowed to veto your choice of the men who will be living here."

"You'd do that anyway, love."

She smiled and laughed softly. "So, when do we leave?"

"Perhaps a month. The session will start on January 13, but I we will need time to find proper lodging, for me to figure out what I need to do. I don't expect to just walk up to the Capitol and knock on the door, after all."

"So we'll be celebrating Christmas in Austin?"

"I'd prefer to be doing so here in our home, but I don't think we can delay our departure that long."

Annie frowned. "Alas, I don't expect that to be the last sacrifice I will be making, now that I am the wife of a politician."

The rain was pouring down, but Saul barely noticed. He made no effort to shield himself from it, simply letting the water drip down onto his exposed face as it dribbled off the leaves of the magnolia tree under which they were sheltering. One of the three survivors who remained with him was trying to keep the campfire going, but it was a losing battle. In the distance, flashes of lightning were visible, accompanied by low rolls of thunder.

They had not moved from the campsite for four days. In all that time, Saul had not said a word to his men. He had hardly moved from his position, sitting with his back to the trunk of the tree. At times he had slept, but mostly he remained awake. The men came and went to collect firewood and perform other routine chores, to which they had long been accustomed by their long time in the wilderness. All three of the men still with him were veterans from the beginning of the campaign, men who had served in the U.S.C.T. units during the war. Almost all of the slaves liberated from the plantations or freed during their brief occupation of New Iberia had died in the slaughter around the hotel, with the few survivors having scattered to the four winds.

Seven men had escaped with Saul. Two had died three days later in a skirmish with a pursuing militia unit. One had become separated from the tiny band a few weeks later and had not been seen since. Saul assumed that he had gotten lost, but it was possible that the man had simply set off on his own, no longer seeing a purpose in remaining with him.

There had to be other survivors, Saul knew. There was no way to communicate with any of them and certainly not instruct them to gather together in one place so as to resume the fight. Perhaps they had escaped in small bands like his own, or perhaps only as individuals. Some were doubtless trying to make their way north to the border between Arkansas and Missouri, though Saul expected few if any to make it. Others might have thought to head towards New Orleans and vanish into the free black population of the city, though the police would probably be on the lookout for them.

The four men remaining with him were all that he had left. Each man had a rifle, though only two seemed likely to be in working order and there was no ammunition in any event. Each man had a bayonet or knife, and two had machetes taken from sugar plantations. That was all. Not long ago, he had commanded a well-armed force of over two hundred men. It pained him to reflect on how far he had fallen.

The danger of capture by pursuing Confederate cavalry or Louisiana militia at least seemed to have abated. In the days immediately after the recapture of New Iberia, trackers with hunting dogs specially trained to sniff out black men had combed through the swamps and forests around the town. It had only been with difficulty that Saul and his men had evaded them. Now, they were far west of New Iberia, perhaps as far as a hundred miles, and there did not seem to be anyone following them. Five men in such a vast wilderness could easily conceal themselves for as long as they wished.

To what end, Saul was no longer sure. His men would follow him wherever he choose to lead them, but what was the point? The rebellion had been crushed in New Iberia. It was useless to deny it. Saul might have escaped, but he was powerless. Would could five men with knives do against the might of the Confederacy?

On a few occasions, when truly desperate for food, they had stolen produce and meat from the slave quarters of plantations in the middle of the night. When they had said who they were, the slaves had been more than willing to part with their food and had sworn that they would not say a word about it to their masters or anyone else. In some of these cases, the slaves had expected Saul to slaughter the whites on the plantations and set them all free. Some had begged him to take them with him, but without the means to defend themselves, a larger group would only have been easier for the Confederates to track. It must have been disappointing when Saul and his remaining survivors had moved on, leaving them enslaved.

He looked around at the four men still with him. The man trying to keep the fire lit had finally made some progress, forming a small canopy with sticks and his coat to shield the flames from the rain. The wet wood released a large amount of smoke, which ordinarily would trouble Saul as it might reveal their location. Yet they were far enough away from New Iberia, and such a long time had passed, that he felt perfectly safe. Besides, he realized that he might actually prefer to be caught and killed by the Confederates, as it would be better to die fighting that to starve to death out in the woods.

As the first man struggled to keep the fire going, another man began to cook two skinned rabbits that he had caught in traps. The sweet smell of roasting meat was soon noticeable. It would be the first meat any of them had eaten in several days. Saul could feel the pangs of hunger in his stomach and knew that his body was famished, but yet strangely felt little desire to eat anything.

An hour passed and the man finished cooking the rabbits. Using his bayonet, he cut off a piece, so small that Saul could have eaten it with two or three bites.

"Here, boss," the man said, offering it to Saul. "You eat first."

"No," Saul replied.

"You're hungry. You need to eat."

"Don't tell me what to do. You eat it."

The man glanced uncertainly at his comrades. Saul did not like this at all, for it suggested that he considered Saul's orders a suggestion only, rather than something he was required to do instantly without thinking.

"I said you eat it!" Saul said, more loudly.

The man devoured the cooked piece of rabbit in a matter of seconds. When he finished, he quickly distributed the rest of the meat to his three comrades. He held out more meat to Saul, who turned his head away and ignored it.

Saul did not want to eat. He wished that Ferguson was there, or Troy, or Lowell. He could have discussed the question with them in a way that he could not with these four men. Ferguson and Troy had died in New Iberia and Saul assumed that Lowell had been executed by the Confederates in New Orleans. His remaining followers would not have understood a philosophical conversation, or would simply have agreed with whatever he said. In a very real sense, he was alone.

Saul tilted his head back, letting the rain drip down onto his closed eyes. He reflected on the long path that had led him to this nondescript magnolia tree in the middle of nowhere. A slave on a plantation, he had become a soldier fighting for the freedom of his people. Protected by his mother's magic, he fought the Confederate slaveholders in battle after battle. Even when the war ended and the bluecoats had gone home, he had remained in the field. A great many of the slaveholders had fallen under his gun and knife.

Then Morgan had emerged like a sinister knight on a dark horse. Saul had matched wits with him and proven to be a formidable enemy, before the treachery of Silas had proven his undoing. The thought of Silas made Saul tense with a physical feeling of hatred. How differently things might have turned out but for that man's disloyalty. He remembered the look of stark terror on the criminal's face as he was being buried alive and felt a welcome sense of satisfaction.

All had seemed lost, when Lowell had arrived. One of the good white men, of whom Saul had seen so few in the world, he had given the insurgents the chance to restore their fortunes and, for a few weeks, they struck terror into the heart of the Confederacy by capturing New Iberia and setting its slaves free. The fighting had been fierce and no one could accuse Saul and his men of being weak or cowardly. They had fought as hard and as well as any men on Earth could have fought.

What tormented Saul was the question of whether things could have ended differently. What if they have moved more quickly and sparked a larger uprising among the slaves on the surrounding plantations? Could their declared free zone have become a reality? Perhaps it was better if his efforts had been doomed from the beginning, he thought bitterly. In that case, he could not blame himself for their failure. On the other hand, it also meant that slavery was never going to be destroyed.

Only one thing brought Saul any consolation. When they had taken food from the slave quarters of the plantations, all of the slaves had known who he was. Indeed, they had gazed upon him in wonder, as if he was some sort of angel rather than a man. They had hurriedly told him some of what they had heard about him, including fanciful stories of him killing huge numbers of slaveholders with his bare hands. Somehow, the story of his mother's magic that had given him immunity to bullets had become known among the slaves on the plantations across southern Louisiana.

He remembered the words of Morgan during their strange conversations under the flag of truce in New Iberia. The Confederacy could not leave Saul alive not because they really thought he could free the slaves on his own, but simply because of the fear that he caused in the hearts of the white South.

He wasn't really a man any longer, Saul realized. He might as well have died in New Iberia. Now, he had become a representation of something much larger than himself. He was a shadow, like the ghosts in the stories told by old slaves on the plantations to frighten the children into obeying their parents. He could do the Confederacy no harm any longer merely as a man. As a specter, however, he could continue to haunt its swamps and forests.

What would he do? He could take his four remaining men and make for the Missouri border, but it was several hundred miles away. Even if the Confederate had given up on trying to find survivors from New Iberia, chances were that they would be caught by regular slave patrols long before they got close to the border. Nor was trying to escape into New Orleans an option, as too many people knew what he looked like. He could hardly remain in the wilderness indefinitely.

Perhaps the answer lay in finding a Confederate patrol of some kind and launching a hopeless attack, so as to die under the bullets of the enemy. After thinking about it a moment, Saul shook his head. The fact that he had survived the battle in New Iberia would certainly send a shock through the Confederacy, but they would then have his body and unquestionable proof that he was dead.

Worse was the possibility that, if he choose such a course, Saul might be taken prisoner. The very thought of this made him nauseous. He could imagine be carted through the streets of New Orleans as white mobs spat on him and pummeled him with rotten vegetables. He could imagine the sound of their laughter, their relief that the black man who had terrorized them had been reduced to a captive animal, to be toyed with for an appropriate length of time before being taken to a humiliating execution at the gallows. Everything he had achieved was now entangled with the fear he had engendered in the whites. Were he to be captured and disgraced, all that would be lost.

The more he thought about it, the more he realized that there was only one thing for him to do.

Saul stood, his muscles aching after having remained stationary for four days. His men looked up at him, wondering if he would say something. Without a word, he stepped forward and took the musket from the hands of one of his men. He twisted off the bayonet and tossed the musket away. Turning it towards his own belly, he considered how quickly and powerfully he would have to pull the blade backwards into his body in order to kill himself. It would be easier to thrust forwards, as that required less thought, but he did not have that option.

"Boss, no!" one of the men cried out.

Saul ignored him. As soon as he was dead, the men would no longer matter. He wondered what it would be like. Would it be what the Christians had always said to him, passing through a tunnel of light until coming into the presence of God? He had never really grasped what the voodoo priests and priestesses believed about death, although they seemed to go to a good deal of trouble with funeral rites and maintenance of graves. In any case, he was about to find out about death in the most effective manner possible.

He was surprised, however, to find that he could not bring himself to do it. His mind commanded his hand to yank the blade backwards into his stomach, but his hand refused to obey. It was frustrating. Suicide would be his final act as a truly free man. He would have thought it would be as easy as an apple falling from a tree. Yet he could not do it.

"Here," he said, holding the bayonet out towards one of his men. "You do it."

The man folded his arms and shook his head. "I won't, boss."

"Yes, you will. I order it."

"What for?" The man's voice was surprisingly defiant.

"I can't explain it to you," Saul said. "Just trust me. It needs to be done."

"What about the magic, boss?" another of the men said. "They say you can't be killed by no man."

Saul hadn't considered this. His mother's magic protected him from the weapons of any enemy. He fervently believed this and he felt his belief had been vindicated by so many battles in which he had never been harmed. Still, the incantation had referred to enemy weapons. This would be the act of a friend, one of his own men. Saul did not think his magic would do anything to prevent it from happening.

"The magic keeps me from harm when I want to be kept from harm," he said. "It won't stop this from happening."

"What will we do, boss?" one of the men asked resignedly.

Saul decided that he owed them at least some direction. "You use your own judgement. Head north for the border. Go to New Orleans. You have choices that I don't have. But you can't never tell nobody about it. You may talk about me and tell folks that you was one of my men, but you can't never tell nobody that you saw me die. Bury me here and never tell a soul where my body is."

He held the bayonet out towards the man again. This time, he took it. Saul leaned back against the tree, bracing himself, telling himself that it would only hurt for a moment and then he would be embraced by the light. The man stood uncertainly, but then his face grew determined and he stepped forward towards Saul.

"Do it fast," Saul said. "Don't hold back."

"Goodbye, boss," the man said sadly.

The man pushed Saul's head back against the tree, exposing the neck. With a single, clean movement, he slashed the bayonet across Saul's throat. It felt like white hot fire against the most tender parts of his skin. He could feel blood pouring down onto his chest. The man who had cut his throat stepped back, his eyes wide with fear and wonder. Instinctively, Saul reached up to grip his throat in an attempt to stem the flow of blood, but the sticky red liquid simply passed between his fingers.

He felt the life ebb out of him as more and more of his blood flowed from his body and down onto the ground. He slowly sank into a half-sitting, half-lying position. His mind fought through the pain to think clearly. He had fought against the Confederacy to destroy slavery and free his people. He did not live long enough to see it happen, but others would follow in his wake. His example would inspire thousands of others. Sooner or later, slavery would be expunged from the land and those who had enslaved the blacks would face judgement. This thought was the last conscious idea that passed through his mind as life fled from his body.

So died Saul. And in so dying, he ensured that he would live forever.

EPILOGUE

1907
May 31, Morning
Jamestown, Virginia

Congressman Robert Lowell sat on the deck of the river steamer that the Confederate government had provided for them, the *CSS Reliable*. He was enjoying a cup of coffee and a breakfast of pastries before disembarking for his second day at the Jamestown Exposition. It was a lovely spring day, with the air clear and fresh and a general feeling of satisfaction and pleasure among the other people in the ship. Although he was technically in Virginia for political work, the whole thing had more the air of a vacation than anything else.

When the president had asked him to serve as a member of the United States official delegation to the exposition commemorating the three hundredth anniversary of the Jamestown Settlement, Lowell thought the request odd. Though the arrest, trial, and pardon of his father might have happened four decades before, it remained one of those events in recent history about which everyone had an opinion. Had his father been a hero who had struck a great blow against slavery or had he been a renegade who should have been hanged as originally planned? His inclusion in the delegation had generated quite a bit of chatter in certain circles, which had spilled over into the newspapers. Was the president intending to send an insulting message to the Confederates or was he giving the South the chance to acknowledge that bygones were bygones?

The Confederates, for their part, had been nothing but polite to him since his arrival four days before. With most of the rest of the delegation, he had arrived in Richmond on the express train that linked the city with Philadelphia. Enough business was done between the two governments that official trains passed back and forth between the respective capitals at least once a week. The Southerners had even allowed the delegation to be accredited as diplomats, which meant that they had been exempt from the usual customs check at the border.

They had been put up in the Spottswood Hotel the night they arrived in Richmond, where the Confederates organized a welcoming party for them, complete with champagne and a dinner of oysters and grilled sea bass. The following day, they boarded the *Reliable*, which had taken them down to Jamestown. Each night had seen a lovely dinner in the ship's dining hall. Lowell was not entirely comfortable with the idea that taxpayer money was being used to provide such luxurious treatment, especially when so many people across the Confederacy lived in poverty, but their instructions were adamant that they were not to be disagreeable to their hosts in any way.

The previous day, the delegation had disembarked from the ship to begin their tour of the exposition. The whole affair had the feeling of a grand festival. Crowds of people wandered through every part of the exposition, poking their heads into each different pavilion in turn. The chorus of voices was chaotic and charming. Here he was listening to a father fend off the sobbing pleas of a son to purchase him an overpriced sausage on a stick. There a man waiting in line was loudly complaining that the event's organizers had not provided a sufficient number of bathrooms. Everywhere was the sound of music, projected throughout the whole area by a series of interconnected electrical speakers provided free of charge by a German company named Siemens.

The first day had been taken up with visiting the reconstruction of the Jamestown colony, half a mile from the actual site, which had been very well done. The Confederates had clearly gone to a great deal of trouble to make sure it was historically accurate, complete with reenactors dressed in what the organizers assumed was clothing that matched the historical period. Access to the real remains of Jamestown was more tightly controlled, as organizers of the exposition feared that people might damage the archeologically sensitive area, but Lowell and some of the other Northerners had been taken on a guided tour the day before.

It had been fascinating and enjoyable. Of course, as he had been educated in the United States, Lowell's teachers had focused much more on the arrival of the Pilgrims and Puritans in Massachusetts than the establishment of the Jamestown colony in Virginia. When, as a young boy, he has raised his hand to point out that Virginia had actually been settled some years earlier than Massachusetts, his teacher had scornfully replied that the Virginia colony had been established only because a few foolish Englishmen had thought they might make money there from finding gold, even though the region had none. The settlers of Massachusetts, the teacher had proudly concluded, had by contrast been motivated by a high-minded pursuit of religious freedom.

The story told in the pavilions that Confederate and Virginia state governments had set up about Jamestown, of course, was a very different tale. In their version, the Jamestown settlers were forward-looking agents of progress whose brave actions had opened up the American continent for future generations. One of the lecturers speaking during the tour had tried to be polite to his Northern guests but felt it necessary to say that the trials and tribulations faced by the settlers in Jamestown had been far worse than those faced by the Pilgrims in Massachusetts. Lowell had found the comment amusing, as if the two sides were engaged in some sort of competition. Reflecting on it on his way back to their lodgings on the ship, he thought that such vying perspectives explained why the holiday of Thanksgiving was widely celebrated in the United States, yet not at all in the Confederacy.

Lowell sipped his coffee, which was fast becoming lukewarm, and concentrated on the newspaper for a few minutes. The lead story dealt with diplomatic tensions between Britain and Russia regarding the border between Canada and Alaska. This was especially sensitive due to the gold mines known to be in the area. Another news item that Lowell noticed included a rumored agreement between Japan and Russia to divide Manchuria between them, the merger of two of the largest labor unions in Britain, and a report on the fragile health of Emperor Maximilian of Mexico. Lowell smiled as he reflected on the fact that the world was a very interesting place.

His breakfast complete, Lowell rose from his chair and walked towards the gangplank. It was only a little past nine o'clock, meaning that he would have plenty of time to explore the pavilions. He had decided to do so on his own, planning to meet up with the other members of his group later in the day. At one o'clock the official delegations of the various attending nations were scheduled to gather to listen to a speech by Confederate President Alexander Pendleton. Until then, Lowell could wander to his heart's content.

He descended the gangplank onto the soft Virginia soil and proceeded up towards the pavilions. The various exhibit areas had been contributed by governments, organizations, or businesses from each of the North American nations. Each of the eleven states of the Confederacy had funded a pavilion which showcased its history and not so subtly advertised the economic opportunities an aspiring businessman might discover were they to visit. To no one's surprise, Virginia's was the largest and most elaborate. This only made sense, seeing as they were the host state of the entire event, but it also underlined the fact that Virginia remained the most populous and influential of all the Confederate states.

One pavilion had been sponsored directly by the Richmond government, the highlight of which had been the actual copy of the 1901 Constitution, which was created in the wake of the constitutional crisis of 1899. In fact, as Lowell and the other members of the Union delegation fully realized, that constitution was the true reason any of them were here. The entire Jamestown Exposition was effectively an enormous public relations effort by the Confederate government to convince the world that it was stable and secure and that the events of eight years before would never happen again. The effort that other nations had put into recruiting and paying for illustrious members to serve in the official delegations was, in turn, meant to display support for the Confederate government within the other countries. It was in the interest of everyone, after all, for the Confederacy to be governed in a calm and steady manner.

It was an open secret that the Confederate government was largely behind the financing of the exposition. Despite public pronouncements to the contrary, there was no way that the event was going to turn a profit. Attendance had been high, but this was largely because ticket prices had been comparatively low. The officials in Richmond were perfectly happy to swallow their financial losses if it meant that they had an opportunity to tell the world that their government could be trusted. Political implications aside, Lowell was happy to enjoy the showcase.

One of the pavilions had been set up by the Orphan Society, which Lowell had visited earlier in the day. It told the story of the exiled Kentucky Confederates, including President John C. Breckinridge, and how they had prospered in the new nation up to the time when Kentucky had become a part of the Confederacy in 1890. Lowell found it illuminating, though he wondered whether the Orphan Society still served much of a purpose. Many people at the pavilion had suggested the same thing and rumors abounded that the organization would wrap itself up in a few years.

Of particular interest to Lowell, given his family's abolitionist tradition, was the marquee set up by the Confederate African Association. Lowell had walked through and studied its exhibits with great interest. In several displays and models, it told the story of blacks in North America, beginning with the arrival of the first African slaves at Jamestown in 1619. The last display in the chronological procession through which visitors walked was an oversized copy of the last clause in the tenth article in the Confederate Constitution of 1901, whose simple wording belied its momentous import.

All persons held as slaves in the Confederate States of America shall be free from slavery and all forms of involuntary servitude as of January 1, 1905.

Lowell remembered reading the newspaper the morning after the actual text of the new Confederate constitution had been revealed to the world. He reflected sadly that his father, long dead from tuberculosis, would have rejoiced at the news. Indeed, by helping Saul's rebellion in the years immediately after the end of the War for Southern Independence, his father had helped bring about the abolition of slavery in the Confederacy, as the actions of the Saulite rebels had the most important contributing factors in pushing the Southerners to the momentous action. His father had died thinking that he had failed, but time had proven that the opposite was true.

Of course, the legal abolition of slavery in the Confederacy had certainly not meant anything approaching equality of the races in the Southern nation. This point was brought home to Lowell as he walked past the next pavilion, where a professor from a university in Atlanta was giving a lecture. Half a minute of listening told Lowell that the topic was some sort of bogus scientific research suggesting that people descended from Africans were intellectually inferior to those of European descent, thereby justifying the limitations on the voting rights of black Confederates.

Lowell moved on, not wishing to listen. He had always made a point to read the arguments of the opposing side, something inculcated in his youth by both his mother and father, and so knew full well the claims of the "Jernigan School" of Confederate sociologists. He knew that they were being used to justify the strict laws governing relations between the races that had been enacted by the Confederate Congress and the individual states since the 1901 Constitution was implemented. Lowell found it all very distasteful, though it reminded him of the work that still had to be done before racial justice could truly prevail on the American continent. Blacks were still far from equal to whites in the United States, after all.

As be moved on, he saw something even more repugnant than the lecture by the racist sociologist. A group of people, evenly divided between men and women, were standing inside a roped-off area that Lowell quickly realized had been set aside for demonstrations. Each of them was holding a sign saying the same thing.

No Amnesty For Saulite Murderers!

As people passed by the protest zone, the people called out to them, expressing with their shouted voices the same sentiments expressed in their printed signs. Lowell walked by, studying them carefully, unnerved by the ferocious hatred he could see in their eyes. He wondered what they might have done to him had they known who he was.

Wishing to put these troubling scenes out of his mind, Lowell walked on. The Pacific Republic had several interesting exhibits, including one dealing with their innovative system of "national parks" intended to preserve wilderness areas. Lowell had read some newspaper accounts of the joint ventures between the governments of the Pacific Republic and the United States to jointly run some of these parks when the area intended for conservation overlapped the border between the two nations. This struck him as a pleasant example of cooperation, but then the relationship of his country with the Pacific Republic had not been nearly as acrimonious as that with the Confederacy, for no blood had been spilled during the separation.

Lowell was surprised to see that even the little country of Deseret, ruled by the enigmatic Mormon theocracy, had funded a pavilion. He stepped inside and looked around, finding the exhibits to be oversized paintings depicting the different stages of Mormon history in America, beginning with the alleged religious revelations of Joseph Smith, moving through the persecution experienced by the Mormon people, their settlement in Utah, and the official establishment of Deseret. Lowell found it all very interesting. He found the religion of Mormonism faintly ridiculous, but also disliked the prejudice against the Mormons by most of the rest of the North American population. Perhaps it was best that they had their own little republic in which they could practice their strange faith in peace.

He left the Deseret exhibit and moved along towards the series of pavilions set up by the Republic of Texas, which Lowell was especially excited to see. The first one had a working replica of an oil rig steadily churning away, surrounded by a series of exhibits highlighting the technology being used to exploit the vast reserves of oil that had been discovered beneath the soil of Texas a decade earlier. Coming from a family whose wealth was now tied up in the steel industry, Lowell found it all fascinating. His firms were already doing a good deal of business in Texas and this seemed likely to increase in the coming years as more oil fields came on line.

Lowell was leaving the oil industry pavilion and walking towards one apparently focused on the cattle trade when he heard a voice call from behind him.

"You would be Congressman Lowell?"

He turned around and was stunned to see a face he knew only from newspaper photographs. It was Thaddeus McFadden, President of the Republic of Texas. Lowell was taken aback at coming face-to-face with one of the most illustrious men of his time, who had led the movement for Texan independence and played such an important role in the constitutional crisis of 1899. The man, about his own age, looked as striking as the pictures of him in the newspapers.

"You're Congressman Lowell, aren't you?" McFadden asked. "Of Massachusetts, yes?"

"I am the man, sir," Lowell said, extending his hand as McFadden approached. The Texan had a firm handshake, which almost made Lowell wince.

"I am honored to meet you, Congressman."

"The honor is all mine, Mr. President," replied Lowell. "Normally men say this merely as a pleasantry, but I believe it is undeniably true in this case."

"Nonsense," McFadden said in response. "Are you enjoying the exposition?"

"I am," Lowell said. "The Confederates have pulled out all the stops to ensure a successful event, I must say. I don't want to think about how much all of this is costing them."

"Have you seen the British pavilion? The one with the airplane?"

"I have," Lowell said, his eyes brightening. "I found it amazing, to put it mildly. It is the very plane that first flew in Australia, or so they claim. I can't imagine that they would lie about something like that. Very thoughtful of them to bless this little event with such a unique thing to see."

"Indeed," McFadden said with a smile. "I hope that we Americans will soon be producing such wonders. They say that if development on these heavier-than-air flying vehicles continues, they might one day carry passengers in the same way trains do today."

"Quite an amazing world we live in, Mr. President."

McFadden glanced over at a covered area with picnic tables, where drinks were being served. "Congressman, would you be interested in sitting down for a pint of beer with me?"

Lowell preferred wine to ale, but was delighted to be considered for such an invitation by the likes of McFadden and so did not hesitate. "Certainly, Mr. President."

They strolled over to the refreshment stand and McFadden placed the order for two beers, paying for it without asking Lowell. If the bartender had any clue who either of them was, he didn't show it. McFadden took the ales and nodded towards an empty table, at which they sat.

"If I'm not mistaken, the steel company controlled by your family does a lot of business with different oil companies in Texas, yes?"

"That's correct," Lowell said.

"If you encounter any difficulty in doing business with my country, I want you to personally let me know how I can be of assistance. There is not yet any trade agreement between Texas and the United States. Until there is, I don't want any red tape getting in the way. Texas currently lacks the ability to manufacture steel on its own in any large quantities and so we rely on companies such as yours."

"Thank you, sir."

"Oil will be the lifeblood of Texas. It's already led to an economic boom, but I worry that the wealth will be concentrated into the hands of the very few. The resources of Texas belong to the Texan people as a whole and not to a few select individuals."

"The Texan people?" Lowell said. "Black as well as white?"

"Black as well as white. Of course, there are comparatively few blacks in Texas. Many more Tejanos. But everyone has equal rights in Texas. Our constitution saw to that. Still, there is the letter of the law and there is reality, isn't there?"

"Quite."

"If the oil continues to flow and I can somehow ensure that the economic benefits fall to all Texans, my country can become one of the most prosperous places on Earth. I am determined to see this happen, you understand. Any help you can give me would be most welcome."

"I am very pleased to see what has happened in Texas, Mr. President. But I hope you don't underestimate the challenges you face."

"I don't," McFadden said quickly. "Many people in my country continue to oppose me. Our Confederate neighbors are still not very happy with us for leaving. And then, of course, there is the world as a whole. We are moving towards great instability and danger, I think. This news of the League of the Three Emperors, or whatever they are calling it, is deeply unsettling."

"I agree fully," Lowell replied. "I sit on the House Foreign Relations Committee and we have been receiving extensive briefings from our State Department. Russia is powerful enough on its own. Combined in an alliance with the Germans and the Japanese, and with the oft-stated expansionist aims of the new czar, they have the potential to be a grave threat to the world."

Lowell had thought on this matter for the last two months, ever since word arrived that the treaty establishing the League of the Three Emperors had been signed in St. Petersburg. It was another reason why relations between the Union and the Confederacy had warmed considerably. Both countries, formerly bitter enemies, knew that they might one day need to turn to one another for assistance in an uncertain world.

"The Russians do not like us Texans," McFadden said with a wry grin. "What with Baku and Romania they had a near-monopoly on oil before the big strike in East Texas ten years ago. I've even had the Texas Rangers tell me that Russian agents are paying oil workers to sabotage our production facilities."

"That is unsettling," Lowell said.

McFadden finished the last swallow of his beer. "In any case, Lowell, I have been very pleased to make your acquaintance. Perhaps you would do me the favor of visiting me in Austin sometime? It is important that the various republics of America maintain friendly relations with one another. Texas and the United States have common interests and no potential conflicts. We are natural friends."

"I don't disagree," Lowell replied. "I should have to clear any such visit with the State Department, of course."

"Naturally." He extended his hand across the table. "I must get back to the Texas pavilions. I like to greet the visitors there personally. I find that little touches go a long way."

Lowell shook the president's hand and, with a nod, the Texan soon vanished into the crowd, heading back in the direction from which they had come. Lowell sat at the table for a few more minutes, slowly finishing his own glass of beer. He listened to the chatter among the people sitting around him, who were expressing their various opinions about the quality of each exhibit. The prevailing consensus appeared to be that the British display of the airplane was by far the most interesting.

He checked his watch. It was nearly one o'clock. He tossed back the last bit of beer and rose from the table, beginning to move in the direction of the main amphitheater that had been set up for nightly theatrical productions. President Pendleton would speak there today, followed by the heads of the different delegations. Lowell sighed deeply, steeling himself for what would be a long and dull afternoon of unnecessarily protracted speeches, all of which would say more or less the same thing. He would much rather have continued exploring the exhibits, but there was official work to be done, even if it involved nothing more than sitting in a chair and occasionally clapping.

Lowell arrived at the amphitheater and stepped into the box set aside for the use of the United States delegation. Other members drifted in over the next half hour or so, including the Governor of Iowa, the mayor of Chicago, and a few fellow members of Congress. A few captains of industry and academics had also been included. A single black man, the head of the Union of Black Railroad Employees, had also come along, though Lowell thought this was more for appearances than anything else. The head of the delegation, Secretary of State Whitelaw Reid, was already sitting on the stage near where the Confederate president was going to speak.

He waited, chatting politely with the other members of the delegation for the next few minutes. President Pendleton soon arrived on the stage, but took a seat with the others rather than take the podium. Apparently he was waiting for more of the seats to fill before he began his speech.

An Episcopalian minister from Richmond, decked out in his traditional white robes, arrived on the stage and moved towards the podium. Lowell realized with disappointment that the speeches were going to be preceded by some sort of religious blessing. He didn't mind this much, though he himself was not especially religious. He only regretted that the time would be dragged out even longer than he had expected.

"Almighty God," the minister began. "We humbly beseech Thee to hold up the example of this great exposition as an example to the world of the peace and friendship that can prevail between the various peoples of North America. We ask that You bless and keep the state of peace that now prevails between us for all time to come."

Lowell nodded, thinking the sentiments worthy enough, if a bit obvious. He then found himself wondering, for the first time since he had arrived, if the goodwill manifested by the exposition was real or a façade. The more he thought about it, the more the question troubled him.

THE END

ACKNOWLEDGMENTS

My thanks go out to the staff of the United States Senate History Office, the staff of the Royal Welch Fusiliers Museum, the staff of the Austin Public Library, the staff of the Round Rock Public Library, and countless other people who helped me complete this project in different ways.

Thank you to Brian Crawford and Phil McBride, both excellent writers themselves, for generously reading through the manuscript, pointing out numerous errors, and making many suggestions to improve the quality of this book. Thanks to my friend and colleague Willow Clark for the cover art.

Thank you to my friend Gareth Horwood for his constant encouragement and for giving me a place to write when my house was overrun with loud little girls.

Thank you to my parents, Lonnie and Barbara, for always being encouraging and helping the project in various ways. And to my daughters, Evelyn and Amelia, for always being an inspiration.

And thanks most of all to my brilliant, beautiful and amazing wife Jill, who is not only a wonderful (if occasionally ruthless) editor, but has always provided a nurturing and supportive home environment that allows me to pursue my writing in the midst of so many other pressures of life.

ABOUT THE AUTHOR

Jeff Brooks was born in Richmond, Virginia, and grew up in Dallas, Texas. He lives in Manor, Texas, just outside the state capital of Austin. He graduated from Texas State University with a double bachelor's degree in history and political science and a master's degree in history. He also studied at the University of Kent in Canterbury, England. Aside from his writing, he teaches American history to 8th graders at Kelly Lane Middle School. He is a certified wine sommelier and a devoted fan of Chelsea Football Club.

Jeff met his wife Jill at a wine tasting in 2009. They married in the Bahamas in 2011. In 2013, their daughter Evelyn was born. A second daughter, Amelia, followed in 2016.

Made in United States
North Haven, CT
03 February 2024

48300867R00433